THREE COMPLETE NOVELS
BY
V.C. ANDREWS®

Heaven
Dawn
Ruby

POCKET BOOKS

New York   London   Toronto   Sydney   Tokyo   Singapore

Following the death of Virginia Andrews, the Andrews family worked with a carefully selected writer to organize and complete Virginia Andrews' stories and to create additional novels, such as *Dawn* and *Ruby*, inspired by her storytelling genius.

Heaven was written by Virginia Andrews.

This book consists of works of fiction. Names, characters, places and incidents are products of the author's imagination or are used fictitiously. Any resemblance to actual events or locales or persons, living or dead, is entirely coincidental.

 POCKET BOOKS, a division of Simon & Schuster Inc.
1230 Avenue of the Americas, New York, NY 10020

Heaven copyright © 1985 by Vanda Productions, Ltd.
Dawn copyright © 1990 by The Virginia C. Andrews Trust
Ruby copyright © 1994 by The Virginia C. Andrews Trust

ISBN: 0-671-01688-1

First Pocket Books hardcover printing October 1997

10 9 8 7 6 5 4 3 2 1

V.C. Andrews is a registered trademark of the
Virginia C. Andrews Trust.

POCKET and colophon are registered trademarks of
Simon & Schuster Inc.

Printed in the U.S.A.

CONTENTS

Heaven

Dawn

Ruby

Heaven

PART ONE

In the Willies

PROLOGUE

Whenever the summer winds blow I hear the flowers whispering, and the leaves singing in the forest, and I see again the birds on wing, the river fish jumping. I remember, too, the winters; how the bare tree branches made tortured sounds as the cold winds whipped them about, forcing limbs to scrape the shedlike cabin that clung precariously to the steep mountainside of a range called by the West Virginian natives, the Willies.

The wind didn't just blow in the Willies, it howled and shrieked, so everyone living in the Willies had good reason for looking anxiously out their small dirty windows. Living on the mountainsides was enough to give anyone the willies—especially when the wolves howled like the wind and the bobcats screeched and the wild things of the forests roamed at will. Often small pets would vanish, and once every decade or so an infant disappeared or a toddler wandered off and was never seen again.

With special clarity I remember one particular cold February night that revealed to me my own beginning. It was the eve of my tenth birthday. I lay close to the wood stove on my floor pallet, tossing and turning, hearing the wolves yowl at the moon. I had the unfortunate habit of sleeping lightly, so the slightest movement in the tiny cabin jolted me awake. Every sound was magnified in our isolated cabin. Granny and Grandpa snored. Pa staggered home drunk, bumping into furniture as he stumbled over sleeping bodies on the floor before he crashed down on the squealing springs of his big brass bed, waking up Ma and making her angry again so she raised her voice in shrill complaint because again he'd spent too much time in Winnerrow, in *Shirley's Place*. At that time I didn't even know why *Shirley's Place* was such a bad place, and why Pa's going there caused so much trouble.

Our cabin floor, with half-inch spacings between each crookedly laid board, let in not only cold air but also the snortings of the sleeping pigs, dogs, cats, and whatever else took retreat under it.

Out of the black suddenly came a different kind of noise. Who was moving in the darkness of the dim red glow near the stove? I strained to see it was Granny, bent over, her long gray hair streaming, making her seem a witch sliding along the rough wooden planks as quietly as possible. It couldn't be the outhouse she was heading for; Granny was the only one of us allowed to use the "hockeypot" when nature called. The rest of us had to trek two hundred yards to the outhouse. Granny was in her mid-fifties. Chronic arthritis and various other undiagnosed aches and pains made life miserable for Granny, and the loss of most of her teeth made her seem twice her age. Once, so I had been told by those old enough to remember, Annie Brandywine had been the beauty queen of the hills.

"Come, girl," Granny whispered hoarsely, her gnarled hand on my shoulder, "it's time ya stopped cryin out in t'night. I'm hopin maybe ya won't be doin it no more once ya know t'truth bout yerself. So, before yer pa wakes up agin, ya an *me* are goin somewheres, an fore we come back, ya'll have somethin t'cling ta when he glares his eyes an slings his fists." She sighed like the south wind blowing gently, whispering the tendrils of hair around my face to make them tickle like ghosts that were coming—through her.

"You mean we're going outside? Granny, it's miserably cold out there," I warned even as I got up and pulled on a cast-off pair of Tom's too-big shoes. "You aren't planning on going far, are you?"

"Gotta," said Granny. "Hurts bad t'hear t'words my Luke yells at his own firstborn. Even worse, it makes my blood run cold t'hear ya scream right back when he can strike out an end what ain't hardly begun yet. Girl, why do ya have t'answer back?"

"You know, you know," I whispered. "Pa hates me, Granny, and I don't know why. Why does he hate me so much?"

There was enough moonlight coming through a window to allow me to see her dear old wrinkled face.

"Yes, yes, time ya knew," she mumbled, tossing me a heavy black shawl she'd knitted herself, then wrapping her own narrow, bent shoulders in another just as dark and drab. She led me to the door, swung it open, letting in the cold wind before she shut it again. In their bed beyond the tattered faded red curtain, Ma and Pa grumbled as if the wind half woke them. "We got a trip t'make, ya an me, down t'where we plant our kinfolk. Been atryin t'make it with ya fer many a year. Kin't keep puttin it off. Time runs out, it does. Then it's too late."

So on this cold, snowy, miserable, dark night she and I set off through the black piny woods. A solid sheet of ice lay rippling on the river, and the wolves sounded closer now. "Yep, Annie Brandywine Casteel sure knows how t'keep secrets," Granny said as if to herself. "Not many do, ya know, not many born like me . . . ya listenin, girl, are ya?"

"Can't help but hear you, Granny. You're shouting directly in my ear."

She had me by the hand, leading me a far way from home. Crazy to be out here, it was. Why, on this freezing winter's night, was she going to give up one of her precious secrets, and to me? Why me? But I loved her enough to assist her down the rough mountain trail. It seemed like miles we traveled in the dark cold of night, that old moon overhead shining down on us with evil intentions.

The treat she had in store for me was a graveyard, stark and eerie in the light of the pale bluish winter moon. The wind blew wild and fierce and snapped her thin white hair and blended it with my own before she spoke again. "Onliest thin I kin give ya, child, onliest thin worth havin, is what I'm gonna tell ya."

"Couldn't you have told me in the cabin?"

"Nah," she scoffed, stubborn as she could sometimes be, set in her ways like an old tree with too many roots. "Ya wouldn't pay no tention iffen I told ya there. *Here,* ya'll always rememba."

She hesitated as her eyes fixed on a slim little tombstone. She raised her arm and pointed her gnarled finger at the granite headstone. I stared at it and tried to read what was engraved there. How very odd for Granny to bring me here during the night, where maybe the ghosts of those who lay here roamed about looking for living bodies to inhabit.

"Ya gotta fergive yer pa fer bein what he is," intoned Granny, huddling close to me for warmth. "He's what he is, and he kin't help it no more than t'sun kin help from risin or settin, no more than t'skunks kin help from makin their stinks, an no more than ya kin help bein what ya are."

Oh, that was an easy thing for Granny to say. Old people didn't remember what it was like to be young and afraid.

"Let's go home," I said, shivering and pulling at Granny. "I've heard and read tales about what goes on in graveyards on nights when the moon is full and the hour is after midnight."

"Know betta than to be skerred of dead thins that kin't move or speak."

Yet she drew me tighter into her embrace and forced me to stare again at the narrow sunken grave. "Ya jus listen an don't say nothin till I'm finished. I got a tale t'tell that's gonna make ya feel betta. There's a good reason why yer pa speaks mean when he looks at ya. He don't really hate ya. In my mind I done put t'pieces togetha, an when my Luke looks at ya he sees *not* ya but someone else . . . an, chile, he really is a lovin man. A good man underneath it all. Why, he had a first wife he loved so much he near died when she did. He met her down in Atlanta. He was seventeen an she was only fourteen an three days, so she tole me lata." Her thin voice dropped an octave. "Beautiful as an angel, she was, an oh, yer pa did love her so. Why, he swept her offen her feet, when she was runnin away from home. Headin fer Texas, she was. Runnin from Boston. Had a fancy suitcase with her, full of clothes t'likes of what ya've neva seen. All kinds of pretty stuff in that suitcase, suits an silky thins, silvery brush, comb an a silver mirror, an rings fer her fingas, an jewels fer her ears, an she come here t'live, cause she went an made t'mistake of marryin up with a man not her kind . . . cause she loved him."

"Granny, I've never heard of Pa having a first wife. I thought Ma was his first and only wife."

"Didn't I tell ya t'stay quiet? Ya let me finish tellin this in my own way. . . . She was from a rich Boston family. Come t'live with Luke an Toby an me. I didn't want her when she come. Didn't like her at first. Knew she wouldn't last, right from t'first, knew that. Too good fer t'likes of us, an t'hills, an t'hardships. Thought we had bathrooms, she did. Shocked her when she knew she'd have t'trek ta t'outhouse, an sit on a board with two holes. Then durn if Luke didn't go an build her a pretty lil outhouse all her own, painted it white, he did, an she put in it fancy rolled paper on a spindle, an even offered t'let me use her pink store-bought paper. Her *bathroom*, she called it. She hugged an kissed Luke fer doin that fer her."

"You mean Pa wasn't mean to her like he is to Ma?"

"Shut up, girl. Yer makin me lose track. . . . She came, she stole my heart, maybe Toby's, too. She tried so hard t'do her best. Helpin out with t'cookin. Tryin t'make our cabin pretty. An Toby an me, we gave em our bed, so they could start their babies in t'right way an not on t'floor. She'd have slept on t'floor, she woulda, but wouldn't let her. All

Casteels are made in beds . . . I'm ahopin an prayin anyways that's true. Well . . . one day she's laughin an happy cause she's gonna have a baby. My Luke's baby. An I feel so sorry, so blessed sorry. Was always ahopin she'd go back t'where she come from fore t'hills took her, t'way they do delicate folks. But she made him happy when she was here. Made him happier than he's been since." Granny stopped talking abruptly.

"How did she die, Granny? Is this her grave?"

She sighed before she continued. "Yer pa was only eighteen when she passed on, an she was still only fourteen when he had t'bury her in this cold ground an walk away an leave her alone in t'night. He knew she hated t'cold nights without him. Why, chile, he laid on her grave all t'first night t'keep her warm, an it was February . . . an that's my tale of her who came as an angel t'the hills, t'live an love yer pa, an make him happier than he's eva been, an likely he'll neva be that happy agin, from t'looks of it."

"But why did you have to bring me out here to tell me all of this, Granny? You could have told me in the cabin. Even if it is a sad and kind of a sweet story . . . still, Pa's meaner than hell, and she must have taken all the best of him into the grave with her, and left only the worst for the rest of us. Why didn't she teach him how to love others? Granny, I wish she'd never come! Not ever come! Then Pa would love Ma, and he'd love me, and not her so much."

"Oh," said Granny, appearing stunned. "What's wrong with ya, girl, what's wrong? Ain't ya done guessed? That girl that yer pa called his angel, she was *yer ma!* She's the one who birthed ya, an by t'time ya come, she could hardly speak . . . an she named ya Heaven Leigh, she did. An ya kin't truly say, kin ya, that ya ain't proud of that name that everybody says suits ya jus fine, jus fine."

I forgot the wind. I forgot my hair snapping around my face. Forgot everything in the wonder of finding out just what and who I was.

When the moon slipped from behind a dark cloud, a random beam of light shone for an instant on the engraved name:

ANGEL
BELOVED WIFE OF
THOMAS LUKE CASTEEL

Strange how it made me feel to see that grave. "But where did Pa find Sarah? And how did he do it so quick?"

Granny, as if eager to spill it all out while she had the chance, began to talk faster. "Well, yer pa needed a wife t'fill his empty bed. He hated his lonely nights, an men gets cravins, chile, *physical* cravins yer gonna find out bout one day when yer old enough. He wanted a wife t'give him what his angel had, an she tried, give Sarah credit fer that. She made ya a good motha, treated ya like ya were her own. Nursed ya, loved ya. An Sarah gave Luke her body willingly enough, but she had nothin of his angel's spirit t'give him, an that leaves him still yearnin fer t'girl who would have made him a betta man. He *was* betta then, chile Heaven—even if ya don't believe it. Why, in t'days when yer angel ma were alive he'd set out fer work early each mornin, drivin his old pickup truck down t'Winnerrow where he was learnin all about carpentry an how t'build houses an such. He used t'come home full of nice talk about buildin us all a new house down in t'valley, an when he had that house, he were gonna work t'land, raise cows, pigs, an horses . . . yer pa, he's always had a keenin fer animals. Loves em, he does, like ya do, chile Heaven. Ya get that from him."

Odd how I felt when Granny took me back to the cabin, and from beneath a clutter of old junk, and many old cartons in which we kept our pitifully few clothes, she dragged out something wrapped about in an old quilt. From that she extracted an elegant suitcase, the kind mountain folks like us could never afford. "Yers," she whispered so the others wouldn't wake up and intrude on this most private moment. "Belonged t'yer ma. Promised her I'd give it t'ya when t'time were right. Figure it's as right as it'll eva be t'night, now . . . so look, girl, look. See what kind of ma ya had."

As if a dead mother could be compressed and put into a fancy, expensive suitcase!

But when I looked, I gasped.

There before me in the dim firelit room were the most beautiful clothes I'd ever seen. Such delicate lacy things I hadn't dreamed existed . . . and at the very bottom I found something long, and carefully wrapped in dozens of sheets of tissue paper. I could tell from Granny's expression she was tense, watching me closely, as if to savor my reaction.

In the dim glow of the woodfire burning I stared at a doll. A doll? What I'd expected least to find. I gazed and gazed at the doll with the silvery-gold hair bound up in a fancy way. She wore a wedding veil, the filmy mist flowing out from a tiny jeweled cap. Her face was exceptionally pretty, with beautifully shaped bowed lips, the upper cleft ridge fitting so precisely into the bottom center indentation. Her long dress was made of white lace, lavishly embroidered with tiny pearls and sparkling beads. A bride doll . . . veil and everything. Even her white shoes were lace and white satin, with sheer stockings fastened to a tiny garter belt, as I saw when I took a peak under the skirts and veil.

"It's her. Yer ma. Luke's angel that was named Leigh," whispered Granny, "jus t'way yer ma looked when she came here afta she married up with yer pa. Last thin she said before she died was, 'Give what I brought with me to my little girl . . .' An now I have."

Yes, now she had.

And in so doing, she'd changed the course of my life.

1

The Way It Used to Be

If Jesus died almost two thousand years ago to save us all from the worst we had in us, he'd failed in our area, except on Sundays between the hours of ten A.M. and noon. At least in my opinion.

But what was my opinion? Worthy as onion peelings, I thought, as I pondered how Pa had married Sarah two months after my mother died in childbirth—and he'd loved his "angel" so much. And four months after I was born and my mother was buried, Sarah gave birth to the son Pa had so wanted when I came along and ended my mother's brief stay on earth.

I was too young to remember the birth of this first son, who was christened Thomas Luke Casteel the Second, and they put him, so I've been told, in the cradle with me, and like twins we were rocked, nursed, held, but not equally loved. No one had to tell me that.

I loved Tom with his fire-red hair inherited from Sarah, and his flashing green eyes, also inherited from his mother. There was nothing in him at all to remind me of Pa, except later he did grow very tall.

After hearing Granny's tale of my true mother on the eve of my tenth birthday, I determined never, so help me God, never would I tell my brother Tom any different from what he already believed, that Heaven Leigh Casteel was his own true whole-blood sister. I wanted to keep that special something that made us almost one person. His thoughts and my thoughts were very much alike because we'd shared the same cradle, and had communicated silently soon after we were born, and that had to make us special. Being special was of great importance to both of us, I guess because we feared so much we weren't.

Sarah stood six feet tall without shoes. An Amazon mate very suitable for a man as tall and powerful as Pa. Sarah was never sick. According to Granny (whom Tom sometimes jokingly called Wisdom Mouth), the birth of Tom gave Sarah a mature bustline, so full it appeared matronly when she was still fourteen.

"An," informed Granny, "even afta givin birth, Sarah would get up soon as it was ova, pick up what chore she'd left unfinished, jus as if she hadn't undergone t'most awful ordeal we women have t'suffa through without complaint. Why, Sarah could cook while tryin t'encourage a newborn baby t'suckle." Yeah, thought I, her robust good health must be her main attraction for Pa. He didn't seem to admire Sarah's type of beauty much, but at least she wasn't likely to die in childbirth and leave him in a pit of black despair.

One year after Tom came Fanny, with her jet-black hair like Pa's, her dark blue eyes turning almost black before she was a year old. An Indian girl was our Fanny, browner than a berry, but very seldom happy about anything.

Four years after Fanny came Keith, named after Sarah's long-dead father. Keith had the sweetest pale auburn hair, you just had to love him right from the beginning—especially when he turned out to be very quiet, hardly any bother at all, not wailing, screaming, and demanding all the time as Fanny had—and still did. Eventually Keith's blue eyes turned topaz, his skin rivaled the peaches-and-cream complexion lots of people said I had, though I didn't truly know since I wasn't given much to peering into our cracked and poorly reflecting mirror.

Keith grew to be an exceptionally good little boy who appreciated beauty so much that when a new baby came along the year after he was born, he would sit for hours and hours just gazing at the delicate little girl who was sickly from the very beginning. Pretty as a tiny doll was this new little sister that Sarah allowed me to name, and Jane she became, since at that time I'd seen a Jane on a magazine cover, too pretty to believe.

Jane had soft wisps of pale golden-red hair, huge aqua eyes, long dark curling lashes that she'd flutter as she lay discontentedly in the cradle gazing at Keith. Occasionally Keith would reach to rock the cradle, and that would make her smile, a smile of such disarming sweetness you'd do anything just to see that smile come out like sunshine after the rain.

After Jane was born she began to dominate our lives. To bring a smile to Jane's angelic face became the loving and dutiful obligation of all of us. To make her laugh instead of wail was my own special delight. Time to rejoice when Jane could smile instead of whine from mysterious aches and pains she couldn't name. And in this, as in everything else, what I enjoyed doing was what Fanny had to spoil.

"Ya give her t'me!" screamed Fanny, running with her long, skinny legs to kick my shins before she darted away and called from a safe place in our dirt yard, "She's *our* Jane—not yers! Not Tom's! Not Keith's! OURS! Everythin here is *OURS*, not yers alone! Heaven Leigh Casteel!"

From then on Jane became *Our Jane*, and was called that until eventually all of us forgot that once upon a time our youngest, sweetest, frailest, had only one name.

I knew about names and what they could do.

My own name was both a blessing and a curse. I tried to make myself believe such a "spiritual" name had to be a blessing—why, who else in the whole wide world had a name like Heaven Leigh? No one, no one, whispered the little bluebird of happiness who lived now and then in my brain, singing me to sleep and telling me that everything, in the long run, would work out just fine . . . just fine. Trouble was, I had an old black crow roosting in my brain as well, telling me such a name tempted fate to do its worst.

Then there was Pa.

In my secret and putaway heart there were times when I wanted more than anything in the world to love the lonely father who sat so often staring sullenly into space, looking as if life had cheated him. He had ebony-dark hair, inherited from a true Indian ancestor who'd stolen a white girl and mated with her. His eyes were as black as his hair, and his skin kept a deep bronze color winter and summer; his beard didn't show through shadowy dark the way most beards did on men with such dark hair. His shoulders were wonderfully wide. Why, you could watch him in the yard swinging an ax, chopping wood, and see the most complicated display of muscles all big and strong, so that Sarah, bending over a washtub, would look up and stare at him with such love and yearning in her eyes it would almost break my heart to know he never seemed to care whether or not she admired and loved him, or cried every time he didn't come home until early morning.

Sometimes his moody, melancholy air made me doubt my mean

thoughts. I watched him the spring when I was thirteen, knowing about my own true mother, and saw him sitting slouched in a chair, staring into space, as if dreaming of something; I, in the shadows, longed to reach out and touch his cheek, wondering if it would be bristly—I'd never touched his face. What would he do if I dared? Slap *my* face? Yell, shout, no doubt that's exactly what he'd do—and yet, yet, there was in me a deep need to love him and be loved by him. All the time that aching need was there, waiting to ignite and burst into a bonfire of love and affection.

If only he'd see me, do or say one thing to encourage me to believe he did love me at least a little.

But he never even looked at me. He never spoke to me. He treated me as if I weren't there.

But when Fanny came flying up the rickety steps of the porch and hurled herself onto his lap, shouting out how glad she was to see him, he kissed *her*. My heart pained to see the way he cuddled her close so he could stroke her long, shiny dark hair. "How ya been, Fanny girl?"

"Missin ya, Pa! Hate it when ya don't come home. Ain't good here without ya! Please, Pa, this time stay!"

"Sweet," he murmured, "nice t'be missed—maybe that's why I stay away."

Oh, the pain my father delivered when he stroked Fanny's hair and ignored mine. Worse than the pain he gave from slaps and ugly words when once in a while I made him see me, and forced him to respond to me. Deliberately I strode forward, coming out of the shadows into the light, carrying balanced on my hips a huge basket of clothes I'd just taken from the rope lines and folded. Fanny smirked my way. Pa didn't move his eyes to indicate he knew how hard I worked, though a muscle near his lips twitched. I didn't speak but passed on by, as if he hadn't been gone two weeks and I'd seen him only minutes ago. It did shrivel me some to be ignored, even as I ignored him.

Fanny never did any work. Sarah and I did that. Granny did the talking; Grandpa whittled; and Pa came and went as he pleased, selling booze for the moonshiners, and sometimes helping them make it, but it was outwitting the Feds that gave Pa his greatest pleasure, and made him his biggest money—according to Sarah, who was terrified he'd be caught and thrown in jail, because the professional liquor brewers didn't care for the competition overproof alcohol gave them. Often he'd go and stay a week or two, and when he was gone Sarah allowed her hair to go dirty, and her meals were worse than usual. But when Pa walked in the door and threw her a careless smile or word, she came alive, to hurry and bathe, to put on the best she had (a choice of three dresses, none really good). It was her fervent desire to have makeup to wear when Pa was home, and a green silk dress to match the color of her eyes. Oh, it was easy to see that Sarah had all her hopes and dreams pinned on that day when real cosmetics and a green silk dress came into her life and made Pa love her as much as he'd loved that poor dead girl who'd been my mother.

Our cabin near the sky was made of old wood full of knotholes to let in the cold and heat, or let out our cold or heat, whichever would make us most miserable. It had never known paint, and never would. Our roof was made of tin that had turned rusty long before I was born, and had wept a million tears to stain the old silvery wood. We had drainpipes and rain barrels to catch the water in which we took baths and washed our hair once we had heated it on the cast-iron stove we nicknamed Ole Smokey. It belched and spat out so much vile smoke we were always half crying and coughing when we were shut up in there with the windows down and the only door to the outside closed.

Across the front of our mountain cabin was the obligatory front porch. Each spring saw Granny and Grandpa leave the cabin, to decorate our sagging, dilapidated porch with their twin rockers. Granny knitting, crocheting, weaving, making braided rugs, as Grandpa whittled. Sometimes Grandpa fiddled for the barn dances held once a week, but the older Grandpa grew the less he liked to fiddle and the more he liked to whittle.

Inside were two small rooms, with a tattered curtain to form a kind of flimsy door for the "bedroom." Our stove not only heated our place but also cooked our food, baked our biscuits, heated our bathwater. Once a week before we went to church on Sundays, we took baths and washed our hair.

Next to Ole Smokey sat an ancient kitchen cabinet outfitted with metal bins for flour, sugar, coffee, and tea. We couldn't afford real sugar, coffee, or tea, but we did use gallon cans of lard for our gravy and biscuits. When we were extraordinarily lucky we had honey enough for our wild berries. When we were blessed beyond belief we had a cow to give us milk, and always there were chickens, ducks, and geese to supply us with eggs, and fresh meat on Sundays. Hogs and pigs roamed at will, to snuggle down under our house and keep us awake with all *their* bad dreams. Inside, Pa's hunting hounds had the run of our home, since all mountain folk knew dogs were durn important when it came to supplying a steady flow of meat other than domestic fowl.

Animals we had aplenty when you counted the stray cats and dogs who came to give us hundreds of kittens and puppies. Why, our dirt yard was full of wandering animals, and anything else that could stand the clutter and noise of living with Casteels—the scum of the hills.

In what we called our bedroom was one big brass bed with a saggy old stained mattress over coiled springs that squeaked and squealed whenever there was activity on that bed. Sometimes what went on in there was embarrassingly close and loud; the curtain did little to muffle sound.

In town and in school they called us hill scum, hill filth, and scumbags. Hillbillies was the nicest thing they ever called us. Of all the folks in the mountain shacks, there wasn't one family more despised than ours, the Casteels, the worst of the lot. Despised not only by valley folk but by our own kind, for some reason I never understood. But . . . we were the family with five Casteel sons in prison for major and minor crimes. No wonder Granny cried at night; all her sons had been so disappointing. She had only her youngest left, Pa, and if he gave her joy I never knew of it. On him she'd placed all her expectations, waiting for that wonderful someday when he proved to the world that Casteels *were not* the worst scum of the hills.

Now, I've heard tell, though it's hard to believe, that there are kids in the world who hate school, but Tom and I couldn't wait for Mondays to roll around, just so we could escape the confines of our small mountain cabin with its smelly, cramped two rooms, its far walk to the stinking old outhouse.

Our school was made of red brick and sat smack in the heart of Winnerrow, the nearest valley village, set deep in the Willies. We walked seven miles to and seven miles fro as if they were nothing, always with Tom close at my side, Fanny tagging along behind, meaner than ten vipers, with Pa's black eyes and Pa's own temper. She was pretty as a picture, but mad at the world because her family was so "stinking rotten poor," as Fanny succinctly put it.

". . . an we don't live in a pretty painted house like they do in Winnerrow, where they got real bathrooms," Fanny shrilled, always complaining about things the rest of us accepted lest we be miserable. "Inside bathrooms—kin ya imagine? Heard tell some houses got two, *THREE*—each with hot an cold runnin water, kin ya believe such as that?"

"Kin believe most anythin bout Winnerrow," answered Tom, skipping a pebble over the river water that was our bathing hole in the summers. Without that river running we'd have been much dirtier than we were. The river and its little ponds, pools, and freshwater springs made life better in a thousand ways, making up some for all that would have been intolerable but for cool, tasty spring water, and a swimming hole as good as any city pool.

"Heaven, ya ain't listenin!" yelled Fanny, who had to have center stage all of the time. "An what's more, they got kitchen sinks in Winnerrow. *Double* sinks! Central heating . . . Tom, what's central heating?"

"Fanny, we got t'same thin in Ole Smokey that sets clean smack in t'middle of our cabin."

"Tom," I said, "I don't think that's really what central heating means."

"As fer as I'm concerned, that's exactly what I want it t'mean."

If I seldom agreed with Fanny about anything else, I did agree that it would be paradise unlimited to live in a painted house with four or five rooms, to have all the hot and cold water at one's will just by turning on a faucet—and a toilet that flushed.

Oh, gosh, to think of central heating, double sinks, and flushing toilets made me realize just how poor we really were. I didn't like to think about it, to feel sorry for myself, to be inundated with worries about Keith and Our Jane. Now, if Fanny would only wash her clothes, that would help a little. But Fanny never would do anything, not even sweep the front porch, though she was pretty crazy about sweeping the dirt yard free of leaves. Because it was a fun thing to do, was my sour reasoning. Out there she could watch Tom playing ball with his buddies, while Sarah and I did the real work, and Granny did the talking.

Granny had good reasons for not working as hard as Sarah. Granny had her own problems getting up once she was down, and getting down once she was up. The time it took for her to get from here to there seemed an eternity as she held on to what furniture we had. There just wasn't enough furniture to take Granny everywhere she wanted to go easily.

Sarah taught me when I was old enough, and Granny was too feeble to help (and Fanny flatly refused to do anything even when she was three, four, or five), how to diaper babies, how to feed them, give them baths in a small metal washtub. Sarah taught me a thousand things. By the time I was eight I knew how to make biscuits, melt the lard for the gravy, add the flour with water before I blended it into the hot grease. She taught me how to clean windows and scrub floors and use the washboard to force dirt out of filthy clothes. She also taught Tom to do as much as he could to help me, even if other boys did call him a sissy for doing "women's work." If Tom had not loved me so much, he might have objected more.

A week came when Pa was home every night. Sarah was happy as a bluebird, humming under her breath and shyly glancing at Pa often, as if he'd come courting and wasn't just a husband tired of running moonshine. Maybe somewhere out on a lonely highway a Federal revenue man was waiting for Luke Casteel, ready to pitch him into jail along with his brothers.

Out in the yard I scrubbed away on dirty clothes, as usual, while Fanny skipped rope and Pa pitched the ball for Tom to swing at with his one and only plaything, a ballbat left over from Pa's childhood. Keith and Our Jane hung around me, wanting to hang up the washed clothes—neither one could reach the rope lines.

"Fanny, why don't you help Heavenly?" yelled Tom, throwing me a worried glance.

"Don't want to!" was Fanny's answer.

"Pa, why don't you make Fanny help Heavenly?"

Pa hurled the ball so hard it almost hit Tom, who took a wild swing and, off balance, fell to the ground. "Don't ever pay attention to women's work," said Pa with a gruff laugh. He turned toward the house, in time to hear Sarah bellow our evening meal was ready: "Come an git it!"

Painfully Granny rose from her porch rocker. Grandpa struggled to rise from his. "Gettin old is worse than I thought it would be," groaned Granny once she was on her feet and trying to make it to the table before all the food was gone. Our Jane ran to her to be led by the hand, for Granny could do that if not much else. She groaned again. "Makes me think that dyin ain't so bad after all."

"Stop saying that!" stormed Pa. "I'm home to enjoy myself, not to hear talk about death and dying!" And in no time at all, almost before Granny and Grandpa were comfortable in their chairs at the table, he got up, finished with the meal that had taken Sarah hours to prepare, and out into the yard he went, jumping into his pickup truck to head to God knows where.

Sarah, wearing a dress she'd ripped apart, then sewn back together in a different fashion, with new sleeves and pockets added from her bag of scrap fabrics, stood in the doorway staring out, softly crying. Her freshly washed hair scented with the last of her lilac water shone rich and red in the moonlight, and all for nothing when those girls in *Shirley's Place* wore real French perfume, and real makeup, not just the rice powder that Sarah used to take the shine from her nose.

I determined I was not going to be another Sarah—or another angel found in Atlanta. Not me. Not ever me.

2

School and Church

The cock-a-doodle-do of our solitary rooster with his harem of thirty hens woke us all. The sun was only a hazy rim of rose in the eastern sky. With the crow of the cock came the mumbling of Ma waking up, of Granny and Grandpa turning over, of Our Jane beginning to wail because her tummy always ached in the mornings. Fanny sat up and rubbed at her eyes. "Ain't gonna go t'school t'day," she informed grouchily.

Keith sprang immediately to his feet and ran to fetch Our Jane a cold biscuit she could nibble on to calm those hunger pains that hurt her more than they hurt any of the rest of us. Placated, she sat on her floor pallet and nibbled on her biscuit, her pretty eyes watching each one of us hopefully for the milk she'd soon be crying for.

"Hey, Ma," said Tom, coming in the door, "cow's gone. Went out early to milk her . . . she's gone."

"Damn Luke t'hell an back!" shrieked Sarah. "He knows we need that cow fer milk!"

"Ma, maybe Pa didn't sell her. Somebody coulda stole her."

"He sold her," she said flatly. "Said yesterday he might have ta. Go see iffen ya kin round up that goat."

"Milk, milk, milk!" wailed Our Jane.

I hurried to Our Jane, drawing her into my arms. "Don't cry, darling.

Why, in ten minutes flat you'll be drinking the best kind of milk, fresh from a nanny goat."

Our morning meal consisted of hot biscuits made fresh each day, covered with lard gravy. Today we were also having grits. Our Jane wanted her milk more than she wanted anything else. "Where is it, Hev-lee?" she kept asking.

"It's coming," said I, hoping and praying it was.

It took Tom half an hour to come back with a pail of milk. His face was flushed and hot-looking, as if he'd run a long, long way. "Here ya are, Our Jane," he said with triumph, pouring milk into her glass, and then into the pitcher so Keith could enjoy the milk as well.

"Where'd ya get it?" asked Ma suspiciously, sniffing the milk. "That cow belongs now t'Skeeter Burl, ya know that . . . an he's mean, real mean."

"What he don't know won't hurt him," answered Tom, sitting down to dig into his food. "When Our Jane and Keith need milk, I go astealing. An yer right, Ma. Our cow is now pastured in Skeeter Burl's meadow."

Sarah threw me a hard look. "Well, that's t'wager, ain't it? An yer pa lost, like always."

Pa was a gambling man, and when Pa lost we all lost, not only the cow. Each day for the past several weeks, one by one our barnyard fowl had been disappearing. I tried to convince myself that they'd be back once Pa had a winning streak. "I'll collect the eggs," called Sarah, heading for the door while I dressed for school. "Got to before he wagers all our hens! One day we'll wake up to no eggs, no nothin!"

Sarah was given to pessimism, whereas Tom and I were always thinking somehow our lives would turn out fine, even without cows, goats, or chickens and ducks.

It seemed to take forever for Our Jane to grow old enough to go with us to Winnerrow and attend first grade. But finally, this fall, she was six, and she was going if Tom and I had to drag her there every day. And that's what we had to do, literally drag her along, holding fast to her small hand so she couldn't escape and dash back to the cabin. Even as I tried to tug her along at a faster pace, she dragged her small feet, resisting in every way she could, as Keith encouraged and assured her, "It's not so bad, not so bad," and that's all he could say in favor of school. The cabin was where Our Jane wanted to stay, with Sarah, with her ragged old doll with the stuffing half fallen out. Right from the beginning she hated school, the *hard* seats without cushions, sitting still, having to pay attention, though she loved being with other children her age. Our Jane's attendance at school was irregular because of her frail health—and her determination to stay home with her ma.

Our Jane was a dear, darling doll, but she could wear on your nerves with her caterwauling, and all the food she spat up that smelled sickly sour. I turned to scold her, knowing that she was going to make us late, and that again everyone in the school would mock us for not even knowing how to tell time. Our Jane smiled, stretched out her frail, slender arms, and immediately my chastising words froze unspoken on my tongue. I picked her up and lavished on her pretty face all the kisses she had to have. "Feeling better, Our Jane?"

"Yes," she whispered in the smallest voice possible, "but don't like walkin. Makes my legs hurt."

"Give her to me," said Tom, reaching to take her from my arms. Even Tom, loudmouthed, brash, and tough, proud to be all boy, turned sweet and tender with Our Jane. Definitely my smallest sister was gifted in ways of grabbing your heart and never giving it back.

Tom held her in his arms, staring down at her pretty little face, all screwed up to yell if he dared to put her down. "You're just like a tiny, pretty doll," Tom said to her before he turned to me. "You know, Heavenly, even if Pa can't afford to give you or Fanny dolls for Christmas or birthdays, you have something even better, Our Jane."

I could have disagreed with that. Dolls could be put away and forgotten. No one could ever forget Our Jane. Our Jane saw to it that you didn't forget her.

Keith and Our Jane had a special relationship, as if they, too, were "heartfelt twins." Sturdy and strong, Keith ran beside Tom, staring up at his small sister with adoration, just as he ran at home to wait on his little sister who'd immediately smile through her tears when he turned over to her whatever she wanted. And she wanted whatever *he* had. Keith, kindly, sweetly, gave in to her demands, never complaining even when too many "wants" of Our Jane would have had Tom openly rebellious.

"Yer a dope, Tom, an ya too, Keith," stated Fanny. "Durn if I would carry no girl who kin walk as good as I kin."

Our Jane began to wail. "Fanny don't like me . . . Fanny don't like me . . . Fanny don't like me . . ." And it might have gone on all the way to school if Fanny hadn't reluctantly reached out and taken Our Jane from Tom's arms. "Aw, ya ain't so bad. But why kin't ya learn t'walk, Our Jane, why kin't ya?"

"Don't wanna walk," said Our Jane, hugging her arms tight around Fanny's neck and kissing Fanny's cheek.

"See," said Fanny proudly, "she loves me best . . . not ya, Heaven, nor ya, Tom . . . loves me best, don't ya, Our Jane?"

Disconcerted, Our Jane looked down at Keith, at me, at Tom, then screamed: "Put me down! Down! Down!"

Our Jane was dropped into a mud puddle! She screamed, then started to cry, and Tom chased after Fanny to give her a good wallop. I tried to calm Our Jane and dry her off with a rag I had for a handkerchief. Keith broke into tears. "Don't cry, Keith. She's not hurt . . . are you, darling? And see, now you're all dry, and Fanny will say she's sorry . . . but you really should try to walk. It's good for your legs. Now catch hold of Keith's hand, and we'll all sing as we go to school."

Magic words. If Our Jane didn't like walking, she did like to sing as much as we all did, and together she, Keith, and I sang until we caught up with Tom, who had chased Fanny into the schoolyard. Six boys had formed a line for Fanny to hide behind—and Tom was outclassed by boys much older and taller. Fanny laughed, not at all sorry she'd dropped Our Jane and soiled her best school dress so it clung damply to her thin legs.

With Keith waiting patiently, in the school rest room I again dried Our Jane off; then I saw Keith to his classroom, pried him loose from Our Jane, then led Our Jane to the first grade. Seated at the table with five other little girls her age, she was the smallest there. What a shame all the other girls had nicer clothes, though not one had such pretty hair, or such a sweet smile. "See you later, darling," I called. Her huge scared eyes stared woefully back at me.

Tom was waiting for me outside Miss Deale's classroom. Together we entered. Every student in there turned to stare at our clothes and our feet; whether we were clean or dirty, it didn't matter. They always snickered. Day in and day out, we had to wear the same clothes, and every day they looked us over scornfully. It always hurt, but we both tried to ignore them as we took our seats near the back of the class.

Seated in front of our classroom was the most wonderful woman in the entire world—the very kind of beautiful lady I hoped and prayed I would be when I grew up. While all her students turned to mock us, Miss Marianne Deale lifted her head to smile her welcome. Her smile couldn't have been warmer if we'd come adorned in the best clothes the world had to offer. She knew we had to walk farther than any of the others, and that Tom and I were responsible for seeing that Keith and Our Jane made it safely to school. She said a million nice things with her eyes. With some other teacher perhaps Tom and I wouldn't have developed such a love for school. She was the one who made our school days a real adventure, a quest for knowledge that would take us, eventually, out of the mountains, out of a poverty-ridden shack, into the bigger, richer world.

Tom and I met eyes, both of us thrilled to be again in the presence of our radiant teacher who had already given us a bit of the world when she inspired in us the love of reading. I was nearer the window than Tom, since looking outside always gave Tom compelling itches to play hooky despite his desire to finish high school and earn a scholarship that would take him through college. If we couldn't win our way to college with good grades, we'd work our way through. We had it all planned. I sighed as I sat. Each day we managed to go to school was another small battle won, taking us closer to our goals. Mine was to be a teacher just like Miss Deale.

My idol's hair was very much the texture and color of Our Jane's, pale reddish blond; her eyes were light blue, her figure slim and curvy. Miss Deale was from Baltimore and spoke with a different accent than any of her students. Truthfully, I thought Miss Deale was absolutely perfect.

Miss Deale glanced at a few empty seats before she looked again at the clock, sighing as she stood up and made the roll call. "Let us all stand and salute the flag," she said, "and before we sit again, we will all say silent prayers of gratitude to be alive and healthy and young, with all the world waiting for us to discover, and to improve."

Boy, if she didn't know how to start the day off right no one did. Just to see her, to be with her, gave both Tom and me reason to feel the future did hold something special for both of us. She had respect for her students, even us in our shabby clothes, but she never gave an inch when it came to order, neatness, politeness.

First we had to hand in our homework. Since our parents couldn't afford to buy our books, we had to use the schoolbooks to complete our homework during school hours. Sometimes this was just too much, especially when the days grew shorter and darkness fell before we reached home.

I was scribbling like mad from the chalkboard when Miss Deale stopped at my desk and whispered, "Heaven, you and Tom please stay after class. I have something to discuss with the two of you."

"Have we done something wrong?" I asked worriedly.

"No, of course not. You always ask that. Heaven, just because I single out you and Tom does not always mean I plan to reprimand you."

The only times Miss Deale seemed to be disappointed in either Tom or me was when we turned sullen and quiet from her questioning about how we lived. We became defensive of both Ma and Pa, not wanting her to know how poorly we were housed, and how pitiful were our meals compared to what we heard the city kids describing.

Lunchtimes in school were the worst. Half the valley kids brought brown lunch bags, and the other half ate in the cafeteria. Only we from the hills brought nothing, not even the change it took to buy a hot dog and a cola drink. In our high mountain home we ate breakfast at dawn, a second meal before darkness drove us into bed. Never lunch.

"What ya think she wants?" Tom asked as we met briefly during the lunch hour, before he went to play ball and I went to skip rope.

"Don't know."

Miss Deale was busy checking papers as Tom and I hung back after school, worried about Keith and Our Jane, who wouldn't know what to do if we weren't there when they were dismissed from their classrooms. "You explain," Tom whispered, and then dashed off to collect Keith and Our Jane. We couldn't depend on Fanny to look out for them.

Suddenly Miss Deale looked up. "Oh, I'm sorry, Heaven . . . have you been standing there long?"

"Only a few seconds," I lied, for it had been more than that. "Tom ran to fetch Our Jane and Keith and bring them here. They'll be afraid if one or the other of us doesn't show up to walk them home."

"What about Fanny? Doesn't she do her share?"

"Well," I began falteringly, trying to be protective of Fanny just because she was my sister, "sometimes Fanny gets distracted and forgets."

Miss Deale smiled. "I realize you have a long walk home, so I won't wait for Tom to return. I've spoken to the school-board members about the two of you, hoping to convince them to allow you to take books home to study, but they are adamant, and said if they give you two special privileges, they will have to give all the students free books. So I am going to allow you to use *my* books."

I stared at her in surprise. "But won't you need them?"

"No . . . there are others I can use. From now on, you can use them, and please take as many books from the library as you care to read in one week. Of course you'll have to respect those books and keep them clean, and return when they're due."

I was so thrilled I could have shouted. "*All* the books we can read in a week? Miss Deale, we won't have arms strong enough to carry so many!"

She laughed, and, strangely, tears came to her eyes. "I could have guessed you'd say something like that." She beamed at Tom as he came in carrying Our Jane, who appeared exhausted, and leading Keith by the hand. "Tom, I think you already have your arms full, and won't be able to carry home books."

Dazed-looking, he stared at her. "Ya mean we kin take home books? Not have to pay for them?"

"That's right, Tom. And pick up a few for Our Jane and Keith, and even Fanny."

"Fanny won't read em," said Tom, his eyes lighting up, "but Heavenly and I sure will!"

We went home that day with five books to read, and four to study. Keith did his bit by carrying two books so neither Tom nor I would refuse to carry Our Jane when she grew tired. It worried me to see how white she grew after only a few steps uphill.

Tagging along behind came Fanny with her boyfriends swarming like bees around the sweetest flower. I had only a devoted brother. Keith lagged about twenty yards behind Fanny and her friends, reluctant to stay with us, but not for the same reasons as Fanny. Keith was in love with nature, with the sights, sounds, and smells of earth, wind, forest, and, most of all, animals. I glanced behind to check, and saw he was so absorbed in studying the bark of a tree he didn't hear me calling his name. "Keith, hurry up!"

He ran a short way before he stopped to pick up a dead bird, examining it with careful hands and observant eyes. If we didn't constantly remind him where he was, he would be left far behind, and never find his way home. Strange how absentminded Keith was, never noticing where he was, only where the objects of his interest grew, lived, or visited.

"Which is heavier, Tom, the books or Our Jane?" I asked, lugging along six.

"The books," he said quickly, setting down our frail sister so I could empty my arms of books and pick up Our Jane.

"What are we gonna do, Ma?" Tom asked when we reached our cabin, where the smoke belched out and reddened our eyes immediately. "She gets so tired, yet she needs to go to school."

Sarah looked deep into Our Jane's tired eyes, touched her pale face, then gently picked up her youngest and carried her into the big bed and laid her down. "What she needs is a doctor, but we kin't afford it. That's what makes me so damned mad with yer pa. He's got money fer booze, an money fer women . . . but none fer doctors to heal his own."

How bitter she sounded.

* * *

Every Sunday night I had nightmares. The same one repeated over and over, until I grew to hate Sunday nights. I dreamed I was all alone in the cabin, snowed in and alone. Every time the dream came I woke up crying.

"It's all right," comforted Tom, crawling over from his place on the floor near the stove and throwing his arms about me after one of my worst nightmares. "I get those bad dreams, too, once in a while. Don't cry, we're all here. Ain't no place for us to go but to school and back, and to church and back. Wouldn't it be nice if we *never* had to come back?"

"Pa doesn't love me like he loves you, Fanny, Keith, and Our Jane," I sobbed, and even that made me feel weak and ashamed. "Am I so ugly and unbearable, Tom? Is that why Pa hates me so?"

"Naw," scoffed Tom, looking embarrassed, "it's somethin about yer hair he dislikes. Heard him tell Sarah that once. But I think yer hair is beautiful, really do. Not so hatefully red as mine, nor so pale as Our Jane's. Or so black and straight as Fanny's. You've got an angel look, even if it is black. I think you are, no doubt, the prettiest girl in all the hills, and Winnerrow as well."

There were many pretty girls in the hills and in the valley. I hugged Tom and turned away. What did Tom know about judging beautiful girls? Already I knew there was a world beyond the hills—a huge, wonderful world I was going to know one day.

"I'm sure glad I'm not a girl," shouted Tom the next day, shaking his head in wonder at a sister who went so easily from frowns to laughter, "made happy by silly compliments!"

"You didn't mean what you said last night?" I asked, crestfallen. "You're not gonna like me either?"

He whirled about and made an ugly face. "See—yer almost as pretty as this face of mine—and I'd marry ya when I grow up—if I could."

"You've been saying that since you learned how to talk."

"How would ya know?" he shouted back.

"Tom, you know Miss Deale doesn't want you to say *yer* or *ya*. You must remember your diction and your grammar. Say instead *you are* or *you*. You must learn to speak properly, Tom."

"Why?" he asked, his green eyes sparkling with mischief. He tugged the red ribbon from my ponytail and set my hair free to blow in the wind. "Nobody round here cares about grammar and diction, not Ma, not Pa, not anybody but *ya* and Miss Deale."

"And who do you love most in the whole wide world?" I asked.

"Love you first, Miss Deale second," Tom said with a laugh. "Can't have you, so I'll settle for Miss Deale. I'm gonna order God t'stop her from growing old and ugly. Then I can catch up and marry her, and she'll read to me every book in the whole wide world."

"You'll read *your own* books, Thomas Luke Casteel!"

"Heavenly," (he was the only one to combine my two names in this flattering way) "the others in the school whisper about you, thinking you know more than you should at your age, and that's my age too. I don't know as much. How come?"

"I get the A's, and you get the B's and C's because you play hooky too much—and I don't play hooky at all." Tom was as thirsty for knowledge as I was, but he had to be like others of his sex once in a while, or fight them each day so they wouldn't call him teacher's pet. When he came back to the cabin from his wild days of fun in the woods or on the river, he'd spend twice as much of his free time poring over the books Miss Deale allowed us to bring home.

Other words Miss Deale had said to Tom and me lingered in my head, to comfort me when my pride was injured, my self-confidence wounded. "Look," she'd said, her pretty face smiling, "you and Tom are my very best students. The very kind every teacher hopes for."

The day Miss Deale gave us permission to take books home, she gave us the world and all it contained.

She gave us treasures beyond belief when she put in our hands her favorite classics. *Alice's Adventures in Wonderland, Through the Looking Glass, Moby Dick, A Tale of Two Cities,* and three Jane Austen novels— and they were all for me. On the days that followed Tom had his own selection, boy books, the Hardy Boys series, seven of them, and just when I'd begun to think he'd select nothing but fun books, he picked up a thick volume of Shakespeare, and that made Miss Deale's blue eyes glow.

"You don't, perchance, hope to be a writer one day, do you, Tom?" she asked.

"Don't know yet what I want to be," he said in his most careful diction, nervous as he always was around someone as educated and pretty as Miss Marianne Deale. "Get all kinds of notions about being a pilot; then next day I want to be a lawyer so I can get to be president one day."

"President of our country, or of a corporation?"

He blushed and looked down at his large feet that kept shuffling about. How awful his shoes looked. They were too big, too old and worn. "I guess President Casteel would sound kinda stupid, wouldn't it?"

"No," she said seriously, "I think it sounds fine. You just set your mind on what you want to be, and take your time about it. If you work to obtain your goal, and realize from the very beginning that nothing valuable comes easily, and still forge ahead, without a doubt you'll reach your goal, whatever it is."

Because of Miss Marianne Deale's generosity (we learned later she put down her own money as deposit so we could take those books home), in books we had the chance to look at pictures of the ancient world, and in books we traveled together to Egypt and India. In books we lived in palaces and strode the narrow crooked lanes in London. Why, we both felt that when we got there eventually, we wouldn't even feel strange in a foreign land, because we'd been there before.

I loved historical novels that brought the past to life much better than history books did. Until I read a novel about George Washington I thought him a dull, stodgy sort of president . . . and to think he'd once been young and handsome enough to cause girls to think he was charming and sexy.

We read books by Victor Hugo, by Alexandre Dumas, and thrilled to know adventures like that were possible, even if they were horrible. We read classics, and we read junk; we read everything, anything that would take us out of that godforsaken cabin in the hills. Maybe if we'd had movies, our own TV set, and other forms of entertainment, we wouldn't have grown so fond of those books Miss Deale allowed us to take home. Or maybe it was only Miss Deale, being clever when she "allowed" only *us* to take home precious, expensive books that she said others wouldn't respect as much as we did.

And that was true enough. We read our books only after we washed our hands.

I suspected that Miss Marianne Deale liked our pa more than a little. God knows she should have had better taste. According to Granny, his "angel" had taught Pa to speak proper English, and with his natural good looks, many an aristocratic woman fell for the charms of Luke Casteel, when he cared enough to be charming.

Every Sunday Pa went with us to church, sat in the midst of his large family, next to Sarah. Petite and dainty Miss Deale sat primly across the aisle and stared at Pa. I could guess she was marveling at Pa's dark good looks, but surely she should consider his lack of knowledge. From all I'd heard from Granny, Pa had quit school before he was finished with the fifth grade.

Sundays rolled around so fast when you didn't have the kind of good clothes you needed, and I was always thinking I'd have a pretty new dress before another showed up; but new garments of any kind were difficult to come by, when Sarah had so much to do. So there we were again, in the very last pew, all in our best rags that others would throw out for trash. We'd stand, and we'd sing along with the best and richest in Winnerrow, along with all the other hillbillies dressed no better or worse than we were, who reveled in coming to church.

In God you had to trust, and in God you had to believe or feel a fool.

On this particular Sunday after church services were over, I tried to keep Our Jane neat while she licked the ice cream just outside the pharmacy, not so far from where Pa had parked his truck. Miss Deale had bought cones for all five of the Casteel children. She stood about ten yards away, staring at where Ma and Pa were having a tiff about something, which meant any moment Pa might whack her, or Sarah would belt him one. I swallowed nervously, wishing Miss Deale would move on, or look elsewhere, but she stood watching, listening, almost transfixed.

It made me wonder what she was thinking, though I never found out.

Not a week passed without her writing at least one note to Pa concerning Tom or me. He was seldom home, and when he was, he couldn't read her neat, small handwriting; even if he could, he wouldn't have responded. Last week she had written:

Dear Mr. Casteel,
  Surely you must be very proud of Tom and Heaven, my two best students. I would like very much, at a time convenient for both of us, to meet you to discuss the possibilities of seeing that they both win scholarships.

Yours sincerely,
Marianne Deale

The very next day she'd asked me, "Didn't you give it to him, Heaven? Surely he wouldn't be so rude as not to respond. He's such a handsome man. You must adore him."

"Sure do adore him," I said cynically. "Sure could chisel him into a fine museum piece. Put him in a cave with a club in his hand, and a red-haired woman at his feet. Yep, that's where Pa belongs, in the *Smithsonian*."

Miss Deale narrowed her sky-blue eyes, stared at me with the oddest expression. "Why, I'm shocked, really shocked. Don't you love your father, Heaven?"

"I just adore him, Miss Deale, I really do. Specially when he's visiting *Shirley's Place*."

"Heaven! You shouldn't say things like that. What can you possibly know about a house of ill-rep—" She broke off and looked embarrassed. Her eyes lowered before she asked, "Does he really go there?"

"Every chance he gets, according to Ma."

The next Sunday Miss Deale didn't look at Pa with admiration; in fact, she didn't cast her eyes his way one time.

But even if Pa had fallen from Miss Deale's grace, she still was waiting for all five of us in the pharmacy while Ma and Pa chatted with their hill friends. Our Jane ran to our teacher with wide-open arms, hurling herself at Miss Deale's pretty blue skirt. "Here I am!" she cried out in delight. "Ready for ice cream!"

"That's not nice, Our Jane," I immediately corrected. "You should wait and allow Miss Deale to offer you ice cream."

Our Jane pouted, and so did Fanny, both with wide, pleading eyes fixed doglike on our teacher. "It's all right, Heaven, really," Miss Deale said, smiling. "Why do you think I come here? I like ice-cream cones, too, and hate to eat one all alone . . . so, come, tell me which flavors you want this week."

It was easy to see Miss Deale pitied us, and wanted to give us treats, at least on Sundays. In a way it wasn't fair, to her or to us, for we were so damned needing of treats, but we also needed to have pride in ourselves. Time after time pride went down in defeat when it came to choosing between chocolate, vanilla, or strawberry. Lord knows how long it would have taken us if there had been more flavors.

Easily Tom could say he wanted vanilla; easily I could say chocolate; but Fanny wanted strawberry, chocolate, *and* vanilla, and Keith wanted what Our Jane was having, and Our Jane couldn't make up her mind. She looked at the man behind the soda fountain, stared wistfully at the huge jars of penny candy, eyed a boy and a girl sitting down to enjoy an ice-cream soda, and hesitated. "Look at her," whispered Fanny; "kin't make up her mind cause she wants it all. Miss Deale, don't give it all t'her—unless ya give it all to us, too."

"Why, of course I'll give Our Jane anything she wants, all three flavors if she can manage a triple cone, and a chocolate candy bar for later, and a bag of candy for all of you to take home. Is there anything else you'd like?"

Fanny opened her mouth wide, as if to blab out all we wanted and needed. I quickly intervened. "You do too much already, Miss Deale. Give Our Jane her small vanilla cone, which will drip all over her before she eats it anyway, and a chocolate bar that she and Keith can share. That's more than enough. We have plenty of what we need at home."

What an ugly face Fanny made behind Miss Deale's back. She groaned, moaned, and made a terrible fuss before Tom hushed her up with his hand over her mouth.

"Perhaps one day you'll all have lunch with me," Miss Deale said casually after a short silence as all of us watched Our Jane and Keith lick their cones with so much rapture it could make you cry. No wonder they loved Sundays so much; Sundays brought them the only treats they'd known so far in life.

We'd no sooner finished our cones than Ma and Pa showed up in the doorway of the drugstore. "C'mon," called Pa, "leaving for home now—unless you want to walk."

Then he spied Miss Deale, who was hurriedly buying penny candy that Our Jane and Fanny were selecting with the greatest possible care, pointing to this piece, that piece. He strode toward us, wearing a cream-colored suit that Granny said my mother had bought for him on their two-week honeymoon in Atlanta. If I hadn't known differently, I would have thought Pa a handsome gentleman with culture, the way he looked in that suit.

"You must be the teacher my kids talk about all the time," he said to her, putting out his hand. She pulled away, as if all my information about his visiting *Shirley's Place* had killed her admiration for him.

"Your eldest son and daughter are my best students," she said coolly, "as you should know since I've written you many times about them." She didn't mention Fanny or Keith or Our Jane, since they weren't in her class. "I hope you are proud of both Heaven and Tom."

Pa looked totally astounded as he glanced at Tom, then flicked his eyes my way. For two solid years Miss Deale had been writing him notes to tell him how bright she thought we were. The Winnerrow school was so delighted with what Miss Deale was doing for deprived hill kids (sometimes considered half-wits) they were allowing her to "advance" along with us, from grade to grade.

"Why, that's a very nice thing to hear on a beautiful Sunday afternoon," said Pa, trying to meet her eyes and hold them. She refused to look at him, as if afraid once she did, she couldn't look away. "I always wanted to go on to acquire a higher education myself, but never had the chance," extolled Pa.

"Pa," said I, speaking up loud and sharp, "we've decided to walk home . . . so you and Ma can leave and forget about us."

"Don't wanna walk home!" cried Our Jane. "Wanna ride!"

Near the doorway of the store Sarah stood watching with her eyes narrowed suspiciously. Pa bowed slightly to Miss Deale and said, "It's been a pleasure to meet you, Miss Deale." He leaned to sweep Our

Jane up in one arm, lifted Keith with the other, and out the door he strode, seeming to everyone in the store the only cultivated, charming Casteel the world had ever seen. Not one pair of lips was left together, all gaping as if at a miracle not to be believed.

And again, despite all I'd said to warn her, something admiring lit up the gullible sky-blue eyes of my teacher.

It was a rare kind of perfect day, with birds flying overhead, and autumn leaves softly falling. I was like Keith, caught up in nature. I only half heard what Tom was saying until I saw Fanny's dark eyes widen with surprise. "NO! Yer wrong. Weren't Heaven that good-looking new boy was staring at! It was me!"

"What boy?" I asked.

"The son of the new pharmacist who's come to run the drugstore," explained Tom. "Didn't ya notice the name Stonewall? He was in the store when Miss Deale bought us the cones, an by gosh, he sure seemed taken by ya, Heavenly, he sure did."

"Liar!" yelled Fanny. "Nobody ever stares at Heaven when I'm there, they don't!"

Tom and I ignored Fanny and her screaming voice. "Heard tell he's gonna be comin t'our school tommorra," Tom continued. "Made me feel funny t'way he looked at ya," he went on in an embarrassed way. "Sure will hate t'day when ya marry up an we're not close anymore."

"We'll always be close," I said quickly. "No boy is ever going to convince me I need him more than I need an education."

Yet, in bed that night, curled up on the floor near Ole Smokey, I stared through the dimness to where I could imagine seeing a brand-new pretty blue dress, never worn by anyone else, hanging on a wall nail. Foolishly, as only the young can believe, I thought that if I wore beauty it would somehow change the world about me. I woke up knowing I wanted a new dress more than anything—and wondering, too, if that new boy would like me even if I never had anything new to wear.

3

Logan Stonewall

Tom, Fanny, Our Jane, Keith, and I had hardly hit the schoolyard on Monday morning when Tom was pointing out the new boy, the very one he'd spotted staring at me in the drugstore. When I turned to look toward the ball field where the boys were already playing, my breath caught. He stood out from all the others, this new boy in better clothes than the valley boys wore. The morning sun behind him put a sort of fiery halo above his dark hair, so I couldn't really see his face that was in shadow, yet I knew from the way he stood, tall and straight, not slouched like some mountain boys who were ashamed of their height, that I liked him right from the beginning. It was silly, of course, to like a complete stranger just because he had a certain kind of confidence that wasn't arrogance, only visible strength and poise. I glanced at Tom, and knew why I immediately liked a boy I'd never seen before. Logan and Tom both had the same kind of natural grace and ease with themselves that came from knowing who and what they were. I looked again at Tom. How could he stride so proudly beside me when he was a Casteel?

I longingly wished I had his poise, his confidence, his ability to accept, though I might have if I'd had my father's love—as he had.

"He's staring at you again," whispered Tom, giving me a sharp nudge, causing Fanny to shrill in her too-loud voice, "He is NOT starin at Heaven! He's starin at *ME!*"

Fanny embarrassed me again. But if that new boy heard, he didn't show any signs. He stood out like a Christmas tree in his sharply creased gray flannel slacks and his bright green sweater worn over a white shirt and a gray-and-green-striped tie. He had on regular Sunday hard shoes, polished to a shine. All the valley boys wore jeans and knit tops, and sneakers. No one, ever, came to school dressed up as Logan Stonewall was.

Did he see us staring? He must have, for suddenly, alarmingly, he came our way! What would I say to someone so dressed up? I tried to shrink into my shoes. Each step that brought him closer put panic in my heart. I wasn't ready yet to meet anyone wearing gray flannel slacks (something I wouldn't have known if Miss Deale hadn't once worn a gray suit to school of the same fabric; she was always trying to educate me on fabrics, clothes, and such). I tried to scurry away with Keith and Our Jane before he saw the shabbiness of my worn, colorless dress with the hem half out and my scuffed, almost soleless shoes, but Our Jane resisted.

"Don't feel good," she wailed. "Wanna go home, Hev-lee."

"You can't go home again," I whispered. "You'll never finish first grade if you stay out sick all the time. Maybe I can bring you and Keith a sandwich this noon—and some milk."

"Tuna fish!" Keith sang out happily, and with thoughts of half a tuna fish sandwich, Our Jane let go of my hand and with slow small steps entered the classroom where all the first graders seemed to have fun—all but Our Jane.

I hurried after my two charges, but not so fast that Logan Stonewall didn't catch up in the hall just outside the first grade. I turned to see him shaking hands with Tom. Logan was good-looking in the kind of way I'd seen in books and magazines, like someone with years and years of cultured background that had given him what none of us in the hills had—quality. His nose was slender and straight, his lower lip much fuller and more shapely than his upper one, and even from six feet away I could see his dark blue eyes smiling warmly at me. His jaw was squarish and strong, and a dimple in his left cheek played in and out as he smiled my way. His demeanor of assurance made me feel awkward, afraid I'd do and say everything wrong, and then he'd turn for sure to Fanny, and if she said and did *everything* wrong, it wouldn't matter. Boys always fell for Fanny.

"Hi there, stranga," greeted Fanny, skipping forward and smiling up into his face. Fanny had never bothered to accompany Our Jane or Keith to their respective classrooms before. "Yer t'best-lookin boy I eva did see."

"That's Fanny, my sister," explained Tom.

"Hi, Fanny . . ." But Logan Stonewall didn't do more than glance at Fanny. He waited for Tom to introduce me.

"And this is my sister, Heaven Leigh." There was so much pride in Tom's voice, as if he didn't see my shapeless ugly dress, or think I had any reason to be ashamed of my shoes. "And that small girl who's peeking out of the first-grade door is my youngest sister, who we call Our Jane, and across the hall, that amber-haired boy grinning at us is my brother, Keith. Go sit down, Keith; you too, Our Jane."

How could Tom act so natural around a boy as citified and well dressed as Logan Stonewall? I was all aflutter with excitement as those smiling sapphire eyes looked at me as I'd never been looked at before. "What a pretty name," said Logan, his eyes meeting mine. "It suits you very well. I don't think I've ever seen more heavenly blue eyes."

"I've got *black* eyes," shouted Fanny, stepping in front of me to block his view. "Anybody kin have blue eyes . . . like Heaven's. I like yer color blue betta."

"Cornflower-blue eyes, Miss Deale calls the color of Heavenly's eyes," informed Tom with evident pride, "and there isn't another girl fer ten miles around with eyes that same shade of blue that *I* call heavenly blue."

"I believe you . . ." murmured Logan Stonewall, still staring at me.

I was only thirteen; he couldn't have been more than fifteen, or at the most sixteen, yet our eyes seemed to cling and strike a gong that would resound throughout the rest of our lives.

It was only the school bell ringing.

I was saved from having to say anything by the bustling scurry of kids rushing to their homerooms and seating themselves before the teacher came in. Tom was laughing when he sat behind his desk. "Heavenly, I never saw you turn so many shades of red. Logan Stonewall is just another boy. Better dressed than most, and better looking, but only another boy."

He wasn't feeling what I was feeling, yet he narrowed his eyes and stared at me in an odd way, until he turned and bowed his head, and I bowed mine.

Miss Deale came in, and before I could figure out what I'd say to Logan when next I saw him, it was lunchtime. I had to keep my promise about the sandwich and milk. I sat at my desk as all the others left for lunch. Miss Deale looked up. "Why, Heaven, do you want to speak with me about something?"

I wanted to plead for a sandwich to give to Keith and Our Jane, but somehow I just couldn't. Standing, I smiled and hurried out, staring at the floor of the corridor, just praying to find a quarter . . . and that's when Logan's gray shoes came into view. "I waited for you to come out with Tom." He looked earnest even as his eyes still smiled. "Will you have lunch with me?"

"I never eat lunch."

My answer made him frown. "Everybody eats lunch. So come along, and we'll have hamburgers, shakes, and french fries."

Did that mean he was going to pay for my lunch as well as his own? My pride reared high. "I have to take care of Our Jane and Keith during the lunch hour . . ."

"Okay, they're invited, too," he said nonchalantly, "and I might as well include Tom and Fanny, in case you're thinking of them."

"We can afford to pay for our own lunches."

For a second he didn't seem to know what to say. He shot me another quick glance, then shrugged. "All right, if you want it that way."

Oh, gosh . . . I didn't want it that way! But my pride was as high as any mountain in the Willies.

He walked beside me toward the lower-grade classrooms. Any moment, I thought, he'd regret his invitation. Both Our Jane and Keith were waiting near the first grade, each seeming terribly anxious before Our Jane came flying into my arms, half sobbing. "Kin we eat now, Hev-lee? My tummy hurts."

About the same time, Keith began jabbering about the tuna fish sandwich I'd promised. "Did Miss Deale send us another one?" he asked, his small face bright and eager. "Is it Monday today? Did she send us milk?"

I tried to smile at Logan, who was taking all of this in and looking thoughtfully at Our Jane, then at Keith. Finally he turned to me and smiled. "If you'd rather have tuna fish sandwiches, maybe the cafeteria will have a few left if we hurry there."

There wasn't anything I could do now that Keith and Our Jane began running toward the cafeteria like foxes on the scent of chickens. "Heaven," said Logan with earnestness, "I've never allowed a girl to pay for her own lunch when I invite her. Please allow me to treat you."

We no sooner entered the cafeteria than I could hear the whispers and speculations—what was Logan doing with the crummy Casteels? Tom was there, as if Logan had invited him earlier, and for some reason that made me feel much better. Now I could smile and help Our Jane sit at a long table. Keith crowded as close to her side as possible and looked around shyly. "Everybody still want tuna fish sandwiches and milk?" asked Logan, who had asked Tom to go with him to help bring back our lunches. Our Jane and Keith stuck to their preference, while I agreed to try the hamburger and cola drink. I looked around while Tom and Logan were gone, trying to see Fanny. She wasn't in the cafeteria. That gave me another worry. Fanny had her own ways of gaining a meal.

All about us, people kept whispering, not seeming to care if I heard or not. "What's he doing with *her*? She's just a hillbilly. And his family has to be rich."

Logan Stonewall drew many an eye as he came back with Tom, both of them smiling and happy to deliver tuna sandwiches, hamburgers, french fries, and shakes, and milk too. Both Our Jane and Keith were overwhelmed by all the food, wanting to sip my shake, taste my hamburger, try the french fries, so I ended up with the milk and Our Jane drank my cola, closing her eyes tight with delight. "I'll buy you another," Logan offered, but I refused to allow him to do that. He'd already done more than enough.

I found out he really was fifteen. He smiled with pleasure when I whispered my age. He had to know my birthdate, as if that mattered, and it seemed it did; his mother believed in astrology. He told me how he'd managed to have himself assigned to the study hall where I sat each day to do my homework. I always tried to finish it there so I could take novels home instead of schoolbooks.

For the first time in my life I had a real boyfriend, one who didn't presume I was easy just because I lived in the hills. Logan didn't mock my clothes or my background. However, from day one Logan made enemies in our school, because he was different, too good-looking, his clothes too "citified." His poise was too annoying, his family too rich, his father too educated, his mother too haughty. It was presumed by the other boys he was a sissy. Even that first day Tom said that one day Logan would have to prove himself. The other boys tried all their silly, but not so harmless, pranks. They put tacks in his shoes in the gym; they tied his shoelaces together so he'd be late to his next class after gym; they put glue in his shoes, and backed away when he grew angry and threatened to beat the culprit.

Before his first week was over Logan was placed two grades above Tom's and my level. By that time he, too, wore jeans and plaid shirts, but more expensive designer jeans, and shirts that came from some place in New England called Bean's. He still stuck out despite the clothes. He was too soft-spoken and polite when others were rude, loud, and rough. He refused to act like the other boys, refused to use their foul language.

* * *

On Friday I skipped study hall, much to Tom's amazement. He couldn't stop questioning me as we strolled home in bright September sunshine. It was still warm enough so Tom could dive into the river, clothes and all—though he did pull off his worn sneakers. I fell on the grassy bank with Our Jane cuddled near my side, and Keith gazed up at a squirrel perched on a tree limb. I said without thought to Tom as he splashed around, "I wish to God I'd been born with silvery-gold hair"; then I bit down hard on my tongue from the way Tom turned to stare at me. He shook his head to throw off the water as a dog would. Fortunately, Fanny had dropped far, far behind as we trudged home, and even from where we were, we could hear her faint lilting giggles coming over the hills and through the woods.

"Heavenly, do ya know now?" Tom asked in the oddest hesitant whisper.

"Know what?"

"Why ya want silvery-blond hair when what ya got is fine, jus fine?"

"Just a crazy wish, I guess."

"Now wait a minute, Heavenly. If ya an me are gonna stay friends, an more than just brother and sister, ya gotta be on the square. Do ya or don't ya know who had that silvery-gold color of hair?"

"Do *you* know?" I tried to evade.

"Sure I know." He came out of the water, and we headed toward home. "Always have known," he said softly, "since t'first time I went t'school. Boys in the rest room told me about Pa's first city wife from Boston with her long silvery-gold hair, an how everybody jus knew she couldn't last livin up in t'hills. Jus kept on hopin *ya*'d neva find out, an stop thinking I was so durn wonderful. Cause I ain't that wonderful. Got no Boston blood in me, no rich genes that's been cultured an civilized—like you got. I got one hundred percent dumb hillbilly genes, despite what you and Miss Deale think."

It hurt to hear him say such things. "Don't you talk like that, Thomas Luke Casteel! You heard Miss Deale talk on that subject the other day. The most brilliant parents in the world often give birth to idiots . . . and idiots can give birth to genius! Didn't she say that it was nature's way to equalize? Didn't she say that sometimes when parents are too smart, they seem to use up all the brain fodder on themselves and leave none of it for their children? Remember all she said about nothing in nature being predictable? The only reason you don't get all the A's I do is because you play hooky too much! You must keep on believing what Miss Deale said about all of us being unique, born for a purpose only we can fulfill. Thomas Luke, you keep remembering that."

"You keep remembering it too," he said, gruffly, turning to give me a hard look, "and stop crying out in the night to be different than what you are. I like what you are now." His green eyes were soft and luminous in the dim shade of the piny woods. "You're my fair gypsy sister, ten times more important to me than my whole sister, Fanny, who doesn't really give a damn about anybody but herself. She doesn't love me as you do, and I can't love her as much as I can love you. You're the only sister I got who can put her mind on a star in another universe." He looked so sad then, making me hurt inside.

"Tom, I'm gonna cry if you say one more thing! It makes me ache to think someday you might go away and I'll never see you again."

He shook his head, making his red hair ruffle in layers. "I'd never go anywhere you didn't want me to go, Heavenly. It's you and me together, all our lives through. You know, like they say in books, through thick and thin, through rain and snow . . . through the dark of night."

Laughing, I answered, "That's the mail, silly." Tears were in my eyes as I reached to take his hand and squeeze it. "Let's just promise never, so help us God, will we ever go separate ways, or be angry with one another, or feel differently about each other than we feel now."

He had me then in his arms, holding me as if I were made of spun glass and any second I'd break. He choked when he said, "Someday you'll get married—I know you say you won't, but Logan Stonewall is already looking with calf eyes at you."

"How can he love me when he doesn't know me?"

His face bowed into my hair. "All he needs to do is look at your face, your eyes—that's enough. Everything about you is written on your face, shining in your eyes."

I pulled away and brushed at my tears. "Pa never sees what you do, does he?"

"Why do you let him hurt you so much?"

"Oh, Tom . . . !" I wailed, falling into his arms and really beginning to cry. "How am I ever going to have any confidence in myself when my own father can't stand to look at me? There must be something evil he sees in me that makes him hate me."

He stroked my hair, my back, and there were tears in his eyes when I looked, as if my pain were his. "Someday Pa's gonna find out he don't hate ya, Heavenly. I know that day's comin soon."

I yanked away.

"No, it's not ever coming! You know it as much as I know it. Pa thinks I killed his angel by being born, and in a thousand years he won't forgive me! And if you want to know what I think, I think my mother was damned lucky to escape him! For sooner or later he'd have been as mean to her as he is to Sarah now!"

We were both shaken by this kind of frankness. He pulled me back and tried to smile, but he only looked sad. "Pa doesn't love Ma, Heavenly. He's miserable with Ma. From all I've heard, he did love your mother. He married mine only because she was pregnant with me, and he tried for once to do the right thing."

"Because Granny made him do the right thing!" I flared with hot bitterness.

"Nobody kin make Pa do what he sets his mind against, remember that."

"I'm remembering," I said, with thoughts of how Pa refused to let himself really look at me.

Again it was Monday, and we were all in school. Miss Deale expounded on the joys of reading Shakespeare's plays and sonnets, but I was dying to get on to study hall.

"Heaven," said Miss Deale, her baby-blue eyes fixed on me, "are you listening, or daydreaming?"

"Listening!"

"What was the poem I just discussed?"

For the life of me I couldn't remember one word she'd said in the last half hour, and that was not my way. Oh, I had to stop thinking of that darn Logan. Yet, when I was in the study hall and Logan was seated to my right, I began feeling the strangest kind of sensations whenever our eyes met. His hair wasn't a true brown or black, but a blend with auburn highlights, with a little gold where the summer sun had streaked it. Really, I had to force myself not to glance his way again, since every time I did he was staring at me.

Logan smiled before he whispered: "Who in the world was ingenious enough to give you such a name as Heaven? I've never known of anyone with that name before."

I had to swallow twice so I could say it just right. "My father's first wife named me minutes after I was born, and then Leigh because that was *her* Christian name. Granny said she wanted to give me something *uplifting,* and Heaven is about as uplifting as a name can get."

"It's the most beautiful name I have ever heard. Where is your mother now?"

"Dead in a cemetery," I said bluntly, forgetting to be charming and coquettish, something Fanny never forgot. "She died minutes after I was born, and because she did, my father can't forgive me for taking her life."

"Absolutely no talking in this room!" shouted Mr. Prakins. "The next one who speaks will receive fifteen hours' detention after school!"

Logan's eyes softened with compassion and sympathy. And the minute Mr. Prakins left the room, Logan again whispered: "I'm sorry it happened that way, but you said it wrong. Your mother isn't dead in a cemetery—she's passed into the great beyond, into a better place, into heaven."

"If there is a heaven or a hell, I've been thinking it's right here on earth."

"How old are you anyway, one hundred and twenty?"

"You know I'm thirteen!" I flared angrily. "Just feeling two hundred and fifty today."

"Why?"

"Because it's better than feeling thirteen, that's why!"

Logan cleared his throat, glanced at Mr. Prakins, who kept his eyes on us through a glass wall, and risked another whisper. "Would it be all right if I walked you home today? I've never talked to anyone as old as two hundred and fifty, and you've got my curiosity aroused. I'd sure like to hear what you have to say."

I nodded, feeling a bit sick as well as exuberant. Now I'd tricked myself into a situation that might disappoint him with only ordinary answers. What did I know about wisdom, old age, or anything else?

Still, he showed up on the edge of the schoolyard, where all the boys walking home with hill girls waited until their choices showed up. And there stood Fanny.

She spun about, flinging her hair over her face, then tossed it back, whipping around to make it fan out in a circle; grinning broadly when she saw Logan, as if she thought he was coming for her. A short distance from Fanny stood Tom and Keith. Tom seemed surprised to find Logan waiting near our trail. Ours was just a faint path through the underbrush that led to the woods, and eventually to only our cabin nearest the sky. The minute Fanny saw Logan and me heading for our trail she let out a whoop so loud and embarrassing I wanted to drop dead.

"Heaven, what ya doin with that new boy? Ya know ya don't like boys! Ain't ya done said a million times yer neva gonna be nothin but a dried-up ole schoolteacher?"

I tried to ignore Fanny, though my face turned beet-red. What kind of sisterly loyalty was she showing anyway? I knew better than to expect tact. I tried to smile at Logan. It was always best to ignore Fanny, if possible.

Logan stared at her with disapproval, as did Tom.

"Fanny, please don't say one more word," I said uncomfortably. "Just run along home, and start the wash for a change."

"I neva have t'walk home with only a brotha," Fanny said to Logan in a sneering way before she turned on her most brilliant smile. "Boys don't like Heaven, they always like me. Ya'll like me, too. Ya wanna hold my hand?"

Logan glanced at me, at Tom, and then said seriously to Fanny, "Thank you, but right now I'm intent on seeing Heaven home, and hearing all that she has to tell me."

"Ya should hear me sing!"

"Another time, Fanny, I'll listen to you sing."

"Our Jane sings . . ." said Keith faintly.

"She sure does!" exclaimed Tom, seizing Fanny by the arm and pulling her along with him. "Come along, Keith. Our Jane is home waiting for you." That's all Keith needed to hear to hurry after Tom, for Our Jane had missed school today due to another tummyache and a fever.

Fanny broke away from Tom and came running back to scowl and yell before she stuck out her tongue. "Yer selfish, Heaven Leigh Casteel! Mean, skinny, an ugly too! Hate yer hair! Hate yer silly name! *Hate yer everythin! I do!* Ya just wait till I tell Pa what yer doin! Pa won't like ya fer takin charity from some strange city boy who pities ya—eatin his hamburgers an stuff, an teachin Our Jane an Keith t'beg!"

Oh, now Fanny was at her worst, jealous, spiteful, and apt to do just what she threatened, and Pa would punish me!

"Fanny," called Tom, running to catch her. "You can have my new watercolor set if you keep yer trap shut about Logan taking all of us to lunch . . ."

Instantly Fanny smiled. "All right! I want that colorin book Miss Deale gave ya, too! Don't know why she don't give me nothin!"

"You don't know why?" sneered Tom, giving her what she asked for even though I knew he wanted that paint set and that coloring book so much it hurt. He'd never had a box of brand-new watercolors before, or a coloring book about Robin Hood. Robin Hood, this year, was his favorite hero from a book. "When you learn to behave yerself in t'cloakroom, maybe Miss Deale will be generous with you, for a change."

Again I could have died from embarrassment!

Crying, Fanny fell down on the mountain trail that was gradually spiraling upward through tall trees that appeared to touch the sky. She pounded her small tough fists on the grass, screamed because a stone was hidden there and it drew blood. Sucking on that, she sat up and stared at Tom with huge pleading eyes. "Don't tell Pa, please, please."

Tom promised.

I promised. Though I still wanted to vanish and not see Logan's wide eyes drinking all this in, as if never in his life had he witnessed such a stupid, ill-mannered scene. I tried to avoid meeting his eyes until he smiled and I saw understanding. "You sure got one family that might age you dramatically *inside*—outside, you look younger than springtime."

"Yer stealin words from a song!" yelled Fanny. "Ya ain't supposed t'court a gal with song words!"

"Oh, dry up!" ordered Tom, seizing her arm again and running so she had to race with him or have her arm pulled off. This gave me my chance to be alone with Logan.

Keith was again bringing up the rear of our little parade, though he'd stopped to stare up at a robin, mesmerized and not likely to move for at least ten minutes—if the bird didn't fly away.

"Your sister is really something else," said Logan when finally we were as good as alone on the trail. Keith was far behind us and so quiet. I kept my thoughts to myself. Valley boys thought all hill girls were easy for any boy hoping to experiment with sex. As young as she was, Fanny had caught the hill spirit and its easy sexuality that came much earlier than it did in low places. Perhaps it was due to all the copulating we saw going on in our yards and in our one- or two-room shacks. There was no need for sex education in our hills; sex hit you in the face the moment you knew a man from a woman.

Logan cleared his throat to remind me he was there. "I'm ready to hear all your years of accumulated wisdom. I'd take notes, but I find it difficult to write while walking. But next time, I could bring along a tape recorder."

"You're making fun of me," I complained before I justified myself. "We happen to live with our grandparents. Grandpa never says anything that's not absolutely necessary, and seldom does he find words necessary. My granny rambles on and on incessantly, talking about how good all the old times were, and how rotten things are now. My stepmother fusses and fumes because she's got more than she can do . . . and sometimes when I go home to that cabin, and face up to all the problems, I feel not two hundred and fifty but one thousand years old—only without any wisdom from living that long."

"Hey," he said with a smile, "a girl who knows how to talk honestly. I like that. I understand. I'm an only child, and I've grown up with uncles, aunts, and grandparents, too, so I do understand. But you've got the edge on me with two brothers and two sisters."

"Is it an edge of advantage or disadvantage?"

"Whatever you make it. From my point of view, Heaven Leigh, it's an advantage to have a large family so you're never lonely. Lots of time I'm lonely, wishing I had brothers, sisters. I think Tom's great, loads of fun and a good sport; and Keith and Our Jane are beautiful kids."

"And Fanny, what do you think of her?"

He blushed and looked uncomfortable before he spoke slowly, cautiously. "I think she's going to grow up to be an exotic beauty."

"That's all you think?" He had to know about Fanny and all her promiscuous ways with the boys in the cloakroom.

"No, it's not all I think. I think of all the girls I've ever seen, and all the girls I hope to see, the one I see named Heaven Leigh is the one with the potential to be more beautiful than any other. I think this Heaven is exceptionally honest and forthright . . . so if you don't mind, and I hope you don't, I'd like to walk you home every day from now on."

I felt so happy! Soaring high, laughing before I ran on ahead and called back, "Logan, see you tomorrow. Thanks for seeing me home."

"But we haven't reached there yet!" he called, taken aback by my abrupt flight.

I couldn't let him see where we lived, how we lived. Why, he'd never want to speak to me again if he really knew our circumstances. "On another day, a better day, I'll invite you in," I called, standing at the edge of a clearing in the dappled sunlight. He was across the small bridge covering our narrow stream. Behind him was a field of wild yellow grass, and the sun had snagged in his hair and eyes. If I live to be a thousand, I'll never forget the way he smiled, then waved and called back, "Okay. I've staked my claim. Heaven Leigh Casteel is, from this day on, mine."

All the rest of the way home I sang to myself, happier than I'd ever been, forgetting all about my promise to myself that I positively would not fall in love until I was thirty.

"Yer lookin mighty happy," commented Sarah, glancing up from the washboard with a weary sigh. "Day gone good?"

"Oh, yes, Ma, it went fine."

Fanny stuck her head out of the cabin door. "Ma, Heaven's gone an got herself a valley boyfriend—an ya know what kind *they* are."

Again Sarah sighed. "Heaven, ya ain't gone an let him . . . have ya?"

"Ma!" I cried out in protest. "You know I wouldn't!"

"She would too!" screamed Fanny from the doorway. "She's shameful in t'cloakroom with t'boys, really shameful!"

"Why, you big liar!" I started to go for her, but Tom shoved Fanny out onto the porch, where she fell and immediately started howling. "Ma, it's not Heavenly who carries on. Fanny's t'most indecent-acting girl in t'entire school, an that's sayin a whole lot."

"Yeah," muttered Sarah, turning the wash over to me, "sure would be sayin a lot. Guess I know who's t'one who's t'worst, without yer havin t'tell me. It's my Indian Fanny with her wild devil ways, her flirtin eyes that's gonna get her inta t'same mess I'm in soona or lata. Heaven, ya stick t'yer guns, an say no, NO, NO! . . . Now take off that dress, an get t'work on t'wash. Ain't feelin so good lately. Jus don't understand why I'm tired all t'time."

"Maybe you should see a doctor, Ma."

"Will, when they got free ones."

I finished the wash, and with Tom's willing help hung the clothes up to dry. When we finished it looked like a yard rag sale. "Ya like Logan Stonewall?" asked Tom.

"Yes, I think so . . ." I answered, blushing several times.

He looked sad, as if Logan might put a wall of difference between us, when nothing could, not ever.

"Tom, maybe Miss Deale will give you another watercoloring set . . ."

"It doesn't matter. I'm not gonna be an artist. Probably won't end up much of nothing, if you're not there to help me believe in myself."

"But we're always going to be together, Tom. Didn't we swear to stay together through thick and thin?"

His green eyes looked happier, then shaded. "But that was before Logan Stonewall walked you home."

"You walk Sally Browne home sometimes, don't you?"

"Once," he admitted, blushing, as if he didn't know I knew about that, "but only because she's something like you are, not silly and giggly."

I didn't know what to say then. Sometimes I wished to be like the other girls, full of silly laughter about nothing at all, and not always so burdened down with responsibilities that made me feel older than my years.

Later that same night I gave Fanny a good scolding about her behavior and the consequences. She didn't have to explain again. Already she'd confessed to me, on a rare occasion when we were like sisters needing each other, that she hated school and the time it took from having fun with the other girls her age. Even at the tender age of not quite twelve, she wanted to make out with much older boys who might have ignored her but for her insistence. She liked the boys to undress her, to slip their hands into her panties and start those exciting sensations only they could give her. It had distressed me to hear her say that, and distressed me even more to *witness* how she acted in the cloakroom with boys.

"Won't do it no more, really I won't let them," promised Fanny, who was sleepy and agreeable to any suggestion, even an order from me to stop.

The very next day, despite Fanny's vow, it happened all over again when I went to Fanny's class to pick her up and head her back home. I forced my way into the cloakroom and tore Fanny away from a pimply-faced valley boy.

"Yer sister ain't stuck-up and prissy like ya!" the boy hissed.

And all the time I could hear Fanny giggling.

"Ya leave me alone!" Fanny screamed as I dragged her away. "Pa treats ya like yer invisible, so naturally ya kin't know how good it feels t'like boys and men, and if ya keep on pesterin me not t'do this an not t'do that, I'm gonna let em do *anythin* they want—an I won't give a damn if ya tell Pa. He loves me an hates *ya* anyway!"

That stung, and if Fanny hadn't come running to throw her slender arms about my neck, crying and pleading for my forgiveness, I might have forever turned my back on such a hateful, insensitive sister. "I'm sorry, Heaven, really sorry. I love ya, I do, I do. I just like what *they* do. Kin't help it, Heaven. Don't want t'help it. Ain't it natural, Heaven, ain't it?"

"Yer sister Fanny is gonna be a whore," said Sarah later, her voice dull and without hope as she pulled bed pallets from boxes for us to put on the floor. "Ya kin't do nothin bout Fanny, Heaven. Ya jus look out fer yerself."

Pa came home only three or four times a week, as if timing how long our food would last, and he'd come in bringing as much as he could afford to buy at one time. Just last week I'd heard Granny telling Sarah that Grandpa had taken Pa out of school when he was only eleven in order to put him to work in the coal mines—and Pa had hated that so much he'd run away and hadn't come back until Grandpa found him hiding out in a cave. "And Toby swore to Luke he'd neva have t'go down inta them mines agin, but he sure would make more money iffen he did once in a while . . ."

"Don't want him down there," Sarah said dully. "Ain't right t'make a man do somethin he hates. Even iffen t'Feds catch him soona or lata peddlin moonshine, he'd die fore he'd let em lock him up. Ratha see him dead than shut up like his brothas . . ."

It made me look at the coal miners differently than I had before.

Many of them lived beyond Winnerrow, scattered a bit higher on the hills, but not really in the mountains like we were. Often at night when the wind was still, I'd lie awake and think I could hear the pickaxes of those dead miners who'd been trapped underground, all trying to dig their way out of the very mountain that was topped by our own cabin.

"Can you hear them, Tom?" I asked the night when Sarah went to bed crying because Pa hadn't been home in five days. "Chop, chop, chop . . . don't you hear em?"

Tom sat up and looked around. "Don't hear nothin."

But I did. Faint and far away, chop chop chop. Even fainter, help help help! I got up and went out to the porch, and the sound was louder. I shivered, then called to Tom. Together we drifted to where the sound came from—and there was Pa in the moonlight, shirtless and sweaty, swinging an ax to fell another tree so we could have firewood, come this winter.

For the first time in my life I looked at him with a kind of wondering pity. Help help help echoed in my brain—had it been him crying out, had it been? What kind of man was he anyway, that he would come in the night to chop wood without even stopping in the cabin to say hello to his wife and children?

"Pa," called out Tom, "I kin help ya do that."

Pa didn't pause in his swing that sent wood chips flying, just yelled: "Go back and get your rest, boy. Tell your ma I've got a new job that keeps me busy all day, and the only spare time I have is at night, and that's why I'm chopping down trees for you to split into logs later on." He didn't say a word to indicate he saw me beside Tom.

"What kind of job have ya got now, Pa?"

"Workin on a railroad, boy. Learnin how t'drive one of them big engines. Pulling coal on the C and O . . . come down t'the tracks tomorrow about seven and you'll see me pull out . . ."

"Ma sure would like t'see ya, Pa."

I thought he paused then, the ax hesitating before it slammed again into the pine. "She'll see me . . . when she sees me." And that was all he said before I turned and ran back to the cabin.

On my coarse pillow stuffed with chicken feathers I cried. Didn't know why I cried, except all of a sudden I was sorry for Pa—and even sorrier for Sarah.

4

Sarah

Another Christmas came and went without real gifts to make it memorable. We were given only small necessities like toothbrushes and soap. If Logan hadn't given me a gold bracelet set with a small sapphire I wouldn't even have remembered that Christmas. I had nothing to give him but a cap I'd knitted.

"It's a terrific cap," he said, pulling it down over his head. "I've always wanted a bright red hand-knitted cap. Thank you very much, Heaven Leigh. Sure would be nice if you'd knit me a red scarf for my birthday that's coming up in March."

It surprised me that he wore the cap. It was much too large, and he didn't seem to notice that I'd dropped a couple of stitches and that the wool had been handled so much it was more than a bit soiled. No sooner was Christmas over than I started on the scarf. I had it finished by Valentine's Day. "It's too late for a red scarf in March," I said with a smile when he wrapped it around his neck—and he was still wearing that red cap to school every day. If anything could have made me like him more than his devotion to that awful red cap, I don't know what it would have been.

I turned fourteen in late February. Logan gave me another gift, a lovely white sweater set that made Fanny's dark eyes blaze with envy. The day after my birthday Logan met me after school where the mountain trail ended; he walked me to the clearing before the cabin, and every day after until it was spring. Keith and Our Jane learned to love and trust him, and all the time Fanny plied her charms, but Logan continued to ignore her. Oh, falling in love at age fourteen was so exhilarating I could have laughed and cried at the same time, I was so happy.

The glorious spring days sailed too quickly by now that love was in the air, and I wanted time for romancing, but Granny and Sarah were relentless in their demands for my time. There was planting to do as well as all the other chores that were my duty, but not Fanny's. Without the large garden in the back of our cabin we wouldn't have been as well nourished as we were. We had cabbages, potatoes, cucumbers, carrots, collards for the fall, and turnip greens, and, best of all, tomatoes.

On Sundays I looked forward to seeing Logan again in church. When we were in church and he was seated across the aisle from me, meeting and holding my eyes and sending so many silent messages, how could I help but forget the desperate poverty of our lives? Logan shared so much of what was in his father's pharmacy with us; small things he thought commonplace filled all of us with delight, like shampoo in a bottle, perfume we could spray on, and a razor and blades for Tom, who began to grow more than auburn fuzz over his lip.

One Sunday afternoon we planned to go fishing after church, though Logan didn't tell his parents who he was chumming with. I could tell from their stony faces when we occasionally met on the streets of Winnerrow that his parents didn't want me, or any Casteel, in their son's life. What they wanted didn't seem to matter nearly as much to Logan as it did to me. I wanted them to like me, and yet they always managed, somehow, to avoid the introductions Logan wanted to make.

I was thinking about Logan's parents as I furtively brushed my hair while Fanny was in the yard tormenting Snapper, Pa's favorite hound. Sarah sat down heavily behind me and pushed back long strands of red hair from her face before she sighed. "I'm really tired. So blessed tired all t'time. An yer Pa's neva home. When he is he don't even look t'see my condition."

What she said made me start, made me want to look and see what Pa was missing. I whirled around to stare at her, realizing that I very seldom really looked at Sarah, or else I would have seen before this that she was pregnant . . . again.

"Ma!" I cried. "Haven't you told Pa?"

"Iffen he really looked at me, he'd know, wouldn't he?" Iridescent tears of self-pity formed in her eyes. "Last thin in t'world we need is anotha mouth t'feed. Yet we're gonna have anotha, come fall."

"What month, Ma, what day?" I cried, unsettled by the thoughts of another baby to take care of, just when Our Jane was finally in school and not quite as troublesome as she'd been, and Lord knows it had been difficult enough with only a year separating her and Keith.

"I don't count days t'tell doctors. Don't see a doctor," whispered Sarah, as if her strong voice were weakened by the coming baby.

"Ma! You've got to tell me when so I can be here if you need me!"

"I jus hope an pray this one will be black-haired," she mumbled as if to herself. "T'dark-eyed boy yer pa's been wanting—a boy like him. Oh, God, hear me this time an give t'me an Luke his look-alike son, an then he will love me, like he loved her."

It made me hurt to think about that. What good did it do for a man to grieve too long—if he did—and when had he started that baby? Most of the time I could tell what they were doing, and it had been a long time since the bedsprings had creaked in that rhythmical, telling way.

Gravely I told Tom the news while we were on the path to the lake where we would meet Logan to fish. Tom tried to smile, to look happy, and finally managed a weak grin. "Well, since there's nothin we kin do about it, we'll make the best of it, won't we? Maybe it will be the kind of boy that will make Pa a happier man. And that would be nice."

"Tom, I didn't mean to hurt you by repeating that."

"I ain't hurt. I know every time he looks at me he wishes I looked more like him than Ma. But as long as you like my looks, I'll be satisfied."

"Oh, Tom, all the girls think you're devilishly handsome."

"Ain't it funny how girls always put *devilishly* up front to make *handsome* not quite so meaningful?"

I turned to hug him. "It's those teasing green eyes, Tom." I bowed my head so my forehead rested on his chest just under his chin. "I feel so sorry for Ma, all worn out and so big and clumsy-looking, and you know, up until today, I never even noticed. I feel so ashamed. I could have done so much more to help her."

"Ya do enough already," Tom mumbled, pulling away when Logan stepped into view. "Now smile, act happy, for boys don't like girls with too many problems."

All of a sudden Fanny appeared, darting out from the shadows of the trees. She ran straight to Logan and threw herself at him as if she were six instead of a girl of thirteen, already beginning to develop rapidly. Logan was forced to catch her in his arms or be bowled over backward.

"My, yer gettin more handsome by t'day," crooned Fanny, trying to kiss him, but Logan put her down and shoved her away forcefully, then came over to me. But Fanny was everywhere that day with her loud voice to scare off the fish, with her incessant demands for attention, so the Sunday afternoon that could have been fun was spoiled, until finally around twilight Fanny took off for parts unknown, leaving Logan, Tom, and me standing with three small fish not worth carrying home. Logan threw them back into the water, and we watched them swim away.

"I'll see ya at the cabin," said Tom before he darted off, leaving me alone with Logan.

"What's wrong?" asked Logan as I sat staring at the way the setting sun was reflecting all sorts of rosy colors on the lake. I knew soon it would turn crimson as the blood that would spill when Sarah's newest baby came into the world. Memories of other births came fleetingly into the dark crevices of my mind. "Heaven, you're not listening to me."

I didn't know if I should or should not tell Logan about something so personal, yet it came out voluntarily, as if I couldn't keep anything secret from him. "I'm scared, Logan, not just for Sarah and her baby, but for all of us. Sometimes when I look at Sarah and see how desperate she is, I don't know how long she can put up with her kind of life, and if she goes—and she's always talking about leaving Pa— then she'll leave behind a new baby for me to take care of. Granny can't do anything much but knit or crochet, or sew braided rugs together."

"And already you have more than enough to do, I understand. But, Heaven, don't you know everything always works out? Didn't you hear Reverend Wise's sermon today about the crosses we all have to carry? Didn't he say God never gives us one too heavy?"

That's what he'd said, all right, but right now Sarah was feeling that her cross weighed a ton, and I could hardly blame her.

We walked slowly toward the cabin, reluctant to part. "You're not going to ask me in . . . again?" asked Logan in a stiff way.

"Next time . . . maybe."

He stopped walking. "I'd like to take you home with me, Heaven. I've told my parents how wonderful you are, and how pretty, but they'll have to see you and know you to appreciate the truth of what I've been saying."

I backed off, sad for him and sad for me, wondering why he didn't let the poverty and shame of the Casteels drive him away. That's when he stepped up very quickly, grabbed me, and gave me a peck on my mouth. I was startled by the feel of his lips, by the way he looked in the strange light of the early evening. "Good night . . . and don't you worry, for I'll be here when you need me." And with that he was off down the trail, heading for the clean and pretty streets of Winnerrow, where he'd climb stairs to the apartment over Stonewall's Pharmacy. In bright, cheerful modern rooms with running water and flushing toilets, two of them, he'd watch TV this evening with his parents. I stared at the place where he had disappeared, wondering what it would be like to live in clean rooms, with a color television. Oh, a thousand times better than here, I knew that, just knew that.

If I hadn't been thinking romantically of Logan, and his kiss, I wouldn't have drifted so unaware into the cabin—and been so surprised when it exploded all around me.

Pa was home.

He paced the small space of the front room, throwing Sarah glares hard enough to drive knives through her. "Why did you let yourself get pregnant again?" he bellowed, slamming his fist into the palm of his other hand; then he whirled to bang his fists on the nearest wall, causing cups to jump from the shelf nearby and fall to the floor and break. And we had just enough cups, none to spare.

Pa was terrible in his anger—frightening as he whipped around with energy too great to confine in such a small space. "I'm working night and day now to keep you and your kids going . . ." he stormed.

"Ya had nothin t'do with em, did ya?" screamed Sarah, her long red hair loose from the ribbon that usually held it back.

"But I gave you those pills to take!" yelled Pa. "I paid good money for those things, hoping you'd have sense enough to read the directions!"

"I took em! Didn't I tell ya I took em? Took em all, waitin fer ya t'come home, an ya didn't—an when ya did, all t'pills were gone!"

"You mean you took them all at one time?"

She jumped up, started to speak, and then fell back into the chair she'd just left, one of the six hard straight chairs that gave no one real comfort. "I fergit . . . kept fergittin, so I swallowed all so I wouldn't fergit . . ."

"Oh, God!" Pa moaned. His dark eyes glared at her with scorn and contempt. "Dumb! And I read the directions to you!" With that he slammed out the door, leaving me to sit on the floor near Tom, who held Keith and Our Jane on his lap. Our Jane had her small face hidden against Tom, crying as she always cried when her parents fought. Fanny was on her bed pallet rolled up in a tight knot, her hands over her ears and her eyes squinched tight. Granny and Grandpa just sat rocking on and on, staring blankly into space, as if they'd heard all this many times before and they'd hear it many times again in the future. "Luke'll come back and take kerr of ya," Granny comforted weakly when Sarah continued to cry. "He's a good boy. He'll fergive ya when he sees his new baby."

Groaning, Sarah got up and began to prepare our last meal of the day. I hurried to assist. "Sit down, Ma, or go and rest on the bed. I can handle this meal by myself."

"Thank ya, Heaven . . . but I gotta do somethin t'keep from thinkin. An I used t'love him so much. Oh, God, how I used t'love an want Luke Casteel, neva knowin, or guessin, he don't know how t'love anyone betta than himself . . ."

Fanny hissed at me that night, soon after supper was over: "Gonna hate that new baby! We don't need it. Ma's too old t'have babies . . . it's me who needs my own baby."

"You don't need your own baby!" I flared sharply. "Fanny, you're just brainwashing yourself to think having a baby means you'll be grown-up and free—a baby will tie you down worse than youth, so watch out how you play with your boyfriends."

"You don't know nothin! It don't happen t'first time! Yer ten times more a kid than me or else ya'd know what I really mean."

"What do you really mean?"

She sobbed, clutching at me. "Don't know . . . jus want so much we don't have it hurts. There's gotta be somethin I kin do t'make my life betta. Don't have no real boyfriend like ya got. They don't love me like Logan loves ya. Heaven, help me, please help me."

"I will, I will," I pledged as we clung together, not knowing what I could do but pray.

Hot August days seemed to grow shorter much too fast. The last weeks of Sarah's pregnancy passed more or less painfully for her, and for all of us, even though Pa showed up more often than he had, and he'd stopped yelling and pacing, and seemed resigned to the fact that Sarah might have five or six more kids before she was through.

She clumped heavily around the mountain cabin, her red, callused hands often clasped over the mound that carried her fifth baby, which she was not anticipating with much joy. Mumbled prayers stayed on her lips, or else she bellowed out orders. The sweetness of Sarah at her best seldom showed anymore. Then, worse than anything, the loudmouthed meanness we'd unhappily grown accustomed to was replaced by an alarming silence.

Instead of yelling and screaming abuse at Pa, at all of us, she just shuffled along, like an old lady, and Sarah wasn't more than twenty-eight. She hardly glanced at Pa when he came home, not even bothering to ask where he'd been, forgetting about *Shirley's Place;* forgetting to ask if he was still earning "clean" money, or selling that moonshine which was "dirty" money. Sarah seemed locked up in herself, struggling to make some decision.

Day by day Sarah grew quieter, more withdrawn, less devoted to all of us. That hurt, to have no mother at all now, especially when Our Jane and Keith needed her so badly. Her glare hardened whenever Pa came in the door once or twice a week. He was working in Winnerrow, doing honest work, but she refused to believe that, as if she were looking for a reason to hate and distrust him. Sometimes I heard him telling Sarah about his work, looking uneasy because she didn't ask. "Doin odd jobs fer t'church an t'rich ladies with banker husbands who don't wanna dirty their lily-white hands."

Sure, many a dollar Pa earned doing handyman chores for rich folks, and Sarah shouldn't dispute him. Pa could do any sort of handyman job.

Our Jane felt Sarah's depression, and seemed to get sick even more than usual that summer. She was the one who caught all the colds the rest of us easily threw off; then she had chicken pox; and no sooner was that over than Our Jane fell into a patch of poison ivy and cried for one solid week night and day—driving Pa out in the middle of the night, again, to visit *Shirley's Place.*

There were good days when Our Jane felt well. When she was smiling and happy, there wasn't a more beautiful child in the whole wide world than Our Jane, the supreme ruler in the cabin of the Casteels. Oh, indeed, all the valley folks said, how beautiful were all the children of the wicked, cruel, sullen, and stormy Luke Casteel, and his wife Sarah, who, according to jealous women, was not just plain but huge and downright ugly.

One day when Keith, who seldom wanted anything, asked for crayons, it happened that the only ones in the cabin at the time were the ones given to Fanny by Miss Deale months ago. (So far Fanny had not once opened the box to color anything.)

"NO!" Fanny screeched. "Keith kin't have my brand-new crayons!"

"Give him your crayons or he might not speak again," I urged, keeping a wary eye on the little quiet brother who had Grandpa's own silent way of sitting and doing nothing much. Still, Grandpa saw so much more than the rest of us. Who else could whittle each hair on a squirrel's tail? Who else had eyes that didn't just look, but really saw?

"I don't kerr if he neva says nothin!" yelled Fanny.

Tom took her crayons and gave them to Keith as Fanny screamed and threatened to drown herself in the well.

"SHUT UP!" bellowed Pa, striding in the door and surveying his raucous children. He winced as if the noise we made pained his head.

"Ya made 'em, didn't ya?" was Sarah's only welcome. She clamped her lips together and didn't say another word. Pa glowered her way and dumped his supply of food on our scrubbed plank table. I hurriedly checked it over, trying to calculate how long that fifty-pound sack of flour would last, that five-gallon tin of lard, the bags of pinto and navy beans. I'd make soup to stretch the cabbages and ham . . .

Bang went the front door. Dismayed, I looked up. Pa was striding across the yard toward his old truck. Gone again.

My heart sank.

Every time Pa walked out and left Sarah needing, she did something terrible to one of us, or to herself. And I could hardly blame him sometimes for not wanting to stay. Not only did Our Jane and the rest of us wear on Pa's nerves, he and Sarah wore on each other's nerves too. Sarah had lost not only what looks she had but her sweet personality as well.

Early mornings turned winterlike and squirrels raced around, hurrying to store their nuts for the winter, and Tom was helping Grandpa find the wood he needed to whittle, and that was no easy chore, for it had to be a certain kind, not too hard, and not so soft it would break easily with much handling. Both Pa and I were in the yard, alone for a change. "Pa," I began in a tentative way, "I'm doing the best I can for this family . . . can't you do at least one thing for me, like say a kind word now and then?"

"Haven't I told ya before t'leave me alone!" His piercing eyes glared my way before he turned his back. "Now git before I give you what you deserve."

"What do I deserve?" I asked fearlessly, my eyes no doubt an everlasting reminder of all he'd had once and lost. *Her.*

Starlings sat like miniature dark soldiers on the clotheslines. Puffy, sleepy birds, eyes closed, anticipating the coming cold and waiting for the warming sun. Mountain snow would soon be falling in the nights. I sighed as I stacked the wood, knowing no matter how we tried we'd never have enough to keep really warm. There was an ax half jutting from a felled tree trunk, an ax I thought Pa might use on me if I said one more word. I shut up and hefted the logs he'd split neatly onto the pile.

"There," Pa said to Sarah when she came to the door, "that should hold you until I'm home again."

"Where ya goin this time, so late?" called Sarah, who'd washed her hair and tried to make herself pretty for a change. "Luke, gets mighty lonesome fer a woman without a man, jus ole folks an kids fer company."

"See ya soon," Pa called back, hurrying toward his pickup truck. "Got me a job to finish, an then I'll come home t'stay all night."

He didn't come home for an entire week. I sat on the porch steps late one night and stared at the grim, stormy sky. Sour thoughts made me miserable. There had to be a better place than here for me. Somewhere, a better place. An owl hooted, followed by the howl of a roaming wolf. The night held a thousand sounds. The autumn wind from the north shrieked and whistled around the forest trees, whipped around the trembling cabin and tried to blow it away, but all the people huddled close together for warmth held the house down, or so I thought.

I stared at the horned moon half hidden by dark clouds—the same moon that rode high over Hollywood and New York City, London and Paris. I blinked my eyes and tried to see across the hills, the ocean, then closed my eyes the better to see my future. Someday I'd like to have a real bed of my own to sleep in, with goosedown pillows and satin comforters.

I'd have closets, too, full of new dresses I'd wear once, like Queen Elizabeth, and I'd burn them as she had hers burned, so she'd never see them worn by anybody else. And shoes by the dozens I'd have, in all colors, and I'd eat in fancy restaurants where tall, slim candles glowed . . . but right now I had only a hard, cold step to sit on. And tears were freezing on my cheeks and eyelashes.

I began to shiver, to cough; still, I wouldn't go inside and lie in that crowded room between Fanny and Our Jane. Tom and Keith slept next to the pallet used by Granny and Grandpa.

While the others lay sleeping more or less peacefully, there came the whisper of old feet moving slowly. Raspy breathing, grunts and groans, as Granny settled down by my side on the step.

"Ya'll catch yer death in this night cold, an maybe ya'll think that will make yer pa sorry, but is that gonna make ya happy in yer grave?"

"Granny, Pa doesn't have to hate me like he does. Why can't *you* make him understand it wasn't my fault my mother died?"

"He knows it ain't yer fault—down underneath he knows it. But if he admits it, he's gotta blame himself fer marryin up with her, an bringin a gal like her ta this kind of place she weren't used ta. She tried, oh, she did try to do her best, an I'd see her out here scrubbin, ruinin her pretty white hands, brushin back that hair of hers that was somethin t'see . . . an she'd go runnin t'that suitcase of hers, full of all sorts of pretties, an she'd rub on cream from a tube, tryin, always tryin, to keep those hands young an pretty."

"Granny, you know I can't bear to look in that suitcase and see all her pretty things. What good are clothes like that way up here where nobody ever comes? But I had a dream about the doll the other night— that she was me, and I was her. Someday I'm going to go to Boston and find my mother's family. I owe it to them to let them know what happened to their daughter, for surely they must think she's alive, living happily somewhere."

"Yer right. Neva thought of it myself, but yer right." Her thin old arms hugged me briefly, and there was no strength in them, none at all. "Ya jus set yer mind on what ya want, an ya'll get it, ya will."

Life in the mountains was harder on Granny than on any of us. Nobody but me seemed to notice how much more difficult it had become for Granny to get up and down. Often she'd stop walking to clutch at her heart. Sometimes her face would go chalky gray, and she'd gasp. It didn't do any good to suggest a doctor; she didn't believe in doctors, or any medicine she didn't concoct herself from roots and herbs she sent me out to find.

With Sarah acting glum and grim, each day was an ordeal to survive, except when I was with Logan, and then one terrible day when the sun was truly hot, I found him down by the river and Fanny was racing up and down the riverbank without a stitch on! Laughing and teasing him to try and catch her. "An when ya do . . . I'll be yers, all yers," she taunted. I stood frozen, horrified by Fanny's actions, as I turned my eyes on Logan and waited to see what he'd do.

"Shame on you, Fanny!" he called to her. "You're just a kid who deserves a good spanking."

"Then ya catch me an give it t'me!" she challenged.

"No, Fanny," he yelled, "you're just not my type." He turned to head back toward Winnerrow, or so I thought, and that's when I stepped out from behind the tree that had shielded me from his view.

He tried to smile and succeeded only in looking embarrassed. "I wish you hadn't seen and heard that. I was waiting for you when Fanny showed up, and she just tore off her dress, and she wore nothing underneath . . . it wasn't my fault, Heaven, I swear it wasn't."

"Why are you explaining?"

"It's not my fault!" he cried, his face red.

"I know it wasn't . . ." I said stiffly. I knew Fanny and her need to take from me anything I really wanted for myself. Still, from all I'd heard, most boys wanted loose girls with no modesty and no inhibitions, like my younger sister Fanny, who would undoubtedly live ten exciting lives while I struggled through one.

"Hey," said Logan, reaching to tilt my bowed head so my lips were near his, "it's *your* type I want, and your type I need. Fanny's pretty and bold . . . but I like my girls shy, beautiful, and sweet, and if I don't manage somehow to marry Heaven, I don't want to go there, not ever."

This kiss he gave me did ring a few bells. I could hear them chiming like wedding bells ringing in the future. Mrs. Logan Grant Stonewall . . . me.

Instantly I was happy. In some things Fanny was right. Life did have to go on. Everybody needed a chance at living and loving. Now it was my turn.

Now Sarah took to talking to herself, walking in some unhappy dream.

"Gotta escape, gotta get away from this hell," she mumbled. "Ain't nothin but work, eat, sleep, wait an wait fer him t'come home—an when he does, ain't no satisfaction, ain't none at all."

Don't say that, Sarah, please don't . . . what would we do without you?

"Done dug my own grave with my own desire," Sarah confessed to herself on another day. "Coulda had some otha man, coulda . . ."

"I'd leave, but fer t'kids." She said this to herself day and night; then she'd stare hard at Pa when he came home on weekends, only to see he'd grown more handsome (damn him, she'd mutter), and her heart would jump up in her emerald eyes, and like a stupid stopped clock whose hands had to say the same thing over and over again, back came her love for him.

Only too obviously, too painfully, Sarah's small world grew darker, grimmer. And it was I who bore most of the brunt of Sarah's frustration. Exhausted at the end of the day, I fell to my floor pallet and sobbed silent tears into my hard pillow. Granny heard, and Granny laid a comforting hand on my shoulder.

"Sssh, don't cry. Sarah don't hate ya none, chile. It's yer pa that makes her mad, but yer here and he's not. She can't yell out at him when he's not here, or hit out at him—couldn't even iffen he was here. Nobody ya don't love kin be hurt if ya yell and scream—an she's been yellin an screamin fer years an years, an he don't hear or kerr—an she don't go nowhere, so she's strikin out at ya."

"But why did he marry her in the first place if he didn't love her, Granny?" I sobbed. "Just so I'd have a stepmother to hate me?"

"Aw, Lawdy knows t'whys an t'wherefors of what makes men like they are," wheezed Granny, turning over and hugging Grandpa, whom she called Toby, with great affection. Giving him more love with one kiss and one stroking hand on his grizzly face than any of us ever did. "Ya jus make sure t'marry t'right one, like I did, that's all. An wait till yer old enough t'have good sense. Say fifteen."

In the hills, a girl who reached sixteen without being engaged was almost beyond hope, bound to be an old maid.

"Listen t'em whisperin," mumbled Sarah, keening her ears from behind the faded thin red curtain, "talkin bout me. Girl's cryin agin. Why am I so mean t'her, why not Fanny who causes all the trouble? *He* likes Fanny, hates *her*—why not jump on Fanny? Our Jane, Keith? An most of all Tom."

I pulled in a deep fearful breath. Oh, the pity of Sarah thinking about turning against Tom!

It was terrible the day when Sarah lashed Tom with a whip, as if in striking him she could get back at Pa for never being what she wanted him to be. "Didn't I tell ya t'go inta town an earn money? Didn't I?"

"But, Ma, nobody wanted to hire me! They got boys who have riding lawn mowers with vacuums that pulls in t'leaves. They don't need a hill boy who hasn't got even a push mower!"

"Excuses! I need money, Tom, money!"

"Ma . . . I'll try again tomorrow," cried Tom, throwing up his arms and trying to protect his face. "I'll never get a job if I look swollen and bloody, will I?"

Frustrated momentarily, Sarah stared down at the floor—unfortunately. Tom had forgotten to wipe his feet. "Didn't look, did ya? T'floors clean! Jus scrubbed it! An look at it now, all muddy!"

Wham! She slammed her heavy fist into Tom's astonished face, spun him back against the wall, jarring from the shelf above our precious jar of stolen honey that fell on his head and spilled the sticky stuff all over him.

"Thanks a heap, Ma," said Tom with a funny grin. "Now I got all t'honey I kin eat."

"Oh, Tommy . . ." she sobbed, immediately ashamed. "I'm sorry. Don't know what gets inta me . . . don't ya go hatin yer ma who loves ya."

A nightmare with a capricious red-haired witch included had come to live in our house. A nightmare that didn't go when the sun dawned, when noon flared bright and cheerful; the stringy-haired, loud-mouthed, ugly witch showed no mercy, not even to her own.

It was September. Soon we'd be going back to school, and any day Sarah's baby could come, any day. Still Sarah didn't go as she threatened time and again, thinking she'd really hurt Pa when she took away his look-alike dark-haired son. Pa stayed more and more in town.

All the hours blurred one into the other, horrible hours less than hell but far from paradise. Over the summer, we had grown noticeably larger, older, needing more, asking more questions. But as Sarah's unborn child swelled out her front, the oldest among us grew weaker, quieter, less demanding.

It was building, building toward something. That something kept me tossing and turning all night, so when I got up in the morning it was as if I hadn't slept at all.

5

Bitter Season

Logan was waiting for me halfway down the trail to the valley to walk me to the first day of school. The weather was turning chilly in the hills, but it was still pleasantly warm in the valley. Miss Deale was still our teacher, since the school board continued to allow her to advance with her class. I was enchanted by her, as always; still, I kept drifting off . . .

"Heaven Leigh," called the sweet voice of Miss Deale, "are you daydreaming *again?*"

"No, Miss Deale. I don't daydream in class, only at home." Why did everyone always titter, as if I did daydream?

It thrilled me to be back in school where I'd see Logan every day, and he'd walk me home and hold my hand, and with him I could momentarily forget all the problems that beset me in the cabin.

He walked beside me on the way home, both of us eagerly discussing our plans for the future, as Tom led the way with Our Jane and Keith, and Fanny lagged way back, accompanied by her many boyfriends.

All I had to do was to look around and see that soon our mountain nights would be freezing the water in the rain barrels, and all of us needed new coats and sweaters and boots that we couldn't afford. Logan held my hand, glancing at me often, as if he couldn't stop admiring. Slowly, slowly, we strolled. Now Our Jane and Keith were skipping, laughing, as Tom ran back to check on what Fanny was doing with those boys.

"You're not talking to me," Logan complained, stopping to pull me down onto a rotting log. "Before we know it we'll reach your cabin yard, and you'll dash ahead, turn to me, and wave good-bye, and I'll never get to see the inside of your home."

"There's nothing to see," I said with my eyes lowered.

"There's nothing to be ashamed of, either," he said softly, squeezing my fingers before he released my hand and tilted my face toward his. "If you're going to stay in my life, and I can't picture life without you, someday you'll have to let me in, won't you?"

"Someday . . . when I'm braver."

"You're the bravest person I've ever known! Heaven, I've been thinking about us a lot lately; about how much fun we have together, and how lonely the hours are when we're not together. When I'm finished with college, I'm thinking about becoming a scientist, a brilliant one, of course. Wouldn't you be interested in delving into the mysteries of life along with me? We could work as a team like Madame Curie and her husband. You'd like that, wouldn't you?"

"Sure," I said without thought, "but wouldn't it be boring, shut up in a lab day in and day out? Is it possible to have an outdoor lab?"

He thought me silly, and hugged me close. I put my arms around his neck and pressed my cheek against his. It felt so good to be held like this. "We'll have a glass lab," he said in a low, husky voice, with his lips close to mine, "full of live plants . . . will that make you happy?"

"Yes . . . I think so . . ." Was he going to kiss me again? If I tilted my head just a little to the right, would that eliminate the problem of his nose bumping against mine?

If I didn't know how to manage a kiss, he sure did. It was sweet, thrilling. But the moment I was home all my elation was lost in the tempestuous seas of Sarah's miseries.

That Saturday dawned a bit brighter, a little warmer, and, eager to escape the sour hatefulness of Sarah at her worst, Tom and I went to meet Logan, and behind us tagged Our Jane and Keith. We were all good friends, trying to make Keith and Our Jane as happy as possible.

Hardly had we reached the river where we intended to fish when over the hills came Sarah's bellowing hog call, beckoning us back. "Good-bye, Logan!" I cried anxiously. "I have to get back to Sarah; she might need me! Tom, you stay and take care of Our Jane and Keith."

I saw Logan's disappointment before I sped away to respond to Sarah's demand that I wash the clothes instead of wasting my time playing around with a no-good village boy who'd only ruin my life.

No good to love playing games and having fun when Sarah couldn't sit comfortably or stand for longer than seconds, and the work never ended. Feeling guilty to have escaped for a few minutes, I lifted the washtub onto the bench, carried hot water there from the stove, and began scrubbing on the old rippled board. Through the open window that tried to let out the stench from Ole Smokey, inside the cabin I could hear Sarah talking to Granny.

"Used t'think it were good growin up in these hills. Felt freer than bein some city gal who'd have to lock away all her sexual feelins till she was sixteen or so. Went t'school only three years, hardly ever learned anythin. Didn't like spellin, readin, writin, didn't like nothin but t'boys. Fanny an me, no different. Couldn't keep my eyes offen boys. When I first saw yer son my heart did likkity-splits an flip-flops, an he were a man, almost. I were jus a kid. Used t'go t'all t'barn dances, every last one, an I'd hear yer Toby playin his fiddle, an see yer son dancin with all t'prettiest gals, an somethin deep inside me told me I jus had t'have Luke Casteel or die tryin." Sarah paused and sighed, and when I took a peek in the window, I saw a tear coursing its way down her reddened face.

"Then there goes Luke off t'Atlanta an meets up with that city gal, an he ups an marries her. My face, when I saw it sometimes in mirrors, looked coarse as a horse as compared t'hers. But didn't make no difference, Annie, it didn't. Married or not, I still wanted Luke Casteel . . . wanted him so bad I'd do jus anythin t'get him."

Grandpa was on the porch rocking, whittling, paying no mind. Granny was rocking, not even seeming to be listening as Sarah talked on and on. "Luke, he didn't look at me, though I tried t'make him."

I kept on scrubbing dirty clothes, keening my ears to hear better. Near me was a rain barrel full of frogs croaking. Clothes I'd already washed were flapping on the line drying. Another peek inside showed me that Sarah was working near the stove, cutting biscuits with an inverted small glass, and in her low monotone she continued as if she had to tell someone or burst—and Granny was the best kind of listener. Never asking questions, just accepting, as if nothing she said would change anything. And no doubt it wouldn't.

I was all ears, and I kept sliding closer and closer to the window in order to hear better.

"I hated everythin bout her, that frail gal he called his angel; hated how she walked an how she talked—like she was betta than us—an he doted on her like some jackass fool; tryin t'act fancypants like she did. Still, we all went runnin afta, specially when she got herself knocked up; we thought he'd want t'screw around on t'side, an he paid us no mind at all. I decided I'd get him one way or nother. He couldn't have her then, so he took me three times, an what I prayed fer happened. He put in me a baby. He didn't love me, I knew that. Maybe he didn't even like me. He seemed bothered every time he were with me, an even called me angel once when he was ridin me. When I tole him I had his kid comin, he started turnin money ova t'me fer t'baby I had in my womb. An jus when I thought I'd have t'up an marry some otha man, that city girl obliged me by dyin . . .''

Oh, oh! How awful for Sarah to be glad my mother died!

Sarah talked on in her flat, emotionless way, and I could hear the faint squeak of Granny's rocker going back and forth, back and forth.

"When he came t'me t'ask me t'marry him so his baby could have its father, I thought in a month or so he'd ferget all bout her—but he didn't. He ain't yet. I tried t'make him love me, Annie, truly I did. Was good t'his baby named Heaven. Gave him Tom, then Fanny, Keith, an Our Jane. Ain't had no otha man since I married up. Would neva have nother if only he'd love me like he loved her—but he won't do it—an I kin't talk t'him no more. He won't listen. He's got his mind set on doin somethin crazy, an won't let me say nothin t'keep him from tryin. Gonna go an leave us all, that's what he's plannin t'do someday soon. Leave me here to wash, cook, clean, suffa . . . an take kerr of anotha baby. I'd stay foreva if only he'd love me. But when he turns on me an shouts out ugly words, they eat on my soul, tellin me I'm sendin him t'his ruin, makin of him a mean, ugly animal that hits out at his own kids—wishin they were hers, not mine. I know. I see it in his eyes. He won't eva love me, not even like me. Ain't nothin I got that he admires. Cept my good health, an he's ruinin that. By God, he's ruinin that!''

"Why ya keep sayin that, Sarah? Ya seem healthy nough.''

"Neva thought that dead wife would take his heart in t'grave with her, neva did think that,'' Sarah whispered brokenly, as if she hadn't heard Granny's question. "Don't kerr no more bout him, Annie. Don't kerr no more bout nothin. Not even my own kids. I'm jus here, puttin in time . . .''

What did she mean? Panic hit me hard. I almost tipped over the washtub and the scrubbing board I was leaning so hard against the rim.

The next day Sarah paced the floor again, mumbling to herself and anyone who chose to listen. "Gotta escape, gotta get away from this kind of hell. Ain't nothin but work, eat, sleep, wait an wait fer him t'come home—an when he does, ain't no joy, no happiness, no satisfaction.''

She'd said all that a thousand times, and she was still here. It had been building so long I thought it could never happen, though I'd had ugly dreams of seeing Sarah murdered and bloody. I dreamed of Pa in his coffin, shot through the heart. Many times I wakened suddenly, thinking I'd heard a gunshot. I'd glance at the walls, see the three long rifles, and shudder again. Death and killings and secret burials were all part of mountain living, which was always close to mountain dying.

Then the day came . . . what we'd all been nervously anticipating. It started early on a Sunday September morning when I was up and putting on water so we'd have some hot water for quick washups before going to church. Out of the bedroom came howls of distress, loud, sharp, full of pain. "Annie, it's comin! Annie, it's Luke's dark-haired son acomin!"

Granny scuttled around lamely, but her legs hurt and her breath came in short gasps, making my help more than necessary. And right from pain one she seemed to know this birthing was going to be different, and more complicated than the others. Tom ran to hunt up Pa and bring him home as Grandpa reluctantly got up from his porch rocker and set off in the direction of the river, and I ordered Fanny to take care of Keith and Our Jane, but not to take them too far from the cabin. Granny and Sarah needed my help. This labor was taking much longer than it had when Our Jane came into the world on the same bed where all of us had been born. Exhausted, Granny fell into a chair and gasped out instructions while I boiled the water to sterilize a knife to cut the umbilical cord. I tried to stop all the blood that flowed from Sarah like a red river of death.

And finally, after hours and hours of trying, with Pa in the yard waiting with Grandpa, Tom, Keith, and Our Jane, and Fanny nowhere to be found, while Sarah's face was white as paper, through all that blood emerged painfully, and slowly, a baby. A little bluish baby lying exceptionally still and strange-looking.

"A boy . . . a girl?" wheezed Granny, her voice as weak and thin as the wind that fanned our worn curtains. "Tell me, girl, is it Luke's look-alike son?"

I didn't know what to say.

Sarah propped herself up to look. She stared and stared, trying to brush back her hair that was wet with sweat. Her color came back as if she had gallons of blood to spare. I gingerly carried the baby over to Granny so she could tell me just what kind of baby this was.

Granny looked where some type of sex parts should be, and neither she nor I saw any.

I could hardly accept what my eyes told me. Shocking to see a baby with nothing between its legs. But what did it matter that this child was neither girl nor boy when it was dead and the top of its head was missing? A monster baby, icky with running sores.

"STILLBORN!" screamed Sarah, jumping out of bed and seizing the baby from my arms. She hugged it close, kissed its poor half-face a dozen or more times before she threw back her head and howled out her anguish like one of those mountain wolves that screamed at the moon.

"It's Luke an his damned whores!" Wild and crazy, she ran like a fury to where Pa sat outside, and she called his name just once before she shoved the baby into his arms. He held the baby with expertise, then stared down with incredulity and horror.

"SEE WHAT YA DID!" yelled Sarah, her single shapeless garment stained with the fluids of childbirth. "YA AN YER ROTTEN BLOOD AN WHORIN WAYS DONE KILLED YER OWN CHILD! AN MADE IT A FREAK, TOO!"

Pa yelled out his rage. "YOU'RE THE MOTHER! WHAT YOU PRODUCE AIN'T GOT A DAMN THING T'DO WITH ME!" He threw the dead child onto the ground, then ordered Grandpa to give it a decent burial before the hogs and dogs got to it. And away he strode, to jump into his truck and head to Winnerrow to drown his sorrows, if he had any, in moonshine, and later he'd no doubt stagger into *Shirley's Place.*

Oh, how terrible was this Sunday when I had to bathe a dead child in the tin tub, and get *it* ready for burying while Granny took care of Sarah, who suddenly lost all her strength and began to cry like any ordinary woman would. Gone the Amazon fighting strength, only a woman after all, a sobbing bereaved mother on her knees asking God why a baby had to be cursed by his father's sins.

Poor little thing, I kept thinking as I washed away all the blood and froth of birth from the pitiful tiny body that lay so limp and still. I didn't even have to be careful to keep its half-head above water, but I did just the same. I dressed it in clothes that both Our Jane and Keith had worn, maybe Fanny, Tom, and me as well.

Sarah finally fell flat on her face on the soiled bed, gripping the mattress in her clawing fingers, crying as I'd never known her to cry before.

I didn't even notice Granny until I was finished with the dead baby. Not until I looked at her two or three times did I realize that she wasn't knitting, crocheting, darning, braiding, weaving, or even rocking. She was just sitting very still with her eyes half closed. On her thin white lips was a faint smile. It scared me, that funny happy smile; she should be looking sad and mournful.

"Granny . . ." I whispered fearfully, laying down the stillborn child all dressed and clean, "are you all right?"

I touched her. She fell to one side. I felt her face, and she was already turning cold, her flesh hardening.

Granny was dead!

Shocked into death by the birth of a monster baby, or by years and years of struggling to endure a life of hardships! I cried out, and felt an awful blow to my own heart. I knelt by her rocking chair to hold her close. "Granny, when you get to heaven, please tell my mother I'm really trying hard to be like her. Tell her that, will you, please?"

A scraping sound moved our way, drifting in from the porch. "What ya doing with my Annie?" asked Grandpa, coming back from the river where he'd gone to avoid knowing what men never wanted to know— only fitting for men to disappear until birthing was over. The way of the men of the hills, to flee from women's screams of suffering, and pretend to themselves they never suffered at all.

I looked up, my face streaked with tears, not knowing how to tell him. "Grandpa . . ."

His faded blue eyes widened as he stared at Grandma. "Annie . . . yer all right, ain't ya? Git up, Annie . . . why don't ya git up?" And of course he had to know when her eyes were staring backward into her head. He stumbled forward, all his agility fleeing as if his life had flown the moment he knew his better half was dead.

On his knees he took Granny from my arms and cuddled her against his heart. "Oh, Annie, Annie," he sobbed, "been so long since I said I loved ya . . . kin ya hear me, Annie, kin ya? Meant t'do betta by ya. Had me t'best intentions. Neva knew it'd turn out this way . . . Annie."

It was awful to see his suffering, his terrible grief to lose a good and faithful wife who'd been with him since he was fourteen years old. How strange to know I'd never see him and Grandma cuddled up together on their bed pallet, with her long white hair spread out to pillow his face.

It took both Tom and me to pry Granny's body from Grandpa's arms, and all the time Sarah just lay on her back, tears gone now as she stared blankly at a wall.

We all cried at the funeral, even Fanny, all but Sarah, who stood frozen as stiff and empty-eyed as any cigar-store Indian.

Pa wasn't even there.

Dead drunk down at *Shirley's Place*, I had to presume, when his last child and his only mother were buried. Reverend Wayland Wise was there with his poker-faced wife, Rosalynn, to say the words for an old woman whom everybody had liked, if not respected.

Not one of ours would go into the ground without a proper funeral, with all the right words said to see this old woman and this stillborn child into heaven.

"And the Lord giveth, and the Lord taketh away," intoned the Reverend. He tilted his face toward the sun. "Lord God, hear my prayer. Accept this beloved wife, mother, grandmother and true believer, along with this tiny new soul, into heaven—fling *WIDE* your pearly gates, *THROW EM OPEN! Gather in this Christian woman, Lord, this child, Lord, for she was honest, plain, true to her faith, and the child is innocent, pure, and blameless!"*

We trudged home in single file, still crying.

The people of the mountains were there to grieve with us, to suffer the departure of Annie Brandywine Casteel, one of their own, and with us they trooped back to the house, and sat with us, and sang with us, and prayed with us for hours on end. And when it was done, they brought out the moonshine, the guitars and banjos and fiddles, and they struck up a lively tune as the hill women brought out the treats to serve.

The next day, when the sun was shining, I went again to the graveyard to stand with Tom and stare down at Granny's raw grave, and that tiny one barely a foot long. My heart was broken to see "Child Casteel" buried near my own mother. There wasn't a date put on her tombstone.

"Don't look at it," whispered Tom. "Your mother's been dead so long, and it's Granny we're going to miss most. Didn't know until her chair was empty just how much she added t'our lives—did ya know?"

"No," I whispered, shamefaced. "I just accepted her presence like she'd live forever. We're going to have to do more for Grandpa, he's so lost and alone-looking."

"Yeah," agreed Tom, catching my hand and leading me away from a sorrowful place that did little to communicate love to us. "We gotta appreciate Grandpa while he's still with us, an not save our caring for his funeral day."

A week later Pa came home looking sober and very grim. He pushed Sarah into a chair, pulled up a second one, and spoke in a strained voice while Tom and I paused outside the window to spy and eavesdrop. "Went t'see a doctor in the city, Sarah. That's where I been. He told me I was sick, real sick. Told me I was spreading my disease all over, and I'd have to stop what I was doing or I'd go insane before I die too young. Told me I can't have sexual relationships with any woman, not even my wife. Told me I needed shots to cure what I got, but we don't have that kind of money."

"What ya got?" demanded Sarah in a cold, hard voice, not at all sympathetic.

"Got syphilis in its first stages," Pa confessed in a hollow voice. "Wasn't yer fault ya lost that baby, was mine. An so I'll say this one time, and that's all. I'm sorry."

"T'LATE T'BE SORRY!" yelled Sarah. "T'late t'save my baby! Ya killed yer ma when ya killed my last little one! Hear that! *YER MA IS DEAD!*"

Even I, who hated him, was shocked at how Sarah yelled that out, for if Pa loved anyone but himself, it had been Granny. I heard him suck in his breath, kind of groan, and then he sat down heavily enough to make the chair crack . . . and Sarah hadn't even finished punishing him.

"Ya had t'play around, when I were here all t'time, jus yearnin fer ya t'need me. I HATE YA, LUKE CASTEEL! Hate ya even more fer neva lettin go a dead woman ya should have let alone anyway!"

"Yer turning against me?" he said bitterly. "Now—when my ma is gone an I'm sick?"

"YER DAMNED RIGHT!" she screamed, jumping up and beginning to throw his clothes into a cardboard carton. "Here's all yer rotten, stinkin clothes—NOW GIT! Git before ya make all of us as rotten sick as ya are! Neva want t'see ya agin! Not eva!"

He stood up, seeming humbled, glancing around the cabin as if he'd never see it again, and I was scared, so darn scared. I trembled as Pa stopped by Grandpa's chair and laid a gentle hand on his shoulder. "Sorry, Pa. Really sorry I wasn't here on her funeral day."

Grandpa said nothing, only bowed his head lower, and the tears from his eyes fell slowly, slowly, to wet his knees.

I watched silently as Pa again got into his old truck and sped off, kicking up dry dirt and scattering dead leaves, creating a whirl of dust and litter. He was gone, and he'd taken his dogs with him. Now we had only cats who hunted just for themselves.

When I ran to tell Sarah that Pa had really gone and this time he'd taken his dogs, she cried out and sank slowly to the floor. I knelt beside her. "Ma, it's what you wanted, isn't it? Ya drove him out. You said you hated him . . . why are you crying when it's too late?"

"SHUT UP!" she roared in Pa's own ugly way. "Don't kerr! It's betta so, betta so!"

Better so? Then why did she cry even more?

Whom did I have to talk to now but Tom? Not Grandpa, whom I'd never loved as much as Granny, mainly because he was so content in his locked-in small world, and he didn't seem to need anyone but his wife, and she was gone.

Still, I helped him to the table each morning when Sarah stayed in bed, and each evening, and said what I could to ease him along until he grew accustomed to being without a wife. "Your Annie has gone to heaven, Grandpa. She told me many a time to look out for you after she was gone, and I will. And think of this, Grandpa. Now she doesn't ache and pain anymore, and in paradise she can eat anything she wants, and not feel sick after every meal. I guess that's her reward . . . isn't it, Grandpa?"

Poor Grandpa . . . he couldn't speak. Tears streaked from his pale, tired eyes. When he had eaten a little, I helped him back to the rocker Granny had used, the one with the best cushions to make it more bearable for painful hips and joints. "Ain't nobody to call me Toby no more," he said in the saddest way.

"I'll call you Toby," I said quickly.

"So will I," volunteered Tom.

Grandpa said more after Granny died than I'd heard him say since I was born.

"Oh, God, life's gettin dreary!" cried Fanny. "If somebody else dies, I'm takin off!"

Sarah looked up, stared at Fanny for the longest time before she disappeared into the second room, where I heard the bedsprings squeal in protest as she threw herself down and cried again.

For when Granny's spirit left our cabin, all the love that held us together seemed to go with her.

6

The End of
the Road

For the first time since Granny had given it to me, when everyone was fast asleep I tiptoed to that secret place where I had hidden my mother's suitcase. I pulled it out from under all the old boxes full of junk and carefully, while sitting behind Ole Smokey so Fanny couldn't wake up and see, I took out the doll.

The magical-beautiful bride doll that represented to me my mother.

I held that long, hard bundle for a long time, thinking back to the winter's night when Granny had given it to me. I'd been in and out of the suitcase a dozen times to fondle this or that, but I'd not unwrapped the doll since. Many a time I'd wanted to stare at the pretty face surrounded by all that lovely pale hair, but I'd feared doing so would make me feel sick inside for a mother who must have deserved better than she got. Granny's frail voice came as a whispery ghost to echo in my ears:

"Go on, chile. Ain't it time ya looked good t'see what's inside? Been awonderin many a year why ya don't want t'play with it, an wear t'fancy clothes."

I felt her thin white hair whispering across my face, felt the cold winter winds blowing as I took out the fancy bride doll and un-wrapped her. In the glow of the fire I stared at her face. How lovely she was in her marvelous white lace gown and veil, with tiny buttons that fastened right up to the chin, with white filmy stockings, white satin-

and-lace shoes that could be taken off and put back on. She wore a blue satin garter, for something blue, and held a tiny white-and-gold Bible with silk orange blossoms and white satin ribbons dangling, for something new.

Even her underwear was exquisitely made, a tiny bra to cup small hard breasts, and defiantly there was a cleft where most dolls remained neutered between the thighs.

Why was this doll made differently, more realistically?

It was part of the mystery of my mother, the doll and what it had to signify in her life. Someday I'd find out. I kissed her small face and saw the cornflower-blue eyes up so close there were faint specks of green and gray and violet—like my own eyes! My very own eyes!

In the morning, while Fanny was visiting a friend, and Tom was out showing Keith and Our Jane how to fish with more skill, I remembered when Granny told me how Pa had wanted to chop up everything my mother had left behind, so she'd taken the suitcase and its contents and hidden them away. Now I'd lost Granny. My best connection to the past. Pa would never talk to me the way she had. Grandpa no doubt hadn't even taken notice of the girl his son called angel.

"Oh," I sighed as Tom came in. "Look, Tom, here is a doll that Granny said belonged to my real mother. A bride doll made to look like her when she was only a girl the same as me. See what's written on her bare foot." I held it so he could see, once I had her decently dressed again, but for stockings and shoes.

A Tatterton Original Portrait Doll
Issue, One

"Put her stockins an shoes on, an hide her quick," whispered Tom. "Fanny's comin with Our Jane and Keith, an that's your face if ever I saw it. No good lettin Fanny ruin somethin so beautiful."

"You're not surprised?"

"Sure, but I found it long ago, and put it back like Granny told me to do. . . . Now quick, before Fanny comes in."

As fast as I could I pulled on the stockings, stuffed on the shoes, and rewrapped the suitcase in the filthy old quilt, and in the nick of time hid it again, only then brushing away the tears from my cheeks.

"Still cryin fer Granny?" asked Fanny, who could display grieving emotions one second and be laughing the next. "She's betta off, she is, than sittin in here all day an doin nothin but hurtin an complainin. Anywhere but here is a betta place."

My doll made up for so much. Made up, I thought at the time, for

Sarah's meanness, for Pa's illness, for the fact that I hadn't seen Logan for a week. Where was he? Why didn't he wait to walk me home anymore? Why hadn't he come to say he was sorry about Granny? Why didn't he and his parents go to church anymore? What kind of devotion was he showing now that he'd kissed me?

Then I guessed. His parents had to know about Pa's disease, and they didn't want their one and only son coming to see hill scum like me. I wasn't good enough, even if *I* didn't have syphilis.

Putaway thoughts. Better to think about the doll, and the secret of why my mother, at such a late age, would want a doll made to look like herself.

Nothing short of death would keep *us* from church, and proudly we trudged onward, wearing our old rags, the best we had, with Sarah leading the way now that Pa had the truck and didn't come to drive us there. I held Grandpa's large, bony hand in mine, and actually pulled him along, just as I had to tug on Our Jane, who held with her other hand to Keith.

Every head in the church turned to stare our way, as if one family with so much trouble had to be unworthy sinners.

They were singing as we entered, singing in their glorious voices that had so much practice when they attended church three times a week, and we only went on Sundays.

> "Rock of Ages, cleft for me,
> Let me hide myself in thee . . ."

Hide, how appropriate that word was. We should all run away and hide until Pa was well again, and Sarah could laugh once more, and Our Jane stopped crying for a granny who'd gone away and didn't give her hugs anymore. But there was no place to hide.

Then, the next day, Logan showed up by my locker, smiling at me with his eyes even when his lips stayed in a straight line. "Did you miss me the week I was gone? I wanted to tell you my grandmother was sick and we'd be flying to see her, but there wasn't time before the plane left."

I stared at him with huge wistful eyes. "How is your grandmother now?"

"Fine. She had a small stroke, but seemed to feel much better when we left."

"That's nice," I said in a choked way.

"What did I say wrong? Something, I can tell! Heaven, haven't we sworn to always be honest with one another? Why are you crying?"

My head bowed and then I was telling him about Granny, and he said all the right words to console me. I cried awhile on his shoulder, and with his arm still about my shoulder we headed up the trail toward home. "And what about the baby your stepmother was expecting?" asked Logan, appearing happy that Tom and Fanny stayed out of sight with Our Jane and Keith.

"It was stillborn," I answered stiffly. "Granny died the same day . . . guess all of us went kind of numb, losing two, and on the same day."

"Oh, Heaven, no wonder you looked so funny when I said my grandmother recovered. I'm sorry, so damned sorry. Someday, I hope, someone will tell me the right words to say at moments like this. Right now I feel inadequate . . . except I know I'd have loved your granny just as much as you did."

Yes, Logan would have loved Granny, even if she would have embarrassed his parents. As Grandpa would still embarrass them, if ever . . .

The next day Miss Deale beckoned me to stay after class for a few minutes. "You go for Our Jane and Keith," I whispered to Tom before I stepped up to her desk. I was eager to meet with Logan, and anxious to avoid a teacher who could sometimes ask too many questions I didn't know if I should answer.

She looked at me for long moments first, as if she saw changes in my eyes as Logan had. I knew my eyes were shadowed underneath, knew I was losing weight, but what else could she be seeing? "How are things going with you now?" she asked, staring directly into my eyes as if to keep me from lying.

"Fine, just fine."

"Heaven, I heard about your grandmother, and I'm so very sorry you had to lose someone you loved so much. I see you in church often, so I know you have the same kind of faith your grandmother did, and you do believe we all have eternal souls."

"I want to believe that . . . I do . . ."

"Everyone does," she said softly, laying her hand on mine. I sighed heavily and tried not to cry. And without meaning to be a tattletale and show lack of family loyalty, I had to speak when I didn't know what others might have already told her. "Granny died, I guess, from heart failure," I said before my tears came. "Sarah had a baby that was stillborn and sexless, and Pa's gone, but other than that, we're all just fine."

"Sexless . . . Heaven, all babies are one sex or the other."

"I thought the same thing myself, until I helped deliver this one.

Don't you tell a soul, please, for it would hurt Sarah if others knew—but this last baby didn't have any genitals."

She paled. "Oh . . . I'm so sorry to have been so tactless. I did hear a few rumors, but I try never to listen to them. Of course nature sometimes creates oddities. Since all your father's children are so beautiful, I naturally presumed your mother would have another perfect child."

"Miss Deale, it's a wonder you haven't heard about me. Sarah is not my mother. My father has been married twice. I am his first wife's child."

"I know," she whispered in a low voice. "I've heard about your father's first wife, and how lovely she was, and how young when she died." She blushed and looked uncomfortable, then began to pick invisible lint from her expensive knit suit. "I presumed you love your stepmother very much, and like to pretend she is your mother."

"Used to like doing that." I smiled. "I've got to run along now, or else Logan will be walking another girl home. Thank you, Miss Deale, for being a good friend; for growing with us in school; for making Tom and me feel good about ourselves. Why, Tom and I said just this morning, school would sure be a bore without our wonderful Miss Deale."

Chuckling and tearfully smiling, she touched my hand and excused me with: "You're prettier each time I see you, Heaven—but set your goals now. Don't give them up just to become another girl who rushes into marriage too soon."

"Don't you worry that I'll not head for my goals!" I sang out, backing toward the door. "It'll be a rare fine day when I'm thirty before I go into some man's kitchen to bake his biscuits and wash his dirty clothes—and have his babies once a year!" And out of the classroom I ran, hurrying to where I thought Logan would be waiting.

This particular day in the valley was sunny, mild, with fat white clouds heading for London, Paris, and Rome as I ran to where six or seven boys clustered in a tight gang, yelling.

"Yer a sissy city boy!" one bully called Randy Mark yelled at a filthy, dirty boy who I gasped to see was Logan! Oh, they'd finally gotten him—and he'd said they never would. There he was on the ground, wrestling with another boy his age. Already Logan's shirt sleeve was torn, his jaw red and puffy, and his hair fell over his forehead.

"Heaven Casteel is just another whore in t'makin like her sister—even if she won't let us, she lets *you!*"

"She does not!" roared Logan, red-faced and so angry he seemed to give off smoke even as he managed to snatch a good leg lock on Randy before he twisted that leg ruthlessly. "You take back everything nasty you said about Heaven! She's the most honorable, decent girl I've met in my whole life!"

"Cause ya don't know rotten apples from good!" screamed another boy.

Who had started this, and what had been said? I glanced around to see one of the girls in my class who always laughed at my shabby clothes, and she was grinning slyly. I ran to where Tom crouched, ready to jump into the fight. "Tom," I cried, "why don't you help Logan?"

"I would if it wouldn't convince all the others he doesn't know how to fight. Heavenly, Logan's gotta do this himself, or he'll never live it down that I had to help."

"But hill boys don't fight fair, you know that!"

"Don't matter. He's gotta do it their way, or forever be picked on."

Fanny was jumping up and down, terribly excited, as if Logan were fighting for her honor, not mine. Keith pulled Our Jane over to the swings and began to push her back and forth so she wouldn't cry to see one of her friends hurt. How sensitive Keith was, I had time to think before I looked back at the pair on the ground.

It was awful to stand there and watch those boys take on Logan one after the other, not giving him time to catch his breath before a new boy jumped into the dirt ring they'd drawn and began throwing blows. By this time Logan was bloody, his face bruised and swollen, and his left eye was all but closed. I clutched at Tom, almost crying. "Tom, you *have* to help him now!"

"No . . . hang on . . . he's doing fine."

How could he say that when Logan looked ten times worse than any of the others? "They're killing him, and you say he's doing fine!"

"They're not gonna kill him, silly. They're just testin t'see if he's got what it takes."

"WHAT DOES IT TAKE?" I yelled, ready to pitch in myself and help, but Tom caught and held me.

"Don't you dare shame him by helpin," he whispered urgently. "As long as he keeps slingin blows an fightin back, they'll respect him. Once you or I help, it's all over for him."

As I stood there and watched, cringing every time Logan was hit, and yelling savagely every time he delivered a blow, he quickly glanced my way, dodged the next blow, and delivered a swift uppercut. I screamed encouragement, feeling as vicious as any girl there.

Now Logan was on top, and the boy underneath was screaming. "Now apologize . . . take back what you said about my girl!" ordered Logan.

"Yer girl's a Casteel . . . ain't none of em no good!"

"Take it back, what you said, or I'll break your arm." Logan gave that arm a vicious twist. The boy beneath him yelled for mercy. "I take it back."

"Apologize to her. While she's here and can hear."

"Ya ain't like yer sister Fanny!" screamed a boy about to have his arm broken. "But *she's* sure gonna be one damned whore, t'whole town knows it!"

Fanny ran to give him several hard kicks while all the others laughed. Only then did Logan release the boy's arm, turning him over before he slammed his fist into the boy's jaw. Instantly everyone stopped yelling and stared down at the unconscious face as Logan stood up, brushed off his clothes, and glared at everyone there but Tom and me.

Funny how they all disappeared, leaving me, Tom, and Fanny standing together as Keith and Our Jane continued to use the yard swings and paid no attention to the fight. Tom ran to pound Logan on the back. "Boy, buddy, you were great, really great! You threw that right hook just perfect. Timed your leg twist just right . . . couldn't have done it better myself."

"Thanks for giving me the lessons," murmured Logan, looking dazed and terribly exhausted. "Now, if you don't mind, I'm going into the school and wash up. If I went home looking like this, my mom would faint." He smiled my way. "Heaven, hang around, will you, until I'm back?"

"Sure." I stared at all his bruises, and his black eye. "Thanks for defending my honor . . ."

"Why, he defended *all* our honors, dummy!" shrieked Fanny. Then, so help me, she ran to throw her arms about Logan and kissed him squarely on his swollen, bleeding lips.

I should have done that.

Logan walked off toward the school as Tom grabbed Fanny's arm, called Our Jane and Keith, and all of them headed for our trail. All alone in the schoolyard I waited for Logan to come out of the boys' rest room.

On the swing Our Jane had used I shoved myself higher and higher, hanging back and dangling so my hair would fan and almost sweep the ground. I hadn't felt so happy since before Granny died. I closed my eyes and flew ever higher on the swing.

"Hey . . . you up there in the sky, come on down so I can walk you home before dark, and we can talk."

Logan looked somewhat cleaner, somewhat less damaged, as I dragged my feet and brought the swing to a stop. "You're not really hurt, are you?" I asked with concern.

"No, not really hurt." His one eye peered at me. "Do you really care if I am?"

"Of course I care."

"Why?"

"Well . . . I don't know why, except, well, you did call me your girl. Am I your girl, Logan?"

"If I said so, then you must be. Unless you have some objections."

I was up now, and he had my hand, gently urging me toward the mountain trail that spiraled steeply up, up, up.

Winnerrow had only one main street, and all the others branched off from that. Even placed in the middle of town, the school backed up to the mountain range. There wasn't any way the town could escape the surrounding Willies. "You haven't answered," urged Logan when we'd strolled on for fifteen minutes without speaking, only holding hands and glancing often at one another.

"Where'd you go last weekend?"

"My parents wanted to see the college where I'll be going. I wanted to call and tell you, but you have no telephone, and I didn't have time to walk to your place."

There it was again. His parents didn't want him to see me, or he could have found time. I turned and put my arms about his waist and pressed my forehead against his dirty torn shirt. "I'm thrilled to be your girl, but I've got to warn you now, I don't intend to get married until I've had the chance to live and grow on my own, and to become somebody. I want my name to mean something after I'm dead."

"Looking for immortality?" he teased, holding me closer and bowing his face into my hair.

"Something like that. You see, Logan, a psychiatrist came to our class one day and he said there are three kinds of people. One, those who serve others. Two, those who give to the world by producing those who serve others. Three, the last kind, those who can't be satisfied unless they achieve on their own, not by serving others but by their own merits and talents, producing, and not through their children, either. I'm the third kind. There's a niche in this world meant for me and what innate talents I have . . . and I won't find it if I marry young."

He cleared his throat. "Heaven, aren't you getting way ahead of this situation? I'm not asking you to be my wife, just my girl."

I drew sharply away. "Then you don't really want to marry me someday?"

His hand spread helplessly. "Heaven, can we predict the future and who we'll want when we're twenty, twenty-five, or thirty? Take what I offer now, and let the future take care of itself."

"What are you offering now?" I asked suspiciously.

"Just me, my friendship. Just me, and the now-and-then right to kiss you, hold your hand, touch your hair, and take you to the movies, and listen to your dreams because you listen to mine, and be silly once in a while, build a past we'll enjoy remembering—that's all."

That was enough.

Hand in hand we continued to stroll, and it was sweet to reach the cabin near twilight that flattered the tiny house nestled on the hillside. He had only one good eye anyway, and I knew he couldn't truly see the shoddiness of how we lived until he went inside.

I turned and cupped his face between my palms. "Logan, would it be all right, and not too much like Fanny, if I kissed you just once for being so exactly what I want?"

"I think I could bear up."

Slowly my arms slid up around his neck—how awful his eye looked now that we were inches apart—I closed my eyes and puckered my lips, and kissed that swollen eye, his cut cheek, and finally his lips. He was trembling by this time. So was I.

I was scared to say another word, so afraid realities would spoil the sweetness of what we had. "Good night, Logan. See you tomorrow."

"Good night, Heaven," he whispered, as if he'd lost his voice. "Sure has been a great day, sure has been . . ."

In that part of the day Granny used to call the gloaming I watched until Logan was out of sight, disappearing into darkness, before I turned away and entered the cabin that immediately depressed my soaring spirits. Sarah had stopped making any attempt to keep the cabin clean, or even tidy. Meals that had been adequate before had become haphazard affairs of bread and gravy without greens or vegetables, and seldom did we have chicken or ham anymore. Slab bacon was a memory food better not to think about. Our garden out back where Granny and I had spent so much time pulling weeds and planting seeds was neglected. Ripe vegetables were left to rot in or on the ground. No salt pork or ham was in the smokehouse to flavor our bean soup or collard greens, spinach, or turnips, now that Pa never came home. Our Jane was in a finicky mood, refusing to eat or throwing up what she did, and Keith cried constantly because he never had enough to eat, and Fanny did nothing but complain.

"Somebody but me should do something!" I yelled, turning in circles. "Fanny, you go to the well and fill the bucket, and bring it in with water to the brim, not just a few cupfuls, which is your lazy way. Tom, go to the garden and pull up whatever is there we can eat. Our Jane, stop that wailing! Keith, entertain Our Jane so she'll stay quiet and I can think."

"Don't ya give me orders!" screamed Fanny. "I don't have t'do nothin ya say! Jus cause ya had a boy fight fer ya don't mean yer queen of this hill!"

"Yes, you do have to obey Heaven," backed Tom, who gave Fanny a shove toward the door. "Go to the spring and bring back really good water."

"But it's dark out there!" wailed Fanny. "Ya know I'm skerred of t'dark!"

"Okay, I'll fetch the spring water, you pick the vegetables, and stop back-talking . . . or I'll be the *king* of the hill and give yer bottom ten solid wacks!"

"Heaven," Tom whispered from where he lay on his floor pallet that night looking at me with so much compassion, "someday, I kin feel in my bones, it's all gonna turn out fine for all of us. Ma will go back t'how she was, an start cookin good meals again. She'll clean up t'house and you won't have so much to do. Pa will come home cured, an nicer to us than before. We'll grow up, graduate from high school, go t'college, be so smart we'll make piles of dough, an we'll ride around in big cars, live in mansions, have servants, an we'll sit an laugh at how tough we thought we had it, never suspecting all this was good fer us. Makes us determined, hardy, better kids than those who have it easy—that's what Miss Deale says, anyway. The best often comes out of t'worst."

"Don't feel sorry for me. I know it's going to be better, someday." I brushed away weak tears.

He crawled over to cuddle in the pallet beside me, his strong young arms feeling good, warm, safe. "I kin hunt up Pa, an you talk to Ma."

"Ma," I said the very next evening, hoping to cheer her with casual talk before I got down to serious matters, "only a few short hours ago I thought I had fallen in love."

"Yer a damned fool if ya do," muttered Sarah, glancing at my figure, which was definitely taking on a woman's shape. "Ya git offen this mountain—git far from here before ya let some man put his kid in ya," she warned. "Ya run fast an ya run far before ya become what I am."

Distressed, I threw my arms about Sarah. "Ma, don't say things like that. Pa'll come home soon, and he'll bring all the food we need. He always comes home before we're really hungry."

"Yeah, sure he does." Sarah's expression turned ugly. "In the nick of time our dear Luke comes back from whorin an boozin, an he throws his bags on the table like he's bringin us solid gold. An that's all he does fer us, ain't it?"

"Ma . . ."

"I AIN'T YER MA!" yelled Sarah, red-faced and looking ill. "Never was! Where's all t'brains ya think ya got? Kin't ya see ya don't look like me?"

She stood with bare feet braced wide, her long red hair in complete disarray, not washed since the baby was born dead, not combed or brushed either, nor had Sarah bathed in more than a month. "I'm gettin out of this hellhole, an if ya got any brains at all, ya'll run soon afta."

"Ma, please don't go!" I cried out in desperation, trying to catch hold of her hands. "Even if you aren't my real ma, I love you, I do! I always have! Please don't go and leave us here alone! How can we go to school and leave Grandpa? He doesn't walk as well as he did when Granny was alive. He can't chop wood anymore. He can hardly do anything. Please, Ma."

"Tom kin chop t'wood," she said with deadly calm, as if she'd decided to leave, no matter what happened to us.

"But Tom has to go to school, and it takes more than one to chop enough wood and kindling to last through the entire winter, and Pa is gone."

"Ya'll get by. Don't we always?"

"Ma, you can't just up and leave!"

"I kin do anythin I damn well please—will serve Luke right!"

Fanny heard and came running. "Ma, take me with you, please, please!"

Sarah shoved Fanny away, backed off to stare at us all with calm indifference. Who was this dead-faced woman who didn't care? She wasn't the mother I'd always known. "Good night," she said at the curtain that was her bedroom door. "Yer Pa'll come when ya need him. Don't he always?"

Maybe it was the fruit in the middle of the table that tickled my nostrils and made me come awake.

Why, look at all that food stacked there. Where had it come from, when last night our cupboard had been bare? I picked up an apple and bit it as I went to call Sarah and tell her that Pa had come home during the night and brought us food. In the doorway, holding back the flimsy curtain, I froze, my teeth deep into the red apple, my eyes wide and shocked . . . no Sarah. Just a rumpled bed with a note left on the mattress.

During the night while we slept, Sarah must have slipped out into the dark, leaving a note we were supposed to pass on to Pa when he returned—if ever he returned.

I shook Tom awake to show him the note. He sat up and rubbed at his eyes, and read it over three times before comprehension dawned. He choked, tried not to cry. He and I were both fourteen now. Birthdays came and went without parties or any kind of celebrations to mark our years.

"What y'all doin up so early?" grumbled Fanny, grouchy as she always was when she came out of sleep and found her bones stiff from hard floorboards and not enough padding between her skeleton and the floor. "I don't smell no biscuits bakin, no bacon fryin . . . see no gravy in t'pan."

"Ma's gone," I said in a small voice.

"Ma wouldn't do that," said Fanny, sitting up and looking around. "She's in t'outhouse."

"Ma don't leave notes to Pa when she does that," Tom reasoned. "All her things are gone—what little she had."

"But t'food, t'food, I see food on t'table!" screeched Fanny, jumping up and running to grab a banana. "Bet ya Pa came back an brought all this here stuff . . . an he an Ma are out somewhere fightin."

When I gave it more thought, it seemed very likely that Pa had slipped into the cabin at night, left the food, then drove off without a word to anyone; and perhaps finding the food there, and knowing Pa hadn't bothered to stay or even greet her, had given Sarah the final motivation to leave, thinking now we had food to provide for us until he came back again.

How oddly Our Jane and Keith took the absence of Sarah, as if they'd always lived on unstable ground and Sarah had never given either one enough loving attention to make any difference. Both came running to me, staring up into my face. "Hev-lee," cried Our Jane, "ya ain't goin nowhere, are ya?"

How fearful those big aqua eyes. How beautiful the small doll face that looked up into mine. I tousled her reddish blond hair. "No, darling, I'm staying. Keith, come closer so I can give you a big hug. We're going to have fried apples and sausage for breakfast today, with our biscuits . . . and see, Pa brought us margarine. Someday we're going to eat real butter, aren't we, Tom?"

"Well, I sure hope so," he said as he picked up the package of oleo. "But I'm glad right now we have this. Hey, do you really think Pa came in the night, like Santa Claus, and left all this stuff?"

"Who else would?"

He agreed. As hateful and mean as Pa was, he did try to see that we were kept fed, and as warm as possible.

Now life got down to basics. Sarah had run out and Granny was dead.

Grandpa couldn't do anything but sit and stare, and whittle. I went to his rocker where he'd slept bent over and miserable-looking all night, took his hand, and helped him to stand. "Tom, see that Grandpa visits the outhouse while I fix breakfast, and after he's eaten, give him more wood to whittle, for durn if I can stand seeing him doing nothing at all."

I guess that breakfast on such a heartrending day made it somewhat easier, when we had hot sausages to eat and fried apples and taters, and biscuits with what had to taste as good as butter.

"Wish we had a cow," said Tom, who worried about none of us drinking enough milk. "Wish Pa hadn't gambled away our last one."

"Ya could steal one," contributed Fanny, who knew all about stealing. "Skeeter Burl's got t'one that used t'be ours. Pa don't have no right to gamble away our cow—so steal it back, Tom."

I felt hollow inside, beset with worries far too heavy for my years; when I gave it more thought, I realized there was many a girl my age with a family of her own. Still, those girls didn't desire a college education as I did. They were happy to live out their lives being wives and mothers, and living in shacks, and if their men beat them once a week, they thought it their due.

"Heaven, aren't ya comin?" Tom asked as he readied himself for school.

I glanced again at Grandpa, at Our Jane who was feeling poorly. She'd barely tasted the best breakfast we'd had in weeks.

"You go on, Tom, with Fanny and Keith. I can't leave Our Jane when she's not feeling well. And I want to see that Grandpa doesn't just sit and rock and forget to walk around."

"He's all right. He can take care of Our Jane."

I knew, even as he said that, he didn't believe it; he blushed and bowed his head and looked so miserable I felt like crying again. "In a few days we'll all adjust, Tom. Life will go on, you'll see."

"I'll stay home," Fanny volunteered. "An I'll take kerr of Our Jane an Grandpa."

"A perfect solution," Tom agreed happily. "Fanny's not ever going to finish high school. She's old enough to do somethin simple."

"Okay," I said as a test. "Fanny, first you'll have to give Our Jane a cool bath. You'll have to see that she drinks eight glasses of water a day, and make her eat a little food off and on, and walk Grandpa back and forth to the outhouse, and do what you can to clean up and keep this place tidy."

"Goin t'school," stated Fanny. "I ain't no slave t'Grandpa, ain't no motha t'Our Jane. I'm goin where t'boys are."

I might have known.

Reluctantly Tom backed toward the door. "What should I tell Miss Deale?"

"Don't you tell her Sarah ran off and left us!" I flared hotly. "You just say I'm staying home to help out with all there is to do when Grandpa's feeling bad and Our Jane is sick. That's all you tell her, understand?"

"But she could help."

"How?"

"I don't know how, but I'll bet she could think of something."

"Thomas Luke, if you hope to reach your goals in life, you can't go around begging for help. You rise above all difficulties and find your own solutions. Together you and I will see this family through, and find ways to stay healthy. You say anything you have to say to keep Logan and Miss Deale unaware that Ma has walked out on us . . . for she might come back any minute, once she realizes what she did was wrong. We wouldn't want to shame her, would we?"

"No," he breathed, appearing relieved. "She sure could come back once she thinks more about how wrong it is to go."

He took Keith's right hand, and Fanny took Keith's left hand, and off they set toward the school, leaving me standing on the porch with Our Jane in my arms. She wailed to see Keith trudging dutifully toward school, while I longed to be there with them.

First thing I did after bathing Our Jane and putting her into the big brass bed was to hand Grandpa his whittling knives and his pieces of prime wood. "Whittle something Granny would like, say a doe with big sad eyes. Granny had a special liking for does—didn't she?"

He blinked once or twice, glanced at the empty rocking chair he refused to use even though it was the best one, and two fat tears slid down his wrinkled cheeks. "Fer Annie," he whispered when he picked up his favorite knife.

I turned my attention back to Our Jane, and dosed her fever as I thought Granny would have done, with herbal medicine, and then I set about doing all that Sarah used to do before she turned on us.

Tom seemed stricken when he came from school to see if Ma had returned and found she hadn't. "I guess it's up t'me now t'be the man in t'family," he said, as if overwhelmed by all he'd have to do. "Won't be no money comin in if somebody doesn't go out an make it. Yard jobs are hard t'find when ya don't have t'right equipment. Stores don't give away food staples, an what we got won't last nearly long enough. An we sure could all use new shoes. Heavenly, ya kin't go t'school wearin shoes without toes."

"I can't go to school, shoes or not," I said tonelessly, wiggling my toes that stuck out of shoes much too small, so I'd had to cut them. "You know I can't leave Grandpa alone, and Our Jane isn't well enough to go back to school. Tom, if only we had money enough to take her to a doctor."

"Doctors kin't help what she's got," mumbled Grandpa with his head bowed low. "Somethin inside Our Jane don't work right, an ain't no doctor kin give her what she needs."

"But how do you know that, Grandpa?" I challenged.

"Annie had a youngun once, same as Our Jane. Put him in a hospital, they did. Cost me an Annie all our savins . . . an didn't do one bit of good. Sweetest boy I eva had up an died on Easter Sunday. Tole myself he was like Christ on t'cross, too good an too sweet fer this mean ole world."

There went Grandpa talking just like Granny, when he'd never said much of anything when she lived. "Grandpa, don't say things like that!"

"No, Grandpa," put in Tom, holding fast to my hand. "Doctors can save people from dying. Medicine gets better year by year. What killed your son doesn't have to kill Our Jane."

Tom stared at me with wide, frightened eyes as we readied ourselves for bed after a meal of more fried taters, more sausage, and biscuits and gravy, and apples for desert. All the energy drained from his eyes. "What are we gonna do, Heavenly?"

"Don't you worry, Tom. You, Fanny, Keith, and Our Jane will go to school. I'll stay home and take care of Grandpa, and do the wash, and cook the meals. I know how," I finished defiantly.

"But it's you who loves school, not Fanny."

"Don't matter. Fanny's not responsible enough to stay home and run things."

"She acts that way on purpose," said Tom, tears in his eyes. "Heavenly, no matter what you say, I am gonna tell Miss Deale. Maybe she can think of something that will help."

"No! You can't do that. We've got our pride, Tom, if we don't have anything else. Let's save something we can cherish."

Pride was important to both of us. Perhaps because it was something free, something that made us feel important. We, Tom and I, had to prove ourselves to the world, and also to ourselves. Fanny wasn't included in our pact. Fanny already had proven herself untrustworthy.

7

Coping

Tom hurried home each day to help me with the wash, with the floor scrubbing, with taking care of Our Jane; then he'd chop wood, always he had to chop wood. Sometimes we all ran about madly, trying to round up hogs and pigs that had escaped our frail fence rails, our chickens which were one by one being killed off by bobcats or foxes, or stolen by vagabonds.

"Did Logan ask about me again today?" I quizzed when I'd missed three days of school.

"He sure did. Got me after school and wanted to know where you are. How ya are. Why ya don't come. I told him Sarah is still sick, an Our Jane, too, an ya had to stay home an take care of everybody. Boy, ya never saw anybody look so unhappy as he did."

I was happy to know that Logan really cared, and at the same time I felt angry to be so mired in our troubles. With a pa who had syphilis. With a stepmother who ran out on her responsibilities. Oh, life wasn't fair!

I was angry at the world, at Pa most of all, for he'd started all of this. And what did I go and do but turn on the person I loved most. "Stop saying *yer* instead of *your*—and *ya* instead of *you!*"

Tom grinned. "I love *you*, Heavenly. Now, did I say that right? I appreciate what *you* do to make this a family . . . did I say that correctly? I'm glad *you are* what you are, different from Fanny."

I sobbed, turned, and fell into his arms, thinking he was the best thing in my life—and how could I tell him now that I wasn't wonderful, special, or anything but a cynical, hateful person who hated my life, and the man who'd made it what it was?

Two weeks after Sarah left I just happened to glance out a front window and there was Tom trekking home with more books, and beside him was Logan! Tom had broken his word and told Logan of our desperate situation!

Instantly I went on the defensive and ran to the door, blocking both Tom's and Logan's entrance. "Let us in, Heavenly," ordered Tom. "It's mighty cold out here for you to stand there in the way like a human wall."

"LET EM IN!" shrieked Fanny. "YER LETTIN OUT T'HEAT!"

"You don't want to come in here," I said hostilely to Logan. "City boys like you would shiver with disgust."

I saw his lips tighten with surprise; then came his voice of calm determination. "Heaven, step aside. I am coming in. I am going to find out just why you don't go to school anymore—and Tom's right, it is cold out here. My feet feel like ice."

Still I wouldn't move. Behind Logan Tom signaled wildly for me to stop acting like a fool, and let Logan in. "Heavenly . . . you'll waste all our wood if you keep holding that door open."

I started to push the door shut, but Logan forced me backward and entered with Tom close behind him. It took both of them to shove the door closed when the wind was so strong behind it. For a lock we had a board that dropped down and secured the door as a latch.

His face cold and red, Logan turned to me apologetically. "I'm sorry I had to do that, but I no longer believe Tom when he says Our Jane is sick and Sarah isn't feeling well. I want to know what's going on."

He had on dark glasses. Why, on a dull gray winter day when the sunlight was frail and hardly existent? He wore a warm winter jacket that reached his hips, while poor Tom had only secondhand sweaters, worn in layers that at least kept his upper torso warm, if not his bottom half.

I stepped aside, resigned. "Come in, Sir Logan, said the maiden in distress, and enjoy what you see."

He stepped closer, turned his head, seeming to peer around, while Tom hurried over to the stove and began to warm his hands, his feet, before he even bothered to take off a few sweaters. Fanny, crouched as close to the stove as possible, was not about to give up her place or her bed pallet, though she did set about combing her hair in a big hurry, and she fluttered her long black lashes and smiled at Logan invitingly. "Come sit here with me, Logan."

Tom ignored her, as did Logan. "Well," said Tom cheerfully, "this is home to us, Logan."

Obviously Logan didn't know what to say, so he said nothing.

"You really don't need sunglasses in here, Logan," said I, moving to pick up Our Jane; then I sat to rock her back and forth in Granny's old rocker. The minute I did that, the squeaking of the floor encouraged Grandpa to reach for his whittling and begin another rabbit. His eyesight for near work was very good, but once you were six feet away, he couldn't see much. I suppose I must have looked to him like Granny when she was young and holding a child on her lap. Keith ran to climb up on my lap as well, though he was getting too big and heavy for this kind of cuddling. Still, the three of us together warmed each other.

It was so embarrassing to have Logan here, at our poorest time. I busied myself wiping Our Jane's runny nose, and I tried to put her tousled hair in order. I didn't notice what Logan did until he was seated near the table, and he had his head turned my way. "It's a long, cold walk up this mountain, Heaven. The least you could do is make me feel welcome," he said with reproach in his voice. "Where's Sarah? I mean your mother."

"We don't have an indoor bathroom," I said harshly. "She's out there."

"Oooh . . ." His voice was weak, his face flushed from my frank information. "Where's your pa?"

"Working somewhere."

"I wish I could have known your granny. And I'm still sorry."

So was I.

So was Grandpa, who stopped whittling and looked up, a fleeting shaft of sorrow wiping away the contentment he'd just found in some memory image.

"Tom, I've got my hands full. Would you please boil some water so we can serve Logan hot tea, or cocoa?"

Tom stared at me with astonishment and spread his hands wide. He knew we didn't have tea or cocoa.

Still, he rummaged about in the almost empty cabinet, and came up with some of Granny's sassafras, giving Logan worried looks before he put the water on to boil.

"No, thank you, Tom, Heaven. I've got only a short time to stay, and it's a long trek back to Winnerrow. I want to get there before dark since I don't know my way like you do, being a *city boy*." Logan smiled my way, then leaned forward. "Heaven, tell me how you are. Surely your mother can look out for Our Jane when she's sick. And Fanny's stopped going to school—why?"

"Oh," said Fanny, looking more alert, "ya missed me, huh? Why, ain't that sweet of ya. Who else misses me? Anybody been askin where I am?"

"Sure," Logan said in an offhand way, still staring at me, "all of us wonder why the two prettiest girls in the school stay away."

What could I say to embellish bleak lives of hunger and cold? All he had to do was look around to see how poorly we lived. Why did he just keep his head turned toward me, refusing to stare at a room with no creature comforts but those rolled-up straw mattresses we put on the floor? "Why are you wearing dark glasses, Logan?"

He stiffened. "I guess I never told you I wear contacts. That last fight I had, well, a fist hit me in the eye, and the lens cut my iris, and now my ophthalmologist wants me to keep strong light out of my eyes, and when you favor one eye, you have to favor the other as well, or wear an eyepatch. I prefer the shades."

"Then you can hardly see a thing, can you?"

He flushed. "Not much, to be honest. I see you as a dim figure . . . and I think you've got Our Jane and Keith on your lap."

"Logan, she's not Our Jane t'ya . . . only t'us," Fanny spoke up. "Ya kin call her jus Jane."

"I want to call her what Heaven calls her."

"Kin ya see me?" Fanny asked, standing up, and when she did, she had on only her panties with several of Granny's old shawls about her shoulders . . . and beneath those shawls she was bare from the waist up. Her tiny breasts were just beginning to poke out like hard green apples. Fanny carelessly let the shawl fall open as she rose and sauntered about barefooted. Oh, the shame of her doing that, in front of Logan . . . and Tom!

"Go put on clothes," ordered Tom, red-faced. "Ya ain't got enough of anything fer anyone t'notice anyway."

"But I will have!" screamed Fanny. "Have bigga an betta than Heaven eva will!"

Logan stood to go. He waited for Tom as if he needed help finding the door—when it was right in front of him. "If you can't talk to me when I walk all this way, Heaven, I'm not coming again. I thought you knew I am your friend. I came to prove that I care, and I worry when I don't see you for so long. Miss Deale worries. Just tell me this before I go . . . are you all right? Do you need anything?" He paused for my answer, and when I didn't give it, he asked: "Do you have enough food? Wood? Coal?"

"We don't have enough of nothin!" yelled Fanny loudmouth.

Logan kept his eyes on me, not on Fanny, who'd covered herself again and was now curled up as if half asleep.

"What makes you think we wouldn't have enough to eat?" I asked, pride making my voice haughty.

"I just want to make sure."

"We're fine, Logan, just fine. And of course we have wood and coal—"

"WE DO NOT!" cried Fanny. "We've neva had coal! Wish t'God we did. Heard tell it burns hotter than wood!"

Quickly I spoke. "As you know, Logan, Fanny is a greedy soul and out to get all she can, so ignore anything she says. We're fine, as you can plainly see. I do hope your damaged iris will heal soon and you can take off those dark glasses."

Now he appeared offended and stayed close behind Tom, who led the way out. "Good-bye, Mr. Casteel," he said to Grandpa. "See you later, Keith, Our Jane . . . and keep your clothes on, Fanny." He turned one last time to me, reaching out as if to touch me, or perhaps it was a motion to draw me to him. I sat on, determined not to contaminate his life with Casteel troubles. "I hope soon you'll be coming back to school, Heaven." And he flicked his hand to include Fanny and Keith and Our Jane. "If you ever do need anything, or just want something, remember my dad has a store full of things, and what we don't have there, we can get elsewhere."

"How nice for you," was my sarcastic reply, showing no gratitude at all. "Must make you feel grand and rich . . . why, it's a wonder you'd even bother with a hillbilly girl like me."

I pitied him as he stood there in the open door, staring at me, not knowing what to say. "Good-bye, Heaven. I risked the good health of my vision coming to see you when the sun on the snow up here is not what I'm supposed to see—yet I came anyway. I'm sorry I did now. I wish you luck, but I'll not be coming again just to be insulted."

Ooooh, don't go away feeling hurt, Logan . . . please . . . but I didn't say those words. I just rocked on and on and allowed him to slam out the door, with Tom chasing after, to see him through the woods where he might get lost, and down the safest trail to the valley, where he'd never lose himself, even wearing those damned glasses.

"Boy, were you hateful to Logan," said Tom when he returned. "Durn if I didn't feel sorry for him, trekking all this way up here, almost blind, t'meet with a hateful girl who snapped her eyes at him, and lied her crazy head off . . . ya know we don't have anything much. An he could help."

"Tom, do you want everyone to know that Pa has . . . you know."

"No . . . but do we have to tell him about Pa?"

"We'd have to give some reason why he isn't here, wouldn't we? I guess Logan presumes he's still coming and going, and more or less providing."

"Yeah, I guess yer right," agreed Tom, sinking into dialect when he was discouraged and hungry. "Back to t'fishin lines, t'traps, so keep yer fingers crossed." And with briefly warmed hands and feet, he again left the cabin to search for food. Never could we keep our laying hens when our cooking pot called them to early deaths.

Life not only grew a thousand times more difficult after Sarah left, it also grew impossibly complicated. Pa didn't come home. That meant no money to buy what we needed to keep us going. Our kerosene was so low we had to use candles.

Hours passed that seemed like bits of eternity, waiting for life to begin when Tom came home with Fanny and Keith, and sometimes Our Jane. I wanted to convince myself that Grandpa didn't matter, and I could go to school when Our Jane recovered, and he'd take care of himself just fine. But all I had to do was look at him and see how lost he was without Granny. "Go on," said Grandpa one day when I had the cabin tidy but was wondering what we'd eat tonight. It was almost Thanksgiving. "I don't need ya. Kin do fer myself."

Maybe he could, but the next day Our Jane came down with another cold. "Hongry . . ." she wailed, running to tug on my shiftlike garment. "Wanna eat."

"Sure, honey. You just go back to bed and rest, and in no time at all, supper will be ready." How easily I said that, how lightly, when there wasn't anything in the house to eat but some stale biscuits left over from breakfast, and a half-cupful of flour. Oh, why hadn't I rationed the food we'd had when Sarah left? Why was it I thought Pa would always show up, as if by magic, just when our supplies ran out? Where was he anyway?

"Tom, is it possible to fish after dark?" I asked.

He looked up from his reading, startled. "You want me to go out in the dark and fish?"

"You could also check your rabbit traps."

"I already checked them before I came home from school. Nothing. And at night, how could I find what I hide so well?"

"That's why you've got to fish now," I said in a whisper near his ear, "or there's nothing to eat but two biscuits, and I'll be lucky if I can scrape enough lard out of the can to make the gravy." I was whispering, for if Our Jane heard, or Keith did, there'd be such a clamor none of us could stand it. Our Jane's stomach had to be fed on time or it hurt. Hurting tummy made her wail, and when she was wailing, it was impossible to do anything.

Tom got up and took a rifle down from the wall. He checked it for buckshot. "Deer season just opened, so maybe I kin draw a bead on somethin . . . doe or not."

"Ya mean we ain't got nothin t'eat if ya don't shoot a deer?" shouted Fanny. "Jesus Christ, we'll starve t'death iffen we have t'depend on yer shootin!"

Tom stalked to the door, threw Fanny a hard, long look of disgust, then smiled at me. "Go on, get your gravy ready—and in half an hour I'll be back with meat—if I'm lucky."

"What if you're not?"

"I won't come home until I can bring something."

"Well," said Fanny, rolling over on her back and staring into a small cheap mirror, "guess we won't eva see Tom agin."

Tom slammed the door and left.

Fishing and hunting were both part of our daily routine now. Part of my time during the day was spent outdoors, setting traps, baiting fish lines. Tom made the snares to catch rabbits or squirrels. We had already hunted for mushrooms that Granny had taught us how to distinguish from deadly toadstools. We had picked berries until our hands turned bloody from the briars, searched for wild bean and pea pods in the woods, dug for turnips that could be found near the edge of Winnerrow. We stole spinach, lettuce, collards, and other things from Winnerrow backyard gardens. When real cold winter came, the berry bushes stopped producing. The peas and beans dried up. The rabbits and squirrels disappeared in their hidden hibernation places, and weren't attracted to our snares and boxes now that we didn't have decent bait. And mushrooms didn't favor freezing cold nights any more than we did. And that was why our larder of food had been reduced to almost nil.

"Heaven," complained Fanny, "cook what ya got. We kin't sit around an wait all night fer Tom t'come back with nothin. Ya got beans an peas hidden somewhere, I jus know ya have."

"Fanny, if just once in a while you'd do more to help, maybe I would have a hidden store of beans and peas . . . but I don't have anything but lard scrapings and two dry old biscuits." All this said in a low voice that the keen ears of Our Jane and Keith couldn't hear.

For once Grandpa's ears perked up. He craned his neck and peered my way. "Taters planted in t'smokehouse floor."

"Used all those last week, Grandpa."

Our Jane let out a terrible shriek. "Gotta eat!" she howled. "Hurts! Tummy hurts so bad . . . Hev-lee, when we gonna eat?"

"Now," I said, running to pick her up and sit her at the table on a chair raised by two blocks of wood placed on the seat. I kissed the sweet place on the back of her slender neck and ruffled her soft hair. "Come, Keith. You and Our Jane can eat first tonight."

"What ya mean, *they* kin eat first? What about me?" cried Fanny. "I'm a member of this family much as they are!"

"Fanny, you can wait until Tom comes back."

"If he's gotta shoot somethin first, I'll be old an in my grave fore he does!"

"O you of little faith," said I, busy heating up the little lard I had, putting water and a little flour in a small bowl and mixing it until the lumps disappeared, before I added it to the hot lard, shaking into it salt and pepper, stirring and stirring so it wouldn't go lumpy. I tasted, sprinkled in more salt, stirred some more, actually feeling the hungry eyes of Our Jane and Keith devouring it while it still heated in the pan. Grandpa rocked on and on, eyes glazed, thin hands clutched on the chair arms, not expecting to eat again today. If Our Jane and Keith suffered most, second most had to be Grandpa, who was losing weight so rapidly I could have cried for him.

"Annie could sure make t'best blueberry pies," Grandpa mumbled wistfully, his eyes closed, his thin lips quivering.

"Ya only got two biscuits fer six of us?" asked Fanny. "What ya gonna do, give us each a crumb?"

"Nope. Gonna give Keith and Our Jane each a half, and Grandpa gets the other half, and you, Tom, and me will split the last half into three portions."

"*A crumb!* Jus what I thought! Grandpa don't need a whole half fer himself!"

Grandpa shook his head. "Ain't hongry, Heaven chile. Ya give my half t'Fanny."

"No! I did that this morning. Fanny can eat her portion or forget about eating until tomorrow, or when Tom comes back with meat."

"I'm not waitin fer Tom!" stormed Fanny, throwing herself into a chair by the table. "I'm eatin now! I'm three times bigga than Our Jane. She don't need a whole half."

I was doing everything as slowly as possible, not that there was much to do. Two cats had returned today, a black one and a white one, both perched high on a shelf near pots and pans, and both were staring down at me with hope in their hungry eyes, needing food as much as we did. And there I was, staring up at them, wondering if anybody ever ate cats.

Then I was staring down at Pa's old hunting hound that had returned with the cats. Oh, how awful to even contemplate eating pets we loved. Yet that's just what I was doing.

Suddenly Fanny was beside me, whispering and pointing at old Snapper, the hound Pa loved best of all. Sixteen years old, and almost blind, and yet he could always forage for himself and come home looking fat and well fed. "He's got meat on those ole bones," Fanny said in an intense way. "Sure would like t'eat meat agin. Ya kin do it, Heaven, know ya kin. Slit his throat, like they do hogs. Fer Our Jane, fer Keith—an Grandpa—why, we could all eat . . ."

At that point Snapper opened his sleepy hooded eyes and stared at me soulfully. I glanced again at where Our Jane and Keith sat, each moaning.

"Betta an ole dog than us," Fanny crooned more urgently. "All ya gotta do is bash in his head." She handed me the hatchet we used for chopping kindling for Ole Smokey. Even now it was belching out foul black smoke that stung our eyes.

"Go on. I know ya kin do it," encouraged Fanny, shoving me toward Snapper. "Take him out first—then give it t'him." Snapper suddenly jumped to his feet, as if sensing my intention, and ran for the door. Fanny let out a shriek of dismay and ran after. At that moment the door opened, and, hell-bent to escape our murdering intentions, Snapper disappeared in the night.

Tom strode in, grinning at us, his rifle on his shoulder, and slung on the other a sack heavy with something in it.

His grin faded when he saw the hatchet in my hand, and my look of shame and guilt. "You were goin t'kill Snapper?" Incredulity was in his voice. "But I thought you loved that dog."

"I do," I sobbed.

"But ya didn't have faith, did ya?" he asked bitterly. "I ran all t'way there and back."

He hurled his lumpy bag on the table. "Two dead chickens inside. Course Race McGee is gonna wonder who shot inta his henhouse, and iffen he ever finds out he'll kill me, but at least I'll die with a full stomach."

We ate well that night, devouring an entire chicken, and saving the other for the next day. But the day after, when both chickens were eaten, we were again faced with the same problem. No food. Tom whispered not to worry, where there was a will there was also a way.

"It's time now to forget honor and honesty, and steal," Tom figured. "Didn't see a deer. Nary a coon in sight. Woulda shot an owl, but they didn't hoot. Every night, along bout twilight, when folks in Winner-row are settling down at their tables t'eat, you, me, an Fanny gonna sneak down t'the valley and steal what we can."

"What a wonderful idea!" cried Fanny, quite delighted. "They don't hang shotguns on their walls down there, do they?"

"Don't know," answered Tom, "but we're gonna sure find out."

It was a fearsome, scary thing that we set out to do the next twilight, while we still had chicken in our stomachs to give us courage. We wore dark clothes, soot on our faces, and trudged through all the cold until we came to a small outlying farm where the meanest man alive lived. What was worse, he had five giant sons, and four huge daughters, and a wife who would have made even Sarah look weak and dainty.

Fanny, Tom, and I clung to the protection of dense scrubs and fir trees until we saw every member in that family settle down in the kitchen to make such a racket it would surely cover any noise we might make. They had a yard full of dogs, same as we used to have, and cats and kittens.

"Soothe the dogs," ordered Tom in a hissy, scary whisper, "so Fanny and I can raid the henhouse and not use my rifle." He gestured to Fanny. "You grab for the feet, two for each hand, and I'll grab my four. That should hold us for a while."

"Do they peck ya?" asked Fanny, looking strange.

"Nah, ain't ya eva heard about being chickenhearted? They don't put up much fight, jus lots of squawking."

Tom had assigned me the chore of diverting the most vicious-looking dogs I'd ever seen. I had a way with animals, and most of the time they trusted and liked me . . . but that great big dog looked half English bull, and from the mean look in his eyes he hated me on sight. I had with me a tiny bag of chicken necks, tail ends, and feet.

Inside, the McLeroys were eating and fussing, while I threw out a chicken foot and said softly, "Nice doggy . . . you don't hate me, and I can't hurt you . . . so eat the chicken foot . . . go on, eat."

He sniffed the dried yellow foot with disgust, then growled. That seemed to be a signal to all the other dogs. There must have been seven or eight of them left in the yard to protect the fenced-in pigs, chickens, and other farm animals. All of a sudden all the dogs were coming my way! Snarling, barking, showing the sharpest-looking teeth I'd ever seen. "Stop it this minute!" I ordered sharply. "STOP! You hear?"

Inside the kitchen a woman was bellowing out almost the same words. The dogs stopped, seeming undecided. While they were, I tossed them the chicken necks and tails and the rest of the feet. They ran to gobble up what they could, not nearly enough, then came at me with tails wagging for more.

About that time a terrible squawking came from the henhouse—and the dogs took off, running toward the chicken coop.

"STOP!" I ordered. "FIRE!" One dog hesitated and looked back at me as I leaned over and set fire to a pile of dead leaves left for some lazy son or daughter to sweep up and put in a mulch pit.

"Ma!" bellowed a giant of a man in overalls. "There's someone settin our yard on fire!"

I ran.

Never had I run so fast, with all the dogs at my heels. Perhaps I ran twenty feet before the swiftest hound was almost on me. I shinnied as fast as possible up a tree, and sat on a thick limb staring down at dogs gone crazy now that I'd shown fear. "Go way!" I ordered in a firm voice. "I'm not afraid of you!"

Out of the darkness came old Snapper running to my defense, and into that pile of younger, stronger dogs he threw his strength just as Farmer McLeroy came on the run with a rifle!

Immediately he fired his gun over the heads of the dogs. They scattered in all directions, leaving me to cringe up there, trying not to draw attention to myself.

Unfortunately, the moon was out. "Ain't that ya, Heaven Casteel?" asked the giant farmer. He could have been one of Sarah's relatives, his hair was so red. "Ya t'one who's been stealin my chickens?"

"I'm the one your dogs chased up this tree, just cause I went huntin for Pa's favorite hound. He's been missing for weeks, and just a few days he came home . . . now he's gone again."

"Get down here!" he snapped.

I gingerly lowered myself to the ground, hoping and praying Fanny and Tom had stolen the chickens and were well on the way home.

"Where'd ya hide em?"

"Hide what?"

"My chickens."

"Do you think I could shinny up that tree holding chickens? Mr. McLeroy, I've only got two hands."

Behind him loomed three huge sons, all with bushy heads of red hair. All wore thick, coarse beards, and two had flashlights they aimed at my face, and one traveled slowly down to my feet, then up again. "Hey, looky, Pa, she's done gone an grown up t'look like her ma, t'pretty city one."

"She's a chicken thief!"

"Do you see any chickens on me?" I asked, bold as brass.

"Well, we ain't felt ya all ova yet," said a boy hardly older than Logan. "Pa, I'll do t'searchin."

"You will not!" I snapped. "All I was doing was looking for my pa's dog, and that's not against the law!"

Boy, was I learning how to lie, giving Tom and Fanny time to run to safety in the hills.

Those giants let me go near the edge of the woods, convinced I wasn't a chicken thief—just a big liar.

Tom and Fanny had managed to get away with five chickens, and Tom had pocketed six eggs, though only three remained unbroken when he reached the cabin. "We'll save two hens," I said when I reached there, flushed and breathless, "so they can lay eggs and Our Jane and Keith can have eggs every day."

"Where were you all that time?"

"Up a tree, dogs underneath."

We became pretty good at stealing, never robbing from the same place twice. We'd leave Grandpa in charge of our two youngest and set off each night, learning all kinds of sneaky ways to grab what we could. In the gloom of winter twilight, we waited for women to empty car trunks of bags of groceries. Some of the women made four and five trips inside . . . and that gave us the chance to run fast, seize a bag, and quickly leave. It was stealing, out and out, yet we reasoned we were saving our lives, and one day we'd pay those women back.

One evening each of us managed to grab a bag, barely escaping before a woman yelled out, "Help, thieves!" And what I had in my bag was only paper toweling, waxed paper, and two bundles of toilet tissue. Fanny doubled over laughing. "Dummy, ya gotta go fer t'*heavy* bags."

For the first time in our lives we had real toilet paper, paper toweling, and waxed paper—whatever to do with it? Didn't have anything to wrap up and save in a refrigerator.

Tom and I lay side by side on our floor pallets, thinking now that Grandpa should use the bed to comfort his old bones with softness for a change. "It makes me feel bad," Tom whispered. "Stealing from people who work hard to earn money. I gotta get a job, even if I don't come home till midnight. An I can always do a little stealing from rich folks' gardens. They don't need extras anyway."

Trouble was, valley folks didn't trust hill boys not to steal, and finding a job wasn't easy. In the end all of us had to sneak again and again to Winnerrow and steal. Then came the day when Tom stole a pie he saw cooling on a window ledge and ran all the way back to the cabin to share the pie with us. I'd never seen such a delicious-looking pie, with crust fluted perfectly even all around the edges, and juice bubbling up out of holes punched in a flower design on the top crust.

It was a tart apple pie that tasted so good I didn't really want to scold him for becoming an expert thief.

"Oh, it's all right," laughed Tom with twinkling eyes. "This pie we just finished off was made by your boyfriend's mother, an ya jus know Logan would give up anything to make his Heaven's family happy."

"Who's Logan?" mumbled Grandpa, while the taste of the pie still warmed my mouth and thrilled my taste buds.

"Yeah," growled a familiar deep voice from the doorway, "who's Logan? And where the hell is my wife? Why is this place such a pigsty?"

Pa!

He strode in, carrying over his shoulder a huge burlap bag with bulky things inside that had to be food supplies, and he hurled all that he'd brought onto the tabletop.

"Where t'hell is Sarah?" he yelled again, glaring at each of us in turn.

Not one of us could find words to tell him. Pa stood tall and lean, his bronze face clean-shaven and paler than usual, as if he'd undergone a great ordeal, and had lost at least ten pounds, and yet he looked fresher, cleaner, and, in a way, healthier than when I'd seen him last. He appeared a dark-haired giant, reeking of whiskey and that strange, overpowering scent that was strictly male. I shivered to know he was back; at the same time, I was overcome with relief. As mean as he was, he'd save us from starvation, now that real winter was upon us, and every day snow would be falling, and the wind would be whistling around our frail cabin, finding all kinds of ways to get in and chill our bones.

"Ain't nobody here who knows how t'talk?" he asked sarcastically. "Thought I sent my kids to school. Don't they learn nothin? Not even how to greet their own pa, and say they're glad to see him home again?"

"We're glad," said Tom, while I got up and turned again to the stove, ready to do my best to cook another meal, now that we had plenty, from the looks of that bag. And I was, in my own way, trying to hurt Pa as he so often hurt me with his indifference.

"Where's my wife?" he bellowed again. "SARAH!" he shouted. "I'm back!" His yell could have been heard down in the valley . . . but it didn't bring Sarah.

He checked the bedroom, standing with his hands holding the curtains spread apart, his legs wide, as he looked in and didn't understand. "In the outhouse?" he asked, turning again to Tom. "Where is Ma?"

"I'll be only too happy to tell you," I spoke up when Tom floundered.

He flashed his dark eyes my way. "I asked Tom. Answer me, boy—where the hell is your mother?"

As if I'd been born for this moment, this chance to sting his pride—I was ready to pounce. I could tell from his expression he thought now Sarah might possibly be dead—as Granny had died when he was absent—and for a moment I hesitated before I went on, speaking harshly.

"Your wife's left you, Pa," I said, glaring at him. "She couldn't stand more grief and suffering after her baby was stillborn. Couldn't take this cabin and never having enough, with a husband who had to have his fun, while she had none. So she's gone, and she left you a note."

"I DON'T BELIEVE YOU!" he roared.

No one said anything, just stared at him, even Fanny.

Then it was Grandpa who found the strength to rise from his rocker and face his son. "Ya ain't got no wife now, son."

His voice seemed full of pity for this son who'd lost twice, and would no doubt lose all of his life, and it wouldn't be anybody's fault but his own. That was my mean thought on the night that Pa showed up after being gone almost a month.

"Yer Sarah packed up her thins an left in t'night," Grandpa concluded with great difficulty, for easy words had long ago departed.

"Somebody fetch her note," Pa whispered, as if he'd lost his strength now, and was suddenly as old as Grandpa.

Silently, with vicious pleasure, I stepped toward the highest shelf, where we placed our valuables that were so few, and from a chipped sugar bowl Granny had once told me Pa had bought new for his angel I took out the brief note, folded four times into a tiny hard wad.

"Read it t'me," ordered Pa, gone numb and strange-looking.

"Dear husband [I read],

"Can't stay no longer with a man who just don't care enough about anything. Going where it's better. Good luck and goodbye.

"Much as I loved ya, hate ya now.

Sarah"

"And that's all, ALL?" bellowed Pa, snatching the note from my hand and trying to read the scratchy, childish handwriting. "She runs off and leaves me with five kids, and she wishes me good luck?" He balled up her note and hurled it into the open door of the stove. His long fingers raked through his dark mane of hair. "Goddam her to hell!" he said dully, before he jumped up and bellowed, shaking his fist at the cabin ceiling. "When I find her I'm gonna wring her damned neck, or cut out her heart—if I can find it. To go when there's no woman here, to leave little children on their own—damn you, Sarah, I expected better, I did!"

In a flash he was out the door, leaving me to think he was going this very minute to hunt up Sarah and kill her, but in a minute or two he was back, hurling down on our table more supplies. He brought in two sacks of flour, salt, slab bacon, beans, dried peas, a huge tin of lard, bundles of tied spinach, apples, potatoes, orange yams, bags of rice, and lots more we'd never had before, such as boxes of crackers and cookies, and peanut butter and grape jelly.

Our tabletop was covered, seeming enough to last a year. And when he had it all spread out, he turned to all of us and spoke to no one in particular.

"I'm sorry your granny is dead. Sorrier your ma ran out on me, and that means all of you as well. I'm sure she's sorry to hurt you just to get to me." He paused before he continued.

"I'm going this day and not coming back until I'm cured of what I've got. I'm almost well, and would like t'stay an take care of ya, but stayin would do more harm t'ya then my leavin. An I've got a job that suits my condition. So you go easy on this food, fer there won't be more coming from me until I get back."

Aghast, I wanted to cry out and tell him not to leave, that we just couldn't survive the rest of this bitterly cold winter without him.

"Don't none of ya have any idea where she went?"

"Oh, Pa!" cried Fanny, trying to run into his arms, but he held up his hand to stay her.

"Don't touch me," he warned. "Don't understand much what I got, but it's a nasty thin t'have. See how I had a man put everything in sacks? Burn all the sacks when I'm gone. I've got a friend who will try and find Sarah, and make her come back. Hold on till she does, or I do . . . hold on."

As bad as he was, as evil and cruel as he could sometimes be, still he'd work long enough selling somebody's moonshine to buy us basic food supplies, a few treats, and enough clothes to keep us covered, if not well, at least warmly.

For I was staring at the used clothes that Fanny was pawing through and squealing over. Sweaters and skirts, blue jeans for Tom and Keith, and underwear for all of us, and five pairs of shoes, though he'd had to guess at our shoe sizes. Tears welled up in my eyes. No coats or boots or hats, and we needed those things. Still, I was grateful to see the heavy ugly sweaters, gone nubby from others' wearing them.

"Pa!" yelled Tom, running after him. "Ya can't leave us all alone! I'm doing what I can to help, but it ain't easy when nobody in Winnerrow trusts a Casteel, an already Heavenly can't go to school—and I've gotta go, Pa! Gotta go or stop breathing! Pa! Are ya listenin? Hearin me?"

Pa strode on, closing his ears to the pitiful words of a son I knew he loved. And the wails of Fanny crying surely must have followed him for many days. But a daughter named Heaven didn't plead or cry, or say a word. I just felt the cold, clammy hand of fate squeezing the blood out of my heart. Alone, just as in my nightmares.

Alone in the cabin. Without parents, without any way to support ourselves.

Alone when the wind blew, when the snow fell, when the trails to the valley disappeared beneath ice and snow.

We didn't have snowshoes, coats, skis, none of the things that would take us swiftly to the valley, to school, or to church. And that pile of food, as high as it looked now, would disappear soon enough. What then?

Pa stood near his truck, staring at us in turn, at all but me. It hurt that even now he couldn't bring himself to meet my eyes.

"Take care," he said, and disappeared in the dark. We heard the roar of his old truck as it took off and sped down the dark trails to wherever it was that he went.

As Sarah would have done, I did, too. I set about putting things away, not a tear in my eye, my lips set in a thin grim line as I faced up to the responsibilities of running this cabin until Pa came home again.

8

Squalor and Splendor

For a brief and wonderful moment before Pa stalked out into the night, leaving us alone again, hope had lit up all our hearts, lifted us high only to plunge us into even deeper despair once he was gone, and we were, again, left alone.

Snagged in our nightmare, we stood in a tight group and listened to the lonely night sounds when we could no longer hear his truck driving away. We had food on the table to show he'd cared a little, if not enough. I damned him for not staying, damned him for a thousand reasons.

I stared at the table covered with what he'd brought, and though it seemed a great deal—would it last until he came back again?

Out into our primitive wooden box on the porch that served us well enough as a refrigerator during the winters we put what meat we wouldn't use today. In some ways it was a blessing this was winter and not summer when we'd have to gobble down everything before it spoiled in the heat. When Granny was alive, with Sarah and Pa, there had been nine of us, and there was never enough left to spoil.

I didn't realize until later that Pa had come on Thanksgiving Day to bring us our Thanksgiving Day dinner.

Hunger dictated our menus. Only too soon all that Pa had brought to last until he came again dwindled down to nothing but beans, peas, and the eternal staple of our lives, biscuits and gravy.

The howling wind added nothing to our happiness, nor did the cold that kept us all huddled around Ole Smokey. Hours and hours Tom and I spent in the yard chopping wood, felling small trees, and searching to find dead branches broken off during windstorms.

Life in the cabin flipped backward into that same familiar nightmare that even the brightest morning light couldn't dispel. I stopped hearing the early-morning birdsongs (those few brave birds that dared to stay), stopped watching the glory of winter sunsets. No time to linger out of doors when we might catch our deaths, and there'd be no one wise enough to make us well again. No time to linger near a window where it was drafty. Only too much time to crowd near the fire and think bitter thoughts.

Up at dawn every morning, I continued the daily struggle to do all the things that Sarah had once done. Not until this stepmother was gone did I realize how much I'd been spared, even when she was her laziest. Tom tried, really tried to help, but I kept insisting that he continue with his schooling, though Fanny was only too happy to stay home.

Trouble was, Fanny stayed home not to help out with the work but to steal out and meet with the kind of boys who'd never go anywhere in this world but to jail, or to early graves—the ones who incessantly played hooky, were already hooked on booze, pool, gambling . . . and girls.

"Don't need no education," Fanny flared scornfully, "already got enough!" A zillion times she said that as she admired herself in that silver mirror that had been my mother's; unfortunately, Fanny had immediately seized it from my hand when foolishly I took it out of its hiding place, and she tried to claim it for her own. It was tarnished, and she didn't recognize it as valuable. Rather than battle her for it then and there, and allow biscuits to burn in the oven, I decided that later on, while she slept, I'd reclaim my mirror and hide it in a better place. At least she hadn't found the suitcase with the doll yet.

"Worst thin is, t'school's warmer than here. Heaven, why ya have t'have so much pride? Ya done stuck some of it on me, so onliest time I kin yell out t'truth is when yer near t'say it's a lie, or I'd go yellin out t'everybody we're hongry! Cold! Miserable an dyin!"

Fanny cried real tears. "There's gonna come a day when I'm neva gonna be hongry or cold agin . . . ya wait an see!" she sobbed brokenly. "Hate this place! All t'thins I have t'do t'keep from cryin all t'time. Hate cryin! Hate not havin what city girls do! . . . Heaven, let go yer pride so I kin let go of mine."

I hadn't known she had any until this startling minute. "It's all right,

Fanny," I said softly; "go on and cry. I figure a good cry sets you free to have pride . . . and that will help us to be better people, stronger people. Granny always said that."

The moon was riding high before Tom came home from school, the fierce wind blowing him in the door and slamming it behind him before he threw two squirrels on the table, tiny gray ones he quickly skinned while I hid Our Jane's eyes and Keith stared wide-eyed and teary to see his "friends" stripped of their pretty fur. Soon I had the meat boiling to make a stew, adding the last of our carrots and potatoes. Keith crouched in a corner and said he wasn't hungry.

"You have to eat," Tom said softly, going to pick him up and carry him to the table. He plopped Keith down beside Our Jane on her cushion. "If you don't eat, then Our Jane won't eat, and she's already weak and too thin . . . so eat, Keith, show Our Jane you like Heavenly's stew."

Day after day passed and Logan didn't come again, nor did Tom see him in the school hallways. Tom wasn't as old as Logan, so they weren't in the same classes.

Ten days after Logan's visit Tom told me, "Logan's gone away with his parents somewhere." He had made a real effort to find out what had happened to Logan Stonewall. "His pa's got another pharmacist working in his store until they come home. Maybe somebody in the family died."

I hoped not, yet I sighed in relief. My worst fear was that Logan would move away, forget about me, and even if he didn't, he'd stay so angry he'd never look my way again. Better to believe Logan was off on a vacation, or even attending a funeral or visiting a sick grandmother, than disappearing because he didn't like me anymore. Soon he'd be coming home again. Someday better than now he'd show up, we'd meet, I'd say I was sorry, he'd smile, say he understood, and everything would be fine between us.

There was mending and sewing to do. Once Sarah had picked up fabric at sales, ugly, cheap stuff that nobody else wanted; by ripping apart old dresses and using them for patterns she'd fashioned wearable clothes, even if they weren't fitted properly and looked hideous. I didn't know how to make dresses for Our Jane or Fanny, much less for myself. Tom's shirts grew ragged, and there was no money to buy him new ones. I sewed on patches; sewed up rips with clumsy large stitches that soon pulled out. I pulled together split seams, tried to weave threads so they filled tiny holes. I took apart old dresses I'd outgrown and tried to put together a new dress for Our Jane, who could be made very happy by something new and pretty. It was freezing cold in the cabin, and as much as I hated to, I went to the magical suitcase, hunted through all the beautiful summer clothes, and pulled out a soft pink pullover sweater. It had three-quarter sleeves, and still was much too big for Our Jane to wear as a dress. But the moment she spied it, she wanted that sweater in the worst way. "Now, hold on until I make it fit."

And make it fit I did, by running thin elastic through the neckline to draw up the shoulders. Now Our Jane had a full-length pretty, warm pink sweater-dress.

"Where'd ya get that kind of fabric?" asked Fanny, coming in from the woods, immediately suspicious when she saw Our Jane skipping happily about in the cabin, showing off her new dress. "I neva saw that pink thin before . . . where'd ya get it, huh?"

"I found it blowing wild on the wind," answered Tom, who had a terrific imagination for embroidering his own hunting tales. "There I was, lying flat on my belly, buried deep in t'snow, waitin fer a wild turkey t'poke up his head so we'd have a tasty Christmas meal. Had my beady dead eye on t'bush it was hidin behind, my rifle cocked an aimed, my eye slotted an sure, an here comes this pink thing flyin through t'air. Almost shot it dead, I did, but it landed on a bush, an durn if it weren't a sweater-dress with Our Jane's name on the tag."

"Yer lyin," proclaimed Fanny. "Biggest, stupidest lie ya eva told—an ya done tole a million."

"Ya otta know, havin told yer own ten zillion."

"Grandpa, Tom's callin me a liar! Make him stop!"

"Stop, Tom," Grandpa said dully. "Ya shouldn't tease yer sista Fanny."

That's the way it went, Fanny and Tom fighting, Keith and Our Jane staying quiet, Grandpa whittling and staying off his feet which he constantly said were sore from corns, bunions, and other scaly things that I thought soap and water would cure. Grandpa didn't favor soap and water too much; even on Saturday night we had to force him to take a bath. Grandpa tried hard not to do anything but whittle.

Fanny used any excuse to keep from doing her share of the work even if she didn't go to school, so eventually I just gave up on Fanny and decided if being ignorant was her goal and her style, she was already college-degreed. It was Tom who had to finish his education, and to that we were both dedicated.

"All right," he said to me with a touching sad smile, "I'll go on, an really try to learn enough for two, so I can teach you when I'm home.

But wouldn't it be better if I could tell Miss Deale, and then she could write assignments for you to complete—wouldn't it be, Heavenly?"

"If you make sure she doesn't know we are alone up here, suffering, hungry, cold, miserable. We don't want her to know that, do we?"

"Would it be so awful? Maybe she could help . . ." he said tentatively, as if afraid I'd blow.

"Look, Tom, Miss Deale earns what Logan calls a pittance, and she'd spend it all on us, she's so generous. We can't let her do that. Besides, didn't she give all of us a lecture one day in class, saying poverty and hardships made for strong backbones and hearty characters? Boy, are we going to end up with iron spines and sturdy, unbreakable characters!"

He stared at me with great admiration. "Boy, you sure got character right now, and an iron spine as well! If you had any more, we really might starve to death."

Each and every day Tom trudged off to school, his homework completed to perfection. Nothing stopped him, not the cold drenching rains, the sleet, the wind, or the cold. Like the mail, he went, regardless. He walked to and fro, never having the appropriate clothing to wear. He needed a new winter jacket to keep him warm, no money for that. He needed new shoes and high boots to keep his feet dry, for the shoes Pa had brought didn't fit anybody. Sometimes, to escape the dreary sameness of the cabin, Fanny trailed behind Tom, sitting in class and learning nothing, but it did give her time to flirt with the boys. Keith went to school when Our Jane was so sick she didn't scream to see him go.

We still took baths on Saturday nights, with the tin tub pulled close to the fire. Our hot water, drawn from the well, heated on the stove so we could also wash our hair. We were getting ready for the only fun event we had left to enjoy: going to church.

Every Sunday morning when the weather was halfway decent, at dawn we set out, wearing our pitiful best.

Tom carried Our Jane half the way. I'd help her walk the rest, or pick her up myself. If she hadn't had visions of ice-cream cones in her head, I don't think she would have gone so willingly. Keith skipped and danced alongside whoever was in control of his most beloved possession, his sister. Fanny always raced on ahead. Way behind, the last of all, trudged Grandpa, slowing us down more than Our Jane did. Grandpa used a walking cane now, and often Tom had to drop back to help Grandpa over some fallen tree or boulder. The last thing we needed was for Grandpa to fall and break a bone.

It took one or two hours for Grandpa to make the descent into the valley, and that meant four of us were out in the cold that long just to keep him company. The fifth, Fanny, was snug inside the church long before we got there, hidden in some dark cubbyhole, enjoying forbidden adult delights. Tom hunted her up immediately, smacked the boy she was with, dragged Fanny away, made her straighten her skirt, and we all arrived late, as usual the last to enter, and were the objects of the all-over scrutiny that told us again we were the worst of the hill folks, the scummiest of the scum, the Casteels.

But to go to that small white church with the high steeple gave us hope. It was born in us to believe, to have faith, to trust.

As arduous as these Sunday excursions were for all of us, going to church gave us not only pleasure but much to talk about during our long lonely times. To sit in the back pew and look around and see all the prettily dressed people, to feel just a small part of the human race for a few hours, helped us to endure the tortures of the rest of the week.

I tried to avoid Miss Deale, who didn't always come to church, but this particular day she was there, turning to smile at us with relief in her pretty eyes, welcoming us with her gestures to sit next to her. Sharing the hymnbook with me, in glorious celebration of life Miss Deale raised her beautiful voice and sang. Our Jane lifted her small face and gazed at Miss Deale with such rapt adoration it made tears come to my eyes. "How ya do that?" she whispered once we were seated and Reverend Wise was at the podium.

"We'll discuss singing after church," whispered Miss Deale, leaning to lift Our Jane and hold her on her lap. From time to time I'd see her gazing down at Our Jane, touching her silky hair, tracing a delicate finger over Our Jane's sweet cheek.

To stand and hold the hymnbooks and sing was the best part of all. The worst came when we had to sit still and listen to all those frightening sermons about deeds that were so sinful. Christmas was just around the corner, inspiring Reverend Wayland Wise to be his most fervent, which meant his fire-and-brimstone sermons that gave me nightmares as bad as being in hell.

"Which one of you hasn't sinned? RISE UP and let us stare in awe, in admiration—and disbelief! We are *ALL* sinners! Born from sin! Born through sin! Born into sin! And we will *DIE* in sin!"

Sin was all around us, inside us, lurking in the corners, in the dark side of our natures, sure to catch us.

"GIVE AND YE SHALL BE SAVED!" yelled Reverend Wise, pounding his fist on the podium and making it shake. "Give and ye shall be delivered from *Satan's arms!* Give to the poor, the needy, the beset and bereft . . . and from the river of your gold all goodness shall flow back into your own lives. GIVE, GIVE, GIVE!"

We had a little change that Tom had earned doing odd jobs for valley wives, but it sure was gonna hurt giving up any of it in hopes of that river of gold flowing uphill to us.

Sitting on Miss Deale's lap, Our Jane coughed, sneezed, needing someone to help her blow her nose, to go to the bathroom. "I'll do that," I whispered, leading her out to where she could again be held in thrall by the pretty ladies' room with its row of pure white basins, its liquid soaps, its paper hand towels. She entered a tiny compartment where she could sit and not smell "bad" odors, and then had the pleasure of flushing the toilet. A real compulsion she had to keep dropping in paper so she could watch it go down, flushing and flushing. When we returned, I refused to let her sit on Miss Deale again and wrinkle that pretty suit. Our Jane complained her feet hurt in shoes that were too small, and it was too cold in here, and why did that man up there yell and take so long to finish talking? And when did we stand to sing again? Our Jane loved to sing, though she couldn't carry a tune.

"Sssh," I cautioned, lifting my sweetest little one up on my lap. "It will soon be over, and we'll sing again, and then we can have ice cream in the store."

For an ice-cream cone Our Jane would have walked on red-hot coals.

"Who's gonna pay for it?" Tom whispered worriedly. "We can't let Miss Deale do it again. And we won't have any cash left if we drop our change into t'collection plate."

"Don't drop it in. Just pretend you do. We're the poor, the needy, the beset and bereft—and rivers don't flow upward, do they?"

Tom reluctantly agreed, though he would have been willing to gamble on God's generosity. We did have to keep what money we had left to buy Keith and Our Jane their ice cream, if nothing else. At least we could do that for them.

The collection plate was passed down our aisle. "I'll pay for all of us," whispered Miss Deale when Tom reached into his pocket. "You keep what you have for yourselves"—and darn if she didn't drop in two whole dollars!

"Now," I whispered when the last hymn was over and Miss Deale was standing and collecting her purse, pulling on her fine leather gloves, picking up her personal hymnbook and Bible, "head fast for the door, and don't hesitate for anything!"

Our Jane resisted, dragging her feet. Quickly I swept her up, and she let out a howl. "ICE CREAM! Hev-lee, ICE CREAM!" And that gave Miss Deale the chance to catch up with us as we slipped by Reverend Wise and his grim wife.

"Stop, wait a minute!" called Miss Deale, hurrying after us, her high heels clicking on the slippery pavement.

"It's no use, Tom," I whispered as he tried to support Grandpa and keep him from falling. "Let's make up good excuses so she won't fall and break a leg."

"Oh, thank goodness," gasped Miss Deale when we turned to wait for her. "What do you mean hurrying off when you know I promised Our Jane and Keith ice cream? Don't the rest of you still like treats?"

"We'll always adore ice cream!" Fanny declared fervently, as Our Jane stretched her arms toward her ice-cream godmother. Like a burr Our Jane clung to our teacher.

"Now let's all go where it's warm, and sit and relax, have some fun." Miss Deale turned and led the way back toward Stonewall's Pharmacy, with Keith skipping along, clinging to her free hand, and Fanny was almost as childish-acting as Keith and Our Jane . . . and just a few minutes ago she'd been ready to seduce some pimply-faced valley boy if he'd give her a quarter.

"And how is your father?" called back Miss Deale, turning into the drugstore. "I haven't seen him lately."

"He'll come home one day," I said in a forbidding way, hoping and praying she'd never hear about his disease.

"And your mother, Sarah, why didn't she come today?"

"She's home, not feeling so well, just resting."

"Tom told me you've been ill; you look fine, though much thinner."

"I'll be coming back to school, soon . . ."

"And Keith and Jane, when will they be coming back?" she persisted, her sky-blue eyes narrowing suspiciously.

"Both have been kinda sickly lately . . ."

"Heaven, I want your honesty. I'm your friend. A friend is someone you can depend on, *always*, who is there to help when you need it. A friend understands. I want to help, need to help, so if there's anything at all that I can do, I want you or Tom to tell me what you need. I'm not rich, but I'm not poor, either. My father left me a small inheritance when he died. My mother still lives in Baltimore, and isn't feeling too well lately. So, before I go home for the Christmas holidays, I want you to tell me what I can do to help make your lives happy and more bearable."

Here was my golden chance. Opportunity seldom knocked twice on any door—but pride tightened my throat and froze my tongue, and because I didn't speak out, neither did Tom, or Grandpa. Fanny the bold and shameless had, fortunately or unfortunately, wandered away to flip through pages of magazines.

And while I stood just inside the door, debating the wisdom of confessing everything, Miss Deale turned to stare at Grandpa sitting so dejectedly on a padded bench behind a small table. "Poor dear man, he misses his wife, doesn't he?" she asked with so much compassion. "And you must miss her just as much." Then she was meeting my eyes and smiling warmly. "I've just had the most marvelous idea—ice cream is fine, but not a real meal. I'm planning to have lunch in a restaurant. And I hate eating alone, it makes everyone stare—please do me the honor of joining me, and that will give you time to tell me what's been going on in your lives."

"We'd love to!" Fanny shouted eagerly. Suddenly she was there, her smile a yard wide. She had the nose of a bloodhound for a free meal.

"Thank you very much, but I'm afraid we can't accept," I said briskly, caught in my own snare of devilish stubbornness, all the time wishing I could throw away my pride and be like Fanny. "It was very nice of you to ask, more than kind, but we have to get home before dark."

"Don't ya listen t'her, Miss Deale," yelled Fanny. "We're hungry since Pa went away! Ma's gone, Granny's dead, an it will take Grandpa t'rest of this day t'make t'trip back. An when we get there we won't have nothin much t'eat. An it *will be* dark fore we reach there!"

"But Pa's coming back any day," I hurriedly added. "Isn't he, Tom?"

"Yeah, any day," confirmed Tom, looking wistfully at the restaurant across the street. It was one we'd often stared into, wishing that just once we could sit at a round table with a crisp white tablecloth, with a crystal vase holding a single red rose, with waiters wearing black and white, and pretty chairs with red velvet seats; oh, how lovely the combination of white, red, and gold. How clean and perfumy it must smell in there, not to mention how warm it had to be, and how delicious the food would surely be.

"And your mother is gone . . . ?" questioned Miss Deale with a strange look on her pretty face. "Now, I've heard rumors about town that say she has gone for good. Is that true?"

"Don't know," I answered shortly. "She may change her mind and come back. She's like that."

"SHE AIN'T LIKE THAT!" yelled Fanny. "She's neva comin back! She left a note an said so. Pa read it an got madder'n hell! Then he ran out t'get her . . . an we're suffering, Miss Deale, all of us . . . ain't got no ma, ain't got no pa, an not eva got enough food t'eat, or warm clothes t'wear, an half t'time no wood t'burn—why, it's awful, downright awful!"

I could have shot Fanny dead on the spot. Fanny had screamed out our humiliating condition right in the drugstore where perhaps twenty pairs of ears heard every word she said.

I stood with my face flushed, wishing I could sink through the floor or go up in smoke, so embarrassed and ashamed to have all our secrets exposed. It was like being naked in public. I wanted to stop Fanny, who went on and on telling more about our lives and family secrets. Then I glanced over at Grandpa, and back at Keith and Our Jane, and sighed heavily. What was pride when compared to seeing huge eyes sunken in deep, hungry hollows? What kind of fool was I to reject the kindness of this wonderful, caring woman? An idiot, I decided. Fanny had ten times more sense.

"Come now, Heaven, if Fanny wants to eat in a restaurant, and Tom looks as if he would as well, and Jane and Keith are so thin, should you vote against the majority? You are outvoted, and it's decided. The Casteel family are my dinner guests this Sunday, and every Sunday until your father is back to take care of you all."

Oh, I had to swallow to keep from crying. "Only on the condition that you allow us to repay you someday when we can."

"Why, of course, Heaven."

Fate had stepped in, wearing an expensive suit with a mink collar— and when fate came dressed like that, who could resist?

Like Moses leading his starving horde, Miss Deale strode across Main Street, with Our Jane clinging devotedly to her gloved hand. Prouder than one of those peacocks I'd never seen, she entered that fancy restaurant where men in black and white stared at us as if we were circus freaks they fervently hoped would vanish. Other diners stared, wrinkled their noses, and looked contemptuous, but Miss Deale smiled at everyone.

"Why, good afternoon, Mr. and Mrs. Holiday," she greeted pleas- antly, nodding to a handsome-looking couple dressed as finely as she was, "how nice to see you again. Your son is doing marvelously in school. I know you're proud of him. It's so wonderful to have a family to dine with me." She sailed like a ship knowing its home port, despite the ragged line behind her, heading toward the best table in the restaurant.

Once there, she arrogantly gestured to an astonished older man to seat us properly as she explained to us, "This table has the best view of your mountain."

I was overwhelmed, scared, embarrassed. In a fancy gold chair with crimson velvet covering the seat and back, I sat as if in a dream of royal riches. Our Jane's nose was running again. Tom quickly grabbed at Keith and asked directions to the nearest men's room. Fanny smiled at everyone as if she truly belonged here, no matter how shabby she looked. Before Fanny would even sit, as the waiter held her chair, she tugged off her three sweaters one by one. Every pair of eyes in the place watched with astonishment and dismay, no doubt thinking Fanny would strip to her skin—as did I. However, Fanny stopped at her shabby dress and smiled brilliantly at Miss Deale.

"Neva felt so happy in my whole miserable life as I do right now."

"Why, Fanny, that's sweet, and hearing you say that makes me feel just as happy."

Keith was not as fond of flushing as was Our Jane, and he and Tom came rushing back as if afraid they'd miss something wonderful. Tom beamed at me happily. "Some Christmas treat, right, Heavenly, right?"

Oooh, yes! Christmas was only five days away. I stared at the tall, splendid tree in the corner, at the poinsettias placed around the room. "Ain't it pretty, though, Heaven?" Fanny said much too loudly. "When I'm rich an famous I'll *lunch* like this every day, every day in t'year!"

Miss Deale beamed at all of us in turn. "Now, isn't this nice? Much better than you going your way and me going mine. You can each tell me what you'd like most. We'll start with you, Mr. Casteel."

"I'll jus have what t'rest of ya does," muttered Grandpa, appearing overwhelmed and ill at ease. He kept trying to hide his mouth with his hand, afraid others would see his missing teeth, his watery eyes still downcast, as if still awed to be seated where he was.

"Miss Deale," Fanny said without hesitation, "ya pick out t'best there is, what *ya* like most, an that's what we all want. An dessert. Jus leave out t'collards, t'biscuits an gravy."

Even after that Miss Deale managed to keep her compassionate expression.

"Yes, Fanny," she concluded, "a very good idea, I must say, for me to select what I like most for all of you. Now, is anyone here who doesn't like beef?"

Beef! We never had beef at home, and it would put color in the cheeks of Our Jane and Keith.

"Love beef!" Fanny cried with loud, lusty passion. Grandpa nodded, Our Jane sat looking wide-eyed all around, and Keith had his eyes on his small sister, while Tom just glowed.

"Anything you like will suit us just fine," I said humbly, everlast-ingly grateful to be here, and at the same time so afraid we'd shame her yet with our bad table manners.

Miss Deale lifted her napkin, which was folded like a flower, and shook it open, then slipped it over her lap. I quickly did the same, even as I kicked Fanny's shin under the table, and helped Keith with his napkin, as Miss Deale helped Our Jane with hers. Grandpa somehow managed to catch on and did the same; so did Tom. "Now, for the first course we should have salad or soup. The entrée will be meat and vegetables. If you'd rather have seafood, lamb, pork, speak up now."

"We'll have beef," stated Fanny, almost drooling.

"Fine, everybody agreed?"

We all nodded, even Our Jane and Keith.

"Now . . . we'll have to decide if we want our beef roasted rare, medium, or well done—or would you rather have steak?"

Baffled again, Tom and I met eyes. "Roast beef," I whispered. In my favorite books all the really romantic men ate roast beef.

"Good, I adore roast beef myself, medium rare, I think, for all of us. And we'll have potatoes . . . and for vegetables—"

"Don't want none," Fanny informed quickly. "Jus give me t'meat, t'taters, an t'dessert."

"That's not a well-balanced meal," Miss Deale went on without even glancing up from her menu as the waiter took ours away and delicately brushed them off. "We'll all have a tossed salad, and green beans. We should enjoy that, don't you agree, Mr. Casteel?"

Grandpa nodded dumbly, appearing so intimidated I doubted he'd be able to eat anything. As far as I knew, Grandpa had never eaten "out."

It wasn't a meal . . . it was a feast!

Huge plates of salad were put before us. We just stared for a few minutes before I lifted my eyes to watch which fork Miss Deale used, and then I picked up mine. Tom did the same, but Fanny just plucked out what she wanted with her fingers until I nudged her under the table again. Our Jane picked at hers, and Keith looked troubled as he did his best to swallow strange food without crying. Miss Deale buttered two hot rolls and handed one each to Our Jane and Keith. "Try that with your salads; it helps a lot."

To my dying day I'll remember that salad full of green leaves we'd never seen before, and tomatoes at this time of the year, and teeny ears of corn, and green peppers, and raw mushrooms, and so many other things I couldn't name. Tom, Fanny, and I devoured our salad in short order, reaching often to seize up hot bread from a covered basket, and three times it had to be replaced. "Real butter," I whispered to Tom, "it has to be."

Before Our Jane, Keith, and Grandpa could finish their salads, the "entrée" arrived.

"Do ya eat like this every day?" asked Fanny, her dark eyes glowing with happiness. "Why, it's a wonda ya don't weigh a ton."

"No, I don't eat like this every day, Fanny. Sunday is my day to treat myself, and from now on, when I'm in town, it will be your day to enjoy with me."

It was too good to believe. Why, we could live all week on what we ate today, and with great determination I decided I'd eat everything, even though it did appear an enormous amount. I think Fanny, Tom, and even Our Jane and Keith made the same decision. Only Grandpa had trouble with the beef since he had so few teeth.

I felt like crying I was so happy to see Our Jane eating with real enjoyment. In no time Keith cleaned his plate, even if he did overdo it when he leaned over to put his head in his plate so he could lick up the last bit of the dark sauce.

Miss Deale's hand on my arm restrained my scolding. "Let him sop up his gravy with the roll, Heaven; it does my heart good to see all of you enjoy your meal." She smiled radiantly.

When we'd all emptied our plates, leaving them so clean they sparkled, she said, "And of course you'll all be wanting dessert."

"We'd love dessert!" shouted Fanny, making other diners turn to stare at us again. "I want that fancy chocolate cake," she said, pointing to the dessert cart.

"And you, Mr. Casteel?" asked Miss Deale in the softest of voices, her eyes looking so kind. "What will you have for dessert?"

I could tell Grandpa was uncomfortable, no doubt suffering from gas when his stomach surely was not accustomed to so much food all at once, and chewing took him forever.

"Anythin . . ." he mumbled.

"I think I'll have chocolate pie," Miss Deale said. "But I know Our Jane and Keith will love the kind of chocolate pudding they serve here, and Mr. Casteel, Heaven, Tom, all of you select what you want, for it would really make Fanny and me feel miserable to be eating sweets if everyone doesn't join us."

Pie, cake, chocolate pudding? Which one? I chose the pie because Miss Deale had to know best. Fanny's huge piece of cake topped with whipped cream and a cherry enchanted me even as I quickly devoured the pie. But Grandpa, Tom, Our Jane, and Keith were served the chocolate pudding in fancy footed dishes that made me wish I'd chosen differently.

As if paradise had finally found its way into her mouth, Our Jane spooned her chocolate pudding onto her tongue so fast she was finished before Keith. She beamed the broadest smile of her life on Miss Deale. "That was GOOD!" she said. Several people seated near us smiled.

It had gone fairly well up until now, but for Keith licking his plate. I should have known our luck couldn't hold out.

Abruptly, without the slightest warning, Our Jane gagged, turned greenish, then suddenly threw up, right on Miss Deale's wine-colored wool skirt! Some splattered on the crisp tablecloth, some on me.

Our Jane's eyes turned huge, dark, before she began to wail, loud, terrified cries. She tried to bury her face in my lap as I apologized and dabbed at the mess on Miss Deale's skirt with my huge white napkin.

"Oh, Heaven, don't look so distressed," said Miss Deale calmly, not appearing disturbed in the least even as she mopped at her smelly skirt. "I'll send this to the cleaner's, and it will come back as good as new. Now, everybody stop looking worried, be calm, and I'll pay the check while all of you put your warm clothes back on; then I'll drive you home."

The other diners turned their eyes away, ignored the scene. Even the waiters didn't seem disturbed, as if they'd correctly presumed the moment we came in the door that we'd ultimately do something like this.

"I did a bad thin," sobbed Our Jane as Miss Deale signed the check. "Didn't wanna, Hev-lee. Couldn't help it, Hev-lee."

"Just tell Miss Deale you're sorry."

But Our Jane was too shy to speak, and again she wailed.

"It's all right, Jane dear. I remember doing the same thing when I was your age. Things like that happen to all of us, don't they, Heaven?"

"Yes, yes," I said eagerly, grasping at the straw. "Especially when you have a tiny stomach not used to so much."

"I neva threw up on nobody," proclaimed Fanny. "My stomach knows how t'behave."

"Yer tongue don't," threw in Tom.

I carried Our Jane out to Miss Deale's expensive black car. Light snow began to drift down as Miss Deale drove higher and higher, up into the misty clouds where we lived. All the way home I fretted, fearful Our Jane's queasy stomach might let loose again and ruin the interior of the magnificent car; but Our Jane managed to keep what else she'd eaten down, and we arrived home without soiling anything else.

"I don't know how to thank you enough," I said humbly, standing on the sagging porch, my sister still in my arms. "I'm terribly sorry about your beautiful suit. I hope the stain comes out."

"It will, I know it will."

"Please ask us agin next Sunday," implored Fanny; then she opened the cabin door and disappeared inside, slamming it behind her. In a second the door popped open and she called out, "An thanks a heap, Miss Deale. Ya sure know how t'throw a party."

Bang went the door.

"You're one in a million," Tom said gruffly, leaning to kiss Miss Deale's cold cheek. "Thanks for everything. If I live t'be a hundred and ten, I'll never forget today, and you, and your meal, the best I've ever eaten, no disrespect to you, Heavenly."

Of course, now was the time to invite Miss Deale inside and show *our* hospitality. But to let her in would give her too much information, and that I couldn't do. Though I could sense she was waiting for an invitation, and the chance to see how we really lived. The cabin as viewed from the outside was pitiful enough, but for her to see the inside would keep her sleepless.

"Thanks again, Miss Deale, for all that you've done. And please forgive Fanny for being too aggressive, and Our Jane is terribly sorry, even if she can't say so. I'd ask you in, but I left the house in a terrible mess . . ." Boy, that was no lie.

"I understand. Maybe your father is inside, wondering where you are. If so, I'd like to speak with him."

Fanny stuck her head out again. "He ain't in here, Miss Deale. Pa's sick an—"

"He *was* sick," I interrupted hastily. "He's much better, and is due home tomorrow."

"Oh, that's a relief to hear." She smiled and hugged me close, and her perfume filled my nostrils as her soft hair tickled my face. "You're so brave and so noble, but too young to endure so much. I'll be back tomorrow afternoon, shortly after school is over, to deliver your presents to put under your Christmas tree."

I didn't tell her we didn't have a Christmas tree. "We can't let you do that," I protested weakly.

"Yes, you can; you must. Expect me tomorrow about four-thirty."

Again Fanny put her head out the door; obviously she'd been listening through the flimsy door. "We'll be waitin. Don't ferget."

Miss Deale smiled, started to speak, but seemed to change her mind before she touched my cheek gently. "You're such a lovely girl, Heaven. I would hate to think you won't finish high school, when you have such a gift for learning."

Suddenly a small, frail voice spoke up, when I never expected to hear Keith volunteer anything. "Yes," whispered Keith, clinging close to my skirt. "Our Jane is sorry."

"I know she is." Miss Deale lightly touched Our Jane's round cheek, then ruffled Keith's pretty hair before she turned to leave.

In the cabin that was almost as cold as outside, Tom stuffed more wood into Ole Smokey. I sat down and rocked Our Jane, feeling the cold winds blowing in through the openings in the walls, seeping up through the floor cracks, coming in through the ill-fitting window frames. For the first time this cabin seemed totally unreal, not home at all. I had the vision of the restaurant with its soft white walls, its crimson carpet, its fancy furniture; that was the world I wanted for all of us. And to think it was the best meal of my life made me realize just how miserable we all were, so much I began to cry.

Tonight I was going to say my longest, most sincere prayer, down on my knees. I was going to stay there for hours and hours, and this time God would hear me and answer my prayer, and send Pa home again.

Yet I was up at dawn the next morning, singing as I began my day with cooking, with seeing Tom off to school, and right away I set in to make the cabin as clean and tidy as possible, enlisting Fanny's help.

"Ya kin't make it pretty!" she complained. "Ya kin scrub, dust, sweep, an still it'll stink!"

"No, it won't. Not when you and I are finished; this place is gonna shine, really shine—so get busy, lazybones, and do your share, or no more treats for you!"

"She won't slight me, I know she won't!"

"Do you want her to sit in a dirty chair?"

That did it. Fanny made an effort to help, though it wasn't more than an hour before she fell down and rolled up to go back to sleep. "Makes t'time go fasta," she mumbled, and when I looked Grandpa was dozing in his rocker, also waiting for the miracle of Miss Deale who would come at four-thirty.

Four-thirty came and went without Miss Deale showing up.

It was almost dark when Tom came home with a note from Miss Deale.

Dearest Heaven,
  When I returned home last night, there was a telegram under my door. My mother is in a hospital and seriously ill, so I'll be

flying to be with her. If you need me for any reason whatsoever please call the number below, and reverse the charges.

I am sending a delivery boy to your home with everything I think you need. Please accept my gifts to children I love as my own.

Marianne Deale

She'd written a number with the area code, perhaps forgetting we didn't have a telephone. I sighed and looked up at Tom. "Did she have anything else to say?"

"Lots. Wanted to know when Pa was coming home. Wanted to know what we needed, and what size clothes we all wore, and shoe sizes. She pleaded with me, Heavenly, to let her know what we needed most. How could I tell her when the list would be a mile long? We need everything, most of all food. An ya know, I stood there like a jackass an wished t'God I could be like Fanny, an shout it all out, an have no pride . . . an feel no humiliation, just take what I could—but I couldn't, an she's gone. The only friend we have, gone."

"But she's sending gifts anyway."

He laughed. "Hey . . . where's all that pride?"

Three days passed, and that box of presents didn't arrive.

On the day before Christmas Eve Tom came home with bad news. "Went to the store Miss Deale told me about, to ask where were the things she wanted them to deliver, and they said they didn't deliver in this county. I argued with them, but they insisted we'd have to wait until she was back again, and paid an extra fee. Heavenly, they must not have told her that, or she would have taken care of it. I know she would have."

I shrugged, trying to appear indifferent. It was all right, we'd manage. But my heart went bleak.

Real winter mountain weather chose this day to attack with such ferocity we were left totally unprepared. We ran about stuffing rags in the cracks we could reach. We stuffed rags under the doors, in between the floorboards, around the rattly window glass. Our cabin looked like a loosely knitted raggy scarf inside, giving fleas, roaches, and spiders good nesting places, even if they were cold. Sunsets were always fleeting in the mountains, and night always fell with alarming swiftness. With the night came the smothering cold to settle down on the mountains like an ice blanket. Even when we rolled up mattresses used for bedding and slept in the middle of the roll, all of us failed to keep warm when the floor near the stove was so cold. Grandpa slept in the big brass bed when he could remember to leave his rocker, and that's where I wanted to keep his old, tired bones, off the floor where it was hard and cold.

"No," Grandpa objected stubbornly. "Ain't a right thin t'do, when younguns need t'bed more than me. No back talk now, Heaven girl, ya do as I say. Ya put Jane an Keith in t'bed, an if t'rest of ya crowd in y'all should keep each other warm."

It hurt to take the bed from Grandpa, but he could be stubborn about the oddest things. And always I'd believed him to be so selfish. "T'bed was for t'younguns," he insisted, "t'frailest," and of course that had to be Our Jane and Keith.

"Now, ya wait a minute!" bellowed Fanny, using her bull-moose voice. "If younguns deserve soft, warm beds, I'm next in line. Plenty of room fer me, too."

"If there's plenty of room for you, then there's plenty of room for Heavenly as well," insisted Tom.

"And if there's room for me, Tom, there should be room for just one more," I contributed.

"But there ain't enough room fer Tom!" yowled Fanny.

There was.

Tom found room at the foot of the bed, his head on the portion where Our Jane and Keith lay, so he wouldn't have longer legs thrusting bare feet that close to his face—and cold feet at that.

Tom, before he could go to bed, had to chop more wood in order to get enough to build a hotter fire to melt the ice for water. Ole Smokey kept coughing out more evil-smelling smoke.

It was Tom who got up in the night to add more wood to the fire. Wood was running low. Every spare moment after school, until the night was dark, and all Saturday and Sunday found Tom outside chopping wood for an old stove that devoured wood the way elephants ate peanuts.

He'd chop with determined dedication until his arms and back ached so much he couldn't sleep without tossing and turning and crying out in pain. Muscles aching so badly, he slept lightly. I got up to rub his back with hot castor oil that Granny used to swear by, good for any ailment under the sun. Enough of it could cause an abortion, and that I didn't doubt. Enough castor oil inside, and *all* that was in would melt and flow away. However, it did help Tom's aching muscles.

When I wasn't hearing Tom groaning, I heard other things in the night: the wheezing rattle in Grandpa's chest, the small incessant coughs of Our Jane, the rumblings of hunger in Keith's tummy; but most of all I heard footsteps on the rickety porch.

Pa coming home?

Bears on the porch?

Wolves coming nearer and nearer to eat us all?

It was Tom's fervent belief that Pa would not abandon us to starve and freeze to death. "No matter what ya think, he loves us, Heavenly, even you." I was curled up on my side, with my feet on the small of Tom's back, but I had my head turned so I could stare up at the low ceiling, the unseen sky beyond, praying that Pa would come home again, healthy and strong, pleading for our understanding.

The next day was Christmas Eve. In our cupboard was only about half a cup of flour, a tablespoon or so of lard, and two dried apples. I woke that morning with a sense of doom that weighed me down so much I could hardly move about. I stood staring at what food I had left, tears streaking my face; Our Jane could eat all the gravy I made and still she wouldn't have enough. The floor squeaked behind me as Tom slipped his arms around my waist.

"Don't cry, Heavenly, please don't. Don't give up now. Something will turn up to save us. Maybe we can sell some of Grandpa's whittled animals in town, and if we can do that, we'll have money to buy lots of food."

"When the snow is over," I whispered hoarsely, my hunger pains a dull throb that never let up.

"Look," he said, turning to the window and pointing at a bright streak in the leaden gray sky, "it's brightening. I can almost see the sun breaking through. Heavenly, God hasn't forgotten about us. He's sending Pa home, I can feel it in my bones. Even Pa wouldn't leave us here to starve alone, you know that."

I didn't know anything anymore.

9

Christmas Gift

It seemed Tom and I could have traveled a hundred miles on a sunny day in less time than it took us to creep to the smokehouse on Christmas Eve, holding one to the other, as the wind howled in our ears, blew snow in our faces to almost blind us. But when we headed back, we had in our pockets a dozen of Grandpa's best wooden carvings that he'd never miss, they'd been so long in the smokehouse.

The relief of feeling the porch beneath my feet allowed me to open my eyes for the first time and see how white our world was, not from new snow but from the old snow the wind banked around our crouched cabin. Tom fought to open the door, and then he shoved me through and quickly followed.

Stumbling inside, at first I couldn't focus my eyes, they were so heavily lidded with snow caught on my lashes. Fanny was screaming, and there was so much other noise. Startled, I looked around—only to freeze in shock and then feel the instant flaring hope.

Pa! Come home for Christmas Day . . . ? Our prayers answered, at last, at last!

He stood in the dim firelit room, gazing down at where Keith and Our Jane were huddled together for warmth. Even with Fanny dancing around and yelling her head off they slept on and on, as did Grandpa in his rocker.

Pa didn't seem to hear or see Tom and me as we quietly slipped into the room, keeping as far from him as possible. Something in his stance, in his manner as he gazed down at the two youngest, put me on guard.

"Pa," Tom cried joyfully, "ya've come back to us!"

Pa turned, his expression blank, as if he didn't know that large, flame-haired boy. "I've come t'bring a Christmas gift," he said dully, with no joy in his eyes.

"Pa, where ya been?" asked Tom, while I stood back and refused to greet him, just as he refused to look my way and acknowledge my presence.

"Nowhere ya'd care to hear about."

That's all he'd say before he fell to the floor beside Grandpa's rocker, and now Grandpa woke up enough to smile weakly at his son, and only too soon both he and Pa were snoring.

Bags and sacks and boxes of food were on the table. We could eat again, yet it wasn't until I was in bed that night that I wondered what wonderful gift Pa had brought home, so huge he couldn't carry it in. Clothes? Toys? He never brought us toys or candy, yet hopefully I longed for all of that.

Tomorrow was Christmas Day.

"Thank you, God," I whispered full of gratitude when I got up to pray on my knees by the bed; "you sent him in the nick of time, you truly did."

On Christmas morning I was cooking mushrooms that Tom had found in a shallow woodsy ravine just yesterday, when Pa got up from the floor, went out briefly to use the outhouse, then strode back inside, unshaven and stale-looking, and plucked Our Jane and Keith from their warm, snug bed. He held them both easily in his strong arms, looking at each with affection, while they stared at him with wide, kind of frightened eyes, as if they no longer knew him. They were *my* children now, not his. He didn't love them as I did, or else he wouldn't leave them for so many days without enough food. Holding my tongue by sheer force of will, I kept on cooking the mushrooms.

For an extra treat today we'd have eggs, but I'd save the bacon until Pa went away again. I'd not waste even a thin slice on him.

"Hurry up with the meal, girl," barked Pa. "Got company coming."

Company?

"Where's the Christmas gift?" asked Tom, striding in from an hour of chopping wood.

Pa ambled to the nearest window, not noticing it was sparkling clean, and stared out. "Get these two dressed, and quick!" he ordered without meeting my eyes as he put Our Jane and Keith down on the floor.

Why did his eyes shine like that? Who was the company? Sarah? Could it be Sarah—was she our gift? How wonderful, absolutely wonderful!

Our Jane and Keith flew to me, as if I represented their mother, their security, their hopes and their dreams, and quickly enough I wiped both their faces. Soon I had them both dressed in their best, which was poor enough.

Life would get better now, I thought. I still possessed that childish optimism that refused to be dreary or depressed during the day. Steadfastly I held tight to hope, despite what I saw in Pa's eyes, sensed in the air, felt in my bones. Something—something bad. His cold, hard eyes glanced my way briefly before they lingered on Tom, Fanny, and, last of all, Keith and Our Jane.

Of all his five children he preferred Tom, and next Fanny. "Hi there, darlin," he said to her with a sweet smile. "Got another hug fer yer pa?"

Fanny laughed. She had a smile and a hug for anyone who noticed she was alive. "Pa, I prayed every night, every day, ya'd come back. Missed ya so much it hurt." She pouted her full lower lip and asked where he'd been.

I heard a car drive up outside and pull to a stop. I moved to the window to see in that car a stout man and his wife waiting, it seemed, for Pa's signal. Glancing at Pa, I could tell he was having a difficult time making up his mind as he lifted Fanny onto his lap and stroked her long black hair. "Now, you kids gotta face some hard facts," he began in a short, gruff way, with pain in his eyes. "Yer ma ain't never coming back. Hill folks are like that. Once they make up their minds, put action behind it, ain't nothing short of death can make em undo a decision. Not ever. What's more, don't want to ever see her again. If she shows her face here—I'll use my shotgun and blow it off." He didn't smile to show he was only joking.

Not one of us spoke.

"Now, I've found nice rich folks who can't have kids of their own, and they want one so much they're willin to pay good money for what they want. They want a young child. So it's gonna be either Keith or Our Jane. Now, don't none of ya yell out or say no, cause it has t'be done. If ya want t'see them grow up healthy and strong, and have nice things I can't afford to give them, ya keep yer mouths shut, and let this couple make their choice."

I went cold inside. All the hopes that had lit up were snuffed out in the harsh winds of knowing what Pa was going to do. Pa was Pa and would never, never change. A no-good, filthy, rotten, drunken Casteel! A man without soul or heart, not even for his own.

"It's my way to give Keith or Our Jane the best kind of Christmas gift—an don't none of ya go yellin an cryin an spoilin it. Ya think I don't love none of ya, but I do. Ya think I ain't been worried about what's goin on in this cabin, but I've worried. Been sick inside, sick outside, tryin to find a way to save ya all. An one dark night when I was sicker than any starvin dog in a gutter, it came t'me."

He bestowed on Fanny a charming smile, gave another to Tom, Keith, and Our Jane, but he didn't even look at me. "Already told yer grandpa. He thinks it's a good thing to do."

Fanny slowly left Pa's lap and backed up to where I was holding Our Jane, and Tom had both his hands on Keith's narrow, frail shoulders.

"Pa," said Fanny, looking pale and concerned for once, "what ya plannin on doin?"

Again Pa smiled in his most winning way. (I thought he looked exceptionally cunning.) "I got t'thinkin about just how willin rich folks are to pay for what they want. Me, I got more kids than I can take care of. Some want kids an can't have any. There's lots of rich folks out there, wantin what I got plenty of—an so I'm sellin."

"Pa," Tom said stoutly, beginning to tremble, "yer just jokin, ain't ya?"

"Shut up, boy," warned Pa in a low, intense tone. "I'm not joking. Dead serious. Got my mind set on this being the best thing. The only way out. At least one of ya will be saved from starvin."

This was our Christmas present? Selling Keith or Our Jane?

I felt sick. My arms clutched Our Jane tighter to my breasts as I buried my face in her soft curling hair.

Pa moved to the door to let in that couple from the black car.

A fat lady wearing high-heeled pumps entered, followed by a fatter man. Both wore warm, heavy coats with fur collars, and gloves, and big, happy smiles on their faces that soon faded when they saw the hostility on *our* faces. Then they turned in a slow circle to stare with abject horror at all the poverty.

No Christmas tree here. No gifts, no trimmings, no packages spread around. Nothing at all to indicate this was anything but another day to suffer through.

And here was Pa planning on selling his own.

Beyond belief, those city folks' expressive, shocked eyes said. "Oh, Lester," cried the rather pretty fat woman, getting down on her knees to try and cuddle Keith to her enormous bosom, "did you hear what he said as we came up the steps? We can't let this dear, lovely child starve! Look at his eyes, so huge and pretty. Look at this fine silky hair. And he's clean. Sweet-looking. And that dear little girl the older one is holding—isn't she just a darling, isn't she, Lester?"

Panic was all I could feel. Oh, why had I bathed and shampooed them yesterday? Why didn't they look dirty so she wouldn't want them? I sobbed and held Our Jane tighter as she clung to me with trembling fear. Maybe Our Jane or Keith would be better off—but would I, would I? They were mine, not hers. She hadn't stayed up with them all night, and walked the floors, or spoon-fed them, taking hours and hours that could have been spent outdoors playing.

Go way, go way, I wanted to scream, but what did I say? This:

"Our Jane is only seven years old." My voice was hoarse as I determined to save Our Jane from this woman, this man. "Neither she nor Keith has ever been away from home. They can't be separated from each other; they'll cry and scream, be unhappy enough to die."

"Seven," murmured the woman, appearing shocked. "I thought she was younger. I wanted a younger child. Lester, can you believe she's seven—and how old is the little boy?"

"Eight!" I cried. *"Too old* to adopt! And Our Jane is sickly," I went on with hope in my heart. "Actually, she's never been what anyone could call healthy. She throws up often, has every disease that rolls around, colds all the time and high fevers . . ." And on and on I would have gone, trying to ruin Our Jane's chances, because I couldn't bear to see her go, for her own good or not—but Pa scowled and ordered me to shut up.

"Then we'll take the little boy," spoke up the fat man called Lester, pulling out his bulging leather wallet. "I always wanted a son, and that boy there is a good-looking young man, and well worth the price you're asking, Mr. Casteel. Five hundred, right?"

Our Jane began to scream.

"NO! NO! NO!" she yelled right in my ear.

She wiggled free from my tight embrace and ran to join Keith, throwing her arms about him, and continued to scream, terrible screams expressing the kind of anguish a child should never know. Keith saw her pain, joined in, and clung to his sister.

More desperate words from me: "Keith is not what you'd want in a son. He's very quiet, uneasy in the dark, scared most of the time— can't bear to be without his sister. You don't want to go, do you, Keith?"

"Don't wanna go!" cried Keith.

"NO, NO, NO!" wailed Our Jane.

"Oh, Lester . . . isn't this heartbreaking, just heartbreaking? We can't separate such two little dears. Lester, why not take *both*? We can afford both, and then they won't cry or miss their family so much, if they have each other. An you'll have your son, an I'll have my daughter, an we'll all be so happy, our family of four."

Oh, God! In trying to save each of them, I'd lost both!

But there was hope, for Lester was hesitant, however insistent his wife. If only Pa would keep quiet, but he said in a sad, caring way: "Now, that's what I call real quality, a woman with a heart of gold, willing to give to two instead of one," and that's all it took for Lester to make his decision, and then he was pulling out papers and was adding another line or two before he signed, and Pa bent over to painstakingly form his own signature.

As difficult as Pa made writing seem, and as painfully slow as he was, I knew when he was finished there would be a signature as beautiful as any. Like many ignorant people, to Pa appearances meant more than content.

During all of this, I'd backed to the stove and picked up the heavy iron poker. Once I had it in both my hands, I raised it high and had the courage to actually hiss when I yelled at Pa. "Ssstop thisss! I won't let you do thisss! Pa, the authorities will come and put you in jail if you sell your own flesh and blood! Keith and Our Jane are not hogs or chickens for sale, they're your own children!"

Pa moved like lightning, even as Tom hurried to protect me. With one painful twist of my arm, I had to release the poker or have my arm broken. The poker fell to the floor with a clatter.

The stout woman looked my way, alarmed. "Mr. Casteel, you did say you'd talked this over with the other children. They agreed, didn't they?"

"Yes, of course they agreed," lied Pa. His charm, his sincerity, created some mesmerizing aura of integrity that convinced that married pair easily enough. "Ya know how younguns are, agreeing one moment, squabbling the next. Soon as they enjoy what this money buys, all left here in this cabin will know I did the right thing."

NO! NO! my mind was screaming. Don't believe him, he's a liar! But I was speechless, caught up in the horror of knowing I might never again see my little brother and sister.

Before it could even be absorbed, Keith and Our Jane were sold, like hogs at the market, and that man named Lester said to Pa: "We hope you realize, Mr. Casteel, that this sale is legally binding, and you can never seek to recover your two children once we leave. I'm an attorney, and I've written a contract that says you are fully cognizant of what you're doing, and the consequences of this act, and this contract that states firmly that you did willingly, without altercation or argument or persuasion, or force, agree to sell your two youngest children to me and to my wife, and you do irrevocably give up all rights to see them again, or contact them in any way in the future."

I cried out. Pa might not even know what *irrevocably* meant!

No one heeded me, but Tom moved to my side and pulled me into his arms. "It's not going to happen, Heavenly," he whispered. "After hearing all that, Pa surely won't go through with it."

"And," the lawyer went on, "you hereby grant to us"—pointing to his name, and where his wife had signed—"the right to make all decisions considering the future of your two children, named Keith Mark Casteel and Jane Ellen Casteel, and if you seek to legally or illegally take them from me and from my wife, there will be a suit for which you will have to pay all court and attorney fees, and all the expenses accrued by the children while they are in our care, and of course there will be various other expenses, such as medical and dental ones, for we intend to take both children as soon as possible to doctors for physicals and dental checkups, and we will be sending them to school, and buying them new clothes, and books, and toys, and the proper furniture for their rooms. And there will be various other items I'm forgetting about now . . ."

Oh, my God.

Pa would never have enough money to buy them back! Not in a thousand years!

"I understand completely," said Pa, appearing not in the least troubled. "That's one of the reasons I'm doing what I am. Our Jane needs medical attention, and perhaps Keith does as well. So even if my eldest girl is emotional, she did speak truthfully, so you know exactly what you are getting."

"A dear, a sweet little dear who will turn out just fine," crooned the fat lady, who held fast to Our Jane's frail arm to prevent her from pulling away and running back to me. "A wonderful little boy," she added, patting Keith on the head, for he stood as always, as close to Our Jane as possible, his hand holding hers. If she didn't escape, he wouldn't either.

I was crying now. I was losing the brother and sister I'd helped raise. All the memories of how they'd looked and behaved as babies and little toddlers came flooding back, filling me with fresh tears. Visions flashed behind my eyes: All of us on the hills teaching Our Jane to walk, and how cute she'd looked on her bowed legs and baby toes, her arms out for balance. Tom and I guiding Keith's first toddling steps as well. My voice instructing them how to speak clearly, correctly, and Fanny always so jealous because they loved me best, and Tom second best.

I'd gone numb now, held frozen by the forbidding glance Pa threw my way, warning me not to speak again as he pocketed more money than he'd ever had before in his life.

One thousand dollars.

Excitement made his dark eyes glow like hot coals.

"Fanny, it's beginning to rain," said Pa, showing concern for those two in their rich, warm clothes when he'd shown none for us. "Fetch that ole umbrelly we got somewhere so the lady won't ruin her nice hairdo."

Pa scooped up Keith and Our Jane and ordered them to stop screaming, and I ran for a quilt to wrap them with.

I dashed back, carrying the best quilt we had, hand-sewn years ago by Granny. "They don't have coats, hats, boots, or anything," I said to the lady urgently. "Please be good to them—give them lots of orange juice and other fruit. And meat, especially red meat. We've never had enough meat, even chicken and pork. Our Jane loves fruit and won't eat much of anything else. But Keith has a good appetite, even if he does catch cold often, and they both have nightmares, so leave on a little light so the dark won't frighten them . . ."

"Shut up," hissed Pa again.

"Why, child, I'll be good to your brother and sister," the lady said kindly, touching my cheek lightly and appearing sorry for me. "Aren't you a dear one, just like a little mother. Now, don't you worry yourself about these two. I'm not a cruel woman, nor is my husband a cruel man. We're going to be kind, give them all new clothes, and Christmas morning is waiting for them at our house, everything their hearts can desire. We didn't know if we'd take the boy or the girl, so we bought things both sexes can use . . . a rocking horse, a tricycle, a dollhouse, lots of trucks, cars, and clothes . . . not enough for two, but they can share until we go shopping again. We'll do that tomorrow, buy everything they can possibly need. So you feel good about this, honey. Don't cry. Don't worry. We'll do our best to make wonderful parents, won't we, Lester?"

"Yes," Lester said shortly, eager to leave. "Let's get a move on, dear. It's growing late, and we have a long drive ahead."

Now Pa handed the woman Our Jane, and the man carried Keith, who had given up fighting and was now only screaming, as was Our Jane.

"Hev-lee . . . Hev-lee!" sobbed Our Jane, stretching out her slender arms toward me. "Don't wanna go, don't wanna . . ."

"Hurry, Lester. I can't bear to see this child cry." Out the door in a hurry went the two carrying the screaming children, with Pa running in servile attendance, holding the torn old umbrella over the head of the lady and Our Jane.

I sank to the floor and sobbed.

Tom ran to a window, and despite my will not to look, I jumped up and hurried to stand beside him, and then Fanny was crouched down on her knees, staring out and saying: "Wish they'd chosen me. Oh, holy Jesus on the cross, I wish I could have all that stuff on Christmas morning! Why didn't they want me instead of Our Jane, who cries all t'time? An Keith ain't much better, an he wets t'bed. Why didn't ya tell em that, Heaven, why didn't ya?"

I wiped away tears and tried to gain control of my emotions. I tried to tell myself it wasn't so bad, not really, to lose Our Jane and Keith if they were to have so many fine things—oranges to eat, and toys to play with—and a doctor to make Our Jane well.

Then I was flying toward the door and the porch so I could call out breathlessly, just as the black car prepared to drive off, "And be sure to send them both to good schools—please!"

The lady rolled down a window and waved. "Please don't worry, darling," she called. "I'll write you from time to time and let you know how they are, but there won't be a return address. And I'll send you photographs." And up went the window again, smothering Our Jane's loud, anguished wails, and those of Keith.

Pa didn't even bother to enter the cabin again to find out what his children thought about the "Christmas gift" he'd just given.

He ran, as if from me and my accusing eyes; me and all the angry words I had ready to scream in his face. He jumped into his old truck and drove off, leaving me to think he'd soon throw away his thousand dollars on whores, booze, and gambling. And in bed tonight he wouldn't give one single thought to Our Jane, to Keith, to any of us.

Like a flock of chickens paralyzed by strange events beyond our understanding, we huddled, with Grandpa sitting quietly and whittling as if nothing untoward had happened, and then we met eyes. Soon even Fanny began to cry. She wrapped her arms about me and sobbed. "They'll be all right, won't they? People do love all little children, even those not their own, don't they?"

"Yes, of course they do," I said, trying to choke back fresh tears and save my anguish for later, when I was alone. "And we'll see them again. If the lady writes long letters we'll hear how they are, and one day Our Jane and Keith can write themselves, and won't that be wonderful . . . won't it be . . . wonderful." I broke anew, tears flooding down my face before I could manage to ask a very important question. "Tom, did you notice their license plates?"

"Sure did," he answered in a gruff, hoarse voice. "Maryland. But I didn't have time to catch the last three numbers. First were nine-seven-two. Remember that." Tom always noticed things like that. I never did.

Now the little ones I'd worried about were gone. No wailing in the night and in the morning. No wet beds and quilts, not so much washing to do, plenty of room in the brass bed now.

How empty the small cabin, how sad all the hours, minutes, and seconds after Our Jane and Keith went away. And maybe in the long run they would be better off—especially since those people appeared so rich—but what about us? Love, wasn't that worth anything? Wasn't blood the tie that bound, not money?

"Grandpa," I said in my constantly hoarse voice, "we got room for you in the bed now."

"Not proper or healthy t'put t'old in with t'young," Grandpa mumbled again and again, his gnarled hands quivering as if with some ancient ague. His faded old eyes pleaded with me to understand. "Luke's a good boy, chile, he is. He meant well. Though ya don't know it. He wanted t'help, that's all. Now, don't ya go thinkin bad about yer pa, when he did all he knew what t'do."

"Grandpa, you'd say good things about him no matter what he did, cause he's your son, the only one you've got left. But from this day forward, he's not my father! I'm not calling him Pa from now on. He's Luke Casteel, an ugly, mean liar, and someday he's going to pay for all the suffering he's put us through! I hate him, Grandpa, hate his guts! Hate him so much I feel sick inside!"

His poor old withered face went dead white, when already it was pale and sickly, crosshatched with a million wrinkles, and he really wasn't that old. "T'Good Book says t'honor thy motha an thy fatha . . . ya remember that, Heaven girl."

"Why doesn't the Good Book say honor thy children, Grandpa, why doesn't it?"

Another storm blew in, and turned into a blizzard. Snow banked as high as the top of our windows, covering the porch. Ice sheeting prevented us from looking through the wavy cheap glass even when Tom went out to shovel some of the snow away. Luckily, Pa had brought enough food to see us through another few days.

Heartbreak ruled the cabin without the cheerful chirping of Our Jane and the sweet quiet of Keith. I forgot all about the trouble Our Jane had been, forgot the plaintive wails, the tempestuous stomach that was so difficult to please. I remembered only the tender young body, the sweetness of the back of her neck where her curls turned damp when she slept. Two angels they'd appeared when they cuddled in the bed and closed their eyes; I remembered Keith and how he liked to be rocked to sleep, wanting to hear bedtime stories I'd read a thousand times or more. I remembered his sweet good-night kisses, his strong legs; I heard his small voice saying his prayers, saw him next to Our Jane, both on their knees, their small feet bare, pink toes curled; they never had the proper kind of pretty nightclothes. I sobbed, felt sicker, meaner, angrier, and everything I remembered formed steel bullets that sooner or later would gun down the man who'd taken so much from me.

Poor Grandpa forgot how to talk. Now he was as silent as he'd been when Granny was alive, and he didn't whittle, didn't fiddle, only stared into space and rocked to, fro, to, fro. Once in a great while he'd mumble some prayer that was never answered.

We all said prayers that were never answered.

In my sleep I dreamed of Our Jane and Keith waking up to a fantasy of what I believed the merriest of all Christmas mornings. I saw them in pretty red flannel nightclothes playing in an elegant living room where a magnificent Christmas tree spread over all the new toys and new clothes underneath. Laughing with the silent merriment of dreams, my youngest brother and sister raced about ripping open all their gifts, riding in miniature cars, Our Jane small enough to crawl inside the dollhouse; and long colorful stockings were full of oranges, apples, candy and chewing gum, and boxes of cookies; and finally came a meal served on a long table with a white tablecloth, sparkling with crystal and gleaming with silver. A huge golden-brown turkey arrived on a silver platter, surrounded by all the things we'd eaten that time in the restaurant, and there was pumpkin pie straight from one of the glossy magazines I'd seen. Oh, the things my dreams gave to Our Jane and Keith.

Without Keith and Our Jane to distract me, I heard more from Fanny, who continually grouched about not being the child chosen to go with those rich people in their fine clothes and long car.

"It coulda been *me* an not Our Jane that rich lady wanted," she said for the hundredth time, "if I'd have had time t'wash my hair an take a bath. Ya used all t'hot wata on them, Heaven! Selfish, ya are! Them rich folks didn't like me cause I looked messy—why didn't Pa tell us t'get ready?"

"Fanny!" I exclaimed, quite out of patience. "What's wrong with you? To go away with strangers you don't even know. Why, only God above knows what will happen to—" And then I broke and started to cry.

Tom came to comfort me. "It's gonna be all right. They truly did look rich and nice. A lawyer has to be intelligent. And think of this, wouldn't it have been terrible if Pa had sold them to folks as poor as we are?"

As was to be expected, Grandpa took his son's side. "Luke only does what he thinks is best—and ya hold yer tongue, girl, when next ya see him, or he might do somethin awful t'ya. This ain't no fittin' place fer kids nohow. Betta off they'll be. Stop cryin, an accept what can't be changed. That's what life is about, standing firm against t'wind."

I should have known that Grandpa, like Granny, wouldn't be any help when it came to Pa. Always she'd had excuses to explain her son's brutal behavior. A good man—at heart. Underneath all that cruelty, a frustrated gentleman who couldn't find the right way.

A monster only a parent could love, was my opinion.

I stood as far as I could from the old man who disappointed me in so many ways. Why couldn't Grandpa be stronger and stand up for all our rights? Why didn't he open his silent mouth and put his tongue to good use? Why did all his thoughts come out in the form of charming little wooden figures? He could have told his son he couldn't sell his children. But he hadn't said a word, not a word.

How bitter I felt to think my grandfather went to church every Sunday he could, to sing and stand up and say prayers with bowed head, and then he came back to a home where small children were whipped, starved, brutalized, and then sold.

"We'll run away," I whispered to Tom when Fanny was asleep and Grandpa was in his pallet. "When the snow melts, before Pa comes back again, we'll put on all our clothes and run to Miss Deale. She must be back from Baltimore by now. She has to be. She'll tell us what to do, and how to get back Our Jane and Keith."

Yes, Miss Deale would know, if anyone did, just how to thwart Pa and keep him from selling us all to strangers. Miss Deale knew a thousand things that Pa would never know; she had connections.

It snowed for three days without letup.

Then suddenly, dramatically, the sun broke out from behind clouds. The bright light pouring in almost blinded us when Tom threw open the front door to stare out.

"It's over," Grandpa murmured weakly. "That's t'way of our Lord, t'save his own jus when we think we kin't live on another hour."

How were we saved? Not saved at all by sunlight, only warmed a bit. I turned again to the old chipped and rickety cabinet that held our pitiful store of food. Again, nothing to eat but a few of the nuts harvested in the fall.

"But I like nuts," Tom said cheerfully, setting down to munching on his two. "And when the snow has melted enough, we can put on our warmest clothes and escape. Wouldn't it be nice to head west, into the sun? End up in California, living on dates and oranges, drinking coconut milk. Sleeping on the golden grass, staring up at the golden mountains . . ."

"Do they have golden streets in Hollywood?" asked Fanny.

"Spect everything is golden in Hollywood," mused Tom, still standing and looking outside. "Or else silver."

Grandpa said nothing.

We lived in capricious country. Spring could come as quickly as a lightning bolt and do just as much damage. Springlike days would warm up the earth in December, January, and February, trick the flowers into blooming ahead of time, fool the trees into leafing out; then winter would come back and freeze the flowers, kill off the new baby leaves, and when real spring came, those flowers and trees wouldn't repeat their performances since they'd been deceived once, wouldn't be deceived again, or at least not this season.

Now the sun turned the mounds of heaped snow into slushy mush that soon melted and flooded the streams, causing bridges to be swept away . . . and trails were lost in the woods. There was no way to escape now that the bridge was gone. Exhausted and exceedingly tired from his long quest to find a way out, Tom came home to report the loss of the nearest bridge.

"The current's running fast and strong, or else we could swim across. Tomorrow will be a better day."

I put down *Jane Eyre*, which I was reading again, and drifted over to stand beside Tom, both of us silent until Fanny ran to join us. "Let's swear a solemn vow now," Tom whispered so Grandpa wouldn't hear, "to run the first chance we get. To stay together through thick and thin, one for all and all for one . . . Heavenly, we've said this to each other before. Now we have to add Fanny. Fanny, put your hand on top of mine. But first cross your heart and hope to die if ever you let us be split apart."

Fanny seemed to hesitate, and then with rare sisterly camaraderie her hand covered mine, which rested on top of Tom's. "We do solemnly swear . . ."

"We do solemnly swear . . ." repeated Fanny and I.

"To always stay together, to care for one another through joys and suffering . . ."

Again Fanny hesitated. "Why do ya have t'mention sufferin? Yer makin this sound like a weddin, Tom."

"All right, through thick and thin, through good and bad, until we have Our Jane and Keith with us again—is that good enough for you two?"

"It's fine, Tom," I said as I repeated his vows.

Even Fanny was impressed, and more like a real sister than she'd ever been as she snuggled up beside me, and we talked about our futures out in the big world we knew nothing about. Fanny even helped Tom and me search the woods for berries as we waited for the swollen river to go down and the bridge to be restored.

"Hey," Tom said suddenly, hours later, "just remembered. There's another bridge twenty miles away, and we can reach it if we're determined enough. Heavenly, if we all have to hike twenty miles or more, we're gonna need more than one hazelnut apiece, I can tell ya that right now."

"Think we can make it on two nuts apiece?" asked I, who'd been holding back just for an emergency like this.

"Why, with all that energy, we could probably walk to Florida," Tom said with a laugh, "which might almost be as good as California."

We dressed in our best, put on everything we owned. I tried not to think of leaving Grandpa all alone. Fanny was eager to escape a cabin where only sadness and old age and hopelessness had come to stay. Guiltily, with reluctant determination, we kissed Grandpa good-bye. He stood up feebly, smiled at us, nodding as if life never held any surprises for him.

In my hand I held my mother's suitcase that finally Fanny had seen, though her excitement had been lessened by the knowledge we were leaving . . . for somewhere.

"Good-bye," called all three of us in unison, but I hung back when Tom and Fanny raced outside. "Grandpa," I said in an embarrassed voice, really hurting inside, "I'm sorry to be doing this to you. I know it's not right to leave you alone, but we have to do it or be sold like Keith and Our Jane. Please understand."

He looked straight ahead, one hand holding a knife, the other his bit of wood to shave, his thin hair trembling in the drafts. "We'll come back one day when we're grown-up and too old for Pa to sell."

"It's all right, chile," whispered Grandpa, his head bowed low so I couldn't see his tears. "Ya jus take kerr."

"I love you, Grandpa. Maybe I've never said that before, don't know why now that I didn't, cause I always have."

I stepped closer to hug and kiss him. He smelled old, sour, and felt brittle in my arms. "We wouldn't leave you if there was any other way, but we have to go to try and find a better place." Again he smiled through tears, nodded as if he believed, and sat again to rock. "Luke will come back soon with food—so don't ya worry none. Forgive me for saying nasty things I didn't mean."

"What nasty things did ya say?" bellowed a rough voice from the open doorway.

10

Too Many Farewells

Pa towered in the open doorway, glowering at us. He was wearing a thick red jacket that reached his hips. Brand-new. His boots were better than any I'd ever seen him wear, as were his pants; his hat had a furry band across the top that ended in earmuffs. With him he had more boxes of food. "I'm back," he said casually, as if he'd just left yesterday. "Brought food with me." And then he turned to leave, or so I thought.

Trip after trip he made to his truck to bring things in. What was the use of our trying to run now, when his long legs could catch up and swiftly bring us back again—if he didn't chase us in his truck?

More than anything, now Fanny didn't want to escape. "Pa!" she cried, happy and excited, dancing around him and trying to find a way to hug and kiss him before he had all the supplies in from the truck.

Many times she tried to throw herself into his arms, and then succeeded. "Oh, Pa! Ya've come to save us agin! Knew ya would, knew ya loved me! Now we don't have t'run away! We were hungry an cold an goin t'find food or steal it, an waitin fer t'snow t'melt an t'bridges t'come back, an I'm so durn happy we don't have t'do none of that!"

"Runnin away t'find food, huh?" asked Pa with his lips tight, his eyes narrow. "Can't run nowhere I can't find ya. Now sit and eat, an get ready for the company that's comin."

It was going to happen again!

Fanny's face lit up as if an electric switch had been pushed. "Oh, Pa, it's me this time, ain't it? Ain't it? Jus let it be me!"

"Get yourself ready, Fanny," Pa ordered as he fell into a chair and almost tipped it over backward. "Found ya a new ma and pa, jus like ya asked me t'do, an as rich as t'ones who took Jane and Keith."

This information made her squeal in delight. She hurried to heat a pot of water on the stove. While that was warming she pulled out the old aluminum basin we all used for a bathtub. "Oh, I need betta clothes!" Fanny bewailed as the water began to boil. "Heaven, kin't ya do somethin with a dress of yours, so it'll look good on me?"

"I'm not doing anything to help you leave," I said, my voice so cold it chilled my throat, while I felt hot tears in my eyes. Fanny cared so little about leaving us and breaking her vow.

"Tom, run fetch me more water," she called in her sweetest voice, "enough t'fill up t'tub an rinse my hair!" And Tom obeyed, though reluctantly.

Maybe Pa read my thoughts. He glanced my way, caught my full hard glare, and perhaps saw for the first time why he hated me, who was so different from his angel. You bet I was different. I would have had better sense than to fall for an ignorant mountain man who lived in a shack and ran bootleg moonshine. He seemed to read my mind as his lips pulled back in a sneer that showed one side of his upper teeth so he no longer looked handsome.

"Yer gonna do something now, little gal? Go on. Do it. I'm waiting."

Unconsciously I'd picked up the poker again.

Tom came in, quickly set down the pail of water, then sprang forward to keep me from using the poker. "He'll kill you if you do," he whispered urgently, pulling me back from harm's way.

"Got ya a real champion, haven't ya?" Pa asked, looking at Tom with scorn. Casually he stood up, yawned, as if nothing at all had happened to make either one of us hate him. "They'll be coming any minute. Hurry up there, Fanny girl. Ya'll soon know just how much yer pa loves ya when ya see who's gonna take ya in and treat ya betta than gold."

Hardly were the words out of his mouth when a car pulled into our dirt yard. Only this was not a strange car, it was a car we knew very well, having seen it many times on the streets of Winnerrow. It was a long, black, shiny Cadillac that belonged to the wealthiest man in Winnerrow, the Reverend Wayland Wise.

At last, at last! Miss Deale had found a way to save us!

Squealing more, Fanny hugged her arms over her small breasts and shot me a smug, delighted look. "ME! They want ME!"

In a moment she was dressed in what used to be *my* best.

Pa flung open the door and cordially invited inside the Reverend and his thin-faced wife, who didn't smile, didn't speak, only looked sour and unhappy. She didn't stare at what must have been a shock to someone so affluent, but then I reckoned she must have expected to see such living conditions. As for the handsome Reverend, he didn't waste one moment.

I was wrong to have presumed that Miss Deale had sent him to save us, much less that God was going to work one of his miracles. Fanny knew much more about reality than I. God's man already knew which one of Pa's remaining three he wanted, though, when the Reverend looked us over up close, his eyes lingered long and lusting on me.

I backed away, terribly frightened by the holy man. I shot an angry glance at Pa, to see him shaking his head, as if he didn't want *me* living too near his home.

Confirmed when Pa said: "My eldest is a troublemaker, quick to answer back, stubborn, hardheaded, and mean, Reverend Wise, Mrs. Wise. Take my word for it, this younger girl, Fanny, is far the better choice. Fanny is easygoin, beautiful, and sweet. Why, I call her my dove, my doe, my lovely, lovin Fanny."

What a lie! He never called any of us by pet names.

This time there would be no caterwauling, no fighting, no holding back. Fanny couldn't have been happier. Her smile was dazzling she was so happy. The Reverend handed out boxes of chocolate candy to all three of us, and also gave Fanny a beautiful red coat just her size, with a black fur collar. Fanny was won over. That's all it took!

She didn't even wait to hear about the beautiful room of her own they said they'd have decorated to suit her fancy, or other things they planned to give her, like dancing and music lessons.

"I'll be what ya want!" cried Fanny, her dark eyes shining. "Be anythin ya want! I'm ready, willin, eager t'go! An thank ya fer comin, fer wantin me, thank ya, thank ya."

Fanny ran and threw her arms about the Reverend. "Blessed are ya—blessed am I! Two million times I say, thank ya! I'll never be hungry or cold again. Already I love ya, I do, I do—fer choosin me an not Heaven."

Fanny! Fanny! I silently screamed. Have you forgotten already our pledge to stick together through thick and thin? God didn't plan it this way, for families to be split and given one to this person and one to that. *Fanny, you've been like my own.* "Ya see, ya see," Pa exclaimed proudly. "Best choice, this one. A lovin, sweet girl ya'll never be ashamed of."

He threw me another of those sneering looks as I stared straight ahead, ashamed of Fanny, fearful for Fanny. What did a thirteen-year-old know about anything? Tom stood beside me, holding my hand, his face pale, his eyes dark with his own frightened pain.

Five little Indians we were playing.

All disappearing one by one. Two left.

Who'd it be next time, Tom or me?

"I'm sure proud they chose me," Fanny pronounced happily again as if she couldn't get over the wonder of it. When she was wearing her new red coat, she whispered in a breathless, touching way, "I'm gonna live in a big rich house, an ya kin come t'see me." She sniffled once or twice, enough to show at least a little regret, before she threw several beseeching looks at me and Tom. Then she picked up her two-pound box of chocolates and smiled before she turned and led the way out to the big car. "See ya in town," she called without looking back, not even at Pa.

Paperwork finished, the Reverend paid his five hundred in cash, accepted Pa's carefully written receipt, and turned to follow Fanny, with his wife a step or two behind him. And, like a true gentleman, the Reverend helped both Fanny and his wife into his car. All sat on the front seat, Fanny in the middle.

Bang! went the heavy car door.

The sharp pain came again, not as bad as it had been for Our Jane and Keith. Fanny wanted to leave, and hadn't screamed and howled and kicked her legs and flailed her arms—the little ones had wanted to stay. Who could say which decision was right?

And Fanny was only going to Winnerrow. Our Jane and Keith were way off in Maryland, and Tom could remember only three of the license-plate numbers. Would that be enough to lead us to them . . . someday?

Now it was my time to miss Fanny, my tormentor, my now-and-then friend and sister. Fanny, also my shame when I was in school and heard her giggles coming from the cloakroom. Fanny with her sex ready, her uninhibited inheritance from the hills.

This time Pa didn't go after Fanny left. As if the information Fanny gushed when first he came in had put him on guard, and he'd not leave to find Tom and me gone when he came back again. Both Tom and I were anxious to see him go so we could escape before we too were sold. We waited without speaking, sitting side by side on the floor not far from the stove. We sat so close I felt his heat, as he must have felt mine. I heard his hard breathing, as surely he heard mine.

In no way was Pa going to give us a chance to run. He ensconced himself in a hard chair on the other side of the stove, tipping it backward before he half lowered his lids, and seemed to be waiting. I tried to convince myself days would pass before someone else came. Time for us to escape. Plenty of time . . .

No such luck.

A muddy maroon-colored pickup truck just as old and beat up as Pa's pulled to an abrupt stop in our yard, putting panic in my heart that was echoed in Tom's eyes. He reached again for my hand, squeezed it hard, as we both backed to the wall. Fanny'd only been gone two hours, and here was another buyer.

Footfalls on the porch steps. Heavy feet crossing the porch. Three loud raps, then another three. Pa's eyes opened; he jumped up, sprang to the door, threw it open. Now we could see a burly, short man who stepped inside, looked over the cabin with a frown on his grizzly bearded face. He saw Tom, who was already a head taller than he was.

"Don't cry, Heavenly, please don't," pleaded Tom. "I won't be able t'stand it if you do." He squeezed my fingers again, touched my tears with his free hand, then lightly kissed me. "Ain't nothin we kin do, is there? Not when people like Reverend Wise and his wife don't see nothin' wrong in buyin kids. It's been done before, ya know it and I know it. Ain't gonna be t'last time it happens either, ya know that."

I threw myself into his arms, held tight. I was not going to cry, not going to let it hurt so bad this time. Best thing to do, really it was. Nobody could be more heartless than Pa, nobody more shiftless and rotten. Everybody sure would be better off. Sure we would. Nicer houses, more and better food to eat. Sure was going to be wonderful to know we were all eating three meals a day like everybody else in this free land called the United States.

That's when I broke and began to bawl.

"Tom, run! Do something!"

Pa moved to block any chance of Tom's escaping, though he didn't try. We had only one door, and the windows were too high and too small.

Pa didn't see my tears, refused to see the anguish on Tom's face before he hurried over to shake the hand of the burly man wearing worn, dirty overalls. His face was heavyset, what could be seen of it. His dense grizzly beard hid everything but his bulbous nose and his small, squinty eyes. His thick salt-and-pepper hair made his head seem to sit atop his broad shoulders without a neck; then came his bulging chest, his huge, swollen beer belly—all half concealed beneath those loose-fitting overalls.

"I come t'git him," he said without preliminaries, looking straight at

Tom, not even glancing at me. He was about three feet away, and between him and us was Pa. "If he's what ya said he is, that is."

"Take a look at him," said Pa, not smiling this time. He was all business with this farmer. "Tom is fourteen years old and already he's almost six feet tall. Look at those shoulders, those hands and feet; that's how you judge what kind of man a boy's gonna make. Feel his muscles, made strong from swinging an ax, and he can pitch hay as good as any full-grown man."

Sick, it was cruel and sick, treating Tom like a prize calf to be sold.

That farmer with the red face yanked Tom closer, held him as he looked into Tom's mouth, checked over his teeth, felt his muscles, his thighs and calves, asked him intimate questions about elimination problems, if he had any. Other embarrassing questions that Pa answered when Tom refused to reply. As if Pa could possibly know, or even care, whether or not Tom had headaches or early-morning lusts.

"He's a healthy boy, he must be sexually aware. I was at his age, eager and ready to do my damndest fer the girls."

What did he want with Tom anyway, stud services?

The burly farmer stated his occupation; he was a dairy farmer named Buck Henry. Needed help, he did. Needed someone young and strong and eager to earn good wages. "Don't want nobody weak, shiftless, or lazy, or unable to take orders."

Pa took umbrage at that. "Why, my Tom has never had a lazy day in his life." He looked proudly at Tom, while Tom scowled and seemed miserable, and tried to stay at my side.

"Good, strong-looking boy," Buck Henry said with approval. He handed Pa the five hundred in cash, signed the papers Pa had ready, accepted his receipt, seized Tom by the arm, pulled him toward the door. Tom tried to drag his feet, but Pa was behind him shoving him on, and kicking his shins when he moved too slowly. Grandpa rocked on and on, whittling.

At the door Tom broke. "I don't want to go!" he yelled, fighting to free himself.

Pa moved quickly to position himself directly behind me; though I tried to escape, I moved too late. Pa caught me by my hair. His large hands moved downward to rest lightly on my shoulders, his fingers spread in such a way all he had to do was move them slightly and he'd have a choking grip on my neck and throat.

It seemed to chill Tom to see me held like a chicken about to have its neck wrung.

"Pa!" he yelled. "Don't you hurt her! If you sell Heavenly like the rest of us—you find her the best parents! If you don't I'll come back one day and make you regret you ever had a child!" His wild eyes met mine. "I'll come back, Heavenly!" he cried. "I promise I won't forget our pledge. I love what you've tried to do for me, and for all of us. I'll write often, keep you so much in touch you won't even miss me—and I'll get to you wherever you are! I make this solemn vow never to be broken."

My eyes felt strained, swollen, as if I had two discolored, dreary suns behind the blackest of all moons. "Tom . . . write, please, please. We'll see each other again—I know we will. Mr. Henry, where do you live?"

"Don't tell her," warned Pa, tightening his fingers about my throat. "This one means nothing but trouble, and don't let Tom write. At least not to this one named Heaven. She should have been called Hell."

"Pa!" screamed Tom. "She's the *best* you got, and you don't know it."

Tom was outside now and the door had been left open. I managed to call out, my voice hoarse, "There's always a bridge up ahead, Thomas Luke, you keep remembering that. And you'll achieve your dream, I know!"

Turning, he heard and understood, waved, smiled, then got in the truck and kept his head out of the window, yelling back to me. "No matter where you go or who tries to keep us apart, I'll find you, Heavenly! I'll never forget you! Together we'll find Keith and Our Jane, just like we planned to do!"

The dirty old truck drove off, headed toward the rough road, and disappeared, and I was alone with Pa and Grandpa. Feeling numb, in a state of shock so despairing I sank to the floor when Pa released me.

Already I sensed just what lay ahead for Tom.

No more education for Tom, no more fun hunting and fishing for Tom, or baseball playing, or fooling around with his buddies, just work, work, and more work.

Tom with his brilliant mind, his dreams and aspirations, would be buried out in the middle of cow pastures, living a farmer's life, the kind he'd often said he'd never put up with.

But what lay ahead for me frightened me just as much.

11

My Choice

Tom was gone.

I was without a soul to love me. Who would ever call me Heavenly again?

Tom took with him all the laughter, all the excitement, brightness, courage, encouragement, and good humor he'd given to a grim, struggling household. The fun side of myself disappeared in that pickup truck with license plates so covered with mud I couldn't read them. And I'd tried so hard. I'd thought before, foolishly, that I'd been alone after Keith and Our Jane left. Now I was truly the only one left, and I was the one Pa hated.

I tried to comfort myself by believing I was also the only one who did anything useful in the cabin, like cooking and cleaning, and caring for Grandpa—certainly Pa wouldn't want to leave Grandpa here alone. . . .

I willed Pa to go, to slam out the door, jump into his truck, and drive for Winnerrow, or wherever he went now that he had to stay out of *Shirley's Place*.

He didn't go.

He positioned himself near the only door to our shack like a guard dog, to keep me imprisoned until he had me sold, too.

He didn't speak, just sat sullen and quiet, and when night fell he moved his chair closer to the stove, his large feet propped up, his eyes half closed, a look of misery on his face.

All through the remainder of the week after Tom left with Buck Henry I tried to find the strength to run off alone if ever I had the chance—that meant when I had to use the outhouse.

Without Tom, Keith, Our Jane, I had no heart, no spirit, no will to run anywhere to save myself from what had to be my certain fate. If only I could send a message to Miss Deale. Was she back yet? I prayed each night for Miss Deale or Logan to come to my rescue.

No one came.

I was the one Pa hated, and I would be the one he'd turn over to the very worst kind of people. No rich folks for me. Not even anyone as good as Buck Henry. Very likely he'd sell me to that madam who ran *Shirley's Place*.

The more my thoughts dwelled on my fate, the angrier I grew. He couldn't do this to me! I wasn't a dumb animal to be sold off and forgotten. I was a human being with an eternal soul, with the inalienable right to life, liberty, and the pursuit of happiness. Miss Deale had said that so often it was imprinted on my brain. Then, to myself, I had to grin bitterly, for in that class of hers there dwelled a spirit that reached out to me, telling me to hold on, she was coming to the rescue. It was almost as if I heard Miss Deale calling out encouragement, her voice coming closer and closer over the hills.

Hurry, Miss Deale, I wanted to yell across the mountains. This is my needing time, Miss Deale! All pride gone now, vanished, conquered! Without shame I'll take from you! Come, come fast to save me, for it won't be long now!

I prayed, then got up from my knees, moved to the kitchen cabinet, and peered inside. Life went on despite everything, and meals had to be prepared.

Hope was in Grandpa's reddened, watery eyes when he came back from his necessity trip with more tree branches. He carefully seated himself in his rocker. He didn't pick up his whittling knife, only fixed his eyes on me. *Don't leave me,* his eyes were pleading. *Stay,* they begged silently, even as he motioned me close and whispered, "I'm all right, chile. I know what yer thinkin. Ya wanna run. So go when ya get t'chance—steal out when Luke's asleepin."

I loved him for saying that. Loved him so much I forgave him for keeping quiet when the others were sold, knowing even as I thought this that I had to love somebody or curl up and die. "You won't hate me if I leave you here alone? You'll understand?"

"Nope, won't understand. Jus want ya to have what ya want. In my heart I know yer pa's doin what he thinks is best. In yer heart ya think he's doin what's worst."

It seemed Pa had slept his last sleep in some distant unknown place. He didn't doze, didn't even close his eyes all the way. His cold, dark eyes never left me. Not that he met my challenging glares; he only gazed with hooded eyes at some part of me, my hair, my hands, my feet, my middle, anywhere but my face.

Seven days passed, and Pa stayed on and on.

Then one day Logan came to our door, come like a prince to save me!

I opened it expecting to see Grandpa coming from the outhouse. "Hi," Logan said, smiling broadly and then flushing. "Been thinkin a lot about you lately, wondering why you, Tom, and the others don't come to school now that the weather's not so bad. Why are all of you staying away? What you been up to?"

He hadn't seen Fanny—why not?

I yanked him in the door when once I would have shoved him out, or thought of a million reasons why he couldn't come in. "Pa's chopping wood out back," I whispered frantically, "and Grandpa's in the outhouse, so I won't have much time. Pa comes in to check on me every few minutes. Logan, I'm in trouble, big trouble! Pa is selling us off, one by one. Our Jane and Keith first, then Fanny, next Tom . . . and soon it'll be me."

"Who ya talkin to, girl?" bellowed Pa from the door. I shrank inside my skin as Logan turned to face the powerful brute who was my father.

"My name is Logan Stonewall, sir," said Logan in a polite yet firm way. "My father is Grant Stonewall, and he owns Stonewall Pharmacy, and Heaven and I have been good friends ever since we came to Winnerrow to live. It's been troubling me why Heaven, Tom, Fanny, Keith, and Our Jane don't go to school anymore, so I came to check on all of them."

"Why they go or don't go is none of yer damned business," snapped Pa. "Now take yerself out of here. We don't need nosy people checking on what we do or don't do."

Logan turned again to me. "I guess I should go home before the sun goes down. Please take care of yourself. By the way, my teacher said that Miss Deale will be back next week." He gave Pa a long, significant look, making my heart thrill. He did believe me, he did!

"You tell that teacher to stay away and mind *her* own goddamned business," roared Pa, moving toward Logan in a threatening manner. "Now you've had your say, so *git.*"

Calmly Logan swept his eyes around the cabin, drinking in all the poverty that was only too plain to see. I knew he was trying to keep pity and shock from showing in his eyes, but I saw it there, nevertheless. Logan's dark blue eyes met mine, giving me some silent message

I didn't know quite how to interpret. "I hope to see you again in a few days, Heaven. I'll tell Miss Deale you're not sick. Now tell me where Tom is, and Fanny, Our Jane, and Keith."

"They've gone t'visit relatives," said Pa, throwing open the door, standing aside, and motioning for Logan to go or be thrown out.

Logan glared at Pa. "You take good care of Heaven, Mr. Casteel."

"Get out," Pa said with disgust, and slammed the door behind Logan.

"Why'd that boy come?" he asked when I turned back to the stove, and Grandpa came stumbling in from the other room. "Did ya send fer him in some way, did ya?"

"He came because he cares, and Miss Deale cares, and the whole world is going to care when they know what you've done, Luke Casteel!"

"Thanks fer warning me," he said with a sneer. "I'm skerred, real skerred."

He was worse after that, even more vigilant.

I kept hoping and praying Logan would run into Fanny, and she'd tell him what was going on, and Logan would do something before it was too late. Yet, at the same time, I suspected Pa might have warned the Reverend to keep Fanny close until he had a chance to get rid of me.

I'd read in the newspapers about adopted children selling for ten thousand dollars, and Pa was stupid enough not to ask for that much. But five times five hundred meant he'd have more money than he'd ever had in his entire life; a fortune to any hillbilly in the Willies who couldn't think as high as a thousand.

"Pa," I said on the tenth day after Tom had gone, "how can you go to church every Sunday for most of your life, and do what you've done?"

"Shut up," he said, his eyes hard as flat river stones.

"I DON'T WANT TO SHUT UP!" I flared. "I want my brothers and sisters back! You don't have to take care of us. Tom and I found a way to support ourselves."

"Shut up!"

Oh, I hate you! my wild inner voice raged, even as my instinct warned me to keep quiet or be severely punished.

"Others sell their kids," he said suddenly, taking me off guard, that he would speak—to me—as if trying to explain himself, when I'd thought he'd never do such a thing. "I'm not t'first, won't be t'last. Nobody talks bout it, but it happens all t'time. Poor people like us have more kids than the rich ones who can afford kids, an we who can't afford em, most of us don't know how t'keep from havin em. . . . When there's nothin else betta t'do on a cold winter's night but go t'bed an take what pleasure ya kin with yer woman—we make our own gold mines, our kids, our pretty younguns. So why not take advantage of the laws of nature's balance?"

It was more than he'd said to me in my entire life. And he *was* well now, his cheeks were flushed with healthy color, no longer gaunt. Strong, high cheekbones—damned handsome face! If he died, would I feel sorry? No, I told myself over and over, not in a million years.

Late one night I overheard him talking to Grandpa, saying all sorts of melancholy things about his life going to pot, kids holding him back, keeping him from reaching the goal he'd set for himself. "When I get all the money, Pa, it won't be too late. I'm going on t'do what I always wanted, and woulda done but fer *her* . . . an em . . ."

I stopped crying that night. Tears didn't do any good.

I stopped praying for God to send back my brothers and sisters, stopped thinking Logan would be able to save me. I stopped betting on Miss Deale, and fate that had killed her mother, and lawyers who were holding her in Baltimore. I had to plan my own escape.

Sunday the sun came out. Pa ordered me to dress in my best, if I had any best. My heart jumped, thinking he'd found a buyer. His hard eyes mocked me. "It's Sunday, girl, churchgoing time," he said, as if several Sundays hadn't come and gone without any Casteel showing up.

Hearing the word "church," Grandpa immediately brightened. With stiff joints and many grunts and groans he managed to pull on his only fairly decent clothes, and soon we were ready for our trip into Winnerrow and church.

The church bell chimed clear, resonant tones, giving me a certain false serenity, the sense that God was in his heaven and all was right with the world; as long as the church stood, the bell kept ringing, the people kept coming, kept singing, kept believing.

Pa parked our truck far from the church (others had taken all the close parking places), and we walked the rest of the way, with him holding my arm in a viselike grip.

Those already in the church were singing when we entered.

> "Bringin in the sheaves,
> Bringin in the sheaves,
> We shall go rejoicin,
> Bringin in the sheaves . . ."

Sing, sing, sing. Make the day brighter, make it less cold, less forbidding. I closed my eyes, saw Our Jane's sweet small face. Kept them closed, heard Miss Deale's soaring soprano. Still keeping my eyes closed, I felt my hand clasped in Tom's, felt Keith tugging on my skirt, and then came that loud, commanding voice. I opened my eyes and stared up at him, wondering how he could buy a child and then call her his own.

"Ladies, and gentleman, will you please stand and turn to page one hundred and forty-seven in your hymnbooks, then all together sing our most beloved hymn of all," instructed Reverend Wayland Wise.

"And we walk with him,
And we talk with him,
And he tells us we are his own,
And the voice we hear singin
In our ears,
No other has ever known . . ."

Singing made my heart lighter, happier, until I caught sight of Fanny sitting in the front pew next to Rosalynn Wise. Fanny didn't even glance around to see if any member of her "former" family was seated in a back pew. Maybe she hoped we wouldn't be there.

I sucked in my breath when she turned her head in profile. Oh, how beautiful she looked in that white fur coat, with a hat to match, and a fur muff to stuff her hands into; even though the church was stifling hot, still Fanny kept on all that fur and made sure that everyone behind glimpsed the muff at least once. She managed this by standing up from time to time, and excusing herself for one reason or another; then off to the right she'd stroll to a small hidden chamber, and in there she did something or other that took a few minutes, then slowly, slowly, she sauntered back to her pew, to primly take her place beside her new "mother."

Of course this gave everyone a good view of all the new clothes Fanny wore. Including white boots with fur trim at the top.

When the services were over, Fanny stood with Reverend Wise and his tall wife to shake hands with all the congregation, who considered themselves deprived if they didn't have the chance to shake the hand of the Reverend or his wife before they left to somehow endure six entire days of solid sinful living, only to come again to be forgiven. For it seemed the more you sinned during the week, the more the Lord above loved you for giving him so much to forgive.

If the Lord loved sinners so much, he must really be thrilled to have Luke Casteel in his church. Why, if I were truly lucky he might glue Pa's feet to the floor and never let him go.

Inch by slow inch we followed in the wake of everyone else. No one spoke to us, though a few mountain folk nodded. The cold wind whistled inside each time someone passed through the wide double doors. Everyone but me wanted to touch the hand of the spokesman of God here on earth, the handsome, smooth-talking Reverend Wise, and if not him, his wife . . . or his newly adopted daughter.

Like a lovely princess was Fanny in her costly white fur and bright green velvet dress, displayed every time Fanny put one leg or another forward, shuffling like an idiot dancer just to show off. For one brief moment I forgot my loss, my predicament, and enjoyed Fanny's gain.

But lo, when Fanny's own family showed up, she turned away, whispered something into the ear of Rosalynn Wise, and disappeared in the crowd.

Pa sailed right on by, heading straight for the door without even pausing to turn his eyes on the Reverend or his wife. He had me by the arm, holding it with steely fingers. Nobody looked at the Casteels, or what was left of us.

Grandpa followed Pa's lead obediently, his gray, almost bald head bowed and subservient, until I tore my arm away from Pa and dashed back to deliberately hold up the line as I fixed my most penetrating glare on Rosalynn Wise.

"Will you kindly tell Fanny when you see her next that I asked about her?"

"I will." Her voice was cold and flat, as if wishing I had followed Pa's example and ignored her as he had. "And you tell your father not to come to this church, an we would all greatly appreciate if *no* Casteel ever came to services again."

Shocked, I stared at the woman whose husband had just given his sermon about the Lord loving sinners and welcoming them into his home. "You have a Casteel living in your home, don't you?"

"If you are referring to our *daughter*, her name has been legally changed to Wise. Louisa Wise is her name now."

"Louisa is Fanny's middle name!" I cried. "You can't just change her names when her father is still living."

Someone shoved me from behind.

Suddenly I was forced by many hands out to the wooden steps. Alarmed and angry, I spun around to yell something or other about hypocrites, when I saw Logan Stonewall directly in front of me. But for him I would have confronted Reverend Wise himself, shouted out the whole truth to everyone here—but Logan was staring at me, through me. He didn't speak. He didn't smile either.

It was as if he didn't want to see me! And I, who'd thought nothing could hurt me more after losing Sarah, Granny, Our Jane, Keith, and Tom, felt my heart plunge into a deep well of darkness. Of hopelessness.

What had happened between the time he came to see me and now?

Logan, Logan, I wanted to cry out, but pride reared its head, and I didn't say a word, just lifted my chin and strode on by the Stonewall family, who stood off in a separate little group of three.

Pa seized hold of my arm again and dragged me away.

That night, lying on the floor close to belching Ole Smokey, I heard the creak of the old pine floorboards as Pa got out of the brass bed and paced the small space of the other room. He stole as quietly as one of his Indian ancestors to where I lay very still. With my eyes half lidded, I could just see his bare feet, his bare legs. Pretending to turn in my sleep, I rolled over on my side, presenting him with my back, and curled up tighter in the old stained quilt.

Did he kneel on the floor by the stove just so he could touch my hair? I felt something moving lightly over my head. He'd never touched me before. I froze, almost stopped breathing. My heart beat wildly; my eyes, unable to stay closed, popped open wide and staring. Why was he touching me?

"Soft," I heard him murmur, "like hers . . . silky, like hers . . ."

Then his hand was on my shoulder that had somehow worked its way free of the covering; that hand that had always battered me cruelly slid tenderly down my upper arm, and then back up, lingering where my shoulder joined my neck. For long, long moments I felt scared, holding my breath and waiting, waiting for something horrible to happen.

"Luke . . . what ya doin?" Grandpa asked in an odd voice.

Pa snatched his hand away.

Pa hadn't hit me! Hadn't hurt me! I kept thinking as I lay there marveling at the kindness of that hand on my shoulder and arm. Why, after all these years, had he touched me lovingly—why?

Grandpa's frail voice woke me near dawn. He was at the stove, heating water, giving me a few extra moments of sleep. I'd overslept, perhaps from worrying so late into the night.

"I saw ya, Luke! I won't have it. I won't! Ya leave that chile be. There's a whole town of women t'take once ya know it's safe, but right now ya don't need a woman, or a girl."

"She's mine!" Pa raged. "And I'm well now!" His face was red when

I dared to take a peek. "Born of my seed . . . and I'll do what I damn well like with her. She's old enough, plenty old enough. Why, her ma wasn't but a little older when she married up with me."

Grandpa's voice turned to a thin wind from the north. "I remember a night when all the world went dark fer ya, an it'll go even darker if ya touch that girl. Get her away from here, out of temptation's reach. She's no more fer ya than the other one was."

Monday night Pa disappeared while I slept. He came back near dawn. I felt drugged when I woke up, heavy-hearted, dull-spirited, yet I got up to do what I always did, opening the iron stove door, shoving in more wood, putting on water to boil. Pa watched me closely, seeming to weigh my mood, or judge what I might do. When I looked again, Pa seemed reflective, as if trying to pull himself together, before he said in a strange, tight kind of voice, with better pronunciation than usual:

"You, my sweet young thing, are going to have a choice. A choice not many of us have." He moved so I had to look at him or be trapped in a corner. "Down in the valley are two childless couples who have seen you from time to time, and it seems they both admire you, so when I approached them, saying you needed new parents, both couples were eager to have you. Soon they'll be coming. I could sell you to the highest bidder, but I won't."

My eyes clashed with his defiantly, yet I could find nothing to say that would prevent him from doing what he wanted to do.

"This time, I'm allowing you to choose just which set of parents you want."

A certain kind of indifference fell like a cloak over me. Over and over again Grandpa's words echoed in my mind: "Get her away from here . . ." Even Grandpa didn't want me. As Fanny had shouted out, anyone, any place, would be better than here.

Any house!

Any parents!

Grandpa wanted me to go. There he sat whittling on a figure, as if a thousand grandchildren could be sold away, and still he'd just sit and whittle.

Thoughts of Logan Stonewall flitted like doomed moths to the candle of my burning despair. He wouldn't even meet my eyes. Wouldn't even turn his head to stare after me, as I'd hoped he would do. And even if his parents beside him had made him shy or embarrassed, still he could have managed a secret signal, but he hadn't made any. Why not? He'd trudged all the way up the mountainside. Had seeing inside the cabin shocked him to such an extent his feelings for me had changed?

I don't care, I said to myself over and over. Why should I care? He wouldn't believe me when I told the truth.

For the first time I truthfully believed maybe life would be better living with decent town folks. And when I was safely away from this place I'd find a way to search for those I loved.

"You better get dressed," Pa said after I'd wiped the table clean and put away the floor bed pallets. "They'll be coming soon."

I sucked in my breath, tried to meet his eyes, and failed. Better so, I told myself, better so. Without zest I looked through the boxes to find the best of what clothes I had. Before I put them on, I swept the cabin floor—and not once did Pa move his eyes from me.

I made the bed, just as if this were another ordinary day. Pa didn't move his eyes from whatever I did. He made me self-conscious. Made me nervous. Made me clumsy and slow when usually I felt graceful and swift. Made me feel so many emotions I grew confused, reeling with my long-lived hatred for him.

Two shiny new cars crawled into our dirt yard and parked one behind the other. A white car, a black car. The black one was long and luxurious-looking, the white one smaller, snazzier, with red seats.

I was wearing the only dress Fanny hadn't taken, a simple shiftlike garment that had once been blue and was now gray from years of washings. Underneath I had on one of the two pairs of underpants I owned. I needed to wear a bra now, but I didn't own one. Quickly I brushed my hair; then I remembered the suitcase. I had to take that suitcase with me!

Soon I had retrieved the cherished suitcase that held the treasures of my mother, and around it I wrapped several of Granny's handmade shawls.

Pa's dark eyes narrowed when he saw me with the suitcase that had been *hers*. Still, he didn't say a word to stop me from taking my mother's belongings. I would have died to save them from his destruction. Maybe he guessed that.

Twice Pa seemed to rip away his eyes from staring at my mouth. Was he seeing how much I looked like her, his dead angel? Inwardly I shivered. My own mother's lips, the doll mirrored—a doll in a wedding gown—a doll who looked no older than I did now.

Deep in my thoughts, I didn't hear the raps on the door. Didn't glimpse the two couples who came in until they were there, in the middle of our largest room. Ole Smokey coughed and spat out smoke. Pa shook hands, smiling, acting like a genial host. I looked around, trying to see something I'd forgotten.

Then came the silence. The long, awful silence as four sets of eyes turned on me, the item up for sale. Eyes that swept over me from head to feet, took my measurements, studied my face, hands, body, while I was caught in a web of darkness so intense I could hardly see them at all.

Now I knew how Tom must have felt. Tom—I could feel him beside me, giving me strength, whispering his encouraging words. *It'll be all right, Heavenly . . . don't it all work out in t'end, don't it?*

Pa spoke loud and sharp, making my eyes focus on an older couple who stood slightly in front of a younger one who held back considerately for the middle-aged couple to have the first chance at the sale merchandise. I edged backward toward a corner not so far from where Grandpa sat whittling.

Look at me, Grandpa, see what your good-hearted son is doing! Stealing from you the only one you have left that loves you! Say something to stop him, Toby Casteel . . . say it, say it, say it!

He said nothing, only whittled.

The gray-haired man and woman before me were tall and very distinguished, both wearing gray coats with suits underneath, as if they came from a foreign world, with education and intelligence an aura all around them. They didn't stare around the way the younger man and woman did at the shocking poverty and the pitifulness of Grandpa whittling and acting as if no one had come to call.

Their bearing was arrogant, regal, their eyes kind as they looked at me pressed back against the wall, with panic in my face and heart. What my eyes must have shown flicked a shimmer of pity in the man's blue eyes, but the woman refused to show anything. She could have been thinking about the weather. I sighed again, swallowing the lump in my throat, or tried to, feeling trapped. I wished time would speed up, and it would be two years from now. But right at this moment my heart was thudding madly, drumming out a tune of fright in the cage of my ribs, making me feel weak in the knees and queasy in the stomach. I wanted Grandpa to glance upward and meet my eyes and do something to stop this, but I'd never succeeded in forcing Grandpa to do anything when Pa was around.

They don't like me, don't like me, I kept thinking about the older couple, who refused to smile encouragement my way that would make me feel right about choosing them. With the kind of desperate hope that had been Fanny's, I darted a quick glance at the younger pair.

The man was tall and good-looking, with dark brown straight hair and light brown eyes. Beside him stood his wife, almost as tall as he was. Six feet, or very near it, she had to be, even without those high heels. Her hair was a huge mass of auburn red, darker and richer than

Sarah's hair had been. Sarah had never been to a beauty parlor, and only too obviously this woman's hair couldn't survive without one. Hair teased to such exaggerated fullness it seemed quite solid. Her eyes were a strange pale color, so light they seemed not to have any color at all, only huge pupils swimming in a colorless sea. She had that porcelain-white skin that often came with naturally red hair, flawless and made up to perfection. A pretty face? Yes. Very pretty.

She had the look of the hill people . . . something there . . .

Unlike the older couple who wore those heavy gray tailored coats, she wore a hot-pink suit, so tight it appeared painted on. She sashayed about, staring at everything, even leaning to peer into the oven that she opened. Why did she do that? Straightening up, she smiled at everyone and at no one in particular, turning about to stare brazenly at the old brass bed that I had just made, staring up at the baskets on the ceiling, gaping at the pitiful attempts to give the cabin comforts and coziness. Her face wore myriad expressions, changing fleetingly, as if all struggled to survive new impressions that wiped out former gasps, shocks, shudders . . . and other unspoken surprises. With two long-nailed lacquered fingers she picked up the cloth I had used to wipe off the table, held it gingerly two seconds, then dropped it to the floor as if she'd touched a loathsome disease. Her bright pink lips froze in the smile she tried to maintain.

And all the time the good-looking young husband kept his eyes glued on me. He smiled as if to reassure me, and that smile of his lit up his eyes. For some reason that made me feel better—he, at least, approved of what he saw.

"Well," said Pa, planting his big feet wide apart, his huge fists on his hips, "it's up t'ya, girl, up t'ya . . ."

From one couple to the other I stared. How could I know from appearances? What was I supposed to look for? The auburn-haired woman in the bright pink knit smiled winningly, and that made her even prettier. I admired her long painted nails, her earrings big as half-dollars; admired her lips, her clothes, her hair. The older, gray-haired woman met my eyes without blinking and she didn't smile. Her earrings were tiny pearls and not impressive at all.

I thought I saw something hostile in her eyes that made me draw back and look at *her* husband—and he wouldn't meet my gaze. How could I tell if there was no eye contact? The soul was read through the eyes—deceiving eyes if they didn't meet yours squarely.

Again I turned to the younger couple, who wore the "in" kind of clothes and not the tailored, expensive type of the older couple, the kind of clothes that would never go out of style. Stuffy, dowdy clothes, Fanny would say. At that time I knew nothing at all about comparing real wealth with tacky nouveau riche.

And all this only made me feel less than human in my shapeless garment, drooping low on one shoulder because the neckline was much too large, with its jagged hemline that I was always meaning to fix but never had time to tend to. Even as I stood there, I felt wispy wild hair tickling my forehead, so automatically I reached up to brush it away. This drew everyone's attention to my reddened, chapped hands with short, broken fingernails. I tried to hide my hands that scrubbed clothes every day of my life and did all the dishwashing. Who'd want me when I was such a mess?

Neither pair would.

Fanny had been chosen quickly, eagerly. Fanny hadn't ruined her hands, and Fanny's long, straight hair was heavy enough to stay in place. I was too ordinary, too ugly, and too pathetic—who could ever want me—if Logan couldn't bear to meet my eyes anymore? How could I have dared to think that perhaps one day he might even love me?

"Well, girl," Pa said again, frowning and showing his disapproval because I was taking so long. "I said ya'd have yer pick, an if ya don't make it soon, I'll do it fer ya."

Troubled, sensing something of an undercurrent and not under-standing what it was, I tried to guess what was behind the older pair's withdrawn, cold attitude, their eyes resting on me but apparently not wanting to really see me. That made me see them as dull, staid, perhaps cold, and all the time the auburn-haired woman with the colorless eyes was smiling, smiling, and Sarah had been red-haired and so loving—at least until the babies started dying.

Yes, the younger couple would be exciting and less strict. And that was how I made my hasty decision.

"Them," I said, indicating the redhead and her handsome husband. The wife seemed a bit older, but that was all right, she was still young enough, and the longer I stared the prettier she became.

Those colorless sea eyes with round black fish swimming took on a glistening glow—of happiness? She hurried to me, gathered me in her embrace, smothered my face against her voluptuous bosom. "Ya'll neva regret it, neva," she said, half laughing, glancing triumphantly at Pa, then at her husband. "I'm gonna make ya t'best motha there is, t'very very best there is . . ."

Then, as if she'd touched red-hot coals, she dropped her arms and stepped back from me, glancing down to see if I'd dirtied her hot-pink suit before she brushed it off vigorously.

She wasn't really so pretty on close inspection. Her darkly fringed pale eyes were set a bit too close together, and her ears were small and lay close to her head, making them almost not there. And yet, when you didn't pick her apart bit by bit, altogether she made a woman marvelous to behold.

Truthfully, I'd never seen a woman with so much exaggerated femininity, radiating sexuality with her heaving bosom, her full buttocks, her tiny waist that must have struggled to support all it had to. Her knit top was strained so much it appeared thin over the stress areas. Her pants emphasized the wide V of her crotch—making Pa stare at her with a queer smile, not of admiration but of contempt.

Why was he smiling like that? How could he feel contemptuous of a woman he didn't know—did he know her? Of course, he'd have to have seen her before to set this thing up.

Again, fearfully alarmed, I looked at the older couple, too late. Already they had turned and were heading for the door. I felt a sinking sensation.

"Thank you, Mr. Casteel," said the older gentleman, stepping outside, assisting his wife over the doorsill, and, as if with relief, they both headed for their long black car. Pa hastened after them, leaving the door open behind him, said a few words in a low tone, and then hurried back.

No sooner was Pa in the door than he grinned at me in the most mocking way.

Had I chosen wrong? Panicky butterflies were on the wing again, battering my brain with doubts, buffeting my heart with indecision that came too late.

"My name is Calhoun Dennison," said the good-looking husband, stepping forward and taking my trembling hand firmly between both of his, "and this is my wife, Kitty Dennison. Thank you for choosing us, Heaven."

His voice was soft, barely above a whisper. I'd never heard a man with such a soft voice before. Was his an educated voice? It had to be, since all the uneducated roared and shouted, yelled and bellowed.

"Oh, Cal, ain't she jus darlin, jus darlin?" asked Kitty Dennison in a voice slightly on the shrill side. "Ain't it gonna be fun dressin her up an makin her look pretty, ain't it, though?"

I was breathing hard. Beside me Grandpa was quietly crying. *Grandpa, Grandpa, you could have said something before—why wait until it's too late to show you care?*

"An weren't it easy, Cal?" laughed Kitty, hugging and kissing him, and making Pa turn away as if revolted by her display. "Thought she might want them in their big, rich car an heavy, expensive coats, but it were easy, so easy."

Again I felt panic.

"Honey," Kitty Dennison said to me when she had finished playing with her man, "ya run along an put on yer coat, but don't ya botha t'pack any of yer clothes. Gonna buy ya everythin new, brand-new. Don't wanna carry no filthy germs inta my clean home . . ." She gave the cabin another look, this time clearly showing her repugnance. "Kin't wait t'get ya outa here."

With lead in my legs, I pulled my old coat from the nail in the bedroom, put it on, and, daring her disapproval, I picked up the suitcase I'd swathed about with Granny's old shawls. I wasn't going to leave my mother's things here to rot, especially not that beautiful bride doll.

"Ya remember, now," called Kitty Dennison, "jus bring yerself, nothin else."

I strolled out of what we called the bedroom into full view, wearing my shabby old coat, lugging my unsightly bundle, and stared defiantly at Kitty Dennison. Her pale eyes glittered strangely. "Didn't I tell ya not t'bring anythin?" shrilled Kitty Dennison, irritation on her face. "Kin't take that filthy stuff inta my clean house, ya kin't."

"I can't leave here without what I hold dearest in the world," I said with determination. "My granny made these shawls, and they're clean. I just washed them."

"Ya'll have t'wash em again, then," said Kitty, somewhat placated but still looking angry.

I paused beside Grandpa, leaning to kiss the top of his balding head. "Take care, Grandpa. Don't fall and break your bones. I'll write often, and somebody can always . . ." And here I hesitated, not wanting those strangers to guess that Grandpa couldn't read or write. "Well, I'll write."

"Ya done been a good girl, t'best. Couldn't have wanted anyone betta." He sobbed, dabbed at his tears with a handful of his shirttail, and continued brokenly, "Ya go an ya be happy, ya hear?"

"Yes, I hear, and please do take care of yourself, Grandpa."

"Ya be good now, ya hear."

"I'll be good," I swore. I blinked back my own tears. "Good-bye, Grandpa."

"Bye . . ." said Grandpa. Then he picked up a new stick and began to shave off the bark.

When, if ever, has he really looked at me? I was going to cry, and I didn't want Pa to see me cry. I stared him straight in the eyes, and for a change his dark eyes locked with mine in silent combat. *Hate you, Pa. Not saying good-bye to you and take care. I'm going and I don't care.* Nobody needs me here. Nobody has ever needed me but Tom, Keith, and Our Jane . . . not Fanny, not Granny, not really, and certainly not Grandpa, who has his whittling.

"Now, don't ya cry, girl," Kitty said in a strong voice. "Ya've seen me before, an jus didn't know it. I've seen ya in church when I come t'visit my ma an pa who live in Winnerrow. There ya sits with all yer kinfolks, lookin like an *angel*, truly like an *angel*."

Pa's head jerked upward. His hard, dark eyes clashed with Kitty's. He didn't say a word, not a word, leaving me floundering again in uncertainty. There was something unspoken between them, something that hinted that they knew each other more than just casually. It terrified me that she was the kind of woman Pa went after—different from my real mother.

"Really did envy that red-haired ma of yers," Kitty gushed on, as if Pa didn't matter a hoot to her—and that made me even more suspicious. "Since ya were knee-high onta a grasshopper, I've been watchin yer ma luggin all her brood t'church an back. Envied her then, really did. Wanted her kids so bad, cause they were all so pretty." Her loud, shrill voice turned dull and cold.

"Kin't have none of my own." Her strange eyes filled with bitterness and fixed on Pa in a hard, accusing way. Oh, oh, oh . . . she did know him!

"There's some who might say that's my good luck, not to have no kids of my own . . . but I got me one now . . . an she's an *ANGEL*, a real live angel; even if she don't have silvery-blond hair, she's still got t'angel face and t'angel-blue eyes . . . ain't that right, Cal?"

"Yeah," agreed Cal. "She's sure got the look of innocence, if that's what you mean."

I didn't know what either one was talking about. I feared the battle of unspoken recognition between Pa and Kitty. I'd never seen this woman before, and she wasn't the kind anyone would easily overlook. I glanced again at her husband, who was staring around the cabin. His pity showed when he looked at Grandpa sitting like a limp rag doll in his rocker. Eyes blank, his hands idle now. What was he thinking, if anything? Had Granny and Grandpa ever thought? Did minds close off as age came on? Did old ears go deaf just so they wouldn't have to hear what might make them miserable?

"First name is Kitty. Not a nickname. Wouldn't want to be no Katherine, or Katie, or Kate, or Kit. An, honey, ya kin call him Cal, like

I does. Now, when yer livin with us yer gonna enjoy all t'big color TV sets we got. *Ten* of em." She flashed her eyes again at Pa, as if to show him just what kind of rich man she'd captured. Pa seemed indifferent.

Ten TV sets? I stared at her disbelievingly. Ten? Why have ten when one would be enough?

Shrilly Kitty laughed. She hadn't even heard my silent question. "Knew that would give ya a jolt. Cal here runs his own TV repair and sale shop, an some dummies turn in their old sets fer nothin or almost nothin, so he kin bring em home an fix em up good as new, an he sells em as new t'poor folks who don't know no different. Got me a smart man, a handsome, clever man, best kind of man t'have. Turns a tidy profit, too, don't ya, Cal?"

Cal looked embarrassed.

Kitty laughed again.

"Now ya hurry up an say all yer good-byes, Heaven," said Kitty, assuming an air of authority and looking with distaste at the contents of the cabin again, as if to make sure Pa saw how little she thought of his home and his money-making abilities. "Say good-bye to yer *fatha,* an we'll set off. Gotta get home soon as possible."

I could only stand there, not looking at Pa, not wanting to look at Pa.

It was Kitty who was holding up our leave-taking. Kitty who addressed Pa, not me. "I keep *my* house spick an span, everythin in its place. An everythin's got its place, believe ya me. Not like this shack of yers."

Pa leaned back against a wall, pulled out a smoke, and lit it. Kitty turned to me. "Kin't stand dirt an messiness. An yer pa done said ya knew how t'cook. I pray t'God he didn't tell us no lie."

"I can cook," I answered in a small voice. "But I've never made anything complicated." An edge of panic was in my voice as I realized this woman might expect fancy meals when all I really knew how to make well were fluffy biscuits and tasty lard gravy.

Pa wore an odd look, half sad, half full of satisfaction, as he looked from me back to Kitty and Cal Dennison. "Ya done made the right choice," he said solemnly, then turned to smother either a sob or laughter.

That it could be laughter put fears in me I hadn't felt before. I sobbed, my tears beginning to flow fast. I sailed right on by Pa, saying nothing. Nor did he speak to me.

At the door I turned and looked back. Something sweet and sour was in my throat; it hurt me to leave this shabby house that had known my first steps, and Tom's and Fanny's, and it hurt too much to think of Keith and Our Jane.

"O, Lord, give me my day in the future," I whispered before I turned and headed for the steps.

The late-winter sun shone hot on my head as I strode toward the nice-looking white car with the red seats. Pa drifted out to the porch, his hunting hounds back again, as if he'd rented them out and reclaimed them so they could crowd about his legs. Cats and kittens perched on the roof, on lidded rain barrels, peered out from under the porch, and the pigs were rooting with snorts and grunts. Chickens roamed at will, a rooster chasing a hen with obvious intent on reproducing himself. I stared in amazement. Where had they come from? Were they really there? Was I seeing them only in my imagination? I rubbed at my eyes that were smeary with tears. It had been ever so long since I saw the hounds, the cats, the pigs and chickens. Had Pa brought them all here in his pickup truck, planning to stay awhile and take care of his father?

The sky was full of those stringy long clouds slowly forming into fat billowing ones that painted pictures of happiness and fulfillment up ahead.

Cal and Kitty Dennison got into their car, using the front seat, and telling me I could have the back one all for myself. Stiff, anxious, I twisted about to stare back at what I knew so well, and once believed I'd want to forget as quickly as possible.

Say good-bye to poverty and growling stomachs that were never really satisfied.

Say good-bye to the old smelly outhouse, the belching kitchen stove, the worn and tattered bed pallets on the floor.

Say good-bye to all the miseries, as well as all the beauty of the hills: the wild berries, the flaming leaves of autumn, the babbling brook and freshwater streams where trout jumped, and fishing with Tom and Logan.

Say good-bye to memories of Keith and Our Jane and Tom and Fanny.

Say good-bye to all the laughter and all the tears. Going to a better place, a richer place, a happier place.

No reason to cry—why was I crying?

Up there on the porch Pa wasn't crying, just staring off into space with the blank look still on his face.

Cal turned the key and gunned the motor, and away we sped, causing Kitty to squeal and fall backward on the seat. "Slow down, ya damn fool!" she cried. "I know it were horrible, an t'stink will cling t'us fer weeks, but we got us a daughter, an that's what we came fer."

A shiver rippled down my spine.

It was all right. All right.

Going away to a better life, a better place, I kept repeating.

Yet all I thought about was what Pa had done. Sold his children for five hundred dollars apiece. I hadn't seen the papers signed in this last transaction, or heard the sale price. Pa's soul would rot in hell. Not for one moment did I doubt that.

From what I'd heard between Kitty and her husband, they were heading for Winnerrow, where I'd always wanted to live in some pretty painted house not so far from Stonewall Pharmacy. There I would finish high school, go on to college. And I'd see Fanny often, see Grandpa when he went to church.

But what was this?

Why was Cal taking the right turn and heading his car past Winnerrow? I swallowed over another of those burning throat lumps.

"Didn't Pa say you were from the valley?" I asked in a low, scared voice.

"Sure, kid," said Kitty, twisting about in the front seat and smiling back at me. "I was born an raised in that crummy town of Winnerrow," she went on in a voice turned more country, her dialect all hillbilly and slurry. "Couldn't wait t'get away from there. Ran off one day when I were thirteen with a truck driver, we wed up, an then I found out he was already married, but not until years lata. Made me sick, made me hate men, most, men; then I met up with my sweet Cal. Loved him on first sight. We've been married five years, an we wouldn't have been down this way at all cept we had t'get away from all t'stink of havin our house redecorated inside an out. Fresh paint makes me vomit. Get so sick of bad odors, perm lotions an such. Gonna have white wall-t'-wall in every room. All white-on-white wallpaper, gonna be so pretty, so clean-lookin. Cal, now, he done said it's gonna be sterile, like a hospital, but it won't be, ya jus wait an see. Gonna pretty it up with all my thins. Won't it be pretty when all my beautiful thins are put in there fer color contrast, ain't it gonna be, Cal?"

"Sure."

"Sure what?"

"Sure it will be pretty."

She patted his cheek, then leaned to kiss him.

"Now that we're away from yer ole man," intoned Kitty, her sharp chin again resting on her folded arms, "I kin be more honest. Knew yer ma, yer *real* ma. Not that Sarah woman. Now, yer real ma was some looker. Not jus pretty, but beautiful—an I hated her guts."

"Oh," I breathed, feeling sick, unreal. "Why did you hate her?"

"Thought she had a real catch in Luke Casteel. Thought Luke

Casteel should have been mine when I was a kid an didn't know no betta. What a damned idiot I was then, thinkin a handsome face an a strong, beautiful body was all there was t'it. Now I hate him—hate *his* guts!"

This should make me feel good, yet it didn't. Why would Kitty want the daughter of the man she hated?

I'd been right, she had known Pa a long time. Her dialect was just as bad as his, and all the others in our area.

"Yeah," continued Kitty in a strange, soft voice like a cat's purr. "Saw yer real ma every time she came inta Winnerrow. Every hotshot man in town had t'hots fer Luke's angel. Nobody could understand how she would marry t'likes of Luke. Love made her blind, was my thinkin. Some women are like that."

"Shut up, Kitty." Cal's voice, full of warning.

Kitty ignored him. "An there I was with t'hots fer yer big, handsome pa. Oh, every girl in town wantin an waitin fer him t'get inta her pants."

"Kitty, you've said enough."

The warning in his voice was more intense. Kitty threw him an impatient look, jerked around, and switched on the car radio. She fiddled with the dial until she found country music. Loud, twangy guitar music filled the car.

Now we couldn't talk.

Miles and miles and miles slid by like a long ribbon picture postcard that had no end. Out of the hills, down into the flatlands.

Soon the mountains became distant shadows. Miles and miles later, afternoon light faded away. Sun going down, turning twilight time. Where had all the hours gone? Had I fallen asleep without knowing it? Farther away than I'd ever been before. Little farms, big farms, small villages, gasoline stations, long stretches of barren land with patches of red dirt.

Deep twilight came to smear the sky rosy with violet and orange, with bright gold edging all those heavenly colors. Same sky I'd seen in the hills, but the country look that I was accustomed to was left behind. Gasoline stations by the dozens rose up, and quick-food places with colorful neon lights, imitating the sky, or trying to and failing.

"Ain't it somethin," said Kitty, staring out her window, "t'way t'sky lights up? Like drivin when it's twilight time. Heard say it's t'most dangerous time of all, makes people feel unreal, caught up in dreams . . . always had me a dream of having lots of kids, all pretty."

"Please don't, Kitty," pleaded her husband.

She shut up, left me to my own thoughts. I'd seen twilight skies many a time, but I'd never seen a city at night. Fatigue forgotten, I stared at everything, feeling a true hillbilly for the first time in my life. This was no Winnerrow, but the biggest city I'd ever seen.

Then came the golden arches, and the car slowed, as if drawn there magnetically without discussion between husband and wife. Soon we were inside, seated at a tiny table. "What ya mean, ya ain't neva ate at McDonald's before?" asked Kitty, amused and disgusted at the same time. "Why, I bet ya ain't even had Kentucky Fried."

"What's that?"

"Cal, this girl *is* ignorant. Really *ig–nor–ant*. An her pa tole us she was smart."

Pa had said that? It made me feel funny to hear he had. But he'd say anything to gain another five hundred dollars.

"Eating in joints like this doesn't make anybody smart, Kitty. Just less hungry."

"Why, I bet ya ain't neva been t'a moving-picture show, have ya?"

"Yes I have," I answered quickly. "Once."

"Once! Did ya hear that, Cal? This smart girl has been t'a movie *once*. Now, that is somethin, really somethin. What else ya done that's smart?"

How to answer that when it was asked in such a mocking, sarcastic tone?

Suddenly I was homesick for Grandpa, for the miserable cabin and its familiar space. Again those unwanted sad pictures flashed behind my eyes. Our Jane and Keith saying "Hev-lee." I blinked once or twice, glad I had the wonderful doll with me. When Kitty saw her, she'd be impressed, really impressed.

"Now . . . say what ya think of t'burger," quizzed Kitty, dispatching hers in mere seconds, and applying hot-pink lipstick to lips that wore a perpetual stain. She handled the tube expertly despite her inch-long nails, shiny with polish that matched her pink clothes exactly.

"It was very good."

"Then why didn't ya eat all of it? Food costs good money. When we buy ya food we expect ya t'eat it all."

"Kitty, you talk too loud. Leave the girl alone."

"I don't like yer name, either," Kitty flared, as if annoyed at Cal's defense. "It's a stupid name. Heaven's a place, not a name. What's yer middle name—somethin jus as dumb?"

"Leigh," I answered in a tone of ice. "My mother's Christian name."

Kitty winced. "Damn!" she swore, slamming her fists one into the other. "Hate that name!" She swung her seawater eyes to her husband and met his mild look with fierce anger. "That was *her* name, that

Boston bitch who took Luke! Goddam if I eva want t'hear it said aloud again, ya hear?"

"I hear. . . ."

Kitty's mood swung in a different direction, from anger to thoughtfulness, as Cal got up and headed for the men's room. "Always wanted a girl I could call Linda. Always wanted t'be named Linda myself. There's somethin sweet an pure about Linda that sounds so right."

Again I shivered, seeing those huge, glittery rings on Kitty's large, strong hands. Were they real diamonds, rubies, emeralds—or fakes?

It was a relief to be in the car again, on the road speeding toward some distant home. A relief, that is, until Kitty told Cal she was changing my name. "Gonna call her Linda," she said matter-of-factly. "Like that name, really I do."

Immediately he barked, "No! Heaven suits her best. She's lost her home and her family; for God's sake, don't force her to lose her name as well. Leave well enough alone."

There was some forceful quality in his voice this time that stilled Kitty's incessant chatter for a peaceful five minutes, and, best of all, Cal reached to turn off the radio.

In the backseat I curled up and tried to stay awake by reading the road signs. By this time I'd noticed that Cal was following all the signs that directed us toward Atlanta. Overpasses and underpasses, through cloverleafs and down expressways, under train trestles, over bridges crossing rivers, through cities large, small, and medium, going onward toward Atlanta.

I gasped to see the skyscrapers rearing up black in the night, glittering with lit windows, wearing clouds like wispy scarfs. I gasped at store windows on Peachtree Street, stared at policemen standing right in the middle of everything and not afraid, and some were on horseback. Pedestrians were strolling the avenues as if it were midday and not long after nine. Back home I'd be on the floor sound asleep by this time. Even now I had to rub at my eyes, gritty with sleep. Maybe I did sleep.

All of a sudden a loud voice was singing. Kitty had the radio on again and was snuggled up close to Cal, doing something that made him plead for her to stop. "Kitty, there's a time and a place for everything—and the time and place isn't right for this. Now take your hand away."

What was Kitty doing? I rubbed at my eyes, then leaned forward to find out. Just in time to see Cal pull up his fly zipper. Oh—was that nice? Fanny would think so. Quickly I slid backward, alarmed that Kitty might have seen me peek at what was, really, none of my business. Again I stared out the window. The big city with all its majestic skyscrapers had disappeared. Now we were driving down streets not so wide or so busy.

"We live in the suburbs," Cal explained briskly. "Subdivision called Candlewick. The houses are split-levels and almost alike, six different styles, you take your pick. And then they build them for you. You can be an individual only with the way you decorate outside and in. We hope you will enjoy living here, Heaven. We want to do our best by you and give you the kind of life we'd give our own, if we could have children. The school you'll be attending is within walking distance."

Snorting, Kitty mumbled, "Mind. Mind. What the hell difference does it make? She's goin t'school if she has t'crawl there. Damned if ah want some ignorant kid spoilin my reputation."

I sat up straighter, tried to keep sleep from stealing my first view of my new home, and with interest I studied the houses that were, as Cal had said, almost alike, but not quite. Nice houses. No doubt every one had at least one bathroom, maybe more. And all those wonderful electrical conveniences city folks couldn't live without.

Then the car pulled into a driveway, and a garage door was sliding magically upward, and then we were inside the garage, and Kitty was yelling for me to wake up. "We're home, kid, home."

Home.

I quickly opened the car door and left the garage to stand and stare at the house in the pale moonlight. Two stories. How sweet it looked snuggled in the midst of lush shrubbery, mostly evergreens. Red brick with white blinds. A palace in comparison to the shack in the hills I'd just left. A pretty house with a white front door.

"Cal, ya put her dirty thins in t'basement where they belong, if they belong." Sadly I watched my mother's wonderful suitcase, much better than any bag Kitty owned, disappear . . . though of course Kitty couldn't know what was under all those dark knitted shawls.

"C'mon," Kitty called impatiently. "It's goin on eleven. An I'm really pooped. Ya got yer whole life long t'stare at t'outside, ya hear?"

How final she made that sound.

PART TWO

Candlewick Life

12

A New Home

Kitty flicked a switch near the door, and the entire house lit up. What I saw made me gasp.

It was so wonderful, this clean and modern house. It thrilled me to know I was going to live here. The whiteness—all this pure snowy *cleanliness!*—and elegance! I shivered again, seeing cleansing snow that would never melt with sunlight, wouldn't be turned into slush by tromping feet. Deep inside me, all along, I'd known there had to be a better place for me than the cabin with all its dirt and unhappiness.

From second one I thought of this as Kitty's house. The authoritative air she took on, the way she ordered Cal to take my "nasty thins" to the basement, told me clearly that this was her house, not his. There was not one thing to indicate a man lived in all this feminine prettiness, nothing masculine at all here, also giving me the notion that Kitty was the boss in this house.

While Cal followed her instructions, Kitty went around switching on other lamps, as if dim corners terrified her. I soon knew my judgment was wrong. Kitty was looking for flaws in the new paint job.

"Well, now, it sure is betta than yer shack in t'hills, ain't it, kid? Betta by heck than anythin in Winnerrow . . . hick town. Couldn't wait t'escape it. Don't know why I keep goin back." A frown of displeasure darkened her pretty face. Soon she began complaining that the workmen, left on their own, had done a great many "wrong" things.

She saw her home differently than I did—to her it was not wonderful at all.

"Would ya jus look an see where they put my chairs? An my lamps? Nothin's right! I tole em where I wanted everythin, I did! Ya kin bet yer life they're gonna hear about this—"

I tried to see what she saw, but I thought everything looked perfect.

Kitty glanced at me, saw my awed expression, and smiled with tolerant indulgence. "Well, c'mon, tell me what ya think."

Her living room was larger than our entire cabin—but the most surprising thing about this room was the colorful zoo it contained. Everywhere, on the windowsills, in corner cabinets, on the tables, lining the white carpet up the stairs, sat animals made into fancy stands to hold plants; animal faces and forms made picture frames, lamps, baskets, candy dishes, footstools.

Live plants sprouted from the backs of giant green ceramic frogs with bulging yellow eyes and scarlet tongues. There were huge golden fish with gaping mouths and frightened sea-blue eyes bearing more plants. There were blue geese, white and yellow ducks, purple and pink polka-dotted hens, brown and tan rabbits, pink squirrels, hot-pink fat pigs with cute curly tails. "C'mon," said Kitty, grabbing my hand and pulling me into the center of that domestic zoo, "ya gotta see em up close t'appreciate all t'talent it takes t'make em."

I was speechless.

"C'mon, say somethin!" she demanded.

"It's beautiful," I breathed, impressed with all this white, the wallpaper that looked like white silk tree rings, the white lounging chairs, the white sofa, the white lampshades over huge fat white shiny bases. No wonder Kitty had been so appalled by the cabin with all its generations of filth. Here, there was a fireplace with a carved white wooden mantel and frame, and a white marble hearth, and tables of a rich-looking dark wood I was to find out later was rosewood, and glass and brass tables, too. Not a speck of dust anywhere. No fingerprints. Not a thing out of place.

She stood beside me, as if to see her glorious living room through my naive country eyes, while I was afraid to step on that white carpet that had to dirty more quickly than a dog could wag his tail. I glanced down at my clumsy, ugly old shoes, and right away pulled them off.

My feet sank deep into the pile as I drifted dreamlike from one object to the other, marveling. Fat cats, skinny cats, slinky, sneaky, slithering cats. Dogs sitting, standing, sleeping; elephants and tigers, lions and leopards, peacocks, pheasants, parakeets, and owls. A mind-boggling array of animals.

"Ain't they somethin, though, my creations? Made em, I did, with my own hands. Baked em in my huge class kiln. Gotta little one upstairs. I hold classes ever Saturday. Charge each student thirty dollars, an got thirty who come regular. None of my students is as good as I am, of course, an that's a good thin, keeps em comin back, hopin t'outmaster t'master. Did ya notice all t'fancy decorations, t'flower garlands I put on em? Ain't they somethin, ain't they?"

Still overwhelmed, I could only nod in agreement. Oh, yes, I had to be impressed that Kitty could create such wonders as those carousel horses galloping around a white lamp base. I said again, my voice full of admiration, "So beautiful, all of them."

"Knew ya'd think so." Proudly she picked up and displayed what I might have overlooked. "Teachin makes fer lots of cash; won't take no checks, then there's no taxes t'pay. Could teach ten times as many if I'd give up my beauty-salon business, but I jus can't see myself doin that when I earns so much when t'celebrities come t'town an wants their hair done. Do everythin from bleach an tint jobs to perms and pedicures, my eight girls do. Save myself fer special customers, an in my shop I sell thousands of what ya see all around ya. Clients love em, jus love em."

She stood back and crossed her strong arms over her high-rise bosom and beamed at me. "Ya think ya could do as well, do ya, do ya?"

"No. I wouldn't know where to begin," I confessed.

Cal came in from a back door and stood back and looked at Kitty with a certain kind of disgust—as if he didn't admire her "creations" or didn't like all the hours she spent teaching.

"Would ya say I'm an artist, would ya?"

"Yes, Kitty, a real artist . . . did you go to school and study art?"

Kitty scowled. "There's some things ya jus know how t'do, born knowin, that's all. I'm just gifted that way—ain't I, honey?"

"Yes, Kitty, you *are* gifted that way." Cal strolled toward the stairs.

"Hey!" yelled Kitty. "Yer fergettin this kid has t'have new clothes. Kin't let her sleep in our new-painted house in those ole rags she's got on. She stinks, kin't ya smell her? Cal, ya get yerself back in that car an drive ta t'K mart that stays open all night, an get this chile some decent clothes—specially nightgowns—an ya make sure they're all too large. Don't want her growin out of stuff before they're worn out."

"It's almost eleven," he said in that cold, distant voice that I had heard before in the car, and was already beginning to recognize as his disapproving voice.

"I *KNOW* that! Ya think I kin't tell time? But no kid is sleepin in my clean house without a bath, without a shampoo, without a delousin, an, most specially, without new clothes—ya hear!"

Cal heard. He whirled about, grumbling under his breath, and disappeared. Pa would never let a woman tell him what to do and where to do it, much less when. What kind of leash did Kitty have about Cal's neck that he would obey, even grudgingly?

"Now, ya come along with me, an I'll show ya everythin, just everythin, an yer gonna love it all, ya will, know ya will." She smiled and patted my cheek. "Knew yer pa. Guess ya know that by now. Knew he couldn't do nothin fer ya, not like I'm gonna do. Gonna give ya all t'thins I wanted when I was a kid like ya. Advantages I neva had are gonna be yers. It's yer good luck t'have picked me, an my Cal . . . an yer Pa's *bad* luck. Serves him right, too, to lose everythin . . . every one of his kids." Again she smiled her strange smile. "Now, tell me what ya like t'do most."

"Oh . . . I love to read!" I answered quickly. "My teacher, Miss Deale, used to give Tom and me lots of books to bring home, and for birthdays and such she'd give us our very own books—brand-new ones. I brought a few with me, my favorite ones—and they're not dirty, Kitty, really they're not. Tom and I taught Keith and Our Jane to love books and respect them as friends."

"*Books* . . . ?" she asked, distaste on her face. "Ya mean that's what ya'd rather have, more than anythin? Ya must be crazy." And with that she spun on her heel and seemed eager to lead me into the dining room, though my vision was smeary with fatigue, my impressions becoming vague from too many changes all at once.

Yet I had to view the dining room with its large oval glass-top table, sitting atop a fancy gold-colored pedestal formed by three golden dolphins that obligingly fanned their tails to support the thick, heavy glass. I was swaying on my feet, exhausted. I tried desperately to listen to Kitty, to see all the objects that Kitty kept pointing out.

Next we visited the spanking-white kitchen. Even the white floor tiles shone. "Expensive vinyl," she explained, "t'best money kin buy." I nodded, not knowing the best from the worst. Through sleepy eyes I beheld the modern-day wonders I'd dreamed about all my life: the dishwasher, the double porcelain sinks, the gleaming chrome fixtures, the large kitchen range with two ovens, all the white cabinets, the long countertops, the round table and four chairs. Everywhere possible, to keep all the white from being monotonous, were more of Kitty's works.

She'd taken animal forms and made them into different kinds of containers. Ceramic baskets were really flour, sugar, tea, and coffee canisters; a pink pig held utensils too large to fit inside a drawer; and a magenta horse was sitting down as a human would, holding pink paper napkins.

"Now what ya think, really think?" demanded Kitty.

"It's pretty, so clean, colorful, and pretty," I whispered, my voice gone hoarse.

We returned to the front foyer, where Kitty again checked over the living room and then narrowed her eyes. "They done put em in t'wrong places!" she shrieked. "Would ya look where they put my elephant end tables? An I jus noticed! In t'corners—in t'dammed corners—where ya kin't even see em! Heaven, right now we got t'put this place t'orda."

It took an hour to move everything to where Kitty wanted it to be. The large ceramic pieces were surprisingly heavy. I was tired enough to drop. Kitty stared at my face, seized hold of my hand, and pulled me toward the stairs. "Give ya a betta tour tomorra. Yer gonna love it. Right now we gotta get ya ready fer bed."

All the way up the stairs Kitty rambled on about her famous movie-star clients, all stars who insisted only she could do their hair right. "They come t'perform in shows, an always they ask fer me. Why, I've seen things ya jus wouldn't believe—Lord, haven't I? Secrets, I've got 'em by t'million—won't tell a soul, not a single soul. Closemouthed, I am." Kitty paused, turned me around, and stared deep into my eyes. "What's wrong with ya? Kin't you hear? Aren't ya listenin?"

She was a blurred image. So exhausted I could sleep on my feet, I made an effort to be more enthusiastic about Kitty's rich clients, and also an honest excuse about it being a long day, and I wasn't hearing or seeing too well.

"Why ya talk like that?"

I winced. All my life I'd fought not to talk the way she did, as all hill folks talked, slurring their conjunctions so they ran into nouns, verbs, whatever, and she was criticizing me. "Miss Deale always insisted we should not slur our words and contractions."

"Who t'hell is Miss Deale?"

"My teacher."

Kitty snorted. "Neva had no use fer school or teachers. Nobody uses yer kind of Yankee talk. Ya'll make enemies, ya will, with that accent. Ya learn t'talk like t'rest of us, or suffer t'consequences."

What consequences?

"Yes, Kitty."

We'd reached the top of the stairs. Walls were wavering before my eyes. Suddenly Kitty turned to seize me by the shoulders; then she began to bang my head against the nearest wall. "WAKE UP!" yelled Kitty. "Ya wake up an hear this—I'm not Kitty t'ya! Yer t'call me *Mother!* Not Momma, not Mommy, not Mom or Motha—and, least of all, not *Ma!* But Moth-her, understand?"

I was dizzy, my head hurt. She was amazingly strong. "Yes, Mother."

"Good, that's a nice girl, good girl—now let's take that bath."

Oh, I must never become too tired again, and risk the wrath of a woman who could turn on me in a second, and for no apparent reason.

Down a short hall toward an open door that revealed shiny black wallpaper with gold designs Kitty led me. "Now, here's t'master bathroom," informed Kitty, stepping inside first and dragging me along by the arm. "That thing ova there is called a commode by fancy folks, but I'm not fancy—it's a toilet. Ya lift t'lid before ya sit down, an ya flush every time ya use it—an don't ya fill it with paper or it'll stop up an flood ova, an it'll be yer goddam job t'clean it up. In fact, this whole house is yers t'keep clean. I'll explain how t'keep my plants alive, watered an fed, dusted, my planters shiny, all my stuff dusted, clean, vacuumed, an ya'll do t'laundry, but first t'bath."

Here I was, my most fervent wish come true, an indoor bathroom, with hot and cold running water, a bathtub, a basin, mirrors on two walls—now I was too tired to enjoy any of it.

"Are ya listenin, girl—are ya?" came Kitty's shrill voice through my ever-thicker fog of fatigue. "All this paint, wallpaper, an carpet is brand-new, as ya kin plainly see. I want it t'stay that way. It's yer duty t'see it stays this way, brand-new—ya hear?"

Blindly I nodded.

"An ya might as well know from the beginnin, I expect ya t'work out t'expense of stayin here, an t'cost of what ya eat, by doin t'chores I assign. I'm sure ya don't know t'least thing about housework, an that's goin t'waste a good deal of my valuable time, but ya'll learn fast if ya hope t'live here." She paused again and stared deep into my eyes.

"Ya do like it here, don't ya?"

Why did she keep asking, when I hadn't had time to do more than glance around? And the way she talked was already putting me on guard, stealing my hope that this would be a home, rather than a jail.

"Yes," I said, trying to show more enthusiasm. "Everything is beautiful."

"Yeah, ain't it?" Kitty smiled softly. "Got another bathroom on t'first level. Jus as pretty—save it fer guests. Like t'keep it spotless, shinin. That'll be yer job."

All the time Kitty was reaching for bottles and jars hidden behind mirrored doors that slid open, and soon she had quite a collection on the counter shelf that was pink marble, to match the oval bathtub. Black and pink and gold, everything in the "master bath." More rainbowed fish swimming on the black and gold walls . . .

"Now," continued Kitty, all business, "t'first thing we gotta do is scrub all that filth from yer skin. Wash that dirty, buggy hair. Kill t'lice yer bound t'have. Kill all t'nasty germs. That pa of yers has got t'have everythin, an ya've been wallowin in his filth since t'day ya were conceived. Why, t'tales they tell about Luke Casteel in Winnerrow would curl hair betta than perms. But he's payin t'price fer all that fun now . . . payin a heavy price." She seemed glad, smiling her scary secret smile.

How did she know about Pa's disease? I started to say he was well now, but I was too tired to speak.

"Oh, fergive me, honey. Yer feelins hurt? But ya gotta understand I jus don't like yer pa."

That confirmed my choice. Anyone who didn't like Pa had to have good judgment. I sighed, then smiled at Kitty.

"Grew up in Winnerrow, parents still live there," she continued; "in fact, they wouldn't live nowhere else. People get like that when theys neva go nowhere. Skerred livin, that's what I call it. Fraid if they leaves home no big city is gonna know they exist. In Atlanta, where I work, they'd be just nobody important. Don't know how t'do nothin like I do. Don't have no talents like mine. Now, we don't *live* in Atlanta, like we said before, but in this subdivision twenty miles away; both Cal an I work, an there we have'ta fight t'world. That's what it is, ya know, a daily battle out there, me an him against t'world. He's mine an I love him. I'd kill t'keep him." She paused, eyeing me thoughtfully with hard, narrowed eyes.

"My shop is in a big, fancy hotel that draws all t'rich folks. Kin't buy a house here in Candlewick unless ya make more than thirty thousand a year, an with both Cal and me working, we double that some years. Why, honey, yer gonna love it, just love it. Ya'll go t'school in a three-storied building where they have an indoor swimming pool, an auditorium where they show movies, an of course ya'll be much happier there than in that lil old second-rate school . . . an jus think, yer right in time t'start t'new semester."

It made me hurt to think of my old school, and to remember Miss Deale. It was there I'd learned about the rest of the world, the better world, the different world that cared about education, books, paintings, architecture, science . . . not just existing from day to day. And I hadn't even been able to say good-bye to Miss Deale. I should have been nicer, more grateful for her caring. I should have thrown away my pride. I tried to stifle a sob. Then there was Logan, who might not have spoken because his parents were there that last time at church. Or some other reason. Now not only my beloved teacher but Logan too seemed unreal, like dreams I'd never have again. Even the cabin had gone fuzzy in my mind, and I'd left only hours ago.

Grandpa would be sound asleep by this time. And here the stores were still open and people were still shopping. Like Cal, off somewhere buying me new clothes that would be too large. I sighed heavily; some things never changed.

With leaden legs, I waited for Kitty to finish filling the fancy pink tub with water.

Steamy vapor clouded all the mirrors, filled my lungs, misted the air so Kitty seemed miles and miles away, and into fantasy land Kitty and I had drifted, up in the clouds near the moon—black, foggy night full of golden fish drifting with us. I felt drunk from lack of energy, swaying on my feet, and heard, as if truly from the moon, Kitty ordering me to undress and drop everything into the trash can she'd lined with a plastic bag, and out into the garbage would go everything I had on, to be thrown in the city dump and eventually burned.

Clumsily I began to undress.

"Yer gonna have everything new. Spendin a fortune on ya, girl, so ya think of that whenever ya feel homesick fer that pigsty cabin ya called home. NOW STRIP DOWN, *INSTANTLY!* Ya gotta learn t'move when I speak, not jus stand there like ya don't hear or understand— understand?"

With fingers made awkward from fear and fatigue, I began to work on the buttons of my old dress. Why weren't my fingers working better, faster? Somehow I managed to unfasten two, and even as I did this, Kitty pulled from a cabinet drawer a plastic apron. "Stand on this and drop yer clothes down around yer feet. Don't let anything ya wear touch my clean carpet or my marble countertops."

Naked, I stood on the plastic apron, with Kitty eyeing me up and down. "Why, bless my soul, yer not a little girl afta all. How old are ya anyway?"

"Fourteen," I answered. My tongue felt thick, my thoughts thicker, my eyes so sleepy they had grit in them, and even as I tried to obey Kitty, I blinked, yawned, and swayed.

"When will ya be fifteen?"

"February twenty-second."

"Ya had yer first monthly bloody time yet?"

"Yes, started when I was almost thirteen."

"Well, now, neva would have guessed. When I was yer age I had boobs, big ones. Made t'boys hot jus t'look my way, but all of us kin't be that lucky, kin we?"

Nodding, I wished Kitty would leave me alone to take my first bath in a real porcelain tub. Apparently Kitty had no intention of getting out, or giving me a moment to use the bathroom alone.

I sighed again and moved toward the pink toilet seat, realizing that she didn't intend to leave.

"NO! First ya have t'cover t'seat with paper." And even that body function had to wait for Kitty to spread tissues all over the seat, and then she turned her back. What good did that do when she could still hear, and there were mirrors everywhere to reflect everything even if they were cloudy from steam?

Then Kitty sprang into action. She squatted down near the tub and informed me as she tested the water temperature, "Hot water is what ya have'ta sit in. Gotta scrub ya with a brush, put sulfur an tar soap on that hair of yers t'kill all those nits ya must have."

I tried to speak and tell Kitty I bathed more often than most hill people did, and once a week I washed my hair (only this morning), but I was without energy, without will to speak and defend myself. All kinds of confused emotions were churning within me, making me more tired and weak.

Funny how sick I felt. Silent screams stuck in my throat, tears froze behind my eyes, and, as Fanny often did, I wanted to yell and scream and throw some kind of tantrum, kick out and hurt somebody just so I wouldn't hurt so much inside; but I did nothing but wait for the tub to fill.

And fill it did. With scalding water.

All that was pink in the small room suddenly seemed red—and in that hellish misty red I saw Kitty taking off her pink knit top and pants. Underneath she wore a pink bikini bra and panties so small they hardly covered what they should.

Warily I edged away, watching Kitty move to pour something from a brown bottle into the tub. The stench of Lysol.

I knew the smell from school, when I'd stayed late to help Miss Deale, and the cleaning ladies and men had used Lysol in the rest rooms. I'd never heard of anyone taking a bath in Lysol.

Somehow a pink towel had found its way into my hand, a towel so large and thick I felt I could hide safely behind it. Not that anyone in the cabin had ever cared much about modesty, but I was ashamed to let Kitty see how thin I was.

"Put down the towel! Ya shouldn't touch my clean towel. All t'pink ones belong t'me, an only I use em, ya hear?"

"Yes, ma'am."

"Yes, *Mother*," she corrected. "Neva call me anything but Mothther . . . say it like that."

I said it like that, still clutching the towel and dreading the feel of that hot water.

"Black velvet towels belong to Cal, not ya, rememba that. When my pink ones fade almost white, I'll turn em ova t'ya. Right now ya kin use some ole ones I brought home from my salon."

I nodded, my eyes riveted on the steam coming from the tubful of water.

"Now I've got everything ready." She flashed me a smile of assurance. "Now, slide yer feet along on t'plastic apron, an make it move with ya, so when yer near nough ya kin step inta t'tub."

"The water's too hot."

"Of course it's hot."

"It will burn me."

"How t'hell ya think ya kin come out clean without scaldin t'filth from yer skin? How? Huh? Now, get in!"

"It's too hot."

"It . . . is . . . not . . . too . . . hot."

"Yes, it is. It's steaming hot. I'm not used to hot water, only barely warm."

"I *knows* that . . . that's why I gotta scrub ya off with hot, real hot."

Kitty closed in.

The dense fog of steam almost hid the long-handled pink brush in her right hand. She smacked the palm of her left hand with that brush. The threat was unmistakable.

"Nother thin. When I tell ya t'do somethin—*anythin*—ya'll do it without question. We have paid out good money to buy ya, an now yer our property t'do with as we will. I took ya in cause once I was idiot nough t'love yer pa so much I let him break my heart. Made me pregnant, he did, made me think he loved me, and he didn't. Tole him I'd kill myself iffen he didn't marry up with me . . . an he laughed an said, 'Go ahead,' then walked out. Took off fer Atlanta, where he met up with yer ma an married her . . . HER! An me, I'm stuck with a baby, so I gave myself an abortion, an now I kin't have a baby. But I got HER baby . . . even iffen ya aren't a baby now, yer still his. But don't ya go thinkin cause I was sweet on yer pa once, I'm gonna let ya run my life. There are laws in this state that would put ya away if they found out yer so bad yer own pa had to sell ya."

"But . . . but . . . I'm not bad. Pa didn't have to sell me."

"Don't stand there an argue with me! GET in t'tub!"

I neared the tub gingerly, obeying Kitty by slipping my bare feet in such a way the plastic apron slid with me. I was doing everything I could to give that water time to cool off. First I closed my eyes and balanced on one leg as I tentatively extended my foot over heat-shimmering water. It was like dangling my foot over hell. Uttering a small cry, I jerked back my foot and turned to Kitty, pleading with my eyes, even as she snatched the pink towel away and hurled it toward the dirty-clothes hamper.

"Mother, it really is too hot."

"It *is not too hot.* I always bathe in hot water, an if I kin stand it, so kin ya."

"Kitty . . ."

"Mother—say it."

"Mother, why does the water have to be so hot?"

Perhaps Kitty liked the submissive tone in my voice, for she changed almost as if a magician had pushed a switch.

"Oh, honey," she crooned, "it's truly fer yer own good, really it is. T'hot will kill all t'germs. I wouldn't make ya do anythin that would hurt ya." Her seawater eyes turned soft, her tone as well; she appeared kind, motherly, persuading me I'd been mistaken. Kitty was a good woman needing a daughter to love. And I so wanted a mother to love me.

"See," Kitty said, testing the water by putting in her hand and arm up to her elbow, "it's not as hot as ya think. Now, step in like a good girl, an sit down, an let *Mother* scrub yer skin cleaner than it's eva been in yer whole life."

"Are you sure your bathwater is this hot?"

"Not lyin, honey baby. I do take baths in hot water like that all t'time." Kitty shoved me closer. "Once yer in an t'shock is ova, it feels good, real good; makes ya relax an feel sleepy. See, I'll pour in some pretty pink bubble bath. Ya'll like that. Ya'll come out smellin like a rose, looking like one, too."

Kitty had to let out some water in order to put in the bubble bath so she could again let the hot water gush in and make the pink crystals foam—and this, unfortunately, took away water that might have cooled down a bit from all I'd done to hesitate.

There it was before me, one of the dreams I'd prayed someday to enjoy, a perfumy bubble bath in a pink tub with mirrors all around . . . and I wasn't going to enjoy it.

I just knew it was going to burn.

"It'll be all right, sweetheart, really it will be. Would I ask ya t'do somethin that would hurt ya? Would I? I was a girl like ya once, an I neva had t'chance t'enjoy what-all I'm gonna do fer ya. One day in t'future ya'll go down on yer knees an give thanks ta t'Lord fer savin ya from t'depths of hell. Think of t'hot water as *holy water*. That's how I do it. Think of cold thins like ice, tons of crushed ice, sittin in ice an sippin cola drinks, think of that. It won't hurt. Neva hurt me, an I've got baby-soft skin."

Kitty moved suddenly. She caught me off balance, and in a flash, instead of hovering above the water to test it again, I was facedown in the water!

The scalding water seared me like liquid hot coals from Ole Smokey. I shoved upward blindly, pulled up my knees, balancing on my hands, trying blindly to fight my way out of the tub; but Kitty held me down, grasped my shoulders with strong hands, and twisted me over so I was sitting in the water. Now I could scream!

Time and time again I let go, howling, flailing my arms as Our Jane would, as Fanny would, yelling, "Let me go, let me go!"

Wham!

Kitty's hand slapped me!

"SHUT UP! Damn ya! Shut up! Don't ya be yellin when my Cal comes in, an make him think I'm bein mean. I ain't, I ain't! I'm doin what I have t'do, that's all."

Where was Cal . . . why didn't he come back and save me?

It was terrible, so terrible I couldn't find another scream, not when I was gasping, choking, crying, struggling to push Kitty away, to stop that brutal brush from taking off all my red, seared skin. I was stinging all over—and inside as well. The Lysol water was seeping into my most private parts. My eyes pleaded with Kitty to have mercy, but Kitty grimly set about scrubbing off the germs, the contamination, the Casteel filth.

It seemed I could hear Reverend Wayland Wise preaching, chanting me into paradise as I lingered on the verge of unconsciousness. Shock had taken over. My mouth was open, my eyes as well, and Kitty's face above me was a pale mean moon, bent on destruction.

On and on the bath lasted, until at last the water began to cool, and Kitty poured dark-looking shampoo from an orange bottle onto my hair. If my scalp hadn't already been burned, perhaps it wouldn't have stung so much, but it hurt, really hurt! I found strength to struggle and nearly pulled Kitty into the tub.

"STOP IT!" yelled Kitty, slapping me hard. "Yer actin like a damned fool! It's not that hot!" And there she went and put in her arms, thrusting her face close to mine. "See, it's not hot. I'm not screamin."

Oh, oh, oh . . . it *was* hot.

It was the worst experience of my life to flip and turn, kick and struggle, and never get away from Kitty, who managed to lather up every strand of my hair with that dreadful-smelling soap that was almost black. That was the worst thing anyone could do to my hair. It was long and fine, and screwing it around like that would mat it so badly it would never untangle. I tried to tell Kitty that.

"Shut up, damn ya! Ya think I don't know what hair is, an how t'wash it? I'm a professional! A professional! Been doin this all my adult life. People pay t'have me wash their hair, an yer complainin. One more yelp out of ya, an I'm turnin on t'hot water agin, an I'll hold ya down an take t'skin from yer face."

I tried to stay still while I allowed Kitty to do what she would.

After my hair was lathered it had to set to kill whatever was hidden in its depths, and during that time Kitty picked up the long-handled brush again and scrubbed my already tortured skin. Whimpering, I managed to stay in the water that gradually cooled more, and now I didn't have to wiggle or whimper, not that any of what I'd done had prevented Kitty from completing a thorough scrubdown and inspection of all my crevices that might conceal running sores.

"I don't have sores, Mother . . . I really don't, not ever . . ."

Kitty didn't care. She was intent on what she felt she had to do, even if it killed me.

Dream of hell, that's what this was—steaming vapors of hellfires, looming pale white face that wasn't pretty now that her hair was in damp strings, hanging all around that hateful moon that had a red slash that kept crooning about how babyish I was acting.

Oh, my God, oh, my God, oh, my God, I whispered, though I didn't hear any words coming from my throat. I felt as if I'd been cooked for dinner, a chicken in the pot, now being scrubbed with a brush and making skin already red and tender sting like fire.

I turned into Our Jane and began to cry, helplessly, uncontrollably. The Lysol in the water crept into my eyes, burned them. Reaching blindly, I found the cold-water spigot and turned it on, threw a handful of water in my face, relieving the pain in my eyes.

Strangely, Kitty didn't object. She seemed intent on finishing her inspection of the cleft between my buttocks. On hands and knees, I kept throwing cold water on my face, chest, shoulders, back.

"Now I'm gonna rinse off all t'suds," Kitty crooned tenderly, patting my raw bottom as if I were a baby. "Germs all gone now, all gone. Clean baby, clean, sweet, nice, obedient baby. Turn ova, let Mother rinse ya off."

Deep in my private hell, I turned to sprawl helplessly in the tub, my feet lifted and hanging over the side to lend some relief and coolness to the rest of me.

"I'm gonna be real careful not to get any of this in yer eyes, but yer gonna have t'do yer part by holdin still. Stuff done killed yer lice, if ya had any. Yer a new person, almost. Ya want that, don't ya? Ya want us t'do nice thins fer ya, don't ya? Want Cal an me t'love ya, don't ya? We kin't if ya don't cooperate, kin we? It's yer duty t'be clean, t'do what we want. Stop cryin. Don't tell dear Cal it hurt, that'll make *him* cry. He's weak, tenderhearted, ya know. All men are. Babies more than they're lil boys. Ya kin't tell em that, makes em mad, but that's t'truth. Scared of women, all of em are, every last man in this old mean world, terrified of mommy, of wifey, of daughta, of sista, of auntie, of granny, of lovey-dovey girlfriends. Got pride, they have. Too much of it. Feared of rejection, like we don't get it all t'time. They want ya, kin't leave ya alone, but when they got ya, they wish they didn't have ya, or, worse than anythin, wish they didn't need ya. So they go around thinkin they kin find nother woman who's different.

"Ain't none of us different. So be sweet t'him, make him think he's got ya sold on how big, strong, an wonderful he is, an ya'll be doin me a big favor, so then I kin do ya a big favor."

Kitty kneaded deeper and deeper into my mass of matted hair. "I saw t'shack ya lived in. I know what ya are underneath that sweet, innocent face. Same look yer ma had. Hated her then. Ya make sure I don't end up hatin *ya*."

Now the water was cold, soothing my burning skin, my sore scalp, and Kitty was smiling. Smiling, and fanning away the steam.

By the time I was out and standing on a plain white mat that Kitty pulled from the linen closet, I was trembling with relief to be alive. Every bit of me stung, every bit was red, even the whites of my eyes when I glanced in the long mirrors. But I was alive—and I was clean. Cleaner than I'd ever been in my entire life—about that Kitty was right.

"Ya see, ya see," soothed Kitty, hugging and kissing me. "It's all ova, all ova, an yer betta than new. Look new, ya do. Look spick an span an sweet. An, honey, now I'm gonna smooth on some nice pink

lotion that will help take t'burn from yer poor red skin. Didn't mean
t'scare ya. Didn't know yer skin were so tender, but ya gotta realize I
had t'do somethin drastic to remove all t'years of accumulated filth.
T'stink of those hockeypots an outhouses was ground inta yer skin,
clingin t'yer hair; even if ya couldn't smell it, I could. Now yer cleaner
than a newborn babe."

Smiling, she picked up a big pink bottle with a gold label and gently
smoothed on lotion that felt cooling.

Somehow I managed to smile gratefully. Kitty wasn't so bad, not
really. She was like Reverend Wayland Wise, shouting and putting the
fear of God's retaliation into everyone to make them better. God and
hot water, about the same thing.

"Don't ya feel wonderful, betta than eva before? Haven't I saved ya
from t'gutter, haven't I? Don't ya feel reborn, fresh, brand-new? Ready
now t'face the world that would condemn ya but fer me?"

"Yes . . ."

"Yes what?"

"Yes, Mother."

"Ya see," said Kitty, towel-drying my hair, wrapping it in a clean
faded pink towel before she used another towel to dry my almost raw
body, "ya survived. If yer skin is a little red, it's still there. Yer hurtin,
but all medicine meant to heal is nasty. Ya have t'suffa t'be cleansed an
made whole an decent."

Kitty's hypnotic voice in the fading mists lulled me into a sense of
security as the pain eased. Then she began to comb my still-damp hair.

Ouch!

It hurt!

My hair was matted in thick wads to my scalp—wads that Kitty was
determined to untangle even if she had to pull out every strand.

"Let me do it," I cried, snatching the comb from her hands. "I know
how."

"*YA* know how? Have ya spent years an years of yer life standin on yer
feet until they ache up ta yer waist? Have ya studied hair? Have ya—
have ya?"

"No," I whispered, really trying to work out the tangles with my
fingers before I attempted again to use the comb, "but I know my own
hair. When it's washed you have to be careful not to bunch it up and
screw it around, like you just did."

"Are ya tryin t'tell me my own business?"

At that moment a door slammed downstairs. Cal's soft voice called
out. "Honey, where are you?"

"Up here, darlin love. Helpin this poor chile rid herself of filth. Soon as I've finished with her, I'm comin t'take care of ya." She hissed in my ear. "Now, don't ya go complainin t'him, ssssista. What we do when we're alone is none of his damned business . . . understand?"

Nodding, I clutched at my body towel and backed off.

"Darling," Cal called from the other side of the locked bathroom door, "I've bought new clothes for Heaven, including a couple of nightgowns. Didn't know her size, so I just guessed. Now I'm going downstairs again to make up the sofa bed."

"She's not goin t'sleep downstairs," Kitty called in that strange, flat way.

His voice sounded shocked. "What do you mean? Where else can she sleep? That second bedroom is jam-packed with all your ceramic junk that should be in your workshop. You knew she was coming. You could have had it all moved out, but no, you wouldn't do that. You wanted to put the kid on the sofa—and now you don't. What's with you, Kitty?"

Kitty smiled at me as if her lips were stiff. Silently she moved to the door, holding my fearful gaze with her commanding eyes. "Not a word, darlin dear, not a word, ya hear, not a single word t'him . . ."

Throwing back her red hair, she managed to look seductive when she unlocked and opened the door just a crack. "She's a terribly modest little thing, sweetheart love. Jus hand me one of those nightgowns an soon we'll be seeing ya."

Bang!

She slammed the door and tossed me a thin nightgown with a dainty print.

I'd never owned a nightgown before, but I'd always anticipated this momentous step of drawing a sleeping garment over my head. The height of luxury to have special clothes just to sleep in, when nobody saw you once you went to bed. But as soon as I had it on, the thrill was over.

The stiffness of the new fabric chafed my raw skin. The lace ruffling about the neck and sleeves felt like sandpaper.

"Ya remember, now. All yer towels, washcloths, an toothbrushes will be white—or near white. Mine are t'hot-pink ones. Cal has black—and don't ya eva ferget." She smiled, opened the door, led me down the hall a short way, then showed me the very fancy large bedroom beside the bath.

Cal was in there, just beginning to unzipper his pants. Quickly he zippered again and blushed as we came in. I bowed my head low to hide my embarrassment.

"Really, Kitty," he began with a sharp edge to his voice, "haven't you learned about knocking first? And where do you plan to put her in here—in our bed?"

"Yeah," quipped Kitty without hesitating. I glanced up in time to see her expression—odd, so odd. "She's gonna sleep in t'middle. Me on one side, ya on t'otha. Ya know how wild an obscene these hill girls are, an this is one I'm gonna have t'tame by seein that she is neva left alone when she's lyin down."

"Good God in heaven!" stormed Cal. "Have you gone crazy?"

"I'm t'only one here with good sense."

What a fearful thing to hear.

"Kitty, I just won't have it! She sleeps downstairs, or we take her back!"

He was standing up to her—hooray!

"What do ya know about it? Ya were raised in a big city, an this girl here has no morals, unless we give em t'her. An startin tonight, our lessons are beginnin. When I have her straightened out, she kin use t'sleep sofa downstairs—but not until then."

That's when he caught a glimpse of my face, though I'd tried to keep myself hidden behind Kitty. "My God, what have you done to her face?"

"Washed it."

He shook his head disbelievingly. "You've taken off her skin! Kitty, goddam you for doing that! You should be ashamed." He turned kind eyes on me and held out his arms. "Come, let me see if I can't find some medication to put on all that raw red skin."

"Ya leave her alone!" yelled Kitty. "I've done what I had t'do, an ya know I'd neva hurt anythin. She was dirty, smelly; now she's cleansed, an in our bed she's going to sleep til I kin trust her t'be alone in t'night."

What did Kitty think I was going to do?

Cal looked cold, seeming to retreat, as if anger made him ice instead of fire, like Pa. Striding out to the bathroom, slamming the door hard, leaving Kitty to hurry in there and say whatever she had to as I sighed, gave in to necessity, and crawled into the big bed. I no sooner lay down than I was asleep.

Cal's loud voice woke me up. An innate sense of timing told me I'd been asleep only a few minutes. Keeping my eyes closed, I heard them arguing.

"Why the hell did you put on that black lace nothing nightgown? Isn't that kind of gown your way of letting me know what you want? Kitty, I can't perform with a child in the bed, and between us."

"Why, of course I don't expect ya ta."

"Then why the hell the black lace nightgown?"

I opened my eyes a crack and took a peek. There was Kitty stuffed into a tight black mist of a gown that barely shaded her nudity. Cal stood there in his jockey shorts, a huge bulge in the crotch that made me hastily close my eyes again.

Please, God, I prayed, don't let them do it in the bed—not with me here, please, please.

"This is my way t'teach ya some self-control," Kitty replied primly, and crawled into the bed beside me. "Ya don't have any, ya know. It's all ya want from me, an ya ain't gonna have any till I got this girl trained t'way I want her t'be."

I listened, amazed that he took what she dished out. Pa never would have. What kind of man was Kitty's husband? Wasn't a man always the boss in his family? I felt a bit sick that he didn't fight back and stand up to her.

Cal slipped into the bed on the opposite side of me. I stiffened when I felt the brush of his bristly skin against my arm. I felt angry that he hadn't gone downstairs and made up the sleep sofa himself, overridden her desires and staked his own bed for his own reasons; yet, for some reason, I pitied him.

I knew already who was the real man in this family.

His low voice rolled over me. "Don't push me too far, Kitty," Cal warned before he turned on his side and tucked his arm under his head.

"I love ya, sweetheart darlin, I do. An t'sooner this girl learns her lessons, t'sooner ya an me kin have this bed all fer ourselves."

"Jesus Christ," was the last thing he said.

It was awful to sleep between a man and his wife, and know he was resenting my presence. Now he'd never learn to like me, and I'd been depending on his favor. Without it, how could I manage to endure Kitty and her strange behavior and swings of mood? Maybe this was Kitty's way to see that he never liked me. What a hatefully mean thing to do.

Mother, Mother, I lay sobbing, desperately wanting that long-dead mother who was buried on the mountainside where the wolves cried at the moon and the wind sang in the leaves. Oh, to be home again, back with Granny alive, with Sarah cutting out biscuits, with Grandpa whittling, and Tom, Fanny, Keith, and Our Jane running in the meadows.

I was suspecting already . . . paradise lived in Winnerrow. Hell was up ahead.

No, didn't have to be that way. Not if I could make Kitty like and trust me.

Not if I could somehow convince Kitty I wouldn't do anything dangerous or wicked when I slept alone downstairs on the sofa bed. I closed out the pain of my raw skin and again fell into deep, merciful sleep.

13

Fevered Dreamer

As if I still lived in the cabin high in the Willies, my mental rooster crowed.

I woke up stiff and aching; it hurt every time I moved. Visions of the night before and the hot bath made me think I'd had a nightmare, but my burning skin was proof I hadn't dreamed that scalding bath.

Five o'clock, my body clock said. I thought of Tom, and how he would be outside chopping wood or hunting now; seldom did I awaken to find Tom sleeping—back in the Willies where my heart ached to be. Disoriented, I blindly reached to find the soft sweetness of Our Jane, and touched a strong arm bristly with hair. I bolted more wide awake, stared around, reluctant to look at Kitty or her husband sprawled asleep on the wide bed. Frail morning light poured in through the open drapes.

Moving stiffly, I carefully crawled over Cal, thinking him the better choice to risk awakening. I slipped out of bed and looked around, admiring so much of what I saw, while some things left me bothered; such as the careless way Kitty had dropped all her clothes on the floor and just left them there. Why, we didn't do that in the cabin. All the fine ladies I'd read about in novels had never dropped their clothes on the floor. And Kitty had made such a fuss about everything being neat and clean! Then, I reasoned, Kitty had no worries about finding roaches and other vermin in her floor-scattered clothes, which had always been on my mind when I hung a garment on a nail. Still . . . she shouldn't do that. I picked up her clothes and hung them neatly in her closet, amazed at all the other clothes I saw there.

Quietly leaving the bedroom, I eased the door behind me, breathed a sigh of relief. Oh, I couldn't keep sleeping between husband and wife . . . it just wasn't right.

How silent this house was. I stepped down the hall and into the bathroom, and saw myself in the long wall-length mirror. Oh, my poor face! It was red and swollen, and when I touched it, it felt soft in some places, hard and irritated in others. The rash of small red dots burned like fire. Some of the larger patches were even bloody, as if I'd scratched them in the night. Helpless tears coursed down my face . . . would I ever be pretty again?

What had Granny always said? "Ya takes what ya get an makes t'most of it . . ."

Well, I would have to accept what couldn't be helped now. Though it hurt to pull off my brand-new nightgown, hurt to raise my arms, hurt to move my legs. In fact, every move I made hurt my skin. How had I managed to sleep so soundly? Fatigue so deep even pain didn't reach me? But the night had delivered not so much rest as seething bad dreams about Tom, Keith, and Our Jane, leaving unpleasant impressions to trouble my mind as first I used that pink seat, and hesitated before flushing it. Next I set about frantically trying to untangle the impossible mess of my hair.

Through the thin walls that separated the bath from the bedroom drifted Kitty's grunts and groans, as if the new day gave Kitty immediate problems. ". . . Where t'hell are my bedroom slippers? Where t'hell is that dumb kid? She'd betta not use all t'hot water— she'd betta not!"

Cal's calm, soft voice consoled Kitty as if she were a small child and had to be indulged. "You go easy on her, Kitty," he cautioned. "You're the one who wanted her, you keep remembering that. Though why you insist on her sleeping in our bed is beyond comprehension. A girl her age needs her own room, to decorate, to dream in, to keep her secrets."

"Ain't gonna be no secrets!" fired Kitty.

He continued as if she hadn't spoken, and my hopes rallied. "I was against this from the first. Still, I feel sorry for her. Especially after what you did last night. And when I think of that pitiful cabin, all those attempts to make it cozy, I realize how blessed we are to have what we do. Kitty, even if you don't want to move out your pottery wheel and all the other junk, we could manage to put a twin bed in our second bedroom, and a nice dresser. A bedside table and a lamp, and maybe a desk where she could do her homework. C'mon, Kitty . . . what do you say?"

"I say NO!"

"Honey, she appears to be a nice girl, very sweet."

He was trying to persuade her, maybe with kisses and hugs. Why, from the noises they made, I could almost see what he was doing.

A slap! A hard hand striking soft flesh! "Ya thinks she's pretty, don't ya? Yer noticin already, huh? But ya kin't have her, ya keep rememberin that! I got patience, an I got tolerance, but don't ya go foolin around with no kid who's gonna be our daughta."

How loud she yelled.

"Don't you ever slap me again, Kitty," Cal said in a hard, cold voice. "I put up with a lot from you, but I draw the line at physical violence. If you can't touch me with love and tenderness, don't touch me at all."

"Honey, it didn't hurt, did it?"

"That's not the issue, whether or not it hurt. The issue is, I don't like violent women, or ones that shout and raise their voices. And the walls are paper-thin. I'm sure Heaven thinks you treat her fine, just like a mother always treats a daughter she loves. Putting her to bed with her parents. She's a teenager, Kitty, not an infant."

"Ya jus don't understand, do ya?" Kitty sounded more than grouchy. "I know how hill gals are; ya don't. Ya kin't begin to know t'evil stuff they do—an they don't need no man t'be there, neither. An if ya want peace in this house, ya'll let me do it my way."

Not a word from Cal to defend me. Not a word about the boiling bath and all the damage it had done—why not? Why was he timid around Kitty when she was in the house, when he'd stood up to her in the car?

The bedroom door opened. The slippy-slop of Kitty's feathered slippers sounded on the hall floor, coming this way. I panicked. Quickly I seized one of the faded old towels and swathed it about my sore body.

Kitty came in without knocking, threw me a hard glance, then without a word whipped off her flimsy black nightgown, kicked off her pink slippers, and sat down naked on the toilet. I started to leave, but she ordered me back. "Do somethin fer yer head . . . it looks awful!" she said flatly.

I bowed my head, trying not to see or hear anything. Diligently I worked with as much careful speed as my tangled hair would allow.

Soon Kitty was in the shower, singing country tunes in a loud voice. All the time I kept trying to unsnarl my hair.

Kitty came out of the shower, drying her body with a lush pink towel, scowling my way. "Neva wanta come in here agin an see what I just saw in that toilet—ya hear?"

"I'm sorry. But I was afraid if I flushed it, it would awaken you and your husband. Tomorrow morning I'll use the downstairs bath."

"Ya betta," mumbled Kitty. "Now ya hurry up an finish, then put on one of t'nice dresses Cal bought fer ya t'wear. This aftanoon, Cal an me's gonna show ya around, go t'Atlanta, let ya see my shop, how pretty it is, how much my girls love me. Tomorrow we'll go t'church, an Monday ya'll start school with all t'other kids yer age. Sacrificin my ceramic classes fer yer sake, ya keep that in mind. Could make plenty t'day, but won't, jus t'get ya started right."

I again set diligently to work on my hair as Kitty made up her face and dressed all in pink. She picked at her bush of auburn hair with a funny-looking wire thing, then turned to beam at me. "What say?"

"You look beautiful," I answered truthfully. "I never saw anyone so beautiful."

Kitty's pale eyes glistened. Her smile spread to show large, even white teeth. "Neva guess, would ya, that I'm thirty-five?"

"No," I breathed. Older than Sarah, imagine that, and Kitty looked so much younger.

"Cal's only twenty-five, an that worries me some, bein ten years olda than my own husband. Caught me a fine man, I did, a real fine man, even if he is younga—but don't ya tell nobody my age, ya hear?"

"They wouldn't believe me if I did."

"Why, ain't that sweet of ya," Kitty said in a new and softer voice. She stepped closer to give me a quick hug, a swift kiss on my raw cheek. "Didn't really want t'make yer skin look so red an raw. Does it really hurt?"

I nodded, and then Kitty was finding ointment to touch lightly on my face with great kindness. "Guess sometimes I overdo thins. Don't want ya t'hate me. Want more than anythin fer ya t'love me like ya would yer own mother. Honey, I'm sorry—but ya gotta admit, we done killed all t'bad stuff ya had clingin t'ya like moss on a rotten tree."

She said everything I had been secretly praying to hear, and impulsively I hugged Kitty back, kissed her cheek very carefully so as not to spoil that perfect makeup job. "And you smell so good," I whispered tearfully, overcome with relief.

"Ya an me are gonna get along fine, jus fine, we are, we are," enthused Kitty, smiling happily. Then, to show she meant right, she took the comb from my hand and began to work on my tangled hair.

With gentleness and great adroitness she soon had my hair a smooth-flowing cascade. Next she picked up a brush she said I could use from now on, and she brushed and brushed, using it in mysterious ways. Dipping it in water, shaking off most, curling hair over her fingers . . . and when I again looked into the mirror, I saw a beautiful head of shining dark curling hair around a white patchwork face and two huge blue eyes.

"Thank you," I whispered gratefully, loving Kitty for being kind, and more than willing to forget the torture of last night.

"Okay. Now let's head fer t'kitchen an t'tour I promised ya. Gotta be quick about all of this. Got so much t'do."

Together we descended the stairs. Cal was already in the kitchen. "I've got the coffee water boiling, and I'm fixing breakfast today," Cal said in a cheerful voice. He was busy frying bacon and eggs in separate skillets, so he couldn't turn his head. "Good morning, Heaven," he greeted, laying the bacon carefully on paper toweling, spooning hot grease over the sunny-side ups. "Do you like toast best, or English muffins? I'm an English muffin fan, especially with currant jelly or orange marmalade."

It wasn't until we all sat down at the pretty round table to eat that he really saw me again. His eyes widened with pity to see my face, not even noticing how lovely my hair looked. "Good Lord in heaven, Kitty, it's an awful shame to take a pretty face and make it look like a clown. What the hell is that white stuff smeared all over her?"

"Why, honey, it's t'same stuff ya woulda used."

He appeared thwarted, disgusted, and turned to pick up the newspaper. "Please refrain from washing her face again, Kitty. Let her do it herself," he said from behind the newspaper, as if so angry he couldn't bear to look at Kitty.

"She'll be all right agin, give her time," stated Kitty matter-of-factly, sitting down and picking up a section of the paper he'd laid aside. "Okay, Heaven, eat up. Got a lot t'do today, all of us. Gonna show ya t'time of yer life ain't we, honey?"

"Yeah," he said gruffly, "but it would have been nicer for Heaven if she didn't have to be seen as she is."

Despite my face, once I had the ointment wiped off I did have a wonderful time seeing Atlanta and the hotel where Kitty had her beauty salon, all decorated in pink, black, and gold, where rich ladies sat under slick white hoods banded in pink and gold, where eight pretty girls worked, and everyone there was a blonde.

"Ain't they pretty, though, ain't they?" asked Kitty, looking so proud. "Jus love bright golden hair that looks sunny an cheerful . . . not dull silvery-blond hair that's hardly no color at all."

I winced, knowing she was referring to my mother's hair.

She introduced me to everyone, while Cal stayed out in the hotel lobby, as if Kitty didn't want him in here with all these girls.

Then they took me shopping again. Already I was wearing a pretty new blue coat that Cal had chosen, and it fitted perfectly. Unhappily, all that Kitty selected for me—skirts, blouses, sweaters, underwear— she bought a size too large, and I hated the heavy, clumsy white saddle shoes she thought I should wear. Even the valley girls in Winnerrow wore better than those. I tried to tell Kitty this, but she had her own memories of what kind of shoes she'd worn. "Don't ya say anotha word! Kids don't wear fancy shoes t'school—they don't!"

Yet, when we were again back in the car, I had to feel happy with so many new clothes, more than I'd had in all my life. Three pairs of shoes. Nicer ones to wear tomorrow when we went to church.

We ate again in a fast-food place that seemed to disgust Cal. "Really, Kitty, you know I hate this kind of greasy junk."

"Ya like t'throw good money around just t'show off. Me, I don't kerr what I eat if it's cheap enough."

Cal didn't reply, only frowned and turned very quiet, letting Kitty do all the talking as he drove and she explained the sights. "This is t'school where ya'll be goin'," she said as Cal drove slowly past a huge red-brick building that was surrounded by several acres of lawn and playing fields. "Ya kin ride t'yellow buses on rainy days, but walk on sunny ones—Cal darlin honey, did we buy her all she needs fer school?" she shouted.

"Yes."

"Why ya mad at me?"

"I'm not deaf. You don't have to shout."

She snuggled closer to him as I leaned back and tried not to see how she kissed him even as he drove through traffic. "Honey sweetheart, love ya, I do. Love ya so much it hurts."

He cleared his throat. "Where is Heaven sleeping tonight?"

"With us, honey—ain't I done tole ya how it is with hill girls?"

"Yes . . . ya done tole me," he said with sarcasm, and then said no more, not even when we settled down that night so I could watch my first color television show. It was so thrilling it took my breath away. How beautiful all those colorful dancing girls, how little they wore, and then the scary movie came on, and Cal disappeared.

I hadn't even noticed when he left. "That's what he does when he's mad," said Kitty, getting up to switch off the TV. "Goes t'hide in t'basement, an pretends t'work. We're goin up now. Ya'll take anotha bath, wash yer hair yerself, an I won't enta while yer in there." She paused and looked thoughtful. "Right now I gotta go down an do some sweet-talkin t'my man." She giggled, and headed toward the kitchen, leaving me to enjoy my bath in the pink tub.

I hated to sleep again between Kitty and Cal. Hated the way she teased and tormented him, giving me the impression she didn't really love him half as much as he loved her. Did Kitty really hate men?

Sunday I was up first again. On bare feet I padded down the stairs, hurried through the kitchen, hunted for the door to the basement, and found it in a small back hall. Once I was down there in the dimness, I searched and searched among all the clutter that Kitty *didn't* keep neat and clean, until I found my suitcase put high on a shelf over a workbench. Granny's shawls were neatly folded in a pile beside it. I climbed up on the bench to pull down the suitcase, wondering if Cal had opened it.

Everything inside was exactly as I'd left it. I'd stuffed in six favorite books given to me by Miss Deale . . . even a nursery-rhyme book that Keith and Our Jane had loved for me to read at bedtime. Tears filled my eyes just to see that book . . . "Tell us a story, Hev-lee . . . make it last, Hev-lee. Read it again, Hev-lee."

I sat down at the workbench, pulled out a notepad, and began a letter to Logan. Quickly, with a high sense of peril all around, I scribbled out my desperate situation, how I needed to find Tom, Keith, and Our Jane, would he please do what he could to find out where Buck Henry lived? I gave him the Maryland license plate's first three numbers. When I finished the letter I gathered up a few other things, then hurried to the front door to see the address. I had to dash down to the corner to find the street name. When I was back in the door I'd left open, I felt a fool, for there were magazines neatly stacked with Kitty's name, and the address and zip-code number. I rifled through a small desk to find an envelope and stamps.

Now all I had to do was find an opportunity to mail my first letter. Down in the basement my beautiful bride doll slept peacefully, awaiting that wonderful day when she and I, with Tom, Keith, and Our Jane, would head for Boston, leaving Fanny to enjoy herself in Winnerrow.

I tiptoed up the stairs, then on toward the bathroom, my letter stashed under the corner of the hall rug. I closed the bathroom door behind me and breathed a sigh of relief. The letter to Logan was my highway to freedom.

"Why, looky there, Cal, our lil gal is all dressed, ready fer church. So let's be on time fer a change."

"You look very pretty this morning," said Cal, sweeping his eyes over my new dress, and my face that had lost its redness, and most of the swelling had gone down.

"She'd look betta if she'd let me trim and shape that hair," said Kitty, eyeing me critically.

"No, leave her hair alone. I hate hair so placed and perfect. She's like a wildflower."

Kitty scowled and stared long and hard at Cal before she entered the kitchen and whipped breakfast together so fast I couldn't believe it would taste so good. Omelets. Why, I'd never known eggs could be so light and fluffy. Orange juice . . . oh, I prayed Our Jane, Keith, and Tom were drinking orange juice now, too.

"Ya like my omelet?"

"It's delicious, Mother. You really know how to cook."

"I jus hope *ya* do," she said flatly.

The church we attended was like nothing I'd seen before, a stone cathedral, tall, splendid, dark inside. "Is it Catholic?" I whispered to Cal as we were entering and Kitty was talking to a woman she knew.

"Yes, but she's a Baptist," he whispered back. "Kitty is trying hard to find God and tries all religions at least once. Right now she's pretending to be Catholic. Next week we may be Jewish, or Methodist, and once we even went to a ceremony worshiping Allah. Don't say anything to make her feel foolish. The fact that she goes to church at all surprises me."

I loved the dark interior of that cathedral with all its candles burning, with its niches and holy statues, and the priest up there in his long robes saying words I couldn't understand, and I imagined he spoke of God's love for mankind, not his desire to punish them. The songs they sang I'd never heard before, yet I tried to sing along, while Kitty just moved her lips and I heard not a sound. Cal did as I did.

Before we could leave, Kitty had to visit the ladies' room, and that was when I ran to mail my letter to Logan. Cal watched me with a sad look. "Writing home already?" he asked when I returned. "I thought you liked it here."

"I do. But I have to find out where Tom is, and Our Jane and Keith. Fanny will be okay with Reverend Wise, but I have to keep in touch with my family or else we'll grow apart, so it's better to start now. People move about . . . I might never find them if I let too much time pass."

Gently he tilted my face up toward his. "Would it be so awful if you just forgot your old family and accepted your new one?"

Stinging tears filled my eyes. I blinked them away, or tried to. "Cal, I think you've been wonderful . . . and Kitty—I mean Mother—is trying . . . but I love Tom, Our Jane, and Keith . . . even Fanny. We're blood kin, and have suffered through so much together, and that ties us together in ways happiness doesn't."

Compassion flickered through his light brown eyes. "Would you like me to help you find your brothers and sisters?"

"Would you?"

"I'll be happy to do what I can. You give me what information you have, and I'll do my best."

"Do yer best what?" asked Kitty, looking hard at both of us. "What ya two whisperin about, huh?"

"Doing my best to see that Heaven always stays happy in her new home, that's all," he said easily.

She kept her frown as she strode toward their white car, and we again headed for a place to eat, more fast food that didn't waste good money. Now Cal wanted to see a movie, but Kitty didn't like movies. "Kin't stand sittin in t'dark with so many strangas," she complained. "An t'kid's gotta get up early so she kin start school tomorra."

Just the word *school* made me happy. A big-city school—what was that going to be like?

More television watching that night, and for the third time I was put in the middle of their bed. This time Kitty put on a red nightgown edged with black lace. Cal didn't even glance her way. He slipped into the bed, snuggled up close to me. His strong arms embraced me tightly as he nestled his face in my hair. I felt terribly frightened. And surprised.

"Get out t'bed!" yelled Kitty. "Won't have no kid seducin my man! Cal—take yer arm offa her!"

I thought I heard him chuckle as I headed downstairs, to open up the sleep sofa that Cal had shown me how to use. In my arms I had sheets, blankets, and a wonderfully soft goosedown pillow. For the first time in my life—a bed all my own. A room all my own, filled to overflowing with such a colorful zoo it's a wonder I was able to sleep at all.

The moment my eyes opened I thought of that new school, where there'd be hundreds or even thousands of new kids and I wouldn't know even one. Although my clothes were ever so much better than they used to be, I'd already seen enough in Atlanta to know the clothes I had now weren't what most girls my age wore. They were cheap copies of better dresses, skirts, blouses, and sweaters. Lord, don't let them laugh at me in my too-large clothes, I prayed silently as I took a quick bath and pulled on the best of what Kitty had selected.

Something must have happened in Kitty's bedroom that night, something that made her grouchier than usual in the morning. In the kitchen her pale eyes raked over me from head to feet. "Been easy on ya so far—but t'day begins yer *real* life. I expect ya t'be up early, an cookin every mornin from now on, not fiddlin in t'bathroom with yer hair fer hours on end."

"But, Mother, I don't know how to use a stove like that."

"Didn't I show ya how yesterday—t'day before?"

From the range to the dishwasher to the garbage disposal to the refrigerator she showed me again how to do everything. Then once more she led me down to the basement, where there was a pink washer and dryer set in a little alcove all its own, with shelves to hold more of Kitty's animal collection, and cabinets for boxes and plastic bottles of soap and detergents, softeners, bleaches, waxes, polishers, cleansers, window cleaners, toilet cleaners, brass and copper polish, silver polish—why, it went on forever. I wondered how they had any money left for food.

Food had been the main objective in our lives, back home in the hills; none of these cleaning products had even been imagined, or considered in the least necessary. Only lye soap for everything from shampoos to baths to scrubbing filthy clothes on the washboard. No wonder Kitty considered me a heathen.

"An ova there," said Kitty, pointing to a large space full of technical-looking equipment, "is where Cal has his home workshop. Likes t'fiddle away his time down here, he does. Now, don't ya botha none of his stuff. Some of it could be dangerous. Like that electric saw and all those carpentry tools. Fer gals like ya, not used t'stuff like that there all, only thin ya kin do is stay away. Keep that in mind, ya hear?"

"Yes."

"Yes what?"

"Yes, Mother."

"Now back t'business. Ya think ya kin wash an dry our clothes widout tearin em up or burnin em?"

"Yes, Mother."

"Ya betta mean it."

Back in the kitchen we found Cal had put on water for the coffee, and he was now sitting down to peruse the morning newspaper. He put it aside and smiled when we joined him. "Good morning, Heaven. You're looking very fresh and pretty for your first day at a new school."

Kitty whipped around. "Didn't I tell ya she'd look all right soon enough?" she quibbled, sitting down, snatching up a section of the morning paper. "Gotta see what celebrity is comin t'town . . ." she mumbled.

I stood in the middle of the kitchen, not knowing quite what to do. Kitty looked up, her eyes hard, cold, ruthless. "Okay, girl, cook."

Cook. I burned the thinly sliced bacon I'd never fried before. Our kind came in thick slabs, not done up in narrow slices and wrapped in fancy packages.

Kitty's eyes narrowed as she watched without comment.

I burned the toast, not knowing I'd moved the lever to dark when I'd wiped away fingerprints with the sponge Kitty had given me earlier, telling me I had to keep all chrome appliances free of spots and fingerprints.

The sunny-side ups that Cal wanted I fried too long. He barely ate his rubbery eggs. The coffee was the final straw. In a flash Kitty was up and across the slick kitchen floor, delivering to my face a stunning slap!

"ANY DAMN FOOL KIN TOAST BREAD!" she screamed. "AN IDIOT FOOL KIN FRY BACON! I should have known, should have!" She dragged me to the table and shoved me down. "I'll do it t'day, but t'morra it's you from then on—an if ya do what ya did t'day, I'll *BOIL* ya in wata next time! Cal, ya take yerself off t'work, buy anotha breakfast somewhere. I'll have t'stay home from work anotha hour t'enroll this kid in school."

Cal put a kiss on Kitty's rouged cheek. Not a long, passionate one, only a dutiful peck. "Take it easy on the girl, Kitty. You're expecting an awful lot when you know she's not accustomed to modern gadgets. Give her time and she'll do just fine. I can tell by her eyes that she's intelligent."

"Kin't tell by her cookin, kin ya?"

He left.

Alone with Kitty I felt a fresh wave of anxiety. Gone was the considerate woman who'd brushed my hair and curled it over her fingers. I'd already learned to fear the irrational, tempestuous swings of Kitty's moods, learned enough not to be fooled by her attempts at caring. Yet, with surprising patience, Kitty taught me all over again how to operate the kitchen range, the dishwasher, the trash compactor; and then she was instructing me on just how I had to stack the dishes, *precisely* stack them.

"Don't eva wanna look in these cabinets an see one thin out of place, ya understand?"

I nodded. She patted my cheek, hard. "Now run along an finish dressin, fer it's off-t'-school time."

The brick building had looked huge from the outside. Inside, I feared I'd be lost. Hundreds of adolescent children swarmed, all wearing wonderful clothes. Mine didn't fit at all. Not another girl had on the ugly kind of saddle shoes I wore, with white socks. The principal, Mr. Meeks, smiled at Kitty as if overwhelmed to see such a voluptuous woman in his office. He beamed at her bosom, which was on his eye level, and darn if he could raise his eyes long enough to see she had a pretty face as well.

"Why, of course, Mrs. Dennison, I'll take good care of your daughter, of course, why, of course . . ."

"Gonna go now," said Kitty at the door that would take her out into the hall. "Do what teachers tell ya t'do, an walk home. I've left ya a list of what t'do when I'm not there. Ya'll find t'cards on t'kitchen table. Hope t'come home t'a cleana, betta house—understand?"

"Yes, Mother."

She beamed at the principal, then sashayed down the hall, and darn if he didn't follow out to the hall to watch her departure. I realized from the way he stared after her that Kitty was the woman of many men's fantasies, all her feminine differences exaggerated.

It was hard that first day. I don't know if I imagined the hostility, or if it was real. I felt self-conscious with my long, wild hair, my cheap, ill-fitting clothes (better than any I'd owned before, and yet I wasn't happy), my obvious distress at not knowing where to go or how to find the girls' room. A pretty-looking girl with brown hair took pity on me and showed me around between classes.

I was given tests to see which class my country education had prepared me for. I smiled to read the questions. Why, Miss Deale had covered all this a long time ago. And then I was thinking of Tom, and tears slipped from my eyes. I was placed in the ninth grade.

Somehow I found my way around the school, and managed to get through a day that was exceptionally long and tiring, and slowly, slowly, I walked home. It wasn't nearly as cold here as it had been in the mountains, nor was it as pretty. No white water bubbling over rocks, and no rabbits, squirrels, and raccoons. Just a cold winter's day, a bleak gray sky, and strange faces to tell me I was an alien in this city world.

I reached Eastwood Street, turned in at 210, used the key Kitty had given me, took off my new blue coat, hung it carefully in the hall closet, then hurried into the kitchen to stare at the five-by-eight cards on the kitchen table. I could almost hear Kitty saying, "Read those ova. List of instructions. Read em an learn yer duties."

"Yes."

"Yes what?"

"Yes, Mother."

I shook my head to clear it, then sat to read the cards in the sunless kitchen that didn't look so cheerful without all the lights on. I'd been warned to use the lights as little as possible when I was home alone, and never was I to look at TV unless either Kitty or Cal was looking too.

The lists of what to do and not to do filled four cards.

DO'S

1. Every day, after every meal, wipe up the countertops, scrub the sinks.
2. After every meal, use another sponge to wipe off the refrigerator door, and keep everything inside neat and tidy, and check the meat and vegetable compartments to see nothing is rotten, or needing to be thrown out. It's up to you to see everything is used before it goes bad.
3. Use the dishwasher.
4. Grind up the soft garbage in the disposal, and never forget to turn on the cold water when it's running.
5. Washed dishes are to be removed immediately, put in cupboards in exact placement. Never stack cups one inside the other.
6. Silverware is to be neatly arranged in trays for forks, knives, spoons, not tossed in the drawer in a heap.
7. Clothes have to be sorted before washing. All whites with whites. Darks with darks. My lingerie goes in a mesh bag— use gentle cycle. My *washable* clothes, use cold water, and cold water soap. Wash Cal's socks by themselves. Wash sheets, pillowcases, and towels by themselves. Your clothes wash last, by themselves.
8. Dry clothes as instructed on the dryer I showed you how to use.
9. Hang clothes in closets. Mine in mine, Cal's in his. Yours in the broom closet. Fold underwear and put in correct drawers. Fold sheets and cases like what you find in the linen closet. Keep everything neat.

10. Every day wipe up kitchen and baths with warm water containing disinfectant.
11. Once a week, scrub kitchen floor with liquid cleanser I showed you, and once a month remove buildup of wax, then reapply wax. Once a week, scrub bathroom floors, clean grout in shower stall. Scrub out tub after every bath you take, I take, and Cal takes.
12. Every other day run the vacuum over all the carpets in the house. Move the furniture aside once a week and sweep under everything. Check under chairs and tables for spiders and webs.
13. Dust everything, every day. Pick things up.
14. First thing after Cal and me are gone, clean up the kitchen. Make the bed with clean linens, change towels in bathrooms.

The cards fell from my hand. I sat on, stunned. Kitty didn't want a daughter, she wanted a slave! And I'd been so ready to do anything to please her if only she'd love me, and be like a mother. It wasn't fair for fate to always rob me of a mother just when I thought I had one.

Hot, bitter tears coursed down my cheeks as I realized the futility of my dream of winning Kitty's love. How could I live here or anywhere without someone who loved me? I brushed at my tears, tried to stop them, but they came, like a river undammed. Just to have someone who needed me, who really loved me enough to be caring, was that too much to ask? If Kitty could only be a real mother, gladly I'd do everything on her list, and more—but she was making demands, issuing orders, making me feel used without consideration. Never saying please, or would you?—even Sarah had been more considerate than that.

So I sat on, doing nothing, feeling more betrayed by the moment. Pa must have known what Kitty was, and he'd sold me to her, without heart, without kindness, forever punishing me for what I couldn't help or undo.

Bitterness dried my tears. I'd stay only until I could run, and Kitty'd rue the day she took me in to do more work in one day than Sarah had done in a month!

Ten times more work here than in the cabin, despite all the cleaning equipment. Feeling strange, weak, I stared at the cards lying on the table, forgetting to read the last one, and when I tried to find it later on, I couldn't.

I'd ask Cal, who seemed to like me, what Kitty could have written on that last card. For if I didn't know what not to do, ten to one I'd be sure to do it, and Kitty would somehow know.

For a while I just sat on in the kitchen, everything clean and bright around me, while my heart ached for an old rickety cabin, dim and dirty, for familiar smells and all the beauty of the outside world. No friendly cats here to rub against my legs, or big dogs that wagged furious tails to show how mean they were. Only ceramic animals of unnatural colors holding kitchen utensils, cat faces grinning from the wall, pink ducks parading toward an unseen pool. Dizzy, that's how I felt from seeing so many colors against all the white.

When next I glanced at a clock, I jumped up. Where had the time gone? I began to race around—how to finish before Kitty was home again? Those panicky butterflies were on wing again, battering my self-confidence. I'd never be able to please Kitty, not in a million years. There was something dark and treacherous in Kitty, something slippery and ugly hidden beneath all those wide smiles, lurking in those seawater eyes.

Thoughts of my life as it had been came like ghosts to haunt me— Logan, Tom, Keith, Our Jane . . . and Fanny—are they treating you like this, are they?

I vacuumed, dusted, went carefully from plant to plant and felt the dirt, all damp. I returned to the kitchen to try and begin the evening meal, which Kitty said should be called *dinner* because Cal insisted the main meal of the day was dinner and not *suppa*.

About six Cal came in, looking fresh enough to make me wonder if he did anything all day, and then he was smiling broadly. "Why are you looking at me like that?"

How could I tell him that he was the one I instinctively trusted, that without him here I couldn't stay on another minute? I couldn't say that during our first time alone together. "I don't know," I whispered, trying to smile. "I guess I expected you to look . . . well, dirty."

"I always shower before I come home," he explained with a small, odd smile. "It's one of Kitty's rules—no dirty husband in her house. I keep a change of clothes to put on after I'm finished for the day. Then, too, I am boss, and I have six employees, but I often like to pitch in and do the trouble-shooting in an old set."

Feeling shy with him, I gestured to the array of cookbooks. "I don't know how to plan a meal for you and Kitty."

"I'll help," he said instantly. "First of all, you've got to stay away from starches. Kitty adores spaghetti, but it makes her gain weight, and if she gains a pound she'll think it's your fault."

We worked together, preparing a casserole that Cal said Kitty would like. He helped me slice the vegetables for the salad as he began to talk. "It's nice having you here, Heaven. Otherwise I'd be doing this by myself, as before. Kitty hates to cook, though she's pretty good at it. She thinks I don't earn my way, for I owe her thousands of dollars and I am in hock up to my neck, and she holds the purse strings. I was just a kid when I married her. I thought she was wise, beautiful, and wonderful; she seemed to want to help me so much."

"How'd you meet her?" I asked, watching how he tore the lettuce and sliced everything thin and on an angle. He showed me how to make the salad dressing, and it was as if his busy hands set free his tongue, almost as if he were talking more to himself than to me as he chopped and sliced. "You trap yourself sometimes, by thinking desire and need is love. Remember that, Heaven. I was lonely in a big city, twenty years old, heading for Florida during spring break. I met Kitty quite by accident, in a bar my first night here in Atlanta. I thought she was absolutely the most beautiful woman I'd ever seen." He laughed hard and bitterly. "I was naive and young. I had come for the summer from my home in New England while I was still going to Yale, had two more years to go before I graduated. Alone in Atlanta I felt lost. Kitty was lost too, and we found we had a lot in common. After a while, we married. She set me up in business. I'd always planned to be a history professor, can you imagine? Instead I married Kitty. Haven't been on a university campus since. I've never been home again, either. I don't even write to my parents anymore. Kitty doesn't want me to contact them. She's ashamed, afraid they might find out she didn't finish high school. And I owe her at least twenty-five thousand dollars."

"How'd she make so much money?" I asked, half forgetting what I was doing.

"Kitty goes through men like castor oil, leaving them weak emotionally and drained financially. She told you she married first when she was thirteen? Well, she's had three other husbands, and each has provided for her very well—in order to get out of a marriage each must have found abominable after a while. Then, to give her credit, her beauty salon is the best in Atlanta."

"Oh," I said, with my head bowed low. His confession was not what I'd expected. Yet it felt so good to have someone talk to me as if I were an adult. I didn't know if I should ask what I did. "Don't you love Kitty?"

"Yes, I love her," he admitted gruffly. "When I understand what makes her what she is, how can I not love her? There's one thing, though, I want to say now, while I have a chance. There are times when Kitty can be very violent. I know she put you into hot water on your first night here, but I didn't say anything since you weren't permanently harmed. If I'd said something then, she would be worse the next time she has you alone. Just be careful to do everything as she wants. Flatter her, say she looks younger than I do . . . and obey, obey, and be meek."

"But I don't understand!" I cried. "Why does she want me, except to be her slave?"

He looked up, appearing surprised. "Why, Heaven, haven't you guessed? You represent to her the child she lost when she aborted your father's baby and ruined herself so she can never have another child. She loves you because you are part of him, and hates you for the same reason. Through you, she hopes one day to get to him."

"To hurt him through me?" I asked.

"Something like that."

I laughed bitterly. "Poor Kitty. Of all his five children, I am the one he despises. She should have taken Fanny or Tom—Pa *loves* them."

He turned to put his arms about me, and tenderly he held me the way I'd always wanted to be held by Pa. I choked up and clung to this man who was almost a stranger; my need to be loved was so great I grasped greedily, then felt ashamed and so shy I almost cried. He cleared his throat and let me go. "Heaven, above all, never let Kitty know what you just told me. As long as you are valuable to your father, you have value for Kitty. Understand?"

He cared. I could see it in his eyes, and with trust that he'd always keep confidences to himself, I had the courage to tell him about the suitcase in the basement and what it contained. He listened as Miss Deale would have listened, with compassion and understanding.

"Someday I'm going back there, Cal, to Boston, to see my mother's family. And I'll have the doll with me, so they'll know who I am. But I can't go unless I have found—"

"I know," he said with a small laugh, his eyes sparkling at last. "You must take with you Tom, Keith, and Our Jane. Why on earth do you call your little sister Our Jane?"

He laughed again when I told him. "Your sister Fanny sounds like a real character. Will I ever meet Fanny?"

"Why, I sure hope so," I said with a worried frown. "She's living now with Reverend Wise and his wife, and they call her Louisa, which is her middle name."

"Aaah, the good Reverend," he said in a solemn, slow way, looking thoughtful, "the richest, most successful man in Winnerrow."

"You don't like him?"

"I am always suspicious of any man that successful—and that religious."

It was good to be with Cal in the kitchen, working alongside him and learning just by watching what he did. I'd never in a million years have believed a week ago that I could feel so comfortable with a man I hardly knew. I was shy, yet so eager to have him for my friend, for a substitute father, for a confidant. Every smile he gave me told me he'd be all of that.

Our casserole baked in the oven, the timer went off, and my biscuits were ready, and Kitty didn't come home, nor did she call to explain why she was late. I saw Cal glance at his watch several times, a deep frown putting a pucker of worry between his eyes. Why didn't he call and check?

Kitty didn't return home until eleven, and Cal and I were in the living room watching TV. The remainder of the casserole had long ago dried out, so it couldn't taste nearly as good to her as it had to us. Still, she ate it with relish, as if lukewarm food gone dry didn't matter. "Ya cooked this all yerself?" she asked several times.

"Yes, Mother."

"Cal didn't help ya none?"

"Yes, Mother, he told me not to prepare starchy foods, and he helped me with the salad."

"Ya washed yer hands in Lysol water first?"

"Yes, Mother."

"Okay." She studied Cal's expressionless face. "Well, clean up, girl; then let's all go t'bed afta our baths."

"She's sleeping down here from now on," Cal said, steel in his voice as he turned cold eyes her way. "Next week we are going shopping and we are going to buy new furniture and replace all that clutter in our second bedroom. We will leave the potter's wheel and what you have locked in the cabinets, but we're adding a twin bed, a chair, a desk, and a dresser."

It scared me the way she looked at him, at me, it really did.

Still, she agreed. I really was going to have a room of my own, a real bedroom—as Fanny had with Reverend Wise.

Days of school and hard work followed. Up early, late to bed, I had to clean up after Kitty's dinner, even if she came home at midnight. I found out that Cal liked me by his side when he watched television. Every evening he and I prepared dinner, and ate it together if Kitty wasn't there. I was adjusting to the busy school schedule, and making a few friends in school who didn't think I talked strange, though they never said what they thought of my too-large, cheap clothes, or my horrible clunky shoes.

Finally it was Saturday, and I could sleep late, and Kitty had given her permission for Cal and me to shop for furniture that would be mine alone to use.

And because of this shopping trip that loomed up bright and promising, all the early hours of Saturday I rushed about to finish the housework. Cal had half the day off and would be home by noon, expecting to eat lunch. What did city folks eat for lunch when they ate home? So far I'd eaten lunch only in school. Poor Miss Deale had tried so many times to share the contents of her lunch bag with an entire class of underfed children. I had never eaten a sandwich before she forced one upon me. The ham, lettuce, and tomato was my favorite, though Tom and Keith had liked peanut butter and jelly well enough—and, more than any other kind, tuna fish.

Almost I could hear Tom saying: "That's why she brings six, you know. How could a petite lady like Miss Deale eat six sandwiches? So we really do help her out, don't we, when we eat up?"

I sighed, sad to think I'd left without saying thank you to Miss Deale, and sighed again when I thought of Logan, who had not yet answered my first letter.

Thoughts of yesterdays slowed me down, so I had to rush about to check over downstairs, the living and dining rooms again, before I finished upstairs. I kept hoping to find shelves of books, or books put away in cabinets, but I didn't find even one book. There wasn't even a Bible. There were plenty of magazines, confession stories that Kitty hid in table drawers, and pretty house magazines she put on top of the coffee table in a neat stack. But not one book.

In the small room Kitty had converted into a home ceramic hobby room, the one that was going to be mine, shelves lined the wall, and on those shelves were tiny animals and miniature people, all small enough to fit inside her little kiln. There were also cabinets lining one entire wall, all locked. I stared at those locked doors, wondering what secrets they held.

Downstairs again, I carefully stacked the dirty dishes in the washer, filled the compartments with detergent, then stood back and fearfully waited for the thing to blow up, or discharge the dishes like bullets. But the darn thing still worked after almost a week of hill-scum handling. I felt strangely exhilarated, as if in learning to push the right buttons I had gained control over city living.

Scrubbing the floor was nothing new, except this one had to be waxed, and that required more reading of directions on the bottle. I watered the many live green plants, and found that some of Kitty's plants were silk, not real at all. Lord God above, don't let her see I watered a few before I knew they weren't real.

Noon came before I'd finished doing even one quarter of what was listed on those cards. It took so much time to figure out how to operate all the machines, and wrap the cords back like they'd been, and put the attachments on, and take them off, and put them away in neat order. Oh, gosh, at home all this had been done with one old broom.

I was tangled up in vacuum cord when the door from the garage banged and Cal appeared in the back hall, staring at me in a strange, intense way, as if trying to see what I was really feeling. "Hey, kid," he said after his survey, his eyes sort of unhappy, "there's no need to work like a slave. She's not here to see. Slow down."

"But I haven't cleaned the windows yet, and I haven't washed the bric-a-brac, and I haven't—"

"Sit down. Take a breather. Let me fix our lunch, and then we'll go shopping for the furniture you need—and how about a movie for a treat? Now, tell me what you want for lunch."

"Anything will suit me fine," I said guiltily. "But I should finish the housework . . ."

He smiled bitterly, still eyeing me in that odd way. "She won't be home until ten or eleven tonight, and there is a special movie I think you need to see. Do you good to have some fun for a change. I presume you haven't had much. All life in mountain country isn't unpleasant, Heaven. Some mountains can deliver beauty, graceful living, peace, and even wonderful music . . ."

Why, I knew that.

It hadn't all been bad. We'd had our fun, running and laughing, swimming in the river, playing games we made up, chasing each other. Bad times came when Pa was home. Or when hunger took over.

I shook my head again to clear it of memories that could make me sad. I couldn't believe he'd want to take me to the movies, not when . . . "But you have *ten* TV sets, two and three in some rooms."

Again he smiled. He was twice as handsome when he smiled, though his smiles never lasted long enough to make him seem truly happy. "They don't all work. They're just used as pedestals to hold Kitty's works of art." He grinned ironically when he said that, as if he didn't admire his wife's artistic endeavors nearly as much as he should. "Anyway, a television is not like a movie theater, where the screen is huge, and the sound is better, and there are real people there to share your pleasure."

My eyes locked with his a moment, then lowered. Why was he challenging me with his eyes? "Cal, I've never been to a movie, not even once."

He reached to caress my cheek, his eyes soft and warm. "Then it's time you did go, so run on up and get ready, and I'll throw together a couple of sandwiches. Wear that pretty blue dress I bought for you—the one that's going to fit."

It did fit.

I stared in a mirror that had known only Kitty's kind of beauty, and felt so pretty now that my face had healed and there were no scars. And my hair shone as it never had before. Cal was kind and good to me. Cal liked me, and that proved there were men who could like me, even if Pa didn't. Cal was going to help me find Tom, Keith, Our Jane. Hope . . . I had hope . . . a soaring kind of hope.

In the long run, it would all work out for the best. I was going to have my own bedroom with brand-new furniture, new blankets, real pillows—oh, glory day, who'd ever have dreamed Cal could be like a real father! Why, I could even see Tom smiling as I ran down the stairs, to see the first movie of my life.

My own father had refused to love me, but that didn't hurt so much now that I had a new and better father.

14

When There's Music

Cal's ham, lettuce, and tomato sandwiches were delicious. And when he held the new blue coat for my arms to slip into, I said, "I can keep my head low so people won't notice I'm not really your daughter."

He shook his head sadly and didn't laugh. "No. You hold your head high, feel proud. You have nothing to be ashamed of, and I'm proud to escort you to your first movie." His hands rested lightly on my shoulders. "I hope to God Kitty will never do anything to spoil your face."

There was so much he left unsaid as we both just stood there, caught in the mire of what Kitty was, and what Kitty could do. He sighed heavily, caught hold of my arm, and guided me toward the garage. "Heaven, if ever Kitty is unnecessarily hard on you, I want you to tell me. I love her very much, but I don't want her to harm you, physically or emotionally. I have to admit she can do both. Never be afraid to come to me for help when you need it."

He made me feel good, made me feel that at last I had the right kind of father. I turned around and smiled; he flushed and quickly looked away. Why would my smile make him embarrassed?

All the way to the furniture store I sat proudly beside him, filled with happy anticipation to have so much pleasure in one day, new furniture *and* a movie. All of a sudden Cal changed from sad to lighthearted, guiding me by my elbow when we entered the store full of so many different types of bedroom sets I couldn't decide. The salesman looked from me to Cal, pondering, so it seemed, our relationship. "My daughter," Cal said proudly. "She'll choose what she likes." The trouble was, I liked it all, and in the end it was Cal who chose what he considered appropriate for me. "This bed, that dresser, and that desk," he ordered, "the ones that aren't too girlish and will see you through to your twenties and beyond."

A small flutter of panic stirred in my chest—I wouldn't be with him and Kitty when I was in my twenties, I'd be with my brothers and my sisters, in Boston. I tried to whisper this when the salesman stepped away. "No," Cal denied, "we have to plan for the future as if we know what it is; to do otherwise cancels out the present and makes it meaningless."

I didn't understand what he meant by that, except I liked the feeling that he wanted me permanently in his life.

Just thinking of how pretty *my* room was going to look must have put stars in my eyes. "You look so pretty—like someone just plugged in your cord of happiness."

"I'm thinking of Fanny in Reverend Wise's house. Now I'll have a room as nice as hers must be."

Just for saying that he bought a bedside table and a lamp with a fat blue base. "And two drawers in the table that lock, in case you have secrets . . ."

Strange how close this shopping expedition made us, as if creating a pretty room together gave us a special bond. "What movie are we going to see?" I asked when we were back in the car.

Again he was staring at me with that quizzical, self-mocking look fleeting through his golden-brown eyes. "If I were you, I shouldn't think it would matter."

"Not to me, but it must to you."

"You'll see." He'd say nothing more.

It was exciting driving to the movie theater, seeing all the crowds on the street. So much better than it had been with Kitty to spoil the fun with the tensions she caused. I'd never been inside a theater before. I was trembling with excitement, seeing so many people all in one place, all spending money as if they had barrels of it. Cal bought popcorn, cola drinks, two candy bars, and only then did we settle down side by side in the near dark. I'd never thought it would be this dark in a movie theater.

My eyes widened when the colorful picture began with the woman on the mountaintop singing. *The Sound of Music!* Why, this was a movie that Logan had wanted to see with me. I couldn't feel unhappy about that, not when Cal was sharing the single big box of buttery, salty popcorn. It was hot, and I couldn't eat enough. Occasionally we'd both reach into the box at the same time. To sit there, to eat and drink and feast my eyes on the beauty of the movie, filled me with so much delight I felt as if I were living in a picture book with sound, movement, dancing, and singing. Oh, truly this had to be the most exhilarating day of my entire life.

On and on I sat spellbound, my heart bursting with happiness, a kind of magic enveloping me so I felt I was in that movie. The children were Tom, Fanny, Keith, and Our Jane . . . and me. That's the way we should have been, and I wouldn't have cared at all if Pa had blown a whistle, and hired a nun to tutor us. Oh, if only my brothers and sisters could be here with us!

After the movie Cal drove me to an elegant restaurant called the Midnight Sun. A waiter pulled out my chair and waited for me to sit, and all the time Cal was smiling at me. I didn't know what to do when the waiter handed me a menu, except to stare at him in a helpless way. All of a sudden I was inundated with need for Tom, for Our Jane, for Keith and Grandpa, so much so I was near tears . . . but he wasn't seeing that. Cal was seeing something beautiful written on my face, as if my very youth and inexperience made him feel ten times more a man than Kitty did. "If you'll trust me, I'll order for both of us. But first tell me which you like most. Veal, beef, seafood, lamb, chicken, duck, what?"

Images of Miss Deale came again, she in her pretty magenta suit, smiling, appearing so proud to have us . . . when nobody else wanted to know we existed. I thought of her gifts—had they ever arrived? Were they back there on the porch of the cabin, with no one there to wear the clothes? Eat the food?

"Heaven, what meat do you want?"

Oh, my God . . . how did I know? I frowned, concentrating on the complicated menu. I'd had roast beef when Miss Deale took us to a restaurant not nearly as fine as this one.

"Try something you've always wanted to eat and never have," Cal softly prompted.

"Well," I mused aloud, "I've had fish caught in the river near the cabin—had pork—eaten many a chicken—and had roast beef once, and it was really good, but I guess I'll have something brand-new— you choose it."

He laughed and ordered salad and veal cordon bleu, for two. "Children in France grow up on wine, but I guess we'll wait a few years before you try that." He'd encouraged me to order escargot, and only after I had finished my six did he explain that they were snails in hot garlic butter, and the bit of French bread I was using to sop up the delicious sauce hesitated in my hand that was suddenly trembling.

"Snails?" I asked, feeling queasy, sure he was teasing me. "Nobody, even the dumbest hill folks, eats things as nasty as snails."

"Heaven," he said with a warm smile in his eyes, "it's going to be fun teaching you about the world. Just don't say anything about this to my wife. She's stingy about restaurants, thinks they charge too much. Do you realize that since the day I married her we have not once eaten out except in fast-food joints? Kitty just doesn't appreciate gourmet cooking, and doesn't really understand what it is. She thinks she does. If she spends half an hour preparing a meal, she thinks that's gourmet food. Haven't you noticed how fast she puts a meal together? That's because she refuses to tackle anything complicated. Warm-up food, I call what she cooks."

"But you said Kitty was a wonderful cook before!"

"I know, and she is, if you like her breakfast menu . . . that's what she cooks best, and country food that I don't like."

That very day I began to fall in love with city life and city ways that were far, far different from mountain ways, or even valley life.

We were barely in the door when Kitty came home from her nighttime ceramic class, irritable as she stared at us. "What ya two do all day?"

"We went shopping for the new furniture," Cal said casually.

She narrowed her eyes. "What store?"

He told her, and her scowl came. "How much?"

When he named a figure, she clasped her long-nailed hand to her forehead, seeming appalled. "Cal, ya damn fool—ya should buy her only cheap stuff! She don't know good from bad! Now, ya send that all back if it comes when I'm gone. If I'm here, I'll send it back!"

My heart sank.

"You will not send it back, Kitty," he said, turning to head for the stairs, "even if you are here. And you might as well know I ordered the best mattress, the best pillows and bed linens, and even a pretty coverlet with a dust ruffle to match the curtains."

Kitty screamed: "YER TEN TIMES A DAMNED FOOL!"

"All right, I'm a damned fool who will pay for everything with my own money, not yours. Good night, Heaven. Come, Kitty, you sound tired—after all, it was your idea that we drive to Winnerrow and find ourselves a daughter. Did you think she'd sleep on the floor?"

I could hardly contain myself when the furniture arrived two days later. Cal was there to direct where things should go. He expressed a desire to have the room wallpapered. "I hate so much white, but she never asks me what color I'd like."

"It's fine, Cal. I love the furniture." Together, when the deliverymen had gone, he and I made the bed with the pretty new flowered sheets, and then we spread on the blankets, and topped everything off with the pretty quilted coverlet.

"You do like blue?" he asked. "I get so damned tired of hot pink."

"I love blue."

"Cornflower blue, like your eyes." He stood in the middle of my small room, now prettier than I could have imagined, and seemed too big and too masculine for all the dainty things he'd chosen. I turned in circles and stared at accessories I hadn't known he'd ordered. A set of heavy brass duck bookends for the books I'd stuffed in the broom closet with my clothes. A desk blotter, pencil cup, and pen and pencil set, and a small desk lamp, and framed pictures for the wall. Tears came to my eyes, he'd bought so much.

I sobbed, "Thank you," and that's all I could manage before I lost my voice and cried all the tears I'd saved up through the years, flat on my face on that narrow twin bed that was so pretty, and Cal sat awkwardly on the side of the bed and waited for me to finish. He cleared his throat. "I've got to get back to work, Heaven, but before I go, I have another surprise. I'll lay it here on your desk, and you can enjoy it after I'm gone."

The sound of his feet departing made me turn over and sit up, and once more I called out, "Thank you for everything." I heard his car drive off, and I was still sitting on the bed . . . and only then did I look at the desk.

A letter lay on the dark blue of the desk blotter . . . a single letter.

I don't even remember how I got there and when I sat, except I did sit, and I stared for the longest time at my name written on that envelope. Miss Heaven Leigh Casteel. In the upper left-hand corner was Logan's name and address. Logan!

He hadn't forgotten me! He did care enough to write! For the first time I used a letter opener. What nice handwriting Logan had, not as scrawly as the way Tom wrote, or as precisely perfect as Pa's small script.

Dear Heaven,

You just can't know how much I've worried about you. Thank God you wrote, so now I can go to sleep knowing you're all right.

I miss you so much it hurts. When the sky is bright and blue,

I can almost see your eyes, but that only makes me miss you more.

To be honest, my mom tried to keep your letter hidden so I'd never read it, but one day I found it stashed in her desk when I was hunting for stamps, and for the first time in my life, I was really disappointed in my own mother. We fought, and I made her admit she'd hidden your letter from me. Now she admits she was wrong, and has asked me, and you, to forgive her.

I see Fanny often, and she's fine, looking great. She's a terrible showoff, and to be honest again, I think that Reverend Wise may have his hands fuller than he thought.

Fanny says she wasn't sold! She says your father *gave* all his children away to save them from starving. I hate to believe either one of you, yet you've never lied to me before, and it's you I do believe. I haven't seen your father—but I have seen Tom. He came into the store and asked if I had your address so he can write. Your grandfather is living in a rest home in Winnerrow.

I have no idea how to help you find Keith and Our Jane. Keep on writing, please. I still haven't met anyone I like nearly as much as I do Heaven Leigh Casteel.

And until I see you again, I'm not even going to look.

My love as always,
Logan

I cried again I was so happy.

Shortly after Logan's letter came I turned fifteen. I knew better now than to call attention to myself and didn't say a word to Kitty or Cal, but somehow Cal knew and gave me an incredible gift—a brand-new typewriter!

"It will help with your homework." His smile was wide, so pleased with my overwhelmed response. "Take typing in school. It never hurts to know how to type."

That typewriter, as much as I loved it, wasn't the biggest thrill of my fifteenth birthday. Oh, no. It was the huge card that came in the mail, bright with pretty flowers, sweet with a verse, and thick with a silk scarf and a letter from Logan.

Still, I longed to hear from Tom. He had my address now; why wasn't he writing?

In a whole school of girls I managed to make two good friends who repeatedly invited me to visit their homes. Neither one understood why I always had to refuse. Then, to my dismay, discouraged or put off, they began, bit by bit, to drift away. How could I tell anyone that Kitty flatly denied me friends who might take time away from the housework I had to do every day? The boys who asked me for dates I had to reject too, though not altogether for the same reasons. It was Logan I wanted to date, not them. I was saving myself for Logan and not once did I question that he was doing the same thing.

The house I slaved to keep clean and tidy never stayed that way when Kitty could come in to devastate ten hours of work with her careless habits. The plants I watered and dusted and fertilized withered from too much care, and then Kitty yelled at me for being stupid. "Any damn fool kin keep a plant living . . . any damn fool!"

She found her water-spotted silk plants and slapped me for being an idiot hill-scum girl who didn't have brains. "Yer thinkin bout boys, kin see it in yer eyes!" she yelled when she caught me idling one afternoon when she came home unexpectedly. "Don't ya sit in t'livin room when we ain't home! TV is off limits fer ya when yer alone! Ya stay busy, ya hear?"

I was up early every day to prepare breakfast for Kitty and Cal. She seldom came home for the evening meal before seven or eight o'clock, and by that time Cal and I had eaten. For some reason this didn't annoy her. Almost with relief she fell into a kitchen chair and broodingly stared at her plate until I dished up the food she wolfed down in mere seconds, without appreciation for all the trouble I took to learn her favorite dishes.

Before I could go to bed I had to put the kitchen in order, check all the rooms to see that everything was in its proper place and no magazines or newspapers cluttered the tabletops or lay on the floor. In the morning I hurried to make my bed before Kitty came in to check, then rushed downstairs to begin breakfast. Before I left for school, I washed clothes while I made the beds, put the dirty dishes in the washer, wiped up all fingerprints, smudges, spills, and such, and only when I had the door locked behind me did I begin to feel free.

Now I was well fed and my clothes were warm and adequate, and yet there were times when I thought longingly of home and forgot the hunger, the awful cold, the deprivations that should have scarred me forever. I missed Tom so much it hurt. I ached for Our Jane and Keith, for Grandpa and even Fanny. Logan's letters helped me not to miss him so much.

I was riding the school bus now that it was raining every day and Kitty didn't want to buy me a raincoat or boots. "Soon it'll be summer," she said, as if there'd be no spring to mention, and that made me homesick again. Spring was a season of miracles in the mountains, when life got better and the wildflowers came out to coat the hills with beauty Candlewick would never know. In school I studied with much more determination than other students, on a mad hurry-hurry schedule to get back home and dig into housework.

The many TVs were a constant temptation calling to me. It was lonely in the empty house, and despite Kitty's warning never to turn on a TV when I was alone, I soon was a soap-opera addict. I dreamed about the characters at night. Why, they had even more problems than the Casteels, though none were financial, and all of ours had been related to money problems—or so it seemed now.

Day after day I checked the mailbox waiting for Logan's letters that came regularly, always anticipating that long-awaited letter from Tom that didn't show up. One day, out of pure frustration from not hearing from Tom, I wrote to Miss Deale, explaining how we'd been sold and pleading with her to help me find my brothers and sister.

The weeks passed, and still no letter came from Tom. The letter I'd written to Miss Deale came back stamped Addressee Unknown.

Then Logan stopped writing! My first thought was he had another girl. Sick at heart, I stopped writing to him. Every day that passed without hearing from Logan made me think that nobody loved me enough to last long enough to do me any good, except Cal. Cal was my savior, the only friend I had in the world, and more and more I depended on him. The quiet house came alive when he came in the door and the television was snapped on and housework could be forgotten. I began to long for him as the hour of six drew near and my dinner was almost ready to serve. I took pains to set the table prettily, to plan menus I knew he'd enjoy. I spent hours and hours preparing his favorite dishes, not caring anymore if Kitty grew fat from the pasta dishes he preferred and I liked, too. When the clock on the mantel struck six, my ears keened to hear the sound of his car in the drive. I ran to take his coat when he came in the back door, loving the ceremony of his greeting that was the same each day:

"Hi there, Heaven. What's new?"

His smiles brightened my life; his small jokes gave me laughter. I began to see him as bigger than life, and forgot all his weaknesses when it came to Kitty. Best of all, he listened, really listened, when I talked to him. I saw him as the kind of father I'd always wanted, always needed, the one who not only loved me, but also appreciated what I was. He understood, never criticized, and always, no matter what, he was on my side. Though with Kitty that never helped much.

"I write and write, and Fanny never answers, Cal. Five letters I've written to her since I've been here, and not even a postcard in return. Would you treat your sister like that?"

"No," he said with a sad smile, "but then, my family members never write to me, so I don't write to them—not since I married Kitty, who doesn't want any competition for my affections."

"And Tom doesn't write, even though Logan gave him this address."

"Maybe Buck Henry doesn't give him the time to write letters, or prevents him from mailing the ones he might write."

"But surely he could find a way—?"

"Hold on. One day you'll see a letter in our box from Tom, I'm sure of it."

I loved him for saying that; loved him for making me feel pretty, for saying I was a good cook, for appreciating all I did to keep the house clean. Kitty never saw anything I did unless it was wrong.

Weeks passed during which Cal and I became closer and closer, like a true father and daughter. (Often Kitty didn't come home until ten or eleven at night.) I knew that Cal was the best thing in my Candlewick life, and for him I was going to do something special. He had a yen for all kinds of fancy egg dishes, so for the first time in my life I was going to prepare what he often asked Kitty to make—a cheese soufflé. An amusing lady on TV was teaching me all about gourmet cooking.

The perfect time was Saturday, before our trip into Atlanta to see a movie.

I fully expected it to fail, as most of my experiments did—and then I was drawing it from the oven, amazed to see it looked right. Golden brown, high and light! I'd done it right! If I could have patted myself on the back, I would have done so. I ran to the china cabinet, wanting to serve it on the royal dishes it deserved. Then I stepped halfway down the basement stairs, leaned over, and called in my most demure voice, "Lunch is served, Mr. Dennison."

"Coming right up, Miss Casteel," he called back. We sat in the dining room, where he stared with admiration at my high and wonderful cheese soufflé. "Why, it's beautiful, Heaven," said Cal, tasting it, "and delicious," closing his eyes to savor it. "My mother used to make cheese soufflés just for me—but you shouldn't have gone to so much trouble."

Why did he look uneasy sitting in his own dining room, as if he'd never eaten in here before? I looked around, feeling very uneasy. "Now you'll have lots of dishes to clean up before we head for town and fun . . ."

Oh, that was all.

No one moved more swiftly than I did that afternoon. I stacked the pretty china in the dishwasher; while it washed, I ran upstairs to bathe and dress. Cal was ready and waiting, smiling at me, seeming relieved to have the dining room restored to a museum piece. I was ready to step out the door before I remembered. "One moment, and I'll be back. Wouldn't want Kitty to come home and find her china not put back *exactly* in place."

As I finished doing this and that, he decided to go back to the basement to put his own tools away—that's when the doorbell rang. We so seldom had guests the sound of the bell startled me, and I quickly went to the door. The mailman smiled at me.

"A certified letter for Miss Heaven Leigh Casteel," he said cheerfully.

"Yes," I said eagerly, staring at the pack of letters in his hand, so many.

He extended a clipboard with a paper. My hand trembled when I made my crooked signature.

Once I had the door closed, I sank down onto the floor. The sun through the fancy diamond windows near the door fell on the envelope of a letter I was sure was from Tom—but it wasn't. Strange handwriting.

Dearest Heaven,

I hope you don't mind my familiarity. I'm sure you will forgive me this when you hear my good news. You don't know my name, and I can't sign this letter. I am the woman who came with her husband to become the mother of your darling little sister and brother.

If you recall, I promised to write and keep you in touch. I remember your great love and concern for your brother and sister, and I have to admire and respect you for that. Both children are very well, and have, I believe, adapted to this family, and have stopped missing their mountain family so much.

Your father didn't want to give me your address; however, I persisted, believing I should keep my promise. Our Jane, as you used to call her, has recovered from an operation to correct a diaphragmatic hernia. You can look this up in a medical encyclopedia, and find out exactly what it was that made that dear child so frail. You'll be happy to know she is now gaining weight and has a good appetite. She is as healthy and normal as any seven-and-a-half-year-old girl. Every day she and Keith have all the fruit juice they want. And I do leave night-lights on in both of their rooms. They attend a good private school, and are driven there each day, and picked up when school is over. They have many friends.

Keith shows great artistic talent, and dear Jane loves to sing and listen to music. She is taking music lessons, and Keith has his own easel, and equipment for drawing and painting. He is especially good at drawing animals.

I hope I have answered all questions, and given you enough information to keep you from worrying. Both my husband and I love these two children as if they were our own. And I believe they love us as much in return.

Your father says he has found good homes for all of his children, and I pray this is true.

Under separate cover I am sending you photographs of your brother and sister.

My best wishes to you.

R.

That's the way she signed her letter, with just an initial, no address to give me a clue. My heart thudded madly as I stared at the envelope again, trying to read fingerprints, hidden numbers and street names. It had been postmarked in Washington, D.C. What did that mean? Had they moved from Maryland? Oh, thank God the doctors had found out what was wrong with Our Jane and had cured her!

For the longest time I just sat there, thinking about Keith and Our Jane—and the kind of lady who'd been thoughtful enough to write. Again and again I read the letter. I brushed tears from my eyes as I read it through. Oh, it was wonderful to hear that Our Jane was well and happy, and she and Keith had everything—but it wasn't good to hear they'd forgotten me and Tom, not good at all.

"Heaven," said Cal from a few feet away, "would you rather sit on the floor and read letters all day than go to the movies?"

In a moment I was up, showing him the letter, eagerly telling him the contents even as he read them for himself. He appeared as delighted as I felt. Then he began to look through his own mail. "Why, here's another envelope for Miss Heaven Leigh Casteel," he said with a broad grin, handing a heavy brown envelope to me.

A dozen snapshots were inside, and three photographs taken at a professional portrait shop.

Oh, dear God—snapshots of Keith and Our Jane playing on the grass in a garden behind a huge, beautiful house. "Polaroid shots," said Cal, looking over my shoulder. "What beautiful children."

I stared at the lovely children in expensive-looking play clothes, both sitting in a sandbox with a bright awning overhead. Behind them was a swimming pool, the chairs and tables placed on flagstone borders. The same man and wife were there, wearing swimsuits, smiling lovingly at Keith and Our Jane. It was summer where they were! Summer! Did that mean Florida? California? Arizona? I studied the other snapshots that showed Our Jane laughing as Keith pushed her on a swing playyard set. Others taken in her pretty bedroom with all the dolls and toys. Our Jane sleeping in a fancy little bed, all ruffled, with a pink canopy overhead. Keith in his blue room full of all kinds of toys and picture books. Then I opened a large, elaborate cardboard folder to see Our Jane really dressed up, in pink organdy with ruffles, her hair curled, looking as if she belonged in the movies, smiling at whoever was snapping her picture; and there was another of Keith dressed in a cute blue suit, wearing a small tie, and a third portrait showing them together.

"It cost money to take portraits like those," Cal said from over my shoulder. "See how they're dressed. Heaven, they are very beloved children, well cared for and happy. Why, look at the shine in their eyes. Unhappy children couldn't fake smiles like that—smiles that light up their faces. Why, in some ways you should thank God your father *did* sell them."

I didn't realize how much I was crying until Cal blotted my tears by holding me against his chest. "There, there . . ." he crooned, cuddling me in his arms, giving me his handkerchief to blow my nose. "Now you can sleep at night without crying and calling out for them. Once you hear from Tom, your whole world will brighten. You know, Heaven, there are very few Kittys in this world. I'm just sorry you had to be the one to suffer at her hands . . . but I'm here. I'll do what I can to protect you from her." He held me close, closer, so I felt every curve of my body pressed against his.

Alarm filled me. Was this right? Should I pull away to let him know he shouldn't? But it had to be right, or he wouldn't be doing it. Still, I felt uneasy enough to push him away, though I smiled tearfully into his face, and turned so we could leave, but not before I carefully hid the letter and the photographs. For some reason I didn't want Kitty to see how lovely Pa's other two children were.

That Saturday was even more special than the others had been. Now I could really enjoy myself, knowing Our Jane and Keith weren't really suffering . . . and someday I'd know about Tom, too.

It was ten-thirty when Cal and I drove back from Atlanta, both of us rather tired from trying to do too much: see a three-hour movie, eat in a restaurant, and do some shopping. Clothes for me that Cal didn't want Kitty to see. "I hate those saddle shoes as much as you do. However, don't let her see these new ones," he warned before we drove into the garage. "Sneakers are fine for gym, and the Mary Janes she bought for church are just too young for you now. I'll keep these locked in one of my workshop cabinets, and give you a duplicate key. And if I were you, I'd never let my wife see that doll or anything that once belonged to your mother. I'm ashamed to say that Kitty has an abnormal hatred for a poor dead girl who couldn't have known she was taking from Kitty the one man she could truly love."

That hurt, really hurt. I turned big sad eyes his way. "Cal, she loves you. I know she does."

"No, she doesn't, Heaven. She needs me once in a while, to show off as her 'prize catch'—a college man—'her man,' as she so often puts it. But she doesn't love me. Underneath all those exaggerated feminine curves is hidden a small, cold soul that hates men . . . all men. Maybe your father made her that way, I don't know. I pity her, though. I've tried for years and years to help her overcome her traumatic childhood. She was beaten by her father, by her mother, and forced to sit in hot water to kill her sins, and handcuffed to her bed so she wouldn't run off with some boy. Then, the moment she was set free, she ran off with the first man she met. Now I've given up. I'm just hanging around until one day I can't take any more—then I'll go."

"But you said you loved her!" I cried out. Didn't you stay when you loved? Could pity be the same as love?

"Let's go in," he said gruffly. "There's Kitty's car. She's home, and there will be hell to pay. Don't say anything. Let me do the talking."

Kitty was in the kitchen pacing the floor. "Well!" she shouted when we came in the back way. "Where ya been? Why ya look so guilty? What ya been doin?"

"We went to the movies," said Cal, stalking by Kitty and heading for the stairs. "We ate dinner in the kind of restaurant you seem to hate. Now we're going to bed. I suggest you say good night to Heaven, who must be as tired as I am, after cleaning this house from top to bottom before noon."

"She ain't done one damn thin on my lists!" snapped Kitty. "She went off with ya an left this house a mess!"

She was right. I hadn't really done much housecleaning, since nothing ever seemed to get messy and dirty, and Kitty seldom bothered to check.

I tried to follow where Cal led, but Kitty reached out and seized my arm. Cal didn't look back.

"Ya damned stupid kid," she hissed. "Ya put my best china in t'washer, didn't ya? Don't ya know I neva use my Royal Dalton and Lenox unless there's company? It's not fer every day! Ya done chipped my plates, two of em! Ya done stacked my cups, broke a handle! Cracked anotha! Didn't I tell ya neva t'stack my cups, but t'hang em up?"

"No, you never told me that. You just said don't stack them."

"I did tell ya! I warned ya! Ya don't do what I say not t'do!"

Slap slap slap.

"How many times do I have t'tell ya?"

Slap slap slap.

"Didn't ya see t'hooks under t'shelves—didn't ya?"

Sure, I'd seen the hooks, and hadn't known what they were for. She hadn't had the cups hung from the hooks. I tried to explain, to apologize, promising to pay for the plates. Her eyes grew scornful. "How ya gonna do that, dummy? Those dishes cost eighty-five dollars a place settin—ya got that kind of dough?"

I was shocked. Eighty-five dollars! How could I know the fancy dishes in the dining-room breakfront were only for looking at, never for using?

"Yer a damned fool—that's my best—took me foreva payin fer all those cups, saucers, plates, an thins—now ya gone an ruined my thins—goddam Jesus Christ idiot hill-scum trash!"

Her pinching grasp hurt my arm. I tried to tug free. "I won't do it again, Mother. I swear I won't!"

"Yer damned right ya won't do it again!" Wham! She punched my face, once, twice, three times!

I staggered backward, off balance, feeling my eye beginning to swell as my nose began to bleed from blows she threw like a boxer. "Now ya git upstairs an stay in that room all day tomorra—with t'door locked. No church an no food until ya kin come down an make me believe yer really sorry t'have ruined my best thins that should be hand-washed."

Sobbing, I ran for the stairs, for the little room with the furniture Cal and I had chosen, hearing Kitty swearing behind me, saying such awful things about hill-scum trash I felt those words would be forever engraved on my brain. In the hall I collided with Cal. "What's wrong?" he asked with alarm, then caught me and forced me to hold still so he could see my face. "Oh, God," he groaned when he saw my injuries. "Why?"

"I chipped her best plates . . . broke a handle off a cup . . . put her wooden-handled knives in the washer . . ."

He strode off, descended the stairs, and down there I heard him raise his voice for the first time. "Kitty, because you were abused as a child is no reason for you to abuse a girl who tries to do her best."

"Ya don't love me," she sobbed.

"Of course I do."

"NO YA DON'T! Ya think I'm crazy! Ya'll leave me when I'm ole an ugly. Ya'll marry some otha woman, younga than me."

"Please, Kitty, let's not go through this again."

"Cal . . . didn't mean t'do it. Neva mean t'hurt her. Or hurt ya. I know she's not really bad . . . it's jus somethin about her . . . somethin about me, don't understand it . . . Cal, I got me yearnins t'night."

Oh, God, what went on beyond their bedroom wall had taught me only too well why he stayed on and on, despite all the ways she had of castrating him.

In that bedroom with the door shut and locked, he was putty in her hands. She didn't blacken *his* eyes, or make *his* nose bloody. What she did for him made him smile in the morning, made his eyes bright, his steps light.

The next morning was Sunday, and Kitty forgave me for chipping her china, forgave me for breaking a cup handle and ruining an expensive knife . . . now that she had Cal under her thumb again. Yet when Cal and I were in the car, waiting for her to finish checking to see what I'd failed to do, he said without looking my way, "I promise to do all I can to help you find Tom. And when you're ready to go to Boston to see your mother's parents, I'll do some detective work myself, or hire others to find your mother's family. They must have been very wealthy, for I hear a Tatterton Toy Portrait Doll costs several thousand dollars. Heaven, you must show that doll to me one day—the day you fully trust me."

To prove how much I did trust him, while Kitty napped upstairs that very afternoon Cal and I entered the basement. First I had to put in a load of Kitty's clothes, and while the washer spun I opened my precious suitcase of dreams and lovingly lifted out the doll. "Turn your back," I ordered, "so I can straighten her gown, put her hair in order . . . and then look, and tell me what you think."

He seemed stunned to see the bride doll with her long silver-gold hair. For long moments he couldn't speak. "Why, that's you with blond hair," he said. "How beautiful your mother must have been. But you are just as lovely . . ."

Hurriedly I wrapped the doll again, tucked her away. For some reason I felt deeply disturbed. After seeing the doll, why did Cal look at me as if he'd never seen me before?

There was so much I didn't know. So much to keep me awake at night in the small room with so much space still taken up by all the things Kitty refused to move out. Again Kitty and Cal were arguing, over me.

"Stop telling me no!" said Cal in a low but intense voice. "Last night you said you wanted me every day, every night. Now you shove me away. I'm your husband."

"Kin't let ya. She's right next door. Where ya wanted her."

"YOU put her in our bed! But for me she'd still be here between us!"

"I went in there—walls ain't thick enough. Makes me self-conscious t'know she kin hear."

"That's why we have to get rid of all your stuff. Then we could put her bed on the other wall, much farther away. You do have a huge kiln in your classroom. And all the other junk should go as well."

"It's not junk! Ya stop callin my thins junk!"

"All right. They're not junk."

"T'only time I kin get a rise out of ya is when ya defend her—"

"Why, Kitty, I didn't know you wanted a rise out of me."

"Yer mockin me. Yer always mockin me by sayin that, when ya knows what I mean . . ."

"No, I wish to God I knew what you really are up to. I wish I knew who and what you are, what thoughts go on beneath all that red hair—"

"Ain't red! Auburn! Titian . . ." she flared hotly.

"All right, call it whatever you want. But I know this: if ever you hit Heaven again, and I come home to see her nose bleeding, her face bruised, her eyes black . . . I'll leave you."

"Cal! Don't say thins like that! I love ya, I do! Don't make me cry . . . kin't live without ya now. I won't hit her, promise I won't. Don't wanna anyway . . ."

"Then why?"

"Don't know. She's pretty, young—an I'm gettin old. Soon I'll be thirty-six, and that's not far from forty. Cal, life ain't gonna be no good afta forty."

"Of course it will." His voice sounded softer, more understanding. "You're a beautiful woman, Kitty, getting better each year. You don't look a day over thirty."

She yelled: "I wanna look *twenty!*"

"Good night, Kitty," he said with disgust in his voice. "I won't see twenty again, either, but I'm not grieving about it. What did you have when you were twenty but insecurity? You know who and what you are now; isn't that a relief?"

No, apparently knowing who and what she was was the horror of being Kitty.

However, to celebrate Kitty's traumatic thirty-sixth birthday, that summer Cal reserved rooms in a fine hotel near a beach, and in August, the month of the lion, all three of us were under a beach umbrella. Kitty was the sensation of the beach in her skimpy pink bikini. She refused to leave the shade of an umbrella bright with red stripes. "Skin's delicate, burns easy . . . but ya go on, Heaven, Cal. Don't mind me. I'll just sit here an suffa while ya two have fun."

"Why didn't you tell me you didn't want to come to the shore?"

"Ya didn't ask."

"But I thought you liked to swim and sunbathe."

"That's how much ya know about me—nothin."

Nobody had any fun when Kitty didn't.

It was a flop of a holiday, when it could have been so much fun if Kitty had only shared the water with us, but Kitty made her birthday vacation a torture.

The day we returned from vacation, Kitty sat me down at the kitchen table with her large box of manicuring equipment and began to give me my first manicure. I felt ashamed of my short, broken fingernails as I admired her long, perfectly groomed ones, with all the cuticles pushed back, and never a chip   never! My ears perked up when she began her lecture on how to have nails as nice as hers. "Ya gotta stop chewin on yers, an learn how t'be a woman. Don't come naturally t'hill girls, all t'gracious ways a woman has t'have. Why, it takes time an trainin t'be a woman, takes a lot of patience with men."

The air-conditioning made a soft, hypnotic whir as she continued.

"They're all t'same, ya know, even t'sweet-talkin ones. Like Cal. All want one thing, an bein a hill gal, ya know what it is. All is dyin t'slam their bangers inta yer whammer, an afta they done it, if ya start a baby, they won't want it. They'll say it's not theirs, even if it is. If they gives ya a disease, they don't kerr. Now, ya heed my advice, an don't listen t'no sweet-talkin boy—or man—includin mine."

Kitty finished painting my nails bright rose. "There. They do look betta now that yer not scrubbin on washboards no more an usin lye soap. Knuckles done lost all t'redness. Face done healed—an are ya harmed, are ya?"

"No."

"No what?"

"No, Mother."

"Ya love me, don't ya?"

"Yes, Mother."

"Ya wouldn't take nothin from me that was mine, would ya?"

"No, Mother."

Kitty rose to leave. "Got anotha hard day of bein on my feet. Slavin t'make others look pretty." She sighed heavily and looked down at her five-inch heels. She had remarkably small feet for such a tall woman; like her waist, they appeared to belong to someone petite and frail.

"Mother, why don't you wear low-heeled shoes to work? It seems a pity to make yourself suffer in high heels like that."

Kitty stared with disdain at my bare feet. I tried to tuck them under the full skirt that fell to the floor when I was sitting.

"Shoes ya wear tell people what yer made of—an I'm made of t'right stuff, *steel*. Kin take t'pain, t'sufferin—*an ya kin't*."

Hers was a crazy way of thinking. I vowed never again to mention her miserable, too-small shoes that curled her toes so they could never straighten out. Let her feet hurt . . . why should I care?

Summer days were full of work and cooking, and Saturday treats. Soon there were signs of autumn, and school supplies showed up in store windows, with sweaters and skirts, coats and boots. I'd been here eight months, and although Logan had begun writing to me again, still there was no word from Tom. It hurt so much I began to think it was better to stop hoping I'd ever hear from him . . . and then there it was, in the mailbox! Just one letter.

Oh, Thomas Luke, it's so good to see your handwriting, so good, please let me find only happy things inside.

With his letter in my hand, it was almost as if I had Tom beside me. I hurried to sit and carefully rip open his letter so as not to tear his return address. He wrote with the flavor of the hills, but something new had been added . . . something that took me quite by surprise, and despite myself, I felt jealous.

Dear Heavenly,

Boy, I sure do hope you get this letter. Been writing my fool head off to you, and you never answer! I see Logan from time to time and he nags at me to write to you. I do, but I don't know what happens to my letters, so I'll keep trying. Heavenly, first of all I want you to know that I'm all right. Mr. Henry is not cruel, not mean as you no doubt think, but he can sure drive you to do your very best.

I live in his farmhouse which has twelve rooms. One of them is mine. It's a nice room, clean and kind of pretty in a plain way. He has two daughters, one named Laurie, age thirteen, and one named Thalia, age sixteen. Both are pretty, and so nice I don't really know which one I like best. Laurie is more

fun; Thalia is serious, and gives everything more thought. I've
told them both about you, and they say they're dying to meet
you one day soon.

Logan told me about Our Jane's operation, and how well she's
doing, and that Keith is happy and well. You know that's a load
off my mind. Trouble is, according to Logan, you say little about
yourself. Please write and tell me all that has happened since last
you and I were together. I miss you so bad it hurts. I dream about
you. I miss the hills, the woods, the fun things we used to do. I
miss our talks about our dreams, miss so many things. One thing
I don't miss is being hungry, cold, and miserable. I have lots of
warm good clothes, too much to eat, especially milk to drink
(imagine)—and cheese and more cheese.

I'd write a letter two thousand pages long if I didn't have so
many chores to finish before bedtime. But don't worry, please
don't. I'm fine, and we will meet again someday soon. I love you,

Your brother,

Tom

I sat thinking about Tom long after I finished the letter. Then I hid
his letter away with those from Logan. Had Kitty somehow kept Tom's
letters from me? That wasn't really possible since I was home every
day while she worked, and I brought in the mail almost every day. I
stared around my cluttered room, knowing Kitty had been in here and
moved things about. It wasn't really my room as long as Kitty kept her
"thins" locked behind those cabinet doors, and obviously she checked
over all my belongings. Her huge pottery wheel was shoved into a
corner, and she had shelves everywhere filled with little knickknacks
where my books would have fitted nicely. Kitty had no use for books
on her shelves. I sat down at my small desk and began to answer Tom's
letter. All the lies I'd told Logan would also convince Tom that Kitty
was an angelic mother, the best ever . . . but I didn't have to tell lies
about Cal, who *was* the best father possible.

He's truly wonderful, Tom. Every time I look at him, I think to
myself, that's how Pa should have been. It feels so good to
know that at last I have a real father I can love, who loves me.
So stop worrying about me. And don't forget one day you're
going to be president—and not of a dairy firm either.

Now I'd heard from Tom, and knew Our Jane and Keith were happy,
and Logan wrote that Fanny was having the time of her life—so what
did I have to worry about? Nothing. Nothing at all . . .

15

Heartthrobs

Early-morning light in the city found me awake about six, when once I'd risen at dawn to begin my day. Downstairs in the second bath I took a quick shower, put on clean clothes, and began breakfast. I was looking forward to returning to school and renewing my neglected friendships. Unbeknownst to Kitty, I had a brand-new outfit that fit perfectly. Cal had paid far too much for it, but I wore it with so much pride. I saw the boys staring at me with ten times more interest now that my figure wasn't hidden by loose fabric. For the first time in my life I began to feel some of the power that women had over the opposite sex, just from being female, and pretty.

I could lose myself in class listening to the teacher talk about monumental people who left their marks on history. Did historians skip over character faults, just to inspire students like me to always strive harder? Would I leave my mark? Would Tom? Why did I feel so driven to prove myself? Miss Deale had always made the people in the past seem human, fallible, and that had given both Tom and me hope.

I made new friends who didn't understand, as my old friends hadn't, why I couldn't invite them home. "What's she like, that mother? Boy, she sure is stacked. And yer father—wow! What a man!"

"Isn't he wonderful?" I said with pride. Funny the way they looked at me. The teachers treated me with special consideration, as if Kitty had told them I was a dimwit hill girl who couldn't have much sense. I

studied like crazy to prove her wrong, and soon enough I earned the
teachers' respect. I was especially good at typing. I spent hours and
hours typing letters—when Kitty wasn't home. When she was, the
clickity-clack of the typewriter made her head ache. Everything made
Kitty's head ache.

Cal saw to it that I had dozens of pretty dresses, skirts and blouses,
slacks, shorts, swimsuits, clothes that Cal and I selected when we went
shopping in Atlanta, clothes that he kept locked in one of his basement
lockers that Kitty thought held only dangerous tools. Kitty feared his
electronic equipment almost as much as she feared insects. In a small
hall closet meant for storing cleaning equipment my too-large ugly
dresses, selected by Kitty, hung with the vacuum cleaner, the mops,
brooms, pails, and other clutter. There was a closet in my bedroom, but
that was kept locked.

Even though I had the clothes, still I had to decline the invitations
that came my way, knowing I had to scurry home and finish cleaning
that white house that needed so much everlasting care. Housework
was robbing me of my youth. I resented the hundreds of houseplants
that needed so much attention; resented the ornate elephant tables
with their silly fake jewels that had to be carefully washed and
polished. If only one tabletop weren't cluttered I could have made one
clean swipe with my dustcloth, but I had to lift and move, shift and be
careful not to scratch the wood; then run to fold Kitty's underwear,
hang her dresses, blouses, put the towels in the linen closet and be
sure only the folded ends showed in front. A thousand rules Kitty had
to keep her house a display piece. And only her "girls" ever came to
admire it.

Saturday afternoons more than made up for all the abuses Kitty felt
were my due. The hard, brutal slaps that came so readily over any
trifling mistake, the cruel words meant to destroy my self-confidence,
were more than paid for by the movies, by delicious restaurant meals,
by trips to amusement parks when the days weren't rainy or cold. In
the park Cal and I threw peanuts to the elephants, and scattered
cracked corn to the wild ducks, swans, and geese that came running up
from the zoo lake. I'd always had a way with animals, and Cal was
charmed with my ability to "talk" to chickens, ducks, geese, even
elephants.

"What's your secret?" he teased when I had a wild-looking zebra
nuzzling my cupped palm looking for treats. "They don't come
running to me as they run to you."

"I don't know," I answered with a small, wistful smile, for Tom used
to ask the same thing. "I like them, and maybe they can tell in some

mysterious way." Then I told him about the days of stealing, when a certain farmer's dogs hadn't been charmed with my abilities.

Real autumn came with brisk cold winds to blow away the leaves, and wistful thoughts of the hills and Grandpa kept coming back. A letter from Logan had given me the address of where Pa had put him, and that was enough for me to write Grandpa. He couldn't read, but I thought someone might read my letter to him. I wondered if Fanny ever visited him, if Pa went to Winnerrow now and then to visit her and his father. I wondered so many things I sometimes walked around in a daze, as if the best part of me were still in the Willies.

I planted tulips, daffodils, irises, crocuses, all with Cal's help, as Kitty sat in the shade supervising. "Do it right. Don't ya mess up my six hundred dollars' worth of Dutch bulbs. Don't ya dare, hill scum."

"Kitty, if you call her that again, I'll dump all these worms we've dug up in your lap," Cal threatened.

Instantly she was on her feet and running into the house, making both Cal and me laugh as our eyes met. With his gloved hand he reached out and touched my face. "Why aren't you afraid of worms, roaches, spiders? Do you speak their language, too?"

"Nope. I hate all those things as much as Kitty does, but they don't scare me nearly as much as she does."

"Do I have your promise you will call me at work if things get rough here? Don't you allow her to do one more thing to you—do I have that promise?"

I nodded, and for a brief moment he held me tight against him, and I could hear the loud thumping of his heart. Then I glanced up and saw Kitty at the window staring out at us. Pulling away, I tried to pretend he'd only been comforting my wounded hand. . . .

"She's watching us, Cal."

"I don't care."

"I do. I can call you, but it takes time for you to drive home, and by that time she could peel the skin from my back."

For the longest time he stared at me, as if all along he'd not believed she was capable of that and now he did. The shock was still in his eyes when we put our gardening tools away and entered the house to find Kitty sound asleep in a chair.

Then came the nights. Eventually I didn't have to try not to listen, for eventually Cal stopped making any attempts to reason with Kitty, and stopped kissing her passionately, only pecks on her cheek, as if he no longer desired her. I felt his inner rage and frustration building, too. Along with mine.

Thanksgiving Day I roasted my first store-bought turkey so Kitty could invite all her "girls" and brag about *her* cooking. "Weren't nothin t'it," she said over and over again when they praised all her housekeeping and cooking skills. "An I've got so little time, too. Heaven helps some," she admitted generously as I waited on the table, "but ya knows how young gals are . . . lazy, an interested in nothin but boys."

Christmas came with stingy gifts from Kitty, and expensive secret gifts from Cal. He and Kitty attended many a party, leaving me home to watch TV. It was only then that I learned that Kitty had a drinking problem. One drink started off a chain reaction so she'd have to drink more, more, more, and many a time Cal had to carry her in the door, undress her, and put her to bed, sometimes with my help.

It felt odd to undress a helpless woman with the help of her husband, an intimacy that left me feeling uneasy. Still, an unspoken but strong bond united Cal and me. Cal's eyes would meet mine . . . mine would meet his. He loved me, I knew he loved me . . . and at night when I snuggled down in my bed, I felt his protective presence guarding my sleep.

One fine Saturday in late February he and I celebrated my sixteenth birthday. For one year and more than one month I'd been living with him and Kitty. I knew Cal wasn't quite like a real father, nor quite like an uncle, nor quite like any man I'd ever known. He was someone who needed a friend and family to love as badly as I did, and he was settling for the closest, the most available female. He never scolded or criticized me, never spoke harshly to me as Kitty usually did.

We were friends, Cal and I. I knew I loved him. He gave me what I'd never had before, a man who loved me, who needed me, who understood me, and for him I would gladly have died.

He bought me nylons and high-heeled shoes for birthday gifts, and when Kitty wasn't home, I practiced wearing them. It was like learning to walk all over again on longer, newer legs. With nylons on, and high heels, I was very conscious of my legs, thinking they looked great, and unconsciously I'd stick them out so everyone could admire them. It made Cal laugh. Of course, I had to hide the shoes and nylons along with all my other new clothes down in the basement where Kitty never went alone.

Spring came quickly to Atlanta. Because of all the effort Cal and I had put into the yard, we had the most spectacular garden in Candlewick. A garden that Kitty couldn't enjoy because honeybees hovered over the flowers, and ants crawled on the ground, and inchworms swung from fine gossamer threads to catch in her hair.

Once Kitty almost broke her neck brushing one from her shoulder, screaming all the while.

Kitty was afraid of dim places where spiders or roaches might hide. Ants on the ground sent her into panic; ants in the kitchen almost gave her heart attacks. A fly on her arm made her scream, and if a mosquito was in the bedroom she didn't sleep a wink, only kept us all up, complaining about the buzzing of that "damned thin!"

Afraid of the dark, was Kitty. Afraid of worms, dirt, dust, germs, diseases, a thousand things that I never gave a thought to.

When Kitty grew too overbearing with her many demands, I escaped to my room, threw myself down, and reached for a book brought home from the school library . . . and lost myself in the world of *Jane Eyre* or *Wuthering Heights.* Over and over I read those two books before I went to the library and hunted up a biography of the Brontë sisters.

Bit by bit I was edging back Kitty's parade of tiny ceramics with my treasured collection of books. I'd brought the doll up from the basement, and every day I took her out of the bottom dresser drawer and stared into her pretty face, determined one day to find my mother's parents.

Once in a while I even wore a few of my mother's clothes, but they were old, frail, and I decided it was better to leave them stretched out as flat as possible, and save them for the day when I went to Boston.

Tom wrote long letters, and Logan wrote now and then, hardly telling me anything. Still I kept writing to Fanny, even if she didn't respond. My world was so tight, so restricted, I began to feel strangely out of touch with everyone . . . everyone but Cal.

Yet in many ways my life had become easier. Housework that had terrified me once with all its complexities of instructions was no longer so overwhelming. I could have been born with a blender in one hand and a vacuum in the other. Electricity was part of my life now, and honestly, it seemed it always had been. Every day Cal seemed more and more my savior, my friend, my companion, and my confidant. He was my tutor, my father, my date to the movies and restaurants; he had to be now that the boys in the school had stopped asking me to dances and movies. How could I leave him alone when once he had said: "Heaven, if you have movie dates who will I go with? Kitty hates movies, and I enjoy them, and she hates the kind of restaurants I like. Please don't abandon me in favor of kids who won't appreciate you as I do . . . allow me to take you to the movies. You don't need them, do you?"

How guilty that question made me feel, as if I were betraying him even to think about having a date. I tried many a time to think that

Logan was as faithful to me as I was to him . . . and yet I couldn't help but wonder—was he? After a while I just stopped looking at boys, knowing better than to encourage them and perhaps alienate the only truly dependable friend I had.

To please Cal, I did as he wanted, went where he wanted, wore what he wanted, styled my hair to please him. And all the time my resentment against Kitty grew and grew. Because of her he was turning to me. He was wonderful, and yet it made me feel strange, guilty, especially when that odd burning look came into his eyes, as if he liked me so much—perhaps too much.

My school chums began to look at me in odd ways. Did they know Cal took me out? "Ya got a boyfriend on t'outside?" asked Florence, my best chum. "Tell me bout him—do ya let him, ya know, go all t'way?"

"No!" I stormed. "Besides, there isn't anyone."

"There is too! Kin tell from yer blush!"

Had I blushed?

I went home to dust and vacuum, to water the hundreds of plants, to do endless chores, and all the time I thought about why I'd blushed. There was something exciting going on in my body, waking it up, sending unexpected thrills to my groin at the most unexpected moments. Once I glimpsed myself in the bathroom mirror, wearing nothing but a bikini bra and panties, and that alone sent a sexual thrill through me. It scared me and made me feel unwholesome that I could be thrilled just to see myself scantily clad. I'd never have the enormous bosom Kitty was so proud of, but what I had seemed more than adequate. My waist had slimmed down to a mere twenty-two inches, though it seemed I'd never grow any taller than five feet six and a half. Tall enough, I told myself. Plenty tall enough. I didn't want to be a giant like Kitty.

Months ahead of her dreaded thirty-seventh birthday, Kitty started staring at calendars, seeming so cursed by the onset of middle age that she sank into a state of deep depression. When Kitty was depressed, Cal and I had to mirror her feelings, or be accused of being insensitive and uncaring. He was wild with frustration from wanting her all the time, as she provoked and teased him and then yelled NO, NO, NO! "Nother time . . . tomorra night . . ."

"Why don't you tell me never, for that's what you mean!" he shouted. He stalked off, down to the basement to whir his electrical saw, to do damage to something instead of to her.

I followed Kitty into the bathroom, hoping I could talk as one woman to another, but she was preoccupied with staring into the mirror. "Hate gettin old," she moaned, peering closer into a hand mirror, while the theatrical lights all around showed every tiny line she considered very noticeable.

"I don't see any crow's-feet, Mother," I said quite honestly, liking her much better now that she was acting more or less like a normal human being. If sometimes I slipped up and called her Kitty, she didn't demand that I correct myself. Still, I was warily suspicious, wondering why she didn't demand my respect as she had before.

"Got t'go home soon," she murmured, staring more intensely into the mirror. "Ain't right t'Cal what I'm doin." She grinned broadly to see all her teeth, checking for yellow, for bad gums, going over her hair carefully looking for gray. "Gotta put my feet on home ground—let em all back there see me again while I still look good. Looks don't last foreva like I used t'think they would. When I was yer age, I thought I'd neva grow old. Didn't worry bout wrinkles back then; now all I do is think about em, look t'find em."

"You look too closely," I said, feeling sorry for her. I also felt edgy, as I always felt when I was shut up in a room alone with her. "I think you look ten years younger than your actual age."

"BUT THAT DON'T MAKE ME LOOK YOUNGA THAN CAL, DO IT?" she shouted with bitterness. "Compared t'me, he looks like a kid."

It was true. Cal did look younger than Kitty.

Later that same day, when we were eating in the kitchen, Kitty again spoke mournfully about her age. "When I was younga, used t'be t'best-lookin gal in town. I was, wasn't I, Cal?"

"Yes," he agreed, forking into the apple pie with a great deal of enthusiasm. (I'd studied cookbooks for months just to make him his favorite dessert.) "You certainly were the best-looking girl in town."

How did he know? He hadn't known her then.

"Saw a gray hair in my eyebrow this mornin," Kitty moaned. "Don't feel good about myself no more, don't."

"You look great, Kitty, absolutely great," he said, not even looking at her.

How terrible she was making middle age seem even before she got there. Truthfully, when Kitty was all dressed up, with her makeup on, she was a magnificent-looking woman. If only she could act as pretty as she could look.

I'd been with Kitty and Cal for two years and two months when she informed me: "Soon as ya finish school this June we'll be headin back t'Winnerrow."

It thrilled me to think of going back where I happily anticipated seeing Grandpa again, and Fanny. And the prospect of meeting the strange, cruel parents of Kitty intrigued me. She hated them. They had made her what she was (according to Cal), and yet she was going back to stay in their home.

In April Kitty came from a shopping trip bearing gifts for me—three new summer dresses that fitted this time, expensive dresses from an exclusive shop, and this time she allowed me to select really pretty new shoes, pink, blue, and white, a pair to match each dress.

"Don't want my folks thinkin I don't treat ya right. Buyin em early, for t'best is all picked ova. Stores rush summa at ya in winta, shove winta at ya in summa; ya gotta move quick or be left out altogetha."

For some reason her words took the thrill away from the beautiful clothes that were bought only to prove something to parents Kitty said she hated.

Days later, Kitty took me to her beauty salon in the big hotel for the second time, and introduced me to her new "girls" as her daughter. She seemed very proud of me. The shop was larger, more elaborate, with crystal chandeliers, and hidden lights to make everything sparkle. She had European ladies who gave facials in tiny cubicles, using magnifying optical glasses through which the specialists could peer and find even the smallest flaws in the clients' complexions.

Kitty put me in a pink leather chair that raised and lowered, tilted back, and swiveled, and for the first time in my life I had a professional shampoo, trim, and set. I sat there with the plastic apron about my neck and shoulders, staring into the wide mirror, scared to death when Kitty came in to inspect me that she'd say I looked horrible, and pick up the shears and make my hair even shorter. I sat tense and ready to jump from the chair if she chopped off too much. All eight of her "girls" stood around to admire Kitty's artistry with hair. She didn't hack it up. She carefully layered, snipped, and when she was done, she stood back and smiled at all her "girls."

"Didn't I tell ya my daughta is a beauty? Ain't I done improved on nature? Hey, ya, Barbsie, ya saw her when she first came—ain't she done improved? Kin't ya tell she's been fed right, treated good? She's my own kid, an mothers like me shouldn't brag bout their own, but jus kin't help it when she's so beautiful—an mine, all mine."

"Kitty," said the oldest of her girls, a woman about forty, "I didn't know you had a child."

"Didn't want any of ya t'disrespect me fer marryin so young," Kitty said with the sincerity of truth. "She's not Cal's, but don't she look like him, though, don't she?"

No, I didn't look like him. I took offense, and added another block to my tower of resentments that was bound to topple one day.

I could tell from all the faces of her girls they didn't believe her, yet she went on insisting I was hers, even when she'd told them differently before. Later, when I had the chance, I told Cal about that. He frowned and looked unhappy.

"She's slipping, Heaven. Living a fantasy life. Pretending you are the baby she destroyed. That baby would have been only a little older if she hadn't aborted it. Be careful to do nothing to set her off . . . for Lord knows she's unpredictable."

Like a time bomb with a long fuse . . .

Waiting for my match.

However, when Kitty improved my looks, I was childishly overwhelmed with gratitude, as I was for the least kind thing she did for me. I took all her small deeds and treasured them as if I had precious jewels to keep me forever safe. For each kindness, I took off a heavy block of hostility, and yet the very next word she said could make my tower even higher.

I woke up with what I thought was a brilliant idea. I would do something wonderful for Kitty—perhaps just to hide the resentment I felt growing day by day. Now that she wasn't awful, I feared her even more. There was something in her eyes, those pale, more than strange eyes.

Cal called early the morning we planned to surprise Kitty with a spring party. "Isn't it too much work? We can't really keep it a surprise," he added with some exasperation. "She doesn't like surprises. I'll have to tell her. If she comes home with a hair out of place, or chipped fingernail polish, she'd never forgive me, or you. She'll want to look perfect, and wear her best dress, and have her hair done—so have the house spotless, and maybe then she'll feel pleased to show off."

He made out the guest list, including all Kitty's girls and their husbands, and her ceramic students (which included both sexes) and their spouses. He'd even given me one hundred dollars so I could buy Kitty a gift I chose myself. A hot-pink leather handbag that cost sixty-five dollars had been my choice. With the money left over I purchased party decorations . . . wasting money, Kitty would say later on, but I dared her wrath anyway.

Cal called the afternoon of the party, which we thought could be a kind of graduation party for her students. "Look, Heaven, don't bother making a cake. I can buy one at the bakery, and it won't be so much trouble."

"Oh, no," I said quickly. "Bakery cakes aren't nearly as tasty as a cake made from scratch, and you know how she's always talking about her mother's cakes, and how difficult cakes are to make right. She mocks my cooking, and baking a scratch cake will have to prove something, won't it? Besides, I've already baked one. You won't believe your eyes when you see all the sweet pink roses and little green leaves I put on the top and sides. If I say so myself, it's the most beautiful-looking cake I've ever seen—and also the first one I've seen that I can eat." I sighed because I'd never had a party of my own, with guests; none of us had, back in the Willies. Even our birthdays had been celebrated by staring in Winnerrow store windows at cakes probably made of cardboard. I sighed as I admired the lovely cake. "I just hope it'll taste as wonderful as it looks."

He laughed, assured me it would be delicious, and we both hung up.

The party was to begin at eight. Cal would eat in town, as would Kitty, who would then rush home to dress for her "surprise" party.

In my own room I took out my mother's bride doll, sat her on my bed so she could watch as I began to dress, pulling over my head a wonderful dress of cornflower-blue georgette. To me the doll represented my mother, and through those glassy eyes the soul of my mother was looking at me with admiration, love, and understanding. I found myself talking to the doll as I brushed my hair and arranged it in a new style that was more adult. Along with pretty new shoes and stockings, the dress had been a gift from Cal on my seventeenth birthday.

By six o'clock I was ready for the party. I felt silly to be ready so early, like a child who just couldn't wait to dress up. Once more I checked over the house. I'd strung gay paper ribbons from the dining-room chandelier, and Cal had hung balloons after Kitty had left this morning. How festive the house looked; yet I grew tired when there was nothing left to do but sit and wait for guests to arrive. In my room again I stared out the window. The early evening grew darker exceptionally quickly as storm clouds gathered overhead, blackening the sunset. Soon a light rain was falling. Rainy days always made me sleepy. I carefully lay on my bed, spreading my skirt so it wouldn't wrinkle, and then cuddled my bride doll in my arms, and into sweet dreams of my mother I easily slid.

She and I were running in the hills, she with her shining pale hair, me with my long dark hair—then I had her color of hair and she had mine, and I didn't know who I was. We laughed in the silent way of dreams . . . and froze in a time frame . . . froze, froze . . .

I bolted wide awake. Seeing first the bulging yellow eyes of another green frog planter. What had awakened me? I rolled my eyes without turning my head. That golden fish? That elephant table that wasn't as perfect as some downstairs? All the junk went into my room, those ceramics not fit to be seen or sold. Why did everything have its glassy stare fixed on me?

A loud roll of thunder rumbled overhead. Almost immediately a bolt of lightning zigzagged through the room. I hugged my doll closer.

Abruptly the sky opened. It wasn't a pleasant summer drizzle that fell. I sat up and peered out the blurry window to see the street below was flooded, the houses across the street out of focus and distant-appearing, as if they were in another world. Again I curled up on my bed, forgetful of my beautiful georgette dress. With my "mother" doll in my arms, I drifted off again.

The rain was a loud drumming sound, shutting out all other noise. The thunder overhead rumbled like those fabled giant bowling balls heard by Rip Van Winkle, all rolling at once, colliding in thundering crashes, creating fierce electrical bolts that lit up the darkness every few seconds. Like a magic movie director I fitted all nature's noises into my dream scenes . . .

In the misty dream more beautiful than reality, Logan and I were dancing in a forest green and shadowy. He was older, so was I . . . something was building between us, some electrical excitement that made my heart beat faster, louder . . .

Out of the dark loomed a figure, not in misty white like a ghost, but in hot pink. Kitty!

I sat up, rubbed my eyes.

"Well . . ." drawled Kitty's deadliest flat voice when the thunder stilled momentarily, "looky what hill-scum crud is doin now. All dressed up an on t'bed."

What was I doing so terrible that Kitty would look like the wrath of God come to end the world?

"Do ya hear me, idiot?"

This time I jerked as if slapped. How could she treat me like this when I'd slaved all day to make a party for her? Enough! I'd had enough! I was tired, at last, of being called so many ugly names, sick and tired and fed up. This time I wasn't going to be cowed, or weak. No! I wasn't hill-scum crud!

My rebellion rose like a giant fire—maybe because she glared her eyes so hard, and that reminded me of all the times she'd slapped without cause. "Yeah, I hear you, bigmouth!"

"WHAT'S THAT YA SAID?"

"I said, *BIGMOUTH, I HEAR YOU!*"

"WHAT?" Louder now, more demanding.

"Kitty *BIGMOUTH.* Kitty *LOUDMOUTH.* Kitty who yells NO every night to her husband so I have to hear it. What's wrong with you, Kitty? Have you lost your sexual appetite now that you're growing old?"

She didn't hear me. She was distracted by what I held in my arms. "What t'hell ya got there? Caught ya, didn't I? Lyin there on yer side, like I ain't done tole ya one million times not t'do nasty stuff like that!"

She snatched the doll from my arms, quickly turned on all the lights in my room, and stared down at the doll. I jumped up to rescue my doll.

"It's her! *HER!"* she screamed, hurling my irreplaceable heirloom doll at the wall. "Luke's *damned angel!"*

I scurried to pick up the doll, almost tripping because I forgot I was wearing high-heeled sandals. Oh, thank God she wasn't broken, only her bridal veil had fallen off.

"GIVE ME THAT THIN!" ordered Kitty, striding to take the doll from me. She was again distracted by my dress, her eyes raking down my length to see my nylons, my silver sandals. "Where ya get that dress, them shoes?"

"I decorate cakes and sell them to neighbors for twenty dollars apiece!" I lied with flair, so angry that she would sling my doll at the wall and try to ruin the most precious thing I owned.

"Don't ya lie t'me, an say stupid thins like that! An give me that doll."

"NO! I will not give you this doll."

She glared at me, dumbfounded that I would answer her back, and in her own tough tone of voice she said, "Ya kin't say no t'me, hill scum, an hope t'get by wid it."

"I just said no, Kitty, and I am getting by with it. You can't buffalo me anymore. I'm not afraid of you now. I'm older, bigger, stronger— and tougher. I'm not weak from lack of nourishing strength, so I do have that to thank you for, but don't you ever dare lay a hand on this doll again."

"What would ya do iffen I did?" she asked in a low, dangerous voice.

The cruelty in her eyes stunned me so much I was speechless. She hadn't changed. All this time when I'd lived apparently in peace, she'd been brewing some kind of hatred inside her. Now it was out, spewing forth from her pale gimlet eyes.

"What's t'matta, hill scum, kin't ya hear?"

"Yeah, I hear you."

"What did ya say?"

"I said, *Kitty*, YEAH, I hear you."

"*WHAT?*" Louder now, more demanding.

Aggressively, no longer willing to play humble and helpless, I held my head high and proud, flaring back: "You're not my mother, Kitty Setterton Dennison! I don't have to call you Mother. Kitty is good enough. I've tried hard to love you, and forget all the awful things you've done to me, but I'm not trying anymore. You can't be human and nice for but a little while, can you? And I was stupid enough to plan a party, just to please you, and give you a reason for having all that china and crystal . . . but the storm is on, and so are you, because you just don't know how to act like a mother. Now it's ugly, mean time again. I can see it in your watery eyes that glow in the darkness of this room. No wonder God didn't allow you to have children, Kitty Dennison. *God knew better.*"

A lightning flash lit up Kitty's pale face gone dead white as the lights flickered on and off. She spoke in short gasps. "I come home t'fix myself up fer t'party—an what do I find but a lyin, tricky, nasty-minded bit of hill-scum filth who don't appreciate anythin I've done."

"I do appreciate all the good things that you've done, that's what this party is all about, but you take away my good feelings when you hit out at me. You try to destroy what belongs to me, while I do all I can to protect what belongs to you. You've done enough harm to me to last a lifetime, Kitty Dennison! I haven't done anything to deserve your punishment. Everybody sleeps on their sides, on their stomachs—and no one thinks it is sinful but you. Who told you the right and wrong positions for sleeping? God?"

"YA DON'T TALK T'ME LIKE THAT WHEN YER IN MY HOUSE!" Kitty screamed, livid with rage. "Saw ya, I did. Breakin my rules, ya were. Ya knows ya ain't supposed t'sleep on yer side huggin anything . . . an ya went an done it anyway. YA DID!"

"And what is so bad about sleeping on my side? Tell me! I'm dying to know! It must be tied up somehow to your childhood, and what was done to you!" My tone was as hard as hers, aggressive too.

"Smartmouth, ain't ya?" she fired back. "Think yer betta than me, cause ya gets A's in school. Spend my good money dressin ya up, an what fer? What ya plannin on doin? Ya ain't got no talents. Kin't half cook. Don't know nothin bout cleanin house, keepin thins lookin pretty—but ya think yer betta than me cause I didn't go no higher than t'fifth grade. Cal done told ya all bout me, ain't he?"

"Cal's told me nothing of the kind, and if you didn't finish school I'm sure it was because you couldn't wait to sleep with some man, and run off with the first one who asked you to marry him—like *all* hill-scum girls do. Even if you did grow up in Winnerrow, you're not one whit better than any scumbag hill-crud girl."

It was Kitty's fault, not mine, that Cal was beginning to look at me in ways that made me uneasy, forgetting he was supposed to be my father, my champion. Kitty's fault. My rage grew by leaps and bounds that she would steal from me the one man who'd given me what I needed most—a real father. Yet it was she who found her voice first.

"HE TOLE YA! I KNOW HE DID, DIDN'T HE?" she screamed, high and shrill. "Ya done talked about me t'my own husband, tole him lies, made him so he don't love me like he used ta!"

"We don't talk about you. That's too boring. We try to pretend you don't exist, that's all."

Then I threw on more fuel, thinking that I'd already started the blaze, so I might as well heap on all the rotten wood I had been saving since the day I came. Not one harsh word she'd said had been forgotten or forgiven, not one slap, one bloody nose or black eye . . . all had been stored to explode now.

"Kitty, I'm never going to call you Mother again, because you never were and never will be my mother. You're Kitty the hairdresser. Kitty the fake ceramic teacher." I spun around on the heel of one silver slipper and pointed at the line of wall cabinets. And I laughed, really laughed, as if I enjoyed this, but I wasn't enjoying myself, only putting on a false front of bravado.

"Behind those locked cupboard doors you've got professional molds, Kitty, thousands of *bought* molds! With shipping labels still on the boxes they came in. You don't *create* any of these animals! You buy the molds, pour in the clay slip—and you display them and label them as one of a kind, and that's fraud. You could be sued."

Kitty grew unnaturally quiet.

That should have warned me to shut up, but I had years of frustrated rage locked up within, and so I spewed it out, as if Kitty were a combination of Pa and everything else that had managed to spoil my life.

"Cal told ya that," came Kitty's deadly flat statement. "*Cal . . . done . . . betrayed . . . me.*"

"Nope." I reached for a drawer in my desk and pulled out a tiny brass key. "I found this one day when I was cleaning in here, and just couldn't help opening the cabinets you always keep locked."

Kitty smiled. Her smile couldn't have been sweeter.

"What do ya know about art, hill scum? *I made t'molds.* I sell t'molds t'good customers—like myself. I keep em locked up so sneaks like ya won't steal my ideas."

I didn't care.

Let the sky fall, let the rain swell the ocean and wash over Candlewick, carry it to the bottom of the sea, to sleep forever next to lost Atlantis . . . what did I care? I could leave now that the weather was hot. I could hitchhike—who'd care? I'd live. I was tough. Somehow or other I'd make my way back to Winnerrow, and when I was there I'd tear Fanny away from Reverend Wise, find Tom, save Keith and Our Jane . . . for I'd thought of a way we could all survive.

To prove my strength, my determination, I turned and stuffed my doll far under the bed, then deliberately fell on the bed and curled up on my side, reaching for a pillow that I hugged tight against me. It hit me then—the thing I'd not thought of before—just what was the evil thing Kitty presumed I did. The girls in school talked about it sometimes, how they pleasured themselves, and foolishly I threw my leg over the pillow and began to rub against it.

I didn't do that more than two seconds.

Strong hands seized me under my armpits, and I was yanked from the bed. I screamed and tried to fight Kitty off, tried to twist around so my hands could rake Kitty's face or do some other damage that would force her to let me go. It was as if I were a struggling kitten in the jaws of a powerful tiger. I was carried and dragged down the stairs, into the dining room I'd made pretty with party decorations—she picked me up, plunked me down on the hard glass-top dining-room table.

"You're putting fingerprints on your clean tabletop," I said sarcastically, idiotically dauntless in the face of the worst enemy I was likely to ever have. "I'm finished with shining your glass tabletops. Finished with cooking your meals. Finished with cleaning your stupid house that has too many gaudy animals in it."

"SHUT UP!"

"I DON'T WANT TO SHUT UP! I'm going to have my say for once. I HATE YOU, KITTY DENNISON! And I could have loved you if you'd given me half a chance. I hate you for all you've done to me! You don't give anyone half a chance, not even your own husband. Once you have anybody loving you, you do something ugly so that person has to turn on you and see you for what you are—INSANE!"

"Shut up." How calmly she said that this time. "Don't ya move from that table. Ya sit there. Ya be there when I come back."

Kitty disappeared.

I could run now. Flee out the door, say good-bye to this Candlewick house. On the expressway I could catch a ride. But this morning's papers had spewed ugly photos on the front page. Two girls found raped and murdered alongside the freeway.

Swallowing, I sat frozen, snared by indecision, regretting, too late, all the things I'd said. Still . . . I wasn't going to be a coward and run. I was going to sit here, show her I wasn't afraid of anything she did—and what worse thing could she do?

Kitty came back, not carrying a whip or a stick or a can of Lysol to spray in my face. She carried only a thin long box of fireplace matches.

"Goin home, back t'Winnerrow fer a visit," said Kitty in her most fearsome monotone. "Goin so ya kin see yer sista Fanny, an yer grandpa. So I kin see my sista, Maisie, my brotha, Danny. Goin back t'touch my roots again, renew my vows t'neva get like em. Gonna show ya off. Don't want ya lookin ugly, like I might neglect ya. Ya've grown up prettier than I thought. Hill-scum boys will try and get ya. So I'm gonna save ya from yer worst self in a way that won't show. But ya'll know from this day on not t'disobey me. Neva again. An if ya eva want t'find out where yer lil sister Our Jane is, and what happened t'that little boy named Keith, ya'll do as I say. I knows where they are, an who has em."

"You know where they are, you really do?" I asked excitedly, forgetting all I'd said to anger Kitty.

"Does t'sky know where t'sun is? Does a tree know where t'plant its roots? Of course I know. Ain't no secrets in Winnerrow, not when yer one of em . . . an they thinks I am."

"Kitty, where are they, please tell me! I've got to find them before Our Jane and Keith forget who I am. Tell me! Please! I know I was ugly a moment ago, but you were, too. Please, Kitty."

"Please what?"

Oh, my God!

I didn't want to say it. I wiggled about on the slippery tabletop, gripping the edge so hard the glass if it hadn't been beveled would have sliced off my fingers.

"You're not my mother."

"Say it."

"My real mother is dead, and Sarah was my stepmother for years and years . . ."

"Say it."

"I'm sorry . . . Mother."

"An what else?"

"You will tell me what you know about Keith and Our Jane?"

"Say it."

"I'm sorry I said so many ugly things . . . Mother."

"Sayin sorry ain't enough."

"What else can I say?"

"Ain't nothin ya kin say. *Not now.* I seen ya doin it. I heard what ya said t'me. Called me a fake. Called me a hill scumbag. Knew ya'd turn against me soona or lata, t'minute I had my back turned ya'd do somethin nasty. Had t'lay on yer side, wiggle round an round, an pleasure yerself, didn't ya? Then ya had t'tell me off . . . an now I gotta do what I kin t'rid ya of evil."

"And then you'll tell me where Keith and Our Jane are?"

"When I finish. When yer saved. Then . . . maybe."

"Mother . . . why are you lighting the match? The lights have come back on. We don't need candles before it's really dark."

"Go get t'doll."

"Why?" I cried, desperate now.

"Don't ask why—jus do as I say."

"You'll tell me what you know about Keith and Our Jane?"

"Tell ya everythin. Everythin I know."

She had one of the long matches lit now. "Fore it burns my fingas, fetch t'doll."

I ran, crying as I fell to my knees and reached under the bed and dragged out the doll that represented my dead mother, my young mother whose face I'd inherited. "I'm sorry, Mother," I cried, lavishing her hard face with kisses, and then I ran again. Two steps from the bottom I tripped and fell. I got up to limp as fast as I could toward Kitty, the pain in my ankle so terrible I felt like screaming.

Kitty stood near the living-room fireplace. "Put her in there," she ordered coldly, pointing to the andirons that held the iron grate. Logs were stacked there, kindling laid by Cal just for looks, for Kitty didn't like wood smoke dirtying and "stinkin up" her clean house.

"Please don't burn her, Ki—Mother . . ."

"T'late t'make up fer t'harm ya done."

"Please, Mother. I'm sorry. Don't hurt the doll. I don't have a photograph of my mother. I've never seen her. This is all I have."

"Liar!"

"Mother . . . *she* couldn't help what my pa did. She's dead—you're still alive. You won in the end. You married Cal, and he's ten times the man my father is, or ever could be."

"Put that nasty thin in there!" she commanded.

I stepped backward, causing her to step threateningly forward. "If ya eva wanna know where Keith an Our Jane is . . . ya have t'give that hateful doll t'me of yer own free will. Don't ya make me snatch it from ya—or ya'll neva find yer lil brotha an sista."

My own free will.

For Keith.

For Our Jane.

I handed her the doll.

I watched Kitty toss my beloved bride doll onto the grate. Tears streaked my face as I fell to my knees and bowed my head and said a silent prayer . . . as if my mother herself lay on her funeral pyre.

With horror I watched the fine lace dress with pearls and crystal beads burst into instant flame, the silvery-gold hair catching fire; the wonderfully alive-looking skin seemed to melt; two small licks of flames consumed the long, dark curling lashes.

"Now ya listen, scumbag," said Kitty when it was over, and my irreplaceable portrait doll lay in ashes. "Don't ya go tellin Cal what I did. Ya smile, ya act happy when my guests show up. STOP that cryin! It were only a doll! Only a doll!"

But that heap of ashes in the fireplace represented my mother, my claim to the future that should have been hers. How could I prove who I was, how, how?

Unable to refrain, I reached into the hot ashes and plucked from them a crystal bead that had rolled free from the hearth. It sparkled in my palm like a teardrop. My mother's tear. "Oh, I hate you, Kitty, for doing this!" I sobbed. "It wasn't necessary! I hate you so much I wish it had been YOU in the fire!"

She struck! Hard, brutally, over and over again until I was on the floor, and still she was slapping my face, slamming her fists into my stomach . . . and I blacked out.

Mercifully blacked out.

16

My Savior, My Father

Shortly after the party was over and all Kitty's friends were gone, Cal found me lying facedown on the floor in the room where I slept; no longer could I think of it as my room. He stood in the doorway silhouetted by the hall light behind him. I felt too sore and raw to move. My beautiful new dress was torn and dirty. And even though he was there I continued to lie in a crumpled heap and cry. It seemed I was always crying for what I'd had once and lost. My pride, my brothers and sisters, my mother—and her doll.

"What's wrong?" Cal asked, stepping into the room and falling down on his knees beside me. "Where have you been? What's the matter?"

I cried on and on.

"Heaven darling, you've got to tell me! I tried to slip away from the party earlier, but Kitty clung to my arm like a burr. She kept saying you didn't feel well, that you were having cramps. Why are you on the floor? Where were you during the party?" He turned me over gently and gazed lovingly into my swollen and discolored face before he stared at my torn dress and nylons full of runs. An expression of such rage flashed through his eyes it frightened me. "Oh, my God," he cried out, clenching his fists. "I should have known! She's hurt you again, and I didn't save you from her! And that's why she treated me so possessively tonight! Tell me what happened," he demanded again, reaching to cradle me in his arms.

"Go way," I sobbed. "Leave me alone. It's going to be all right. I'm not really hurt . . ."

I sought for the right words to soothe his anxiety and my own misery, which by this time I was thinking I'd brought on myself. Maybe I *was* hill-scum filth, and *did* deserve everything Kitty had done. My own fault. Pa couldn't love me. If your own father couldn't love you, who could? *Nobody* could love me. I was lost, all alone . . . and never would anybody love me, never love me enough.

"No, I won't go away." He lightly touched my hair, his lips traveling all over my sore, puffy face. Perhaps he thought it was that way only from crying, not from a battering. There were no lights on for him to see well. Did he think his small kisses could ease the pain? Yet they did, a little. "Does it hurt that much?" he asked with pity in his voice. He looked so sad, so loving.

His fingertips on my swollen eye were so tender. "You look so beautiful lying here in my arms, with the moonlight on your face. You seem half a child, half a woman, older than sixteen, but still so young, so vulnerable and untouched."

"Cal . . . do you still love her?"

"Who?"

"Kitty."

He seemed dazed. "Kitty? I don't want to talk about Kitty. I want to talk about you. About me."

"Where's Kitty?"

"Her girlfriends," he began in a mocking, sarcastic voice, "decided that Kitty really needed a special gift." He paused and smiled ironically. "They've all gone to watch male strippers, and I was left here to sit with you."

"As if I'm a baby . . . ?"

I stared at him with tears wetting my face. His smile grew tighter, more cynical. "I'd rather be right where I am, with you, than any other place in the world. Tonight, with all those other people, drinking and eating, laughing over silly jokes, I realized something for the first time. I felt all alone because you weren't there." His voice deepened. "You came into my life, and truthfully I didn't want you. I didn't want to take on the role of a father, even if Kitty did feel she had to be a mother. But now I'm so damned scared Kitty will hurt you in some horrible way. I've tried to be here as much as possible. And yet I haven't saved you from anything. Tell me what she did today."

I could tell him. I could make him hate her. But I was scared, not only of Kitty but of him, a grown man who appeared at this very minute totally infatuated with a kid of seventeen. Limply I lay in his arms, completely exhausted, listening to his heart pound.

"Heaven, she slapped you, didn't she? She saw you wearing an expensive new dress and tried to tear it off, didn't she?" he asked in a voice thick with emotion. Deep in my own thoughts I didn't even notice that he'd raised my hand to press it against his heart. Beneath his shirt I could feel the steady heartbeats, thumping, making it seem I was already part of him. I wanted to speak and tell him I was almost his daughter, and he shouldn't be looking at me the way he was. But no one had ever looked at me with love before—love I had needed for so long. Why was it making me afraid of him?

He both comforted me and frightened me, made me feel good and made me feel guilty. I owed him so much, perhaps too much, and I didn't know what to do. A funny glazed look came into his eyes, as if I had unknowingly pushed some switch, perhaps because I lay so submissively in his embrace. Much to my surprise, his lips were making a trail all around my throat, savoring the taste and feel of my flesh. I shivered again, wanting to tell him to stop, afraid if I did he wouldn't love me. If I drove him away I wouldn't have anyone to protect me from Kitty, or to care any longer what happened to me . . . and so I didn't say stop.

I had journeyed away from tears into unknown territory, where I lay trapped, not knowing what to do, or what to feel . . . It wasn't wrong, was it, this sweet tenderness he showed when he brushed his lips over mine, gently touching me as if afraid he'd frighten me with too bold an approach—and then I saw his face.

He was crying! "I wish you weren't just a beautiful child. I wish you were older."

Those tears glistening in his eyes filled my heart with pity for him. He was as trapped as I was, in debt to Kitty up to his hairline; he couldn't just walk out on all the effort and years of learning electronics. I couldn't pull away and slap his face when he'd given me the only kindness I'd ever had from a man, and saved me from a life that could have been so much worse here in Candlewick.

Still, I whispered, "Noooo," but it didn't stop him from kissing where he wanted to kiss, or fondling where he wanted to fondle. I quivered all over, as if God above were looking down and condemning me to eternal hell, as Reverend Wise had said he would, and where Kitty reminded me every day that I was sure to go. It surprised me that he would want to nuzzle his face against my breasts while his tears poured like hot rain and he sobbed in my arms.

What had I done or said to make him think what he had to be thinking? Guilt and shame washed over me. Was I truly innately wicked, as Kitty was always saying? Why had I brought this on myself?

I wanted to cry out and tell him what Kitty had done, burned my mother's doll—but perhaps he'd think that a trivial, silly sorrow, to see a doll burned. And what were a few slaps when I'd endured so much more?

Save me, save me! I wanted to scream.

Don't do anything else to take away my pride, please, please! My body betrayed me. It felt good, what he was doing. It felt good to be held, rocked, cuddled, and caressed. A precious thing he made me feel one second, an evil, wicked thing the next. All my life long I'd been starved for hands that touched kindly, lovingly. All my life yearning for a father to love me.

"I love you," he whispered, kissing my lips again, and I didn't ask how he loved me, as a daughter or as something more. I didn't want to know. Not now, when for the first time in my life I felt valuable, worthy enough for a fine man like him to love and desire . . . even if something deep within me was alarmed.

"How sweet and soft you are," he murmured when he kissed my bared breasts.

I closed my eyes, tried to not think about what I was allowing him to do. Now he'd never leave me alone with Kitty. Now he'd find ways to keep me forever safe, and force Kitty to tell him where Keith and Our Jane were.

Thank God caressing my thighs and abdomen and buttocks under my torn dress seemed to satisfy him enough. Perhaps because I began to talk, to make him remember who I was. In a burst of words I gushed it all out, about the doll, the burning, how Kitty had forced me by saying she knew where Keith and Our Jane were. "Do you really think she does know?" I asked.

"I don't know what she knows," he said shortly, bitterly, coming back to himself as the dazed look in his eyes went away. "I don't know if she knows anything but how to be cruel."

He met my wide, frightened eyes. "I'm sorry. I shouldn't be doing this. Forgive me for forgetting who you are, Heaven."

I nodded, my heart pounding as I watched him take from his shirt pocket a tiny box wrapped in silver and tied with blue satin ribbon. He put it in my hand. "I have a gift to congratulate you for being such a

good student, and making me so proud of you, Heaven Leigh Casteel."
He opened the box and lifted the lid on the smaller black velvet box
inside, which revealed a dainty gold watch. His eyes met mine,
pleadingly. "I know you're living for the day when you can escape this
house, and Kitty, and me. So I give you a calendar watch, to count the
days, hours, minutes, and seconds until you can find your brother and
little sister. And I swear I'll do all I can to find out what Kitty knows.
Please don't run from me."

Truth was in his eyes. Love for me was there as well. I stared and
stared, until finally I had to accept, and I held out my arm and allowed
him to fasten the watch about my wrist. "Naturally," he said bitterly,
"you can't let Kitty see this watch."

He leaned to kiss my forehead tenderly, cupping my face between
his palms before he said, "Forgive me for trespassing where I should
never go. Sometimes I need someone so badly, and you're so sweet, so
young and understanding, and as starved for affection as I am."

He didn't notice that I'd sprained my ankle, since I took great pains
to see that I didn't walk until he had left the room and my bedroom
door was closed. I couldn't fall asleep. Cal was so close, dangerously
close, and we were alone in the house. He was in the other room, a few
feet away. Right through the walls I could almost sense his need for
me, and my terrible fear that need would override his sense of decency
made me get up, pull a robe over my nightgown, and painfully make
my way down the stairs and into the living room, where I lay on the
white sofa and waited for Kitty to come home.

All night long the rain was a steady drumming, slashing against the
windowpanes, pelting the roof, rolling thunder and far-off flashes,
keeping me always on edge. However, I had a purpose in mind. I
meant to confront Kitty, and this time come out the winner. Somehow
or other I had to force her to tell me where Keith and Our Jane were. I
clutched in my hand a tiny crystal bead with a few threads of charred
white lace I'd found in the fireplace. Yet as I sat there on her sofa, in
her spanking-clean white house, with her rainbowed creatures all
around me, I felt outnumbered, overwhelmed. I fell into sleep and
missed Kitty's stumbling steps when she came home dead drunk.

Her loud voice coming from the bedroom woke me up.

"Done had me a good time!" Kitty bellowed. "Best damned party
eva! Gonna do it every year from now on—an ya kin't stop me!"

"You may do as you damn well please," answered Cal as I drifted
nearer and nearer the stairs. "I don't care anymore what you do, or
what you say."

"Then yer leavin me . . . are ya, are ya?"

"Yes, Kitty. I am leaving you," he said, to my surprise and joy.

"Ya kin't, ya know. Yer stuck wid me. Once ya go ya ain't got nothin. I'll take yer shop, an all these years ya done been married up t'me go down t'drain, an yer penniless agin . . . unless ya go home to Mommy an Daddy an tell em what a damn fool ya are."

"You do have a sweet and convincing way with words, Kitty."

"I love ya. Ain't that all that counts?" Kitty said, her voice sounding suddenly vulnerable.

I stared upward, wondering what was happening. Was he stripping off her clothes, full of desire just because this time she was going to let him?

When I heard Cal in the downstairs bath the next morning, I got up and started breakfast. Cal was whistling in the shower. Was he happy now?

Kitty came from upstairs apparently a changed woman, smiling at me as if she hadn't burned my most beloved possession and punched me in the face. "Why, honey baby," she crooned, "why'd ya stay upstairs durin t'party ya gave me, huh, why did ya? Missed ya, I did. Wanted ya there t'show ya off t'all my friends. Why, all t'girls were dyin t'see ya, an ya were shy an didn't show up an let em see my pretty daughta gets betta-lookin every day. Really, honey doll, ya do gotta get used t'monthly cramps, an ferget all about em—or else yer neva gonna enjoy bein a woman."

"You tell me where Keith and Our Jane are!" I shouted. "You promised to tell me!"

"Why, honey, what ya talkin bout? How would I know?" She smiled, so help me, she smiled as if she'd completely forgotten all she'd done. Was she pretending? Oh, she had to be! She wasn't that crazy! Then came the more dreadful thought—maybe she really was insane!

Cal strode in and threw Kitty a look of disgust, though he didn't say anything. Behind her back his eyes met mine, sending me a silent warning. *Do nothing. Say nothing.* Let Kitty play her pretend game, and we'd play ours. A knot formed in the pit of my stomach. How could I live through day after day of this? My eyes lowered to watch the eggs sizzling in the pan.

It was May now, and the hustle and bustle of preparing for exams was in the air. I studied hours on end so I'd earn good grades. Very late in the month, a weird kind of northeaster blew in and chased away spring warmth, and suddenly it was unseasonably cold. Furnaces that had been shut down in March were started up again. Sweaters put in mothballs came out with woolen skirts. On the coldest Friday in May I'd ever known, I stayed late for a conference with Mr. Taylor, my biology teacher. He asked me if I'd please take our class hamster, Chuckles, home for the weekend.

The dilemma I faced showed up clearly in my troubled expression as I stood by the hamster's large wire cage, wanting to shout out the truth about Kitty and her diabolical hatred of all living animals, when under any other circumstances I would have been delighted to be in charge of the pregnant hamster that was the biology-class pet.

"Oh, no," I said quickly when he persisted. "I've told you. Mr. Taylor, my mother doesn't approve of pets in her house. They're messy, smelly, and she's always sniffing the air for odors she doesn't recognize."

"Oh, come now, Heaven," said Mr. Taylor, "you're exaggerating, I know you are. Your mother is a lovely, gracious woman, I can tell from the way she smiles at you."

Yeah, how sweet and kind were the smiles of Kitty Dennison. How dumb men could be, really. Even book-smart ones like Mr. Taylor.

My teacher's voice took on a persuading tone while the wild northeast winds whipped around the school building, making me shiver even with the heat on. On and on he wheedled: "The city orders us to turn off the heat on weekends, and all the other students are gone. Do you want the poor little expectant mother to stay in a freezing room so we'll find her dead on Monday? Come, dear, share the responsibility of loving a pet . . . that's what love is all about, you know, responsibilities and caring."

"But my mother hates animals," I said in a weak voice, really wanting to have Chuckles for an entire weekend.

He must have seen some yearning in my expression, for he went on cajoling. "Gets mighty cold in here," he said, watching my face in a calculating way. "Even if Chuckles has food and water, mighty cold for a wee dear caged expectant mother."

"But . . . but . . ."

"No buts. It's your duty. Your obligation. I'm leaving this weekend with my family, or else I'd take Chuckles home with me. I could leave her in my home alone with plenty of food in her cage, and her bottle of water . . . but she might give birth any day. And I want you there with the movie camera I taught you how to use to show the class the miracle of birth, in case it happens while she's with you."

And so I was persuaded against my better judgment, and in Kitty's spick-and-span white-and-pink house, among all the brilliant ceramic critters, tan-and-white Chuckles was established in the basement, a place Kitty never went now that she had a slave to do the clothes washing and drying.

However, Kitty was not in the least predictable. Her mood swings were startling, dramatic, and, most of all, dangerous. With much trepidation I bustled about making a clear and clean place, out of drafts, for the big cage. Under a sunny high window seemed to me just perfect. I found an old standing screen with its black lacquer peeling off, and I set it up. Now Chuckles would be protected not only from drafts but from Kitty's cruel seawater eyes if ever she dared to enter the basement. There was absolutely no reason for her to come to where I had Chuckles cozily established against a distant wall. I felt only a small apprehension for Chuckles' safety.

"Now, you take it easy down here, Chuckles," I warned the small animal, who sat up on her haunches and nibbled daintily on the slice of apple I gave her. "Try not to use your treadmill so much. In your condition, you might overdo it."

The darn wheel squeaked and squealed, and even after I took the wheel out and oiled the moving parts, it still made a certain amount of noise when I spun it with my fingers. Chuckles ran madly about in her cage, wanting her exercise wheel back. Once I put it back in the cage, Chuckles instantly jumped in and began to run in the wheel—it still squealed, but not very much.

Upstairs in the back hall I pressed my ear against the closed basement door. All was silent down there. I opened the door and listened. Still I couldn't hear anything. Good. I descended the stairs, five, six, then seven of them, paused to listen. Only then could I hear a faint sound . . . but it was all right. Kitty would never enter the basement alone, and she couldn't do anything if Cal was at his workbench. I had finished with the laundry, so why should she check?

In another few minutes I had a few old chairs put one on each side of the screen, so it wouldn't topple over and fall on the cage. I tested it, found it stable enough, and once more told Chuckles to be a good girl, " . . . and please don't have your babies before I have the camera set up and ready."

Chuckles went right on spinning in the treadmill.

It was another of those strange evenings, with Kitty not working overtime as she used to do. There was a distraught look in her pale eyes. "Got another migraine," she complained in a whiny tone. "Goin t'bed early," she announced after an early supper. "Don't want t'hear t'dishwasher goin, ya hear? Makes t'house vibrate. I'm gonna swallow some pills an sleep an sleep an sleep.''

Wonderful!

Saturday began like any other Saturday. Kitty got up grouchy, tired, rubbing at her puffy, reddened eyes, complaining of feeling drugged. ''Don't know if I kin make it t'my classes,'' she mumbled at the breakfast table, while I dutifully tended to the sausages, browning them just right, with a bit of water added to keep them moist. ''All t'time tired, I am. Life ain't good no more. Kin't understand it.''

''Take the day off,'' suggested Cal, unfolding the morning paper and beginning to read the headlines. ''Go back to bed and sleep until you can get up and not feel tired.''

''But I should go t'my classes. Got my students waitin . . .''

''Kitty, you should go to a doctor.''

''Ya know I *hate* doctors!''

''Yes, I know, but when you have constant headaches that indicates trouble, or the need for eyeglasses.''

''Ya know I'm not gonna wear any damn spectacles an make myself look like an ole lady!''

''You could wear contacts,'' he said as if disgusted, and he glanced at me. ''I'll be working all day, until at least six. I just hired two new men who need training.'' He was telling me not to expect too much in the way of entertainment tonight.

Kitty rubbed at her eyes again, staring at the plate I put before her as if she didn't recognize her favorite morning meal of sausages, fried eggs, and grits. ''Don't have no appetite fer nothin . . .'' She stood up, turned, saying she was going back to bed and sleep until she woke up without head pains. ''An ya kin call an make my excuses.''

All morning I cleaned and scrubbed, and didn't hear or see Kitty. I ate lunch alone. In the afternoon I dusted, vacuumed downstairs, quickly saw to the needs of Chuckles, who very obviously didn't want me to go and leave her alone. She indicated this in playful, touching ways, sitting up and begging, acting cuter whenever I turned to leave. Oh, but for Kitty I'd bring Chuckles home every night, keep her in my room. ''It's all right, darling,'' I said, scratching her soft, furry head, and that made soft sounds of contentment in her throat. ''You play as much as you want to. The demon in the house has drugged herself with Valium, and that keeps you safe, safe.''

Cal didn't take me to the movies that Saturday; he and I watched television, neither one of us talking very much.

* * *

Sunday.

Kitty's loud singing woke me early.

"Feel good," she shouted to Cal as I got up and quickly strode down the hall toward the stairs and the downstairs bath. "Feel like goin t'church. HEAVEN," she bellowed as she heard me pass her open door, "get yer lazy butt down in t'kitchen fast, an fix breakfast. We're goin t'church. All of us. Gonna sing praises ta t'Lord fer chasin away my headaches . . ."

Why, she sounded just like her old self!

Feeling tired myself, burdened with too much to do, I dashed about trying to do everything before Kitty came down. I started for the bathroom to take a quick shower before I began breakfast. No, better to put the water on for the coffee first, and shower while it heated. After the shower, I'd check on Chuckles as the bacon fried slowly.

But someone had already put the water in the kettle, and it was hot and steaming. I headed for the bath, presuming Cal had been downstairs and was eager for his two cups of morning coffee.

My robe and nightgown I hung on a hook on back of the bathroom door, before I turned to step into the tub.

That's when I saw Chuckles!

Chuckles—in the tub—all bloody! A long string of intestines spewed out of her mouth; her tiny babies strung out from the other end! I fell to my knees sobbing, heaving up the contents of an almost empty stomach so it splashed into the tub to blend with the blood and other sickening contents.

Behind me the door opened.

"Makin a mess agin, are ya?" asked a harsh voice from the doorway. "Screamin an yellin like yer seein somethin ya didn't expect. Now go on, take yer bath. Not gonna let no dirty hill-scum gal go inta my church widout a bath."

Wide-eyed with horror, with hate, I stared at Kitty. *"You killed Chuckles!"*

"Are ya losin yer mind? I ain't killed no Chuckles. Don't even know what yer talkin bout."

"LOOK IN THE TUB!" I yelled.

"Don't see nothin," said Kitty, staring directly down at the pitiful dead animal and all the bloody mess there. "Jus use t'stopper an fill up t'tub while I watch. Ain't gonna take no hill filth inta my church!"

"CAL!" I screamed as loud as possible. "HELP ME!"

"Cal's in t'shower," said Kitty pleasantly, "doin what he kin to cleanse away *his* sins. Now ya do t'same—cleanse yers!"

"You're crazy, really crazy!" I screamed.

Calmly Kitty began to fill the tub. I leaped to my feet and snatched for a towel to shield my nudity. And in reaching, I took my eyes off of Kitty for one brief second.

Enough time. Like a baseball bat Kitty slung her stiffened arm so it struck and hurled me toward the tub. I stumbled, staggered off balance, and again Kitty moved, but this time I managed to dodge, and, screaming, I headed for the stairs, calling Cal's name as loudly as I could.

"YA COME BACK HERE AN TAKE YER BATH!" shrieked Kitty.

I pounded on the door of the upstairs bath, screaming for Cal to hear me, but he was in there with the water going full blast, singing at the top of his voice, and he didn't hear. Any minute I expected Kitty to climb the stairs and force me to sit in that tub of filth and death. Daring embarrassment, I turned the knob on the door. Cal had locked it! Oh, damn, damn!

Sliding to the floor, I waited for him to come out. The minute he turned off the water I was up and calling again. Tentatively he cracked open the door, still dripping water from his hair, with a towel swathed about his hips. "What's wrong?" he asked with great concern, drawing me into his arms and bowing his damp face into my hair as I clung to him for dear life. "Why are you acting so frightened?"

I gushed it all out, Chuckles in the basement, how Kitty had used something to wrap about her middle and squeeze the life out of a harmless, helpless little creature.

His face turned grim as he released me and reached for his robe, and, with me in tow, headed for the downstairs bathroom. In the doorway I waited, unable to look at poor Chuckles again. Kitty had disappeared. "There's nothing in the tub, Heaven," he said, coming back to me. "Clean as a whistle . . ."

I looked myself. It was true. The dead hamster and her young were gone. Sparkling-clean tub. Still wearing nothing but a towel, I tagged behind Cal to visit the basement. Empty cage with a wide-open door.

"What ya two doin down there?" called Kitty from above. "Heaven, now ya take yer shower, an hurry up. Don't wanna be late fer church."

"What did you do with Chuckles?" I shrieked when I was in the back hall.

"Ya mean that rat I killed? I threw it away. Did ya want t'save it? Cal," she said, turning to him and looking sweeter than sugar, "she's mad cause I killed a nasty ole rat in t'tub. An ya know I kin't put up with filth like rats in my house." Her deadly cold eyes riveted on me with warning.

"Go on, Heaven," urged Cal. "I'll talk to Kitty."

I didn't want to go. I wanted to stay and fight it out, make Cal see Kitty for what she was, a psycho who should be locked up. Yet I felt too weak and sick to do more than obey. I showered, shampooed, even fixed breakfast, as Kitty protested over and over again, growing more and more vehement, that she'd never seen a hamster, didn't even know what one looked like, would never go alone into the basement no time, no how.

Her pale eyes swung to me. "Hate ya fer tryin t'turn my man against me! I'll go ta t'school authorities an tell em what ya did ta that poor lil critter—an tryin t'put t'blame on me. It were yers, weren't it? I'd neva do nothin so mean . . . ya did it jus t'blame me! Ya kin stay here until ya finish school—then get out! Ya kin go t'hell fer all I kerr."

"Chuckles was pregnant, Kitty! Maybe that made her more than you could stand!"

"Cal, would ya hear this girl lie? I neva saw no hamster—did ya?"

Could Cal believe I could do anything so horrible? No, no, his eyes kept saying. Let it pass this time, please, please.

Why didn't he look for evidence in the garbage can? Why didn't he come right out and accuse Kitty? Why, Cal, why?

The nightmare continued in the church.

> "Amazing grace . . .
> How sweet the sound . . ."

Everybody was singing reverently. How spaced out I felt standing beside Kitty, dressed in my best new clothes. We looked so fine, so respectably Christian and God-fearing, and all the time the memory of a dear little dead hamster was in my head. Who would believe me if I told?

Kitty dropped her tithe in the passed plate; so did Cal. I stared at the plate, then at the bland face of the deacon who passed it. I refused to put in one penny. "Ya do it," whispered Kitty, giving me a sharp elbow nudge. "Ain't gonna have no friends of mine thinkin yer a heathen, an ungrateful fer all yer blessins."

I stood up and walked out of the church, hearing behind me all sorts of murmurs. Kitty's insanity was coloring everything, making me stare at people and wonder what they were really like inside.

Down the street I started walking fast, leaving Kitty and Cal still in the church. I hadn't gone two blocks before Cal's car was pulling up behind me, with Kitty leaning out to call, "C'mon, kid, don't be silly.

Ya kin't go nowhere when ya ain't got more than two bucks—an that belongs ta t'Lord. Get in. Feelin betta, I am. Mind's clear as a bell, though all night an all mornin early it near gave me a fit."

Was she trying to tell me she hadn't known what she was doing when she murdered Chuckles?

Reluctantly I got into the car. Where could I go with only two dollars in my purse?

All the way home from church I thought about what to do. She had felt she had to kill Chuckles. Only crazy people did sadistic things like that. And how was I ever going to find a reasonable excuse for Chuckles' death when next I saw Mr. Taylor?

"You can't tell him," said Cal when we had the chance to be alone, while Kitty was again sleeping to rid herself of a fresh assault of "cluster headaches." "You've got to make it seem that Chuckles died in childbirth . . ."

"You're protecting her!" I cried angrily.

"I believe you, but I also want you to finish high school. Can you do that if we go now to the authorities and try to have her committed? She'll fight us. We'll have to prove her insane, and you know as well as I do that Kitty shows her worst self only to you and me. Her 'girls' think she's wonderful, generous, and self-sacrificing. Her minister adores her. We have to convince her to see a psychiatrist, for her own good. And, Heaven, we can play our own game until then, and in the meanwhile I'm putting away extra dollars so you'll have enough money to escape this hellhole."

I stepped to the door, then said in a calm voice, "I'll help myself, in my own way, in my own time."

He stood for a moment looking back, like a small boy who'd lost *his* way, before he closed another door, softly.

17

Saving Grace

Our lives in Candlewick took an unexpected turn after Chuckles died. Mr. Taylor naively accepted my excuse about Chuckles dying in childbirth. One day passed, and in the cage I'd brought back there was another hamster, also pregnant (and little different from the one Kitty had killed), again named Chuckles. It hurt, really hurt, to see that one life more or less really didn't make any difference.

I'm not going to love this one, I told myself. I'm going to be careful not to love anything while Kitty is still in my life.

After this incident, as if the murder had done something to shame her spirit, Kitty slipped into a deep, prolonged silence, sitting for hours in her bedroom just staring into space and combing and brushing her hair, teasing it until she had it standing straight out like a wire brush; then she'd smooth it down again, and repeat and repeat the entire process until it was a wonder she had any hair left.

She seemed to have undergone a drastic personality change. From loud and abrasive she became brooding and too quiet, reminding me somewhat of Sarah. Soon she stopped brushing her hair and doing her nails and face. She no longer cared how she looked. I watched her throw out the best of her lingerie, including dozens of expensive bras. She cried, then fell into a dark pit of reflection. I told myself she deserved whatever she was going through.

For a week Kitty made excuses for not going to work, for staying in bed, staring at nothing. The more Kitty withdrew, the more Cal lost *his* abstract quality, forgot his moodiness, and took on a new, confident air. For the first time, he seemed in control of his life as Kitty gave up control in hers.

Strange, so strange, I couldn't stop wondering about what was going on. Could it be guilt, shame, and humiliation, so Kitty didn't have the nerve to face another day? Oh, God, let her change for the better—for the better, Lord, for the better.

School ended, hot summer began.

Temperatures soared over ninety, and still Kitty was like a walking zombie. On the last Monday in June, I went to find out why Kitty wasn't up and ready to rule over her beauty-salon domain. I stared at Kitty lying on the bed, refusing to look my way or respond to her name. She lay there as if paralyzed. Cal must have thought she was still sleeping when he got up. He came from the kitchen when I called to tell him Kitty was desperately ill. He called an ambulance and had her rushed to the hospital.

At the hospital she was given every test known to medical science. That first night at home, alone with Cal, was very uncomfortable. I more than suspected Cal desired me, and wanted to be my lover. I could see it in the way he looked at me, feel it in the long, uncomfortable silences that came suddenly between us. Our easy relationship had flown, leaving me feeling empty, lost. I held him off by setting a daily routine that wore both of us out, insisting we spend every second we could with Kitty in her private room in the hospital. Every day I was there doing what I could, but Kitty didn't improve, except that she did begin to say a few words. "Home," she kept whispering, "wanna go home."

Not yet, said her doctors.

Now the house was mine to do with as I pleased. I could throw out the hundreds of troublesome houseplants that were so much work, could put some of those gaudy ceramic pieces in the attic, but I did none of this. I carried on exactly as I'd been taught by Kitty, to cook, to clean, dust, and vacuum, even if it did wear me out. I knew I was redeeming my sinful acts with Cal by working slavishly. I blamed myself for making him desire me in a way that wasn't right. I was dirty, as Kitty had always said I was. The Casteel hill-scum filth coming out. And then, contrarily, I'd think, NO! I was my mother's child, half Bostonian—but—but—and then I'd lose the battle.

I *was* the guilty one.

I was bringing this on myself. Just as Fanny couldn't help being what she was, I couldn't either.

Of course I'd known for a long time about Cal's smoldering passion for me, a girl ten years younger than he, thrust at him in a thousand ways by Kitty herself. I didn't understand Kitty, probably never would, but since that horrible day when she burned my doll his need and desire had become ten times more intense. He didn't see other women, he didn't really have a wife, and certainly he was a normal man, needing release of some kind. If I kept rejecting him, would he turn from me and leave me totally alone? I both loved and feared him, wanted to please him and wanted to reject him.

Now he could take me out more often in the evenings, with Kitty in the hospital, the object of every medical test an army of doctors could dream up, and still they could find nothing wrong with her. And she'd say nothing to give them any clue to her mysterious ailment.

In a small hospital office, Kitty's team of doctors talked to Cal and me, seeking clues, and neither of us knew what to say.

All the way home from the hospital Cal didn't say a word. Nor did I. I felt his pain and his frustration, his loneliness—but for me. Both of us from different backgrounds, struggling to live with our battle scars delivered by Kitty. In the garage he let me out, and I ran for the stairs, for the safety of my room, where I undressed, put on a pretty nightie, and wished I could lock the door. No locks in Kitty's house, except in the bathrooms. Uneasily I lay on my bed, frightened that he'd come up, talk to me, force me . . . and I'd hate him then! Hate him as much as I hated Pa!

He did none of that.

I heard his stereo downstairs playing his kind of music, not Kitty's. Spanish music . . . was he dancing by himself? Pity overwhelmed me, a sense of guilt, too. I got up, pulled on a robe, and tentatively headed for the stairs, leaving an unfinished novel on my nightstand. It was the music that drew me irresistibly down the stairs, I kept telling myself.

Going nowhere in reality, poor Cal, marrying the first woman who appealed to him. Loving me was another mistake, I knew that. I pitied him, loved him, distrusted him. I felt choked with my own needs, my own guilts and fears.

He wasn't dancing alone, though the music played on and on. He was just standing and staring down at the Oriental rug, not seeing it, either, I could tell by the glaze in his eyes. I drifted through the door and stood beside him. He didn't turn to speak, to give any kind of sign that he knew I was there; he just continued to stare as if he were looking into all the tomorrows with Kitty as his wife, useless to him, except as a burden to care for. And he was only twenty-seven.

"What's that song you're playing?" I asked in a low, scared voice, forcing myself to touch his arm and give him comfort. He did better than just tell me, he sang the lyrics softly; and if I live to be two hundred and ten, I'll never forget the sweetness of that song and the way he looked at me when he sang the words about a stranger in paradise.

He took my hand in his, staring down into my eyes, his luminous and deep in a way I hadn't seen them before, appearing lit by the moon and stars, and something else, and in my mind I saw him as Logan, the perfect soul mate who would love me all the days of my life, as I wanted and needed to be loved.

I think the music got to me as much as his voice and his soft eyes, for somehow my arms stole up around his neck when I didn't send them there. I didn't willfully place one hand on the back of his neck, my fingers curling into his hair, the other cupping his head to gently pull it down to where he could find my lips eagerly waiting for his kiss. No, it just happened. Not my fault, not his, either. Fault of the moonlight snared in his eyes, the music in the air, the sweetness of our lips meeting, all that made it happen.

His hand cupped my head, treasured it, slid down my back, shaping it to fit his need, and then it was on my hip, hesitating there before he moved it to caress my buttocks, fleetingly, lightly, his hand darting to briefly touch my breasts, discovering me again, trying to wake me up as his lips found mine.

I shoved him away.

"Stop!" I slapped his face. Cried out "NO, NO!" and ran up the stairs, slamming my door behind me, wishing again it had a lock, wishing I had more of what came naturally to Fanny, and despising myself for even thinking that. For I loved him now.

Loved him so deeply, so much, it hurt to think of my hand striking his beloved face. A tease, the boys in Winnerrow would call me, or much worse. Cal, I'm sorry, I wanted to scream out. I wanted to go to him in his room, but I was held back by all the words Kitty had said to make me feel foul, unclean, unwholesome.

Again, some powerful force pulled me to the top of the stairs. I looked down. He was still there, glued like a statue to the floor in the living room, the same music still playing. I drifted down the stairs, caught up in some romantic notion of sacrificing myself to please him. He didn't turn or speak when I reached his side. My hand slid into his tentatively, tightened around his fingers. He failed to respond. I whispered, "I'm sorry I slapped you."

"Don't be. I deserved it."

"You sound so bitter."

"I'm just a fool standing here and thinking of my life, and all the stupid things I've done—and the dumbest of all was to allow myself to think you loved me. But you don't love me. You just want a father. I could hate Luke as much as you do for failing you when you needed him; then maybe you wouldn't be needing of a father so much."

Again my arms went around him. I tilted my head backward, closed my eyes, and waited for his kiss . . . and this time I wasn't going to run. It was wrong and I knew it, but I owed him so much, more than I could ever repay. I wasn't going to tease him, then scream no, as Kitty had been doing for years. I loved him. I needed him.

Not even when he swept me up and carried me into his room and laid me on his bed and began doing all those frightening wrong things did I realize what I'd started, and it was too late to stop him this time. His face was smeary with bliss, his eyes glazed, his actions making the bedsprings creak, and I was bounced, my breasts jiggling with the pure animal force of his lovemaking. So this was what it was all about. This thrusting in and out, this hot, searing pain that came and went—and if my conscious mind was shocked and didn't know how to respond, my unconscious physical side had innate knowledge, moving beneath his thrusts as if in other lives I'd done this ten thousand times with other men I'd loved. And when it was over, and he was curled up on his side holding me clutched tight in his embrace, I lay stunned with what I'd allowed him and myself to do. Tears were on my cheeks, streaming down to wet the pillow. Kitty had burned the best of me when she burned my doll in the fire.

She'd left only the dark side of the angel who went to the hills and died there.

He woke me up in the night with small kisses on my face, on my bared breasts, and asked his question. NO, NO, NO, I could almost hear Kitty yelling, as she'd screamed at him so many times when he must have asked her the same thing. I nodded and reached for him, and again we joined as one. When we finished I, again, lay stunned and sickened by my actions, by my too-enthusiastic response. Hill scum! I could hear Kitty shouting. Trashy no-good Casteel, I heard all of Winnerrow shouting. *Just what we expected from a Casteel, a no-good scumbag Casteel.*

The days and nights swiftly passed and I couldn't stop what had begun. Cal overrode all my objections, saying I was being silly to feel guilt or shame when Kitty was getting what she deserved, and I was doing no worse than many girls my age, and he loved me, really loved me, not like some rawboned boy who'd only use me. Nothing he said took away the shame, or the knowledge that what I was doing with him was wrong, totally wrong.

He had two weeks alone with me that seemed to make him very happy, as I pretended to have let go of my shame and guilt. Then one morning Cal drove off early to bring Kitty home. I had the house sparkling and filled with flowers. She lay on her bed blankly staring at all I'd done to make the house pretty, and she showed no signs of recognizing where she was. Home was where she'd said she wanted to be . . . perhaps just so she could pound on the floor overhead with a walking cane, and demand our attention. Oh, how I learned to hate the sound of that cane pounding on the floor that was the living-room ceiling.

Once every week one of Kitty's beauty-salon operators came and shampooed and set her red hair, gave her a manicure and a pedicure. I suspected Kitty was the best-looking invalid in town. At times I was touched by Kitty's helplessness, lying in her pretty pink nightclothes, her hair long and thick, and beautifully groomed. Her "girls" seemed devoted to Kitty, coming often to sit, chat, and laugh while I served them treats I made on Kitty's best china, then raced about trying to keep the house clean, be a companion to Cal, and also keep his books and, using Kitty's checkbook, pay household bills.

"She wouldn't like me doing this," I said with a worried frown, then chewed on the end of a ballpoint pen. "You should be doing this, Cal."

"I don't have time, Heaven."

He took the stack of bills from the small desk that had been Kitty's and put them back in a filing cabinet. "Look, it's a beautiful summer day, and it's been almost a month of constant caring for Kitty. We need to do some serious thinking about what to do with Kitty. Paying those nurses to help you is costing a fortune. And when you go back to school, I'll need another nurse . . . around-the-clock nursing. Have you heard from her mother yet?"

"I wrote and told her Kitty was very ill. But she hasn't replied yet."

"Okay . . . when she does, I'll call and talk to her. She owes Kitty a great deal. And perhaps before school starts, we can work out some permanent solution." He signed and glanced at Kitty before he said, "At least she does seem to enjoy the TV." I'd never seen him look so miserable.

Was this retribution—did Kitty deserve to be stricken with whatever she had? She'd asked for it, and God in his mysterious ways did prevail after all. And my own exhaustion made me say yes, going back to Winnerrow and turning Kitty over to her mother was a fine idea, and it would give me the chance to see Fanny, check on Grandpa . . . and hunt up Tom, to say nothing of Logan. Beyond that I couldn't think. For how could I even look at Logan now?

Finally a letter came from Reva Setterton, Kitty's mother.

"I hate going back there," he said after he read the short letter that showed no real concern for a sick daughter. "I can tell from the way they look at me they think I married her for her money, but if we don't stay with them, they'll think you and I have some kind of relationship going on."

He wasn't looking at me when he said this; still, I heard something wistful and yearning in his voice that made me feel guilty again. I swallowed, quivered, and tried not to think about what he might be implying.

"Besides, you need a break. You work too hard waiting on her, even when the nurse is here. If we stay I'll go broke from paying for nurses. And I can't let you quit school to tend to her. The worst thing is, nothing at all seems wrong with Kitty but her desire to stay home and watch TV."

"Come back to life and love him before it's too late," I yelled at Kitty that day, trying to make her understand she was losing her husband. She'd driven him to me with her coldness, her cruelty, her inability to give.

Later when he was home: "Cal," I began in a low, scared voice, not wanting to desert him now when he had no one, "Kitty wouldn't want to be there all day and night without moving if something weren't terribly wrong."

"But I've had the best doctors in the country look at her. They've made every test they can think of, and found nothing."

"Remember when those doctors gave you their diagnosis? They did admit sometimes the body is as much a mystery to them as it is to us. Even though the neurologists said she seems perfectly healthy, they don't know what's going on inside her brain, do they?"

"Heaven, taking care of her is ruining both our lives. I don't have you as much as I need you. I thought at first it was a blessing in disguise." He laughed, short and hard. "We've got to take Kitty back to Winnerrow."

Helplessly I met his eyes, not knowing what to say.

* * *

Kitty was in her bed, wearing a hot-pink nightgown under a hot-pink bedjacket trimmed with row upon row of tiny pleated ruffles. Her red hair was growing longer and longer, and appeared remarkably healthy.

Her muscle tone didn't seem as flabby as it had, nor did her eyes seem quite as stark or apathetic as they turned our way when we entered together. "Where ya been?" she asked weakly, showing little interest.

Before one of us could answer, she fell asleep, and I was stricken with the pity of such a strong, healthy woman lying still all the remaining days of her life.

I was also filled with excitement, with relief, with a rare kind of anticipation, as if Winnerrow had once given me something besides pain.

"Cal . . . there are times when I think she's getting better," I said after we left Kitty's room.

His brown eyes narrowed. "What makes you think that?"

"I don't know. It's nothing she does, or doesn't do. It's just that when I'm in her room, dusting the things on top of her dresser, I feel she's watching me. Once I glanced up and I could swear I saw some fleeting emotion in her eyes, and not that blank look she usually wears."

Alarm sprang into his eyes. "That's all the more reason to move fast, Heaven. Loving you has made me realize I never loved her. I was just lonely, trying to fill the void in my life. I need you; I love you so much I'm bursting with it. Don't pull away and make me feel I'm forcing you." His lips on mine tried to give me the same kind of passion he experienced; his hands did what they could to bring me to the pitch of excitement he reached so easily—why couldn't I let go of the sense I was drowning myself? Going under each time we made love.

He possessed me with his body, with his will, with his needs, so much that he began to frighten me as much as Kitty once had. Not that he'd ever hurt me physically . . . only mentally and morally I felt damaged beyond repair. Regardless, I loved him, and I had that same insatiable, aching hunger to be cherished tenderly.

Going home would save me, save him, save Kitty, I convinced myself.

I'd find Tom, see Grandpa, visit Fanny, find Keith and Our Jane. I brainwashed myself with this litany I repeated over and over. I made of Winnerrow a kind of refuge, believing it held all the solutions.

PART THREE

Return to Winnerrow

18

~~~

Winnerrow Family

Cal and I made a bed for Kitty in the backseat, loaded our suitcases in the trunk, and set off on a fine sunny day in mid-August, a few days before her thirty-seventh birthday. Kitty had been incapacitated for two months, and seemed likely to stay that way from the vacant way she acted.

Yesterday her "girls" had shampooed and set her hair, had given her a fresh manicure and pedicure, and this morning I'd given her a sponge bath, put on her pretty pink bra, then dressed her in a brand-new pink summer pantsuit. I'd styled her hair as best I could, and done a pretty good job before I put on her makeup so she looked pretty. But for the first time during a trip, Kitty didn't say a word. She just lay as if dead, like the doll she'd burned so ruthlessly.

All the things we should have said on this return to West Virginia remained unsaid as Cal and I sat in the front seat with enough room between us to have put Kitty, if she could have sat up. Soon Kitty and Cal would be established with her family and no longer could he come to me with his needs. Pray God that the Settertons never learned about what we had done together. It troubled me so much I felt almost ill. Was Cal thinking the same thing? Was he regretting now his declarations of love for a hill-scum girl?

This was our moment of truth, or soon would be. His eyes stayed on the road ahead, mine on the passing landscape. In another few weeks school would be starting again, and before that we had to decide what to do with Kitty.

I couldn't help but compare this summer's trip with the winter one, more than two years ago. All that had been impressive then had now become commonplace. McDonald's golden arches no longer commanded my awe or admiration, and hamburgers no longer pleased my palate since I'd eaten in the best restaurants in Atlanta. What was Cal going to do with me now? Could he turn off his love and need, as Kitty could so easily turn off what she used to be? I sighed and forced myself to think of the future, when I'd be on my own. I had already taken my SAT exams and applied to six different universities. Cal had said he'd go with me to college, and acquire his own degree while I began my higher education.

It wasn't until we were halfway to Winnerrow that I knew why Miss Deale had come to our range of mountains, to give the best of her talents to those who needed it most. We were the forgotten, the underprivileged of the coal-mining regions. A long time ago I'd told Tom in jest I'd be another Miss Deale; now, looking around, I knew I wanted more than anything to be her kind of inspiring teacher. Now that I was sixteen, Logan would be in college, home for summer vacation, but soon to leave. Would he see guilt and shame on my face? Would he see something to tell him I was no longer a virgin? Granny had always said she could tell when a girl was "impure." I couldn't tell Logan about Cal, could never tell anybody, not even Tom. I sat on and on, feeling heavy with the burden of shame I carried.

Miles and miles and miles slipped by. Then we were in the hill country, steadily climbing, winding around and around. Soon the gasoline stations became more widely spaced. The grand new sprawling motels were replaced by little cabins tucked away in shadowy dense woods. Shoddy, unpainted little buildings heralded yet another country town off the beaten track, until those too were left behind us. No fast expressway to take us up into the Willies. How scary that name sounded now.

I was seeing the countryside as my true mother must have seen it seventeen years ago. She'd be only thirty-one if she'd lived. Oh, what a pity she had to die so young. No, she hadn't *had* to die. Ignorance had killed her, the stupidity of the hills.

How had my mother had the nerve to marry Luke Casteel? What insanity had driven her away from a cultivated place like Boston, so she'd end up here where education and culture were scorned, and the general opinion was *who t'heck kerrs . . . life's short . . . grab what ya kin an run, run, run*. Running all through life, trying to escape poverty, ugliness, brutality, and never succeeding.

I glanced back at Kitty. She appeared to be sleeping.

A fork in the road ahead. Cal made a right turn that took us away from the dirt road leading to our small, pitiful cabin in the high country. How familiar everything seemed now, as if I'd never left. It all came rushing back, filling me with memories, tingling my nostrils with the familiar scents of honeysuckle and wild strawberries, and raspberries ripe on the vine.

I could almost hear the banjos playing, hear Grandpa fiddling, see Granny rocking, Tom running, hear again Our Jane wailing, while Keith stayed in close, loving attendance. Out of all this mountain ignorance, all this stupidity, still came the gifts of God, the children, not blighted by their genes, as some might have thought, but blessed in many ways.

Mile by mile I was growing more impatient, more excited.

Then came the broad green fields on the outskirts of Winnerrow; neat farms with fields of summer crops that soon would be harvested. After the farms came the houses of the poorest in the valley, those not much better off than true hillbillies. Beyond them, higher up, were the shacks of the coal miners dotting the hills along with the moonshiners' cabins.

The deepest part of the valley was reserved for the affluent, where all the richest mountain silt was driven downward by the heavy spring rains, to end up eventually in the gardens of Winnerrow families, providing fertile soil for those who needed it least, producing lavish flowers and gardens, so the rich grand houses of Winnerrow could grow the best tulips, daffodils, irises, roses, and every other flower to flatter their beautifully painted Victorian homes. No wonder they called it Winnerrow. All the winners in this area lived on Main Street, and all the losers in the hills. On Main Street, long ago, the owners of the coal mines had constructed their lavish homes, and the owners of the long-ago gold mines that had stopped producing. Now those homes were owned by the cotton-factory owners or their superintendents.

Down Main Street Cal drove carefully, past all the pastel homes of the richest, backed by the lesser homes of the middle class, the ones who worked in the mines, holding down some overseer or manager position. Winnerrow was also blessed, or cursed, with cotton gins that made the fabric for bed and table linens, fancy knobby bedspreads, carpets and rugs. Cotton mills with all their invisible airborne lint breathed into many a worker's lungs, so they coughed up their lungs sooner or later (as did the coal miners), and no one ever sued the mill owners—or the mine owners. Couldn't be helped. A living had to be made. Was just the way things were. *Ya took yer chances.*

All this was in my mind as I stared at the fine homes that had commanded my childhood admiration, and in some ways, I had to admit, they still did. See all the porches, the remembered voice of Sarah was saying in my head. Count the floors by the windows, the first, second, and third. See all the cupolas, some houses with two, three, four. Houses pretty as picture postcards.

I turned again to check on Kitty. This time her eyes were open. "Kitty, are you all right? Do you need anything?"

Her pale seawater eyes moved my way. "Wanna go home."

"You're almost there, Kitty . . . almost there."

"Wanna go home," she repeated, like a parrot speaking the only phrase she knew. Uneasily I turned away. Why was I still afraid of her?

Cal slowed, then pulled into a curving driveway leading to a fine home painted soft yellow and trimmed with white. Three levels of gingerbread grandeur, perhaps built around the turn of the century, with porches on the ground and second level, and a small balcony on the third that must be the attic. The porches went around the house on four sides, Cal explained as he drew the car to a slow stop, got out, and opened the back door so he could lift Kitty from the backseat and carry her toward the high porch where her family stood motionless and waiting.

Why didn't her family come running to welcome Kitty home? Why did they just stand up there, bunched together, watching Cal with Kitty in his arms? Kitty had told me they'd rejoiced when she ran off and married at the age of thirteen. "Neva did love me, none of em," I could remember Kitty saying more than once. And apparently from their lack of enthusiasm, they were not glad to see her again, especially sick and helpless—but could I blame them, could I? If she could do what she had to me . . . what had she done to them? They were very generous to agree to take her back, more than generous.

Hesitatingly, I just sat there, reluctant to leave the cool isolation and safety of the car.

Up the five broad steps of the porch Cal carried Kitty, to stop at the top between the white balustrades. That family stared at Kitty as I finally made up my mind that Cal needed some support, and it seemed I was the only one he was going to get it from.

It was like the story Granny used to tell of how she and Grandpa had just waited when Pa brought home the bride he called his angel, and they hadn't wanted her . . . not at first. *Oh, Mother, how painful it must have been for you. How painful it could be for Kitty.*

I ran to catch up, seeing the way they flicked their eyes at me. They weren't friendly eyes, nor were they hostile; all four stood staring as if Cal carried some unwanted alien in his arms. It was clear they didn't really want her, but still they had agreed to take her in and do their best . . . "until it's all over, one way or nother . . ."

The large, formidable-looking woman whom Kitty resembled had to be her mother, Reva Setterton, dressed in tissue-thin bright green silk, with huge gold buttons parading single file down to her hem. Her shoes were also green, and of course, foolishly, that impressed stupid me.

"Where can I put her?" Cal asked, shifting Kitty's weight, as Kitty stared at her mother with a blank expression.

"Her old room is ready an waitin," said the woman, who quirked her thin lips in an imitation smile, then thrust forth her strong, reddened hand and briefly shook mine in a limp halfhearted way. Her auburn hair had wide streaks of white, making it appear that a peppermint stick had melted and formed a fat blob on her head. The short, portly man at her side had a horseshoe ring of gray hair around his pinkish bald pate. Cal introduced him as Porter Setterton, "Kitty's father, Heaven."

"I'm going to take her right up to her room," said Cal. "It's been a long trip. Kitty had to be uncomfortable and cramped in the backseat. I hope I sent enough money to rent all she'll need."

"We kin take kerr of our own," said Kitty's mother, giving her daughter another hard look of contempt. "She don't look sick—not wid all that gook on her face."

"We'll talk about that later," informed Cal, heading for the house while I was eyed up and down by Kitty's sister, Maisie, a pale, insipid imitation of what Kitty must have been when she was seventeen. The pimply-faced, sandy-haired young man named Danny couldn't take his eyes off of me. I guessed his age to be about twenty.

"Ya must have seen us lots of time," said Maisie, stepping up and trying to act friendly. "We sure did see ya an yer family. Everybody always stared at t'hill—I mean t'Casteels."

I stared at Maisie, at Danny, trying to remember, and couldn't place them anywhere. Whom had I ever seen in church but the Reverend, his wife, and the prettiest girls and best-looking boys? Miss Deale . . . and that was about it. The best-dressed had also drawn my eyes, coveting what they wore for myself. Now I was wearing clothes much better than any I'd ever seen in Winnerrow's one and only church.

So far Danny hadn't said one word. "I've got to go and help Kitty," I said, glancing back at the car. "We have our things in the trunk of the car . . . and we'll be needing them to take care of her."

"I'll bring em up," offered Danny, finally moving, as I turned to follow Reva Setterton into the house, closely followed by Maisie, as Mr. Setterton followed Danny to Cal's car.

"Ya sure got some dilly of a name," Maisie said as she trailed up the stairs behind me. "Heaven Leigh. Sure is pretty. Ma, why'd ya go an name me somethin so dumb as Maisie? Ain't ya got no imagination?"

"Shut yer mouth, an be grateful I didn't name ya Stupid."

Squelched, Maisie blushed and hung her head. Perhaps Kitty's tales of a nightmare childhood, told long ago to Cal, had been true after all.

What I could see of the house seemed spacious, neat, and rather pretty, and I was soon led to a bedroom where Kitty had already been put on a hospital bed and was stretched out in her modest pink nightgown. As Cal pulled up the sheet he glanced at me, smiled, then addressed Kitty's mother. "Reva, I truly appreciate your offer to take Kitty in and do what you can for her. I've been paying nurses around the clock. But if you can manage with one night nurse, I'll send you a weekly check to pay for her services, and the expenses of Kitty's medical needs."

"We ain't poor," stated Reva. "Done already said we kin take kerr of our own." She glanced around the pretty room. "You kin call me Reva, girl," she said to me. "This used t'be Kitty's room—ain't so bad, is it? Kitty always made it seem we had her in a pigsty. A jail, she used t'call it. Couldn't wait t'grow up an run off with some man . . . first one who'd take her . . . an now look at her. That's what comes of sinnin, an neva doin what she should of . . ."

What could I say to that?

In fifteen minutes I had Kitty refreshed with a sponge bath and slipped into a clean, pretty pink gown. She stared at me sleepily, with a kind of wonder in her fuzzy gaze, then drifted off into sleep. What a relief to see those strange eyes closed.

Downstairs in a pleasant living room we all sat while Cal explained Kitty's strange illness that no doctor could diagnose. Reva Setterton's lips curled upward to display contempt. "Kitty was born complainin bout everythin. Neva could fix nothin up right enough fer her t'like. She neva liked me, her pa, or nobody else—unless they were male an handsome. Maybe this time I kin make up fer all my failures in t'past . . . now that she kin't answer back, an make me madder'n hell."

"True, true," volunteered Maisie, clinging like a burr to my side. "Ain't nothin but trouble when Kitty comes t'stay. Don't like nothin we do or nothin we say. Hates Winnerrow. Hates all of us, yet she keeps comin back . . ." And on and on Maisie rattled, following me to my room, watching me as I unpacked, and she soon was gasping at the display of all the fancy lingerie and pretty dresses that had filled my closet once Kitty was too sick to care how much money Cal spent on me.

"Bet she's awful hard t'live with," pried Maisie, falling flat on the yellow bedspread and staring at me with admiring green eyes. She lacked something that Kitty used to have, the vitality, and the toughness. "Kitty's never been much of a sister. She was off an married up time I was old nough t'remember. Neva liked Ma's cookin. Now she'll have t'eat it, like or not." Maisie smirked like a satisfied cat. "Neva likes nothin we do or say. She's a queer one, our Kitty. But it makes me feel sad t'know she's lyin on a bed, unable t'move. What did it t'her?"

That was a good question, a very good question that the doctors had asked many times.

When Maisie left, I sank into a tub chair covered with a chintz yellow print and gave it more thought. How had it all begun? After Chuckles was killed? I thought backward, closing my eyes and concentrating, trying again to find a clue. Perhaps it had started the day when Kitty came storming home, furious because half her clients had shown up late for appointments. "Damn crappy women!" Kitty had bellowed. "As if they thinks they're betta than me, an kin keep me waitin like I don't have nothin betta t'do. I'm hungry, got me t'worst kind of appetite—an I keep losin weight! Wanna eat, an eat, then eat some more."

"I'm hurrying as fast as I can," I'd answered, racing from sink to stove.

"Goin up t'take a bath . . . ya be finished time I'm back."

Clickity-clack went her high heels up the stairs.

I could almost see Kitty up there, ripping off her pink uniform, letting it fall to the floor, stripping off her undergarments, letting them fall as well. Clothes that I'd have to pick up, wash, and take care of. I heard the water in the tub running. Heard Kitty singing in a loud voice, the same song she always sang when she was bathing.

"Down in t'valley . . . valley so low . . . owww, owww . . .
Late in t'evenin . . . hear t'train blow . . . owww, owww . . ."

Over and over again, until the song ate into my brain, chewed on my nerves. Just those two lines, repeated until I wanted to stuff my ears with cotton.

Then the scream.

That long, horrible scream.

I'd gone flying up the stairs, expecting to find Kitty had slipped in the tub and cracked her head on the tile . . . and all I found was Kitty standing nude before a bathroom mirror, staring with wide, appalled eyes at her naked right breast. "Cancer, got me a breast cancer."

"Mother, you'll have to go to a doctor. It could be just a benign cyst, or a benign tumor."

"What t'hell does 'benign' mean?" she'd yelled. "They're gonna cut it off, slice me with one of those scalpel knives, mutilate me . . . an no man will want me then! I'll be lopsided, half a woman, an I've neva had my baby! Neva gonna know what it feels like t'nurse my own child! . . . Done tole me, they have, I don't have no cancer. But I know I do! Jus know I do!"

"You've already been to a doctor . . . Mother?"

"Yes, damn you, YES! What do they know? When yer on yer deathbed, that's when they know!"

It had been crazy and wild, the way Kitty had carried on, screaming until I had to call Cal, asking him to come home immediately, and then I'd gone back up the stairs to find Kitty lying on her wide bed, eyes fixed on the ceiling, just staring at nothing.

Darn if I could really remember . . .

After our first meal in the Setterton home, which was really very good, I helped Reva and Maisie with the dishes; then all three of us joined Mr. Setterton on the porch. On a glider I managed to remind Cal of that day while Reva Setterton bustled about upstairs, forcing food down Kitty's mouth. "She ate it," she said when she was back, sitting stiffly in a reed rocker. "Ain't nobody in my house gonna starve t'death."

"Reva, a few months ago, Kitty said she found a lump in her breast. And she said she went to a doctor who reported she didn't have a malignant growth—but how can we know if she really went? However, when she was in the hospital for two weeks, they went over her thoroughly and they didn't find anything suspicious."

For some odd reason, Kitty's mother got up and left the porch.

"An that's all, all?" asked Maisie, her green eyes wide. "What a dope to clam up until she knew . . . but then again, she's sure got some great ones, ain't she? With that kind, could hardly blame her for not wantin t'know."

"But," said Cal, sitting close at my side, "her doctors checked her over, Maisie."

"Wouldn't make no difference t'Kitty," Maisie said with surprising complacency. "Breast cancer runs in our family. Got a whole long history of it. Ma's had both hers taken off. Wears fake ones now. That's why she walked away. Kin't stand t'hear people talk about it. Neva would know it, though, would ya? Our ma's mom had one off. Pa's ma had one off, then died before they could cut off t'other. Always Kitty's been scared t'death of losing what she's so proud of." Maisie looked thoughtfully down at her own small breasts. "Ain't got much myself, compared t'hers, but I'd sure hate losing one—sure would."

Could this be it, explained so simply?

Something neither the doctors nor I nor Cal had thought of. Her secret to brood over. The reason why Kitty had retreated into a solitary world—where cancer didn't exist.

Two hours passed, and that was enough for me to sense that something about Cal was different now that he was in the home of Kitty's parents; something that put a distance between us. I didn't quite understand what it was, though I felt relieved and grateful, sensing he no longer needed me as much as he had. Maybe it was pity for Kitty that softened his eyes when he sat beside her bed and tried to hold her hand. I stood in the doorway and watched him trying to console Kitty before I turned and walked away.

What had happened between Cal and me would stay my most shameful, terrible secret.

When I was downstairs and on the porch wondering what to do next, I thought of Tom. Was this the day I'd feast my eyes on him—and Fanny as well?

And Logan—when will I see you again? Will you know me now, be happy I'm back . . . or will you turn away as you did that last time, when your parents were beside you? He'd never said a word to explain his action, as if he thought I hadn't noticed.

That first night Maisie and I slept together in her room, and Cal was given a cot to sleep on in the room with Kitty. Very early the next morning I was up and fully dressed while the others were still in bed. I had one foot on the step going down when Cal called from behind me, "Heaven, where are you going?"

"To visit Fanny," I said in a whisper, fearing to turn and meet his eyes, feeling a thousand times more ashamed in Winnerrow than I'd felt in Candlewick.

"Let me go with you. Please."

"Cal," I implored, "if you don't mind, I'd like to do this myself. My relationship with Fanny has always been difficult. With you there, she might not talk honestly. And I need to hear the truth and not a pack of lies."

His voice was gruff. "How swiftly you run, Heaven, the moment you are on familiar territory. Are you running *from* me? Using any excuse to escape me? You don't need an excuse; I don't own you. You go on, and I'll stay here to tend to Kitty, and make plans for her care with her parents—but I'll miss you while you're gone."

It hurt to hear the pain in his voice; still, it felt good to escape the house and leave all that behind. Each step I took away from the Setterton home made me younger, happier.

I was going to see Fanny.

My feet chose a roundabout way so I'd have to pass by Stonewall Pharmacy. My pulse quickened as I neared the familiar store. I was just strolling by, truthfully not expecting to see Logan just because I was thinking about him and wondering what kind of boy he was by this time. I glanced inside the wide glass windows, my heart almost in my mouth, and didn't see him. I sighed, and then I caught the interested stare of two dark blue eyes belonging to a handsome young man who was stepping out of a sporty dark blue car. I froze, staring back at— Logan Grant Stonewall.

Oh, gosh!

He seemed caught in the same dream I was, both of us staring, disbelieving.

"Heaven Leigh Casteel . . . is that you, or am I dreaming?"

"It's me. Is that you, Logan?"

His face instantly brightening, he came quickly to me, grasping both my hands and holding them tightly as he stared into my eyes, then pulled in his breath. "You've grown up . . . really grown up to be so beautiful." He blushed, stammered, and then smiled. "I don't know why I'm surprised; I always knew you'd grow more beautiful."

I was shy, snared in a spider's web of my own making, wanting to fling myself into his arms as he held them out inviting me to do just that. "Thank you for answering all my letters . . . or most of them."

He looked disappointed because I didn't make the next move. "When I got your note saying you were bringing Kitty Dennison back here, I wrote and told Tom."

"So did I," I whispered, still staring at how handsome he was, how tall and strong-looking. I felt shamed and sick that I'd not held Cal off, to wait for this clean, pure, shining kind of love that would have been so right. I lowered my eyes, terrified he might see something that I didn't want him to see. I trembled with the guilt I felt, then backed off a foot or more so as not to contaminate him with my sins. "Sure will be wonderful to see Tom again," I said weakly, trying to pull my hands from his grip as he stepped forward to hold them even tighter.

"Not so wonderful to see *me* again?" Gently he tugged me closer, until he released my hands only to slide his arms about my waist. "Look at me, Heaven. Don't look down. Why are you acting as if you don't love me anymore? I've been waiting so long for this day, wondering what I'd say, and what you'd say, and how we'd act . . . and now you're not meeting my eyes. All the time you've been gone I've thought of no one else. Sometimes I go to your cabin and wander about in those abandoned rooms, thinking of you and how tough you had it, and how brave you were, never complaining or feeling sorry for yourself. Heaven, you're like a rose, a wild, beautiful rose, sweeter and more lovely than any other. Please, put your arms around me. Kiss me, say you still love me!"

Everything I'd ever dreamed he'd say, he said, and again I was flooded with guilt—if he knew the truth—and yet I couldn't resist the pleading in his eyes, or the urging of my own romantic nature that said, yes, Logan! I flung my arms about him and felt myself lifted up and swung around. My head lowered so I could put my lips on his, and I kissed him so passionately I think it took his breath away, though he returned my kiss with even more fervor. His eyes shone when we separated, and he was breathing heavily.

"Oh, Heaven, this is the way I knew it would be . . ." he whispered breathlessly.

Now we were both speechless, our young bodies calling to each other. He pulled me against him so I could feel his excitement. It reminded me of Cal. This wasn't what I wanted! I tried to draw away, cringing as I shoved against him, shuddering and overwhelmed with a wild kind of terror, not only of Logan but of every man. Don't touch me that way! I wanted to yell. Just kiss me, embrace me, and let that be enough!

Of course he didn't understand my resistance. I could tell from the startled way his eyes widened, but he let me go. "I apologize, Heaven," he said in a low, humble way. "I suppose I forgot it's been two years and eight months since we'd seen each other—but in your letters you sounded as if we'd never feel like strangers . . ."

I tried to sound normal and not terrified. "It's been great seeing you again, Logan, but I'm in kind of a hurry . . ."

"You mean you're leaving? And we're only going to have these few minutes together? Heaven, didn't you hear me say I love you?"

"I have to go, really I do."

"Wherever you're going, I'm going too."

NO! *Leave me alone, Logan! You don't want me now!*

"I'm sorry, Logan. I'm going to see Fanny, and then Grandpa . . . and I think it's best if I see Fanny alone. Perhaps tomorrow . . . ?"

"No perhaps, definitely a date. Early tomorrow, say eight o'clock, so we can spend the day together. You said a lot in your letters, but not nearly enough. Heaven—"

I whirled around, trying to smile. "I'll see you tomorrow early. See you all day, if that's what you want."

"*If* that's what I want? Of course that's what I want! Heaven, don't look at me like that! As if I frighten you! What's wrong? Don't tell me nothing is! You've changed! You don't love me now, and you haven't got the nerve to tell me!"

I sobbed, "That's not true."

"Then what is it?" he demanded, his young face taking on a more mature look. "If we don't talk about it, whatever it is will put up a wall that sooner or later we'll never be able to climb."

"Good-bye, Logan," I threw out, hurrying away.

"Where?" he called out, sounding desperate. "Here or the Setterton place?"

"Come there. Any time after seven," I said with a nervous laugh. "I'll be up early to help with Kitty."

If only I'd come back to him still innocent, still a girl he could teach . . . and yet, even so, it felt good, really good, to walk away knowing his eyes were following me with admiration so strong I could almost feel it reaching out and touching me. His devotion warmed my heart. Then I heard him running to catch up. "What will it hurt if I walk you to the parsonage, then disappear? I can't wait until tomorrow to hear the truth. Heaven . . . you told me that day in your cabin that your pa sold Keith and Our Jane, Fanny and Tom—were you sold?"

"Yes," I said shortly, putting too much misdirected anger in my voice because he could still doubt, even now. "Sold, like an animal, for five hundred bucks! I was carted away to work like a slave for a crazy woman who hates Pa as much as I do!"

"Why are you yelling at me? I didn't sell you! I'm terribly sorry that you've suffered—but damned if I can see that you have! You look terrific, wearing expensive, beautiful clothes, like a debutante, and you come and tell me you've been sold and treated like a slave. If all slaves end up looking like beauty queens, maybe all girls should be sold into slavery."

"What an insensitive remark to make, Logan Stonewall!" I snapped, feeling as mean as Kitty at her worst. "I used to think you were so kind and understanding! Just because you can't see my scars doesn't mean I don't have them!" Now I was crying, my words breaking. And only a few minutes ago he had been so sweet. Unable to say more, and angry at myself for always losing my control and breaking into childish tears, I turned away again.

"Heaven . . . don't turn away. I'm sorry. Forgive me for being insensitive. Give me another chance. We'll talk it out, like we used to do."

For his own good, I should run off and never see him again, and yet I couldn't let go of a boy I'd loved from the moment I'd first seen him. And with differences forgotten for the moment, side by side we walked until we came to the fine house of Reverend Wayland Wise.

He held my hand as I stared at the parsonage.

A pure white house, a pious house, a grand house, surrounded by two acres of beautiful flower gardens and manicured lawns. This house made Kitty's home in Candlewick seem a shack. I sighed. Sighed again for Fanny, who was now a young lady of sixteen and four months, and Tom, like me, was seventeen, and Keith would soon be twelve, Our Jane eleven. Oh, to see them again, to know they were healthy, happy.

But first Fanny.

Now that I was here, I could only stand and stare at the grandest house in all of Winnerrow. Corinthian columns lined the long porch. The steps up were made of intricately laid red bricks. Red geraniums and red petunias grew in huge terra-cotta planters. On the porch were sturdy-looking white wicker chairs with high fancy peacock backs.

In the huge old trees birds were chirping; a yellow canary in a white wicker cage hung from the porch ceiling began its cheerful song. It startled me to hear that singing from such a high place; the bird had been put there, I guessed, to keep it safe from cats and drafts. All her life Fanny had wanted a canary in a white cage; now she had one.

But for the singing of the birds, there were no other noises.

How silent this great house that gave no hint of its inhabitants.

How was it that such a lovely house could appear so threatening?

19

Found Casteels

Several times I jabbed at that doorbell. As I stood and waited for what seemed an eternity, I grew more than impatient. Every so often I looked to see if Logan had gone away as I hoped he would, but he hadn't. He leaned against a tree, smiling when I glanced his way.

Faint footsteps sounded inside the house. I stiffened and listened more closely. Slow, sneaky steps . . . then the heavy oak door opened just a wee slot. Dark sloe eyes peered out at me, glittering narrowed eyes that appeared suspicious, unfriendly. Only Fanny had almost black eyes like that, only Fanny—and Pa. "Go way," said the voice that was undeniably Fanny's.

"It's me—Heaven," I called excitedly. "I've come to see you, to find out how you are. You can't send me away."

"Go way," Fanny whispered more insistently. "Kin do what I want. An I don't wanna see ya! Don't know ya anymore! Don't need ya anymore! I'm Louisa Wise now. I've got everythin I eva wanted. An I don't want ya comin round t'mess it up."

She could still sting me with her mean, selfish words and ways. Always I'd believed that, underneath all her hostility and jealousy, Fanny loved me. Life had warped her in ways different than it had me.

"Fanny, I'm your sister," I pleaded in a low voice, ashamed Logan would overhear her "welcome." "I need to talk to you, to see you, and know if you've heard anything about Keith and Our Jane."

"Don't know nothin," whispered Fanny, opening the door a bit wider. "Don't wanna know nothin. Jus go way, leave me alone."

I could see my younger sister had grown into a very pretty girl with long black hair and a figure shapely enough to break many a man's heart. That Fanny would break many hearts without remorse had always been my expectation. Still, I was hurt that Fanny would refuse to let me enter the house, and showed no interest at all in how *I'd* been, or where I'd been.

"Have you seen Tom?"

"Don't wanna see Tom."

I winced, again stung. "I wrote you time and time again, Fanny Casteel! Didn't you receive my letters?" I demanded, forcefully holding the door open so she couldn't slam it in my face. "Damn you, Fanny! What kind of person are you anyway? When people are kind and thoughtful enough to write letters, the least you can do is answer—unless you just don't give a damn!"

"Guess ya got t'picture," snapped Fanny in reply.

"Now, you wait a minute, Fanny! You can't slam the door in my face! I'm not going to let you!"

"Ya neva wrote me, not once!" she cried, then turned to look over her shoulder with alarm. Her voice lowered to a whisper again. "Ya gotta go, Heaven." Urgency was in her eyes, a look of fright. "They're upstairs sleepin. The Reverend an his wife hate t'be reminded of who I am. They've done warned me not t'eva talk t'ya, or any otha Casteel. Neva have heard from Pa since I came." She wiped at a tear that came to the corner of one eye and slid like a dewdrop on her cheek. "I used t'think Pa loved me best; seems he don't." Another tear formed that she didn't wipe away. "Glad ya look good." Her eyes swept over my face before her full red lips thinned a bit.

"Gotta go now. Don't want em t'wake up an scold me fer talkin t'ya. Ya jus take yerself out of here, Heaven Leigh—don't wanna know ya; wish I'd never known ya; kin't remember nothin good about ya an those ole days when we were younguns in t'hills. Only remba stinks an hunger, an cold feet, an neva enough of anythin."

Quickly I thrust my foot in the door when Fanny would have slammed it shut with more force than my hands alone could resist. "You wait a minute, Fanny Louisa Casteel! I've thought about you night and day for more than two long years—you can't tell me to go away! I want to know how you've been, if you've been treated fairly. I care about you, Fanny, even if you don't care about me. I remember the good times when we lived in the hills, and try to forget all the bad.

I remember when we used to snuggle up together to keep warm, and I love you, even if you always were a damned pain in the neck."

"Ya get off this porch," sobbed Fanny, crying openly now. "Kin't do nothin fer ya, kin't."

She brutally kicked my foot out of the way and slammed the door. The inside lock was turned, and I stood alone on the porch.

Almost blind with tears, I stumbled down the steps, and Logan was there, sweeping me into his arms and trying to comfort me. "Damn her for talking like that to you—damn her!"

I yanked away, hurting so much from Fanny's indifference I could hardly keep from screaming. What good did it do to dole out so much love to people who turned against you the moment they no longer needed you?

What did I care if I'd lost Fanny? She'd never been a loving sister anyway . . . why did I hurt so much? "Go away, Logan!" I yelled, swinging my fists at him when he tried to embrace me again. "I don't need you—don't need anybody!"

I turned from him, but he seized me by my arm and swung me around so his strong arms drew me against him. "Heaven!" he cried. "What's wrong? What have I done?"

"Let me go," I pleaded weakly.

"Now, look," he urgently pleaded, "you're taking out your anger on me when it's Fanny who hurt you. She's always been a hateful sister— hasn't she? I guess I knew all the way here she'd act like she did. I'm sorry you're so hurt, but do you have to turn on me? I wanted to hang around and be here when you needed me. *Need me, Heaven!* Don't slap out at me! I haven't done anything but admire, respect, and love you. I could never really believe your pa would sell his kids. I guess I do now. Forgive me for not fully believing until today."

I yanked away. "You mean in all this time you haven't talked to Fanny about me?"

"I've tried many a time to talk to her about you . . . but you know how Fanny is. She takes everything and turns it around until she makes herself believe it's her I want to hear about, and not you. Fanny doesn't care about anyone but herself." He blushed and stared down at his feet. "I've found out it's better to leave Fanny alone."

"She still comes on strong, right?" I asked bitterly, guessing that Fanny must have been her usual aggressive self with him . . . and I wondered if he'd fallen, like all the others.

"Yeah," he said, raising his eyes. "Takes a lot of resisting to hold Fanny off . . . and the best way to do that is to stay miles away."

"From temptation?"

"Stop! I do what I can to keep girls like Fanny out of my life. Since you went away, I keep hoping someday a girl named Heaven will be the one to really love me. Somebody sweet and innocent; somebody who knows how to care and how to give. Somebody I can respect. How can I respect anyone like Fanny?"

Oh, God help me! How could he respect me . . . now?

We walked away from Reverend Wise's home and didn't even glance back. Obviously Fanny had adjusted well to *her* new life.

"Logan, now Fanny's ashamed of her old family," I said with tears in my voice. "I thought she'd be glad to see me. There were times when she and I did nothing but fight, but we're blood kin, and I love her just the same."

Again he tried to hold me, to kiss me. I held him off and turned my face aside.

"Do you happen to know where my grandfather is?" I asked in a small voice.

"Sure I know. I visit him from time to time so I can talk to him about you, and often I help sell his whittled animals. He's good, you know, really an artist with that knife of his. And he's expecting you. His eyes lit up when I told him you were coming. He said he was going to take a bath, wash his hair, and put on clean clothes."

Again my throat constricted . . . Grandpa was going to take a bath without urging? On his own going to wash his hair and change his clothes?

"Have you seen or heard from Miss Deale?"

"She isn't here anymore," he said, keeping my hand tightly in his. "She left before you did, remember? Nobody's heard from her since. I go by our old school every once in a while, just for old times' sake, and sit on a swing and remember how it used to be. Like I said before, I've even been up to your cabin, and walked in your empty rooms—"

"Oh, why did you do that!" I cried, so ashamed.

"I went there to understand, and I think I do. To think that someone as smart and beautiful as you could come from such as that cabin, and Tom as well, fills me with awe, and so much respect. I don't know if I could have come out of that with all your courage, and all your drive, and when I see Tom—"

"You've seen Tom? When?" I asked eagerly.

"Sure, and soon you'll see him too." He smiled sadly when he saw my expression. "Don't cry. He's fine, and quite a guy, Heaven. You just wait and see."

We were approaching Martin's Road, which was one of the lesser, poorer areas, about twelve blocks from where Fanny lived in the grandest house of all. "Mrs. Sally Trench runs a nursing home, and she's the one who takes care of your grandpa. I've heard that your father sends money once a month to pay for his stay there."

"I don't care what my father does." But it surprised me to know *he* could be that caring . . . sending money to support an old man he'd seldom noticed.

"Of course you care about your father, but you won't admit it. Maybe he did take the wrong road out, but you're alive and well. Fanny seems happy enough to me, and so does Tom. And when you find Keith and Our Jane, no doubt you'll be amazed at how well they both are. Heaven, you've got to learn to expect the best, not the worst; that's the only way you'll give yourself a chance to be happy instead of miserable."

My heart felt heavy, my soul wounded, as I glanced his way. Once I'd believed that kind of philosophy . . . now I didn't. I had tried his way of thinking with Kitty and Cal, doing my best to please both of them, and fate had tricked me, maybe tricked all of us. How could I restore the trusting innocence I'd lost? How could I turn back the clock and this time say no to Cal?

"Heaven . . . I'm never going to love anyone as much as I love you! I know we're both young and inexperienced and the world is full of others who might attract us later on, but right this minute you've got my heart in your hand, and you can throw it down, step on it, and crush it. Don't do that to me."

I couldn't speak, made dumb from all the guilt I felt, all the shame of not being the girl he thought I was.

"Please, look at me. I need you to love me, and now you don't let me touch you, hold you. Heaven, we're not kids anymore. We're old enough now to feel adult emotions—and share adult pleasures."

Another man who wanted to take from me!

"My family gives me lots to worry about. I wonder how I managed to grow at all," I managed to say.

"Seems to me you did a super job of growing—and shaping up." His tentative, troubled smile faded as his eyes went serious, and for a moment I thought I saw in those stormy blue eyes all the devotion and love an ocean could hold. For me, for me! An eternity of love, caring, and faithfulness. A deep throb stabbed me and made me feel for a moment there was hope, when there couldn't be, not ever.

"What's the matter?" he asked when I began to stride onward at a faster pace. "Have I said something wrong? Again? Remember the day we pledged ourselves to each other?"

I remembered just as much as he did that wonderful day when we'd

lain by the river and made our childish vows to love each other forever.
Now I knew nothing lasted forever.

Then it had been easy to make pledges, thinking neither he nor I
would or could ever change. Now everything *had* changed. I wasn't
worthy of him anymore, if ever I had been. Funny how being a hill
scumbag wasn't nearly as humiliating as being what I was since first I
had allowed Cal to touch me, just another trampy girl who'd allowed
herself to be used by a man.

"I guess you've never had any girlfriend but me?" Bitterness was in
my voice that he didn't seem to notice.

"Just dates, casual dates."

We'd reached Martin's Road. And there on the corner was a huge
monster of a house, painted a sickly sea-foam green, like froth on the
sea, like Kitty's eyes.

The yard about the house was wide, mowed to perfection. It was
hard to picture Grandpa shut up in such a big house as that. Every last
one of the old rockers on the porch was empty. Why wasn't Grandpa
on that grand front porch, whittling?

"If you want, I'll wait out here while you visit with him," Logan said
thoughtfully.

I stared at all those tall thin windows, all those steps there had to be
inside, and Grandpa might now be as feeble and lame as Granny had
been.

The home was on a treelined street. All the houses looked well kept
up. Each had a front lawn, and morning newspapers lay on porch
steps, or near the doors. Husbands in morning disarray were out
walking dogs on leashes.

Many a night I'd visited Winnerrow in dreams when all the streets
were dim, empty, and dogs didn't bark, and birds didn't sing, and not
a sound was to be heard. Terrible dreams in which I walked alone,
always alone, searching for Our Jane, Keith, and Tom. Never for
Grandpa, as if my subconscious had truly believed he'd always be in
that hill cabin, somehow surviving, just because I wanted him to.

Logan spoke again. "I've heard that your grandfather helps with the
cleaning to pay for his room and board, when your father forgets or is
late paying Sally Trench."

The sun, hardly over the horizon, was already blazing-hot, smothering
the valley. No refreshing cool breezes blew as they did up in the Willies.
And to think all my life I'd believed the valley represented paradise.

"Let's go," Logan said, taking me by the elbow and guiding me
across the street and up the brick walk. "I'll wait out here on the porch.
Take your time. I've got all day—all my life—to spend with you."

A fat, frowsy-looking woman in her mid-fifties responded to my timid knock, stared at me with intense interest, then swung the screen door wide and admitted me.

"I've been told my grandfather, Mr. Toby Casteel, is staying here with you," I announced.

"Sure, honey, he's here—an ain't ya a pretty thin, though. Really a pretty thin, ya are, ya truly are. Love that color hair, those pretty lips— kissin lips, ya could say." She sighed, glanced in a nearby window, and scowled at her own reflection before she turned back to me. "Dear old man, got a soft spot in my heart fer such as him. Took him in when nobody else would. Put him in a nice room, an fed him betta meals than he's eva had before. Lay ya ten t'one on that, twenty t'one. Bettin fool, I am. Have t'be. Kin't stay in this kinda business if ya don't gamble. People's tricky, real tricky. Younguns come an put their parents in here an say they'll pay, an they don't. They go, neva show up agin, an some old daddy or momma sits all their lives away, awaitin an awaitin fer visitors who neva come, an letters nobody writes. It's a shame, a cryin shame, what kids kin do t'parents once they're too old to do em any good."

"I understood my father sends money every month."

"Oh, he does, he does! A fine man, yer father, a real fine lookin an actin man. Why, I rememba him from way back when he were a kid, an all t'gals were hot t'catch him. Kin't say I blame em none—but he sure turned out a lot different than most folks thought he would—he sure did."

What did she mean? Pa was a rotter through and through, and all of Winnerrow had to know that.

She grinned, showing false teeth so white they appeared chalky. "Nice place, ain't it? Yer Heaven Casteel, ain't ya? Saw yer mom once or twice, a real beauty, really too fine fer this hateful world, an I guess God must've thought t'same thing. Ya got t'same kind of look as she had, tender, like ya kin't take much." She rested her small but friendly eyes on me before she frowned again. "Get ya gone from this place, honey. Ya ain't meant fer t'likes of what we are."

She would have rambled on all day if I hadn't asked to see my grand-father. "I haven't got much time. I'd like to see my grandfather now."

The woman led me through the dim foyer of the house. I glimpsed old-fashioned rooms with beaded lampshades, browning portraits hanging from ceiling moldings on heavy twisted silken ropes, before I was led up the steep stairs. This huge house seemed terribly old now that I was inside. All the glory of new paint and refurbishings was on the outside. There was nothing fresh and clean inside but the scent of Lysol.

Lysol . . .
Take yer bath now, hill scum.
Use plenty of Lysol, stupid.
Gotta rid ya of Casteel filth.
I shivered.

We passed a room on the second floor that seemed a page straight from a thirties Sears catalog.

"Ya kin have five minutes with him," I was informed as the woman became more businesslike. "I've got sixteen people t'feed three meals a day, an yer grandpa has t'do his share of t'work."

Grandpa hadn't ever done his share of the housework!

How abruptly some personalities could change. Up three more flights of steep, twisting stairs. The buttocks under that flimsy cotton dress seemed twin wild animals fighting each other—I had to look away. Oh, how had Grandpa managed to climb these stairs, even once? How did he ever go outside? The higher we went, the older the house appeared. Up here no one cared if the paint was chipped and peeling off, if roaches scuttled all over the floor. Spiders spun webs in dim corners, draped them from chair to table, from lamp to base. What a fright all this would give Kitty! . . .

On the top level, we followed a narrow hall with many closed doors, to reach the door at the very end, and when it was opened, it revealed a pitifully small, shabby room, with a sagging old bed, a small dresser—and there sat Grandpa in a creaky old rocker. He'd aged so much I hardly recognized him. It broke my heart to see the second rocker—both chairs had been taken from our pitiful cabin in the Willies, and Grandpa was talking as if Granny sat in her rocker. "Ya work t'hard on yer knittin," he murmured. "Gotta get ready fer Heaven girl who's comin . . ."

It was unbelievably hot up there.

There was no beautiful scenery all around, no dogs, cats, kittens, pigs, hogs, or chickens to keep my grandpa company. Nothing here at all but a few pieces of beat-up old furniture. He was so lonely he'd turned on his imagination, and put his Annie in that empty rocker.

As I stood in the open doorway hearing that landlady stomp away, an overwhelming pity washed over me.

"Grandpa . . . it's me, Heaven Leigh."

His faded blue eyes turned to stare my way, not with interest as much as with surprise at hearing a different voice, seeing a different face. Had he reached a certain kind of miserable plateau where nothing really mattered?

"Grandpa," I whispered again, tears welling, my heart aching to see him like this. "It's me, Heaven girl. That's what you used to call me—don't you remember? Have I changed so much?"

Slow recognition came. Grandpa tried to smile, to show happiness, his pale eyes lighting up, opening wider. I threw myself into his arms that slowly opened to receive me . . . and just in the nick of time. While he silently cried, I held him in my arms and wiped away his tears with my handkerchief.

"Now, now," soothed Grandpa, finding a rusty voice to use while smoothing my rumpled hair, "don't ya cry. We ain't sufferin, not Annie, not me. Neva had it so good before, huh, Annie?"

Oh, dear God! . . . He was looking at the empty rocker and seeing Granny! He even reached to pat where her hand would have been if she'd been sitting there. Then, almost with relief, he leaned over to spread sheets of old newspapers on the floor at his feet, and began with his sharp knife to shave a piece of tree limb free of bark. It was so good to see those hands busy.

"Lady here pays me an Annie t'work, help wid t'cookin, an t'make these critters," Grandpa said in a low whisper. "Hate t'see em go. Neva thought I'd let even one go, but it means nice thins fer Annie. She kin't hear so good nowadays, either. Gonna buy her a hearin aid. But I kin hear good, real good. Don't need no glasses yet. . . . That is ya, Heaven girl, that really ya? Yer lookin good, like yer ma who came. Annie . . . where did Luke's angel come from? Kin't seem t'rememba much of nothin lately . . ."

"Granny's looking fine, Grandpa," I managed to say as I knelt by his side and put my cheek on his old gnarled hand when it was momentarily still. "Are they good to you here?"

"It's not so bad," he said vaguely, looking lost and bewildered when he moved his eyes over the room. "An I'm mighty glad t'see ya lookin so fine an pretty; pretty as yer own true ma. An here ya are, Luke's angel's Heaven. Gladdens this heart t'see yer face lookin like yer ma come back t'life."

He paused, looked at me uneasily before he went on. "Know ya don't love yer pa, know ya don't even want t'hear bout him, but still he's yer fatha, an there's nothin t'be done bout that now. My Luke's done gone an got himself some kind of crazy, dangerous job, so I hear tell, but don't know what it is, cept he's makin lots of money. Luke set Annie and me up here with his money, didn't leave us t'starve."

How grateful he seemed for nothing! This horrible small room! And then I felt shamed, for he was better off here than alone in the cabin.

"Grandpa, where is Pa?"

He stared at me blankly, then lowered his eyes to his whittling.

"Like t'dead risin from t'grave," he muttered. "Like God tried once an made a mistake, an's tryin again t'do it right. *God help her.*"

It sure did make me feel strange, his saying that. I knew he didn't realize he'd said those frightening words aloud. Still, I felt sort of doomed. And even worse, he kept on speaking in that strange, mumbling way, as if to his Annie. "Would ya look at her, Annie, just would ya?"

"Grandpa, stop mumbling! Tell me where Pa is! Tell me where I can find Keith, Our Jane! You see Pa . . . he must have told you where they are."

Vacant stare into nowhere. No voice to answer a question like that. It was no use.

In time he said all there was to say, and I stood to go.

"I'll be coming back soon, Grandpa," I said at the door. "Take care, now. You hear?"

Then I joined Logan on the porch.

There was someone with him. A tall young man with dark auburn hair who turned when he heard the clickity-clack of my heels. I stared . . . and then my knees went weak.

Oh, my God!

It was Tom!

My brother Tom, standing and grinning at me, just the way he used to do . . . only thing was, in two years and eight months he'd grown to look almost exactly like Pa!

Tom stepped toward me, grinning broadly and holding out his arms. "I can't believe my eyes!" I ran to him then and was caught up in his strong embrace, and we were hugging, kissing, laughing, crying, both trying to talk at once.

Soon all three of us walked down Main Street with arms locked, me in the middle. We stopped at a park bench that just happened to face the church, and of course the parsonage was across from the church. Fanny could have looked out and seen us there, even if she was too cowardly to join her own family reunion.

"Now, Tom," I gushed, "tell me everything your letters didn't."

Tom glanced at Logan and seemed a little embarrassed. Immediately Logan was on his feet, making excuses that he had to hurry back home. "Sorry about this, Logan," Tom apologized, "but I've only got ten minutes to visit with my sister, and years of filling in to do, but I'll see you again in about a week."

"See you tomorrow in church," Logan said to me in a significant way.

Logan left, while I feasted my eyes on Tom. His sparkling green eyes locked with mine. "Good golly, if you ain't a sight for sore eyes."

" 'If you aren't' is the way you should say it."

"I should have known. Still the schoolteacher!"

"You're no skinnier than you used to be, but so much taller, and so good-looking. Tom, I never guessed you'd grow to look like Pa."

What did he hear in my voice to take the smile from his eyes and lips? "You don't like the way I look now?"

"I like the way you look, of course I do. You're handsome—but did you have to grow up to look so much like Pa?" I almost shouted. Now I'd gone and hurt his feelings when I hadn't meant to do that. "I'm sorry, Tom," I choked, laying my hand on his huge one. "It's just that you took me by surprise."

He had an odd look on his face. "There's many a woman who thinks Pa is the best-looking man alive."

Frowning, I glanced away. "I don't want to talk about him, please. Now, have you heard anything about Keith and Our Jane?"

He turned his head so I saw his profile, and again I felt stunned that he could be so much like Pa. "Yeah. I heard they are fine, and Our Jane is alive and well. If Pa hadn't done what he did, no doubt she'd be dead."

"Are you making excuses for him?"

Again he turned to me and grinned. "You sound just like you used to. Don't hold on to hate, Heavenly . . . let go of it before it eats you up and makes you worse than he is. Think of those who love you, like me. Don't go spoiling everything good that will come along in the future because you had a cruel father. People change. He's taking care of Grandpa, isn't he? Never thought he'd do that, did you? And Buck Henry isn't nearly as mean as he looked that first time we saw him; as you can see, I'm not starved, not sick, not worked to death. And I'll be graduating from high school same time as you do."

"Your hair isn't as red as fire anymore . . ."

"Sorry about that, but I'm glad. Tell me if my eyes still shine with devilment."

"Yes, they still do."

"Then I haven't changed so much after all, have I?"

He had a clean, honest face, with clear, shining eyes without secrets, while I had to duck my head and hide my eyes, so scared he'd see my terrible secret. If he knew, he wouldn't respect me as he always had. He'd think I was no better than Fanny, and maybe even worse.

"Why are you hiding your eyes, Heavenly?"

I sobbed and tried to meet his gaze again. If only I could tell him everything right now, and say it all so that he'd see I had been as trapped by my Candlewick circumstances as Fanny had been by her hill genes. I began to tremble so much that Tom reached to pull me into his arms where I could rest my head on his shoulder. "Please don't cry cause you're so happy to see me, and make me cry, too. I haven't cried since the day Buck Henry bought me from Pa. But I sure did cry a lot that night, wondering what had happened to you after he drove me away. Heavenly, you are all right, aren't you? Nothing bad happened, did it?"

"Of course I'm all right. Don't I look all right?"

He studied my face as I tried to smile and conceal all the guilt and shame I felt. What he saw apparently satisfied him, for he smiled as well. "Gee, Heavenly, it's great to be here with you. Now tell me everything that's happened to you since the day I went away—and say it all fast, cause I'll have to go in another few minutes."

The urgency in his voice made me look around—was Buck Henry with him?

"You first, Tom. Tell me everything you didn't in your letters!"

"Don't have time," he said, jumping to his feet and pulling me up as I saw a familiar stocky figure coming down the street. "That's him looking for me. Just one fast hug, and I've got to go. He's here in town buying vet supplies for two sick cows. Next time you've got to tell me more about your life in Candlewick. Your letters say so little. Too much talk about movies and restaurants and clothes. By gosh, it seems to me all of us were blessed the day Pa sold us off."

There were shadows in the emerald depths of his eyes, dark shadows I suddenly noticed, putting doubts in my mind as to his happiness; but before I could question, he was off, calling back: "I'm joining Mr. Henry, but be looking for me next Saturday, and I'll bring Laurie and Thalia with me . . . and we'll all have lunch or dinner together—maybe both if we're lucky!"

I stood staring after him, so sad to see him going already; he was the one and only person who might understand, if only I could tell him. Tears were streaking my face as I watched him join that man I just couldn't believe Tom could like. Still, he looked fine. He seemed happy, big, and strong. The shadows in his eyes were only there because of the shadows he caught from me, as always he'd been my reflection.

Next Saturday I'd see him again. I could hardly wait for the day!

20

～

The Love of a Man

Cal was waiting for me when I finally returned to the Setterton home. "Heaven!" he cried when he saw me on the steps. "Where the devil have you been? I've been worried sick about you."

He was the man who loved me, who'd given me so much happiness when he gave me kindness and care, who gave me shame when he gave me love; and added all together, it totaled up to feeling trapped. As I surrendered to his quick embrace and his hasty kiss, I was enveloped in a heavy fog of despair. I loved him for what he'd done to save me from the worst of Kitty's meanness, and yet I wished desperately that he'd just stayed my father, and not become my lover.

"Why are you looking at me like that, Heaven? Can you love me only in Candlewick, and not in Winnerrow?"

I didn't want to love him in the way he wanted me to! I couldn't let him overwhelm me again with his needs. I whispered hoarsely, "I saw Tom today, and Fanny, and Grandpa."

"And you're crying? I thought you'd be happy."

"Nothing is ever quite what you think it's going to be, is it? Tom has grown to be as tall as Pa, and he's only seventeen."

"And how was Grandpa?"

"So old and pitiful, and pretending Granny's still alive, sitting in the rocker next to him." I half laughed. "Only Fanny was predictable. She

2 9 6

hasn't changed at all in personality, except she has turned into a beauty."

"I'm sure she can't hold a candle to her sister," he said in a low, intimate voice, lightly touching my breast. At that moment Maisie opened the screen door, and her eyes were huge. She'd seen! Oh, God!

"Kitty's been callin fer ya," said Maisie in a small voice. "Ya betta run on up an see what she wants. Ma kin't do nothin right fer her."

Sunday morning we were all up early preparing to go to church. Kitty had to wait until Monday to see the doctors. "We're all goin t'church," said Reva Setterton when she saw me in the hall. "Ya hurry an eat yer breakfast so ya kin go. I done took kerr of my daughta early, so she's all right t'leave alone fer a few hours."

Cal was in his bedroom doorway, staring at me in a disturbing way. Did he realize now that it was better that he and I never be alone again? Surely he had to know Logan was the right one for me, and he'd let me go without making further demands. I pleaded with my eyes, begging him to restore our proper relationship . . . but he frowned and turned away, seeming hurt.

"I'll stay here with Kitty; the rest of you go on," I said. "I don't like to leave her alone." Instantly Cal turned to follow Kitty's family out the door. He glanced back to give me a long, appraising look before his lips quirked in a wry small smile.

"Be good to your *mother*, Heaven."

Was that sarcasm I heard in Cal's voice?

Here I was, stuck in this house, when Logan would be waiting for me in the church. How stupidly blind of me to presume Reva Setterton would stay home with her daughter, and how indifferent she'd been to suggest leaving her alone.

Slowly I climbed the stairs to check on Kitty.

Kitty lay on the wide bed, her face scrubbed so clean it shone. Not only was it red and chafed, as mine had been after that bath in scalding water, her thick red hair had been parted in the middle and was tightly braided in two long plaits that just reached the swell of her bosom. Her mother had put her in a plain white cotton nightgown such as old ladies wore, buttoned up to the throat, the very kind of nightgown Kitty despised, a plain, cheap nightgown. I'd never seen Kitty look so unattractive.

Her mother was wreaking her own revenge, as Kitty had hers when she put me in boiling water . . . and yet I felt an overwhelming rage rising. I hated Reva Setterton for doing this to a helpless woman! How cruel when Kitty was so defenseless. Like a protective mother I gathered what I needed to undo what Reva had done. I pulled out Kitty's prettiest nightgown, and took off the plain ugly one, before I soothed her chafed skin all over with lotion; then gently I eased the lacy pink nightie over her head. Then I began to undo her tightly bound hair. When I had it styled as best I could, I carefully soothed her irritated face with moisturizer and began to apply her makeup.

As I worked to repair the damage I talked on and on. "Mother, I'm just beginning to understand how it must have been for you. But don't you worry. I just put a good moisturizing lotion all over your body, and cream to help your face. I know I won't make your face up as well as you do it yourself, but I'll try. We're taking you to the hospital tomorrow, and the doctors are going to give your breasts a more thorough examination. It isn't necessarily true that you have to inherit tumors, Mother. I hope to God you really told me the truth, and you did go, as you said you did—did you really go?"

She didn't answer, though it seemed she was listening, and a tear formed in the corner of her left eye. I went on talking, using blusher, eyebrow pencil, adding lipstick and mascara; and when I'd finished, she looked like herself again. "You know something, Kitty Dennison, you are still a beautiful woman, and it's a damned shame you're lying there and not caring anymore. All you had to do was reach out and tell Cal you love him, and need him, and stop saying no so much, and he'd have been the best husband in the world. Pa wasn't meant to be any woman's husband. You should have known that. He's a born rogue! The best thing that ever happened to you was when he walked out and Cal walked in. You hate my mother, when you should have pitied her—look what he did to her."

Kitty began to cry. Silent tears slid down her face and ruined her freshly applied makeup.

Early Monday morning an ambulance drove Kitty to the hospital. I rode beside her, and with me was Cal, while her mother and father stayed home. Maisie and Danny had gone on a hayride into the mountains.

For five hours Cal and I sat on hard, uncomfortable hospital chairs and waited for the verdict on Kitty. Sometimes I held his hand, sometimes he held mine. He was wan, restless, chain-smoking. When Kitty had ruled her house, he'd never smoked; now he couldn't leave cigarettes alone. Finally a doctor called us into an office, and we sat side by side as he tried to tell us without emotion:

"I don't know how it was overlooked before, except sometimes a tumor is very difficult to find when a woman has such large breasts as your wife, Mr. Dennison. We did a mammogram of her left first, since for some reason women seem to have them more frequently on that side than the other, and then her right. She does have a tumor, set deep under the nipple in the most unfortunate place, for it's difficult to discover there. It's about five centimeters in size. That's very large for this type of tumor. We are absolutely sure your wife has known about this tumor for some time. When we tried to do the mammogram, she suddenly came out of her lethargy and fought us. She screamed and yelled, and shouted out 'Let me die!'"

Stunned, both Cal and I. "She can talk now?" he asked.

"Mr. Dennison, your wife could always talk. She chose not to. She knew she had a growth. She's told us she'd rather be dead than have her breast removed. When women feel this strongly about losing a breast, we don't push the issue; we suggest alternatives. She's refused chemotherapy, for it would cause the loss of her hair. She wants us to try radiation . . . and if that fails, she says she is ready to 'meet her Maker.'" He paused, and something that I couldn't read flickered through his eyes. "In all honesty I have to tell you that her tumor has gone beyond the size that can be treated by radiation . . . but since that's all she'll do to help herself, we have no alternative but to do our best—unless you can convince her otherwise."

Cal stood up and seemed to quiver. "I have not once in my life convinced my wife of anything. I'm sure I can't now, but I'll try."

He did his best. I was with him when he pleaded at her bedside. "Please, Kitty, have the operation. I want you to live." She clammed up again. Only when she glanced at me did her pale green eyes shimmer, with hate or something else, I couldn't tell.

"You go home now," ordered Cal, settling in the only chair in her room. "Even if it takes me a month, I'll convince her."

It was three o'clock on Monday, and my heels made clicking sounds on the pavement. I wore blue button earrings Cal had given me only a week ago. He gave me so much, everything he thought I could possibly want. He'd even given me Kitty's jewelry box, but I couldn't force myself to use anything that belonged to her. The sweetness of this beautiful afternoon made me feel younger and fresher than I had since that first day Kitty had made me feel like hill scum. Whatever happened to Kitty would be of her own making, in a way, for she could have saved that breast if she'd acted sooner, and ended up with only a tiny scar that no man would ever notice.

With every step I took I prayed Cal would convince Kitty to have that operation. I prayed, too, that she'd see him for the fine man he was, and when she did, I knew he'd let go of me. It was Kitty he loved, had always loved, and she'd treated him so poorly, as if she couldn't love any man after what Pa had done to harm her.

Pa! Always full circle back to Pa!

Footsteps were following. I didn't look around. "Hey," called a familiar voice. "I waited for you yesterday."

Why did my steps quicken when all along I'd hoped he'd seek me out? "Heaven, don't you run. You can't run fast enough and you can't run far enough to escape me."

I spun around and watched Logan approach. He'd grown to be everything I'd ever dreamed he could be—and it was too late to claim him now for my own. Much too late.

"Go away!" I flared. "You don't want me now!"

"Now, you wait a minute," he growled, catching up and grabbing me by the arm, forcing me to walk with him. "Why are you acting like this? What have I done? One day you love me, the next day you push me away . . . what's going on?"

My heart ached so much I felt weak. Yes, I loved him, had always loved him; would always love him; and yet I had to say what I did. "Logan, I'm sorry, but I keep remembering how you ignored me that last Sunday before Pa sold me to the Dennisons. I wanted your help, and you looked right through me, and you were all I had after Miss Deale went away. You were my white knight, my savior, and you did nothing, absolutely nothing! How can I ever really trust you after that?"

Pain was in his eyes as he reddened. "How dumb can you be, Heaven? You think you're in this world all by yourself with your problems, while nobody else has any. You knew I had trouble with my eyes that year. What do you think I was doing while you were starving up there on your mountaintop? Down in the valley I was almost going blind, so I had to be flown to a special hospital to have eye surgery! That's where I was! Far from here, stuck in a hospital with my head held in a clamp, my eyes heavily bandaged until they healed. Then I had to wear dark glasses and take it easy until my retinas were securely attached again. That day when you thought I saw you in church, I was only *trying* to see, and all I got were blurry images—and I was looking for you! You were the reason I was there at all!"

"Do you see all right now?" I asked with a lump in my throat.

He smiled, then stared into my eyes until *my* vision blurred.

"I'm seeing you with twenty-twenty eyes. Say I'm forgiven for that long-ago Sunday?"

"Yes," I whispered. I swallowed all the tears that wanted to come again, bit on my lip before I bowed my head and rested my forehead briefly on his chest. I said a silent prayer for God to let him forgive me when or if I ever had to tell him. Useless to him now that I wasn't what he believed me to be—untouched, no longer a virgin. Yet I couldn't bring myself to tell him, not here.

With resolve I began to lead him toward the woodsy area of Winnerrow.

"Where are we going?" he asked, his fingers intertwining with mine. "To see your cabin?"

"No, you've already gone there by yourself and discovered all I wanted to hide from you. There's another place I should have shown you years ago."

Hand in hand we strolled on toward the overgrown trail that would take us up to the graveyard. I glanced at him from time to time; several times our eyes met and locked, forcing me to tear my eyes away. He did love me. I could tell. Why hadn't I been stronger, shown more resistance? I sobbed and stumbled, and quickly he reached to balance me. I ended up in his arms. "I love you, Heaven," he whispered hoarsely, his warm, sweet breath on my face before he kissed me. "All last night I lay awake thinking about how wonderful you are, how faithful and devoted you stay to your family. You're the kind of woman a man can trust; the kind you can leave alone and know will stay faithful."

Gone numb from the misery I felt, I tried not to let too much sunshine come into the shadows of my heart as he rambled on and on, making me familiar with his parents, his aunts and uncles and cousins, until we came to the riverbank where we'd sat for so many hours a long time ago. Here time had stood still. Logan and I could have been the same adolescents falling in love for the first time. We sat again, perhaps in the very same place, so close our shoulders brushed, his thigh next to mine. I stared at the water that rippled over the stones. And only then did I begin the most difficult story of my life. I knew he'd hate me when it was over.

"My granny used to say my real mother came to that spring over there," I said, pointing to the water that jetted from a crack in the rock face, "and she'd fill our old oak bucket with the spring water since she thought the well water wasn't as good for drinking, or for making soup, or for the dyes Granny used to make to color old stockings she'd braid into a rug to fit under a cradle and keep out the drafts. She was fixing up the cabin as best she could for my birth . . ."

He sprawled on the grass at my side, playing idly with long tendrils of my hair. It was romantic sitting there with Logan, as if we were both brand-new, and nobody had ever loved before but us. I could see us in my mind's eye, young and fresh, unwrinkled and bright, in the prime flowering of our lives—but other bees had already flown to me. . . . He played with my hands, first one, then the other, kissing my fingertips and palms before he folded my fingers on the kiss gifts he'd put in my hands. "For all the days when I wanted you so much, and you were gone." He pulled me down so my upper half lay on his chest, and my hair was a dark shawl that tented both our faces as we kissed, and then I lay with my cheek on his chest, his arms enfolding me. If only I were what he thought I was, then I could really enjoy this. I felt like a dying person on the last picnic of my life; the sun in all its glory couldn't keep the rain from my conscience.

I closed my eyes, wishing he'd talk on forever and wouldn't give me the chance to ruin his dream—and mine.

"We'll marry while the roses are still in bloom, the year I graduate from college. Before the snow falls, Heaven."

I shook my head, half caught up in his fantasy. My eyes closed, my breath regulated to coincide with his. He was caressing my back, my arms—and then, tentatively, my breast. I jumped, cried out as I jerked away and sat up. My voice shook as I said, "Let's go now. You have to see, if you're to understand who and what I am."

"I already know who and what you are. Heaven, why are your eyes so wide and frightened-looking? I wouldn't hurt you, I love you."

He wouldn't, not when he knew the truth. It was Cal who knew what I'd been through and Cal who understood. I was a Casteel, born rotten, and Cal didn't care, not the way the perfectionist Stonewalls would. Time and again Logan had turned from Fanny because she was wild and too free with herself.

Logan's bright eyes clouded with worry, seeming to sense I had a secret that wouldn't make him happy. I felt so small, so tainted, so alone.

"I've got a strange desire," I said in a small, quivery voice. "If you don't mind, Logan, I'd like to see my mother's grave again. When she died she left me a portrait doll I couldn't save from a fire, and I needed it to prove who I am when I return to Boston to find my mother's family!"

"You plan to go there?" he cried in a deep, troubled voice. "Why? When we marry, my family will be your family!"

"Someday I've got to go there. It's something I feel I have to do, not only for myself but also for my mother. She ran from her parents and they never heard from her again. They can't be too old, and must have worried about her for so many years. Sometimes it's better to know the truth than to go on forever wondering, speculating . . ."

He drew away from me now, though he matched his steps to mine as we climbed upward.

Soon the leaves would flame into a witch's brew of bright colors, and autumn would flare briefly in the mountains. Down in the valley where the wind didn't blow, two Stonewall parents would resent this Casteel girl who wasn't worthy enough for an only son. I reached for his hand, loving him as only the very young can love. Instantly he smiled and stepped closer. "Must I say I love you ten million times before you believe me? Should I go down on my knees and propose? You can't tell me anything that would make me stop loving and respecting you!"

Oh, yes, there was something I could say, and everything would change. I held his hand tighter, leading him on, always ascending, curving around tall pines, thick oaks and hickories, until all the trees turned to evergreens . . . and then we were there, in the cemetery. Room for only a few more now. Newer, better graveyards down lower, where it wasn't so much trouble to haul up machines to mow the grass, and men to dig the graves.

No one mowed the grass where my young mother lay, all alone and off to one side. Just a narrow mound that was beginning to sink, a cheap headstone in the form of a cross.

ANGEL
BELOVED WIFE OF
THOMAS LUKE CASTEEL

I released Logan's warm hand and sank to my knees, and bowed my head and said my prayer that someday, some wonderfully kind day, I would see her in paradise.

Along the way here I'd plucked a single red rose from the garden of Reverend Wayland Wise, and this I put in a cheap glass jar I'd buried at the foot of her grave years ago. No water nearby to put in the jar to keep the rose alive and fresh. A red rose left to wither and turn brown. As she had withered and died before I ever had a chance to know her.

The wind whipped up and lashed the long arms of the evergreens as I knelt there and tried to find the will to say what I had to.

"Let's go now," Logan said uneasily, glancing up at the late-day sun that began a swift descent behind the mountaintops.

What was he sensing?

The same thing I was?

All the little evening sounds bounced back and forth, echoing across the valleys, singing with the wind through the canyons, through the summer leaves, whispering the tall grass that hadn't been cut in years.

"It looks like rain . . ."

Still I couldn't tell him.

"Heaven, what are we doing here? Did we come just so you could kneel and cry, and forget the pleasures of being alive and in love?"

"You're not listening, Logan. Or looking, or understanding. This is the grave of my real mother who died when I was born, died at the tender age of fourteen."

"You've told me about that before," he said softly, kneeling beside me and placing his arm over my shoulder. "Does it still hurt so much? You didn't know her."

"Yes, I do know her. There are times when I wake up and I feel as she must have felt. She's me, and I'm her. I love the hills, and I hate them. They give so much, and they rob you of so much. It's lonely here, and beautiful here. God blessed the land and cursed the people, so you end up feeling small and insignificant. I want to go, and I want to stay."

"Then I'll make up your mind for you. We're going back to the valley, and in two years we'll be married."

"You don't have to marry me, you know that."

"I love you. I've always loved you. There's never been anyone but you. Isn't that reason enough?"

Tears were streaking my face now, falling to make raindrops on the red rose. I glanced up at the storm clouds swiftly drawing closer, shuddered, and started to speak. He drew me against him. "Heaven, please don't say anything that will spoil what I feel for you. If what you're planning to say is going to hurt, don't say it, please don't say it!"

And I went and said it, as I'd planned all along, to say it here, where she could hear.

"I'm not what you think I am—"

"You're all I want you to be," he said quickly.

"I love you, Logan," I whispered with my head bowed low. "I guess ever since the day we met I've loved you, and yet I let another—"

"I don't want to hear about it!" he flared hotly.

Because he jumped to his feet, I jumped to mine, and then we faced each other. The wind snapped my long hair so it brushed his lips. "You know, don't you?"

"What Maisie's been spreading around? No, I don't believe anything so ugly! I can't believe gossip! You're mine, and I love you . . . don't you try to convince me there's a reason I can't love you!"

"But there is!" I cried desperately. "Candlewick wasn't the happy place I wanted you to believe when I wrote those letters. I lied about so much . . . and Cal was—"

He wheeled about and ran!

Ran for the path to take him back to Winnerrow, calling back, "No! No! I don't want to hear more! I don't want to hear—so don't tell me! *Never* tell me!"

I tried to catch up, but he had much longer legs, and my little heels dug into the mushy earth and slowed me. I headed back up the trail, to visit again the cabin that stunned me with its bleakness. There on the wall was the pale place where Pa's tiger poster used to hang, and underneath, when Tom and I were babies, our cradle had sat. I stared at the cast-iron stove covered with rust where it wasn't green with fungus, and gazed with tears in my eyes at the primitive wooden chairs fashioned long ago by some dead Casteel. The rungs were loose, some were missing, and all the little things we'd done to pretty this place were gone. Logan had seen all of this! I cried then, long and bitterly, for all I'd never had, and all I might still lose. In the silence of the cabin the wind began to howl and shriek, and the rain came down. Only then did I get up from the floor to make my wet way back to Winnerrow, which was no home at all.

Cal was on the porch of the Setterton home, pacing back and forth. "Where have you been that you come back wet, torn, and so dirty?"

"Logan and I visited my mother's grave . . ." I whispered hoarsely as I sat wearily on the top step, not caring that it was still raining.

"I thought you were with him." He sat beside me, as heedless of the rain as I; he bowed his head into his hands. "I've been with Kitty all day, and I'm beat. She won't eat. They're putting intravenous tubes in her arm, and beginning the radiation treatments tomorrow. She didn't go to a doctor as she told you she had. That lump has been growing steadily for two or three years. Heaven, Kitty would rather die than lose what represents her femininity to her."

"What can I do to help?" I whispered.

"Stay with me. Don't leave me. I'm a weak man, Heaven, I've told you that before. When I saw you walking with Logan Stonewall, it made me feel old. I should have known that youth would call to its own, and I'm the old fool caught in my own trap."

He tried to sit beside me. I jumped up, a wild panic in my heart. He didn't love me, not as Logan did. He only needed me to replace Kitty.

"Heaven!" he cried. "Are you turning away from me too? Please, I need you now!"

"You don't love me!" I cried. "You love her! You always have! Even when she was cruel to me, you made excuses for her!"

Wearily he turned, his shoulders sagging as he headed for the front door of the Setterton home. "You're right about some things, Heaven. I don't know what I want. I want Kitty to live, and I want her to die and get off my back. I want you, and I know it's wrong. I should never, never have let her talk me into taking you into our home!"

Bang!

Always doors were being slammed in my face.

21

Without a Miracle

A week passed. Every day I tended to Kitty in the hospital. I hadn't seen Logan since the day he ran from me and left me in the rain, and I knew that in just one more week he'd be returning to college. Many a time I strolled by Stonewall Pharmacy, hoping to catch a glimpse of him, even as I tried to convince myself he'd be better off without someone like me. And I'd be better off without someone who'd never forgive me for not being perfect. Too flawed, Logan must have been thinking—too much like Fanny. If Cal noticed I was miserable from not seeing Logan anymore, he didn't say anything.

Hours spent in the hospital at Kitty's bedside made all the days seem exceptionally long. Cal sat on one side, I on the other. He held her hand most of the time, while I kept my hands folded on my lap. As I sat there, almost feeling her suffering as my own, I pondered the complexities of life. At one time I would have rejoiced to see Kitty helpless and unable to deliver slaps and insulting words to take away my self-esteem. Now I was full of compassion, willing to do almost anything to ease her pain, when there was little enough I could do to make her comfortable. Still, I tried, thinking I was redeeming myself, forgetting, as I struggled to find myself worthy and clean again, just what Kitty had done to make me hate her.

There were nurses to give her medications, but I was the one who gave her baths. She gave me signs to hint she'd rather have me do for her all the pampering things the nurses didn't have time for, such as smoothing lotion all over her body, or brushing and styling her hair as she wanted. Often as I teased, then smoothed with a pick, I thought I could have truly loved her if she'd given me half a chance. I made up her face twice a day, dabbed on her favorite perfume, painted her nails, and all the time she watched me with those strange pale eyes. "When I die ya gotta marry Cal," she whispered once.

I looked up, startled, and started to question, but she closed her eyes again, and when she did that, she wouldn't speak even if she were still awake. *Oh, God, please let her get well, please!* I prayed over and over. I loved Cal and needed him as a father. I couldn't love him in the way he wanted me to.

Other times, as I tended to her needs, I rambled on and on, talking as much to myself as to her; talking about her family and their great concern for her welfare (even though they didn't have any), trying to lift her spirits and give her hope as well as courage to fight the thing that was controlling her life now. Often her eyes were shiny with tears. Other times those dull seawater eyes riveted on me without expression. I sensed something in Kitty was changing, for better or for worse, I couldn't tell.

"Don't look at me like that, Mother," I said with a kind of nervous resentment. I was afraid Maisie might have visited and told her tales of seeing some touch or small bit of affection between Cal and me. *But it wasn't my fault, Kitty, not really,* I wanted to say as I pulled on her pretty new gown and arranged her arms so she didn't appear so lifeless.

No sooner had I finished with Kitty than her mother came in, scowling disapprovingly, her large, strong arms folded as shields across her fake swelling bosom, her scowl deep and menacing. "She'd look betta widout all that paint on," she grumbled, giving me another sour look. "She's done taught ya rotten ways, ain't she? Done made ya inta what *she* is. Gave ya all her own faults, ain't she? An I licked her many a time t'take t'evil out of her. Neva did. Neva could. She's got it in her yet, festerin, killin her . . . an t'Lord in t'end always wins, don't he?"

"If you mean we all have to die, yes, Mrs. Setterton, that's true. But a good Christian like you should believe in life after death—"

"Are ya mockin me, girl? Are ya?"

In her eyes I saw some of Kitty's meanness shining forth. My indignation rose. "Kitty likes to look pretty, Mrs. Setterton."

"Pretty?" she queried, staring down at Kitty as if seeing an abomination. "Don't she have no color gowns but pink?"

"She *likes* pink."

"Jus goes t'show she's got no taste. Redheads like her don't wear pink. Done tole her that all her life, an still she wears it."

"Everyone should wear whatever color they like. It's her choice," I insisted.

"Ya don't have t'make her look like a clown, do ya?"

"No, I paint her face so she looks like a movie star."

"A *whore* is more like it!" Reva Setterton stated flatly before she turned her stony eyes on me. "Know what ya are now. Maisie done tole me. That man of hers, knew he couldn't have been no good or he wouldn't have wanted *her*. She's no good, neva was even when she were a baby—an neitha arc ya! I don't want ya in my house! Don't ya show up there agin, hill-scum filth! Take yerself ta t'motel on Brown Street, where all yer kind of trash hangs out. I've made her man move all yer stuff out along with his."

Astonishment and anger widened my eyes before my shame and guilt made me blush. She saw and smiled cruelly. "Don't wanna see ya agin, not eva—ya hide when ya see me comin!"

Trembling, I spread my hands wide. "I have to keep visiting Kitty. She needs me now."

"Ya hear me, scumbag! Come no more t'my place!" And out of the room she stormed, having come and looked at Kitty without one word of sympathy or encouragement or compassion. Had she come just to let me know what she thought of me?

Kitty was staring at the door, an unhappy pale fire in her eyes.

Tears coursed a crooked way down my cheeks as I turned again to Kitty, arranging her bedjacket so she looked neat, before I fiddled again with her hair. "You look lovely, Kitty. Don't believe what you just heard. Your mother is a strange woman. Maisie was showing me the family photograph albums, and you look a great deal like your mother when she was your age . . . except you are prettier, and no doubt all your life she's been jealous of you." (Why was I being so kind, why, when she'd been so cruel? Perhaps because Reva Setterton might have done many of the things to Kitty that Kitty had done to me.)

"Git out now," Kitty managed when I was through with her.

"Mother!"

"*Not yer motha.*" Some terrible pain fleeted through her eyes, the agony of frustration so horrible I had to duck my head and hide my pity. "Always wanted t'be a motha, more than anythin else wanted my own baby. Ya were right when ya told me what ya did. Ain't fit t'be a motha. Neva was. Ain't fit t'live."

"Kitty!"

"Leave me be!" she cried weakly. "Got t'right t'die in peace—an when t'time comes, I'll know what t'do."

"No, you don't have the right to die! Not when you have a husband who loves you! You've got to live! You have Cal, and he needs you. All you have to do is will your body to fight back. Kitty, please do that for Cal. Please. He loves you. He always has."

"Git out!" she yelled with a bit more strength. "Go t'him! Take kerr of him when I'm gone. Soon I will be! He's yers now. My gift t'ya! Only took him fer my man cause he had somethin about him that made me think of Luke—like Luke coulda been if he'd been brought up by some nice family in t'city." She sobbed low in her throat, a hoarse, raw sound that tore at my heart. "When first I saw him afta he came an sat at my table, I squinted my eyes an pretended he *were* Luke. All t'time I been married t'him, I could only let him take me when I played my pretend game—an made him Luke."

Oh, Kitty, you fool, you fool!

"But Cal's a wonderful man! Pa's no good!"

The pale fire flared hotter. "Heard that all my life bout myself, an I'm not bad, I'm not! I'm not!"

I couldn't take any more. I went out into the fresh September air.

What kind of trick did love play on common sense? Why one man when there were thousands to choose from? Yet here was I, hoping to find Logan. Almost wild to find him and have him tell me he understood and forgave me. But when I passed Stonewall Pharmacy, Logan wasn't to be seen. In the drizzling rain I stood in the shadow of a huge elm and stared across the street at the windows of the apartment over the corner store. Was he up there looking down at me? Then I saw his mother at one of the windows just before she pulled the cord and closed the draperies, shutting me out. I knew she'd like to keep me forever out of her son's life. And she was right, right, right . . .

I walked toward Brown Street, to the only motel in town. The two rooms Cal had rented were both empty. After I'd refreshed myself and put on dry clothes, I went out into the rain again and walked all the way back to the hospital, where I found Cal sitting dejectedly on a waiting-room sofa, staring moodily at a magazine held loosely in his hand. He glanced up when I came in.

"Any change?" I asked.

"No," he answered gruffly. "Where have you been?"

"I was hoping I'd see Logan."

"Did you see him?" he asked dryly.

"No . . ."

He reached for my hand and held it firmly. "What do we do, and how do we live with something like this? It could last six months, a year, longer. Heaven, I thought her parents were a solution. They're not. They're withdrawing their financial support. It's you and I or no one, until she's well, or gone . . ."

"Then it's you and I," I said, sitting down to hold his hand in mine. "I can go to work."

He didn't say anything. We continued to sit, our hands joined, as he stared at the wall.

For two weeks we lived in that motel. I didn't see Logan. I was sure he'd gone back to college by now, without even saying good-bye to me. School started, and that told me only too clearly I might never again enter a classroom and college was only a dream cloud drifting off into the sunset. And the job I'd thought would be so easy to find when I could type ninety words a minute didn't materialize.

The first real signs of winter came, and although I'd seen Tom twice, his visits were too short for us to really say all we needed to say. Always Buck Henry was waiting for him, glaring when he saw me, and forcing Tom to hurry, hurry. I went every day to visit Grandpa, hoping just once Pa would be there, but he never was. I tried time and again to see Fanny, but she wouldn't even come to the door anymore. A black maid responded to my demands. "Miss Louisa don't talk t'strangers," was what she said every time, refusing to recognize I was her sister, not a stranger.

I hated the motel, the way people looked at Cal and me, though he had his room and I had mine, and not since we'd come to Winnerrow had he made love to me. When we went to church, we drove to another town and prayed there, knowing by this time that the Reverend Wise wouldn't allow us in his.

One morning I woke up cold. The strong north wind was blowing leaves from the trees and fanning out the curtains as I got up and began to dress. A walk before breakfast was on my mind.

It was a cloudy, rainy day, with fog covering the hills. I stared upward toward our cabin; through the mists I saw snow on the mountain peaks. Snowing up there, raining down here . . . and here was where I'd longed to be so many times.

I heard footsteps following, making me walk faster; a tall figure came to walk beside me. I expected to see Cal, but it was Tom! Instantly my heart gladdened. "Thank God you're back again! I waited and waited last Saturday praying you'd show up. Tom, are you all right?"

He laughed as he turned to hug me, thinking all my concern for his welfare was silly and unnecessary. "I can stay a whole hour this time. I thought we could have breakfast together. Maybe Fanny will join us and it will be like old times, almost."

"I've tried to visit Fanny, Tom, and she refuses to talk to me. A black maid comes to the door, so I never even see her, and she doesn't stroll the streets."

"We gotta try," said Tom, frowning. "I don't like what I'm hearing in whispers. Nobody sees Fanny anymore, not like they used to before you came. There was a time when Fanny was everywhere showing off her new clothes, and bragging about all the Wises give her. Now she doesn't even attend church on Sundays, or go to any of their social events—and neither does Rosalynn Wise."

"To avoid me, I suspect," I guessed with some bitterness, "and Mrs. Wise stays home to see that Fanny stays in her room. Soon as I'm gone, Fanny will come out of hiding."

At the restaurant that served truck drivers, we ate a hearty breakfast, laughing as we reminisced about all our poor meals when we lived in the Willies. "Have you decided yet which sister you want?" I asked when he insisted on picking up the check.

"Nope." He threw me a small, shy grin. "Like em both. However, Buck Henry says if I marry Thalia, he'll send me on to college and leave Thalia the farm. If I select Laurie, I'll have to make it on my own . . . and so I've decided not to marry either, and leave soon as I finish high school, and set out on my own." Until now his tone had been light; suddenly he was serious, his voice heavy. "When you leave for Boston, how about taking me along?"

I reached for his hand, and laughed to think he'd say the very words I'd been hoping to hear. People in Boston wouldn't be as prejudiced as they were here; they'd see our true worth. There I could easily find a job, and then I could mail Cal money to help pay for Kitty's care. He had put the house in Candlewick up for sale, but even if he did sell it, that money wouldn't last if she didn't recover soon, or . . .

"Don't look like that, Heavenly. Everything will work out, you'll see." Arms linked, we strolled on toward the nursing home to visit Grandpa.

"He ain't here," said Sally Trench when she responded to Tom's loud knocking. "Yer father done come an took him away."

"Pa's been here!" cried Tom, seeming unbelievably happy. "Where did he take Grandpa?"

Sally Trench didn't know. "Left about half an hour ago," she informed us before she slammed the door.

"Pa could still be in town, Heavenly!" Tom cried excitedly. "If we hurry, maybe we can find him!"

"I don't want to see him, not ever!" I flared.

"Well, I do! He's the only one who can tell us where to find Keith and Our Jane."

Both of us began to run. Winnerrow was an easy city to search, one main street with twelve side roads. As we ran we looked in store windows, questioned those we saw walking. The sixth man we asked had seen Pa. "Think he was goin t' t'hospital."

Why would he go there? "You go on alone," I said tonelessly when Tom insisted.

Helplessly Tom spread his large, callused hands. His expression was miserable. "Heavenly, I've got to be honest. I've been lying to you all the time. In those letters, and those pictures I enclosed, those were only school friends named Thalia and Laurie. Buck Henry doesn't have any children but ones who're buried in a churchyard. That fine house belongs to Laurie's mother and father, six miles down the road. Buck Henry's house might once have been nice, but now it's run-down and needs repairing. He's a slave driver who works me twelve to fourteen hours a day."

"You mean you lied? All those letters when I lived in Candlewick— all lies?"

"All lies. Lies made up to make you feel good about me." His eyes pleaded. "I knew what you had to be thinking, and I didn't want you to worry, but now I have to say I hate that farm! Hate Buck Henry so much sometimes I feel if I don't escape I might kill him . . . so please understand why I'm going to run away from him and find Pa. I have to do this."

To help Tom have what he wanted, to see Keith and Our Jane again, I'd do anything, even face the man I hated most in the world. "Hurry!" Tom kept urging, and soon we were both running toward the hospital.

"Maybe Cal will be with Kitty by this time," I gasped breathlessly when we were in the hospital lobby looking around.

"Sure," said a nurse when Tom asked about Luke Casteel, "he was here . . ."

"But where is he now?"

"Why, I don't know . . . been an hour ago since he asked the room number of Mrs. Dennison."

Pa had come to see Kitty . . . or me?

Grasping my hand tighter, Tom began to pull me along.

All the nurses and attendants had grown to know me by this time, and they greeted me by name as I took over and led Tom toward an elevator that would take us up to Kitty's room. I felt strange, almost numb, and so fearful of what I'd say and do when I saw Pa. Still, when I was in Kitty's room, and she was pale and weak-looking, and Cal was kneeling by the side of her bed crying, it took me moments to adjust to the disappointment of *not* seeing Pa, and then I was again shocked to see how happy Kitty looked. She lay on the narrow bed, beaming at me, at Tom. Why?

"Yer pa done come t'see me," she whispered in a frail voice I could hardly hear. "He asked bout ya, Heaven; he said he hoped t'see ya. Said he were sorry fer what he did in t'past, an hoped I'd fergive him. Ya know, neva thought in a million years I'd hear Luke Casteel sound—Cal, what way did he sound?"

"Humble," Cal said in a hoarse voice.

"Yeah, that's it. He were humbled, sorry-soundin." Her eyes were bright, as if she'd seen a miracle. And for days she hadn't spoken. "He looked at me, Heaven, an he neva did that before. When I loved him, an woulda died fer him, he neva saw me . . . jus took me like I was a thin, an left. But he done changed, he has . . . an he's gone an left this here note fer ya."

Hers was a feverish kind of happiness, frenzied, as if she had to hurry, hurry. For the first time I saw she was dying, dying right before our eyes, maybe had been for months before we even came here, and both Cal and I had grown too accustomed to her erratic swings of moods to recognize they were manifestations of depression, of frustrations . . . and fearful secret anxieties about that lump. Her thin hand seemed gaunt, her nails long and witchy, as she handed me the envelope with my name on the outside. But her smile, for the first time, seemed warm, loving.

"Did I say thank ya fer all ya've been doin fer me, Heaven? Got me a daughta, at last—an ain't it somethin, though, ain't it, that Luke would come t'see me? Were ya t'one who sent fer him—were ya? Ya must have, cause he came in an he looked around, like he expected t'see ya. So go on, Heaven, go on, read what he says in his letta."

"This is Tom, my brother," I finally said.

"It's good to see you, Tom," said Cal, standing up and shaking his hand.

"Why, yer like Luke when he was yer age!" Kitty cried with delight, her pale eyes glowing strangely. "All ya need is black hair and black eyes . . . an ya'd be jus like yer pa! Ya would, ya would!"

She was touching, this devil-woman with her red hair and her long pink nails that had raked my skin many a time. Images of how she used to be flashed in and out of my brain; my ears rang with all the insults she'd thrown my way without regard for my feelings; and here she was putting tears in my eyes when I should have been feeling glad God was delivering to her just what she deserved. Yet I was crying. I sat in the chair that Cal pulled out for me and, with tears streaming to wet my blouse, I opened the letter from Pa and began to silently read.

"Daughta, read it *aloud*," whispered Kitty.

Again I glanced at her, sensing something different; then I began in a small voice:

"Dear Daughter,

"Sometimes a man does what he feels is necessary and lives to find out his problems could have been solved in better ways. I ask you to forgive me for things that can't be changed now.

"Our Jane and Keith are happy and healthy. They love their new parents, and Fanny loves hers.

"I have married again, and my wife insists that I try and put my family back together again. I have a fine home now, and earn a great deal of money. There is very little hope that I can buy back Keith and Our Jane, or Fanny, but I am hoping you and Tom will come to live with us. Your grandfather will also be there.

"Maybe this time I can be the kind of father you can love instead of hate.

Father"

There was an address and a telephone number beneath his name, but I could hardly read by this time. He'd never called me daughter before, never referred to himself as my father before—why now? I balled up the note and hurled it into the trash can near Kitty's bed.

Anger overrode all my other emotions. How could I trust a man who'd sell his children? How did I know for sure Tom and I would be all right in his care? What could he possibly do to earn a lot of money? Or had he married it? How could I believe anything he said? How could he know that Keith and Our Jane were truly happy where they were? Or Fanny? How could I know until I found out for myself?

Tom ran to retrieve the balled-up letter, and carefully he smoothed it out and read it silently. Each line he read made his face brighter.

"Why did ya do that?" asked Kitty with softness in her eyes. "It were a nice letta, it were, weren't it, Cal? Heaven, ya take it up an save it, cause there'll come a day when ya'll need t'see him again—" And then she failed and began to cry.

"Tom, let's go." I turned to leave.

"Wait a minute," whispered Kitty. "Got somethin else fer ya." She smiled weakly and took a small envelope from under her pillow. "Had a good talk wid yer pa—an he gave me this here t'keep fer ya, an give t'ya when t'time comes. It's my way of tryin t'make up fer what I did . . ." She floundered, glanced at Cal, then added, "I think t'time is now."

I was trembling as I took the second small envelope. What could Pa say in this one to make up for all he'd done? Maybe Our Jane and Keith were fine—but how could I be sure, when that horrible farmer had worked Tom like a slave, as Kitty had worked me? Then I glanced up and saw Tom with his eyes fixed on me, as if I held his life in his hands . . . and maybe I did. Oh, what harm would it do to read more lies?

Again I read his small handwriting. My eyes widened even as my heart began to race.

Pa'd come to the hospital hoping to find *me*.

Your grandpa has told me you have your heart set on going to Boston to find your mother's parents. If that is your choice, to go there instead of coming to live with me and my wife, enclosed is a plane ticket I bought for you to use, and I have called your Boston grandparents to tell them you might be coming. Here is their address and telephone number. Write to me to let me know how things go.

My muscles tightened from the shock I felt. Why was he doing this? To get rid of me a second time? There were two addresses at the bottom of the letter, one written hurriedly in pencil. I stared at the names: Mr. and Mrs. James L. Rawlings.

I looked up. "Heaven," Cal said softly, "it was Kitty who persuaded your father to put the names of the couple who bought Our Jane and Keith in that note you hold. Now you know where they are, and someday you can go to see them."

I couldn't speak, could hardly think.

Tom was reading over my shoulder. "Heavenly, you see, you see, he's not as bad as you think! Now we can visit Our Jane and Keith. But I remember that contract the lawyer made Pa sign . . . we can never take them away—" He stopped short, staring at my face. I felt odd, my knees weak, all my emotions draining into the floor. I'd so wanted to find Keith and Our Jane, and now it appeared I could. But the plane ticket in my hand seemed blackmail to force me to stay out of their lives. Trembling still, I jammed the small envelope and its contents into my pocket, and said good-bye to Kitty before I strode out into the hallway, leaving Tom still talking to Cal.

Let Cal stay. I didn't care.

In the hall outside of her room I called "Tom!" impatiently, tired of waiting when he continued to talk in a low voice with Cal. "I'm not going to wait forever."

I turned and walked away. Tom hurried to catch up, and outside the hospital I headed for the motel, thinking that right now, today, I'd head for Boston . . .

"Are you going with me to Boston, Tom?"

His long strides shortened to keep in step with me. He had his head lowered against the wind and rain. "Heavenly, we've got to talk."

"We can talk as we walk to the motel. I'll pack my things. Kitty's happy . . . did you see her face? Cal didn't even look at me. Why aren't you delighted to be going with me?"

"Everything has changed! Pa's different! Can't you tell by his letters? He went to see that woman, and she sees he's changed—why can't you? Heavenly, I want to go with you, you know I do, and Mr. Dennison said he'd pay my way, if that's what I wanted . . . but first I have to see Pa. I'm sure he's gone on to the Setterton home to look for you, and perhaps he's already been to visit Buck Henry, and suspects I am with you. We can catch him if we hurry."

"NO!" I flared, feeling my face burn with anger. "You go if you feel you have to, but I never want to see him again! He can't write two short notes and wipe the slate clean!"

"Then promise to stay put until you hear from me!"

I promised, still feeling numb from all that had happened to confuse my hatred. "Tom . . . you will go with me to Boston? Come with me, and together, after we're established, we'll go for Keith and Our Jane."

He was striding away from me! Turning at the corner to wave and smile. "Heavenly, hold on. Don't you dare go anywhere until you hear from me!"

I watched Tom walk away with a certain joy in his stride, as if he believed he'd find Pa, and with Pa he'd have a better life than with Buck Henry.

In the motel room, I lay down and gave in to a weird crying spell that left me weak and completely drained. I resolved before I slipped into sleep never to cry again. When the telephone rang I woke up to answer it, and heard Tom on the other end saying he'd found Pa, and now they both were coming to see me. "Heavenly, he was in Stonewall

Pharmacy asking for you, and for me. He's changed. You're not going to believe it when you see him! He's sorry for all the mean things he did and said, and he's going to say that when he sees you . . . so you be there when we drive up. Promise?"

I hung up without promising.

Tom had betrayed me!

Again I left the motel, to sit alone in the park. It wasn't until dark, when I felt Tom would have given up, that I returned to the motel and fell into the bed.

Tom wasn't going with me to Boston—he'd rather stay with Pa, and after all the vows we'd made to one another!

And Logan had flown off to college without making any effort to see me again. What did I have left but my mother's parents in Boston? Even Cal seemed indifferent to me now that he was so taken up with Kitty. I needed someone. Maybe this was Fate's way of seeing I went on to Boston to my grandparents.

I was packing my clothes when Cal came in and told me that he knew about Tom finding Pa, and Pa driving Tom to the motel to pick me up, only I'd gone. "They looked all over town for you, Heaven. Tom presumed you'd already flown to Boston, and he looked so hurt. Anyway, he and your father gave up their search. Where were you?"

"Hiding in the park," I admitted. Cal didn't understand; still, he held me and rocked me as if I were six instead of seventeen. "If they call to check on me, you tell them you haven't seen me," I pleaded.

"Yes," he agreed, his eyes troubled as they tried to meet mine. "I do think, though, you should see Tom again, and talk to your father. Heaven, maybe he has changed. Maybe he is sorry. Maybe you don't have to fly to Boston, and will like living with your father and his new wife."

I turned my back. Pa hadn't changed.

Cal left me alone, and I continued to pack, thinking of what a sorry mess I'd let myself in for when I chose Kitty Dennison and her husband. I had almost packed all my clothes when Cal opened the door and stared at me, his eyes narrowed. "You're still going to Boston?"

"Yes."

"What about me?"

"What about you?"

He blushed, had the decency to bow his head. "The doctors examined Kitty a little while ago. I know this sounds incredible, but she's better! Really better. Her white-cell count is almost normal. Her platelet count is rising. The tumor has shrunk just a bit, and if this keeps up they think she will live. Heaven, that visit from your father gave her the will to go on. Now she says it was always me she loved most, and she didn't know it until she was on the brink of death—what can I do? I can't turn away from my wife when she needs me so much, can I? So perhaps it is for the best that you go on to Boston with my prayers and all my love—and someday you and I will meet again, and maybe then you can forgive me for taking advantage of a young and sweet and beautiful girl."

Stunned, I widened my eyes in astonishment. "You never loved me!" I yelled accusingly, brokenly. "You used me!"

"I *do* love you! I will always love you! I hope wherever you go you'll always love *me* just a little. You were there when I needed someone. Go and forget Kitty and what was done, and don't step into Tom's life when he'll have everything going fine for him. Fanny is happy where she is. Leave Keith and Our Jane where they are. Your mother's people in Boston might object if you come with others. And forget me. I made my bed when I married Kitty. It doesn't have to be your bed too. Go now, while I have the strength to do the right thing. Go before she leaves that hospital a well woman, and her old self returns to seek you out and destroy you for taking what she thinks belongs solely to her. Kitty'll never truly change. She's been on the brink of death, afraid of what's on the other side . . . but once she recovers, she'll come after you. So, for your own sake . . . go now, today."

I didn't know what to say, or what to do. I could only stare with teary vision as he paced back and forth.

"Heaven, when your father was in the room with Kitty, she was the one who pleaded for him to tell you where Our Jane and Keith are. It was her gift to you to make up for all she's done."

I didn't understand, and yet my heartthrobs hurt so much I wanted to run from my body. "How can I believe anything Kitty says, or Pa?"

"Your father sensed you were running from him, and he guessed you'd never see him again, so he turned over to Tom more photographs of Our Jane and Keith so he could give them to you. I saw them, Heaven. They've grown since the last pictures sent to you. They have parents who adore them, and they live in a fine home, and attend one of the best schools in the country. If you have an idea of going there, remember you will take with you sad memories they might want to forget . . . think of that before you walk into their new lives. Give them time to grow up a bit more, Heaven, and give yourself time to mellow."

He said many things that I refused to hear.

Cal gave me cash that Pa had given him to pass on to me. I stared at the bills in my hand. A stack of twenty-dollar bills—amounting to five hundred dollars, the price Kitty and Cal had paid for me. My wide bleak eyes raised to meet Cal's—and he turned away.

That was all I needed to really decide me. I'd go! I'd never come back! Not even to see Logan again! I was finished with Winnerrow and the Willies, and everybody who'd said they loved me.

The first flight to Atlanta, from where I could transfer to a plane for Boston, was the next day at nine. Cal drove me to the airport, and carried my bags for me. He seemed nervous, anxious to get away, before he kissed me good-bye; then his stark eyes fleetingly swept over my face, scanned down to my shoes, then up again, slowly, slowly. "Your plane takes off in twenty minutes. I'd like to stay and wait with you . . . but I really should get back to Kitty."

"Yes, you really should," I said dryly. I wasn't going to say good-bye, wasn't . . . yet I did. "Good-bye . . . good-bye . . ." I wasn't going to cry or hurt inside to see him walk away without looking back, yet I did, though I saw him slow and hesitate before he shrugged, stood taller, and then walked off even faster. Going back to Kitty, and whatever the future held.

Twenty minutes to wait. How could I pass the time? I didn't have anyone now that Logan had run from me, now that Tom preferred Pa to me; and Fanny had long ago decided she didn't need me. . . . New doubts washed over me in great fearful waves. How did I know my mother's family would want me? But I had five hundred dollars, and even if things didn't work out right in Boston, I'd find a way to survive.

"Heaven! Heaven!" I heard a familiar voice call. Turning, I stared at the lovely young girl running my way. Was that Fanny? Fanny running in a slow and awkward way? "Heaven," she gasped, throwing her arms about me. "Tom came an tole me ya were leavin, an I couldn't let ya go way thinkin I don't kerr, when I do, I do! So skerred we'd be late an miss ya! Sorry I was mean t'ya, but they don't want me t'talk to ya!" She drew away and, with a broad, happy smile, threw open her heavy fur coat to display her bulging middle. Then she whispered in my ear. "Got t'Reverend's baby in there. It's gonna be so sweet, I jus know it is. His wife is gonna pass it off as her own, an give me ten grand fer it . . . then I'm headin on t'New York!"

Nothing could surprise me anymore. I could only stare at her. "You'd sell your own baby, for ten thousand?"

"Ya'd neva do that, would ya?" she asked. "Don't ya make me sorry

I said yes when Tom came an said I had t'come an say good-bye.'' Tears shone in her dark eyes. "Do what I feel I gotta, jus as ya do.''

She backed off, and only then did I see Tom, who was smiling at me in the sweetest, most loving way. He stepped forward to take me in his arms. "Cal Dennison called and told me you were leaving for Boston today, Heavenly . . . and he asked me not to bring along Pa.''

Yanking away, I cried out, "You're not coming with me, are you?''

He spread his large hands wide in a supplicating gesture. "LOOK AT ME! What do you think your grandparents will feel when they see you've brought your half brother with you? They won't want me! I'm all hillbilly! Like Pa! Haven't you said that many times since you came back here? I'm not refined and dainty the way you are, with culture and manners. Heavenly, I'm thinking of *your* welfare when I say I've got to stay with Pa, even though I'd much rather go with you.''

"You're lying! You'd rather stay with Pa!''

"Heavenly, please listen! You can't go to your mother's family hauling along all your hillbilly relatives! I want your life to turn out right, and it won't if I go with you!''

"Tom, PLEASE! I need you!''

He shook his head, his wild red hair flying. "If you need me later on, after you're settled in, write and I'll come, I swear that. But for now, start out fresh.''

"He's right,'' vouched Fanny, coming closer and looking around nervously, as anxious to leave as Cal had been. "It was Tom who made me come, an I'm glad I did. I love ya, Heaven. Didn't want t'close t'door in yer face . . . but I do what I hav'ta. Mrs. Wise is takin me away so my baby kin be born where nobody will know who we are; an when it's ova, she'll go back t'Winnerrow with *her own* baby, an she'll tell everyone it's hers, an I was jus a no-good Casteel an ran off with a no-good fella.''

"And you won't care?''

"Nope. Kin't affort ta.'' She smiled and backed off. "Tom, we gotta git back fore I'm missed. Ya promised me, ya did.''

Fanny, who'd always said she wanted a baby so much, was selling hers, just as Pa had sold his.

Again I turned to Tom. "So you're going to stay with Pa and his new wife. Why don't you tell me about her—one of the girls from *Shirley's Place?*''

He flushed and looked uneasy. "No, not that kind at all. Right now I've got to drive Fanny back home. Good luck, Heavenly. Write . . .'' And with those words he kissed my cheek and seized Fanny by the arm and hurried her away.

"Good-bye, good-bye!" I was calling again, waving frantically to Fanny, who turned and smiled through her tears. Oh, how I hated good-byes! Would I ever see Fanny or Tom again?

And why was Tom turning around to smile at me in that odd, sad kind of way? I watched him and Fanny until they were out of sight, then turned and sat again, thinking now I had ten more minutes before my flight.

It was a small airport with a nice little park outside where I could watch the planes as they landed. I paced back and forth in the frail autumn sunlight, with the wind whipping my hair and stealing all the neatness and making it wild again. I almost felt I was back in the hills.

My eyes swam in tears.

Then it was time for me to go to my plane, which was boarding passengers. For the first time in my life I was boarding a small plane, climbing the ramp, taking a seat and buckling my seat belt, as if I'd done this many times before. In Atlanta I transferred to another, larger plane that would land in Boston.

I'd begin a new life in a new place. My past would be unknown.

Strange that Kitty could be so happy just because my pa came to see her one time, and brought her roses, and said he was sorry, when Cal had bought her roses a hundred times, and he'd said he was sorry a million times, and that hadn't given her peace or happiness—or the will to survive. Who would have ever believed Pa could inspire that kind of lasting love?

But I'd asked myself that before, and hadn't found the answer. Why ask again?

I closed my eyes and determined to stop thinking about the past and clear the way for the future. Kitty and Cal would go back to Candlewick when she was released from the hospital, and they'd live on in her pink-and-white house, and somebody else would water all those plants. I reached in my pocket for a tissue to dry my eyes and blow my nose. To distract myself I opened the Winnerrow newspaper that I'd picked up in the airport just before I left and casually flipped through its pages.

It had only four sheets. On the fourth one I stared at an old photograph of Kitty Setterton Dennison, taken when she was about seventeen years old. How pretty she'd been, so fresh-faced and eager and sweet-looking. It was an obituary!

> Kitty Setterton Dennison, age 37, died today in the Winnerrow Memorial Hospital. The deceased is survived by her husband, Calhoun R. Dennison, her

parents, Mr. and Mrs. Porter Setterton, her sister, Maisie Setterton, and her brother, Daniel Setterton. Funeral services will be held at the Setterton family home on Main Street, on Wednesday, 2 P.M.

It took me a while before all that sank in.

Kitty was dead. Had died the day before I left Winnerrow. Cal had driven me to the airport, and he must have known and didn't tell me!

Why?

He'd rushed away . . . why?

Then I guessed why.

I bowed my face into my hands and sobbed again, not so much for Kitty as for the man who'd finally gained the freedom he'd lost at the age of twenty.

Freedom at last, I could almost hear him shouting, to be what he wanted, do what he wanted, how he wanted—and he didn't want me to deprive him of what he had to have.

What kind of crazy world was this anyway, that men could take love, then throw it back? Cal wanted to go on alone.

Bitterness overwhelmed me.

Maybe that's the way I should be, more like a man, take 'em and leave 'em and not care so much. I'd never have a husband; only lovers to hurt and discard, as Pa had done. Sobbing, I folded the paper and stuffed it into the pocket on the back of the seat in front of me.

Then, once more, I slipped a photograph out of a large brown envelope, the one Tom had handed me just before he pulled Fanny away, and at the time I hadn't even considered it important. "Hold on to this," he'd said in a low whisper, as if he hadn't wanted Fanny to know. There they were, Our Jane and Keith, looking older, stronger, happier. I stared and stared at Our Jane's sweet, pretty face, and then it came to me who she looked like. Annie Brandywine Casteel! Granny born again in Our Jane, just as I could see a bit of Grandpa in Keith's good-looking young face. Oh, they did deserve the best, the very best, and for now I'd do nothing to bring unhappy memories to them.

My tears dried. I knew without doubt that someday Fanny would reach her goals, no matter what she had to do to gain them.

What about me? I knew now that every event in anyone's life changed some facet of them—what was I now? Even as I thought that, my spine stiffened. From this day forward I'd step boldly, without fear or shame, not timid, nor shy, nor to be taken advantage of. If you gave me nothing else, Kitty, you did give me true knowledge about my strength; through thick and thin, through hell and back, I'd survive.

Sooner or later I'd come out the winner.

And as for Pa, he'd see me again. He still had a huge debt to pay, and pay he would before I quit this world that had shown me so little mercy.

As for now—Boston. The home of my mother. Where I'd change, as if magically, into all that my mother had been—and more.

Dawn

Momma once told me that she and Daddy named
me Dawn because I was born at the break of day.
That was the first of a thousand lies Momma and
Daddy would tell me and my brother Jimmy. Of
course, we wouldn't know they were lies, not for a
long time, not until the day they came to take us
away.

1

Another New Place

The sound of dresser drawers being opened and closed woke me. I heard Momma and Daddy whispering in their room, and my heart began to thump fast and hard. I pressed my palm against my chest, took a deep breath, and turned to wake Jimmy, but he was already sitting up in our sofa bed. Bathed in the silvery moonlight that came pouring through our bare window, my sixteen-year-old brother's face looked chiseled from granite. He sat there so still, listening. I lay there listening with him, listening to the hateful wind whistle through the cracks and crannies of this small cottage Daddy had found for us in Granville, a small, run-down town just outside of Washington, D.C. We had been here barely four months.

"What is it, Jimmy? What's going on?" I asked, shivering partly from the cold and partly because deep inside I knew the answer.

Jimmy fell back against his pillow and then brought his hands behind his head. In a sulk, he stared up at the dark ceiling. The pace of Momma's and Daddy's movements became more frenzied.

"We were gonna get a puppy here," Jimmy mumbled. "And this spring Momma and I were gonna plant a garden and grow our own vegetables."

I could feel his frustration and anger like heat from an iron radiator.

"What happened?" I asked mournfully, for I, too, had high hopes.

"Daddy came home later than usual," he said, a prophetic note of doom in his voice. "He rushed in here, his eyes wild. You know, bright and wide like they get sometimes. He went right in there, and not long after, they started packing. Might as well get up and get dressed," Jimmy said, throwing the blanket off him and turning to sit up. "They'll be out here shortly tellin' us to do it anyway."

I groaned. Not again, and not again in the middle of the night.

Jimmy leaned over to turn on the lamp by our pull-out bed and started to put on his socks so he wouldn't have to step down on a cold floor. He was so depressed, he didn't even worry about getting dressed in front of me. I fell back and watched him unfold his pants so he could slip into them, moving with a quiet resignation that made everything around me seem more like a dream. How I wished it were.

I was fourteen years old, and for as long as I could remember, we had been packing and unpacking, going from one place to another. It always seemed that just when my brother, Jimmy, and I had finally settled into a new school and finally made some friends and I got to know my teachers, we had to leave. Maybe we really were no better than homeless gypsies like Jimmy always said, wanderers, poorer than the poorest, for even the poorest families had some place they could call home, some place could return to when things went bad, a place where they had grandmas and grandpas or uncles and aunts to hug them and comfort them and make them feel good again. We would have settled even for cousins. At least, I would have.

I peeled back the blanket, and my nightgown fell away and exposed most of my bosom. I glanced at Jimmy and caught him gazing at me in the moonlight. He shifted his eyes away quickly. Embarrassment made my heart pitter-patter, and I pressed my palm against the bodice of my nightgown. I had never told any of my girlfriends at school that Jimmy and I shared even a room together, much less this dilapidated pull-out bed. I was too ashamed, and I knew how they would react, embarrassing both Jimmy and me even more.

I brought my feet down on the freezing-cold bare wood floor. My teeth chattering, I embraced myself and hurried across the small room to gather up a blouse and a sweater and a pair of jeans. Then I went into the bathroom to dress.

By the time I finished, Jimmy had his suitcase closed. It seemed we always left something else behind each time. There was only so much room in Daddy's old car anyway. I folded my nightgown and put it neatly into my own suitcase. The clasps were as hard as ever to close and Jimmy had to help.

Momma and Daddy's bedroom door opened and they came out,

their suitcases in hand, too. We stood there facing them, holding our own.

"Why do we have to leave in the middle of the night again?" I asked, looking at Daddy and wondering if leaving would make him angry as it so often did.

"Best time to travel," Daddy mumbled. He glared at me with a quick order not to ask too many questions. Jimmy was right—Daddy had that wild look again, a look that seemed so unnatural, it sent shivers up and down my spine. I hated it when Daddy got that look. He was a handsome man with rugged features, a cap of sleek brown hair and dark coal eyes. When the day came that I fell in love and decided to marry, I hoped my husband would be just as handsome as Daddy. But I hated it when Daddy was displeased—when he got that wild look. It marred his handsome features and made him ugly—something I couldn't bear to see.

"Jimmy, take the suitcases down. Dawn, you help your momma pack up whatever she wants from the kitchen."

I glanced at Jimmy. He was only two years older than I was, but there was a wider gap in our looks. He was tall and lean and muscular like Daddy. I was small with what Momma called "China doll features." And I really didn't take after Momma, either, because she was as tall as Daddy. She told me she was gangly and awkward when she was my age and looked more like a boy until she was thirteen, when she suddenly blossomed.

We didn't have many pictures of family. Matter of fact, all I had was one picture of Momma when she was fifteen. I would sit for hours gazing into her young face, searching for signs of myself. She was smiling in the picture and standing under a weeping willow tree. She wore an ankle-length straight skirt and a fluffy blouse with frilly sleeves and a frilly collar. Her long, dark hair looked soft and fresh. Even in this old black and white photo, her eyes sparkled with hope and love. Daddy said he'd taken the picture with a small box camera he had bought for a quarter from a friend of his. He wasn't sure it would work, but at least this picture came out. If we'd ever had any other photos, they'd been either lost or left behind during our many moves.

However, I thought that even in this simple old photograph with its black and white fading into sepia and its edges fraying, Momma looked so pretty that it was easy to see why Daddy had lost his heart to her so quickly even though she was only fifteen at the time. She was barefoot in the picture, and I thought she looked fresh and innocent and as lovely as anything else nature had to offer.

Momma and Jimmy had the same shimmering black hair and dark eyes. They both had bronze complexions with beautiful white teeth that allowed them ivory smiles. Daddy had dark brown hair, but mine was blond. And I had freckles over the tops of my cheeks. No one else in my family had freckles.

"What about that rake and shovel we bought for the garden?" Jimmy asked, careful not to let even a twinkle of hope show in his eyes.

"We ain't got the room," Daddy snapped.

Poor Jimmy, I thought. Momma said he was born all crunched up as tightly as a fist, his eyes sewn shut. She said she gave birth to Jimmy on a farm in Maryland. They had just arrived there and gone knocking on the door, hoping to find some work, when her labor began.

They told me I had been born on the road, too. They had hoped to have me born in a hospital, but they were forced to leave one town and start out for another where Daddy had already secured new employment. They left late in the afternoon one day and traveled all that day and that night.

"We were between nowhere and no place, and all of a sudden you wanted to come into this world," Momma told me. "Your daddy pulled the truck over and said, 'Here we go again, Sally Jean.' I crawled onto the truck bed where we had an old mattress, and as the sun came up, you entered this world. I remember how the birds were singing.

"I was looking at a bird as you were coming into this world, Dawn. That's why you sing so pretty," Momma said. "Your grandmomma always said whatever a woman looked at just before, during, or right after giving birth, that's what characteristics the child would have. The worst thing was to have a mouse or a rat in the house when a woman was pregnant."

"What would happen, Momma?" I asked, filled with wonder.

"The child would be sneaky, cowardly."

I sat back amazed when she told me all this. Momma had inherited so much wisdom. It made me wonder and wonder about our family, a family we had never seen. I wanted to know so much more, but it was difficult to get Momma and Daddy to talk about their early lives. I suppose that was because so much of it was painful and hard.

We knew they were both brought up on small farms in Georgia, where their people eked out poor livings from small patches of land. They had both come from big families that lived in run-down farmhouses. There just wasn't any room in either household for a newly married, very young couple with a pregnant wife, so they began what would be our family's history of traveling, traveling that had not yet ended. We were on our way again.

Momma and I filled a carton with those kitchenwares she wanted to take along and then gave it to Daddy to load in the car. When she was finished, she put her arm around my shoulders, and we both took one last look at the humble little kitchen.

Jimmy was standing in the doorway, watching. His eyes turned from pools of sadness to coal-black pools of anger when Daddy came in to hurry us along. Jimmy blamed him for our gypsy life. I wondered sometimes if maybe he wasn't right. Often Daddy seemed different from other men—more fidgety, more nervous. I would never say it, but I hated it whenever he stopped off at a bar on his way home from work. He would usually come home in a sulk and stand by the windows watching as if he were expecting something terrible. None of us could talk to him when he was in one of those moods. He was like that now.

"Better get going," he said, standing in the doorway, his eyes turning even colder as they rested for a second on me.

For a moment I was stunned. Why had Daddy given me such a cold look? It was almost as if he blamed me for our having to leave.

As soon as the thought entered my mind, I chased it away. I was being silly! Daddy would never blame me for anything. He loved me. He was just mad because Momma and I were being so slow and dawdling, instead of hurrying out the door. As if reading my mind, Momma suddenly spoke.

"Right," she said quickly. Momma and I started for the door, for we had all learned from hard experience that Daddy was unpredictable when his voice turned so tight with anger. Neither one of us wanted to invoke his wrath. We turned back once and then closed the door behind us, just like we had closed dozens of doors before.

There were few stars out. I didn't like nights without stars. On those nights shadows seemed so much darker and longer to me. Tonight was one of those nights—cold, dark, all the windows in houses around us black. The wind carried a piece of paper through the street, and off in the distance a dog howled. Then I heard a siren. Somewhere in the night someone was in trouble, I thought, some poor person was being carried off to the hospital, or maybe the police were chasing a criminal.

"Let's move along," Daddy ordered and sped up as if they were chasing us.

Jimmy and I squeezed ourselves into the backseat with our cartons and suitcases.

"Where we going this time?" Jimmy demanded without disguising his displeasure.

"Richmond," Momma said.

"Richmond!" we both said. We had been everywhere in Virginia, it seemed, but Richmond.

"Yep. Your daddy's got a job in a garage there, and I'm sure I can land me a chambermaid job in one of the motels."

"Richmond," Jimmy muttered under his breath. Big cities still frightened both of us.

As we drove away from Granville and the darkness fell around us, our sleepiness returned. Jimmy and I closed our eyes and fell asleep against each other as we had done so many times before.

Daddy had been planning our new move for a little while because he had already found us a place to live. Daddy often did things quietly and then announced them to us.

Because the rents in the city were so much higher, we could afford only a one-bedroom apartment, so Jimmy and I still had to share a room. And the sofa bed! It was barely big enough for the two of us. I knew sometimes he awoke before me but didn't move because my arm was on him and he didn't want to wake me and embarrass me about it. And there were those times he touched me accidentally where he wasn't supposed to. The blood would rush to his face, and he would leap off the bed as if it had started to burn. He wouldn't say anything to acknowledge he had touched me, and I wouldn't mention it.

It was usually like that. Jimmy and I simply ignored things that would embarrass other teenage boys and girls forced to live in such close quarters, but I couldn't help sitting by and dreaming longingly for the same wonderful privacy most of my girlfriends enjoyed, especially when they described how they could close their doors and gossip on their own phones or write love notes without anyone in their families knowing a thing about it. I was even afraid to keep a diary because everyone would be looking over my shoulder.

This apartment differed little from most of our previous homes—the same small rooms, peeling wallpaper, and chipped paint. The same windows that didn't close well. Jimmy hated our apartment so much that he said he would rather sleep in the street.

But just when we thought things were as bad as they could be, they got worse.

Late one afternoon months after we had moved to Richmond, Momma came home from work much earlier than usual. I had been hoping she would bring something else for us to have for dinner. We were at the tail end of the week, Daddy's payday, and most of our money from the previous week was gone. We had been able to have one or two good meals during the week, but now we were eating leftovers. My stomach was rumbling just as much as Jimmy's was, but before either of us could complain, the door opened and we both turned, surprised to see Momma come in. She stopped, shook her head, and started to cry. Then she hurried across the room to her bedroom.

"Momma! What's wrong?" I called after her, but her only answer was to slam the door. Jimmy looked at me and I at him, both of us frightened. I went to her door and knocked softly. "Momma?" Jimmy came up beside me and waited. "Momma, can we come in?" I opened the door and looked inside.

She was facedown on the bed, her shoulders shaking. We entered slowly, Jimmy right beside me. I sat down on the bed and put my hand on her shoulder.

"Momma?"

Finally she stopped sobbing and turned to look up at us.

"Did you lose your job, Momma?" Jimmy asked quickly.

"No, it's not that, Jimmy." She sat up, grinding her small fists against her eyes to wipe the tears away. "Although I won't be havin' the job all that much longer."

"Then what is it, Momma? Tell us," I begged.

She sniffed and pushed back her hair and took each of our hands into hers.

"You're gonna have either a new brother or sister," she declared.

My pounding heart paused. Jimmy's eyes widened and his mouth dropped open.

"It's my fault. I just ignored and ignored the signs. I never thought I was pregnant, because I didn't have no more children after Dawn. I finally went to a doctor today and found out I was a little more n' four months pregnant. Suddenly I'm gonna have a child, and now I won't be able to work, too," she said and began to cry again.

"Oh, Momma, don't cry." The thought of another mouth to feed dropped a black shadow over my heart. How could we manage it? We didn't have enough as it was.

I looked to Jimmy to urge him to say something comforting, but he looked stunned and angry. He just stood there, staring.

"Does Daddy know yet, Momma?" he asked.

"No," she said. She took a deep breath. "I'm too old and tired to have another baby," she whispered and shook her head.

"You're mad at me, ain'tcha, Jimmy?" Momma asked him. He was so sullen, I wanted to kick him. Finally he shook his head.

"Naw, Momma, I ain't mad at you. It's not *your* fault." He swung his eyes at me, and I knew he was blaming Daddy.

"Then give me a hug. I need one right now."

Jimmy looked away and then leaned toward Momma. He gave her a quick hug, mumbled something about having to get something outside, and then hurried out.

"You just lay back and rest, Momma," I said. "I almost have the dinner all made anyway."

"Dinner. What do we have to eat? I was going to try to pick up something tonight, see if we could charge any more on our grocery bill, but with this pregnancy and all, I clean forgot about eating."

"We'll make do, Momma," I said. "Daddy gets paid today, so tomorrow we'll eat better."

"I'm sorry, Dawn," she said, her face wrinkling up in preparation for her sobs again. She shook her head. "Jimmy's so mad. I can see it in his eyes. He's got Ormand's temper."

"He's just surprised, Momma. I'll see about dinner," I repeated and went out and closed the door softly behind me, my fingers trembling on the knob.

A baby, a little brother or sister! Where would a baby sleep? How could Momma take care of a baby? If she couldn't work, we would have even less money. Didn't grown-ups plan these things? How could they let it happen?

I went outside to look for Jimmy and found him throwing a rubber ball against the wall in the alley. It was mid-April, so the chill was out of the air, even in the early evening. I could just make out some stars starting their entrance onto the sky. The neon lights above the doorway of Frankie's Bar and Grill at the corner had been turned on. Sometimes, on his way home on a hot day, Daddy would stop in there for a cold beer. When the door was opened and closed, the laughter and the music from the jukebox spilled out and then died quickly on the sidewalk, a sidewalk always dirtied with papers and candy wrappers and other refuse that the wind lifted out of overflowing garbage cans. I could hear two cats in heat threaten each other in an alleyway. A man was shouting curses up at another man, who leaned out a two-story window about a block south of us. The man in the window just laughed down at him.

I turned to Jimmy. He was as tight as a fist again, and he was heaving all his anger with each and every throw of the ball.

"Jimmy?"

He didn't answer me.

"Jimmy, you don't want to make Momma feel any worse than she already does, do you?" I asked him softly. He seized the ball in the air and turned on me.

"What's the use of pretending, Dawn? One thing we definitely don't need right now is another child in the house. Look at what we're eating for dinner tonight!"

I swallowed hard. His words were like cold rain falling on a warm campfire.

"We don't even have hand-me-downs to give to a new baby," he continued. "We're gonna have to buy baby clothes and diapers and a crib. And babies need all sorts of lotions and creams, don't they?"

"They do, but—"

"Well, why didn't Daddy think of that, huh? He's off whistlin' and jawin' with those friends of his who hang around the garage, just as if he's on top of the world, and now here's this," he said, gesturing toward our building.

Why hadn't Daddy thought of that? I wondered. I had heard of girls going all the way and becoming pregnant, but that was because they were just girls and didn't know better.

"It just happened, I guess," I said, fishing for Jimmy to give his opinion.

"It doesn't just happen, Dawn. A woman doesn't wake up one morning and find out she's pregnant."

"Don't the parents plan to have it?"

He looked at me and shook his head.

"Daddy probably came home drunk one night and . . ."

"And what?"

"Oh, Dawn . . . they made the baby, that's all."

"And didn't know they had?"

"Well, they don't always make a baby each time they . . ." He shook his head. "You'll have to ask Momma about it. I don't know all the details," he said quickly, but I knew he did.

"It's going to be hell to pay when Daddy gets home, Dawn," he said, shaking his head as we walked back inside. He spoke in a voice just above a whisper and gave me a fearful chill. My heart pounded in anticipation.

Most of the time when trouble came raining down over us, Daddy would decide we had to pack up and run, but we couldn't run from this. Because I always cooked dinner, I knew better than anyone that we didn't have anything to spare for a baby. Not a cent, not a crumb.

When Daddy arrived home from work that night, he looked a lot more tired than usual and his hands and arms were all greasy.

"I had to pull out a car transmission and rebuild it in one day," he explained, thinking the way he looked was why Jimmy and I were staring at him so strangely. "Somethin' wrong?"

"Ormand," Momma called. Daddy hurried into the bedroom. I busied myself with the dinner, but my heart started to pound so hard I could barely breathe. Jimmy went to the window that looked out on the north side of the street and stood staring as still as a statue. We heard Momma crying again. After a while it grew quiet and then Daddy emerged. Jimmy pivoted expectantly.

"Well, now, you two already know, I reckon." He shook his head and looked back at the closed door behind him.

"How we gonna manage?" Jimmy asked quickly.

"I don't know," Daddy said, his eyes darkening. His face began to take on that mad look, his lips curling in at the corners, some whiteness of his teeth flashing through. He ran his fingers through his hair and sucked in some breath.

Jimmy flopped down in a kitchen chair. "Other people plan kids," he muttered.

Daddy's face flared. I couldn't believe he had said it. He knew Daddy's temper, but I recalled what Momma said: Jimmy had the same temper. Sometimes they were like two bulls with a red flag between them.

"Don't get smart," Daddy said and headed for the door.

"Where're you going, Daddy?" I called.

"I need to think," he said. "Eat without me."

Jimmy and I listened to Daddy's feet pound the hallway floor, his steps announcing the anger and turmoil in his body.

"Eat without him, he says," Jimmy quipped. "Grits and black-eyed peas."

"He's going to Frankie's," I predicted. Jimmy nodded in agreement and sat back, staring glumly at his plate.

"Where's Ormand?" Momma asked, stepping out of her bedroom.

"He went off to think, Momma," Jimmy said. "He's probably just trying to come up with a plan and needs to be alone," he added, hoping to ease her burden.

"I don't like him going off like that," Momma complained. "It never comes to no good. You should go look for him, Jimmy."

"Go look for him? I don't think so, Momma. He don't like it when I do that. Let's just eat and wait for him to come back." Momma wasn't happy about it, but she sat down and I served the grits and black-eyed peas. I had added some salt and a little bit of bacon grease I had saved.

"I'm sorry I didn't try to get us something else," Mommy said, apologizing again. "But Dawn, honey, you did real fine with this. It tastes good. Don't it, Jimmy?"

He looked up from his bowl. I saw he hadn't been listening. Jimmy could get lost in his own thoughts for hours and hours if no one pestered him, especially when he was unhappy.

"Huh? Oh. Yeah, this is good."

After supper Momma sat up for a while listening to the radio and reading one of the used magazines she had brought back from the motel she worked in. The hours ticked by. Every time we heard a door slam or the sound of footsteps, we anticipated Daddy coming through the door, but it grew later and later and he didn't reappear.

Whenever I gazed at Momma, I saw that sadness draped her face like a wet flag, heavy and hard to shake off. Finally she stood up and announced she had to go to bed. She took a deep breath, holding her hands against her chest, and headed for her bedroom.

"I'm tired too," Jimmy said. He got up and went to the bathroom to get ready for bed. I started to pull out the sofa bed, but then stopped, thinking about Momma lying in her bed, worried and frightened. In a moment I made up my mind—I opened the door quietly and left to look for Daddy.

I hesitated outside the door of Frankie's Bar and Grill. I had never been in a bar. My hand trembled as I reached out for the doorknob, but before I could pull it, the door swung open and a pale-skinned woman with too much lipstick and rouge on her face stepped out. She had a cigarette dangling from the corner of her mouth. She paused when she saw me and smiled. I saw she had teeth missing toward the back of her mouth.

"Why, what you doing coming in here, honey? This ain't no place for someone as young as you."

"I'm looking for Ormand Longchamp," I replied.

"Never heard of him," she said. "You don't stay in there long, honey. It ain't a place for kids," she added and walked past me, the stale odor of cigarettes and beer floating in her wake. I watched her for a moment and then entered Frankie's.

I had seen into it once in a while whenever someone opened the door, and I knew there was a long bar on the right with mirrors and shelves covered with liquor bottles. I saw the fans in the ceiling and the sawdust on the dirty brown wood slab floor. I had never seen the tables to the left.

A couple of men at the end of the bar turned my way when I stepped in. One smiled, the other just stared. The bartender, a short stout bald-headed man, was leaning against the wall. He had his arms folded across his chest.

"What do you want?" he asked, coming down the bar.

"I'm looking for Ormand Longchamp," I said. "I thought he might be in here." A glance down the bar didn't produce him.

"He joined the army," someone quipped.

"Shut up," the bartender snapped. Then he turned back to me. "He's over there," he said and gestured with his head toward the tables on the left. I looked and saw Daddy slumped over a table, but I was afraid to walk farther into the bar and grill. "You can wake him up and take him home," the bartender advised.

Some of the men at the bar spun around to watch me as if it were the evening's entertainment.

"Let her be," the bartender commanded.

I walked between the tables until I reached Daddy. He had his head on his arms. There were five empty bottles of beer on the table and another nearly emptied. A glass with just a little beer in it was in front of the bottle.

"Daddy," I said softly. He didn't budge. I looked back at the bar and saw that even the men who had continued to watch me had lost interest. "Daddy," I repeated a little louder. He stirred, but didn't lift his head. I poked him gently on the arm. "Daddy." He grunted and then slowly lifted his head.

"What?"

"Daddy, please come home now," I said. He wiped his eyes and gazed at me.

"What . . . What are you doing here, Dawn?" he asked quickly.

"Momma went to bed a while ago, but I know she's just lying there awake waiting for you, Daddy."

"You shouldn't come in a place like this," he said sharply, making me jump.

"I didn't want to come, Daddy, but—"

"All right, all right," he said. "I guess I can't do nothing right these days," he added, shaking his head.

"Just come home, Daddy. Everything will be all right."

"Yeah, yeah," he said. He gazed at his beer a moment and then pushed back from the table. "Let's get you outta here. You shouldn't be here," he repeated. He started to stand and then sat down hard.

He looked down at the bottles of beer again and then put his hand in his pocket and took out his billfold. He counted it quickly and shook his head.

"Lost track of what I spent," he said, more to himself than to me, but when he said it, it sent a cold chill down my back.

"How much did you spend, Daddy?"

"Too much," he moaned. "Afraid we won't be eating all that well this week, either," he concluded. He pushed himself away from the table again and stood up. "Come on," he said. Daddy didn't walk straight until we reached the door.

"Sleep tight!" one of the men at the bar called. Daddy didn't acknowledge him. He opened the door and we stepped out. I was never so happy to confront fresh air again. The musty smell of the bar had turned my stomach. Why would Daddy even want to walk in there, much less spend time there? I wondered. Daddy appreciated the fresh air, too, and took some deep breaths.

"I don't like you going in a place like that," he said, walking. He stopped suddenly and looked at me, shaking his head. "You're smarter and better than the rest of us, Dawn. You deserve better."

"I'm not better than anybody else, Daddy," I protested, but he had said all he was going to, and we continued to our apartment. When we opened the door, we found Jimmy already in the pull-out bed, the covers drawn so high, they nearly covered his face. He didn't turn our way. Daddy went right to his bedroom, and I crawled under the covers with Jimmy, who stirred.

"You went to Frankie's and got him?" he asked in a whisper.

"Yes."

"If I had been the one, he'd be furious," he said.

"No, he wouldn't, Jimmy, he'd . . ."

I stopped because we heard Momma moan. Then we heard what sounded like Daddy laughing. A moment later there was the distinct sound of the bedsprings. Jimmy and I knew what that meant. In our close quarters we had grown used to the sounds people often make whenever they make love. Of course, when we were younger, we didn't know what it meant, but when we learned, we pretended that we didn't hear it.

Jimmy drew the blanket up toward his ears again, but I was confused and a bit fascinated.

"Jimmy," I whispered.

"Go to sleep, Dawn," he pleaded.

"But, Jimmy, how can they—"

"Just go to sleep, will you?"

"I mean, Momma's pregnant. Can they still . . . ?" Jimmy didn't respond. "Isn't it dangerous?"

Jimmy turned toward me abruptly.

"Will you stop asking those kind of questions?"

"But I thought you might know. Boys usually know more than girls," I said.

"Well, I don't know," he replied. "Okay? So shut up." He turned his back to me again.

It quieted down in Momma and Daddy's room, but I couldn't stop wondering. I wished I had an older sister who wouldn't be embarrassed with my questions. I was too embarrassed to ask Momma about these things because I didn't want her to think Jimmy and I were eavesdropping.

My leg grazed Jimmy's, and he pulled away as if I had burned him. Then he slid over to his end of the bed until he was nearly off. I shifted as far over to mine as I could, too. Then I closed my eyes and tried to think of other things.

As I was falling asleep, I thought of that woman who had come to the bar door just as I was about to open it to enter. She was smiling down at me, her lips twisted and rubbery, her teeth yellow and the cigarette smoke twirling up and over her bloodshot eyes.

I was so glad I had managed to get Daddy home.

2

Fern

One afternoon during the first week of Momma's ninth month while I was preparing dinner and Jimmy was struggling over some homework on the kitchen table, we heard Momma scream. We rushed into the bedroom and found her clutching her stomach.

"What is it, Momma?" I asked, my heart pounding. "Momma!" Momma reached out and seized my hand.

"Call for an ambulance," she said through her clenched teeth. We didn't have a telephone in the apartment and had to use the pay phone on the corner. Jimmy shot out the door.

"Is this supposed to happen, Momma?" I asked her. She simply shook her head and moaned again, her fingernails pressing so hard and so sharply into my skin, they nearly caused me to bleed. She bit down on her lower lip. The pain came again and again. Her face turned a pale, sickly yellow.

"The hospital is sending an ambulance," Jimmy announced after charging back in.

"Did you call your daddy?" Momma asked Jimmy through her clenched teeth. The pain wouldn't let go.

"No," he replied. "I'll go do it, Momma."

"Tell him to go directly to the hospital," she ordered.

It seemed to take forever and ever for the ambulance to come. They put Momma on a stretcher and carried her out. I tried to squeeze her

343

hand before they closed the door, but the attendant forced me back. Jimmy stood beside me, his hands on his hips, his shoulders heaving with his deep, excited breaths.

The sky was ominously dark and it had begun to rain a colder, harder rain than we had been having. There was even some lightning across the bruised, charcoal-gray clouds. The gloom dropped a chill over me, and I shuddered and embraced myself as the ambulance attendants got in and started away.

"Come on," Jimmy said. "We'll catch the bus on Main Street."

He grabbed my hand and we ran. When we got off the bus at the hospital, we went directly to the emergency room and found Daddy speaking with a tall doctor with dark brown hair and cold, stern green eyes. Just as we reached them, we heard the doctor say, "The baby's turned wrong and we need to operate on your wife. We can't wait much longer. Just follow me to sign some papers and we'll get right to it, sir."

Jimmy and I watched Daddy walk off with the doctor, and then we sat on a bench in the hall.

"It's stupid," Jimmy suddenly muttered, "stupid to have a baby now."

"Don't say that, Jimmy," I chided. His words made my own fears crash in upon me like waves.

"Well, I don't want a baby who threatens Momma's life, and I don't want a baby who'll make our lives more miserable," he snapped, but he didn't say anything more about it when Daddy returned. I don't know how long we had been sitting there waiting before the doctor finally appeared again, but Jimmy had fallen asleep against me. As soon as we set eyes on the doctor, we sat up. Jimmy's eyelids fluttered open, and he searched the doctor's expression as frantically as I did.

"Congratulations, Mr. Longchamp," the doctor said, "you've got a seven pound, fourteen ounce baby girl." He extended his hand and Daddy shook it.

"Well, I'll be darned. And my wife?"

"She's in the recovery room. She had a hard time, Mr. Longchamp. Her blood count was a little lower than we like, so she's going to need to be built up."

"Thank you, Doctor. Thank you," Daddy said, still pumping his hand. The doctor's lips moved into a smile that didn't reach his eyes.

After we went up to maternity, all three of us gazed down at the tiny pink face wrapped in a white blanket. Baby Longchamp had her fingers curled. They looked no bigger than the fingers on my first doll. She had a patch of black hair, the same color and richness as Jimmy's and Momma's hair and not a sign of a freckle. That was a disappointment.

It took Momma longer than we expected to get back on her feet after she came home. Her weakened condition made her susceptible to a bad cold and a deep bronchial cough, and she couldn't breast-feed like she had planned, so we had another expense—formula.

Despite the hardships Fern's arrival brought, I couldn't help but be fascinated with my little sister. I saw the way she discovered her own hands, studied her own fingers. Her dark eyes, Momma's eyes, brightened with each of her discoveries. Soon she was able to clutch my finger with her tiny fist and hold on to it. Whenever she did that, I saw her struggle to pull herself up. She groaned like an old lady and made me laugh.

Her patch of black hair grew longer and longer. I combed the strands down the back of her head and down the sides, measuring their length until they reached the top of her ears and the middle of her neck. Before long, she was stretching with firmness, pushing her legs out and holding them straight. Her voice grew louder and sharper, too, which meant when she wanted to be fed, everyone knew it.

With Momma not yet very strong, I had to get up in the middle of the night to feed Fern. Jimmy complained a lot, pulled the blanket over his head, and moaned, especially when I turned on the lights. He threatened to sleep in the bathtub.

Daddy was usually grouchy in the morning from his lack of sleep, and as the sleepless nights went on, his face took on a gray, unhealthy look. Early each morning he would sit slumped in his chair, shaking his head like a man who couldn't believe how many storms he had been in. When he was like this, I was afraid to talk to him. Everything he said was usually gloom and doom. Most of the time that meant he was thinking of moving again. What scared me to the deepest place in my heart was the fear that one day he might just move on without us. Even though sometimes he scared me, I loved my father and longed to see one of his rare smiles come my way.

"When your luck turns bad," he would say, "there's nothing to do but change it. A branch that don't bend breaks."

"Momma looks like she's getting thinner and thinner and not stronger and stronger, Daddy," I whispered when I served him a cup of coffee one early morning. "And she won't go to the doctor."

"I know." He shook his head.

I took a deep breath and made the suggestion I knew he wouldn't want to hear. "Maybe we should sell the pearls, Daddy."

Our family owned one thing of value, one thing that had never been used to mend our hard times. A string of pearls so creamy white they took my breath away the one time I'd been allowed to hold them. Momma and Daddy considered them sacred. Jimmy wondered, as I did, why we clung to them so tenaciously. "The money it would bring in would give Momma a chance to really get well," I finished weakly.

Daddy looked up at me quickly and shook his head.

"Your momma would rather die than sell those pearls. That's all we got that ties us, ties you, to family."

How confusing this was to me. Neither Momma nor Daddy wanted to return to their family farms in Georgia to visit our relatives, and yet the pearls, because they were all we had to remind Momma of her family, were treated like something religious. They were kept hidden in the bottom of a dresser drawer. I couldn't recall a time Momma had even worn them.

After Daddy left I was going to go back to sleep, but changed my mind, thinking that it would only make me feel more tired. So I started to get dressed. I thought Jimmy was fast asleep. He and I shared an old dresser Daddy had picked up at a lawn sale. It was on his side of the pull-out bed. I tiptoed over to it and slipped my nightgown off. Then I pulled out my drawer gently, searching for my underthings in the subdued light that spilled in from the bulb in the stove when the stove door was left down. I was standing there naked trying to decide what I should wear that would be warm enough for what looked to be another bitterly cold day, when I turned slightly and out of the corner of my eye caught Jimmy gazing up at me.

I know I should have covered up quickly, but he didn't see I had turned slightly and I couldn't help but be intrigued by the way he stared. His gaze moved up and down my body, drinking me in slowly. When he lifted his eyes higher, he saw me watching him. He turned quickly on his back and locked his eyes on the ceiling. I quickly drew my nightgown up against my body, took out what I wanted to wear, and scurried across the room to the bathroom to dress. We didn't talk about it, but I couldn't get the look in his eyes out of my mind.

In January Momma, who was still thin and weak, got a part-time job cleaning Mrs. Anderson's house every Friday. The Andersons owned a small grocery two blocks away. Occasionally Mrs. Anderson gave Momma a nice chicken or a small turkey. One Friday afternoon Daddy surprised Jimmy and me by coming home much earlier from work.

"Old man Stratton's selling the garage," he announced. "With those two bigger and more modern garages being built only blocks away, business has begun to drop off something terrible. People who are buying the garage don't want to run it as a garage. They want the property to develop housing."

Here we go again, I thought—Daddy loses a job and we have to move. When I told one of my friends, Patty Butler, about our many moves, she said she thought it might be fun to go from school to school.

"It's not fun," I told her. "You always feel like you've got ketchup on your face or a big mole on the tip of your nose when you first walk into a new classroom. All the kids turn around and stare and stare, watching my every move and listening to my voice. I had a teacher once who was so angry I had interrupted her class, she made me stand in front of the room until she was finished with her lesson, and all the time the students were goggling me. I didn't know where to shift my eyes. It was so embarrassing," I said, but I knew Patty couldn't understand just how hard it really was to enter a new school and confront new faces so often. She had lived in Richmond all her life. I couldn't even begin to imagine what that was like: to live in the same house and have your own room for as long as you could remember, to have relatives nearby to hold you and love you, to know your neighbors forever and ever and be so close to them, they were like family. I hugged my arms around myself and wished with all my heart that one day I might live like that. But I knew it could never happen. I'd always be a stranger.

Now Jimmy and I looked at each other and turned to Daddy, expecting him to tell us to start packing. But instead of looking sour, he suddenly smiled.

"Where's your ma?" he asked.

"She's not back from work yet, Daddy," I said.

"Well, today's the last day she's gonna work in other people's houses," he said. He looked around the apartment and nodded. "The last time," he repeated. I glanced quickly at Jimmy, who looked just as astonished as I was.

"Why?"

"What's happening?" Jimmy inquired.

"I got a new and much, much better job today," Daddy said.

"We're going to stay here, Daddy?" I asked.

"Yep and that ain't the best yet. You two are gonna go to one of the finest schools in the South, and it ain't gonna cost us nothing," he announced.

"Cost us?" Jimmy said, his face twisted with confusion. "Why should it cost us to go to school, Daddy? It's never cost us before, has it?"

"No, son, but that's because you and your sister been going to public schools, but now you're going to a private school."

"A private school!" I gasped. I wasn't sure, but I thought that meant very wealthy kids whose families had important names and whose fathers owned big estates with mansions and armies of servants and whose mothers were society women who had their pictures taken at charity balls. My heart began to pound. I was excited, but also quite frightened of the idea. When I looked at Jimmy, I saw his eyes had shadowed and grown deep and dark.

"Us? Go to a fancy private school in Richmond?" he asked.

"That's it, son. You're getting in tuition free."

"Well, why is that, Daddy?" I asked.

"I'm going to be a maintenance supervisor there and free tuition for my children comes with the job," he said proudly.

"What's the name of this school?" I asked, my heart still fluttering.

"Emerson Peabody," he replied.

"Emerson Peabody?" Jimmy twisted his mouth up as if he had bitten into a sour apple. "What kind of a name is that for a school? I ain't going to no school named Emerson Peabody," Jimmy said, shaking his head and backing up toward the couch. "One thing I don't need is to be around a bunch of rich, spoiled kids," he added and flopped down again and folded his arms across his chest.

"Now, you just hold on here, Jimmy boy. You'll go where I tell you to go to school. This here's an opportunity, something very expensive for free, too."

"I don't care," Jimmy said defiantly, his eyes shooting sparks.

"Oh, you don't? Well, you will." Daddy's own eyes shot sparks, and I could see he was maintaining his temper. "Whether you like it or not, you're both gonna get the best education around, and all for free," Daddy repeated.

Just then we heard the outside door opening and Momma start coming down the hallway. From the sound of her slow, ponderous footsteps, I knew she was exhausted. A sensation of cold fear seized my heart when I heard her pause and break out in one of her fits of coughing. I ran to the doorway and looked at her leaning against the wall.

"*Momma!*" I cried.

"I'm all right. I'm all right," Momma said, holding her hand up toward me. "I just lost my breath a moment," she explained.

"You sure you're all right, Sally Jean?" Daddy asked her, his face a face of solid worry.

"I'm all right; I'm all right. There wasn't much to do. Mrs. Anderson had a bunch of her elderly friends over is all. They didn't make no mess to speak of. So," she said, seeing the way we were standing and looking at her. "What are you all standing around here and looking like that for?"

"I got news, Sally Jean," Daddy said and smiled. Momma's eyes began to brighten.

"What sort of news?"

"A new job," he said and told her all of it. She sat down on a kitchen chair to catch her breath again, this time from the excitement.

"Oh, children," she exclaimed, "ain't this wonderful news? It's the best present we could get."

"Yes, Momma," I said, but Jimmy looked down.

"Why's Jimmy looking sour?" Momma asked.

"He doesn't want to go to Emerson Peabody," I said.

"We won't fit in there, Momma!" Jimmy cried. Suddenly I was so angry at Jimmy, I wanted to punch him or scream at him. Momma had been so happy she had looked like her old self for a moment, and here he was making her sad again. I guess he realized it because he took a deep breath and sighed. "But I guess it don't matter what school I go to."

"Don't go putting yourself down, Jimmy. You'll show them rich kids something yet."

That night I had a hard time falling asleep. I stared through the darkness until my eyes adjusted, and I could faintly see Jimmy's face, the usually proud, hard mouth and eyes grown soft now that they were hidden by the night.

"Don't worry about being with rich kids, Jimmy," I said, knowing he was awake beside me. "Just because they're rich doesn't mean they're better than us."

"I never said it did," he said. "But I know rich kids. They think it makes them better."

"Don't you think there'll be at least a few kids we can make friends with?" I asked, my fears finally exploding to the surface with his.

"Sure. All the students at Emerson Peabody are just dying to make friends with the Longchamp kids."

I knew Jimmy had to be very worried—normally, he would try to protect me from my own dark side.

Deep down I hoped Daddy wasn't reaching too hard and too far for us.

A little more than a week later Jimmy and I had to begin attendance at our new school. The night before, I had picked out the nicest dress I had: a cotton dress of turquoise blue with three-quarter sleeves. It was a little wrinkled, so I ironed it and tried to take out a stain I had never noticed in the collar.

"Why are you working so hard on what to wear?" Jimmy asked. "I'm just wearing my dungarees and white polo shirt like always."

"Oh, Jimmy," I pleaded. "Just tomorrow wear your nice pants and the dress shirt."

"I'm not putting on airs for anyone."

"It's not putting on airs to look nice the first day you go to a new school, Jimmy. Couldn't you do it this once? For Daddy? For me?" I added.

"It's just a waste," he said, but I knew he would do it.

As usual, I was so nervous about entering a new school and meeting new friends, I took forever to fall asleep and had a harder time than usual waking up early. Jimmy hated getting up early, and now he had to get up and get himself ready earlier than ever because the school was in another part of the city and we had to go with Daddy. It was still quite dark when I rose from my bed. Of course, Jimmy just moaned and put the pillow over his head when I poked him in the shoulder, but I flicked on the lights.

"Come on, Jimmy. Don't make it harder than it has to be," I urged. I was in and out of the bathroom and making the coffee before Daddy came out of his bedroom. He got ready next, and then the both of us nagged Jimmy until he got up looking more like a sleepwalker and made his way to the bathroom.

When we left for school, the city looked so peaceful. The sun had just come up and some of the rays were reflected off store windows. Soon we were in a much finer part of Richmond. The houses were bigger and the streets were cleaner. Daddy made a few more turns, and suddenly the city seemed to disappear entirely. We were driving down a country road with farmhouses and fields. And then, just as magical as anything, Emerson Peabody appeared before us.

It didn't look like a school. It wasn't built out of cold brick or cement painted an ugly orange or yellow. Instead, it was a tall white structure that reminded me more of one of the museums in Washington, D.C. It had vast acreage around it, with hedges lining the driveway and trees everywhere. I saw a small pond off to the right as well. But it was the building itself that was most impressive.

The front entrance resembled the entrance to a great mansion. There were long, wide steps that led up to the pillars and portico, above which were engraved the words EMERSON PEABODY. Right in front was a statue of a stern-looking gentleman who turned out to be Emerson Peabody himself. Although there was a parking lot in front, Daddy had to drive around to the rear of the building, where the employees parked.

When we turned around the corner, we saw the playing fields: football field, baseball field, tennis courts, and Olympic-size pool. Jimmy whistled through his teeth.

"Is this a school or a hotel?" he asked.

Daddy pulled into his parking spot and turned off the engine. Then he turned to us, his face somber.

"The principal's a lady," he said. "Her name's Mrs. Turnbell, and she meets and speaks to every new student who comes here. She's here early, too, so she's waiting in her office for both of you."

"What's she like, Daddy?" I asked.

"Well, she's got eyes as green as cucumbers that she glues on you when she talks to you. She ain't more n' five feet one, I'd say, but she's a tough one, as tough as raw bear meat. She's one of them blue bloods whose family goes back to the Revolutionary War. I gotta take you up there before I get to work," Daddy said.

We followed Daddy through a rear entrance that took us up a short stairway to the main corridor of the school. The halls were immaculate, not a line of graffiti on a wall. The sunlight came through a corner window making the floors shine.

"Spick and span, ain't it?" Daddy said. "That's my responsibility," he added proudly.

As we walked along, we gazed into the classrooms. They were much smaller than any we had seen, but the desks looked big and brand-new. In one of the rooms I saw a young woman with dark brown hair preparing something on the blackboard for her soon-to-arrive class. As we went by, she looked our way and smiled.

Daddy stopped in front of a door marked PRINCIPAL. He quickly brushed back the sides of his hair with the palms of his hands and opened the door. We stepped into a cozy outer office that had a small counter facing the door. There was a black leather settee to the right and a small wooden table in front of it with magazines piled neatly on top. I thought it looked more like a doctor's waiting room than a school principal's. A tall, thin woman with eyeglasses as thick as goggles appeared at the gate. Her dull light brown hair was cut just below her ears.

"Mr. Longchamp, Mrs. Turnbell has been waiting," she said.

Without a friendly sign in her face, the tall woman opened the gate and stepped back for us to walk through to the second door, Mrs. Turnbell's inner office. She knocked softly and then opened the door only enough to peer in.

"The Longchamp children are here, Mrs. Turnbell," she said. We heard a thin, high-pitched voice say, "Show them in."

The tall woman stepped back, and we entered right behind Daddy. Mrs. Turnbell, who wore a dark blue jacket and skirt with a white blouse, stood up behind her desk. She had silver hair wrapped in a tight bun at the back of her head, the strands pulled so tightly at the sides, that they pulled at the corners of her eyes, which were piercing green, just as Daddy said. She didn't wear any makeup, not even a touch of lipstick. She had a complexion even lighter than mine, with skin so thin, I could see the crisscrossing tiny blue veins in her temples.

"This here's my kids, Mrs. Turnbell," Daddy declared.

"I assumed that, Mr. Longchamp. You're late. You know the other children will be arriving shortly."

"Well, we got here as soon as we could, ma'am. I—"

"Never mind. Please be seated," she said to us and indicated the chairs in front of her desk. Daddy stood back, folding his arms across his chest. When I looked back at him, I saw a cold sharpness in his eyes. He was holding back his anger.

"Should I stay?" he asked.

"Of course, Mr. Longchamp. I like the parents to be present when I explain to students the philosophies of the Emerson Peabody School, so everyone understands. I was hoping your mother would be able to come as well," she said to us.

Jimmy glared back at her. I could feel the tension in his body.

"Our momma's not feeling that well yet, ma'am," I said. "And we have a baby sister she has to mind."

"Yes. Be that as it may," Mrs. Turnbell said and sat down herself. "I trust you will take back to her everything I tell you anyway. Now, then," she said, looking at some papers before her on her desk. Everything on it was neatly arranged. "Your name is Dawn?"

"Yes, ma'am."

"Dawn," she repeated and shook her head and looked up at Daddy. "That's the child's full Christian name?"

"Yes, ma'am."

"Very well, and you are James?"

"Jimmy," Jimmy corrected.

"We don't use nicknames here, James." She clasped her hands and leaned toward us, fixing her gaze on Jimmy. "Those sort of things might have been tolerated at the other institutions you attended, public institutions," she said, making the word *public* sound like a curse word, "but this is a special school. Our students come from the finest families in the South, sons and daughters of people with heritage and position. Names are respected; names are important, as important as anything else.

"I'll come right to the point. I know you children haven't had the same upbringing and advantages as the rest of my students have had, and I imagine it will take you two a little longer to fit in. However, I expect that very shortly you two will adjust and conduct yourselves like Emerson Peabody students are supposed to conduct themselves.

"You will address all your teachers as either sir or ma'am. You will come to school dressed neatly and be clean. Never challenge a command. I have a copy of our rules here, and I expect both of you to read and commit them all to memory."

She turned toward Jimmy.

"We don't tolerate bad language, fighting, or disrespect in any form or manner. We expect students to treat each other with respect, too. We frown on tardiness and loitering, and we will not stand for any sort of vandalism when it comes to our beautiful building.

"Very soon you will see how special Emerson Peabody is, and you will realize how lucky you are to be here. Which brings me to my final point: In a real sense, you two are guests. The rest of the student body pays a handsome fee to be able to attend Emerson Peabody. The board of trustees has made it possible for you two to attend because of your father. Therefore, you have an added responsibility to behave and be a credit to our school.

"Am I understood?"

"Yes, ma'am," I said quickly. Jimmy glared at her with defiance. I held my breath, hoping he wouldn't say anything nasty.

"James?"

"I understand," he said in a somber tone.

"Very well," she said and sat back. "Mr. Longchamp, you may resume your duties. You two will go out to Miss Jackson, who will provide you with your class schedules and assign a locker to each of you." She stood up abruptly, and Jimmy and I stood up, too. She stared at us a moment longer and then nodded. Daddy started out first.

"James," she called just as we reached the door. He and I turned back. "It would be nice if you shined your shoes. Remember, we are often judged by our appearance." Jimmy didn't reply. He walked out ahead of me.

"I'll try to get him to do it, ma'am," I said. She nodded and I closed the door behind me.

"I gotta get to work," Daddy said and then left the office quickly.

"Well," Jimmy said. "Welcome to Emerson Peabody. Still think it's going to be peaches and cream?"

I swallowed hard; my heart was pounding.

"I bet she's that way with every new student, Jimmy."

"Jimmy? Didn'tcha hear? It's James," he said with an affected accent. Then he shook his head.

"We're in for it now," he said.

3

Always a Stranger

The first day at a new school was never easy, but Mrs. Turnbell had made it harder for us. I couldn't get the trembles out of my body as Jimmy and I left the principal's office with our schedules. In some schools the principal assigned a big brother and a big sister to help us get started and find our way around, but here at Emerson Peabody we were thrown out to sink or swim on our own.

We weren't halfway down the main corridor when doors began to open and students began to enter. They came in laughing and talking, acting like any other students we had seen, only how they were dressed!

All of the girls had on expensive-looking, beautiful winter coats made of the softest wool I had ever seen. Some of the coats even had fur trim on the collars. The boys all wore navy blue jackets and ties and khaki-colored slacks and the girls wore pretty dresses or skirts and blouses. Everyone's clothes looked new. They were all dressed as if this were their first day, too, only it wasn't. They were in their regular everyday school clothes!

Jimmy and I stopped in our tracks and stared, and when the students saw us, they stared, too, some very curious, some looking and then laughing to each other. They moved about in small clumps of friends. Most had been brought to the school in shiny clean buttercup-yellow buses, but we could see from gazing out the opening doors that some of the older students drove to school in their own fancy cars.

No one came over to introduce him or herself. When they approached us, they went to one side or the other, parting around us as if we were contagious. I tried smiling at this girl or that, but none really smiled back. Jimmy just glared. Soon we were at the center of a pool of laughter and noise.

I looked at the papers that told us the times for the class periods and realized we had to move along if we weren't going to be late the very first day. In fact, just as we got our lockers opened and hung up our coats, the bell rang to signal that everyone had to go to homeroom.

"Good luck, Jimmy," I said when I left him at the beginning of the corridor.

"I'll need it," he replied and sauntered off.

Homeroom at Emerson Peabody was the same as it was anywhere else. My homeroom teacher, Mr. Wengrow, was a short, stout, curly-haired man who held a yardstick in his hand like a whip and tapped it on his desk every time someone's voice went over a whisper or he had something to say. All of the students looked up at him attentively, their hands folded on their desks. When I entered, every head turned my way. It made me feel like I was a magnet and their heads and bodies were made of iron. Mr. Wengrow took my schedule sheet. He read it, pressed his lips together, and entered my name in his roll book. Then he tapped his yardstick.

"Boys and girls, I'd like to introduce you to a new student. Her name is Dawn Longchamp. Dawn, I'm Mr. Wengrow. Welcome to 10Y and to Emerson Peabody. You can take the next to last seat in the second row. And Michael Standard, make sure your feet aren't on the back of her chair," he warned.

The students looked at Michael, a small boy with dark brown hair and an impish grin. There was some tittering as he straightened in his seat. I thanked Mr. Wengrow and walked back to sit at my desk. Everyone's eyes were still on me. A girl wearing thick blue-framed glasses across from me offered me a smile of welcome. I smiled back. She had bright red hair tied in a ponytail, that hung listlessly down her back. I saw she had long thin pale arms and thin pale legs that were covered all over with pale red freckles. I thought about Momma telling me how awkward and gangly she was when she was my age.

I heard the public address system click on. Mr. Wengrow straightened into attention and glared around the room to be sure everyone was being attentive. Then Mrs. Turnbell came on and commanded everyone to rise for the Pledge of Allegiance, after which she made a series of announcements about the activities of the day. When she was finished and the public address system clicked off, we were permitted to sit down, but almost as soon as we did, the bell rang to begin the first-period class.

"Hi," the girl with the red ponytail said. "I'm Louise Williams." When she stood next to me, I realized how tall she was. She had a long bony nose and thin lips, but her timid eyes held more warmth than anyone else's had yet at this school. "What do you have first?" she asked.

"Phys ed," I said.

"Mrs. Allen?"

I looked at my schedule card.

"Yes."

"Good. You're in my class. Let me see your schedule," she added, practically ripping it out of my hand. "Oh, you're in a lot of my classes. You'll have to tell me all about yourself, who your parents are and where you live. What a nice dress. It must be your favorite; you look like you're wearing it out. Where did you go to school before? Do you know anyone here yet?" She fired one question after another at me before we even reached the door. I just shook my head and smiled.

"Come on," Louise said, urging me along.

From the way the other girls ignored Louise as we passed through the corridor to our first class, I gathered that she wasn't very popular. It was always hard to break the ice in a new school, but usually there were cracks to find. Here, the ice around me seemed solid, except for Louise, who talked a streak from homeroom to our first class.

By the time we reached the gymnasium, I knew that she was very good in math and science and only fair in history and English. Her daddy was a lawyer in a family firm that went back just ages and ages, and she had two brothers and a sister who were still in grade school.

"Mrs. Allen's office is over there," Louise said, pointing. "She'll assign you a locker and give you a gym suit and a towel for your shower." With that, she hurried off to change.

Mrs. Allen was a tall woman about forty years old. "All the girls must take showers after class," she insisted as she handed me a towel. I nodded. "Come on," she said. She looked stern as we walked toward the locker room. The loud chatter eased up when we entered, and all the girls turned our way. It was a mixed class with girls from three different grades. Louise was already in her uniform.

"Girls, I would like you all to meet a new student, Dawn Longchamp. Let's see," Mrs. Allen said, "your locker is over there"—she pointed across the room—"next to Clara Sue Cutler."

I gazed at the blond girl with the chubby face and figure who was standing at the center of a small clique. None of them were in uniform yet. Mrs. Allen's eyes narrowed as she led me across the locker room.

"What's taking you girls so long?" she asked and then sniffed. "I smell smoke. Have you girls been smoking?" she demanded with her hands on her hips. They all looked at one another anxiously. Then I saw some smoke coming out of a locker.

"It's not a cigarette, Mrs. Allen," I said. "Look."

Mrs. Allen squinted and moved to the locker quickly.

"Clara Sue, open this locker immediately," she demanded.

The chubby girl sauntered over to it and worked the combination. When she opened it, Mrs. Allen made her stand back. There was a lit cigarette burning on the shelf.

"I don't know how that got in there," Clara Sue said, her eyes wide with what was obviously fake amazement.

"Oh, you don't, don't you?"

"I'm not smoking it. You can't say I'm smoking," Clara Sue protested haughtily.

Mrs. Allen lifted the burning cigarette out of the locker, holding it between her forefinger and thumb as though it were a cylinder of disease.

"Behold, girls," she said, "a cigarette that smokes itself."

There was some giggling. Clara Sue looked very uncomfortable.

"All right, everyone get dressed and quickly. Miss Cutler, you and I will have a talk about this later," she said, then pivoted and left the locker. The moment she was gone, Clara Sue came at me, her face red and bloated with anger.

"You stupid idiot!" she screamed. "Why did you tell her?"

"I thought it was a fire," I explained.

"Oh, brother. Who are you, Alice in Wonderland? Now you got me in trouble."

"I'm sorry, I . . ."

I looked around. All the girls were glaring at me. "I didn't mean it. Honest. I thought I was helping you."

"Helping?" She shook her head. "You helped me into trouble, that's what you did."

Everyone nodded and the group broke up so everyone could finish dressing. I looked to Louise, but even she turned away. Afterward, the girls were very stand-offish in the gym. Every chance she got, Clara

Sue glared hatefully at me. I tried to explain again, but she wasn't interested.

When Mrs. Allen blew the whistle to end the period and send us to the showers, I tried to get Louise's attention.

"You got her in trouble," was all she would say.

Here I was only an hour or so in a new school and already I had made enemies when all I wanted to do was make some new friends. As soon as I saw Clara Sue, I apologized again, making it sound as sincere as I could.

"It's all right," Clara Sue suddenly said. "I shouldn't have blamed you. I just lost my temper. It was my own fault."

"Really, I wouldn't have pointed out the smoke if I'd thought you were smoking. I don't tattletale."

"I believe you. Girls," she said to those nearest, "we shouldn't blame Dawn. That's your name, right? Dawn?"

"Uh-huh."

"Do you have any brothers or sisters?"

"A brother," I said quickly.

"What's his name, Afternoon?" a tall beautiful girl with dark hair asked. Everyone laughed.

"We better get moving or we're going to be late for our next class," Clara Sue announced. It was easy to see that many of the girls looked up to her as a leader. I couldn't believe I'd had the bad luck to begin by getting her in trouble. Of all the girls to get in trouble, I thought, and breathed a sigh of relief, grateful for her forgiveness. I took off my gym uniform quickly and followed everyone to the showers. They were nice showers, clean stalls with flower-print shower curtains, and the water was warm, too.

"You better get a move on in there," I heard Mrs. Allen call.

I stepped out of the shower and wiped myself dry as quickly as I could. Then I wrapped the towel around my body and rushed to my locker. It was wide open. Had I forgotten to lock it? I wondered. I discovered the answer very quickly. Except for my shoes, all my clothes were gone.

"Where are my clothes?" I cried. I turned around. All the girls were looking my way and smiling. Clara Sue was standing by the sink, brushing her hair. "Please. This isn't funny. Those are my best clothes."

That made everyone laugh. I looked to Louise, but she turned away quickly, slammed her locker shut, and hurried out of the locker room. Soon everyone but me was leaving.

"Please!" I cried. "Who knows where my clothes are?"

"They're being washed," someone called back.

"Washed? What does that mean? Washed?"

I spun around, the towel still tucked in over my body. I was alone in the locker room. The bells were ringing. What was I going to do?

I started looking everywhere, under benches, in corners, but I found nothing until I went into the bathroom and checked the stalls.

"Oh, no!" I cried. They had thrown my clothes into the toilet. There was my pretty dress, my bra, and my panties. Even my socks, soaking with toilet paper floating around it all for good measure. And the water was discolored. Someone had urinated in there, too!

I fell back against the stall door and sobbed. What was I going to do?

"Who's left in here?" I heard Mrs. Allen ask.

"It's me," I bawled. She stepped into the bathroom.

"Well, what are you . . ."

I pointed down at the toilet, and she gazed into the stall.

"Oh, no . . . who did this?"

"I don't know, Mrs. Allen."

"I don't have any trouble guessing," she said sternly.

"What will I do?"

She thought a moment, shaking her head.

"Fish them out and we'll put them in the washer and dryer with the towels. In the meantime, you will have to wear your gym uniform."

"To classes?"

"There's nothing else you can do, Dawn. I'm sorry."

"But . . . everyone will laugh at me."

"It's up to you. You will miss a few classes by the time this is all washed and dried out. I'll go to see Mrs. Turnbell and explain what happened."

I nodded and lowered my head in defeat as I walked back to my locker to put on my gym uniform.

As the morning went on, I found most of my teachers to be kind and sympathetic once they heard what had happened, but the rest of the students thought it was very funny, and everywhere I looked I found them smiling and laughing at me. It was always hard to face new students whenever I went to a new school, but here, before I even got a chance to meet anyone and anyone got a chance to know me, I was the laughingstock.

When Jimmy saw me in the hallway and I told him what had happened, he was outraged.

"What did I tell you about this place?" he said loud enough for most of the students around us in the hallway to hear. "I'd just like to know who did it, that's all. I'd just like to get my hands on her."

"It's all right, Jimmy," I said, trying to calm him down. "I'll be all right. After the next class my clothes should be washed and dried." I didn't mention the fact that my dress would be wrinkled and need ironing. I didn't want him to get any angrier than he was.

The warning bell for the next class rang.

Jimmy scowled so hard at the students who were staring at us that most turned their heads away as they rushed to get to class.

"I'll be all right, Jimmy," I insisted again before starting toward my math class.

"I'd like to know who did it!" he called after me. "Just so I could wring her neck." He said it loud enough for everyone who was left in the hallway to hear.

As soon as I entered class, the teacher called me to his desk.

"You're Dawn Longchamp, I assume," he said.

"Yes, sir." I looked at the class, and of course, all the students were looking at me, smiles on their faces.

"Well, we'll introduce ourselves later. Mrs. Turnbell wants to see you immediately," he said.

"The Longchamp girl is here," Mrs. Turnbell's secretary announced as I entered the reception room. I heard Mrs. Turnbell say, "Send her in." The secretary stepped back and I entered.

Mrs. Turnbell's gaze was icy as she asked me to explain what had happened.

With my stomach jumping up and down and my voice shaking, I told her how I had come out of the shower and found my clothing in the toilet.

"Why would anyone do that to a new girl?" she asked. I didn't respond. I didn't want to get into any more trouble with the other girls, and I knew that was exactly what would happen if I mentioned the smoke.

But she knew already!

"You don't have to explain. Mrs. Allen told me how you turned in Clara Sue Cutler for smoking."

"I didn't turn her in. I saw smoke coming from this locker and—"

"Now, listen to me," Mrs. Turnbell ordered, leaning over her desk, her pale face going first pink, then red. "The other students at this school have been brought up in fine homes and have a head start on how to get along with other people. But that doesn't mean I will allow you and your brother to come in here and disrupt everything. Do you understand?"

"Yes, ma'am," I said hoarsely, tears choking me. Coldly Mrs. Turnbell eyed me and shook her head.

"Going around to class in a gym uniform," she muttered. "You march right out of here and go directly to the laundry and wait for your clothing to be washed and dried."

"Yes, ma'am."

"Go on. Get dressed and back to your classes as soon as possible," she commanded with a wave of her hand.

I hurried out, wiping the tears away as I ran through the hallway and down to the laundry. When I put on my dress again, it was so wrinkled it looked like I had been sitting on it. But there was nothing I could do.

I hurried up to make my English class. When I got there several students looked disappointed to see me in regular clothing again. Only Louise looked relieved. When our gazes met, she smiled and then looked away quickly. At least for now, my ordeal had ended.

After English class, Louise caught up with me at the doorway.

"I'm sorry they did that to you!" she cried. "I just want you to know I wasn't part of it."

"Thank you."

"I should have warned you right away about Clara Sue. For some reason most of the girls do what she tells them to."

"If she did this, it was a very mean thing to do. I told her I was sorry."

"Clara Sue always gets her way," Louise said. "Maybe she won't bother you anymore. Come on, I'll go with you to lunch."

"Thank you," I said. A few other students said hello to me and smiled, but for the most part Louise was the only raft for me to cling to in unfamiliar waters.

The cafeteria was fancier than any I'd ever seen. Here the seats and tables looked plush and comfortable. The walls were painted light blue, and the tiled floor was an off white. The students picked up their trays and silverware at an area just before the serving counter and proceeded to the awaiting cashier.

I saw Clara Sue Cutler sitting with some of the other girls from our gym class. They all laughed when they set eyes on me.

"Let's sit over there," Louise said, indicating an empty table away from them.

"Just a minute," I said and marched up to Clara Sue's table. The girls all turned in surprise.

"Hi, Dawn," Clara Sue said, with a cat-who-has-eaten-the-canary look on her spiteful face. "Shouldn't you have ironed that?"

Everyone laughed.

"I don't know why you did this to me," I fired back in a hard voice as I eyed them all coldly. "But it was a terrible thing to do to someone, especially someone who has just entered your school."

"Who told you I did?" she demanded.

"No one told me. I know."

The girls stared. Clara Sue's big blue eyes narrowed to slits and then widened with an apparent softness.

"All right, Dawn," she said in a voice of amnesty. "I guess we broke you into Emerson Peabody. You're forgiven," she said with a queenly gesture. "In fact, you may sit here, if you like. You, too, Louise," she added.

"Thank you," I said. I was determined to mend fences and not disrupt Mrs. Turnbell's precious little school. Louise and I took the two empty seats.

"This is Linda Ann Brandise," Clara Sue said, indicating the taller girl with soft, dark brown hair and beautiful almond-shaped eyes. "And this is Margaret Ann Stanton, Diane Elaine Wilson, and Melissa Lee Norton."

I nodded at all of them and wondered if I was the only girl in the school without a formal middle name.

"Did you just move here?" Clara Sue asked. "You're not a sleep-over, I know."

"Sleep-over?"

"Students who stay in the dorms," Louise explained.

"Oh. No, I live in Richmond. Do you sleep over, Louise?"

"No, but Linda and Clara Sue do. I'm going to get my lunch," Louise declared and then pulled herself up. "Coming, Dawn?"

"I just need to get a container of milk," I said, putting my lunch bag on the table.

"What's that?" Louise asked.

"My lunch. I have a peanut butter and jelly sandwich." I opened my purse and found my milk money.

"You made your own lunch?" Clara Sue asked. "Why would you do that?"

"It saves money."

Louise stared at me, her watery, pale blue eyes blinking as she struggled to understand.

"Saves money? Why do you want to save money? Did your parents cut off your allowance?" Linda inquired.

"I don't have an allowance. Momma gives me money for milk, but other than that . . ."

"Money for milk?" Linda laughed and looked at Clara Sue. "What does your father do, anyway?"

"He works here. He's a maintenance supervisor."

"Maintenance?" Linda gasped. "You mean . . . he's a janitor?" Her eyes widened when I nodded.

"Uh-huh. Because he works here, my brother, Jimmy, and I get to go to Emerson Peabody."

The girls turned to each other and suddenly laughed.

"A janitor," Clara Sue said, as though she couldn't believe it. They laughed again. "I think we'll let Louise and Dawn have this table," she purred. Clara Sue lifted her tray and stood up. Linda and the others followed suit and started away.

"I didn't know your father was a janitor here," Louise said.

"You never gave me a chance to tell you. He's a supervisor because he's very good at fixing and maintaining all sorts of engines and motors," I said proudly.

"How nice." She looked around and then slipped her hands around her books and lifted them off the table. "Oh! I just remembered. I have to talk to Mary Jo Alcott. We have a science project to do together. I'll see you later," she said quickly and walked across the cafeteria to another table. The girls there didn't seem so happy to greet her, but she sat down anyway. She pointed at me and they all laughed.

They were snubbing me because they thought I was beneath them just because Daddy was the janitor. Jimmy was right, I thought. Rich kids were spoiled and horrible. I glared back at them defiantly, even though tears burned like fire under my eyelids. I rose and walked proudly to the lunch line to get some milk.

I looked around for Jimmy, hoping that he had been luckier than me and had made at least one friend by now, but I didn't see him anywhere. I returned to my table and began to unfold my bag when I heard someone say, "There any free seats here?"

I looked up at one of the handsomest boys I had ever seen. His hair was thick and flaxen blond like mine. It waved just enough to be perfect. His eyes were cerulean blue and they sparkled with laughter. His nose was straight and neither too long nor too narrow, nor too thick. He was just a little taller than Jimmy, but he had wider shoulders and stood straight and confidently. When I looked more closely at him, I saw that just like me, he had a tiny patch of freckles under each eye.

"They're all free," I said.

"Really? Can't imagine why," he said and sat down across from me. He extended his hand. "My name's Philip Cutler," he said.

"Cutler?" I pulled my hand back quickly.

"What's wrong?" His blue eyes sparkled wickedly. "Don't tell me some of those catty girls have warned you against me already?"

"No . . ." I turned and looked at the table of girls with Clara Sue at the center. They were all looking our way.

"I . . . your sister . . ."

"Oh, her. What'd she do?" His gaze darkened as he glanced back their way. I saw how it infuriated Clara Sue.

"She . . . blames me for getting her in trouble this morning in gym class. I . . . didn't you see me walking through the school in my gym uniform?"

"Oh, that was you? So you're the famous new girl—Dawn. I did hear about you, but I was so busy this morning, I didn't catch sight of you."

The way he smiled made me wonder if he was lying. Did Clara Sue put him up to this?

"You're probably the only one in the school who didn't," I said. "I was even called down to the principal's office and bawled out, even though it wasn't my fault."

"That doesn't surprise me. Mrs. Turnbell thinks she's a prison warden instead of a principal. That's why we call her Mrs. Turnkey."

"Turnkey?" I had to smile. It fit.

"And all this was my bratty sister's fault, huh?" He shook his head. "That figures, too."

"I've tried to make friends, apologize, but . . ." I glared at the girls. "They all turned on me when they found out what my father does."

"What's he do—rob banks?"

"He might as well for all they would care," I shot back. "Especially your sister."

"Forget her," Philip advised. "You can't let my sister get to you. She's a spoiled brat. She deserves whatever she gets. Where are you from?"

"Many places. Before Richmond, Granville, Virginia."

"Granville? I've never been there. Was it nice?"

"No," I said. He laughed, his teeth white and perfect. He looked at my bag and sandwich. "A bag lunch?"

"Yes," I said, anticipating his ridicule, too. But he surprised me.

"What do you have?"

"Peanut butter and jelly."

"Looks a lot thicker than the peanut butter sandwiches they give you here. Maybe I'll get you to bag me a lunch, too," he said. He looked serious about it for a moment, and then he laughed at my expression. "My sister is the biggest busybody here. She loves snooping in other people's business and then spreading rumors."

I studied him for a moment. Was he saying these things just to win my confidence or did he really mean it? I couldn't imagine Jimmy speaking so hatefully about me.

"What grade are you in?" I asked, trying to change the subject.

"Eleventh. I got my driver's license this year and my own car. How would you like to go for a ride with me after school?" he asked quickly.

"A ride?"

"Sure. I'll show you the sights," he added, winking.

"Thank you," I said. "But I can't."

"Why not? I'm a good driver," he pursued.

"I . . . have to meet my father after school."

"Well, maybe tomorrow, then. Hey," he said when I hesitated, searching for another excuse, "I'm perfectly harmless, no matter what you've heard."

"I haven't—" I broke off in confusion and felt my cheeks start to burn.

He laughed.

"You take everything so serious. Your parents gave you the right name. You're definitely as fresh as the birth of a new day," he said. I blushed even harder and looked down at my sandwich.

"So, do you stay in the dorms or live nearby?" he asked.

"I live on Ashland Street."

"Ashland? Don't know it. I'm not from Richmond, though. I'm from Virginia Beach."

"Oh, I've heard of it, but I've never been there. I heard it's very pretty there," I said and bit into my sandwich.

"It is. My family owns a hotel there: the Cutler's Cove Hotel, in Cutler's Cove, which is just a few miles south of Virginia Beach," he said sitting back proudly.

"You have a whole place named after your family?" I asked. No wonder Clara Sue was so swollen with her own importance, I thought.

"Yep. We've been there ever since the Indians gave it up. Or so my grandmother says."

"Your grandmother lives with you?" I asked enviously.

"She and my grandfather used to run the hotel. He died, but she still runs it with my parents. What does your father do, Dawn?"

"He works here," I said and thought, here I go again.

"Here? He's a teacher? And you let me say all those things about Mrs. Turnkey and—"

"No, no. He's a maintenance supervisor," I said quickly.

"Oh." Philip smiled and released a sigh of relief. "I'm glad of that," he said.

"You are?" I couldn't help sounding surprised.

"Yes. The two girls I know here whose fathers are teachers are the biggest snobs—Rebecca Clare Longstreet and Stephanie Kay Sumpter. Ignore them at all costs," he advised.

Just then I saw Jimmy come in. He was walking all by himself. He stopped in the doorway and gazed around. When he saw me, he flashed a look of surprise at the sight of Philip as well. Then he headed quickly to my table. He slapped his bag on top and flopped into a seat.

"Hi," Philip said. "How's it going?"

"Stinks," Jimmy said. "Just got bawled out for putting my feet on the rung of the seat ahead of me. I thought she would keep me there right through lunch."

"Gotta watch that around here. If Mrs. Turnbell comes by and sees a student doing something like that, she bawls out the teacher first, and that makes the teacher get even madder," Philip explained.

"This is Philip Cutler," said Dawn. "Philip, my brother, Jimmy."

"Hi," Philip said, extending his hand. Jimmy looked at it suspiciously a moment and then shook quickly.

"What do they think this place is, gold?" Jimmy said, getting back to his problem.

"Did you make any friends yet, Jimmy?" I asked hopefully.

He shook his head.

"I gotta get my milk." He got up quickly and went to the lunch line. The boys in front of him looked nervous when he approached.

"Jimmy's not overjoyed about being here, I gather," Philip said, looking his way.

"No, he's not. Maybe he's right," I added.

Philip smiled.

"You've got the clearest, prettiest eyes I've ever seen. The only one whose eyes come close is my mother."

I felt myself blush from my neck to my feet. I was absolutely beguiled by his flattering words, by the admiring look in his eyes. For a moment I couldn't speak. I had to shift my eyes away while I took another bite of my sandwich. I chewed quickly and swallowed, then turned back to him.

Some boys passing by said hello to him and then looked at me curiously. Finally two of his friends flopped down beside him.

"Aren't you going to introduce us to your famous new friend,

Philip?" asked a tall thin boy with peach-colored hair and brown eyes. He had a crooked smile that brought the corner of his mouth up.

"Not if I can help it," Philip said.

"Aw, come on. Philip likes to keep everything to himself," the tall boy told me. "Very selfish guy."

"My name's Dawn," I said quickly.

"Dawn. You mean like 'it dawned on me'?" He and his companion laughed hard.

"I'm Brandon," the tall boy finally said. "And this idiot beside me is Marshall." The shorter boy beside him only nodded. His eyes were very close together and he had his dark brown hair cut very short. He wore a smirk, rather than a smile. I recalled Momma once telling me never to trust anyone whose eyes were too close together. She said their mommas, just before giving birth, must have been surprised by snakes.

Jimmy returned and Philip introduced him to the other boys, but he sat quietly eating his sandwich. Philip was the only one who would talk to him, but Jimmy obviously didn't care. I saw from the way he looked at Marshall from time to time that he didn't like him much, either.

The bell rang to end the lunch period.

"Going to gym class?" Brandon asked Philip. "Or do you have other plans?" he added, gazing at me and smiling. I knew what he meant, but I tried to look like I didn't understand.

"I'll meet you," Philip said.

"Don't be late," Marshall quipped, speaking out of the corner of his mouth. The two boys went off, laughing.

"Where are you heading, Dawn?" Philip asked.

"Music."

"Good. I'll walk along with you. It's on the way to my gym class," he said. We started away from the table. When I looked to the side, I saw how Clara Sue and her friends were staring at us and whispering. They looked so hateful. Why? I wondered. Why did they have to be this way?

"Where's your next class, Jimmy?" I asked.

"I gotta go the other way," he said and scurried off before I could say a word. He elbowed his way through the crowd of students heading out the doors to the corridors and disappeared quickly.

"Have you been going to this school all your life?" I asked. Philip nodded. As we went along, I noticed many girls and boys nod and say hello to Philip. He was obviously very popular.

"My sister and I even attended the kindergarten associated with it."
He leaned toward me. "My parents and my grandmother make sizable
contributions to the school," he added, but he didn't sound arrogant
about it. It was just a statement of fact.

"Oh." Everyone around me seemed so sophisticated and so
wealthy. Jimmy had been right. We were like fish out of water. My
daddy only worked here, and what would I wear tomorrow? What
would Jimmy wear? If we stood out like sore thumbs now, what would
happen tomorrow?

"We both better get a move on before we're thrown to Mrs.
Turnkey," he said and smiled. "Think about going for a ride with me
tomorrow, okay?"

I nodded. When I looked back, I saw Clara Sue and her friends
walking slowly behind us. Clara Sue looked very unhappy about the
attention her brother was giving me. Maybe he was sincere. He was so
handsome and I felt like doing something to annoy her.

"I'll think about it," I said loud enough for the girls to hear.

"Great." He squeezed my arm gently and walked off, turning once
to smile back. I returned a smile, making sure Clara Sue could see, and
then I entered the music suite just as the bell beginning the class rang.

My music teacher, Mr. Moore, was a rosy-faced man with dimples in
his cheeks and hair as curly as Harpo Marx's. He had the sweetest
disposition of any of my teachers I had met so far, and when he smiled,
it was a smile full of warmth and sincerity. I saw that shy students shed
their bashfulness when he coaxed them and willingly stood up to sing
a few notes solo. He walked around the classroom with his tuning
harmonica teaching us the scales, explaining notes, making music
more interesting than even I imagined it could be. When he got to me,
he paused and twitched his nose like a squirrel. His hazel brown eyes
brightened.

"And now for a new voice," he said. "Dawn, can you sing Do re, mi,
fa, so, la, ti, do? I'll give you a start," he began, bringing his harmonica
to his lips, but I started before he had a chance to toot. His eyes
widened and his bushy reddish-brown eyebrows lifted. "Well, now, a
discovery. That's the best rendition of the scales cold I have heard in
years," he said. "Wasn't that perfect, boys and girls?" he asked the
class. When I looked around, I saw a sea of faces full of envy. Louise
was especially jealous of the compliment Mr. Moore had given me.
Her face was lime. "I think we might have found our solo singer for
our next concert," Mr. Moore mused aloud, squeezing his round chin

between his right forefinger and thumb as he looked at me and nodded. "Have you been in chorus before, Dawn?"

"Yes, sir."

"And do you play an instrument of any kind?" he inquired.

"I have been teaching myself the guitar."

"Teaching yourself?" He looked around the classroom. "Now, that's motivation, boys and girls. Well, we're going to have to see how far along you've come. If you're very good, you can put me out of a job," he said.

"I'm not very good, sir," I said.

He laughed, his cheeks trembling with his chuckles.

"There's something refreshing," he said, speaking to the rest of the class, "modesty. Ever wonder what that was, boys and girls?" He laughed at his own joke and went on with the day's lesson. When the bell ending the period rang, he asked me to remain a moment.

"Bring your guitar in with you tomorrow, Dawn. I'd like to hear you play," he said, his face serious and determined.

"I don't have a very good guitar, sir. It's second-hand and—"

"Now, now. Don't you be ashamed of it, and don't let any of the students here make you feel that way. I have an idea that it's a lot better than you think anyway. Besides, I can supply you with a very good guitar when the time comes."

"Thank you, sir," I said. He sat back in his seat and contemplated me a moment.

"I know the students are supposed to call their teachers sir and ma'am," he said. "But when we're working alone, could you manage to call me Mr. Moore?"

I smiled.

"I'll try."

"Good. I'm glad you're here, Dawn. Welcome to Emerson Peabody. Now you better hurry off to your next class."

"Thank you, Mr. Moore," I said and he smiled.

I started for my next class, but stopped when I saw Louise waiting for me.

"Hi," I said, seeing she wanted to be friends again. But that wasn't her first concern.

"I saw Philip Cutler sitting with you at lunch," she said, unable to hide the note of jealousy. "You'd better be careful. He's got a bad reputation with girls," she said, but her voice was still filled with envy.

"A bad reputation? He seems very nice. A lot different from his sister," I said pointedly. "What do they say that's so bad?"

"It's what he wants to do, even on a first date," she replied, her eyes big.

"What does he want to do?" I asked. She stepped back.

"What do you think?" She looked to the side to be sure no one could overhear. "He wants to go all the way."

"Did you go out with him?"

"No," she said, her eyes wide. "Never."

I shrugged.

"I don't think you should let people decide what you should and should not think about someone. You should decide for yourself. Besides, it's not fair to Philip," I added, his dazzling blue eyes still hovering in my thoughts.

Louise shook her head. "Don't say I didn't warn you," she advised.

"At least he didn't make me sit alone at lunch." My point, like an accurate arrow, hit the bull's eye.

"I'm sorry I left you . . . can we have lunch together tomorrow?" she asked.

"Probably," I said without sounding very definite about it. I was still feeling the scratches she and her catty friends had drawn across my heart. But that satisfied her enough to give me the benefit of another warning.

"If you think Clara Sue Cutler doesn't like you now, wait until she hears what Mr. Moore said."

"What do you mean?"

"She thinks she's going to sing the solo at the concert. She did last year," Louise said and punctured my balloon of happiness just as it was starting to inflate.

4

A Kiss

At the end of the school day I met Jimmy in the lobby. He was very unhappy because his math teacher had said she thought he was so far behind, he might have to take the class over again.

"I warned you about missing all that school, Jimmy," I chastised softly.

"Who cares?" he replied, but I could see he was upset.

While we were talking, all the other students were hurrying out to catch buses or get into their cars. Those who slept in the dorms sauntered out slowly.

"All these rich kids got money to burn," Jimmy muttered, seeing some of them heading for their own cars. "Come on," he said, heading toward the stairway. "Let's see how long we've got to wait for Daddy."

I followed Jimmy down to the basement where Daddy's office was. There was a workroom right next to Daddy's office, which wasn't a big office, but he did have a nice wooden desk and two chairs in it. There were shelves on the walls and a large, hanging light in a dark blue metal shade draped at the end of a wire and chain just over the desk.

Jimmy sat down behind Daddy's desk and slumped back in the seat. I brought the other chair closer and opened my textbooks to begin doing some of my homework. Thoughts about the day whirled confusingly through my brain, and when I looked up, I caught Jimmy staring at me.

"Did you ever find out who did that to you?" he asked.

"No, Jimmy," I lied. "Let's just forget about it. It was all a misunderstanding." I didn't want him getting into trouble on account of me.

"Misunderstanding?" He shook his head. "They're all snobs here. The girls are stuck up and the boys are jerks. All they talk about are their cars and their clothes and their record collections. How come that guy named Philip was sitting with you in the cafeteria?" he asked.

"Philip? He came over and asked if any of the seats were free," I said, making it sound like nothing, when all along I had thought it wonderful. "When he found out they all were, he sat down."

"Funny, how he got so friendly so fast." Jimmy's eyes grew small as his mind worked overtime.

"He's just being nice." I myself had been unsure about trusting Clara Sue's brother, but for some reason I had to defend Philip to Jimmy. Philip was the only friendly soul at this school so far. I thought of his full lips curving into a lopsided smile and his blue eyes holding my own gaze hypnotically as he'd asked me to ride in his car. Just remembering made me shiver a little.

"Now that I think about it, I don't trust him," Jimmy suddenly concluded. He nodded, confirming his theory. "This all might be part of some joke because of what happened to you this morning. Maybe somebody made a bet with him that he couldn't get you to like him right away or something. What if he does something to embarrass you?"

"Oh, that can't be true, Jimmy. He's too nice to do anything like that!" I cried a little too desperately.

"If I'm right, you're going to be very sorry. If he hurts you," he added, "he'll have to deal with me."

I smiled to myself, thinking how good it was to have a brother who was so protective.

Just then Daddy appeared in the doorway. Unlike the end of his day's work at all of his other jobs, Daddy didn't look tired and dirty. His hands were as clean as they had been in the morning, and there were no smudges on his clothes.

I waited, holding my breath, expecting that by now he had found out about the gym class incident, but if he did know, he didn't say a word. And he didn't seem to notice how wrinkled my dress was.

"So?" he said. "How did your day go, kids?" He shot a very quick smile at me and stroked my hair for the most fleeting moment.

I glanced at Jimmy. We had decided we wouldn't tell Daddy what had happened to me, but all of a sudden I longed to bury my face in his chest and while safe in his arms cry a waterfall of tears. Even with the memories of Philip and music class to warm me, most of the day had been awful; now it was a blur of laughing faces swimming before my eyes. I knew I couldn't tell him, though—Daddy's temper was fiery and unpredictable. What if he said something and got fired, or even worse—what if Mrs. Turnbell convinced him everything was my fault?

"This place is just what I expected it to be: full of spoiled rich kids and teachers who look down on you," Jimmy said.

"Nobody's looking down on me," Daddy replied gruffly.

Jimmy looked away and then glanced at me as if to say Daddy wouldn't know if they did.

"Yeah, yeah. When can we get out of this place?" Jimmy demanded.

"We're leaving right now. I just want to enter some figures into my record book here," he said, pulling a black and white notebook out of a side desk drawer.

"You like this job, don't you, Daddy?" I asked as we were leaving. I looked pointedly at Jimmy so he would understand how much this all meant to our family.

"Sure do, baby. Well, let's get ourselves home to your momma and see what her day was like."

When we arrived at our apartment, it was very quiet. At first I thought Momma and little Fern were out, but when we peered into her bedroom, we found them both curled up together asleep.

"Ain't that a picture?" Daddy whispered. "Let's just let them sleep," he said. "Jimmy, what'dya say me and you go get some ice cream for dessert tonight? I feel like celebrating a little."

As soon as Daddy and Jimmy left, I took off my dress so Momma wouldn't see how wrinkled it was, and I started to prepare dinner. Fern woke up first and cried out for me. When I walked in to get her, Momma opened her eyes.

"Oh, Dawn. Are you all back?" she asked and struggled to sit up. Her face looked flushed and her eyes were glassy.

"Daddy and Jimmy went to get some ice cream. Momma, you're still not feeling well."

"I'm fine, honey. Just a bit tired from a full day with Fern. She's a good baby, but she's still a handful for anyone. How was your day at school?"

"Did you go to the doctor?" I asked.

"I did something even better. I went out and bought the ingredients for this tonic," she said and pointed to a bottle on the night table beside her bed.

"What is this, Momma?" I turned the bottle of dark liquid around and around in my hands. Then I opened it and smelled it. It stank.

"It's all sorts of herbs and such, my granny's formula. You'll see. I'll be better now in no time. Now let's not talk any more about me. Tell me about the school. How was it?" she asked, some excitement and brightness coming back into her eyes.

"It was okay," I said, swinging my eyes away so she couldn't see my lie. At least some of it was good, I thought. I put the bottle of herbal medicine down and took little Fern in my arms. Then I told Momma about Mr. Moore and some of the other teachers, but I didn't tell her about Clara Sue Cutler and the other girls, nor did I talk about Philip.

Before I was finished Momma closed her eyes and brought her hands to her chest. It looked like she was having trouble taking a deep breath.

"Momma, I'm staying home from school and watching Fern until this homemade medicine works or you go to the doctor!" I cried.

"Oh, no, honey. You can't start missin' days at a new school right off on account of me. If you stay home, I'll just be so upset, I'll get sicker and sicker."

"But, Momma . . ."

She smiled and took hold of my right hand while I held Fern in my left arm. As long as I held little Fern, she was content just sucking on her thumb and listening to me and Momma speak. Momma pulled me closer to her until she was able to reach out and stroke my hair.

"You look so pretty today, Dawn honey. Now, I don't want you worrying and denying yourself things on account of me. I can mend myself. I been in worse spots than this, honey, believe me. Your daddy got you and Jimmy into a fancy school where you're going to get advantages we never expected either of you would have. You just can't go on like you had to in the other places," she insisted.

"But, Momma . . ."

Suddenly her eyes grew dark and intense and her face was more serious than I'd ever seen it. She squeezed my hand so tight the bones in my fingers seemed to rub against each other, but the changes in her scared me so much I couldn't pull my hand away.

"You belong in this school, Dawn. You deserve this chance."

Momma's eyes glazed over a little, as though she wandered through an old memory. Her painful grip on my hand never loosened. "You should mix with the rich and the blue-blooded," she insisted. "There ain't one girl or boy at that school better than you, you hear?" she cried.

"But, Momma, the girls at this school wear clothes I'll never even get to try on and talk about places I'll never go. I'll never fit in with them. They seem to know so much."

"You deserve those same things, Dawn. Never forget it." With that her iron grip tightened even more, making me cry out a little. My whimper seemed to make her wake up, her eyes cleared, and she let my hand go.

"All right, Momma. I promise, but if you don't get better soon—"

"I'll go to a fancy doctor, just like I promised I would. That's a new promise," she proclaimed and raised her hand like a witness taking the stand in a courtroom. I shook my head. She saw I didn't believe her. "I will. I will," she repeated and lowered herself back to the pillow. "You better feed the baby before she starts letting you know you're late with her food. She can holler something awful when she's a mind to."

I hugged Fern to me and then took her out to feed her. Daddy and Jimmy returned and I whispered to Daddy that Momma was sicker than ever. A worried frown drew Daddy's dark brows together.

"I'll go talk to her," he said. Jimmy looked in, too, and then returned. He just stood by quietly and watched me feed Fern. Whenever Jimmy was worried and frightened about Momma, he would become as silent and as still as a statue.

"Momma's so pale and thin and weak, Jimmy," I said, "but she won't let me stay home from school to mind Fern."

"Then I'll stay home," he said through his clenched teeth.

"That would make her even angrier and you know it, Jimmy."

"Well, what are we going to do, then?"

"Let's see if Daddy gets her to go to a doctor," I said.

When he returned, he told us Momma had promised she would definitely go if the formula didn't work.

"Stubbornness runs in her family," Daddy explained. "One time her daddy slept on his shack roof just so he could get this woodpecker that was peckin' away at the shingles every mornin'. Took him two days, but he wouldn't come off that roof."

Daddy's stories had us all laughing again, but every once in a while I would look at Momma and then exchange a glance of worry with Jimmy. To me Momma looked like a wilting flower. I saw little things about her that filled my balloon of worry with more and more concern. I knew if it continued, I would burst into a panic.

The next day Philip Cutler surprised me at my locker right before the homeroom bell rang.

"Going to let me take you for a ride today?" he asked, whispering in my ear.

I had thought about it all night. It would be the first time I had ever gone for a ride with a boy.

"Where would we go?"

"I know a spot on this hill that overlooks the James River. You can see for miles and miles. It's beautiful. I've never taken anyone there," he added, "because I haven't met anyone I thought would appreciate it like I do. Up until now, that is."

I looked into his soft blue eyes. I wanted to go, but my heart felt funny, as if I were betraying someone. He saw the hesitation in my face.

"Sometimes you just sense things," he said. "I wouldn't ask any of these other girls because they're so spoiled they wouldn't be satisfied just looking at nature or scenery. They'd want me to take them to a fancy restaurant or something. Not that I don't want to take you to one," he added quickly. "It's just that I thought you might appreciate this the way I do."

I nodded slowly. What was I doing? I couldn't just go off with him without asking Daddy first, and I had to get back home to help Momma with Fern. And what if Jimmy was right and this was all some sort of secret prank engineered by Philip's sister and her friends?

"I've got to be home early enough to help Momma with dinner," I said.

"No problem. It's only a few minutes from here. Is it a date? I'll meet you in the lobby just after the bell rings."

"I don't know."

"We'd better start for class," he said, taking my books in his arms. "Come on, I'll walk you."

As the two of us walked side by side down the corridor, we turned a number of heads. His friends all smiled and said hello to me. At my homeroom doorway he handed me my books.

"So?" he asked.

"I don't know. I'll see," I said. He laughed and shook his head.

"I'm not asking you to marry me. Not yet anyway," he added. My heart fluttered and I felt as though Philip had been able to read my every thought. I hadn't been able to stop myself from making up stories—my own private fairy tale—before I fell asleep last night. I had imagined handsome Philip Cutler and me becoming the ideal couple, pledging undying love for each other, and becoming engaged. We would live in his hotel, and I would bring Momma and Daddy and Fern, and even Jimmy would come eventually because Philip would make him a manager or something. At the end of my fantasy Philip forced Clara Sue to be a chambermaid.

"I'll be after you all day," he promised and went off to his own class. His blue eyes seemed so sincere. This couldn't be a joke, I thought. Please, don't let it be a trick.

When I turned to enter homeroom, I saw the looks of surprise on the faces of some of the girls who had obviously seen me with Philip. Louise's eyes were as round as half-dollars and I could see that she couldn't wait to ask me questions.

"He wants me to go for a ride with him after school," I told her finally. "Do you think his sister put him up to it?" I asked, fishing for some clues.

"His sister? Hardly. She's mad at him for even talking to you."

"Then maybe I'll go," I murmured dreamily.

"Don't do it," she warned, but I could see the excitement in her own eyes.

Every time I passed from one class to the next, Philip was waving and asking, "Well?" Just after I sat down in my math class, he popped his head in the door and looked at me, raising his eyebrows, questioning. I could only laugh. He disappeared quickly when the teacher turned toward him.

The only sour incident occurred when I found Clara Sue waiting for me at the doorway to my next class. Linda was standing beside her.

"I heard that Mr. Moore is considering you for the solo at the concert," she said, her eyes small and watchful.

"So?" My heart was pounding.

"He's considering me, too."

"That's nice. Good luck," I said and started into the room, but she grabbed my shoulder and spun me around.

"Don't think you can come here and take over everything, you little charity case!" she cried.

"I'm not a charity case!"

Clara Sue inspected me from head to toe, releasing a disdainful sniff. "Stop deluding yourself, Dawn. You don't belong here. You're an outsider. You're not one of us. You never have been and you never will be. You're just poor white trash from the wrong side of the tracks. Everyone in school knows that."

"Yeah," Linda threw in. "You're nothing but poor white trash."

"Don't you dare say such things to me!" I protested angrily, fighting back the tears I could feel forming in the corners of my eyes.

"Why not?" Clara Sue asked. "They're true. Can't bear to hear the truth, Dawn? Well, it's about time you did. Who do you think you're fooling with your wide-eyed 'Miss Innocence' act?" she sneered. "If you think my brother is interested in *you*, you're nuts."

"Philip likes me. He does!" I declared.

Clara Sue raised an eyebrow. "I'll bet he does."

There was an undertone to her words . . . an undertone I didn't like. "What are you talking about?"

"My brother *loves* girls like you. He turns girls like you into mothers once a month."

Linda laughed loudly.

"Really?" I pushed my way to Clara Sue. "Well, I'll just tell Philip you said so." My words wiped away Clara Sue's smile, and for an instant she looked panicked. Without giving her a chance to retaliate, I left Clara Sue and her hateful words.

Philip did sit with me and Jimmy at lunch and spent a lot of time convincing Jimmy he should join the intramural basketball program. Jimmy was reluctant, but I could see that reluctance chipping away. I knew he liked basketball.

"So?" Philip asked me as we started for class. "Have you decided yet?"

I hesitated and then told him what had happened between Clara Sue and me in the morning. I didn't tell him exactly what she had said, however, just that she warned me against him.

"That little . . . *witch* is the only word that fits her. Wait until I get my hands on her."

"Don't, Philip. She'll just hate me more and try to make more trouble for me."

"Then come with me for a ride," he said quickly.

"That sounds like blackmail."

"Yeah," he said, smiling, "but it's nice blackmail."

I laughed. "Are you sure you can get me home early?"

"Absolutely." He raised his hand. "On my honor."

"All right," I said. "I'll ask my daddy."

"Great. You won't regret it," Philip assured me. I was so nervous about it, however, that I almost forgot to show Mr. Moore my guitar. I was really walking in a daze when I entered his classroom and took my seat.

"Is there really a guitar in there or is that just the case?" he asked when I didn't mention it.

"What? Oh, it's a guitar!" I exclaimed. He laughed and asked me to play. Afterward he said I had done very well for someone without any formal lessons.

The kind look in his eyes made me reveal my secret hope. "My dream is to learn how to play the piano and have one of my own some day."

"I'll tell you what," he said, sitting forward and bracing his elbows on his desk so he could rest his chin on his clenched hands. "I need another flute player. If you'll take up the flute for the school orchestra, I'll spend three afternoons a week after school teaching you the piano."

"You will?" I nearly jumped out of my desk.

"We'll start tomorrow. Is it a deal?" he said, extending his hand over the desk.

"Oh, yes," I said and reached out to shake. He laughed and told me I should meet him in the music rooms right after the last class of the day tomorrow.

I couldn't wait to run down and tell Daddy. When I told Jimmy, I was worried he would be upset that he would have to wait alone for Daddy in Daddy's office those afternoons. He surprised me with an announcement of his own.

"I've decided to join the intramural basketball program," he said. "One of the boys in my math class needs another guy on his team. And then I might join the cross-country team in the spring."

"That's wonderful, Jimmy. Maybe we can make friends here; maybe we just met the wrong people yesterday."

"I didn't say I was making friends," Jimmy replied quickly. "I just figured I could kill some time twice a week."

Daddy wasn't around, so I asked Jimmy to tell him I had gone for a ride and Philip would take me home.

"I wish you wouldn't get involved with that guy," Jimmy said.

"I'm not getting involved, Jimmy. I'm just going for a ride."

"Sure," Jimmy said and slumped down sadly in a chair. I ran back upstairs to meet Philip. He had a pretty red car with soft furry white sheepskin covers on the seats. He opened the door for me and stepped back.

"Madam," he said with a sweeping bow.

I got in and he closed the door. The car was even prettier inside. I ran my hand over the soft covers and looked at the black leather dashboard and gearshift.

"You have a beautiful car, Philip," I told him when he got behind the steering wheel.

"Thank you. It was a birthday gift from my grandmother."

"A birthday gift!" How rich his grandmother must be, I thought, to give him a car as a present. He shrugged, smiled coyly, and started the engine. Then he shifted into gear and we were off.

"How did you find this wonderful place, Philip?" I asked as we headed away from the school and in the opposite direction from where I lived.

"Oh, I was just cruising by myself one day and came upon it. I like to go for rides and look at the scenery and think," he said. He made a turn off a main street and headed quickly down a road without many houses on it. Then he turned again, and we began to climb up a hill. "It's not much farther," he said. We passed a few houses as we continued to climb, and then Philip turned down a rather deserted road that ran along a field and into a patch of trees. The road was only gravel and rock.

"You found this accidentally?"

"Uh-huh."

"And you haven't taken any other girl from Emerson Peabody up here?"

"Nope," he said, but I was beginning to have my doubts.

We drove through the small forest and came out on a clear field. There really wasn't any more road, but Philip continued over the grass until we came to the edge of the hill and could look out over the James River. Just as he promised, it was a spectacular view.

"Well?"

"Beautiful, Philip!" I exclaimed, drinking in the scene. "You were right."

"And you should see it at night with the stars out and the lights of the city. Think I can get you out at night?" he asked, with a crooked smile.

"I don't know," I answered quickly, but I harbored a hope. That would be more like a real date, my first real date. He edged closer to me, his arm over the top of the seat.

"You're a very pretty girl, Dawn. The moment I saw you, I said to myself, there's the prettiest girl I've seen at Emerson Peabody. I'm going to get to know her as fast as I can."

"Oh, lots of the girls at Emerson Peabody are prettier than me." I wasn't trying to be falsely modest. I had seen so many pretty girls with beautiful, expensive clothing. How could I compare to them? I wondered.

"They're not prettier to me," he said. "I'm glad you transferred to our school." His fingers grazed my shoulder. "Have you had many boyfriends?" I shook my head. "I don't believe that," he said.

"It's true. We haven't been able to stay in one place long enough," I added. He laughed.

"You say the funniest things."

"I'm not trying to be funny, Philip. It's true," I repeated, widening my eyes for emphasis.

"Sure," he said, moving his fingers to my hair and tracing a strand with his forefinger. "You have the tiniest nose," he said and leaned forward to kiss the tip of my nose. It took me by such surprise, I sat back.

"I couldn't help it," he said and leaned forward again, this time to kiss my cheek. I looked down as his left hand settled on my knee. It sent a tingle up my thigh. "Dawn," he whispered softly in my ear. "Dawn. I just love saying your name. You know what I did this morning? I got up with the sunrise, just so I could see the dawn."

"You didn't."

"Yes, I did," he said and brought his lips to mine. I had never kissed a boy on the lips before, although I had dreamt about it. Last night I had fantasized about kissing Philip, and here I was doing it! It felt like dozens of tiny explosions all over my body, and my face grew hot. Even my ears tingled.

Because I didn't back away, Philip moaned and kissed me again, harder this time. Suddenly I felt the hand that had been on my knee traveling up over my waist until his fingers settled around my breast. The moment they did, I pulled back and pushed him away at the same time. I couldn't help it. All the things I had heard about him flashed before my mind, especially Clara Sue's horrible threat.

"Easy," he said quickly. "I'm not going to hurt you."

My heart was pounding. I pressed my palm against my chest and took a deep breath.

"Are you all right?"

I nodded.

"Didn't you ever let a boy touch you there before?" he asked. When I shook my head, he tilted his skeptically. "Really?"

"Honest, no."

"Well, you're missing it all then," he said, inching toward me again. "There's nothing to be afraid of," he coaxed, bringing his hand back to my waist.

"Haven't you at least been kissed like that before?" he asked. His fingers started moving up my side. I shook my head. "Really?" He brought his hand firmly to the side of my breast. "Just relax," he said. "You don't want to be the only girl your age at Emerson Peabody who's never been kissed and touched like this, do you? I'll do it slowly, okay?" he said, barely inching forward over the top of my breast.

I took a deep breath and closed my eyes. Once again he pressed his lips to mine.

"That's it. Easy," he said. "See." The tips of his fingers surrounded a button on my blouse. I felt it open and then felt his fingers against my skin, moving like a thick spider in and under my bra. When the tips of his fingers found my nipple, I felt a surge of excitement that took my breath away.

"No," I said pulling back again. My heart was pounding so hard, I was sure he could hear it. "I . . . we'd better start back," I said. "I've got to help Momma with dinner."

"What? Help your mother with dinner? You're kidding. We just got here." He stared at me a moment.

"You don't have some other boyfriend already, do you?"

"Oh, no!" I said, nearly jumping out of my seat. He laughed and traced my collarbone with the tip of his forefinger. I felt his hot breath on my cheek. "Will you come back here with me one night?"

"Yes," I said with abandon. He was so handsome, and despite my fears, his touch had made my stomach feel like butterflies were flying around in it.

"Okay, I'll let you slip out of my hands this time then," he said and laughed. "You're really cute, you know." He leaned over and kissed me quickly again. Then he lowered his eyes to my opened blouse. I quickly buttoned it.

"Actually, I'm glad you're shy, Dawn."

"You are?" I thought he would hate me because I wasn't as sophisticated as most of the girls he knew at Emerson Peabody.

"Sure. So many girls are know-it-alls these days. There's nothing fresh and honest about them. Not like there is about you. I want to be the one who teaches you things, makes you feel things you've never felt before. Will you let me? Will you?" he pleaded with those soft blue eyes.

"Yes," I said. I wanted to learn new things and feel new things and be just as grown-up and sophisticated as the girls he knew at Emerson Peabody.

"Good. Now, don't bring any other boys up here behind my back," he added.

"What? I wouldn't."

He laughed and got back behind the steering wheel.

"You're definitely something else, Dawn. Something good," he added.

I gave him the directions to take me home and finished buttoning my blouse.

"Our section of town isn't very nice," I said, preparing him. "But we're only living there until Daddy can find something better."

"Yeah, well," he said, looking at the houses along the streets in my neighborhood, "for your sake I hope that's not much longer. Don't you have any family here?" he asked.

"No. Our family is all in Georgia, on farms," I replied. "But we haven't seen them for a while because we've been traveling a lot."

"I've taken trips here and there, but summers, when most of the other kids go off to Europe or to other parts of the country, I have to remain in Cutler's Cove and help with our hotel," he said, smirking unhappily. He turned to me.

"It's expected that someday I'll be the one to take it over and run it."

"How wonderful, Philip."

He shrugged.

"It's been in our family for generations. It was started as just an inn way back when there were whalers and fishermen from everywhere. We've got paintings and all sorts of antiques in the attic of the hotel, things that belonged to my great-great-grandfather. Our family's just about the most important one in town, founding fathers."

"It must be wonderful to have all of that family heritage," I said. He caught the note of longing in my voice.

"What were your ancestors like?"

What would I tell him? Could I tell him the truth—that I hadn't ever seen my grandparents, much less known what they were like? And how could I explain never seeing or knowing or ever hearing from any cousins, uncles, or aunts?

"They were . . . farmers. We used to have a big farm with cows and chickens and acres and acres," I said, but I looked out my window when I said it. "I remember riding on the hay wagon when I was just a little girl, sitting up front with my grandfather, who held me in his arm while he held on to the reins. Jimmy would be in the hay, looking up at the sky. My grandfather smoked a corncob pipe and played the harmonica."

"So that's where your musical talent comes from."

"Yes." I continued spinning the threads of my fantasy, nearly forgetting as I went on that my words were as false as false could be. "He knew all the old songs and would sing them to me, one after the other, as we went along in his wagon, and at night, too, on the porch of our big farmhouse, while he rocked and smoked and my grandmother crocheted. The chickens would run loose in the front yard, and sometimes I would try to catch one, but they were always too fast. I can still hear my grandfather laugh and laugh."

"I don't really remember too much about my grandfather, and I've never been very close to my grandmother. Life's more formal at Cutler's Cove," he explained.

"Turn here," I said quickly, already regretting my lies.

"You're the first girl I've driven home," he said.

"Really? Philip Cutler, is that the truth?"

"Cross my heart. Don't forget, I just got my license. Besides, Dawn, I can't lie to you. For some reason, it would be like lying to myself." He reached over and stroked my cheek so softly I could barely feel the tip of his finger. My heart dipped. Here he was being so thoughtful and truthful, and I was making up stories about my imaginary family, stories that made him sad about his own life, a life I was sure had to be a thousand times more wonderful than mine.

"Down this street," I pointed. He turned onto our block. I saw him grimace when he saw the cluttered lots and the sloppy front yards. "That's our apartment building just ahead, the one with the toy red wagon on the sidewalk."

"Thank you," I said as soon as he pulled up.

He leaned over to kiss me, and when I leaned toward him, he brought his hand up to my breast again. I didn't pull away.

"You taste real good, Dawn. You're going to let me take you for another ride soon, right?"

"Yes," I said, my voice barely above a whisper. I gathered my books into my arms quickly.

"Hey," he said, "what's your telephone number?"

"Oh, we don't have a phone yet," I said. When he looked at me strangely, I added, "We just didn't get around to it yet."

I got out of the car quickly and ran to my front door, positive he saw through my foolish lie. I was sure he never wanted to see me again.

Daddy and Momma were sitting at the kitchen table. Jimmy, who was on the couch, peered over a comic book at me.

"Where you been?" Daddy asked in a voice that made me start.

I looked at him. His eyes didn't soften, and there was that darkness around his face again, a darkness that made my heart pound hard and loud. "I went for a ride. But I got home early enough to help with dinner and Fern," I added in my own defense.

"We just don't like you riding around with boys yet, Dawn," Momma said, trying to calm the treacherous waters of Daddy's anger.

"But why, Momma? I bet the other girls my age at Emerson Peabody go for rides with boys."

"That don't matter none," Daddy snapped. "I don't want you riding around with this boy anymore." Daddy looked up at me and his handsome face was lit with a fiery rage—my mind raced, searching desperately for a reason for Daddy's anger.

"Please, Dawn," Momma said. It was followed with a cough that nearly took her breath away.

I looked toward Jimmy. He had the comic book up high, so I couldn't see his face and he couldn't see mine.

"All right, Momma."

"That's a good girl, Dawn," she said. "Now we can start on dinner." Her hands were shaking, but I didn't know what caused it—her coughing or the tension in the room.

"Aren't you home early, Daddy?" I asked. I had hoped to beat him and Jimmy home anyway.

"I left a little early. It don't matter. I ain't as crazy about this job as I thought I was," he said to my surprise. Had he found out what the girls had done to me? Did that turn him against the school?

"Did you have a fight with Mrs. Turnbell, Daddy?" I asked, suspecting his temper had reared its ugly head.

"No. There's just so much to do. I don't know. We'll see." He gave me a look that said there'd be no more talk about it. Since Daddy had started working at Emerson Peabody, these looks and his temper had disappeared. Suddenly it was all returning and I was frightened.

That night, after Fern had been put to sleep and Momma and Daddy went to bed, Jimmy turned to me after crawling under the covers.

"I didn't do anything to get them hot and bothered about you going for a ride with Philip." Jimmy's dark eyes begged me to believe him. "I just told Daddy. Next thing I knew, we were rushing home. Honest."

"I believe you, Jimmy. I guess they're just worried. We don't need any more problems," I said.

"Of course, it don't bother me all that much that you won't be going for rides with Philip," he said. "All those rich kids are spoiled and always get what they want," he said bitterly, staring at me, his dark gaze catching my own and holding it tightly.

"There are a lot of bad poor people, too, Jimmy."

"At least they got an excuse. Dawn"—he paused—"be careful." With that, Jimmy turned over, moving as far away from me as he could and still be in the same bed with me.

I didn't fall asleep for the longest time. All I could think about was not being able to go out with Philip—or even ride with him. The idea of it made me want to dig a well to cry my tears into—a well that would have been filled up in no time if Jimmy hadn't been there trying to sleep.

Why couldn't I have this one thing I wanted? I'd had little enough until now, my brain cried, and I'd tried so hard to keep my family happy—to make smiles appear on my Daddy's face. How could they take this away, too?

Philip was special. I relived his kiss, the way he brought his lips to mine, the deep blue in his eyes, the way my face glowed and the excitement that flashed through my body when his fingers touched my breast. Just thinking about it warmed me and made the butterflies in my stomach wake up all over again.

It would have been exciting parking with him on that hill at night with the lights below us and the stars above us. When I closed my eyes, I imagined him in the dark moving closer, bringing his hands back to my breasts and his lips to mine. The image was so vivid, I felt a wave of warmth travel up my body as if I had lowered myself gently into a tepid bath. When it reached my neck, I moaned. I didn't realize I had done so aloud until Jimmy spoke.

"What?" he asked.

"I didn't say anything," I said quickly.

"Oh. Okay. Night," he repeated.

"Night," I said and turned over so I could force myself to sleep and forget.

5

My Brother's Keeper

Philip came to school extra early the next morning just so he could meet me before all the other students had arrived. Daddy went right to work on an electrical problem they were having in the gymnasium, and Jimmy and I went to his office as usual. A few minutes after we had arrived, Philip came to the door.

"Morning," he said and smiled at both Jimmy's and my look of surprise. "I had to get to the library early this morning and thought I'd see if you were here."

"The library don't open this early," Jimmy replied, busting Philip's flimsy excuse to bits.

"Sometimes it is," Philip insisted.

"I've got to go to the library, too," I said. "I'll join you."

Jimmy scowled as I got up.

"See you later, Jimmy," I said and walked upstairs with Philip.

"I was thinking about you a lot last night," Philip said. "I wanted to call you every five minutes last night to see how you were. Are you going to get a phone soon?"

"Oh, Philip," I said, spinning on him, "I don't think so. Jimmy would just hate me for saying all this, but I have to be truthful. We're a very poor family. The only reason Jimmy and I are in this school is on account of my daddy having this job. That's why I wear these plain clothes and Jimmy just wears a pair of dungarees and a shirt. He'll

387

wear the same shirt twice a week at least. I've got to wash everything right away so we can wear it again. We're not just living in that ugly neighborhood temporarily. It's the nicest place we've ever lived!" I cried and started away.

Philip reached out quickly and seized my arm.

"Hey." He spun me about. "I knew all that."

"You did?"

"Sure. Everyone knows how you got into Emerson Peabody."

"They do? Of course they do," I realized bitterly. "I'm sure we're on everybody's gossip list, especially your sister's."

"I don't listen to gossip, and I don't care whether you're here because your father's rich or because your father works here. I'm just happy you're here," he said. "And as for belonging here—you belong here more than most of these spoiled kids. I know your teachers are happy you're here, and Mr. Moore is walking on a cloud because he finally has a very talented student to teach," Philip declared. He looked so sincere. His eyes shone bright with determination, and his gaze was so soft and warm upon me that I shivered.

"You're probably just saying all these nice things to make me feel better," I said softly.

"I'm not. Really." He smiled. "Cross my heart and hope to fall in a well full of chocolate sauce." I laughed. "That's better. Don't be so serious all the time." He looked around and then drew closer, practically pressing his body to mine. "When can you and I take a ride again?"

"Oh, Philip, I can't take any more rides with you." Uttering the words hurt so much, but I couldn't disobey Momma and Daddy.

"Why not?" His eyes grew small. "Did my sister or her friends say something else to you about me, because whatever they said, it's a lie," he added quickly.

"No, it's not that." I looked down. "I had to promise Momma and Daddy I wouldn't."

"Huh? How come? Someone say something to your father about me?" he demanded. I shook my head.

"It's not you, Philip. They think I'm too young yet, and I can't do anything about it right now. We have too many problems."

He stared hard at me and then suddenly smiled.

"Well, then," he said, refusing to be defeated. "I'll just wait until they give you permission. I might even speak to your father."

"Oh, no, Philip. Please don't. I don't want to make anyone unhappy, least of all Daddy."

Despite my words, part of me wanted Philip to talk to Daddy. I was so flattered that he wouldn't give up on me or take no for an answer. He was my knight in shining armor who wanted to whisk me off into the sunset and give me everything I had always dreamed of.

"Okay," he said. "Take it easy. If you don't want me to talk to him I won't."

"Even though Daddy won't let me ride with you now, I want you to know I will go for a ride with you as soon as they say it's all right," I added in a rush. I didn't want to lose Philip. He was becoming a special part of my life that I liked very much. When I saw that his eyes brightened hopefully, I felt much better.

We heard the doors opening and saw some other students beginning to arrive. Philip looked toward the library.

"I do have to get some research material for my term paper. It wasn't a total fib," he said, smiling. He started backing away. "See you later."

He kept backing up until he backed into a wall. We both laughed. Then he turned and hurried toward the library. I took a deep breath and turned to the front doors. The rest of the student body was charging in, and I caught sight of Louise. Louise waved, so I waited for her.

"Everyone's talking about you," she said, rushing over to me, her pale, freckled face flushed with excitement.

"Oh?"

"They all know you went for a ride with Philip after school. Linda just told me there's a lot of gossip at the dorms."

"What are they saying?" My heart was racing like a train at the thought of all these rich girls talking about me.

Louise looked back at the growing crowd of arriving students and nodded toward the girls' room. I followed her in.

"Maybe I shouldn't tell you," Louise said.

"Of course you should. If you want to be my friend, like you keep saying you want to be. Friends don't hide things from each other. They help each other."

"Clara Sue's telling everyone that her brother wouldn't be interested in a girl like you, a girl from such a poor family, if he hadn't found out that you have a reputation. . . ."

"Reputation? What kind of a reputation?"

"A reputation for going all the way on the first date," she admitted finally and bit her lower lip quickly as if to punish herself for permitting the words to fall out of her mouth. "She told the girls Philip told her you two . . . did it yesterday. She said her brother bragged."

I could see the way she eyed me that she wasn't convinced it was all a lie.

"It's a disgusting, hateful lie!" I shouted. Louise only shrugged.

"Now Linda and the other girls are saying the same things. I'm sorry, but you wanted to know."

"I never met a girl as horrible as Clara Sue Cutler," I said. I felt the fury in my face, but I couldn't help it. One moment the world was bright and beautiful. There were birds singing and the sky was blessed with soft, clean white clouds that made you feel happy to be alive and able to see them, and the next moment, a storm came rushing in, flooding the blue with dirty dark gray and drowning the sunlight and the laughter and the smiles.

"They want me to spy on you," Louise whispered. "Linda just asked me."

"Spy? What do they mean?"

"Tell them anything you tell me about things you do with Philip," she explained. "But I would never tell them anything you told me in confidence," she said. "You see you can trust me," she added, but I wondered if she had told me what the girls were saying because she really wanted to help me or because she wanted to see me made sad.

Jimmy was right about rich people, I thought. These rich, spoiled girls were much more conniving than the girls I had known at my other schools. They had more time to spend on intrigues and seemed to swim in a pool of jealousy. There were more green eyes here, and everyone was so conscious of what each wore and had. Of course, girls were proud of their nice clothes and their jewelry everywhere I had been, but here they flaunted it more, and if one had something special, the others tried to have something even better very quickly.

I was no threat to them as far as clothes and jewelry went; yet it must be bothering them a great deal that Philip Cutler cared about me. They couldn't get him to care about them, no matter how expensive their clothes were and how dazzling their jewels were.

"So what did happen yesterday?" Louise asked.

"Nothing," I said. "He was very polite. He took me for a ride and showed me wonderful scenery and then he took me home."

"He didn't try to . . . do anything?"

"No," I said and quickly swung my eyes away. When I looked back at her, I could see her disappointment. "So Clara Sue had better stop spreading her lies."

"She's just ashamed her brother likes you," Louise said rather nonchalantly.

How horrible, I thought, to be considered so much lower than someone else just because your parents weren't rich. It was on the tip of my tongue to say she could tell Clara Sue not to worry anymore anyway, since my parents had forbidden me to go riding with Philip, but before I could say anything, we heard the bell for homeroom.

"Oh, no," I said, realizing the time. "We're going to be late."

"That's all right," Louise said. "I've never been late before. Old Turnkey won't keep us after school for just one lateness."

"We had better get going anyway," I said, heading for the door. Louise stopped in the doorway when I opened it.

"I'll tell you what they say about you," she said, her watery eyes watching me from under her lashes, "if you want me to."

"I don't care what they say about me," I lied. "They're not worth caring about." I hurried on to homeroom with Louise right beside me, her shoes clicking as we flew down the hallway. My heart, which had been made of feathers, had suddenly grown as heavy as lead.

"You girls are late," Mr. Wengrow said the moment we came through the doorway.

"I'm sorry, sir," I said first. "We were in the bathroom and—"

"Gossiping and you didn't hear the bell," he concluded and shook his head. Louise hurried to her desk, and I slipped into mine. Mr. Wengrow made some notations and then slapped his yardstick on the desk in anticipation of the morning's announcements.

Another day at Emerson Peabody had only just begun, and already I felt as if I had been on a roller coaster for hours and hours.

A little more than halfway through the third period, I was called out of my social studies class to see Mrs. Turnbell. When I came to her office, her secretary glared at me and spoke curtly, telling me to take a seat. I had to wait at least another ten full minutes and wondered why I had been told to come right away if I couldn't go right in. I was missing valuable class time just sitting there. Finally Mrs. Turnbell buzzed her secretary, who then told me to go in.

Mrs. Turnbell was sitting behind her desk, looking down and writing. She didn't even look up when I entered. I stood there for a few moments, waiting, clutching my books to my chest tightly. Then, still without looking at me, she told me to take the seat in front of her desk. She continued to write for a few moments after I had sat down. Finally her cold green eyes lifted from the papers before her and she sat back in her seat.

"Why were you late for homeroom today?" she demanded without any greeting first.

"Oh. I was talking to a friend in the bathroom, and we got so involved, I lost track of time until the second bell rang, but as soon as it had, I ran to my homeroom," I said.

"I can't believe I have another problem with you so soon."

"It's not a problem, Mrs. Turnbell. I—"

"Do you know that your brother has been late twice for classes since you two were entered in this school?" she snapped.

I shook my head.

"And now you," she added, nodding.

"It's my first lateness. Ever," I added.

"Ever?" She raised her dark and somewhat bushy eyebrows skeptically. "In any case this is not the place to begin developing bad habits. This is especially not the place," she emphasized.

"Yes, ma'am," I said. "I'm sorry."

"I believe I explained our rules to you and your brother on your first morning here. Tell me, Miss Longchamp, was my explanation adequate?" She kept on without allowing me to answer. "I told you that both of you had an extra burden and an extra responsibility since your father was employed here," she continued. Her words stung and made the tears that had flown into my eyes feel hot.

"When a brother and sister have the same bad habits," she went on, "it is not hard to determine that they have them because they come from the same background."

"But we don't have bad habits, Mrs. Turnbell. We—"

"Don't be insolent! Are you questioning my judgment?"

"No, Mrs. Turnbell," I said and bit down on my lower lip to keep myself from adding any words.

"You will report to detention immediately after school today," she snapped.

"But . . ."

"What?" She raised her eyes and glared at me.

"I have a piano lesson with Mr. Moore after school and—"

"You're going to have to miss this one, but you have only yourself to blame," she said. "Now, return to your class," she commanded.

"What happened?" Louise asked when I saw her on the way to the cafeteria.

"I got detention for being late to homeroom," I moaned.

"Really? Detention for being late only once?" She tilted her head. "I guess I'm next, only . . ."

"Only what?"

"Clara Sue and Linda have been late to class twice this week, and the Turnkey hasn't even called them down to reprimand them. Usually it's after three latenesses."

"I think she's clumped my brother's two and my one together," I reasoned sourly.

Philip was waiting for me at the entrance to the cafeteria. He saw the sad look on my face, and I told him what had happened.

"That's so unfair," he said. "Maybe you should have your father speak to her."

"Oh, I couldn't ask Daddy to do that. What if she got mad at him and had him fired and all on account of me!"

Philip shrugged.

"It's still not fair," he said. He looked down at the paper bag I had clutched in my hand. "And what gourmet sandwich did you make for yourself today?" he asked.

"I . . ." All I had in my bag was an apple I had grabbed on the way out. Fern had gotten up earlier than usual, and between taking care of her and making breakfast, I had just forgotten to make any sandwiches until it was time to leave. I couldn't make Daddy late for work, so I made a sandwich quickly for Jimmy and threw an apple into a paper bag for myself. "I just have an apple today," I said.

"What? You can't just have an apple for lunch. Let me buy you lunch today."

"Oh, no, I don't have much of an appetite anyway and—"

"Please. I never bought a girl lunch before. All the girls I ever knew could buy me lunch twice over," he added, laughing.

"If I can't take you for rides, at least let me do this."

"Well . . . okay," I said. "Maybe just this once."

We found a table off to the side and got into the lunch line. The girls who sat with Louise and the older girls all gazed with curiosity, especially the ones at Clara Sue's table. I saw the way she nodded and whispered. Ironically, my being with Philip helped confirm the ugly rumors she was spreading about me. I knew all their eyes would be glued to Philip and me when we approached the cashier, and they would all know he had bought me lunch. The thought of what she'd say then made me feel like ripping those golden strands out of Clara Sue's head.

"So," Philip said, turning to me after we sat down and started to eat, "there's no chance of your getting out for a ride soon, huh?"

"I told you, Philip—"

"Yeah, yeah. Listen, how about this," he said. "I'll come by your place about seven tonight. You sneak out. Tell your parents you're going to study with a friend or something. They won't know the difference and—"

"I don't lie to my parents, Philip," I said.

"It won't be a lie, exactly. I'll study something with you. How's that?"

I shook my head.

"I can't," I said. "Please don't ask me to lie."

Before he could say anything else, we suddenly heard a commotion and turned in Jimmy's direction. Some boys had gone over to Jimmy's table and said something to him, and whatever they had said had set him off like a firecracker. In seconds he was up and at them, pushing and wrestling with boys bigger than him. It drew the attention of the entire cafeteria.

"They're ganging up on him," Philip said, and shot off to jump into the fray. Teachers rushed in; cafeteria staff came around the counter. It only took a few moments to break it up, but to me it seemed like ages. All the boys involved were marched out of the cafeteria just as the bell rang for the students to return to class.

I was on pins and needles most of the afternoon. Whenever the bell rang to change classes, I, along with most everyone else, walked past Mrs. Turnbell's office to see what was happening. Louise, who was as good as a news service, found out that four boys, as well as Jimmy and Philip, had been brought to the office and kept sitting in the outer office while Mrs. Turnbell questioned each of them privately. Daddy had been called into Mrs. Turnbell's office, too.

By the day's end the verdict was known. All the boys except Jimmy were assigned detention for roughhousing in the cafeteria. Jimmy was declared the cause of it all and was suspended three days and put on probation.

I had ten minutes before I had to report to detention, so I rushed down to Daddy's office looking for him and Jimmy. As soon as I reached the basement, I could hear Daddy's shouting.

"How do you think this looks—my son being suspended? I got to have the respect of my men. Now they'll be laughing at me behind my back!"

"It wasn't my fault," Jimmy protested.

"Not your fault? You're always in trouble. Since when's it not your fault? Here they're doing us a favor letting you and Dawn attend the school—"

"It ain't no favor to me!" Jimmy snapped back. Before he could say another word, Daddy's hand came flying up and slapped him across the face. Jimmy fell back and saw me standing in the doorway. He looked at Daddy and then rushed out past me.

"Jimmy!" I cried and hurried to catch up with him. He didn't stop until he reached the exit. "Where are you going?" I asked.

"Out of here and for good," he said, his face beet red. "I knew it wouldn't be any good. I hate it here! *I hate it!*" he screamed and ran off. *"Jimmy!"*

He didn't turn back, and the clock was ticking against me. I couldn't be late for detention, too, especially after all this. Feeling as if I were bound and gagged, more frustrated than I'd ever been in my life, I lowered my head and hurried up the stairs and to the detention room, my tears flowing freely.

Everything had started to look like it would work out—my music, piano lessons, Philip, and now, just as if it had all been made of soap bubbles, it burst around me, splashing alongside my tears on the floor.

As soon as detention ended, I hurried downstairs to Daddy, hoping that he had calmed down. Cautiously I entered the office. He was sitting behind his desk with his back to the door, staring at the wall.

"Hi, Daddy," I said. He turned around, and I tried to judge his mood.

"I'm sorry about what happened, Daddy," I said quickly, "but it's not all my and Jimmy's fault, either. Mrs. Turnbell has been out to get us. She didn't like us from the start. You must have seen that in her face the first day," I protested.

"Oh, I know it bent her out a whack to have her told my children get to go here, but it's not the first time Jimmy's been in a ruckus, Dawn. And he's been late to class, too, and snippy with some of his teachers! Seems no matter what you do for him, he's going to be bad."

"It's harder for Jimmy, Daddy. He hasn't had the chance to be a real student until now, and these rich boys have been picking on him something terrible. I know. Up until now, he's taken all they've thrown at him and held his temper, just because he wanted to please you . . . and me," I added. I wouldn't dare tell him what some of the nastier girls were doing to me.

"I don't know," Daddy said, shaking his head. "He's bound for trouble's doors, I think. Takes after my brother Reuben, who, the last time I heard, was in jail."

"In jail? For what?" I asked, astounded with this sudden bit of information. Daddy had never mentioned his brother Reuben before.

"Stealing. He was always into one thing or another all his life."

"Is Reuben older or younger than you, Daddy?"

"He's older, by little more than a year. Jimmy even looks like him and sulks just the way he used to." Daddy shook his head. "Don't look good," he added.

"He won't be as bad as Reuben!" I cried. "Jimmy's not evil. He wants to be good and do well in school. I just know he does. He just needs a fair chance. I can talk to him and get him to try again. You'll see."

"I don't know. I don't know," he repeated and shook his head. Then he rose with a great effort. "Shouldn't have come here," he mumbled. "It was bad luck."

I followed Daddy out, walking in the coolness of his shadow. Maybe it was bad luck to try to do things that are beyond you. Maybe we just belonged in the poor world, gazing dreamily at the rich people as they went by, and looking hungrily in store windows. Maybe we were meant to always struggle to make ends meet. Maybe that was our terrible destiny, and we couldn't do anything about it.

"How come you never told me about Reuben before, Daddy?"

"Well, he was in trouble so much, I just put him out of mind," Daddy explained quickly.

We stepped out into the dreariest day I had seen in a long time, I thought. The sky was a bitter gray with a layer of clouds moving rapidly under another, thicker layer. The wind was cooler and sharper.

"Looks like it's going to be a cold rain soon," Daddy said. He started the car. "Can't wait for spring."

"When did you hear about your brother Reuben, Daddy?" I asked as we started away.

"Oh, about two years ago or so," he said casually. Two years ago? I thought. But how could he? We weren't near the family then.

"Do they have phones on the farm?" I asked incredulously. From all I had been able to learn about the farms back in Georgia, they sounded too poor to afford phones, especially if we couldn't.

"Phones?" He laughed. "Hardly. They don't have running water or electricity. The homestead, if you can call it that, has a hand pump and there's an outhouse. At night they use oil lamps. Some of them crackers think a phone's the devil's own invention and never in their lives have put their ear against one or want to."

"Then how did you hear about your brother only two years or so ago, Daddy?" I asked quickly. "Did you get a letter?"

"A letter. Hardly. There ain't a one of them who can write more than his name, if that much."

"Then how did you learn about Reuben?" I asked again. For a moment he didn't respond. I didn't think he was going to, so I added, "You didn't go back there yourself one time without us, did you, Daddy?"

The way he looked at me told me I had hit the mark.

"You're getting pretty smart, Dawn. It's not easy keeping something under the covers when you're around. Don't say nothing about it to your ma, but I did go back one time for a few hours. I was working close enough to make the drive and return the same night and I did it without saying nothing."

"Well, if we were that close, why didn't we all go, Daddy?"

"I said *I* was close. I woulda had to go hours back to get you and then hours back to where I was and then hours to the farm," he explained.

"Who did you see on the farm, Daddy?"

"I saw my ma. Pa died a while back. Just keeled over in a field one day clutching his heart." Tears came into Daddy's eyes, but he quickly blinked them back. "Ma looked so old," he added, shaking his head. "I was sorry I went. It near broke my heart to look at her sitting there in her rocker. Pa's death and Reuben's going to jail and problems with some of my other brothers and sisters grayed her skin as well as her hair. She didn't even recognize me, and when I told her who I was, she said, 'Ormand's in the house churnin' up some butter for me.' I used to do that for her all the time," he added, smiling.

"Did you see your sister Lizzy?"

"Yeah, she was there, married with four of her own kids, two not a year apart. She's the one told me about Reuben. I didn't stay there long, and I never told your ma because it was all bad news, so don't you go blabbing now."

"I won't. I promise. I'm sorry I didn't get to see Grandpa, though," I said sadly.

"Yeah, you would have liked him. He probably would have got out his harmonica and stumped out something for you, and then maybe the two of you would have sung and played something together," Daddy said, dreaming aloud.

"You must have told me about his playing the harmonica before, Daddy, because that stuck in my mind."

"Must have," he said. He started to hum something I imagined his father played, and I didn't say anything and he didn't say anything until we were home, but I wondered about Daddy and what other secrets he had.

Jimmy hadn't been home yet, so Momma didn't know a thing about the troubles at school. Daddy and I looked at each other after looking at her and silently decided to keep it all to ourselves.

"Where's Jimmy?" she asked.

"He's with some new friends," Daddy said. Momma took a look at me and saw the lie, but she didn't question it.

But when Jimmy didn't come home for supper, we had to tell

Momma about the fight and his getting into trouble. She nodded as we spoke.

"I knew it anyway," she said. "Neither of you are worth a pig's knuckle when it comes to telling white lies—or any lies for that matter." She sighed. "That boy's just not happy, might never be," she added with a tone of prophetic doom.

"Oh, no, Momma. Jimmy's going to be something great yet. I just know it. He's very smart. You'll see," I insisted.

"Hope so," she said. She started to cough again. Her cough had changed, become deeper, shaking her entire body silently sometimes. Momma claimed that meant she was getting better, driving it down and out, but I didn't feel good about it, and I still longed for her to go to a real doctor or a hospital.

After I cleaned the dishes and put everything away, I practiced a song. Daddy and Fern were my audience, with Fern very attentive whenever I sang. She clapped her little hands together whenever Daddy clapped his hands. Momma listened from her bedroom, calling out once in a while to tell me how good I sounded.

It grew dark and the cold rain Daddy had forecast came, the drops splattering our windows. They sounded like thousands of fingers being tapped against the glass. There was thunder and lightning, and the wind whipped around the apartment house, whistling through all the cracks and crannies. I had to put another blanket on Momma when her teeth started chattering. We decided we would let little Fern sleep in her clothes this night. I felt so sorry and worried for Jimmy because he was still out there somewhere, wandering about in the dark, stormy night—I thought my heart might break. I knew he didn't have any money with him, so I was sure he had gone without any supper. I had wrapped him up a plate of food that was ready to be warmed up the moment he returned.

But the night wore on and he didn't come home. I stayed awake as long as I could, staring at the door and listening for Jimmy's footsteps in the hallway, but whenever I heard footsteps, they were going upstairs or into another apartment. Once in a while I went to a window and gazed out through the cloudy glass and into the rainy darkness.

I finally went to sleep, too, but sometime in the middle of the night, I awoke to the sound of the front door opening.

"Where were you?" I whispered. I couldn't see his eyes or much of his face in the darkness.

"I was going to run away," he said. "I even got as far as fifty miles outside of Richmond."

"James Gary Longchamp, you didn't?"

"I did. I hitched a couple of rides, and the second one letting me out at a roadside restaurant. All's I had on me was some change, so I got a cup of coffee. The waitress took pity on me and brought me a roll and butter. Then she started asking me questions. She has a boy about my age, too, and works all the time because her husband was killed in a car accident about five years ago.

"I was going to go out and keep hitchhiking, but it started to rain so hard, I couldn't get out. The waitress knew this truck driver who was heading back to Richmond, and she asked him to take me along, so I came back. But I ain't staying, and I ain't going back to that snob school, and you shouldn't either, Dawn," he said with determination.

"Oh, Jimmy, you've got a right to be upset. Rich kids aren't better than the poor kids we've known, and we've been treated unfairly just because we're not rich like the others, but Daddy didn't mean to harm us by getting us into Emerson Peabody. He was only trying to do something good for us," I said. "You have to admit that the school is beautiful and full of new things, and you told me yourself some of your teachers were very nice and very good. You've already started doing better schoolwork, haven't you, and you like playing on the intramural team, right?"

"We're still like fish out of water there, and those other kids are never going to accept us or let us live in peace, Dawn. I'd rather be in a regular public school."

"Now, Jimmy, you can't really mean that," I whispered. I touched his hand, which was still very cold. "You must have been freezing out there, James Gary. Your hair is soaked. And so are your clothes. You could have caught pneumonia!"

"Who cares?"

"I care," I said. "Now get out of those wet clothes quickly," I ordered and went for a towel. When I returned, he was wrapped in the blanket, his wet clothing on the floor. I sat beside him and began to wipe his hair dry. When I was finished, I saw the outline of his smile in the dark.

"I never met another girl like you, Dawn," he said. "And I'm not just saying that because you're my sister. I guess I came back because I didn't want to leave you all alone with this mess. I got to thinking about you having to go back to that school and how you'd have no one to protect you."

"Oh, Jimmy, I don't need protection, and besides, if I do, Daddy will protect me, won't he?"

"Sure," he said, pulling his hand back. "Just like he protected us today. I tried to tell him it wasn't my fault, but he wouldn't listen. All he could do was yell at me for being no good and letting him down. And then he goes and hits me."

He flopped back on his pillow.

"He shouldn't have hit you, Jimmy. But he said you reminded him of his brother Reuben, who's in jail now."

"Reuben?"

"Yes," I said, lowering myself to lie beside him. "He told me all about him and why he was so afraid when you got into trouble. He says you look like Reuben and even act like him sometimes."

"I don't remember him mentioning anyone named Reuben," he said.

"Me neither. Daddy's been back to his home," I whispered even lower, and told him what Daddy had said about his visit.

"I was thinking of heading for Georgia myself when I left here," he said, his voice full of wonder.

"Were you? Oh, Jimmy," I said, sitting up and looking down at him, "can't you try again, just once more, just for me? Ignore those nasty boys and just do your work."

"It's hard to ignore them when they get ugly and disgusting." He looked away from me.

"What did they say to you, Jimmy? Philip wouldn't tell me." Jimmy was silent. "It had to do with me and Philip, didn't it?" There was a long painful silence between us.

"Yeah," he finally said.

"They knew they could get you angry that way, Jimmy." And it was all because of Clara Sue Cutler, I thought, and her vicious jealous streak. I never disliked anyone as much as I disliked her. "They were deliberately baiting you, Jimmy."

"I know, but . . . I can't help getting angry when anyone says bad things about you, Dawn," he confessed, gazing at me with eyes so full of hurt it made my heart ache. "I'm sorry if you're mad," he finished.

"I'm not mad at you. I like the way you look after me, only I don't want to cause you any trouble."

"You didn't," he said. "But it's just like you to think it was all your fault. All right," he said after a moment and after a deep sigh, "I'll sit out my suspension and go back and try again, but I don't think it's going to matter. We just don't belong there. At least, I don't," he added.

"Sure you do, Jimmy. You're just as smart and strong as any of them."

"I don't mean I'm not as good as them. I'm just not their kind.

Maybe you are, Dawn. You can get along with anyone. I bet you could make the devil repent."

I laughed.

"I'm glad you came back, Jimmy. It would have broken Momma's heart if you hadn't, and Daddy's, too. Little Fern would have been crying for you every day."

"And you?" he asked quickly.

"I was crying already," I admitted. He didn't say anything. After a moment he took my hand and squeezed it gently. It seemed like it had been so long since he had wanted to touch me. I brushed back the strands of hair that had fallen over his forehead. I felt like kissing him softly on the cheek, but I didn't know how he would react. We were so close, my breast grazed his arm, but unlike all the other times, he didn't jump as if he had been stuck with a pin. Suddenly I felt him shudder.

"Aren't you warm enough, Jimmy?"

"I'll be all right," he said, but I put my arm around him and held him, rubbing his naked shoulder.

"You'd better get under the blanket yourself and go back to sleep, Dawn," he said, his voice cracking.

"All right. Night, Jimmy," I whispered and risked kissing him on the cheek. He didn't pull away.

"Good night," he said, and I lay back. For a long time I stared up into the darkness, my emotions in a turmoil. When I closed my eyes, I still saw Jimmy's naked shoulders glistening in the darkness, and the feel of his soft cheek still lingered on my lips.

6

Opening Night

Daddy started to yell at Jimmy first thing in the morning.

"Why'd you run away for?" he shouted.

"You always do," Jimmy shot back. They glared at each other, but when Momma came out, she was so happy Jimmy had come home that for once Daddy stopped.

"I'll go around and get all your schoolwork from your teachers, Jimmy," I said quickly. "In the meanwhile you'll be able to help Momma with Fern."

"Just what I wanted to be, a baby-sitter," he moaned.

"It's your own fault," Daddy said. Jimmy went into a sulk. I was glad when it was time for Daddy and me to go to school.

"Jimmy's going to try again, Daddy," I told him after we started off. "He promised me last night after he came home."

"Good," Daddy grunted. Then he turned to me and looked at me so strangely. "It's nice of you to care so much about your brother."

"Didn't your family care about each other, Daddy?" I asked.

"Nothing like you and Jimmy," he said, but I could see from the way his eyes narrowed that he didn't want to talk about it.

I couldn't imagine not caring about Jimmy. No matter how happy I could be, if Jimmy wasn't happy, I wasn't. So much had happened to us so quickly at Emerson Peabody, it left my head spinning. I thought the best thing I could do now was concentrate on my schoolwork and my music and put all the bad things behind me. Jimmy really did try harder, too. When he returned, he became more involved with his intramural sports and even did passingly well in his classes. It was beginning to look like we would be all right.

However, once in a while, when I was passing through the corridors, I would see Mrs. Turnbell standing off to the side watching me. Jimmy said he felt as if she were haunting him, he saw her watching him so often. I smiled and greeted her politely whenever I could and she nodded back, but she looked like she was waiting for something to confirm her belief that we couldn't live up to the demands a school like Emerson Peabody made on its students, students who she believed were more special than us.

Of course, Philip was still upset that I couldn't go out on dates with him, and that I wouldn't sneak out to do it. He kept after me to ask Daddy or to meet him secretly. In my heart I hoped everything would improve when spring came. Unfortunately, winter held on stubbornly, keeping the floorboards cold, the skies gray, and the trees and bushes bare. But when the air finally turned warm and the trees and flowers budded, I was filled with a sense of renewed hope and happiness. I drew strength and pleasure from everything that blossomed around me. Bright sunshine and bright colors made even our poor neighborhood look special. Daddy wasn't talking about quitting his job anymore, Jimmy was doing well in school, and I was finally involved in music the way I had always dreamt I would be.

Only Momma's persistent illness depressed us, but I thought that with the coming of spring, with her walking outside on sunny days and keeping the windows open for more fresh air, she would surely improve. Spring had a way of renewing all faith. It always had for me, and now, more than ever, I prayed it would do wonders for us again.

One bright afternoon after I was finished with my piano lesson, I found Philip waiting for me at the door of the music suite. I didn't see him and almost bumped into him because I was walking with my books cradled in my arms and my eyes down. My body was still filled with the music. The notes I had played continued to play repeatedly in my head. When I played the piano, it was as if my fingers had dreams of their own. Ten minutes after I had gotten up from the piano stool, I could still sense how they held on to the feel of the piano keys. The tips tingled with the memory of the touch, and they wanted to repeat their movements over the keyboard, drawing out the notes and weaving them into melodies and tunes.

"Penny for your thoughts," I heard and looked up at Philip's smiling, gentle eyes. He was leaning against the corridor wall nonchalantly, his arms crossed over his chest. His golden hair was brushed back and shiny, still a little wet from the shower he had just taken after baseball practice. Philip was one of the starting pitchers on the school's varsity team.

"Oh, hi," I said stopping abruptly with surprise.

"I hope you were thinking about me," he said.

I laughed.

"I was just thinking about my music, about my piano lessons."

"Well, I'm disappointed, but how's it going?"

"Mr. Moore's pleased," I said modestly. "He just gave me the solo to sing at the spring concert."

"He did? Wow!" Philip said, straightening up. "Congratulations."

"Thank you."

"We had a shortened practice today, and I . . . I knew you would still be here."

The halls were practically empty. Once in a while someone came out of a room and walked off, but other than that, we were alone for what was really the first time in a long time.

He drew closer until he had my back to the wall and put his hands on the wall to cage me in.

"I wish I could drive you home," he said.

"So do I, but—"

"What if I come by your house tonight, and we don't go for a ride? We just sit in my car."

"I don't know, Philip."

"You won't be lying then, will you?"

"I'll have to tell them where I'm going and—"

"You tell them everything? All the time?" He shook his head. "Parents expect you to do secret things sometimes. They do," he said. "How about it?"

"I don't know. I . . . I'll see," I said. There was such frustration in his eyes. "Maybe one night."

"Good." He looked around and drew closer.

"Philip, someone could see us," I said when he brought his lips closer.

"Just a quick congratulations kiss," he said and brought his lips to mine. He even brought his hand to my breast.

"Philip," I protested. He laughed.

"All right. So," he said, standing straight again, "are you nervous about singing at the concert?"

"Of course. It will be the first time I've ever sung by myself in front of so many people, and so many well-to-do people who have heard and seen really talented performers. Louise told me your sister's going to be jealous and angry about it. She expected to get the solo."

"She had it last year. Besides, she sounds like a foghorn."

"Oh, no, she doesn't," I said, looking up quickly. "But I wish she would stop saying nasty things about me. If I do well on a test, she tells people I cheated. She hasn't let up on me since I arrived. One of these days I'm going to have it out with her." Philip started to laugh. "It's not funny."

"I was laughing at how bright and intense your eyes become when you're angry. You can't hide your true feelings."

"I know. Daddy says I would be a terrible poker player."

"I'd like to play strip poker with you someday," he said, smiling licentiously.

"Philip!"

"What?"

"Don't say things like that," I said, but I couldn't help imagining it. He shrugged.

"Can't help it sometimes. Especially when I'm around you."

Could he hear my heart pounding? I saw some students coming around the corner behind us.

"I've got to get down to Daddy's office. He and Jimmy are probably waiting for me," I added and started down the stairway.

"Dawn. Wait."

I turned back to him. He joined me on the stairs.

"Do you think . . . I mean, since it's such a special occasion and all . . . that you can get your father and mother to let me take you to the concert at least?" he asked hopefully.

"I'll ask," I said.

"Great. I'm glad I waited around to see you," he added and leaned forward to kiss me. I thought he was going to kiss me quickly on the cheek, but he kissed me on the neck instead. He did it and was on his way before I had a chance to respond. The students coming down the corridor saw him and the boys howled. My heart didn't seem to fit my chest. It beat too fast, too fierce, too loud, and my pulse raced too excitedly. I was afraid Daddy and Jimmy would see the redness in my cheeks and know I had been kissed.

Surely there was something very special between me and Philip, I thought, if his merely kissing me or looking at me or speaking softly to me could set my body on fire, make me tingle and make me dizzy. I took a deep breath and sighed. Daddy and Momma just had to let him take me to the concert; they just had to, I thought. I had done what they had wanted and not nagged them to go out on dates, even though girls my age all around me were allowed to do so. It wasn't fair; they had to understand.

I could understand them being a little afraid for me when I had first started at Emerson Peabody. But I believed I had grown considerably during these last few months anyway. Success with my music and my schoolwork had given me a new sense of confidence. I felt older, stronger. Surely if I saw that in myself, Momma and Daddy could see it as well.

Confident they would give me permission, I hurried down to the basement to meet Daddy and Jimmy and give them the news about my solo. I had never seen Daddy so excited and proud.

"You hear that, Jimmy boy!" he exclaimed, slapping his hands together. "Your sister's a star."

"I'm not a star yet, Daddy. I've got to do it well," I said.

"You will. What good news," Daddy said. "Something good to bring home to your momma."

"Daddy," I said as he gathered his things for us to leave. "Do you think since this is a special occasion that Philip Cutler could pick me up and take me to the concert?"

Daddy stopped in his tracks. His smile evaporated slowly and his eyes darkened for a moment and grew small. As I stared at him, hoping, a little warmth crept back into his gaze.

"Well, I don't know, honey. I . . . we'll see."

When we got home, Momma was lying in bed awake, one eye on Fern, who sat on a blanket on the floor playing with her toys. The late afternoon sunlight played peekaboo with some lazy clouds, but Momma had the shades drawn so even when the sun peeped out, it didn't drop any warm, happy rays into the room. When I entered, Momma sat up slowly and with great effort.

She had obviously not brought a brush to her hair all day. The strands hung down randomly on the sides and some curled up and spiraled about on top. She used to wash her hair almost every day, so that it had gleamed like black silk.

"A woman's hair is her crowning jewel," she had told me many times. Whenever she had been too tired to brush her hair herself, she always asked me to do it.

Momma never needed much makeup. She always had a smooth complexion with pink lips. Her eyes sparkled like polished black onyx. I wanted so much to look like her and thought it was unfair of nature to have skipped a generation while most other children looked exactly like their parents.

Before she became sickly, Momma would stand perfectly straight and walk with her shoulders back, as proud as the mythical Indian princess Daddy always compared her to. She moved gracefully, swiftly, passing through the day like a streak of ebony paint stroked through a milk-white canvas. Now she sat hunched over, her head down, her arms resting limply on her legs, and she looked at me with sad, glassy eyes, the onyx dulled, the silk hair turned into a rough cotton, her complexion faded, pale, and her lips nearly colorless. Her cheekbones were far more prominent and her collarbone looked as if it would pop right through her thin layer of skin.

Before I could say anything about Philip, Fern reached up for me and started to cry my name.

"Where's your daddy and Jimmy?" Momma asked, looking behind me.

"They went to pick up some groceries. Daddy thought I should come right in to help you with Fern."

"I'm glad," she said, fighting for a deep breath. "The baby tired me out today."

"It's not just the baby, Momma," I chastised gently.

"It's coming along, Dawn," she replied. "Could you get me a glass of water, honey? My lips feel parched."

I went out with Fern and got Momma her water. Then I handed her the glass and watched as she drank. Her Adam's apple bobbed like a float on a fishing line.

"For months you've been promising you would go to a real doctor and not rely on backwoods medicines and such if you didn't get better quickly. Well, you're not getting better that fast, and you're not living up to your promise." I hated speaking to her so firmly, but I thought I had to now.

"It's just one of them stubborn coughs. I had a cousin back in Georgia who had a cold for nearly a year before it upped and left her."

"Well, she suffered for a year for no reason," I insisted. "Just like you're suffering, Momma."

"All right, all right. You're getting worse than Grandma Long-champ. Why, when I was pregnant with Jimmy, she wouldn't let up on me a minute. Everything I did was wrong. It was a relief giving birth, just so I could get her off my back."

"Grandma Longchamp? But, Momma, I thought you gave birth to Jimmy at a farmhouse on the road."

"What? Oh, yeah, I did. I meant until I left the farm."

"But didn't you and Daddy leave right after you got married?"

"Not exactly right after. Soon after. Quit questioning me so closely, Dawn. I'm not thinking straight just yet," she snapped. It wasn't like her to be so short with me, but I imagined it was because of her illness.

I thought I should change the topic. I didn't want to make her unhappy while she was still suffering so.

"Guess what, Momma?" I said, bouncing Fern in my arms. "I'm going to sing the solo at the concert," I said proudly.

"Why, bless my soul. Bless my soul." She pressed her palms against her chest. Even when she wasn't coughing, she seemed to have trouble breathing every once in a while, especially when something caught her by surprise or she moved too quickly. "Ain't that wonderful. I knew you'd show those rich folks they ain't no better than you. Come here so I can give you a real hug," she said.

I put little Fern down on the bed, and Momma and I embraced. Her thin arms held me to her as tightly as she could, and I could feel her ribs through her shift dress.

"Momma," I said, the tears filling my eyes. "You've lost so much weight, much more than I realized."

"Not so much and I shoulda lost a few pounds here and there. It'll come back on faster than you can shake a stick, you'll see. One thing about women my age, when they wanna gain weight, they just gotta smell food. Sometimes just looking at it will add a pound here and there," she joked. She kissed me on the cheek. "Congratulations, Dawn honey. Did you tell your daddy?"

"Yes."

"I bet his chest blew out some," she said, shaking her head.

"Momma, I got something to ask about the concert."

"Oh?"

"Since it is a special occasion and all, do you think it would be all right for Philip Cutler to pick me up and take me? He promises to drive carefully and—"

"Did you ask your daddy?" she responded quickly.

"Uh-huh. He said we'll see, but I think if it's all right with you, it's all right with him."

Suddenly she looked so troubled and old staring back at me.

"It's not a long ride, Momma, and I really want to go with Philip. Other girls my age go for rides and on dates, but I haven't complained. . . ."

She nodded. "I can't hold you back from growing up, Dawn. And I don't want to, but I don't want you to get serious with this boy . . . any boy yet. Don't be like me and give up your youth."

"Oh, Momma, I'm not getting married. I'm just going to the spring concert. Will it be all right?" I pleaded.

It was as if it took all her strength to do it, but she nodded.

"Oh, thank you, Momma." I hugged her again.

"Dawn, up," Fern called impatiently, jealous of all the affection Momma and I were passing between us. "Dawn, up."

"Her Highness is calling," Momma said, and then lay back against her pillow. I watched her with my heart in a turmoil: happy about my being about to go out on a date, but sad and aching with the sight of how slowly and painfully Momma spoke and moved.

Mr. Moore decided to double up my lessons for the rest of the week. Finally it was the day of the concert. At lunchtime Mr. Moore played the piano and I sang. Twice my voice cracked. He stopped playing and looked up at me.

"Now, Dawn," he said. "I want you to take a deep breath and calm yourself down before we go on."

"Oh, Mr. Moore, I can't do this!" I cried. "I don't know why I thought I could. But to sing a solo in front of all those people, most of whom go to the opera and to Broadway in New York City and know real talent—"

"*You* are real talent," Mr. Moore said. "Do you think I would put you out on that stage alone if I didn't think so? Don't forget, Dawn, when you go out there, I go, too. Now, you're not going to let me down, are you?"

"No, sir," I said, nearly in tears.

"Remember when you told me once you wished you could be like a bird, high on a tree, singing freely into the wind and not worrying about who hears it and who doesn't?"

"Yes. I still do."

"Well, then, close your eyes and see yourself perched on that branch and then sing into the wind. After a while, just like a baby bird, you'll get your wings and fly. You'll soar, Dawn. I just know it," he said. Gone was his cherub smile and his impish grin; gone was the playful happy twinkle in his eyes. Instead, his face was stone serious, and his words and eyes filled me with confidence.

"Okay," I said softly, and we began again. This time I sang my heart out, and when we were finished, his face was flushed with satisfaction. He got up and kissed me on the cheek.

"You're ready," he said.

My heart was pounding with excitement and happiness as I hurried out of the music suite.

As soon as the last bell rang, I ran to find Jimmy and Daddy. I was paralyzed with nervousness and wanted to go straight home to get ready for the concert, scheduled for 8:00 P.M.

When we arrived home, Momma was lying in bed, her face more flushed than usual, and shivering something terrible. Fern had gotten into some of the kitchenware, but I could see Momma didn't know. We all gathered around her bed, and I felt her forehead.

"She's shivering, Daddy," I said, "but she feels feverish."

Momma's teeth chattered, and she turned her eyes to me and forced a smile.

"It's . . . just . . . a cold," she claimed.

"No, it's not, Momma. Whatever's been eating at you is getting worse."

"I'll be all right!" she cried.

"You will if you go to a doctor, Momma."

"Dawn's right, Sally Jean. We can't let this go on anymore. We're going to wrap you up real good and take you over to that hospital so they can look at you and give you some medicine fast," he said.

"*Nooo!*" Momma cried. I tried to comfort her while Daddy gathered her warmest clothing. Then I helped him dress her. When I looked at Momma without her clothes, I was shocked at how thin she had gotten. Her ribs poked so hard against her skin, and all her bones looked like they were going to pop out. There were fever blotches all over her, too. I kept myself from crying and worked at getting her ready. When it came time to take her out, we discovered she couldn't walk on her own. Her legs ached too much.

"I'll carry her," Daddy said, barely holding back his own tears. I hurriedly dressed Fern. Momma didn't want us to, but we were all going to go along. Neither Jimmy nor I wanted to remain home and wait.

When we arrived I went in first and told the emergency room nurse about Momma. She had an attendant roll out a wheelchair, and we got Momma into it quickly. The hospital security guard helped get Momma in. He looked at Daddy oddly, like someone trying to remember someone he had known years ago. Daddy didn't notice anything but Momma.

While we waited, Jimmy went to the gift store and brought back a lollypop for Fern. It kept her occupied, but it also smeared her face green. She had a baby's gibberish now, mixed with a real word or two, and often looked at other people waiting in the lobby and started blubbering at them. Some smiled; some were so worried about their loved ones, they could only stare blankly.

Finally, well over an hour later, a doctor sought us out. He had red hair and freckles and looked so young, I thought he couldn't bring anyone bad news. But I was wrong.

"How long has your wife had this cough and run fevers, Mr. Longchamp?" he asked Daddy.

"A while, on and off. She seemed to be getting better, so we didn't think much of it."

"She has consumption and very bad, too. Her lungs are so congested, it's amazing she can breathe," he said, not hiding his annoyance at Daddy.

But it wasn't Daddy's fault. Momma was the stubborn one, I wanted to shout. Daddy looked overwhelmed. He lowered his head and nodded. When I gazed at Jimmy, I saw him standing stiffly, his hands clenched into fists, his eyes burning with anger and sorrow.

"I've rushed her into intensive care," the doctor continued, "and put her on oxygen. She looks like she's lost a great deal of weight," he added and shook his head.

"Can we see her?" I asked, tears streaming down my face.

"Just for five minutes," he said. "And I mean five minutes."

How could a man so young be so firm? I wondered. However, it made me feel he was a good doctor.

Silently, with only little Fern repeating "lolly, lolly," and reaching for the rest of her lollypop, we walked to the elevator. Fern was intrigued with it as Jimmy pushed two and it lifted us up. Her eyes went from side to side. I pressed her closely to me and kissed her soft pink cheek.

We followed the sign that directed us to the intensive care unit. When we opened the door, the head nurse came around her desk quickly to greet us.

"You can't bring a baby in here," she declared.

"I'll wait out here, Daddy," I said. "You and Jimmy go in first."

"I'll come out after a minute or two," Jimmy promised. I saw how much he wanted and needed to see Momma. There was a small couch and a chair in a special waiting room outside of intensive care. I took Fern in there and let her crawl around on the couch while we waited. Just about two minutes later Jimmy appeared. His eyes were red.

"Go on," he said quickly. "She wants to see you."

I handed Fern to him and hurried into the room. Momma was lying in the last bed on the right. She was in an oxygen tent. Daddy stood at the right of the bed holding her hand. When I came up beside her, Momma smiled and reached out to take my hand, too.

"I'll be all right, honey," she said. "You just do a wonderful singing job tonight."

"Oh, Momma, how can I sing with you lying here in the hospital?" I cried.

"You sure better," she said. "You know how proud me and your daddy are, and it's gonna make me a whole lot better knowing my little girl's singing for all those fancy people. Promise me you'll do it, Dawn, and not let my getting sick stop you. Promise."

"I promise, Momma."

"Good," she said. Then she beckoned me closer. "Dawn," she said, her voice barely audible. I drew as close to the tent as I could. She was squeezing my hand as firmly as she was able to. "You must never think badly of us. We love you. Always remember that."

"Why should I think badly of you, Momma?"

She closed her eyes.

"Momma?"

"I'm afraid your five minutes are up, and the doctor was very explicit about that," the intensive care nurse said.

I looked back at Momma. She had her eyes closed tightly, and her face looked more flushed than before.

"Momma!" I cried under my breath. I looked at Daddy. Tears were flowing freely down his face now, and he was staring at me so hard, I felt terrible for him.

We obeyed the nurse and started away. As soon as we left the intensive care unit, I turned to Daddy.

"Why did Momma say that, Daddy? What did she mean by 'you must never think badly of us'?"

"Part of her fever, I guess," he said. "She's a bit delirious. Let's go home," he said, and we went to fetch Jimmy and little Fern.

When we got home, we didn't have time to worry about Momma, although she was on our minds. We were too busy getting ready for the concert and trying to find a baby-sitter for Fern.

As hard as I tried, I couldn't bear the thought of making my singing debut without Momma present. Yet I'd promised her I would do my best, and I wasn't going to let her down.

I didn't have time to take a shower or shampoo my hair. Instead I brushed my hair a hundred times, giving it a soft, silky sheen, adding a blue ribbon for a nice dash of color.

At least I didn't have to worry about what I should wear. One of the good things about being in the school band and chorus was that we got to wear uniforms when we performed. The school uniform consisted of a white and black wool sweater and black skirt. After I put it on, I stood up and straightened my skirt. Then I stood back and gazed at myself, imagining myself standing there before all those fine people. I knew I had developed a young girl's figure and I filled out the school sweater better than most girls my age. For the first time I thought my fair skin, blond hair, and blue eyes were attractive. Was it terrible to suddenly become infatuated with yourself? I wondered. Would this bring me bad luck? I was afraid, but I couldn't help it. The girl in the mirror smiled with satisfaction.

Daddy came in then and told me that Mrs. Jackson, an old lady who lived down the hall from us, would be willing to watch Fern tonight. He also told me that he had given the hospital Mrs. Jackson's number in case we needed to be reached. After telling me that, Daddy took a step back, giving me a long admiring look.

"You look real beautiful, honey," Daddy said. "Real grown-up."

"Thank you, Daddy."

He held something in his hand.

"Before we left the hospital, your momma asked me to give you these to wear tonight, since it's such a special occasion."

He held out the precious string of pearls.

"Oh, Daddy," I said, nearly breathless. "I can't; I shouldn't. That's our insurance policy."

"No, no, Sally Jean said you must wear them," he insisted and put them on me. I looked down at the pearls gleaming soft and white and perfect and then gazed at myself in the mirror.

"They'll bring you luck," Daddy said and kissed me on the cheek. We heard a knock on the front door.

"It's Philip," Jimmy called from the other room. Daddy stepped back, his face suddenly serious again.

Philip was dressed in a blue suit and matching tie and looked very handsome.

"Hi," he said. "Boy, you look great."

"Thank you. So do you. Philip," I said. "This is my father."

"Oh, yes, I know. I've seen you around the school, sir," Philip said. "Waved to you once in a while."

"Yes," Daddy said, his eyes growing smaller and smaller.

"How's Mrs. Longchamp?" Philip asked. "Jimmy just told me that you had to take her to the hospital earlier."

"She's very sick, but we're hopeful," Daddy said. He looked from him to me, his face so somber.

"Well, we'd better get started," Philip said softly.

"Okay," I said. I grabbed my coat, and Philip moved forward quickly to help me put it on. Daddy and Jimmy stared, Daddy looking very troubled. Just as Philip and I reached the front door, I heard Jimmy call my name.

"I'll be right with you, Philip," I said. Philip went out, and I waited for Jimmy.

"Just wanted to wish you luck," he said and leaned forward quickly to kiss me on the cheek. "Good luck," he whispered and hurried back to the apartment. I stood there a moment, bringing my fingers to my cheek, and then I turned and went out into the night. It was full of stars. I hoped one was twinkling just for me.

7

Twinkle, Twinkle Little Star

When the Emerson Peabody School came into view, my heart began to pound so hard, I thought I might faint. That's how nervous I was, and when we turned into the school driveway and we saw the lines of expensive cars arriving, I couldn't stop myself from trembling.

The parents and guests were dressed tonight as though they were attending a performance at the Metropolitan Opera House. The women wore magnificent furs and diamond earrings. Under their warm, extravagant coats they wore silk dresses in the most beautiful colors I'd ever seen. The men were all in dark suits. Some people arrived in long limousines and had their doors opened by uniformed chauffeurs.

Philip drove us around to the side entrance used by the students performing in the concert. He stopped near the door to let me out.

"Wait," Philip said when I reached for the door handle. I turned back, and he simply stared for a moment. Then he leaned forward, brought his lips to mine, and kissed me.

"Dawn," he whispered. "I spend every night dreaming of kissing you and holding you. . . ."

He started to kiss me again, but I heard the sound of the other students arriving. We were in the parking lot under the tall bright lights.

"Philip, they'll see us," I said and pulled back even though I was giddy with the nearness of him.

"Most of the girls around here wouldn't care," he said. "You're so bashful."

"I can't help it."

"It's all right. There's always later," he said, winking. "Good luck," he said.

"Thank you," I replied. It was barely a whisper.

"Wait!" he exclaimed. Then he jumped out and ran around the car to open my door for me as I gathered myself together.

"A star should be treated like a star," he said, reaching in to take my hand.

"Oh, Philip. I'm far from a star. I'm going to fall flat on my face!" I cried, looking at the crowd of impressed students who stared.

"Nonsense, Miss Longchamp. By the end of the evening we'll have to fight off the autograph seekers. Good luck. I'll be sitting out there rooting for you." He held on to my hand.

"Thank you, Philip." I took a deep breath and looked toward the doorway. "Here I go," I said. Philip didn't release my hand.

"See you right after the concert," he said. "We'll get something to eat and then . . . we'll go to my favorite spot and look at the stars. Okay?"

He pleaded with his eyes and held on to my hand tightly.

"Yes," I whispered and felt as if I had surrendered myself to him already, just by agreeing to go.

He smiled and let go. Then he started toward the auditorium. I watched him for a moment, my heart still pounding. All three of the men in my life had kissed me and filled me with confidence. Buoyed by their good wishes and affection, I turned toward the entrance. I suddenly felt a little like Sleeping Beauty awakened by the kiss of the prince.

I entered the school with some of the other members of the chorus. We all headed down the corridor toward the music suite and the backstage area. We were to put our coats in the music suite and then go prepare for the concert: warming up our instruments and our voices.

"Hi, Dawn," Linda said, approaching me. "Are those real pearls?" she asked as soon as I had taken off my coat. At the word *pearls* other girls gathered around us, including Clara Sue.

"Yes, they are. They're my mother's and they're our family heirloom," I emphasized, looking down at them myself. I was terrified the string would break and I would lose them.

"It's so hard to tell real pearls from fake pearls nowadays," Clara Sue said. "At least, that's what my mother told me once."

"These are real," I insisted.

"They really don't go with what you're wearing," Linda said, smirking, "but if they're some sort of family good-luck piece, I suppose it's all right."

"Why don't we go to the girls' room and freshen up. We've got a few minutes yet," Clara Sue suggested. As usual, when Clara Sue made a suggestion, the others quickly agreed.

"What's the matter," Linda said to me as they started out, "you too good to join us?"

"I hardly think I'm the one who's stuck-up, Linda."

"So?"

"There's plenty of time," Melissa Lee said.

They all stared at me.

"Oh, all right," I said, actually surprised at their desire to include me. "I guess I should brush my hair."

The bathroom was crowded. Girls were making last-minute adjustments on their hair and freshening lipstick. Everyone was talking excitedly. There was an electricity in the air. I went to a mirror to check myself and suddenly realized all of Clara Sue's friends were around me.

"I love your hair tonight," Linda told me.

"Yes, I never saw it looking so radiant," Clara Sue said. The others nodded, these silly smiles on their faces.

Why were they all being so nice to me? I wondered. Did they always follow Clara Sue's lead like a bunch of sheep? Was it that Philip wanted me to be his girlfriend? Maybe he told Clara Sue once and for all to be nice to me.

"Do you smell something, girls?" Clara Sue suddenly asked. Everyone started sniffing. "Someone needs some perfume."

"What's that supposed to mean, Clara Sue?" I said, realizing all this friendliness was phony.

"Nothing. We're just thinking of you. Right, girls?" she said.

"Yeah," they replied in chorus, and on that cue everyone brought out a can of stink-bomb spray from behind her back and aimed it at me. A cloud of horrible putrescence hit me. I screamed and quickly covered my face and hair. The girls laughed and kept spraying over my uniform. They were in hysterics, some holding their stomachs, they were laughing so hard. Only Louise looked pained. She stepped back as if I might explode like a bomb.

"What's the matter?" Clara Sue asked. "Don't you like expensive perfume, or are you so used to cheap stuff you can't stand it?"

That made everyone laugh harder.

"What is this?" I cried. "How can I get it off?" Every time I spoke, it made the crowd of horrid girls laugh more. I rushed forward to the sink and started to wet a paper towel. Then I began wiping my sweater frantically.

"Who's the poor idiot who has to stand and sit beside her tonight?" Linda asked the dreadful audience. Someone screamed.

"That's not fair. Why should I be the one to suffer?"

The laughter continued.

"It's getting late," Clara Sue announced. "We'll meet you on the stage, Dawn," she called as they all started out, leaving me to my horrible fate at the sink. I scrubbed at my sweater and skirt so hard the paper towel tore into shreds, but mere water had no effect.

Becoming more frantic, I took off the pearls carefully and then pulled my sweater off and shook it out. I didn't know what to do. Finally I sat down on the floor and cried. Where would I get another school uniform now? How could I go on stage smelling like this? I would have to stay in the bathroom and then go home.

I cried until I had no more tears and my head and throat ached. I felt as if a heavy blanket of defeat had been thrown over me. It weighed far too much for me to simply throw it off. My shoulders shook with my sobs. Poor Daddy and Jimmy. They were probably already out there in their seats anxious for me. Poor Momma lying in her hospital room and watching the clock, thinking soon I would be out on that stage.

I looked up when someone came in, and I saw it was Louise. She gazed at me quickly and then looked down at the floor.

"I'm sorry," she said. "They made me do it, too. They said if I didn't, they would make up stories about me, just like they made them up about you."

I nodded.

"I should have expected something like this, but I was too excited to see through their false smiles," I said, standing up.

"Would you do me a favor? Would you go back to the music suite and get my coat for me? I can't put this back on," I said, indicating my sweater. "The odor is too strong."

"What are you going to do?"

"What can I do? I'll go home."

"Oh, no, you can't. You just can't," she said, nearly in tears herself.

"Please, get me my coat, Louise."

She nodded and left, her head down. Poor Louise, I thought. She wanted to be different—she wanted to be nice—but the girls wouldn't let her, and she wasn't strong enough to stand against them.

Oh, why were girls like Clara Sue so cruel? They had so much—all the fancy clothes they wanted; they could get their hair done, their nails done, even their toenails! Their parents took them on wonderful trips, and they lived in big houses with enormous rooms of their own with big soft beds and floors of plush carpet. They never went to sleep in cold rooms, and they always had anything and everything they wanted to eat. If they ever got sick, they knew they had the best doctors and medical care available. Everyone respected their parents and their family names. They shouldn't be filled with jealousy. Why in the world did they resent me—me who'd had so little compared to them. My heart hardened against them as I stood there in the bathroom, became as small and as sharp as theirs.

A few moments later Louise returned, only she didn't have my coat; she had another school uniform.

"Where did you get that?" I asked, smiling through my tears.

"Mr. Moore. I found him in the hall and told him what had happened. He just went to the storage room quickly and got this out. It smells a little like mothballs, but—"

"Oh, that's far better than this!" I exclaimed, tossing the spoiled sweater aside and slipping out of my skirt as fast as I could. I slipped the new sweater on quickly and put on Momma's pearls. The sweater was a little tighter, clinging to my bosom and my ribs firmly, but as Momma always said, "Beggars can't be choosers."

"Does my hair smell? I don't think they got much spray on it." I leaned down so she could check.

"It's all right."

"Thank you, Louise." I hugged her to me. We heard all the instruments being tuned. "Let's hurry," I said and started out.

"Wait," Louise called. She picked up my smelly sweater and skirt with her right thumb and forefinger and held them away from herself. "I have an idea."

"What idea?"

"Follow me," she said. We left the bathroom. Everyone was in the backstage area warming up. Louise hurried back to the music suite. I followed, curious. "Keep your eyes on the hallway," she said.

She went to Clara Sue's beautiful soft blue cashmere coat and shoved my smelly sweater into it, closing the coat around it.

"Louise!" I couldn't help smiling. Louise was not usually this brave, and Clara Sue deserved it.

"I don't care. Besides, she won't blame it on me; she'll blame it on you," Louise said so nonchalantly, it made me laugh.

We hurried to the backstage area and our instruments. The girls who had been in the bathroom when I had been betrayed looked with curiosity as I entered. They soon realized I had another sweater and skirt on. Even so, Linda and Clara Sue pretended I still smelled awful.

Mr. Moore announced it was time for us to take our positions on the stage. We all marched out behind the closed curtains. I could hear the murmur of the audience as people took their seats.

"Ready, everyone?" Mr. Moore asked. He stopped beside me and squeezed my arm softly. "Are you all right?"

"Yes," I said.

"You'll do fine," he said and then took his position. The curtain was opened and the audience responded with loud applause. The stage lights made it hard to look out at the crowd and distinguish faces easily, but after a while my eyes got used to the lights and I could see Jimmy and Daddy gazing up.

The chorus sang three songs, and then Mr. Moore nodded toward me. I stepped out to the front of the stage, and Mr. Moore went to the piano. The hush in the audience was deep, and I felt the warm lights on my face.

I didn't even remember beginning. Everything came naturally. Suddenly I had my head back, and I was singing to the world, singing into the wind, and hoping my voice would be carried all the way to Momma, who would close her eyes and hear me, as far away as she was.

"Somewhere, over the rainbow, way up high . . ."

When I sang my final note, I closed my eyes. For a moment I heard nothing, just a great silence, and then there was a thunder of applause. It rolled in from the audience like a wave rushing to shore, building and building until it hit with a crescendo that overwhelmed me. I looked at Mr. Moore. He was smiling from ear to ear and had his hand out and toward me.

I curtsied and stepped back. Looking through the audience, I found Daddy again and saw him clapping so hard his whole body shook. Jimmy was clapping, too, and smiling up at me. Someone squeezed my arm and then someone else and soon everyone in the chorus was congratulating me.

The entire chorus sang another song, and then the band played three numbers. The evening ended with the band playing "The Star-Spangled Banner" and then the Emerson Peabody school song. The moment the last note was sounded, the band and the chorus cheered and everyone congratulated everyone else, but girls and boys were coming to me especially. Boys shook my hand and girls hugged me. Some of the girls who had been in the bathroom earlier hugged me, too, all looking sorrowfully guilty. I accepted their hugs and squeezed them just as hard. My heart was too full and had no room for hate and anger at this moment.

"I don't think that was anything special," Clara Sue said, coming up behind me. "I'm sure I would have done a lot better, but Mr. Moore took pity on you and gave you the solo."

"You're a despicable person, Clara Sue Cutler," I said. "Someday you'll have no one but yourself."

When we all emerged in the hallway, we were greeted by our parents and friends. Daddy and Jimmy were standing by, both smiling proudly.

"You did good, Dawn. Just like I thought." Daddy hugged me to him and held me tightly. "Your momma will be awfully proud of you."

"I'm glad, Daddy."

"You were great," Jimmy said. "Better than you sound in the shower," he kidded. He kissed me again on the cheek. I looked past him and saw Philip standing by, waiting for his chance. When Jimmy stepped back, Philip approached.

"I knew you were headed for stardom," he said. He looked at Daddy, who lost his smile again. "You've got a talented daughter, sir."

"Thank you," Daddy said. "Well, I guess we all better head home and relieve Mrs. Jackson."

"Oh, Daddy," I said after Philip had taken my hand, "Philip is taking me to have some pizza. Can you look after Fern until I get back? We won't be long."

Daddy looked uncomfortable. For a moment I thought he would say no. My heart pounded in anticipation, teetering on the brink of disaster. Philip looked as if he were holding his breath. Daddy gazed at him a moment and then looked at me and finally smiled.

"All right, sure," he said. "Jimmy, are you going with them?"

Jimmy stepped back as if he had been punched.

"No," he said quickly. "I'm going home with you."

"Oh." Daddy looked disappointed. "Well, okay then. Be careful and come home early. I just gotta check on how things are being cleaned up, Jimmy. And then we can go."

"I'll go with you, Daddy," he said. He looked at me and then at Philip. "See you later," he added quickly and followed Daddy down the hall.

"Come on," Philip said, pulling me along. "Let's beat the crowd out of here."

"I've got to get my coat," I said, and he followed me to the music suite. When we arrived, we found a small group of girls gathered around Clara Sue. I had forgotten what Louise had done to her coat. She looked up at me hatefully.

"This wasn't funny," she said. "This was an expensive coat, probably worth more than your entire wardrobe."

"What's she talking about?" Philip asked.

"Something stupid that happened earlier," I said. I just wanted to get away from all of them and their stupidity. Suddenly all that seemed so immature. I grabbed my coat and we left. After we got into his car and started away, Philip insisted I tell him all about the bathroom incident. As I did, he grew angrier and angrier.

"She's so spoiled, and she hangs around with spoiled girls," he said. "Jealous, spoiled girls. My sister has become the worst of all of them. When I get my hands on her . . ." He nodded and then he suddenly laughed. "I'm glad you gave it back to her."

"I didn't," I said and told him about Louise.

"Good for her," he replied. Then he looked at me and smiled. "But let's not let anything ruin this night, your night—your opening night, I should say.

"Dawn, you were so good. You've got the prettiest voice I've ever heard!" he exclaimed. I didn't know how to react to such lavish praise. It was all so overwhelming. I felt a warmth in my heart and sat back. It was wonderful . . . the applause, Daddy's happiness and Jimmy's pride, and now Philip's affection. I couldn't believe how lucky I was. If only my luck would spread to Momma, I thought, and help her get better quicker. Then we would have everything.

A number of students from Emerson Peabody came to the restaurant to get pizza. Philip and I had a booth toward the rear, but anyone entering the restaurant could see us. Most of the students who attended the concert came by to tell me how much they'd enjoyed my singing. They heaped so many compliments on me, I really did begin to feel like a star. Philip sat across from me smiling, his blue eyes twinkling with pride. Of course, the girls who came by all made it their business to say hello to him, too, and bat their eyelashes. Suddenly Philip looked at me with such longing.

"Why don't we order our pizza to go," he said. "We can eat it under the stars."

"Okay," I said, my heart pounding.

Philip told our waitress, who then brought our pizza in a box. I felt every other student's eyes on us as we got up and left the restaurant.

After we drove off, Philip decided we should have a piece of pizza on the way. The aroma was driving us crazy. I held his piece for him and fed him carefully as he drove. We laughed at the string of cheese he had to gobble. Finally we drove down his secret road and parked in the darkness with the stars blazing in the sky before us.

"Oh, Philip, it's everything you promised. I feel like I'm on top of the world!" I cried.

"You are and you should be," he said. He leaned toward me and we kissed, a very long kiss. Before it ended I felt the tip of his tongue press against mine. It shocked me at first and I started away, but he held me firmly and I let him continue.

"Didn't you ever French kiss?" he asked.

"No."

He laughed.

"I do have a lot to teach you. Did you like it?"

"Yes," I whispered, as if it were a sin to admit it.

"Good. I don't want to go too fast," he said, "or scare you like I did the last time we were here."

"I'm all right. My heart is just pounding," I confessed, frightened it would cause me to faint.

"Let me feel it?" he said, bringing his fingers to my breast slowly. But then suddenly his hand was at the bottom of my sweater, his fingers gliding underneath and coming up to my bra. I couldn't help getting tense.

"Easy," he whispered into my ear. "Relax. You'll enjoy it. I promise."

"I can't help being nervous, Philip. I never did this with any other boy but you."

"I understand," he said. "Easy," he whispered in a soothing voice. "Just keep your eyes closed and lean back. That's it," he said when I closed my eyes. He slipped his fingers under the elastic material and gently lifted it from my naked bosom. I felt a rush of heat just before he brought his lips to mine again.

I moaned and leaned back. Contradictory voices were crying out. One, sounding like my mother, demanded that I stop, that I push him away. For some reason Jimmy's angry eyes flashed before me. I recalled the way Daddy had gazed sadly at Philip when I had asked him if we could go for pizza.

Philip started to lift my sweater.

"Philip, I don't think—"

"Easy," he repeated, lowering his head so he could bring his lips to my breast. When they touched me, I felt as though I would burst with excitement. I felt the tip of his tongue begin to explore.

"You're delicious," he said, "so fresh, so soft."

His other hand began to make its way under my skirt. Wasn't this all happening too quickly? I thought. Did the other girls my age let boys touch them under their clothes like this? Or was I being the bad girl they gossiped and lied about?

I envisioned Clara Sue's hateful face before me when she said, "My brother makes girls like you mothers once a month."

Philip's fingers found the bottom of my panties. I twisted my legs away from him.

"Dawn . . . you don't know how long I've dreamt of this. This is my night . . . your night. Relax. I'll show you . . . teach you." He brought his lips to the nipple of my breast and I felt myself sinking back, giving in like someone losing consciousness. His other hand was in my panties. How do girls resist? How do they stop it once the feelings get so strong? I wanted to stop it, but I felt so helpless. I was drifting, losing myself in his kisses and his touch and the way it brought heat to my breasts and into my thighs.

"I want to teach you so much," he whispered, but just at that moment the light from another car's headlights exploded over us, and I screamed.

Philip pulled back instantly, and I sat up to straighten my clothing. We turned to see the second car pull very close to ours.

"Who is it?" I asked, unable to hide my fear. I rushed to bring down my sweater.

"Aw, it's just one of the other guys from the baseball team," Philip said. "Damn it." We could hear the radio playing in his friend's car, and we could hear the laughter of girls. Our precious, private place had been invaded; our moment violated. "They're probably going to bug us soon," Philip said angrily.

"I thought this was your special place, Philip," I said. "I thought you found it accidentally."

"Yeah, yeah," he said. "I made the mistake of telling one of the guys about it one day, and then he told someone else."

"It's getting late anyway, Philip, and with Momma sick . . . I'd better get back."

"Maybe we can go someplace else," he said, not hiding his disappointment and frustration. "I know other spots."

"We'll come back some other time," I promised and squeezed his arm. "Please. Take me home."

"Damn," he repeated. He started the car and backed away before his friends could bother us. They beeped their horn, but we didn't pay any attention. Philip drove me home quickly, barely looking at me.

"I should have come right up here instead of taking you for the pizza," he said, almost in a growl.

We made the turn on our street, but as we were approaching the house, I thought I saw Daddy and Jimmy rushing down the sidewalk toward our car. Drawing closer, I was sure of it and sat up quickly.

"It's Daddy! And Jimmy! Where are they going so late?" I cried. Philip sped up until he pulled alongside, just as Daddy got behind the steering wheel.

"What is it, Daddy? Where are you going this time of night?"

"It's Momma," he said. "The hospital called Mrs. Jackson just now. Momma ain't doin' so good."

"Oh, no!" I felt my throat close up and the tears come rushing over my eyes. I got out of Philip's car quickly and into Daddy's.

"I hope everything will be all right," Philip called out. Daddy just nodded and started away.

As soon as we reached the hospital, we rushed to the entrance, where the security guard came forward to stop us. I recognized him as the same one who had been at the emergency room when we had brought Momma in.

"Where you all heading?" he asked. He spoke gruffly, demanding an answer, and just like the first time, looked closely at Daddy.

"The hospital just phoned about my wife, Sally Jean Longchamp. They told us to come right over."

"Just a minute," the security guard said, holding his hand up. He went to the central desk and spoke to the receptionist. "All right," he said, returning. "Go on up. The doctor's waiting for you." He followed us to the elevator and watched us go in, still staring hard at Daddy.

When we arrived at the door to the intensive care unit, Daddy paused. The young-looking, red-haired doctor who had examined Momma in the emergency room was off to the side talking softly with a nurse. They both turned when we approached. I felt the lump crawl up in my throat, and I bit down on my lower lip. There were shadows deep and dark in the young doctor's eyes. Suddenly they looked more like the eyes of an old man, a more experienced doctor who had seen a great many more very sick patients. He stepped up to Daddy and shook his head as he came forward.

"Wha . . . what?" Daddy asked.

"I'm sorry," the young doctor said. The nurse he had been speaking to joined him.

"Momma!" My voice cracked. My tears were stinging.

"Her heart just gave out. We did the best we could, but she was so far gone with this lung congestion . . . the strain . . . it was all just too much for her," he added. "I'm sorry, Mr. Longchamp."

"My wife's . . . dead?" Daddy asked, shaking his head to deny whatever the young doctor would say. "She ain't . . . ."

"I'm afraid Mrs. Longchamp passed away a little over ten minutes ago, sir," he replied.

"Nooo!" Jimmy screamed. "You're a liar, a dirty liar!"

"Jimmy," Daddy said. He tried to embrace him, but Jimmy pulled away quickly. "She ain't dead. She can't be dead. You'll see; you'll see." He started for the intensive care door again.

"Wait, son," the young doctor said. "You can't . . ."

Jimmy thrust open the door, but he didn't have to go in to see where Momma had been lying and see her bed was now empty, the mattress stripped. He stood there staring incredulously.

"Where is she?" Daddy asked softly. I embraced him around the waist and held on tightly. He had his arm around my shoulder.

"We have her down here," the doctor said, pointing to a door about halfway down the hall.

Daddy turned slowly. Jimmy came up beside him, and he reached for him. This time Jimmy didn't pull away. He drew closer to Daddy, and the three of us moved down the hallway slowly. The nurse led the way and stopped at the door.

I couldn't feel myself moving; I couldn't feel myself breathing. It was as if we had all slipped into a nightmare and were being carried away by it. We're not here, I hoped. We're not about to go into this room. It's a terrible dream. I'm home in bed; Daddy and Jimmy are home in bed.

But the nurse opened the door, and in the dimly lit room I saw Momma lying on her back, her black hair resting around her face, her arms at her sides, the palms up. Her fingers were curled inward.

"She's at peace," Daddy muttered. "Poor Sally Jean," he said and moved to the side of the gurney.

Everything in me broke loose. I cried harder than I had ever cried. My body shook and my chest ached. Daddy took Momma's hand into his and held it and simply stared down at her. Her face looked so peaceful. No more coughing, no more struggle. When I looked at her more closely, I thought I saw a slight smile on her lips. Daddy saw it, too, and turned to me.

"She must've heard you singing, Dawn. Just before she passed on, she must've heard."

I looked at Jimmy. He was crying now, but he stood so still, his eyes firmly fixed on Momma. His tears ran down his cheeks freely and dripped off his chin. A part of him was fighting the show of emotion and a part of him was just letting go. The struggle dazed him. Then he wiped the tears away with the back of his hand and turned away. He started for the door.

"Jimmy!" I cried. "Where are you going?"

He didn't answer. He just kept walking.

"Let him be," Daddy said. "He's like my side of the family. He's got to be alone when he hurts real bad." He looked back at Momma. "Good-bye, Sally Jean. I'm sorry I wasn't more of a husband for you; sorry the dreams we started with never took shape. Maybe now you'll realize some of them." He leaned down and kissed Momma for the last time. Then he turned, put his hand around my shoulder, and started out. I wasn't sure whether he was leaning on me for support or I was leaning on him.

When we left the hospital, we looked for Jimmy, but he was nowhere in sight.

"He ain't here," Daddy said. "We might as well go home, Dawn."

Poor Jimmy, I thought. Where could he be? It wasn't right for him to be all alone now, I thought. No matter how strong the Longchamps were when it came to hard times, everyone needed comfort and love when he or she was cast so deeply into the pool of tragedy as we were. I was sure he was feeling the same deep pain I was, feeling as if his heart had been ripped out, as if he were made hollow and so weak and light, a gust of wind could wipe him away. He probably didn't care anymore, didn't care what happened to him or where he would go.

Despite his hard shell, Jimmy had always suffered something terrible whenever Momma was unhappy or sick. I knew that many times he ran off just so he wouldn't have to see her unhappy or exhausted. Perhaps he had become real acquainted with loneliness and solitude and had retreated to some dark spot to cry with his shadow. The thing was I needed him as much as I hoped he needed me.

After we had stepped out of the hospital, I noticed that all the stars were gone. Clouds had come rolling in and swept away the brightness and the light. The world was dismal, dark, somber, and unfriendly.

Daddy embraced me and we went on to the car. I rested my head against his shoulder and lay there with my eyes closed all the way home. We didn't say anything to each other until we drove down our street.

"It's Jimmy," he said as we pulled up in front of the apartment building. I sat up quickly. Jimmy was sitting on the stoop. He saw us, but he didn't get up. I got out of the car slowly and approached him.

"How did you get home, Jimmy?" I asked.

"I ran all the way," he said, looking up at me. The small light at the doorway threw enough illumination over him for me to see the redness in his face. His chest was still heaving. I could imagine just what it had been like for him running all those miles, pounding the pavement to drive away the blackbird of sorrow that had made a nest in his heart.

"We made all the arrangements, son," Daddy said. "You might as well come inside now. There ain't nothing else we can do."

"Please come inside, Jimmy," I pleaded. Daddy went to the door. Jimmy looked up at me, and then he stood up and we went into the apartment house.

Thankfully, Fern was fast asleep. Mrs. Jackson was very sympathetic and offered to come in early in the morning to help with Fern, but I told her I could do it all. I needed and wanted to keep myself busy.

After she left, the three of us stood there silently, almost as if none of us knew what to do next. Daddy went to his bedroom door, and then he broke into heavy sobbing. Jimmy looked at me and we both embraced him. We held each other tightly and cried until we were all too exhausted to stand. Never before had the three of us welcomed sleep as much.

Of course, we couldn't afford a fancy funeral. Momma was buried in a cemetery just outside of Richmond.

Some of the people Daddy worked with at the school attended, as well as Mrs. Jackson. Mr. Moore came and told me that the best thing I could do for my mother's memory was continue with my music. Philip brought Louise.

I had no idea what we would do now. The school gave Daddy a week off with pay. Daddy went over his accounts and said with a little tightening here and there we could afford to give Mrs. Jackson something to watch Fern while Jimmy and I were at school, just so we could finish off the year, but Jimmy, more than ever, didn't want to return to Emerson Peabody. We didn't have many more days to go to complete the semester. I begged Jimmy to reconsider and at least finish up, and I think he might have relented and done it, too, if we hadn't woke up one morning a few days later to a loud knocking on our door. There was something in the way the knocking echoed through our apartment that sent chills up and down my spine and made my heart pound.

It was a knocking that would change our lives forever and forever, a knocking at the door that I would hear in a thousand dreams to come, a knocking that would always wake me, no matter how deeply I slept or how comfortable I was.

I was just getting up and had put my robe on to go out to the kitchen and make breakfast. Little Fern was stirring in her crib. Although she was too young to understand the nature of the tragedy that had befallen us, she sensed some of it in our voices, in the way we moved about, and in the expression in our faces. She didn't cry as much or want to play as much, and whenever she looked for Momma and didn't find her, she would turn toward me and look at me with sad, inquisitive eyes. It made my heart sick, but I tried not to cry. She had seen enough tears.

The knocking at the door frightened her, and she pulled herself up in her crib and began to cry. I hoisted her up and into my arms.

"There, there, Fern," I cooed softly. "It's all right." I could hear Momma saying the same words to her time and time again. I squeezed Fern tightly to me and started out, just as Daddy came to his doorway. Jimmy sat up in the pull-out. We all looked at one another and then at the door.

"Who can that be this early?" Daddy muttered and ran his hand through his messed hair. He scrubbed his face with his dry palms to wake himself a bit more and then started across the living room to the doorway. I stood back beside Jimmy and waited. Fern stopped crying and turned toward the door, too.

Daddy opened the door, and we saw three men—two policemen and a man I recognized as the security guard at the hospital.

"Ormand Longchamp?" the taller of the two policemen said.

"Yeah?"

"We have a warrant for your arrest."

Daddy didn't ask what for. He stepped back and sighed as if something he had always expected had finally taken place. He lowered his head.

"I recognized him the first time I seen him at the hospital," the security guard said. "And when I heard the reward still stood—"

"Recognized who? Daddy, what is this?" I cried, my voice filled with panic.

"We're arresting this man on the charge of kidnapping," the taller policeman said.

"Kidnapping?" I looked to Jimmy.

"That's stupid," Jimmy said.

"Kidnapping? My daddy didn't kidnap anyone!" I cried. I turned back to Daddy. He still hadn't responded in his own defense. His silence frightened me. "Who could he have kidnapped?" I asked.

The security guard spoke up first. He was proud of his achievement.

"Why, he kidnapped you, honey," he said.

8

Daddy . . . a Kidnapper?

Chilled with fear, I sat alone in a small room without windows in the police station. I couldn't stop shivering. Once in a while my teeth chattered. I embraced myself and gazed around the room. The walls were a faded beige, and there were ugly scuff marks along the bottom of the door. It looked like someone had been kicking at it, trying to get out. The room's light came from a single bulb in a silver-gray fixture dangling at the end of a chain from the center of the ceiling. The bulb threw a pale white glow over the short, rectangular light metal table and chairs.

The police had brought all of us here in two cars: a car for Daddy and a car for Jimmy, Fern, and me; but once we arrived, they separated all of us. Jimmy and I were sure this was all a terrible mistake, and soon they would realize it and return us to our home, but this was the first time I had ever been inside a police station, and I was more afraid than I'd ever been before.

Finally the door opened and a short, plump policewoman entered. She wore a uniform jacket with a dark blue skirt, a white blouse, and a dark blue tie. Her reddish-brown hair was cut short and she had bushy eyebrows. Her eyelids drooped so that she looked sleepy. She was carrying a notepad under her arm and went around the table to the other side. She sat down, put the pad on the table, and looked up at me without smiling.

"I'm Officer Carter," she said.

"Where's my little sister and where's my brother?" I demanded. I didn't care who she was. "I want to see my daddy, too," I added. "Why did you put us all into separate rooms?"

"Your daddy, as you call him, is in another room being questioned and booked for kidnapping," she said sharply. She leaned forward with both her arms on the table. "I'm going to complete our investigation, Dawn. I have some questions to ask you."

"I don't want to answer questions. I want to see my sister and my brother," I repeated petulantly. I didn't like her, and I wasn't going to pretend I did.

"Nevertheless, you will have to cooperate," she proclaimed. She straightened up sharply in her seat, bringing her shoulders back.

"It's all a mistake!" I cried. "My daddy didn't kidnap me. I've been with my momma and daddy forever and ever. They even told me how I was born and what I was like as a baby!" I exclaimed. How could she be so stupid? How could all these people make such a horrible error and not see it?

"They kidnapped you as a baby," she said and gazed down at her pad. "Fifteen years, one month and two days ago."

"Fifteen years?" I started to smile. "I'm not fifteen yet. My birthday isn't until July tenth, so you see—"

"You were born in May. They changed it as part of the cover-up of their crime," she explained, but so nonchalantly it turned my blood cold. I took a deep breath and shook my head. I was already fifteen? No, I couldn't be, none of this could be true.

"But I was born on a highway," I said, hot tears burning into my eyes. "Momma told me the whole story a hundred times. They didn't expect it, I was delivered in the back of the pickup truck. There were birds and—"

"You were born in a hospital in Virginia Beach." She gazed at her pad again. "You weighed seven pounds and eleven ounces."

I shook my head.

"I have to confirm something," she said. "Would you please unbutton your blouse and lower it."

"What?"

"No one will intrude. They know why I am in here. Please," she repeated. "If you don't cooperate," she added when I didn't move, "you will only make things harder on everyone, including Jimmy and the baby. They have to remain here until this investigation is completed."

I lowered my head. The tears were escaping now and zigzagging down my cheeks.

"Unbutton your blouse; lower it," she commanded.

"Why?" I looked up, grinding the tears away with my small fists.

"There is a small birthmark just below your left shoulder, isn't there?"

I stared at her, the cold wave rushing over me and streaming down my body, turning me into a statue made of ice.

"Yes," I said, my voice barely audible.

"Please. I have to confirm that." She stood up and came around the table.

My fingers were cold and stiff and far too clumsy to manipulate the buttons on my blouse. I fumbled and fumbled.

"Can I help you?" she offered.

"No!" I said sharply and succeeded in opening my blouse. Then I lowered it over my shoulders slowly, closing my eyes. I sobbed and sobbed. I jumped when she put her finger on my birthmark.

"Thank you," she said. "You can button your blouse again." She went back to her seat. "We have footprints to match . . . just to finish the confirmation, but Ormand Longchamp has confessed anyway."

"*No!*" I cried. I buried my face in my hands. "I don't believe it, none of it. *I can't believe it!*"

"I'm sure it's a shock to you, but you're going to have to believe it," she said firmly.

"How did all this happen?" I demanded. "How . . . Why?"

"How?" She shrugged and looked at her pad again. "Fifteen years ago, Ormand Longchamp and his wife worked at a resort in the Virginia Beach area. Sally Jean was a chambermaid, and Ormand was a handyman at this hotel. Soon after you were brought home from the hospital, Ormand and"—she looked at the pad again—"Sally Jean Longchamp stole you and a considerable amount of jewelry."

"They wouldn't do such a thing!" I moaned through my tears.

She shrugged again, her pale face indifferent, her dull eyes unfeeling, as if she had seen this happen time after time and was used to it.

"No . . . no . . . no . . ." I'm in the middle of a nightmare, I told myself. Soon it will end and I will wake up in my bed back at our apartment. Momma won't be dead, and we will all be together again. I'll hear Fern squirming in her crib, and I'll get up and make sure she's warm and comfortable. Maybe I'll peek out at Jimmy and see his head silhouetted in the darkness as he sleeps soundly on the pull-out. I'll just count to ten slowly, I told myself, and when I open my eyes . . . one . . . two . . .

"Dawn."

"Three . . . four . . . five . . ."

"Dawn, open your eyes and look at me."

"Six . . . seven . . ."

"I'm supposed to prepare you for your return to your real family now. We are going to leave the station shortly and . . ."

"Eight . . . nine . . ."

"Get into a police car."

"Ten!"

I opened my eyes, and the unobstructed harsh light burned away all hope, all dreams, all prayers. Reality came thundering down over me.

"*No!* Daddy!" I screamed. I stood up.

"Dawn, sit down."

"I want Daddy! I want to see Daddy!"

"Sit down this moment."

"*Daddy!*" I screamed again. She had her arms around me, holding my arms down at my sides and forcing me back into the chair.

"If you don't stop this, I'll have a straitjacket put on you and deliver you that way, do you hear?" she threatened.

The door opened and two police officers stepped in.

"Need any help?" one asked. I gazed up at them, my eyes on fire with the terror and the anger and the frustration. The younger officer looked sympathetic. He had blond hair and blue eyes and reminded me of Philip.

"Hey," he said. "Take it easy, honey."

"I've got this under control," Officer Carter replied. She didn't ease her embrace, but I let my arms relax.

"Yeah, you look like you're doing a terrific job," the younger policeman said.

She released me and stood up.

"You want to do this, Dickens?" she asked the young policeman.

I caught my breath and subdued my sobs, my shoulders heaving as I gasped for air. The young policeman looked down at me with his soft blue eyes.

"It's a raw deal for a kid this age. She's about my sister's age," he said.

"Oh, boy," Officer Carter said. "A social worker in disguise."

"We'll be right outside when you're ready," Patrolman Dickens said, and they left the room.

"I told you," Officer Carter said, "that if you aren't cooperative, you will just prolong the difficulties, especially for your stepbrother and stepsister. Now, are you going to behave, or do I have to leave you in here for a few hours thinking about it?"

"I want to go home," I moaned.

"You are going home, to your real home and your real parents."

I shook my head.

"I need to do that footprint now," she said. "Take off your shoes and socks."

I sat back in my chair and closed my eyes.

"Damn," I heard her say and a moment later felt her taking off my shoes. I didn't resist, nor did I open my eyes. I was determined to keep them closed until all this had ended.

Some time later, when it was all over, the two policemen who had been waiting outside returned and stood by as Officer Carter completed her report. She looked up from her notepad.

"The captain wants us to get started," Patrolman Dickens announced.

"Terrific," Officer Carter said. "You want to go to the bathroom, Dawn? This is the time."

"Where are we going?" I asked, my voice seemingly drifting away from me. I felt as if I were floating. I was in a daze, time and place were lost. I had even forgotten my name.

"You're going home, to your real family," she replied.

"Come on, honey," Patrolman Dickens said, taking my arm gently and helping me to my feet. "Go on. Use the bathroom and wash your face. You have funny little streaks across your cheeks from crying, and I know once you wash them off, you'll feel better."

I looked at his warm smile and kind eyes. Where was Daddy? Where was Jimmy? I wanted to hold Fern in my arms and kiss her soft, pudgy cheeks until they were red. I would never complain about her whining and crying again. In fact, I wanted to hear her whine. I wanted to hear her chanting: "Dawn, up. Dawn, up," and see her reaching for me.

"This way, honey," the patrolman said. He directed me toward the bathroom. I washed my face. The cold water on my cheeks did restore some of my energy and awareness. After I had used the bathroom, I came out and looked at the policemen expectantly.

Suddenly another door across the hall opened, and I saw Daddy sitting in a chair, his head down to his chest.

"*Daddy!*" I screamed and ran toward the opened door. Daddy lifted his head and gazed out at me, his eyes vacant. It was as though he were hypnotized and didn't see me standing there. "Daddy, tell them this isn't true; tell them it's all been a horrible mistake." He started to speak to me, but shook his head and looked down instead.

"*Daddy!*" I screamed again when I felt someone's hands on my shoulders. "*Please, don't let them take us all away!*"

Why wasn't he doing anything? Why didn't he show some of his temper and strength? How could he let this go on?

"Come on, Dawn," I heard someone say behind me. The door to the room Daddy was in started to close. He looked up at me.

"I'm sorry, honey," he whispered. "I'm so sorry."

Then the door was closed.

"Sorry?" I pulled out of the grip on my shoulders and pounded on the door. "*Sorry? Daddy? You didn't do what they said, you didn't!*"

The grip on my shoulders was firmer this time. Officer Dickens pulled me back.

"Let's go, Dawn. You've got to go."

I turned and looked into his face, the tears streaming down my own.

"Why didn't he help me? Why did he just sit there?" I asked.

"Because he's guilty, honey. I'm sorry. You've got to go now. Come on."

I looked back at the closed door once. It felt as if I had a hole in my chest where my heart had been. My throat ached and my legs felt wobbly. Officer Dickens practically carried me to the front door of the police station, where Officer Carter was waiting with my little suitcase.

"I threw whatever I thought was yours into this suitcase," she explained. "There didn't seem to be that much."

I stared down at it. My little suitcase, how I used to take such care packing it so I could get everything I owned into it for our frequent journeys from one world to another. Suddenly panic seized my heart. I went to my knees and opened it to search the little compartment. When my fingers found Momma's picture, I breathed relief. I cradled it in my hands and then pressed it to my bosom. Then I stood up. They started me forward again.

"Wait," I said stopping. "Where's Jimmy?"

"He's already gone to a home for wayward children until he gets placed," Officer Carter said.

"Placed? Placed where?" I asked frantically.

"With a foster family who might adopt him," she said.

"And Fern?" I held my breath.

"Same thing," she said. "Let's go. We have a long ride."

Jimmy and little Fern must be so frightened, not knowing what lay ahead of them. Was this all my fault—all because of me? Fern had been calling out for Momma, and now she would be calling out for me.

"But when will I see them? How will I see them?" I looked to

Patrolman Dickens. He shook his head. "Jimmy . . . Fern . . . I must see them . . . please."

"It's too late. They're gone," Patrolman Dickens said softly. I shook my head. Officer Carter moved me forward to the waiting patrol car. Patrolman Dickens took my suitcase from her and put it into the car trunk. Then he got in behind the steering wheel quickly, and the other policeman opened the rear door for me and Officer Carter. He didn't say anything.

Officer Carter directed me into the backseat. Between the backseat and the front seat was a metal grate, and the doors had no handles on them. I couldn't get out until someone opened the doors. I was like a criminal being transported from one jail to another. Officer Carter was on my right and the second patrolman was on my left.

The speed with which it was all happening kept me in a daze. I didn't start to cry again until the patrol car shot off and I realized Daddy, Jimmy and Fern were really gone and I was all alone, being carried off to another family and another life. A panic came over me when I understood what was about to happen. When would I ever see Daddy again, or Jimmy, or little Fern?

"It isn't fair," I muttered. "This isn't fair." Officer Carter heard me.

"Imagine how your real parents must have felt when they discovered you were missing—that their employees had taken you and run off? Think that was fair?"

I stared at her and shook my head. "It's a mistake," I muttered.

How could my daddy and mommy have done such a terrible thing to someone? Daddy . . . steal me from another family? Not care about that mother's sorrow and that father's pain?

And Momma with all her stories and memories of us growing up . . . Momma working so hard so that we would have enough . . . Momma getting sicker and thinner, but not caring about herself as long as Jimmy and I and Fern had clothes to wear and food to eat. Momma knew sorrow and tragedy from her own life. How could she hurt some other Momma?

"There's no mistake, Dawn," Officer Carter said dryly. Then she repeated, "Dawn," and shook her head. "I wonder what they'll do about that?"

"What?" My heart started to pound again. It was thumping like a drum in a marching band, the throb pulsating all through my body.

"Your name. That's not your real name. They stole you after you had been brought home and you had already been named."

"What's my name?" I asked. I felt like an amnesiac slowly regaining her memory, returning from a world where everyone's face was blank, just eyes, a nose, and a mouth, like faces etched on white paper.

Officer Carter opened her notebook and turned a few pages.

"Eugenia," she replied after a moment. "Maybe you're better off being Dawn," she added dryly and started to close her notebook again.

"Eugenia? Eugenia what?"

"Oh, how stupid of me to not give you all of it." She opened her notebook again. "Eugenia Grace Cutler," she declared.

My thumping heart stopped.

"Cutler? You didn't say Cutler?"

"Yes, I did. You're the daughter of Randolph Boyse Cutler and Laura Sue Cutler. Actually, honey, you're going to be pretty well off. Your parents own a famous resort, the Cutler's Cove Hotel."

"Oh, no!" I cried. It couldn't be! It just couldn't be!

"Don't be so upset. You could be a lot worse off."

"You don't understand," I said, thinking of Philip. "I can't be a Cutler. I can't!"

"Oh, yes, you can and yes, you are. It's about as confirmed as it could be."

I couldn't speak. I sat back, feeling as if I had been punched in the stomach. Philip was my brother. Those resemblances between us that I had thought were wonderful, that I had thought had been planted by destiny to bring us together as boyfriend and girlfriend instead were brother and sister resemblances.

And Clara Sue . . . horrible Clara Sue . . . was my sister! Fate was forcing me to trade Jimmy and Fern for Philip and Clara Sue.

So much of what had been a mystery to me in the past was now falling in place. No wonder Momma and Daddy never wanted to return to their families. They knew they were being hunted as criminals and must have expected the police would search for them there. And now I understood why Momma cried out to me from her hospital bed after I told her Philip was taking me to the concert. I could see why she said, "You must never think badly of us. We love you. Always remember that."

It was all true. My stubborn insistence that it was not would have to be put aside. I would have to face it, even though I could not understand it. Would I ever?

I sat back and closed my eyes again. I was so tired. The crying, the pain, the agony of leaving Jimmy and Fern and Daddy behind, Momma's death, and now this news weighed down on me. I felt drained, listless, a shell of myself. My body had been turned into smoke, and I was caught in a breeze that was carrying me wherever it wanted.

Jimmy's face and Fern's face fell away, peeling off like leaves blown from tree limbs. I could barely see them anymore.

The patrol car rushed on, carrying us toward my new family and my new life.

The trip seemed to take forever. By the time we arrived in Virginia Beach, the cloudy night sky had cleared a little bit. Stars peeked out through every available opening, but I took no comfort in their twinkling. Suddenly they seemed more like frozen tears, tiny drops of ice melting very slowly out of a black and dismal sky.

For most of the ride the police officers had talked to each other and rarely said anything to me. They barely looked at me. Never had I felt so alone and lost. I dozed on and off, but I welcomed sleep because it was a short escape from the horror of what was happening. Every time I woke, I held on to some hope for an instant, hope this had all been a dream. But the dreary sound of the car tires, the dark night washing past the windows, and the quiet conversation of the police officers brought home the terrible reality time after time.

I couldn't help but be curious about the new world I had been literally dragged into, but they were going so fast, buildings and people whizzed by before I could absorb what I had seen. In moments we were on a highway and away from the busier areas. I knew the ocean was just out there in the darkness somewhere, so I studied the scenery until the land gave way to a vast mirrored sea of dark blue. In the distance I could see the tiny lights of fishing boats and even pleasure ships. Shortly after that the coastline of Virginia Beach itself was announced by a road sign and in moments, we were driving through the seaside resort with its neon lights, its restaurants, motels and hotels.

Soon I caught sight of a large road sign that indicated we were about to enter Cutler's Cove. It wasn't much of a village, just a long street with all sorts of small stores and restaurants. I couldn't see much because we passed through it so quickly, but what I did see looked quaint and cozy.

"According to our directions, it's just up here," Officer Dickens said.

I thought about Philip, who was still back at school, and wondered if he had been told any of this yet. Perhaps his parents had phoned him. How had he taken the news? Surely he was just as confused by the lightning revelations.

"Looks real nice for a new start," the policeman next to me said, finally acknowledging what we were doing and why we were in the car heading for the Cutler's Cove Hotel.

"That's for sure," Officer Carter said.

"There it is," Officer Dickens announced, and I sat forward.

The coastline curved inward at this point, and I saw that there was a beautiful length of sandy white beach that sparkled as if it had been combed clean. Even the waves that came up came up softly, tenderly, as if the ocean were afraid of doing any damage. As we passed the entrance to the beach, I spotted a sign that read, RESERVED FOR CUTLER COVE HOTEL GUESTS ONLY. Then the patrol car turned right up a long drive, and I saw the hotel ahead, sitting on a little rise, the manicured grounds gently rolling down before it.

It was an enormous three-story Wedgwood blue mansion with milk-white shutters and a large wraparound porch. Most of the rooms were lit up, and there were Japanese lanterns along the top of the porch and above the spiraling stairway built out of bleached wood. The foundation was made from polished stone. Bathed in the ground lights, it sparkled as if it had been built out of pearls. Guests were meandering about the beautiful grounds upon which there were two small gazebos; wooden and stone benches and tables; fountains, some shaped like large fish, some simple saucers with spouts in the middle; and gardens full of beautiful flowers capturing almost all the colors of the rainbow. The walkways were bordered with short hedges and lit by well-spaced footlights.

"Somewhat better than what you've been used to, huh?" Officer Carter said. I just glared at her. How could she be so callous? I didn't answer her; I turned away and gazed out the window as the patrol car wound its way around the circular drive.

"Keep going," Officer Carter said. "Round back. That's where we were told to go."

Round back? I thought. Where were my new parents, my real parents? Why hadn't they rushed to Richmond to claim me instead of having policemen bring me as if I were a criminal? Weren't they excited about meeting me? Perhaps they were as nervous about it as I was. I wondered if Philip had told them things about me. Had Clara Sue? She would get them to hate me for sure.

The patrol car stopped, but my heart wouldn't stop pounding, thumping against my chest as if there were a tiny little drummer inside me beating his drumsticks against my bones. I could barely breathe, and I couldn't stop trembling. Oh, Momma, I thought, if you hadn't gotten sick and been taken to the hospital, I wouldn't be here now. Why was fate so cruel? This can't be happening; you and Daddy just

couldn't have been baby kidnappers. There has to be another explanation, one my true parents might know and be willing to tell me. Please
let it be so, I prayed.

As soon as we stopped, Officer Dickens got out quickly and opened
the door for us.

"After I get them to sign this," Officer Carter said, indicating papers
on her clipboard, "I'll come right out."

Sign this? I thought, looking at the document. I was being treated as
if I were something delivered and actually taken to the delivery
entrance.

I stood there, staring at the back entrance of the hotel. All it was was
a small door with a screen door. There were four wooden steps leading
up to it. Officer Carter started toward the door, but I didn't follow. I
stood there holding my suitcase.

"Come along," she commanded. She saw my hesitation and put her
hands on her hips. "This is your home, your real family. Let's go," she
snapped and reached out to take my hand.

"Good luck, Dawn," Officer Dickens called.

Officer Carter tugged me, and I followed her to the door. Suddenly it
was opened and a nearly bald-headed, tall man, with skin so pale he
could be an undertaker, stood looking out at us. He was dressed in a
dark blue sport jacket, matching tie, white shirt, and slacks. He stood
at least six feet tall. As we drew closer, I saw he had bushy eyebrows, a
long mouth with thin lips, and a nose that was an eagle's beak. Could
this be my real father? He looked nothing like me.

"Please come right this way," he said, stepping back. "Mrs. Cutler is
awaiting you in her office. My name is Collins. I'm the maître d'," he
added. He looked at me with curious dark brown eyes, but he did not
smile. He gestured ahead with his long arm and long, slightly brown
fingers, moving so gracefully and quietly it was as if he moved in slow
motion.

Officer Carter nodded and headed down the short, narrow entryway
that brought us to what was obviously the rear of the kitchen where
the storage rooms were. Some doors were opened, and I saw cartons of
canned goods and boxes of grocery items. Collins pointed to the left
when we reached the end of the corridor.

Why were they sneaking me in? I wondered. We turned a corner and
moved down another long hallway.

"I hope we get there before I have to retire from the police force,"
Officer Carter quipped.

"Just right down here," Collins replied.

Finally he stopped at a door and knocked softly.

"Come in," I heard a firm female voice say. Collins opened the door and peered inside.

"They've arrived," he announced.

"Show them in," the woman said. Was it my mother?

Collins stepped back so we could enter. Officer Carter walked in first, and I followed slowly. We were in an office. I looked around. There was a pleasant lilac scent, but I saw no flowers. The room had an austere and simple look. The floor had hardwood slats that were probably the original floor. There was a tightly woven dark blue oval rug in front of the aqua chintz settee, which was at right angles to the large, dark oak desk on which everything was neatly arranged. Presently, the only light in the room came from a small lamp on the desk. It cast an eerie yellowish glow over the face of the elderly woman who gazed at us.

Even though she was seated, I could see that she was a tall, stately looking woman with steel-blue hair cut and styled in soft waves that curled under her ears and just at the base of her neck. Pear-shaped diamond earrings dangled from each lobe. She wore a matching pear-shaped diamond necklace set in gold. Although she was thin and probably didn't weigh more than one hundred and fifteen pounds, she looked so stern and secure, she seemed much larger. Her shoulders were pulled back in the bright blue cotton jacket she wore over her white frilly collar blouse.

"I'm Officer Carter and this is Dawn," Officer Carter said quickly.

"What has to be done?" the elderly woman, who I thought must be my real grandmother, demanded.

"I need this signed."

"Let me see it," my grandmother said and put on her pearl-framed glasses. She read the document quickly and then signed it.

"Thank you," Officer Carter said. "Well." She looked at me. "I'll be on my way. Good luck," she muttered and left the office.

Without speaking to me, my grandmother rose and came around her desk. I saw she wore an ankle-length matching blue skirt and eggshell-white leather shoes designed for someone who had to do a great deal of walking. They looked more like men's shoes. The only imperfection in her appearance, if it could be called that, was a slight roll in her nylon stocking on her right foot.

She turned on a pole lamp in the corner, so that there was more light, and then with her stone-cold gray eyes she stood staring at me for a long moment. I searched her face for evidence of myself and thought my grandmother's mouth was firmer and longer than mine and her eyes didn't show a trace of blue.

Her complexion was almost as smooth and as perfect as a marble statue's. There was just a tiny brown age spot on the top of her right cheek. She wore a touch of rose-red lipstick and just a brush of rouge on her cheeks. Not a strand of her hair was out of place.

Now that there was more light in the room, I gazed about and saw the walls were paneled in rich wood. There was a small bookcase behind and to the right of the desk. But above the rear wall was a large portrait of who I thought had to be my real grandfather.

"You have your mother's face," she declared. Queenly stiff, she moved behind her impressively wide desk. "Childlike," she added, disdainfully, I thought. There was just the slightest lift in the corner of her mouth when she ended her sentences. "Sit down," she snapped. After I had done so, she crossed her arms over her small bosom and leaned back in her chair, but kept her posture so straight I thought her back was a sheet of cold steel.

"I understand your parents have been drifters all these years and your father never settled on a solid job anywhere," she declared harshly. I was surprised she had called them my parents, and had referred to Daddy as my father.

"Worthless," she continued. "I knew it the day I set eyes on him, but my husband had a soft spot for lost souls and hired him and his ragtag wife," she said with disgust.

"Momma wasn't a ragtag wife!" I snapped back.

She didn't reply. She stared at me again, delving into the depths of my eyes as if to drink up my essence. I was beginning to get very upset with the way she glared at me, studying me as if she were searching for something in my face, looking me over with very interested gimlet eyes.

"You don't have the nicest manners," she finally replied. She had a habit of nodding after saying anything she thought was absolutely true. "Weren't you ever taught to respect your elders?"

"I respect people who respect me," I said.

"You have to earn respect. And I must say you have not yet earned it. I can see you will have to be retrained, redeveloped; in a word, brought up properly," she proclaimed with a power and an arrogance that made my head spin. As small-framed as she was, she had the strongest gaze I had ever seen a woman have, much sterner and stronger than even Mrs. Turnbell's frightening green look. These eyes were piercing, cold, so sharp they could cut and draw blood.

"Did the Longchamps ever tell you anything about this hotel or this family?" she demanded.

"No, nothing," I replied. The tears in my eyes burned, but I wouldn't let her see how painful they were or how horrible she was making me feel. "Maybe this is all a mistake," I added, even though I harbored little hope after seeing Daddy at the police station. I sensed if it were somehow a mistake, she would be able to correct it. She looked like she had the power to rearrange time.

"No, no mistake," she said, sounding almost as sad about it as I was. "I'm told you're a good student in school despite the life you've been leading. Is that so?"

"Yes."

She sat forward, resting her hands on the top of the desk. She had long thin fingers. A gold watch with a large face dangled loosely on her tiny wrist. It, too, looked like something a man would wear.

"Since the school year is just about over, we won't bother to send you back to Emerson Peabody. It's all been somewhat embarrassing for us anyway, and I don't think it would do either Philip or Clara Sue any good if you returned under these conditions. We have time to decide what to do about your schooling. The season has begun and there is much to do here," she said. I glanced at the door, wondering where my real father and mother were and why they were leaving all these decisions up to her.

I had always dreamt about meeting my grandparents, but my real grandmother didn't fit any of my visions. This wasn't the kind of grandmother who made cookies and comforted me when life was hard. This wasn't the soft and lovable grandmother of my dreams, the grandmother I had imagined would teach me things about life and love and cherish me as much as she did her own daughter, love me even more.

"You will have to learn all about the hotel, from the ground up," my grandmother lectured. "No one is permitted to be lazy here. Hard work makes good character, and I'm sure you need hard work. I have already spoken to my house manager about you, and we have let one of our chambermaids go to provide a position for you."

"Chambermaid?" That's what Momma had done here, I thought. Why did my grandmother want me to do the same thing?

"You're not a long-lost princess, you know," she said curtly. "You're to become part of this family again, even though you were part of it only for a short while, and to do so properly you will have to learn all about our business and our way of life. Each one of us works here, and you will be no exception. I expect you're a lazy thing," she continued, "considering—"

"I am not lazy. I can work just as hard as you can or anyone can," I declared.

"We'll see," she said. She nodded slightly, staring at me intently again. "I've already discussed your living arrangements with Mrs. Boston. She is in charge of our quarters. She will be here momentarily to show you your room. I will expect you to keep it neat and tidy. Just because we have a servant looking after our rooms doesn't mean we can be sloppy and disorganized."

"I've never been sloppy, and I've always helped Momma clean and organize our apartments," I said.

"Momma? Oh . . . yes . . . well, let that be the rule and not the exception." She paused, almost smiling, I thought, because of the way she lifted the corners of her mouth.

"Where are my father and mother?" I asked.

"Your mother," she said, making the word sound obscene, "is having another one of her emotional breakdowns . . . conveniently," Grandmother Cutler said. "Your father will see you shortly. He's very busy, very busy." She sighed deeply and shook her head. "This situation is not easy for any of us. And it has all occurred at the wrong time," she said, making me feel as if I were to blame for Daddy having been recognized and the police finding me. "We are right in the middle of the start of a new season. Don't expect anyone to have time to cater to you. Do your work, keep your room clean, and listen and learn. Do you have any questions?" she asked, but before I could respond, there was a knock on the door.

"Come in," she called and the door was opened by a pleasant-looking black woman. She had her hair pinned up neatly and tied in a bun. She wore a white cotton chambermaid's uniform with white stockings and black shoes. She was a small woman, barely my height.

"Oh, Mrs. Boston. This is . . ." My grandmother paused and looked at me as if I had just come in. "Yes," she said, listening to a voice only she could hear, "what about your name? It's a silly name. We'll have to call you by your real name, of course . . . Eugenia. Anyway, you were named after one of my sisters who had passed away from smallpox when she was no older than you are."

"My name is not silly, and I don't want to change it!" I cried. Her eyes shifted quickly from me to Mrs. Boston and then back to me.

"Members of the Cutler family do not have nicknames," she replied firmly. "They have names that distinguish them, names that bring them respect."

"I thought respect was something that had to be earned," I whiplashed. She pulled herself back as if I had slapped her.

"You will be called Eugenia as long as you live here," she declared firmly. Her voice was cold and uncaring, as if I were without ears to hear.

"Show *Eugenia*," my grandmother said, "her room, Mrs. Boston. And"—she gazed at me quickly, a look of disgust on her face—"take her the back way."

"Yes, ma'am." Mrs. Boston looked to me.

"My name fits me," I said, unable to hold back my tears now and recalling how many times Daddy had told me about my birth, "because I was born at the break of day." Surely that couldn't have been a lie, too, not the story about the birds and the music and my singing.

My grandmother smiled so coldly it sent a chill up my spine.

"You were born in the middle of the night."

"No," I protested. "That's not true."

"Believe me," she said. "I know what is true and what is not true about you." She leaned forward, her eyes appearing long and catlike. "For your whole life you've lived in a world of lies and fantasy. I told you," she continued, "we don't have time to cater to you and pretend. We're in the middle of the season. Now, pull yourself together immediately. Members of the family do not show their emotions or their problems to the guests. As far as the guests are concerned, everything is always wonderful here. I don't want you going out and through the lobby crying hysterically, Eugenia.

"I have to return to the dining room," my grandmother said, rising. She came around her desk and paused before Mrs. Boston. "After you show her to her room, take her to the kitchen and get her something to eat. She can eat with the kitchen staff," she said. "Then take her to Mr. Stanley so he can find her a chambermaid's uniform. I'd like her to begin work tomorrow."

She turned back to me, pulling her shoulders back and holding her head so high, it was as if she were looking down at me from a great height. Despite my desire to do so, I couldn't look away. Her eyes pulled and held mine fixed in her glare.

"You are to get up at seven A.M. promptly, Eugenia, and go to the kitchen for your breakfast. Then report directly to Mr. Stanley, our house manager, and he will assign you your duties. Is that all clear?" she asked. I didn't respond. She turned to Mrs. Boston. "See that she remembers all this," she added and walked out.

Although the door clicked softly closed, it sounded like a gunshot to me.

Welcome to your real family and real home, Dawn, I told myself.

9

My New Life

"**G**rab your suitcase and follow me, Eugenia," Mrs. Boston commanded in a tone of voice my grandmother had been using.

"My name is Dawn," I declared firmly.

"If Mrs. Cutler wants you called Eugenia, that's what you'll be called here. Cutler's Cove is her kingdom and she's the queen. Don't expect nobody to go against her wishes, not even your daddy," Mrs. Boston added and then widened her eyes and leaned toward me to whisper, "And especially not your mother."

I turned away and quickly wiped the tears from my eyes. What sort of people were my real parents? How could they be so afraid of my grandmother? Why weren't they dying of curiosity about me and making it their business to see me right away?

Mrs. Boston led me out the rear door and down the dimly lit corridor that ran behind the kitchen.

"Where are we going now?" I asked. I was tired of being dragged around like some stray dog.

"The family lives in the old section of the hotel," Mrs. Boston explained as we walked.

When we paused at the end of the corridor, I was able to see the hotel lobby. It was lit by four large chandeliers and had a light blue carpet and pearl-white papered walls with a blue pattern. Behind the reception counter were two middle-aged women greeting guests. All were quite well dressed, the men in suits and jackets, the women in pretty dresses and bedecked with jewels. Once they entered the lobby, they milled about in small groups chatting.

I caught sight of my grandmother standing by the dining room entrance. She glanced our way once, her eyes like ice, but as soon as some guests approached, her face brightened and softened. One woman held on to her hand as they spoke. They kissed each other, and then my grandmother followed all the guests toward the dining room, throwing a gaze like a snowball back at us before disappearing into the dining room herself.

"Let's move along . . . quickly," Mrs. Boston said urgently, stung by my grandmother's sharp, cold look. We turned down a long corridor and finally reached what was clearly the older section of the hotel.

We passed a sitting room that had a fieldstone fireplace and warm-looking antique furniture—soft cushion chairs in hand-carved wood frames, a dark pine rocking chair, a thick cushioned couch with pinewood end tables and a thick, eggshell-white rug. I saw that there were many paintings on the walls, and there were pictures and knickknacks on the mantel above the fireplace. I thought I glimpsed a picture of Philip standing beside the woman who must be our mother, but I couldn't pause long enough to see her clearly. Mrs. Boston was practically trotting.

"Most of the bedrooms are on the second floor, but there is one bedroom downstairs off the small kitchen. Mrs. Cutler told me that one's to be yours," she said.

"What was it, a servant's bedroom?" I asked. Mrs. Boston didn't respond. "After I earn respect, I will be able to sleep upstairs," I grumbled. I don't know if Mrs. Boston heard me or not. If she had, she didn't acknowledge it.

We went through the small kitchen and then passed through a short hallway to my bedroom on the right. The door was opened. Mrs. Boston turned on the light as we entered.

It was a very small room with a single bed against the wall on the left. The bed had a simple light-brown headboard. At the foot of the bed was a slightly stained cream-colored oval rug. There was a single-drawer night table beside the bed with a lamp on it. To the right was a dresser and a closet, and directly ahead of us was the room's only window. Right now I couldn't tell what the window looked out on, for it was dark and there were no lights at this side of the hotel grounds. The window had no curtains, just a pale yellow shade.

"Do you want to put your things away now, or would you rather go to the kitchen and get something to eat?" she asked. I placed my little suitcase on the bed and looked around sadly.

There were many times we had moved into an apartment so small that Jimmy and I didn't have much more room than this to share, but somehow, because I was with a loving family, because I was with people who cared about me and about whom I cared, the size of my room didn't matter as much. We made do, and besides, I had to keep a cheerful face to help keep Jimmy cheerful and Daddy happy. But there was no one to keep happy here, no one to care about right now but myself.

"I'm not hungry," I said. My heart felt like an iron weight, and my stomach was all twisted and tight.

"Well . . . Mrs. Cutler wanted you to eat," she said and looked troubled. "I'll stop by later and take you to the kitchen," she decided, nodding. "But don't forget, I got to bring you to Mr. Stanley and get you a uniform. Mrs. Cutler told us."

"How could I forget?" I said. She stared at me a moment and pressed her lips together firmly. Why was she so annoyed with me? I wondered. Then it occurred to me—my grandmother had said she had let someone go to make a position for me.

"Who was fired so I could have this job?" I asked quickly. The expression on Mrs. Boston's face confirmed my suspicions.

"Agatha Johnson, who had been working here five years."

"I'm sorry," I said. "I certainly didn't want her fired."

"Nevertheless, that poor girl is gone and walking the streets looking for something new. And she got a little boy to raise," she said with disgust.

"Well, why did she have to fire her? Couldn't she keep her on along with me?" I asked. My grandmother had put me in a horrible position, fixing it so the help would resent me for being discovered and returned as much as she apparently did.

"Mrs. Cutler runs a very tight ship," Mrs. Boston said. "No excess, no waste. Whoever don't pull his load goes. She got just as many chambermaids as she needs, just as many waiters and busboys, just as many kitchen help and service people. Not a single one more. That's why this hotel goes on and on while other places have peeled off over the years."

"Well, I'm sorry," I repeated.

"Um," she said, still without much sympathy. "I'll be back in a while," she added and left.

I sat down on the bed. The mattress was old and had lost any firmness it might have had and the springs squeaked with complaint.

Even my little weight was too much. I took a deep breath and opened my suitcase. The sight of my simple belongings brought back a flood of memories and feelings. How my heart ached. The tears started to flow. I sat there and let them run down my cheeks and drip off my chin. Then I saw something white peeking out of the cloth pocket inside my suitcase. I reached inside and pulled out Momma's wonderful string of pearls. They had been in my dresser drawer at home—because of the confusion after the concert and Momma's death, I had never given them back to Daddy to put away. The policeman who had packed my bag must have thought they were mine. Now I hugged them to me, crying ten oceans of tears as memories came crashing over me, dragging me down to drown within their depths. How I longed for Momma now to hold me and stroke my hair, to see Jimmy's face full of pride and anger, to have Fern's eyes light up at the sight of me and her little arms reach up to be held. The pearls brought back all of this and more till my heart was an aching ruin.

Daddy, how could you do this? How could you do this? I screamed inside.

Suddenly there was a knock on my door. I quickly hid the pearls in a drawer, wiped my face with the back of my hands, and turned.

"Who is it?"

The door opened slowly and a handsome man dressed in a tan sport jacket and matching slacks peered in. His light brown hair was brushed back neatly at the sides, but he had a small, soft wave in the front. There was a tinge of gray at his temples. His rich, dark tan emphasized the blue in his eyes. I thought he looked as debonair and as elegant as a movie star.

"Hello," he said, gazing in at me. I didn't respond. "I'm your father," he said as if I should have known. He stepped in. "Randolph Boyse Cutler." He held out his hand for me to shake. I couldn't imagine ever being introduced to Daddy and shaking his hand like a stranger. Daddies were supposed to hug their daughters, not shake their hands.

I gazed up at him. He was tall, at least six feet two or three, but he was slim. He had Philip's gentle smile and soft mouth. Everyone was telling me that the man standing before me was my real father, so I searched for resemblances to myself. Had I inherited his eyes? His smile?

"Welcome to Cutler's Cove," he said squeezing my fingers gently. "How was your trip?"

"My trip?" He was acting as though I had been away for a holiday or something. I was about to say, "Horrible," when he spoke.

"Philip has already told me a lot about you," he said.

"Philip?" Just pronouncing his name brought tears to my eyes. It took me back to the world I had been ripped from, a world that had begun to be friendly and wonderful before Momma's death, a world full of stars and hope and kisses that carried promises of love.

"He told me about your beautiful singing voice. I can't wait to hear you sing," he said.

I couldn't see myself ever singing again, for my singing came from my heart, and my heart had been shattered into so many pieces, it would never be strong again and certainly it would never be filled with music.

"I'm glad to see you're such a pretty girl, too. Something else Philip warned me about. Your mother's going to be pleased," he said and looked at his watch as if he had a train to catch.

"Naturally, this has all been something of an emotional shock for her, so I'll have to take you to see her tomorrow sometime. She's under some medication, in her doctor's care, and he advises us to go slowly. You can imagine what it was like for her to learn that the baby she had lost fifteen years ago had been found, but I'm sure she's as excited about finally seeing you as I have been," he added quickly.

"Where is she now?" I asked, thinking she might be in a hospital. Even though I hated being here, I couldn't help but be curious about her and what she looked like.

"In her room, resting."

She was in her room? I thought. Why wasn't she excited about seeing me? How could she put it off?

"In a day or so, when I get some free time, I would like to spend some of it with you and let you tell me what your life has been like up until now, okay?"

I looked down so he wouldn't see the way my eyes had filled with tears.

"I imagine all this must have come as a terrible shock, but in time we'll make it all up to you," he said.

Make it up to me? How could anyone do that?

"I want to find out what happened to my baby sister and my brother," I heard myself say before I even realized I was going to say the words. He pressed his lips in and shook his head.

"That's out of our hands. They're not really your brother and sister, so we don't have any right to demand information about them. I'm afraid you will have to forget them."

"I'll never forget them! Never!" I cried. "And I don't want to be here.

I don't, I don't . . ." I started to sob. I couldn't help it. The tears overflowed my lids and my shoulders shook.

"There, there. Everything will be fine," he said, touching my shoulder tentatively and then pulling back as if he had done something forbidden.

This man, my real father, was suave and handsome, but he was still a stranger. There was a wall between us, a thick wall, not only built out of time and distance, but built out of two entirely different ways of life. I felt like a visitor in a foreign land with no one to trust and no one to help me understand the strange new customs and ways.

I took a deep breath and fumbled through my purse for a tissue.

"Here," he said, obviously anxious to do something. He handed me his soft silk handkerchief. I wiped my eyes quickly.

"Mother has told me about your first meeting and how she intends to take a special interest in you. With all she has to do around here, you should be flattered," he added. "When Mother takes personal interest in someone, he or she usually succeeds."

He paused, maybe to hear me say how grateful I was, but I wasn't and I wouldn't lie.

"My mother was the first to learn about you, but she's usually the first to learn about anything around here," he continued. Perhaps he's as nervous as I am, I thought, and has to keep talking. He shook his head and widened his smile. "She never thought she would have to pay out the reward money and, like the rest of us, had given up all hope long ago.

"Well," he said, looking at his watch again. "I've got to return to the dining room. Mother and I visit with the guests at dinner. Most of our guests are regulars who return year after year. Mother knows them all by name. She has a wonderful memory for faces and names. I can't keep up with her."

Whenever he spoke about his mother, his face brightened. Was this the same elderly woman who had greeted me with eyes of ice and words of fire?

There was a knock on the door, and Mrs. Boston appeared.

"Oh," she said, "I didn't know you was here, Mr. Cutler."

"That's all right, Mrs. Boston. I was just leaving."

"I come to see if Eugenia wanted something to eat yet."

"Eugenia? Oh, right. I had forgotten your real name for a moment," he said, smiling.

"I hate it!" I cried. "I don't want to change my name."

"Of course you don't," he said. I breathed relief until he added,

"Right now. But after a while I'm sure Mother will convince you. One way or another she usually gets people to see what would be best."

"I won't change my name," I insisted.

"We'll see," he replied, obviously unconvinced. He looked around the room. "Do you need anything?"

Need anything? I thought. Yes. I need my old family back. I need people who really love me and really care about me and who don't look at me as if I were some unwashed and polluted person who could contaminate them and their precious world. I need to sleep where my family sleeps, and if the woman upstairs is my real mother, I need her to treat me like her real daughter and not have to have doctors and medicine before she can face me.

I need to go back to the way things were, as bad as they seemed. I need to hear Jimmy's voice and be able to call him through the darkness and share my fears and my hopes with him. I need my little sister calling for me, and I need a daddy who comes to greet me with a hug and a kiss—not one who stands in the doorway and tells me I have to change my name.

But there was no point in telling my real father any of this. I didn't think he would understand.

"No," I said.

"Okay, then, you should go with Mrs. Boston and eat something. Take her right along, Mrs. Boston," he said, heading out. He turned back to me. "I'll speak to you again soon," he said and left.

"I'm not hungry," I repeated as soon as he was gone.

"You got to eat something, child," she said. "And you got to do it now. We have a schedule to meet. Mrs. Cutler, she cracks a whip around here."

I saw she wasn't going to leave me alone, so I stood up and followed her back to the hotel and to the kitchen. When we reached the stairway, I looked up. My real mother was up there somewhere, in her room, unable to face seeing me yet. The very idea made it sound like I was a monster with fangs and claws. What would she be like when we finally did meet? Would she be more loving and thoughtful than my grandmother? Would she insist I be moved upstairs immediately so I could be near her?

"Come along," Mrs. Boston said, seeing I had paused.

"Mrs. Boston," I said, still gazing up the stairs, "if you call my grandmother Mrs. Cutler, what do you call my mother? Doesn't everyone get confused?"

"No one gets confused."

"Why not?"

She gazed upstairs to be sure no one was near us and could overhear. Then she leaned toward me and whispered.

"They call your mother little Mrs. Cutler," she said. "Now, let's go. We got lots to do."

The kitchen seemed like bedlam to me. The waiters and waitresses who served the guests in the dining room were lined up in front of a long table to pick up their trays of food.

The food was delicious, but Mrs. Boston stood behind me waiting impatiently for me to finish. As soon as I rose from the table, we were off to see Mr. Stanley.

He was a slim man about fifty with thin brown hair and a narrow face with small eyes and a long mouth. There was something birdlike about him and the way he moved in short, jerky motions. He stood back with his arms folded and considered me after Mrs. Boston had introduced us.

"Hmm," he said, his head bobbing. "She could fit into Agatha's old uniform."

I wanted Agatha's old uniform even less than I wanted her job, but Mr. Stanley was very efficient and didn't wish to carry on any conversation. He chose the uniform, found me some white shoes my size with white socks, and distributed it all to me as though I were entering the army. I even had to sign for it.

"Whatever anyone breaks here, they pay for," he said. "What they lose, they pay for, too. Things don't walk away from this hotel as easily as they do from the others. That's for sure," he said proudly.

"When you get here in the morning, you'll go to the east wing with Sissy."

"You know how to get back to your room?" Mrs. Boston asked as we left. I nodded. "Okay, then, I'll see you in the morning," she said. I watched her walk off and then I started back.

After I reached the old wing, I paused at the living room and entered so I could look at the family pictures on the mantel. There was Clara Sue when she was a little girl, and there was Philip, standing together in front of one of the small gazebos. I found the picture of Philip and our mother I had only glimpsed before, but just as I reached up to bring it closer to me, my grandmother appeared in the doorway. I jumped when she spoke.

"If I were you, Eugenia, I would get a good night's rest," she said, her eyes moving from me to the pictures. "You have to get yourself into the daily schedule."

I put the picture back quickly.

"I told you," I said defiantly, "my name is Dawn." I didn't wait for her response. I hurried away and to my little room, shutting the door after I entered. I stood there listening to see if she had followed me, but I heard no footsteps. Then I let out the breath I was holding and turned to my little suitcase.

I took out the picture of Momma as a young girl and placed it on the little table. As I looked at her, I recalled her final words to me.

"You must never think badly of us. We love you. Always remember that."

"Oh, Momma!" I cried. "Look what has happened to us! Why did you and Daddy do this?"

I reached into the drawer where I had hidden the pearls and removed them. Holding them made me feel closer to Momma, but I couldn't wear them. I just couldn't. Not here. Not in this horrible place that was my new home. The pearls had been meant to be worn on happy occasions, and my current situation certainly didn't qualify. I looked at the pearls one last time and then hid them away again. No one at Cutler's Cove would know about their existence. The pearls were my last link to my family. They were the only thing that gave me some feeling of comfort, and they would be my secret. If I ever felt lonely or needed to remember happier times, I'd just take them out of their drawer and hold them. Maybe one day I'd wear them again.

Finally, exhausted from what had to be one of the worst days of my life, I put away the rest of my things and dressed for bed. I crawled under the cover that smelled clean, but felt rough, and the pillow was too soft. I hated this room more than any of the awful apartments we had lived in.

I stared up at the cracked white ceiling. The cracks zigzagged across, looking like threads pasted up there. Then I turned over and switched off the light. With the night sky now overcast and no lights outside my window, it was pitch dark in my room. Even after my eyes grew used to it, I could barely make out the dresser and the window.

It was always hard to get used to a new place when we were traveling and moving from one town to another. First nights were scary, only then Jimmy and I had each other to comfort each other. Now, alone, I couldn't help but listen to every creak in the antique wing of the old hotel and shudder. I had to get used to every sound until nothing surprised me.

Suddenly, though, I thought I heard someone crying. It was muffled, but it was clearly the sound of a woman crying. I listened hard and heard my grandmother's voice, too, although I couldn't make out any words. The crying stopped as suddenly as it had started.

Then the silence and the darkness became heavy and ominous. I strained to hear the sounds of the hotel, just so I would have the comfort that came from hearing other people's voices. I could hear them, but they seemed so distant, like voices on a radio far, far away, and they didn't make me feel any safer or any more comfortable. But after a while my exhaustion overcame my fear, and I fell asleep.

I had arrived at what was my real home, only I didn't feel any sense of belonging. How long, I wondered, would I be a stranger in my own house and to my own family?

My eyes snapped open when I heard someone at the door. For a moment I forgot where I was and what had happened. I expected to hear Fern cry out and see her bounce up and down impatiently in her crib. But instead, when I sat up, I confronted my grandmother. Her hair was brushed back as perfectly as it had been when I had first met her, and she was wearing a dark gray cotton skirt with a matching blouse and jacket. Pearl earrings dangled from her lobes, and she wore the same rings and watch. She smirked with disapproval.

"What is it?" I asked. The look on her face and the way she had burst in my room jumped my heart right up against my throat.

"I had a suspicion you were still in bed. Didn't I make clear what time you were to get up and dressed?" she asked sharply.

"I was very tired, but I didn't fall right asleep because I heard someone crying," I told her. She drew her shoulders up and made her eyes small.

"Nonsense. No one was crying. You were probably already asleep and dreaming."

"It wasn't a dream. I heard someone crying," I insisted.

"Must you always contradict me?" she snapped. "A young girl your age should learn when to speak and when to be quiet."

I bit down on my lower lip. I wanted to snap back at her. I wanted to demand she stop treating me this way, but fate had pulled me through a knothole and stretched me out thin and flat. I trembled. It was as if I had lost my voice and everything would be trapped forever inside me, even tears. She glanced at her watch.

"It's seven," she said. "You must get dressed and go to the kitchen immediately if you want any breakfast. If any member of the staff wants breakfast, he or she has to eat it earlier than the guests. See to it that you get yourself up in the morning from now on," she commanded. "At your age, you shouldn't be dependent upon others to fulfill your responsibilities."

"I always get up early, and I always fulfill my responsibilities," I shot back at her. My anger finally exploded like a balloon filled with too much air. She stared a moment. I remained in bed, holding my blanket against my chest to keep down the pounding of my broken heart.

She studied me for a moment, and then her glance went to my little nightstand. Suddenly her face grew fiery red.

"Whose picture is that?" she demanded stepping forward.

"It's Momma," I said.

"You brought Sally Jean Longchamp's picture into my hotel and put it out for anyone to see?"

In a flash, far faster than I ever imagined someone as old as she could move, she seized my precious photograph.

"How dare you bring this here?"

"No!" I cried, but in an instant she tore it in two. "That was my picture, my only picture!" I cried through my tears. She pulled herself up to her full height.

"These people were kidnappers, child-stealers, thieves. I told you," she said through her clenched teeth, her lips pulled back until they were pencil thin, "I don't want any contact with them. Wipe them from your memory."

She threw Momma's picture into the small wastebasket. "Be in the kitchen in ten minutes. The family must set a good example for the staff," she added and stepped back out, closing the door as she did so.

The tears flowed down my cheeks.

Why was my grandmother being so horrible to me? Why couldn't she see the pain I was in having been ripped from the family I thought was mine? Why wasn't I given a little time to adjust to a new home and a new life? All she could do was treat me as if I were someone who had been brought up to be wild and useless. It made me furious. I hated this place; I hated being here.

I got up and quickly got dressed in a pair of jeans and a blouse. Not thinking about anything else but getting away from this horrible place, I ran out of my room and out the side entrance. I didn't care about breakfast; I didn't care about being late for my new work. All I could think of was my grandmother's hateful eyes.

I walked on, my head down, not caring where I ended up. I could walk off a cliff, for all I cared. After a while I did look up, however, and found myself standing in front of a tall, stone archway. The words carved into it read Cutler's Cove Cemetery. How appropriate, I thought. I felt as though I'd rather be dead.

I gazed through the dark portal at the stones gleaming like so many bones in the morning sunlight and found myself drawn in like someone who had been hypnotized. I discovered a path to the right and walked down it slowly. It was a well-cared-for cemetery, with the grass neatly cut and trimmed and the flowers well weeded. Before long I found the Cutler section and looked upon my ancestors' stones: the graves of the people who had to be my great-grandfather and great-grandmother, aunts and uncles, cousins. There was a large monument marking my grandfather's grave, and right behind that and to the right was a very small stone.

Curious, I walked over to the small stone and then stopped in my tracks as I was able to read what it said. I blinked disbelieving eyes. Was I reading correctly, or was the morning light playing tricks on me? How could this be? Why would this be? It didn't make sense. It just didn't make sense!

Slowly I knelt at the tiny monument, running my fingers over the carved letters as I read the few words.

EUGENIA GRACE CUTLER

INFANT

GONE BUT NOT FORGOTTEN

My stomach tightened even further as I looked at the dates which fit my own birth and disappearance. There was no denying the fact. This grave was *mine.*

Suddenly the ground beneath my knees felt as though it were burning. I felt icicles dripping down the back of my neck. I stood up quickly on trembling legs, tearing my eyes away from the evidence of my nonexistence. There wasn't any doubt in my mind as to who had had that grave created: Grandmother Cutler. She'd certainly be happier if my little body was really in there. But why? Why was she so anxious to have me buried and forgotten?

Somehow I had to face up to this hateful old woman and show her I was not a lowly creature to be spit upon and tormented. I wasn't dead. I was alive, and nothing she could do would deny my existence.

When I returned to the hotel and my room, I reached into the wastebasket and took out Momma's torn picture. It had been ripped through her beautiful smile. It was as if my grandmother had ripped through my heart. I hid the torn pieces under my underwear in the dresser. I would try to tape it together, but it would never be the same.

I changed into my uniform and went directly to the kitchen. By the time I arrived, it was already filled with waiters, other chambermaids, kitchen help, and the bellhops and receptionists. The conversations stopped and every face turned my way. I felt just the way I used to feel whenever I entered a new classroom. I imagined most of them knew who I was by now.

Mrs. Boston called to me, and I joined her and the other chambermaids. I could see they resented me for taking someone's job, someone who really needed it. Nevertheless, she introduced me to everyone and pointed out Sissy. I sat down beside her.

She was a black girl who was five years older than I was even though she didn't look a day older. I was an inch or so taller. She had her hair chopped short, cut evenly around as if someone had put a bowl over her head and snipped it.

"Everyone's chattering about you," she said. "People always knew about the missing Cutler baby, only everyone thought you was dead. Mrs. Cutler even had that memorial put up on the family cemetery," she added.

"I know," I said. "I've seen it."

"You have?"

"Why did they do it?"

"I heard that Mrs. Cutler had it made years later after she came to the conclusion you weren't going to be found alive. I was too little to go to the service, of course, but my grandmother told me no one but the family went anyway. Mrs. Cutler told everyone the day you was kidnapped was the same as if it was the day you died."

"No one mentioned it to me," I said. "I just came upon it by accident when I wandered into the cemetery and found the family section."

"I suppose they'll be digging it up now," Sissy said.

"Not if my grandmother has her way," I mumbled.

"What's that?"

"Nothing," I said. I was still shaking from the sight of the small stone with that name on it. Even though it wasn't the name I accepted, it was meant to be me; it was the same thing. I was glad to get to work and put my mind on other things.

After breakfast we went with the other chambermaids to Mr. Stanley's office. He gave out the assignments, new rooms that had to be prepared, rooms that had to be cleaned because guests were checking out. Sissy and I had to do what was called the east wing. We had fifteen rooms. We alternated rooms down the corridor. Just before lunch my father came to get me.

"Your mother is ready to meet you, Eugenia," he said.

"I told you . . . my name's Dawn," I retorted. Now that I had seen the gravestone, the other name was even more despicable.

"Don't you think Eugenia has a more distinguished sound to it, honey?" he asked as we walked. "You were named after one of my mother's sisters. She was only a young girl when she died."

"I know, but I didn't grow up with that name, and I don't like it."

"Maybe you will. If you give it a chance," he suggested.

"I won't," I insisted, but he didn't seem to hear or care.

We turned into the old section of the hotel and headed for the stairway, my pulse throbbing harder and harder with each forward step.

The upstairs had new-looking wallpaper with light blue polka dots, and the corridor had a plush cream carpet. A large window at the far end made it airy and bright.

"This is Philip's room," my father explained as we came to a door on the right, "and the next door is Clara Sue's. Our bedroom suite is right down here on the left. Your grandmother's suite is just around the corner."

We paused outside the closed door to his and my mother's bedroom, and my father took a deep breath, closing and opening his eyes as if he had a weight on his chest.

"I must explain something to you," he began. "Your mother is a very delicate woman. The doctors say she has frayed nerves, and so we try to keep tension and pressure away from her. She comes from a fine old southern family, aristocrats, and she was well protected all her life. But that's why I love her. To me she's like . . . a work of art, fine china, fragile, beautiful, exquisite," he said. "She's someone who needs to be protected, cherished, and held dearly. Anyway, you can imagine what all this has done to her. She's a little afraid of you," he added.

"Afraid of me? Why?" I asked.

"Well . . . bringing up our two children has been a strain on her as it is. To suddenly be confronted by a long-lost child who has lived an entirely different sort of life . . . it frightens her. All I ask is that you be patient.

"All right," he said, taking another deep breath and reaching for the doorknob, "here we go."

It was like entering another world. First we stepped into a sitting room with a burgundy velvet carpet. All of the furniture, although shiny, clean, and new-looking, was obviously antique. Later I would learn how valuable it was. It was all original and dated back to the turn of the century.

On the left was a fieldstone fireplace with a long, wide mantel. Atop it at the center was a silver frame with a picture of a young woman holding an umbrella and standing on the beach. She was dressed in a light-colored dress with a long hem. On both ends of the mantel were slim vases with a single rose in each.

Above the mantel was a painting of what must have been the original Cutler's Cove Hotel. There were people gathered on the lawn and people sitting on the wraparound porch. A man and a woman stood together at the front door. I wondered if they weren't supposed to be my grandparents. The sky behind and above the hotel was dotted with small puffy clouds.

To my immediate left was a piano. There was a sheet of music on it, but it looked as though it had been placed there simply for show. In fact, the entire sitting room looked unused, untouched, like a room in a museum.

"Right this way," my father said, indicating the double doors before us. He took hold of both handles and opened both doors with one graceful motion. I stepped forward into the bedroom and nearly gasped in astonishment. It was so big, I thought it was larger than most of the apartments I had lived in. The thick sea-blue carpet rolled on forever until it reached an enormous canopy bed at the far end. There were large windows on each side of the bed, with white lace curtains draped over them. The walls were covered with dark blue velvet. To the right was a long milk-white marble vanity table with cherry-red streaks running through it. There were two high-back matching cushioned chairs. Vases filled with jonquils were spaced along the table. A floor-to-ceiling mirror ran the entire wall behind the vanity table, which made the bedroom look even longer and wider.

A door on the left opened to a walk-in closet bigger than the room I now slept in. There was another closet down from that. The bathroom was on the right. I had only a glimpse of it, but I was able to see the gold fixtures in the sinks and the enormous tub.

My mother was almost lost in the enormous bed. She sat up against two jumbo fluffy pillows. She was wearing a bright pink silk robe with a lace cotton nightie. As we drew closer, she looked up from her magazine and put a chocolate back into the box that was beside her on the bed. Even though she was still in bed, she wore pearl earrings and lipstick and eyeliner. She looked as if she could get out of bed, slip into a fancy dress, and go dancing.

"Laura Sue, we're here," my father sang, stating the obvious. He stopped and turned to me, gesturing for me to come farther forward. "Isn't she a pretty girl?" he added when I stepped up beside him.

I looked at the woman I had been told was my real mother. Yes, there were resemblances, I thought. We were both blondes, my hair the same shade of yellow and as bright as the morning sun. I had her blue eyes, and I had her peaches-and-cream complexion. She had a graceful neck and slight shoulders, and her hair rested softly on those shoulders and looked as if it had been brushed a thousand strokes, it was so soft and shiny.

She looked me over quickly, her eyes darting from my feet to my head, and then she gasped deeply as if trying to catch her breath. She brought her hand to the heart-shaped locket between her breasts and fingered it nervously. There was an enormous diamond ring on her hand, the stone so large it looked awkward and out of place on her slim, short finger.

I took a deep breath, too. The room was permeated with the scent of the jonquils, for there were vases of them on the end tables and one on the table in the far corner.

"Why is she in a chambermaid's uniform?" my mother asked my father.

"Oh, you know Mother. She wanted her to get used to the hotel life immediately," he replied. She grimaced and shook her head.

"Eugenia," she finally said in a whisper, directing herself to me. "Is it really you?" I shook my head, and she looked confused. She turned quickly to my father. A worried frown drew his eyebrows together.

"I must tell you, Laura Sue, that Eugenia has known only Dawn as her name, and she is a little uncomfortable being called anything else," he explained. A puzzled expression flashed through her face and creased her brow. She battered her eyelashes and pursed her lips.

"Oh? But Grandmother Cutler named you," she said to me, as if that meant it had been written in stone and could never be changed or challenged.

"I don't care," I said. Suddenly she looked frightened, and when she looked to my father this time, it was to ask for help.

"They named her Dawn? Just Dawn?"

"However, Laura Sue," my father said, "Dawn and I did just agree she would give Eugenia a chance."

"I never said I agreed," I said quickly.

"Oh, this will be so difficult," my mother said, shaking her head. Her hand hovered near her throat; her eyes darkened. Something frightening burgeoned in my heart just from watching her reactions. Momma had been deathly ill, but never looked as weak and helpless as my real mother did.

"Whenever anyone calls her Eugenia, she won't know they're calling her. You can't call yourself Dawn now," she said to me. "What would people think?" she moaned.

"But it's my name!" I cried. She looked as if she would cry herself.

"I know what we will do," she said suddenly, clapping her hands together. "Whenever we introduce you to anyone who is important, we will introduce you as Eugenia Grace Cutler. Around here, in the family's quarters, we will call you Dawn, if you like. Doesn't that sound sensible, Randolph? Won't Mother think so?"

"We'll see," he replied, not sounding happy. But my mother put on a pained expression, and he relaxed and smiled. "I'll speak to her."

"Why can't you just tell her that's what you want?" I asked my mother. At this point I was more curious than angry. She shook her head and brought her hand to her breast.

"I . . . can't stand arguments," she said. "Must there be arguments, Randolph?"

"Don't concern yourself with this, Laura Sue. I'm sure Dawn and I and Mother will work it all out."

"Good." She took a deep breath. "Good," she repeated. "That's settled," she said.

What was settled? I glanced at my father. He smiled at me as if to say let it be. My mother was smiling again, looking like a little girl who had been promised something wonderful like a new dress or a day at the circus.

"Come closer, Dawn," she said. "Let me get a real good look at you. Come, sit by the bed." She indicated a chair I should bring up with me. I did so quickly and sat down. "You are a pretty girl," she said, "with beautiful hair and beautiful eyes." She reached out to stroke my hair, and I saw her long, perfect pink fingernails. "Are you happy to be here, to be home?"

"No," I said quickly, perhaps too quickly, for she blinked and brought herself up as if I had slapped her. "I'm not used to it," I explained, "and I miss the only people I ever knew as my family."

"Of course," she said. "You poor, poor thing. How horrible this all must be for you." She smiled, a very pretty smile, I thought, and when I looked up at my father, I saw how much he adored her. "I knew you only for a few hours, held you in my arms for only a little while. My nurse, Mrs. Dalton, knew you longer than I did," she whined. She turned her sad eyes toward my father, and he nodded sadly.

"Whenever I am able to see you, you must spend as much time with me as you can, telling me all about yourself, where you have been, and what you have done. Did they treat you well?" she asked, grimacing as if preparing to hear the worst things: stories about being locked in closets or starved and beaten.

"Yes," I said firmly.

"But they were so poor!" she exclaimed.

"Being poor didn't matter. They loved me and I loved them," I declared. I couldn't help it. I missed Jimmy and little Fern so much it made me tremble inside.

"Oh, dear," my mother said turning to my father. "This is going to be just as difficult as I imagined it would be."

"It will take time," he repeated. "Don't work yourself into a panic, Laura Sue. Everyone will help, especially Mother."

"Yes, yes, I know." She turned back to me. "Well, I'll do what I can for you, Dawn, but I'm afraid my strength hasn't returned yet. I hope you will understand."

"Of course she will," my father said.

"After a while, when you've learned how to behave in society, we will have a little party to celebrate your homecoming. Won't that be nice?" she asked, smiling.

"I know how to behave in society," I replied, wiping the smile from her face.

"Well, of course you don't know how, dear. It took me ages and ages to learn the proper etiquette, and I was brought up in a nice home surrounded by nice things. People of position were continually coming and going. I'm sure you don't know the proper way to greet someone, or how to curtsy and look down when someone gives you a compliment. You don't know how to sit at a formal dinner table, what silverware to use, the proper way to eat soup, butter your bread, reach for things. There is so much for you to learn now. I'll try to teach you as much as I can, but you must be patient, okay?"

I looked away. Why were these things important to her now? What about us really getting to know each other? What about a true mother-daughter relationship? Why wasn't she more interested in what I wanted and needed?

"And we can talk about womanly things, too," she said. I raised my eyes with interest.

"Womanly things?"

"Of course. We can't have you looking like this all the time."

"She's working in the hotel this summer, Laura Sue," my father reminded her gently.

"So? She can still look like a daughter of mine should look."

"What's wrong with the way I look?" I asked.

"Oh, dear, honey, your hair should be cut and styled. I'll have my beautician look at you. And your nails," she said, grimacing. "They need a proper manicure."

"I can't make beds and clean rooms and worry about my nails," I declared.

"She's right, Laura Sue," my father said gently.

"Does she have to be a chambermaid?" my mother asked my father.

"Mother thinks it's the best place to begin."

She nodded with a look of deep resignation as if whatever my grandmother thought or said was gospel. Then she sighed and contemplated me again, shaking her head gently.

"In the future please change into something pleasant before coming to see me," she told me. "Uniforms depress me, and always shower and wash your hair first. Otherwise, you will bring in the dust and grime."

I guess I was a windowpane, easy to read, for she saw the pain in my heart.

"Oh, Dawn dear, you must forgive me if I sound insensitive. I have not forgotten how hard this is for you, too. But just think of all the wonderful and new things you will have and be able to do. You will be a Cutler in Cutler's Cove and that's an honor and a privilege. Someday there will be a line of proper suitors begging for your hand in marriage, and all that has happened to you will seem like a bad dream.

"Just like it seems to me," she added and took another deep breath. It was more like she was gasping for air.

"Oh, dear, it's getting hot," she announced, practically in the same breath. "Could you turn on the fan, please, Randolph?"

"Of course, dear."

She fell back against the pillow and fanned herself with her magazine.

"This is all so overwhelming," she said. "Randolph, you've got to help me with this!" she cried, her voice thin and high, sounding as if she were on the verge of hysterics. "It's hard enough for me to look after Clara Sue and Philip."

"Of course I will, Laura Sue. Dawn will not be a problem."

"Good," she said.

How could she think I would be a problem for her? I wondered. I wasn't a baby who needed constant care and watching.

"Does everyone know about her, Randolph?" she asked, staring up at the ceiling. When she spoke about me like this, it was as if I weren't in the room with her.

"It's getting around Cutler's Cove, if that's what you mean."

"Heavens. How will I go about? Everywhere I go, people will have questions and questions. I can't stand the thought of that, Randolph," she moaned.

"I'll answer the questions, Laura Sue. Don't worry."

"My heart is pounding so, Randolph. It just started and I feel my pulse throbbing in my neck," she said, bringing her fingers to her throat. "I can't catch my breath."

"Now, take it easy, Laura Sue," my father advised. I looked at him in anticipation. What was happening? He nodded and tilted his head toward the door.

"I'd better be going," I said. "I've got to get back to work."

"Oh . . . oh, yes, sweetheart," she said, turning back to me. "I need a little nap now anyway. Later we will talk again. Randolph, please ask Dr. Madeo to come back."

"Now, Laura Sue, he was just here not an hour or so ago and—"

"Please. I think I need him to change my medicine. It's not helping."

"All right," he said with a sigh. He followed me out. I looked back once and saw her lying back with her eyes closed, her hands still pressed to her bosom.

"She'll be all right," my father assured me as we stepped out. "Just one of her spells. They come and go. It's part of her nervous condition. Why, in a day or two, she will be up and about, dressed in one of her beautiful dresses and standing in the dining room doorway alongside Mother, greeting guests. You'll see," he said, patting me on the shoulder.

My father assumed my sad and troubled look came from my worrying about my mother, but she was still a stranger to me. True, we looked somewhat alike, but I did not feel any warmth between us and couldn't imagine calling her Mother. She hadn't even made an effort to kiss me. Instead, she had made me feel dirty and unschooled, a wild thing brought in from the streets, someone to be made over and trained like a stray dog.

I looked away. Not money, not power and position, not all the honor associated with being a Cutler could replace one loving moment I had lived as a Longchamp. But no one wanted to see this or understand, least of all my real parents.

Oh, Momma! Oh, Daddy! I cried in the darkness of my tormented thoughts. Why did you do this? I had been better off not knowing the truth. It would have been better for all of us if that memorial stone to a stolen baby remained untouched, lingering forever in the darkness on a quiet cemetery, just another lie.

But to me the world was full of lies, and one more now seemed not to matter.

10

A New Brother, a Lost Love

For the next few days I barely saw my father. Every time I did see him, he appeared frenzied, rushing from one place to another like a worker bee while my grandmother sauntered coolly about the hotel like the queen. Whenever my father saw me, he promised to spend more time with me. I felt like a pebble in his shoe. He would pause to shake me out and then hurry off, forgetting from one time to the next that he had seen me and said the same things.

My mother didn't come down from her room for days. Then one day she appeared at the dining room door, greeting the guests as they entered. She was dressed in a beautiful turquoise gown and had her hair brushed and curled so it lay just over her shoulders. She wore a diamond necklace that glittered so brightly it was blinding in the light from the overhead chandelier, and I thought she was one of the most beautiful women I had ever seen. She looked as if she had never been sick a single day in her life. Her complexion couldn't have been more rosy, her eyes brighter, her hair more healthy and rich.

I stood off in a corner of the lobby and watched how she and my grandmother greeted people, both of them smiling warmly, patting hands, accepting kisses on the cheeks, and kissing other women and men. It seemed as though everyone who stayed at the hotel was an old friend. Both my mother and my grandmother looked radiant and alive, energized by the crowd of guests filing past them.

But when it was over, when all the guests had entered, my grandmother gave my mother a strange, stern look and then walked into the dining room. My mother didn't see me watching her at first. She looked as though she would burst into tears. My father came out to fetch her. Just before she turned to accompany him into the dining room, she looked my way.

I thought she had the oddest expression, one that even frightened me a bit. She looked as though she didn't recognize me. Her eyes were filled with curiosity, and she tilted her head slightly. Then she whispered something to my father. He turned, saw me, and waved. My mother continued into the dining room, but my father came across the lobby.

"Hi," he said. "How are you doing? You getting enough to eat?"

I nodded. He had asked me the same question three times in two days.

"Well, tomorrow you will have more to do and more fun. Philip and Clara Sue are coming home. School's out."

"Tomorrow?" I had forgotten the date. Time had lost its meaning for me.

"Uh-huh. I'd better get back in there. Lunch is about to begin. As soon as I get that free moment, we'll talk," he added and left me quickly.

Tomorrow Philip was coming, I thought. I was afraid of seeing him. How would he feel about all this? Would he be embarrassed? Maybe he wouldn't be able to look me in the face. How many times had he recalled kissing me, touching me? Did it disgust him now? None of this was his fault, nor was it mine. We didn't deceive each other; we had been deceived.

And then there was Clara Sue to think about. I would never be able to face the reality of her being my sister, I thought, and with the way she hated me . . . tomorrow . . . just the thought of it made me sweat and tremble.

Later that day I went exploring through the hotel. After I finished working with Sissy, afternoons usually belonged to me. The only problem was that there was usually nothing to do. I was all alone, without anyone to talk to. Sissy always had other jobs to do, and there was no one else my age among the guests since the summer season hadn't started yet. Part of me was looking forward to Philip and Clara Sue's arrival. Granted, things would be awkward at first, but we'd all adjust. We had to. After all, we were a family.

Family. It was the first time the word had entered my mind with regards to the new people in my life. We were a *family*. Philip, Clara

Sue, Grandmother Cutler, my real mother and father, and *me*, were a family. There would never be any changing of that. We belonged to each other, and no one would ever be able to take them away from me.

Although the thought of the Cutlers as my real family gave me a sense of comfort and security I had never thought possible, it also made me feel guilty. I instantly envisioned Daddy and Momma, Jimmy and Fern. They were my family, too, no matter what anyone said. I would always love them, but that didn't mean I couldn't learn to love my real family, too, did it?

Not wanting to dwell on my two families anymore, at least for the moment, I concentrated on my exploration trek. I went from room to room, floor to floor, really paying attention to my surroundings. The extravagance and opulence of Cutler's Cove was dazzling. There were plush carpets, Oriental rugs, rich tapestries, sleek leather sofas and chairs, lamps with glittering shades of Tiffany glass, polished bookshelves with rows upon rows of books.

There were paintings and sculptures; delicate figurines and vases overflowing with lush, fragrant flowers. The beauty of it all left me speechless, but the most amazing thing of all was that I belonged here. This was my new world. I had been born into the wealth of the Cutler family, and now I had been returned to it. It was going to take some getting used to.

Each room outshined the next one that I stepped into, and soon I lost track of where I was. Trying to get my bearings so that I could return to the hotel's lobby, I rounded a corner. Yet instead of stairs, there was only a door in the wall. There were no other rooms. Intrigued by my discovery, I opened the door. It creaked on its hinges, and a musty smell drifted out. Darkness stretched before me. I reached out a hand, searching for a light switch. Finding one, I turned it on. The bath of light put me at ease and gave me the courage to walk down what seemed to be an unused corridor.

I reached the end and another door. Biting my lip I opened it and stepped inside. Surrounding me were packed boxes, trunks, and covered piles of furniture. I was in some sort of storage room. Suddenly I became excited. The perfect place to learn about one's family—one's past—was by going through what was left behind by one's ancestors.

Eagerly I knelt before a trunk, not caring about the dust on the floor, consumed only by thoughts of what I would discover. I couldn't wait!

Trunk after trunk was opened as the afternoon flew by. There were photos of Grandmother Cutler as a young woman, looking just as stern as ever. There were photos of my father from the time he was a child until he married my mother. There were photos of my mother, too, but for some reason she didn't look happy. In her eyes there was a sad faraway look. I turned to the back of the photos of her, noting the dates. The photos had been taken after I had been kidnapped. No wonder she looked the way she did.

There were photos of Clara Sue and Philip and photos of the hotel in its various stages of growth as Cutler's Cove became more and more prosperous.

A look at my watch showed me that it was six o'clock. Dinner would be in half an hour and I was a mess! A mirror across the room provided a reflection of my dusty self. I'd have to hurry to get myself ready. Gathering up the folders the photos had been in, I prepared to put them back in the trunk I had opened. As I was about to replace the folders, I noticed a folder I had missed in the bottom of the trunk. Although I knew I was cutting things close timewise, I couldn't resist taking a peek. Putting aside the other folders, I scooped up the one I had missed. After pouring out the contents, I was stunned.

There were newspaper clippings . . . newspaper clippings of my kidnapping!

Forgetting about having to be ready for dinner, I pored over the clippings. Each account was exactly the same, telling no more and no less than what was already known. Photos of Daddy and Momma, along with my real mother and father, accompanied the articles. I looked into their young faces, searching for answers, trying to understand how they all felt.

Reading about myself . . . about my kidnapping . . . was strange. A part of me still hadn't wanted to believe that Momma and Daddy had done such a terrible thing. Yet in my hands, in black and white newsprint, I held the proof. There was no longer any denying what had happened.

"So there you are! Just what do you think you're doing up here?" a steely whisper demanded.

There was no mistaking that voice. Startled, I fell to the floor, the newspaper clippings scattering from my hand. I turned around and my blood chilled as I stared up into the angry wrath of Grandmother Cutler.

"I asked you a question," she hissed. "What are you doing up here?"

"I was just looking," I managed to answer.

"Looking? Only *looking?* Don't you mean *snooping!* How dare you rummage through things that don't belong to you." She gave an indignant snort. "I shouldn't be surprised. You were raised by a thief and kidnapper."

"Don't you say such things about Momma and Daddy," I said, instantly coming to their defense.

Grandmother Cutler ignored me. "Look at this mess!"

Mess? What mess? The trunks were only open . . . their contents as neatly arranged as when I had found them. All that needed to be done was a closing of the trunk lids.

I felt like contradicting her, but one look at her face made me change my mind. Her face was turning red; she was barely controlling herself.

"I'm sorry," I said, nervously playing with the pearls I had chosen to wear around my neck that morning. When I had woken up this morning, I had suddenly missed Momma more than I ever had. Putting on the pearls had made me feel better. I knew I had broken my promise to myself, but I had been unable to help it. Besides, I'd kept the pearls hidden under my blouse. Momma would have liked seeing me wear them.

Grandmother Cutler's eyes suddenly bulged. *"Where did you get those?"*

Shocked, I looked up at her, shivering as she drew closer. "Get what?" I didn't know what she was talking about.

"Those pearls," she hissed.

Puzzled, I looked at the pearls. "These? I've always had them. They belonged to my family."

"Liar! You stole them, didn't you? You found those pearls in one of the trunks."

"I did not!" I hotly answered. How dare she accuse me of stealing. "These pearls belonged to my momma. My daddy gave them to me to wear on the night of the concert." I gave Grandmother Cutler a defiant look, despite the fact that I was quivering inside. She wasn't going to scare me. "These pearls are mine."

"I don't believe you. You've never worn them before. If they're so *special,*" she sneered, "then why is this the first time I'm seeing them around your neck?"

I was about to answer when Grandmother Cutler raced forward. With lightning speed she reached for the pearls, ripping them from my neck. Momma's beautiful pearls, each one individually knotted, didn't scatter or break. But they were still gone. She held them up in one hand, triumphantly tightening a fist. "They're *mine* now."

"No!" I protested, jumping to my feet and grabbing for her fist. "Give them back!" I couldn't lose Momma's pearls. I couldn't! They were all I had left of her after Grandmother Cutler had hatefully torn up her photo. "I'm telling you the truth. I swear I am."

Grandmother Cutler gave me a vicious shove, pushing me to the floor. I landed on the dusty attic floor with an "oomph," my bottom aching with soreness.

"Don't you ever raise a hand to me again! Do you understand?"

Glaring at her defiantly, I refused to answer. My silence only infuriated her further.

"Do you understand?" she repeated, snatching up a handful of my hair and twisting it painfully. "When I ask you a question, I expect an answer."

Tears sprang to my eyes, desperate to be free, but I wouldn't release them. I wouldn't give Grandmother Cutler the satisfaction. I wouldn't!

"Yes," I said, gritting my teeth. "I understand."

Amazingly, my answer returned her to some semblance of normalcy. She let go of my hair, and I rubbed my aching head. "Good," she purred. "Good." She gave a look at the open trunks. "Fix this place as you found it." She swept up the fallen newspaper clippings. "These will be burned," she stated, sending me a glare I had already become familiar with.

"You know I'm telling the truth," I told her. "You know those pearls belonged to Sally Jean Longchamp."

"I know nothing of the sort. All I know," she spat out, "is that I haven't seen these pearls since the day you disappeared."

"What are you saying?" I gasped.

She gave me a smug look. "What do you think I'm saying?"

"Those pearls belonged to my momma!" I cried out. "They did! I won't believe what you're insinuating. I won't!"

"I've always believed in the truth, Eugenia. Sally Jean and Ormand Longchamp stole these pearls. There's no escaping that fact, just like there's no escaping the fact that they stole you."

What she was saying couldn't be true. It couldn't! How could I bear this final stain against Momma and Daddy's memory? It was just too much to bear!

With her final words Grandmother Cutler left, taking away my last connection to my past. I waited for my tears to fall, but they didn't. That was because I had realized something. It didn't matter what had come with me from my former life. I had my memories and my memories of life with Daddy and Momma, Jimmy and Fern, were something that Grandmother Cutler could never take away.

The following morning I threw myself into my work, trying desperately not to think about what was soon to come or what had happened the previous day. I didn't linger around the other chambermaids and staff at lunch, either. Most of them were still very incensed about my taking Agatha's job. If I tried to speak or act friendly, one of them brought up Agatha and asked if anyone had heard anything about her. A few times I felt like standing up and shouting at them: "I didn't fire her! I didn't ask to be made a chambermaid! I didn't even ask to be brought back here! You're all so cruel and heartless. Why can't you see that?"

The words were tickling the tip of my tongue, but I was afraid to scream them, for I knew the moment I did, I would be even more isolated than I was now. Not even Sissy would speak to me, and my grandmother would have another reason to chastise me and make me feel lower than an insect. Not that I could feel much lower being stuffed away in some cubbyhole of a room in a distant part of the hotel as if I were a disgrace and an embarrassment my grandmother wanted hidden and forgotten.

I was beginning to feel like someone caught in limbo—not really accepted as a Cutler yet, and not accepted by the staff. My only real companion was my own shadow. Loneliness draped itself over me like a shroud. I felt invisible.

I was spending my break after lunch in my room alone when there was a knock on my door and Mrs. Boston appeared, her arms laden with a pile of clothing and a bag of shoes and sneakers.

"Little Mrs. Cutler asked me to bring this down to you," she said as she entered my bedroom.

"What is it?"

"I just finished getting Miss Clara Sue's room in order. That girl's the worst when it comes to being neat and organized. You would think a young lady from a good family like this would take a little more pride in her things and her living quarters, but that girl . . ." She shook her head and dropped everything at the foot of my bed.

"This here is everything Clara Sue don't use no more. Some of it is from a year or so back, so even though she's a mite bigger than you everywhere, this stuff might fit.

"Some of it she never even wore. That's how spoiled she is. Why, just look here," she added, reaching into the pile. She lifted a blouse up. "See, this still has the tag on it."

It did look brand-new. I began to sift through the things. It would certainly not be the first time I had worn used clothing. It was just the idea that it was Clara Sue's clothing, Clara Sue's hand-me-downs, that disturbed me. I couldn't help remembering all the terrible things she had done to me at school.

On the other hand, my mother, whom I really hadn't spoken to since our first meeting, was thinking about me. I supposed I should be grateful.

"My mother picked all this out for me?" I asked. Mrs. Boston nodded and raised her hands.

"She didn't pick it out exactly. She asked me to gather all the things I knew Clara Sue didn't use or want and see if you could make use of it."

I tried on one of the sneakers. Clara Sue was a year younger than me, but she was a lot bigger. The old sneakers and shoes were a perfect fit. All of the blouses and skirts would fit, too. There was even a bag of underwear.

"Everything in that is far too small for her now," Mrs. Boston said. I was sure all the panties would fit, but the year-old bra was still too big for me.

"You can sort out what works and what don't. Let me know what you don't want. There are plenty of poor people I know who would really appreciate most of this," she said, raising her eyebrows. "Especially Agatha Johnson."

"Well, I don't have time to work on this right now," I snapped. "I have to go to the card room. I'm supposed to clean it up between one and two while most of the guests are away." I put the clothing aside. Mrs. Boston grimaced and then left. I followed her out and went to do my afternoon chores.

I had just finished polishing the last table in the card room and put back the chairs when I heard Philip call, "Dawn." I turned and found him standing behind me in the doorway. He wore a light blue shirt with a button-down collar and khaki-colored slacks. With his hair brushed neatly, every strand in place, he looked his usual unperturbed self.

I had lost interest in my own appearance from the day I had arrived at Cutler's Cove. In the morning I would simply pin up my hair and then tie a bandanna around it the way the other chambermaids did. My uniform was dirty from cleaning the card room.

It was the first dark rainy day since I had arrived at the hotel. The brooding sky had made this particular day even more dreary and tedious for me. The air was cool and clammy, and I worked harder and faster to keep the chill out of my bones.

"Hello, Philip," I said, turning about completely.

"How are you?" he asked.

"All right, I guess," I replied, but my lips began to tremble and my shoulders started to shake. When I looked at him now, it made me think that my days at Emerson Peabody were all part of some dream, a dream that had turned into a nightmare the day Momma died.

"I set out looking for you as soon as I arrived," Philip said, not taking a step closer. "I haven't even unpacked. I just threw down my things and asked Mrs. Boston where I could find you. She told me Grandmother put you downstairs and started you working as a chambermaid," he added. "That's my grandmother—I mean, *our* grandmother—for you."

He paused again. The silences between our sentences were deep, and the small distance between us seemed like miles. Rapid and dramatic events had made him feel like a stranger to me. I was having trouble thinking of things to say and how to say them.

But suddenly he smiled the same way he always had with that twinkle in his eyes, that impish grin in his face. He shook his head.

"I can't think of you as my sister. I can't. This is too much," he said.

"What can we do, Philip? It's true."

"I don't know." He kept shaking his head. "So," he said, stepping closer, "how do you like the hotel? It's quite a place, isn't it? The grounds are beautiful. When it's not raining like this," he added.

"I've only been able to explore the inside of the hotel. I haven't had much of a chance to explore outside," I said. "Mostly, I've been working and spending time alone in my room."

"Oh." His smile widened. "Well, now that I've arrived, you will have more to do. I'll show you every nook and cranny. I'll re-explore everything with you, show you my favorite places, my old hiding places . . ."

For a moment we let our gazes lock. My face felt hot, my heart raced. What did he see when he looked at me? Did he still think me the nicest and prettiest girl he had met?

"On your day off," he continued quickly, "we'll walk along the beach and look for seashells and—"

"I don't have a day off," I said.

"What? No day off? Of course you do. Everybody gets a day off. I'll speak to Mr. Stanley right away about it."

I shrugged and put my polishing cloth and polish in my little cart. He came closer.

"Dawn," he said, reaching for my hand. When his fingers touched mine, I pulled away instinctively. I couldn't help it. What had once been thrilling now seemed as soiled as the linens I changed every morning. It felt wrong to look deeply into his eyes, wrong to hear him speak softly to me, wrong to have him care about me. I even felt guilty talking to him alone in the card room.

"Not a day has passed when I didn't think about you and what a horror you've been going through. I wanted to call you, even to leave school and come home to see you, but Grandmother thought it would be better to wait," he said, and I looked up at him sharply.

"Grandmother?"

"Yes."

"What did you tell her about us?" I asked quickly.

"Tell her?" He shrugged as if it had all been so simple and so harmless. "Just how you and I had become such good friends and what a wonderful person you were and how beautifully you sang. She asked me about your mother and father, and I told her about your mother's illness and death and how surprised I was to learn what they had done."

"I don't know why they did what they did or why any of this happened," I said, shaking my head. I looked away to hide the tears in my eyes.

"Grandmother felt the same way. It had been a terrible surprise to her, too, when it happened," he said. I spun around.

"Why . . . why did you call your grandmother? Why didn't you speak with . . . your father or mother?" It was still hard for me to think of them as my parents, too.

"Oh, I've always gone to Grandmother for most things," he replied, smiling. "She's always been in charge. At least, as long as I can remember, and . . . you've met Mother," he said, raising his eyes toward the ceiling. "She's having a hard enough time about it all as it is. Father would only ask Grandmother for advice anyway if I had called him. She's quite a woman, isn't she?"

"She's a tyrant," I snapped.

"What?" He kept his smile.

"She wants to change my name from Dawn to Eugenia, only I won't agree. She's insisting everyone in the hotel call me Eugenia, and they're all afraid to do otherwise."

"I'll talk to her. I'll get her to understand, you'll see."

"I don't care if she understands or not. I won't change my name to please her," I declared firmly.

He nodded, impressed with my determination. We stared at each other again.

"Don't worry," he said, moving closer. "It will be all right."

"It will never be all right," I moaned. "I try to keep busy so I won't think about Jimmy and Fern and what's happened to them." I looked up at him hopefully. "Have you heard anything? Do you know anything?"

"No. Sorry. Oh, before I forget, regards from Mr. Moore. He says no matter what, you must continue with your music. He said to tell you he wants to come hear you sing at Carnegie Hall someday."

I smiled for the first time in a long time.

"I haven't felt much like singing or playing piano these days."

"You will. After a while. Dawn," Philip said, this time seizing my hand and holding on to it tightly. He went on, his eyes soft as they saw my distress. "It's not all that easy forgetting about you the way you were, even when I see you here."

"I know," I said, looking down.

"No one can blame me, can blame you for feeling the way we do about each other. Let's just keep it our secret," he said. I looked up surprised. His eyes darkened with sincerity. "As far as I'm concerned, you're still the most beautiful girl I have ever met."

He pressed my hand more firmly and drew close as though he wanted me to kiss him on the lips. What did he expect me to do? To say?

I pulled my hand out of his and stepped back.

"Thank you, Philip, but we have to try to think of each other differently now. Everything's changed."

He looked disappointed.

"This isn't easy for me, either, you know," he said sharply. "I know you've suffered, but I've suffered, too. You can't imagine what it was like at school," he added, his forehead creasing. Then, easy as a mask to take off, he threw away his anger and put on his dreamy-eyed romantic look.

"But whenever I grew sad about it, I forced myself to think about all the wonderful things you and I could do here at Cutler's Cove. I meant what I said before. I want to show you the hotel and the grounds and the town and catch you up on our family history," he said, his voice full of energy and excitement.

"Thank you," I said. "I'll look forward to that," I added. He stepped back, still holding that sexy smile, but for me it was as if we were gazing at each other over a great valley, the distance between us widening and widening until the Philip I had known dwindled into a memory and burst like a soap bubble. He was gone. Then the gap dwindled, and he was replaced by this new Philip, my older brother.

Good-bye to my first and what I thought would be my most wonderful romantic love, I thought. Good-bye to being swept off my feet and floating alongside warm, soft white clouds. Our passionate kisses shattered and fell with the raindrops, and no one could tell which were my tears and which were the drops of rain.

Four elderly men came in and took up seats at a corner table. They were there for their daily game of gin rummy. Philip and I watched them for a moment and then turned back to each other.

"Well, I'd better get to my unpacking. I haven't even seen Mother yet. I can just imagine how this has all left her—headaches, nervous breakdowns." He shook his head. Then he laughed. "I wish I was here when she first set eyes on you. That must have been something. You can tell me all about it later, when we're alone," he said, his eyebrows rising.

"I'll start working with dinner tonight. Everybody's a slave driver around here I'll come looking for you as soon as I get free," he said as he backed away, "and we'll go for a walk or something. Okay?"

"Okay."

He turned and hurried off. I stared after him a moment and then returned to my work.

Afterward I returned to my room as usual to rest. The rain had settled into a steady drizzle, and my room was dingy and dark, even though I had the lamp on. I waited for Philip and listened keenly for footsteps in the corridor. Soon I heard some and looked up expectantly when the door was opened. It was Clara Sue. For a moment we just glared at each other. Then she brought her hands to her hips and smirked, shaking her head.

"I can't believe it. I just can't believe it," she said.

"Hello, Clara Sue." Accepting her as my sister was a hard pill to swallow, but what choice did I have?

"You don't know how embarrassing all this was for me and Philip at school!" she exclaimed, widening her eyes.

"I've already spoken to Philip. I know about the gossip he had to endure, but—"

"Gossip?" She laughed, hard and mirthless; then her face turned hard, determined. "That was only part of it. He sat in a corner by himself and refused to have anything to do with anybody. But I wasn't going to let this spoil my fun," she said, coming a little farther into the room. She looked at the bland walls and the window without any curtains to warm them. "This used to be Bertha's room, my black nanny. Only it was a lot nicer then."

"I haven't had a chance to decorate," I said dryly. She stepped back quickly when she saw some of her hand-me-downs on my bed.

"Hey, isn't that one of my blouses and one of my skirts?"

"Mrs. Boston brought it to me after she cleaned up your room."

"What kind of people did you live with? Ugh. Stealing babies. No wonder you looked so . . . unwashed and Jimmy was so goofy."

"Jimmy wasn't goofy," I snapped. "And I never looked unwashed. I admit we were poor, but we were not dirty. I said I didn't have much clothing, but what I did have, I cleaned and washed regularly." She shrugged as if I couldn't say anything that would dispute her statements.

"Jimmy was weird," she insisted. "Everyone said so."

"He was shy and gentle and loving. He wasn't weird. He was just afraid, that's all. Afraid of not being accepted by a school full of snobs." I couldn't stand talking about Jimmy this way, acting as if he were dead. That made me more angry than the things she was saying.

"Why are you defending him so strongly? He wasn't really your brother," she retorted. Then she embraced herself and shook her head. "It must have been horrible and disgusting, like being forced to live with strangers."

"No, it wasn't. Momma and Daddy were always—"

"They weren't your momma and daddy," she snapped. "Don't call them that. Call them what they were—kidnappers, baby snatchers!"

I looked away, the tears stinging behind my eyes. I wouldn't let her see me cry, but what could I say? She was right, and she enjoyed driving the nails of ridicule into me.

"The worst thing of all was you and Philip," she said grimacing and twisting her mouth as if she had gulped castor oil. "No wonder he sat alone, sulking. He felt so dirty and stupid wanting to be his sister's boyfriend. And everybody knew!" She grimaced again, her face much chubbier than mine, ballooning in the cheeks. We shared hair color and eyes, but our mouths and our figures were so different.

"He can't be blamed for something he didn't know," I said softly. How long would we have to make excuses and defend our actions? I wondered. Who else would bring it up here?

"So what? It was still disgusting. How far did you two go?" she asked, stepping closer again. "You might as well tell me. Besides, I warned you about Philip, so I won't be surprised by anything you say. I'm your sister now, and you don't have anyone else you can trust," she added and swung her eyes to me. They were full of expectation.

I stared at her. Could I ever trust her? Did she mean it? She saw the hesitation in my face.

"I'm glad Mrs. Boston brought you all my old clothing," she said. "I'd much rather you have it than throw it out or give it to the help. And I'm sorry about the things I did to you," she added quietly, "but I didn't know who you were, and I didn't think it was right then that Philip should like you so much. I must have had a prem . . . prem . . ."

"Premonition?"

"Yes," she said. "Thank you. I know you're smart and I'm glad." She pushed aside some of the clothing and sat on my bed. "So, you can tell me," she said, her face lighting with anticipation. "I know he took you to his favorite spot. You must have kissed and kissed, right?"

"Not exactly, no," I said, sitting down beside her. Maybe it would be wonderful to have a sister close to my age, I thought. Maybe I could forgive her for all the terrible things she had done, and we could learn to really get to like each other and share thoughts and dreams as well as clothes and other things. I had always wanted a sister near my age. Girls needed other girls to confide in.

She looked at me with inquisitive eyes, urging me on with her soft, sympathetic look.

"Was Philip your first boyfriend?" she asked. I nodded. "I haven't had a real boyfriend yet," she said.

"Oh, you will. You're a very pretty girl."

"I know that," she said, shaking her head. "It's not that I couldn't have a boyfriend. There have been a number who have wanted to be, but I didn't like any one enough. And none of them were as nice as Philip or as good-looking as he is. All my friends have crushes on him and were jealous of you."

"I thought so," I said.

"You know Louise had a terrible crush on Jimmy." She laughed. "I found this love letter she wrote to him but never had the nerve to mail. It was full of 'I love you' and 'You're the nicest boy I have ever met and the best-looking.' And she even wrote love words in French! I stole it and showed it to all the other girls."

"You shouldn't have done that. It must have been painful for her," I said. She blinked her eyes quickly and sat back on her hands.

"She's a freak anyway. You were the only one who ever paid her any attention. And anyway," she said, sitting up, "I used the letter to make her do things, like spy on you and get her to cooperate when we sprayed you with that stuff."

"It was a horrible trick, Clara Sue, no matter how much you didn't like me."

She shrugged.

"I said I was sorry. Look, you ruined one of my best coats," she retorted. "I had to throw it out."

"You threw it out? Why didn't you just clean it?"

"What for?" She smiled slyly. "It's easier to get Daddy to buy me a new one. I just told him someone stole it, and he sent me money for a new one." She sat forward eagerly. "But let's forget about all that and talk about Philip and you. What else did you two do besides kiss?"

"Nothing," I said.

"You don't have to be afraid to tell me," she urged.

"There's nothing to tell."

She looked very disappointed.

"You let him touch you and stuff, right? I'm sure he wanted to. He did it to one of my friends last year, slipped his hand right under her sweater, even though he denies it."

I shook my head quickly. I didn't want to hear these things about Philip, and I couldn't imagine him doing anything to a girl that she didn't want him to do anyway.

"I don't blame you for being embarrassed about it, now that the truth is out," Clara Sue said. She narrowed her eyes, eyes which became as cold metallic gray as our grandmother's eyes. "Look, I saw him kiss you in the car the night of the concert. It was a movie star kiss, a long kiss, with tongues touching, right?" she asked, her voice nearly a whisper. I shook my head vehemently, but she nodded, believing what she wanted to believe.

"He came looking for you as soon as he got here, didn't he? I heard him drop his suitcases and go rushing out of his room. Did he find you?" I nodded. "Well, what did he say? Was he angry? Did he feel like a fool?"

"He's understandably upset."

"I'll bet. I hope he doesn't forget you are his sister now," she added curtly. She gazed at me a moment. "He didn't kiss you again on the lips, did he?"

"Of course not," I said, but she looked skeptical. "We both understand what's happened," I added.

"Um." Her eyes brightened with a new thought. "What did my father say when he met you?"

"He said . . . he welcomed me to the hotel," I said, "and he told me he would have a long talk with me, but he hasn't yet. He's been very busy."

"He's always very busy. That's why I get whatever I want. He'd rather give it to me than be bothered.

"What do you think of Mother?" she asked. "You must have quite an opinion of her." She laughed anticipating. "If one of her fingernails breaks or Mrs. Boston leaves a hairbrush out of place, she has a breakdown. I can just imagine what she was like when she heard about you."

"I'm sorry she's so nervous and sick so often," I said, "because she is very beautiful."

Clara Sue nodded and folded her arms under her bosom. She was becoming a full-figured girl quickly, her baby fat already softening into what I knew most boys would consider a voluptuous look.

"Grandmother says she got sick right after you were kidnapped, and the only thing that saved her and made her happy at all again was my birth," she said, obviously proud of that. "They had me as quickly as they could to overcome their grief about losing you, and now you're back," she added, not disguising her note of disappointment. She gazed at me a moment and then smiled again.

"Grandmother made you into a chambermaid, huh?"

"Yes."

"I'm one of the receptionists now, you know," she boasted. "I get dressed up and work behind the counter. I'm letting my hair grow longer this year. Grandmother told me to go to the beautician tomorrow and have it styled," she said, gazing at herself in the mirror. She glanced quickly at me. "All the chambermaids usually cut their hair short. Grandmother likes them to."

"I'm not cutting my hair short," I said flatly.

"If Grandmother tells you to, you will. You'll have to, otherwise your hair will be dirty every day anyway. It looks dirty right now."

I couldn't argue with that. I hadn't washed it for days, not caring about my looks. It was easier to wear the bandanna.

"That's why I don't do menial jobs," Clara Sue said. "I never did. And now Grandmother thinks I'm pretty enough to be at the front desk and old enough to handle the responsibilities."

"That's very nice. You're very lucky," I said. "But I'd rather not be meeting a lot of people and forcing smiles anyway," I added. It wiped the condescending leer from her face.

"Well, I'm sure everyone's embarrassed about all this, and for now they're just trying to hide you from the public," she said curtly.

I shrugged. It was a very good theory, but I didn't want to show her that what she said might be true.

"Maybe."

"I still can't believe it." She stood up and looked down at me sharply. "Maybe I'll never believe it," she said. She tilted her head to one side and thought for a moment. "Maybe there's still a chance it's not so."

"Believe me, Clara Sue, I wish more than you that it wasn't."

That took her back a pace. Her eyebrows lifted.

"What? Why not? You certainly weren't better off living like a pauper. Now you're a Cutler and you live in Cutler's Cove. Everybody knows who we are. This is one of the finest hotels on the coast," she bragged with what I was beginning to recognize as a family arrogance she had inherited from Grandmother Cutler.

"Our lives were hard," I admitted, "but we cared about each other and loved each other. I can't help missing my little sister Fern and Jimmy."

"But they weren't your family, dummy," she said, shaking her head. "Whether you like it or not, we're your family now." I looked away. "Eugenia," she added. I spun around on her self-satisfied smile.

"That's not my name."

"Grandmother says it is, and whatever Grandmother says around here, goes," she crooned, moving toward the door. "I've got to get dressed and start my first shift at the front desk." She paused at the door. "There are a number of kids our age who come to the hotel every season. Maybe I'll introduce you to one or two of the boys, now that you can't chase after Philip anymore. After work change into something nice and come to the lobby," she added, throwing her words out as someone would throw a bone to a dog. Then she left, closing the door behind her. It clicked shut, sounding more like the door of a prison cell to me.

And when I looked around my dull and tedious room with its bland walls and worn furniture, I felt so empty and alone, I thought I might as well have been placed in solitary confinement. I folded my hands in my lap and dropped my head. Talking about family with Clara Sue made me wonder about Jimmy. Had he been given to a foster family yet? Did he like his new parents and where he had to live? Did he have a new sister? Maybe they were kinder people than the Cutlers, people who understood how terrible it had been for him. Was he worrying about me, thinking about me? I knew he must be, and my heart hurt for the pain he was surely feeling.

At least Fern was still young enough to make a quicker adjustment, I thought, even though I couldn't help but believe she missed us terribly. My eyes filled with tears just thinking about her waking up in a strange new room and calling for me, and then crying when a complete stranger came to pick her up. How terrified she must be, I thought.

Now I understood why we had always left so quickly in the middle of the night and why we'd moved so often. Daddy must have been spooked or thought he or Momma had been recognized. Now I knew why we couldn't go too far South those times and why we couldn't return to Daddy's and Momma's families. All the time we were fugitives and never knew it. But why had they taken me? I couldn't stand not knowing everything.

An idea came to me. I opened the top drawer of my night table and found some hotel stationery and began to write a letter I hoped would find its way.

Dear Daddy,

As you know by now, I have been returned to my rightful home and real family, the Cutlers. I do not know what has become of Fern and Jimmy, but the police told me that they would be farmed out to foster families, most likely two different families. So now we are all apart, all alone.

When the police came for me and accused you of kidnapping me, my heart sank because you did nothing to defend yourself, and at the police station all you could say was you were sorry. Well, being sorry is not enough to overcome the pain and the suffering you have caused.

I do not understand why you and Momma would have taken me from the Cutlers. It couldn't have been because Momma wasn't able to have any more children. She had Fern. What possessed you to do it?

I know it doesn't seem all that important to know the reason anymore, since it has been done and is over with now, but I can't stand living with this mystery and pain, a pain I am sure Jimmy feels as well wherever he is. Won't you please try to explain why you and Momma did what you did?

We have a right to know. Keeping secrets can't mean anything to you anymore now that you are locked in prison and Momma is gone.

But it matters to us! Please write back.

Dawn

I folded it neatly and put it in a Cutler's Cove envelope. Then I left my room and went to the one person I hoped would be able to get this letter to Daddy: my real father.

I knocked on my father's office door and opened it when I heard him call. He was seated at his desk, a pile of papers and a stapler before him. I hesitated in the doorway.

"Yes?" The way he squinted at me, I thought for a moment he had forgotten who I was.

"I must talk to you. Please," I said.

"Oh, I haven't got much time at the moment. I have fallen behind on my paperwork, as you can see. Grandmother Cutler gets so upset when things aren't running on time."

"It won't take long," I pleaded.

"All right, all right. Come in. Sit down." He lifted the pile of papers and moved them to the side. "So, have you seen Philip and Clara Sue yet?"

"Yes," I said. I took the seat in front of the desk.

"Well, I imagine it will be quite an experience for the three of you to get to know each other as brother and sisters, now that you knew each other as school chums, eh?" he asked, shaking his head.

"Yes, it will."

"Well," he said, sitting up. "I'm sorry I don't have more time to spend with you right now . . ." He gestured at his office as if the responsibilities and the work were hanging on his walls. "Until we get things rolling in their proper rhythms, there is always so much to do.

"However," he said, "I've planned a night out for all of us. I'm just waiting on Laura Sue to decide which night. Then your mother and I, and Philip and Clara Sue and you will go to one of the finest seafood restaurants in Virginia. Doesn't that sound nice?"

"Yes, it does," I said.

"Well," he said, laughing softly, "you don't sound very excited about it."

"I can't help it. I know that in time, I'm supposed to get used to my new life, my real family, and forget all that has happened. . . ." I looked down.

"Oh, no," he said, "no one expects you will completely forget the past. I understand. It will take time," he said, sitting forward and stroking his ruby pinky ring as he spoke.

"So, what can I do for you?" he asked. His understanding tone of voice encouraged me.

"I can't understand why they did it. I just can't."

"Did it? Oh, you mean the Longchamps. No, of course not," he replied, nodding. "It's hard enough for other adults to understand these things, much less young people."

"And so I wrote a letter," I added quickly and produced the envelope.

"A letter?" His eyes widened and his eyebrows jumped. "To whom?"

"To my daddy . . . I mean, to the man I always thought was my daddy."

"I see." He sat back, thoughtful, his eyes narrowing and taking on some of that metallic tint I saw so often in my grandmother.

"I want him to tell me why he and Momma did this. I've got to know," I said with determination.

"Uh-huh. Well, Dawn." He grinned and lowered his voice to a loud whisper. "Don't tell my mother I keep calling you that," he said, half in jest and half seriously, I thought. His grin faded and his eyes turned severe. "I was hoping you would not try to keep in contact with Ormand Longchamp. It will only make things more difficult for everyone, even for him."

I looked down at the envelope in my hands and nodded. Tears blurred my vision. I rubbed at my eyes as a child would, feeling a child in a crazy adult world. My heart began to feel like a fist made of stone clenched in my chest.

"I just can't start a new life without knowing why they did it," I said. I looked up sharply. "I just can't."

He gazed at me quietly for a moment.

"I see," he said, nodding.

"I was hoping you would find out where they sent him and get this letter to him for me."

My suggestion surprised him. He raised his eyebrows and gazed quickly at the door as if he feared someone might be listening at the keyhole. Then he brought his left forefinger and thumb to his pinky ring and began to turn it and turn it as he nodded and thought.

"I don't know," he muttered. "I don't know whether or not that would create complications with the authorities," he said.

"It's very important to me."

"How do you know he will tell you the truth anyway?" he asked quickly. "He lied to you, told you terrible stories. I don't mean to be the one who hardens your heart against him," he added, "but what is true is true."

"I just want to try," I pleaded. "If he doesn't write back or if he doesn't tell me, I'll put it aside forever and ever. I promise."

"I see." Suddenly he picked up his pile of papers and put it down in front of him again, practically blocking me out of his vision. "Well, I don't know," he mumbled. "I don't know. I have all this work . . . Grandmother Cutler wants things running smoothly," he repeated. He started to staple papers. It seemed to me he wasn't even looking at what he was putting together.

"We shouldn't just run off doing things, half-cocked. There are responsibilities, obligations . . . preparation," he chanted.

"I don't know who else to ask, who else could do it for me," I said, my voice full of pleading. "Please!" I cried vehemently.

He stopped and looked at me.

"Well . . . all right," he said, nodding. "I'll see what I can do."

"Thank you," I said, handing him the envelope. He took it and looked at it. I had already sealed it. He put it in his top desk drawer quickly. As soon as it was gone, his face changed. The worried look disappeared and he smiled.

"Well, now," he said, "I've been meaning to talk to you about your wardrobe. Laura Sue and I discussed it last night. There are a number of things Clara Sue doesn't wear anymore that might fit you. Mrs. Boston will bring them down to your room later today, and you can go through them and see what's good and what's not."

"She already has," I said.

"Oh, good, good. Laura Sue wants to take you shopping in a day or so for whatever else you need. Is there anything else I can do for you right now?"

I shook my head. "Thank you," I said and stood up.

"It's a blessing, a miracle that you have been returned to us," he said. Then he rose from his chair and came around his desk to walk me to the door.

"Oh. Philip told me how well you play the piano," he said.

"I just started to learn. I'm not that good."

"Still, it would be nice if you came up and played something for Laura Sue and me on the piano."

I was just getting ready to answer him when he looked back down at his desk and said, "I'm sorry, I'm just so busy. Soon I'll spend lots of time with you."

Busy with what, I wondered, stapling papers? Why didn't he have a secretary do that? "Everything will be fine. Just give it time," he advised and opened the door for me.

"Thank you," I said.

And then he leaned over and kissed me on the cheek. It was a tentative, quick peck. He squeezed my hand in his, too, and then he closed the door between us quickly as if he were afraid someone would see that he had kissed me and spoken with me.

His bizarre manner, my grandmother's unexpected harshness, my mother's strange infirmities, all left me in a daze, floundering in despair. How was I ever going to swim in this new ocean of turmoil and confusion?

And who would be my raft and keep me afloat now?

11

Betrayed

At first I wasn't going to wear any of Clara Sue's hand-me-downs, but I wanted to look pretty again and feel like a girl instead of a tired, haggard maid. I expected Philip might come looking for me to take me for a walk through the hotel as soon as he finished his work in the dining room; so after dinner I returned to my room and tried on different blouse and skirt combinations, finally settling on a light blue, short-sleeved cotton blouse with pearl buttons and a dark blue pleated skirt. There was a pair of pretty white flat-heeled shoes in the bag. They had some slight smudges on the sides, but other than that, they looked nearly new.

Then I unpinned my hair and brushed it down. It really had to be washed and trimmed; there were a lot of split ends. I thought about Clara Sue going to a beautician, having all the brand-new clothes she wanted whenever she wanted them, and always being treated as though she were someone special. Would Grandmother Cutler eventually accept me and treat me the same way? I couldn't help imagining myself going to a beautician and wearing a new dress. I, too, would rather be working behind the reception desk than cleaning rooms.

I decided to tie a ribbon under my hair to lift it in the back. Momma used to say I shouldn't cover my ears. I could hear her even now. "You got beautiful ears, baby. Let the world see 'em." It brought a smile to my face, recalling. My eyes brightened. I was glad that Philip's arrival had made me long to be pretty again. It was good to have something to look forward to and not live in a dismal dark state all the time.

Even after getting into nice clothes and brushing my hair, however, I thought I still looked pale and sickly. My eyelids drooped and the brightness that had once radiated down from my light hair and warmed my smile had been dulled by sorrow, pain, and torment. All the expensive clothing, even a professional beautician, couldn't make the outside cheerful, if the inside was still melancholy, I thought. I pinched my cheeks as Momma used to pinch her own sometimes to make them look rosy.

When I looked at myself in the mirrors now, however, I suddenly wondered why I was doing all this. Philip wasn't my boyfriend anymore. Why did it matter how pretty I looked? Why was it still so important to please him? If anything, I was playing with forbidden fire. Just then I heard footsteps in the corridor. I went to the door and peered out, surprised to see someone in a staff uniform approaching.

"Your father asked me to have you come upstairs to your parents' rooms and play the piano for your mother." With that the short clerk hurried away. Well, I thought, being commanded to appear before them and perform isn't the loving attention I've been hoping for, but it's a start. Maybe by the end of the summer we'd be a close family, I hoped as I wandered through the hotel toward the section where the rest of my family lived.

I found Philip and Clara Sue at our mother's bedside, sitting in chairs they had brought up close. My mother was propped up against two large fluffy pillows. She had unpinned her hair, and it lay softly over her petite shoulders. She wore a gold nightie under her robe and still wore her earrings and diamond necklace, as well as all her makeup. I saw that Philip held her hand in his. Clara Sue sat back, her arms folded, her face in a smirk.

"Oh, how pretty you look, Dawn!" my mother exclaimed. "Clara Sue's clothes are a perfect fit."

"That skirt is so out of style, it isn't funny," Clara Sue inserted.

"Nothing that fits well and looks good is out of style," Father said in my defense. Clara Sue shifted her feet and squirmed in her seat. I could see she didn't like the way Father was gazing at me. "Aren't we lucky to have two pretty daughters?" he remarked. "Clara Sue and Dawn."

When I looked at Philip, I saw him staring at me intently, a slight smile on his face. Clara Sue looked at him, too, and then looked quickly at me, her eyes flashing with envy.

"I thought we weren't supposed to be calling her Dawn," Clara Sue reminded. "I thought we were supposed to call her Eugenia. That's what Grandmother said."

"When we're alone, it's all right," Mother replied. "Isn't it, Randolph?"

"Of course," he said and squeezed my hand gently after flashing a look at me that said, "Please, humor her for now."

"Grandmother's not going to like it," Clara Sue insisted. She glared at me. "You were named after her dead sister. It was a sacred gift. You should be grateful that you have a name like that instead of something stupid."

"My name is not stupid."

"Dawn for a name?" Clara Sue responded. Her laughter mocked me.

"Shut up," Philip snapped.

"Oh, please, Clara Sue!" Mother cried. "No controversy tonight. I'm so exhausted." She turned to me to explain. "It's always overwhelming when the summer people first come and we have to remember everyone's name and make them feel at home. None of us are permitted to be tired, or unhappy, or sick when Grandmother Cutler requires us to be present," she added, a note of bitterness in her voice. She tossed an icy glance at Father, but he rubbed his hands together and smiled as if he hadn't heard her.

"Well, now," he said. "Here we are, all of us, finally together. We have a great deal for which to be thankful. Isn't it wonderful? And what better way to make Dawn part of the family than to have her play something for us," Father said.

"Something soothing, please, Dawn," Mother pleaded. "I couldn't stand any rock and roll right now," she moaned, swinging her eyes at Clara Sue, who looked uncomfortable and very unhappy about being here.

"I don't know any rock and roll," I said. "There's a piece Mr. Moore, my music teacher, taught me. It was one of his favorites. I'll try to remember it," I said.

I was happy that they were all going to remain in the bedroom with Mother while I went out to the piano in the sitting room. At least I didn't have to play with Clara Sue glaring at me, I thought. But when I sat down, Philip came in and stood by my side, staring at me so intently, I felt myself begin to tremble.

I tested the notes the way Mr. Moore had instructed and I found the piano in tune.

"That's quite a song," Clara Sue quipped, hoping to make fun of me; but no one laughed.

"Relax," Philip said. "You're with your family now," he added, touching my shoulder. He gazed back at the doorway and quickly planted a kiss on my neck. "For good luck," he said quickly when I looked up surprised.

Then I closed my eyes and tried to shut the world out just the way I used to back at Emerson Peabody. With the first note I slipped softly into my musical kingdom, a land where there were no lies and sickness, no dreary skies and hateful days, a world full of smiles and love. If there was a wind, it was gentle, just strong enough to caress the leaves. If there were clouds, they were mushy white and as soft as downy silk pillows.

My fingers touched the ivory and began to move over the keyboard as though they had a mind of their own. I felt the notes flow from the piano up my arm, the music circling about me protectively, creating a cocoon of security. Nothing could touch me, not jealous eyes or ridiculing laughter. Resentment, bitterness, derogatory words of any kind were forgotten for the moment. I even forgot Philip was standing nearby.

When I was finished, it was a letdown. The music lingered like a shadow calling to me to go on. My fingers tingled and hovered over the keys, my eyes remained closed.

I opened them at the sound of the ovation. Father had come into the doorway to clap, and Philip applauded beside me. I heard my mother's gentle applause, too, and Clara Sue's quick salvo.

"Wonderful," my father said. "I'll speak to Mother. Maybe we'll have you play for the guests."

"Oh, I couldn't."

"Sure you could. What do you think, Laura Sue?" he called.

"It was beautiful. Dawn!" she cried. I got up. Philip was beaming, his eyes dancing with happiness. I returned to my mother's bedroom, and she surprised me by holding her arms out. I approached her and let her embrace me. She kissed me softly on the cheek, and when I pulled back, I saw tears in her eyes, but there was something in the way she gazed at me that made me tremble and hesitate. I sensed she saw something else in me, something I did not know existed. She was looking at me, but not exactly at me.

I questioned her with my eyes, searching her face for understanding. Now that I was this close to her, I saw how tiny her eyelashes were, how diminutive were her facial features, features I had inherited. Her eyes were dazzling, I thought, unable to take my gaze from the soft blue that twinkled with mystery as well as jeweled beauty. I spotted some faint freckles under them, just where mine were. Her skin was so translucent, I could see the tiny blue veins at the corners of her eyes, mapped out along her temples.

How delightfully sweet she smiled—her hair filled with the fragrance of jasmine. And how silky and soft her cheek had felt against mine. No wonder my father loved her so, I thought. Despite her nervous condition, she maintained a healthy, vibrant appearance, and she was as precious and lovely as any woman could be.

"That was so beautiful," she repeated. "You must come up often and play for me. Will you?"

I nodded and then glanced at Clara Sue. Her face was red and swollen with envy, her eyes burning, her mouth firm, her lips so taut they caused little patches of whiteness to appear in the corners. She clenched her fingers into puffy little balls in her lap and continued to glare at me.

"I've got to see Grandmother," she said, standing up quickly.

"Oh, already?" Mother cried mournfully. "You've just returned from school, and we haven't had time to gossip like we do. I so enjoy hearing about your friends at school and their families."

"I don't gossip," Clara Sue snapped unexpectedly, swinging her eyes at me and then back to Mother quickly.

"Well, I just meant—"

"Grandmother says we're very busy now, and we don't have time to lollygag around."

"Oh, how I hate those expressions," Mother said, grimacing. "Randolph?" she appealed.

"I'm sure Grandmother didn't mean for you to hurry right back. She knows you're up here visiting with us."

"I promised," Clara Sue insisted. Father sighed and then shrugged slightly at Mother. She took a deep breath and fell back against the pillow as if she had heard a death sentence. Why did she take everything so tragically? Had her condition begun when I had been stolen away? I felt sorry for her and terribly saddened, for it made Daddy and Mommy's action seem that much more terrible.

"I'm tired anyway," Mother suddenly said. "I think I'll retire for the evening."

"Very good, honey," Father said. Philip stepped forward.

"I can show you around a bit now," he told me. Clara Sue turned on us sharply, her eyes blazing.

"She's been here for days; you don't have to show her around," she complained.

"She's been working constantly and hasn't had time to really look over the hotel. Right, Dad?"

"Oh, yes, yes. We've all been so busy. Anyway, I'm making plans for our family outing—dinner at the Seafood House in Virginia Beach next week. If your mother feels up to it, that is," he added quickly.

"I'm working Tuesday night," Clara Sue interjected.

"Well, I'll speak to the boss and see if I can't get your schedule adjusted," Father said, smiling, but Clara Sue didn't return his smile.

"Grandmother hates when we do that. She wants the hotel to run like a clock," Clara Sue insisted, her hands on her hips. Whenever she nagged or whined, she scrunched up her nose, widening her nostrils and making herself look like a little hog.

"We'll see," Father said, still not showing any fluster. I couldn't imagine why not. Clara Sue needed discipline if anyone ever did, I thought.

"I've got to go," Clara Sue repeated and stormed out.

"Oh, how I hate the summer season," Mother said. "It makes everyone so tense. I wish I could go to sleep and wake up in September." She actually had two small tears shining in the corners of her eyes.

"Now, now, dear," Father said, going to her side. "Don't let anything bother you this summer, remember? Remember what Doctor Madeo said: You've got to develop a tougher skin, ignore things that disturb you and think about only pleasant things. Now that Dawn is back and she is so talented and beautiful, we have even nicer things to think about."

"Yes," Mother said, smiling at him through her tears. "I did enjoy her piano playing."

"We've had some talented performers play here over the years, Dawn," Father said. "It will be wonderful to add you to the list someday soon."

I looked from his smiling face to my mother's and saw that hers had become serious, even sorrowful again as she gazed intently at me. Once more I saw something confusing in her eyes, but I didn't give myself a chance to think about it.

The next day there was an air of excitement running throughout the hotel. Everywhere I looked the staff was busy working, taking extra care to make the hotel look spic and span. In the kitchen the cook, Nussbaum, was cooking up a feast, and outside the gardeners were tending to the grounds with meticulous care.

"What's going on?" I asked Sissy as I saw her zoom by with an armful of fine lace tablecloths.

Sissy stopped dead in her tracks. She stared at me, her eyes widening. "Don't you know?" she asked. "Don't you know what day today is?"

"No, I don't," I honestly admitted. "Is today a special day?"

"It sure is!" Sissy proclaimed. "Today is Mrs. Cutler's birthday. Tonight there's going to be a big party with decorations, a birthday cake, and tons of guests and presents."

After delivering the news Sissy continued on her way, leaving me to grapple with a dilemma. Today was Grandmother Cutler's birthday, and I hadn't even known. But even if I had, what difference would it have made? I knew how she felt about me—her feelings were obvious. Why should I care that today was her birthday? Yet suddenly I remembered Momma always telling me to treat others the way you would like them to treat you. Although I wanted to be just as mean and thoughtless to Grandmother Cutler as she had been to me, I kept remembering Momma's words. I sighed. I suppose I could turn my cheek the other way just this once. Maybe this was the chance I had been waiting for. Maybe this could be the first step in making things right between myself and Grandmother Cutler. I had hardly any money saved up to buy her a nice present. What was I going to do?

I supposed I could ask my father for some money to buy a present, but that wouldn't be the same as getting Grandmother Cutler something myself. Besides, knowing her, she'd be awfully suspicious if I bought something I really couldn't afford. Then I came up with a solution. A brilliant solution! I would give Grandmother Cutler a gift from my heart and upon which a price tag could never be placed.

I would sing her a song. This would be a step toward smoothing things out between us. Yes, my song would make everything right!

I eagerly dashed off to my room to practice, unable to wait for Grandmother Cutler's birthday party that evening.

That night I dressed with extra special care. First, I took a long, luxuriating shower, shampooing my hair and then conditioning it. When my hair was finally dry it was soft and fluffy, falling down my back in silky, cascading waves.

Surveying my wardrobe, I chose to wear a white pleated skirt with a pink silk blouse and a sweater vest of pink and white. Taking a look at myself in a mirror, I thought I looked very nice and hurried down to the hotel lobby. That's where Grandmother Cutler would be greeting her guests and accepting her gifts.

The lobby was already decorated with colorful streamers and balloons. A sign that read HAPPY BIRTHDAY stretched from one end of the lobby to the other. A line of guests was already waiting to meet with my grandmother. At its end were Clara Sue and Philip. Each had a gaily wrapped package in their hands. Philip's was tiny while Clara Sue's was huge. For a moment I felt embarrassed being empty handed. Then I reminded myself that I had a gift for Grandmother Cutler, too.

"What are you doing here?" Clara Sue sniffed disdainfully. She inspected me from head to toe. "Why does that outfit look so familiar? Oh, yes!" she laughed gaily. "It was mine before I decided to throw it out. Shall we call you 'Second-Hand Dawn' from now on? It seems like you're always settling for seconds. Clothing, family." She laughed cruelly.

Philip gave Clara Sue a dark look. "You sound jealous, Clara Sue. Could it be that your outfit looks much better on Dawn than it ever did on you?" he said, coming to my defense.

"Thank you," I said to Philip. "And thank you, Clara Sue." I was determined not to let Clara Sue's pettiness bother me. "I never owned anything so pretty before."

"It must be hard getting used to silk when you've only worn burlap for years," Clara Sue said sweetly.

I bit my tongue and turned to Philip. "What did you buy for Grandmother?"

"Perfume," he proudly boasted. "It's her favorite. It costs a hundred dollars a bottle."

"I bought her a handmade vase," Clara Sue threw in, shoving herself between me and Philip. "It was made in China. What did you get her?"

"I didn't have enough time or money to buy her a present," I admitted, "so I'm going to sing her a song."

"A song?" Clara Sue looked at me blandly. "A *song*? You've got to be kidding!"

"Yes, a song. What's wrong with that?" I could feel myself turning red. Maybe I should have brought Grandmother Cutler *something*. There was still time. I could get a bouquet of flowers in the hotel gift shop.

"You can't be serious!" Clara Sue exclaimed. "What's the matter? You too cheap?"

"I'm not cheap!" I told her. "I told you why I don't have a present. Besides, it's the thought that counts."

"Some thought," Clara Sue snorted. "An off-key tune. Whooppee!"

"That's enough, Clara Sue," Philip ordered sharply. "Dawn's right. It's the thought that counts."

I gave Philip a grateful smile as we moved closer up. "Thanks for the vote of confidence."

He gave me a wink. "Don't worry. You'll knock her socks off."

After half an hour we reached Grandmother Cutler. Both my parents were at her side, looking exceptionally nice. My father gave me a smile while my mother stared at me nervously.

Philip was the first to approach Grandmother. She opened his present slowly, being careful not to rip the paper. After finding the bottle of perfume, she dabbed some on her wrists and neck, inhaling the scent while giving Philip a big smile.

"Thank you, Philip. You know how much I adore this scent."

Clara Sue was next, and Grandmother once again opened the package slowly, removing a very pretty vase with an Oriental design from a mass of pink tissue paper.

"It's exquisite, Clara Sue," she raved. "Exquisite! It will look lovely in my bedroom."

Clara Sue nudged me in the side. "Let's see you top that with your dinky little song," she whispered before heading to kiss Grandmother Cutler on the cheek.

Now it was my turn. Butterflies fluttered around my stomach, but I ignored them as I stepped up to Grandmother Cutler, a tentative smile on my face.

"This is a surprise," she said, looking down at me from the ornately carved chair she sat upon. She held out her hands, expecting a gift to be placed in them. "Well?" she coldly asked.

I nervously cleared my throat. "My gift isn't wrapped, Grandmother."

She looked at me strangely. "It isn't?"

"No." I took a deep breath. "I'm going to sing you a song. That's my present to you."

Taking a deep breath, I launched into the song I had chosen to sing. It was my very favorite, "Over the Rainbow," the song I felt I sang with the most confidence. Suddenly I was no longer in Cutler's Cove, but over the rainbow. In the land of *my* dreams. I was back with Momma and Daddy, and Jimmy and Fern. We were all together, safe and happy. Nothing would ever tear us apart.

When I finished the song, there was a tear in my eye. The crowd broke into applause and I smiled at everyone. My parents and Philip were even clapping, although Clara Sue wasn't. I turned to Grandmother Cutler. She was also clapping, but it wasn't because she was proud of me. Oh no! She was only doing this for appearance, because others were around. Her eyes glared at me icily and although there was a smile on her lips, her face was devoid of emotion. Frozen solid and as sleek as a chunk of granite.

The guests started heading to the dining room, talking among themselves. Many of them complimented me as they walked by. Soon only my family was left.

"What did you think of my song?" I asked Grandmother Cutler meekly.

"Is that all?" she asked in her iciest tone as she rose from her seat. "If so, please step to one side. I have guests to entertain."

"That's all," I whispered. I stood still, speechless. How could everything have gone so wrong? I looked to my parents, to Philip and Clara Sue, but no one came to my defense. No one. Once again I was all alone.

Grandmother Cutler turned to the rest of my family. "Shall we adjourn to the dining room?" She led the way out, not even looking at me.

Not able to say anything, fearing I would break down and cry, I turned away and fled. As long as I lived I would never, ever forget this horrible evening.

The following day Philip found me alone in the lobby, still feeling sorry for myself.

"Shake away that frown and forget about last night," he said. "You'll win over Grandmother. Wait and see. In the meantime, you need some cheering up." He grabbed my hand, pulling me after him as he headed outside.

The clouds had parted, and the sunlight was now streaming down in warm rays and making everything look bright and new. The grass smelled fresh and was Kelly green, as were the leaves on bushes and trees.

I did look at everything as though for the first time. Up until now I had spent most of my time in the hotel working or sitting in my room. Philip's excitement opened my eyes and made me realize just how beautiful and big the Cutler's Cove Hotel and grounds were.

To the left was a huge sparkling blue swimming pool with a bright white and blue cabana at the far end and a children's wading pool at the near end. A number of guests had come out to greet the returning sun and were bathing and sunning themselves on the lounge chairs that were set up along the sides of the pool. Pool boys were circulating about, setting up the cushions and providing guests with towels or whatever they needed. The lifeguard sat in his high chair at the far end overseeing the swimmers.

There were pretty little walkways off to the right, circling through gardens and fountains. At the center was a large bright green gazebo. Some guests were seated at a table playing cards, and others were simply relaxing on the benches, talking softly, enjoying the afternoon.

We walked down one of the fieldstone pathways. I paused to smell the scent of the tulips, and Philip broke off a white gardenia and put it into my hair.

"Perfect," he said, standing back.

"Oh, Philip, you shouldn't do that," I said gazing about quickly to see if anyone had noticed. No one was looking our way particularly, but my heart fluttered beneath my breast.

"No big deal. We own the place, remember?"

He took my hand again, and we continued down the pathway.

"We have a baseball field over there," Philip said, pointing to the extreme right. I could see the high-back stop fence. "There's a staff softball team. Sometimes we play the guests; sometimes we play the staffs from other hotels."

"I didn't realize how beautiful and spacious it was back here," I said. "When I arrived at the hotel, it was already dark, and I haven't done much exploring on my own."

"Everyone's jealous of how much land we own and what we've been able to do with it over the years," he said proudly. "We offer guests much more than the average beach resort can," he added, sounding like a true son of a hotel family. He saw the smile on my face. "I sound like an advertising brochure, huh?"

"That's all right. It's good to be excited about your family's business."

"It's your family's business now, too," he reminded me. I looked about again. How long would it take before I had such a feeling? I had to keep telling myself that if I hadn't been stolen right after my birth, I would have grown up here and been used to it.

We stopped at one of the fountains. He stared at me a moment, his blue eyes growing darker and more thoughtful and then suddenly lighting up with the exciting thought that had occurred behind them.

"Come on," he said, seizing my hand again, "I want to show you something secret." He tugged me so hard, I nearly fell over.

"Philip!"

"Oh, sorry. You all right?"

"Yes," I said laughing.

"Come on," he repeated, and we ran around the side of the old section until we came to a small cement stairway that led down to a faded white and chipped wooden door with a black iron handle. The door's hinges were rusted, and it was so off kilter that when he scurried down the steps and started opening it, it scraped along the cement and he had to jiggle and lift it to get it to open.

"Haven't been here since school began," he explained.

"What is it?"

"My hideaway," he said with furtive eyes. "I used to come here whenever I was unhappy or just when I wanted to be alone."

I gazed through the doorway into a pitch-dark room. A whiff of cold, damp air came out to greet us.

"Don't worry, there's a light. You see," he said, entering slowly. He reached back for my hand. This time a tingle traveled through my fingers when they became laced with his. I followed.

"Most buildings in Cutler's Cove don't have basements, but ours, because it was built up here, does," he explained. "Years and years ago, when Cutler's Cove was just a rooming house, this was where the caretaker lived." He stopped and reached up through the darkness for a cord that dangled from the sole light fixture. When he pulled it, the naked bulb cast a pale white glow over the room, revealing cement walls and a cement floor, some shelving, a small wooden table with four chairs, two old dressers, and a bed in a metal frame. There was only a stained old mattress on the bed.

"There's a window here," Philip said, pointing, "but it's kept boarded up to keep field animals out. Look," he said, indicating the shelves, "there are still some of my toys down here." He went to the shelves and showed me little trucks and cars and a cap pistol quite rusted. "There's even a bathroom down here," he said and pointed to the right rear of the underground room.

I saw a narrow doorway and went to it. There was a small sink, toilet, and tub. Both the tub and sink had ugly brown stains, and there were cobwebs everywhere.

"Needs a good cleaning, but everything works," Philip declared, coming up beside me. He knelt down and turned the water on in the tub. Brown, rusted liquid came gushing out. "Hasn't been used for some time, of course," he explained. He let the water run until it began to clear up.

"So," he said, standing. "How do you like my hideaway?"

I smiled and gazed around. It wasn't that much worse than some of the places Momma and Daddy, Jimmy and I had lived in before Fern had been born, I thought, but I was too embarrassed to tell Philip.

"Use it whenever you want, whenever you want to get away from the turmoil," he said as he walked over to the bed and flopped down on the mattress. He bounced on it, testing the springs. "I'm going to bring down some bedding and some clean dishes and towels." He lay back on the mattress, his hands behind his head, and gazed up at the beams in the ceiling. Then he swung his eyes to me, gazing intently, his full sensual lips open.

"I couldn't help thinking about you all the time, Dawn, even after I had found out about us and I knew it was wrong to think of you this way." He sat up quickly. I couldn't take my eyes from his. They were so magnetic, demanding. "I like to think of you as two different people: the girl with whom I had found magic and . . . my new sister. But I can't just forget the magic," he added quickly.

I nodded and looked down.

"I'm sorry," he said and got up. "Am I embarrassing you?"

I looked into his soft blue eyes again, unable to stop myself from recalling that first day at school when he had come to sit with me in the cafeteria, when I had thought him the handsomest boy I had ever met.

"How am I ever going to get used to the idea that you're my sister?" he complained.

"You'll have to." Standing this close to him made me shiver. Those were the lips that had pressed so warmly against mine. If I closed my eyes, I could feel his fingers traveling gently over my breasts. The memory made them tingle. He was right about one thing—our new relationship was so surprising and so new, it was hard to accept it yet.

"Dawn," he whispered. "Can I just hold you, just for a moment, just to—"

"Oh, Philip, we shouldn't. We should try to—"

He ignored me and brought his hands to my shoulders to pull me toward him. Then he gathered me in his arms and held me there against him. His breath was warm on my cheek. He clutched me as if I were the only one who could save him. I felt his lips graze my hair and forehead. My heart pounded as he held me tighter, my breasts brought firmly to his chest.

"Dawn," he whispered again. I felt his hands coming around my shoulders. Electric tingles seized madly up and down my arms, and all those nerves that a girl my age wasn't supposed to have burned with fire. I must stop him, I thought. This is wrong. I screamed inside myself, but suddenly he seized my wrists and held them against my sides. Then he kissed my neck and started to travel down to my breasts.

He let go of my wrists and brought his hands to my bosom quickly. As soon as he did, I stepped back.

"Philip, stop. You mustn't. We'd better go." I started toward the door.

"Don't go. I'm sorry. I told myself I wouldn't dream of doing that when I was alone with you, but I couldn't help it. I'm sorry," he said.

When I looked back at him, he did look like someone in torment.

"I won't do it again. I promise," he said. He smiled and stepped toward me. "I just wanted to hold you to see if I could hold you the way a brother should hold a sister, to comfort you or greet you, but not . . . to touch you that way."

He bowed his head remorsefully.

"I guess I shouldn't have brought you here so soon."

He waited, his eyes hopeful that I would disagree and want to forget the truth.

"Let's leave, Philip," I said. When his arms had encircled me and held me fast, I had become an instrument of desire for romantic fulfillment. Now I was scared, too, of what was inside me.

He reached up quickly and pulled the light cord dropping a sheet of darkness over us. Then he seized my arm.

"In the darkness we can pretend we're not brother and sister. You can't see me; I can't see you." His grip tightened.

"Philip!"

"Just kidding," he said and laughed. He released his hold on me, and I retreated to the door.

I hurried out and turned to wait for him to close the door and follow. As soon as he did, we started up the cement stairs. But just as we did so, a shadow moved over us, and we both looked up into the disapproving eyes of Grandmother Cutler.

Bloated with anger, she glared down at us and looked so much bigger and taller.

"Clara Sue thought you two would be here," she spat. "I'm returning to my office. Eugenia, I want to see you there within five minutes. Philip, Collins needs you in the dining room immediately."

She spun on her heels and walked off briskly.

My heart felt as if it would crack open my chest, and my face felt so hot and flushed, I thought my cheeks would burn. Philip turned back to me, his face filled with fear and embarrassment. What had happened to the strong, confident look he had worn so often back at school? He looked so feeble and weak. He gazed after Grandmother and then back at me.

"I . . . I'm sorry. I'd better get going," he stammered.

"Philip!" I cried, but he lunged up the remaining steps and rushed off.

I took a deep breath and continued up the stairs. A heavy-looking, bruised gray cloud slipped over the warm afternoon sun, putting a chill in my heart.

Clara Sue smiled smugly at me from the receptionist's desk as I walked through the lobby toward Grandmother Cutler's office. She was obviously still jealous and upset by the way Father and Mother had reacted to my playing the piano the other day, I thought, as well as to the crowd's applause for my singing at Grandmother Cutler's birthday party. I knocked on Grandmother's office door. I found her seated behind her desk, her back straight, her shoulders stiff, and her arms on the arms of the chair. She looked like a high court judge. I stood before her, a tight wire inside, stretched so taut I thought I might break and cry.

"Sit down," she commanded icily and nodded toward the chair before her desk. I slipped into it, clutching the arms tightly in my palms, and gazed nervously at her.

"Eugenia," she said, only moving her head slightly forward, "I'm going to ask you this just once. Just what is there between you and your brother?"

"Between us?"

"Don't force me to define every one of my words and speak unspeakable things," she snarled and then quickly relaxed again. "I know that when you were at Emerson Peabody, before Philip learned the truth of your identity, he fancied you one of his girlfriends, and you, understandably, were attracted to him. Did anything happen for which this family should feel shame?" she asked, raising her eyebrows inquisitively.

It was as if my heart stopped beating and waited for my mind to stop reeling. A gush of heat rushed up my stomach and over my breasts, circling my throat in a fiery ring that choked me. I felt feverish. At first my tongue refused to form words, but as the silence stretched and became uncomfortably thick, I vanquished my throat lumps and caught my breath.

"Absolutely nothing," I said with a voice so deep I hardly recognized it as my own. "What a horrible thing to ask!"

"It would be far more horrible if you had something to confess," she retorted. Her sharp, penetrating gaze rested on me with deep concentration.

"Philip is a healthy young man," she began, "and like all young men, he is not unlike a wild horse just finding his legs. I think you have the worldly experience to understand my point." She waited for me to acknowledge her, but I simply stared, my heart pounding, my teeth coming down on my lower lip. "And you are not without attractive feminine characteristics, the sort most men find irresistible," she added disdainfully. "Therefore," she concluded, "most of the responsibility for proper behavior will depend on you."

"We've done nothing wrong," I insisted, now unable to keep the tears that burned behind my eyelids from emerging.

"And that's the way I want to keep it," she replied, nodding. "I am forbidding you from this day forward to spend any time alone with him, do you hear? You are not to go into any hotel rooms by yourselves or invite him into your room without a third party present."

"That's not fair. We're being punished when we haven't done anything wrong."

"It's for preventative purposes," she said and in a little more reasonable tone added, "until you are both able to conduct yourselves more like a normal brother and sister. You must keep in mind how unusual the circumstances have been and are. I know what's best."

"You know what's best? Why do you know what's best for everyone else? You can't tell everyone how to live, how to act, even when to speak to each other," I stormed, my anger now rising like an awakened giant. "I won't listen to you."

"You will only make things more difficult for yourself and for Philip," she threatened.

I gazed about the room frantically and wondered where were my mother and my father? Why wasn't at least my father here to participate in this discussion? Were they merely puppets? Did my grandmother pull their strings and run their lives, too?

"Now, then," she said, shifting herself in the seat and shifting her tone of voice as if the issue had been settled, "I have given you sufficient time to adjust yourself to your new surroundings and your new responsibilities, yet you persist in hanging on to some of your old ways."

"What old ways?"

She leaned forward and uncovered something on her desk.

"That silly name, for one," she said. "You have succeeded in confusing my staff. This nonsense has got to end. Most girls who had lived the kind of hand to mouth existence you were forced to live would be more than grateful for all you have now. I want to see some signs of that gratitude. One way you can do that is to wear this on your uniform; it's something most of my staff does anyway."

"What is it?" I leaned forward, and she turned the nameplate toward me. It was a tiny brass plaque with EUGENIA written boldly in black.

Instantly my heart became a thumping heavy lead drum in my chest. My cheeks became so inflamed, it felt as if my skin were on fire. All I could think was that she was trying to brand me, to make me a conquest, a possession, to prove to everyone in the hotel that she would have her way whenever she wanted.

"I'll never wear that," I said defiantly. "I'd rather be sent to live with some foster family."

She shook her head and pulled the corners of her mouth in as if I were some pitiful creature.

"You'll wear it; you won't go live with any foster family, though goodness knows, I would gladly send you if I thought that would end the turmoil.

"I was hoping that by now you had seen that this is your life and that you should live according to the rules set down for you. I was hoping that in time you would somehow fit in here and become part of this distinguished family. Because of your squalid background and upbringing, I see now that you will not fit in as quickly as I'd wished— particularly since despite some qualities and talents to recommend you, you cling to your wild and unrefined ways."

"I'll never change my name," I said resolutely. She glared at me and nodded.

"Very well. You are to return to your room and remain there until you change your mind and agree to put this nameplate on your uniform. Until then you will not report to work and you will not go to the kitchen to eat. No one will bring you anything to eat, either."

"My father and mother won't let you do this," I said. That made her smile. "They won't!" I cried through my tears. "They like me; they want us to be a family," I bawled. The hot drops streaked down my face.

"Of course we will be a family; we are a family, a distinguished family, but in order for you to become part of it, you must cast off your disgraceful past.

"Now, after you put on your nameplate and accept your birthright—"

"I won't." I ground the tears out of my eyes with my fists and shook my head. "I won't," I whispered.

She ignored me.

"After you put on your nameplate," she repeated, hissing through clenched teeth, "you will return to your duties." She stopped talking and scrutinized me.

"We'll see," she said with such cold confidence, it made my knees shake. "Everyone in the hotel will know you are being insubordinate," she added. "No one will talk to you or be friendly until you conform. You can save yourself and everyone else a great deal of grief, Eugenia." She held out the nameplate. I shook my head.

"My father won't let you do this," I said, half in prayer.

"Your father," she said with such vehemence it widened my eyes. "That's another problem you cling to stubbornly. You have learned what terrible things Ormand Longchamp has done, and yet you want to remain in contact with him." I looked up sharply. She sat back and opened her desk drawer to take out the letter I had written to Daddy and had given to my father to send. My heart jumped and then plunged. How could my father have given it to her—I'd told him how important it was to me. Oh, was there no one I could trust in this hateful place?

"I forbid you to communicate with this man, this child stealer." She tossed the letter across her desk. "Take this and yourself back to your room. Don't even come out to eat. When you are ready to become part of this family, this hotel, and this great heritage, return and ask for your nameplate. I don't want to set eyes on you again until you do that. You're excused," she said and turned to some papers on her desk.

For a long moment my legs wouldn't respond to my command to stand. I felt paralyzed in the chair. Her strength seemed so formidable. How could I hope to defeat such a person? She ruled the hotel and the family like a queen, and I, still the most lowly family member, had been returned to her kingdom, in many ways more of a prisoner than Daddy, who was in jail.

I rose slowly, my legs shaking. I wanted to run out of her office and charge out of the hotel, but where would I run to? Where would I go? Who would take me in? I never knew any of Daddy or Momma's relatives in Georgia, and they, as far as I knew, never even heard of me or Jimmy or Fern. If I just ran off, Grandmother would send the police after me, I thought. Or maybe she wouldn't; maybe she would be glad. Still, she couldn't help but inform the police, and a girl like me in a strange place would soon be found and returned.

Everyone would consider me the ungrateful one, too, the unwashed wild thing who had to be trained, broken, and forced to be a young lady. Grandmother would look like the abused yet loving matriarch of the family. No one would want anything to do with me until I obeyed her and changed into what she wanted me to be.

I started out of her office, my head down. Who could I turn to?

Never did I miss Jimmy more than I did at this moment. I missed the way he narrowed his eyes when he gave something deep thought. I missed the confident smile he had when he was sure what he was saying was right. I missed the warmth in his dark eyes when he looked at me lovingly. I remembered the way he promised to always be there whenever I needed him, and how he swore he would always protect me. How I missed the security that came from the feeling that he was nearby watching over me.

I opened the office door and without looking back walked out. The hotel lobby was growing crowded. People were coming in from their afternoon activities. Many milled about talking excitedly. I saw some children and teenagers standing with their parents. Like all of the guests, they were well dressed, happy, affluent-looking people. Everyone was bubbly and cheerful. They were enjoying their holiday together. For a moment I stood there and looked longingly and enviously at these happy families. Why were they so lucky? What had they done to be born into that sort of world, and what had I done to be tossed and turned about in a storm of confusion: mothers and fathers who were not real parents, brothers and sisters who were not real brothers and sisters.

And a grandmother who was a tyrant.

With my head down I walked through the lobby and did the only thing that I could do: return to my room, which had now become my prison. But I was determined. I would rather die than give up my name, even though it was a lie.

Sometimes we need our lies more than we need the truth, I thought.

12

Answered Prayers

On the way to my room I paused when I reached the stairway that led up to my parents' suite. I was still feeling cold because of my father's betrayal, but I thought my mother should at least know what my grandmother was doing to me. After only a short hesitation, I scampered up the steps and met Mrs. Boston, who had just brought my mother her supper.

"Doesn't she feel well?" I asked, and Mrs. Boston looked at me as if to say, "When does she?"

After she left I knocked softly and entered my mother's bedroom.

"Dawn. How nice," she said, looking up from her tray of food. It had been placed on a bed table, and she was propped up against her pillows as usual; and as usual, she had her face all made up as though she were going to throw off her covers and jump into a pair of shoes to attend a party or a dance. She wore a soft-looking silk nightgown with a silver lace collar. Her fingers and wrists were laden with rings and bracelets. Gold drop earrings dangled from her lobes.

"Did you come to play me some dinner music on the piano?" she asked, smiling softly. She did have an angelic face with eyes that betrayed just how fragile she was. I was tempted to do only what she asked—play the piano and leave without telling her about the horrible events.

"I was going to come down and join everyone for dinner, but when I began to get dressed, I was suddenly stricken with an ugly headache. It's diminished some now, but I don't want to do anything that would bring it back," she explained.

"Come, sit by me a moment and talk to me while I eat," she said and nodded toward a chair.

I brought the chair closer to the bed. She continued to smile and began to eat, cutting everything up into tiny pieces and then pecking at the food like a small bird. She rolled her eyes as if the effort it took to chew exhausted her. Then she sighed deeply.

"Don't you sometimes wish you could skip eating, just go to sleep and wake up nourished? Meals can be such ordeals, especially in a hotel. People are so involved with their food. It's absolutely the most important thing for most of them. Have you noticed?"

"I will be skipping my meals," I began, taking a cue from her complaint. "But not because I want to skip them."

"What?" She started to widen her smile, but saw the intensity in my eyes and stopped. "Is something wrong? Oh, please, don't tell me something's wrong," she pleaded, dropping her fork and pressing her palms to her bosom.

"I have to tell you," I insisted. "You're my mother, and there just isn't anyone else."

"Are you sick? Do you have some obnoxious stomach cramps? Your time of month?" she said, nodding hopefully, and continued pecking at her food with her fork, scrutinizing each piece before stabbing it quickly to bring it to her mouth. "Nothing bores me more and disgusts me so much. During my period, I don't budge from this bed. Men don't know how lucky they are not to have to go through it. If Randolph gets impatient with me then, I just remind him of that, and he shuts right up."

"It's not my period. I wish it were only that," I replied. She stopped chewing and stared.

"Did you tell your father? Has he sent for the doctor?"

"I'm not sick, Mother. Not in that sense, anyway. I just came from a meeting with Grandmother Cutler."

"Oh," she said, as if one sentence explained everything.

"She wants me to wear a nameplate on my uniform with the name Eugenia on the plate," I said. I skipped the part about Philip, not only because I didn't want to confuse her, but I couldn't stand talking about it myself.

"Oh, dear." She looked down at her food and then dropped the fork again and pushed the tray away. "I can't eat when there is so much controversy. The doctor says it would damage my digestion, and I would have bad stomachaches."

"I'm sorry. I didn't mean to ruin your dinner."

"Well, you did," she said with surprising sharpness. "Please, don't talk about these things anymore."

"But . . . Grandmother Cutler has told me to remain in my room until I wear the nameplate, and she has forbidden me to eat. The kitchen staff certainly won't serve me if she tells them not to."

"Forbidden you to eat?" She shook her head and looked away.

"Can't you speak to her for me?" I pleaded.

"You should have gone to your father," she said, still not looking at me.

"I can't. He won't do anything to help me anyway," I moaned. "I gave him a letter to mail to . . . to the man who had pretended to be my daddy, and he promised he would, but instead, he gave the letter to Grandmother Cutler."

She nodded, slowly, and turned back to me, now a different sort of smile on her face. It was more like a smirk of disgust.

"It doesn't surprise me," she said. "He makes promises easily and then forgets he made them. But why did you want to mail a letter to Ormand Longchamp after you learned what he had done?"

"Because . . . because I want him to tell me why he did it. I still don't understand, and I never had a real chance to speak with him before the police scooted me off and brought me back here. But Grandmother Cutler won't let me have any contact with him," I said and held up the envelope.

"Why did you give it to Randolph?" Mother asked, her eyes suddenly small and suspicious.

"I didn't know where to send it, and he promised he would find out and do it for me."

"He shouldn't have made such a promise." She was thoughtful for a moment, her eyes taking on a glazed, far-off look.

"What should I do?" I cried, hoping she would assume her role as my mother and be in charge of what happened to me. But instead, she looked down in defeat.

"Wear the nameplate and take it off when you're not working," she replied quickly.

"But why should she be able to tell me what to do? You're my mother, aren't you?" I cried.

She looked up, her eyes sadder, darker.

"Yes," she said softly. "I am, but I am not as strong as I used to be."

"Why not?" I demanded, frustrated by her weakness. "When did you become sick? After I was kidnapped?" I wanted to know more.

She nodded and fell back against her pillows.

"Yes," she said, looking up at the ceiling. "My life changed after that." She sighed deeply.

"I'm sorry," I said. "But I don't understand. That's why I wrote to the man I grew up thinking was my daddy. Where was I kidnapped from? The hospital? Had you brought me home?"

"You were here. It happened late at night when we were all asleep. One of the suites that we keep shut up across the hall was your nursery. We had set it up so nicely." She smiled at the memory. "It was so pretty with new wallpaper and new carpet and all the new furniture. Every day during my pregnancy, Randolph bought another infant's toy or something to hang on the walls.

"He had hired a nurse, of course. Her name was Mrs. Dalton. She had two children of her own, but they were fully grown and off making their own lives, so she was able to live here."

Mother shook her head.

"She lived here only three days. Randolph wanted to keep her on duty after you were stolen. He was always hopeful you would be found and returned, but Grandmother Cutler discharged her, blaming her for being so negligent. Randolph was heartbroken over it all and thought it was wrong to blame her, but there was nothing he could do."

She took a deep breath, closed her eyes, and then opened them and shook her head.

"He stood right there in that doorway," she said, "and cried like a baby himself. He loved you so." She turned to me. "You never saw a grown man act so silly over a baby when you were born. If he could have spent twenty-four hours a day with you, he would have.

"You know, you were born with nearly a full head of hair, all golden. And you were so small, almost too small to take right home. For a long time afterward, Randolph used to say he wished you had been too small. Then maybe we'd still have you.

"Of course, he wouldn't give up searching and hoping. False alarms sent him traveling all over the country. Finally Grandmother Cutler decided to put an end to the hope."

"She made the memorial stone," I said.

"I didn't think you knew about that," Mother said, her eyes wide with surprise.

"I saw it. Why did you and Father let Grandmother Cutler do such a thing? I wasn't dead."

"Grandmother Cutler's always been a strong-willed woman. Randolph's father used to say she was as tenacious as tree roots and as hard as bark.

"Anyway, she insisted we do something to face facts and go on with our lives."

"But wasn't it terrible for you? Why would you do such a thing?" I repeated. I couldn't imagine a mother agreeing to bury her own child symbolically without knowing for sure that the child was dead.

"It was a quick, simple ceremony. No one but the family, and it worked," she said. "After that, Randolph stopped hoping, and we went on to have Clara Sue."

"You let her force you to give up," I said. "To forget me," I added, not without some note of accusation.

"You're too young to understand these things, honey," she replied in her own defense. I glared at her. There were some things that didn't require you to be old to understand and appreciate. One of them was a mother's love for her child, I thought. Momma wouldn't have let someone force her to go to the funeral of her missing child.

It was all so strange.

"If I was so small, wasn't it dangerous for them to kidnap me?" I asked.

"Oh, sure. That's why Grandmother Cutler insisted you were probably dead," she replied quickly.

"If you had a sleep-in nurse, how did they get me anyway?" I still couldn't believe I was talking about something terrible Daddy and Momma had done.

"I don't remember all the details," Mother said and rubbed her forehead. "My headache's coming back. Probably because you forced me to recall so many horrible memories."

"I'm sorry, Mother," I said. "But I have to know."

She nodded and sighed.

"But let's not talk about it anymore," she suggested and smiled. "You're here now; you've been returned. The horror is behind us."

"The monument is still there," I said, remembering what Sissy had told me.

"Oh, dear, how morbid you can be."

"Why did they steal me, Mother?"

"No one has told you that?" She looked at me slyly, her head tilted. "Grandmother Cutler didn't tell you?"

"No," I said. My heart paused. "I was afraid to ask her anything like that."

Mother nodded understandingly.

"Sally Longchamp had just given birth to a stillborn baby. They simply substituted you for the dead baby.

"That's another reason why Grandmother Cutler wants your name changed so much, I guess."

"What is?" I asked, my voice so weak it was barely audible.

"Not many people remember anymore. Randolph never knew. I just happened to know because . . . I just happened to know. And of course your grandmother knew. There wasn't much she didn't know if it happened anywhere near or on the hotel grounds," she added acridly.

"What?" I repeated.

"The dead Longchamp baby was a girl, too. And they were going to name it Dawn."

I could see there wasn't much point to my continuing to plead for my mother to intercede between me and my grandmother. Mother's attitude was to do what Grandmother Cutler wanted because in the long run that was the easiest route to take. She told me that somehow Grandmother Cutler always managed to get her way anyway. It was futile to fight.

Of course, I didn't agree. The things she had told me about Momma and Daddy and my kidnapping left me stunned. No matter how terrible it must have been for Momma to give birth to a stillborn, it was still horrible of them to steal me from my real parents. What they had done was selfish and cruel, and when my mother described my father crying in the doorway, my heart ached for him.

I returned to my little room and plopped down on the bed to stare up at the ceiling. It had begun to rain, another summer storm rushing in from the ocean. The staccato beats on the building and windows were military drums to take me into dreams, into nightmares, to exactly where I didn't want to go. I envisioned Momma and Daddy sneaking up the stairs at night when everyone was asleep. Although I had not met her, I imagined Nurse Dalton dead asleep in the nursery suite, perhaps her back to the door. I pictured Daddy tiptoeing into the suite and scooping me up in his arms. Perhaps I had just started to cry when he handed me to Momma, who pressed me dearly to her bosom and kissed my cheeks, giving me the sense of comfort and security again.

Then, with me wrapped firmly in my blanket, they stole down the stairs and through the corridor outside my room to the rear door. Once out in the night they easily made their way to their awaiting vehicle, with infant Jimmy asleep in the backseat, unaware that he was soon to have a new sister.

In moments they were all in the car and off into the night.

I pressed my eyelids tightly shut when I then imagined Nurse Dalton finding the crib empty. I saw my parents come rushing out of their room, my grandmother charging out of hers. Philip was awakened by the shouting and sat up terrified. Surely, he had to be comforted, too.

The hotel was in an uproar. My grandmother was shouting orders at everyone. Lights were snapped on, the police were called, staff members were ordered out and about the grounds. Moments after the little beach town of Cutler's Cove came to life, all the inhabitants discovered what had happened. Sirens were sounded. Police cars were everywhere. But it was too late. Momma and Daddy were some distance away by then, and I, just a few days old, didn't know the difference.

My heart felt as if it would split in two. The ache traveled up and down my spine. Maybe I should give up, I thought. My name was a lie; it belonged to another little girl, one who had never had the chance to open her eyes and see the dawn, one who had been taken from one darkness to another. My body shook with my sobs.

"You don't have to lie there crying," Clara Sue said. "Just do what Grandmother tells you to do."

I spun around. She had come sneaking into my room, not knocking, but opening the door as softly as a spy. She stood there with a terribly satisfied grin of self-satisfaction on her face and leaned against the doorjamb. Obviously intending to tease and torment me, she nibbled on a chocolate-covered pastry.

"I want you to knock before you come into my room," I snapped and ground the tears out of my eyes quickly. I wiped my cheeks with the back of my hands as I sat up.

"I did knock," she lied, "but you were crying so loud, you couldn't hear me. You don't have to go hungry," she lectured and took another bite of her pastry, closing her eyes to telegraph how delicious it was.

"That stuff will make you even fatter," I said in a sudden burst of nastiness. Her eyes popped open.

"I'm not fat," she insisted. I only shrugged.

"Pretend what you want, if it makes you happy," I said casually. My tone infuriated her more.

"I'm not pretending. I have a full figure, a mature woman's figure. Everyone says so."

"They're just being polite. How many people have the nerve to tell someone she's fat, especially the owner's daughter?"

She blinked, finding it hard to refute the logic.

"Look at all the clothing you've outgrown, and some of it you hadn't even worn yet," I said, nodding toward my closet. She stared at me, her eyes growing smaller with anger and frustration, making her cheeks look even fuller. Then she smiled.

"You just want me to give you the rest of this so you won't be hungry."

I shrugged again and pulled myself up in the bed to lean back against my pillow. "Of course not," I said. "I wouldn't eat sweets instead of real food."

"You'll see. After a day you're going to be so hungry your stomach will growl and ache," she promised.

"I've been hungry, far hungrier than you've ever been, Clara Sue," I retorted. "I'm used to going without food for days and days," I said, relishing the effect my exaggeration was having on her. "There were days when Daddy couldn't find any work, and we had only a few crumbs left for all of us. When your stomach starts to ache, you just drink loads of water and the ache goes away."

"But . . . this is different," she insisted. "You can smell the food being cooked, and all you have to do to get it is wear the nameplate."

"I won't do it and I don't care anyway," I said with unexpected sincerity. It made her eyebrows lift. "I don't care if I waste away in this bed."

"That's stupid," she said, but she backed up as if I had some infectious disease.

"Is it?" I shifted my eyes to her and glared. "Why did you tell Grandmother Cutler stories about Philip and me? You did, didn't you?"

"No. I just told her what everyone at school knew—that Philip was your boyfriend for a little while, and you and he went on a date."

"I'm sure you told her more."

"I didn't!" she insisted.

"It doesn't matter anyway," I said and sighed. "Please leave me alone." I lowered myself down onto the bed and closed my eyes.

"Grandmother sent me to see if you had changed your mind before she makes a big announcement about you to the staff."

"Tell her . . . tell her I won't change my name, and she can bury me right where she put up the monument," I added. Clara Sue's eyes nearly bulged. She backed into the doorway.

"You're just being a stubborn little brat. No one's going to help you. You'll be sorry."

"I'm sorry already," I said. "Please close the door on your way out."

She stared at me in disbelief and then shut the door and was gone.

Of course, she was right. It would be harder to go hungry here, where there was so much and where the aromas of the wonderful foods threaded their way through the hotel, drawing the guests like flies to the dining room for delicious entrées and sumptuous desserts. Just the thought of it made my stomach churn in anticipation. I thought the best thing to do was to try to sleep.

I was emotionally and mentally exhausted anyway. The rainstorm continued and the musty, damp scent chilled me. I slipped out of my uniform, wrapped my blanket around my body, and turned away from the tear-streaked window. I heard the growl of thunder. The whole world seemed to tremble, or was it just me? After a few moments I fell asleep and didn't wake up until I heard shouting in the hall followed by many loud footsteps. A moment later my door was thrown open, and my grandmother burst in, followed by Sissy and Burt Hornbeck, chief of the hotel's security.

I pulled my blanket around myself and sat up.

"What is it?" I gasped.

"All right," my grandmother snapped and tugged Sissy forward by the wrist so she could stand at her side and face me. Burt Hornbeck stepped up on the other side of her and stared at me. "I want you to say it all in her presence with Burt as a witness." Sissy looked down and then looked up at me slowly, her eyes wide and bright with fear. Yet there was a glint of sadness and pity in them, too.

"Say what?" I asked. "What is this?"

She turned on Sissy.

"You alternated rooms, correct?" my grandmother demanded with a prosecutor's clipped, sharp tone of voice. Sissy nodded. "Speak up," my grandmother commanded.

"Yes, ma'am," Sissy said quickly.

"You took the odd number and she took the even?"

"Uh-huh."

"Then she would have been the one to clean room one-fifty?" she pursued. I looked from her to Burt Hornbeck. He was a stout, forty-year-old man with dark brown hair and small brown eyes. Whenever I had seen him before, he had always smiled warmly at me. Now he looked stern, angry, a moon locked in orbit around my grandmother's blazing face of fury and anger.

"Yes, ma'am," Sissy said.

"So we alternated rooms and I did the even numbers. What does this mean?" I asked.

"Get out of bed," she ordered. I looked at Burt. I was wearing only my bra and panties. He understood and directed his gaze at the window while I rose, keeping the blanket as tightly wrapped around me as I could.

"Are you naked?" my grandmother asked, as if to be so was a sin in her hotel.

"No. I'm wearing underwear. What do you want?"

"I want the return of Mrs. Clairmont's gold necklace, and I want it now," she said, her eyes fixed on me with such fire. She stuck out her palm, her long thin fingers straight.

"What necklace?" I looked at Burt Hornbeck, but he didn't change expression.

"There's no point in denying it now. I have managed to keep Mrs. Clairmont, one of my lifelong guests, I might add, quiet about this entire manner, but I have promised her the return of her necklace. She will get it back," she insisted, her shoulders hoisted, her neck so stiff it looked carved out of marble.

"I didn't take her necklace!" I cried. "I don't steal."

"Sure you don't steal," she said with ridicule and a birdlike nod. "You lived with thieves all your life and you don't steal."

"We never stole!" I cried.

"Never?" She twisted her lips into a cold, sharp mocking smile. My eyes fled before the onslaught of hers. My knees began to click together nervously even though I had nothing to fear. I was innocent. Swallowing first, I repeated my innocence and looked at Sissy. The poor, intimidated girl swung her eyes away quickly.

"Tear this place apart, Burt," she ordered, "from top to bottom until you locate that necklace."

Reluctantly he moved toward the small dresser.

"It's not here. I told you . . . I swear . . ."

"Do you realize," she said slowly, her eyes now like two hot coals in a stove, "how embarrassing this can be for Cutler's Cove? Never, never in the long and prestigious history of this hotel, has a guest had anything stolen out of his or her room. My staff has always consisted of hardworking people who respect other people's property. They know what it is to work here; they think of it as an honor."

"I didn't steal it," I moaned, the tears now streaming down my cheeks. Mr. Hornbeck had everything out of my drawers and was turning the drawers over. He looked behind them in the dresser, too.

"Sissy," my grandmother snapped, "take her bed apart. Strip off the sheets and pillowcase and turn that mattress over."

"Yes, ma'am," she said and moved instantly to carry out my grandmother's orders. She gazed up at me, her eyes asking my forgiveness as she began to tear off my bed sheet.

"I won't leave here until I have that necklace back," my grandmother insisted, folding her arms under her small bosom.

"Then you will sleep here tonight," I said. Mr. Hornbeck turned to me, surprised at my defiance, his eyebrows raised in a question mark. I could see the doubt flash across his brow—perhaps I was innocent. He turned to my grandmother.

Her puckered, now prune-colored mouth drew up like a drawstring purse. I watched and waited for her sardonic smile to come and break her parchment skin. I expected her voice to crackle, cackle, witchlike.

"You won't fool anyone with this defiance," she finally said. "Least of all me."

"I don't care what you or anyone else thinks—I didn't steal any gold necklace," I insisted.

Sissy had the bed stripped down. She pulled off the mattress, and Mr. Hornbeck searched under the bed. He looked up at my grandmother and shook his head.

"Look in those shoes," my grandmother told Sissy. She got down on her knees and searched every pair. My grandmother made her sift through all my garments and look in socks and pants pockets while Mr. Hornbeck searched the remainder of the room. When both came up empty-handed, she scrutinized me closely with her suspicious eyes. Then she turned to Mr. Hornbeck.

"Burt, step outside a moment," she said. He nodded and left quickly. At this point I was shivering from the fright and the indignity. My grandmother stepped toward me.

"Drop that blanket," she commanded.

"What?" I looked at Sissy, who was standing on the side looking as frightened as I was.

"Drop it!" she snarled.

I released the blanket and she gazed upon me, giving my body such close scrutiny, I couldn't help from blushing. Her eyes lifted to mine, and I felt as if she were delving the depths of my soul, trying to absorb my very being into her own so she could control me.

"Take off your brassiere," she said. I stepped back, my heart pounding. "If you don't do it now, I'll have to have the police from town come here and take you down to the station for an even more embarrassing strip search. Do you want that?"

Memories of the police station where I had been questioned and told of Daddy's crime returned vividly. I shook my head and my tears flowed again, but she was unfeeling, unsympathetic, her metallic eyes cold and determined.

"I'm not hiding any necklace," I said.

"Then do what I say," she snapped back.

I looked at Sissy, and she looked down, ashamed for me. Slowly I brought my hands behind my back and unfastened my bra. Then I slipped it down my arms and quickly folded my arms across my bosom to shield it from her probing eyes. I stood there trembling. She stepped forward and checked the inside of my bra, of course finding nothing.

"Lower those panties," she said, not satisfied. I took a deep breath. Oh, the horror of her, I thought. I couldn't stop crying. My body shook with sobs.

"I can't stand here all day and wait," she said.

I closed my eyes to block out the embarrassment, and I brought my panties to my knees. As soon as I did so, she demanded I turn around.

"All right," she said. I pulled up my panties and put on my bra. Then I wrapped the blanket around myself again. I was shaking as much as I would had I been left out naked in the middle of a winter storm. My teeth wouldn't stop clicking against each other, but she didn't appear to notice or care.

"If you have hidden this necklace somewhere in this hotel, I will eventually know about it," she said. "Nothing, absolutely nothing happens here without my knowing about it one way or another, one time or another. And this is a unique necklace with rubies and small diamonds. You can't hope to sell it without it being known."

"I didn't take the necklace," I said, holding my sobs back and keeping my eyes closed. I shook my head vehemently. "I didn't."

"If I leave here now, and we discover you have the necklace, I will have to turn you over to the police. Do you understand? Once I leave, I can no longer cover for your crime," she warned.

"I didn't steal it," I repeated.

She pivoted and seized the door handle.

"You can't imagine the embarrassment I have to face now. You are defiant and stubborn, refusing to listen and do the things I have told you. Now thievery has been added to the list. I won't forget it," she threatened. She gazed at Sissy. "Let's go," she said.

"I'm sorry," Sissy mumbled quickly and rushed out after her. I collapsed on my naked mattress and cried until my tears dried up. Then I remade my bed and crawled under the blanket, stunned by the events that had just occurred. It all seemed much more like a nightmare than reality. Had I been dreaming?

The emotional tension exhausted me. I must have drifted off into a sleep of escape, because when I opened my eyes, I saw the rain had stopped, although there was still a wet chill in the air and the world outside was pitch dark—no stars, no moon, just the sound of the wind rushing in and over the hotel and grounds, swishing around the building.

I sat up with my back to the headboard, keeping the blanket wrapped around me. Then I decided to get up and get dressed. I needed to talk to someone and Philip was the first person who came to mind. But when I went to open the door, I found it locked. I pulled on the handle, disbelieving.

"No!" I cried. "Open this door!"

I listened, but all I heard was silence. I turned the handle and pulled. The door wouldn't budge. Being locked in this small room suddenly filled me with panic. I was sure my grandmother had done it to add salt to my wounds, to punish me this way because she hadn't found the necklace in my room as she had expected.

"Someone open this door!"

I pounded the door with my small fists until they grew red and my arms ached. Then I listened. Someone had heard me. I could hear footsteps in the hallway. Maybe it was Sissy, I thought.

"Who's there?" I called. "Please, help me. The door is locked."

I waited. Although I didn't hear anyone speak, I sensed someone was there. I could feel someone's presence on the other side of that door. Was it my mother? Or Mrs. Boston?

"Who's there? Please."

"Dawn," I finally heard my father say. He spoke through the crack between the door and the jamb.

"Please, unlock the door and let me out," I said.

"I told her you didn't take the necklace," he said.

"No, I didn't."

"I didn't think you would steal."

"I didn't!" I cried. Why wasn't he opening the door? Why was he speaking through a crack? He must be standing right up against it, I thought, with his lips to the opening.

"Mother will get to the bottom of it," he said. "She always does."

"She's a very cruel person," I said. "To do what she did and then lock me in my room. Please, open the door."

"You mustn't think that, Dawn. Sometimes she appears hard to people, but after she makes her point, people usually see she's right and fair and they're happy they've listened to her."

"She's not a god; she's just an old lady who runs a hotel!" I cried. I waited, expecting him to unlock the door, but he said nothing and did nothing. "Father, please open the door," I pleaded.

"Mother just wants to do the right things, bring you up the right way, correct all the wrong things you've been taught."

"I don't have to be locked up in here," I moaned. "I didn't live like some animal. We weren't thieves, dirty, and stupid," I said.

"Of course you weren't, but there is much you have to learn that's new. You're part of an important family now, and Grandmother Cutler just wants you to adjust.

"I know it's hard for you, but Mother's been in this business for more years than even I've been alive, and her instincts about people and things are excellent. Look what she's built here and how many people come back every year," he said in a soft, reasonable tone of voice through the crack.

"I'm not going to wear that dumb nameplate," I insisted, my eyes burning with determination.

He was silent again, this time for so long that finally I thought he had left.

"Father?"

"When you were stolen away from us, you weren't just taken away from your mother and me; you were also taken away from Grandmother Cutler," he said, his voice now louder. "When you were stolen, her heart broke, too."

"I can't believe that," I declared. "Wasn't she the one who decided to put a monument in the cemetery with my name on it?" I couldn't believe I was talking to him through a door, but in a way it made it easier for me to say what I wanted.

"Yes, but she did that only to save my sanity. I thanked her for it later on. I couldn't work; I was no good to Laura Sue or to Philip. All I did was call police departments and chase around the country whenever there was a slight lead. So you see, it wasn't such a terrible thing."

Not a terrible thing? To symbolically bury a child who wasn't dead? What sort of people were these? What kind of family had I inherited?

"Please, open the door. I don't like being locked in."

"I have an idea," he said instead of opening the door. "People who don't know me well call me Mr. Cutler and other people, close friends and family, call me Randolph."

"So?"

"Think of Eugenia the way I think of Mr. Cutler and Laura Sue thinks of Mrs. Cutler. How's that? Your friends are always going to call you by your nickname."

"It's not a nickname; it's my name."

"By your informal name," he said, "but Eugenia could be your . . . your hotel name. How's that?"

"I don't know." I stepped back from the door, my arms folded under my breasts. If I didn't agree, they might never open the door, I thought.

"Just do this little compromise, and you'll bring peace and tranquillity back. We're right in the middle of the season, and the hotel is full, and—"

"Why did you give her my letter to Ormand Longchamp?" I snapped.

"She still has that letter?"

"No," I said. "I have it. She returned it and forbid me to have anything to do with him. She likes to forbid things," I said.

"Oh, I'm sorry, I . . . I thought she was going to get the letter delivered. We had discussed it, and although she wasn't happy about it, she said she would get the police chief of Cutler's Cove to take care of it. I guess she got so upset, she—"

"She was never going to have the letter delivered," I said. "Why couldn't you do it yourself?"

"Oh, I guess I could. It's just that Mother and the police chief are good friends, and I thought . . . I'm sorry," he said. "I'll tell you what," he said quickly. "If you agree to wear the nameplate, I'll take the letter to the chief myself and see to it that it's delivered. How's that? Is it a deal? I'll even make sure there's a receipt so you can see that it was delivered."

For a moment I was caught in a storm of confusion raging through my mind and heart. The kidnapping had put an ugly stain on Momma and Daddy. I could never forgive them for what they had done, but deep inside I still clung to the hope that there was some explanation. I had to have Daddy tell me his side of it.

Now I had to pay a price to have any contact with him. One way or another Grandmother Cutler got her way at Cutler's Cove, I thought. But this time I was going to get something, too.

"If I agree, will you find out what has happened to Jimmy and Fern?"

"Jimmy and Fern? You mean the Longchamps' real children?"

"Yes."

"I'll try. I promise, I'll try," he said, but I recalled what Mother had said about his promises and how easily he made them and then forgot them.

"Will you really try?" I asked.

"Sure."

"All right," I said. "But people who want to can call me Dawn."

"Sure," he said.

"Will you open the door?"

"Where's the letter?" he replied.

"Why?"

"Slip it under the door."

"What? Why won't you open the door?"

"I don't have the key," he said. "I'll go get it and tell Mother about our agreement."

I slipped the letter under, and he took it quickly. Then I heard him walk off, leaving me feeling as though I had just made a deal with the devil.

I sat down on the bed to wait, but suddenly I heard the turning of the key in the lock. The door opened and I faced Philip.

"How come your door's locked?"

"Grandmother did it. She thinks I stole a necklace."

He shook his head.

"You better get out of here. Grandmother doesn't want us to be alone together. Clara Sue told her stories and—"

"I know," he said, "but I can't help it this time. You must come with me."

"Come with you? Where? Why?"

"Just trust me," he said in a loud whisper. "Hurry."

"But—"

"Please, Dawn," he pleaded.

"How come you had the key to my room?" I demanded.

"Had the key?" He shook his head. "It was in the door."

"It was? But . . ."

Where had my father gone? Why did he lie about the key? Did he have to get permission before opening the door to let his own daughter out?

Philip seized my hand and pulled me out of the room. He started down the corridor to the side exit.

"Philip!"

"Quiet," he ordered. We rushed out and around the building. When I saw he was leading me to the little cement stairway, I stopped.

"Philip, no."

"Just come, will you. Before someone sees us."

"Why?" I demanded, but he tugged me forward.

"Philip, why are we going in there?" I demanded.

Instead of answering, he opened the door and dragged me into the darkness with him. I was about to shout angrily when he reached up and pulled the light cord.

The contrast between pitch darkness and blazing brightness hurt my eyes. I closed them and then opened them.

And there, standing before us, was Jimmy.

13

A Piece of the Past

"**J**immy! What are you doing here?" I asked, half in shock, half in delight. I had never been so happy to see anyone as I was to see him. He stared at me, his dark eyes twinkling impishly. I could see just how happy he was to set his eyes on me, too, and that warmed my heart.

"Hi, Dawn," he finally said.

We both faced each other awkwardly for a moment, and then I embraced him. Philip watched us with a half smile on his face.

"You're drenched to the bone," I said, pulling back and shaking out my palms.

"I got caught in it just outside of Virginia Beach."

"How did you get here?"

"Hitched all the way. I'm getting to be real good at it," he said, turning to Philip.

"But how . . . why?" I squealed, unable to cloak my joy.

"I ran away. Couldn't take it anymore. I'm on my way to Georgia to find our . . . to find my relatives and live with them. But I thought I'd stop by here and see you one more time."

"One of the guys came into the hotel looking for me," Philip explained. "They said someone from Emerson Peabody wanted to see me outside. I couldn't imagine . . . anyway, there he was."

"I thought I should get a hold of Philip and have him find you. I didn't want to take any chances. I'm not going back," he declared firmly, pulling back his shoulders.

"I told him he could stay here in the hideaway for a few days," Philip said. "We'll get him some food, warm clothing, and some money."

"But, Jimmy, won't they just come after you?"

"I don't care if they do, but they probably won't. No one really cares," he said, his eyes small and determined and full of anger. "I didn't know when you and I would ever see each other again, Dawn. I had to come," he said.

Our gazes locked warmly on each other's, and in that gaze I saw all our happier times together, saw his smile, and something inside me became warm. Suddenly I felt safer here at Cutler's Cove.

"I'm going back to the hotel and sneak into the kitchen to get him something to eat," Philip said. "I'll also get him some dry clothes and a towel. We've just got to be careful that no one discovers him," Philip emphasized. He turned to Jimmy. "My grandmother would blow her stack. Don't go out without checking carefully to see that no one's around, okay?"

Jimmy nodded.

"Give me about fifteen minutes to get the food and the clothing," he said and hurried out.

"You'd better start taking off those wet clothes, Jimmy," I advised. It was as if we had never been apart and I was still looking after him.

He nodded and pulled off his shirt. His wet skin gleamed under the light. Even in the short time we had been apart, he looked changed— he was older, bigger, with broader shoulders and thicker arms. I took his shirt and draped it over a chair as he sat down to take off his soaked sneakers and socks.

"Tell me what happened to you after we were taken to the police station, Jimmy. Do you know anything about Fern?" I added quickly.

"No, I never saw her after we were brought to the station. They took me to what they called a holding house where there were other kids waiting to be assigned to foster homes. Some were older, but most were younger than me. We slept on bunk beds not much bigger or nicer than this one," he said, "and we were crowded four in a room. One little boy kept whimpering all night. The others continually shouted at him to shut up, but he was too frightened. I got into a fight with them because they wouldn't stop terrorizing the kid."

"Why doesn't that surprise me?" I said, smiling.

"Well, it made them feel big to bully him," he said angrily. "Anyway, one thing led to another, and I was put in the basement of the house to sleep. It had a dirt floor and lots of bugs and even rats!

"A day later I was told they had already found a home for me. I think they were determined to get rid of me first. The others were jealous, but that was only because they didn't know where I was going.

"I went home with this chicken farmer, Leo Coons. He was a stout, grouchy man with a face like a bulldog, and he had a scar across his forehead. It looked like someone had hit him with an ax. His wife was half his size, and he treated her like another kid. They had two daughters. It was his wife who encouraged me to run away. Her name was Beryle, and I couldn't believe she was only in her thirties. She had gray hair and looked as worn down as an old pencil. Nothing she did made Coons happy. The house was never clean enough; the food never tasted right. Complain, complain, complain was all he did.

"I had a nice room, but he had come to the holding house to get a foster kid my age to make into a slave. First thing he did was show me how to candle eggs and had me up before dawn working alongside his two daughters, both older than me, but both as skinny as scarecrows and both with big, sad dark eyes that reminded me of frightened puppy dogs.

"Coons moved me from one job to the next—shoveling chicken manure, lugging feed. We worked before the sun rose until an hour or so after it went down.

"At first I didn't care what happened to me; I was that depressed, but after a while I got so tired of the work and hearing Coons shouting this and shouting that . . .

"What did it, I suppose, was the night he hit me. He was complaining about the supper, and I said I thought it was pretty good, too good for him. He hit me with the back of his hand, but so hard, I fell off the chair.

"I was going to just punch and kick at him, but Dawn, this guy is big and he's as hard as bricks. Later that night Beryle came to me and told me the best thing I could do for myself was run away like the others. Seems he's done this before—go fetch a foster kid and make him work until he drops. They don't care back at the home, because they get so many kids, they're glad anyone comes to get one."

"Oh, Jimmy . . . if Fern was given to mean people . . ."

"I don't think so. It's different with babies. Lots of good people want babies because they can't have their own for one reason or another. Don't look so glum," he said, smiling. "I'm sure she's all right."

"It's not that, Jimmy. What you just said reminded me of something terrible. They tell me that's why Momma and Daddy stole me—she had a baby right before, and the baby was born dead."

His eyes widened, and then he nodded as if he had always known it.

"So Daddy talked her into taking you," he concluded. "It was just like him. I don't doubt any of it. Now look what a mess he got us all in. I mean, I'm in. You ain't in such a mess, I guess."

"Oh, Jimmy," I said, sitting beside him quickly. "I am. I hate it here."

"What? With this big, fancy hotel and all? Why?"

I began by describing my real mother and her continuous nervous condition. Jimmy listened intently, his eyes full of wonder as I related the story of my kidnapping and how it had affected her and made her into some kind of invalid soaked in luxury.

"But weren't they glad to see you when you were brought here?" he asked. I shook my head.

"As soon as I arrived here, I was made a chambermaid and put into a little room away from the family. You won't have much trouble imagining how mean Clara Sue has been," I said. Then I told him about being accused of stealing and related the horrible search I had been put through.

"She made you take off your clothes?"

"Strip to the bone. Afterward, she locked me in my room."

He stared at me in disbelief.

"What about your real father?" he asked. "Did you tell him what she did?"

"He's so strange, Jimmy," I said and told him how he had come to the door and refused to do anything until I had agreed to the compromise over my name. "Then he left, claiming he had to get the key, but Philip said the key was in the door when he came to fetch me to bring me to you."

He shook his head.

"And here I thought you were living high on the hog."

"I don't think my grandmother's ever going to let up on me. For some reason she hates me, hates the sight of me," I said. "I just can't get it through my head that Daddy did this. I can't." I shook my head and stared down at my hands in my lap.

"Well, I can," Jimmy said sharply, drawing my eyes to his. Fiery anger filled his eyes. "You don't want to believe it; you never liked believing bad things about him, but you gotta now."

I told Jimmy about my letter to Daddy.

"I hope he writes back and tells me his side of it."

"He won't," Jimmy insisted. "And even if he does, it'll be all lies."

"Jimmy, you can't go on hating him like this. He's still your real father, even if he's not mine."

"I don't want to ever think of him as my father. He's dead with my mother," he declared, his eyes burning with such fury, it brought an ache to my heart. I couldn't keep the tears trapped under my eyelids; they burned so.

"No sense in crying about it, Dawn. There's nothing we can do to change things. I'm going down to Georgia and maybe live with Momma's side of the family, if they'll have me. I don't mind working hard, as long as it's for my own family."

"I wish I was going with you, Jimmy. I still feel those people are more my family than these people, even though I never met them."

"Well, you can't. If you came with me, we'd be hunted down for sure."

"I know." My tears kept coming. Now that Jimmy was here, I couldn't help myself.

"I'm sorry you're not happier, Dawn," he said and slowly brought his arm up and around my shoulders. "Whenever I lay awake thinking about how terrible all this was, I would cheer myself a bit by thinking you were safe and comfortable in a new and richer life. I thought you deserved it and maybe it was good it all happened. I didn't mind what happened to me as long as it meant you would have better things and be with better people."

"Oh, Jimmy, I could never be happier if you were unhappy, and just thinking about poor little Fern in a strange place—"

"She's little enough to forget and start new," he said, his eyes dark with a wisdom beyond his years, a wisdom forced upon him by hard times. He was older in mind and body. Hard, cruel times had dragged him out of childhood.

He sat inches from me, his arm still around my shoulders, his face so close I could feel his breath on my cheeks. It made me dizzy, confused. I was trapped on a runaway merry-go-round of emotions. Jimmy, whom I had thought to be my brother, was now just a boy who cared for me, and Philip, a boy who had cared for me, was now my brother. Their kisses, their smiles, and the way they touched and held me had to have different meaning.

Just a little while ago I would have felt strange and guilty about the feelings that passed through me when Jimmy touched me. Now, when the tingle traveled up and down my spine and made me shudder pleasantly, I didn't know what to do, what to say. He cupped my face between his palms and tenderly kissed away my tears. I felt so warm all over. Before this I would have forced that warmth to stop its journey to my heart. Now it rushed over the highways along my skin and curled up comfortably inside my breast.

His face remained close to mine, his serious eyes so delving, worried, and intense. A lump came in my throat as I wondered where the boy was I used to know. Where was that brother, and who was this young man staring so long into my eyes? Greater than any pain or ache or hurt I had ever felt before or since was the pain caused me by the suffering I saw in his tortured eyes.

We heard Philip's footsteps on the cement stairway, and Jimmy pulled his arm off my shoulders and continued to take off his sneakers and socks.

"Hi," Philip said, coming in. "Sorry the food's not hot, but I wanted to rush in and out of the kitchen before someone caught me and wondered what I was doing."

"Food's food. I don't care whether it's hot or cold at this point," Jimmy said, taking the covered dish from Philip. "Thanks."

"I brought you some of my clothes—should fit—and this towel and blanket."

"Get the wet clothes off and dry yourself before you eat, Jimmy," I advised. He went into the bathroom and slipped out of his pants and underwear, wiped himself down, and returned in Philip's clothes. The shirt was a little big and the pants too long, but he rolled up the cuffs. Philip and I stood by and watched him gobble the food, scooping one mouthful into his mouth before he had swallowed the one he already had.

"Sorry, but I'm starving," he said. "I didn't have any money to stop to eat."

"That's all right. Look, I'm going to have to get back to the hotel. Grandmother saw me go in before and probably will be keeping an eye out for me to be sure I'm mixing with the others."

"In the morning I'll put aside some food as I serve breakfast, and later, as soon as I can get loose, I'll bring it down to you, Jimmy."

"Thanks."

"Well," Philip said, standing and looking at us. "See you later. Have a good night."

We watched him go.

"I don't understand," Jimmy said almost as soon as Philip disappeared up the cement stairway. "Why was he worried about his grandmother seeing him in the hotel?"

I told him what Clara Sue had told Grandmother Cutler and what she had forbidden. Jimmy lay back in the bed, his hands behind his head, listening. His eyes grew small and the tight smile around his lips became a serious and intense look.

"Of course, I was worried about all that, too," he said. "I was wondering what it was going to be like for you. You were starting to get stuck on him in school."

I was going to tell him how it was harder for Philip to adjust, how he still wished I could be his girlfriend, but I thought it might make Jimmy upset and cause more problems. "It hasn't been easy," I simply said. Jimmy nodded.

"Here you have to work at thinking about him as your brother, and here I was your brother and you got to work at forgetting I was," he said.

"I don't want to forget, Jimmy."

He looked sad, disappointed.

"Do you want me to forget? Do you want to forget me?" Perhaps he did; perhaps it was the only way he could start new, I thought mournfully.

"I don't want you to feel dirty about it or ever let anyone make you feel that way," he said firmly.

I nodded and sat beside him on the bed. Neither of us said anything for a few moments. This old section of the hotel creaked and moaned as the sea breeze poked and prodded, slipping itself into every crack and cranny, and we could hear music from the jukebox in the recreation room spilling out into the night and being carried off by the same sea breezes.

"I'll tell the relatives that Momma and Daddy are both dead. They don't have to know all the ugly details, and I'll try to start a new life," Jimmy said with a far-off look in his eyes.

"I hate thinking about you being in a new life without me, Jimmy."

He smiled the soft and gentle smile I recalled so fondly.

"Let's just lie here together one more time like we used to lie together," he said. "And you talk me to sleep like you always did by telling me about all the good things we're going to have someday." He shifted over to make room for me.

I lowered myself beside him, resting my head against his arm and closed my eyes. For a moment I threw myself back through time, and we were lying together on one of our poor pull-out beds in one of our run-down apartments. Rain pounded the dilapidated building, and the wind scratched at the windows, threatening to poke them in.

But Jimmy and I cuddled together, taking solace in the warmth and closeness of our bodies. We closed our eyes, and I began to spin the rainbows. I did it now.

"We will have good things happen to us, Jimmy. We've been through a storm of trouble, but after every storm, the clouds part and the sun returns with its warmth and its promise.

"You'll go off and find Momma's relatives like you planned, and they'll welcome you with open arms. You'll meet uncles and aunts and cousins.

"And maybe they're not as bad off as we always thought. Maybe they got a good farm. And you're a strong, willing worker, Jimmy, so you'll be a great help to them. Before you know it, the farm will become something special, and people from all around will ask: Who's that new young man who came to help and made your farm so good?

"But you'll have to promise to write to me and . . ."

I turned to him. His eyes were closed, and he was breathing softly. How tired he had been. He must have walked miles and miles and been in the rain for the longest time, suffering just to get down here to see me one more time.

I leaned over and pressed my lips to his warm cheek.

"Good night, Jimmy," I whispered as I had done so many nights before. I hated to leave him all alone in so strange a place, but from what he had described to me, he had been in more horrible places.

I paused in the doorway and looked back. It did seem more like a dream to see Jimmy lying there. It was almost like a wish come true. I slipped out of the hideaway and up the stairs, checking carefully to be sure no one was looking my way. It looked all clear so I made my way around the building. Just as I entered and started down the corridor, I saw the door to my room open, and Clara Sue stepped out.

"What are you doing in there?" I demanded, approaching quickly.

She looked flustered for a moment and then smiled.

"Grandmother sent me to unlock your door," she said. "Who did it?"

"I don't know," I said quickly. She smirked.

"If I find out and tell Grandmother, she'll fire her."

"I don't know who did it," I repeated. "I shouldn't have been locked in there anyway."

She shrugged.

"If you weren't such a brat, Grandmother wouldn't have to do these things," she said and hurried off. I thought she was in quite a rush to get away from me. After I watched her go, I went into my room.

I got undressed, put on my robe, and went to the bathroom. I really was very tired and looked forward to crawling under the covers. But when I returned and pulled back my blanket to slip in and under, I discovered what Clara Sue had been doing in my room. It was as if I had been made to swallow a glassful of ice water. It sent a painful shiver through my heart.

There on my sheet was a gold necklace with rubies and diamonds.

Clara Sue had taken it out of Mrs. Clairmont's room and placed it here so I would be blamed. Now what would I do? If I returned it, everyone was sure to think I had stolen it originally and my grandmother had frightened me into returning it. No one would believe Clara Sue had done this, I thought.

The sound of footsteps drove me into a panic. What if she had gone and told Mr. Hornbeck she had seen me with the necklace and was returning with my grandmother? I looked about frantically for a place to hide it and realized that this was just what Clara Sue would want me to do. They would search again and find it hidden and be convinced I had stolen it.

I froze, unable to decide on anything. Fortunately, the sound of the footsteps died away. I let out my breath and scooped up the necklace. It felt hot and forbidding in my hands. I had the urge to open the window and heave it out into the night, but then, what would happen if someone found it the next morning near my window?

Should I take it to my father? My mother? Maybe I should find Philip and give it to him. He would certainly believe me when I told him what Clara Sue had done, I thought, but merely walking through the hotel with it in my possession frightened me. I could be stopped if Clara Sue had gone to tell someone.

It should be returned to Mrs. Clairmont somehow, I thought. Perhaps it was a very precious, meaningful piece of jewelry for her, a necklace with special memories. Why should she suffer just because Clara Sue was so jealous and spiteful?

I decided to get dressed and take a chance of carrying it through the hotel. I slipped it into my uniform pocket and hurried out. It wasn't that late. Guests were enjoying the grounds, playing cards, visiting in the lobby, some listening to a string quartet in the music suite. There was a good chance Mrs. Clairmont wasn't in her room, I thought. I went directly to the linen closet and got the master key for the section Sissy and I worked in. Then I hurried to the corridor.

My heart was pounding so hard, I was sure I would faint just after entering Mrs. Clairmont's room. I envisioned them finding me on the floor with the necklace in my palm. I brushed the sweat off my forehead and walked quickly to her door. Fortunately, there was no one around. I knocked and waited. If she were in there, I thought I would pretend I had knocked on the wrong door. No one answered, so I slipped the master key into the lock and turned. The small clicking sound never seemed so loud. In my mind I thought it had echoed throughout the hotel and was surely going to bring people running.

I waited, listening. It was quiet and dark within. I didn't want to take any more chances than I had to, so I simply leaned in and tossed the necklace at the dresser. I heard it land safely, and then I quickly closed the door and locked it, my fingers trembling so badly as I did so, I had to do it twice.

Just as I turned and started down the corridor, I heard voices. Terrified of being discovered on the floor, I spun around and headed in the opposite direction, never looking back to see who it was. I rushed away, but this path took me back into the lobby of the hotel.

It took my father three times to call "Eugenia" before I realized he was calling me. I stopped midway across the lobby and turned to see him beckoning. Had Clara Sue reported seeing me with the necklace? I approached him slowly.

"I was just on my way to see you," he said. "I wanted to be sure Clara Sue went directly to your room with the key and unlocked your door."

"There was a key in the door," I said pointedly.

"There was? I didn't see it. Well," he said, smiling quickly, "at least that unpleasantness is all over. You'll be happy to know your grandmother likes our little compromise," he added, smiling. And then he reached into his jacket pocket and produced my hateful nameplate. I stared down at it.

It hadn't looked as large when my grandmother first showed it to me. It wouldn't have surprised me to learn that she had had it redone so she could make it bigger. It would be her way of showing me that she always got her way and if I challenged her, I would only suffer more for it.

I plucked it out of his palm slowly. It felt like a small block of ice in my hands.

"You want me to pin it on for you?" he asked when I hesitated.

"No, thank you. I can do it myself." I did so quickly.

"And that's that," he said beaming. "Well, I've got to get back to work. See you tomorrow. Have a good night's sleep," he said and left me standing there, feeling as if I had just been branded.

But it didn't bother me as much as it ordinarily might have. Just knowing that Jimmy was close by brought me comfort. In the morning right after I had done my work, I would go to him and we would talk and spend almost the whole day together. Of course, I would have to show myself around the hotel every once in a while so no one would come looking for me.

For the first night since I had arrived at Cutler's Cove, I went to sleep easily and looked forward eagerly to the once familiar sunrise.

*   *   *

The next morning Grandmother Cutler made an appearance in the kitchen while the staff was having its breakfast. She greeted everyone as she crossed the room to come toward the table I was at. After she reached us, she paused to be sure I was wearing her precious nameplate. When she saw it pinned on my uniform, she pulled herself up and her eyes twinkled with satisfaction.

I didn't dare look defiant or upset. If she confined me to my room again, I wouldn't be able to see Jimmy, or if I snuck out against her wishes, I might cause him to be discovered. I went on with Sissy, and we did our assignments. I worked so hard and fast that even Sissy remarked about it. As I came out of my last room, I found Grandmother Cutler waiting. Oh, no, I thought, she is going to give me another assignment, and I won't be able to go to Jimmy. I held my breath.

"Apparently, Mrs. Clairmont's necklace has miraculously turned up," she said, her metallic eyes glued to me.

"I never took it," I said firmly.

"I hope nothing is ever taken from here again," she retorted and continued down the corridor, her shoes clicking.

I didn't return to my room to change out of my uniform. Taking great care, I made my way out the back of the hotel and scurried around to Philip's hideaway.

It was such a bright warm summer's day, I wished I could take Jimmy out of the dark basement room and walk with him through the gardens with their rainbow colors of flowers and sparkling fountains. He had looked so pale and tired to me the night before. He needed to be in the warm sunlight. Bright sunshine on my face always cheered me, no matter how hard and troubled the day was.

Just as I reached the cement stairway, I saw some guests standing and talking nearby, so I waited for them to wander off before descending. When I opened the door and slipped in, I found Jimmy well rested and eagerly waiting for me. He was sitting on the bunk bed and beamed a wide, happy smile.

"Philip was already here with some breakfast, and he gave me twenty dollars for my trip to Georgia," he told me and then sat back and laughed.

"What?"

"You look funny in that uniform and bandanna. Your nameplate looks like a medal your grandmother pinned on you."

"I'm glad you like it," I said. "I hate it," I added and shook my hair loose as soon as I pulled off the bandanna. "Did you sleep all right?"

"I don't even remember your leaving, and when I woke up this morning, I forgot where I was for a moment. Then I fell asleep again. Why did you sneak away?"

"You fell asleep pretty quickly, so I decided to let you get your rest."

"I didn't wake up again this morning until Philip arrived. That's how tired I was. I'd been traveling all day and all night for two days. I slept on the side of the road for a couple of hours night before last," he admitted.

"Oh, Jimmy, you could have been hurt."

"I didn't care," he said. "I was determined to get here. So what does a chambermaid do? Tell me about this hotel. I didn't see much of it last night. Is it a nice place?"

I described my work to him and the layout of the hotel. I went on to tell him about some of the staff, especially Mrs. Boston and Sissy, but he was mostly interested in my mother and father.

"What's exactly wrong with her?"

"I don't know for sure, Jimmy. She doesn't look sick. Most of the time she looks beautiful, even when she's in bed with her headaches. My father treats her like a fragile little doll."

"And so your grandmother really runs the hotel?"

"Yes. Everyone is afraid of her, but they're afraid to say anything bad about her even to each other. Mrs. Boston says she's tough but fair. I don't think she's been very fair to me," I said sadly. I told him about the memorial stone. He listened wide-eyed as I described what I knew of my symbolic funeral.

"But how do you know the stone's still there?" he asked.

"It was as of the time I arrived. No one's told me otherwise."

"They wouldn't. They'd just remove it, I'm sure."

He sat back on the bed with his shoulders against the wall and looked thoughtful.

"It took a lot of nerve for Daddy to steal a baby right out from under the nurse's eyes," he said.

"That's what I thought," I said, happy he found trouble believing it, too.

"Of course, he might have been drinking—"

"Then he wouldn't have been as careful, and he would surely have been heard."

Jimmy nodded.

"You don't believe he would do such a thing, either, do you, Jimmy? Not deep down in your heart."

"He confessed. They had him cold, Dawn. And he didn't try to deny it to us." He lowered his eyes sadly. "I guess I should be getting on my way."

My heart stopped, my thoughts taking frantic flight, wanting to go off with Jimmy and escape this prison. I felt trapped and needed to seek out the wind so it could fan my hair and sting my skin and make me feel free and alive again.

"But, Jimmy, you were going to stay here a few days and rest up."

"I'll just get caught here and make trouble for you and Philip."

"No, you won't!" I cried. "I don't want you to go yet, Jimmy. Please stay." He lifted his eyes to gaze into mine. Swelling up in both of us was a turmoil of whirling emotions.

"Sometimes," Jimmy said in the softest, warmest voice I ever heard him speak, "I used to wish you weren't my sister."

"Why?" I said and held my breath.

"I . . . thought you were so pretty, I wished you could be my girlfriend," he confessed. "You were always after me to choose this friend of yours or that to be my girlfriend, but I didn't want anybody else but you." He looked away. "That's why I was so jealous and angry when you started getting interested in Philip."

For a moment I didn't know what to say. My first impulse was to put my arms around him and lavish a million kisses on his face. I wanted to draw his head down against my breast and cuddle it there.

"Oh, Jimmy," I said, my eyes tearing something awful again, "it just isn't fair. All this mix-up. It's not right."

"I know," he said. "But when I learned that you were not really my sister, I couldn't help feeling happy as well as sad. Of course, I was unhappy about your being taken away, but what I was hoping . . . aw, I shouldn't hope," he added quickly and looked away again.

"No, Jimmy. You can hope. What do you hope? Please tell me." He looked down, his face red. "I won't laugh."

"I know you wouldn't laugh, Dawn. You would never laugh at me; I just can't help feeling ashamed thinking it, much less saying it."

"Say it, Jimmy. I want you to say it," I replied in a much more demanding tone. He turned and looked at me, his gaze moving up and down my face as if he wanted to capture me in his mind forever and ever.

"I was hoping that if I ran away and stayed away long enough, you would stop thinking of me as your brother, and someday I would come back and you might think of me as . . . as a boyfriend," he said, all in one breath.

For a moment it was as if the world had stopped on its axis, as if every sound in the universe had died, as if birds were frozen in midair, and cars and people. There was no wind; the ocean became like glass, the waves up and ready to fall, the tide stuck just at the shore. Everything waited on us.

Jimmy had uttered the words that had lingered unspoken in both our hearts for years and years, for our hearts knew the truth long before we did, and kept feeding us feelings we thought were unclean and forbidden.

Could I ever do what he dreamt I would: look into his face and not see him as my brother, not see every touch, every kiss as a sin?

"You can see now why I have to get going," he said sternly and stood up.

"No, Jimmy." I reached out and seized his wrist. "I don't know whether or not I can ever do what you hope, but we're not going to find out if we're apart. We're just going to always wonder and wonder until the wondering becomes too much and we stop caring."

He shook his head.

"I'll never stop caring about you, Dawn," he said with such firmness, it washed away any shred of doubt. "No matter how far away I am or how much time passes. Never."

"Don't run off, Jimmy," I pleaded. I held on to his wrist, and his body finally relaxed. He lowered himself back to the bunk, and we sat there beside each other, neither speaking, me holding his wrist, him staring ahead, his chest lifting and falling with his own excitement.

"My heart's pounding so much," I whispered and lowered my forehead against his shoulder. Now, whenever we touched, it sent a streak of warmth through my body. I felt feverish.

"Mine, too," he said. I brought my palm to his chest and pressed it against his heart to feel the thumping; and then I lifted his hand and brought it to my breast so he could feel mine.

The moment his fingers were pressed to my bosom, he closed his eyes tightly, just like someone in pain.

"Jimmy," I said softly, "I don't know whether I could ever be your girlfriend, but I don't want to wonder forever."

Slowly, almost a millimeter at a time, he turned his face to mine. Our lips were inches apart. It was I who moved toward him first, but then he moved toward me, and we kissed on the lips for the first time like any boy and girl might kiss. All our years as brother and sister came raining down around us, threatening to drown us in dark and gloomy guilt, but we held on to each other.

When we parted, he stared at me with a face sculptured in seriousness, not a line creasing softly, his dark eyes searching mine quickly for some sign. I smiled and his body relaxed.

"We haven't been properly introduced," I said.

"Huh?"

"I'm Dawn Cutler. What's your name?" He shook his head. "Jimmy what?"

"Very funny."

"It isn't funny, Jimmy," I replied. "We are meeting for the first time in a way, aren't we? Maybe, if we pretend—"

"You always want to pretend." He shook his head again.

"Try it, Jimmy. Just try it once. For me. Please."

He sighed.

"All right. I'm James Longchamp of the renowned southern Longchamps, but you can call me Jimmy."

I giggled. "See? It wasn't that hard to do." I lay down on my side and looked up at him. His smile widened, spreading through his face and brightening his eyes.

"You're so crazy, but so special," he said, running his fingers up my arm. He touched my neck, and I closed my eyes. I felt him lean over, and then I felt his lips on my cheek and a moment later pressing against mine again.

His hands moved over my breasts. I moaned and reached up to bring him down to me. All the while as we kissed and caressed, I kept smothering the voice that tried to scream out that this was Jimmy, my brother, Jimmy. If he had similar thoughts about me, they were driven down, too, held underwater by the building passion and excitement as our bodies touched and our hands and arms held us tightly to each other.

I was back on that merry-go-round of emotions, only it was spinning faster than ever, and I was getting so dizzy, I thought I would become unconscious. I never even realized he had unbuttoned my uniform and his fingers had traveled under my bra until I felt the tips slip over my firming nipples. I wanted him to stop, and I wanted him to go on.

I opened my eyes and looked into his face. His eyes were closed; he looked lost in a dream. A smothered groan escaped his lips—more like a moan. As the skirt of my uniform traveled up my thighs, he slipped himself between my legs, and I felt that male part of him grow hard against me. It sent a panic up through my bosom.

"Jimmy!"

He stopped and opened his eyes. Suddenly they were filled with shock as he realized what he had done and what he was doing. He pulled back quickly and turned away. My heart was drumming against my chest, making it hard for me to catch my breath. As soon as I had, I put my hand on his back.

But he pulled away as if my hand were on fire, keeping his back to me.

"It's all right, Jimmy," I said softly. He shook his head.

"I'm sorry."

"It's all right. I just got frightened. It wasn't because of who we were to each other. I would have gotten frightened no matter who you were."

He turned and looked at me skeptically.

"Really," I said.

"But you can't stop thinking of me as your brother, can you?" he asked, his anticipation of disappointment making his eyes darker and bringing creases to his forehead.

"I don't know, Jimmy," I said honestly. It looked as though he might cry. "It's not something that I can do quickly, but . . . I'd like to try," I added. That pleased him and his smile returned. "Will you stay a little longer?"

"Well," he said, "I do have some pressing engagements with my business associates in Atlanta, but I suppose I could manage a few more days. . . ."

"See," I said quickly, "pretending isn't so hard for you either."

He laughed and lay back beside me again.

"It's the effect you have on me, Dawn. You always kept the gloom and doom out of my eyes." He traced my lips with his forefinger and grew serious again. "If only something good could come out of all this. . . ."

"Something good will, Jimmy. You'll see," I promised. He nodded.

"I don't care what your real parents and your grandmother say, Dawn has to be your name. You bring sunshine into the darkest places."

We both closed our eyes and started to bring our lips toward each other's again, when suddenly the hideaway door was thrust open and we turned to see Clara Sue standing in the hideaway doorway, her hands on her hips, a gleeful smile of satisfaction on her twisted lips.

14

Violations

"**W**ell, isn't this a pleasant surprise," Clara Sue purred, sauntering farther in. "I came here expecting to find you with Philip, but instead it's your . . ." She stared a moment and then smiled. "What should we call him? Brother? Boyfriend?" She laughed. "Maybe both?"

"Shut up," Jimmy snapped, the blood rushing to his face.

"Clara Sue, please," I pleaded. "Jimmy's had to run away from a terrible foster father. He's had a horrible time, and now he's on his way to Georgia to live with relatives."

She whipped her eyes to me and flared them with hate. Then she put her hands on her hips.

"Grandmother sent me to find you," she said. "Some kids had a food fight in the coffee shop, and we need all the chambermaids to help clean up." She gazed again at Jimmy, a sly smile returning to her twisted lips. "How long are you going to keep him hidden here? Grandmother would sure be angry if she knew," she said, her threatening note clear.

"I'm leaving," Jimmy said. "You don't have to worry."

"I'm not the one who has to be worried," she sneered.

"Jimmy, don't go yet," I said, pleading with my eyes for him not to leave.

"It's all right," Clara Sue suddenly said in a much softer, kinder tone of voice. "He can stay. I won't tell anyone. It might be fun."

"It's not fun," Jimmy said. "I don't want to get people in trouble on account of me."

"Does Philip know about all this?" Clara Sue demanded.

"He brought him down here," I said, replacing the sneer on her face with a look of indignation. Her hands flew back to her hips.

"Nobody tells me anything," she moaned. "You come and everyone forgets I'm part of the family. You better get inside before Grandmother sends someone else to look for you, too," she warned, her eyes turning cold and hard again.

"Jimmy, you won't run off, will you?" I said. He looked at Clara Sue and then shook his head.

"I'll wait," he said. "As long as she promises not to tell and get you in trouble."

I looked imploringly at Clara Sue. I wanted to tear into her for trying to get me into trouble with the necklace, but I had to keep my tongue glued to the roof of my mouth. In order to protect Jimmy, I had to remain under her thumb.

"I said I wouldn't tell, didn't I?"

"Thank you, Clara Sue." I turned back to Jimmy. "I'll return as soon as I can," I promised and started out. Clara Sue lingered behind me, staring at Jimmy. He ignored her and returned to the bunk.

"Boy, wouldn't Louise Williams like to know he's here. She would come right away." She laughed, but Jimmy didn't look at her or say anything, so she turned and followed me out.

"Please help us, Clara Sue," I pleaded as we walked up the cement stairway. "Jimmy's had a terrible time living with a cruel man. He hitched rides and didn't eat for days. He needs to rest up."

She didn't say anything for a moment, and then she smiled.

"Lucky Mrs. Clairmont found her necklace," she said.

"Yes, lucky." There was no love lost between us as we stared hatefully at each other.

"All right, I'll help you," she said, her eyes narrowing. "As long as you help me, too."

"What can I do for you?" I asked, surprised. Mother and Father bought her anything she wanted. She lived upstairs in a warm, cozy suite, and she had a nice job in the hotel and could dress up and be pretty and clean all day.

"I'll see. You better hurry to the coffee shop before Grandmother blames me for not finding you and demands to know what kept me."

I started obediently toward the front of the building, feeling like a puppet whose strings were in Clara Sue's hateful fingers.

"Wait!" she cried. "I know something you can do for me right away."

I turned back with dread.

"What?"

"Grandmother's upset about the way I keep my room. She thinks I make too much work for Mrs. Boston and I'm too messy and disorganized. I don't know why she worries so much about Mrs. Boston. She's just another one of the help around here," she said, wagging her head. "Anyway, when you're finished in the coffee shop, go up to my room and straighten it up. I'll be there later and see how you did.

"And don't take anything!" she added, smiling. "No necklaces." She pivoted on her heels as if she were my drill instructor and went in the opposite direction. I felt the heat rise in my neck. How could she think to make me her personal maid? I wanted to chase after her and pull out her hair, but I gazed toward the hideaway and thought about poor Jimmy. All I would do was create a commotion and drive him away. Frustrated and fuming, I plodded on to help the others clean up the coffee shop.

Clara Sue hadn't exaggerated. It was a mess with ketchup and French fries, milk and mustard, ice cream and soda all splattered on the walls and tables. I had seen a food fight at a cafeteria in one of the schools Jimmy and I attended, but it didn't seem as bad a mess as this. Of course, I didn't have to clean the school mess up, but now I could feel sorry for the custodial staff.

"It's some of those spoiled rich kids who come here," Sissy muttered as soon as I arrived and began washing down one of the tables. There were pieces of food everywhere. I had to step around puddles of milk and ketchup splashed on the floor. "They thought it was funny, even after it was all over and there was this mess. They run off through the hotel laughing and giggling. Mrs. Cutler was fit to be tied. She says the younger families ain't what the older ones used to be. The older ones is more classy and wouldn't have children this bad. That's what she told us."

Grandmother appeared in the doorway shortly afterward and watched us work. When we were finished, she and Mr. Stanley inspected the coffee shop to be sure it had been restored properly. I thought I would go up and do Clara Sue's room right away, but Mr. Stanley told Sissy and me to go right to the laundry and help wash and dry linens. That took more than two hours. I worked as hard and as fast as I could, realizing Jimmy was all alone, shut up in the hideaway, waiting for my return. I was afraid he might leave before I arrived.

As soon as we finished in the laundry, I started out to visit him, but Clara Sue caught me going down the corridor toward the exit. She had come looking for me.

"You've got to go right to my room," she demanded urgently. "Grandmother is coming up later this afternoon to see how I fixed it up."

"Well, why can't you do it?"

"I have to entertain the children of some important guests. Besides, you're better at cleaning up. Just do it. Unless you don't want me to help you and Jimmy," she said, smiling.

"Jimmy needs something for lunch!" I cried. "I won't leave him without food all day."

"Don't worry. I'll see that he gets it," she said.

"You have to be careful no one sees you sneak food to him," I warned.

"I think I'm better at being careful than you are, Eugenia," she commented and walked off laughing.

Grandmother Cutler was right about one thing—Clara Sue was a slob. Her clothing was scattered all about—panties and bras draped over chairs, shoes under the bed and in front of the closet instead of inside it, skirts and blouses on the floor, blouses hanging on the headboard and on the back of the vanity table chair. And the vanity table! Makeup and creams were left open. There were streaks of cream and powder over the table. Even the mirror was spotted.

Her bed was unmade and covered with fashion and fan magazines. I found an earring under the bedspread and searched everywhere in vain for its mate. She had her jewelry strewn about, some of it on her desk, some on her vanity table, and some on the top of the dresser.

All the dresser drawers were open, and some had panties and stockings leaking out. When I started to put things into the drawers, I saw they were all mixed up—stockings with panties, T-shirts with stockings. I shook my head. There was so much to do. No wonder Grandmother Cutler was angry.

And when I opened the closet door! Clothing hadn't been properly hung, so skirts and pants, blouses and jackets were half on and half off hangers, some of the clothing fallen to the floor in heaps. Clara Sue had no respect for her possessions, I thought. It all came too easily.

It took me more than two more hours to do up her room, but when I was finished, it was clean, organized, and spotless. I was exhausted, but I headed out quickly and snuck around the back of the hotel to see Jimmy.

When I entered the hideaway, however, he wasn't there. The

bathroom door was open, so I could see he wasn't in it. He had gotten disgusted waiting for me, I thought mournfully, and he had run off again. I flopped down on the bunk bed. Jimmy was gone; perhaps I would never see him or hear from him again. I couldn't keep the tears from rushing out—all my frustrations, fatigue, and unhappiness ganged up on me. I cried hysterically, my shoulders heaving, my chest aching. The dark, damp room closed in on me as I bawled. All our lives we were trapped in small, run-down places. I didn't blame Jimmy for fleeing from this one. I made up my mind I wouldn't come here again.

Finally, exhausted from crying, I stood up and wiped my tear-streaked cheeks with the back of my hands, which were dusty and dirty from all the cleaning I had done. Head bowed, I started for the door, but just before I reached it, Jimmy came in.

"Jimmy! Where were you? I thought you had run off for Georgia without saying good-bye!" I cried.

"Dawn, you should have known I wouldn't do that to you."

"Well, where were you? You could have been seen and . . ." There was a strange look in his eyes. "What happened?"

"Actually, I was running away," he said, lowering his head with a look of embarrassment. "I was running away from Clara Sue."

"What?" I followed him to the bunk bed. "What did she do? What happened?"

"She came down with some lunch for me and stayed while I ate, talking nonsense to me about Louise and the other girls and asking me all sorts of nasty questions about you and me and how we lived together. I got angrier and angrier, but I kept my temper down because I didn't want her to make any more trouble for you.

"Then . . ." He shifted his eyes from me and sat down.

"What then?" I asked sitting beside him.

"She got cute."

"What do you mean, Jimmy?" My heart started to race.

"She wanted me to . . . kiss her and stuff. I finally told her I had to get out for a while and ran out. I hid out by the baseball field until I was sure she would be gone and then I snuck back. Don't worry. No one saw me or paid any attention to me."

"Oh, Jimmy."

"It's all right," he said, "but I think I'd better go before she does make things worse."

I looked down, my tears building again.

"Hey," he said, reaching out to lift my chin. "I don't remember you ever being this unhappy."

"I can't help it, Jimmy. After you go, I'm just going to feel so terrible. When I first came in here and I thought you had left—"

"I can see." He laughed and got up to go into the bathroom. He ran the water over a washcloth and returned to clean my cheeks. I smiled at him, and he leaned forward to plant a soft kiss on my lips. "All right," he said, "I'll stay one more night and leave sometime tomorrow."

"I'm glad, Jimmy. I'll sneak back and eat dinner with you," I said excitedly, "and later I'll come down and . . . stay with you all night. No one will know," I quickly added when he took on a look of worry.

He nodded.

"Be careful. I feel like I'm making so much trouble for you, and you've got more than your share because of us Longchamps."

"Don't ever say that, Jimmy. I know I'm supposed to be happier here because I'm a Cutler and my family's well off, but I'm not and I'll never stop loving you and Fern. Never. I don't care. I'll never stop," I insisted. Jimmy had to laugh.

"All right," he said. "Don't stop."

"I'm going to go get washed and changed and show my face about the hotel, so no one suspects anything," I said. "I'll eat with the staff, but I won't eat much. I'll save my appetite to eat with you." I stood up and looked down at him. "Are you going to be all right?"

"Me? Sure. It gets a little stuffy in here, but I'll keep that door partly open. And later, after it gets good and dark, I might sneak over to that big pool and jump in."

"I'll jump in with you," I said. I headed for the door and turned back just as I reached it. "I'm glad you came, Jimmy, so glad."

He beamed the widest, brightest smile at me, which wiped away all the frustration and fatigue I had to suffer to keep him here. Then I hurried out and away, cheered by the promise of once again spending a night with Jimmy. But as soon as I entered the old section of the hotel, I heard my grandmother and Mrs. Boston talking in the corridor. They had just come down from upstairs where they had inspected Clara Sue's room. I stood just outside the doorway and waited until I saw Grandmother walk by, her face so firm, it looked like a chiseled bust of her. How straight she stood, I thought, her posture so perfect when she walked. She radiated so much confidence and authority, I was sure not even a fly would cross her path.

As soon as she passed, I reentered and started down the corridor, but just as I went by the sitting room, Mrs. Boston stuck her head out and called to me.

"Now, you tell me the truth," she said as I approached. She lifted her eyes toward the family suites above. "It was you who cleaned and fixed up Miss Clara Sue's room, right?"

I hesitated. Would she get me into more trouble now?

"She never did nothing that good, not that child." Mrs. Boston folded her arms under her bosom and peered at me suspiciously. "Now, what she give you to get you to do that, or what she promise you, huh?"

"Nothing. I just did her a favor," I said, but shifted my eyes too quickly. I was never a very good liar and hated trying.

"Whatever it is she promised you, you shouldn't have done it. She's always getting someone to do things for her. Mrs. Cutler is trying to get her to take more responsibility for herself. That's why she ordered her to fix up her room before dinner."

"She told me Grandmother Cutler was mad because she was leaving too much for you to do."

"Well, goodness knows, that's true, too. That girl makes enough of a mess for two of me. Always has, from the day she was born," she said. It made me think.

"Mrs. Boston, you were here when I was stolen away, right?" I asked quickly.

Her eyes grew smaller, and there was a slight tremble in her lips. "Yes."

"Did you know the woman who had been my nurse for that short time . . . Nurse Dalton?"

"I knew her before and knew her after. She's still living, but she needs a nurse herself these days."

"Why's that?"

"She's an invalid, suffering from diabetes. She lives with her daughter just outside of Cutler's Cove." She paused and looked at me askance. "Why you asking questions? There's no sense dragging up bad times."

"But how could my daddy . . . I mean Ormand Longchamp steal me right out from under my nurse's nose? Don't you remember the details?" I pursued.

"I don't remember no details. And I don't like dragging up bad times. It happened; it's over and done. Now I got to get going and finish up my work." She started away.

Puzzled by the way she reacted to my questions, I stood there and watched her walk off.

How could she forget the details of my kidnapping? If she once knew and still knew Nurse Dalton, she surely knew the way it had happened. Why was she so nervous when I asked her questions? I wondered.

If anything, it made me want to pursue the answers even harder.

I hurried on to get out of my dirty uniform and clean up. I wanted to take a long, hot shower and wash my hair so it smelled fresh and clean for Jimmy. I'd choose one of the nicer outfits from Clara Sue's hand-me-downs and brush out my hair so it shone the way it used to before all this happened. This could be the last night Jimmy and I spent together for years, I thought. What I wanted to do was bring back happier memories, help him to recall the times when we were all cheerful and hopeful. I needed to bring back the memories as much for myself as for him.

As soon as I got into my room, I stripped off my uniform and tossed it in the corner. I took off my underthings and my shoes and socks. Then I wrapped a towel around my body and went to the little bathroom. It always took a few minutes to get the water hot, so I turned it on and stood back to wait when all of a sudden the bathroom door was thrust open behind me.

I gasped and quickly scooped up the towel to wrap around myself again. Philip, smiling coyly, eyes big and bright, stepped in and closed the door behind me.

"Philip, what are you doing? I'm taking a shower!" I cried.

"So? Go ahead. I don't mind." He folded his arms across his chest and leaned back against the door provocatively.

"You get out of here, Philip, before someone comes along and hears you in here."

"No one's coming along," he said calmly. "Grandmother's busy with guests; Father's in his office, Clara Sue's with her friends, and Mother . . . Mother is debating whether or not she is well enough tonight to come to the dining room. We're safe," he said, smiling again.

"We're not safe. I don't want you in here. Please . . . go," I begged.

He continued to gaze at me, his eyes moving from my feet to my head, drinking me in with pleasure. I tightened the towel around my body, but it was too small to be an adequate covering. When I brought it higher to cover my breasts, it came up too far on my thighs, and when I lowered it, most of my bosom was revealed.

Philip's tongue moved across his lips as if he had just finished eating something delicious. Then he grinned wickedly and took a step toward me. I backed up until I was against the wall.

"What are you doing, getting all cleaned and dressed for Jimmy?"

"I'm . . . getting ready for dinner. I did a lot of work today, and I'm not very clean. So go. Please."

"You're clean enough for me," he said. I cringed as he drew closer. In a moment he had me pinioned in his arms, with his palms flat against the wall to prevent my escape. His lips brushed my cheek.

"Philip, are you forgetting who we are now and what has happened?"

"I'm not forgetting anything, especially," he said, kissing my forehead and moving his lips toward mine, "our night under the stars when we were rudely interrupted by my idiot friends. I was about to teach you things, things you should know by your age. I'm a very good teacher, you know. You'll be grateful, and you don't want to learn these things from just anybody, do you?" He dropped his right hand to my shoulder.

"You've had a taste of what it's like," he said softly, his eyes fixed on me. "How can you not want more?"

"Philip, you can't. We can't. Please . . ."

"We can as long as we know when to stop, and I promise I know that. I keep my promises, too. I'm keeping my promise to help you with Jimmy, aren't I?" he said, raising his eyebrows to drive home his point.

Oh, no, I thought. Not Philip, too. Both he and Clara Sue were taking advantage of Jimmy's troubles to get me to do things.

"Philip, please," I pleaded. "This doesn't feel right anymore. I can't help it. I'm just as sorry as you are that it's turned out this way, believe me; but there is nothing we can do about it but accept it."

"I accept it. I accept it as another challenge," he said, slipping his hand farther down to run his fingers along the top of my towel. I clutched it desperately.

"But it's not fair," he said, his face suddenly turning dark and angry. "You knew how much I wanted to touch you and hold you, and you led me to believe it would happen."

"But it's not my fault."

"It's nobody's fault . . . or maybe it's your other father's fault, but who cares right now? As I said," he continued, working his forefinger in and under the top of my towel, "we don't have to go as far as ordinary, unrelated men and women do. It won't mean anything then, but I had promised you I would show you—"

"I don't need to be shown."

"But I do," he said, forcing the towel down against my inadequate grip. I tried twisting away, but that only helped him get a better grip and the towel slipped off my breasts. His eyes widened with appreciation.

"Philip, stop!" I screamed. He gripped the inside of my elbows, pinning my arms back.

"If anyone hears you, we'll all get into trouble," he warned, "you, me, and Jimmy especially." He brought his lips to my nipples, moving quickly from one to the other and then back again.

I closed my eyes to try to deny this was happening. Once I had dreamt of him holding me and loving me, but this was twisted and harsh. My poor confused body responded to his caresses—stirred in places it had not been stirred before, but my mind screamed *No!* I felt like someone sinking into warm, soothing quicksand. For a few seconds it felt good, but it promised only trouble.

I continued to twist and squirm under his pincerlike fingers. The tip of his tongue drew a line from one breast to another and then he began to lower his body, kissing his way down my stomach until he reached the towel that was barely around my waist. I held it in the tip of my fingers. He bit the towel and tugged at it like a mad dog.

"Philip, stop, please," I pleaded.

With one strong pull, he drew the towel away from my body and dropped it at my feet. Then he gazed up at me, his eyes mad with desire. The glint in them was enough to set my heart racing even faster and pounding even harder than it already was.

Unable to get around him because he had me trapped against the wall, I brought my hands to my face as soon as he released my arms to embrace my thighs and draw them to his face. I felt my legs crumble and slid down the wall to the floor, keeping my face covered.

"Dawn," he said, his breathing heavy and hard. "It feels so good holding you. We don't have to think about anything else."

All I could do was cry as his hands moved over my body, exploring, caressing.

"Doesn't this feel good? Aren't you happy?" he whispered. I took my hands off my face when he took his hands from me and started unbuttoning his pants. It sent an electric bolt of fear up my spine. With all my strength, I tried pushing him away so I could drive him back enough for me to lunge for the door and make a quick exit. But he seized my wrists and turned them until I was on my back on the wooden floor.

"Philip!" I cried. "Stop before it's too late."

In one swift motion he slipped himself between my legs.

"Dawn . . . don't be so frightened. I can't help wanting to be with you. I thought I could, but you're too pretty. It doesn't have to mean anything," he said, gasping his words.

I clenched my hands into small fists and tried to pummel his head, but it was like a small bird slapping its wings against the snoot of a fox. He didn't even acknowledge it; instead, he moved himself more comfortably against me, his lips catching the soft flesh of my breast between them and nibbling his way over my bosom.

Suddenly I felt his hardness press itself firmly against me until he forced in that swollen, rigid male sex part of him that had to be satisfied. It drove into my tight and resisting flesh, which tore and bled.

I screamed, not caring anymore if we were discovered and if Jimmy were found. The shock of feeling him inside me drove away any concern for anything but my own violated being. My piercing screech was enough to cause his retreat.

"All right," he pleaded. "Stop. I'll stop." He drew back and stood up, quickly pulling up his underwear and pants and buckling his belt. I turned over on my stomach and cried into my arms, my body shaking.

"Wasn't it good for you?" he asked softly, kneeling beside me. I felt his palm on my lower back. "At least now you have an idea of what it will be like."

"Go away. Leave me alone, Philip. Please!" I cried through my tears.

"It's just the shock of it all," he said. "All girls have the same reaction." He stood up. "It's all right," he repeated, more to convince himself, it seemed, than to convince me.

"Dawn," he whispered. "Don't hate me for wanting you."

"Just leave me alone, Philip," I demanded in a much sterner tone. There was another long pause and then I heard him open the bathroom door and leave.

I turned over to be sure he was gone. This time I made sure the door was locked. Then I gazed down at myself. There were red blotches over my breasts and stomach where he had nibbled and sucked on me. I shuddered. His violation of me, although short, left me feeling unclean. The only way I could stop myself from sobbing was to step into the shower and let the now hot water run over my body, practically scalding my flesh. I endured the heat, feeling it was cleansing me and washing away the memory of Philip's fingers and kisses. I scrubbed myself with such intensity, I brought about new red blotches, making my skin scream with pain. All during my shower my tears mixed in with the water, seeming to fall as freely. What had once held the promise of romantic ecstasy and wonder had now turned sordid and depraved. I scrubbed and scrubbed.

Finally, exhausted from the effort to wash away what had just happened, I stepped out of the shower and dried myself. I returned to my bedroom and, feeling more tired than I could ever remember, lay down. I couldn't cry anymore. I closed my eyes and fell asleep, awakening when I heard a gentle rapping at my door.

He's returned, I thought, my heart racing again. I decided to remain still and see if he would believe I was already gone. The knocking got louder, and then I heard, "Dawn?"

It was my father. Had Philip, upset about my rebuffing him gone to him and told him about Jimmy? I got up slowly, my arms and legs as sore as they would be had I been working out in a farm field all day. I put on my robe and opened the door.

"Hi," he said. His smile quickly wilted. "Aren't you feeling well?"

"I'm . . ." I wanted to tell him all of it, wanted to shout it out as a way of getting rid of the memory. I wanted to scream about all my violations, this sexual one only being the most recent. I wanted to demand retribution, demand love and concern, demand to be treated like a human being at least, if not a member of the family. But I could only look down and shake my head.

"I'm very tired," I said.

"Oh. I'll see about getting you a day off."

"Thank you."

"I have something for you," my father said and reached into his breast pocket to pull out an envelope.

"What's that?"

"The receipt of delivery from the prison. Ormand Longchamp has your letter," he said. "I did what I promised."

I took the receipt slowly from his hand and gazed upon the official signature. Daddy had received my letter and most likely had already set his eyes upon my words. At least now I could look forward hopefully to receiving his reply.

"But you mustn't be upset if he doesn't write back," my father advised. "I'm sure by now he's ashamed and would have a hard time facing you. Most likely, he doesn't know what to say."

I nodded, staring down at the official receipt.

"It's still hard for me to understand," I said, squeezing back my tears. I looked up at him sharply. "How could he have stolen me right out from under my nurse's nose?"

"Oh, he was very clever about it. He waited until she had left the nursery to go visit Mrs. Boston in her room. It wasn't that she neglected you. You had fallen asleep, and she had taken a break. She and Mrs. Boston were good friends. He must have been hiding in the corridors, watching and waiting for his opportunity. When it came he went in and took you and snuck out the back way."

I looked up sharply.

"Nurse Dalton had gone to Mrs. Boston's room?" He nodded. But why didn't Mrs. Boston tell me this when I asked her how Daddy could have taken me right out from under Nurse Dalton's eyes? I wondered. That was such an important detail; how could she forget it?

"We didn't know you had been taken until Mrs. Dalton returned and discovered you gone," my father continued. "At first she thought we had taken you into our room. She came to our door, frantic.

"'What do you mean?' I said. 'We don't have her.' We didn't think Grandmother Cutler would take you to her suite, but Mrs. Dalton and I ran out to see, and then the realization hit me, and I went running through the hotel. But it was far too late.

"One of the staff members had seen Ormand Longchamp in the family section of the hotel. We put two and two together and came to the realization about what he had done. By the time we contacted the police, he and his wife were gone from Cutler's Cove, and of course, we had no idea in what direction they had headed.

"I jumped into my car and went tearing about, hoping to be lucky and come upon him, but it was futile." He shook his head.

"If he should write you, whatever he tells you in a letter," my father said, his face turning as sour and angry as I imagined it could, "it can't justify the terrible thing he did. Nothing can.

"I'm sorry his wife died and he's had such a hard life, but perhaps they were being punished for the horrible crime they committed."

I turned away because the tears had begun to sneak out the corners of my eyes and zigzag down my cheeks.

"I know it's been especially difficult for you, honey," he said, putting his hand softly on my shoulder, "but you're a Cutler; you'll survive and become all you were meant to become.

"Well," he continued, "I've got to get back to the job. You should try to eat something," he said, and I remembered Jimmy. I had to get food to him. "Tell you what," my father said. "I'll stop by the kitchen and have someone fix you a plate and send it on down. Okay?"

I could bring that food to Jimmy, I thought.

"Yes, thank you."

"If you still don't feel too well later, let me know, and I'll have the hotel doctor look in on you," he said and left.

I gazed in the mirror to see how bad I looked. I couldn't let Jimmy know what had happened between Philip and me. If he found out, he would become enraged and go after him, only getting himself into terrible trouble. I had to make myself look good for him so he couldn't sense that anything terrible had happened to me. There were still some blotches on my neck and right around my collarbone.

I went to the closet and found a pretty blue skirt and white blouse that had a wide collar and would hide most of the blotches. Then I brushed out my hair and tied a ribbon around it. I put on a little lipstick, too. I wished I had some rouge to make my pale cheeks look healthier, I thought.

I heard a knock on my door and opened it to accept my tray of food from one of the kitchen staff. I thanked him and closed the door, waiting to hear his footsteps disappear. Then I opened the door slowly and peered out. When I was certain all was clear, I hurried down the corridor and out the exit, carrying the warm tray of food to Jimmy.

"I'm stuffed," Jimmy announced and then looked up from his plate. "One thing you have here is great food, huh?" He sighed. "But I feel like a cooped-up chicken in here, Dawn. I can't stay much longer."

"I know," I said sadly and looked down. "Jimmy . . . Why can't I go with you?"

"Huh?"

"Oh, Jimmy, I don't care about the food or the beautiful grounds. I don't care how important my family is in this community or how wonderful people think the hotel is. I'd rather go with you and be poor and live with people I can love.

"Daddy's and Momma's relatives won't know anything if we don't tell them. We'll tell them about Momma dying, but we'll make up another reason for Daddy's being in prison."

"Oh, I don't know, Dawn . . ."

"Please, Jimmy. I can't stay here."

"Oh, things are bound to get better for you, a whole lot better than they would be in Georgia. Besides, I told you, if you ran off with me, they'd surely send someone after us, and we'd only be caught."

I nodded and looked into his soft, sympathetic eyes.

"Doesn't all this seem like one long, terrible nightmare sometimes, Jimmy? Don't you just hope you will wake up and it will all have been a horrible dream? Maybe if we wish hard enough . . ."

I closed my eyes.

"I wish I could lock out all the bad things that had happened to us and put us in a magical place where we could live out our deepest, most secret dreams, a place where nothing ugly or sordid could touch us."

"So do I, Dawn," he whispered. I felt him lean toward me, and then

I felt his breath on my lips before I felt his lips. When we kissed, my body softened, and I thought how right it would have been for Jimmy to be the one to have taken me from girlhood innocence into a woman's world. I had always felt safe with him, no matter where we went or what we did, because I sensed how much he cared for me and how important it was to him that I be happy and secure. Tragedy and hardship had tied us together as brother and sister, and now it seemed only right, even our destiny, that romantic love bind us even tighter.

But Philip's attack had stolen away the enchantment that comes when a girl willingly casts off her veil of innocence and enters maturity hand in hand with someone she loves and someone who loves her. I felt stained, polluted, spoiled. Jimmy felt me tense up.

"I'm sorry," he said quickly, thinking it was his kiss that had done it.

"It's all right, Jimmy," I said.

"No, it's not all right. I'm sure you can't stop seeing me beside you on one of our pull-out couches. I can't stop seeing you as my sister. I want to love you; I do love you, but it's going to take time—otherwise we won't feel clean and right about it," he explained.

He tried to look away, but slowly he was drawn back to me, his eyes so full of torment. It made my heart pound to see how much he loved and wanted me and yet his deep sense of morality kept him chained back. My impulses, my unleashed sexuality thrashed about like a spoiled child, demanding satisfaction, but the wiser part of me agreed with Jimmy and loved him more for showing his wisdom. He was right—if we rushed into things, we would suffer regret. Our confused consciences could turn us away from each other afterward, and our love would never grow to be pure and good.

"Of course you're right, Jimmy," I said, "but I always loved you as much as a sister could love her brother, and now I promise to learn to love you the way a woman should love a man, no matter how long it takes me and how long I have to wait."

"Do you mean that, Dawn?"

"I do, Jimmy."

He smiled and kissed me softly again, but even that short, gentle peck on the cheek sent an electric thrill through my body.

"I should leave tonight," he said.

"Please don't, Jimmy. I'll stay with you all night," I said. "And we'll talk until you can't keep your eyelids open."

He laughed.

"All right, but I should leave early in the morning," he said. "The truckers get started early, and they're the best chance I got to get rides."

"I'll get you breakfast when I go to eat with the rest of the staff. That's early. And we'll have a little more time together.

"But do you promise that when you get to Georgia, you'll write and tell me where you are?" I asked. Just the thought of his leaving and being so far away from me now made me feel sick inside.

"Sure. And as soon as I earn enough money on my own, I'll come back to see you."

"Promise?"

"Yes."

We lay together on the bunk, me snuggled in his arm, and talked about our dreams. Jimmy had never had his mind set on being anything before, but now he talked about joining the air force when he was old enough and maybe becoming a pilot.

"But what if there was a war, Jimmy? I'd feel terrible and worry all the time. Why don't you think about being something else, like a lawyer or a doctor or—"

"Come on, Dawn. Where am I going to get enough money to go to a college?"

"Maybe I'll get enough money to send you to college."

He was quiet and then he turned to me with his dark eyes so sad and heavy.

"You won't want me to be your boyfriend if I'm not somebody big and important. Is that it, Dawn?"

"Oh, no, Jimmy. Never."

"You won't be able to help it," he predicted.

"That's not true, Jimmy," I protested.

"Maybe it's not true now, but after you've been living here a while, you'll get to feel that way. It happens. These rich, old southern families plan their daughters' lives—what they will be, who they will marry—"

"It won't happen to me," I insisted.

"We'll see," he said, convinced he was right. He could be so stubborn sometimes.

"James Gary Longchamp, don't tell me what I will and will not be like. I am my own person, and nobody—not a tyrant grandmother or anybody else—is going to mold me into someone else. She can call me Eugenia until she gets red in the face."

"All right," he said, laughing. He kissed me on the cheek. "Whatever you say. I don't think she's going to be a match for your temper anyhow. I wonder who you get that from? Your mother got a temper?"

"Hardly. She whines instead of yells. And she gets everything she wants anyway. She doesn't have to be mad at anyone."

"What about your father?"

"I don't think he's capable of getting angry. Nothing seems to bother him. He's as smooth as fresh butter."

"So then you inherited your grandmother's temperament. Maybe you're more like her than you think."

"I don't want to be. She's not what I imagined my grandmother would be like. She's . . ."

We heard the sets of footsteps on the cement stairway before the door was thrust open. A moment later the hideaway was illuminated, and we looked up at two policemen. I grabbed Jimmy's hand.

"See," Clara Sue said from behind them, "I told you I wasn't lying."

"Let's go, kid," one of the policemen said to Jimmy. He stood up slowly.

"I ain't going back there," he said defiantly. The policeman moved forward. Jimmy stepped to the side. When the policeman reached out to grab him, Jimmy ducked and scooted to the side.

"Jimmy!" I cried.

The other policeman moved swiftly and seized him around the waist, lifting him off the ground. Jimmy flared out, but the second policeman joined the first, and they restrained him quickly.

"Let him go!" I screamed.

"You can come along quietly, or we'll put handcuffs on you, kid," the policeman holding him from behind said. "What's it going to be?"

"All right, all right," Jimmy said, his face red with embarrassment and anger. "Let go."

The policeman loosened his grip, and Jimmy stood by, his head lowered in defeat.

"Move on out," the other policeman commanded.

I turned to Clara Sue, who stood in the doorway.

"How could you do this?" I screamed. "You mean, selfish . . ."

She stepped back to let the policemen and Jimmy pass. Just as Jimmy reached the door, he turned back to me.

"I'll come back, Dawn. I promise. Someday I'll come back."

"Move it," the policeman commanded, pushing him. Jimmy stumbled forward through the door.

I ran after them.

"Jimmy!" I cried. I started running up the steps and stopped when I reached the top.

My father stood beside my grandmother, and Clara stood just behind them both.

"Go directly to your room, Eugenia," my grandmother commanded. "This is a terrible disgrace."

"Go on," my father said a little softer, but his face dark with disappointment. "Go to your room."

I looked after Jimmy and the policemen. They were nearly at the front of the building.

"Please," I said. "Don't let them take him back. He had a horrible time living with a mean man. Please—"

"It's not our problem," my grandmother said.

"We can't do anything," my father confirmed. "And it's against the law to harbor a fugitive."

"He's not a fugitive. No," I said, shaking my head. "Please . . ." I turned in Jimmy's direction, but he had already gone around the building. *"Jimmy,"* I called. I started after him.

"Eugenia!" my father cried. "Get back here."

I ran, but by the time I had reached the front of the hotel, the policemen had shoved Jimmy into the back of the patrol car and slammed the door. I stood by watching as they got in. Jimmy peered out the window.

"I'll be back," he mouthed.

The roof light began, and the patrol car was started up.

"Jimmy!"

I felt my father's hand on my shoulder, restraining me.

"How utterly embarrassing," my grandmother said from somewhere behind me. "That my guests should see this."

"You'd better get inside," my father advised.

My body shook with sobs as the police car pulled away, taking Jimmy back into the night.

15

Secrets Revealed

I felt my father's fingers grip my shoulders softly as the lights from the police patrol car disappeared on the street below. My grandmother stepped forward to face me. Her lips were tight and thin, and her eyes were wide and maddening with rage. Under the lanterns and the bright porch lights, her skin was ghostly white. With her shoulders raised and her neck lowered between them, she looked like a hawk about to pounce on a mouse, and right now I felt like some sort of trapped creature.

"How could you do such a thing?" she hissed. She turned sharply to my father. "I told you she was no better than a wild animal brought in from the streets. She's sure to bring them all here if we don't put an immediate stop to it. She has to be sent away to some private school that specializes in this sort of person."

"I'm not a wild animal! You're a wild animal!" I screamed.

"Eugenia," my father snapped. I spun out of his hands.

"I'm not Eugenia! I'm not! I'm Dawn, Dawn!" I insisted, pounding my sides with my own small fists.

I looked up and saw the guests who had gathered at the front entrance and on the porch gawking down at me, some of the elderly women shaking their heads and the men nodding their agreement. Suddenly Philip pushed his way through and gazed at us in confusion.

"No," I said. "You shouldn't have let them take him," I added and began to sob. "You shouldn't have."

"Eugenia," he said softly, stepping toward me.

"Get her inside," my grandmother commanded through her teeth. "Now!" She turned away and smiled up at her guests. "It's all right, everyone. Just a misunderstanding. Nothing to alarm anyone."

"Please, Eugenia," my father said, reaching out to take my hand. "Let's go inside," he pleaded.

"No!" I backed farther away. "I'm not going inside. I hate it; I hate it!" I screamed and turned and ran down the driveway.

"Honestly, Daddy, you're always treating Dawn with kid gloves," I heard Clara Sue say. "She's a big girl. She's made her bed! Now let her lie in it."

Her words put more force into my stride. Clara Sue was such a liar. As I ran, the tears streamed down and blew off my cheeks. I felt as though my chest would explode, but I didn't stop running. I reached the street and turned right, running down the sidewalk, half the time with my eyes closed, sobbing.

I ran and ran until the pain in my side became a sharp knife cutting deeper and deeper, forcing me to slow down to a trot and then a walk, my hand on my ribs, my head down, gasping for breath. I had no idea where I was headed or where I was. The street had turned to the left, bringing me closer to the ocean, and the pounding surf seemed right beside me. Finally I stopped by some large rocks and leaned against them to rest and catch my breath.

I gazed out at the moonlit sea. The sky was dark, deep, even cold, and the moon looked sickly yellow. Occasionally the spray from the surf reached me and sprinkled my face.

Poor Jimmy, I thought, spirited off into the night like some common criminal. Would they force him to return to that mean farmer? What had we done to deserve this? I bit down on my lower lip to prevent myself from sobbing any more. My throat and chest ached so much from crying.

Suddenly I heard someone calling. It was Sissy wandering through the streets looking for me.

"Your daddy sent me after you," she said.

have seen."

"I did see. I seen it all from the side of the porch. Who was he?"

"He was my . . . the boy I thought was my brother. He had run off from a cruel foster parent."

"Oh."

"And there was nothing I could do to help him," I wailed helplessly, standing back and wiping my cheeks. "Nothing." I sighed deeply and lowered my head. How frustrated and defeated I felt. Sissy was right: I had to return to the hotel. Where else would I go?

"I hate Clara Sue," I said through my clenched teeth. "She told my grandmother Jimmy was hiding out here and got her to call the police. She's a mean, spiteful . . . She's the one who stole Mrs. Clairmont's necklace just so I'd be blamed. Afterward, I saw her sneak into my room and put it in my bed."

"But I thought Mrs. Clairmont found it."

"I snuck into her room and put it back, but Clara Sue did it," I repeated. "I know no one will believe me, but she did."

"I believe you. That's one spoiled child for sure," Sissy agreed. "But she will get hers someday. That kind always does, because they hate themselves too much. Come on, honey," Sissy said, putting her arm around my shoulders, "I'll walk you back. You're shivering something terrible."

"I'm just upset, not cold."

"Still, you're shivering," Sissy said, rubbing my arm. We started back to the hotel. "Jimmy's a handsome boy."

"He is handsome, isn't he? And he's very nice. People don't see that at first because he seems so standoffish. That's because he's really shy."

"Ain't nothing wrong with being a little shy. It's the other type I don't like much."

"Like Clara Sue?"

"Like Clara Sue," she agreed, and we both laughed. It felt good to laugh, like finally letting out a breath you had to hold for the longest time. And then an idea came to me.

"Do you know the woman who was my nurse when I was first born—Mrs. Dalton?"

"Uh-huh."

"She lives with her sister, right?" Sissy nodded. "Does she live nearby?"

"Well, back there about four blocks," she said, indicating behind us. "In a little Cape Cod house on Crescent Street. Once in a while my granny sends me over with a jar of this or a jar of that. She's a sick woman, you know."

"Mrs. Boston told me. Sissy, I want to go see her."

"What for?"

"I want to ask her questions about my kidnapping. Will you take me there?"

"Now?"

"It's not that late."

"It's too late for her. She's very sick and would be asleep by now."

"Will you take me in the morning after we do our work? Will you?" I asked. "Please," I begged.

"Okay," she said, seeing how important it was to me.

"Thank you, Sissy," I said.

When we returned to the hotel, my grandmother was nowhere to be seen, but my father greeted us in the lobby.

"Are you all right?" he asked. I nodded and looked down at the carpet. "I think you should just go to your room. We'll have a chance to talk about all this tomorrow when everyone is calmer and can think clearly."

As I was crossing the lobby, I decided what I was going to do. It was time to deal with Clara Sue. She wasn't going to get away with what she had done.

Without even bothering to knock, I stormed into Clara Sue's bedroom, slamming the door behind me.

"How could you?" I angrily demanded. "How could you tell them about Jimmy?"

Clara Sue was on her bed, flipping through a magazine. By her side was a box of chocolates. Despite my angry words, she didn't look up. Instead she continued reading, reaching into the box of chocolates, nibbling one after another and discarding them after one or two bites.

"Aren't you going to say anything?" I asked. I still received no answer, and it infuriated me the way she was so blatantly ignoring me. I swooped down on her and swatted the box of chocolates. It flew off the bed and into the air before crashing to the floor, chocolates scattering everywhere.

I waited for Clara Sue to look up at me. I couldn't wait to confront her about the treacherous thing she had done. But she didn't look up. She only continued reading, ignoring me as though I wasn't there. For some reason this infuriated me even more. I tore her magazine out of her hands, ripping it to shreds, tossing the pieces in the air.

"I'm not leaving, Clara Sue Cutler. I'm staying right here until you look at me."

Finally she looked up, her blue eyes sending me a warning look. "Didn't anyone ever teach you to knock? It's the polite thing to do."

I chose to ignore the look in Clara Sue's eyes. "And didn't anyone ever teach you about trust? About keeping a secret sacred? Jimmy and I trusted you. Why did you do it? Why?"

"Why not?" she purred softly. Then more angrily and with a burst of force as she jumped off her bed, "Why not? Making your life miserable gives me pleasure, Dawn. It makes me happy."

I stared at her in outrage. Without even thinking about it, I brought up my hand and slapped her across the face. "You're nothing but a spoiled selfish brat! I'll never forgive you for this. Never!"

Clara Sue laughed at me, massaging her cheek. "Who wants your forgiveness?" she sneered. "You think you're doing me a favor?"

"We're sisters. Sisters are supposed to be best friends. You didn't want me as a friend, Clara Sue, and now you don't want me as a sister. Why? Why are you so intent on hurting me? What did I ever do to you? Why do you keep doing these nasty things?"

"Because I hate you!" Clara Sue screamed at the top of her lungs. "I hate you, Dawn! I've hated you all my life!"

I was shocked by her anger. It threw me off guard, and I didn't know how to respond. There was such ferocity in her words and her face was bright red, her eyes bulging like the eyes of a madwoman. I'd seen such a look before—on Grandmother Cutler's face. Clara Sue's look chilled me the way Grandmother's had. But I couldn't understand it. Why did they both hate me so? What had I ever done to this family to warrant such ugly emotions?

"How can that be?" I whispered. Part of me wanted to understand Clara Sue's feelings. "How can that be?"

"How can that be?" Clara Sue mimicked cruelly. "How can that be? I'll tell you how. I'll tell you! You've been a part of my life without even being in it! From the day I was born I've lived in your shadow, and I've hated every minute of it!"

"But that wasn't my fault." Part of me was starting to understand. The aftermath of my kidnapping had become a permanent part of life at Cutler's Cove, and Clara Sue had been born into it.

"Oh, wasn't it? I wasn't the first-born, like Philip, or the first daughter, like you. I wasn't even considered the baby of the family. Oh, no! *I was nothing but the baby born to replace you!*" Clara Sue closed the distance between us. "Get out of my room. *Get out!* The sight of you sickens me. But before you go, Dawn, here's a promise. A very special promise that I intend to keep. I will *never* accept you as a part of this family. I will *never* welcome you with open arms or make your life easier. *Never!* Instead I will do everything humanly possible to make your life a living hell. And when that isn't enough, I'll do even more. I will go out of my way to bring you sorrow and heartache. Your unhappiness will bring a smile to my face and make the sun even shinier. I will shatter your dreams until they're nothing more than twisted remnants of your hopes and will bring you only nightmares. *Nothing less will do!*"

I was speechless. "You can't be serious!" I cried. Clara Sue's reasons for turning in Jimmy were now crystal clear, and although I was still very angry at her, part of me pitied her. With everything she had, Clara Sue was miserable. I wanted to help her overcome her unhappiness. Maybe then she wouldn't hate me so much.

Clara Sue's eyes glinted wildly as she stared at me with open amazement. "I don't believe you! I honestly don't believe you! You just don't give up, do you? This isn't some sappy movie where we pour out our hearts to each other, have a good cry, and then kiss and make up. Get your pretty little head out of the clouds, Dawn. Didn't you hear a word I said? We will never be friends, and we will certainly never be sisters. *Ever!*" Clara Sue inched closer, and I backed away from her into the bedroom door. "Never let your guard down with me, Dawn," she warned. "Watch out for me. Always."

With those final words she turned her back on me. I fumbled with the doorknob, anxious to escape from my sister because in my heart I knew that what she had promised was true.

Neither my father nor my grandmother had time to see me the following morning since it was the day of a big check-in and checkout. I was busy with Sissy anyway because we had an additional five rooms to clean and remake. Nevertheless, I anticipated my grandmother's appearance in the kitchen when the staff had its breakfast. I hadn't slept well the night before, and I wasn't in the mood to be yelled at or embarrassed in front of the other workers. I made up my mind to stand up to her, even if it meant being confined to my room without food again.

Because Clara Sue had the early evening shift at the front desk, she always slept late, so I didn't have to face her, but Philip was up and with the other waiters, of course. He avoided me until it was time to go to work. Then he followed me out and called to me.

"Please," he begged when it looked like I wouldn't stop. I turned on him abruptly.

"I have work to do, Philip," I said. "I have to earn my keep," I added bitterly. "And I don't believe Grandmother. I'm not learning the business from the bottom up. I'll always be on the bottom as far as she is concerned." I gazed at him. He looked so different to me now, so cheap and pathetic since he had attacked me. To think I had almost been in love with him!

"Dawn, you have to believe me. I had nothing to do with my grandmother's finding out about Jimmy. She doesn't know I brought him down there to hide him when he first arrived," he said, his eyes showing his fear. So that was it, I thought.

"You're afraid I'll tell her?" He didn't reply, but his face answered. "Don't worry, Philip. I'm not like our precious younger sister. I won't deliberately get you in trouble just to get revenge, although I should," I snapped and pivoted to catch up with Sissy.

During the rest of the morning, whenever I heard footsteps in the corridor, I expected my father or my grandmother. After our work was completed and neither had arrived, I pulled Sissy aside.

"Take me right to Mrs. Dalton's daughter's house, Sissy. Please, before my grandmother finds more work for us."

"I don't know why you want to go see that woman. She don't remember things that well," Sissy said, looking away quickly.

"Why do you say that, Sissy?" I sensed the change in her attitude.

"My granny says so," she said, looking up quickly and then looking down again.

"You told her you were taking me and she didn't like it?" Sissy shook her head. "You don't have to go in with me, Sissy. Just point out the house. And I won't tell anyone you showed me. I promise."

She hesitated.

"My granny says people who dig up the past usually find more bones than they expected, and it's better to let bygones be bygones."

"Not for me, Sissy. I can't. Please. If you don't help me, I'll just go looking anyway until I find the house," I said, screwing my face into a look of determination to impress her.

"All right," she said and sighed. "I'll show you the way."

We left the hotel through a side entrance and quickly went down to the street. It was strange how everything looked different to me in daylight, especially the cemetery. Gone was its foreboding and ominous atmosphere. Today it was just a pleasant, well-manicured resting place, easy to pass.

It was a bright, nearly cloudless day with a soft, warm ocean breeze. The sea looked calm, peaceful, inviting, the tide gently combing the beach and falling back into small waves. Everything looked cleaner, friendlier.

There was a constant line of traffic in the street, but it moved lazily. No one seemed to be in a rush; everyone was mesmerized by the glitter of the sunlight on the aqua water and the flight of terns and sea gulls that floated effortlessly through the summer air.

This might very well have been a wonderful place in which to grow up, I thought. I couldn't help wondering what I might have been like had I been raised in the hotel and Cutler's Cove. Would I have turned out as selfish as Clara Sue? Would I have loved my grandmother, and would my mother have been an entirely different person? Fate and events beyond my control had left these questions forever unanswered.

"There it is, straight ahead of us," Sissy said, pointing to a cozy little white Cape Cod house with a patch of lawn, a small sidewalk, and a small porch. It had a picket fence in front. Sissy looked at me. "You want me to wait here for you?"

"No, Sissy. You can go on back. If anyone asks you where I am, tell them you don't know."

"I hope you're doing the right thing," she said and turned back, walking quickly with her head down as if she were afraid she would set eyes on some ghost in broad daylight.

I couldn't help trembling myself as I approached the front door and rang the buzzer. At first I thought no one was home. I pushed the buzzer again and then I heard someone shout.

"Hold your water. I'm coming; I'm coming."

The door was finally opened by a black woman with completely gray hair. She was in a wheelchair and peered up at me with big eyes, magnified under her thick lenses. She had a soft, round face and wore a light blue housecoat, but her feet were bare. Her right leg was wrapped in a bandage from her ankle up until the bandage disappeared under her dress.

Curiosity brightened her eyes and drew deep creases in her forehead. She pressed her lips together and leaned forward to peer out at me. Then she raised her glasses and wiped her right eye with her small fist. I saw a gold wedding band on her finger, but other than that, she wore no jewelry.

"Yes?" she finally said.

"I'm looking for Mrs. Dalton, the Mrs. Dalton who was a nurse."

"You're looking at her. What do you want?" she asked leaning back in her wheelchair. "I don't work no more, not that I don't wish I could."

"I want to talk to you. My name's Dawn, Dawn Lon . . . Dawn Cutler," I said.

"Cutler?" She studied me. "From the hotel family?"

"Yes, ma'am."

She continued to stare at me.

"You ain't Clara Sue?"

"Oh, no, ma'am."

"Didn't think you was. You're prettier than I remember her to be," she said. "All right, come on in," she added and finally backed her wheelchair up.

"I'm sorry I can't offer you anything. I'm having enough trouble taking care of myself these days," she said. "I live with my daughter and her husband, but they got their own lives and problems. Spend most of my time alone," she mumbled, looking down at the floor and shaking her head.

I paused and looked into the entryway. It was a small one with hardwood floors and a blue and white throw rug. There was a coatrack on the right, an oval mirror on the wall, and a globular overhead light fixture.

"Well, come in if you're coming in," Mrs. Dalton said when she looked up and saw I was still standing in the doorway.

"Thank you."

"Go on into the living room there," she said, pointing after I entered. I went through the doorway on the left. It was a small room with a rather worn dark brown rug. The furniture was vintage, too, I thought. The flower-pattern covering on the couch looked thin in the arms. Across from it was a rocking chair, an easy chair, and a matching settee, all equally tired-looking. There was a square-shaped dark maple table at the center. Against the far wall were paintings— seascapes and pictures of seaside houses. To the left was a glass-door bookcase filled with knickknacks as well as some novels. Over the small fieldstone fireplace hung a ceramic cross, but I thought the nicest thing in the room was an old dark pine grandfather's clock in the left corner.

The room had a pleasant lilac scent. Its front windows faced the sea, and with the curtains drawn back it provided a nice view and made the room bright and cheery.

"Sit down, sit down," Mrs. Dalton commanded and wheeled herself in behind me. I chose the couch. The worn cushions sank in deeply under me, so I sat as far forward as I could. She turned her wheelchair to face me and put her hands in her lap. "Now, then, what can I do for you, honey? There ain't much more I can do for myself," she added dryly.

"I'm hoping you can tell me more about what happened to me," I said.

"Happened to you?" Her eyes narrowed. "Who'd you say you were?"

"I said I was Dawn Cutler, but my grandmother wants me to go by the name I originally had been given when I was born—Eugenia," I added, and I might as well have reached out to slap her across the face. She snapped back in her chair and brought her hands to her sagging bosom. Then she crossed herself quickly and closed her eyes. Her lips trembled, and her head began to shake.

"Mrs. Dalton? Are you all right?" What was wrong with her? Why had my words caused such a reaction? After a moment she nodded. Then she opened her eyes and gazed at me with wonder, her lips still trembling.

She shook her head softly. "You're the lost Cutler baby. . . ."

"You were my nurse, weren't you?"

"Only a few days. I should have known someday I'd set eyes on you. . . . I should have known," she mumbled. "I need a drink of water," she decided quickly. "My lips feel like parchment. Please . . . in the kitchen." She gestured toward the doorway.

"Right away," I said, getting up quickly. I went out to the hallway and followed it to the small kitchen. When I brought back the water, she was slumped to the side in her wheelchair, looking as if she had gone unconscious.

"Mrs. Dalton?" I cried in a panic. "Mrs. Dalton!"

She straightened up slowly.

"It's all right," she said in a loud whisper. "I'm all right. My heart's still strong, although why it still wants to beat in this broken, twisted body is beyond me."

I handed her the water. She sipped some and shook her head. Then she looked up at me with big searching eyes.

"You turned out to be a very pretty girl."

"Thank you."

"But you've been through a few things, haven't you, child?"

"Yes, ma'am."

"Ormand Longchamp was a good father and Sally Jean was a good mother to you?"

"Oh, yes, ma'am," I said, happy to hear their names from her lips. "You remember them well?" I took my seat on the couch again quickly.

"I remember them," she admitted. She swallowed some more water and sat back. "Why did you come here? What do you want from me?" she asked. "I'm a sick woman, advanced diabetes. I'm going to have to have this leg amputated for sure, and after that . . . I might as well be dead anyway," she added.

"I'm sorry for your trouble," I said. "My momma . . . Sally Jean . . . became a sick woman and suffered something terrible."

Her face softened.

"Well, what can I do for you?"

"I want you to tell me the truth, Mrs. Dalton," I said, "every last detail of it you remember, for my daddy . . . the man I called my daddy, Ormand Longchamp, sits in prison, and my mother Sally Jean is dead, but I can't think of them as being the evil people everyone tells me they were. They were always good to me and always took care of me. They loved me with all their hearts, and I loved them. I can't allow such bad things to be said about them. I just can't. I owe it to them to find the truth."

I saw a slight nod in Mrs. Dalton's face.

"I liked Sally Jean. She was a hardworking woman, a good woman who never looked down on nobody and always had a pleasant smile no matter how hard things were for her. Your daddy was a hardworking man who didn't look down on nobody. Never saw me without saying hello and asking how I was."

"That's why I can't think of them as bad people, Mrs. Dalton, no matter what I'm told," I insisted.

"They did take you," she said, her eyes turning glassy.

"I know that, but why . . . how is what I don't understand."

"Your grandmother doesn't know you're here, does she?" she asked, nodding because she anticipated the answer.

"No."

"Nor your real father or mother?" I shook my head. "How is your mother these days?" she asked, pulling the corners of her mouth in.

"Nearly always locked up in her room for one reason or another. She suffers from nervous ailments and gets everything brought to her, although she doesn't look sick to me." I refused to feel sorry for my mother. In her own way she was just as selfish as Clara. "Occasionally she accompanies my grandmother at dinner and greets guests."

"Whatever your grandmother wants," Mrs. Dalton muttered, "she's sure to do."

"Why? How do you know so much about the Cutlers?" I asked quickly.

"I was with them a long time . . . always worked special duty for them when any of them were sick. I liked your grandfather. He was a sweet, gentle man. I cried as much when he died as I did when my own father died. Then I was a maternity nurse for your brother, for you, and for your sister."

"You cared for Clara Sue, too?" She nodded. "Then my grandmother certainly wasn't mad at you for what happened and didn't blame you for my abduction."

"Heavens, no. Who told you that?"

"My mother."

She nodded again. Then she widened her eyes.

"If your grandmother don't know you're here and neither does your parents, who sent you? Ormand?"

"Nobody sent me. Why would my daddy send me?" I asked quickly.

"What do you want?" she asked again, this time more sharply. "I told you I'm sick. I can't sit up and talk long."

"I want to know what really happened, Mrs. Dalton. I spoke to Mrs. Boston—"

"Mary?" She smiled. "How is Mary doing these days?"

"She's fine, but when I asked her about what happened, she didn't tell me you were visiting with her when I was abducted, and she didn't want to talk about it."

"I was with her; she just forgot, that's all. There's nothing more to tell. You were asleep, comfortably. I left the nursery; Ormand took you and then he and Sally Jean run off. You know the rest."

I looked down, the tears building quickly.

"They ain't treating you so good since you been returned, is that it?" Mrs. Dalton asked perceptively. I shook my head and wiped away the tears that had escaped my eyes.

"My grandmother hates me; she's upset I was found," I said and looked up. "And she was the one who put up the money for the reward leading to my recovery. I don't understand. She wanted me found, but she was upset when I was, and it wasn't just because all this time has passed. There's something else. I feel it; I know it. But no one wants to tell me, or no one knows it all.

"Oh, Mrs. Dalton, please," I begged. "My daddy and momma just weren't bad people. Even you just said so. I can't understand them stealing a baby from someone, even if my momma had suffered a stillborn. No matter what I'm told, I can't learn to hate them, and I can't stand thinking about my daddy locked up in some prison.

"My little sister, Fern, and my brother, Jimmy, have been sent to live with strangers. Jimmy just ran away from a mean farmer and hid out in the hotel until Clara snitched on him. The police took him away last night. It was just terrible."

I took a deep breath and shook my head.

"It's like some curse was put on us, and for what? What did we do? We're no sinners," I added vehemently. That widened her eyes again. She brought her hands to the base of her throat and looked at me as if I were a ghost. Then she nodded slowly.

"He sent you," she muttered. "He sent you to me. This is my last chance at redemption. My last chance."

"Who sent me?"

"The Lord Almighty," she said. "All my good churchgoing days don't matter none. It ain't been enough to wash me clean." She leaned forward and grasped my hand firmly into hers. Her eyes were wide, wild. "That's why I'm in this wheelchair, child. It's my penance. I always knew it. This hard life is my punishment."

I sat absolutely still as she stared into my face. After a moment she nodded and released her grip on my hand. She sat back, took a deep breath and looked at me.

"All right," she said. "I'll tell you everything. You was meant to know and I was meant to tell you. Otherwise, He wouldn't have sent you to me."

"Your mother comes from a rich and distinguished old family in Virginia Beach," Mrs. Dalton began. "I remember your father and mother's wedding. Everybody does. It was one of the most gala affairs in Cutler's Cove, and everyone in society was invited, even people from Boston and New York. People thought it was the perfect marriage—two very attractive people from the best families. Why, people here went around comparing it to the marriage of Grace Kelly, the movie star, and that prince in Europe.

"Your father was like a prince here anyway, and there was a number of suitors after your mother's hand. But even back then I heard stories."

"What kind of stories?" I asked when she looked like she wouldn't continue.

"Stories about your grandmother being unhappy about the marriage, not thinking your mother was right for your father. Say what you want about your grandmother, she's a powerful woman with eyes like a hawk. She sees things other people close their eyes to, and she goes and does what has to be done.

"Yes, she's a distinguished lady who wouldn't do anything to embarrass the family. Your grandfather liked your mother. Any man would have. I don't know if she's still as beautiful as she was, but she was like some precious little doll, her features tiny but perfect, and when she batted her eyelashes . . . men would turn into little boys. I seen that firsthand," Mrs. Dalton added, lifting her eyes to me and raising her eyebrows.

"So your grandmother kept her opposition quiet, I guess. I don't know all that went on behind closed doors, mind you, although some of the older staff, people who had been with the Cutlers a long time, people like Mary Boston, had a good idea what was going on and said there was a struggle.

"Not that Mary is the type who goes around gossiping, mind you. She don't. I was always close with Mary, so she told me what she knew. I was already a nurse and had done some special duty at the hotel, taking care of guests who got sick occasionally, and then, as I told you, taking care of Mr. Cutler Senior when he got sick.

"It wasn't no big secret then how your grandmother felt about your mother. She thought she was too flighty and self-centered to be a good hotel man's wife, but your father was head over heels. There was nothing he wanted more.

"Anyway, they got married, and for a while it seemed your mother might make a good hotel man's wife. She behaved, did what your grandmother wanted, learned how to be nice to the guests and be a host . . . She really enjoyed getting all dressed up and wearing all her expensive jewelry so she could be the Princess of Cutler's Cove, and in those days, as it still is, Cutler's Cove was a very special hotel catering to the richest, most distinguished families from up and down the East Coast . . . even Europe!"

"What happened to change things?" I asked, unable to contain my impatience. I knew all about the hotel and how famous it had become. I wanted her to get to the parts I didn't know.

"I'm getting to it, child. Don't forget, I'm not spry, and my mind wanders something awful because of this ailment, this curse, I should say." She waved her hand and then took on a far-off look. I sat obediently, waiting until she turned back to me.

"Where was I?"

"You were telling me about my mother, the wedding, how good things were in the beginning . . . "

"Oh, yeah, yeah. Well, it wasn't long after your brother was born . . ."

"Philip."

"Yeah, Philip, that your mother started to stray a bit."

"Stray?"

"Don't you know what stray means, child? You know what it is when a cat strays, don'tcha?" she asked, leaning toward me.

"I think so. Flirting?" I guessed.

She shook her head.

"She was doing more than just flirting. If your father knew, he didn't let on. 'Least as far as anyone knew, but your grandmother knew. Nothing happens at that hotel, she doesn't know about it the same minute or minutes afterward. It always looked like your grandfather was in charge, but she's the strength, always was, 'least as long as I can remember," she added, blinking quickly.

"I know," I said sadly.

"Anyway, from what I know about it, there comes this entertainer, piano player and singer, as handsome a man as could be. All the young women drooled over him, and he and your mother . . ." She paused and then leaned toward me again as if there were other people in the room and she didn't want to be overheard.

"There was this chambermaid, Blossom, who told me she come upon them out behind the pool house one night. She went out there herself with a man called Felix, who was a handyman. Nothing to look at," she added, twisting her nose, "but Blossom, she'd make love to any man who paused long enough to notice her.

"Anyway, she knew it was your mother, and she got frightened and pulled Felix away. Blossom didn't tell but one or two of her close friends besides me about what she saw, and your mother and her lover didn't know Blossom had been there at the same time, but it wasn't much longer after that, your grandmother found out all of it. She had ears and eyes working for her everywhere in that place, if you know what I mean," Mrs. Dalton said, nodding.

"What did she do?" I asked in a voice barely audible.

"The singer was let go and shortly afterward . . . well, your mother was pregnant."

"With me?"

" 'Fraid so, child. And your grandmother, she got your mother into her office and whipped her with words so bad, she had her begging for mercy. Of course, your mother swore up and down that you was her and Randolph's, but your grandmother was too sharp and knew too much about what went on. She knew dates, times . . . your mother finally confessed and admitted you was most likely not Randolph's child. Besides," she said, her eyebrows up again, "I don't think things was running that smooth between your mother and your father, as smooth as they're supposed to be running between a man and a woman. You understand?"

I shook my head. I didn't.

"Well," she said, "that's another story. Anyway, the only reason I found out about all this was your grandmother was going to force your mother to have an abortion on the sly. She wanted me to take her to someone."

I shook my head, dazed. Randolph Cutler wasn't my father. Once again what I believed to be the truth wasn't. When would this all end? When would the lies stop?

"What was the singer's name?"

"Oh, I don't remember. In those days entertainers came through here like hurricanes. Some stayed a season; some stayed a week on their way to New York or Boston or Washington, D.C. And as I said, he wasn't the first one your mother took behind the pool house."

I couldn't believe what I was hearing about my mother. My poor, sick mother. Ha! What an elaborate farce she had managed to create. How could she have done such a thing to Randolph? How could she have betrayed their love and marriage vows by sleeping with other men? It disgusted me. *She* disgusted me, for her actions were nothing more than those of a selfish woman thinking only of herself and what she wanted.

"Didn't Randolph find out?" I asked.

"He found out your mother was pregnant," she replied. "And that's what saved her from getting an abortion. You see, he thought you were his baby. So Laura Sue begged your grandmother to let her keep the child, go through with the pregnancy, and keep Randolph from knowing of her infidelity.

"Your grandmother didn't want no scandal, but she wasn't happy about keeping another man's child and calling that child a Cutler. She's too proud of her blood and no one *ever* gets the upper hand with her."

"But I was born. She let it happen," I said.

"Yeah, you was born, but right before you was, your grandmother decided she couldn't live with the lie in the hotel after all. I guess it was eating away at her seeing Laura Sue grow bigger and bigger with child, and seeing people fawn over her and talk about a new grandchild, while she knew that child wasn't truly her grandchild. Plus, your mother took every chance she could to gloat in front of your grandmother. That was her big mistake."

"What did she do?" I asked, my heart beginning to pound. I was afraid to breathe too loudly for fear Mrs. Dalton would stop or go off on another subject.

"She confronted Laura Sue. I was already working at the hotel, taking care of her in her last month and staying where I would stay in the nursery after you was born. So I was close by," she added, pulling herself up in the wheelchair and raising her eyebrows.

"You mean you overheard what was said?" I asked. I didn't want to say "eavesdropped." I could see she was sensitive about it.

"I would have found out most of it anyway. They needed me and had to tell."

"Needed you?" I was confused. "Why?"

"Your grandmother had come up with the plan. She rescinded her original agreement with your mother and told her she had to give up the baby. As long as she did that, your grandmother would keep her infidelity a secret, and she could continue to be Princess of Cutler's Cove."

"What did my mother say? There must have been a terrible argument." Despite my mother's illusion of illness, I suspected she could be quite strong-willed when she wanted. When it suited her advantage.

"No argument at all. Your mother was too self-centered and pampered. She was afraid to lose the good life, so she agreed to the ruse."

"Ruse? What ruse?"

"The plan, child. Sally Jean Longchamp had just given birth to a stillborn, as you know. Your grandmother went to her and to Ormand and made a deal with them—they were to abduct the newborn baby. She gave them jewelry and money to help them afford an escape.

"Sally Jean was upset about just losing a child, and here was Grandmother Cutler offering her another one, a child nobody seemed to want anyway. Laura Sue had agreed, and I think they were told that Randolph had too. I can't say for certain about that.

"Your grandmother worked it all out with them and promised to cover their escape well and send the police off in the wrong directions.

"Then she come to me," Mrs. Dalton said and looked down. "I couldn't disagree with her when she said Laura Sue would make a terrible mother. I could see how she was with Philip. She never had any time for him. Too busy lunching or shopping or sunning by the pool. And your grandmother was very upset about the child not being a true Cutler.

"Anyway, she offered me a full year's salary to cooperate. It was a lot of money for just turning my back, and since neither your grandmother nor your mother wanted the baby . . . well, I did as she asked and made myself scarce, went down to Mary Boston's room and waited while Ormand went in and abducted you.

"Mary knew what was happening. She had picked up a hint or two here and there, and then I told her the rest. She never liked your mother. Not many of the staff cared for her, because she was so spoiled and talked down to them.

"Anyway, Mary and I both felt sorry for Sally Jean Longchamp, who had just lost a child she wanted. We thought it was all a good idea. Nobody would be worse off for it.

"Apparently, Randolph still didn't know what was happening and what had happened, so your grandmother continued the ruse by offering a reward. There were times when we thought the police had located Ormand and Sally. Randolph went off to identify the suspects, but it was never them. The rest I guess you know.

"Except," she said, looking down at her hands in her lap, "it got so I regretted my part. No matter how bad a mother Laura Sue would have been and how much Ormand and Sally Jean wanted another child, it was still wrong. They were made into fugitives; you grew up believing you were their daughter, and poor Randolph appeared to be suffering something terrible thinking his newborn baby had been taken.

"I was tempted a few times to tell him the truth, but every time I set out to do that, I lost my courage. Mary kept saying it was for the best anyway. And my daughter . . . she was scared about what might happen if we crossed old Mrs. Cutler, and she and my son-in-law have had enough trouble just caring for me.

"Not long afterward, though, your mother had Clara, and they put that little tombstone in the cemetery to put your memory to rest forever."

"I know; I've seen it."

"I felt terrible about it. I went to look at it myself, and I knew God was watching me. Before long I began to get sick. I got sicker and sicker until you see me now.

"And now you've come back and I'm glad," she said with a sudden burst of energy and strength. "You're my redemption. I can make my peace with the Lord knowing I've told you the truth. I'm sorry, too. I can't right the wrong, but I can tell you I'm sorry I was any part of it.

"You're too young to know and appreciate what forgiveness means, child, but I sure hope someday you can find it in your heart to forgive ole, sick Lila Dalton," she said, smiling softly, hopefully.

"You're not the one who has to ask for forgiveness, Mrs. Dalton," I replied. "You thought you were doing the right thing at the time, even something that would be better for me.

"But," I added, my eyes burning, "Ormand Longchamp shouldn't be sitting in that jail and taking all the blame."

"No, I suppose not."

"Would you tell the truth now, if you were asked to?" I inquired hopefully. "Or are you still afraid of what might happen?"

"I'm too old and too sick to be afraid of anyone or anything anymore," she said. "I'd do what I had to do to make my peace with God."

"Thank you," I said, standing. "For telling me everything. I'm sorry you're so sick, and I hope it does make you feel better."

"That's sweet of you, child. Funny," she said, taking my hand and looking up at me, "you're the grandchild Mrs. Cutler would want the most, and you're the one she gave away."

16

Private Conversations

I returned to the hotel slowly, my head spinning, my whole life whirling by. Every few moments I would stop the wheel of fortune and read off something that now made sense—Momma's last words in the hospital, asking me not to hate her and Daddy, my grandmother's unhappiness at my return, my real mother's cowardice and nervous condition—all of it began to fall into place to create a picture that I didn't like, but that at least made sense.

Lunch had just ended at the hotel. Guests were meandering about the grounds, sitting on the front porch, enjoying the beautiful day. Younger guests were at the tennis courts, and many had gone to the pool. Across the way at the docks other guests were getting into and out of boats that took them for scenic coastal rides. There were smiles and laughter all around me. I was sure I stood out because of the clouds that hovered over me and cast dark shadows over my face.

But I couldn't help it. The bright sunshine, the warm ocean breezes, the happy peal of laughter coming from children, the excitement and energy of the tourists—all of it only pointed up my own sadness. Cutler's Cove was no place to be depressed, I thought, especially not today.

My grandmother was sitting in the lobby smiling and talking to guests. They laughed at something she said and then listened closely as she went on, their attention glued to her as if she were some celebrity. I saw the way other guests were drawn to her, eager to listen. She didn't see that I had entered, so I was able to look at her without her knowing it.

But suddenly she set eyes on me, and her expression frosted. I didn't turn away first. She did. Her smile returned as she continued to talk to her guests. I proceeded through the lobby. I had something to do before I would speak with her, someone else to speak with first.

Clara Sue was behind the front desk. Some of the teenage guests were standing there and talking to her. They all laughed, and then Clara Sue turned my way, her face full of curiosity and without any remorse.

But I didn't care about her right now. Right now she was insignificant to me. I ignored her and walked across the lobby. She made some snide remark about me, I'm sure, because a moment later she and her friends laughed even louder than they had been laughing. I didn't look back. I went to the old section and hurried through the corridor to the stairway.

There I paused, and then I walked up slowly, my eyes fixed ahead of me, my determination building with each step. All I could hear were Momma's last words to me in the hospital; all I could see was Daddy with his head bowed in defeat when the police had arrived.

What I was about to do I was to do for them.

I paused again at the door of my mother's suite, and then I walked in slowly and found her seated at her vanity table, brushing her golden hair and gazing admiringly at herself in the oval mirror. For a long moment she didn't realize I had entered. She was too entranced in her own image. Finally she realized I was standing there staring at her, and she spun around on her stool.

She was dressed in a light blue negligee, but as usual she had on earrings, a necklace, and bracelets. She had been making up her face and wore lipstick, rouge, and eyeliner.

"Oh, Dawn, you frightened me, sneaking in like that. Why didn't you knock? Even though I'm your mother, you've got to learn to knock," she said reproachfully. "Women my age need their privacy respected, Dawn honey," she added and put on her friendly smile that now looked more like a mask to me.

"Aren't you afraid Grandmother will hear you call me Dawn and not Eugenia?" I demanded. She looked more closely at me and saw the angry gleam in my eyes. It unnerved her quickly, and she put her brush down and turned around to get up to go to her bed.

"I'm not feeling too well this morning," she murmured as she crawled over her silk sheets. "I hope you don't have any new problems."

"Oh, no, Mother. All my problems are old ones," I announced, moving closer. She looked up at me curiously and then pulled her blanket over her body and fell back against her fluffy pillows.

"I'm so tired," she said. "It must be this new medication my doctor has prescribed. I'm going to have to have Randolph call him and tell him it's making me too tired. All I want to do is sleep, sleep, sleep. You'll have to leave and let me close my eyes."

"You weren't always like this, Mother, were you?" I asked sharply. She didn't say anything; she kept her eyes closed and her head on the pillow. "Were you, Mother? Didn't you used to be quite a lively young lady?" I asked, stepping up to the bed. She opened her eyes and blazed a wild look at me.

"What do you want? You're acting so strange. I don't have the strength. Go see your father if you have a problem. Please."

"Where shall I find my father?"

"What?"

"Where do I go to find him, my father?" I asked in a sweet, musical voice. "My *real* father."

She closed her eyes and lay back again.

"In his office, I'm sure. Or in his mother's office. You shouldn't have any problem locating him." She waved a hand dismissively.

"Really? I would have thought it would be very hard to find my father. Wouldn't I have to go running about from hotel to hotel, nightclub to nightclub, listening to entertainers?"

"What?" She opened her eyes again. "What are you talking about?"

"I'm talking about my real father . . . finally my *real* father. The one by the pool."

My remark had hit home. I savored the look of unease creeping into her face. For once I wasn't the one who had to answer about the past. I wasn't the one made to feel ashamed. She was.

She stared at me uncomprehendingly and then brought her hands to her bosom.

"You don't mean that Mr. Longchamp? You're not still calling him your father, are you?" I shook my head. "Well, what are you talking about? I can't take this." Her eyelids fluttered. "It's making me feel very faint."

"Don't pass out before you tell me the truth, Mother," I demanded. "I won't leave your side until you do anyway. That I promise."

"What truth? What are you babbling about? What have you been told now? Who have you been speaking to? Where's Randolph?" She gazed at the door as if he were right behind me.

"You don't want him here," I said. "Unless it's time he knew it all. How could you give me up?" I asked quickly. "How could you let someone take your baby?"

"Let . . . someone?"

I shook my head in disgust.

"Were you always this weak and self-centered? You let her force you to give me up. You made your bargain—"

"Who's been filling you with these lies?" she demanded with a surprising burst of energy.

"No one's been filling me with lies, Mother. I have just come from talking with Mrs. Dalton." Her angry scowl wilted. "Yes, Mrs. Dalton, who was my nurse, whom you said Grandmother blamed. You just wanted to shift the blame to someone else. If Grandmother blamed her, why did she give her a year's salary? And why was she rehired to care for Clara Sue?

"There's no sense trying to think of another lie to cover that one," I added quickly when I saw her start to speak. It was better to keep her on her toes. On the defense before she could gather her wits and retaliate with more lies. "Mrs. Dalton's very sick and wants to make her peace with God. She regrets her part in the scheme, and she is willing to tell the truth to anyone now.

"Why did you do it? How could you let anyone have your own child?"

"What did Mrs. Dalton tell you? She's sick; she must be babbling madness. Why did you even go to speak to that woman? Who sent you there?" my mother demanded.

"She's sick, but she's not babbling madness, and there are others here in the hotel who can support her story. I'm the one who is sick," I snapped. "I'm sick of lies, of living a life of lies.

"You lay here in bed pretending to be weak and tired and nervous just to hide yourself from the truth," I said. "Well, I don't care. Do what you want, but don't lie to me anymore. Don't pretend to love me and to have missed me and to pity me for having been taken away to live a poor, hard life. You sent me into that life. Didn't you? *Didn't you?*" I shouted. She winced and looked as if she would burst into tears. "*I want the truth!*" I screamed and pounded my thighs with my fists.

"Oh, God!" she cried and buried her face in her hands.

"Crying and pretending to be sick won't save you this time, Mother. You did a terrible thing, and I have a right to know the truth."

She shook her head.

"Tell me," I insisted. "I won't leave until you do."

Slowly she brought her hands away from her face. It was a changed face, and not just because tears had streaked her makeup and made her eyeliner run. There was a tired, defeated look in her eyes, and her lips trembled. She nodded slowly and slowly turned to me. She looked even younger, more like a little girl who had been caught doing something naughty.

"You mustn't think badly of me," she said in a tiny child's voice. "I didn't mean to do terrible things. I didn't." She pursed her lips and tilted her head as a five-year-old would.

"Just tell me what really happened, Mother. Please."

She glanced toward the doorway and leaned closer to me, her voice in a whisper.

"Randolph doesn't know," she said. "It would break his heart. He loves me very much, almost as much as he loves his mother, but he can't help that. He can't," she said, shaking her head.

"Then you did give me away?" I asked, a sick feeling in the pit of my stomach. Until this moment . . . this moment of truth . . . a secret part of me hadn't wanted to believe what I'd been told. "You *did* let Ormand and Sally Jean Longchamp have me?"

"I had to," she whispered. "She made me do it." She gazed out of the corners of her eyes at the doorway. She was like a little girl trying to shift the guilt onto another little girl. My anger subsided. There was something very pathetic and sad about her. "You musn't blame me, Dawn. *Please!*" she begged. "You mustn't. I didn't want to do it, honest, but she told me if I didn't, she would tell Randolph things about me and have me cast out a disgrace. Where would I go? What would I do? People would hate me. Everyone respects and fears her," she added angrily. "They would believe anything she said."

"So you did make love with another man and got pregnant with me?" I asked softly this time.

"Randolph was always so involved in the hotel. He's in love with the hotel," she complained. "You don't have any idea how hard it was for me in those days," she said, her face twisting. Tears filled her eyes. "I was young and beautiful and full of energy and wanted to do things, but Randolph was always so busy or his mother was always asking him to do this and do that, and if I wanted to go somewhere or do something, he always had to check with his mother. She ruled our lives like some queen.

"I wasn't going to just sit around all the time. *He never had time for me! Never!* It wasn't fair!" she shouted indignantly. "He didn't tell me it would be that way when he courted me. I was fooled. Yes," she said, nodding and liking her theory, "I was tricked, deceived. He was one kind of a man outside the hotel and another inside. Inside, he is what his mother wants him to be, no matter what I say or do.

"So I can't be blamed," she concluded. "It's all really his fault . . . her fault." The tears streaked down her face. "Don't you see? I'm not to blame."

"She told you you would have to give me up and you agreed," I concluded, as if I were a lawyer cross-examining a witness in a trial, but I did feel like it was a trial of sorts, with me acting as attorney for Ormand and Sally Jean Longchamp, as well as myself.

"I had to agree. What else could I do?"

"You could have said no. You could have fought for me and told her I was your child. You could have told her no, no, no!" I shouted wildly, but it was like trying to tell a four-year-old how to behave like an adult. My mother smiled through her tears, nodding.

"You're right. You're right. I was bad. So very bad! But everything's all right now. You're back. Everything's all right. Let's not talk about it anymore. Let's talk about good things, happy things. Please."

She patted me on the hand and took a deep breath, her expression changing as if all that we had been discussing was instantly forgotten and not very important anyway.

"I was thinking that you should have something done with your hair, and maybe we could go shopping for some nice new clothes for you. And new shoes and some jewelry. You don't have to wear all of Clara Sue's hand-me-downs. You can have your own things now.

"Would you like that?" she asked.

I shook my head. She really was a child. Perhaps she had always been like this and that was why my grandmother had her way with her easily.

"But I'm so tired right now," she said. "I'm sure it's this new medicine. I just want to close my eyes for a while." She dropped her head back to the pillow. "And rest and rest." She opened her eyes and looked up at me. "If you see your father, please tell him to call the doctor. I have to change my medicine."

I stared down at her. She did have the face of a little girl, a face to be pitied and pampered.

"Thank you, honey," she said and closed her eyes again.

I turned away. There was no point in screaming at her anymore or making any demands on her. In a way she was an invalid, not as sick as Mrs. Dalton, but just as shut away from reality. I started for the door.

"Dawn?" she called.

"Yes, Mother."

"I'm sorry," she said and then closed her eyes again.

"So am I, Mother," I replied. "So am I."

All my life, I thought as I descended the stairway, I have been carried along by events beyond my control. As an infant, as a child, and as a young girl, I was dependent upon adults and had to do whatever they wanted me to do or, as I had just learned, go along with whatever they wanted done with me. Their decisions, their actions, and their sins were the winds that blew me from one place to the next. Even those who really loved me could turn and go only to certain places. The same was true for Jimmy and certainly for Fern. Events that had been begun even before our births had already determined what and who we would be.

But now all the tragedy of the last few months rushed down over and around me: Momma's death, Daddy's being arrested, having what I thought was my family broken up, being spirited off in the night to this new family, Clara's continuous attempts to hurt me, Philip's raping me, Jimmy's escape and capture, and my learning the truth. I was like someone caught in the middle of a tornado and spun about. Now, like a flag that had suddenly snapped in a violent gust and pulled free of the hinges that held it, I spun on my heels and soared toward the hotel lobby, my head high, my eyes fixed ahead of me, not gazing left or right, not seeing anyone else, not hearing any voices.

My grandmother was still sitting on a settee in the lobby, the small audience of guests surrounding her and listening attentively to whatever she had to say. Their faces were filled with smiles of admiration. Whomever my grandmother singled out for a special word, a touch, beamed like someone blessed by a clergyman.

Something in my face drew the audience back in a wave, made them part and step away as I approached. Slowly, with her soft, angelic smile still firmly settled on her face, my grandmother turned to see what had stolen their attention from the glow of her eyes and the warmth of her voice. The instant she saw me, her shoulders stiffened and her smile retreated, bringing dark shadows to her face, which suddenly seemed more like a hard shell.

I stopped before her, my arms folded under my breasts. My heart was pounding, but I did not want her to see how nervous and frightened I was.

"I want to talk to you," I declared.

"It's impolite to interrupt people like this," she replied and started to turn back to her guests.

"I don't care what's impolite or polite. I want to talk to you right now," I insisted, filling my voice with as much firmness as I could. I did not shift my eyes from her, so she would see just how determined I was.

Suddenly she smiled.

"Well," she said to her admiring circle of guests, "I see we have a little family matter to tend to. Will everyone please excuse me for a few minutes?"

One of the gentlemen at her side moved quickly to help her get up.

"Thank you, Thomas." She glared at me. "Go to my office," she commanded. I glared back and then headed that way while she continued to make excuses for my behavior.

When I entered her office, I looked up at the portrait of my grandfather. He had such a warm, gentle smile. I wondered what it would have been like to know him. How had he put up with Grandmother Cutler?

The door burst open behind me as my grandmother came in like a storm. Her shoes snapped against the wooden floor as she pounded past me and then whipped herself around, her eyes burning in rage, her lips pencil-line thin.

"How dare you? How dare you behave in that manner while I was speaking with my guests? Not even my poorest workers, people who come from the most depressing and lowly backgrounds, act like that. Is there not even a shred of decency in your insolent body?" she ranted. It was as if I had stepped before a coal stove just when the door was open and confronted the raging fire and all its uncovered red heat. I closed my eyes and retreated a few steps, but then I opened them and spit my words back at her.

"You can't speak to me of decency anymore. You're a hypocrite!"

"How dare you? I'll have you shut up in your room; I'll—"

"You won't do anything, Grandmother, but tell the truth . . . finally," I ordered firmly. Her eyes widened in confusion. With a bit of glee I announced my surprise. "I went to see Mrs. Dalton this morning. She's very sick and was happy to finally lift the burden of guilt from her conscience. She told me what really happened after I was born and before."

"This is ridiculous. I won't stand here and—"

"Then I went to see my mother," I added, "and she confessed as well."

Grandmother stared at me a moment, her rage lowering slowly like the flame on a stove, and then she turned and went to her desk.

"Sit down," she ordered and took her own seat. I moved to the chair in front of her desk. For a long moment she and I simply stared at each other.

"What is it you have learned?" she asked in a far calmer tone of voice.

"What do you think? The truth. I found out about my mother's lover and how you forced her to eventually give me up. How you arranged for Ormand and Sally Jean Longchamp to take me and then pretended they had abducted me. How you paid people and got people to go along with your scheme. How you offered a reward just to cover up your actions," I said, all in one breath.

"Who is going to believe such a story?" she replied with such cold control it sent a chill of fear down my spine. She shook her head. "I know how sick Mrs. Dalton is. Did you know that her son-in-law works for the Cutler's Cove Sanitation Company and that I own the Cutler's Cove Sanitation Company? I could have him fired tomorrow just like that," she said, snapping her fingers.

"And if you and I go upstairs together, right now, and confront Laura Sue with this story, she will simply break down and cry and babble so incoherently no one would understand a word. Most likely with me standing beside you, she would not be able to remember anything she had told you." She gave me a look of triumph.

"But it's all true, isn't it?" I cried. I was losing that firmness, that confidence that had put a steel rod in my spine. She was so strong and so sure of herself, she could stand her ground and turn back a herd of wild horses, I thought.

She turned away from me and was quiet for a long moment. Then she looked back.

"You seem to be someone who thrives on controversy . . . harboring that boy here while the police were after him." She shook her head. "All right, I'll tell you. Yes, it's true. My son is not your real father. I begged Randolph not to marry that little tramp. I knew what she was and what she would become, but like all men, he was hypnotized by surface beauty and by her sweet-sounding, syrupy voice. Even my husband was charmed. I watched how she turned her shoulders and dazzled them with her silly little laugh and desperate helplessness," she said, twisting the side of her mouth up in disgust. "Men just love helpless women, only she wasn't as helpless as she pretended to be," she added with a cold smile on her lips. "Especially when it came to satisfying her desires.

"She always knew what she wanted. I didn't want that kind of a woman as part of my family, part of this . . . this hotel," she said, holding her arms out. "But arguing with men who are under a woman's spell is like trying to hold back a waterfall. If you remain under it too long, it will drown you.

"So I retreated, warned them, and then retreated." She nodded, the cold smile returning. "Oh, she pretended to want to be responsible and respectable, but whenever I gave her anything substantial to do, she would complain about the work and the effort, and Randolph would plead for her to be relieved of this or that.

" 'We have enough ornaments to hang on our walls and ceilings,' I told him. 'We don't need another.' But I might as well have directed all my words to the walls in this office.

"It wasn't long that she began to show her true nature—flirting with everything that wore pants. There was no stopping her! It was disgusting! I tried to tell my son, but he was as blind to that as to anything else. When a man is as dazzled by a woman as he was, it's the same as if he had looked directly at the sun. After that, he sees nothing.

"So I gave up and sure enough, as you have undoubtedly learned, she had an affair and got herself into trouble. I could have thrown the little tramp out then. I should have," she added bitterly, "but . . . I wanted to protect Randolph and the family and the hotel's reputation.

"What I did I did for the good of everyone and for the hotel and family, for they are one and the same."

"But Daddy . . . Ormand Longchamp . . ."

"He agreed to the arrangements," she said. "He knew what he was doing."

"But you told him everyone wanted it that way, didn't you? He thought he was doing what my mother and Randolph wanted, right? Isn't that true?" I pursued when she didn't respond.

"Randolph doesn't know what he wants; he never did. I always made the right decisions for him. Marrying her," she said, leaning over the desk, "is the only time he has ever gone against my wishes, and look how it turned out."

"But Ormand believed—"

"Yes, yes, so he thought; but I paid him handsomely and kept the police from finding him. It was his own fault he got caught. He should have stayed farther north and never come to Richmond."

"He doesn't belong in prison," I insisted. "It's not fair."

She turned away again, as though what I had to say was unimportant. But it wasn't!

"I don't care if you can force Mrs. Dalton to recant her story and if you can make my mother look so stupid no one will believe her; they'll believe me or at least it will create enough of a scandal to bring embarrassment. And I'll tell Randolph. Just think how hurt he will be to learn it. You let him go off chasing the hope he would recapture me. You offered that reward."

She studied me a moment. I held my gaze as firmly as I could, but it was like looking directly into the center of a campfire. Finally she softened, seeing my resolution.

"What is it you want? You want to embarrass me, rain down disgrace on the Cutlers?"

"I want you to get Daddy out of jail and stop treating me like dirt. Stop calling my mother a tramp, and stop demanding I be renamed Eugenia," I said determinedly.

I wanted a lot more, but I was afraid to make too many demands. In time I hoped I could get her to do something for Jimmy and for Fern.

She nodded slowly.

"All right." She sighed. "I'll do something about Ormand Longchamp. I'll make some calls to people I know in high places and see about getting him an early parole. I was thinking about doing that anyway. And if you insist on being called Dawn, you can be called Dawn.

"But," she added quickly when I began to smile, "you will have to do something for me."

"What? Do you want me to go back to living with him?"

"Of course not. You're here now and you're a Cutler whether you or I like it or not, but," she purred contentedly, quite pleased with herself, sitting back and contemplating me for a moment, "you don't have to be here all the time. I think it would be much better for all of us . . . Clara Sue, Philip, Randolph, even your . . . your *mother*, if you were away."

"Away? Where would I go?"

She nodded, a curious smile on her face. Obviously, she had thought of something very clever, something that pleased her very much.

"You have a very pretty singing voice. I think you should be permitted to develop your talent."

"What do you mean?" Why was she suddenly so eager to help me?

"I happen to be an honorary member of the board of trustees of a prestigious school for the performing arts in New York City."

"New York City!"

"Yes. I want you to go there instead of returning to Emerson

Peabody. I will make the arrangements today, and you can leave shortly. They have summer sessions, too.

"Of course, it goes without saying that all this and all you have learned will remain here in this office. No one need know anything more than I decided you are too talented to waste your time cleaning rooms in a hotel."

I could see she liked the idea that everyone would consider her as being magnanimous. She would look like a wonderful grandmother doing great things for her new granddaughter, and I would have to pretend to be grateful.

But I didn't want to return to Emerson Peabody, and I did want to become a singer. She would get her way and rid herself of me, but I would have an opportunity I could only dream of before. New York City! A school for performing arts!

And Daddy would be helped, too.

"All right," I agreed. "As long as you do everything you promised to do."

"I always live up to my word," she said angrily. "Your reputation, your name, your family's honor, are all important things. You come from a world where all those things were insignificant, but in my world—"

"Honor and honesty were always important to us," I snapped back. "We might have been poor, but we were decent people. And Ormand and Sally Jean Longchamp didn't betray each other and lie to each other," I retorted. My eyes burned with tears of indignation.

She gazed at me for a long moment again, only this time I thought I saw a look of approval in her eyes.

"It will be interesting," she finally said, speaking slowly, "very interesting to see what kind of a woman Laura Sue's liaison spawned. I don't like your manners, but you have shown some independence and some spunk, and those are qualities I do admire."

"I'm not sure, Grandmother," I replied, "if what you admire is ever going to be important to me."

She pulled herself back as if I had splashed her with ice-cold water, her eyes turning distant and hard again instantly.

"If that's all, I think you had better go. Thanks to you and your meddling, I have a lot to do. You'll be informed as to when you will be leaving," she added.

I stood up slowly.

"You think you can determine everyone's lives so easily, don't you?" I said bitterly, shaking my head.

"I do what I have to do. Responsibility for significant things requires me to make hard choices sometimes, but I do what is best for the family and the hotel. Someday, when you have something important to take care of and it requires you to make either unpleasant or unpopular choices, you will remember me and not judge me as harshly," she said, as if it were important to her that I have a better opinion of her.

Then she smiled.

"Believe me, when you need something or you get into trouble for one reason or another, you won't call on your mother or even my son. You'll call on me, and you will be happy that you can," she predicted.

What arrogance, I thought, and yet it was true—even from my short stay here I could see that she was responsible for Cutler's Cove being what it was.

I spun around quickly and walked out, unsure as to whether I had won or lost.

Later that afternoon Randolph came to see me. It had become more and more difficult to think of him as my father now, and this just when I had begun to adjust to the idea. From the look on his face I could see that my grandmother had told him of her decision to send me to a school for performing arts.

"Mother just told me about your decision to go to New York. How wonderful, although I must say, I will be sad to see you go off when you've really only just arrived," he complained. He did look somewhat upset by the idea, and I thought how sad it was that he didn't know the truth, that I as well as my mother and Grandmother Cutler kept him fooled. Was that fair? How fragile the happiness and peace was in this family, I thought. His devotion to my mother would surely dwindle to nothing if he knew she had been so unfaithful. In a sense everything was built on a lie, and I had to keep that lie alive.

"I've always wanted to go to New York and be a singer," I said.

"Of course you should go. I'm just teasing you. I'll miss you, but I'll come visit you often, and you'll be back for all the holidays. How exciting it's going to be for you. I've already told your mother, and she thinks it's a wonderful idea that you get formal training in the arts.

"She wants to take you shopping for new clothes, of course. I've already arranged for the hotel car to be at your disposal tomorrow morning so the two of you can go from shopping center to shopping center."

"She feels up to it?" I asked, hardly hiding my disdain.

"Oh, I've rarely seen her as chipper as she is now. As soon as I told her about the decision you and Mother made, she sat up and smiled and began to talk excitedly about the shopping. There are few things Laura Sue loves to do more than go shopping," he said, laughing. "And she always wants to go to New York. She will probably be up there visiting you every other weekend," he added.

"What about my work in the hotel tomorrow? I don't want it all to fall on Sissy's shoulders."

"That's all over. No more chambermaid work for you. Just enjoy the hotel and the family until you have to leave for school," he said. "And don't worry about Sissy. We'll assign someone else to help her and hire someone new quickly."

He tilted his head and smiled. "You don't look as happy about it all as I expected. Is something wrong? I know the situation with the Longchamp boy was not pleasant, and I understand why you were so upset, but you shouldn't have let him hide out here." He slapped his hands together as if he could bust the unpleasant memory by clapping. "But it's over. Let's not worry about it anymore."

"I can't help worrying about Jimmy," I said quickly. "He was just trying to get away from a horrible foster family. I tried to tell you, but no one would listen."

"Um . . . well, at least we know the little girl is doing fine."

"You found out about Fern?" I sat up quickly.

"Not much. They don't like giving out that information, but a friend of your grandmother's knew someone who knew someone. Anyway, Fern was taken by a young, childless couple. Their whereabouts are a mystery to us, but we're still looking."

"But what if Daddy wants her back?" I cried.

"Daddy? Oh, Ormand Longchamp? Under the circumstances, I don't think he will be able to get her back when he is released from prison. That will be some time yet anyway," he added. Obviously, Grandmother Cutler had not told him her part of our bargain. There was no way she could without revealing why she would do such a thing.

"Anyway," he continued, "I wanted to stop by to tell you how happy I was for you. I've got to get back to my office. See you at dinner." He knelt down to kiss me on the forehead. "You will probably become the most famous Cutler of all," he said and left.

I lay back against my pillow. How fast it was all happening now. Fern was with a new family. Perhaps she had already learned to call the man Daddy and the woman Momma. Perhaps her memories of

Jimmy and me were already fading. A new home, fine clothing, plenty to eat, and good care would surely erase her earlier life and make it all seem like some vague dream.

I was sure that in a matter of days, Grandmother Cutler would have me carried off to a new life, a life away from her and Cutler's Cove. My great consolation was that I would be in the world of music, and whenever I entered that world, all hardship and misery, all unhappiness and sadness fell away. I made up my mind I would put all my energy and concentration into one thing—becoming a good singer.

That evening I was permitted to sit with my family in the dining room for dinner. The news about my leaving for a performing arts school spread quickly throughout the hotel. Staff members who had previously resented me wished me luck. Even some guests had heard and had something nice to say. My mother made one of her miraculous recoveries. In fact, I had never seen her look more radiantly beautiful. Her hair had a sheen, her eyes were bright and young; she laughed and spoke with more animation than she had ever before demonstrated. To her everything was delicious, people were delightful; it was the most wonderful summer in ages. She rattled on and on about our upcoming shopping spree.

"I have some friends who live in Manhattan," she said, "and first thing in the morning I'm calling them to find out what is in style these days. We don't want you going off and looking like the farmer's daughter," she said and laughed. Randolph found her laughter contagious and was livelier and more charming than ever, too.

Only Clara Sue sat with a dark, dejected look on her face. She glared at me enviously, her emotions confused. She was getting rid of me, which I knew made her happy because once again she would be the little princess and wouldn't have to share the limelight with me in any way; but I was going off to do something very exciting, and I was being pampered, not her.

"I need some new things, too," she complained when she was able to get a word in.

"But you have so much more time, Clara Sue, honey," Mother said. "We'll go shopping for your things closer to the end of the summer. Eugenia is going to New York in a few days. New York!"

"Dawn," I corrected. My mother glanced at me and then at Grandmother Cutler. She saw there was no reprimand pending. "My name is Dawn," I repeated softly.

Mother laughed.

"Of course, if you like and everyone agrees," she said, eyeing Grandmother Cutler again.

"It's what she's used to," Grandmother Cutler said. "If she wants to change her name some time in the future, she can."

Clara Sue looked surprised and upset at the same time. I smiled at her, and she looked away quickly.

Grandmother Cutler and I exchanged a knowing glance. We exchanged a few that evening. Now that our major confrontation was over, I found her acting different toward me, just as she had promised. When some guests stopped by and asked about my singing, she claimed there was an uncle in our family who used to sing and play a violin.

As I gazed around the table, I realized everyone was happy I was leaving, but for different reasons. Grandmother Cutler never wanted me; my mother found me a threat and an embarrassment now; Randolph was sincerely happy for me and my new opportunity; and Clara Sue was happy she was losing her competition for the family's attention. Only Philip, working his waiter's job, cast confused glances in my direction.

After dinner and after I had sat in the lobby with my mother listening to her chat with guests for a while, I excused myself, claiming I was tired. I wanted to write another letter to Daddy describing all that I had learned. I wanted him to know that I didn't blame him for what had been done and that I understood why he and Momma had done it.

But when I opened the door to my room, I found Philip waiting for me. He was lying on my bed, his hands behind his head, looking up at the ceiling. He sat up quickly.

"What are you doing in here?" I demanded. "Get out. *Now!*"

"I wanted to speak to you. Don't worry, I just want to talk," he said, holding his hands up.

"What is it you want, Philip? Don't expect me to forgive you for what you did," I snapped. "I'll never forget what you did to me."

"You told Grandmother something, didn't you? That's why she arranged for you to go to New York so quickly. I'm right, aren't I?" I simply stared at him, not walking in any farther, finding it impossible to be in the same room alone with him after what he had done to me.

"Well, did you?" he asked fearfully.

"No, Philip, I didn't, but I think it's true when people say Grandmother Cutler has eyes and ears all over this hotel." That ought to put a scare in him. "Now leave," I ordered, still standing in the doorway and holding the door open. "The sight of you makes me sick."

"Well, why would she do it? Why would she send you off like this?"

"Haven't you heard? She thinks I'm talented," I said dryly. "I thought you did, too."

"I do, but . . . it all seems so strange . . . right at the beginning of the summer season, just when you've been returned to the family, she sends you off to a special arts school?" He shook his head and narrowed his eyes suspiciously. "There's something going on, something you're not telling me. Does it have to do with Jimmy's being found here, then?"

"Yes," I said quickly, but he didn't look satisfied.

"I don't believe you."

"Too bad. I don't care what you believe or what you think. I'm tired, Philip, and I have a lot to do tomorrow. Please, leave." He didn't move. "Haven't you done enough to me?" I cried. "Just leave me alone."

"Dawn, you must understand what came over me before— sometimes a boy my age loses control. It happens especially when a girl leads him along and then pulls back," he said. I thought his attempt at a justification was pathetic.

"I never led you on, Philip, and I would have expected you to understand why I pulled back." I glared hatefully at him. "Don't you dare place the blame on me. You, and only you, are responsible for your actions."

"You're really mad at me, aren't you?" he asked, the smile on his face turning coy. "You're real pretty when you're angry," he said.

I stared at him in disbelief and recalled the excitement I had felt when we had first met at Emerson Peabody. How different things were then. It was like we were two completely different people. In a real way I suppose we were, I thought. We could never go back to the way things had once been . . . when I had believed in fairy tales and happy endings.

"You mustn't hate me," he said, pretending to plead for understanding. "You *mustn't!*" he insisted.

"I don't hate you, Philip." He smiled. "But I feel sorry for you," I added quickly, wiping the smile off his face. "You can never change what happened between us, and you can never change the way I feel about you. Whatever feelings I had for you died the night you raped me."

"I wasn't lying to you," he protested. "Dawn, I love you. With all my heart and soul. I can't help the way I feel about you."

"Well, you'll just have to! You've got to help it, Philip. I'm your sister. Do you understand? Your *sister!* You've got to get over it. *You* can't love me! I'm sure you won't have trouble finding a new girlfriend."

"I suppose not," he said arrogantly, "but that doesn't mean I won't be thinking about you. I don't want a new girlfriend, Dawn. I want *you*. Only you. Why don't we spend one last night together . . . just talking," he suggested and lay back on my pillow. "For old time's sake."

I couldn't believe him! How could he make such a suggestion? After everything I had just said, Philip still wanted to . . . The thought sickened me. *Philip* sickened me. I could no longer stand to look at him. Just as Clara Sue and I would never have a sibling relationship, neither would Philip and I. I had to get him out of my sight. Before I said something I regretted. Before I did something I regretted. I pretended to hear something in the hallway.

"Someone's coming, Philip. It might be Grandmother. She said she wanted to speak with me later."

"Huh?" He sat up quickly and listened. "I don't hear anyone."

"Philip," I said, looking worried. He got up quickly and came to the door.

"I don't hear anybody," he said. I pushed past him and shoved him out, closing the door and locking it quickly.

"Hey!" he cried. "That's sneaky."

"Sneakiness runs in this family," I said. "Now go away."

"Dawn, come on. I want to make it all up to you, show you I can be warm and loving without attacking you. Dawn? I'll stay here all night. I'll sleep at your door," he threatened.

I ignored him, and after a while he got disgusted and left. I was finally alone with my own thoughts. I pulled the chair up to the little table, took out a pen and paper, and began.

Dear Daddy,

No matter what has happened, I realize I will always call you Daddy. I realize I am writing to you before you even had a chance to respond to my first letter, but I wanted you to know I have learned the truth. I have spoken with the woman who had been my nurse, Mrs. Dalton, and after that I confronted my mother and she confessed.

I then demanded a meeting with Grandmother Cutler and learned it all firsthand. I want you to know that I don't blame you or Momma for anything, and I know that once Jimmy learns the facts, he will feel the same way I do.

They are sending me off to a school for performing arts in New York City. Grandmother Cutler mostly wants to get rid of me, but it's what I always wanted to do, and I think it's best I get away from here anyway.

We still don't know where Fern is, but I hope that someday she will be back with you . . . her real father. I don't know what has become of Jimmy yet, but he ran away from one bad family and was found here and taken back. Perhaps you and he will be together again very soon. Grandmother Cutler has promised to do what she can to get you an early parole.

You always said that I brought you sunshine and happiness. I hope this letter brings some to you during what must be your darkest days. I want you to know that whenever I do sing, I will be thinking of you and your smile and all the love you and Momma gave me.

Love,
Dawn

I sealed the letter with a kiss and put it in an envelope. In the morning I would have it mailed.

I really was very, very tired. Moments after my head touched the pillow and my eyes were closed, I began to drift toward a much welcomed sleep. The sounds of the hotel died away quickly. My short but dramatic life here was coming to an end.

I'm still being whisked away, I thought. I'm not in Daddy's car, and I'm not leaving in the middle of the night, but I'm on the road again, searching, always searching, for a place to call home.

EPILOGUE

Whether it was out of a sense of guilt or merely the excitement of buying clothes, my mother took me off in the hotel limousine and dragged me from store to store. Price was never an object. She bought me more clothing than I had seen in a lifetime: skirts, blouses, jackets, a leather coat and leather gloves, a fur hat, shoes, lingerie, and velvet slippers. We went to a department store to buy makeup, and there she bought me an assortment of powders, lipsticks, blush rouge, and eyeliner. It took two bellhops four trips to bring all our purchases into the hotel.

Clara Sue's eyes nearly popped out of her head when she saw it all. She cried and moaned and demanded Mother go on a similar shopping spree with her.

The day before I was to leave for New York, one of the bellhops came down to my room to fetch me.

"There's a phone call for you at the main desk," he said. "They said to hurry; it's long distance."

I thanked him and rushed out. I was lucky it was early in the morning and Clara Sue was not on duty, I thought. She would have never permitted the call to go through, because it was Jimmy.

"Where are you?" I cried.

"I'm with a new foster family, the Allans, and I'm back in Richmond, but it's all right. I'm going to go to a regular public school,'' Jimmy added quickly.

"Oh, Jimmy, I have so much to tell you I don't know where to begin.''

He laughed.

"Just start at the beginning,'' he said, and I told him all that I had learned, described my meeting with Grandmother Cutler, and explained what had resulted.

"So you see, Jimmy, you shouldn't blame Daddy. He thought he was doing the right thing,'' I said.

"Yeah,'' he said, "I suppose, but it was still dumb,'' he added, only not sounding as hard as he could.

"Will you talk to him when he contacts you, Jimmy?'' I asked, my voice full of hope.

"Let's see if he ever will,'' he replied. "I'm glad Fern was adopted by a young couple. They'll give her lots of love, but I can't wait till we find her again,'' he said. "And I'm glad about your going to a school for performing arts, even though it means I probably won't see you for a long time. But I'll try.''

"I'll try to see you, too, Jimmy.''

"I miss you,'' he said.

"I miss you, too,'' I said, my voice cracking.

"Well, I'd better hang up. They were nice enough to let me make this call. Good luck, Dawn.''

"Jimmy!'' I cried, realizing he was about to hang up.

"What?''

"I know I can think of you differently,'' I blurted. He understood.

"I'm glad, Dawn. It's the same with me.''

"Bye,'' I said. I didn't realize I was crying until a tear dropped from my cheek.

On the morning of my departure the chambermaid staff presented me with a going-away present. Sissy gave it to me in the lobby by the front door as the bellhops were loading my suitcases into the hotel limousine.

"Some people are sorry for the cold way you were treated,'' she said and handed me a tiny package. I unwrapped it and discovered a solid gold mop-and-pail pin.

"We didn't want'cha to forget us,'' Sissy said. I laughed and hugged her.

Grandmother Cutler stood off to the side during all this, watching with her eagle eyes. I could see that she was impressed with the affection the hotel staff had for me.

Clara Sue stood sullenly in the doorway, Philip at her side, a slight smirk on his face.

I hurried down the steps without a farewell glance to either of them. My mother and Randolph were waiting at the limousine. Mother looked fresh and rested. She hugged me and kissed my forehead. I was surprised at how affectionate she was. Was it just for the audience of guests and staff, or had she come to feel something for me?

I looked into her soft eyes, but I couldn't be sure. It was all too confusing.

"Okay, Dawn," Randolph said. "We'll be up to see you as soon as we can get away from the hotel." He kissed me on the cheek. "If you need anything, just call."

"Thank you," I said. The limousine driver opened the door for me and I got in. I sat back and thought how different this was from my arrival in the night in a police patrol car.

We began to pull away from the hotel. I looked back and waved at everyone and saw Grandmother Cutler step out to gaze after me. She looked different, thoughtful. What a strange woman, I thought, and wondered if I would ever get to know her.

Then I turned to look out at the ocean as we came down the driveway. The sun had turned the water into a bright aqua. The little sailboats looked painted against the blue horizon. It was beautiful here, picture perfect, I thought. My heart was full. I was off to do something I had always dreamt of doing, Jimmy sounded happier, and Daddy would soon be freed from prison.

The hotel limousine turned, and we were off toward the airport.

I couldn't help but remember the games Daddy and I used to play when I was very little and we were in the car and off to a new home.

"Come on, Dawn," he would say. "Let's pretend. Where do you want to be this time? Alaska? The desert? On a ship? In an airplane?"

"Oh, let her sleep, Ormand. It's late," Momma would say.

"You tired, Dawn?"

"No, Daddy," I would say, even though I could barely keep my eyes open.

Jimmy was asleep on his side of the car.

"So? Where shall it be this time?" Daddy asked again.

"I think . . . an airplane," I said. "Soaring above the clouds."

"And so it will be. Feel the lift-off," he said and laughed.

A short while later I really was soaring above the clouds.

Sometimes, when we dream hard enough, those dreams come true, I thought.

And I looked ahead toward the long stretch of blue sky and dreamt of thousands of people in an audience listening to me sing.

Ruby

PROLOGUE

During the first fifteen years of my life, my birth and the events surrounding it were a mystery; as much a mystery as the number of stars that shone in the night sky over the bayou or where the silvery catfish hid on days when Grandpere couldn't catch one to save his life. I knew my mother only from the stories Grandmere Catherine and Grandpere Jack told me and from the few faded sepia photographs of her that we had in pewter frames. It seemed that for as long as I could remember, I always felt remorseful when I stood at her grave and gazed at the simple tombstone that read:

GABRIELLE LANDRY
BORN MAY 1, 1927
DIED OCTOBER 27, 1947

for my birth date and the date of her death were one and the same. Every day and every night, I carried in my secret heart the ache of guilt when my birthday came around, despite the great effort Grandmere went through to make it a happy day. I knew it was as hard for her to be joyful as it was for me.

But over and above my mother's sad, sad death when I was born, there were dark questions I could never ask, even if I knew how, because I'd be much too scared it would make my grandmother's face, usually so loving, take on that closed, hooded look I dreaded. Some days she sat silently in her rocker and stared at me for what seemed like hours. Whatever the answers were, the truth had torn my grandparents to pieces; it had sent Grandpere Jack into the swamp to live alone in his shack. And from that day forward, Grandmere Catherine could not think of him without great anger flashing from her eyes and sorrow burning in her heart.

The unknown lingered over our house in the bayou; it hung in the spiderwebs that turned the swamps into a jeweled world on moonlit nights; it was draped over the cypress trees like the Spanish moss that dangled over their branches. I heard it in the whispering warm summer breezes and in the water lapping against the clay. I even felt it in the piercing glance of the marsh hawk, whose yellow-circled eyes followed my every move.

I hid from the answers just as much as I longed to know them. Words that carried enough weight and power to keep two people apart who should love and cherish each other could only fill me with fear.

I would sit by my window and stare into the darkness of the swamp on a warm, spring night, letting the breeze that swept in over the swamps from the Gulf of Mexico cool my face; and I would listen to the owl.

But instead of his unearthly cry of "Who, Who, Who," I would hear him call "Why, Why, Why" and I would embrace myself more tightly to keep the trembling from reaching my pounding heart.

BOOK ONE

1

---\~\~---

Grandmere's Powers

A loud and desperate rapping on our screen door echoed through the house and drew both my and Grandmere Catherine's attention from our work. That night we were upstairs in the *grenier*, the loom room, weaving the cotton jaune into blankets we would sell at the stand in front of our house on weekends when the tourists came to the bayou. I held my breath. The knocking came again, louder and more frantic.

"Go down and see who's there, Ruby," Grandmere Catherine whispered loudly. "Quickly. And if it's your Grandpere Jack soaked in that swamp whiskey again, shut the door as fast as you can," she added, but something in the way her dark eyes widened said she knew this was someone else and something far more frightening and unpleasant.

A strong breeze had kicked up behind the thick layers of dark clouds that enclosed us like a shroud, hiding the quarter moon and stars in the April Louisiana sky. This year spring had been more like summer. The days and nights were so hot and humid I found mildew on my shoes in the morning. At noon the sun made the goldenrod glisten and drove the gnats and flies into a frenzy to find cool shade. On clear nights I could see where the swamp's Golden Lady spiders had come out to erect their giant nets for their nightly catch of beetles and mosquitos. We had stretched fabric over our windows that kept out the insects but let in whatever cool breeze came up from the Gulf.

I hurried down the stairs and through the narrow hallway that ran straight from the rear of the house to the front. The sight of Theresa Rodrigues's face with her nose against the screen stopped me in my tracks and turned my feet to lead. She looked as white as a water lily, her coffee black hair wild and her eyes full of terror.

"Where's your grandmere?" she cried frantically.

I called out to my grandmother and then stepped up to the door. Theresa was a short, stout girl three years older than I. At eighteen, she was the oldest of five children. I knew her mother was about to have another. "What's wrong, Theresa?" I asked, joining her on the galerie. "Is it your mother?"

Immediately, she burst into tears, her heavy bosom heaving and falling with the sobs, her face in her hands. I looked back into the house in time to see Grandmere Catherine come down the stairs, take one look at Theresa, and cross herself.

"Speak quickly, child," Grandmere Catherine demanded, rushing up to the door.

"My mama . . . gave birth . . . to a dead baby," Theresa wailed.

"*Mon Dieu,*" Grandmere Catherine said, and crossed herself once more. "I felt it," she muttered, her eyes turned to me. I recalled the moments during our weaving when she had raised her gaze and had seemed to listen to the sounds of the night. The cry of a raccoon had sounded like the cry of a baby.

"My father sent me to fetch you," Theresa moaned through her tears. Grandmere Catherine nodded and squeezed Theresa's hand reassuringly.

"I'm coming right away."

"Thank you, Mrs. Landry. Thank you," Theresa said, and shot off the porch and into the night, leaving me confused and frightened. Grandmere Catherine was already gathering her things and filling a split-oak basket. Quickly, I went back inside.

"What does Mr. Rodrigues want, Grandmere? What can you do for them now?"

When Grandmere was summoned at night, it usually meant someone was very sick or in pain. No matter what it was, my stomach would tingle as if I had swallowed a dozen flies that buzzed around and around inside.

"Get the butane lantern," she ordered instead of answering. I hurried to do so. Unlike the frantic Theresa Rodrigues whose terror had lit her way through the darkness, we would need the lantern to go from the front porch and over the marsh grass to the inky black gravel highway. To Grandmere the overcast night sky carried an ominous meaning, especially tonight. As soon as we stepped out and she looked up, she shook her head and muttered, "Not a good sign."

Behind us and beside us, the swamp seemed to come alive with her dark words. Frogs croaked, night birds cawed, and gators slithered over the cool mud.

At fifteen I was already two inches taller than Grandmere Catherine who was barely five-feet-four in her moccasins. Diminutive in size, she was still the strongest woman I knew, for besides her wisdom and her grit, she carried the powers of a *Traiteur*, a treater; she was a spiritual healer, someone unafraid to do battle with evil, no matter how dark or insidious that evil was. Grandmere always seemed to have a solution, always seemed to reach back in her bag of cure-alls and rituals and manage to find the proper course of action. It was something unwritten, something handed down to her, and whatever was not handed down, she magically knew herself.

Grandmere was left-handed, which to all of us Cajuns meant she could have spiritual powers. But I thought her power came from her dark onyx eyes. She was never afraid of anything. Legend had it that one night in the swamp she had come face-to-face with the Grim Reaper himself and she'd stared down Death's gaze until he realized she was no one to tangle with just yet.

People in the bayou came to her to cure their warts and their rheumatism. She had her secret medicines for colds and coughs and was said even to know a way to prevent aging, although she never used it because it would be against the natural order of things. Nature was sacred to Grandmere Catherine. She extracted all of her remedies from the plants and herbs, the trees and animals that lived near or in the swamps.

"Why are we going to the Rodrigues house, Grandmere? Isn't it too late?"

"*Couchemal*," she muttered, and mumbled a prayer under her breath. The way she prayed made my spine tingle and, despite the humidity, gave me a chill. I clenched my teeth together as hard as I could, hoping they wouldn't chatter. I was determined to be as fearless as Grandmere, and most of the time I succeeded.

"I guess that you are old enough for me to tell you," she said so quietly I had to strain to hear. "A couchemal is an evil spirit that lurks about when an unbaptized baby dies. If we don't drive it away, it will haunt the family and bring them bad luck," she said. "They should have called me as soon as Mrs. Rodrigues started her birthing. Especially on a night like this," she added darkly.

In front of us, the glow of the butane lantern made the shadows dance and wiggle to what Grandpere Jack called "The Song of the Swamp," a song not only made up of animal sounds, but also the peculiar low whistle that sometimes emerged from the twisted limbs and dangling Spanish moss we Cajuns called Spanish Beard when a breeze traveled through. I tried to stay as close to Grandmere as I could without knocking into her and my feet were moving as quickly as they could to keep up. Grandmere was so fixed on our destination, and on the astonishing task before us that she looked like she could walk through the pitch darkness.

In her split-oak basket, Grandmere carried a half-dozen small totems of the Virgin Mary, as well as a bottle of holy water and some assorted herbs and plants. The prayers and incantations she carried in her head.

"Grandmere," I began. I needed to hear the sound of my own voice. "*Qu'est-ce—*"

"English," she corrected quickly. "Speak only in English." Grandmere always insisted we speak English, especially when we left the house, even though our Cajun language was French. "Someday you will leave this bayou," she predicted, "and you will live in a world that maybe looks down on our Cajun language and ways."

"Why would I leave the bayou, Grandmere?" I asked her. "And why would I stay with people who looked down on us?"

"You just will," she replied in her usual cryptic manner. "You just will."

"Grandmere," I began again, "why would a spirit haunt the Rodrigueses anyway? What have they done?"

"They've done nothing. The baby was born dead. It came in the body of the infant, but the spirit was unbaptized and has no place to go, so it will haunt them and bring them bad luck."

I looked back. Night fell like a leaden curtain behind us, pushing us forward. When we made the turn, I was happy to see the lighted windows of the Butes, our closest neighbor. The sight of it allowed me to pretend that everything was normal.

"Have you done this many times before, Grandmere?" I knew my grandmother was called to perform many rituals, from blessing a new house to bringing luck to a shrimp or oyster fisherman. Mothers of young brides unable to bear children called her to do whatever she could to make them fertile. More often than not, they became pregnant. I knew of all these things, but until tonight I had never heard of a couchemal.

"Unfortunately, many times," she replied. "As did Traiteurs before me as far back as our days in the old country."

"And did you always succeed in chasing away the evil spirit?"

"Always," she replied with a tone of such confidence that I suddenly felt safe.

Grandmere Catherine and I lived alone in our toothpick-legged house with its tin roof and recessed galerie. We lived in Houma, Louisiana, which was in Terrebonne Parish. Folks said the parish was only two hours away from New Orleans by car, but I didn't know if that was true since I had never been to New Orleans. I had never left the bayou.

Grandpere Jack had built our house himself more than thirty years ago when he and Grandmere Catherine had first been married. Like most Cajun homes, our house was set on posts to keep us above the crawling animals and give us some protection from the floods and dampness. Its walls were built out of cypress wood and its roof out of corrugated metal. Whenever it rained, the drops would tap our house like a drum. The rare stranger to come to our house was sometimes bothered by it, but we were as accustomed to the drumming as we were to the shrieks of the marsh hawks.

"Where does the spirit go when we drive it away?" I asked.

"Back to limbo where it can do good God-fearing folks no harm," she replied.

We Cajuns, who were descendants of the Arcadians driven from Canada in the mid-1700s, believed in a spirituality that commingled Catholicism with pre-Christian folklore. We went to church and prayed to saints like Saint Medad, but we clung to our superstitions and age-old beliefs as firmly. Some, like Grandpere Jack, clung to them more. He was often involved in some activity to ward off bad luck and had an assortment of talismans like alligator teeth and dried deer ears to wear around his neck or carry on his belt at times. Grandmere said no man in the bayou needed them more than he did.

The gravel road stretched and turned ahead, but at the pace we were keeping, the Rodrigueses' cypress wood house now bleached a gray-white patina, soon loomed before us. We heard the wailing coming from within and saw Mr. Rodrigues on the front galerie holding Theresa's four-year-old brother in his arms. He sat in a split-oak rocking chair and stared into the night as though he had already seen the evil spirit. It chilled me even more, but I moved forward as quickly as Grandmere Catherine did. The moment he set eyes on her, his expression of sorrow and fear turned to one of hope. It felt good to see how much Grandmere was respected.

"Thanks for comin' so fast, Mrs. Landry. Thanks for comin'," he said, and rose quickly. "Theresa," he cried, and Theresa emerged from the house to take her little brother from him. He opened the door for my grandmother, and after I set the lantern down, I followed her inside.

Grandmere Catherine had been to the Rodrigueses' house before and went directly to Mrs. Rodrigues's bedroom. She lay there, her eyes closed, her face ashen, her black hair spread out over the pillow. Grandmere took her hand and Mrs. Rodrigues looked up weakly. Grandmere Catherine fixed her gaze on Mrs. Rodrigues and stared hard as though searching for a sign. Mrs. Rodrigues struggled to raise herself.

"Rest, Delores," Grandmere Catherine said. "I am here to help."

"Yes," Mrs. Rodrigues said in a loud whisper. She clutched Grandmere's wrist. "I felt it, Catherine. I felt its heartbeat start and stop and then I felt the couchemal slip away. I felt it. . . ."

"Rest, Delores. I will do what has to be done," Grandmere Catherine promised. She patted her hand and turned to me. She nodded slightly and I followed her out to the galerie, where Theresa and the other Rodrigues children waited wide-eyed.

Grandmere Catherine reached into her split-oak basket and plucked out one of her bottles of holy water. She opened it carefully and turned to me.

"Take the lantern and lead me around the house," she said. "Every cistern, every pot with water in it, needs a drop or two of the holy water, Ruby. Make sure we don't miss a one," she warned. I nodded, my legs trembling, and we began our foray.

In the darkness, an owl hooted, but when we turned the corner of the house, I heard something slither through the grass. My heart was thumping so hard, I thought I'd drop the lantern. Would the evil spirit do something to try to stop us? As if to answer my question, something cool and wet slipped past me in the darkness and just grazed my left cheek. I gasped aloud. Grandmere Catherine turned to reassure me.

"The spirit is hiding in a cistern or a pot. It has to hide in water. Don't be afraid," she coached, and then stopped by a cistern used to gather rainwater from the roof of the Rodrigueses' house. She opened her bottle and tipped it so as to spill only a drop or two into it and then closed her eyes and mumbled a prayer. We did the same thing at every barrel and every pot until we circled the house and returned to the front where Mr. Rodrigues, Theresa, and the other two children waited in anticipation.

"I'm sorry, Mrs. Landry," Mr. Rodrigues said, "but Theresa's just told me the children have an old gumbo pot out back. It's surely got some rainwater in it from the downpour late this afternoon."

"Show me," Grandmere ordered Theresa, who nodded and led the way. She was so nervous, she couldn't find it at first.

"We've got to find it," Grandmere Catherine warned. Theresa began to cry.

"Take your time, Theresa," I told her, and squeezed her arm gently to reassure her. She sucked in a deep breath and nodded. Then she bit down on her lower lip and concentrated until she remembered the exact location and took us to it. Grandmere knelt down and dropped the holy water in, whispering her prayer as she did so.

Perhaps it was my overworked imagination; perhaps not, but I thought I saw something pale gray, something that resembled a baby, fly up and away. I smothered a cry, afraid I would frighten Theresa even more. Grandmere Catherine stood up and we returned to the house to offer our final condolences. She set a totem of the Virgin Mary at the front door and told Mr. Rodrigues to be sure it remained there for forty days and forty nights. She gave him another one and told him to put it at the foot of his and his wife's bed and leave it there just as long. Then we started back to our own home.

"Do you think you chased it off, Grandmere?" I asked when we were sufficiently away from the house and none of the Rodrigues family would hear.

"Yes," she said. Then she turned to me and added, "I wish I had the power to chase away the evil spirit that dwells in your grandpere as easily. If I thought it would do any good, I'd bathe him in holy water. Goodness knows, he could use the washing anyway."

I smiled, but my eyes soon filled with tears as well. For as long as I could remember, Grandpere Jack had lived apart from us, lived in his trapper's shack in the swamp. Most of the time, Grandmere Catherine had only bad things to say about him and refused to set eyes on him whenever he did come around, but sometimes, her voice got softer, her eyes warmer, and she would wish he would do this or that to help himself or change his ways. She didn't like me to go poling a pirogue through the swamps to visit him.

"God forbid you turn over that flimsy canoe or fall out. He'd probably be too soaked with whiskey to hear your cries for help and then there are the snakes and gators to contend with, Ruby. He ain't worth the effort of the journey," she'd mutter, but she never stopped me and even though she pretended not to care or want to know about him, I noticed she always managed to listen when I described one of my visits to Grandpere.

How many nights had I sat by my window and looked up at the moon peeking between two clouds and wished and prayed that somehow we could be a family. I had no mother and no father, but only Grandmere Catherine who had been and still was a mother to me. Grandmere always said Grandpere could barely care for himself, much less substitute as a father for me. Still, I dreamed. If they were together again . . . if we were all together in our house, we would be like a normal family. Perhaps then, Grandpere Jack wouldn't drink and gamble. All of my friends at school had regular families, with brothers and sisters and two parents to come home to and love.

But my mother lay buried in the cemetery a half mile away and my father . . . my father was a blank face with no name, a stranger who had come passing through the bayou and met my mother at a *fais dodo*, a Cajun dance. According to Grandmere Catherine, the love they made so wildly and carefree that night resulted in my birth. What hurt me beside my mother's tragic death was the realization that somewhere out there lived a man who never knew he had a daughter, had me. We would never set eyes on each other, never exchange a word. We wouldn't even see each other's shadows or silhouettes like two fishing boats passing in the night.

When I was a little girl I invented a game: the Daddy Game. I would study myself in the mirror and then try to imagine my facial characteristics on a man. I would sit at my drawing table and sketch his face. Conjuring the rest of him was harder. Sometimes I made him very tall, as tall as Grandpere Jack, and sometimes just an inch or so taller than I was. He was always a well-built, muscular man. I decided long ago that he must have been good-looking and very charming to have won my mother's heart so quickly.

Some of the drawings became watercolor paintings. In one of them, I set my imaginary father in a fais dodo hall, leaning against a wall, smiling because he had first set eyes on my mother. He looked sexy and dangerous, just the way he must have looked to draw my beautiful mother to him. In another painting, I had him walking down a road, but turned to wave good-bye. I always thought there was a promise in his face in that picture, the promise of return.

Most of my paintings had a man in them that in my imagination was my father. He was either on a shrimp boat or poling a pirogue through one of the canals or across one of the ponds. Grandmere Catherine knew why the man was in my pictures. I saw how sad it made her, but I couldn't help myself. Lately, she had urged me to paint swamp animals and birds more often than people.

On weekends, we would put some of my paintings out with our woven blankets, sheets, and towels, our split-oak baskets and palmetto hats. Grandmere would also put out her jars of herbal cures for headaches, insomnia, and coughs. Sometimes, we had a pickled snake or a large bullfrog in a jar because the tourists who drove by and stopped loved to buy them. Many loved to eat Grandmere's gumbo or jambalaya. She would ladle out small bowls of it and they would sit at the benches and tables in front of our house and enjoy a real Cajun lunch.

All in all, I suppose my life in the bayou wasn't as bad as the lives some motherless and fatherless children led. Grandmere Catherine and I didn't have many worldly goods, but we had our small safe home and we were able to get by with our loom work and handicrafts. From time to time, although admittedly not often enough, Grandpere Jack would drop by to give us part of what he made trapping muskrats, which was the main way he earned a living these days. Grandmere Catherine was too proud or too angry at him to accept it gracefully. Either I would take it or Grandpere would just leave it on the kitchen table.

"I don't expect no thanks from her," he would mutter to me, "but at least she could acknowledge I'm here leaving her the damn money. It's hard earned, it is," he would declare in a loud voice on the galerie steps. Grandmere Catherine would say nothing in reply, but usually keep on doing whatever she was doing inside.

"Thank you, Grandpere," I would tell him.

"Ah, I don't want your thanks. It's not your thanks I'm asking for, Ruby. I just want someone to know I ain't dead and buried or swallowed by a gator. Someone to at least have the decency to look at me," he often moaned, still loud enough for Grandmere to hear.

Sometimes, she appeared in the doorway if he said something that got to her.

"Decency," she cried from behind the screen door. "Did I hear you, Jack Landry, talk of decency?"

"Ah . . ." Grandpere Jack waved his long arm in her direction and turned away to return to the swamp.

"Wait, Grandpere," I cried, running after him.

"Wait? For what? You ain't seen stubborn until you've seen a Cajun woman with her mind made up. There's nothin' to wait for," he declared, and walked on, his hip boots sucking through the spongelike grass and earth. Usually, he wore his red coat which was a cross between a vest and a fireman's raincoat, with huge sewn in pockets that circled around behind from two sides. They had slit openings and were called rat pockets, for that was where he put his muskrats.

Whenever he charged off in anger, his long, stark white hair would fly up and around his head and look like white flames. He was a dark-skinned man. The Landrys were said to have Indian blood. But he had emerald green eyes that twinkled with an impish charm when he was sober and in a good mood. Tall and lanky and strong enough to wrestle with a gator, Grandpere Jack was something of a legend in the bayou. Few men lived off the swamp as well as he did.

But Grandmere Catherine was down on the Landrys and often brought me to tears when she cursed the day she'd married Grandpere.

"Let it be a lesson to you, Ruby," she told me one day. "A lesson as to how the heart can trick and confuse the mind. The heart wants what the heart wants. But before you give yourself to a man, be sure you have a good idea as to where he's going to take you. Sometimes, the best way to see the future, is to look at the past," Grandmere advised. "I should have listened to what everyone told me about the Landrys. They're so full of bad blood . . . they've been bad since the first Landrys settled here. It wasn't long before signs were posted in these parts saying, No Landrys Allowed. How's that for bad and how's that for listening to your young heart instead of older wisdom?"

"But surely, you must have loved Grandpere once. You must have seen something good in him," I insisted.

"I saw what I wanted to see," she replied. She was stubborn when it came to him, but for reasons I still didn't understand. That day I must have felt a streak of contrariness or bravery, because I tried to probe at the past.

"Grandmere, why did he move away? Was it just because of his drinking, because I think he would stop if he lived with us again?"

Her eyes cut sharply toward me. "No, it's not just because of his drinking." She was quiet a moment. "Although that's good enough a reason."

"Is it because of the way he gambles away his money?"

"Gambling ain't the worse of it," she snapped in a voice that said I should let the matter drop. But for some reason I couldn't.

"Then what is, Grandmere? What did he do that was so terrible?"

Her face darkened and then softened a bit. "It's between him and me," she said. "It ain't for you to know. You're too young to understand it all, Ruby. If Grandpere Jack was meant to live with us . . . things would have been different," she insisted and left me as confused and frustrated as ever.

Grandmere Catherine had such wisdom and such power. Why couldn't she do something to make us a family again? Why couldn't she forgive Grandpere and use her power to change him so that he could live with us once more? Why couldn't we be a real family?

No matter what Grandpere Jack told me and other people, no matter how much he swore, ranted, and raved, I knew he had to be a lonely man living by himself in the swamp. Few people visited him and his home was really no more than a shack. It sat six feet off the marsh on pilings. He had a cistern to collect rainwater and butane lanterns for lights. It had a wood heater for burning scrap lumber and driftwood. At night he would sit on his galerie and play mournful tunes on his accordion and drink his rotgut whiskey.

He wasn't really happy and neither was Grandmere Catherine. Here we were returning from the Rodrigues home after chasing off an evil spirit and we couldn't chase off the evil spirits that dwelt in the shadows of our own home. In my heart I thought Grandmere Catherine was like the shoemaker without any shoes. She can do so much good for others, but she seemed incapable of doing the same sort of things for herself.

Was that the destiny of a Traiteur? A price she had to pay to have the power?

Would it be my destiny as well: to help others but be unable to help myself?

The bayou was a world filled with many mysterious things. Every journey into it, revealed something surprising. A secret until that moment not discovered. But the secrets held in our own hearts were the secrets I longed to know the most.

Just before we reached home, Grandmere Catherine said, "There's someone at the house." With a definite note of disapproval, she added, "It's that Tate boy again."

Paul was sitting on the galerie steps playing his harmonica, his motor scooter set against the cypress stump. The moment he set eyes on our lantern, he stopped playing and stood up to greet us.

Paul was the seventeen-year-old son of Octavious Tate, one of the richest men in Houma. The Tates owned a shrimp cannery and lived in a big house. They had a pleasure boat and expensive cars. Paul had two younger sisters, Jeanne, who was in my class at school, and Toby, who was two years younger. Paul and I had known each other all our lives, but just recently had begun to spend more time together. I knew his parents weren't happy about it. Paul's father had more than one run-in with Grandpere Jack and disliked the Landrys.

"Everything all right, Ruby?" Paul asked quickly as we drew closer. He wore a light blue cotton polo shirt, khaki pants, and leather boots laced tightly beneath them. Tonight he looked taller and wider to me, and older, too.

"Grandmere and I went to see the Rodrigues family. Mrs. Rodrigues's baby was born dead," I told him.

"Oh, that's horrible," Paul said softly. Of all the boys I knew at school, Paul seemed the most sincere and the most mature, although, one of the shyest. He was certainly one of the handsomest with his cerulean blue eyes and thick, *chatin* hair, which was what the Cajuns called brown mixed with blond. "Good evening, Mrs. Landry," he said to Grandmere Catherine.

She flashed her gaze on him with that look of suspicion she had ever since the first time Paul had walked me home from school. Now that he was coming around more often, she was scrutinizing him even more closely, which was something I found embarrassing. Paul seemed a little amused, but a little afraid of her as well. Most folks believed in Grandmere's prophetic and mystical powers.

"Evening," she said slowly. "Might be a downpour yet tonight," she predicted. "You shouldn't be motoring about with that flimsy thing."

"Yes, ma'am," Paul said.

Grandmere Catherine shifted her eyes to me. "We got to finish the weavin' we started," she reminded me.

"Yes, Grandmere. I'll be right along."

She looked at Paul again and then went inside.

"Is your grandmother very upset about losing the Rodrigues baby?" he asked.

"She wasn't called to help deliver it," I replied, and I told him why she had been summoned and what we had done. He listened with interest and then shook his head.

"My father doesn't believe in any of that. He says superstitions and folklore are what keeps the Cajuns backward and makes other folks think we're ignorant. But I don't agree," he added quickly.

"Grandmere Catherine is far from ignorant," I added, not hiding my indignation. "It's ignorant not to take precautions against evil spirits and bad luck."

Paul nodded. "Did you . . . see anything?" he asked.

"I felt it fly by my face," I said, placing my hand on my cheek. "It touched me here. And then I thought I saw it leave."

Paul released a low whistle.

"You must have been very brave," he said.

"Only because I was with Grandmere Catherine," I confessed.

"I wish I had gotten here earlier and been with you . . . to make sure nothing bad happened to you," he added. I felt myself blush at his desire to protect me.

"I'm all right, but I'm glad it's over," I admitted. Paul laughed.

In the dim illumination of our galerie light, his face looked softer, his eyes even warmer. We hadn't done much more than hold hands and kiss a half-dozen times, only twice on the lips, but the memory of those kisses made my heart flutter now when I looked at him and stood so closely to him. The breeze gently brushed aside some strands of hair that had fallen over his forehead. Behind the house, the water from the swamps lapped against the shore and a night bird flapped its wings above us, invisible against the dark sky.

"I was disappointed when I came by and you weren't home," he said. "I was just about to leave when I saw the light of your lantern."

"I'm glad you waited," I replied, and his smile widened. "But I can't invite you in because Grandmere wants us to finish the blankets we'll put up for sale tomorrow. She thinks we'll be busy this weekend and she's usually right. She always remembers which weekends were busier than others the year before. No one has a better memory for those things," I added.

"I got to work in the cannery all day tomorrow, but maybe I can come by tomorrow night after dinner and we can walk to town to get a cup of crushed ice," Paul suggested.

"I'd like that," I said. Paul stepped closer to me and fixed his gaze on my face. We drank each other in for a moment before he worked up enough courage to say what he really had come to say. "What I really want to do is take you to the fais dodo next Saturday night," he declared quickly.

I had never been out on a real date before. Just the thought of it filled me with excitement. Most girls my age would be going to the fais dodo with their families and dance with boys they met there, but to be picked up and escorted and to dance only with Paul all night . . . that sent my mind reeling.

"I'll have to ask Grandmere Catherine," I said, quickly adding, "but I'd like that very much."

"Good. Well," he said, backing up toward his motor scooter, "I guess I better be going before that downpour comes." He didn't take his eyes off me as he stepped away and he caught his heel on a root. It sat him down firmly.

"Are you all right?" I cried, rushing to him. He laughed, embarrassed.

"I'm fine, except for a wet rear end," he added, and laughed. He reached up to take my hand and stand, and when he did, we were only inches apart. Slowly, a millimeter at a time, our lips drew closer and closer until they met. It was a short kiss, but a firmer and more confident one on both our parts. I had gone up on my toes to bring my lips to his and my breasts grazed his chest. The unexpected contact with the electricity of our kiss sent a wave of warm, pleasant excitement down my spine.

"Ruby," he said, bursting with emotion now. "You're the prettiest and nicest girl in the whole bayou."

"Oh, no, I'm not, Paul. I can't be. There are so many prettier girls, girls who have expensive clothes and expensive jewelry and—"

"I don't care if they have the biggest diamonds and dresses from Paris. Nothing could make them prettier than you," he blurted out. I knew he wouldn't have had the courage to say these things if we weren't standing in the shadows and I couldn't see him as clearly. I was sure his face was crimson.

"Ruby!" my grandmother called from a window. "I don't want to stay up all night finishing this."

"I'm coming, Grandmere. Good night, Paul," I said, and then I leaned forward to peck him on the lips once more before I turned and left him standing in the dark. I heard him start his motor scooter and drive off and then I hurried up to the *grenier* to help Grandmere Catherine.

For a long moment, she didn't speak. She worked and kept her eyes fixed on the loom. Then she shifted her gaze to me and pursed her lips the way she often did when she was thinking deeply.

"The Tate boy's been coming around to see you a great deal, lately, hasn't he?"

"Yes, Grandmere."

"And what do his parents think of that?" she asked, cutting right to the heart of things as always.

"I don't know, Grandmere," I said, looking down.

"I think you do, Ruby."

"Paul likes me and I like him," I said quickly. "What his parents think isn't important."

"He's grown a great deal this year; he's a man. And you're no longer a little girl, Ruby. You've grown, too. I see the way you two look at each other. I know that look too well and what it can lead to," she added.

"It won't lead to anything bad. Paul's the nicest boy in school," I insisted. She nodded but kept her dark eyes on me. "Stop making me feel naughty, Grandmere. I haven't done anything to make you ashamed of me."

"Not yet," she said, "but you got Landry in you and the blood has a way of corrupting. I seen it in your mother; I don't want to see it in you."

My chin began to quiver.

"I'm not saying these things to hurt you, child. I'm saying them to prevent your being hurt," she said, reaching out to put her hand over mine.

"Can't I love someone purely and nicely, Grandmere? Or am I cursed because of Grandpere Jack's blood in my veins? What about your blood? Won't it give me the wisdom I need to keep myself from getting in trouble?" I demanded. She shook her head and smiled.

"It didn't prevent me from getting in trouble, I'm afraid. I married him and lived with him once," she said, and then sighed. "But you might be right; you might be stronger and wiser in some ways. You're certainly a lot brighter than I was when I was your age, and far more talented. Why your drawings and paintings—"

"Oh, no, Grandmere, I'm—"

"Yes, you are, Ruby. You're talented. Someday someone will see that talent and offer you a lot of money for it," she prophesied. "I just don't want you to do anything to ruin your chance to get out of here, child, to rise above the swamp and the bayou."

"Is it so bad here, Grandmere?"

"It is for you, child."

"But why, Grandmere?"

"It just is," she said, and began her weaving again, again leaving me stranded in a sea of mystery.

"Paul has asked me to go with him to the fais dodo a week from Saturday. I want to go with him very much, Grandmere," I added.

"Will his parents let him do that?" she asked quickly.

"I don't know. Paul thinks so, I guess. Can we invite him to dinner Sunday night, Grandmere? Can we?"

"I never turned anyone away from my dinner table," Grandmere said, "but don't plan on going to the dance. I know the Tate family and I don't want to see you hurt."

"Oh, I won't be, Grandmere," I said, nearly bouncing in my seat with excitement. "Then Paul can come to dinner?"

"I said I wouldn't throw him out," she replied.

"Oh, Grandmere, thank you. Thank you." I threw my arms around her. She shook her head.

"If we go on like this, we'll be working all night, Ruby," she said, but kissed my cheek. "My little Ruby, my darling girl, growing into a woman so quickly I better not blink or I'll miss it," she said. We hugged again and then went back to work, my hands moving with a new energy, my heart filled with a new joy, despite Grandmere Catherine's ominous warnings.

2

No Landrys Allowed

A blend of wonderful aromas rose from the kitchen and seeped into my room to snap my eyes open and start my stomach churning in anticipation. I could smell the rich, black Cajun coffee percolating on the stove and the mixture of shrimp and chicken gumbo Grandmere Catherine was preparing in her black, cast iron cooking pots to sell at our roadside stall. I sat up and inhaled the delicious smells.

Sunlight wove its way through the leaves of the cypress and sycamores around the house and filtered through the cloth over my window to cast a warm, bright glow over my small bedroom which had just enough space for my white painted bed, a small stand for a lamp near the pillow, and a large chest for my clothing. A chorus of rice birds began their ritual symphony, chirping and singing, urging me to get up, get washed, and get dressed so I could join them in the celebration of a new day.

No matter how I tried, I never beat Grandmere Catherine out of bed and into the kitchen. Rarely did I have the opportunity to surprise her with a pot of freshly brewed coffee, hot biscuits, and eggs. She was usually up with the first rays of sunlight that began to push back the blanket of darkness, and she moved so quietly and so gracefully through the house that I didn't hear her footsteps in the hallway or down the stairs, which usually creaked loudly when I descended. Weekend mornings Grandmere Catherine was up especially early so as to prepare everything for our roadside stall.

I hurried down to join her.

"Why didn't you wake me?" I asked.

"I'd wake you when I needed you if you didn't get yourself up, Ruby," she said, answering me the same way she always did. But I knew she would rather take on extra work than shake me out of the arms of sleep.

"I'll fold all the new blankets and get them ready to take out," I said.

"First, you'll have some breakfast. There's time enough for us to get things out. You know the tourists don't come riding by for a good while yet. The only ones who get up this early are the fishermen and they're not interested in anything we have to sell. Go on now, sit down," Grandmere Catherine commanded.

We had a simple table made from the same wide cypress planks from which our house walls were constructed, as were the chairs with their grooved posts. The one piece of furniture Grandmere was most proud of was her oak armoire. Her father had made it. Everything else we had was ordinary and no different from anything every other Cajun family living along the bayou possessed.

"Mr. Rodrigues brought over that basket of fresh eggs this morning," Grandmere Catherine said, nodding toward the basket on the counter by the window. "Very nice of him to think of us during his troubled times."

She never expected much more than a simple thank-you for any of the wonders she worked. She didn't think of her gifts as being hers; she thought of them as belonging to the Cajun people. She believed she was put on this earth to serve and to help those less fortunate, and the joy of helping others was reward enough.

She began to fry me two eggs to go along with her biscuits.

"Don't forget to put out your newest pictures today. I love the one with the heron coming out of the water," she said, smiling.

"If you love it, Grandmere, I shouldn't sell it. I should give it to you."

"Nonsense, child. I want everyone to see your pictures, especially people in New Orleans," she declared. She had said that many times before and just as firmly.

"Why? Why are those people so important?" I asked.

"There's dozens and dozens of art galleries there and famous artists, too, who will see your work and spread your name so that all the rich Creoles will want one of your paintings in their homes," she explained.

I shook my head. It wasn't like her to want fame and notoriety brought to our simple bayou home. We put out our handicrafts and wares to sell on weekends because it brought us the necessary income to survive, but I knew Grandmere Catherine wasn't comfortable with all these strangers coming around, even though some of them loved her food and piled compliments at her feet. There was something else, some other reason why Grandmere Catherine was pushing me to exhibit my artwork, some mysterious reason.

The picture of the heron was special to me, too. I had been standing on the shore by the pond behind our house at twilight one day when I saw this grosbeak, a night heron, lift itself from the water so suddenly and so unexpectedly, it did seem to come out of the water. It floated up on its wide, dark purple wings and soared over the cypress. I felt something poetic and beautiful in its movements and couldn't wait to capture some of that in a painting. Later, when Grandmere Catherine set her eyes on the finished work, she was speechless for a moment. Her eyes glistened with tears and she confessed that my mother had favored the blue heron over all the other marsh birds.

"That's more reason for us to keep it," I said.

But Grandmere Catherine disagreed and said, "More reason for us to see it carried off to New Orleans." It was almost as if she were sending some sort of cryptic message to someone in New Orleans through my artwork.

After I ate my breakfast, I began to take out the handicrafts and goods we would try to sell that day, while Grandmere Catherine finished making the roux. It was one of the first things a young Cajun girl learned to make. Roux was simply flour browned in butter, oil, or animal fat and cooked to a nutty brown shade without letting it turn so hot that it burned black. After it was prepared, seafood or chicken, sometimes duck, goose, or guinea hen, and sometimes wild game with sausage or oysters was mixed in to make the gumbo. During Lent Grandmere made a green gumbo that was roux mixed only with vegetables rather than meat.

Grandmere was right. We began to get customers much earlier than we usually did. Some of the people who dropped by were friends of hers or other Cajun folk who had learned about the couchemal and wanted to hear Grandmere tell the story. A few of her older friends sat around and recalled similar tales they had heard from their parents and grandparents.

Just before noon, we were surprised to see a silver gray limousine, fancy and long, going by. Suddenly, it came to an abrupt stop and was then backed up very quickly until it stopped again in front of our stall. The rear door was thrown open and a tall, lanky, olive-skinned man with gray-brown hair stepped out, the laughter of a woman lingering behind him within the limousine.

"Quiet down," he said, then turned and smiled at me.

An attractive blond lady with heavily made-up eyes, thick rouge, and gobs of lipstick, poked her head out the open door. A long pearl necklace dangled from her neck. She wore a blouse of bright pink silk. The first several buttons were not done so I couldn't help but notice that her breasts were quite exposed.

"Hurry up, Dominique. I expect to have dinner at Arnaud's tonight," she cried petulantly.

"Relax. We'll have plenty of time," he said without looking back at her. His attention was fixed on my paintings. "Who did these?" he demanded.

"I did, sir," I said. He was dressed expensively in a white shirt of the snowiest, softest-looking cotton and a beautifully tailored suit in dark charcoal gray.

"Really?"

I nodded and he stepped closer to take the picture of the heron into his hands. He held it at arm's length and nodded. "You have instinct," he said. "Still primitive, but rather remarkable. Did you take any lessons?"

"Just a little at school and what I learned from reading some old art magazines," I replied.

"Remarkable."

"Dominique!"

"Hold your water, will you." He smirked at me again as if to say, "Don't mind her," and then he looked at two more of my paintings. I had five out for sale. "How much are you asking for your paintings?" he asked.

I looked at Grandmere Catherine who was standing with Mrs. Thibodeau, their conversation on hold while the limousine remained. Grandmere Catherine had a strange look in her eyes. She was peering as though she were looking deeply into this handsome, well-to-do stranger, searching for something that would tell her he was more than a simple tourist amusing himself with local color.

"I'm asking five dollars apiece," I said.

"Five dollars!" He laughed. "Firstly, you shouldn't ask the same amount for each," he lectured. "This one, the heron, obviously took more work. It's five times the painting the others are," he declared assuredly, turning to address Grandmere Catherine and Mrs. Thibodeau as if they were his students. He turned back to me. "Why, look at the detail . . . the way you've captured the water and the movement in the heron's wings." His eyes narrowed and he pursed his lips as he looked at the paintings and nodded to himself. "I'll give you fifty dollars for the five of them as a down payment," he announced.

"Fifty dollars, but—"

"What do you mean, as a down payment?" Grandmere Catherine asked, stepping toward us.

"Oh, I'm sorry," the gentleman said. "I should have introduced myself properly. My name is Dominique LeGrand. I own an art gallery in the French Quarter, simply called Dominique's. Here," he said, reaching in and taking a business card from a pocket in his pants. Grandmere took the card and pinched it between her small fingers to look at it.

"And this . . . down payment?"

"I think I can get a good deal more for these paintings. Usually, I just take an artist's work into the gallery without paying anything, but I want to do something to show my appreciation of this young girl's work. Is she your granddaughter?" Dominique inquired.

"Yes," Grandmere Catherine said. "Ruby Landry. Will you be sure her name is shown along with the paintings?" she asked, surprising me.

"Of course," Dominique LeGrand said, smiling. "I see she has her initials on the corner," he said, then turned to me. "But in the future, put your full name there," he instructed. "And I do believe, there is a future for you, Mademoiselle Ruby." He took a wad of money from his pocket and peeled off fifty dollars, more money than I had made selling all my paintings up until now. I looked at Grandmere Catherine who nodded and then I took the money.

"Dominique!" his woman cried again.

"Coming, coming. Philip," he called, and the driver came around to put my paintings in the trunk of the limousine. "Careful," he told him. Then he took down our address. "You will be hearing from me," he said as he got into his limousine again. Grandmere Catherine and I stood beside each other and watched the long car go off until it disappeared around the bend.

"Fifty dollars, Grandmere!" I said, waving the money. Mrs. Thibodeau was quite impressed, but my grandmother looked more thoughtful than happy. I thought she even looked a little sad.

"It's begun," she said in a voice barely above a whisper, her eyes fixed in the direction the limousine had taken.

"What has, Grandmere?"

"The future, your future, Ruby. This fifty dollars is just the beginning. Be sure you say nothing about it if your Grandpere Jack should stumble by," she instructed. Then she returned to Mrs. Thibodeau to continue their discussion about couchemals and other evil spirits that lurk about unsuspecting folks.

But I couldn't contain my excitement. I was terribly impatient with the rest of the day, eager to see it hurry along until Paul was to come. I couldn't wait to tell him, and I laughed to myself thinking I could buy him the crushed ice tonight, instead of him buying it for me. Only, I knew he wouldn't let me pay. He was too proud.

The only thing that kept me from exploding with impatience was the business we did. We sold all our blankets, sheets, and towels and Grandmere sold a half-dozen jars of herbal cures. We even sold a pickled frog. All of Grandmere Catherine's gumbo was eaten. In fact, she had to go in and start to make some more for our own dinner. Finally, the sun dropped below the trees and Grandmere declared our day at the roadside had ended. She was very pleased and sang as she worked on our dinner.

"I want you to have my money, Grandmere," I told her.

"We made enough today. I don't need to take your painting money, Ruby." Then she narrowed her eyes on me. "But give it to me to hide. I know you'll feel sorry for that swamp bum and give him some if not all of it one day. I'll put it in my chest for safekeeping. He wouldn't dare look in there," she said.

Grandmere's oak chest was the most sacred thing in the house. It didn't need to be under lock and key. Grandpere Jack would never dare set his hands on it, no matter how drunk he was when he came here. Even I did not venture to open the lid and sift through the things within, for they were her most precious and personal keepsakes, including things that belonged to my mother when she was a little girl. Grandmere promised that everything in it would some day belong to me.

After we had eaten and had cleaned up, Grandmere sat in her rocking chair on the galerie, and I sat near her on the steps. It wasn't as muggy and hot as the night before because there was a brisk breeze. The sky had only a few scattered clouds so the bayou was well lit by the yellowish white light of the moon. It made the limbs of the trees in the swamp look like bones and the still water glisten like glass. On a night like this, sounds traveled over the bayou quickly and easily. We could hear the happy tunes coming from Mr. Bute's accordion and the laughter of his wife and children, all gathered on their front galerie. Somewhere, way in the distance down left toward town, a car horn blared, while behind us, the frogs croaked in the swamp. I had not told Grandmere Catherine that Paul was coming, but she sensed it.

"You look like you're sitting on pins and needles tonight, Ruby. Waiting for something?"

Before I could reply, we heard the soft growl of Paul's motor scooter.

"No need to answer," Grandmere said. Moments later, we saw the small light on his motor scooter, and Paul rode into our front yard.

"Good evening, Mrs. Landry," he said, walking up to us. "Hi, Ruby."

"Hello," Grandmere Catherine said, eying him cautiously.

"We have a little relief from the heat and humidity tonight," he said, and she nodded. "How was your day?" he asked me.

"Wonderful! I sold all five of my paintings," I declared quickly.

"All of them? That is wonderful. We'll have to celebrate with two ice cream sodas instead of just crushed ice. If it's all right with you, Mrs. Landry, I'd like to take Ruby to town," he added, turning to Grandmere Catherine. I saw how his request troubled her. Her eyebrows rose and she leaned back in her rocker. Her hesitation made Paul add, "We won't be long."

"I don't want you to take her on that flimsy motor thing," Grandmere said, nodding toward the scooter. Paul laughed.

"I'd rather walk on a night like this anyway, wouldn't you, Ruby?"

"Yes. All right, Grandmere?"

"I suppose. But don't go anywhere but to town and back and don't talk to any strangers," she cautioned.

"Yes, Grandmere."

"Don't worry, I won't let anything happen to her," Paul assured Grandmere. Paul's assurance didn't make her look less anxious, but he and I started toward town, our way well lit by the moon. He didn't take my hand until we were out of sight.

"Your grandmere worries so much about you," Paul said.

"She's seen a lot of sadness and hard times. But we had a good day at the stall."

"And you sold all your paintings. That's great."

"I didn't sell them so much as get them into a New Orleans gallery," I said, and told him everything that had happened and what Dominique LeGrand had said.

Paul was silent for a long moment. Then he turned to me, his face strangely sad. "Someday, you'll be a famous artist and move away from the bayou. You'll live in a big house in New Orleans, I'm sure," he predicted, "and forget all us Cajuns."

"Oh, Paul, how could you say such a horrible thing? I'd like to be a famous artist, of course; but I would never turn my back on my people and . . . and never forget you. Never," I insisted.

"You mean that, Ruby?"

I tossed my hair back over my shoulder and put my hand on my heart. Then, closing my eyes, I said, "I swear on Saint Medad. Besides," I continued, snapping my eyes open, "it will probably be you who leaves the bayou to go to some fancy college and meet wealthy girls."

"Oh, no," he protested. "I don't want to meet other girls. You're the only girl I care about."

"You say that now, Paul Marcus Tate, but time has a way of changing things. Look at my grandparents. They were once in love."

"That's different. My father says no one could live with your grandfather."

"Once, Grandmere did," I said. "And then things changed, things she never expected."

"They won't change with me," Paul boasted. He paused and stepped closer to take my hand again. "Did you ask your grandmother about the fais dodo?"

"Yes," I said. "Can you come to dinner tomorrow night? I think she should have a chance to get to know you better. Could you?"

He was quiet for a long moment.

"Your parents won't let you," I concluded.

"I'll be there," he said. "My parents are just going to have to get used to the idea of you and me," he added, and smiled. Our eyes remained firmly on each other and then he leaned toward me and we kissed in the moonlight. The sound and sight of an automobile set us apart and made us walk faster toward the town and the soda shop.

The street looked busier than usual this evening. Many of the local shrimp fishermen had brought their families in to enjoy the feast at the Cajun Queen, a restaurant that advertised an all-you-can-eat platter of crawfish and potatoes with pitchers of draft beer. In fact, there was a real festive atmosphere with the Cajun Swamp Trio playing their accordion, fiddle, and washboard on the corner near the Cajun Queen. Peddlers were out and folks sat on cypress log benches watching the parade of people go by. Some were eating beignets and drinking from mugs of coffee and some were feasting on sea bob, which was dried shrimp, sometimes called Cajun Peanuts.

Paul and I went to the soda fountain and confectionery store and sat at the counter to have our ice cream sodas. When Paul told the owner, Mr. Clements, why we were celebrating, he put gobs of whip cream and cherries on top of our sodas. I couldn't remember an ice cream soda that had ever tasted as good. We were having such a good time, we almost didn't hear the commotion outside, but other people in the store rushed to the door to see what was happening and we soon followed.

My heart sunk when I saw what it was: Grandpere Jack being thrown out of the Cajun Queen. Even though he had been escorted out, he remained on the steps waving his fist and screaming about injustice.

"I'd better see if I can persuade him to go home and calm down," I muttered, and hurried out. Paul followed. The crowd of onlookers had begun to break up, no longer much interested in a drunken man babbling to himself on the steps. I pulled on the sleeve of his jacket.

"Grandpere, Grandpere . . ."

"Wha . . . who . . ." He spun around, a trickle of whiskey running out of the corner of his mouth and down the grainy surface of his unshaven chin. For a moment he wobbled on his feet as he tried to focus on me. The strands of his dry, crusty looking hair stood out in every direction. His clothing was stained with mud and bits of food. He brought his eyes closer. "Gabrielle?" he said.

"No, Grandpere. It's Ruby. Ruby. Come along, Grandpere. You have to go home. Come along," I said. It wasn't the first time I had found him in a drunken stupor and had to urge him to go home. And it wasn't the first time he had looked at me with his eyes hazy and called me by my mother's name.

"Wha . . ." He looked from me to Paul and then back at me again. "Ruby?"

"Yes, Grandpere. You must go home and sleep."

"Sleep, sleep? Yeah," he said, turning back toward the Cajun Queen. "Those no good . . . they take your money and then when you voice your opinion about somethin' . . . things ain't what they was around here, that's for sure, that's for damn sure."

"Come on, Grandpere." I tugged his hand and he came off the steps, nearly tripping and falling on his face. Paul rushed to take hold of his other arm.

"My boat," Grandpere muttered. "At the dock." Then he turned and ripped his hand from mine to wave his fist at the Cajun Queen one more time. "You don't know nothin'. None of you remember the swamp the way it was 'fore these damn oil people came. Hear?"

"They heard you, Grandpere. Now it's time to go home."

"Home. I can't go home," he muttered. "She won't let me go home."

I swung my gaze to Paul who looked very upset for me.

"Come along, Grandpere," I urged again, and he stumbled forward as we guided him to the dock.

"He won't be able to navigate this boat himself," Paul declared. "Maybe I should just take him and you should go home, Ruby."

"Oh, no. I'll go along. I know my way through the canals better than you do, Paul," I insisted.

We got Grandpere into his dinghy and sat him down. Immediately, he fell over the bench. Paul helped him get comfortable and then he started the motor and we pulled away from the dock, some of the people still watching us and shaking their heads. Grandmere Catherine would hear about this quickly, I thought, and she would just nod and say she wasn't surprised.

Minutes after we pulled away from the dock, Grandpere Jack was snoring. I tried to make him more comfortable by putting a rolled up sack under his head. He moaned and muttered something incoherently before falling asleep and snoring again. Then I joined Paul.

"I'm sorry," I said.

"For what?"

"I'm sure your parents will find out about this tomorrow and be angry."

"It doesn't matter," he assured me, but I remembered how dark Grandmere Catherine's eyes had become when she asked me what his parents thought of his seeing me. Surely they would use this incident to convince him to stay away from the Landrys. What if signs began to appear everywhere saying, "No Landrys Allowed," just like Grandmere Catherine described from the past? Perhaps I really would have to flee from the bayou to find someone to love me and make me his wife. Perhaps this was what Grandmere Catherine meant.

The moon lit our way through the canals, but when we went deeper into the swamp, the sad veils of Spanish moss and the thick, intertwined leaves of the cypress blocked out the bright illumination making the waterway more difficult to navigate. We had to slow down to avoid the stumps. When the moonlight did break through an opening, it made the backs of the gators glitter. One whipped its tail, splashing water in our direction as if to say, you don't belong here. Farther along, we saw the eyes of a marsh deer lit up by the moonbeams. We saw his silhouetted body turn to disappear in the darker shadows.

Finally, Grandpere's shack came into view. His galerie was crowded with nets for oyster fishing, a pile of Spanish moss he had gathered to sell to the furniture manufacturers who used it for stuffing, his rocking chair with the accordion on it, empty beer bottles and a whiskey bottle beside the chair and a crusted gumbo bowl. Some of his muskrat traps dangled from the roof of the galerie and some hides were draped over the railing. His pirogue with the pole he used to gather the Spanish moss was tied to his small dock. Paul gracefully navigated us up beside it and shut off the motor of the dinghy. Then we began the difficult task of getting Grandpere out of the boat. He offered little assistance and came close to spilling all three of us into the swamp.

Paul surprised me with his strength. He virtually carried Grandpere over the galerie and into the shack. When I turned on a butane lamp, I wished I hadn't. Clothing was strewn all about and everywhere there were empty and partially empty bottles of cheap whiskey. His cot was unmade, the blanket hanging down with most of it on the floor. His dinner table was covered with dirty dishes and crusted bowls and glasses, as well as stained silverware. From the expression on his face, I saw that Paul was overwhelmed by the filth and the mess.

"He'd be better off sleeping right in the swamp," he muttered. I fixed the cot so he could lower Grandpere Jack onto it. Then we both started to undo his hip boots. "I can do this," Paul said. I nodded and went to the table first to clear it off and put the dishes and bowls into the sink, which I found to be full of other dirty dishes and bowls. While I washed and cleaned, Paul went around the shack and picked up the empty cans and bottles.

"He's getting worse," I moaned, and wiped the tears from my eyes. Paul squeezed my arm gently.

"I'll get some fresh water from the cistern," he said. While he was gone, Grandpere began to moan. I wiped my hands and went to him. His eyes were still closed, but he was muttering under his breath.

"It ain't right to blame me . . . ain't right. She was in love, wasn't she? What's the difference then? Tell me that. Go on," he said.

"Who was in love, Grandpere?" I asked.

"Go on, tell me what's the difference. You got somethin' against money, do you? Huh? Go on."

"Who was in love, Grandpere? What money?"

He moaned and turned over.

"What is it?" Paul said, returning with the water.

"He's talking in his sleep, but he doesn't make any sense," I said.

"That's easy to believe."

"I think . . . it had something to do with why he and my Grandmere Catherine are so angry at each other all the time."

"I don't think there's much of a mystery to that, Ruby. Look around; look at what he's become. Why should she want to have him in the house?" Paul said.

"No, Paul. It has to be something more. I wish he would tell me," I said, and knelt beside the cot. "Grandpere," I said, shaking his shoulder.

"Damn oil companies," he muttered. "Dredged the swamps and killed the three-cornered grass . . . killing the muskrats . . . nothin' for them to eat."

"Grandpere, who was in love? What money?" I demanded. He moaned and started to snore.

"No sense talking to him when he's like that, Ruby," Paul said.

I shook my head.

"It's the only time he might tell me the truth, Paul." I stood up, still looking down at him. "Neither he nor Grandmere Catherine will talk about it any other time."

Paul came to my side.

"I picked up a bit outside, but it will take a few days to get this place in shape," he commented.

"I know. We'd better start back. We'll dock his boat near my house. He'll pole the pirogue there tomorrow and find it."

"He'll find his head's got a tin drum inside it," Paul said. "That's what he'll find tomorrow."

We left the shack and got into the dinghy. Neither of us spoke much on the way back. I sat beside Paul. He put his arm around me and I cradled my head against his shoulder. Owls hooted at us, snakes and gators slithered through the mud and water, frogs croaked, but my mind was fixed on Grandpere Jack's drunken words and I heard or saw nothing else until I felt Paul's lips on my forehead. He had shut off the motor and we were drifting toward the shore.

"Ruby," he whispered. "You feel so good in my arms. I wish I could hold you all the time, or at least have you in my arms whenever I wanted."

"You can, Paul," I replied softly, and turned my face to him so that he could bring his lips down to mine. Our kiss was soft, but long. We felt the boat hit the shore and stop, but neither of us made an attempt to rise. Instead, Paul wrapped his arms tighter around me and slipped down beside me, his lips now moving over my cheeks and gently caressing my closed eyes.

"I go to sleep every night with your kiss on my lips," Paul said.

"So do I, Paul."

His left arm pressed the side of my breast softly. I tingled and waited in excited anticipation. He brought his arm back slowly until his hand gently cupped my breast and his finger slipped over my throbbing, erected nipple beneath the thin cotton blouse and bra to undo the top buttons. I wanted him to touch me; I even longed for it, but the moment he did, my electric excitement was quickly followed by a stream of cold fear, for I felt how strongly I wanted him to do more, go further and kiss me in places so intimate, only I had touched or seen them. Despite his gentleness and his deep expressions of love, I could not get around Grandmere Catherine's dark eyes of warning looming in my memory.

"Wait, Paul," I said reluctantly. "We're going too fast."

"I'm sorry," Paul said quickly, and pulled himself back. "I didn't mean to. I just . . ."

"It's all right. If I don't stop you now, I won't stop you in a few

minutes and I don't know what else we will do," I explained. Paul
nodded and stood up. He helped me up and I straightened my skirt
and blouse, rebuttoning the top two buttons. He helped me out of the
boat and then pulled it up so it wouldn't be carried away when the tide
from the Gulf raised the level of the water in the bayou. I took his hand
and we made our way slowly back to the house. Grandmere Catherine
was inside. We could hear her tinkering in the kitchen, finishing up the
preparation of the biscuits she would bring to church in the morning.

"I'm sorry our celebration turned out this way," I said, and wondered
how many more times I would apologize for Grandpere Jack.

"I wouldn't have missed a moment," Paul said. "As long as I was
with you, Ruby."

"Is your family going to church in the morning?" He nodded. "Are
you still coming to dinner tomorrow night?"

"Of course."

I smiled and we kissed once more before I turned and climbed the
steps to the front galerie. Paul waited until I walked in and then he
went to his scooter and drove away. The moment Grandmere Catherine turned to greet me, I knew she had heard about Grandpere Jack.
One of her good friends couldn't wait to bring her the news first, I was
sure.

"Why didn't you just let the police cart him off to jail? That's where
he belongs, making a spectacle of himself in front of good folks with
all those children in town, too," she said, wagging her head. "What did
you and Paul do with him?"

"We took him back to his shack, Grandmere, and if you saw how it
was . . ."

"I don't have to see it. I know what a pigsty looks like," she said,
returning to her biscuits.

"He called me Gabrielle when he first set eyes on me," I said.

"Doesn't surprise me none. He probably forgot his own name, too."

"At the shack, he mumbled a lot."

"Oh?" She turned back to me.

"He said something about someone being in love and what was the
difference about the money. What does all that mean, Grandmere?"

She turned away again. I didn't like the way her eyes skipped guiltily
away when I tried to catch them. I knew in my heart she was hiding
something.

"I wouldn't know how to begin to untangle the mess of words that
drunken mind produces. It would be easier to unravel a spiderweb
without tearing it," she said.

"Who was in love, Grandmere? Did he mean my mother?"

She was silent.

"Did he gamble away her money, your money?" I pursued.

"Stop trying to make sense out of something stupid, Ruby. It's late. You should go to bed. We're going to early Mass, and I must tell you, I'm not happy about you and Paul carting that man into the swamp. The swamp is no place for you. It's beautiful from a distance, but it's the devil's lair, too, and wrought with dangers you can't even begin to imagine. I'm disappointed in Paul for taking you there," she concluded.

"Oh, no, Grandmere. Paul didn't want me to go along. He wanted to do it himself, but I insisted."

"Still, he shouldn't have done it," she said, and turned to me, her eyes dark. "You shouldn't be spending all your time with one boy like this. You're too young."

"I'm fifteen, Grandmere. Some fifteen-year-old Cajun girls are already married, some with children."

"Well, that's not going to happen to you. You're going to do better, be better," she said angrily.

"Yes, Grandmere. I'm sorry. We didn't mean . . ."

"All right," she said. "It's over and done with. Let's not ruin an otherwise special day by talking about your Grandpere anymore. Go to sleep, Ruby. Go on," she ordered. "After church, you're going to help me prepare our Sunday dinner. We've got a guest, don't we?" she asked, her eyes full of skepticism.

"Yes, Grandmere. He's coming."

I left her, my mind in a spin. The day had been filled with so many good things and so many bad. Maybe Grandmere Catherine was right; maybe it was better not to try to fathom the dark things. They had a way of polluting the clear waters, spoiling the fresh and the wonderful bright things. It was better to dwell on the happy events.

It was better to think about my paintings hanging in a New Orleans gallery . . . to remember the touch of Paul's lips on mine and the way he made my body sing . . . to dream about a perfect future with me painting in my own art studio in our big house on the bayou. Surely the good things had a way of outweighing the bad, otherwise we would all be like Grandpere Jack, lost in a swamp of our own making, not only trying to forget the past, but trying to forget the future as well.

3

I Wish We Were a Family

In the morning Grandmere Catherine and I put on our Sunday clothes. I brushed my hair and tied it up with a crimson ribbon and she and I set out for church, Grandmere carrying her gift for Father Rush, a box of her homemade biscuits. It was a bright morning with silky white clouds lazily making their way across the nearly turquoise sky. I took a deep breath, inhaling the warm air seasoned with the salt of the Gulf of Mexico. It was the kind of morning that made me feel bright and alive, and aware of every beautiful thing in the bayou.

The moment we walked down the steps of the galerie, I caught sight of the scarlet back of a cardinal as it flew to its safe, high nest. As we strolled down the road, I saw how the buttercups had blossomed in the ditches and how milk white were the small, delicate flowers of the Queen Anne's lace.

Even the sight of a butcher bird's stored food didn't upset me. From early spring, through the summer and early fall, his fresh kills, lizards and tiny snakes, dried upon the thorns of a thorn tree. Grandpere Jack told me the butcher bird ate the cured flesh only during the winter months.

"Butcher birds are the only birds in the bayou that have no visible mates," he told me. "No female naggin' them to death. Smart," he added before spitting out some tobacco juice and swigging a gulp of whiskey in his mouth. What made him so bitter? I wondered again.

However, I didn't dwell on it long, for ahead of us the church loomed, its shingled spire lifting a cross high above the congregation. Every stone, every brick, and every beam of the old building had been brought and affectionately placed there by the Cajuns who worshipped in the bayou nearly one hundred and fifty years before. It filled me with a sense of history, a sense of heritage.

But as soon as we rounded the turn and headed toward the church, Grandmere Catherine stiffened and straightened her spine. A group of well-to-do people were gathered in a small circle chatting in front of the church. They all stopped their conversation and looked our way as soon as we came into sight, a distinct expression of disapproval painted on all their faces. That only made Grandmere Catherine hoist her head higher, like a flag of pride.

"I'm sure they're raking over what a fool your grandpere made of himself last night," Grandmere Catherine muttered, "but I will not have my reputation blemished by that man's foolish behavior."

The way she stared back at the gathering told them as much. They looked happy to break up to go inside as the time to enter the church for services drew near. I saw Paul's parents, Octavious and Gladys Tate, standing on the perimeter of the throng. Gladys Tate threw a glance in our direction, her hard as stone eyes on me. Paul, who had been talking with some of his school buddies, spotted me and smiled, but his mother made him join her and his father and sisters as they entered the church.

The Tates, as well as some other wealthy Cajun families, sat up front so Paul and I didn't get a chance to talk to each other before the Mass began. Afterward, as the worshippers filed past Father Rush, Grandmere gave him her box of biscuits and he thanked her and smiled coyly.

"I hear you were at work again, Mrs. Landry," the tall, lean priest said with a gently underlying note of criticism in his voice. "Chasing spirits into the night."

"I do what I must do," Grandmere replied firmly, her lips tight and her eyes fixed on his.

"As long as we don't replace prayer and church with superstition," he warned. Then he smiled. "But I never refuse assistance in the battle against the devil when that assistance comes from the pure at heart."

"I'm glad of that, Father," Grandmere said, and Father Rush laughed. His attention was then quickly drawn to the Tates and some other well-to-do congregants who made sizeable contributions to the church. While they spoke, Paul joined Grandmere and me. I thought he looked so handsome and very mature in his dark blue suit with his hair brushed back neatly. Even Grandmere Catherine seemed impressed.

"What time is supper, Mrs. Landry?" Paul asked. Grandmere Catherine shifted her eyes toward Paul's parents before replying.

"Supper is at six," Grandmere told him, and then went to join her friends for a chat. Paul waited until she was out of earshot.

"Everyone was talking about your grandfather this morning," he told me.

"Grandmere and I sensed that when we arrived. Did your parents find out you helped me get him home?"

The look on his face gave me the answer.

"I'm sorry if I caused you trouble."

"It's all right," he said quickly. "I explained everything." He grinned cheerfully. He was the perpetual cockeyed optimist, never gloomy, doubtful, or moody, as I often was.

"Paul," his mother called. With her face frozen in a look of disapproval, her mouth was like a crooked knife slash and her eyes were long and catlike. She held her body stiffly, looking as if she would suddenly shudder and march away.

"Coming," Paul said.

His mother leaned over to whisper something to his father and his father turned to look my way.

Paul got most of his good looks from his father, a tall, distinguished looking man who was always elegantly dressed and well-groomed. He had a strong mouth and jaw with a straight nose, not too long or too narrow.

"We're leaving right this minute," his mother emphasized.

"I've got to go. We have some relatives coming for lunch. See you later," Paul promised, and he darted off to join his parents.

I stepped beside Grandmere Catherine just as she invited Mrs. Livaudis and Mrs. Thibodeau to our house for coffee and blackberry pie. Knowing how slowly they would walk, I hurried ahead, promising to start the coffee. But when I got to our front yard, I saw my grandfather down at the dock, tying his pirogue to the back of the dinghy.

"Good morning, Grandpere," I called. He looked up slowly as I approached.

His eyes were half-closed, the lids heavy. His hair was wild, the strands in the back flowing in every direction over his collar. I imagined that the tin drum Paul predicted was banging away in Grandpere's head. He looked grouchy and tired. He hadn't changed out of the clothes he had slept in and the stale odor of last night's rum whiskey lingered on him. Grandmere Catherine always said the best thing that could happen to him was for him to fall into the swamp. "That way, at least he'd get a bath."

"You bring me back to my shack in the swamp last night?" he asked quickly.

"Yes, Grandpere. Me and Paul."

"Paul? Who's Paul?"

"Paul Tate, Grandpere."

"Oh, a rich man's son, eh? Them cannery people ain't much better than the oil riggers, dredging the swamp to make it wider for their damn big boats. You got no business hanging around that sort. There's only one thing they want from the likes of you," he warned.

"Paul's very nice," I said sharply. He grunted and continued to tie his knot.

"Coming from church, are ya?" he asked without looking up.

"Yes."

He paused and looked back toward the road.

"Your grandmere's still gabbin' with those other busybodies, I imagine. That's why they go to church," he claimed, "to nourish gossip."

"It was a very nice service, Grandpere. Why don't you ever go?"

"This here is my church," he declared, and waved his long fingers at the swamp. "I got no priest lookin' over my shoulder, spitting hell and damnation down my back." He stepped into the dinghy.

"Would you like a cup of fresh coffee, Grandpere? I'm about to make some. Grandmere has some of her friends coming for blackberry pie and—"

"Hell no. I wouldn't be caught dead with those fishwives." He shifted his eyes to me and softened his gaze. "You look nice in that dress," he said. "Pretty as your mother was."

"Thank you, Grandpere."

"I guess you cleaned up my shack some, too, didn't you?" I nodded. "Well, thanks for that."

He reached for the cord to pull and start his motor.

"Grandpere," I said, approaching. "You were talking about someone who was in love and something about money, last night after we brought you home."

He paused and looked at me hard, his eyes turning to granite very quickly.

"What else did I say?"

"Nothing. But what did you mean, Grandpere? Who was in love?"

He shrugged.

"Probably remembered one of the stories my father told me about his father and grandpere. Our family goes way back to the riverboat gamblers, you know," he said with some pride. "Lots of money traveled through Landry fingers," he said, holding up his muddied hands, "and each of the Landrys cut quite a romantic figure on the river. Lots of women were in love with them. You could line them up from here to New Orleans."

"Is that why you gamble away all your money? Grandmere says it's in the Landry blood," I said.

"Well, she ain't wrong about that. I'm just not as good at it as some of my kinfolk was." He leaned forward, smiling, the gaps in his teeth dark and wide where he had pulled out his own when the aches became too painful to manage. "My great, great-grandpere, Gib Landry, was a sure-thing player. Know what that was?" he asked. I shook my head. "A player who never lost because he had marked cards." He laughed. "They called them 'Vantage tools.' Well, they certainly gave an advantage." He laughed again.

"What happened to him, Grandpere?"

"He was shot to death on the *Delta Queen*. When you live hard and dangerous, you're always gambling," he said, and pulled the cord. The motor sputtered. "Someday, when I got the time, I'll tell you more about your ancestors. Despite what she tells you," he added, nodding toward the house, "you oughta know something about them." He pulled the cord again and this time the motor caught and began to rumble. "I gotta get goin'. I got some oysters to catch."

"I wish you could come to dinner at the house tonight and meet Paul," I said. What I really meant was I wish we were a family.

"What do you mean, meet Paul? Your grandmere invited him to dinner?" he asked skeptically.

"I did. She said it was all right."

He stared at me a long moment and then turned back to his motor.

"Got no time for socializin'. Gotta make me a livin'."

Grandmere Catherine and her friends appeared on the road behind us. I saw Grandpere Jack's eyes linger for a moment and then he sat himself down quickly.

"Grandpere," I cried, but he gunned his motor and turned the dinghy to pull away as quickly as he could and head for one of the shallow brackish lakes scattered through the marshes. He didn't look back. In moments, the swamp swallowed him up and only the growl of his motor could be heard as he wound his way through the channels.

"What did he want?" Grandmere Catherine demanded.

"Just to get his dinghy."

She kept her eyes fixed on his wake as if she expected he would reappear. She glared and narrowed her eyes into slits as if she were willing the swamp to swallow him up forever. Soon, the sound of his dinghy motor died away and Grandmere Catherine straightened herself up again and smiled at her two friends. They quickly returned to their conversation and entered the house, but I lingered a moment and wondered how these two people could have ever been in love enough to marry and have a daughter. How could love or what you thought was love make you so blind to each other's weaknesses?

Later that day, after Grandmere Catherine's friends left, I helped her prepare our supper. I wanted to ask her more about Grandpere Jack, but those questions usually put her in a bad mood. With Paul coming for supper, I dared not risk it.

"We're not doing anything special for supper tonight, Ruby," she told me. "I hope you didn't give the Tate boy that impression."

"Oh, no, Grandmere. Besides, Paul isn't that kind of a boy. You wouldn't even know his family was wealthy. He's so different from his mother and his sisters. Everyone in school says they're stuck-up, but not Paul."

"Maybe, but you don't live the way the Tates live and not get to expect certain things. It's just human nature. The higher you build him up in your mind, Ruby, the harder the fall of disappointment is going to be," she warned.

"I'm not afraid of that, Grandmere," I said with such certainty that she paused to gaze at me.

"You've been a good girl, haven't you, Ruby?"

"Oh, yes, Grandmere."

"Don't ever forget what happened to your mother," she admonished.

For a while I feared Grandmere Catherine would hold this cloud of dread over the house up until and through our dinner, but despite her claim that we weren't having anything special, few things pleased Grandmere Catherine as much as cooking for someone she knew would appreciate it. She set out to make one of her best Cajun dishes: jambalaya. While I helped with that, Grandmere made a custard pie.

"Was my mother a good cook, too, Grandmere?" I asked her.

"Oh, yes," she said, smiling at the memories. "No one picked up recipes as quickly and as well as your mother did. She was cooking gumbo before she was nine years old, and by the time she was twelve, no one could clear out the icebox and make as good a jambalaya.

"When your grandpere Jack was still something of a human being," she continued, "he would take Gabrielle out and show her all the edible things in the swamp. She learned fast, and you know what they say about us Cajuns," Grandmere added, "we'll eat anything that doesn't eat us first."

She laughed and hummed one of her favorite tunes. On Sundays we usually gave the house a good once-over anyway, but this special Sunday, I went at it with more energy and concern, washing down the windows until every speck of dirt was gone, scrubbing the floors until they shone, and dusting and polishing everything in sight.

"You'd think the king of France was coming here tonight," Grandmere teased. "I'm warning you, Ruby, don't let that boy expect more of you than there is."

"I won't, Grandmere," I said, but in my secret put-away heart, I hoped that Paul would be very impressed and brag about us to his parents so much they would drop any opposition they might have to his making me his girlfriend.

By late afternoon, our little home nearly sparkled and was filled with delicious aromas. As the clock ticked closer to six, I grew more and more excited. I hoped that Paul would be early, so I sat outside and waited the last hour with my eyes fixed in the direction he would come. Our table was set and I wore my best dress. Grandmere Catherine had made it herself. It was white with a deep lace hem and a lace panel down the front. The sleeves were soft bells of lace that came to my elbows. I wore a blue sash around my waist.

"I'm glad I let out that bodice some," she said when she saw me. "The way your bosom's blossoming. Turn around," she said, and smoothed out the back of the skirt. "I must say, you're turning out to be a real belle, Ruby. Even more beautiful than your mother was at your age."

"I hope I'm as pretty as you are at your age, Grandmere," I replied. She shook her head and smiled.

"Go on now. I'm enough to scare a marsh hawk to death," she said, and laughed, but for the first time, I got Grandmere Catherine to tell me about some of her old boyfriends and some of the fais dodos she had attended when she was my age.

When the clock struck six, I lifted my eyes in anticipation, expecting Paul's motor scooter to rumble moments later. But it didn't and the road remained quiet and still. After a little while Grandmere came to the door and peered out herself. She gazed sadly at me and then returned to the kitchen to do some final things. My heart began to pound. The breeze became more of a wind; all of the trees waving their branches. Where was he? At about seven, I became very concerned and when Grandmere Catherine appeared in the doorway again, she wore a look of fatal acceptance on her face.

"It's not like him to be late," I said. "I hope nothing has happened to him."

Grandmere Catherine didn't reply; she didn't have to. Her eyes said it all.

"You'd better come in and sit down, Ruby. We made the food and want to enjoy it anyway."

"He's coming, Grandmere. I'm sure he's coming. Something unexpected must have happened," I cried. "Let me wait just a little while longer," I pleaded. She retreated, but at seven-fifteen she came to the door again.

"We can't wait any longer," she declared.

Dejected, all my appetite gone anyway, I rose and went inside. Grandmere Catherine said nothing. She served the meal and sat down.

"This came out as good as it ever has," she declared. Then leaning toward me, she added, "even if I have to say so myself."

"Oh, it's wonderful, Grandmere. I'm just . . . worried about him."

"Well, worry about him on a full stomach," she ordered. I forced myself to eat, and, despite my disappointment, even enjoyed Grandmere Catherine's custard pie. I helped her clean up and then I went back outside and sat on the galerie, waiting and watching and wondering what had happened to ruin what would have been a wonderful evening. Almost an hour later, I heard Paul's motor scooter and saw him coming down the road as fast as he could. He pulled up and dropped his scooter roughly to run up to the house.

"What happened to you?" I cried, standing.

"Oh, Ruby, I'm sorry. My parents . . . they forbad me to come. My father ordered me to my room when I refused to have dinner with them. Finally, I decided to climb out the window and come here anyway. I must apologize to your grandmother."

I sank to the steps of the galerie.

"Why wouldn't they let you come?" I asked. "Because of my grandfather and what happened in town last night?"

"That . . . as well as other things. But I don't care how angry they get at me," he said, stepping up to sit beside me. "They're just being stupid snobs."

I nodded. "Grandmere said this would happen. She knew."

"I'm not going to let them keep me away from you, Ruby. They have no right. They—"

"They're your parents, Paul. You've got to do what they tell you to do. You should go home," I said dryly. My heart felt like it had turned into a glob of swamp mud. It was as if cruel Fate had dropped a sheet of dark gloom over the bayou, and just like Grandmere Catherine often said, Fate was a grim reaper, never kind, with little respect for who was loved and needed.

Paul shook his head. Years seemed to melt from him, and he sat there vulnerable, helpless as a child of six or seven, no more comprehending than I.

"I'm not going to give you up, Ruby. I'm not," he insisted. "They can take away everything they've given me, and I still won't listen to them."

"They'll only hate me more, Paul," I concluded.

"It doesn't matter. What matters is that we care for each other. Please, Ruby," he said, taking my hand. "Say that I'm right."

"I want to, Paul." I looked down. "But I'm afraid."

"Don't be," he told me, reaching out to tilt my head toward him. "I won't let anything happen to you."

I stared at him with huge, wistful eyes. How could I explain? I wasn't worried about myself, I was concerned for him because as Grandmere Catherine always told me, defiance of fate just meant disaster for those you loved. Defying it was as futile as trying to hold back the tide.

"All right?" Paul pursued. "Okay?"

"Oh, Paul."

"It's settled then. Now," he said, standing. "I'm going in to apologize to your grandmother."

I waited for him on the steps. He returned a few minutes later.

"Looks like I missed a real feast. It makes me so angry," he said, gazing out at the road with eyes as furious as Grandpere Jack's could get. I didn't feel comfortable with him hating his parents. At least he had parents, a home, a family. He should hold on to those things and not risk them for the likes of me, I thought. "My parents are unreasonable," he declared firmly.

"They're just trying to do what they think is best for you, Paul," I said.

"You're what's best for me, Ruby," he replied quickly. "They're just going to have to understand that." His blue eyes gleamed with determination. "Well, I'd better go back," he said. "Once again, I'm sorry I ruined your dinner, Ruby."

"It's over now, Paul." I stood up and we gazed at each other for a long moment. What did the Tates fear would happen if Paul loved me? Did they really believe my Landry blood would corrupt him? Or was it merely that they wanted him to know only girls from rich families?

He took my hand into his.

"I swear," he said, "I'll never let them do anything to hurt you again."

"Don't fight with your parents, Paul. Please," I begged.

"I'm not fighting with them; they're fighting with me," he replied. "Good night," he said, and leaned forward to kiss me quickly on the lips. Then he went to his motor scooter and drove into the night. I watched him disappear in the darkness. When I turned around, I saw Grandmere Catherine standing in the doorway.

"He's a nice young man," she said, "but you can't rip a Cajun man away from his mother and father. It will tear his heart in two. Don't put all your heart in this, Ruby. Some things are just not meant to be," she added, and turned around to go back into the house.

I stood there, the tears streaming down my face. For the first time, I understood why Grandpere Jack liked living in the swamp away from people.

Despite what had happened on Sunday, I still had high hopes for the Saturday night fais dodo. But whenever I brought it up with Grandmere, she simply replied, "We'll see." On Friday night, I pressed her harder.

"Paul's got to know if he can come by to pick me up, Grandmere. It's not fair to keep him dangling like bait on a fish line," I said. It was something Grandpere Jack would say, but I was frustrated and anxious enough to risk it.

"I just don't want you to suffer another disappointment, Ruby," she told me. "His parents aren't going to let him take you and they would just be furious if he defied them and did so anyway. They would be angry with me, too."

"Why, Grandmere? How can they blame you?"

"They just would," she said. "Everybody would. I'll take you myself," she said nodding. "Mrs. Bourdeaux is going and she and I can sit together and watch the young people. Besides, it's been a while since I heard good Cajun music."

"Oh, Grandmere," I moaned. "Girls my age are going with boys; some have been on dates for more than a year already. It's not fair; I'm fifteen. I'm not a baby anymore."

"I didn't say you were, Ruby, but—"

"But you're treating me like one," I cried, and ran up to my room to throw myself on my bed.

Maybe I was worse off living with a grandmother who was a spiritual treater, who saw evil spirits and danger in every dark shadow, who was always chanting and lighting candles and putting totems on people's doorways. Maybe the Tates just thought we were a crazy family and that was why they wanted Paul to stay away from me.

Why did my mother have to die so young and why did my real father have to desert me? I had a grandfather who lived like an animal in the middle of the swamp and a grandmother who thought I was a small child. My sadness was mixed suddenly with rage. Here I was, fifteen with other girls my age far less pretty than I enjoying themselves on real dates while I was expected to go trailing along with my grandmere to the fais dodo. Never before did I feel like running away as much as I did now.

I heard Grandmere coming up the stairs, her steps heavier than usual. She tapped gently on my door and looked in. I didn't turn around.

"Ruby," she began. "I'm only trying to protect you."

"I don't want you to protect me," I snapped. "I can protect myself. I'm not a baby," I insisted.

"You don't have to be a baby to need protection," she replied in a tired voice. "Strong grown men often cry for their mothers."

"I don't have a mother!" I shot back, and regretted it as soon as the words left my mouth.

Grandmere's eyes saddened and her shoulders slumped. Suddenly, she looked very old to me. She put her hand on her heart and took a deep breath, nodding.

"I know, child. That's why I try so hard to do what's right for you. I know I can't be your mother, too, but I can do some of what a mother would do. It's not enough; it's never enough, but—"

"I didn't mean to say you don't do enough for me, Grandmere. I'm sorry, but I want to go to the dance with Paul very much. I want to be treated like a young woman and not a child anymore. Didn't you want that when you were my age?" I asked. She stared at me a long moment before sighing.

"All right," she said. "If the Tate boy can take you, you can go with him, but you must promise me you will be home right after the dance."

"I will, Grandmere. I will. Thank you."

She shook her head.

"When you're young," she began, "you don't want to face up to what has to be. Your youth gives you the strength to defy, but defiance doesn't always lead to victory, Ruby. More often than not, it leads to defeat. When you come face-to-face with Fate, don't charge headlong into him. He welcomes that; it feeds him and he's got an insatiable appetite for stubborn, foolish souls."

"I don't understand, Grandmere," I said.

"You will," she told me with that heavy, prophetic tone of hers. "You will." Then she straightened up and sighed again. "I guess I'd better iron your dress," she said.

I wiped the tears from my cheeks and smiled.

"Thank you, Grandmere, but I can do it."

"No, that's all right. I want to keep myself busy," she said, then walked out, her head still hanging lower than usual.

All day Saturday, I debated about my hair. Should I wear it brushed down, tied with a ribbon in the back, or should I wear it up in a French knot? In the end I asked Grandmere to help me put my hair up.

"You have such a pretty face," Grandmere Catherine said. "You should wear your hair back more often. You're going to have a lot of nice boyfriends," she added, more to soothe herself than to please me, I thought. "So remember not to give away your heart too quickly." She took my hand into both of hers and fixed her eyes on me, eyes that looked sad and tired. "Promise?"

"Yes, Grandmere. Grandmere," I said, "are you feeling all right? You've looked very tired all day."

"Just that old ache in the back and my quickened heartbeat now and again. Nothing out of the ordinary," she said.

"I wish you didn't have to work so hard, Grandmere. Grandpere Jack should do more for us instead of drinking up his money or gambling it away," I declared.

"He can't do anything for himself, much less for us. Besides, I don't want anything from him. His money's tainted," she said firmly.

"Why is his money any more tainted than any other trapper's in the bayou, Grandmere?"

"His is," she insisted. "Let's not talk about it. If anything sets my heart beating like a parade drum, that does."

I swallowed my questions, afraid of making her sicker and more tired. Instead, I put on my dress and polished my shoes. Tonight, because the weather was unstable with intermittent showers and stronger winds, Paul was going to use one of his family's cars. He told me his father had said it was all right, but I had the feeling he hadn't told them everything. I was just too frightened to ask and risk not going to the dance. When I heard him drive up, I rushed to the door. Grandmere Catherine followed and stood right behind me.

"He's here," I cried.

"You tell him to drive slowly and be sure you're home right after the dancing," Grandmere said.

Paul rushed up to the galerie. The rain had started again, so he held an umbrella open for me.

"Wow, Ruby, you look very pretty tonight," he said, then saw Grandmere Catherine step out from behind me. "Evening, Mrs. Landry."

"You get her home nice and early," she ordered.

"Yes, ma'am."

"And drive very carefully."

"I will."

"Please, Grandmere," I moaned. She bit down on her lip to keep herself silent and I leaned forward to kiss her cheek.

"Have a good time," she muttered. I ran out to slip under Paul's umbrella and we hurried to the car. When I looked back, Grandmere Catherine was still standing in the doorway looking out at us, only she looked so much smaller and older to me. It was as if my growing up meant she was to grow older, faster. In the midst of my excitement, an excitement that made the rainy night seem like a star-studded one, a small cloud of sadness touched my thrilled heart and made it shudder for a second. But the moment Paul started driving away, I smothered the trepidation and saw only happiness and fun ahead.

The fais dodo hall was on the other side of town. All furniture, except for the benches for the older people, was moved out of the large room. In a smaller, adjoining room, large pots of gumbo were placed on tables. We didn't have a stage as such, but platforms were used to provide a place for the musicians, who played the accordion, the fiddle, the triangle, and guitars. There was a singer, too.

People came from all over the bayou, many families bringing their young children as well. The little ones were put in another adjoining room to sleep. In fact, fais dodo was Cajun baby talk for go-to-sleep, meaning put all the small kids to bed so the older folks could dance. Some of the men played a card game called bourré while their wives and older children danced what we called the Two-step.

Paul and I no sooner entered the fais dodo hall than I could hear the whispers and speculations on people's lips—what was Paul Tate doing with one of the poorest young girls in the bayou? Paul didn't seem as aware of the eyes and the whispering as I was, or if he was, he didn't care. As soon as we arrived, we were out on the dance floor. I saw some of my girlfriends gazing at us with green eyes, for just about every one of them would have liked Paul Tate to bring her to a fais dodo.

We danced to one song after another, applauding loudly at the end of each song. Time passed so quickly that we didn't realize we had danced nearly an hour before we decided we were hungry and thirsty. Laughing, feeling as if there were no one else here but the two of us, we headed for refreshments. Both of us were oblivious to the group of boys who followed along, led by Turner Browne, one of the school bullies. He was a stout, bull-necked seventeen-year-old with a shock of dark brown hair and large facial features. It was said that his family went back to the flatboat polers who had navigated the Mississippi long before the steamboat. The polers were a rough, violent bunch and the Brownes were thought to have inherited those traits. Turner lived up to the family reputation, getting into one brawl after another at school.

"Hey, Tate," Turner Browne said after we had gotten our bowls of gumbo and sat at the corner of a table. "Your mommy know you're out slumming tonight?"

All of Turner's friends laughed. Paul's face turned crimson. Slowly, he stood up.

"I think you'd better take that back, Turner, and apologize."

Turner Browne laughed.

"What'cha gonna do, Tate, tell your daddy on me?"

Again, Turner's friends laughed. I reached up and tugged on Paul's sleeve. He was red-faced and so angry he seemed to give off smoke.

"Ignore him, Paul," I said. "He's too stupid to bother with."

"Shut your mouth," Turner said. "At least I know who my father is."

At that, Paul shot forward and tackled the much larger boy, knocking him to the floor. Instantly, Turner's friends let up a howl and formed a circle, around Paul and Turner, blocking out anyone who might have rushed to put a quick end to it. Turner was able to roll over Paul and pin him down by sitting on his stomach. He delivered a punch to Paul's right cheek. It swelled up almost instantly. Paul was able to block Turner's next punch, just as the older men arrived and pulled him off Paul. When he stood up, Paul's lower lip was bleeding.

"What's going on here?" Mr. Lafourche demanded. He was in charge of the hall.

"He attacked me," Turner accused, pointing at Paul.

"That's not the whole truth," I said. "He—"

"All right, all right," Mr. Lafourche said. "I don't care who did what. This sort of thing doesn't go on in my hall. Now get yourselves out of here. Go on, Browne. Move yourself and your crew before I have you all locked up."

Smiling, Turner Browne turned and led his bunch of cronies away. I brought a wet napkin to Paul and dabbed his lip gently.

"I'm sorry," he said. "I lost my temper."

"You shouldn't have. He's so much bigger."

"I don't care how big he is. I'm not going to allow him to say those things to you," Paul replied bravely. With his cheek scarlet and a little swollen, I could only cry for him. Everything had been going so well; we were having such a good time. Why was there always someone like Turner Browne to spoil things?

"Let's go," I said.

"We can still stay and dance some more."

"No. We'd better get something on your bruises. Grandmere Catherine will have something that will heal you quickly," I said.

"She'll be disappointed in me, angry that I got into a fight while I was with you," Paul moaned. "Damn that Turner Browne."

"No, she won't. She'll be proud of you, proud of the way you came to my defense," I said.

"You think so?"

"Yes," I said, although I wasn't sure how Grandmere would react. "Anyway, if she can fix it so your face doesn't look so bad, your parents won't be as angry, right?"

He nodded and then laughed.

"I look terrible, huh?"

"Not much better than someone who wrestled an alligator, I suppose."

We both laughed and then left the hall. Turner Browne and his friends were already gone, off to guzzle beer and brag to each other, I imagined, so there was no more trouble. It was raining harder when we drove back to the house. Paul pulled as close as he could and then we hurried in under the umbrella. The moment we stepped through the door, Grandmere Catherine looked up from her needlework and nodded.

"It was that bully, Turner Browne, Grandmere. He—"

She lifted her hand, rose from her seat, and went to the counter where she had some of her poultices set out as if she had anticipated our dramatic arrival. It was eerie. Even Paul was speechless.

"Sit down," she told him, pointing to a chair. "After I treat him, you can tell me all about it."

Paul looked at me, his eyes wide, and then moved to the seat to let Grandmere Catherine work her miracles.

4

Learning to Be a Liar

"Here," Grandmere Catherine told Paul, "keep this pressed against your cheek with one hand and this pressed against your lip with the other." She handed him two warm cloths over which she had smeared one of her secret salves. When Paul took the cloths, I saw the knuckles on his right hand were all bruised and scraped as well.

"Look at his hand, too, Grandmere," I cried.

"It's nothing," Paul said. "When I was rolling around on the floor—"

"Rolling around on the floor? At the fais dodo?" Grandmere asked. He nodded and then started to speak.

"We were having some gumbo and—"

"Hold those tight," she ordered. While he was holding the cloth against his lip, he couldn't talk, so I spoke for him, quickly.

"It was Turner Browne. He said one nasty thing after another just to show off in front of his friends," I told her.

"What sort of nasty things?" she demanded.

"You know, Grandmere. Bad things."

She stared at me a moment and then looked at Paul. It wasn't easy to keep anything from Grandmere Catherine. For as long as I could remember, she had a way of seeing right into your heart and soul.

"He made nasty remarks about your mother?" Grandmere asked. I

649

shifted my eyes away which was as good as saying yes. She took a deep breath, her hand against her heart and nodded. "They won't let it go. They cling to other people's hard times like moss clings to damp wood." She shook her head again and shuffled away, her hand still on her heart.

I looked at Paul. His sad eyes told me how sorry he was he had lost his temper. He started to take the cloth off his lip to say so, but I put my hand over his quickly. Paul smiled at me with his eyes, even though his lips had to be kept in a straight line.

"Just hold it there like Grandmere said," I told him. She looked back at us. I kept my hand over his and smiled. "He was very brave, Grandmere. You know how big Turner Browne is, but Paul didn't care."

"He looks it," she said, and shook her head. "Your Grandpere Jack wasn't much different and still isn't. I wish I had a pretty penny for every time I had to prepare a poultice to treat the injuries he suffered in one of his brawls. One time he came home with his right eye shut tight, and another time, he had a piece of his ear bitten off. You'd think that would make him think twice before getting into any more such conflicts, but not that man. He was at the end of the line when they passed out good sense," she concluded.

The rain that had been pounding on our tin roof subsided until we could hear only a slight *tap, tap, tap,* and the wind had died down considerably. Grandmere opened the batten plank shutters to let the breeze travel through our house again. She took a deep breath.

"I do love the way the bayou smells after a good rain. It makes everything fresh and clean. I wish it would do the same to people," she said, and sighed deeply. Her eyes were still dark and troubled. I never had heard her sound so sad and tired. A kind of paralyzing numbness gripped me and for a moment, I could only sit there and listen to my heart pound. Grandmere suddenly shuddered and embraced herself.

"Are you all right, Grandmere?"

"What? Yes, yes. Okay," she said, moving to Paul. "Let me look at you."

He took the cloths from his lips and cheek and she scrutinized his face. The swelling had subsided, but his cheek was still crimson and his lower lip dark where Turner Browne's fist had split the skin. Grandmere Catherine nodded and then went to the icebox and chipped out a small chunk to wrap in another washcloth.

"Here," she said, returning. "Put this on your cheek until it gets too cold and then put it on your lip. Keep alternating until the ice melts away, understand?"

"Yes, ma'am," Paul said. "Thank you. I'm sorry all this happened. I should have just ignored Turner Browne."

Grandmere Catherine held her eyes on him a moment and then relaxed her expression.

"Sometimes you can't ignore; sometimes the evil won't leave," she said. "But that doesn't mean I expect to see you in any more fights," she warned. He nodded obediently.

"You won't," he promised.

"Hmm," she said. "I wish I had another pretty penny for how many times my husband has made the same promise."

"I keep mine," Paul said proudly. Grandmere liked that and finally smiled.

"We'll see," she said.

"I better get going," Paul declared, standing. "Thanks again, Mrs. Landry."

Grandmere Catherine nodded.

"I'll walk you to the car, Paul," I said. When we stepped out on the galerie, we saw the rain had nearly stopped. The sky was still quite dark, but the glow from the galerie's dangling naked bulb threw a stream of pale white light to Paul's car. Still holding the ice pack against his cheek, he took my hand with his free hand and we walked over the pathway.

"I do feel terrible about ruining the evening," he said.

"You didn't ruin it; Turner Browne ruined it. Besides, we got in plenty of dancing first," I added.

"It was fun, wasn't it?"

"You know," I said. "This was my first real date."

"Really? I used to think you had a stream of boyfriends knocking on your door, and you wouldn't give me the time of day," he confessed. "It took all the courage I could muster, more courage than it took to attack Turner Browne, for me to walk up to you that afternoon at school and ask to carry your books and walk you home."

"I know. I remember how your lips trembled, but I thought that was adorable."

"You did? Well, then I'll just continue to be the shyest young man you ever did see."

"As long as you're not too shy to kiss me now and then," I replied. He smiled and grimaced with the pain it caused to stretch his lip. "Poor Paul," I said, and leaned forward to kiss him ever so gently on that wounded mouth. His eyes were still closed when I pulled back. Then they popped open.

"That's the best poultice, even better than your grandmother's magical medicines. I'm going to have to come around every day and get another treatment," he said.

"It will cost you," I warned.

"How much?"

"Your undying devotion," I replied. His eyes riveted on me.

"You already have that, Ruby," he whispered, "and always will."

Then he leaned forward, disregarding the pain, and kissed me warmly on the lips.

"Funny," he said, opening his car door, "but even with this bruised cheek and split lip, I think this was one of the best nights of my life. Good night, Ruby."

"Good night. Don't forget to keep that ice on your lip like Grandmere told you to," I advised.

"I won't. Thank her again for me. See you tomorrow," he promised, and started his engine. I watched him back away. He waved and then drove into the night. I stood watching until the small red lights on the rear of his car were swallowed by the darkness. Then I turned, embracing myself, and saw Grandmere Catherine standing on the edge of the galerie looking out at me. How long had she been there? I wondered. Why was she waiting like that?

"Grandmere? Are you all right?" I asked when I approached. Her face was so gloomy. She looked pale, forlorn, and as if she had just seen one of the spirits she was employed to chase away. Her eyes stared at me bleakly. Something hard and heavy grew in my chest, making it ache in anticipation.

"Come on inside," she said. "I have something to tell you, something I should have told you long ago."

My legs felt as stiff as tree stumps as I went up the stairs and into the house. My heart, which had been beating with pleasure after Paul's last kiss, beat harder, deeper, thumped deep down into my very soul. I couldn't remember ever seeing such a look of melancholy and sadness on Grandmere Catherine's face. What great burden did she carry? What terrible thing was she about to tell me?

She sat down and stared ahead for a long time as though she'd forgotten I was there. I waited, my hands in my lap, my heart still pounding.

"There was always a wildness in your mother," she began. "Maybe it was the Landry blood, maybe it was the way she grew up, always close to wild things. Unlike most girls her age, she was never afraid of anything in the swamp. She would pick up a baby snake as quickly as she would pick a daisy.

"In the early days, Grandpere Jack took her everywhere he went in the bayou. She fished with him, hunted with him, poled the pirogue when she was just tall enough to stand and push the stick into the mud. I used to think she was going to be a tomboy. However," she said, focusing her eyes on me now, "she was to be anything but a tomboy. Maybe it would have been better if she had been less feminine.

"She grew quickly, blossomed into a flower of womanhood way before her time, and those dark eyes of hers, her long, flowing hair as rich and red as yours, enchanted men and boys alike. I even think she fascinated the birds and animals of the swamp. Often," she said, smiling at her memory, "I would see a marsh hawk peering down with yellow-circled eyes to follow her with his gaze as she walked along the shore of the canal.

"So innocent and so beautiful, she was eager to touch everything, see everything, experience everything. Alas, she was vulnerable to older, shrewder people, and thus, she was tempted to drink from the cup of sinful pleasure.

"By the time she was sixteen, she was very popular and asked to go everywhere by every boy in the bayou. They all pleaded with her for some attention. I saw the way she teased and tormented some who were absolutely in agony over her smile, her laugh, dying for her to say something promising to them whenever they came around.

"She had young boys doing all her chores, even lining up to help Grandpere Jack, who wasn't above taking advantage of the poor souls, I might add. He knew they hoped to court Gabrielle's favor by slaving for him and he had them doing more for him than they did for their own fathers. It was downright criminal of him, but he wouldn't listen to me.

"Anyway, one night, about seven months after her sixteenth birthday, Gabrielle came to me in this very room. She was sitting right where you're sitting now. When I looked up at her, I didn't need to hear what she was going to say. She was no more than a windowpane, easy to read. My heart did flip-flops; I held my breath.

"'Mama,' she said, her voice cracking, 'I think I'm pregnant.' I closed my eyes and sat back. It was as though the inevitable had occurred, what I had feared and felt might happen, had happened.

"As you know we're Catholics; we don't go to no shack butchers and abort our pregnancies. I asked her who was the father and she just shook her head and ran from me. Later, when Grandpere Jack came home and heard, he went wild. He nearly beat her to death before I stopped him, but he got out of her who the father was," she said, and raised her eyes slowly.

Was that thunder I heard, or was it blood thundering through my veins and roaring in my ears?

"Who was it, Grandmere?" I asked, my voice cracking, my throat choking up quickly.

"It was Octavious Tate who had seduced her," she said, and once again it was as if thunder shook the house, shook the very foundations of our world and shattered the fragile walls of my heart and soul. I could not speak; I could not ask the next question, but Grandmere had decided I was to know it all.

"Grandpere Jack went to him directly. Octavious had been married less than a year and his father was alive then. Your Grandpere Jack was an even bigger gambler in those days. He couldn't pass up a game of bourré even though most times he was the one stuffing the pot. One time he lost his boots and had to walk home barefoot. And another time, he wagered a gold tooth and had to sit and let someone pull it out with a pliers. That's how sick a gambler he was and still is.

"Anyway, he got the Tates to pay him to keep things silent and part of the bargain was that Octavious would take the child and bring it up as his own. What he told his new wife and how they worked it out between them, we never knew, didn't care to know.

"I kept your mother's pregnancy hidden, strapping her up when she started to show in the seventh month. By then it was summer and she didn't have to attend school. We kept her here at the house most of the time. During the final three weeks, she stayed inside mostly and we told everyone that she had gone to visit her cousins in Iberia.

"The baby, a healthy boy, was born and delivered to Octavious Tate. Grandpere Jack got his money and lost it in less than a week, but the secret was kept.

"Up until now, that is," she said, lowering her head. "I had hoped never to have to tell you. You already know what your mother did later on. I didn't want you to think terrible of her and then think terrible of yourself.

"But I never counted on you and Paul . . . becoming more than just friends," she added. "When I saw you two kiss out by his car before, I knew you had to be told," she concluded.

"Then Paul and I are half brother and half sister?" I asked with a gasp. She nodded. "But he doesn't know any of this?"

"As I told you, we didn't know how the Tates dealt with it."

I buried my face in my hands. The tears that burned beneath my lids seemed to be falling inside me as well, making my stomach icy and cold. I shivered and rocked.

"Oh, God, how horrible, oh, God," I moaned.

"You see and understand why I had to tell you, don't you, Ruby dear?" Grandmere Catherine asked. I could feel how troubled she was by making the revelation, how much it bothered her to see me in such pain. I nodded quickly. "You must not let things go any further between the two of you, but it's not your place to tell him what I've told you. It's something his own father must tell him."

"It will destroy him," I said, shaking my head. "It will crack his heart in two, just as it has cracked mine."

"Then don't tell him, Ruby," Grandmere Catherine advised. I looked up at her. "Just let it all end."

"How, Grandmere? We like each other so much. Paul is so gentle and kind and—"

"Let him think you don't care about him anymore like that, Ruby. Let him go and he'll find another girlfriend soon enough. He's a handsome boy. Besides, his parents will only give him more grief if you don't, especially his father, and you will only succeed in breaking the Tates apart."

"His father is a monster, a monster. How could he have done such a thing when he was married for such a short time?" I demanded, my anger overcoming my sadness for the moment.

"I make no excuses for him. He was a grown man and Gabrielle was just an impressionable young girl, but so beautiful, it didn't surprise me that grown men longed for her. The devil, the evil spirit that hovers in the shadows, crept over Octavious Tate day by day, I'm sure, and eventually found entrance into his heart and drove him to seduce your mother."

"Paul would hate him, he would hate his own father if he knew," I said vehemently. Grandmere nodded.

"Do you want to do that, Ruby? Do you want to be the one who puts enmity in his heart and drives him to despise his own father?" she asked softly. "And what will Paul feel about the woman he thinks is his mother? What will you do to that relationship, too?"

"Oh, Grandmere," I cried, and rose off the settee to throw myself at her feet. I embraced her legs and buried my face in her lap. She stroked my hair softly.

"There, there, my baby. You will get over the pain. You're still very young with your whole life ahead of you. You're going to become a great artist and have beautiful things." She put her hand under my chin and lifted my head so she could look into my eyes. "Now do you understand why I dream of you leaving the bayou," she added.

With my tears streaming down my cheeks, I nodded. "Yes," I said. "I do. But I never want to leave you, Grandmere."

"Someday you will have to, Ruby. It's the way of all things, and when that day comes, don't hesitate. Do what you have to do. Promise me you will. Promise," she demanded. She looked so anxious about it, I had to respond.

"I will, Grandmere."

"Good," she said. "Good." She sat back, looking as if she had just aged a year for every minute that passed. I ground the tears from my eyes with my small fists and stood up.

"Do you want something, Grandmere? A glass of lemonade, maybe?"

"Just a glass of cold water," she said, smiling. She patted my hand. "I'm sorry, honey," she said.

I swallowed hard and leaned down to kiss her on the cheek.

"It's not your fault, Grandmere. You have no reason to blame yourself."

She smiled softly at me. Then I got her the glass of water and watched her drink it. It seemed painful for her to do so, but she finished it and rose from her chair.

"I'm very tired, suddenly," she said. "I've got to go to bed."

"Yes, Grandmere. I will soon, too."

After she left, I went to the front door and looked out at where Paul and I had kissed good night.

We didn't know it then, but it was the last time we would ever kiss like that, the last time we would ever feel each other's heart beating and thrill to each other's touch. I closed the door and walked to the stairway, feeling as if someone I knew and loved with all my heart had just died. In a real sense that was true, for the Paul Tate I knew and loved before was gone and the Ruby Landry he had kissed and loved as well was lost. The sin that had given Paul life had reared its ugly head and taken away his love.

I dreaded the days that were now to follow.

That night I tossed and turned and woke from my sleep many times. Each time, my stomach felt as tight as a fist. I wished the whole day and night had just been a bad dream, but there was no denying Grandmere Catherine's dark, sad eyes. The vision of her face lingered behind my eyelids, reminding, reinforcing, confirming that all that had happened and all that I had learned was real and true.

I didn't think Grandmere Catherine had slept any better than I had, even though she had looked so exhausted before going to bed. For the first time in a long time, she was up and about only moments before me. I heard her shuffling past my room and opened the door to watch her make her way to the kitchen.

I hurried to go down to help her with our breakfast. Although the rainstorm of the night before had passed, there were still layers of thin, gray clouds across the Louisiana sky, making the morning look as dreary as I felt. The birds seemed subdued as well, barely singing and calling to each other. It was as if the whole bayou were feeling sorry for me and for Paul.

"Seems a Traiteur should be able to treat her own arthritis," Grandmere muttered. "My joints ache and my recipes for medicine don't seem to help."

Grandmere Catherine was not one to voice complaints about herself. I'd seen her walk miles in the rain to help someone and not utter a single syllable of protest. No matter what infirmity or hard luck she suffered, she always remarked that there were too many who were worse off.

"You don't drop the potato because hills and valleys suddenly appear on your road," she told me, which was a Cajun's way of saying you don't give up. "You bear the brunt; you carry the excess baggage, and you go on." I always felt she was trying to teach me how to live by example, so I knew how much pain she must be suffering to complain about it in my presence this morning.

"Maybe we should take a day off from the road stall, Grandmere," I said. "We've got my painting money and—"

"No," she said. "It's better to keep busy, and besides, we've got to be out there while there are still tourists in the bayou. You know we have enough weeks and months without anyone coming around to buy our things and it's hard enough to scrounge and scrape up a living then."

I didn't say it, because I knew it would only get her angry, but why *didn't* Grandpere Jack do more for us? Why did we let him get away with his lazy, swamp bum life? He was a Cajun man and as such he should bear more responsibility for his family, even if Grandmere was not pleased with him. I made up my mind I would pole out to his shack later and tell him what I thought.

Right after breakfast, I started to set up our roadside stall as usual while Grandmere prepared her gumbo. I saw the strain on her face as she worked and then carried things out, so I ran and got her a chair to sit on as quickly as I could. Despite what she had said, I wished it would rain hard and send us back into the house, so she could rest. But it didn't and just as she had predicted, the tourists began to come around.

About eleven o'clock Paul drove up on his motor scooter. Grandmere Catherine and I exchanged a quick look, but she said nothing more to me as Paul approached.

"Hello, Mrs. Landry," he began. "My cheek is practically all healed and my lip feels fine," he quickly added. The bruise had diminished considerably. There was just a slight pink area on his cheekbone. "Thanks again."

"You're welcome," Grandmere said, "but don't forget your promise to me."

"I won't." He laughed and turned to me. "Hi."

"Hi," I said quickly, and unfolded and folded a blanket so it would rest more neatly on the shelves of the stall. "How come you're not working in the cannery today?" I asked, without looking at him.

He stepped closer so Grandmere wouldn't hear.

"My father and I had it out last night. I'm not working for him anymore and I can't use the car until he says so, which might be never unless—"

"Unless you stop seeing me," I finished for him, then turned around. The look in his eyes told me I was right.

"I don't care what he says. I don't need the car. I bought the scooter with my own money, so I'll just ride around on it. All I care about doing is getting here to see you as quickly as I can. Nothing else matters," he declared firmly.

"That's not true, Paul. I can't let you do this to your parents and to yourself. Maybe not now, but weeks, months, even years from now, you'll regret driving your parents away from you," I told him sternly. Even I could hear the new, cold tone in my voice. It pained me to be this way, but I had to do it, I had to find a way to stop what could never be.

"What?" He smiled. "You know the only thing I care about is getting to be with you, Ruby. Let them adjust if they don't want to drive us apart. It's all their fault. They're snobby and selfish and—"

"No, they're not, Paul," I said quickly. His face hardened with confusion. "It's only natural for them to want the best for you."

"We've been over this before, Ruby. I told you, you're the best for me," he said. I looked away. I couldn't face him when I spoke these words. We had no customers at the moment, so I walked away from the stall, Paul trailing behind me as closely and as silently as my shadow. I paused at one of our cypress log benches and sat down, facing the swamp.

"What's wrong?" he asked softly.

"I've been thinking it all over," I said. "I'm not sure you're the best for me."

"What?"

Out in the swamp, perched on a big sycamore tree, the old marsh owl stared at us as if he could hear and understand the words we were saying. He was so still, he looked stuffed.

"After you left last night, I gave everything more thought. I know there are many girls my age or slightly older who are already married in the bayou. There are even younger ones, but I don't just want to be married and live happily ever after in the bayou. I want to do more, be more. I want to be an artist."

"So? I would never stop you. I'd do everything I could to—"

"An artist, a true artist, has to experience many things, travel, meet many different kinds of people, expand her vision," I said, turning back to him. He looked smaller, diminished by my words. He shook his head.

"What are you saying?"

"We shouldn't be so serious," I explained.

"But I thought . . ." He shook his head. "This is all because I made a fool of myself last night, isn't it? Your grandmother is really very upset with me."

"No, she's not. Last night just made me think harder, that's all."

"It's my fault," he repeated.

"It isn't anyone's fault. Or, at least it isn't our fault," I added, recalling Grandmere Catherine's revelations last night. "It's just the way things are."

"What do you want me to do?" he asked.

"I want you to . . . to do what I'm going to do . . . see other people, too."

"There's someone else then?" he followed, incredulous. "How could you be the way you were last night with me and the days and nights before that and like someone else?"

"There's not someone else just yet," I muttered.

"There is," he insisted. I looked up at him. His sadness was being replaced with anger rapidly. The softness in his eyes evaporated and a fury took its place. His shoulders rose and his face became as crimson as his bruised cheek. His lips whitened in the corners. He looked like he could exhale fire like a dragon. I hated what I was doing to him. I wished I could just vanish.

"My father told me I was a fool to put my heart and trust in you, in a—"

"In a Landry," I coached sadly.

"Yes. In a Landry. He said the apple doesn't fall far from the tree."

I lowered my head. I thought about my mother letting herself be used by Paul's father for his pleasure and I thought about Grandpere Jack caring more about getting money than what had happened to his daughter.

"He was right."

"I don't believe you," Paul shot back. When I looked at him again, I saw the tears that had washed over his eyes, tears of pain and anger, tears that would poison his mind against me. How I wished I could throw myself into his arms and stop what was happening, but I was thwarted and muzzled by reality. "You don't want to be an artist; you want to be a whore."

"Paul!"

"That's all, a whore. Well, go on, be with as many different men as you like. See if I care. I was crazy to waste my time on a Landry," he added and pivoted quickly, his boots kicking up the grass behind him as he rushed away.

My chin dropped to my chest and my body slumped on the cypress log bench. Where my heart had been, there was now a hollow cavity. I couldn't even cry. It was as if everything in me, every part of me had suddenly locked up, frozen, become as cold as stone. The sound of Paul's motor scooter engine reverberated through my body. The old marsh owl lifted his wings and strutted about nervously on the branch, but he didn't lift off. He remained there, watching me, his eyes filled with accusation now.

After Paul left our house, I got up. My legs were very shaky, but I was able to walk back to the roadside stall just as a carload of tourists pulled up. They were young men and women, loud and full of laughter and fun. The men went wild over the pickled lizards and snakes and bought four jars. The women liked Grandmere's hand-woven towels and handkerchiefs. After they had bought everything they wanted and loaded their car, one of the young men paused and approached us with his camera.

"Do you mind if I take your pictures?" he asked. "I'll give you each a dollar," he added.

"You don't have to pay us for our pictures," Grandmere replied.

"Oh, yes, he does," I said. Grandmere Catherine raised her eyebrows in surprise.

"Fine," the young man said and dug into his pocket to produce the two dollars. I took them quickly. "Can you smile?" he asked me. I forced one and he snapped his photos. "Thanks," he said, and got into the car.

"Why did you make him give us two dollars, Ruby? We haven't taken money from tourists in the past." Grandmere asked me.

"Because the world is full of pain and disappointment, Grandmere, and I plan to do all I can from now on to make it less so for us."

She fixed her eyes on me thoughtfully. "I want you to grow up, but I don't want you to grow up with a hard heart, Ruby," she said.

"A soft heart gets pierced and torn more, Grandmere. I'm not going to end up like my mother. I'm not!" I cried and despite my firm and rigid stance, I felt my new wall start to crack.

"What did you say to young Paul Tate?" Grandmere asked. "What did you tell him to make him run off like that?"

"I didn't tell him the truth, but I drove him away, just as you said I should," I moaned through my tears. "Now, he hates me."

"Oh, Ruby, I'm sorry."

"He hates me!" I cried, and turned and ran from her.

"Ruby!"

I didn't stop. I ran hard and fast over the marshland, letting the bramble bushes slap and tear at my dress, my legs, and my arms. I was oblivious to pain; I ignored the ache in my chest and disregarded the puddles and the mud into which I repeatedly stepped. But after a while, the pain in my legs and the needles in my side brought me to a halt, and I could only walk slowly over the long stretch of marshland that ran alongside the canal. My shoulders heaved with my deep sobs. I walked and walked, past the dried domes of grass that were homes to the muskrats and nutrias, avoiding the inlets in which the small green snakes swam. Fatigued and drowning in many emotions, I finally stopped and gasped in air, my hands on my hips, my bosom rising and falling.

After a moment, my eyes focused on a clump of small sycamore trees just ahead. At first, because of its color and size, I didn't see it. But gradually, it formed in my field of vision, seemingly appearing like a vision. I saw a marsh deer watching me with curiosity. It had big, beautiful, but sad looking eyes and it stood as still as a statue.

Suddenly, there was a loud report, the explosion of a high caliber rifle came from the blind, and the deer's knees crumbled. It stumbled a moment in a desperate effort to maintain its stance, but a red circle of blood appeared on its neck and grew larger and larger as the blood emerged. The deer went down quickly after that and I heard the sound of two men cheering. A pirogue shot out from under a wall of Spanish moss and I saw two strangers in the front and Grandpere Jack poling from the rear. He had hired himself out to tourist hunters and brought them to their kill. As the canoe made its way across the pond toward the dead deer, one of the tourists handed the other a bottle of whiskey and they drank to celebrate their kill. Grandpere Jack eyed the bottle and stopped poling so they could give him a swig.

Slowly, I retreated, following my footsteps back. Yes, I thought, the swamp was a beautiful place, filled with wonderful and interesting animal life, with fascinating vegetation, sometimes mysterious and still and sometimes a symphony of nature with its frogs croaking, its birds singing, its gators drumming water with their tails. But it could be a hard, cold place, too, wrought with death and danger, with poisonous snakes and spiders, with quicksand and sticky, sucking mud to draw the unsuspecting intruder down into the darkness beneath. It was a world in which the stronger fed on the weaker and into which men came to enjoy their power over natural things.

Today, I thought, it was like everywhere else on earth, and today, I hated being here.

By the time I returned, the showers had begun and Grandmere Catherine had begun to take in most of our handicraft goods. I hurried to help her with what remained. The rain fell harder and harder, so we had to rush as quickly as we could and we had no time to speak to each other until everything had been safely stored. Then Grandmere got us some towels to wipe our hair and faces. The rain pounded the tin roof and the wind whipped through the bayou. We ran around the house, closing the batten plank shutters.

"It's a real tosser," Grandmere cried. We heard the wind whistle through the cracks in our walls and saw brush and anything else that was loose and light being lifted and driven every which way over the road and lawn. The world outside became very dark. Thunder clapped and lightning scorched the sky. I could hear the cisterns overflowing as sheets of rain came off the roof and collected in the barrels. The drops fell so hard and thick, they bounced when they hit the steps or little walkway in front of the house. For a while it sounded like the tin roof would split. It was as if we had fallen into a drum. Finally, it subsided and just as quickly as it had developed into a heavy downpour, it became a slight drizzle. The sky lightened and moments later, a ray of sunlight threaded itself through the opening in the overcast and dropped a shaft of warm brightness over our home. Grandmere Catherine took a deep breath of relief and shook her head.

"I never get used to those sudden cloudbursts," she said. "When I was a little girl, I used to crawl under my bed."

I smiled at her.

"I can't imagine you as a little girl, Grandmere," I said.

"Well, I was, honey. I wasn't born this old with bones that creaked when I walked, you know." She pressed her hand against the small of her back and straightened up. "I think I'll make a cup of tea. I'd like something warm in my stomach. How about you?"

"All right, Grandmere," I said. I sat at the kitchen table while she put up the water. "Grandpere Jack is doing some guiding for hunters again. I just saw him in the swamp with two men. They shot a deer."

"He was one of the best at it," she said. "The rich Creoles were always after him when they came here to hunt, and none ever left empty-handed."

"It was a beautiful deer, Grandmere."

She nodded.

"And the thing is, they won't care about the meat; they just want a trophy."

She stared at me a moment. "What did you tell Paul?" she finally asked.

"That we shouldn't just be with each other; that we should see other people. I told him because I was an artist, I wanted to meet other people, but he didn't believe me. I'm not a good liar, Grandmere," I moaned.

"That's not a bad fault, Ruby."

"Yes, it is, Grandmere," I retorted quickly. "This is a world built on lies, lies and deceptions. The stronger and the more successful are good at it."

Grandmere Catherine shook her head sadly.

"It looks that way to you right now, Ruby honey, but don't give into the comfort of hating everything and everyone around you. Those you call stronger and successful might seem so to you, but they're not really happy, for there is a dark place in their hearts that they cannot deny and it makes their souls ache. In the end they are terrified because they know the darkness is what they will face forever."

"You've seen so much evil and so much sickness, Grandmere. How can you still feel hopeful?" I asked.

She smiled and sighed.

"It's when you stop feeling hopeful that the sickness and the evil wins over you and then what becomes of you? Never lose hope, Ruby. Never stop fighting for hope," she advised. "I know how much you're hurting now and how much poor Paul is suffering, too, but just like this sudden storm, it will end for you and the sun will be out again.

"I always dreamed," she said, coming over to sit beside me and stroke my hair, "that you would have the magical wedding, the one in the Cajun spider legend. Remember? The rich Frenchman imported those spiders from France for his daughter's wedding and released them into the oaks and pines where they wove their canopy of webs. Over them, he sprinkled gold and silver dust and then they had the candlelight wedding procession. The night glittered all around them, promising them a life of love and hope.

"Someday, you will marry a handsome man who could be a prince and you, too, will have a wedding in the stars," Grandmere promised. She kissed me and I threw my arms around her to bury my head in her soft shoulder. I cried and cried and she petted me and soothed me. "Cry, honey," she said. "And like the summer rains turn to sunshine so will your tears."

"Oh, Grandmere," I moaned. "I don't know if I can."

"You can," she said. She lifted my chin and looked into my eyes, hers those dark, mesmerizing orbs that had seen evil spirits and visions of the future, "you can and you will," she predicted.

The teapot whistled. Grandmere wiped the tears from my cheeks and kissed me again, and then got up to pour us our cups.

Later that night, I sat by my window and looked up at the clearing sky and I wondered if Grandmere was right; I wondered if I would have a wedding in the stars. The glitter of gold and silver dust danced under my eyelids when I lay my head on the pillow, but just before I fell asleep, I saw Paul's wounded face once more and then I saw the marsh deer open its mouth to voice an unheard scream as it crumbled to the grass.

5

Who Is the Little Girl If It's Not Me?

The weeks before summer and the end of the school year took ages and ages to pass. I dreaded every day I attended school, for I knew that some time during the day, I would see Paul or he would see me. During the first few days following our terrible talk, he continued to glare at me furiously whenever he saw me. His once beautiful, soft blue eyes that had gazed upon me with love so many times before were now granite cold and full of scorn and contempt. The second time we approached each other in the corridor, I tried to speak to him.

"Paul," I said, "I'd like to talk to you, to just—"

He behaved as if he didn't hear me or he didn't see me and walked past me. I wanted him to know that I wasn't seeing another boy on the side. I felt dreadful and spent most of my school day with a heart that felt more like a lump of lead in my chest.

Time wasn't healing my wounds and the longer we went on not talking to each other, the harder and colder Paul seemed to become. I wished that I could simply rush up to him one day and gush the truth so he would understand why I said the things I had said to him at my house, but every time I decided I would do just that, Grandmere Catherine's heavy words returned: "Do you want to be the one who puts enmity in his heart and drives him to despise his own father?" She was right. In the end he would hate me more, I concluded. And so

I kept my lips sealed and the truth buried beneath an ocean of secret tears.

Many times I had found myself furious with Grandmere Catherine or Grandpere Jack for not revealing the secrets in their hearts and keeping my family history a deep mystery, a mystery it should no longer have been for me at my age. Now, I was no better than they had been, keeping the truth from Paul, but there was nothing I could do about it. Worst of all, I had to stand by and watch him fall in love with someone else.

I always knew that Suzzette Daisy, a girl in my class, had a crush on Paul. She didn't wait long to pursue him, but ironically, when Paul first began spending more and more time with Suzzette Daisy, I felt a sense of relief. He would direct more of his energies toward caring for her and less toward hating me, I thought. From across the room, I watched him sit with her and eat his lunch and soon saw them holding hands when they walked through the school corridors. Of course, a part of me was jealous, a part of me raged over the injustice and cried when I saw them laughing and giggling together. Then I heard he had given her his class ring which she wore proudly on a gold chain, and I spent a night drenching my pillow in salty tears.

Most of the girls who had once been envious of Paul's affection for me now gloated. Marianne Bruster actually turned to me in the girls' room one June afternoon and blared, "I guess you don't think you're someone special anymore since you were dumped for Suzzette Daisy."

The other girls smiled and waited for me to respond.

"I never thought I was someone special, Marianne," I said. "But thank you for thinking so," I added.

For a moment she was dumbfounded. Her mouth opened and closed. I started past her, but she spun about, flinging her hair over her face, then tossing it back and whipping around to make it fan out in a circle as she grinned broadly at me.

"Well, that's just like you," she said, her hands on her hips, her head wagging from side to side as she spoke. "Just like you to be smart about it. I don't know where you come off being snotty," she continued, now building on her anger and frustration. "You're certainly no better than the rest of us."

"I never said I was, Marianne."

"If anything, you're worse. You're a bastard child. That's what you are," she accused. The others nodded. Encouraged, she reached out to seize my arm and continue. "Paul Tate finally has shown some sense. He belongs with someone like Suzzette and certainly not a low-class Cajun like a Landry," she concluded.

I pulled away and brushed at my tears as I rushed from the girls' room. It was true—everyone thought Paul belonged with someone like Suzzette Daisy and thought they were the perfect couple. She was a pretty girl with long, light brown hair and stately features, but more important, her father was a rich oil man. I was sure Paul's parents were overjoyed at his choice of a new girlfriend. He'd have no trouble getting the car and going to dances with Suzzette.

Yet despite his apparent happiness with his new girlfriend, I couldn't help but detect a wistful look in his eyes when he saw me occasionally and especially at church. Starting a relationship with Suzzette, and the passage of more time since our split-up, finally began to calm him. I even thought he was close to speaking to me, but every time he seemed to be headed in that direction, something stopped him and turned him away again.

Finally, mercifully, the school year ended, and with it my daily contact with Paul, as slight as it had been. Outside of school he and I truly did live in two different worlds. He no longer had any reason to come my way. Of course, I still saw him at church on Sunday, but in the company of his parents and sisters, he especially wouldn't even look in my direction. Occasionally, I would hear what sounded like his motor scooter's engine and go running to my doorway to look out in anticipation and in the hope that I would see him pull into our drive just as he used to so many times before. But the sound either turned out to be someone else on a motorcycle or some old car passing by.

These were my days of darkness, days when I was so sad and tired that I had to fight to get out of bed each morning. Making everything seem worse and harder was the intensity with which the heat and the humidity greeted the bayou this particular summer. Everyday temperatures hovered near a hundred with humidity often only a degree or two less. Day after day the swamps were calm, still, not even the tiniest wisp of a breeze weaving its way up from the Gulf to give us any relief.

The heat took a great toll on Grandmere Catherine. More than ever, she was oppressed by the layers and layers of heavy humidity. I hated it when she had to walk somewhere to treat someone for a bad spider bite or a terrible headache. More often than not, she would return exhausted, drained, her dress drenched, her hair sticking to her forehead and her cheeks beet red; but these trips and the work she did resulted in some small income or some gifts of food for us and with the tourist trade dwindling down to practically nothing during the summer months, there wasn't much else.

Grandpere Jack wasn't any help. He stopped even his infrequent assistance. I heard he was hunting alligators with some men from New

Orleans who wanted to sell the skins to make pocketbooks and wallets and whatever else city folk made out of the swamp creatures' hides. I didn't see him much, but whenever I did, he was usually floating by in his canoe or drifting in his dinghy and guzzling some homemade cider or whiskey, satisfied to turn whatever money he had made from his gator hunting into another bottle or jug.

Late one afternoon, Grandmere Catherine returned from a treater mission more exhausted than ever. She could barely speak. I had to rush out to help her up the stairs. She practically collapsed in her bed.

"Grandmere, your legs are trembling," I cried when I helped her take off her moccasins. Her feet were blistered and swollen, especially her ankles.

"I'll be all right," she chanted. "I'll be all right. Just get me a cold cloth for my forehead, Ruby, honey."

I hurried to do so.

"I'll just lay here a while until my heart slows down," she told me, and forced a smile.

"Oh, Grandmere, you can't make these long trips anymore. It's too hot and you're too old to do it."

She shook her head.

"I must do it," she said. "It's why the good Lord put me here."

I waited until she fell asleep and then I left the house and poled our pirogue out to Grandpere's shack. All of the sadness and days of melancholy I had endured the past month and a half turned into anger and fury directed at Grandpere. He knew how hard it was for us during the summer months. Instead of drinking up his spare money every week, he should think about us and come around more often, I decided. I also decided not to discuss it with Grandmere Catherine, for she wouldn't want to admit I was right and she wouldn't want to ask him for a penny.

The swamp was different in the summer. Besides the waking of the hibernating alligators who had been sleeping with tails fattened with stores, there were dozens and dozens of snakes, clumps of them entwined together or slicing through the water like green and brown threads. Of course, there were clouds of mosquitos and other bugs, choruses of fat bullfrogs with gaping eyes and jiggling throats croaking and families of nutrias and muskrats scurrying about frantically, stopping only to eye me with suspicion. The insects and animals continually changed the swamp, their homes making it bulge in places it hadn't before, their webs linking plants and tree limbs. It made it all seem alive, like the swamp was one big animal itself, forming and reforming with each change of season.

I knew Grandmere Catherine would be upset that I was traveling alone through the swamp this late in the summer day, as well as being upset that I was going to see Grandpere Jack. But my anger had come to a head and sent me rushing out of the house to plod over the marsh and pole the pirogue faster than ever. Before long, I came around a turn and saw Grandpere's shack straight ahead. But as I approached, I slowed down because the racket coming from it was frightening.

I heard pans clanging, furniture cracking, Grandpere's howls and curses. A small chair came flying out the door and splashed in the swamp before it quickly sunk. A pot followed and then another. I stopped my canoe and waited. Moments later, Grandpere appeared on his galerie. He was stark naked, his hair wild, holding a bullwhip. Even at this distance, I could see his eyes were bloodshot. His body was streaked with dirt and mud and there were even long, thin scratches up his legs and down the small of his back.

He cracked the whip at something in the air before him and shouted before cracking it again. I soon understood he was imagining some kind of creature and I realized he was having a drunken fit. Grandmere Catherine had described one of them to me, but I had never seen it before. She said the alcohol soaked his brain so bad it gave him delusions and created nightmares, even in the daytime. On more than one occasion, he had one of these fits in the house and destroyed many of their good things.

"I used to have to run out and wait until he grew exhausted and fell asleep," she told me. "Otherwise, he might very well hurt me without realizing it."

Remembering those words, I backed my canoe into a small inlet so he wouldn't see me watching. He cracked the whip again and again and screamed so hard, the veins in his neck bulged. Then he caught the whip in some of his muskrat traps and got it so entangled, he couldn't pull it out. He interpreted this as the monster grabbing his whip. It put a new hysteria into him and he began to wail, waving his arms about him so quickly, he looked like a cross between a man and a spider from where I was watching. Finally, the exhaustion Grandmere Catherine described set in and he collapsed to the porch floor.

I waited a long moment. All was silent and remained so. Satisfied, he was unconscious, I poled myself up to the galerie and peered over the edge to see him twisted and asleep, oblivious to the mosquitos that feasted on his exposed skin.

I tied up the canoe and stepped onto the galerie. He looked barely alive, his chest heaving and falling with great effort. I knew I couldn't lift him and carry him into the house, so I went inside and found a blanket to put over him.

Then, I pulled in a deep fearful breath and nudged him, but his eyes didn't even flutter. He was already snoring. I went cold inside. All the hopes that had lit up were snuffed out by the sight and the stench rising off him. He smelled like he had taken a bath in his jugs of cheap whiskey.

"So much for coming to you for any help, Grandpere," I said furiously. "You are a disgrace." With him unconscious, I was able to vent my anger unchecked. "What kind of a man are you? How could you let us struggle and strain to keep alive and well? You know how tired Grandmere Catherine is. Don't you have any self-respect?

"I hate having Landry blood in me. I hate it!" I screamed, and pounded my fists against my hips. My voice echoed through the swamp. A heron flew off instantly and a dozen feet away, an alligator lifted its head from the water and gazed in my direction. "Stay here, stay in the swamp and guzzle your rotgut whiskey until you die. I don't care," I cried. The tears streaked down my cheeks, hot tears of anger and frustration. My heart pounded.

I caught my breath and stared at him. He moaned, but he didn't open his eyes. Disgusted, I got back into the pirogue and started to pole myself home, feeling more despondent and defeated than ever.

With the tourist trade nearly nonexistent and school over, I had more time to do my artwork. Grandmere Catherine was the first to notice that my pictures were remarkably different. Usually in a melancholy mood when I began, I tended now to use darker colors and depict the swamp world at either twilight or at night with the pale white light of a half moon or full moon penetrating twisted sycamores and cypress limbs. Animals stared out with luminous eyes and snakes coiled their bodies, poised to strike and kill any intruders. The water was inky, the Spanish moss dangling over it like a net left there to ensnare the unwary traveler. Even the spiderwebs that I used to make sparkle like jewels now appeared more like the traps they were intended to be. The swamp was an eerie, dismal, and depressing place and if I did include my mysterious father in the picture, he had a face masked with shadows.

"I don't think most people would like that picture, Ruby," Grandmere told me one day as she stood behind me and watched me visualize another nightmare. "It's not the kind of picture that will make them feel good, the kind they're going to want to hang up in their living rooms and sitting rooms in New Orleans."

"It's how I feel, what I see right now, Grandmere. I can't help it," I told her.

She shook her head sadly and sighed before retreating to her oak rocker. I found she spent more and more time sitting and falling asleep in it. Even on cloudy days when it was a bit cooler outside, she no longer took her pleasure walks along the canals. She didn't care to go find wild flowers, nor would she visit her friends as much as she used to visit them. Invitations to lunch went unaccepted. She made her excuses, claimed she had to do this or that, but usually ended up falling asleep in a chair or on the sofa.

When she didn't know I was watching, I caught her taking deep breaths and pressing her palm against her bosom. Any exertion, washing clothes or the floors, polishing furniture, and even cooking exhausted her. She had to take frequent rests in between and battle to catch her breath.

But when I asked her about it, she was always ready with an excuse. She was tired from staying up too late the night before; she had a bit of lumbago, she got up too fast, anything and everything but her owning up to the truth—that she hadn't been well for quite some time now.

Finally, on the third Sunday in August, I rose and dressed and went down, surprised I was up and ready before her, especially on a church day. When she finally appeared, she looked pale and very old, as old as Rip van Winkle after his extended sleep. She cringed a bit when she walked and held her hand against her side.

"I don't know what's come over me," she declared. "I haven't overslept like this for years."

"Maybe you can't cure yourself, Grandmere. Maybe your herbs and potions don't work on you and you should see a town doctor," I suggested.

"Nonsense. I just haven't found the right formula yet, but I'm on the right track. I'll be back to myself in a day or two," she swore, but two days went by and she didn't improve an iota. One minute she would be talking to me and the next, she would be fast asleep in her chair, her mouth wide open, her chest heaving as if it were a struggle to breathe.

Only two events got her up and about with the old energy she used to exhibit. The first was when Grandpere Jack came to the house and actually asked us for money. I was sitting with Grandmere on the galerie after our dinner, grateful for the little coolness the twilight brought to the bayou. Her head grew heavier and heavier on her shoulders until her chin rested on her chest, but the moment Grandpere Jack's footsteps could be heard, her head snapped up. She narrowed her eyes into slits of suspicion.

"What's he coming here for?" she demanded, staring into the darkness out of which he emerged like some ghostly apparition from the swamp: his long hair bouncing on the back of his neck, his face sallow with his grimy gray beard thicker than usual, and his clothes so creased and dirty, he looked like he had been rolling around in them for days. His boots were so thick with mud, it looked caked around his feet and ankles.

"Don't you come any closer," Grandmere snapped. "We just had our dinner and the stink will turn our stomachs."

"Aw, woman," he said, but he stopped about a half-dozen yards from the galerie. He took off his hat and held it in his hands. Fishhooks dangled from the brim. "I come here on a mission of mercy," he said.

"Mercy? Mercy for who?" Grandmere demanded.

"For me," he replied. That nearly set her laughing. She rocked a bit and shook her head.

"You come here to beg forgiveness?" she asked.

"I came here to borrow some money," he said.

"What?" She stopped rocking, stunned.

"My dinghy's motor is shot to hell and Charlie McDermott won't advance me any more credit to buy a new used one from him. I gotta have a motor or I can't earn any money guiding hunters, harvesting oysters, whatnot," he said. "I know you got something put away and I swear—"

"What good is your oath, Jack Landry? You're a cursed man, a doomed man whose soul already has a prime reservation in hell," she told him with more vehemence and energy than I had seen her exert in days. For a moment Grandpere didn't reply.

"If I can earn something, I can pay you back and then some right quickly," he said. Grandmere snorted.

"If I gave you the last pile of pennies we had, you'd turn from here and run as fast as you could to get a bottle of rum and drink yourself into another stupor," she told him. "Besides," she said, "we haven't got anything. You know how times get in the bayou in the summer for us. Not that you showed you cared any," she added.

"I do what I can," he protested.

"For yourself and your damnable thirst," she fired back.

I shifted my gaze from Grandmere to Grandpere. He really did look desperate and repentant. Grandmere Catherine knew I had my painting money put away. I could loan it to him if he was really in a fix, I thought, but I was afraid to say.

"You'd let a man die out here in the swamp, starve to death and become food for the buzzards," he moaned.

She stood up slowly, rising to her full five feet four inches of height as if she were really six feet tall, her head up, her shoulders back, and then she lifted her left arm to point her forefinger at him. I saw his eyes bulge with shock and fear as he took a step back.

"You are already dead, Jack Landry," she declared with the authority of a bishop, "and already food for buzzards. Go back to your cemetery and leave us be," she commanded.

"Some Christian you are," he cried, but continued to back up. "Some show of mercy. You're no better than me, Catherine. You're no better," he called, and turned to get swallowed up in the darkness from where he had come as quickly as he had appeared. Grandmere stared after him a few moments even after he was gone and then sat down.

"We could have given him my painting money, Grandmere," I said. She shook her head vehemently.

"That money is not to be touched by him," she said firmly. "You're going to need it someday, Ruby, and besides," she added, "he'd only do what I said, turn it into cheap whiskey.

"The nerve of him," she continued, more to herself than to me, "coming around here and asking me to loan him money. The nerve of him . . ."

I watched her wind herself down until she was slumped in her chair again, and I thought how terrible it was that two people who had once kissed and held each other, who had loved and wanted to be with each other were now like two alley cats, hissing and scratching at each other in the night.

The confrontation with my grandpere drained Grandmere. She was so exhausted, I had to help her to bed. I sat beside her for a while and watched her sleep, her cheeks still red, her forehead beaded with perspiration. Her bosom rose and fell with such effort, I thought her heart would simply burst under the pressure.

That night I went to sleep with great trepidation, afraid that when I woke up, I would find Grandmere Catherine hadn't. But thankfully, her sleep revived her and what woke me the next morning was the sound of her footsteps as she made her way to the kitchen to start breakfast and begin another day of work in the loom room.

Despite the lack of customers, we continued our weaving and handicrafts whenever we could during the summer months, building a stock of goods to put out when the tourist season got back into high swing. Grandmere bartered with cotton growers and farmers who harvested the palmetto leaves with which we made the hats and fans. She traded some of her gumbo for split oak so we could make the baskets. Whenever it appeared we were bone-dry and had nothing to offer in return for craft materials, Grandmere reached deeper into her sacred chest and came up with something of value she had either been given as payment for a treater mission years before, or something she had been saving just for such a time.

Just at one of these hard periods, the second thing occurred to put vim and vigor into her steps and words. The postman delivered a fancy light blue envelope with a lace design on its edges addressed to me. It came from New Orleans, the return address simply Dominique's.

"Grandmere, I've got a letter from the gallery in New Orleans," I shouted running into the house. She nodded, holding her breath, her eyes bright with excitement.

"Go on, open it," she said, slipping into a chair. I sat at the kitchen table while I tore it open and plucked out a cashier's check for two hundred and fifty dollars. There was a note with it.

> Congratulations on the sale of one of your pictures. I have some interest in the others and will be contacting you in the near future to see what else you have done since my visit.
>
> Sincerely,
> Dominique

Grandmere Catherine and I just looked at each other for a moment and then her face lit up with the brightest, broadest smile I had seen her wear for months. She closed her eyes and offered a quick prayer of thanks. I continued to stare incredulously at the cashier's check.

"Grandmere, can this be true? Two hundred and fifty dollars! For one of my paintings!"

"I told you it would happen. I told you," she said. "I wonder who bought it. He doesn't say?"

I looked again and shook my head.

"It doesn't matter," she said. "Many people will see it now and other well-to-do Creoles will come to Dominique's to look for your work and he will tell them who you are; he will tell them the artist is Ruby Landry," she added, nodding.

"Now you listen to me, Grandmere," I said firmly, "we are going to use this money to live on and not bury in your chest for some future thing for me."

"Maybe just some of it," she accepted, "but most of it has to be put away for you. Some day you will need nicer clothing and shoes and other things, and you will need traveling money, too," she said with certainty.

"Where am I going, Grandmere?" I asked.

"Away from here. Away from here," she muttered. "But for now, let us celebrate. Let's make a shrimp gumbo and a special dessert. I know," she said, "we'll make a Kings Cake." It was one of my favorites: a yeast cake ring with colorful sugar glazes. "I'll invite Mrs. Thibodeau and Mrs. Livaudis for dinner so I can brag about my granddaughter until they burst with envy. But first we'll go to the bank and cash your check," she said.

Grandmere's excitement and happiness filled me with joy I hadn't felt in months. I wished that I had someone special with whom to celebrate and thought about Paul. I had seen him only one other time besides church the whole summer and that was when I was in town shopping for some groceries. When I came out of the store, I caught sight of him sitting in his father's car, waiting for him to come out of the bank. He looked my way and I thought he smiled, but at that moment his father appeared and he snapped his head around to face front. Disappointed, I watched him drive off, not looking back once.

Grandmere and I walked to town to cash my check. On the way we stopped at Mrs. Thibodeau's and Mrs. Livaudis's homes to invite them to our dinner of celebration. Then Grandmere began to cook and bake like she hadn't done for months. I helped her prepare and then set the table. She decided to stack the crisp twenty dollar bills at the center of the table with a rubber band around them just to impress her old friends. When they set eyes on it and heard how I had received it, they were astonished. Some people in the bayou worked a whole month for this much money.

"Well, I'm not surprised," Grandmere said. "I always knew she would become a famous artist someday."

"Oh, Grandmere," I said, embarrassed with all the attention, "I'm far from a famous artist."

"Right now you are, but one day you will be famous. Just wait and see," Grandmere predicted. We served the gumbo and the women got into a discussion about varieties of recipes. There were as many gumbo recipes in the bayou as there were Cajuns, I thought. Listening to Grandmere Catherine and her friends argue over what combination of ingredients was the best and what accounted for the best roux amused me. Their spirited talk became even more so when Grandmere decided to bring out her homemade wine, something she saved for only very special occasions. One glass of it went right to my head. I felt my face turn crimson, but Grandmere and her two friends poured themselves glass after glass as if it were water.

The good food, the wine, and the laughter reminded me of happier times when Grandmere and I would go to community celebrations and gatherings. One of my favorites had always been Flocking the Bride. Each of the women would bring a chicken to start the flock for a newlywed, and there was always lots to eat and drink, and lots of music and dancing. Grandmere Catherine, being a Traiteur, was always an honored guest.

After we served the cake and cups of rich, thick Cajun coffee, I told Grandmere to take Mrs. Thibodeau and Mrs. Livaudis out to the galerie. I would clear the table and do the dishes.

"We shouldn't leave the one in whose honor we're celebrating with all the work," Mrs. Thibodeau said, but I insisted. After I cleaned up, I realized we still had the stack of money on the table. I went out to ask Grandmere where she thought I should put it.

"Just run up and put it in my chest, Ruby dear," she said. I was surprised. Grandmere Catherine never let me open her chest or rifle through it before. Occasionally, when she opened it, I looked over her shoulder and gazed in at the finely woven linen napkins and handkerchiefs, the silver goblets, and ropes of pearls. I remembered wanting to sift through all the memorabilia, but Grandmere Catherine always kept her chest sacred. I wouldn't dare touch it without her permission.

I hurried away to hide my new fortune. But when I opened the chest, I saw how empty it had become. Gone were the beautiful linens and all but one silver goblet. Grandmere had bartered and pawned much more than I imagined. It broke my heart to see how much of her personal treasure was gone. I knew that every item had had some special value beyond its money value. I knelt down and gazed at what remained: a single string of beads, a bracelet, a few embroidered scarfs, and a pile of documents and pictures, wrapped in rubber bands. The documents included inoculation certificates for me, as well as Grandmere Catherine's grade school diploma, and some old letters with ink so faded they were barely legible.

I sifted through some of the pictures. She still kept pictures of Grandpere Jack as a young man. How handsome he had been when he was a young man in his early twenties, tall and dark with wide shoulders and a narrow waist. A charming smile flashed brightly from the photograph and he stood so straight and proud. It was easy to see why Grandmere Catherine would have fallen in love with such a man. I found the other pictures of her mother and father, sepia colored and old and faded, but enough left for me to see that Grandmere Catherine's mother, my great-grandmother, had been a pretty woman with a sweet, gentle smile and small delicate features. Her father looked dignified and strong, tight-lipped and serious.

I put back the packets of documents and old family photographs, but before I deposited my money in the chest, I saw the edge of another picture sticking out from the pages of Grandmere Catherine's old leather-bound Bible. Slowly, I picked it up, handling the cracked cover carefully and gently opening the crisp pages that wanted to flake at the corners. I gazed at the old photograph.

It was a picture of a very good-looking man standing in front of what looked like a mansion. He was holding the hand of a little girl who looked a lot like me at that age. I studied the picture more closely. The little girl resembled me so much it was like looking at myself at this young age. In fact, the resemblance was so remarkable, I had to go to my room and find a picture of myself as a little girl. I placed the two side by side and studied them again.

It was me, I thought. It really was. But who was this man and where was I when this picture was taken? I would have been old enough to remember a house like this, I thought. I couldn't have been much less than six or seven at the time. I turned the picture over and saw there was scribbling on the back near the bottom.

Dear Gabrielle,
    I thought you would like to see her on her seventh birthday. Her hair is very like yours and she's everything I dreamed she would be.

Love,
Pierre

Pierre? Who was Pierre? And this picture, it was sent to my mother? Was this my father? Had I been somewhere with him? But why would he be telling my mother about me? She had already died. Could it be he hadn't known at the time? No, that made no sense, for how could he have gotten me even for a short time and not known my mother was dead? And how could I have been with him and not recalled anything?

The mystery buzzed around inside me like a hive of bees making my stomach tingle. It filled me with a strange sense of foreboding and anxiety. I looked at the little girl again and again compared our faces. The resemblance was undeniable. I had been with this man.

I took a deep breath and tried to calm myself so when I went back downstairs and saw Grandmere and her friends, they wouldn't know something had disturbed me, disturbed my very heart and soul. I knew how hard, if not impossible, it would be for me to hide anything from Grandmere Catherine, but fortunately, she was so involved in an argument over crabmeat ravigote, she didn't notice how disturbed I was.

Finally, her friends grew tired and decided it was time for them to leave. Once again, they offered me their congratulations, kissing and hugging me while Grandmere looked on proudly. We watched them leave and then we went into the house.

"I haven't had a good time like that in ages," Grandmere said, sighing. "And look at what a wonderful job you did cleaning up. My Ruby," she said, turning to me, "I'm so proud of you, dear and . . ."

Her eyes narrowed quickly. She was flushed from the wine and the excitement of all her arguments, but her spiritual powers were not asleep. She quickly sensed something was wrong and stepped toward me.

"What is it, Ruby?" she asked quickly. "What's stirred you up so?"

"Grandmere," I began. "You sent me upstairs to put the money in your chest."

"Yes," she said, and then followed that with a deep gasp. She stepped back, her hand on her heart. "You went looking through my things?"

"I didn't mean to snoop, Grandmere, but I was interested in the old pictures of you and Grandpere Jack, and your parents. Then, I saw something sticking out of your old Bible and I found this," I said, holding the picture out toward her. She looked down at it as if she were looking down at a picture of death and disaster. She took it from me and sat down slowly, nodding as she did so.

"Who is that man, Grandmere? And the little girl—it's me, isn't it?" I asked.

She lifted her head, her eyes swollen with sadness and shook her head.

"No, Ruby," she said. "It's not."

"But it looks just like me, Grandmere. Here," I said, putting the picture of me at about seven years old next to the one of Pierre and the little girl. "See."

Grandmere nodded.

"Yes, it's your face," she said, looking at the two, "but it's not you."

"Then who is it, Grandmere, and who is this man in the picture?"

She hesitated. I tried to wait patiently, but the butterflies in my stomach were flying around my heart, tickling it with their wings. I held my breath.

"I wasn't thinking when I sent you up to put the money in my chest," she began, "but maybe it was Providence's way of letting me know it's time."

"Time for what, Grandmere?"

"For you to know everything," she said, and sat back as if she had been struck, the now all too familiar exhaustion settling into her face again. "To know why I drove your grandpere out and into the swamp to live like the animal he is." She closed her eyes and muttered under her breath, but my patience ran out.

"Who is the little girl if it's not me, Grandmere?" I demanded. Grandmere fixed her eyes on me, the crimson in her cheeks replaced by a paleness the color of oatmeal.

"It's your sister," she said.

"My sister!"

She nodded. She closed her eyes and kept them closed so long, I thought she wouldn't continue.

"And the man holding her hand . . ." she finally added.

She didn't have to say it. The words were already settling in my mind.

". . . is your real father."

6

Room in My Heart

"**I**f you knew who my father was all this time, Grandmere, why didn't you tell me? Where does he live? How did I get a sister? Why did it have to be kept such a secret, and why did this drive Grandpere into the swamp to live?" I fired my questions, one after the other, my voice impatient.

Grandmere Catherine closed her eyes. I knew it was her way to gather strength. It was as if she could reach into a second self and draw out the energy that made her the healer she was to the Cajun people in Terrebonne Parish.

My heart was thumping, a slow, heavy whacking in my chest that made me dizzy. The world around us seemed to grow very still. It was as if every owl, every insect, even the breeze was holding its breath in anticipation. After a moment Grandmere Catherine opened her dark eyes, eyes that were now shadowed and sad, and fixed them on me firmly as she shook her head ever so gently. I thought she released a soft moan before she began.

"I've dreaded this day for so long," Grandmere said, "dreaded it because once you've heard it all, you will know just how deeply into the depths of hell and damnation your grandpere has gone. I've dreaded it because once you've heard it all you will know how much more tragic than you ever dreamed was your mother's short life, and I've dreaded it because once you've heard it all, you will know how much of your life, your family, your history, I have kept hidden from you.

"Please don't blame me for it, Ruby," she pleaded. "I have tried to be more than your grandmere. I have tried to do what I thought was best for you.

"But at the same time," she continued, gazing down at her hands in her lap for a moment, "I must confess I have been somewhat selfish, too, for I wanted to keep you with me, wanted to keep something of my poor lost daughter beside me." She gazed up at me again. "If I have sinned, God forgive me, for my intentions were not evil and I did try to do the best I could for you, even though I admit, you would have had a much richer, much more comfortable life, if I had given you up the day you were born."

She sat back and sighed again as if a great weight had begun to be lifted from her shoulders and off her heart.

"Grandmere, no matter what you've done, no matter what you tell me, I will always love you just as I always have loved you," I assured her.

She smiled softly and then grew thoughtful and serious again.

"The truth is, Ruby, I couldn't have gone on; I would never have had the strength, even the spiritual strength I was born to have, if you hadn't been with me all these years. You have been my salvation and my hope, as you still are. However, now that I'm drawing closer and closer to the end of my days here, you must leave the bayou and go where you belong."

"Where do I belong, Grandmere?"

"In New Orleans."

"Because of my artwork?" I said, nodding in anticipation of her response. She had said it so many times before.

"Not only because of your talent," she replied, and then she sat forward and continued. "After Gabrielle had gotten herself into trouble with Paul Tate's father, she became a very withdrawn and solitary person. She didn't want to attend school anymore no matter how much I begged, so that except for the people who came around here, she saw no one. She became something of a wild thing, a true part of the bayou, a recluse who lived in nature and loved only natural things.

"And Nature accepted her with open arms. The beautiful birds she loved, loved her. I would look out and see how the marsh hawks watched over her, flew from tree to tree to follow her along the canals.

"She would always return with beautiful wild flowers in her hair when she went for a walk that lasted most of the afternoon. Gabrielle could spend hours sitting by the water, dazzled by its ebb and flow, hypnotized by the songs of the birds. I began to think the frogs that gathered around her actually spoke to her.

"Nothing harmed her. Even the alligators maintained a respectful distance, holding their eyes out of the water just enough to gaze at her as she walked along the shores of the marsh. It was as if the swamp and all the wildlife within it saw her as one of their own.

"She would take our pirogue and pole through those canals better than your Grandpere Jack. She certainly knew the water better, never getting hung up on anything. She went deep into the swamp, went to places rarely visited by human beings. If she had wanted to, she could have been a better swamp guide than your grandpere," Grandmere added, nodding.

"As time went by, Gabrielle became even more beautiful. She seemed to draw on the natural beauty around her. Her face blossomed like a flower, her complexion was as soft as rose petals, her eyes were as bright as the noonday sunlight streaming through the goldenrod. She walked more softly than the marsh deer, who were never afraid to come right up to her. I saw her stroke their heads myself," Grandmere said, smiling warmly, deeply at her vivid memories, memories I longed to share.

"There was nothing sweeter to my ears than the sound of Gabrielle's laughter, no jewel more sparkling than the sparkle of her soft smile.

"When I was a little girl, much younger than you are now, my grandmere told me stories about the so-called swamp fairies, nymphs that dwelled deep in the bayou and would show themselves only to the purest of heart. How I longed to catch sight of one. I never did, but I think I came the closest whenever I looked upon my own daughter, my own Gabrielle," she said and wiped a single fugitive tear from her cheek.

She took a deep breath, sat back, and continued.

"A little more than two years after Gabrielle's involvement with Mr. Tate, a very handsome, young Creole man came from New Orleans with his father to do some duck hunting in the swamp. In town they quickly learned about your grandpere, who was, to give the devil his due," she muttered, "the best swamp guide in this bayou.

"This young man, Pierre Dumas, fell in love with your mother the moment he saw her emerge from the marsh with a baby rice bird on her shoulder. Her hair was long, midway down her back, and it had darkened to a rich, beautiful auburn color. She had my raven black eyes, Grandpere's dark complexion and teeth whiter than the keys of a brand-new accordion. Many a young man who had chanced by and had seen her had lost his heart quickly, but Gabrielle had become wary of men. Whenever one did stop to speak with her, she would simply toss a thin laugh his way and disappear so quickly he probably thought she really was a swamp ghost, one of my grandmere's fairies," Grandmere Catherine said, smiling.

"But for some reason, she did not run from Pierre Dumas. Oh, he was tall and dashing in his elegant clothes, but later, she would tell me that she saw something gentle and loving in his face; she felt no threat. And I never saw a young man smitten as quickly as young Pierre Dumas was smitten. If he could have thrown off his rich clothes that very moment and gone into the swamp to live with Gabrielle then and there, he would have.

"But the truth was he was already married and had been for a little over two years. The Dumas family is one of the oldest and wealthiest families living in New Orleans," Grandmere said. "Those families guard their lineage very closely. Marriages are well thought out and arranged so as to keep up the social standing and protect their blue blood. Pierre's young wife also came from a well-respected, wealthy old Creole family.

"However, to the great chagrin of Pierre's father, Charles Dumas, Pierre's wife had been unable to get pregnant all this time. The prospect of no children was an unacceptable one to Pierre's father, and to Pierre as well. But they were good Catholics and divorce was not an alternative. Neither was adopting a child, for Charles Dumas wanted the Dumas blood to run through the veins of all of his grandchildren.

"Weekend after weekend, Pierre Dumas and his father, more often, just Pierre, would visit Houma and go duck hunting. Pierre began to spend more time with Gabrielle than he did with Grandpere Jack. Naturally, I was very worried. Even if Pierre wasn't already married, his father would not want him to bring back a wild Cajun girl with no rich lineage. I warned Gabrielle about him, but she simply looked at me and smiled as if I were trying to stop the wind.

" 'Pierre would never do anything to hurt me,' she insisted. Soon, he was coming and not even pretending his purpose was to hire Grandpere Jack to guide him on a hunting trip. He and Gabrielle would pack a lunch and go off in the pirogue, deep into the swamp to places only Gabrielle knew."

Grandmere paused in her tale and stared down at her hands again for a long moment. When she looked up again, her eyes were full of pain.

"This time Gabrielle didn't tell me she was pregnant. She didn't have to. I saw it in her face and soon saw it in her stomach. When I confronted her about it, she simply smiled and said she wanted Pierre's baby, a child she would bring up in the bayou to love the swamp world as much as she did. She made me promise that no matter what happened, I would make sure her child lived here and learned to love the things she loved. God forgive me, I finally gave in and made such a promise, even though it broke my heart to see her with child and to know what it would do to her reputation among our own people.

"We tried to cover up what had happened by telling the story about the stranger at the fais dodo. Some people accepted it, but most didn't care. It was just another reason why they should look down on the Landrys. Even my best friends smiled when they faced me, but whispered behind my back. Many a family I had helped with my healing, contributed to the gossip."

Grandmere took a deep breath before she continued, seeming to draw the strength she needed out of the air.

"Unbeknownst to me, your grandpere and Pierre's father had met to discuss the impending birth. Your grandpere had already had experience selling one of Gabrielle's illegitimate children. His gambling sickness hadn't abated one bit; he still lost every piece of spare change he possessed and then some. He was in debt everywhere.

"A proposal was made some time during the last month and a half of Gabrielle's pregnancy. Charles Dumas offered fifteen thousand dollars for Pierre's child. Grandpere agreed, of course. Back in New Orleans, they were already concocting the fabrications to make it appear the child was really Pierre's wife's. Grandpere Jack told Gabrielle and it broke her heart. I was furious with him, but the worst was yet to come."

She bit down on her lower lip. Her eyes were glazed with tears, tears I was sure were burning under her eyelids, but she wanted desperately to get all of the story told before she collapsed in sorrow. I got up quickly and got her a glass of water.

"Thank you, honey," she said. She drank some and then nodded. "I'm all right." I sat down again, my eyes, my ears, my very soul fixed on her and her every word.

"Poor Gabrielle began to wilt with sorrow. She felt betrayed, but not so much by Grandpere Jack. She had always accepted his bad qualities and weaknesses the same way she accepted some of the uglier and crueler things in nature. For Gabrielle, Grandpere Jack's flaws were just the way things were, the way they were designed to be.

"But Pierre's willingness to go along with the bargain, to do what his father wanted was different. They had made secret promises to each other about the soon-to-be-born child. Pierre was going to send money to help care for the baby. He was going to visit more often. He even said he wanted the child to be brought up in the bayou where he or she would always be part of Gabrielle and her world, a world Pierre professed to love more than his own now that he had met and fallen in love with Gabrielle.

"She was so heartbroken when Grandpere Jack came to her and told her the bargain and how all the parties had agreed, that she did not put up any resistance. Instead, she spent long hours sitting in the shadows of the cypress and sycamore trees gazing out at the swamp as if the world she loved had somehow conspired to betray her as well. She had believed in its magic, worshipped its beauty and she had believed that Pierre had been won over by it as well. Now, she knew there were stronger, harder, crueler truths, the worst one being that Pierre's loyalty to his own world and his own family carried more weight with him than the promises he had made to her.

"She didn't eat well, no matter how I nagged and cajoled. I whipped up whatever herbal drinks I could to substitute for what she was missing and provide the nourishment her body needed, but she either avoided them or her depression overcame whatever value they had. Instead of blossoming in the last weeks of her pregnancy, she grew more sickly. Dark shadows formed around her eyes. She had little energy, became listless and slept most of the day away.

"I saw how big she had gotten, of course, and I knew why, but I never spoke a word of it to Grandpere or to Gabrielle. I was afraid the moment Grandpere knew, he would run out and make a second deal."

"Knew why?" I asked. "What?"

"That Gabrielle was about to give birth to twins."

For a moment my thumping heart stopped. The realization of what she had said thundered through my mind.

"Twins? I have a twin sister?" The possibility had never even occurred to me, even after I had seen how much I resembled the little girl in the picture with Pierre Dumas.

"Yes. She was the baby, the first to be born and the one I surrendered to Grandpere that night. I shall never forget that night," she said. "Grandpere had informed the Dumas family that Gabrielle was in labor. They drove here in their limousine and waited out there in the night. They had brought along a nurse, but I wouldn't permit her to enter my house. I could see the old man's expensive cigar burning in the limousine window as they all waited impatiently.

"As soon as your sister was born, I cleaned and brought her out to Grandpere, who thought I was being very cooperative. He rushed out with the child and collected his blood money. When he returned to the house, I had you cleaned and wrapped and in your weakened mother's arms.

"As soon as he set eyes on you, Grandpere Jack ranted and raved. Why hadn't I told him what to expect? Didn't I realize that I had thrown away another fifteen thousand dollars!

"He decided there was still time and actually went to take you from Gabrielle and run after the limousine. I struck him squarely on the forehead with a frying pan I had kept at my side just for that purpose and I knocked him unconscious. By the time he awoke, I had packed all of his things in two sacks. Then I chased him from the house, threatening to tell the world what he had done if he didn't leave us be. I threw out all his things and he took them and went to live in his trapper's shack. He's been there ever since," she said, "and good riddance to him."

"What happened to my mother?" I asked softly, so softly, I wasn't sure I had spoken.

Finally, Grandmere's tears escaped. They streamed down her cheeks freely, zigzagging to her chin.

"The double birthing, in her weakened state, was too much for her, but before she closed her eyes for the last time, she looked down at you and smiled. I made my promises quickly to her. I would keep you here in the bayou with me. You would grow up much like she had. You would know our world and our lives and some day, when the time was right, you would be told all that I have told you now.

"Gabrielle's last words to me were 'Thank you, *ma mere, ma belle mere.'* "

Grandmere's head dropped as her shoulders shuddered. I got up quickly and went to embrace her, crying with her for a mother I had never seen, never touched, never heard speak my name. What did I know of her? A snip of a ribbon she had worn in her dark red hair, some of her clothes, the few old faded pictures? To never know the sound of her voice, or the feel of her bosom when she embraced me and comforted me, to never bury my face in her hair and feel her lips on my baby cheeks, to never hear that wonderful, innocent laughter Grandmere had described, to never dream, like so many other girls I knew, that I would be as beautiful as my mother—this was the agony left to me.

How was I now to love, even like the man who was my real father but who had betrayed my mother's trust and love and broke her heart so badly she could only pine away?

Grandmere Catherine wiped away her tears and sat back, smiling at me.

"Can you forgive me for keeping all this a secret until now, Ruby?" she asked.

"Yes, Grandmere. I know you did it out of love for me, to protect me. Did my real father ever learn what had happened to my mother and did he ever learn about me?"

"No," Grandmere said, shaking her head. "That is one reason why I have encouraged you in your artwork, and why I wanted you to have your work shown in galleries in New Orleans. I have been hoping that someday, Pierre Dumas might learn of a Ruby Landry and wonder.

"It has brought me great pain and troubled my conscience that you have never met your father and your sister. Now, I feel in my heart that you should and will soon do so. If anything should happen to me, Ruby, you must promise, you must swear here and now, that you will go to Pierre Dumas and tell him who you are."

"Nothing will happen to you, Grandmere," I insisted.

"Nevertheless, promise me, Ruby. I don't want you to stay here and live with that . . . that scoundrel. Promise," she demanded.

"I promise, Grandmere. Now stop this talk. You're tired; you need to rest. Tomorrow, you will be as good as new," I told her.

She smiled up at me and stroked my hair.

"My beautiful Ruby, my little Gabrielle. You're all your mother dreamed you would be," she said. I kissed her cheek and helped her to her feet.

Never did Grandmere Catherine look older going up to her bedroom. I followed to be sure she was all right and I helped her get into bed. Then, as she had done for me so many, many times before, I brought the blanket to her chin and knelt down to kiss her good night.

"Ruby," she said, seizing my hand as I turned to leave. "Despite what he did, there must be something very good in your father's heart for your mother to have loved him so. Seek only that goodness in him. Leave room in your own heart to love that good part of him and you will find some peace and joy someday," she predicted.

"All right, Grandmere," I said, although I couldn't imagine feeling anything toward him but hatred. I turned out her light and left her in darkness groping with the ghosts of her past.

I went out to the galerie and sat in a rocker to stare out at the night and digest all that Grandmere Catherine had told me. I had a twin sister. She lived somewhere in New Orleans and at this moment, she could be looking up at the same stars. Only, she didn't know about me. What would it be like for her when she finally found out? Would she be as happy and as excited at the prospect of meeting me as I was about meeting her? She had been brought up a Creole in a rich Creole's world in New Orleans. How different would that make us? I wondered, not without some trepidation.

And what of my father? Just as I had always thought, he did not know I existed. How would he react? Would he look down on me and not want to acknowledge my existence? Would he be ashamed? How could I ever go to him as Grandmere Catherine expected I would someday? My very presence would complicate his life so much it would be impossible. And yet . . . I couldn't help but be curious. What was he really like, the man who had captured my beautiful mother's heart? My father, the mysterious dark man of my paintings.

Sighing deeply, I gazed through the darkness at that part of the bayou illuminated by the sliver of a pale white moon. I had always felt the depth of the mystery surrounding my life here; I had always heard whispering in the shadows. Truly it was as if the animals, the birds, especially the marsh hawks, wanted me to know who I really was and what had really happened. The dark spots in my past, the hardships of our lives, the tension and the turmoil between Grandmere Catherine and Grandpere Jack forced me to be more mature than I wanted to be at fifteen.

Sometimes, I wanted so badly to be like other young teenage girls I knew, full of silly laughter about nothing at all, and not always burdened down with responsibilities and worries that made me feel so much older than my years. But the same had been true for my poor mother. How quickly her life had flown by. One moment she was like an innocent child, exploring, discovering, living in what must have seemed to her to be an eternal spring; and then, suddenly, all the dark clouds rolled in and her smiles dimmed, her laughter died somewhere in the swamp, and she faded and aged like a leaf drying in the premature autumn of her short life. How unfair. If there is a heaven or a hell, I thought, it's right here on earth. We don't have to die to enter one or the other.

Exhausted, my mind reeling from the revelations, I rose from the rocker and made my way quickly to bed, putting out all the lights behind me as I went, leaving a trail of darkness and returning the world to the demons that feasted so hungrily and so successfully on our vulnerable hearts.

Poor Grandmere, I thought, and said a little prayer for her. She had been through so much trouble and tragedy and yet she cared so for others and especially for me, instead of becoming bitter and cynical. Never did I go to sleep myself loving her more, nor did I ever believe I could go to sleep crying for my dead mother, a mother I had never known, more than I could cry for myself. But I did.

The next morning Grandmere got herself up with a struggle and made her way down to the kitchen. I heard her slow, ponderous footsteps and decided that I would do all that I could to cheer her up again and get her to return to her old, vibrant self. When I joined her at breakfast, I didn't talk about our discussions the night before, nor did I ask her any more questions about the past. Instead, I rattled on about our work and especially about the new painting I was planning.

"It's a painting of you, Grandmere," I said.

"Me? Oh, no, honey. I ain't fit to be the subject of any painting. I'm old and wrinkled and—"

"You're perfect, Grandmere, and very important. I want you sitting in your rocker on the galerie. I'll try to get as much of the house in, too, but you are the subject. After all, how many portraits are there of Cajun spiritual healers? I'm sure, if I do it well, people in New Orleans will pay dearly for it," I added to persuade her.

"I'm not one to sit around all day and model for pictures," she insisted, but I knew she would. It would make it easier for her to rest and her conscience wouldn't bother her so much about not working on her loom or embroidering tablecloths and napkins.

I began the portrait that afternoon.

"Does this mean I've got to wear the same thing every day until you finish that picture, Ruby?" she asked me.

"No, Grandmere. Once I've painted you in something, I don't need to see you in it constantly. The picture is already locked in here," I said, pointing to my temple.

I worked as hard and as fast as I could on her picture, concentrating on capturing her as accurately as I was able. Every day I worked, she fell asleep in her chair midway through the sitting. I thought there was a peacefulness about her and tried to get that feeling in the picture. One day I decided there should be a rice bird on the railing, and then, it came to me that I would put a face in the window looking out. I didn't tell Grandmere, but the face I drew and then painted was my mother's face. I used the old pictures for inspiration.

Grandmere didn't ask to see the painting while I worked on it. I kept it covered in my room at night, for I wanted to surprise her with it when it was finished. Finally, it was, and that night after dinner, I announced it to her.

"I'm sure you made me look a lot better than I do," she insisted, and sat back in anticipation as I brought it out and uncovered it before her. For a long moment, she said nothing, nor did the expression on her face change. I thought she didn't like it. And then, she turned to me as if she were looking at a ghost.

"It's been passed on to you," she said in a whisper.

"What has, Grandmere?"

"The powers, the spirituality. Not in the form it has been passed on to me, but in another form, in an artistic power, a vision. When you paint, you see beyond what is there for other people to see. You see inside.

"I've often felt the spirit of Gabrielle in this house," she said, looking around. "How many times have I paused outside and looked back at the house and seen her gazing out of a window, smiling at me or looking wistfully at the swamp, at a bird, at a deer? And Ruby, she's always looked something like that to me," she said, nodding at the painting. "When you painted, you saw her, too. She was in your vision," she said. "She was in your eyes. God be praised." She lifted her arms for me to go to her so she could embrace me and kiss me.

"It's a beautiful picture, Ruby. Don't sell it," she said.

"I won't, Grandmere."

She took a deep breath and ground away the tiny tears from the corners of her eyes. Then we went into the living room to decide where I should hang the painting.

Summer drew to an end on the calender, but not in the bayou. Our temperatures and humidity hung up there as high as they had been in the middle of July. The oppressive heat seemed to undulate through the air, wave after wave weighing us down, making the days longer than they were, making everything we did, harder than it was.

Throughout the fall and early winter, Grandmere Catherine had her usual treater missions, especially ministering her herbal cures and her spiritual powers to the elderly. They saw her as far more sympathetic to their arthritic pains and aches, their stomach and back troubles, their headaches and fatigue than any ordinary physician would be. She understood because she suffered from the same maladies.

One early February day with the sky a hazy blue and the clouds no more than smokelike wisps smeared here and there from one horizon to the other, a pickup truck came bouncing over our drive, the horn blaring. Grandmere and I were in the kitchen, having some lunch.

"Someone's in trouble," she declared, and got up as quickly as she could to go to the front door.

It was Raul Balzac, a shrimp fisherman, who lived about ten miles down the bayou. Grandmere was very fond of his wife, Bernadine, and had treated her mother for lumbago time after time before she had passed away last year.

"It's my boy, Mrs. Landry," Raul cried from the truck. "My five-year-old. He's burning up something terrible."

"Insect bite?" Grandmere asked quickly.

"Can't find anything on him that says so," Raul replied.

"Be right with you, Raul," she said, and went back to get her basket of medicines and spiritual things.

"Should I come with you, Grandmere?" I asked as she hurried out.

"No, dear. Stay and make us dinner. Prepare one of your good jambalayas," she added, and went to Raul's truck. He helped her in and then quickly drove off, bouncing over the drive as hard as he had when he had arrived. I couldn't blame him for being anxious and frightened, and once again, I was proud of Grandmere Catherine for being the one to whom he came for assistance, the one in whom he placed such trust.

Later in the day, I did what she asked and worked on our dinner while I listened to some of the latest Cajun music on the radio. There was a prediction of another downpour, one that would be full of lightning and thunder. The static on the radio told me the prediction would come true and sure enough, by late afternoon, the sky had turned that purplish dark color that often preceded a violent storm. I was worried about Grandmere Catherine and after I had battened down all the windows, I stood by the door waiting and watching for Raul's pickup. But the rain came before the truck did.

We had hail and then a pounding downpour that sounded like it would drill holes even through the metal roof. Wave after wave of rain was washed over the bayou by the wind that came rushing over the sycamores and cypresses, bending and twisting the branches, tearing leaves and limbs from trees. The distant low, rumbling thunder soon became real boomers, crashing down around the house like boulders and then lighting up the sky with fire. Hawks shrieked, everything that lived struggled to find a hole to crawl in to remain safe and dry. The railings on the porch groaned and the whole house seemed to turn and twist in the wind. I couldn't recall a storm as fierce, nor when I was more frightened by one.

Finally, it began to recede and the heavy drops thinned. The wind slowed down and became less and less severe until it was nothing more than a brisk breeze. Night fell quickly afterward, so I didn't see the resulting damage around the swamp, but the rain trickled on for hours and hours.

I expected Raul was waiting for the storm to stop before bringing Grandmere Catherine home, but as the hours ticked by and the storm dissipated until it was finally nothing more than a sprinkle, the truck still did not appear. I grew more and more nervous and wished that we had a telephone like most of the other people in the bayou, although I imagined the lines would have been down just like they often were after such a storm and the telephone would have been useless.

Our supper was long done. It simmered in the pot. I wasn't all that hungry, being so anxious, but finally, I ate some and then cleaned up. Grandmere had still not returned. I spent the next hour and a half waiting on the galerie, just watching the darkness for the lights of Raul's truck. Occasionally, a vehicle did appear, but it was someone else all the time.

Finally, nearly twelve hours after Raul had come for Grandmere Catherine, his truck turned into the drive. I saw him clearly, and I saw his oldest son, Jean, but I didn't see Grandmere Catherine. I ran down the galerie steps as he came to a stop.

"Where's my grandmere?" I called before he could speak.

"She's in the back," he said. "Resting."

"What?"

I hurried around and saw Grandmere Catherine lying on an old mattress, a blanket over her. The mattress was on a wide sheet of plywood and was used as a makeshift bed for Raul's children when he and his wife went on long journeys.

"Grandmere!" I cried. "What's wrong with her?" I asked as Raul came around.

"She collapsed with exhaustion a few hours ago. We wanted to keep her overnight, but she insisted on us bringing her home and we wanted to do whatever she asked. She broke my boy's fever. He's going to be all right," Raul said, smiling.

"I'm happy about that, Mr. Balzac, but Grandmere Catherine . . ."

"We'll help you get her into the house and to bed," he said, and nodded to Jean. They lowered the rear of the truck and the two of them lifted the mattress and board with Grandmere Catherine off the truck. She stirred and opened her eyes.

"Grandmere," I said, taking her hand, "what's wrong?"

"I'm just tired, so tired," she muttered. "I'll be fine," she added, but her eyelids clamped down shut so quickly alarm filled me.

"Quickly," I said, and rushed ahead to open the door for them. They brought her up to her room and eased her off the mattress and into her own bed.

"Is there anything we can do for you, Ruby?" Raul asked.

"No. I'll take care of her. Thank you."

"Thank her for us again," Raul said. "My wife will send something over in the morning and we'll stop by to see how she is."

I nodded and they left. I took off Grandmere's shoes and helped her off with her dress. She was like someone drugged, barely opening her eyes, barely moving her arms and legs. I don't think she realized I had put her to bed.

All that night I sat at her side, waiting for her to awaken. She moaned and groaned a few times, but she never woke up until morning when I felt her nudge my leg. I was asleep in the chair beside the bed.

"Grandmere," I cried. "How are you?"

"I'm all right, Ruby. Just weak and tired. How did I get home and in bed? I don't remember."

"Mr. Balzac and his son Jean brought you in their truck and carried you in."

"And you sat up all night watching over me?" she asked.

"Yes."

"You poor dear." She struggled to smile. "I missed your jambalaya. Was it good?"

"Yes, Grandmere, although I was too worried about you to eat much. What happened to you?"

"The strain of what I had to do, I suppose. That poor little boy was bitten by a cottonmouth, but on the bottom of his foot where it was hard to see. He was running barefoot through the marsh grass and must have disturbed one," she said.

"Grandmere, you've never been this exhausted after a treater mission before."

"I'll be all right, Ruby. Please, just get me some cold water," she said.

I did so. She drank it slowly and then closed her eyes again.

"I'll just rest some more and then get up, dear," she said. "You go on and have something for breakfast. Don't worry. Go on," she said. Reluctantly, I did so. When I returned to look in on her, she was fast asleep again.

Before lunch, she woke up, but her complexion was waxen, her lips blue. She was too weak to sit up by herself. I had to help her and then she asked me to help her get dressed.

"I want to sit on the galerie," she said.

"I must get you something to eat."

"No, no. I just want to sit on the galerie."

She leaned fully on me to stand and walk. I was never so frightened about her. When she sat back in the rocker, she looked as though she had collapsed again, but a moment later, she opened her eyes and gave me a weak smile.

"I'll just have a little warm water and honey, dear."

I got it for her quickly and she sipped it and rocked herself gently.

"I guess I'm more tired than I thought," she said, and then she turned and gazed at me with such a far-off look in her eyes, a small flutter of panic stirred in my chest. "Ruby, I don't want you to be afraid, but I wish you would do something for me now. It would make me feel less . . . less anxious about myself," she said, taking my hand in hers. Her palms felt cold, clammy.

"What is it, Grandmere?" I could feel the tears aching to emerge from my eyes. They stung behind my lids. My throat felt like closing up for good and my heart shrunk until it was barely beating. My blood ran cold, my legs had turned to lead bars.

"I want you to go to the church and fetch Father Rush," she said.

"Father Rush?" The blood drained from my face. "Oh, why, Grandmere? Why?"

"Just in case, dear. I need to make my peace. Please, dear. Be strong," she begged. I nodded and swallowed back my tears quickly. I would not cry in front of her, I thought, and then I kissed her quickly.

Before I turned to leave, she seized my hand again and held me close.

"Ruby, remember your promises to me. Should something happen to me, you won't stay here. Remember."

"Nothing's happening to you, Grandmere."

"I know, honey, but just in case. Promise again. Promise."

"I promise, Grandmere."

"You'll go to him, go to your real father?"

"Yes, Grandmere."

"Good," she said, closing her eyes. "Good." I gazed at her a moment and then ran down the galerie steps and hurried to town. On the way my tears gushed. I cried so hard, my chest began to ache. I arrived at the church so quickly, I didn't remember the journey.

Father Rush's housekeeper answered the doorbell. Her name was Addie Cochran and she had been with him so long, it was impossible to remember when she wasn't.

"My grandmere Catherine needs Father Rush," I said quickly, an edge of panic in my voice.

"What's wrong?"

"She's . . . she's very . . . she's . . ."

"Oh, dear. He's just at the barber's. I'll go tell him and send him up."

"Thank you," I said, and I turned and ran all the way home, my chest wanting to burst open, the needles in my side poking and sticking me fiercely when I arrived. Grandmere was still on the galerie in her rocker. I didn't realize she wasn't rocking until I reached the steps. She was just sitting still with her eyes half-closed and on her thin white lips was a faint smile. It scared me, that funny, happy smile.

"Grandmere," I whispered fearfully. "Are you all right?"

She didn't reply, nor did she turn my way. I touched her face and realized she was already cold.

Then I fell to my knees on the galerie floor in front of her and embraced her legs. I was still holding on to her and crying when Father Rush finally arrived.

7

The Truth Will Out

Anyone would have thought that the news of Grandmere Catherine's passing must have been caught up in the wind that whipped through the bayou for so many people to have heard about it so quickly; but the loss of a spiritual healer, especially a spiritual healer with Grandmere's reputation, was something special and very important to the Cajun community. Before late morning some of Grandmere Catherine's friends and our neighbors already were arriving. By early afternoon, there were dozens of cars and trucks in front of our house as more and more people stopped by to pay their respects, the women bringing gumbos and jambalaya in big cast iron pots, plus dishes and pans of cake and beignets. Mrs. Thibodeau and Mrs. Livaudis took charge of the wake and Father Rush made the funeral arrangements for me.

Layer after layer of long gray clouds streamed in from the southwest, making for a hazy, peekaboo sun. The heavy air, dark shadows, and the subdued swamp life all seemed appropriate for a day as sad as this one was. The birds barely flitted about; the marsh hawks and herons remained curious but statuelike in their stillness as they watched the gathering that had commenced and continued throughout the day.

No one had seen Grandpere Jack for some time so Thaddeus Bute poled a pirogue out to his shack to give him the dreadful news. He returned without him and mumbled something to the mourners that made people shake their heads and gaze my way with pity. Toward supper Grandpere Jack finally arrived, as usual, resembling someone who had been wallowing in mud. He wore what must have been his best pair of trousers and shirt, but the trousers had holes in the knees and his shirt looked like he had to beat it on a rock in order to soften it enough to slip his arms through the sleeves and button it, wherever there were buttons, that is. Of course, his boots were caked with grime and blades of marsh grass.

He had taken no time to brush down his wild white hair or trim his beard even though he must have known there would be loads of people here. Thick little puffs of hair grew out of his ears and nose. His bushy eyebrows curved up and to the side on his leather tan face, the deeper wrinkles looking like they had a bed of dirt glued there for months. The acrid odors of stale whiskey, swamp earth, fish, and tobacco seemed to arrive at the house long moments before he did. I smiled to myself thinking how Grandmere Catherine would be screaming at him to keep his distance.

But she wasn't going to be screaming at him anymore. She was laid out in the sitting room, her face never so peaceful and still. I sat off to the right of the coffin, my hands folded in my lap, still quite dazed by the reality of what was happening, still disbelieving, hoping it was all a terrible nightmare that would soon end.

The quiet chatter that had begun earlier came to an abrupt pause when Grandpere Jack arrived. As soon as he strode into the house, the people gathered at the doorways parted and stepped back as if they were terrified he might touch them with his polluted hands. None of the men offered theirs to him, nor did he seek any handshakes. Women grimaced after a whiff of him. His eyes shifted quickly from one face to another and then he stepped into the sitting room and froze for a moment at the sight of Grandmere Catherine laid out in her coffin.

He looked at me sharply and then fixed his eyes on Father Rush. For a few moments, it seemed Grandpere Jack didn't trust what his own eyes were telling him or what people were doing here. It looked like the words were on the tip of his tongue and any moment he might ask, "Is she really dead and gone or is this just some scam to get me out of the swamp and cleaned up?" With that skeptical glint in his eyes, he approached Grandmere Catherine's coffin slowly, hat in hand. About a foot or so away, he stopped and gazed down at her, waiting. When she didn't sit up and start screaming at him, he relaxed and turned back to me.

"How you doin', Ruby?" he asked.

"I'm all right, Grandpere," I said. My eyes were bloodshot but dry, for I had exhausted a reservoir of tears. He nodded and then he spun around and glared back at some of the women who were gazing at him with a veil of disgust visibly drawn over their faces.

"Well, what are you all lookin' at? Can't a man mourn his dead wife without you busybodies gaping at him and whispering behind his back? Go on with ya and give me some privacy," he cried.

Outraged and stunned, Grandmere Catherine's friends spun around and, with their heads bobbing, hurried out like a flock of frightened hens to gather on the galerie. Only Mrs. Thibodeau, Mrs. Livaudis, and Father Rush remained in the sitting room with Grandpere Jack and me.

"What happened to her?" Grandpere demanded, his green eyes still lit with fury.

"Her heart just gave out," Father Rush said, gazing warmly at Grandmere. He shook his head gently. "She spent all her energy on helping others, comforting and tending to the sick and the troubled. It finally took its toll on her, God bless her," he added.

"Well, I told her a hundred times if I told her once, to stop parading up and down the bayou to tend to everybody's needs but our own, but she wasn't one to listen. Stubborn to the day she died," Grandpere declared. "Just like most Cajun women," he added, staring at Mrs. Thibodeau and Mrs. Livaudis. They pulled back their shoulders and stiffened their necks like two peacocks.

"Oh, no," Father Rush said, smiling angelically, "you can't keep a soul as great as Mrs. Landry's soul from doing what she can to help the needy. Charity and compassion were her constant companions," he added.

Grandpere grunted. "Charity begins at home I told her, but she never listened to me. Well, I'm sorry she's gone. Don't know who's goin' to send fire and damnation my way. Don't know who's goin' to nag me and chastise me for doin' this or that," Grandpere declared, shaking his head.

"Oh, I expect someone will always be around to chastise you good, Jack Landry," Mrs. Thibodeau replied, nodding at him with her lips tightly pursed.

"Huh?" Grandpere stared at her a moment, but Mrs. Thibodeau had been around Grandmere Catherine too long not to have learned how to stare him down. He ran the back of his hand over his mouth and then shifted his eyes away and grunted again. "Yeah, I suppose," he said. The aromas from the kitchen caught his interest. "Well, I guess you ladies cooked up somethin', didn't you?" he asked.

"There's a spread in the kitchen, gumbo on the stove, and a pot of hot coffee brewing," Mrs. Livaudis said with visible reluctance.

"I'll get you something to eat, Grandpere," I said, rising. I had to do something, keep moving, keep busy.

"Why, thank you, Ruby. That's my only grandchild, you know," he told Father Rush. I snapped my head around sharply and glared at Grandpere. For a moment his eyes twinkled with that impish look and then he smiled and looked away, either not sensing or seeing what I knew or not caring about it. "She's all I got now," he continued. "Only family left. I got to look after her."

"And how do you expect to do that?" Mrs. Livaudis demanded. "You barely look after yourself, Jack Landry."

"I know what I do and I don't. A man can change, can't he? If something tragic like this occurs, a man can change. Can't he, Father? Ain't that so?"

"If it's truly in his heart to repent, anyone can," Father Rush replied, closing his eyes and pressing his hands together as if he were about to offer up a prayer to that effect.

"Hear that and that's a priest talking, not some gossip mouth," Grandpere said, nodding and poking the air between him and Mrs. Livaudis with his thick, long and dirty finger. "I got responsibilities now . . . a place to keep up, a granddaughter to see after, and I'm one to do what I say I'm goin' to do, when I say it."

"If you remember you've said it," Mrs. Thibodeau snapped. She was giving him no ground.

Grandpere smirked.

"Yeah, well, I'll remember. I'll remember," he repeated. He threw another look Grandmere Catherine's way, again as if he wanted to be sure she wasn't going to start screaming at him, and then he followed me out to the kitchen to get something to eat. He plopped his long, lanky body into a kitchen chair and dropped his hat on the floor. Then he looked around as I stirred up the gumbo and ladled a bowl for him.

"Ain't been in this house so long, it's like a strange place to me," he said. "And I built it myself!" I poured him a cup of coffee and then stepped back, folding my arms under my bosom and watching him go at the gumbo, shoving mouthful after mouthful in and swallowing with hardly a chew, the rice and roux running down his chin.

"When was the last time you ate something, Grandpere?" I asked. He paused for a moment and thought.

"I don't know . . . two days ago, I had some shrimp. Or was it some oysters?" He shrugged and continued to gulp his food. "But things are going to change for me now," he said, nodding between swallows. "I'm going to clean myself up, move back into my home, and have my granddaughter take care of me right and proper, and I'm going to do the same for her," he vowed.

"I can't believe Grandmere is actually dead and gone, Grandpere," I said, the tears choking my throat. He gulped some food and nodded.

"Me neither. I would have sworn on a stack of wild deuces that I'd go before she did. I thought that woman would outlive most of the world; she had that much grit in her. She was like some old tree root, just clinging to the things she believed in. I couldn't move her with a herd of elephants, not an inch off her ways."

"Nor could she move you, Grandpere," I quickly replied. He shrugged.

"Well, I'm just a stupid old Cajun trapper, too dumb to know right from wrong, yet I manage to survive. But I meant what I said out there, Ruby. I'm goin' to change somethin' awful and make things right for you. I swear it," he said, holding up his right palm, blotched with grime, the finger ends stained with tobacco. His deeply serious expression dissolved into a smile. "Could you give me another bowl of this. Ain't ate somethin' this good for ages. Beats the hell out of my swamp guk," he said, and chuckled to himself, a slight whistle coming through the gaps in his teeth as his shoulders shook.

I gave him some more and then I excused myself and went back to sit beside the coffin. I didn't like being away from Grandmere Catherine's side too long. Toward evening, some of Grandpere Jack's swamp cronies arrived supposedly to offer comfort and sympathy, but they were soon all going around behind the house to drink some whiskey and smoke their rolled, dark brown cigarettes.

Father Rush, Mrs. Thibodeau, and Mrs. Livaudis remained as long as they could and then promised to return early in the morning.

"You try to get yourself some rest, Ruby dear," Mrs. Thibodeau advised. "You're going to need your strength for the difficult days ahead."

"Your grandmere would be right proud of you, Ruby," Mrs. Livaudis added, squeezing my hand gently. "Now look after yourself."

Mrs. Thibodeau raised her eyes and gazed toward the rear of the house where the laughter was growing louder by the minute.

"If you need us, you just holler," she said.

"You're always welcome at my house," Mrs. Livaudis added before leaving.

Grandmere Catherine's friends and some of the neighbors had cleaned up and had put everything away before they had left. There was nothing for me to do but kiss Grandmere Catherine good night and go to sleep myself. I heard Grandpere Jack and his trapper friends howl and laugh long into the night. In a way I was grateful for the noise. I lay awake for hours, wondering if there was anything else I could have done to have helped Grandmere Catherine, but then I thought, if she couldn't help herself, what could I do?

Finally, my eyelids became so heavy, I had to let them close. Someone was laughing in the darkness. I heard what sounded like Grandpere's howl and then all was still; and sleep, like one of Grandmere Catherine's miracle medicines, brought me some hours of relief and eased the pain in my heart. In fact, when I awoke early the next morning, I felt so relieved from my deep repose, that for a few moments, I actually believed all that had happened had been some terrible nightmare. In moments, I expected to hear Grandmere Catherine's footsteps as she made her way down to the kitchen to start our breakfast.

But I heard nothing but the soft, sweet sounds of the morning birds. Slowly, the reality of what had occurred settled in again and I sat up, wondering where Grandpere Jack had slept when he had finally stopped cavorting with his trapper friends. When I discovered he wasn't in Grandmere Catherine's room, I thought he might have gone back into the swamp; but when I went down, I found him sprawled out on the galerie, one leg dangling over the edge of the porch floor, his head on his rolled up jacket, an empty bottle of cheap whiskey still clutched in his right hand.

"Grandpere," I said, nudging him. "Grandpere, wake up."

"Huh?" His eyes flickered open and then shut. I shook him harder.

"Grandpere, wake up. People will be arriving here any moment. Grandpere."

"What? What's that?" He kept his eyes open long enough to focus on me and then groaned and folded his body into a sitting position. "What the . . ." He looked around, saw the expression of disappointment on my face and then shook his head. "Must have just passed out with grief," he said quickly. "It can do that to you, Ruby. You think you can handle it, but it seeps into your heart and it just takes you over. That's what happened to me," he said, nodding, trying to convince himself as well as me. "I just couldn't handle the tragedy. Sorry," he said, rubbing his cheeks. "I'll go out back and wash myself with the cistern water and then come in for some breakfast."

"Good, Grandpere," I said. "Did you bring any of your other clothes?"

"Clothes? No."

I remembered there were some old things of his in a box upstairs in Grandmere's room.

"You have some clothes still here that might fit," I said. "I'll find them for you."

"Well, that's right nice of you, honey. Right nice. I can see where we're going to make out just fine. You tending after the house and me, and me trappin' and huntin' and guidin' rich city folks through the swamp. I'll make us more money than I ever did. I'll fix up everything that's broke. I'll make this house look as fresh and as new as it did the day I built it. Why, in no time, I'll change . . ."

"Meanwhile, Grandpere, you'd better go and wash like you said you would." If anything, the stench rising from his clothes and hair had grown doubly worse. "It's getting close to the time people will be coming," I said.

"Right, right." He stood up and looked with surprise at the empty whiskey bottle on the floor of the galerie. "I don't know how I got that. Must have been Teddy Turner or someone who laid it on me for a stupid joke."

"I'll throw it away for you, Grandpere," I said, picking it up quickly.

"Thank you, honey. Thank you." He stuck his right forefinger in the air and thought for a moment until it came back to him. "Wash up, that's first," he said, and stumbled off the galerie and around to the back of the house. I went upstairs and found the old carton of clothes. There were a pair of pants and a few shirts, as well as some socks buried under an old blanket. I took everything out, pressed the pants and shirt, and laid the clothes on Grandmere's bed for him.

"I think I'll do just what Catherine would tell me to do with these old clothes I'm wearing," Grandpere said after he came in from washing himself. "I'll burn them." He laughed. I told him to go up and put on the clothes I found. By the time he had come down again, I had some breakfast made and Mrs. Livaudis and Mrs. Thibodeau arrived to help set up the food for our mourners. They ignored Grandpere even though he did look like a new man washed up and in his fresh clothes.

"I got to trim my beard and hair some, Ruby," Grandpere said. "You think if I sit on a rolled over rain barrel out back you could do it for me?"

"Yes, Grandpere," I said. "I'll do it right after you finish your breakfast."

"I thank you," he said. "We're going to do just fine," he added, more for the benefit of Mrs. Thibodeau and Mrs. Livaudis than for me, I thought. "Just fine. Long as people lets us be," he added pointedly.

After he had finished eating, I took the sewing shears and chopped off as much of his long, ratty hair as I could. Much of it was matted and there were lice, so I had to shampoo him with some of Grandmere

Catherine's mixture specially made to get rid of lice as well as crabs and other tiny insects, too. He sat obediently, his eyes closed, a grateful smile on his lips as I worked. I trimmed the beard and cut the excess hair out of his ears and nose. Then I trimmed his eyebrows. When I was finished and I stepped back to look at him, I was surprised and proud of how well I had done. It was possible to look at him now and see why Grandmere Catherine or any woman might have been attracted to him when he was young. His eyes still had a youthful, mirthful glint and his strong cheekbones and jaw gave his face a classic, handsome shape. He gazed at his reflection in a piece of broken glass.

"Well, I'll be. Lookee here now. Who is this? Bet you didn't know your grandpere was a movie star," he said. "Thank you, Ruby." He slapped his hands together. "Well, I'd better go out front and greet some of the mourners, right and proper like," he decided, and went around to take a seat in one of the rockers on the galerie and play the part of a bereaved husband, even though most everyone knew he and Grandmere Catherine hadn't lived together for years.

However, I was beginning to wonder if I couldn't help him change. Sometimes, dramatic events like this made people think harder about their own lives. I could just hear Grandmere Catherine say, "You'd have a better chance of changing a bullfrog into a handsome prince." But maybe all Grandpere Jack needed was another chance. After all, I thought as I cleaned up the gobs of matted hair that had fallen around the barrel, he's the only Cajun family I have left, like it or not.

We had just as many mourners if not more than we had the day before. A steady stream of Cajun folks came from miles and miles away to pay their last respects to Grandmere Catherine, whose reputation had spread much farther through Terrebonne Parish and the surrounding area than I had ever imagined. And so many of the people who arrived had wonderful stories to tell about Grandmere, stories about her earthy wisdom, her miraculous touch, her wonderful remedies, and her strong and always hopeful faith.

"Why, when your grandmother walked into a room of frightened, anxious people concerned over one of their loved ones, it was as if someone lit a candle in the darkness, Ruby honey," Mrs. Allard from Lafayette told me. "We're gonna miss her something terrible."

The people around her nodded and extended their condolences. I thanked them for their kind words and finally got myself up to get something to drink and nibble on some food. It never occurred to me that simply sitting by the coffin and greeting mourners would be so exhausting, but the constant emotional strain took a greater toll than I had imagined it could.

Grandpere Jack, although he wasn't drinking, was holding court vociferously on the front galerie. Every once in a while, he would give out with a shout and rant and rave about one of his pet subjects. "Those damn oil derricks poking their heads above the swamps, changing the landscape from the way it's looked for more than one hundred years, and for what? Just to make some fat Creole oil man wealthy in New Orleans. I say we burn 'em all out. I say—"

I went out back and closed the door behind me. It was nice that all these people came to show their respect and comfort us, but it was beginning to get overwhelming for me. Every time someone came over to squeeze my hand and kiss my cheek, she or he would start up the tears behind my eyes and close my throat until it ached worse than any sore throat ever made it ache. Every muscle in my body was still rope tight from the shock of Grandmere's passing. I took a short walk toward the canal and then felt my head begin to spin.

"Oh," I moaned, bringing my hand to my forehead. But before I could fall backward, a strong pair of arms caught me and held me upright and steady.

"Easy," a familiar voice said. I let myself rest against his shoulder for a moment and then I opened my eyes and looked up at Paul. "You'd better sit down, here, by this rock," he said, guiding me to it. He and I had often sat together on that same rock and thrown little stones into the water to count the ripples.

"Thank you," I said, and let him guide me to it. He sat beside me quickly and put a blade of marsh grass in his mouth.

"Sorry I didn't come yesterday, but I thought there would be so many people around you . . ." He smiled. "Not that there aren't today. Your grandmother was a very famous and beloved woman in the bayou."

"I know. I never fully appreciated how much until now," I said.

"That's usually the way it is. We don't realize how important someone is to us until he or she is gone," Paul replied, the underlying meaning of his words telegraphed through his soft eyes.

"Oh, Paul, she's gone. My grandmere Catherine is gone," I cried, falling into his arms and really beginning to cry. He stroked my hair back and there were tears in his eyes when I looked, as if my pain were his.

"I wish I had been here when it happened," he said. "I wish I had been right beside you."

I had to swallow twice before I could speak again. "I never wanted to send you away from me, Paul. It broke my heart to say the things I said."

"Then why did you?" he asked softly. There was so much hurt in his eyes. I could feel what it must have been like for him and I could see the tears that had emerged. It wasn't fair. Why should the two of us suffer so horribly for the sins of our parents? I thought.

"Why did you, Ruby, why?" he asked again; he begged for the answer. I could understand his turmoil. My words, words spoken right near here, were so unexpected and so abrupt, they had to have made him question reality. Anger was the only way in which he could have dealt with such a surprise, such an unreasonable surprise.

I turned away from him and bit down on my lower lip. My mouth wanted to run away with the words and exonerate me from all blame.

"It's not that I didn't love you, Paul," I began slowly. Then I turned back to him. The memories of our short-lived kisses and words of promise flitted like doomed moths to the candle of my burning despair. "And not that I still don't," I added softly.

"Then what could it have been? What could it be?" he asked quickly.

My heart, so torn by sorrow and so tired of sadness, began to thump like an oil drum, heavy, ponderous, as slowly as the dreadful drums in a funeral procession. What was more important now, I questioned: that there be truth between Paul and me, truth between two people who care for each other with such a rare love, a love that demanded honesty, or that I maintain a lie that kept Paul from knowing the sins of his father and therefore kept peace in his family?

"What was it?" he asked again.

"Let me think a moment, Paul," I said and looked away. He waited impatiently beside me. I was sure his heart was beating as quickly as mine was now. I wanted to tell Paul the truth, but what if Grandmere Catherine had been right? What if, in the long run, Paul would hate me more for being the messenger of such devastating news?

Oh, Grandmere, I thought, isn't there a time when the truth must be revealed, when lies and deceptions must be exposed? I know that when we are little, we can be left to dwell in a world of fantasy and fabrication. Maybe, it's even necessary, for if we were told some of the ugly truths about life then, we would be destroyed before we had a chance to develop the hard crusts we needed to shield us from the arrows of hardship, of sadness, of tragedy, and, alas, the arrows that carried the final dark truths: grandmothers and grandfathers, mommies and daddies die, and so do we. We have to understand that the world isn't filled only with sweet sounding bells, soft, wonderful things, delightful aromas, pretty music, and endless promises. It is also filled with storms and hard, painful realities, and promises that are never kept.

Surely, Paul and I were old enough now, I thought. Surely, we could face truth if we could face deception and live on.

"Something happened here a long time ago," I began, "that forced me to say the words I said to you that day."

"Here?"

"In our bayou, our little Cajun world," I said, nodding. "The truth about it was quickly smothered because it would have brought great pain to many people, but sometimes, perhaps always, when the truth is buried this way, it has a way of coming out, of forcing itself upward into the sunlight again.

"You and I," I said, looking into his confused eyes, "are the truths that were once buried, we are in the sunlight."

"I don't understand, Ruby. What lies? What truths?"

"No one back then when the truth was buried ever dreamed you and I would come to love each other in a romantic sense," I said.

"I still don't understand, Ruby. How could anyone have known years ago about us anyway? And why would it matter then if they had?" he asked, his eyes squinting with confusion.

It was so hard to come right out and say it simply. Somehow, I felt that if Paul came to the understandings himself, if the words were formed in his mind and spoken by him instead of formed in my mind and coming from my lips, it would be less painful.

"The day I lost my mother, you lost yours, too," I finally said. The words felt like tiny, hot embers falling from my lips. The moment I uttered them, that feeling was followed by a chill so cold it was as if someone had poured ice water down the back of my neck.

Paul's eyes rushed over my face, searching for a clearer comprehension.

"My mother . . . died, too?"

His eyes lifted and he took on a far-off look as his mind raced from point A to point B. Then his face turned crimson and he gazed at me again, this time, his eyes more demanding, more frantic.

"What are you saying . . . that you and I . . . that we're . . . related? That we're brother and sister?" he asked, the corners of his mouth pulled up into his cheeks. I nodded.

"Grandmere Catherine decided to tell me only when she saw what was happening between us," I said. He shook his head, still skeptical.

"It was very painful for her to do so. Now that I think back, it wasn't long afterward that age began to creep into her steps and into her voice and heart. Old pains that are revived sting sharper than when they first strike."

"This has got to be a mistake, an old Cajun folktale, some stupid rumor conjured up in a room filled with busybodies," Paul said, wagging his head and smiling.

"Grandmere Catherine never spread gossip, never fanned the flames of idle talk and rumors. You know she hated that sort of thing; she was someone who despised lies and more often than not made people face the truth. She made me do it even though she knew it would break my heart; it was something she had to do, even though it hurt her so much, too.

"But I can't stand your not liking me, your hating me and thinking I wanted to hurt you anymore, Paul. I die every time you look at me furiously at school. Still, almost every night, I go to sleep crying over you. Of course, we can't be in love, but I can't stand our being enemies."

"I never thought of you as an enemy. I just . . ."

"Hated me. Go on, you can say it now. It doesn't hurt for me to hear it now, now that I have suffered through it," I said and smiled through my tears.

"Ruby," Paul said, shaking his head, "I can't believe what you're telling me; I can't believe that my father . . . that your mother . . ."

"You're old enough now to know the truth, Paul. Maybe I'm being selfish by telling it to you. Grandmere Catherine warned me not to, warned me that you would eventually hate me for causing any rift in your family, but I can't stand the lies between us anymore, and especially now, on top of my losing her and my realization that I'm all alone."

Paul stared at me a moment and then he got up and walked down to the edge of the water. I watched him just stand there, kicking some stones into the water, thinking, realizing, coming to terms with what I had told him. I knew that the same sort of tumult that was going on in his heart had gone on in mine, and the same sort of confusion was whirling around in his head. He shook his head again, more vigorously this time, and turned back to me.

"We have all these photographs, pictures of my mother when she was pregnant with me, pictures of me right after I was born, and—"

"Lies," I said. "All pretend, deceptions to hide the sinful acts."

"No, you're wrong. It's all a terrible, stupid mistake, don't you see?"

he said, folding his hands into fists. "And we're being made to suffer for it. I'm sure it can't be true." He nodded, convincing himself. "I'm sure," he said, walking back to me.

"Grandmere Catherine wouldn't lie to me, Paul."

"No, your grandmere wouldn't lie to you, but maybe she thought by telling you this story, she could keep you from getting involved with me and that was good because my family would make such a stink and you and I would suffer. Sure, that's it," he said, comfortable with the theory. "I'll prove it to you. I don't know how I will right now, but I will and then . . . then we'll be together just as we dreamed we would."

"Oh, Paul, how I wish you were right," I said.

"I am," he said confidently. "You'll see. I'll get beat up over you at another fais dodo yet," he added, laughing. I smiled but turned away.

"What about Suzzette?" I asked.

"I don't love Suzzette. I never did. I just had to have someone to . . . to . . ."

"To make me jealous?" I asked, turning back quickly.

"Yes," he confessed.

"I don't blame you for doing that, only you did it very convincingly," I said, smiling.

"Well, I'm . . . good at it."

We laughed. Then I grew serious again and reached up for his hand. He helped me stand. We were inches apart, facing each other.

"I don't want you to be hurt, Paul. Don't put too much hope in your disproving the things Grandmere Catherine told me. Promise me that when you find out the truth . . ."

"I won't find out the lie," he insisted.

"Promise me," I pursued, "promise that if you find out that what Grandmere told me is true, you will accept it as I have and go on to love someone else as much. Promise me."

"I can't," he said. "I can't love anyone else as much as I love you, Ruby. It's not possible."

He embraced me and I buried my face in his shoulder for a moment. He drew me closer. Beneath his shirt, I could feel his steady heartbeat. Then I felt his lips on my hair and I closed my eyes and dreamed we were far away, living in a world where there were no lies and deceit, where it was always spring and where the sunshine touched your heart as well as your face and made you forever young.

The screech of a marsh hawk made me lift my head quickly. I saw it seize a smaller bird, one that might have just learned how to fly, and then go off with its prize, unconcerned that it left some mother bird destroyed, too.

"Sometimes I hate it here," I said quickly. "Sometimes, I feel like I don't belong."

Paul looked at me with surprise.

"Of course you belong here," he said. It was on the tip of my tongue to tell him the rest of it, to tell him about my twin sister and my real father who lived in a big house somewhere in New Orleans, but I shut the lid on the truth. Enough had been revealed for one day.

"I'd better get back inside and continue to greet the people," I said, starting toward the house.

"I'll come with you and stay with you as long as I can," he said. "My parents sent over some food. I gave it to Mrs. Livaudis. They send their regards. They would have come themselves but . . ."

He stopped in the middle of his explanation and smirked.

"I'm not making any excuses for them. My father doesn't like your grandpere," he said.

I wanted to tell him why; I wanted to go on and on and give him all the details Grandmere Catherine had given me, but I thought enough was enough. Let him discover as much of the truth as he was able to himself, as much of it as he was able to face. For truth was a bright light and just like any bright light, it was hard to look into it.

I nodded. He hurried to join me, to thread his arm through mine, and return to the wake to sit beside me where he didn't fully realize or yet believe he belonged. After all, it was his grandmother, too, who had died.

8

It's Hard to Change

Grandmere Catherine's funeral was one of the biggest ever held in Terrebone Parish, for practically all of the mourners who had come to the wake and then some came to the services in church and at the cemetery. Grandpere Jack was on his best behavior and wearing the best clothes he could get. With his hair brushed, his beard trimmed, and his boots cleaned and polished, he looked more like a responsible member of the community. He told me he hadn't been in church since his mother's funeral, but he sat beside me and sang the hymns and recited the prayers. He stood at my side at the cemetery, too. It seemed like as long as he didn't have any whiskey flowing through his veins, he was quiet and respectful.

Paul's parents came to the church, but not to the cemetery. Paul came to the graveside by himself and stood on the other side of me. We didn't hold hands, but he made his close presence known with a touch or a word.

Father Rush began his prayers and then delivered his last blessing. And then the coffin was lowered. Just when I had thought my sorrow had gone as deeply as it could into my very soul; just when I had thought my heart could be torn no more, I felt the sorrow go deeper and tear more. Somehow, even though she was dead, with her body still in the house, with her face in quiet repose, I had not fully understood how final her death was, but now, with the sight of her coffin going down, I could not remain strong. I could not accept that she would not be there to greet me in the morning and to comfort me before bed. I could not accept that we wouldn't be working side by side, struggling to provide for ourselves; I could not accept that she wouldn't be singing over the stove or marching down the steps to go on one of her treater missions. I didn't have the strength. My legs became sticks of butter and collapsed beneath me. Neither Paul nor Grandpere could get to me before my body hit the earth and my eyes shut out the reality.

I awoke on the front seat of the car that brought us to the cemetery. Someone had gone to a nearby brook and dipped a handkerchief into the water. Now, the cool, refreshing liquid helped me regain consciousness. I saw Mrs. Livaudis leaning over me, stroking my hair, and I saw Paul standing right behind her, a look of deep concern on his face.

"What happened?"

"You just fainted, dear, and we carried you to the car. How are you now?" she asked.

"I'm all right," I said. "Where's Grandpere Jack?" I asked. I tried sitting up, but my head began to spin and I had to fall back against the seat.

"He went off already," Mrs. Livaudis said, smirking, "with his usual swamp bums. You just rest there, dear. We're taking you home now. Just rest," she advised.

"I'll be right behind you," Paul said, leaning in. I tried to smile and then closed my eyes. By the time we reached the house, I felt strong enough to get up and walk to the galerie steps. There were dozens of people waiting to help. Mrs. Thibodeau directed I be taken up to my room. They helped me off with my shoes and I lay back, now feeling more embarrassed than exhausted.

"I'm fine," I insisted. "I'll be all right. I should go downstairs and—"

"You just lie here awhile, dear," Mrs. Livaudis said. "We'll bring you something cool to drink."

"But I should go downstairs . . . the people . . ."

"Everything's taken care of. Just rest a bit more," Mrs. Thibodeau said. I did as they ordered. Mrs. Livaudis returned with some cold lemonade. I felt a lot better after I had drunk it and said so.

"If you're up to it then, the Tate boy wants to see how you are. He's chomping at the bit and pacing up and down at the foot of the stairs like an expectant father," Mrs. Livaudis said, smiling.

"Yes, please, send him in," I said, and Paul was permitted to come upstairs.

"How are you doing?" he asked quickly.

"I'm all right. I'm sorry I was so much trouble," I moaned. "I wanted everything to go smooth and proper for Grandmere."

"Oh, it did. It was the most . . . most impressive funeral I've ever seen. No one could remember more people attending one, and you did fine. Everyone understands."

"Where's Grandpere Jack?" I asked. "Where did he go to so quickly?"

"I don't know, but he just arrived a little while ago. He's downstairs, greeting people on the galerie."

"Was he drinking?"

"A little," Paul lied.

"Paul Tate, you'd better practice more if you're going to try to deceive me," I said. "You're no harder to see through than a clean windowpane."

He laughed.

"He'll be all right. Too many people around him," Paul assured me, but no sooner had he uttered the words than we heard the shouting from below.

"Don't you tell me what to do and what not to do in my own house!" Grandpere raved. "You may run the pants off your men at your homes, but you ain't running off mine. Now just get your butts on outta here and make it quick. Go on, get!"

That was followed by a chorus of uproars and more shouting.

"Help me go down, Paul. I've got to see what he's doing," I said. I got out of bed, slipped into my shoes, and went down to the kitchen where Grandpere had a jug of whiskey in his hands and was already swaying as he glared at the small crowd of mourners in the doorway.

"Whatcha all gapin' at, huh? You never seen a man in mourning? You never seen a man who just buried his wife? Quit your gapin' and go about your business," he cried, took another swig, swayed, and wiped his mouth with the back of his hand. His eyes were blazing. "Go on!" he shouted again, when no one moved.

"Grandpere!" I cried. He gazed at me with those bleary eyes. Then he swung the jug against the sink, smashing it and its contents all over the kitchen. The women shrieked and he howled. He was terrible in his anger, frightening as he whumped around with an energy too great to confine in such a small space.

Paul embraced me and pulled me back up the stairs.

"Wait until he calms down," he said. We heard Grandpere scream again and then we heard the mourners flee the house, the women who had brought their families, grabbing up their children and getting into their trucks and cars with their husbands to hightail it away.

Grandpere ranted and raved awhile longer. Paul sat beside me on my bed and held my hand. We listened until it grew very quiet downstairs.

"He's settled down," I said. "I'd better go down and start cleaning up."

"I'll help," Paul said.

We found Grandpere collapsed in a rocker on the galerie, snoring. I mopped up the kitchen and cleared away the pieces of broken jug while Paul wiped down our table and straightened up the furniture.

"You'd better go home now, Paul," I said as soon as we were finished. "Your parents are probably wondering where you are so long."

"I hate to leave you here with that . . . that drunk. They ought to lock him up and throw the key away for doing what he did this time. It's not right that Grandmere Catherine's gone and he's still around, and it's not safe for you."

"I'll be all right. You know how he gets after he has his tantrum. He'll just sleep it off and then wake up hungry and sorry for what he did."

Paul smiled, shook his head, and then reached to caress my cheek, his eyes soft and warm.

"My Ruby, always optimistic."

"Not always, Paul," I said sadly. "Not anymore."

"I'll stop by in the morning," he promised. "To see how things are."

I nodded.

"Ruby, I . . ."

"You had better go, Paul," I said. "I don't want any more nasty scenes today."

"All right." He kissed me quickly on the cheek before rising. "I'm going to talk to my father," he promised. "I'm going to get at the truth of things."

I tried to smile, but my face was like dry, brittle china from all the tears and sadness. I was afraid I might simply shatter to pieces right before his eyes.

"I will," Paul pledged at the doorway. Then he was gone.

I sighed deeply, put some of the food away, and walked upstairs to lie down again. I had never felt so tired. I did sleep through a good part of the rest of the day. If anyone came to the house, I didn't hear them. But early in the evening, I heard pots clanking and furniture being shoved around. I sat up, for a moment, very confused. Then, my wits returning, I got out of bed quickly and went downstairs to find Grandpere on his hands and knees tugging at some loose floorboards. Every cabinet door was thrown wide open and all of our pots and pans had been taken out of the cabinets and lay strewn about.

"Grandpere, what are you doing?" I asked. He turned and gazed at me with eyes I hadn't seen before, eyes of accusation and anger.

"I know she's got it hidden somewhere here," he said. "I didn't find it in her room, but I know she's got it somewhere. Where is it, Ruby? I need it," he moaned.

"Need what, Grandpere?"

"Her stash, her money. She always had a pile set aside for a rainy day. Well, my rainy days have come. I need it to get my motor fixed, to get some new equipment." He sat back on his haunches. "I got to work harder to make a go of it for both of us, Ruby. Where is it?"

"There isn't any stash, Grandpere. We were having a hard time of it, too. I once poled out to your shack to see if I could get you to help us get by, but you were collapsed on your galerie," I told him.

He shook his head, his eyes wild.

"Maybe she never told you. She was like that . . . secretive even with her own. There's a stash here somewhere," he declared, shifting his eyes from side to side. "It might take me a while, but I'll find it. If it's not in the house, it's buried somewhere outside, huh? Did you ever see or hear her diggin' out there?"

"There's no stash, Grandpere. You're wasting your time."

It was on the tip of my tongue to tell him about my art money, but it was also as if Grandmere Catherine were still there, standing right beside me, forbidding me to mention a word about it. In case he decided to look in her chest for valuables, I made a note to myself to move the money under my mattress.

"Are you hungry?" I asked him.

"No," he said quickly. "I'm going out back before it gets too dark and look some more," he said.

After he left, I put back all the pots and pans and then I warmed some food for myself. I ate mechanically, barely tasting anything. I ate just because I knew I had to in order to keep up my strength. Then, I went back upstairs. I could hear Grandpere's frantic digging in the backyard, his digging and his cursing. I heard him ripping through the smokehouse and even banging around in the outhouse. Finally, he grew exhausted with the searching and came back inside. I heard him get himself something to eat and drink. His frustration was so great, he moaned like a calf that had lost its mother. Soon, he was talking to ghosts.

"Where'd you put the money, Catherine? I got to have the money to take care of our granddaughter, don't I? Where is it?"

Finally, he grew quiet. I tiptoed out and looked over the railing to see him collapsed at the kitchen table, his head on his arms. I returned to my room and I sat by my window and gazed up at the horned moon half hidden by dark clouds and I thought, this is the same moon that rode high over New Orleans, and I tried to imagine my future. Would I be rich and famous and live in a big house some day like Grandmere Catherine predicted?

Or was all that just a dream, too? Just another web, dazzling in the moonlight, a mirage, an illusion of jewels woven in the darkness, waiting, full of promises that were as empty and as light as the web itself?

There was no period in my life when I thought time passed more slowly than it did during the days following Grandmere Catherine's funeral and burial. Every time I looked at the old and tarnished brass clock set in its cherry wood case on the windowsill in the loom room and saw that instead of an hour only ten minutes had passed, I was surprised and disappointed. I tried to fill my every moment, keep my hands and my mind busy so I wouldn't think and remember and mourn, but no matter how much work I did and how hard I worked, there was always time to remember.

One memory that returned with the persistence of a housefly was my recollection of the promise I had made to Grandmere Catherine should anything bad happen to her. She had reminded me of it the day she had died and she had forced me to repeat my vow. I had promised not to stay here, not to live with Grandpere Jack. Grandmere Catherine wanted me to go to New Orleans and find my real father and my sister, but the very thought of leaving the bayou and getting on a bus to go to a city that loomed as far away and as strange to me as a distant planet was terrifying. I was positive I would stand out as clearly as a crawfish in a pot of duck gumbo. Everyone in New Orleans would take one look at me and say to himself, "There's an ignorant Cajun girl traveling on her own." They would laugh at me and mock me for sure.

I had never traveled very far, especially on my own, but it wasn't the fear of the journey, nor even the size of the city and the unfamiliarity with city life that frightened me the most. No, what was even more terrifying was imagining what my real father would do and say as soon as I presented myself. How would he react? What would I do if he shut the door in my face? After having deserted Grandpere Jack and then, after having been rejected by my father, where would I go?

I had read enough about the evils of city life to know about the horrors that went on in the slums, and the terrible fates young girls such as myself suffered. Would I become one of those women I had heard about, women who were taken into bordellos to provide men with sexual pleasures? What other sort of work would I be able to get? Who would hire a young Cajun girl with a limited education and only simple handicraft skills? I envisioned myself ending up sleeping in some gutter, surrounded by other downcast and downtrodden people.

No, it was easier to put off the promise and lock myself upstairs in the *grenier* for most of the day, working on the linens and towels as if Grandmere Catherine were still alive and just downstairs doing one of her kitchen chores before joining me. It was easier to pretend I had to finish something she had started while she was off on one of her *treater* missions, easier to make believe nothing had changed.

Of course, part of my day involved caring for Grandpere Jack, preparing his meals and cleaning up after him, which was an endless chore. I made him his breakfast every morning before he left to go fishing or harvesting Spanish moss in the swamp. He was still mumbling about finding Grandmere Catherine's stash and he still spent every spare moment digging and searching around the house. The longer he looked and located nothing, the more he believed I was hiding what I knew.

"Catherine wasn't one to let herself go and die and leave something buried without someone knowing where," he declared one night after he had begun to eat his supper. His green eyes darkened as he focused them on me with suspicion. "You didn't dig somethin' up and hide it where I've already looked, have you, Ruby? Wouldn't surprise me none to learn that Catherine had told you to do just such a thing before she died."

"No, Grandpere. I've told you time after time. There was no stash. We had to spend everything we made. Before Grandmere died, we were depending on what she got from some of her treater missions, too, and you know how much she hated taking anything for helping people." What my eyes must have shown convinced him I was not lying, at least for the time being.

"That's jus' it," he said, chewing thoughtfully, "people gave her things, gave her money, too, I'm sure. I just wonder if she left anything with one of those busybodies, 'specially that Mrs. Thibodeau. One of these nights, I might pay that woman a visit," he declared.

"I wouldn't do that, Grandpere," I warned him.

"Why not? The money don't belong to her; it belongs to me . . . us that is."

"Mrs. Thibodeau would call the police and have you put in jail if you so much as stepped on the floor of her galerie," I advised him. "She's as much as told me so." Once again, his piercing eyes glared my way before he went back to his food.

"All you women are in cahoots," he muttered. "A man does the best he can to keep food on the table, keep the house together. Women take all that for granted. Especially, Cajun women," he mumbled. "They think it's all coming to them. Well it ain't, and a man's got to be treated with more respect, especially in his own home. If I find that money's been hidden on me . . ."

It did no good to argue with him. I saw why Grandmere Catherine made no attempt to change the way he thought, but I did hope that in time, he would give up his frantic search for the nonexistent stash and concentrate on reforming himself the way he had promised and work hard at making a good life for us. Some days he did return from the swamp laden down with a good fish catch or a pair of ducks for our gumbo. But some days, he spent most of his time poling from one brackish pond to the next, mumbling to himself about one of his favorite gripes and then settling down in his pirogue to drink himself into a stupor, having traded his catch for a cheap bottle of gin or rum. Those nights he returned empty-handed and bitter, and I had to make do with what we had and concoct a poor Cajun's jambalaya.

Grandpere repaired some small things around the house, but left most of his other promises of work unfulfilled. He didn't patch the roof where it leaked or replace the cracked floorboards, and despite my not so subtle suggestions, he didn't improve his hygienic habits either. A week would go by before he would take a bar of soap and water to his body, and even then, it was a quick, almost insignificant rinse. Soon, there were lice in his hair again, his beard was scraggly, and his fingernails were caked with grime. I had to look at something else whenever we ate or I would lose my appetite. It was hard enough contending with the variety of sour and rancid odors that reeked from his clothes and body. How someone could let himself go like that and not care or even notice was beyond me. I imagined it had a lot to do with his drinking.

Every time I looked at the portrait I had done of Grandmere Catherine, I thought about returning to my painting, but whenever I set up my easel, I would just stare dumbly at the blank paper, not a creative thought coming to mind. I attempted a few starts, drawing some lines, even trying to paint a simple moss-covered cypress log, but it was as if my artistic talent had died with Grandmere. I knew she would be furious even to hear such a thought, but the truth was that the bayou, the birds, the plants and trees, everything about it in some way made me think of Grandmere and once I did, I couldn't paint. I missed her that much.

Paul came by nearly every day, sometimes just to sit and talk on the galerie, sometimes to sit and watch me work on the loom. Often, he helped with some chore, especially a chore Grandpere should have completed before going out in the swamp for the day.

"What's that Tate boy doin' around here so much?" Grandpere asked me late one afternoon when he returned just as Paul was leaving.

"He's just a good friend, coming around to be sure everything is all right, Grandpere," I said. I didn't have the courage to tell Grandpere I knew all the ugly truths and the terrible things he had done when my mother was pregnant with Paul. I knew how Grandpere's temper could flare, and how such revelations would just send him sucking on a bottle and then ranting and raving.

"Those Tates think they're special just because they make a pile of money," Grandpere muttered. "You watch out for people like that. You watch out," he warned. I ignored him and went in to prepare supper.

Every day, before Paul left, he made a promise to talk to his father about the past, but every day he returned, I could see immediately that he hadn't worked up the courage yet. Finally, one Saturday night, he told me he and his father were going fishing the next day after church.

"It will just be him and me," he said. "One way or the other, I'll get it all discussed," he promised.

That morning I tried to get Grandpere Jack to go to church with me, but I couldn't shake him out of his deep sleep. The harder I shook him, the louder he snored. It would be the first time I had gone to church without Grandmere Catherine and I wasn't sure I could manage it, but I set out anyway. When I arrived, all of Grandmere's lady friends greeted me warmly. Naturally, they were full of questions concerning how I was getting along living in the same house with Grandpere. I tried to make it sound better than it was, but Mrs. Livaudis pursed her lips and shook her head.

"No one should have to live with such a burden, especially a young girl like Ruby," she declared.

"You sit with us, dear," Mrs. Thibodeau said, and I sat in the pew and sang the hymns alongside them.

Paul and his family had arrived late so we didn't talk, and then he and his father wanted to get back as soon as they could and get their boat in the bayou. I couldn't stop thinking about him all day, wondering every other minute whether or not Paul had brought up the past with his father. I expected to see him shortly after dinner, but he didn't come. I sat on the galerie and rocked and waited. Grandpere was inside listening to some Cajun music on the radio and kicking up his heels from time to time as he swung a jug up to his lips. Anyone walking by would have thought a hoeing bee or a shingling party was going on.

It got late; Grandpere Jack settled down into his usual unconscious state, and I grew tired. Without a moon, the sky was a deep black, making the twinkling stars that much brighter. I tried to keep my eyes from closing, but the lids seemed to have a mind of their own. I even dozed off and woke with a start at the cry of a screech owl. Finally, I gave up and went up to bed.

I had just settled my head on the pillow and closed my eyes again, when I heard the front door open and close and then heard soft footsteps on the stairs. My heart began to thump. Who had come into our house? With Grandpere Jack in a stupor, anyone could enter and do what he wanted. I sat up and waited, barely breathing.

First, a tall silhouette appeared on the walls and then the dark figure stepped into my doorway.

"Paul?"

"I'm sorry to wake you, Ruby. I wasn't going to come tonight, but I just couldn't sleep," he said. "I knocked, but I guess you didn't hear and when I opened the door, I saw your grandfather sprawled out on the settee in the sitting room, his mouth wide open, the snoring so loud, it's making the walls vibrate."

I leaned over and turned on the light. One look at Paul's face told me he had learned the truth.

"What happened, Paul? I waited for you until I got too tired," I told him, and sat up, holding the blanket against my flimsy nightgown. He came farther into the room and stood at the foot of my bed, his head bowed. "Did you have the discussion with your father?" He nodded and then lifted his head.

"When I got home from fishing, I just ran into the house and up to my room and shut the door. I didn't go down for dinner, but I just couldn't lie there anymore. I wanted to put my pillow over my face and keep it there until I couldn't breathe," he told me. "I even tried twice!"

"Oh, Paul. What did he tell you?" I asked. Paul sat on the bed and gazed at me silently for a moment. His shoulders slumped and he continued.

"My father didn't want to talk about it; he was surprised by my questions and for a long while just sat there, staring at the water, not speaking. I told him I had to know the truth, that it was important to me, more important than anything else. Finally, he turned to me and said he was going to tell me about it someday; he just didn't think the time had come.

"But I told him it had and I repeated my need to know the truth. At first, he was angry I had found out. He thought Grandpere Jack had told me. He said your grandfather . . . I guess I got to get used to it, even though it makes me sick to the stomach . . . our grandfather," he said, pronouncing the words with a grimace that made it look as if he had swallowed castor oil. "Our grandpere Jack had blackmailed him once before and was trying to figure a way to get money out of him again. Then I told him what Grandmere Catherine had told you and why she had told you, and he nodded and said she was right to do so."

"I'm glad, Paul, glad he told you the truth. Now—"

"Only," Paul added quickly, his eyes growing narrow and dark, "my father's version of the story is a lot different from Grandmere Catherine's version."

"How?"

"According to him your mother seduced him, and he didn't take advantage of her. He claims she was a wild young woman and he wasn't the first to be with her. He said she was hounding him, following him everywhere, smiling and teasing him all the time, and one day, when he was out in the bayou fishing by himself, she came upon him, poling a pirogue. She tore off her clothing and dove into the water naked and then climbed into his boat. That's when it happened. That's when I was made," Paul said bitterly.

My silence bothered him, but I couldn't help it. I was speechless. One part of me wanted to laugh and shout and ridicule such a story. No daughter of Grandmere Catherine's could be such a creature; but another part of me, that part of me that had fantasized such things with Paul told me it might be true.

"I don't believe him of course," Paul said quickly. "I think it happened the way your grandmother told it. He came around here and he seduced your mother, otherwise, why would he have owned up to it so quickly when Grandpere Jack confronted him and why did he pay him any blackmail money?"

I took a deep breath.

"Did you say that to your father?" I asked.

"No. I didn't want to have any arguments about it."

"I don't know how we'll ever know the whole truth about it," I said.

"What's the difference now?" Paul muttered angrily. "The result is the same. Oh, my father complained again and again about how Grandpere Jack came to him and blackmailed him, and how he had to pay him thousands of dollars to keep the matter secret. He said Grandpere was the lowest of the low who belonged with the slimy things in the swamp. He told me how my mother felt sorry for him, especially because of Grandpere Jack, and how she agreed to pretend to be pregnant so my birth would be accepted by the community as the legitimate birth of a Tate. Then he made me promise I wouldn't say anything to my mother. He told me it would break her heart if she knew I discovered she wasn't really my mother."

"I'm sure it would," I said. "He's not wrong about that, Paul. Why hurt her any more than she has been hurt?"

"What about me?" he cried. "What about . . . us?"

"We're young," I said, thinking about Grandmere Catherine's words of wisdom.

"That doesn't mean it hurts any less," he moaned.

"No, it doesn't, but I don't know what else we can do about it, but go on and try to find other people who we can love and care for as strongly as we love and care for each other now."

"I can't; I won't," he said defiantly.

"Paul, what else can we do?"

He fixed his eyes on me, the defiance in his face, the anger and the pain, too.

"We'll just pretend it isn't so," he said, reaching out to take my hand.

I couldn't stop the tingle that had begun around my heart and then shot through my blood to fly through my stomach and my legs and make my breath quicken. Suddenly everything about him, everything about us was forbidden. Just his merely sitting on my bed, holding my hand, gazing at me with such longing was taboo, and just like most anything prohibited, it carried an elevated excitement along with it. It was like teasing fate, testing, exquisitely tormenting our own souls.

"We can't do that, Paul," I said, my voice barely a whisper.

"Why not? Let's ignore that half of ourselves and think only about the other half. It won't be the first time such a thing happened, especially in the bayou," he said. His hand moved up my wrist, the fingers sliding softly over my skin as he lifted himself to sit closer. I shook my head gently.

"You're just upset and angry now, Paul. You're not thinking about what you're saying to me," I told him. My heart was pounding so hard, I thought I would lose my breath.

"Yes, I am. Who knows about us anyway? Just your grandpere Jack and no one would believe anything he would say, and my father and mother who wouldn't want anyone to know the truth. Don't you see? It doesn't matter."

"But we know; it matters to us."

"Not if we don't let it matter," Paul said. He leaned forward to kiss my forehead. Now that we both knew the truth of his origin, his lips felt as hot as a branding iron. I backed away abruptly and shook my head, not only trying to refuse his advances, but refusing the excitement that was building in my own heart.

My blanket fell away and my nightgown dropped so low most of my bosom was visible. Paul's eyes lowered and rose, climbing slowly back to my neck and shoulders and my face.

"Once we do it, once we ignore the ugly past and make love, we will be able to do it easier and easier every time afterward, Ruby," he said. "Don't you see? Why should the other half of ourselves, the better half be denied? We haven't been brought up as brother and sister; we've never thought of ourselves as related.

"If you just close your eyes and forget, if you just let your lips touch mine," he said, drawing close again.

I shook my head, closed my eyes, and sat back as far as I could, but Paul's lips touched mine. I tried to deny him, to slide myself out from under, but he pressed onward, more demanding, his hands finding the bare flesh of my exposed bosom, his fingers turning so the tips would touch my nipples.

"Paul, no," I cried. "Please, don't. We'll be sorry," I said, but I felt myself slipping as the tingle grew into a wave of warm desire. After so much sorrow and so much hardship, my body craved his warm touch, forbidden as it was.

"No, we won't," Paul insisted. His lips grazed my forehead and moved down the side of my face as his hand slipped completely under my nightgown to fully cup my breast. He lifted it to bring his lips to my nipple and I felt myself weaken. I couldn't open my eyes. I couldn't speak. I continued to slide under him and he pressed forward, insistent, driven, unrelenting in his determination to batter down not only my feeble resistance, but all the morals and laws of church and man that not only forbid our erotic touching, but looked down on it with disgust.

"Ruby," he whispered in my ear, sending my mind spinning, my heart racing, "I love you."

"What the hell in tarnation is goin' on here!" we suddenly heard.

Paul snapped back and I gasped. Grandpere Jack was standing in the hallway gazing in at us, his hair sticking up and out, his eyes wide and bloodshot, his body swaying as if a wind were tearing through the house.

"Nothing," Paul said, and stood up, quickly straightening his clothes.

"Nothing! You call that nothing?" Grandpere Jack focused his gaze and stepped through the doorway. He was still drunk, but he recognized Paul. "Who the hell . . . you're the Tate boy, ain't you? The one who's always comin' around here?"

Paul looked down at me and then nodded at Grandpere.

"Figures you'd come around here at night and sneak into the house and into my granddaughter's room. It's in the Tate blood," Grandpere said.

"That's a lie," Paul snapped.

"Humph," Grandpere said and combed his long fingers through his disheveled hair. "Yeah, well, you got no business bein' in my grand-daughter's bedroom this time of night. My advice to you, boy, is to tuck in your tail and git."

"Go on, Paul," I said. "It's better if you go," I added.

He looked down at me, his eyes swimming in tears.

"Please," I whispered. He bit down on his lower lip and then charged out the door, nearly bowling Grandpere Jack over in the process. Paul pounded his way down the steps and out the door.

"Well now," Grandpere Jack said, turning back to me. "Looks like you're a lot older than I thought. Time we thought about finding you a proper husband."

"I don't need anyone finding me a husband, Grandpere, and I'm not ready to marry anyone anyway. Paul wasn't doing anything. We were just talking and—"

"Just talkin'?" He laughed that silent chuckle that made his shoulders shake. "Out in the swamp that kinda talkin' makes new tad-poles," he added, and shook his head. "No, you're right grow'd; I just didn't take a good look at you before," he said, gazing at my uncovered body. I brought the blanket to my chest quickly. "Don't you worry about it none," he said, winking and then he stumbled out and made his way to Grandmere's room where he now slept, whenever he was able to climb the stairs to go to bed.

I sat back, my heart thumping so hard, I thought it would crack open my chest. Poor Paul, I thought. He was so mixed up, so confused, his anger pulling him in one direction, his feeling for me pulling him in another. Grandpere Jack's surprise arrival and accusations didn't help matters any, but it might have saved us from doing something we would have regretted later on, I thought.

I put out the light and lay back again. I had to confess to myself that for a moment, when Paul was so insistent, part of me wanted to give in and do just what he had said: be defiant and seize what fate had made off-limits. But how do you bury such a dark secret in your heart, and how do you keep it from infecting and eventually destroying the purity of any love you might possess for each other? It couldn't be; it wasn't meant to be. It mustn't be, I thought. If anything, I knew now that I couldn't let myself get that close to him again. I didn't have the strength of will to resist the passion either.

As I closed my eyes and tried to sleep again, I realized, this was another reason, maybe even a bigger reason, to find the strength and the courage to leave.

Maybe that was why Grandmere Catherine was so insistent about it; maybe she knew what would happen between Paul and me despite what we had learned about ourselves. I fell asleep with her words echoing in my mind and my promises to her on my lips.

9

Hard Lessons

I didn't see Paul for the remainder of the weekend and I was surprised when I went to school on Monday and didn't see him there either. When I asked his sister Jeanne about him, she told me he wasn't feeling well, but she looked put out that I had asked, especially in front of her friends, and wouldn't say another thing.

After I returned home from school, I decided to take a short walk along the canal before preparing dinner. I strolled down the path through our yard which was abloom with hibiscus and blue and pink hydrangeas. Spring was rushing in this year, the colors, the sweet scents, and the heightened sense of life and birth was all around me. It was as if Nature herself were trying to comfort me.

But my confused and troubled thoughts were like bees buzzing around in a jar. I heard so many different voices telling me to do so many different things. Run, Ruby, run, one voice urged. Get as far from the bayou and from Paul and Grandpere Jack as you can.

Forget running, be defiant, another voice told me. You love Paul. You know you do. Surrender to your feelings and forget what you've learned. Do what Paul wants you to do: live like it was all a lie.

Remember your promise to me, Ruby, I heard Grandmere Catherine urge. Ruby . . . your promise . . . remember.

The warm Gulf breeze lifted strands of my hair and made them dance over my forehead. The same warm breeze combed through the moss on the dead cypress trees in the marsh, making it look like some sprawling green animal, lifting and swaying to catch my attention. On a long sandbar, I saw a cottonmouth coiled over some driftwood soaking up the sun, its triangular head the color of a discolored copper penny. Two ducks and a heron sprung up from the water and flew low over the cattails. And then I heard the distant purr of a motorboat as it sliced through the bayou and wove its way closer and closer until it popped out from around a turn.

It was Paul. The moment he saw me, he waved, sped up, and brought the boat close to the shore, the wakes from the motorboat swelling up through the lily pads and cattails and slapping across the cypress roots along the bank.

"Walk down to the shale there," he called, and pointed. I did and he brought the boat as near as he could before shutting the engine and letting it drift up to me.

"Where were you today? Why didn't you come to school?" I asked. He was obviously not sick.

"I was busy, thinking and planning. Come into my boat. I want to show you something," he said.

I shook my head. "I've got to start on dinner for Grandpere Jack, Paul," I told him, retreating a step.

"You've got plenty of time and you know he'll either be late or not show up until he's too drunk to care," he replied. "Come on. Please," he begged.

"Paul, I don't want anything to happen like it did the other day," I said.

"Nothing will happen. I won't come near you. I just want to show you something. I'll bring you right back," he promised. He held up his hand to take an oath. "I swear."

"You won't come near me and you'll bring me right back?"

"Absolutely," he said, and leaned forward to take my hand as I hopped over the shale and stepped up and into the motorboat. "Just sit back," he said, starting the engine again. He spun the boat around sharply and accelerated with the confidence of an old Cajun swamp fisherman. Even so, I screamed. The best fisherman often ran into gators or sandbars. Paul laughed and slowed down.

"Where are you taking me, Paul Tate?" He steered us through the shadows cast by an overhang of willow trees, deeper and deeper into the swamp before heading southwest in the direction of his father's cannery. Off in the distance I could see thunderheads over the Gulf. "I don't want to get caught in any storms," I complained.

"My, you can be a nag," Paul said, smiling. He wove us through a narrow passage and then headed for a field, cutting his engine as we drew closer and closer. Finally, he turned it off to let the boat drift.

"Where are we?"

"My land," he replied. "And I don't mean my father's land. My land," he emphasized.

"Your land?"

"Yep," he said proudly and leaned back against the side of the boat. "All that you see—sixty acres actually. It's mine, my inheritance." He gestured broadly at the field.

"I never knew that," I said, gazing over what looked like prime land in the bayou.

"My grandfather Tate left it to me. It's held in trust, but it will be mine as soon as I turn eighteen, but that isn't the best of it," he said, smiling.

"Well, what is then?" I asked. "Stop grinning like a Cheshire cat and tell me what this is all about, Paul Tate."

"Better than tell you, I'll show you," he said, and took up the oar to paddle the boat softly through some marsh grass and into a dark, shadowy area. I stared ahead and soon saw the bubbles in the water.

"What's that?"

"Gas bubbles," he said in a whisper. "You know what it means?"

I shook my head.

"It means oil is under here. Oil and it's on my land. I'm going to be rich, Ruby, very rich," he said.

"Oh, Paul, that's wonderful."

"Not if you're not with me to share it," he said quickly. "I brought you here because I wanted you to see my dreams. I'm going to build a great house on my land. It will be a great plantation, your plantation, Ruby."

"Paul, how can we even think such a thing? Please," I said. "Stop tormenting yourself and me, too."

"We can think of such a thing, don't you see? The oil is the answer. Money and power will make it all possible. I'll buy Grandpere Jack's blessings and silence. We'll be the most respected, prosperous couple in the bayou, and our family—"

"We can't have children, Paul."

"We'll adopt, maybe even secretly, with your doing the same thing my mother did—pretending the baby is yours, and then—"

"But, Paul, we'll be living the same sort of lies, the same deceits, and they will haunt us forever," I said, shaking my head.

"Not if we don't let them, not if we permit ourselves to love and cherish each other the way we always dreamed we would," he insisted.

I turned away from him and watched a bullfrog jump off a log. It created a small circle of ripples that quickly disappeared. In a corner of the pond, I saw bream feeding on insects among the cattails and lily pads. The wind began to pick up and the Spanish moss swayed along with the twisted limbs of the cypress. A flock of geese passed overhead and disappeared over the tops of trees as if they had flown into the clouds.

"It's beautiful here, Paul. And I wish it could be our home someday, but it can't and it's just cruel to bring me here and tell me these things," I said, chastising him softly.

"But, Ruby—"

"Don't you think I wish it could be, wish it as much as you do?" I said, spinning around on him. My eyes were burning with tears of anger and frustration. "The same feelings that are tearing you apart are tearing me, but we're just prolonging the pain by fantasizing like this."

"It's not a fantasy; it's a plan," he said firmly. "I've been thinking about it all weekend. After I'm eighteen . . ."

I shook my head.

"Take me back, Paul. Please," I said. He stared at me a moment.

"Will you at least think about it?" he pleaded. "Will you?"

"Yes," I said, because I saw it was the key that would open the door and let us out of this room of misery.

"Good." He started the engine and drove us back to the dock at my house.

"I'll see you at school tomorrow," he said after he helped me out of the boat. "We'll talk about this every day, think it out clearly, together, okay?"

"Okay, Paul," I said, confident that one morning he would awaken and realize that his plan was a fantasy not meant to become a reality.

"Ruby," he cried as I started toward the house. I turned. "I can't help loving you," he said. "Don't hate me for it."

I bit down on my lower lip and nodded. My heart was soaked in the tears that had fallen behind my eyes. I watched him drive off and waited until his motorboat disappeared into the bayou. Then I took a deep breath and entered the house.

The roar of Grandpere's laughter greeted me and was immediately followed by the laughter of a stranger. I walked into the kitchen slowly to discover Grandpere Jack sitting at the table. He and a man I recognized as Buster Trahaw, the son of a rich sugar plantation owner, sat hunched over a large bowl of crawfish. There were at least a half-dozen or so empty bottles of beer on the table that they had drawn out of a case on the floor at their feet.

Buster Trahaw was a man in his midthirties, tall and stout with a circle of fat around his stomach and sides that made it look as if he wore an inner tube under his shirt. All of the features of his plain face were distorted by the bloat. He had a thick nose with wide nostrils, heavy jowls, a round chin, and a soft mouth with thick purple lips. His forehead protruded over his cavernous dark eyes and his large earlobes leaned away from his head so that from behind, he looked like a big bat. Right now, his dull brown hair was matted down with sweat, the strands sticking to the top of his forehead.

As soon as I stepped into the room, his smile widened, showing a mouthful of large teeth. Pieces of crawfish were visible between the gaps and his thick pink tongue was covered with the meat as well. He brought the neck of a beer bottle to his lips and drew on it so hard, his cheeks folded in and out like the bellows of an accordion. Grandpere Jack spun around in his chair when he caught Buster's smile.

"Well, where you been, girl?" Grandpere demanded.

"I went for a walk," I said.

"Me and Buster been here waitin' on you," Grandpere said. "Buster's our guest for dinner tonight," he said. I nodded and went to the icebox. "Can't you say hello to him?"

"Hello," I said, and turned back to the icebox. "Did you bring any fish or duck or anything for the gumbo, Grandpere?" I asked without looking at him. I took out some vegetables.

"There's a pile of shrimp in the sink just waitin' to be shelled," he replied. "She's one helluva cook, Buster. I'd match her gumbo, her jambalaya, and *étouffée* with any in the bayou," he bragged.

"Don't say?" Buster replied.

"You'll soon see. Yes, sir, you will. And look how nicely she keeps the house, even with a hog like me livin' in it," Grandpere added.

I turned and gazed at him suspiciously, my eyes no more than dark slits. He sounded like he was doing a lot more than bragging about his granddaughter; he sounded like someone advertising something he wanted to sell. My suspicious gaze didn't shake him. "Buster here knows about you, Ruby," he said. "He told me he's seen you walking along the road or tending to the stall or in town many times. Ain't that right, Buster?"

"Yes, sir, it is. And I always liked what I saw," he said. "You keep yourself nice and pretty, Ruby," he said.

"Thank you," I said, and turned away, my heart beginning to pound.

"I told Buster here that my granddaughter, she's gettin' to the point when she should think of settlin' down and havin' a place of her own, her own kitchen, her own flock to tend," Grandpere Jack continued. I started to shell the shrimp. "Most women in the bayou end up no better than they were to start, but Buster here, he's got one of the best plantations going."

"One of the biggest and best," Buster added.

"I'm still going to school, Grandpere," I said. I kept my back to him and Buster so neither would see the fear in my face or the tears that were starting to escape my lids and trickle down my cheeks.

"Aw, school ain't important anymore, not at your age. You've already gone longer than I did," Grandpere said. "And I bet longer than you did, huh, Buster?"

"That's for sure," Buster said, then laughed.

"All Buster had to learn was how to count the money comin' in, ain't that right, Buster?"

The two of them laughed.

"Buster's father is a sick man; his days are numbered and Buster's going to inherit the whole thing, ain't you, Buster?"

"That's true and I deserve it, too," Buster said.

"Hear that, Ruby?" Grandpere said. I didn't respond. "I'm talking to you, child."

"I heard you, Grandpere," I said. I wiped my tears away with the back of my hand and turned around. "But I told you, I'm not ready to marry anyone and I'm still in school. I want to be an artist anyway," I said.

"Hell, you can be an artist. Buster here would buy you all the paint and brushes you'd need for a hundred years, wouldn't ya, Buster?"

"Two hundred," he said, and laughed.

"See?"

"Grandpere, don't do this," I pleaded. "You're embarrassing me."

"Huh? You're too old for that kind of thing, Ruby. Besides, I can't be around here watchin' over you all day now, can I? Your grandmere's gone; it's time for you to grow up."

"She sure looks good and grow'd up to me," Buster said and wiped his thick tongue over the side of his mouth to scoop in a piece of crawfish that had attached itself to the grizzle of his unshaven face.

"Hear that, Ruby?"

"I don't want to hear that. I don't want to talk about it. I'm not marrying anyone right now," I cried. I backed away from the sink and from them. "And especially not Buster," I added, and charged out of the kitchen and up the stairs.

"Ruby!" Grandpere called.

I paused at the top of the stairway to catch my breath and heard Buster complain.

"So much for your easy arrangements, Jack. You brought me here, got me to buy you this case of beer and she ain't the obedient little lady you promised."

"She will be," Grandpere Jack told him. "I'll see to that."

"Maybe. You're just lucky I like a girl who has some spirit. It's like breaking a wild horse," Buster said. Grandpere Jack laughed. "Tell you what," Buster said. "I'll up what I was going to give you by another five hundred if I can test the merchandise first."

"What'dya mean?" Grandpere asked.

"I don't got to spell it out, do I, Jack? You're just playin' dumb to get me to raise the ante. All right, I'll admit she's special. I'll give you one thousand tomorrow for a night alone with her and then the rest on our wedding day. A woman should be broken in first anyway and I might as well break in my wife myself."

"A thousand dollars!"

"You got it. What'dya say?"

I held my breath. Tell him to go straight to hell, Grandpere, I whispered.

"Deal," Grandpere Jack said instead. I could see them shaking hands and then opening another bottle of beer.

I hurried into my room and closed the door. If ever I needed proof that all the stories about Grandpere Jack were true, I just got it, I thought. No matter how drunk he got, no matter how many gambling debts he mounted, he should have some feeling for his own flesh and blood. I was seeing firsthand the sort of ugly and selfish animal Grandpere had become in Grandmere Catherine's eyes. Why didn't I have the courage to obey my promise to her immediately? I thought. Why do I always look for the best in people, even when there's not a hint of any there? All my lessons are to be learned the hard way, I concluded.

Less than an hour or so later, I heard Grandpere come up the stairs. He didn't knock on my door; he shoved it open and stood there glaring in at me. He was fuming so fiercely it looked like smoke might pour out of his red ears.

"Buster's gone," he said. "He lost his appetite over your behavior."

"Good."

"You ain't gonna be like this, Ruby," he said, pointing his finger at me. "Your grandmere Catherine spoiled you, probably fillin' you with all sorts of dreams about your artwork and tellin' you you're goin' to be some sort of fancy city lady, but you're just another Cajun girl, prettier than most, I'll admit; but still a Cajun girl who should thank her lucky stars a man as rich as Buster Trahaw's taken interest in her.

"Now, instead of being grateful, what do you do? You make me look like a fool," he said.

"You are a fool, Grandpere," I retorted. His face turned crimson. I sat up in my bed. "But worse, you're a selfish man who would sell his own flesh and blood just to keep himself in whiskey and gambling."

"You apologize for that, Ruby. You hear."

"I'm not apologizing, Grandpere. It's you who have years of apologizing to do. You're the one who has to apologize for blackmailing Mr. Tate and selling Paul to him."

"What? Who told you that?"

"You're the one who has to apologize for arranging the sale of my sister to some Creoles in New Orleans. You broke my mother's heart and Grandmere Catherine's, too," I accused. He stood there sputtering for a moment.

"That's a lie. All of it, a lie. I did what was necessary to do to save the family name and made a little on the side to help us out," he protested. "Catherine just worked you up against me by telling you otherwise and—"

"Just like you're selling me to Buster Trahaw, making a deal with him to come up here tomorrow night," I said, crying. "You, my grandfather, someone who should be looking after me, protecting me . . . you, you're nothing more than . . . than the swamp animal Grandmere said you were," I shouted.

He seemed to swell up, his shoulders rising so he reached his full height, his crimson face turning darker until his complexion was almost the color of my hair, his eyes so full of anger, they seemed luminous.

"I see these busybodies have filled you with defiance and turned you against me. Well, I'm doin' what's best for you by convincing a man as rich and prosperous as Buster to take interest in you. If I make something on the side, too, you should be happy for me."

"I'm not and I won't marry Buster Trahaw," I cried.

"Yes, you will," Grandpere said. "And you'll thank me for it, too," he predicted. Then he turned and left my room, pounding down the stairs.

A short while later, I heard him turn on the radio and then I heard some beer bottles clank and shatter. He was having one of his tantrums. I decided to wait in my room until he fell into his stupor. Afterward, I would leave.

I started to pack a small bag, being as selective as I could about what I would take because I knew I had to travel light. I had my art money hidden under the mattress, but I decided not to take it out until just before I was ready to leave. Of course, I would take the photographs of my mother and the one photograph of my real father and my sister. As I pondered what else to bring, I heard Grandpere's ranting grow more intense. Something else shattered and a chair was smashed. Shortly afterward, I heard something rattle and then I heard his heavy, unsure steps on the stairs.

I cowered back in my bed, my heart thumping. My door was thrown open again and he stood there, gazing in at me, the flames of anger in his eyes fanned by the whiskey and beer he had consumed. He looked around and saw my little bag in the corner.

"Goin' somewheres, are ya?" he asked, smiling. I shook my head. "Thought you might do that . . . thought you might leave me lookin' the fool."

"Grandpere, please," I began but he stepped forward with surprising agility and seized my left ankle. I screamed as he wrapped what looked like a bicycle chain around it and then ran the chain down and around the leg of the bed. I heard him snap on a lock before he stood up.

"There," he said. "That should help bring you to your senses."

"Grandpere . . . unlock me!"

He turned away.

"You'll be thankin' me," he muttered. "Thankin' me." He stumbled out of the door and left me, terrified, crying hysterically.

"Grandpere!" I screamed. My throat ached with the effort and the tears. When I stopped and listened, it sounded as if he had tripped and fallen down the stairs. I heard him curse and then I heard more banging and more furniture shattering. After a while it grew quiet.

Stunned by what he had done, I could only lie there and sob until my chest felt as if it were filled with stones. Grandpere was worse than a swamp animal; he was a monster, for swamp animals would never be as cruel to their own kind, I thought. And there was just so much to blame on the whiskey and beer.

Out of exhaustion and fear, I fell asleep, eagerly accepting the slumber as a form of escape from the horror I had never dreamed.

When I awoke, I felt as if I had slept for hours, but not even two had passed. I had no chance to think that what had happened was just a bad nightmare either, for the moment I moved my leg, I heard the chain rattle. I sat up quickly and tried to slide it off my ankle, but the harder I tugged, the deeper and sharper it cut into my skin. I moaned and buried my face in my hands for a moment. If Grandpere left me chained up like this all day . . . if I were like this when Buster Trahaw returned, I would be defenseless, helpless.

A cold, electric chill cut through my heart. I couldn't remember ever feeling such terror. I listened. All was quiet in the house. Even the breeze barely made the walls creak. It was as if time stood still, as if I were trapped in the eye of a great storm that was about to break over my head. I took a deep breath and tried to calm myself down enough to think clearly. Then I studied the chain and followed the line of it to the leg of the bed.

A surge of relief came over me when I realized that Grandpere Jack in his drunken state had merely wound and locked the chain around the leg, forgetting that I could lift the bed and slide the chain down. I twisted my body until I had my other leg off the bed and then lowered myself awkwardly, painfully, until I was far enough to get the leverage I needed. It took all the strength I could muster, but the bed lifted and I began to nudge the chain down until it fell off the bottom of the leg. I worked the chain around until I unraveled it from my ankle, which was plenty red and sore. Carefully, as quietly as I could, I lay the chain on the floor. Then I picked up my little bag of clothes and precious items, dug my money out from under the mattress, and went to the bedroom door. I opened it a crack and listened.

All was quiet. The butane lantern below flickered weakly, casting a dim glow and making the distorted silhouettes dance over the stairs and the walls. Was Grandpere asleep in Grandmere Catherine's room? I decided not to look, but instead, I slipped out of my bedroom and tiptoed to the stairs. No matter how softly I walked, however, the wooden floors creaked. It was as if the house wanted to betray me. I paused, listened, and then continued down the stairs. When I reached the bottom, I waited and listened. Then I went forward and discovered Grandpere Jack sprawled on the floor by the front door. He was snoring loudly.

I didn't want to risk stepping over him and going out the front, so I turned to the back, but I stopped halfway to the kitchen. I had to do one last thing, take one last look at the picture I had painted of Grandmere Catherine that hung on the wall in the parlor. I walked back softly and paused in the doorway. Moonlight pouring through the uncovered window illuminated the portrait, and for a moment it seemed to me that Grandmere was smiling, that her eyes were full of happiness because I was keeping to my promise.

"Good-bye, Grandmere," I whispered. "Someday, I'll return to the bayou and I'll take your picture back with me to wherever I live."

How I wished I could hug her and kiss her one more time. I closed my eyes and tried to remember the last time I had, but Grandpere Jack groaned and turned over on the floor. I didn't move a muscle. His eyes opened and closed. If he had seen me, he must have thought it was a dream, for he didn't wake up. Not wasting another second, I turned away and walked quickly but quietly through the kitchen and out the back door. Then, I hurried around the corner of the house and headed for the front.

When I reached the road, I stopped and looked back. Something sweet and sour was in my throat. Despite all that had happened and all that would, it hurt me to leave this simple house that had known my first steps. Within those plain old walls Grandmere Catherine and I had made many a meal together, sung together, and laughed together. On that galerie, she had rocked and told me story after story about her own youthful days. Upstairs in that bedroom, she had nursed me through my childhood illnesses and told me the bedtime stories that made it easier to close my eyes and sleep contentedly, always feeling safe and secure in the cocoon of promises she wove with her soft voice and soft, loving eyes. Sitting by my bedroom window on hot summer nights, I had fantasized my future, seen my prince come, envisioned my jeweled wedding with the gold dust in the spiderwebs and the music.

Oh, it was more than an old swamp house I was leaving. It was my entire past, my years of growing and developing, my feelings of joy and feelings of sadness, my melancholy and my ecstasy, my laughter and my tears. How hard it was even now, even after all this, to turn away from it and let dark night shut the door of blackness behind me.

And what of the swamp itself? Could I really tear myself away from the flowers and the birds, from the fish and even the alligators who peered at me with interest? In the moonlight on a limb of a sycamore, sat a marsh hawk, his silhouette dark and proud against the white glow. He opened his wings and held them as if he were saying good-bye for all the swamp animals and birds and fish. And then he closed his wings and I turned and hurried off, the hawk's silhouette still lingering on the surface of my vision.

On the way into Houma, I passed many of the houses of people I knew, people I thought I might never see again. I almost paused at Mrs. Thibodeau's to say good-bye. She and Mrs. Livaudis were such special friends to me and my grandmere, but I was afraid she would try to talk me out of leaving and try to talk me into staying either with her or Mrs. Livaudis. I pledged to myself that someday, when I was finally settled, I would write to both of them.

Few places were still open in town when I arrived. I went directly to the bus station and bought a one-way ticket to New Orleans. I had nearly an hour to wait and spent most of it on a bench in the shadows, fearful that someone would spot me and either try to stop me or tell Grandpere before I left. Twice, I thought about calling Paul, but I was afraid to talk to him. If I told him what Grandpere Jack had done, he was sure to lose his temper and do something terrible. I decided to write him a good-bye note instead. I bought an envelope and a stamp in the station and dug out a piece of paper from my pocketbook.

Dear Paul,

It would take too long to explain to you why I am leaving Houma without saying good-bye. I think the main reason though is I know how much it would break my heart to look at you and then leave. It hurts so much even writing this note. Let me just tell you that more things happened in the past than I revealed that day, and these events are taking me away from Houma to find my real father and my other life. There is nothing I would want more than to spend the rest of my life at your side. It seems like such a cruel joke for Nature to let us fall in love the way we did and then surprise us with the ugly truth. But I know now that if I didn't leave, you would not give up and you would make it painful for both of us.

Remember me as I was before we learned the truth, and I'll remember you the same way. Maybe you're right; maybe we'll never love anyone else as much as we love each other, but we have to try. I will think of you often, and I will imagine you in your beautiful plantation.

Love always,
Ruby

I posted the letter in the mailbox in front of the bus station and then I sat down and choked back my tears and waited. Finally, the bus arrived. It had come from St. Martinville and had made stops and picked up passengers at New Iberia, Franklin, and Morgan City before arriving at Houma, so the bus was nearly filled when I stepped up and gave the driver my ticket. I made my way toward the rear and saw an empty seat on the right next to a pretty caramel skinned woman with black hair and turquoise eyes. She smiled when I sat down, revealing milk white teeth. She wore a bright pink and blue peasant skirt with black sandals, a pink halter, and she had rings and rings of different bracelets on both her arms. She had her hair tied with a white kerchief, a tignon with seven knots whose points all stuck straight up.

"Hello," she said. "Going to the wet grave, too?"

"Wet grave?" I sat down beside her.

"New Orleans, honey. That's what my grandmere called it because you can't bury anyone in the ground. Too much water."

"Really?"

"That's true. Everyone's buried in tombs, vaults, ovens above the ground. You didn't know that?" she asked, holding her smile. I shook my head. "First time to New Orleans then, huh?"

"Yes, it is."

"You picked the best time to visit, you know," she said. I saw how bright her eyes were, how full of excitement she was.

"Why?"

"Why? Why, honey, it's Mardi Gras."

"Oh . . . no," I said, thinking to myself that it was the worst time to go, not the best. I had read and heard about New Orleans at Mardi Gras. I should have realized that was why she was all dressed up. The whole city would be festive. It wasn't the best time to arrive on my real father's doorstep.

"You act like you just stepped out of the swamp, honey."

I took a deep breath and nodded. She laughed.

"My name's Annie Gray," she said, offering her slim, smooth hand. I took it and shook. She had pretty rings on all her fingers, but one ring, the one on her pinky, looked like it was made out of bone and shaped like a tiny skull.

"I'm Ruby, Ruby Landry."

"Pleased to meet you. You got relatives in New Orleans?" she asked.

"Yes," I said. "But I haven't seen them . . . ever."

"Oh, ain't that somethin'?"

The bus driver closed the door and started the bus away from the station. My heart began to race as I saw us drive by stores and houses I had known all my life. We passed the church and then the school, moving over the road I had walked almost every day of my life. Then we paused at an intersection and the bus turned in the direction of New Orleans. I had seen the road sign many times, and many times dreamt of following it. Now I was. In moments we were flying down the highway and Houma was falling farther and farther behind. I couldn't help but look back.

"Don't look back," Annie Gray said quickly.

"What? Why not?"

"Bad luck," she replied.

I spun around to face forward.

"What?"

"Bad luck. Quick, cross yourself three times," she prescribed. I saw she was serious and so I did it.

"I don't need any more of that," I said. That made her laugh. She leaned forward and picked up her cloth bag. Then she dug into it and came up with something to place in my hand. I stared at it.

"What's this?" I asked.

"Piece of neck bone from a black cat. It's gris-gris," she said. Seeing I was still confused, she added, "a magical charm to bring you good luck. My grandmere gave it to me. Voodoo," she added in a whisper.

"Oh. Well, I don't want to take your good luck piece," I said, handing it back. She shook her head.

"Bad luck for me to take it back now and worse luck for you to give it," she said. "I got plenty more, honey. Don't worry about that. Go on," she said, forcing me to wrap my fingers around the cat bone. "Put it away, but carry it with you all the time."

"Thank you," I said, and slipped it into my bag.

"I bet these relatives of yours are excited about seeing you, huh?"

"No," I said.

She tilted her head and smiled with confusion. "No? Don't they know you're comin'?"

I looked at her for a moment and then I looked forward again, straightening myself up in the seat.

"No," I said. "They don't even know I exist," I added.

The bus shot forward, its headlights slicking through the night, carrying me onward toward the future that awaited, a future just as dark and mysterious and as frightening as the unlit highway.

BOOK TWO

10

An Unexpected Friend

Annie Gray was so excited about arriving in New Orleans during the Mardi Gras, she talked incessantly during the remainder of the trip. I sat with my knees together, my hands nervously twisting on my lap, but I was grateful for the conversation. Listening to her descriptions of previous Mardi Gras celebrations she had attended, I had little time to feel sorry for myself and worry about what would happen to me the moment I stepped off the bus. For the time being at least, I could ignore the troubled thoughts crowded into the darkest corners of my brain.

Annie came from New Iberia, but she had been to New Orleans at least a half-dozen times to visit her aunt, who she said was a cabaret singer in a famous nightclub in the French Quarter. Annie said she was going to live with her aunt in New Orleans from now on.

"I'm going to be a singer, too," she bragged. "My aunt is getting me my first audition in a nightclub on Bourbon Street. You know about the French Quarter, don'tcha, honey?" she asked.

"I know it's the oldest section of the city and there is a lot of music, and people have parties there all the time," I told her.

"That's right, honey, and it has the best restaurants and many nice shops and loads and loads of antique and art galleries."

"Art galleries?"

"Uh-huh."

"Did you ever hear of Dominique's?"

She shrugged.

"I wouldn't know one from the other. Why?"

"I have some of my artwork displayed there," I said proudly.

"Really? Well, ain't that somethin'? You're an artist." She looked impressed. "And you say you ain't ever been to New Orleans before?"

I shook my head.

"Oh," she squealed, and squeezed my hand. "You're in for a bundle of fun. You've got to tell me where you'll be and I'll send you an invitation to come hear me sing as soon as I get hired, okay?"

"I don't know where I'll be yet," I had to confess. That slowed down her flood of excitement. She pulled herself back in her seat and scrutinized me with a curious smile on her face.

"What do you mean? I thought you said you're going to visit relatives," she said.

"I am . . . I . . . just don't know their address." I allowed my eyes to meet hers briefly before they fled to stare almost blindly at the passing scenery, which right now was a blur of dark silhouettes and an occasional lit window of a solitary house.

"Well, honey, New Orleans is a bit bigger than downtown Houma," she said, laughing. "You got their phone number at least, don'tcha?"

I turned back and shook my head. Numbness tingled in my fingertips, perhaps because I had my fingers locked so tightly together.

Her smile wilted and she narrowed her turquoise eyes suspiciously as her gaze shifted to my small bag and then back to me. Then she nodded to herself and sat forward, convinced she knew it all.

"You're runnin' away from home, ain'tcha?" she asked.

I bit down on my lower lip, but I couldn't stop my eyes from tearing over. I nodded.

"Why?" she asked quickly. "You can tell Annie Gray, honey. Annie Gray can keep a secret better than a bank safe."

I swallowed my tears and vanquished my throat lump so I could tell her about Grandmere Catherine, her death, Grandpere Jack's moving in and his quickly arranging for my marriage to Buster. She listened quietly, her eyes sympathetic until I finished. Then they blazed furiously.

"That old monster," she said. "He be Papa La Bas," she muttered.

"Who?"

"The devil himself," she declared. "You got anything that belongs to him on you?"

"No," I replied. "Why?"

"Fixin'," she said angrily. "I'd cast a spell on him for you. My great-grandmere, she was brought here a slave, but she was a mama, a voodoo queen, and she hand me down lots of secrets," she whispered, her eyes wide, her face close to mine. *"Ya, ye, ye li konin tou, gris-gris,"* she chanted. My heart began to pound.

"What's that mean?"

"Part of a voodoo prayer. If I had a snip of your grandpere's hair, a piece of his clothing, even an old sock . . . he never be bothering you again," she assured me, her head bobbing.

"That's all right. I'll be fine now," I said, my voice no more than a whisper either.

She stared at me a moment. The white part of her eyes looked brighter, almost as if there were two tiny fires behind each orb. Finally, she nodded again, patted my hand reassuringly and sat back.

"You be all right, you just don't lose that black cat bone I gave you," she told me.

"Thank you." I let out a breath. The bus bounced and turned on the highway. Ahead of us, the road became brighter as we approached more lighted and populated areas en route to the city that now loomed before me like a dream.

"I tell you what you do when we arrive," Annie said. "You go right to the telephone booth and look up your relatives in the phone book. Besides their telephone number, their address will be there. What's their name?"

"Dumas," I said.

"Dumas. Oh, honey, there's a hundred Dumas in the book, if there's one. Know any first names?"

"Pierre Dumas."

"Probably at least a dozen or so of them," she said, shaking her head. "He got a middle initial?"

"I don't know," I said.

She thought a moment.

"What else do you know about your relatives, honey?"

"Just that they live in a big house, a mansion," I said. Her eyes brightened again.

"Oh. Maybe the Garden District then. You don't know what he does for a living?"

I shook my head. Her eyes turned suspicious as one of her eyebrows lifted quizzically.

"Who's Pierre Dumas? Your cousin? Your uncle?"

"No. My father," I said. Her mouth gaped open and her eyes widened with surprise.

"Your father? And he never set eyes on you before?"

I shook my head. I didn't want to go through the whole story, and thankfully, she didn't ask for details. She simply crossed herself and muttered something before nodding.

"I'll look in the phone book with you. My grandmere told me, I have a mama's vision and can see my way through the dark and find the light. I'll help you," she added, patting my hand. "Only, one thing must be to make it work," she added.

"What's that?"

"You've got to give me a token, something valuable to open the doors. Oh, it ain't for me," she added quickly. "It's a gift for the saints to thank them for help in the success of your gris-gris. I'll drop it by the church. What'cha got?"

"I don't have anything valuable," I said.

"You got any money on you?" she asked.

"A little money I've earned selling my artwork," I told her.

"Good," she said. "You give me a ten dollar bill at the phone booth and that will give me the power. You lucky you found me, honey. Otherwise, you'd be wanderin' around this city all night and all day. Must be meant to be. Must be I be your good gris-gris."

And with that she laughed again and again began describing how wonderful her new life in New Orleans was going to be once her aunt got her the opportunity to sing.

When I first saw the skyline of the city, I was glad I had found Annie Gray. There were so many buildings and there were so many lights, I felt as if I had fallen into a star laden sky. The traffic and people, the maze of streets was overwhelming and frightening. Everywhere I looked out the bus window, I saw crowds of revelers marching through the streets, all of them dressed in bright costumes, wearing masks and hats with bright feathers and carrying colorful paper umbrellas. Instead of masks, some had their faces made up to look like clowns, even the women. People were playing trumpets and trombones, flutes and drums. The bus driver had to slow down and wait for the crowds to cross at almost every corner before finally pulling into the bus station. As soon as he did so, our bus was surrounded by partygoers and musicians greeting the arriving passengers. Some were given masks, some had ropes of plastic jewels cast over their heads and some were given paper umbrellas. It seemed if you weren't celebrating Mardi Gras, you weren't welcome in New Orleans.

"Hurry," Annie told me as we started down the aisle. As soon as I stepped down, someone grabbed my left hand, shoved a paper umbrella into my right, and pulled me into the parade of brightly dressed people so that I was forced to march around the bus with them. Annie laughed and threw her hands up as she started to dance and swing herself in behind me. We marched around as the bus driver unloaded the luggage. When Annie saw hers, she pulled me out of the line and I followed her into the station. People were dancing everywhere, and everywhere I looked, there were pockets of musicians playing Dixieland Jazz.

"There's a phone booth," she said, pointing. We hurried to it. Annie opened the fat telephone book. I had never realized how many people lived in New Orleans. "Dumas, Dumas," she chanted as she ran her finger down the page. "Okay, here be the list. Quickly," she said, turning back to me. "Fold the ten dollar bill as tightly as you can. Go on."

I did what she asked. She opened her purse and kept her eyes closed.

"Just drop it in here," she said. I did so and she opened her eyes slowly and then turned to the phone book again. She did look like someone who had fallen into a trance. I heard her mumble some gibberish and then she put her long right forefinger on the page and ran it down slowly. Suddenly, she stopped. Her whole body shuddered and she closed and then opened her eyes. "It's him!" she declared. She leaned closer and nodded. "He does live in the Garden District, big house, rich." She tore off a corner of the page and wrote the address on it. It was on St. Charles Avenue.

"Are you sure?" I asked.

"Didn't you see my finger stop on the page? I didn't stop it; it was stopped!" she said, eyes wide. I nodded.

"Thank you," I said.

"You welcome, honey. Okay," she said, picking up her suitcase. "I got to get me going. You be all right now. Annie Gray said so. I'll send for you when I start singing somewhere," she said, backing away.

"Annie don't forget you. Don't forget Annie!" she cried. Then she spun around once with her right hand high, the colorful bracelets clicking together. She threw me a wide smile as she danced her way off, falling in with a small group of revelers who marched out the door and into the street.

I gazed at the street address on the tiny slip of paper in the palm of my hand. Did she really have some kind of prophetic power or was this incorrect, an address that would get me even more lost than I imagined? I looked back at the opened telephone book, thinking maybe I should know where the addresses for any other Pierre Dumas were, and was shocked to discover, there was only one Pierre Dumas. What sort of magic was required for this? I wondered.

I laughed to myself, realizing I had paid for my company and entertainment. But who knew how much of what Annie had told me was true and how much wasn't? I wasn't one to be skeptical about supernatural mysteries, not with a Traiteur for a grandmother.

Slowly, I walked to the station entrance. For a moment, I just stood there gaping out at the city. I looked around and floundered, filled with trepidation. Part of me wanted to march right back to the bus. Maybe I'd be better off in Houma living with Mrs. Thibodeau or Mrs. Livaudis, I thought. But the laughter and music from another group of revelers coming off a different bus interrupted my thoughts. When they reached me, one of them, a tall man wearing a white and black wolf mask paused at my side.

"Are you all alone?" he asked.

I nodded. "I just arrived."

A light sprang into his light blue eyes, the only part of his face not hidden by the mask. He was tall with wide shoulders. He had dark brown hair and a young voice causing me to think he was no more than twenty-five.

"So did I. But this is no night to be all alone," he said. "You're very pretty, but it's Mardi Gras. Don't you have a mask to go with that umbrella?"

"No," I said. "Someone gave me this as soon as I got off the bus. I didn't come for the Mardi Gras. I came—"

"Of course you did," he interrupted. "Here," he said, digging into his bag and coming up with another mask, a black one with plastic diamonds around its edges. "Put on this one and come along with us."

"Thank you, but I've got to find this address," I said. He looked at my slip.

"Oh, I know where this is. We won't be far from it. Come along. Might as well enjoy yourself on the way," he added. "Here, put on the mask. Everyone must wear a mask tonight. Go on," he insisted, resting his sharp gaze on me. I saw a smile form around his eyes and I took the mask.

"Now you look like you belong," he said.

"Do you really know this address?" I asked.

"Of course, I do. Come on," he said, taking my hand. Perhaps Annie Gray's voodoo magic was working, I thought. I found a stranger who could take me right to my father's door. I took the stranger's hand and hurried out with him to catch up with the group. There was music all around us and people hawking food and costumes and other masks as well. The whole city had been turned into a grand fais dodo, I thought. There wasn't a sad face anywhere, or if there was, it was hidden behind a mask. Above us, people were raining down confetti from the scrolled iron balconies. Columns and columns of revelers wound around every corner. Some of the costumes the women wore were scant and very revealing. I feasted visually on everything, turning and spinning at this carnival of life: people kissing anyone who was close enough to embrace, obvious strangers hugging and clinging to each other, jugglers juggling colorful balls, sticks of fire, and even knives!

As we danced down the street, the crowds began to swell in size. My newly found guide spun me around and threw his head back with laughter. Then he bought some sort of punch for us to drink and a poor boy shrimp sandwich for us to share. It was filled with oysters, shrimp, sliced tomatoes, shredded lettuce, and sauce piquante. I thought it was delicious. Despite my nervousness and trepidation on arriving in New Orleans to meet my real family, I was having a good time.

"Thank you. My name's Ruby," I said. I had to shout even though he was next to me. That's how loud the laughter, the music, and the shouts of others around us were. He shook his head and then brought his lips to my ear.

"No names. Tonight, we are all mysterious," he said in a loud whisper. He followed that with a quick kiss on my neck. The feel of his wet lips stunned me for a moment. I heard his cackle and then I stepped back.

"Thank you for the drink and the sandwich, but I've got to find this address," I said. He nodded, swallowing the rest of his drink quickly.

"Don't you want to see the parade first?" he asked.

"I can't. I've got to find this address," I emphasized.

"Okay. This is the way," he told me, and before I could object, he seized my hand again and led me away from the procession of frolickers. We hurried down one street and then another before he told me we had to take a shortcut.

"We'll go right through this alley and save twenty minutes at least. There's a mob ahead of us."

The alley looked long and dark. It had ash cans and discarded furniture strewn through it, and there was the acrid stench of garbage and urine. I didn't move.

"Come on," he urged, and pulled me behind him, ignoring my reluctance. I held my breath, hoping now to get through it quickly. But less than halfway through the alley, he stopped and turned to me.

"What's wrong?" I asked, a chill so cold in my stomach it was as if I had swallowed an ice cube whole.

"Maybe we shouldn't hurry so. We're losing the best of the night. Don't you want to have fun?" he asked, stepping closer. He put his hand on my shoulder. I stepped back quickly.

"I've got to get to my relatives and let them know I've arrived," I said, now feeling foolish for allowing myself to be pulled into a dark alley with a stranger who wouldn't show me his face nor tell me his name. How could I have been so desperate and trusting?

"I'm sure they don't expect you so soon on a Mardi Gras night. Tonight is a magical night. Everything is different," he said. "You're a very pretty girl." He lifted the mask from his face, but I couldn't see him well in the shadows. Before I could flee, he embraced me and pulled me to him.

"Please," I said, struggling. "I must go. I don't want to do this."

"Sure you do. It's Mardi Gras. Let yourself loose, abandon yourself," he told me, and pressed his lips to mine, holding me so tightly, I couldn't pull away. I felt his hands move down my back and begin to scoop up my skirt. I turned and struggled, but his long arms had mine pinned against my sides. I started to scream and he squelched it by pressing his mouth into mine. When I felt his tongue jet out and rub over mine, I gasped. His hands had found my panties and he was tugging them down as he swung me about. I felt myself growing faint. How could he keep his mouth over mine so long? Finally, he pulled his head back and I gulped air. He turned me around, pressing me toward what looked like an old, discarded mattress on the alley floor.

"Stop!" I cried, twisting and turning to break free. "Let me go!"

"It's party time!" he cried, and laughed that dry cackle again. But this time, as he brought his face toward me, I managed to pull my right hand out from under his arm and claw his cheeks and nose. He screamed and threw me back in a rage.

"You bitch!" he cried, wiping his face. I cowered in the dark as he lifted his head and released another sick laugh. Had I fled from Buster Trahaw only to put myself into a worse predicament? Where was Annie Gray's magical protection now? I wondered as the stranger started toward me, a dark, dangerous silhouette, a character who had escaped from my worst nightmares to invade my reality.

Fortunately, just as he reached out for me, a group of street celebrants turned into our alley, their music reverberating off the walls. My attacker saw them coming, lowered his mask over his face, and ran in the opposite direction, disappearing into the darkness as if he had fled back to the world of dark dreams.

I didn't waste a moment. I scooped up my bag and ran toward the revelers, who shouted and laughed, trying to hold me back so I would join them.

"NO!" I cried and broke loose to tear through them and out of the alley. Once onto a street, I ran and ran to get myself as far away from that alley as I could, my feet slapping the pavement so hard, my soles stung. Finally, out of breath, my shoulders heaving, my side aching, I stopped. When I looked up I was happy to see a policeman on the corner.

"Please," I said, approaching him. "I'm lost. I just arrived and I've got to find this address."

"Some night to come to New Orleans and get lost," he said, shaking his head. He took the slip of paper. "Oh, this is in the Garden District. You can take the streetcar. Follow me," he said. He showed me where to wait.

"Thank you," I told him. Shortly afterward, the streetcar arrived. I gave the driver my address and he told me he would let me know when to get off. I sat down quickly, wiped my sweaty face with my handkerchief, and closed my eyes, hoping my heartbeat would slow down before I stood in my father's doorway. Otherwise, the excitement over what had already happened, and my actually confronting him would cause me to simply faint at his feet.

When the streetcar entered what was known as the Garden District of New Orleans, we passed under a long canopy of spreading oaks and passed yards filled with camellias and magnolia trees. Here there were elegant homes with garden walls that enclosed huge banana trees and dripped with purple bugle vine. Each corner sidewalk was embedded with old ceramic tiles that spelled out the names of the streets. Some of the cobblestone sidewalks had become warped by the roots of old oak trees, but to me this made it even more quaint and special. These streets were quieter, fewer and fewer street revelers in evidence.

"St. Charles Avenue," the streetcar operator cried. An electric chill surged through my body turning my legs to jelly, and for a moment, I couldn't stand up. I was almost there, face-to-face with my real father. My heart began to pound. I reached for the hand strap and pulled myself into a standing position. The side doors slapped open with an abruptness that made me gasp. Finally, I willed one foot forward and stepped down to the street. The doors closed quickly and the streetcar continued, leaving me on the walk, feeling more stranded and lost than ever, clutching my little cloth bag to my side.

I could hear the sounds of the Mardi Gras floating in from every corner of the city. An automobile sped by with revelers hanging their heads out the windows, blowing trumpets and throwing streamers at me. They waved and cried out, but continued on their merry way while I remained transfixed, as firmly rooted as an old oak tree. It was a warm evening, but here in the city, with the streetlights around me, it was harder to see the stars that had always been such a comfort to me in the bayou. I took a deep breath and finally crossed down St. Charles Avenue toward the address on the slip of paper I now clutched like a rosary in my small hand.

St. Charles Avenue was so quiet in comparison to the festive sounds and wild excitement on the inner city streets. I found it somewhat eerie. To me it was as if I had entered a dream, slipped through some magical doorway between reality and illusion, and found myself in my own land of Oz. Nothing looked real: not the tall palm trees, the pretty streetlights, the cobblestone walks and streets, and especially not the enormous houses that looked more like small palaces, the homes of princes and princesses, queens and kings. These mansions, some of which were walled in, were set in the middle of large tracts of land. There were many beautiful gardens full of swelling masses of shining green foliage and heavy with roses and every other kind of flower one could think of.

I strolled on slowly, drinking in the opulence and wondering how one family could live in each of these grand houses with such beautiful grounds. How could anyone be so rich? I wondered. I was so entranced, so mesmerized by the wealth and the beauty, I almost walked right past the address on my slip of paper. When I stopped and looked up at the Dumas residence, I could only stand and gape stupidly. Its outbuildings, gardens, and stables occupied most of this block. All of it was surrounded by a fence in cornstalk pattern.

This was my real father's home, but the ivory white mansion that loomed before me looked more like a house built for a Greek god. It was a two-story building with tall columns, the tops of which were shaped like inverted bells decorated with leaves. There were two galeries, an enormous one before the main entrance and another above it. Each had a different decorative cast iron railing, the one on the bottom showing flowers and the one above, showing fruits.

I strolled along the walk, circling the house and grounds. I saw the pool and the tennis court and continued to gape in awe. There was something magical here. It seemed as if I had entered my dreamland of eternal spring. Two gray squirrels paused in their foray for food and stared out at me, more curious than afraid. The air smelled of green bamboo and gardenias. Blooming azaleas, yellow and red roses, and hibiscus were everywhere in view. The trellises and the gazebo were covered with trumpet vine and clumps of purple wisteria. Redwood boxes on railings and sills were thick with petunias.

Right now the house was lit up, all of its windows bright. Slowly, I made a full circle and then paused at the front gate; but as I stood there gaping, drinking in the elegance and grandeur, I began to wonder what I could have been thinking to have traveled this far and come to this house. Surely the people who lived within such a mansion were so different from me, I might as well have gone to another country where people spoke a different language. My heart sank. A throbbing pain in my head stabbed sharply. What was I doing here, me, a nobody, an orphan Cajun girl who had deluded herself into believing there was a rainbow just waiting for me at the end of my storm of trouble? I knew now that I would have to find my way back to the bus station and return to Houma.

Dejected, my head lowered, I turned from the house and started to walk away when suddenly, seemingly coming from out of the thin air, a small, fire engine red, convertible sports car squeaked to an abrupt stop right in front of me. The driver hopped over the door. He was a tall young man with a shock of shiny golden hair that now fell wildly over his smooth forehead. Despite his blond strands, he had a dark complexion which only made his cerulean eyes glimmer that much more in the glow of the street lamp. Dressed in a tuxedo, his shoulders back, his torso slim, he appeared before me like a prince—gallant, elegant, strong, for the features of his handsome face did seem carved out of some royal heritage.

He had a strong and perfect mouth and a Roman nose, perfectly straight, to go along with those dazzling blue eyes. The lines of his jaw turned up sharply, enhancing the impression that his face had been etched out to duplicate the face of some movie star idol. I was breathless for a moment, unable to move under the radiance of his warm and attractive smile, which quickly turned into a soft laugh.

"Where do you think you're going?" he asked. "And what sort of costume is this? Are you playing the poor girl or what?" he asked, stepping around me as if judging me in some fashion contest.

"Pardon?"

My question threw him into a fit of hysterics. He clutched his side and leaned back on the hood of his sports car.

"That's great," he said. "I love it. Pardon?" he mimicked.

"I don't think it's so funny," I said indignantly, but that just made him laugh again.

"I'd never expect you to choose anything like this," he said, holding his graceful hand out toward me, palm up. "And where did you get that bag, a thrift shop? What's in it anyway, more rags?"

I pulled my bag against my stomach and straightened up quickly.

"These aren't rags," I retorted. He started to laugh again. It seemed I could do nothing, say nothing, gaze at him in no way without causing him to become hysterical. "What's so funny? These happen to be my sole belongings right now," I emphasized. He shook his head and held his wide smile.

"Really, Gisselle, you're perfect. I swear," he said, holding up his hand to take an oath, "this is the best you've ever come up with, and that indignant attitude to go along with it . . . you're going to win the prize for sure. All of your girlfriends will die with envy. Brilliant. And to surprise me, too. I love it."

"First," I began, "my name is not Gisselle."

"Oh," he said, still holding a grin as if he were humoring a mad woman, "and what name have you chosen?"

"My name is Ruby," I said.

"Ruby? I like that," he said, looking thoughtful. "Ruby . . . a jewel . . . to describe your hair. Well, your hair has always been your most prized possession, aside from your real diamonds and rubies, emeralds, and pearls, that is. And your clothes and your shoes," he cataloged with a laugh. "So," he said, straightening up and changing to a serious face, "I'm to introduce you to everyone as Mademoiselle Ruby, is that it?"

"I don't care what you do," I said. "I certainly don't expect you to introduce me to anyone," I added and started away.

"Huh?" he cried. I started to cross the street when he walked quickly behind me and seized my right elbow. "What are you doing? Where are you going?" he asked, his face now contorted in confusion.

"I'm going home," I said.

"Home? Where's home?"

"I'm returning to Houma, if you must know," I said. "Now, if you will be so kind as to let me go, I—"

"Houma? What?" He stared at me a moment and then, instead of releasing me, he seized my other arm at the elbow and turned me fully around so that I would be in the center of the pool of light created by the street lamp. He studied me for a moment, those soft eyes, now troubled and intense as he swept his gaze over my face. "You do look . . . different," he muttered. "And not in cosmetic ways either. I don't understand, Gisselle."

"I told you," I said. "I'm not anyone named Gisselle. My name is Ruby. I come from Houma."

He continued to stare, but still held me at the elbows. Then he shook his head and smiled again.

"Come on, Gisselle. I'm sorry I'm a little late, but you're carrying this too far. I admit it's a great costume and disguise. What else do you want from me?" he pleaded.

"I'd like you to let go of my arms," I said. He did so and stepped back, his confusion now becoming indignation and anger.

"What's going on here?" he demanded. I took a deep breath and looked back at the house. "If you're not Gisselle, then what were you doing in front of the house? Why are you on this street?"

"I was going to knock on the door and introduce myself to Pierre Dumas, but I've changed my mind," I said.

"Introduce yourself to . . ." He shook his head and stepped toward me again.

"Let me see your left hand," he asked quickly. "Come on," he added, and reached for it. I held out my hand and he gazed at my fingers for a moment. Then, when he looked up at me, his face twisted in shock. "You never take off that ring, never," he said, more to himself than to me. "And your fingers," he said, looking at my hand again, "your whole hand is rougher." He released me quickly, as quickly as he would had my hand been a hot coal. "Who are you?"

"I told you. My name is Ruby."

"But you look just like . . . you're the spitting image of Gisselle," he said.

"Oh. So that's her name," I said more to myself than to him. "Gisselle."

"Who are you?" he asked again, now gazing at me as if I were a ghost. "I mean, what are you to the Dumas family? A cousin? What? I demand that you tell me or I'll call the police," he added firmly.

"I'm Gisselle's sister," I confessed in a breath.

"Gisselle's sister? Gisselle has no sister," he replied, still speaking in a stern voice. Then he paused a moment, obviously impressed with the resemblances. "At least, none I knew about," he said.

"I'm fairly sure Gisselle doesn't know about me either," I said.

"Really? But . . ."

"It's too long of a story to tell you and I don't know why I should tell you anything anyway," I said.

"But if you're Gisselle's sister, why are you leaving? Why are you going back to . . . where'd you say, Houma?"

"I thought I could do this, introduce myself, but I find I can't."

"You mean, the Dumas don't know you're here yet?" I shook my head. "Well, you can't just leave without telling them you're in New

Orleans. Come on," he said, reaching for my hand. "I'll bring you in myself."

I shook my head and stepped back, more terrified than ever.

"Come on," he said. "Look. My name's Beau Andreas. I'm a very good friend of the family. Actually, Gisselle is my girlfriend, but my parents and the Dumas have known each other for ages. I'm like a member of this family. That's why I'm so shocked by what you're saying. Come on," he chanted, and took my hand.

"I've changed my mind," I said, shaking my head. "This isn't as good an idea as I first thought."

"What isn't?"

"Surprising them."

"Mr. and Mrs. Dumas don't know you're coming?" he asked, his confusion building. I shook my head. "This is really bizarre. Gisselle doesn't know she has a twin sister and the Dumas don't know you're here. Well, why did you come all this way if you're only going to turn around and go right back?" he asked, his hands on his hips.

"I . . ."

"You're afraid, aren't you?" he said quickly. "That's it, you're afraid of them. Well, don't be. Pierre Dumas is a very nice man and Daphne . . . she is nice, too. Gisselle," he said, smiling, "is Gisselle. To tell you the truth, I can't wait to see the expression on her face when she comes face-to-face with you."

"I can," I said, and turned away.

"I'll just run in and tell them you were here and you're running away," he threatened. "Someone will come after you and it will all be far more embarrassing."

"You wouldn't," I said.

"Of course I would," he replied, smiling. "So you might as well do it the right way." He held out his hand. I looked back at the house and then at him. His eyes were friendly, although a bit impish. Reluctantly, my heart thumping so hard I thought it would take my breath away and cause me to faint before I reached the front door, I took his hand and let him lead me back to the gate and up the walk to the grand galerie. There was a tile stairway.

"How did you get here?" he asked before we reached the door.

"The bus," I said. He lifted the ball and hammer knocker and let the sound echo through what I imagined, from the sound of the reverberation within, was an enormous entryway. A few moments later, the door was opened and we faced a mulatto man in a butler's uniform. He wasn't short, but he wasn't tall either. He had a round face with large dark eyes and a somewhat pug nose. His dark brown hair was curly and peppered with gray strands. There were dime-size brown spots on his cheeks and forehead and his lips were slightly orange.

"Good evening, Monsieur Andreas," he said, then shifted his gaze to me. The moment he set eyes on me, he dropped his mouth. "But Mademoiselle Gisselle, I just saw you . . ." He turned around and looked behind him. Beau Andreas laughed.

"This isn't Mademoiselle Gisselle, Edgar. Edgar, I'd like you to meet Ruby. Ruby, Edgar Farrar, the Dumas' butler. Are Mr. and Mrs. Dumas in, Edgar?" he asked.

"Oh, no, sir. They left for the ball about an hour ago," he said, his eyes still fixed on me.

"Well then, there's nothing to do but wait for them to return. Until then, you can visit with Gisselle," Beau told me. He guided me into the great house.

The entryway floor was a peach marble and the ceiling, which looked like it rose to at least twelve feet above me, had pictures of nymphs and angels, doves and blue sky painted over it. There were paintings and sculptures everywhere I looked, but the wall to the right was covered by an enormous tapestry depicting a grand French palace and gardens.

"Where is Mademoiselle Gisselle, Edgar?" Beau asked.

"She's still upstairs," Edgar said.

"I knew she would be pampering herself forever. I'm never late when it comes to escorting Gisselle anywhere," Beau told me. "Especially a Mardi Gras Ball. To Gisselle, being on time means being an hour late. Fashionably late, of course," he added. "Are you hungry, thirsty?"

"No, I had half of a poor boy sandwich not so long ago," I said, and grimaced with the memory of what had nearly happened to me.

"You didn't like it?" Beau asked.

"No, it wasn't that. Someone . . . a stranger I trusted, attacked me in an alley on the way here," I confessed.

"What? Are you all right?" he asked quickly.

"Yes. I got away before anything terrible happened, but it was quite frightening."

"I'll bet. The back streets in New Orleans can be quite dangerous during Mardi Gras. You shouldn't have wandered around by yourself." He turned to Edgar. "Where is Nina, Edgar?" he asked.

"Just finishing up some things in the kitchen."

"Good. Come on," Beau insisted. "I'll take you to the kitchen and

Nina will give you something to drink at least. Edgar, would you be so kind as to inform Mademoiselle Gisselle that I've arrived with a surprise guest and we're in the kitchen?''

"Very good, monsieur," Edgar said and headed for the beautiful curved stairway with soft carpeted steps and a shiny mahogany balustrade.

"This way," Beau said. He directed me through the entryway, past one beautiful room after another, each filled with antiques and expensive French furniture and paintings. It looked more like a museum to me than a home.

The kitchen was as large as I expected it would be with long counters and tables, big sinks, and walls of cabinets. Everything gleamed. It looked so immaculate, even the older appliances appeared brand-new. Wrapping leftovers in cellophane was a short, plump black woman in a brown cotton dress with a full white apron. She had her back to us. The strands of her ebony hair were pulled tightly into a thick bun behind her head, but she wore a white kerchief, too. As she worked, she hummed. Beau Andreas knocked on the doorjamb and she spun around quickly.

"I didn't want to frighten you, Nina," he said.

"That'll be the day when you can frighten Nina Jackson, Monsieur Andreas," she said, nodding. She had small dark eyes set close to her nose. Her mouth was small and almost lost in her plump cheeks and above her round jaw, but she had beautifully soft skin that glowed under the kitchen fixtures. Ivory earrings shaped like seashells clung to her small lobes.

"Mademoiselle, you changed again?" she asked incredulously.

Beau laughed. "This isn't Gisselle," he said.

Nina tilted her head.

"Go on with you, monsieur. That t'aint enough of a disguise to fool Nina Jackson."

"No, I'm serious, Nina. This isn't Gisselle," Beau insisted. "Her name is Ruby. Look closely," he told her. "If anyone could tell the difference, it would be you. You practically brought up Gisselle," he said.

She smirked, wiped her hands on her apron, and crossed the kitchen to get closer. I saw she wore a small pouch around her neck on a black shoestring. For a moment she stared into my face. Her black eyes narrowed, burned into mine, and then widened. She stepped back and seized the small pouch between her right thumb and forefinger so she could hold it out between us.

"Who you be, girl?" she demanded.

"My name is Ruby," I said quickly, and shifted my eyes to Beau, who was still smiling impishly.

"Nina is warding off any evil with the voodoo power in that little sack, aren't you, Nina?"

She looked at him and at me and then dropped the sack to her chest again.

"This here, five finger grass," she said. "It can ward off any evil that five fingers can bring, you hear?"

I nodded.

"Who this be?" she asked Beau.

"It's Gisselle's secret sister," he said. "Obviously, twin sister," he added. Nina stared at me again.

"How do you know that?" she asked, taking another step back. "My grandmere, she told me once about a zombie made to look like a woman. Everyone stuck pins in the zombie and the woman screamed in pain until she died in her bed."

Beau roared.

"I'm not a zombie doll," I said. Still suspicious, Nina stared.

"I daresay if you stick pins in her, Nina, she'll be the one to scream, not Gisselle." His smile faded and he grew serious. "She's traveled here from Houma, Nina, but on the way to the house, she had a bad experience. Someone tried to attack her in an alley."

Nina nodded as if she already knew.

"She's actually quite frightened and upset," Beau said.

"Sit you down, girl," Nina said, pointing to a chair by the table. "I'll get you something to make your stomach sit still. You hungry, too?"

I shook my head.

"Did you know Gisselle had a sister?" Beau asked her as she went to prepare something for me to drink. She didn't respond for a moment. Then she turned.

"I don't know anything I'm not supposed to know," she replied. Beau lifted his eyebrows. I saw Nina mix what looked like a tablespoon of blackstrap molasses into a glass of milk with a raw egg and some kind of powder. She mixed it vigorously and brought it back.

"Drink this in one gulp, no air," she prescribed. I stared at the liquid.

"Nina usually cures everyone of anything around here," Beau said. "Don't be afraid."

"My grandmere could do this, too," I said. "She was a Traiteur."

"Your grandmere, a Traiteur?" Nina asked. I nodded. "Then she was holy," she said, impressed. "Cajun Traiteur woman can blow the fire out of a burn and stop bleeding with the press of her palm," Nina explained to Beau.

"I guess she's not a zombie girl then, huh?" Beau asked with a smile. Nina paused.

"Maybe not," she said, still looking at me with some suspicion. "Drink," she commanded, and I did what she said even though it didn't taste great. I felt it bubble in my stomach for a moment and then I did feel a soothing sensation.

"Thank you," I said. I turned with Beau to look at the doorway when we heard the footsteps coming down the hall. A moment later, Gisselle Dumas appeared, dressed in a beautiful red, bare shoulder satin gown with her long red hair brushed until it shone. It was about as long as mine. She wore dangling diamond earrings and a matching diamond necklace set in gold.

"Beau," she began, "why are you late and what's this about a surprise guest?" she demanded. She whirled to confront me, putting her fists on her hips before she turned in my direction. Even though I knew what to expect, the reality of seeing my face on someone else took my breath away. Gisselle Dumas gasped and brought her hand to her throat.

Fifteen years and some months after the day we were born, we met again.

11

Just Like Cinderella

"**W**ho is she?" Gisselle demanded, her eyes quickly moving from wide orbs of amazement to narrow slits of suspicion.

"Anyone can see she's your twin sister," Beau replied. "Her name is Ruby."

Gisselle grimaced and shook her head.

"What sort of a practical joke are you playing now, Beau Andreas?" she demanded. Then she approached me and we stared into each other's faces.

I imagined she was doing what I was doing—searching for the differences; but they were hard to see at first glance. We were identical twins. Our hair was the same shade, our eyes emerald green, our eyebrows exactly the same. Neither of our faces had any tiny scars, nor dimples, nothing that would quickly distinguish one of us from the other. Her cheeks, her chin, her mouth, all were precisely the same shape as mine. Not only did all of our facial features correspond, but we were just about the same height as well. And our bodies had matured and developed as if we had been cast from one mold.

But on second glance, a more scrutinizing second glance, a perceptive inspector would discern differences in our facial expressions and in our demeanor. Gisselle held herself more aloof, more arrogantly. There seemed to be no timidity in her. She had inherited Grandmere Catherine's steel spine, I thought. Her gaze was unflinching and she had a way of tucking in the right corner of her mouth disdainfully.

"Who are you?" she queried sharply.

"My name is Ruby, Ruby Landry, but it should be Ruby Dumas," I said.

Gisselle, still incredulous, still waiting for some sensible explanation for the confusion her eyes were bringing to her brain, turned to Nina Jackson, who crossed herself quickly.

"I am going to light a black candle," she said, and started away, muttering a voodoo prayer.

"Beau!" Gisselle said, stamping her foot.

He laughed and shrugged with his arms out. "I swear I've never seen her before tonight. I found her standing outside the gate when I drove up. She came from . . . where did you say it was?"

"Houma," I said. "In the bayou."

"She's a Cajun girl."

"I can see that, Beau. I don't understand this," she said, now shaking her head at me, her eyes swimming in tears of frustration.

"I'm sure there's a logical explanation," Beau said. "I think I'd better go fetch your parents."

Gisselle continued to stare at me.

"How can I have a twin sister?" she demanded. I wanted to tell her all of it, but I thought it might be better for our father to explain. "Where are you going, Beau?" she cried when he turned to leave.

"To get your father and mother, like I said."

"But . . ." She looked at me and then at him. "But what about the ball?"

"The ball? How can you go running off to the ball now?" he asked, nodding in my direction.

"But I bought this new dress especially for it and I have a wonderful mask and . . ." She embraced herself and glared at me. "How can this happen!" she cried, the tears now streaming down her cheeks. She clasped her hands into small fists and slapped her arms against her sides. "And tonight of all nights!"

"I'm sorry," I said softly. "I didn't realize it was Mardi Gras when I started for New Orleans today, but—"

"You didn't realize it was Mardi Gras!" she chortled. "Oh, Beau."

"Take it easy, Gisselle," he said, returning to embrace her. She buried her face in his shoulder for a moment. As he stroked her hair, he gazed at me, still smiling. "Take it easy," he soothed.

"I can't take it easy," Gisselle insisted, and stamped her foot again as she pulled back. She glared at me angrily now. "It's just some coincidence, some stupid coincidence someone discovered. She was sent here to . . . to embezzle money out of us. That's it, isn't it?'' she accused.

I shook my head.

"This is too much to be a coincidence, Gisselle. I mean, just look at the two of you,'' Beau insisted.

"There are differences. Her nose is longer and her lips look thinner and . . . and her ears stick out more than mine do.''

Beau laughed and shook his head.

"Someone sent you here to steal from us, didn't they? Didn't they?'' Gisselle demanded, her fists on her hips again and her legs spread apart.

"No. I came myself. It was a promise I made to Grandmere Catherine.''

"Who's Grandmere Catherine?'' Gisselle asked, grimacing as if she had swallowed sour milk. "Someone from Storyville?''

"No, someone from Houma,'' I said.

"And a Traiteur,'' Beau added. I could see he was enjoying Gisselle's discomfort. He enjoyed teasing her.

"Oh, this is just so ridiculous. I do not intend to miss the best Mardi Gras Ball because some . . . Cajun girl who looks a little like me has arrived and claims to be my twin sister,'' she snapped.

"Looks a little . . .'' Beau shook his head. "When I first saw her, I thought it was you.''

"Me? How could you think that . . . that,'' she said, gesturing at me, "this . . . this person was me? Look at how she's dressed. Look at her shoes!''

"I thought it was your costume,'' he explained. I wasn't happy hearing my clothes described as someone's costume.

"Beau, do you think I'd ever put on something as plain as that, even as a costume?''

"What's wrong with what I'm wearing?'' I asked, assuming an indignant tone myself.

"It looks homemade,'' Gisselle said after she condescended to gaze at my skirt and blouse once more.

"It is homemade. Grandmere Catherine made both the skirt and blouse.''

"See,'' she said, turning back to Beau. He nodded and saw how I was fuming.

"I'd better go fetch your parents.''

"Beau Andreas, if you leave this house without taking me to the Mardi Gras Ball . . .''

"I promise we'll go after this is straightened out," he said.

"It will never be straightened out. It's a horrible, horrible joke. Why don't you get out of here!" she screamed at me.

"How can you send her away?" Beau demanded.

"Oh, you're a monster, Beau Andreas. A monster to do this to me," she cried, and ran back to the stairway.

"Gisselle!"

"I'm sorry," I said. "I told you I shouldn't have come in. I didn't mean to ruin your evening."

He looked at me a moment and then shook his head.

"How can she blame me? Look," he said, "just go into the living room and make yourself comfortable. I know where Pierre and Daphne are. It won't take but a few minutes and they'll come here to see you. Don't worry about Gisselle," he said, backing up. "Just wait in the living room." He turned and hurried out, leaving me alone, never feeling more like a stranger. Could I ever call this house my home? I wondered as I started toward the living room.

I was afraid to touch anything, afraid even to walk on the expensive looking big Persian oval rug that extended from the living room doorway, under the two large sofas and beyond. The high windows were draped in scarlet velvet with gold ties and the walls were papered in a delicate floral design, the hues matching the colors in the soft cushion high back chairs and the sofas. On the thick mahogany center table were two thick crystal vases. The lamps on the side tables looked very old and valuable. There were paintings on all the walls, some landscapes of plantations and some street scenes from the French Quarter. Above the marble fireplace was the portrait of a distinguished looking old gentleman, his hair and full beard a soft gray. His dark eyes seemed to swing my way and hold.

I lowered myself gently in the corner of the sofa on my right and sat rigidly, clinging to my little bag and gaping about the room, looking at the statues, the figurines in the curio case, and the other pictures on the walls. I was afraid to look at the portrait of the man above the fireplace again. He seemed so accusatory.

A hickory wood grandfather's clock that looked as old as time itself ticked in the corner, its numbers all Roman. Otherwise, the great house was silent. Occasionally, I thought I heard a thumping above me and wondered if that was Gisselle storming back and forth in her room.

My heart, which had been racing and drumming ever since I let Beau Andreas lead me into the house, calmed. I took a deep breath and closed my eyes. Had I done a dreadful thing coming here? Was I about to destroy someone else's life? Why was Grandmere Catherine so sure this was the right thing for me to do? My twin sister obviously resented my very existence. What was to keep my father from doing the same? My heart teetered on the edge of a precipice, ready to plunge and die if he came into this house and rejected me.

Shortly after, I heard the sound of Edgar Farrar's footsteps as he raced down the corridor to open the front door. I heard other voices and people hurrying in.

"In the living room, monsieur," Beau Andreas called, and a moment later my eyes took in my real father's face. How many times had I sat before my mirror and imagined him by transposing my own facial features onto the blank visage I conjured before me? Yes, he had the same soft green eyes and we had the same shaped nose and chin. His face was leaner, firmer, his forehead rolled back gently under the shock of thick chestnut hair brushed back at the sides with just a small pompadour at the front.

He was tall, at least six feet two, and had a slim but firm looking torso with shoulders that sloped gracefully into his arms, the physique of a tennis player, easily discernible in his Mardi Gras costume: a tight fitting silver outfit designed to resemble a suit of armor, such as those worn by medieval knights. He had the helmet in his arms. He fastened his gaze on me and his face went from a look of surprise and astonishment to a smile of happy amazement.

Before a word was spoken, Daphne Dumas came up beside him. She wore a bright blue tunic with long, tight sleeves, the skirt of which had a long train and an embroidered gold fringe. It fit closely down to her hips, but was wider after. It was buttoned in front from top to bottom. Over it, she wore a cloak, low at the neck and fastened with a diamond clasp at the right breast. She looked like a princess from a fairy tale.

She was nearly six feet tall herself and stood as correct as a fashion model. With her beautiful looks, her slim, curvaceous figure, she could have easily been one. Her pale reddish blond hair lay softly over her shoulders, not a strand disobedient. She had big, light blue eyes and a mouth I couldn't have drawn more perfectly. It was she who spoke first after she took a good look at me.

"Is this some sort of joke, Beau, something you and Gisselle concocted for Mardi Gras?"

"No, madame," Beau said.

"It's no joke," my father said, stepping into the room and not swinging his eyes from me for an instant. "This is not Gisselle. Hello," he said.

"Hello." We continued to stare at each other, neither able to shift his gaze, he appearing as eager to visually devour me as I was to devour him.

"You found her on our doorstep?" Daphne asked Beau.

"Yes, madame," he replied. "She was turning away, losing her courage to knock on the front door and present herself," he revealed. Finally, I swung my eyes to Daphne and saw a look in her face that seemed to suggest she wished I had.

"I'm glad you came along, Beau," Pierre said. "You did the right thing. Thank you."

Beau beamed. My father's appreciation and approval were obviously very important to him.

"You came from Houma?" my father asked. I nodded and Daphne Dumas gasped and brought her hands to her chest. She and my father exchanged a look and then Daphne gestured toward Beau with her head.

"Why don't you see how Gisselle is getting along, Beau?" Pierre asked firmly.

"Yes, sir," Beau said, and quickly marched away. My father moved in closer and then sat on the sofa across from me. Daphne closed the two large doors softly and turned in expectation.

"You told them your last name is Landry?" my father began. I nodded.

"*Mon Dieu*," Daphne said. She swallowed hard and reached for the edge of a high back velvet chair to steady herself.

"Easy," my father said, rising quickly to go to her. He embraced her and guided her into the chair. She sat back, her eyes closed. "Are you all right?" he asked her. She nodded without speaking. Then he turned back to me.

"Your grandfather . . . his name is Jack?"

"Yes."

"He's a swamp trapper, a guide?"

I nodded.

"How could they have done this, Pierre?" Daphne cried softly. "It's ghastly. All these years!"

"I know, I know," my father said. "Let me get at the core of this, Daphne." He turned back to me, his eyes still soft, but now troubled, too. "Ruby. That is your name?" I nodded. "Tell us what you know about all this and why you have presented yourself at this time. Please," he added.

"Grandmere Catherine told me about my mother . . . how she became pregnant and then how Grandpere Jack arranged for my sister's . . ."—I wanted to say "sale," but I thought it sounded too harsh—". . . my sister's coming to live with you. Grandmere Catherine was not happy about the arrangements. She and Grandpere Jack stopped living together soon afterward."

My father shifted his eyes to Daphne, who closed and opened hers. Then he fixed his gaze on me again.

"Go on," he said.

"Grandmere Catherine kept the fact that my mother was pregnant with twins a secret, even from Grandpere Jack. She decided I was to live with her and my mother, but . . ." Even now, even though I had never set eyes on my mother or heard her voice, just mentioning her death brought tears to my eyes and choked back the words.

"But what?" my father begged.

"But my mother died soon after Gisselle and I were born," I revealed. My father's cheeks turned crimson. I saw his breath catch and his own eyes tear over, but he quickly regained his composure, glanced at Daphne again, and then turned back to me.

"I'm sorry to hear that," he uttered, his voice nearly cracking.

"Not long ago, my grandmere Catherine died. She made me promise that if something bad happened to her, I would go to New Orleans and present myself to you rather than live with Grandpere Jack," I said. My father nodded.

"I knew him slightly, but I can understand why your grandmother didn't want you to live with him," he said.

"Don't you have any other relatives . . . aunts, uncles?" Daphne asked quickly.

"No, madame," I said. "Or at least, none that I know of in Houma. My grandfather talked of his relatives who live in other bayous, but Grandmere Catherine never liked us to associate with them."

"How dreadful," Daphne said, shaking her head. I wasn't sure if she meant my family life or the present situation.

"This is amazing. I have two daughters," Pierre said, allowing himself a smile. It was a handsome smile. I felt myself start to relax. Under his warm gaze the tension drained out of me. I couldn't help thinking he was so much the father I'd always wanted, a soft-spoken, kindly man.

But Daphne flashed him a cool, chastising look.

"Double the embarrassment, too," she reminded him.

"What? Oh, yes, of course. I'm glad you've finally revealed yourself," he told me, "but it does present us with a trifle of a problem."

"A trifle of a problem? A trifle!" Daphne cried. Her chin quivered.

"Well, somewhat more serious, I'm afraid." My father sat back, pensive.

"I don't mean to be a burden to anyone," I said, and stood up quickly. "I'll return to Houma. There are friends of my grand-mere's . . ."

"That's a fine idea," Daphne said quickly. "We'll arrange for transportation, give you some money. Why, we'll even send her some money from time to time, won't we, Pierre? You can tell your grandmother's friends that—"

"No," Pierre said, his eyes fixed so firmly on me, I felt like his thoughts were traveling through them and into my heart. "I can't send my own daughter away."

"But it's not as if she is your daughter in actuality, Pierre. You haven't known her a day since her birth and neither have I. She's been brought up in an entirely different world," Daphne pleaded. But my father didn't appear to hear her. With his gaze still fixed on me, he spoke.

"I knew your grandmother better than I knew your grandfather. She was a very special woman with special powers," he said.

"Really, Pierre," Daphne interrupted.

"No, Daphne, she was. She was what Cajuns call . . . a Traiteur, right?" he asked me. I nodded. "If she thought it was best for you to come here, she must have had some special reasons, some insights, spiritual guidance," Pierre said.

"You can't be serious, Pierre," Daphne said. "You don't put any validity in those pagan beliefs. Next thing, you'll be telling me you believe in Nina's voodoo."

"I never reject it out of hand, Daphne. There are mysteries that logic, reason, and science can't explain," he told her. She closed her eyes and sighed deeply.

"How do you propose to handle this . . . this situation, Pierre? How do we explain her to our friends, to society?" she asked. I was still standing, afraid to take a step away, yet afraid to sit down again, too. I clung so hard to my little bag of possessions, my knuckles turned white while my father thought.

"Nina wasn't with us when Gisselle was supposedly born," he began.

"So?"

"We had that mulatto woman, Tituba, remember?"

"I remember. I remember hating her. She was too sloppy and too lazy and she frightened me with her silly superstitions," Daphne recalled. "Dropping pinches of salt everywhere, burning clothing in a barrel with chicken droppings . . . at least Nina keeps her beliefs private."

"And so we let Tituba go right after Gisselle was supposedly born, remember? At least, that was what we told the public."

"What are you getting at, Pierre? How does that relate to this trifling problem?" she asked caustically.

"We never told the truth because we were working with private detectives," he said.

"What? What truth?"

"To get back the stolen baby, the twin sister who was taken from the nursery the same day she was born. You know how some people believe that missing children are voodoo sacrifices, and how some voodoo queens were often accused of kidnapping and murdering children?" he said.

"I always suspected something like that, myself," Daphne said.

"Precisely. No one's ever proven anything of the sort, however, but there was always the danger of creating mass hysteria over it and causing vigilantes to go out and abuse people. So," he said, sitting back, "we kept our tragedy and our search private. Until today, that is," he added, pressing his hands together and smiling at me.

"She was kidnapped more than fifteen years ago and has returned?" Daphne said. "Is that what we're to tell people, tell our friends?"

He nodded. "Like the Prodigal Son, only this case, it's the Prodigal Daughter, whose fake grandmother got a pang of conscience on her deathbed and told her the truth. Miracle of miracles, Ruby has found her way home."

"But, Pierre . . ."

"You'll be the talk of the town, Daphne. Everyone will want to know the story. You won't be able to keep up with the invitations," he said. Daphne just stared at him a moment and then looked up at me.

"Isn't it amazing?" my father said. "Look at how identical they are."

"But she's so . . . unschooled," Daphne moaned.

"Which, in the beginning, will make her more of a curiosity. But you can take her under your wing just as you took Gisselle," my father explained, "and teach her nice things, correct things, make her over . . . like Pygmalion and Galatea," he said. "Everyone will admire you for it," he told her.

"I don't know," she said, but it was with much less resistance. She gazed at me more analytically. "Maybe scrubbed up with decent clothes . . ."

"These are decent clothes!" I snapped. I was tired of everyone criticizing my garments. "Grandmere Catherine made them and the things she made were always cherished and sought after in the bayou."

"I'm sure they were," Daphne said, her eyes sharp and cold. "In the bayou. But this is not the bayou, dear. This is New Orleans. You came here because you want to live here . . . be with your father," she said, looking at Pierre before looking back at me. "Right?"

I looked at him, too. "Yes," I said. "I believe in Grandmere Catherine's wishes and prophecies."

"Well, then, you have to blend in." She sat back and thought a moment. "It will be quite a challenge," she said, nodding. "And somewhat of an interesting one."

"Of course it will be," Pierre said.

"Do you think I could ever get her to the point where people really wouldn't know the difference between them?" Daphne asked my father. I wasn't sure I liked her tone. It was still as if I were some uncivilized aborigine, some wild animal that had to be housebroken.

"Of course you could, darling. Look at how well you've done with Gisselle, and we both know there's a wild streak in her, don't we?" he said, smiling.

"Yes. I have managed to harness and subdue that part of her, the Cajun part," Daphne said disdainfully.

"I am not wild, madame," I said, nearly spitting my words back at her. "My grandmere Catherine taught me only good things and we went to church regularly, too."

"It's not something people teach you, per se," she replied. "It's something you can't help, something in your heritage," she insisted. "But Pierre's blue blood and my guidance have been strong enough to conquer that part of Gisselle. If you will help, if you really want to become part of this family, I might be able to do it with you, too.

"Although, she's had years and years of poor breeding, Pierre. You must remember that."

"Of course, Daphne," he said softly. "No one expects miracles overnight. As you said so yourself just a moment ago—it's a challenge." He smiled. "I wouldn't ask you if I didn't think you were capable of making it happen, darling."

Placated, Daphne sat back again. When she thought deeply, she pursed her lips and her eyes glittered. Despite the things she had said, I couldn't help but admire her beauty and her regal manner. Would it be so terrible to look and act like such a woman? I wondered, and become someone else's fairy-tale princess? A part of me that wouldn't be denied cried, *Please, please, cooperate, try,* and the part of me that felt insulted by her remarks sulked somewhere in the dark corners of my mind.

"Well, Beau already knows about her," Daphne said.

"Exactly," my father said. "Of course, I could ask him to keep it all a secret, and I'm sure he would die in a duel before revealing it, but things are revealed accidentally, too, and then what would we do? It could unravel everything we've done up until now."

Daphne nodded.

"What will you tell Gisselle?" she asked him, her voice somewhat mournful now. "She'll know the truth about me, that I'm not really her mother." She dabbed at her eyes with a light blue silk handkerchief.

"Of course you're really her mother. She hasn't known anyone else to be her mother and you've been a wonderful mother to her. We'll tell her the story just as I outlined it. After the initial shock, she'll accept her twin sister and hopefully help you, too. Nothing will change except our lives will be doubly blessed," he said, smiling at me.

Was this where I got my blind optimism? I wondered. Was he a dreamer, too?

"That is," he added after a moment, "if Ruby agrees to go along with it. I don't like asking anyone to lie," he told me, "but in this case, it's a good lie, a lie which will keep anyone from being hurt," he said, shifting his eyes toward Daphne.

I thought a moment. I would have to pretend, at least to Gisselle, that Grandmere Catherine had been part of some kidnapping plot. That bothered me, but then I thought Grandmere Catherine would want me to do everything possible to stay here—far away from Grandpere Jack.

"Yes," I said. "It's all right with me."

Daphne sighed deeply and then quickly regained her composure.

"I'll have Nina arrange one of the guest rooms," she said.

"Oh, no. I want her to have the room that adjoins Gisselle's. They will be sisters right from the beginning," my father emphasized. Daphne nodded.

"I'll have her prepare it right away. For tonight, she can use some of Gisselle's night garments. Fortunately," she said, smiling at me with some warmth for the first time, "you and your sister look to be about the same size." She gazed down at my feet. "Your feet look fairly close as well, I see."

"You'll have to go on a shopping spree tomorrow though, darling. You know how possessive Gisselle is with her clothes," my father warned.

"She should be. A woman should take pride in her wardrobe and not be like some college coed, sharing her garments down to her very panties with some roommate." She rose gracefully from the high back chair and shook her head slightly as she gazed at me. "What a Mardi Gras evening this turned out to be." She turned to Pierre. "You're positive about all this. This is what you want to do?"

"Yes, darling. With your full cooperation and guidance, that is," he said, rising. He kissed her on the cheek. "I guess I'll have to make it all up to you doubly now," he added. She looked into his eyes and gave him a small, tight smile.

"The cash register has been ringing for the last five minutes without a pause," she said, and he laughed. Then he kissed her gently on the lips. From the way he gazed at her, I could see how important it was for him to please her. She appeared to bask in the glow of his devotion. After a moment she turned to leave. At the doorway, she paused.

"You will be telling it all to Gisselle?"

"In a few minutes," he said.

"I'm going to bed. This has all been too shocking and has drained me of most of my energy right now," she complained. "But I want to have the strength for Gisselle in the morning."

"Of course," my father said.

"I'll see to her room," Daphne declared and left us.

"Sit down. Please," my father asked. I took my seat again and he sat down, too. "You want something to drink . . . eat?"

"No, I'm fine. Nina gave me something to drink before."

"One of her magical recipes?" he asked, smiling.

"Yes. And it worked."

"It always does. I meant it when I said I have respect for spiritual and mysterious things. You'll have to tell me more about Grandmere Catherine."

"I'd like that."

He took a deep breath and then let it out slowly, his eyes down. "I'm sorry to hear about Gabrielle. She was a beautiful young woman. I had never and have never met anyone like her. She was so innocent and free, a true pure spirit."

"Grandmere Catherine thought she was a swamp fairy," I said, smiling.

"Yes, yes. She might very well have been. Look," he said, growing very serious very quickly, "I know how disturbing and how troubling this all must be to you. In time, you and I will get to know each other better and I'll try to explain it. I won't be able to justify it or turn the bad things that happened into good things. I won't be able to change the events of the past or make mistakes go away, but I hope I will at least get you to see why it happened the way it did. You have a right to know all that," he said.

"Gisselle knows nothing then?" I asked.

"Oh, no. Not a hint. There was Daphne to consider. I had hurt her enough as it was. I had to protect her, and there was no way to do that without creating the fabrication that Gisselle was her child.

"One lie, one mistake, usually creates the need for another and another, and before you know it, you've spun a cocoon of deception around yourself. As you see, I'm still doing that, still protecting Daphne.

"Actually, I was fortunate and am fortunate to have Daphne. Besides being a beautiful woman, she's a woman capable of great love. She loved my father and I believe, she accepted all this because of her love for him, as much as her love for me. In fact, she accepted some responsibility."

His head bowed down into the cradle of his hands.

"Because she was unable to get pregnant herself?" I asked. He lifted his eyes quickly.

"Yes," he said. "I see you know a lot more than I thought. You seem like a very mature girl, perhaps a lot more mature than Gisselle.

"Anyway," he continued, "throughout it all, Daphne has maintained her dignity and poise. That's why I think she can teach you a great deal and why, in time, I hope you will accept her as your mother.

"Of course," he added, smiling, "first, I have to get you to accept me as your father. Any healthy man can make a baby with a woman; but not every man can be a father," he said.

I saw there were tears in his eyes when he spoke. As he talked, I sensed every molecule of his being was striving to reach out and force me to understand even what he himself must have found inexplicable.

I bit down on my tongue to keep from asking any questions. It was difficult to breathe, not to be drowned by everything that was happening so fast.

"What's in your bag?" he inquired.

"Oh, just some of my things and some pictures."

"Pictures?" His eyebrows rose with interest.

"Yes." I opened the bag and took out one of the pictures of my mother. He took it slowly and gazed at it for a long moment.

"She does seem like a fairy goddess. My memory of those days is like the memory of a dream, pictures and words that float through my brain on the surface of soap bubbles ready to burst if I try too hard to remember the actual details.

"You and Gisselle look a lot like her, you know. I don't deserve the good fortune of having two of you to remind me of Gabrielle, but I thank whatever Fate has brought you here," he said.

"Grandmere Catherine," I said. "That's who you should thank." He nodded.

"I'll spend as much time with you as I can. I'll show you New Orleans myself and tell you about our family."

"What do you do?" I asked, realizing I didn't even know that much about him. The way I asked, the way my eyes widened at the sight of all these expensive furnishings in this mansion made him laugh.

"Right now I make my money in real estate investments. We own a number of apartment buildings and office buildings and we're involved in a number of developments. I have offices downtown.

"We are a very old and established family, who can actually trace their lineage back to the original Mississippi Trading Company, a French colonial company. My father did a genealogy which I will have to show you some day," he added, smiling. "And he proved that we can trace our lineage back to one of the hundred *Filles a la Casette* or casket girls."

"What were they?" I asked.

"Women back in France who were carefully chosen from among good middle-class families and each given only a small chest containing various articles of clothing, and sent over to become wives for the Frenchmen settling the area. They didn't have all that much more than you're carrying in your small bag," he added.

"However," he continued, "the Dumas family history isn't filled only with reputable and highly prized things. We had ancestors who once owned and operated one of the elegant gambling houses and even made money on the bordellos in Storyville. Daphne's family has the same sort of past, but she isn't as eager to own up to it," he said.

He rubbed his hands together and stood up.

"Well, we'll have plenty of time to talk about all this. I promise. Right now, I imagine you're tired. You'd like a bath and a chance to relax and go to sleep. In the morning, you can begin your new life, one that I hope will be wonderful for you. May I kiss you and welcome you to what will become your new home and family?" he asked.

"Yes," I said and closed my eyes as he brought his lips to my cheek.

My father's first kiss . . . how many times had I dreamt about it, had I seen him in my dreams approach my bed and lean down to kiss me good night, the mysterious father of my paintings who stepped off the canvas and pressed his lips to my cheek and stroked my hair and drove away all the demons that hover in the shadows of our hearts . . . the father I had never known.

I opened my eyes and looked up into his and saw the tears. His eyes were filled with sorrow and pain, and it seemed he aged a little as he stared at me with much regret.

"I'm glad I've finally found you," I said. In an instant, that sorrow that washed over his beautiful eyes disappeared and his face beamed.

"You must be very special. I don't know why I should be this fortunate." He took my hand and led me out of the living room, talking about some of the other rooms, the paintings, the artworks as we approached the winding stairway.

Just as we reached the upstairs landing, a door was thrust open down right and Gisselle stepped out with Beau Andreas right beside her.

"What are you doing with her?" she demanded.

"Take it easy, Gisselle," our father said. "I'll be explaining it all to you in a moment."

"You're putting her in the room next to mine?" she asked, grimacing.

"Yes."

"This is horrible, horrible!" she screamed, and stepped back into her room before slamming the door.

Beau Andreas, who had come out, looked embarrassed.

"I think I'd better be going," he said.

"Yes," my father told him.

Beau started away and Gisselle jerked open her door again.

"Beau Andreas, how dare you leave this house without me!" she cried.

"But . . ." He looked at my father. "You and your family have things to discuss, to do and—"

"It can wait until morning. It's Mardi Gras," Gisselle declared, and glared at our father. "I've been waiting all year to attend this ball. All my friends are there already," she moaned.

"Monsieur?" Beau said. My father nodded.

"It can wait until morning," he said.

Gisselle swept back the strands of hair she had shaken over her shoulders in her rage and marched out of her room, glaring at me as she walked by to join Beau Andreas. He looked uncomfortable, but let her take his arm, and then the two of them marched down the stairs, Gisselle pounding each step as she descended.

"She has been so looking forward to this ball," my father explained.

I nodded, but my father felt the need to continue to justify her behavior. "It wouldn't do any good to force her to stay. She would be less apt to listen and understand. Daphne does so much better with her when she's like this anyway," he added.

"But I'm sure," he said as we continued toward my new bedroom, "in time she will be overjoyed and excited about getting a sister. She's been an only child too long. She's a bit spoiled. Now," he said, "I have another young lady to spoil, too."

The moment we stepped into my new room, I felt that spoiling had begun. It had a dark pine canopy queen-size bed, the canopy made of fine pearl-colored silk with a fringe border. The pillows were enormous and fluffy looking, the bedspread, pillowcases, and top sheet all in chintz, the flowers full of color and glazed. The wallpaper duplicated the floral pattern in the linens. Above the headboard was a painting of a beautiful young woman in a garden setting feeding a parrot. There was a cute black and white puppy tugging at the hem of her full skirt. On each side of the bed were two nightstands, each with a bell shaped lamp. But beside a matching dresser and armoire, the room had a vanity table with an enormous oval mirror in an ivory frame, the frame covered with hand painted red and yellow roses. And in the corner beside it, an old French birdcage hung.

"I have my own bathroom?" I asked, gazing through the open doorway on my right. The plush bathroom had a large tub, sink, and commode, all with brass fixtures. There were even flowers and birds hand painted on the tub and sink.

"Of course. Twin sister or not, Gisselle is not the sort you share a bathroom with," my father said, smiling. "This door," he added, nodding at the door on my left, "joins the two rooms. I hope the day will soon come when the two of you will move back and forth through it eagerly."

"So do I," I said. I went to the windows and gazed out at the grounds of the estate. I saw that I faced the pool and the tennis court. Through the open window, I could smell the green bamboo, gardenias, and blooming camellias.

"Do you like it?" my father asked.

"Like it? I love it. It's the most wonderful room I've ever seen," I declared. He laughed at my exuberance.

"It will be something fresh to see someone appreciate everything around here again. So often, things are taken for granted," he explained.

"I'll never take anything for granted again," I promised.

"We'll see. Wait until Gisselle works you over. Well, I see you've

been brought a nightgown to use and there's a pair of slippers beside
the bed." He opened a closet and there was a pink silk robe hanging in
it. "Here's a robe, too. You'll find all you need in the bathroom—new
toothbrush, soaps, but should you need anything, just ask. I want you
to treat this house as your home as soon as you can," he added.

"Thank you."

"Well, get comfortable and have a nice sleep. If you get up before the
rest of us do, which is quite possible the morning after Mardi Gras, just
go down to the kitchen and Nina will fix you some breakfast."

I nodded and he said good night, closing the door softly behind him
as he left.

For a long moment I simply stood there gaping at everything. Was I
really here, transported over time and distance into a new world, a
world where I would have a real mother and father, and as soon as she
could accept it, a real sister, too?

I went into the bathroom and discovered the soaps scented with the
fragrance of gardenias and the bottles of bubble bath powder. I drew
myself a hot bath and luxuriated in the silky smoothness of the sweet-
smelling bubbles. Afterward, I put on Gisselle's scented nightgown
and crawled under the soft sheet and down bedspread.

I felt like Cinderella.

But just like Cinderella, I couldn't help feeling trepidation; I couldn't
help being frightened by the ticking of the clock that swung its hands
around to clasp them finally on the hour of twelve, the bewitching
hour.

Would it burst my bubble of happiness and turn my carriage into a
pumpkin?

Or would it tick on and on, making my claim to a fairy-tale existence
that much more secure with each passing minute?

Oh, Grandmere, I thought as my heavy eyelids began to shut, I'm
here. I hope you're resting more comfortably because of it.

12

Blue-Blood Welcome

I awoke to the sweet singing of blue jays and mockingbirds and for the first few moments, forgot where I was. My trip to New Orleans and all that had subsequently followed now seemed more like a dream. It must have rained for a while during the night for although the sun was beaming brightly through my windows, the breeze still smelled of rain and wet leaves as well as the redolent scents of the myriad of flowers and trees that surrounded the great house.

I sat up slowly, drinking in my beautiful new room in the light of day. If anything, it looked even more wonderful. Although the furniture, the fixtures, and everything down to a jewelry box on the vanity table were antique, it all looked brand-new, too. It was almost as if this room had been recently prepared, everything polished and cleaned in anticipation of my arrival. Or that I had gone to sleep for years when all these things were brand-new and woken up without realizing time had stood still.

I rose from bed and went to the windows. The sky was a patchwork quilt of soft vanilla clouds and light blue. Below the grounds people were vigorously at work clipping hedges, weeding flower beds, and mowing lawns. Someone was on the tennis court sweeping off the myrtle leaves and tiny branches that had probably been torn and blown in the rain, and another man was scooping the oak and banana tree leaves out of the pool.

It was a wonderful day to start a new life, I decided. With my heart full of joy, I went to the bathroom, brushed my hair, and got dressed in a gray skirt and blouse I had brought in my little bag. I put all my precious possessions in the nightstand drawer and then slipped on my moccasins and left my room to go down to breakfast.

It was very quiet in the house. All the other bedroom doors were shut tight, but as soon as I reached the top of the stairway, I heard the front door thrust open and slammed closed and saw Gisselle come charging into the house, unconcerned about how much noise she was making or whom she might waken.

She threw off her cloak and a headdress of bright feathers, dropping it all on the table in the entryway, and then started for the stairway. I watched her walk halfway up with her head down. When she lifted it and saw me gazing down at her, she stopped.

"Are you just coming in from the Mardi Gras Ball?" I asked, astounded.

"Oh, I forgot all about you," she said, and followed it with a silly, thin laugh. There was something about the way she wobbled that led me to believe she had been drinking. "That's how good a time I had," she added with a flare. "And Beau was good enough not to mention your shocking appearance all night." Her expression turned sour, indignant as my question to her sunk in. "Of course I'm just coming home. Mardi Gras goes until dawn. It's expected. Don't think you can tell my parents anything they don't know and get me in trouble," she warned.

"I don't want to get you in trouble. I was just . . . surprised. I've never done that."

"Haven't you ever gone to a dance and enjoyed yourself, or don't they have such things in the bayou?" she asked with disdain.

"Yes. We call them fais dodos," I told her. "But we don't stay out all night."

"Fais dodos? Sounds like a good old time, two-stepping to the sounds of an accordion and a washboard." She smirked and continued to climb the stairs toward me.

"They're usually nice dances with lots of good things to eat. Was the ball nice?" I asked.

"Nice?" She paused on the step just below me and laughed again. "Nice? Nice is a word for a school party or an afternoon tea in the garden, but for a Mardi Gras Ball? It was more than nice; it was spectacular. Everyone was there," she added, stepping up. "And everyone ogled me and Beau with green eyes. We're considered the handsomest young Creole couple these days, you know. I don't know how many of my girlfriends begged me to let them have a dance with Beau, and all of them were dying to know where I had gotten this dress, but I wouldn't tell them."

"It is a very pretty dress," I admitted.

"Well, don't expect I'll let you borrow it now that you've stormed into our lives," she retorted, gathering her wits about her. "I still don't understand how you got here and who you are," she added with ice in her voice.

"Your father . . . our father will explain," I said. She flicked me another of her scornful glances before throwing her hair back.

"I doubt anyone can explain it, but I can't listen now anyway. I'm exhausted. I must sleep and I'm certainly not in the mood to hear about you right now." She started to turn but paused to look me over from foot to head. "Where did you get these clothes? Is everything you have handmade?" she asked contemptuously.

"Not everything. I didn't bring much with me anyway," I said.

"Thank goodness for that." She yawned. "I've got to get some sleep. Beau's coming by late in the afternoon for tea. We like reviewing the night before, tearing everyone to shreds. If you're still here, you can sit and listen and learn."

"Of course I'll still be here," I said. "This is my home now, too."

"Please. I'm getting a headache," she said, pinching her temples with her thumb and forefinger. She turned and held her arm out toward me, her palm up. "No more. Young Creole women have to replenish themselves. We're more . . . feminine, dainty, like flowers that need the kiss of soft rain and the touch of warm sunlight. That's what Beau says." She stopped smiling at her own words and glared at me. "Don't you put on lipstick before you meet people?"

"No. I don't own any lipstick," I said.

"And Beau thinks we're twins."

Unable to hold back, I flared. "We are!"

"In your dreams maybe," she countered, and then sauntered to her bedroom. After she entered and closed her door, I went downstairs, pausing to admire her headdress and cloak. Why did she leave it here? Who picked up after her? I wondered.

As if she heard my thoughts, a maid came out of the living room and marched down the corridor to retrieve Gisselle's things. She was a young black woman with beautiful, large brown eyes. I didn't think she was much older than I.

"Good morning," I said.

"Mornin'. You're the new girl who looks just like Gisselle?" she asked.

"Yes. My name's Ruby."

"I'm Wendy Williams," she said. She scooped up Gisselle's things, her eyes glued to me, and then walked away.

I started down the corridor to the kitchen, but when I reached the dining room, I saw my father already seated at the long table. He was sipping coffee and reading the business section of the newspaper. The moment he saw me, he looked up and smiled.

"Good morning. Come on in and sit down," he called. It was a very big dining room, almost as big as a Cajun meeting hall, I thought. Above the long table hung a shoo-fly, a great, wide fan unfurled at dinnertime and pulled to and fro by a servant to provide a breeze and do what it was named for: shoo away flies . . . I imagined it was there just for decoration. I had seen them before in rich Cajun homes where they had electric fans.

"Here, sit down," my father said, tapping the place on his left. "From now on, this is your seat. Gisselle sits here on my right and Daphne sits at the other end."

"She sits so far away," I remarked, gazing down the length of the rich, cherry wood table, polished so much I could see my face reflected in its surface. My father laughed.

"Yes, but that's the way Daphne likes it. Or should I say, that's the proper seating arrangement. So, how did you sleep?" he asked as I took my seat.

"Wonderfully. It's the most comfortable bed I've ever been in. I felt like I was sleeping on a cloud!"

He smiled.

"Gisselle wants me to buy her a new mattress. She claims hers is too hard, but if I get one any softer, she'll sink to the floor," he added, and we both laughed. I wondered if he had heard her come in and knew she had just returned from the ball. "Hungry?"

"Yes," I said. My stomach was rumbling. He hit a bell and Edgar appeared from the kitchen.

"You've met Edgar, correct?" he asked.

"Oh, yes. Good morning, Edgar," I said. He bowed slightly.

"Good morning, mademoiselle."

"Edgar, have Nina prepare some of her blueberry pancakes for Mademoiselle Ruby, please. You'd like that, I expect?"

"Yes, thank you," I said. My father nodded toward Edgar.

"Very good, sir," Edgar said, and smiled at me.

"Some orange juice? It's freshly squeezed," my father said, reaching for the pitcher.

"Yes, thank you."

"I don't think Daphne needs to worry about your manners. Grandmere Catherine did a fine job," he complimented. I couldn't help but shift my eyes away for a moment at the mention of Grandmere. "I bet you miss her a great deal."

"Yes, I do."

"No one can replace someone you love, but I hope I can fill some of the emptiness I know is in your heart," he said. "Well," he continued, sitting back, "Daphne is going to sleep late this morning, too." He winked. "And we know Gisselle will sleep away most of the day. Daphne says she'll take you shopping midafternoon. So that leaves just the two of us to spend the morning and lunch. How would you like me to show you around the city a bit?"

"I'd love it. Thank you," I said.

After breakfast, we got into his Rolls Royce and drove down the long driveway. I had never been in so luxurious an automobile before and sat gaping stupidly at the wood trim, running the palm of my hand over the soft leather.

"Do you drive?" my father asked me.

"Oh, no. I haven't even ridden in cars all that much. In the bayou we get around by walking or by poling pirogues."

"Yes, I remember," he said, beaming a broad smile my way. "Gisselle doesn't drive either. She doesn't want to be bothered learning. The truth is she likes being carted around. But if you would like to learn how to drive, I'd be glad to teach you," he said.

"I would. Thank you."

He drove on through the Garden District, past many fine homes with grounds just as beautiful as ours, some with oleander-lined pike fences. There were fewer clouds now which meant the streets and beautiful flowers had fewer shadows looming over them. Sidewalks and tiled patios glittered. Here and there the gutters were full of pink and white camellias from the previous night's rain.

"Some of these houses date back to the eighteen-forties," my father told me and leaned over to point to a house on our right. "Jefferson Davis, President of the Confederacy, died in that house in 1899. There's a lot of history here," he said proudly.

We made a turn and paused as the olive green streetcar rattled past the palm trees on the esplanade. Then we followed St. Charles back toward the inner city.

"I'm glad we had this opportunity to be alone for a while," he said. "Besides my showing you the city, it gives me a chance to get to know you and you a chance to get to know me. It took a great deal of courage for you to come to me," he said. The look on my face confirmed his suspicion. He cleared his throat and continued.

"It will be hard for me to talk about your mother when someone else is around, especially Daphne. I think you understand why."

I nodded.

"I'm sure it's harder for you to understand right now how it all happened. Sometimes," he said, smiling to himself, "when I think about it, it does seem like something I dreamt."

It was as though he were talking in a dream. His eyes were glazed and far away, his voice smooth, easy, relaxed.

"I must tell you about my younger brother, Jean. He was always much different from me, far more outgoing, energetic, a handsome Don Juan if there ever was one," he added, breaking into a soft smile. "I've always been quite shy when it came to members of the genteel sex.

"Jean was athletic, a track star and a wonderful sailor. He could make our sailboat slice through the water on Lake Pontchartrain even if there wasn't enough breeze to nudge the willows on the bank.

"Needless to say, he was my father's favorite, and my mother always thought of him as her baby. But I wasn't jealous," he added quickly. "I've always been more business minded, more comfortable in an office crunching numbers, talking on the telephone, and making deals than I have been on a playing field or in a sailboat surrounded by beautiful young women.

"Jean had all the charm. He didn't have to work at making friends or gaining acquaintances. Women and men alike just wanted to be around him, to walk in his shadow, to be favored with his words and smiles.

"The house was always full of young people back then. I never knew who would be encamped in our living room or eating in our dining room or lounging at our pool."

"How much younger than you was he?" I asked.

"Four years. When I graduated from college, Jean had begun his first year and was a track star in college already, already elected president of his college class, and already a popular fraternity man.

"It was easy to see why our father doted on him so and had such big dreams for him," my father said, and he made a series of turns that took us deeper and deeper into the busier areas of New Orleans. But I wasn't as interested in the traffic, the crowds, and the dozens and dozens of stores as I was in my father's story.

We paused for a traffic light.

"I wasn't married yet. Daphne and I had really just begun to date. In the back of his mind, our father was already planning out Jean's marriage to the daughter of one of his business associates. It was to be a wedding made in Heaven. She was an attractive young lady; her father was rich, too. The wedding ceremony and reception would rival those of royalty."

"How did Jean feel about it?" I asked.

"Jean? He idolized our father and would do anything he wanted. Jean thought of it all as inevitable. You would have liked him a great deal, loved him, I should say. He was never despondent and always saw the rainbow at the end of the storm, no matter what the problem or trouble."

"What happened to him?" I finally asked, dreading the answer.

"A boating accident on Lake Pontchartrain. I rarely went out on the boat with him, but this time I let him talk me into going. He had a habit of trying to get me to be more like him. He was always after me to enjoy life more. To him I was too serious, too responsible. Usually, I didn't pay much attention to his complaints, but this time, he argued that we should be more like brothers. I relented. We both drank too much. A storm came up. I wanted to turn around immediately, but he decided it would be more fun to challenge it and the boat turned over. Jean would have been all right, I'm sure. He was a far better swimmer than I was, but the mast struck him in the temple."

"Oh no," I moaned.

"He was in a coma for a long time. My father spared no expense, hired the best doctors, but none of them could do anything. He was like a vegetable."

"How terrible."

"I thought my parents would never get over it, especially my father. But my mother became even more depressed. Her health declined first. Less than a year after the tragic accident, she suffered her first heart attack. She survived, but she became an invalid."

We continued onward, deeper into the business area. My father made one turn and then another and then slowed down to pull the vehicle into a parking spot, but he didn't shut off the engine. He faced forward and continued his remembrances.

"One day, my father came to me in our offices and closed the door. He had aged so since my brother's accident and my mother's illness. A once proud, strong man, now he walked with his shoulders turned in, his head lowered, his back bent. He was always pale, his eyes empty, his enthusiasm for his business at a very low ebb.

"'Pierre,'" he said, 'I don't think your mother's long for this world, and frankly, I feel my own days are numbered. What we would like most to see is for you to marry and start your family.'

"Daphne and I were planning on getting married anyway, but after his conversation with me, I rushed things along. I wanted to try to have children immediately. She understood. But month after month passed and when she showed no signs of becoming pregnant, we became concerned.

"I sent her to specialists and the conclusion was she was unable to get pregnant. Her body simply didn't produce enough of some hormone. I forget the exact diagnosis.

"The news devastated my father who seemed to live only for the day when he would rest his eyes on his grandchild. Not long after, my mother died."

"How terrible," I said. He nodded and turned off the engine.

"My father went into a deep depression. He rarely came to work, spent long hours simply staring into space, took poorer and poorer care of himself. Daphne looked after him as best she could, but blamed herself somewhat, too. I know she did, even though she denies it to this day.

"Finally, I was able to get my father interested in some hunting trips. We traveled to the bayou to hunt duck and geese and contracted with your grandpere Jack to guide us. That was how I met Gabrielle."

"I know," I said.

"You have to understand how dark and dreary my life seemed to me during those days. My handsome, charming brother's wonderful future had been violently ended, my mother had died, my wife couldn't have children, and my father was slipping away day by day.

"Suddenly . . . I'll never forget that moment . . . I turned while unloading our car by the dock, and I saw Gabrielle strolling along the bank of the canal. The breeze lifted her hair and made it float around her, hair as dark red as yours. She wore this angelic smile. My heart stopped and then my blood pounded so close to the surface, I felt my cheeks turn crimson.

"A rice bird lighted on her shoulder and when she extended her arm, it pranced down to her hand before flying off. I still hear that silver laugh of hers, that childlike, wonderful laugh that was carried in the breeze to my ears.

" 'Who is that?' I asked your grandfather.

" 'Just my daughter,' he said.

"Just his daughter? I thought, a goddess who seemed to emerge from the bayou. Just his daughter?

"I couldn't help myself, you see. I was never so smitten. Every chance I had to be with her, near her, speak to her, I took. And soon, she was doing the same thing—looking forward to being with me.

"I couldn't hide my feeling from my father, but he didn't stand in my way. In fact, I'm sure he was eager to make more trips to the bayou because of my growing relationship with Gabrielle. I didn't realize then why he was encouraging it. I should have known something when he didn't appear upset the day I told him she was pregnant with my child."

"He went behind your back and made a deal with Grandpere Jack," I said.

"Yes. I didn't want such a thing to happen. I had already made plans to provide for Gabrielle and the child, and she was happy about it, but my father was obsessed with this idea, crazed by it."

He took a deep breath before continuing.

"He even went so far as to tell Daphne everything."

"What did you do?" I asked.

"I didn't deny it. I confessed everything."

"Was she terribly upset?"

"She was upset, but Daphne is a woman of character; she's as they say, a very classy dame," he added with a smile. "She told me she wanted to bring up my child as her own, do what my father had asked. He had made her some promises, you see. But there was still Gabrielle to deal with, her feelings and desires to consider. I told Daphne what Gabrielle wanted and that despite the deal my father was making with your grandfather, Gabrielle would object."

"Grandmere Catherine told me how upset my mother was, but I never could understand why she let Grandpere Jack do it, why she gave up Gisselle."

"It wasn't Grandpere Jack who got her to go along. In the end," he said, "it was Daphne." He paused and turned to me. "I can see from the expression on your face that you didn't know that."

"No," I said.

"Perhaps your grandmere Catherine didn't know either. Well, enough about all that. You know the rest anyway," he said quickly. "Would you like to walk through the French Quarter? There's Bourbon Street just ahead of us," he added, nodding.

"Yes."

We got out and he took my hand to stroll down to the corner. Almost as soon as we made the turn, we heard the sounds of music coming from the various clubs, bars, and restaurants, even this early in the day.

"The French Quarter is really the heart of the city," my father explained. "It never stops beating. It's not really French, you know. It's more Spanish. There were two disastrous fires here, one in 1788 and one in 1794, which destroyed most of the original French structures," he told me. I saw how much he loved talking about New Orleans and I wondered if I would ever come to admire this city as much as he did.

We walked on, past the scrolled colonnades and iron gates of the courtyards. I heard laughter above us and looked up to see men and women leaning over the embroidered iron patios outside their apartments, some calling down to people in the street. In an arched doorway, a black man played a guitar. He seemed to be playing for himself and not even notice the people who stopped by for a moment to listen.

"There is a great deal of history here," my father explained, pointing. "Jean Lafitte, the famous pirate, and his brother Pierre operated a clearinghouse for their contraband right there. Many a swashbuckling adventurer discussed launching an elaborate campaign in these courtyards."

I tried to take in everything: the restaurants, the coffee stalls, the souvenir shops, and antique stores. We walked until we reached Jackson Square and the St. Louis Cathedral.

"This is where early New Orleans welcomed heroes and had public meetings and celebrations," my father said. We paused to look at the bronze statue of Andrew Jackson on his horse before we entered the cathedral. I lit a candle for Grandmere Catherine and said a prayer. Then we left and strolled through the square, around the perimeter where artists sold their fresh works.

"Let's stop and have a cafe au lait and some beignets," my father said. I loved beignets, a donutlike pastry covered with powdered sugar.

While we ate and drank, we watched some of the artists sketching portraits of tourists.

"Do you know an art gallery called Dominique's?" I asked.

"Dominique's? Yes. It's not far from here, just a block or two over to the right. Why do you ask?"

"I have some of my paintings on display there," I said.

"What?" My father sat back, his mouth agape. "Your paintings on display?"

"Yes. One was sold. That's how I got my traveling money."

"I can't believe you," he said. "You're an artist and you've said nothing?"

I told him about my paintings and how Dominique had stopped by one day and had seen my work at Grandmere Catherine's and my roadside stall.

"We must go there immediately," he said. "I've never seen such modesty. Gisselle has something to learn from you."

Even I was overwhelmed when we arrived at the gallery. My picture of the heron rising out of the water was prominently on display in the front window. Dominique wasn't there. A pretty young lady was in charge and when my father explained who I was, she became very excited.

"How much is the picture in the window?" he asked.

"Five hundred and fifty dollars, monsieur," she told him.

Five hundred and fifty dollars! I thought. For something I had done? Without hesitation, he took out his wallet and plucked out the money.

"It's a wonderful picture," he declared, holding it out at arm's length. "But you've got to change the signature to Ruby Dumas. I want my family to claim your talent," he added, smiling. I wondered if he somehow sensed that this was a picture depicting what Grandmere Catherine told me was my mother's favorite swamp bird.

After it was wrapped, my father hurried me out excitedly. "Wait until Daphne sees this. You must continue with your artwork. I'll get you all the materials and we'll set up a room in the house to serve as your studio. I'll find you the best teacher in New Orleans for private lessons, too," he added. Overwhelmed, I could only trot along, my heart racing with excitement.

We put my picture into the car.

"I want to show you some of the museums, ride past one or two of our famous cemeteries, and then take you to lunch at my favorite restaurant on the dock. After all," he added with a laugh, "this is the deluxe tour."

It was a wonderful trip. We laughed a great deal and the restaurant he'd picked was wonderful. It had a glass dome so we could sit and watch the steamboats and barges arriving and going up the Mississippi.

While we ate, he asked me questions about my life in the bayou. I told him about the handicrafts and linens Grandmere Catherine and I used to make and sell. He asked me questions about school and then he asked me if I had ever had a boyfriend. I started to tell him about Paul and then stopped, for not only did it sadden me to talk about him, but I was ashamed to describe another terrible thing that had happened to my mother and another terrible thing Grandpere Jack had done because of it. My father sensed my sadness.

"I'm sure you'll have many more boyfriends," he said. "Once Gisselle introduces you to everyone at school."

"School?" I had forgotten about that for the moment.

"Of course. You've got to be registered in school first thing this week."

A shivering thought came. Were all the girls at this school like Gisselle? What would be expected of me?

"Now, now," my father said, patting my hand. "Don't get yourself nervous about it. I'm sure it will be fine. Well," he said, looking at his watch, "the ladies must all have risen by now. Let's head back. After all, I still have to explain you to Gisselle," he added.

He made it sound so simple, but as Grandmere Catherine would say, "Weaving a single fabric of falsehoods is more difficult than weaving a whole wardrobe of truth."

Daphne was sitting at an umbrella table on a cushioned iron chair on a patio in the garden where she had been served her late breakfast. Although she was still in her light blue silk robe and slippers, her face was made up and her hair was neatly brushed. It looked honey-colored in the shade. She looked like she belonged on the cover of the copy of *Vogue* she was reading. She put it down and turned as my father and I came out to greet her. He kissed her on the cheek.

"Should I say good morning or good afternoon?" he asked.

"For you two, it looks like it's definitely afternoon," she replied, her eyes on me. "Did you have a good time?"

"A wonderful time," I declared.

"That's nice. I see you bought a new painting, Pierre."

"Not just a new painting, Daphne, a new Ruby Dumas," he said, and gave me a wide, conspiratorial smile. Daphne's eyebrows rose.

"Pardon?"

My father unwrapped the picture and held it up.

"Isn't it pretty?" he asked.

"Yes," she said in a noncommittal tone of voice. "But I still don't understand."

"You won't believe this, Daphne," he began, quickly sitting down across from her. He told her my story. As he related the tale, she gazed from him to me.

"That's quite remarkable," she said after he concluded.

"And you can see from the work and from the way she has been received at the gallery that she has a great deal of artistic talent, talent that must be developed."

"Yes," Daphne said, still sounding very controlled. My father didn't appear disappointed by her measured reaction, however. He seemed used to it. He went on to tell her the other things we had done. She sipped her coffee from a beautifully hand painted china cup and listened, her light blue eyes darkening more and more as his voice rose and fell with excitement.

"Really, Pierre," she said, "I haven't seen you this exuberant about anything for years."

"Well, I have good reason to be," he replied.

"I hate to be the one to insert a dark thought, but you realize you haven't spoken to Gisselle yet and told her your story about Ruby," she said.

He seemed to deflate pounds of excitement right before my eyes and then he nodded.

"You're right as always, my dear. It's time to wake the princess and talk to her," he said. He rose and picked up my picture. "Now where should we hang this? In the living room?"

"I think it would be better in your office, Pierre," Daphne said. To me it sounded as though she wanted it where it would be seen the least.

"Yes. Good idea. That way I can get to look at it more," he replied. "Well, here I go. Wish me luck," he said, smiling at me, and then he went into the house to talk to Gisselle. Daphne and I gazed at each other for a moment. Then she put down her coffee cup.

"Well now, you've made quite a beginning with your father, it seems," she said.

"He's very nice," I told her. She stared at me a moment.

"He hasn't been this happy for a while. I should tell you, since you have become an instant member of the family, that Pierre, your father, suffers from periods of melancholia. Do you know what that is?" I shook my head. "He falls into deep depressions from time to time. Without warning," she added.

"Depressions?"

"Yes. He can lock himself away for hours, days even, and not want to see or speak to anyone. You can be speaking to him and suddenly, he'll take on a far-off look and leave you in midsentence. Later, he won't remember doing it," she said. I shook my head. It seemed incredible that this man with whom I had just spent several happy hours could be described as she had described him.

"Sometimes, he'll lock himself in his office and play this dreadfully mournful music. I've had doctors prescribe medications, but he doesn't like taking anything.

"His mother was like that," she continued. "The Dumas family history is clouded with unhappy events."

"I know. He told me about his younger brother," I said. She looked up sharply.

"He told you already? That's what I mean," she said, shaking her head. "He can't wait to go into these dreadful things and depress everyone."

"He didn't depress me although it was a very sad story," I said. Her lips tightened and her eyes narrowed. She didn't like being contradicted.

"I suppose he described it as a boating accident," she said.

"Yes. Wasn't it?"

"I don't want to go into it all now. It *does* depress me," she added, eyes wide. "Anyway, I've tried and I continue to try to do everything in my power to make Pierre happy. The most important thing to remember if you're going to live here is that we must have harmony in our house. Petty arguments, little intrigues and plots, jealousies and betrayals have no place in the House of Dumas.

"Pierre is so happy about your existence and arrival that he is blind to the problems we are about to face," she continued. When she spoke, she spoke with such a firm, regal tone, I couldn't do anything but listen, my eyes fixed on her. "He doesn't understand the immensity of the task ahead. I know how different a world you come from and the sort of things you're used to doing and having."

"What sort of things, madame?" I asked, curious myself.

"Just things," she said firmly, her eyes sharp. "It's not a topic ladies like to discuss."

"I don't want or do anything like that," I protested.

"You don't even realize what you've done, what sort of life you've led up until now. I know Cajuns have a different sense of morality, different codes of behavior."

"That's not so, madame," I replied, but she continued as though I hadn't.

"You won't realize it until you've been . . . been educated and trained and enlightened," she declared.

"Since your arrival is so important to Pierre, I will do my best to teach you and guide you, of course; but I will need your full cooperation and obedience. If you have any problems, and I'm sure you will in the beginning, please come directly to me with them. Don't trouble Pierre.

"All I need," she added, more to herself than to me, "is for something else to depress him. He might just end up like his younger brother."

"I don't understand," I said.

"It's not important just now," she said quickly. Then she pulled back her shoulders and stood up.

"I'm going to get dressed and then I'll take you shopping," she said. "Please be where I can find you in twenty minutes."

"Yes, madame."

"I hope," she said, pausing near me to brush some strands of hair off my forehead, "that in time you will become comfortable addressing me as Mother."

"I hope so, too," I said. I didn't mean it to sound the way it did— almost a threat. She pulled herself back a bit and narrowed her eyes before she flashed a small, tight smile and then left to get ready to take me shopping.

While I waited for her, I continued my tour of the house, stopping to look in on what was my father's office. He had placed my picture against his desk before going up to Gisselle. There was another picture of his father, my grandfather, I supposed, on the wall above and behind his desk chair. In this picture, he looked less severe, although he was dressed formally and was gazing thoughtfully, not even the slightest smile around his lips or eyes.

My father had a walnut writing desk, French cabinets, and ladder-back chairs. There were bookcases on both sides of the office, the floor of which was polished hardwood with a small, tightly knit beige oval rug under the desk and chair. In the far left corner there was a globe. Everything on the desk and in the room was neatly organized and seemingly dust free. It was as if the inhabitants of this house tiptoed about with gloved hands. All the furniture, the immaculate floors and walls, the fixtures and shelves, the antiques and statues made me feel like a bull in a china shop. I was afraid to move quickly, turn abruptly, and especially afraid to touch anything, but I entered the office to glance at the pictures on the desk.

In sterling silver frames, my father had pictures of Daphne and Gisselle. There was a picture of two people I assumed to be his parents, my grandparents. My grandmother, Mrs. Dumas, looked like a small woman, pretty with diminutive features, but an overall sadness in her lips and eyes. Where, I wondered, was there a picture of my father's younger brother, Jean?

I left the office and found there was a separate study, a library with red leather sofas and high back chairs, gold leaf tables, and brass lamps. A curio case in the study was filled with valuable looking red, green, and purple hand blown goblets, and the walls, as were the walls in all the rooms, were covered with oil paintings. I went in and browsed through some of the books on the shelves.

"Here you are," I heard my father say, and I turned to see him and

Gisselle standing in the doorway. Gisselle was in a pink silk robe and the softest looking pink slippers. Her hair had been hastily brushed and looked it. Pale and sleepy eyed, she stood with her arms folded under her breasts. "We were looking for you."

"I was just exploring. I hope it's all right," I said.

"Of course it's all right. This is your home. Go where you like. Well now, Gisselle understands what's happened and wants to greet you as if for the first time," he said, and smiled. I looked at Gisselle who sighed and stepped forward.

"I'm sorry for the way I behaved," she began. "I didn't know the story. No one ever told me anything like this before," she added, shifting her eyes toward our father, who looked sufficiently apologetic. "Anyway, this changes things a lot. Now that I know you really are my sister and you've gone through a terrible time."

"I'm glad," I said. "And you don't have to apologize for anything. I can understand why you'd be upset at me suddenly appearing on your doorstep."

She seemed pleased, flashed a look at Father and then turned back to me.

"I want to welcome you to our family. I'm looking forward to getting to know you," she added. It had the resonance of something memorized, but I was happy to hear the words nevertheless. "And don't worry about school. Daddy told me you were concerned, but you don't have to be. No one is going to give my sister a hard time," she declared.

"Gisselle is the class bully," our father said, and smiled.

"I'm not a bully, but I'm not going to let those namby-pambies push us around," she swore. "Anyway, you can come into my room later and talk. We should really get to know each other."

"I'd like that."

"Maybe you want to go along with Ruby and Daphne to shop for Ruby's new wardrobe," our father suggested.

"I can't. Beau's coming over." She flashed a smile at me. "I mean, I'd call him and cancel, but he so looks forward to seeing me, and besides, by the time I get ready, you and Mother could be half finished. Come out to the pool as soon as you get back," she said.

"I will."

"Don't let Mother buy those horribly long skirts, the ones that go all the way down to your ankles. Everyone's wearing shorter skirts these days," she advised, but I couldn't imagine telling Daphne what or what not to buy me. I was grateful for anything. I nodded, but Gisselle saw my hesitation.

"Don't worry about it," Gisselle said. "If you don't get things that are in style, I'll let you borrow something for your first day at school."

"That's very nice," our father said. "Thanks for being so understanding, honey."

"You're welcome, Daddy," she said, and kissed him on the cheek. He beamed and then rubbed his hands together.

"I have a set of twins!" he cried. "Both grown and beautiful. What man could be luckier!"

I hoped he was right. Gisselle excused herself to go up and get dressed and I walked out to the front of the house with my father to wait for Daphne.

"I'm sure you and Gisselle will get along marvelously," he said, "but there's bound to be a few hills and valleys in any relationship, especially an instant sister relationship. If you have any real problems, come see me. Don't bother Daphne about it," he said. "She's been a wonderful mother for Gisselle, despite the unusual circumstances, and I'm sure she will be wonderful for you, too; but I feel I should bear most of the responsibilities. I'm sure you understand. You seem very mature, more mature than Gisselle," he added, smiling.

What a strange predicament, I thought. Daphne wanted me to come to her and he wanted me to come to him, and each appeared to have good reason. Hopefully, I wouldn't have to trouble either.

I heard Daphne's footsteps on the stairway and gazed up. She wore a flowing black skirt, a white velvet blouse, low black heels and a string of real pearls. Her blue eyes glistened and her smile spread to show even white teeth. She carried herself so elegantly.

"There are few things I like to do better than shop," she declared. She kissed my father on the cheek.

"Nothing makes me happier than seeing you and Gisselle happy, Daphne," he told her. "And now, I can add Ruby."

"Go to work, darling. Earn money. I'm going to show your new daughter how to spend it," she retorted.

"And you won't find a better teacher when it comes to that," he quipped. He opened the door for us and we went out.

I still felt this was all too good to be true and that any moment I would wake up in my little room in the bayou. I pinched myself and was happy to feel the tiny sting that assured me it was all real.

13

⟩⟩—⟨⟨

I Can't Be You

I felt as if I were caught in a whirlwind because of the way my new stepmother went about taking me shopping. As soon as we were finished in one boutique, Daphne whisked me out the door to go to another or to a department store. Whenever she decided something looked nice on me or looked appropriate, she ordered it packed immediately, sometimes buying two, three, and four of the same blouse, the same skirt, even the same pair of shoes, but in different colors. The trunk and the backseat of the car quickly filled up. Each purchase took my breath away and she didn't seem at all concerned about the prices.

Everywhere we went, the salespeople appeared to know Daphne and respect her. We were treated like royalty, some clerks throwing aside anything they were doing the instant Daphne and I marched into their stores. Most assumed I was Gisselle and Daphne did not bother to explain.

"It's not important what these people do and don't know," she told me when a saleslady called me Gisselle. "When they call you Gisselle, just go along for now. The people who matter will be told everything quickly."

Although Daphne didn't have much respect for the salespeople, I noticed how careful they were when they made suggestions, and how concerned they were that Daphne might not approve. As soon as

Daphne settled on a color or a style, all of them nodded and agreed immediately, complimenting her in chorus on the choices she had made for me.

She did seem very informed. She knew the latest styles, the designers by name, and the garments that had been featured in fashion magazines, knowing things about clothes that even the salespeople and store owners didn't know yet themselves. Being chic and up-to-date was obviously a high priority for my stepmother, who became upset if the salesperson brought colors that didn't coordinate perfectly or if a sleeve or hem was wrongly cut. Most of the time between stores and traveling in the car, she lectured to me about style, the importance of appearance, and being sure everything I wore matched and coordinated.

"Every time you go out of the house and into society, you make a statement about yourself," she warned, "and that statement reflects on your family.

"I know that living in the bayou you were used to plain clothes, to practical clothes. Being feminine wasn't as important. Some of the Cajun women I've seen who work side by side with their men are barely distinguishable from them. If it weren't for their bosoms—"

"That's not so, Daphne," I said. "Women in the bayou can dress very pretty when they go to the dances and the parties. They may not have rich jewels, but they love beautiful clothes, too, even though they don't have these expensive stores. But they don't need them," I said, my Cajun pride unfurling like a flag. "My grandmere Catherine made many a gorgeous dress and—"

"You've got to stop doing that, Ruby, and especially remember not to do it in front of Gisselle," she snapped. A small flutter of panic stirred in my chest.

"Stop doing what?"

"Talking about your grandmere Catherine as if she were some wonderful person," she explained.

"But she was!"

"Not according to what we've told Gisselle and what we are telling our friends and society. As far as everyone is to know, this old lady, Catherine, knew you were kidnapped and sold to her family. It's nice that she had remorse on her deathbed and told you the truth so you could return to your real family, but it would be better if you didn't show how much you loved her," she proclaimed.

"Not show how much I loved Grandmere? But—"

"You would only make us look like fools, especially your father," she said. She smiled. "If you can't say anything bad, don't say anything at all."

I sat back. This was too much of a price to pay, even though I knew Grandmere Catherine would tell me to do it. I bit down on my lower lip to keep from voicing any more protest.

"Lies are not deadly sins, you know," she continued. "Everyone tells little lies, Ruby. I'm sure you've done it before."

Little lies? Is that what she considered this story and all the stories that had to follow as a result? Little lies?

"We all have our illusions, our fantasies," she said, and threw me a quick glance of devilment. "Men, especially, expect it," she added.

What kind of men was she talking about? I wondered. Men who expected their women to lie, to fantasize? Could men be that different in the city world from what they were in the bayou?

"That's why we dress up and make up our faces to please them. Which reminds me, you have nothing for your vanity table," she said, and decided to take me to her cosmetic store next and buy me whatever she decided was appropriate for a teenager. When I explained I had never worn any makeup, even lipstick, she asked the saleswoman to give me a demonstration, finally revealing to someone that I wasn't Gisselle. Daphne abbreviated the story, relating it as if it were nothing extraordinary. Nevertheless, the tale flew through the large store and everyone fluttered about us. They sat me before a mirror and showed me how to use the rouge, matched up shades of lipstick to my complexion, and taught me how to pluck my eyebrows.

"Gisselle sneaks on eyeliner," Daphne said. "But I don't think that's necessary."

We went through perfumes next, Daphne actually letting me make the final decision this time. I favored one that reminded me of the scent of the fields in the bayou after a summer rain; although I didn't tell Daphne that was the reason. She approved, bought me some talcum powders, some bubble bath, and fragrant shampoo, besides new hairbrushes and combs, bobby pins, ribbons, nail polish, and files. Then she bought a smart, red leather case for me to put all my toiletries in.

After that, she decided we must get my spring and summer coats, a raincoat, and some hats. I had to model a dozen of each in two different stores before she decided which suited me best. I wondered if she put Gisselle through all this every time she took her shopping. She appeared to anticipate my question when she saw me grimace after she had turned down six coats in a row.

"I'm trying to get you things that are similar but yet distinct enough to draw some differences between you and your twin. Of course, it would be nice for you to have some matching outfits, but I don't think Gisselle would approve."

So Gisselle had some say when it came to her own wardrobe, I concluded. How long would it be before I did, too?

I never thought shopping, especially a shopping spree like this in which everything purchased was purchased for me, would be exhausting; but when we left the last department store in which Daphne had bought me dozens of pairs of undergarments, slips, and a few bras, I was happy to hear her say we were finished for now.

"I'll pick up other things for you from time to time when I go shopping for myself," she promised. I looked back at the pile in the rear of the automobile. It was so high and so thick it was impossible to see through the back window. I couldn't imagine what the total cost had been, but I was sure it was an amount that would be staggering to Grandmere Catherine. Daphne caught me shaking my head.

"I hope you're happy with it all," she said.

"Oh, yes," I said. "I feel like . . . like a princess."

She raised her eyebrows and looked at me with a small, tight smile.

"Well, you are your daddy's little princess, Ruby. You had better get used to being spoiled. Many men, especially rich Creole men, find it easier and more convenient to buy the love of the women around them, and many Creole women, especially women like me, make it easy for them to do so," she said smugly.

"But it's not really love if someone pays for it, is it?" I asked.

"Of course it is," she replied. "What do you think love is . . . bells ringing, music in the breeze, a handsome, gallant man sweeping you off your feet with poetic promises he can't possibly keep? I thought you Cajuns were more practical minded," she said with that same tight smile. I felt my face turn red, both from anger and embarrassment. Whenever she had something negative to say, I was a Cajun, but whenever she had something nice to say, I was a Creole blue blood, and she made Cajuns sound like such clods, especially the women.

"Up until now, I bet you've only had poor boyfriends. The most expensive gift they could probably give you was a pound of shrimp. But the boys who will be coming around now will be driving expensive automobiles, wearing expensive clothing, and casually be giving you presents that will make your Cajun eyes bulge," she said, and laughed.

"Look at the rings on my hand!" she exclaimed, lifting her right hand off the steering wheel. Every finger had a ring on it. There seemed to be one for every valuable jewel: diamonds, emeralds, rubies, and sapphires all set in gold and platinum. Her hand looked like a display in a jewelry shop window.

"Why I bet the amount of money I have on this hand would buy the houses and food for a year for ten swamp families."

"They would," I admitted. I wanted to add and that seems unfair, but I didn't.

"Your father wants to buy you some nice bracelets and rings himself, and he noted that you have no watch. With beautiful jewelry, nice clothes, and a little makeup, you will at least look like you've been a Dumas for your whole life. The next thing I'll do is take you through some simple rules of etiquette, show you the proper way to dine and speak."

"What's wrong with how I eat and talk?" I wondered aloud. My father hadn't appeared upset at breakfast or lunch.

"Nothing, if you lived the rest of your life in the swamps, but you're in New Orleans now and part of high society. There will be dinner parties and gala affairs. You want to become a refined, educated, and attractive young woman, don't you?" she asked.

I couldn't help wanting to be like her. She was so elegant and carried herself with such an air of confidence, and yet, every time I agreed to something she said or did something she wanted me to do, it was as if I were looking down upon the Cajun people, treating them as if they were less important and not as good.

I decided I would do what I had to do to make my father happy and blend into his world, but I wouldn't harbor any feelings of superiority, if I could help it. I was only afraid I would become more like Gisselle than, as my father wished, Gisselle would become more like me.

"You do want to be a Dumas, don't you?" she pursued.

"Yes," I said, but not with much conviction. My hesitation gave her reason to glance at me again, those blue eyes darkening with suspicion.

"I do hope you will make every effort to answer the call of your Creole blood, your real heritage, and quickly block out and forget the Cajun world you were unfairly left to live in. Just think," she said, a little lightness in her voice now, "it was just chance Gisselle was the one given the better life. If you would have emerged first from your mother's womb, Gisselle would have been the poor Cajun girl."

The idea made her laugh.

"I must tell her that she could have been the one kidnapped and forced to live in the swamps," she added. "Just to see the look on her face."

The thought brought a broad smile to hers. How was I to tell her that despite the hardships Grandmere Catherine and I endured and despite the mean things Grandpere Jack had done, my Cajun world had its charm, too?

Apparently, if it wasn't something she could buy in a store, it wasn't significant to her, and despite what she told me, love was something you couldn't buy in a store. In my heart I knew that to be true, and that was one Cajun belief she would never change, elegant, rich life at stake or not.

When we drove up to the house, she called Edgar out to take all the packages up to my room. I wanted to help him, but Daphne snapped at me as soon as I made the suggestion.

"Help him?" she said as if I had proposed burning down the house. "You don't help him. He helps you. That's what servants are for, my dear child. I'll see to it that Wendy hangs everything up that has to be hung up in your closet and puts everything else in your armoire and vanity table. You run along and find your sister and do whatever it is girls your age do on your days off from school."

Having servants do the simplest things for me was one of the hardest things for me to get used to, I thought. Wouldn't it make me lazy? But no one seemed concerned about being lazy here. It was expected of you, almost required.

I remembered that Gisselle said she would be out at the pool, lounging with Beau Andreas. They were there, lying on thick cushioned beige metal framed lounges and sipping from tall glasses of pink lemonade. Beau sat up as soon as he set eyes on me and beamed a warm smile. He was wearing a white and blue terry cloth jacket and shorts and Gisselle was in a two-piece dark blue bathing suit, her sunglasses almost big enough to be called a mask.

"Hi," Beau said immediately. Gisselle looked up, lowering and peering over her sunglasses as if they were reading glasses.

"Did Mother leave anything in the stores for anyone else?" she asked.

"Barely," I said. "I've never been to so many big department stores and seen so much clothing and shoes." Beau laughed at my enthusiasm.

"I'm sure she took you to Diana's and Rudolph Vite's and the Moulin Rouge, didn't she?" Gisselle said.

I shook my head.

"To tell you the truth, we went in and out of so many stores and so quickly, I don't remember the names of half of them," I said with a gasp. Beau laughed again and patted his lounge. He pulled his legs up, embracing them around the knees.

"Sit down. Take a load off," he suggested.

"Thanks." I sat down next to him and smelled the sweet scent of the coconut suntan lotion he and Gisselle had on their faces.

"Gisselle told me your story," he said. "It's fantastic. What were these Cajun people like? Did they turn you into their little slave or something?"

"Oh, no," I said, but quickly checked my enthusiasm. "I had my daily chores, of course."

"Chores," Gisselle moaned.

"I was taught handicrafts and helped make the things we sold at the roadside to the tourists, as well as helping with the cooking and the cleaning," I explained.

"You can cook?" Gisselle asked, peering over her glasses at me again.

"Gisselle couldn't boil water without burning it," Beau teased.

"Well, who cares? I don't intend to cook for anyone . . . ever," she said, pulling her eyeglasses off and flashing heat out of her eyes at him. He just smiled and turned back to me.

"I understand you're an artist, too," he said. "And you actually have paintings in a gallery here in the French Quarter."

"I was more surprised than anyone that a gallery owner wanted to sell them," I told him. His smile warmed, the gray-blue in his eyes becoming softer.

"So far my father is the only one who bought one, right?" Gisselle quipped.

"No. Someone else bought one first. That's how I got the money for my bus trip here," I said. Gisselle seemed disappointed, and when Beau gazed at her, she put her glasses on and dropped herself back on the lounge.

"Where is the picture your father bought?" Beau asked. "I'd love to see it."

"It's in his office."

"Still on the floor," Gisselle interjected. "He'll probably leave it there for months."

"I'd still like to see it," Beau said.

"So go see it," Gisselle said. "It's only a picture of a bird."

"Heron," I said. "In the marsh."

"I've been to the bayou a few times to fish. It can be quite beautiful there," Beau said.

"Swamps, ugh," Gisselle moaned.

"It's very pretty there, especially in the spring and the fall."

"Alligators and snakes and mosquitos, not to mention mud everywhere and on everything. Very beautiful," Gisselle said.

"Don't mind her. She doesn't even like going in my sailboat on Lake Pontchartrain because the water sprays up and gets her hair wet, and she won't go to the beach because she can't stand sand in her bathing suit and in her hair."

"So? Why should I put up with all that when I can swim here in a clean, filtered pool?" Gisselle proclaimed.

"Don't you just like going places and seeing new things?" I asked.

"Not unless she can strap her vanity table to her back," Beau said. Gisselle sat up so quickly it was as if she had a spring in her back.

"Oh, sure, Beau Andreas, suddenly you're a big naturalist, a fisherman, a sailor, a hiker. You hate doing most of those things almost as much as I do, but you're just putting on an act for my sister," she charged. Beau turned crimson.

"I do too like to fish and sail," he protested.

"When do you do it, twice a year at the most?"

"Depends," he said.

"On what, your social calendar or your hair appointment," Gisselle said sharply. Throughout the exchange, my gaze went from one to the other. Gisselle's eyes blazed with so much anger, it was hard to believe she thought of him as her boyfriend.

"You know he has a woman cut his hair at his house," Gisselle continued. The crimson tint in Beau's cheeks rushed down into his neck. "She's his mother's beautician and she even gives him a manicure every two weeks."

"It's just that my mother likes the way she does her hair," Beau said. "I . . ."

"Your hair is very nice," I said. "I don't think it's unusual for a woman to cut a man's hair. I used to cut my grandpere's hair once in a while. I mean, the man I called Grandpere."

"You can cut hair, too?" Beau asked, his eyes wide with amazement.

"Do you fish and hunt as well?" Gisselle inquired, not disguising her sarcasm.

"I've fished, helped harvest oysters, but I've never hunted. I can't stand to see birds or deer shot. I even hate seeing the alligators shot," I said.

"Harvested oysters?" Gisselle said, shaking her head. "Meet my sister, the fish lady," she added.

"When did you first learn what had happened to you as a baby?" Beau asked.

"Just before my grandmere Catherine died," I replied.

"You mean the woman you thought was your grandmother," Gisselle reminded me.

"Yes. It's hard to think like that after so many years," I explained, more to Beau, who nodded with understanding.

"And did you have a mother and a father?"

"I was told my mother died when I was born and my father ran off."

"So you lived with these grandparents?"

"Just my grandmother. My grandfather is a trapper and lives in the swamp away from us."

"So just before she died, she told you the truth?" Beau asked. I nodded.

"How terrible of them to keep the secret all these years," Gisselle said. She gazed at me for a reaction.

"Yes."

"Lucky your fake grandmother decided to tell you or you would never have known your real family. That was nice of her," Beau said, which fired up Gisselle.

"These people she lived with are no better than animals, stealing someone's baby and keeping her! Claudine Montaigne told me about these Cajuns who live in a one-room house, everyone in the family sleeping with everyone else. To them incest is nothing more serious than stealing an apple!"

"That's not so," I said quickly.

"Claudine wouldn't lie," Gisselle insisted.

"There are bad people in the bayou just like there are bad people here," I said. "She might have heard of them, but she shouldn't judge everyone the same. Nothing like that ever happened to me."

"You were just lucky," Gisselle insisted.

"No, really . . ."

"They bought a kidnapped baby, didn't they?" she pursued. "Wasn't that terrible enough?"

I looked at Beau. His eyes were fixed intently on me, waiting for my response. What could I say? Put-away thoughts. The truth was forbidden. The lie had to be upheld.

"Yes," I muttered, and shifted my gaze down to my entwined fingers. Gisselle sat back, contented. There was a moment of silence before Beau spoke.

"You know, you two are going to be the center of attention at school next Monday," he said.

"I know. I can't help being nervous about it," I confessed.

"Don't worry. I'll pick the both of you up in the morning and escort you around all day," he promised. "You'll be a curiosity for a while and then things will settle down."

"I doubt it," Gisselle said. "Especially when everyone learns she's lived like a Cajun all of her life and cooked and fished and made little handicrafts to sell by the road."

"Don't listen to her."

"They'll make fun of her whenever I'm not around to protect her," Gisselle insisted.

"If you won't be around, I will," Beau declared.

"I don't want to be a burden for anyone," I said.

"You won't be," Beau assured me. "Right, Gisselle?" he asked. She was reluctant to answer. "Right?"

"Right, right, right," she said. "I'm tired of talking about this."

"I've got to go anyway," Beau said. "It's getting late. Are we still on for tonight?" he asked her. She hesitated. "Gisselle?"

"Are you bringing Martin?" she countered sharply. He threw a glance my way and then looked at her again.

"Are you sure I should? I mean . . ."

"I'm sure. You'd like to meet one of Beau's friends tonight, wouldn't you, Ruby? I mean, you've fished, harvested oysters, chased alligators . . . I'm sure you had a boyfriend, too, didn't you?"

I looked at Beau. His face had turned troubled and concerned.

"Yes," I said.

"So there's no problem, Beau. She'd like to meet Martin," Gisselle said.

"Who's Martin?" I asked.

"The best looking of Beau's friends. Most of the girls like him. I'm sure you will," she said. "Won't she, Beau?"

He shrugged and stood up.

"You'll like him," Gisselle insisted. "We'll meet you out here at nine-thirty," Gisselle said. "Don't be late."

"Right, boss. Ever see anyone that bossy in the bayou?" he asked me. I looked at Gisselle, who smirked.

"Just an alligator," I said, and Beau roared.

"That's not funny!" Gisselle cried.

"See ya later, alligator," Beau quipped, and winked at me before starting off.

"I'm sorry," I said to Gisselle. "I didn't mean to make fun of you or anything." She pouted for a moment and then broke a small smile.

"You shouldn't encourage him," she advised. "He can be a terrible tease."

"He seems very nice."

"Just another spoiled rich boy," Gisselle insisted. "But, he'll do . . . for now."

"What do you mean, 'for now'?"

"What do you think I mean? Don't tell me you promised to marry every boyfriend you had back in the swamp." Her eyes turned suspicious. "How many boyfriends did you have?" she asked.

"Not that many."

"How many?" she demanded. "If we're going to be sisters, we have to trust each other with the intimate details of our lives. Unless you don't want to be that kind of sister," she added.

"Oh, no. I do."

"So? How many?"

"Really only one," I confessed.

"One?" She stared at me a moment. "Well, it must have been a very hot and heavy romance then. Was it?"

"We cared a great deal for each other," I admitted.

"How much is a great deal?" she pursued.

"As much as we could, I suppose."

"Then you did it with him? Went all the way?"

"What?"

"You know . . . had sexual intercourse."

"Oh, no," I said. "We never went that far."

Gisselle tilted her head and looked skeptical.

"I thought all Cajun girls lost their virginity before they were thirteen," she said.

"What? Who told you such a stupid thing?" I asked quickly. She pulled back as if I had slapped her.

"It's not so stupid. I heard it from a number of people."

"Well, they're all liars then," I said vehemently. "I'll admit that there are many young marriages. Girls don't go off to work or go to college as much, but—"

"So it's true then. Anyway, don't keep defending them. They bought you when you were only a day or so old, didn't they?" Gisselle flared. I shifted my gaze away so she couldn't see the tears in my eyes. How ironic. It was she who had been bought and by a Creole family, not a Cajun. But I could say nothing. I could only swallow the truth and keep it down, only it kept threatening to bubble up and flow out of my mouth on the back of a flurry of hot words.

"Anyway," Gisselle continued in a calmer tone, "the boys will expect you to be a lot more sophisticated than you apparently are."

I looked at her fearfully.

"What do you mean?"

"What did you do with this one devoted boyfriend? Did you kiss and pet at least?" I nodded. "Did you undress, at least partially?" I shook my head. She grimaced. "Did you ever French kiss . . . you know," she added quickly, "touch tongues?" I couldn't remember if that had ever happened. My hesitation was enough to convince her it hadn't. "Did you let him give you hickeys?"

"No."

"Good. I hate them, too. They suck until they're satisfied and we're the ones who walk around with these ugly spots on our necks and breasts."

"Breasts?"

"Don't worry," she said, getting up. "I'll teach you what to do. For now, if Martin or anyone gets too demanding, just tell him you're having your period, understand? Nothing turns them off as fast as that.

"Come on," she said. "Let's go look at the things Mother bought you. I'll help you decide what to wear tonight."

I followed her back to the house, my footsteps on the patio a lot more unsure, my heart beating with a timid thump. Gisselle and I were so identical we could gaze at each other and think we were looking into mirrors, but on the inside, we were more different than a bird and a cat. I wondered what, if anything, we would find to draw us together so we could become the sisters we were meant to be.

Gisselle was surprised by many of the things Daphne had bought me. Then, after she gave it some thought, her surprise turned to jealousy and anger.

"She never buys me skirts this short unless I throw a tantrum, and these colors are always too bright for her. I love this blouse. It's not fair," she wailed. "Now I want new things, too."

"Daphne told me she wanted to buy things that were different from the things you had. She thought you wouldn't like it if we had identical clothes to go along with our identical faces," I explained.

Still pouting, Gisselle held one of my blouses against her and studied it in the mirror. Then she dropped it on the bed and opened the drawers of the armoire to inspect my new panties.

"When I bought a set of these, she thought they were too sexy," she said, holding up the abbreviated light silks.

"I've never worn anything like it," I confessed.

"Well, I'm borrowing this pair of panties, this skirt, and this blouse for tonight," she informed me firmly.

"I don't mind," I said, "but—"

"But what? Sisters share things with each other, don't they?"

I wanted to remind her of the nasty things she had said on the stairway in the morning when I came upon her returning from the ball, how she would never let me borrow her pretty red dress, but I realized that was before my father had had his conversation with her. It did bring about a change in her attitude toward me. Then I recalled something Daphne had said.

"Daphne disapproves of girls sharing things. Even sisters. She said so," I told her.

"You just let me worry about Mother. There are a lot of things she says and then goes and does the exact opposite," Gisselle replied as she went through the blouses to decide if there were any others she wanted to borrow.

And so for the first dinner we would have together as a family, Gisselle and I wore the same style skirt and blouse. She thought it would be amusing for us to brush and tie our hair into French knots as well. We dressed in my room and sat at my vanity table.

"Here," she said, taking a gold ring off her pinky and handing it to me. "You wear this tonight. I'll wear no jewelry, since you have none."

"Why?" I asked. I saw the impish glint in her eyes.

"Daddy wants you on his left, I imagine, and me, as usual on his right."

"So?"

"I'll sit on his left; you sit on his right. Let's see if he knows the difference," she said.

"Oh, he will. He knew I wasn't you the moment he set eyes on me," I told her.

Gisselle didn't know whether to take this as something good or bad. I saw the confusion in her face for a moment and then the decision.

"We'll see," she said. "I told Beau there were differences between us, differences maybe only I can see. I know what," she said, bouncing in her chair. "We'll tease Beau tonight. You'll pretend you're me and I'll pretend I'm you."

"Oh, I couldn't do that," I said, my heart fluttering with the thought of being Beau's girlfriend, even for a few minutes.

"Of course you can. He thought you were me the first time he set eyes on you, didn't he?"

"That was different. He didn't know I existed," I explained.

"I'll tell you exactly how to act and what to say," she continued, ignoring my point. "Oh, this is going to be fun for a change. I mean, real fun, with it all starting at dinner," she decided.

However, just as I predicted, our father knew instantly that we had taken the wrong seats at the dining room table. Daphne, who raised her eyebrows as soon as she saw the two of us in my new clothes, sat down, for the moment confused. But my father threw his head back and roared with laughter.

"What is so funny, Pierre?" Daphne demanded. She had come to dinner dressed formally in a black dress with diamond teardrop earrings and a matching diamond necklace and bracelet. The dress had a V-neck collar that dipped low enough to show the start of her cleavage. I thought she was so beautiful and elegant.

"Your daughters have dressed alike and conspired to test me at their first meal together," he said. "This is Ruby wearing Gisselle's pinky ring and this is Gisselle in Ruby's seat."

Daphne looked from me to Gisselle and then back to me.

"Ridiculous," she said. "Did you think we wouldn't know the difference? Take your proper seats, please," she commanded.

Gisselle laughed and got up. Father's eyes twinkled with delight at me, but then he turned serious, his expression sober when he gazed across the table at Daphne and saw she wasn't amused.

"I hope this is the beginning and the end of such shenanigans," Daphne declared. She directed herself to Gisselle. "I'm trying to teach your sister the proper way to behave at dinner and in the company of others. It's not going to be easy anyway. The last thing I need is for you to set a bad example, Gisselle."

"I'm sorry," she said, and looked down for a moment. Then her head snapped up. "How come you bought her all these short skirts and carried on so much when I wanted them last month?"

"It's what she liked," Daphne said.

I whipped my head around. What I liked? I never was given a chance to offer an opinion. Why did she say that?

"Well, I want some new clothes then, too," Gisselle moaned.

"You can get a few new things, but there's no reason to throw out your entire wardrobe."

Gisselle sat back and looked at me with a smile of satisfaction.

Our meal service began. We ate on a floral pattern set of porcelain china, which Daphne pointed out was nineteenth century. She made everything, down to the napkin holders, sound so expensive and precious, my fingers trembled when I went to lift my fork. I hesitated when I saw there were two. Daphne explained how I was to use the silverware and even how I should sit and hold it.

I didn't know whether or not the meal was something done especially for the occasion of our first dinner together, but it seemed overwhelming.

We began with an appetizer of crabmeat ravigote served in scallop shells. That was followed with grilled cornish game hens with roasted shallots and browned garlic sauce, and Creole green beans. For dessert we were served vanilla ice cream smothered in hot bourbon whiskey sauce.

I saw how Edgar stood just behind Daphne after he served each course, waiting for her to take her first taste and signal approval. I couldn't imagine anyone not being satisfied with anything on the table. My father asked me to describe some of the meals I had in the bayou and I described the gumbos and the jambalayas, the homemade cakes and pastries.

"It doesn't sound like they starved you," Gisselle remarked. I couldn't help sounding enthusiastic over the meals Grandmere Catherine used to make.

"Gumbo is nothing more than a stew," Daphne said. "The food is plain and simple. It doesn't take much imagination. You can see that yourself, can't you, Ruby?" she asked me firmly. I glanced at my father, who waited for my response.

"Nina Jackson is a wonderful cook. I never had such a meal," I admitted. That pleased Daphne and another little crisis seemed to pass. How hard it was for me to get used to belittling and criticizing my life with Grandmere, but I realized that was the currency I would need to pay for the life I now had.

The conversation at the table moved from my description of foods in the bayou to questions Daphne had for Gisselle about the Mardi Gras Ball. She described the costumes and the music, referring to people they all knew. She and Daphne seemed to share opinions about certain families and their sons and daughters. Tired of hearing the gossip, my father began to talk about my artwork.

"I've already inquired about an instructor. Madam Henreid over at the Gallier House has recommended someone to me, an instructor at Tulane who takes pupils on the side. I've already spoken with him and he's agreed to meet Ruby and consider her work," he said.

"How come I never got my singing instructor," Gisselle whined.

"You never really showed that much interest, Gisselle. Every time I asked you to go to the teacher, you had some excuse not to," he explained.

"Well, she should have been brought here," Gisselle insisted.

"She would have come," he said, looking to Daphne.

"Of course she would have come. Do you want your father to call her again?" she asked.

"No," Gisselle said. "It's too late."

"Why?" he asked.

"It just is," she said, pouting.

When dinner was over, my father decided he would show me the room he had in mind for my art studio. He winked at Daphne and had a tight smile on his lips. Reluctantly, Gisselle tagged along. He took us toward the rear of the house and when he threw open the door, there it was—a full art studio, already in place with easels, paints, brushes, clays, everything I would ever need or dreamt of having. For a moment I was speechless.

"I had this all done while you were out shopping with Daphne," he revealed. "Do you like it?"

"Like it? I love it!" I whirled around the room inspecting everything. There was even a pile of art books, going from the most elementary things to the most elaborate and complicated. "It's . . . wonderful!"

"I thought we should waste no time, not with a talent like yours. What do you think, Gisselle?" I turned to see her smirking in the doorway.

"I hate art class in school," she remarked. Then she focused a conspiratorial look on me and added, "I'm going up to my room. Come up as soon as you can. We have some things to prepare for later."

"Later?" my father asked.

"Just girl talk, Daddy," Gisselle said, and left. He shrugged and joined me at the shelves of supplies.

"I told Emile at the art store to give me everything we would need to have a complete studio," he said. "Are you pleased?"

"Oh, yes. There are things here, materials and supplies I have never seen, much less used."

"That's why we need the instructor as soon as possible, too. I think once he sees this studio, he'll be encouraged to take you on as one of his pupils. Not that he shouldn't by just looking at your painting anyway." He beamed his smile down at me.

"Thank you . . . Daddy," I said. His smile widened.

"I like hearing that," he said. "I hoped you felt welcomed."

"Oh, yes, I do. Overwhelmed."

"And happy?"

"Very happy," I said. I stood on my toes to plant a kiss on his cheek. His eyes brightened even more.

"Well," he said. "Well . . ." His eyes watered. "I guess I'll go see what Daphne is up to. Enjoy your studio and paint wonderful pictures here," he added, and walked off.

I stood there in awe of it all for a few moments. The room had a nice view of the sprawling oak trees and garden. It faced west so I could paint the sun on the final leg of its journey. Twilight was always magnificent for me in the bayou. I had high hopes that it would be just as magnificent here as well, for I believed that the things I carried in my heart and in my soul would be with me no matter where I was, where I lived, and what I looked at through my windows. My pictures were inside me, just waiting to be brought out.

After what I thought was only a short while later, I left the studio and hurried up to Gisselle's room. I knocked on the door.

"Well, it's about time," she said, pulling me in quickly and closing the door. "We don't have all that much time to plan. The boys will be here in twenty minutes."

"I don't think I can do this, Gisselle," I moaned.

"Of course you can," she said. "We'll be sitting around the table at the pool when they arrive. We'll have bottles of Coke and glasses for everyone, with ice. As soon as they approach, you introduce me to Martin. Just say I want you to meet my sister, Ruby. Then, you'll take this out from under the table and pour globs of it into the Coke," she said, and plucked a bottle of rum out of a straw basket. "Make sure you pour at least this much into every glass," she added, holding up her thumb and forefinger a good two inches apart. "Once Beau sees you do that, he'll be convinced you're me," she quipped.

"Then what?"

"Then . . . whatever happens, happens. What's the matter?" she snapped, pulling herself back. "Don't you want to pretend you're me?"

"It's not that I don't want to," I said.

"So? What is it?"

"I just don't think I can be you," I said.

"Why not?" she demanded, her eyes darkening and her eyelids narrowing into slits of anger.

"I don't know enough," I replied. That pleased her and she relaxed her shoulders.

"Just don't talk much. Drink and whenever Beau says something, nod and smile. I know I can be you," she added. And then in a voice that was supposed to be imitative, she said, "I just can't believe I'm here. The food is sooo good, the house is sooo big and I'm sleepin' in a real bed without mosquitos and mud."

She laughed. Was I really like that in her eyes?

"Stop being so serious," she demanded when I didn't laugh at her mockery of me. She dropped the bottle of rum into the basket. "Come on," she said, picking it up and seizing my hand. "Let's go tease some stuck-up Creole boys until they beg for mercy."

Trailing along like a kite on a string, I followed my sister out and down the stairs, my heart thumping, my mind in a turmoil. I had never had a day packed with so much excitement. I couldn't begin to imagine what the night would bring.

14

Someone's Crying

"We'll sit over there," Gisselle said, and pointed to lounges on the far end of the pool, near the cabana. It put us far enough away from the outside lights to keep us draped in soft shadows. It was a warm night, as warm as it would be on the bayou, only tonight without the cool breeze that would come up the canals from the Gulf. The sky was overcast; it even felt like it might rain.

Gisselle put the basket with the bottle of rum on the table and I put down the bucket of ice, the Coke, and the glasses. To bolster our courage for Gisselle's prank, she decided we should mix the rum in our Coke before the boys arrived. She did the pouring and it seemed to me she made each drink more rum than Coke. I tried to warn her about the effects of whiskey. After all, I knew about it from painful experiences.

"The man I called Grandpere is a drunk," I told her. "It's poisoned his brain."

I described the time I had poled our pirogue out to see him in the swamp and how he had gone berserk on his galerie. Then I described some of his ranting and raving in the house, how he wrecked things, dug up floorboards, and ended up sleeping in the muck and grime and not caring.

"I hardly think we'll become like that," Gisselle said. "Besides, you don't believe this is the first time I snuck some of our liquor, do you?

All of my friends do it and no one is as bad as that old man you described," she insisted.

When I hesitated to take the glass of rum and Coke from her, she put her fist on her hip and scowled.

"Don't tell me you're going to be an old stick-in-the-mud now and not have fun after I've invited the boys over, especially so you could have a boyfriend."

"I didn't say I wouldn't have some. I just—"

"Just have a drink and relax," she insisted. "Here!" she said, and shoved the drink at me. Reluctantly, I took the glass and sipped, while she took long gulps of hers. I couldn't help grimacing. To me it tasted like one of Grandmere Catherine's herbal medicines.

Gisselle stabbed me with a hard penetrating gaze and then shook her head.

"I guess you didn't have much fun living in the bayou. It sounds like all work and no play, which makes Jack a dull boy," she added, and laughed.

"Jack?"

"It's just an expression. Really," she cried, throwing her hand up dramatically, "you're just like someone from a foreign country. I feel like I've got to do what Mother wants to do: teach you how to talk and walk." She took another gulp of her drink. Even Grandpere didn't swig it down that fast, I thought. I wondered if she was as sophisticated as she was making out to be.

"Hi, there," we heard Beau call, and turned to see two silhouettes come around the corner of the house. My heart began to drum in anticipation.

"Just remember to do what I told you to do and say what I told you to say," Gisselle coached.

"It's not going to work," I insisted in a whisper.

"It better," she threatened.

The two boys stepped onto the pool deck and drew closer. I saw that Martin was a good-looking young man, about an inch or so taller than Beau, with jet black hair. He was leaner, longer-legged, and swaggered more when he walked. They were both dressed in jeans with white cotton shirts with buttoned-down collars. When they stepped into the dim pool of illumination cast by a lantern nearby, I noticed that Martin wore an expensive looking gold watch on his left wrist and a silver ID bracelet on the right. He had dark eyes and a smile that tucked the corner of his mouth into his cheek, creating more of a leer.

Gisselle nudged me with her elbow and then cleared her throat to urge me on.

"Hi," I said. My voice wanted to crack, but I felt Gisselle's hot, whiskey-scented breath on my neck, and I held myself together. "Martin, I'd like you to meet my sister, Ruby," I recited.

I couldn't see how anyone would think I was Gisselle, but Martin looked from me to Gisselle and then to me again with astonishment written on his face and not skepticism.

"Wow, you guys are really identical. I wouldn't know one from the other."

Gisselle laughed stupidly.

"Why, thank you, Martin," she said with a silly twang, "That's a real compliment."

I gazed at Beau and saw a wry smile cocking his lips. Surely, he knew what we were doing, I thought, and yet he said nothing.

"Beau told me your story," Martin said to Gisselle, believing she was me. "I've been to the bayou, even to Houma. I could have seen you."

"That would have been nice," Gisselle said. Martin's smile widened. "We don't have too many good-looking boys out there in the swamps."

Martin beamed.

"This is great," he said, looking from me to her again. "I always thought Beau was real lucky having a girlfriend as pretty as Gisselle, and now there's a second Gisselle."

"Oh, I'm not as pretty as my sister," Gisselle said, batting her eyelashes and twisting her shoulder.

Anger, fanned by the rum that heated my blood, made my heart pound. A terrible fury washed over me as I sat here watching her make fun of me. Unable to hold back, I flared.

"Of course you're as pretty as I am, Ruby. If anything, you're prettier," I countered.

Beau laughed. I shot a furious glance at him and he knitted his eyebrows together with a look of confusion. Then he relaxed, his gaze fixing on the glasses in our hands.

"Looks like the girls have been enjoying themselves some before we got here," he said, turning to Martin and wagging his head toward the straw basket, the ice bucket, and Coke.

"Oh, this," Gisselle said, holding up her glass. "Why this is nothin' compared to what we do in the bayou."

"Oh, yeah," Martin said with interest, "and what did you do in the bayou?"

"I don't want to do anything or say anything that might corrupt you city boys," she quipped. Martin smiled at Beau whose eyes were dancing with amusement.

"I can't think of anything I'd like better than to be corrupted by Gisselle's twin sister," Martin said. Gisselle laughed and extended her arm so Martin could sip from her glass. He sat down quickly and did so. I turned back to Beau. Our eyes met, but he didn't say anything to stop the charade from continuing.

"I'll just mix my own drink. If that's all right with you, Gisselle?" he asked me.

Gisselle fixed a stone stare at me before I could reveal my true identity.

"Of course it is, Beau," I said, and sat back against the lounge. How long did she want to keep this up? Martin turned to me.

"Are your parents going to have the police go to the bayou and get these people?" he asked.

"No," I said. "They're all dead and gone."

"But before they died, they tortured me," Gisselle moaned. Martin's head snapped around so he could face her again.

"What did they do?" he asked.

"Oh, things I can't describe. Especially to a boy," she added.

"They did not!" I cried. Gisselle widened her eyes and shot looks of rage at me.

"Really, Gisselle," she said in her most arrogant, haughty voice, "you don't think I told you everything that happened to me, do you? I wouldn't want to give you nightmares."

"Wow," Martin said. He looked up at Beau who still wore a smart, tight smile on his lips.

"Maybe you shouldn't ask your sister about her previous life," he said, sitting at my feet on the lounge. "You'll only bring up bad memories."

"That's right," Gisselle said. "I'd rather not have bad memories tonight anyway," she added, and ran her hand down Martin's left shoulder and arm. "You've never been with a Cajun girl then, Martin?" she asked coquettishly.

"No, but I've heard about them."

She leaned forward until her lips nearly touched his ear.

"It's all true," she said, and threw her head back to laugh. Martin laughed, too, and took a long gulp from Gisselle's drink, emptying the glass. "Gisselle, can you make us another drink?" she asked me in a voice that dripped with enough sweetness to make my stomach bubble.

It took all my self-control to battle back the urge to throw my own drink into her face and run into the house. But surely, this would end soon, I thought, and Gisselle would be satisfied she had had her little fun, all at my expense. I got up and started to make the drink the way she had instructed. Beau kept his eyes on me. I saw that Gisselle noticed how he was watching me, too.

"I just love that ring you gave my sister, Beau," Gisselle said. "Someday, I hope a handsome young man will think enough of me to give me a ring like that. I'd do just about anything for it," she added.

The bottle slipped out of my hand and hit the table, but didn't break. Beau jumped up.

"Here, let me help you," he said, quickly seizing the neck of the bottle before too much rum spilled.

"Oh, Gisselle, you shouldn't waste good rum like that," Gisselle cried, and laughed again. My hand was still trembling. Beau took it quickly into his and gazed into my eyes.

"You all right?" he asked. I nodded. "Let me finish making the drink," he said, and did so, handing it to Gisselle.

"Thank you, Beau," she said. He smirked at her, but said nothing. "I'm sorry I can't talk about myself, Martin," she said, turning back to him, "but I would love to hear about you."

"Sure," he said.

"Let's take a little walk," she suggested, and rose from the lounge. Martin looked at Beau who simply stared expressionless for a moment. Was he waiting to see how far Gisselle would go? Surely, he didn't believe she was me. Why wasn't he putting an end to it then?

She scooped her arm into Martin's and pulled him close to her, laughing at the same time. Then she fed him some of the rum and Coke like she was feeding a baby. He gulped and gulped, his Adam's apple bouncing with the effort until she pulled the glass from his lips and drank some herself.

"What strong arms you have, Martin," she said. "I thought only Cajun boys had arms like this." She flashed a smile back at me. "And Cajun girls," she added with a laugh. She turned him away and they walked deeper into the shadows, Gisselle's laughter louder and sillier.

"Well," Beau said, sitting on my lounge again. "Your sister has really made herself at home."

"Beau," I began, but he put his fingers on my lips.

"No, don't say anything. I know how hard this has all been for you, Gisselle." He leaned toward me.

"But . . ."

Before I could say anything, he pressed his lips to mine, softly at first and then harder as he wrapped his arm around me and brought me

into the nook between his shoulder and chest. He pressed the palm of
his other hand against the small of my back, lifting me slightly. His
kiss and embrace took my breath away. When our lips parted, I
gasped. He kissed the tip of my nose and then brought his cheek to
mine and whispered.

"You're right," he said. "We shouldn't wait any longer. I can't keep
my hands off you. I've thought of nothing else but touching you and
making love to you," he said, and slid the palm of his right hand over
my hip and up the side of my body until he reached my breast. He
pressed his body against me, driving me back on the lounge.

"Wait . . . Beau . . ."

His lips were over mine again, only this time, he performed the
French kiss Gisselle had described. The feel of his tongue on mine sent
a mixed chill of excitement and fear down my spine. I struggled,
wiggling under him, finally pulling my head back enough to free my
mouth from his.

"Stop," I gasped. "I'm not Gisselle. I'm Ruby. It was all a prank."

"What?"

I saw from the look in his eyes and the silly smile on his face that he
had known. Pressing my hands against his chest, I pushed him away.
He sat back, still pretending a look of amazement and shock.

"You're Ruby?"

"Stop it, Beau. You knew all the time. I know you did. I'm not the
kind of girl Gisselle is making me out to be. You shouldn't have done
that," I admonished. Chastised, he reddened and fired back.

"You played along with the ruse, didn't you?"

"I know and I shouldn't have let her talk me into doing it, but I
didn't think she would let it go this far."

Beau nodded, his body relaxing.

"That's my Gisselle . . . always plotting something outrageous. I
should pretend to be fooled even more," he said. "It would teach her a
lesson."

"What do you mean?" I looked off left and saw that Gisselle and
Martin were out by the gazebo. Beau followed my gaze and we saw
them kissing. His eyes narrowed and his chin tightened.

"Sometimes, she goes too far," he said, his voice now sounding
angry. "Come on," he said, grabbing my hand and standing.

"Where?" I stood up.

"Into the cabana," he said. "It will teach her a lesson."

"But . . ."

"It's all right. We'll just talk. Let her think otherwise though. It will
serve her right," he said and tugged me along. Then he opened the

cabana door and pulled me into the small room, slamming the door behind us so Gisselle and Martin would be sure to hear it. There was a cot against the far wall but neither of us moved from the door. Without any light, it was hard to see anything after the door had been closed.

"This will get to her," Beau said. "We've been in here before and she knows why."

"This is going too far, Beau. She'll hate me," I said.

"She's not exactly being nice to you right now anyway," he replied.

Talking like this in the pitch darkness was both strange and easy, easy because without seeing him, without feeling his eyes on me, I could relax and say what I wanted. I thought that might be true for him, too.

"I'm sorry I got angry at you before," I said. "It really isn't any of your fault. I shouldn't have let her talk me into this."

"You were at a disadvantage. Gisselle loves to take advantage of people whenever she can. It doesn't surprise me. But from now on, don't be anyone but yourself. I haven't known you very long, Ruby, but I think you're a very nice girl who's been through some terrible things and has managed to keep her good nature. Don't let Gisselle ruin it," he warned. A moment later, I felt his hand on my cheek. His touch was soft, but I shuddered with surprise.

"Anyway, you kiss better," he whispered. My heart began to thump again. His hand was on my shoulder and then, I felt his breath on my face and sensed his lips moving closer and closer until they found mine. I didn't resist this time, and when his tongue touched mine, I let my own tongue run over the tip of his. He moaned and then, we heard pounding on the door and parted quickly.

"Beau Andreas, you get yourself out here this minute, you hear. This minute," Gisselle cried. Beau laughed.

"Who is it?" he called through the closed door.

"You know very well who I am," she cried. "Now get out here."

Beau opened the door and Gisselle stepped back. A confused Martin stood beside her. She had her arms folded and she wobbled a bit.

"What do you two think you're doing?" she demanded.

"Ruby," he began, "your sister and I—"

"You know I'm not Ruby and she's not me. You know it, Beau Andreas."

"What?" he said, pretending shock and surprise. He looked at me and stepped back. "I could never have known. This is amazing."

"Just stop it, Beau. It was just a little joke. And you," she said, flicking her bloodshot eyes over me. "You played along real well for someone who said she was scared it wouldn't work."

"What is this?" Martin finally said. "Who's who?"

The three of us turned to him. Beau and Gisselle burst into laughter first and then, feeling lighthearted from the rum and Beau's kisses, I couldn't help but laugh myself.

Gisselle explained the prank to Martin and the four of us began again, this time Martin sitting next to me. Gisselle kept pouring the rum into the Cokes, drinking one almost as quickly as she made it. I drank only a little more, but my head was spinning anyway. Afterward, Gisselle pulled Beau into the cabana, gazing back at me with satisfaction as she closed the door behind them.

I sat back on the lounge, unable to clear my mind of Beau's warm touch and Beau's warm kiss. Was it the effect of the rum that filled me with such warmth?

Martin suddenly embraced me and kissed me and tried to go further, but I pushed him away firmly.

"Hey," he said, his eyes half closed, "what's wrong? I thought we were having fun."

"Despite what you might have heard or believed about girls who come from the bayou, Martin, I'm not like that. I'm sorry," I said.

The rum had definitely gotten to him and he mumbled some apology before falling back on the lounge. Moments later, he was asleep. I waited beside him, but we didn't have to wait long. Suddenly, Beau and Gisselle emerged from the cabana. She was crying about her stomach and heaving so hard, I thought she threw up her lunch as well as her supper. Martin woke up and he and I stood back and watched. She realized what was happening and sobbed with embarrassment.

"I'll take care of her," I told Beau. "You'd better leave."

"Thanks," he said. "This isn't the first time she's done this," he added, and whispered good night after he first whispered, "Yours was the kiss I'll remember tonight."

I was speechless for a moment, watching them walk off, and then Gisselle wailed.

"Oh, I'm going to die!"

"You won't die, but you'll sure wish you had if I remember the way Grandpere felt sometimes," I told her. She moaned again and heaved up some more.

"I've ruined this new blouse," she cried. "Oh, I feel horrible. My head is pounding."

"You'd better go to sleep, Gisselle," I said.

"I can't. I can't move."

"I'll help you into the house. Come on." I embraced her and started her forward.

"Don't let Mother catch us," she warned. "Wait," she said. "Take the bottle of rum in, too." I hated doing all these sneaky things, but I had no choice. With the bottle in the basket in one hand, I helped her up with the other and guided her back to the house, slipping as silently as we could through the door.

It was quiet within. We started up the stairs, Gisselle sniveling to herself. After we reached the landing and started toward her room, I thought I heard something else though. It sounded like someone weeping.

"What's that?" I asked in a whisper.

"What's what?"

"Someone's crying," I said.

"Just get me to my room and forget about it," she said. "Hurry."

We crossed to her door and I helped her in.

"You should take off your clothes and take a shower," I suggested, but she plopped down on her bed and refused to move.

"Leave me alone," she moaned. "Just leave me alone. Hide the bottle in your closet," were her last words.

I stood back and looked at her. She was a deadweight now. There wasn't anything I could do. I wasn't feeling all that well either and reprimanded myself for letting Gisselle talk me into so many rum and Cokes.

I left her lying facedown on her bed, fully dressed, even wearing her shoes, and started for my room. Once again, however, I heard sobbing. Curious, I crossed the hallway and listened. It was coming from a room down right. I walked softly over to the door and leaned my head against it. There was definitely someone within, crying. It sounded . . . like a man.

The click of footsteps on the stairway sent me scurrying back to my room. I went in quickly and immediately hid the basket with the rum in my closet. Then I went to the door and cracked it open enough to peer out. Daphne, dressed in a flowing blue silk robe, stepped so softly she seemed to glide down the hallway to the master bedroom. Just before she got there, however, she paused as though to listen for the sobbing herself. I saw her shake her head and then go into the bedroom. After she closed her door, I closed mine.

I thought about going out again and knocking on that door to see who was crying. Could it have been my father? Thinking it might have been, I went out and approached the door. I listened, but heard nothing this time. Even so, I knocked softly and waited.

"Anyone in there?" I whispered through the crack between the door and the jamb. There was no response. I knocked again and waited.

Still nothing. I was about to turn away when I felt a hand on my shoulder and spun around with a gasp to look into my father's face.

"Ruby," he said, smiling. "Anything wrong?"

"I . . . I thought I heard someone sobbing in this room so I knocked," I said. He shook his head.

"Just your imagination at work, honey," he said. "There hasn't been anyone in that room for years. Where's Gisselle?"

"She just went to sleep," I said quickly. "But I'm almost certain I heard someone," I insisted. He shook his head.

"No. You couldn't have." He smiled. "Gisselle went to bed this early? Must be your good habits are rubbing off already. Well, I'm heading for sleep myself. I've got a busy day tomorrow. Don't forget," he said, "your art instructor will be stopping by at two. I'll be here to meet him also."

I nodded.

"Good night, dear," he said, and kissed me on the forehead. Then he started for the master bedroom. I looked back at the closed door. Could I have imagined it? Was it something that happened because of all the rum I had drunk?

"Daddy?" I said before I crossed to go to my room. He stopped and turned.

"Yes?"

"Whose room was that?" I asked.

He looked at the room and then rolled his dark, shining eyes my way and I saw why they shone—they were full of tears.

"My brother's," he said. "Jean's."

With a sigh he turned and walked away. As if on the legs of a spider, a chill crept up my spine and made me shudder. Fatigued and drowning in many emotions, I returned to my room and got ready for bed. My mind was cluttered with so many different thoughts, my heart full of different feelings. I was so dizzy and tired, I was eager to lay my head upon the soft pillow. When I closed my eyes, a potpourri of the day's images rolled on the backs of my eyelids taking me up and down like a roller coaster. I saw the New Orleans sights I had seen with my father, the myriad of fashions I had waded through with Daphne, my wonderful new art studio, Gisselle's face as she plotted her silly prank and once again, I felt Beau's electrifying kiss when we were in the cabana.

That kiss had frightened me because I had been unable to stop myself from wanting to kiss him back. That unexpected touch of his lips, his tongue forcing my lips to open, shot through me with a jolt of excitement that tore down all my resistance. Did that mean I was bad, that I had too much of the evil Landry blood running through my veins?

Or was it just that Beau had touched something tender and lonely in me, his soft voice whispering to me in the darkness, his assurances restoring a calm to my bedazzled and bewildered soul? Would any young man's kiss have done that or was it just Beau's?

I tried to remember Paul's kisses, but all those memories were clouded and polluted by the discovery of our real relationship. It was impossible to think of him now as my first love and not feel guilty about it, even though it was neither of our faults.

What a long, complex, and troubling day this had been, and yet what a wonderful one, too. Was this the way my life would be from now on?

The questions tired me out. I longed for sleep. As the drowsiness took over and my mind settled, I heard the faint sound of the sobbing again. It came from the darkest corners of my mind and before I fell asleep, I wasn't sure if it was my own sobbing or the sobbing of someone I had yet to meet.

I was surprised at how late I had slept into the next morning. When I finally awoke, I was sure everyone had gone down and had breakfast without me. Ashamed, I shot out of bed and hurriedly washed and dressed, tying my hair in a bandanna rather than spend the time to brush it out properly. But when I bounced quickly down the stairs and popped into the dining room, I found it empty. Edgar was just cleaning away some cups and dishes.

"Is breakfast over?" I asked.

"Breakfast over? Oh, no, mademoiselle. Monsieur Dumas has eaten and gone to work, but you're the first of the ladies to appear," he replied. "What would you like this morning? Some of Nina's eggs and grits?"

"Yes, thank you," I said. He smiled warmly and said he would bring me some fresh orange juice and a pot of hot coffee. I sat down and waited, expecting to hear either Daphne's or Gisselle's footsteps in the hallway at any moment, but I was still the only one at the table by the time Edgar brought me my complete breakfast. He looked in on me every once in a while to see if there was anything else I wanted.

When I was finished, he was there immediately to clear away my dishes. How long would it take, I wondered, for me to get used to being waited on and looked after like this? I couldn't help having the urge to pick up my own dirty dishes and take them into the kitchen. Edgar smiled down at me.

"And how are you enjoyin' New Orleans, mademoiselle?" he asked.

"I love it," I said. "Have you lived here all your life, Edgar?"

"Oh, yes, mademoiselle. My family's been workin' for the Dumas as far back as the Civil War. Of course, they were slaves then," he added, and started for the kitchen. I got up and followed him in to tell Nina how much I had enjoyed her cooking. She looked up with surprise, but was very pleased. She was happy to tell me she had definitely concluded I was no spirit.

"Otherwise, I would be killing a black cat in the cemetery at midnight," she told me.

"My goodness, why?"

"Why? You've got to once a spirit comes haunting. You kill the cat, remove the guts, and cook it all in hot lard with salt and eggs. You eat it as soon as it's lukewarm," she instructed. My stomach started to churn.

"Ugh," I said. "How horrible."

"Then you return to the cemetery the next Friday night and call the cat." Her eyes widened. "When the cat answers, call out the names of the dead people you know and tell the cat that you believe in the devil. When you've seen a spirit once, you'll be sure to see them all the time, so it's best you get to know them and they get to know you.

"Of course," she added as an aside, "this works best in October."

Her talk of spirits made me think about the sobbing I felt sure I had heard in what had been Jean's room.

"Nina, have you ever heard sobbing upstairs coming from what was once my uncle Jean's room?" I asked.

Her eyes, which I thought had become as wide as possible, grew even wider, only now they were full of terror, too.

"You heard that?" she replied. I nodded and she crossed herself quickly. Then she reached out and seized my wrist. "Come with Nina," she commanded.

"What?"

I let her pull me through the kitchen and out the back way.

"Where are we going, Nina?"

She hurried us through the hallway to the rear of the house.

"This is my room," she told me, and opened the door. I hesitated, gasping at the sight.

The walls of the small room were cluttered with voodoo paraphernalia: dolls and bones, chunks of what looked like black cat fur, strands of hair tied with leather string, twisted roots, and strips of snakeskin. The shelves were crowded with small bottles of multicolored powders, stacks of yellow, blue, green, and brown candles, jars of snake heads, and a picture of a woman sitting on what looked like a throne. Around her picture were white candles.

"That be Marie Laveau," Nina told me when she saw I was looking at the picture, "Voodoo Queen."

Nina had a small bed, a nightstand, and a rattan dresser.

"Sit," she said, pointing to the one and only chair. I did so, slowly. She went to her shelves, found something she wanted, and turned to me. She put a small ceramic jar in my hands and told me to hold it. I smelled the contents.

"Brimstone," she said when I grimaced. Then she lit a white candle and mumbled a prayer. She fixed her eyes on me and said, "Someone put a spell on you for sure. You need to keep the evil spirits away." She brought the candle to the ceramic jar and dipped the flame toward the contents so the brimstone would burn. A small stream of smoke twisted its way up. The stench was unpleasant, but Nina looked relieved that I held onto the jar anyway.

"Close your eyes and lean over so the smoke touches your face," she prescribed. I did so. After a moment, she said, "Okay, good." Then she took the jar from me and smothered the fire. "Now you'll be fine. It's good you do what I say and don't laugh at me.

"But I remember you said your grandmere was a Traiteur woman, right?"

"Yes."

"That's good for you, but remember," she warned, "the evil spirits look to go into holy folk first. That is more of a victory." I nodded.

"Has anyone else ever heard sobbing upstairs, Nina?" I asked.

"It is no good to talk about it. Speak of the devil and he'll come through your door smiling and smoking a long, thin black cigar.

"Now we go back. Madame will come down soon for her breakfast," she told me.

I followed her out again and sure enough, when I reentered the dining room, I found Daphne dressed and seated at the table.

"Did you have your breakfast?" she asked.

"Yes."

"Where's Gisselle?"

"I guess she's still upstairs," I said. Daphne grimaced.

"This is ridiculous. Why isn't she up and about like the rest of us?" she said, even though she had just risen herself. "Go up and tell her I want her down here immediately, please."

"Yes, madame," I said and hurried up the stairs. I knocked softly on Gisselle's door and then opened it to find her on her side, still asleep and still dressed in the clothes she had worn last night.

"Gisselle, Daphne wants you to wake up and come down," I said, but she didn't move. "Gisselle." I nudged her shoulder. She moaned and turned over, quickly closing her eyes again. "Gisselle."

"Go away," she cried.

"Daphne wants you to—"

"Leave me alone. I feel horrible. My head is killing me and my stomach feels raw inside."

"I told you this would happen. You drank too much too fast," I said.

"Goody for you," she said, her eyes still shut tight.

"What should I tell Daphne?" She didn't respond. "Gisselle?"

"I don't care. Tell her I died," she said, and pulled the pillow over her head. I stared at her for a moment and saw she wasn't going to budge.

Daphne didn't like my report.

"What do you mean she won't get up?" She slapped the coffee cup down so hard on the saucer, I thought it would shatter. "What did you two do last night?" she demanded, her eyes burning with suspicion.

"We just . . . talked to Beau and his friend Martin," I said. "Out by the pool."

"Just talked?"

"Yes, ma'am."

"Call me Mother or call me Daphne, but don't call me ma'am. It makes me sound years older than I am," she snapped.

"I'm sorry . . . Mother."

She stared at me furiously a moment and then got up and marched out of the dining room, leaving me standing there with my heart thumping. I didn't lie exactly, I thought. I just didn't tell the whole truth, but if I had, I would have gotten Gisselle into trouble. Even so, I felt bad about it. I wasn't happy about being sneaky and deceptive. Daphne was so upset she pounded her way upstairs.

I wondered what I should do and decided to go to the library to pick out a book and spend the day reading until my art instructor arrived. I was flipping through the pages of a book when I heard Daphne scream from the top of the stairs.

"Ruby!"

I put the book back and hurried to the doorway.

"RUBY!"

"Yes?"

"Get up here this instant," she demanded.

Oh, no, I thought, she's discovered Gisselle's condition and wants to hear the whole story. What was I going to do? How would I protect Gisselle and not lie? When I reached the top of the stairway, I looked across the hallway and saw that the door to my room was wide open and Daphne was standing in my room and not in Gisselle's. I approached slowly.

"Get in here," she commanded. I stepped through the doorway. She was standing with her arms folded tightly under her bosom, her back straight, and her shoulders up. The skin around her chin was so taut, it looked like it might tear. "I know why Gisselle can't get up," she said. "You two were just talking last night?"

I didn't reply.

"Humph," she said, and then extended her right arm and pointed at my closet. "What is that in your closet on the floor? What is it?" she shrieked when I didn't respond quickly enough.

"A bottle of rum."

"A bottle of rum," she said, nodding, "that you took from our liquor cabinet."

I looked up quickly and started to shake my head.

"Don't deny it. Gisselle has confessed everything . . . how you talked her into taking the rum outside and showed her how to mix it with Coke."

My mouth gaped open.

"What else went on? What did you do with Martin Fowler?" she demanded.

"Nothing," I said. Her eyes grew smaller and she kept nodding as if she heard a string of sentences in her own mind that confirmed some horrible suspicions.

"I told Pierre last night that you had different values, that you grew up in a world so unlike ours, it would be difficult, if not next to impossible, and I told him you could corrupt Gisselle and influence her more than she would influence you. Don't try to deny anything," she snapped when my lips opened. "I was a young girl once. I know the temptations and how easy it is for someone to influence you and get you to do forbidden things."

She shook her head at me.

"And after we were so nice to you, welcoming you into our home, accepting you, with me devoting so much of my time to setting you up properly . . . why is it you people have no sense of decency, no sense of responsibility? Is it in your blood?"

"That's not true. None of this is true," I wailed.

"Please," she said, closing and opening her eyes. "You're cunning. You've been brought up to be shrewd, just like gypsies. Now take this bottle of rum back down to the liquor cabinet."

"I don't even know where that is," I said.

"I'm not going to waste any more of my time on this. It's upset my breakfast and my day as it is. Do it and don't ever do this again. Your father will hear about this, I assure you," she added, and marched past me.

The tears that were burning behind my eyelids broke free and zigzagged down my cheeks to my chin. I went to the closet and picked up the basket. Then I went next door, barging into Gisselle's room. She was taking a shower and singing. I stomped into the bathroom and screamed at her through the glass door.

"What?" she called back, pretending she couldn't hear me. "What?"

"How could you lie and put the blame on me?"

"Wait a minute," she cried, and rinsed her hair before shutting off the water. "Hand me my towel, please," she said. I put the basket down on the counter and got her her towel. "Now, what is it?"

"You told Daphne I was the one who took the bottle of rum," I said. "How could you?"

"Oh, I had to, Ruby. Please don't be mad. I got into trouble about a month ago when I came home very late with whiskey on my breath. I was almost grounded then. She surely would have grounded me now."

"But you blamed me! Now she thinks terrible things about me!"

"You've just arrived. Daddy is still infatuated with you. You can afford to be blamed a little. They won't do anything to you," she explained. "I'm sorry," she said, scrubbing her hair with the towel. "I couldn't think of anything else to do and it worked. It got her off my back."

I sighed.

"We're sisters," she said, smiling. "We've got to help each other out sometimes."

"Not like this, Gisselle, not by lying," I protested.

"Of course by lying. How else? They're just little lies anyway," she said. I looked up sharply. That was just the way Daphne had put things too, little lies. Was this the foundation upon which the Dumas built their happiness and contentment: little lies?

"Don't worry," she said, "I'll smooth it out with Daddy if he seems too upset with you. I'll make it seem as if I encouraged you to encourage me and he'll just be so confused, he won't do anything to either of us. I've done that sort of thing before," she confessed with an oily and evil smile.

"Relax," she said, wrapping her towel around her nude body. "After you have your art lesson, we'll meet Beau and Martin and go down to the French Quarter. We'll have fun, I promise."

"But . . . what am I to do with this? I don't know where the liquor cabinet is."

"It's in the study. I'll show you," she said. "Come help me pick out something to wear."

I shook my head and sighed.

"What a morning this has been already. I told Nina about the sobbing I heard and she hurried me off into her room to burn brimstone and then this."

"The sobbing?"

"Yes," I said, following her out to her closet. "I thought it came from the room that was Jean's."

"Oh," she said as if it were nothing.

"Have you heard it, too?"

"Of course I have," she said. "What about this skirt?" she asked, plucking one off its hanger and holding it against her. "It's not as short as your skirts, but I like the way it fits my hips. And so does Beau," she added, smiling licentiously.

"It's nice. What do you mean, of course you have heard the sobbing? Why of course?"

"Because it's something Daddy often does."

"What? What does he do?"

"He goes into Uncle Jean's room and cries about him. He's done that for . . . for as long as I can remember. He just can't accept the accident and the way things are."

"But he told me no one was crying in there," I said.

"He doesn't like anyone to know. We all pretend it doesn't happen," she explained. I shook my head sadly.

"It was tragic," I said. "He told me about it. Jean sounded like such a wonderful person, and to die that young with everything ahead of you—"

"Die? What do you mean, die? Did he say Uncle Jean died?"

"What? Well, I just . . . he said he was struck by the mast of the sailboat and . . ." I thought for a moment, recalling the details. "And he became a vegetable, but I just assumed he meant . . ."

"Oh, no," she said. "He's not dead."

"He's not? Well, what happened to him then?"

"He's a vegetable, but he's still quite good-looking. He just walks around without a thought in his head and looks at everyone and everything as though he never saw them or remembered them."

"Where is he?"

"In an institution outside of the city. We only see him once a year, on his birthday. At least, that's all I see him. Daddy might go more often. Mother never goes," she said. "How about this blouse?"

She held it up but I was looking right through it. I waited as she put it on.

"Why aren't there any pictures of Jean around?" I asked.

"Will you stop talking about it? Daddy can't stand it normally. I'm surprised he told you anything. There are no pictures because it's too painful for Daddy," she said. "Now, for the last time, what about this blouse?" She turned to look at herself in the mirror.

"It's very nice," I said.

"Oh, I hate that word," she cried. "Nice. Is it sexy?"

I looked at it seriously this time.

"You forgot to put on your bra," I said.

She smiled. "I didn't forget. A lot of girls are doing that these days."

"They are?"

"Of course. Boy, do you have a lot to learn. Lucky you got out of the swamps," she added.

But right now, I wasn't so sure I was so lucky.

15

A Tour of
Storyville

I sat with Gisselle on the patio and ate some lunch while she nibbled at her breakfast, complaining how sore her stomach still was from all the vomiting she had done last night. She blamed everyone but herself.

"Beau should have stopped me from drinking too much. I was so busy making sure everyone else had a good time, I didn't notice," she claimed.

"I warned you before we began," I reminded her. She smirked.

"It's never done this to me before," she said, but she grimaced in agony.

She had to wear her wide, thick sunglasses because the tiniest light sent ripples of pain up and down her forehead. She had dabbed gobs of rouge on her cheeks and painted her lips thick with lipstick once she saw how pale and wan her complexion was.

The long gray clouds that had made most of the morning dreary had come apart on the journey from one horizon to the other, and a soft sea of blue appeared to accompany the sunshine that rained down upon us to brighten the blossoms of the magnolias and camellias. The blue jays skittered from branch to branch with more spirit and energy, their songs more melodious.

In such a warm, beautiful setting, it was hard to feel unhappy or discouraged, but I couldn't keep the dark foreboding from inching its way into my thoughts. It moved slowly but surely like the shadow of a cloud. Daphne was very disappointed in me. Soon my father would be too, and Gisselle thought it was good for us to lie to both Daphne and him. I felt like going to Nina to ask her to find me a magical solution, some powder or enchanted bone to erase the bad things that had happened.

"Stop sitting there and pouting," Gisselle ordered. "You worry too much."

"Daphne is furious at me, thanks to you," I replied. "And soon Daddy will be, too."

"Why do you keep calling her Daphne? Don't you want to call her Mother?" she wondered. I shifted my gaze away from her and shrugged.

"Of course I do. It's just . . . hard right now. Both of our parents seem like strangers to me. I haven't been living here all my life," I replied, and looked at her. She chewed on my answer as she chewed on her croissant and jam.

"You just called Daddy, Daddy," she said. "Why should that be easier?"

"I don't know," I said quickly, and dropped my gaze so she couldn't see the dishonesty. I couldn't stand living with all this deception. Somehow, someday, it was bound to make our lives more miserable. I felt certain of that.

Gisselle sipped her coffee but continued to stare at me as she chewed lazily.

"What?" I asked, anticipating some question or suspicion.

"What did you do with Beau in the cabana before I came back and knocked on the door?" she demanded. I couldn't help but flush red. Her voice was filled with accusation.

"Nothing. It was Beau's little joke in response to what you did. We just . . . stood there and talked."

"In the dark, Beau Andreas just stood there and talked?" she asked, a wry smile on her face.

"Yes."

"You're not a good liar, sister dear. I'll have to give you lessons."

"That's not something I want to excel at doing," I responded.

"You will. Especially if you want to live in this house," she said nonchalantly.

Before I could reply, Edgar stepped through the French doors and approached us.

"What is it, Edgar?" Gisselle asked petulantly. Because of her hangover, every little noise, every little interruption annoyed her this morning.

"Monsieur Dumas has arrived. He and Madame Dumas want to see you both in the study," he said.

"Tell them we'll be there in a moment. I'm just finishing my croissant," she said, and turned her back on him.

Edgar threw a glance my way, his eyes showing his unhappiness at Gisselle's tone of voice. I smiled at him and his expression softened.

"Very good, mademoiselle," he said.

"Edgar is such a stuffed shirt. He creeps around the house as if he owns it and everything in it," Gisselle complained. "If I put a vase on a table, he'll return it to where it was originally. Once, I changed all the pictures around in the living room just to annoy him. The next day, they were all back in their original places. He's memorized where everything belongs, down to a glass ashtray. If you don't believe me, try moving something."

"I'm sure he's just taking pride in things and how well they're kept," I said. She shook her head and gobbled down her last piece of croissant.

"Let's go get this over with," she declared, and stood up.

As we approached the study, we could hear Daphne complaining.

"Whenever I ask you to come home for lunch or meet me somewhere for lunch, you always have an excuse. You're always too busy to interrupt your precious workday. But all of a sudden, you have all this time to spare to arrange for an art instructor for your Cajun daughter," she decried.

Gisselle smiled at me and grabbed my arm to pull me back so we would delay our entrance.

"This is good. I love it when they have a spat," she whispered excitedly. Not only didn't I want to be an eavesdropper, but I was afraid they would say something to reveal the whole truth.

"I always try to make myself available for you, Daphne. If I can't, it's because of something that can't be helped. And as for coming home today, I thought in light of the circumstances, I had to do something special for her," my father protested.

"Do something special for her in light of the circumstances? What about my circumstances? Why can't you do something special for me? You used to think I was someone special," Daphne retorted.

"I do," he protested.

"But not as special as your Cajun princess apparently. Well, what do you think now after I told you what happened?"

"I'm disappointed of course," he said. "I'm quite surprised." It broke my heart to hear his voice so full of disillusionment, but Gisselle's smile widened with glee.

"Well, I'm not," Daphne emphasized. "I warned you, didn't I?"

"Gisselle," I whispered. "I've got to tell—"

"Come on," she said quickly, and pulled me forward to enter the study. Daphne and our father turned promptly to face us. I could have burst into tears at the sight of his sad and disappointed face. He sighed deeply.

"Sit down, girls," he said, and nodded toward one of the leather sofas. Gisselle moved instantly and I followed, but sat away from her, practically at the other end. Our father stared at us a moment with his hands behind his back and then glanced at Daphne, who pulled her head up and folded her arms under her bosom expectantly. My father turned to me.

"Daphne has told me what happened here last night and what she found in your room. I don't mind either of you having wine at dinner, but sneaking hard liquor and drinking it with boys . . ."

I flashed a look at Gisselle who looked down at her hands in her lap.

"It's not the way young women of character behave. Gisselle," he said, turning to her. "You shouldn't have permitted this to happen."

She pulled off her sunglasses and started to cry, emitting real tears from her eyes at will as if she had some sort of a reservoir of tears stored just under her eyelids to be dipped into at a moment's notice.

"I didn't want to do it, especially right here at our home, but she insisted and I wanted to do what you said: make her feel wanted and loved as soon as I could. Now I'm in trouble," she wailed.

Shocked by what she said, I tried to meet her eyes and hold them, but she refused to look at me, afraid once she did, she couldn't look away.

Daphne widened her eyes and nodded at my father who shook his head.

"I didn't say you were in trouble. I just said I was disappointed in you two, that's all," he replied. "Ruby," he said, turning back to me. "I know that alcoholic beverages were common in your household."

I started to shake my head.

"But we have a different view of that here. There's a time and a place for imbibing and young girls should never do it on their own. Next thing you know, one of your boyfriends gets drunk and everyone gets into the car with him and . . . I just don't like to think what could happen."

"Or what young girls can be talked into doing after they've consumed alcohol," Daphne added. "Don't forget that aspect," she advised my father. He nodded obediently.

"Your mother is right, girls. It's just not a good idea. Now, I'm willing to forgive everyone, put this bad incident aside, as long as I have your solemn promise, both of your solemn promises, that nothing like this will occur again."

"I promise," Gisselle said quickly. "I didn't want to do it anyway. I had a terrible headache this morning. Some people are used to drinking a lot of alcohol and some are not," she added, throwing a glance at me.

"That's very true," Daphne said, glaring at me. I looked away so that no one would see how much I was fuming inside. The heat that built itself up in my chest felt as if it could burn a hole through me.

"Ruby?" my father asked. I swallowed hard to keep my tears from choking me and forced out the words.

"I promise," I said.

"That's good. Now then," he began, but before he could continue, we heard the door chimes. He looked at his watch. "I expect that is Ruby's art instructor," he said.

"Under the circumstances," Daphne said, "don't you think you should postpone this?"

"Postpone? Well . . ." He looked at me and I looked down quickly. "We can't just turn the man away. He's giving his time, traveled here—"

"You shouldn't have been so impulsive," Daphne said. "Next time, I would like you to discuss it with me before you give the girls anything or do anything for them. After all," she said firmly, "I am their mother."

My father pressed his lips together as if to shut up any words in his mouth and nodded.

"Of course. It won't happen again," he assured her.

"Excuse me, monsieur," Edgar said, coming to the doorway, "but a Professor Ashbury has arrived. His card," he said, handing the card to my father.

"Show him in, Edgar."

"Very good, monsieur," he said.

"I don't think you need me for this," Daphne said. "I have some phone calls to return. As you predicted, everyone and anyone who knows us wants to hear the story of Ruby's disappearance and arrival. Telling the story repeatedly is proving to be exhausting. We should have it printed and distributed," she added, spun on her heels and marched out of the study.

"I've got to go take a couple of aspirins," Gisselle said, sitting up quickly. "You can tell me about your instructor later, Ruby," she said, smiling at me. I didn't smile back. As she left the study, Edgar brought in Professor Ashbury, so I had no time to tell my father the truth about what had occurred the night before.

"Professor Ashbury, how do you do?" my father said, extending his hand.

Looking like he was in his early fifties, Herbert Ashbury stood about five-feet-nine and wore a gray sports jacket, a light blue shirt, a dark blue tie, and a pair of dark blue jeans. He had a lean face, all of his features sharply cut, his nose angular and a bit long, his mouth thin and smooth like a woman's.

"How do you do, Monsieur Dumas," the professor said in what I thought was a rather soft voice. He extended a long hand with fingers that enveloped my father's hand when they shook. He wore a beautifully hand crafted silver ring set with a turquoise on his pinky.

"Fine, thank you, and thank you for coming and agreeing to consider my daughter. May I present my daughter Ruby," Daddy said proudly, turning toward me.

Because of his narrow cheeks and the way his forehead sloped sharply back into his hairline, Professor Ashbury's eyes appeared larger than they were. Dark brown eyes with specks of gray, they seized onto whatever he was gazing at and held so firmly he looked mesmerized. Right now they fixed so tightly on my face, I couldn't help but be self-conscious.

"Hello," I said quickly.

He combed his long thin fingers through the wild strands of his thin light brown and gray hair, driving the strands off his forehead, and flashed a smile, his eyes flickering for a moment and then growing serious again.

"Where have you had your art instruction up until now, mademoiselle?" he inquired.

"Just a little in public school," I replied.

"Public school?" he said, turning down the corners of his mouth as if I had said "reform school." He turned to my father for an explanation.

"That's why I thought it would be of great benefit to her at this time to have private instruction from a reputable and highly respected teacher," my father said.

"I don't understand, monsieur. I was told your daughter has had some of her works accepted by one of our art galleries. I just assumed . . ."

"That's true," my father replied, smiling. "I will show you one of her pictures. Actually, the only one in my possession at the moment."

"Oh?" Professor Ashbury said, a look of perplexity on his face. "Only one?"

"That's another story, Professor. First things first. Right this way," he instructed, and led the professor to his office where my picture of the blue heron still remained on the floor against his desk.

Professor Ashbury stared at it a moment and then stepped forward to pick it up.

"May I?" he asked Daddy.

"By all means, please."

Professor Ashbury lifted the picture and held it out at arm's length for a moment. Then he nodded and put it down slowly.

"I like that," he said, then turned to me. "You caught a sense of movement. It has a realistic feel and yet . . . there's something mysterious about it. There's an intelligent use of shading. The setting is rather well captured, too. . . . Have you spent time in the bayou?"

"I lived there all of my life," I said.

Professor Ashbury's eyes lit with interest. He shook his head and turned to Daddy. "Forgive me, monsieur," he said, "I don't mean to sound like an interrogator, but I thought you had introduced Ruby as your daughter."

"I did and she is," Daddy said. "She didn't live with me until now."

"I see," he said, gazing at me again. He didn't seem shocked or surprised by the information, but he felt he had to continue to justify his interest in our personal lives. "I like to know something about my students, especially the ones I take on privately. Art, real art, comes from inside," he said, placing the palm of his right hand over his heart. "I can teach her the mechanics, but what she brings to the canvas is something no teacher can create or teach. She brings herself, her life, her experience, her vision," he said. "Do you understand, monsieur?"

"Er . . . yes," Daddy said. "Of course. You can learn all about her if you like. The main question is do you believe as some already have exhibited they do, that she has talent?"

"Absolutely," Professor Ashbury said. He looked at my picture again and then turned back to me. "She might be the best student I've ever had," he added.

My mouth gaped open and my father's face lit with pride. He beamed a broad smile and nodded.

"I thought so, even though I'm no art expert."

"It doesn't take an art expert to see what potential lies here," Professor Ashbury said, looking at my painting once more.

"Let me show you the studio then," my father said, and led Professor Ashbury and me down the corridor. The professor was very impressed, as anyone would be, I imagined.

"It's better than what I have at the college," he whispered as if he didn't want the college trustees to hear.

"When I believe in something or someone, Professor Ashbury, I commit myself fully," my father declared.

"I can see that. Very well, monsieur," he said with some pomposity, "I accept your daughter as one of my students. Provided, of course," he added, shifting his eyes to me, "she is willing to accept my tutelage completely and without question."

"I'm sure she is. Ruby?"

"What? Oh, yes. Thank you," I said quickly. I was still absorbing Professor Ashbury's earlier compliments.

"I will take you through the fundamentals once again," he warned. "I will teach you discipline, and only when I think you are ready, will I turn you loose on your own imaginative powers. Many are born with talent," he declared, "but few have the discipline to develop it properly."

"She does," my father assured him.

"We'll see, monsieur."

"Come to my office, Professor, and we will discuss the financial arrangements," my father said. Professor Ashbury, his eyes still fixed on me, nodded. "When can she have her first lesson with you, Professor?"

"This coming Monday, monsieur," he replied. "Although she has one of the finest home studios in the city, I might ask her to come to mine from time to time," he added.

"That won't be a problem."

"Très bien," Professor Ashbury said. He nodded at me and left with my father.

My heart was pounding with excitement. Grandmere Catherine had always been so positive about my artistic talent. She had no formal schooling and knew little about art, and yet she was convinced down to her soul that I would be a success. How many times had she assured me of this, and now, an art instructor, a professor at a college, had taken one look at my work and declared me very possibly his best candidate.

Still trembling with joy, I hurried upstairs to tell Gisselle, my heart so full, I had no room for anger anymore. I gushed out all the professor had said. Gisselle, trying on different hats at her vanity table, listened and then turned with a look of puzzlement on her face.

"You really want to spend hours with a teacher after spending most of the day in school?" she asked.

"Of course. This is different. This is . . . what I've always dreamt of doing," I replied.

She shrugged.

"I wouldn't. That's why I never pushed for the singing teacher. We have so little time to have fun. They're always finding things for us to do: teachers pile on the homework, make us study for tests, and then we have to fit our lives to our parents' schedules.

"Once you get to know some of the boys and make some friends, you won't want to waste your time with art instruction," she declared.

"It's not a waste of my time."

"Please," she sighed. "Here," she said, tossing a dark blue beret at me. "Try this on. We're going to the French Quarter to have some fun. You don't want to tag along looking like someone just born," she added.

We heard the sound of a car horn, a funny *bleep, bleep, bleep.*

"That's Beau and Martin. Come on," she said, jumping up. She grabbed my hand and pulled me along, not showing the slightest regret for the things she had said to our father and Daphne about me only a short while ago. Lies did float about this house as lightly as balloons.

"You're not going to lie to us again about which one of you is which, are you?" Martin asked, smiling as he pulled open the door to Beau's sports car for us.

"Now that you're looking at me in broad daylight," Gisselle retorted, "you surely can tell I'm Gisselle." Martin glanced from me to her and nodded.

"Yes, I can," he said, but he said it in such a way to make it hard to tell if he were complimenting her or complimenting me. Beau laughed. Annoyed, Gisselle declared she and I would sit in the back together.

We squeezed tightly into the small rear seat of Beau's sports car and held our berets on our heads as he shot away from the curb. Speeding down the street, we screamed, Gisselle's voice louder and more filled with pleasure and glee than mine which was driven by a pounding heart as we spun around a turn, tires squealing. I imagined we made quite a sight, twins, their ruby red hair dancing and flicking like flames in the wind. People stopped walking to pause and watch us rush by. Young men whistled and howled.

"Don't you just love it when men do that?" Gisselle screamed in my ear. With the sound of the engine and the wind whistling by us, we had to shout to be heard even sitting next to each other.

I wasn't sure what to say. On occasion in the bayou, walking to town, I recalled men driving by in trucks and cars whistling and calling to me like this. When I was younger, I thought it was funny, but I remembered once being frightened when a man in a dirty brown pickup truck not only called to me, but slowed down and followed me along the road, urging me to get into the truck with him. He claimed he would give me a ride to town, but there was something about the way he leered at me that set my heart thumping. I ended up running back toward home and he drove off. I was afraid to tell Grandmere Catherine because I was sure she would stop letting me walk to town by myself.

And yet, I also knew there were girls my age and older who could parade up and down the street day in and day out and never get a second look. It was flattering and threatening at the same time, but my twin sister seemed to draw satisfaction from this attention and looked surprised that I wasn't having a similar reaction.

Our tour of the French Quarter was quite different from the one my father had taken me on, for with Beau, Martin, and Gisselle, I was shown things I hadn't seen even though we were walking on the same streets. Maybe it was because we were there at a later part of the day, but the women I saw lingering in the doorways of jazz clubs and bars now were scantily dressed in what at times looked like no more than undergarments to me. Their faces were heavily made up, some using so much rouge and lipstick and eyeliner, they resembled clowns.

Beau and Martin gawked with interest, their faces frozen in licentious smiles. Every once in a while, one would lean over to the other and whisper something that set them both laughing hysterically. Gisselle was always jabbing one or the other with her elbow and then laughing herself.

The courtyards looked darker, the shadows were deeper, the music was louder. Men and in some places, women, hawked from doorways of sparsely lit bars and restaurants entreating the pedestrians to come in and enjoy the best jazz, the best dancing, the best food in New Orleans. We stopped at a stand to buy poor boy sandwiches and Beau managed to get us all bottles of beer even though no one was of age. We sat at a table on the sidewalk and ate and drank, and when two policemen came walking down the other side of the street, my heart thumped in anticipation of all of us being arrested. But they didn't seem to notice or care.

Afterward, we rushed in and out of stores, amusing ourselves with the souvenirs, the toys, and novelties. Then Gisselle directed us into a small store that advertised the most shocking sexual items I had ever seen displayed. You were supposed to be eighteen or over to go into the store, but the salesman didn't chase us out. The boys lingered over magazines and books, smirking and giggling to themselves. Gisselle made me look at a replica of a man's sex organ made of hard rubber. When she asked the salesman if she could see it, I ran out of the store.

They all followed a few moments later, laughing at me.

"I guess Daddy didn't take you in there when he showed you the French Quarter," Gisselle quipped.

"How disgusting," I said. "Why would people buy those things?"

My question made Gisselle and Martin laugh harder, but Beau just smiled.

At the next corner, Martin asked us to wait while he approached a man dressed in a black leather vest with no shirt beneath. He had tattoos on his arms and shoulders. The man listened to Martin and then the both of them walked deeper into the alleyway.

"What's Martin doing?" I asked.

"Getting us something for later," Gisselle said, then looked at Beau, who smiled.

"Getting what?"

"You'll see," she said. Martin emerged, nodding with satisfaction.

"Where do you want to go now?" he asked.

"Let's show her Storyville," Gisselle decided.

"Maybe we should just go down to the nice stores and arcades at the ocean," Beau suggested.

"Oh, it won't hurt her. Besides, she needs an education if she wants to live in New Orleans," Gisselle insisted.

"What is Storyville?" I asked. In my mind I imagined a place where people sold books and items based on famous tales. "What do they sell there?"

My question threw the three of them into another fit of hysterics.

"I don't see why you should laugh at everything I say and ask," I said angrily. "If any of you came into the bayou and went out in the swamp with me, you'd ask a lot of dumb questions, too. And I assure you, you'd be a lot more frightened than I would be," I added. That wiped the smiles and laughter off their faces.

"She's right," Beau said.

"So what. You're in the city now, not the swamp," Gisselle said. "And I, for one, don't have any intention of ever going to the bayou.

"Come on," she added, grabbing my arm roughly, "we'll take you up some streets and you tell us what you think is sold there."

Her challenge restored the smile to Martin's face, but Beau still looked troubled. Unable to cast off my own curiosity now, I let Gisselle take me along until we reached a corner and looked across the street at what seemed to me to be a row of fancy houses.

"Where are the stores?" I asked.

"Just watch over there," Gisselle pointed. She indicated an imposing four-story structure with bay windows on the side and a cupola on the roof. It was painted in a dull white. A luxurious limousine pulled up at the curb and the chauffeur stepped out quickly to open the door for what looked to be a very distinguished older man. He strutted up the short set of steps to the front of the house and rang the bell. A moment later, the large door was pulled open.

We were close enough to hear the music that poured out and see the woman who greeted the gentleman. She was tall and dark olive in complexion. She wore a dress of red brocade with what had to be imitation diamonds on her neck and wrist. They had to be imitation, they were so big; but what was most curious was she wore tall feathers pluming from her head.

Looking past her, I could see a wide entrance hall, crystal chandeliers, gold mirrors, and velvet settees. A black piano player was running his hands over the keys and bouncing on the stool. Just before the door was closed, I caught sight of a girl wearing nothing more than a pair of panties and a bra and carrying a tray filled with what looked like glasses of champagne.

"What is that place?" I asked with a gasp.

"Lulu White's," Beau replied.

"I don't understand. Is it a party?"

"Only for those who pay for it," Gisselle said. "It's a brothel. A whorehouse," she added when I didn't respond quickly.

I gaped back at the big door. A moment later, it was opened again and this time, a gentleman appeared escorting a young woman in a bright green dress with a neckline that practically plummeted to her belly button. For a moment the girl's face was hidden by a fan of white feathers, but when she pulled the fan back, I saw her face and felt my mouth fall open. She brought the man to his waiting car and gave him a big kiss before he stepped into the rear. As the car pulled away, she looked up and saw us.

It was Annie Gray, the quadroon girl who had ridden on the bus

with me to New Orleans and used voodoo magic to help me find my
father's address. She recognized me immediately, too.

"Ruby!" she called and waved.

"Huh?" Martin said.

"She knows you?" Beau asked.

Gisselle just stepped back, amazed.

"Hello," I called.

"I see you found your way about the city real good, huh?" I nodded,
my throat tight. She looked back at the front door. "My aunt works
here. I'm just helpin' her out some," she said. "But soon, I'm gettin' a
real job. You find your daddy okay?" I nodded. "Hello, boys," she said.

"Hi," Martin said. Beau just nodded.

"I've got to get back inside," Annie said. "You just wait and see. I'll
be singin' someplace real soon," she added, and hurried back up the
steps. She turned in the doorway and waved and then disappeared
within.

"I don't believe it. You know her?" Gisselle declared.

"I met her on the bus," I started to explain.

"You know a real prostitute," she followed. "And you said you
didn't know what was here?"

"I didn't," I protested.

"Little miss goody-goody knows a prostitute," Gisselle continued,
addressing herself to the boys. They both looked at me as if they had
just met me.

"I don't really know her," I insisted, but Gisselle just smiled.

"I don't!"

"Let's go," Gisselle said.

We walked back quickly, no one speaking for quite a while. Every
once in a while, Martin would look at me, smile, and shake his head.

"Where should we go to do it?" Beau asked after we all got back into
his car.

"My house," Gisselle said. "My mother is probably off at a tea party
and Daddy is surely still at work."

"To do what?" I asked.

"Just wait and see," she said. Then she added for the boys, "She
probably knows all about it anyway. She knows a prostitute."

"I told you, I don't really know her. I just sat on a bus with her," I
insisted.

"She knew you were looking for your daddy. Sounds like you two
knew each other real well," Gisselle teased. "You didn't work together
someplace, did you?" she asked. Martin spun around, his face full of
laughter and curiosity.

"Stop it, Gisselle," I snapped.

Beau pulled away from the curb and shot down the street, leaving her laughter falling behind us.

Edgar greeted us all at the doorway when we returned to the house.

"My mother at home?" Gisselle asked him.

"No, mademoiselle," he replied. She threw a conspiratorial glance at Martin and Beau and then we followed her up the stairway to her room.

"What are we doing?" I asked when she cast off her beret and opened the windows as wide as they would go. Beau flopped on her bed and Martin sat at the vanity table smiling stupidly at me.

"Close the door," she ordered. I did so slowly. Then she nodded at Martin who dug into his pocket and produced what to me looked like the cigarettes Grandpere Jack often rolled for himself.

"Cigarettes?" I said, a bit surprised and even a bit relieved. I knew some kids in the bayou who had started smoking when they were ten or eleven. Some parents didn't even mind, but most did. I never liked the taste nor the feeling that my mouth was turning into an ashtray. I also hated the way some of my school friends' clothing reeked of the smoke.

"Those aren't cigarettes. They're joints," Gisselle said.

"Joints?"

Martin's smile widened. Beau sat up, his eyebrows raised, a look of curiosity about me on his face. I shook my head.

"You never heard of pot, marijuana?" Gisselle asked.

I made a small O with my lips. I had never actually seen it this close up, but I did know of it. There were some small shack bars in the bayou in which such things were supposedly taking place, but Grandmere Catherine had warned me about ever going near them. And some of the kids at school talked about it, with some supposedly smoking it. But no one I had been friendly with did.

"Of course, I've heard of it," I said.

"But you never tried it?" she asked with a smile.

I shook my head.

"Should we believe her this time, Beau?" she asked. He shrugged.

"It's the truth," I insisted.

"So this will be your first time," Gisselle said. "Martin." He got up and passed one of the cigarettes to each of us. I hesitated to take mine.

"Go on; it won't bite you," he said, laughing. "You'll love it."

"If you want to hang out with us and the rest of my friends, you can't be a drip," Gisselle said.

I looked at Beau.

"You should try it at least once," he said.

Reluctantly, I took it. Martin lit everyone's and I took a quick puff on mine, blowing the smoke out the moment I felt it touch my tongue.

"No, no, no," Gisselle said. "You don't smoke it like a cigarette. Are you pretending or are you really this dumb?"

"I'm not dumb," I said indignantly. I looked at Beau who had lain back on the bed and inhaled his marijuana cigarette with obvious experience.

"It's not bad," he announced.

"You inhale the smoke and hold it in your mouth for a while," Gisselle instructed. "Go on, do it," she commanded, standing over me with those stone eyes riveted. Reluctantly, I obeyed.

"That's it," Martin said. He was squatting on the floor and puffing on his.

Gisselle put on some music. Everyone's eyes were on me so I continued to puff and inhale, hold the smoke and exhale. I wasn't sure what was supposed to happen, but soon I had a very light-headed feeling. It was as if I could close my eyes and float to the ceiling. I must have had a very funny expression on my face, for the three of them started to laugh again, only this time, without even knowing why, I laughed, too. That made them laugh harder which made me laugh harder. In fact, I was laughing so hard, my stomach started to ache, and no matter how it ached, I couldn't stop laughing. Every time I paused, I looked at one or the other of them and started in again.

Suddenly, my laughing turned to crying. I don't know why it did; it just did. I felt the tears and the expression on my face change. Before I realized it, I was sitting there on the floor, my legs crossed under each other, bawling like a baby.

"Uh-oh," Beau said. He got up quickly and ripped the marijuana cigarette from my fingers. Then he dropped mine and what was left of his own down Gisselle's toilet.

"Hey, that's good stuff," Martin called. "And expensive, too," he added.

"You better do something, Gisselle," Beau said when he saw my crying hadn't ended, but in fact, had gotten worse. My shoulders shook and my chest ached, but I couldn't stop myself. "The stuff was too strong for her."

"What am I supposed to do?" Gisselle cried.

"Calm her down."

"You calm her down," Gisselle said, and sprawled out on her back on the floor. Martin giggled and crawled up beside her.

"Great," Beau said. He approached me and took my arm. "Come on, Ruby. You'd better go lie down in your own room. Come on," he urged.

Still sobbing, I let him help me to my feet and guide me out the door.

"This your room?" he asked, nodding toward the adjacent door. I nodded back and he opened it and led me in. He brought me to my bed and I lay back, my hands over my eyes. Gradually, my sobs grew smaller and wider apart until I was just sniveling. Suddenly, I started to hiccup and I couldn't stop. He went into my bathroom and brought out a glass of water.

"Drink some of this," he said, sitting down beside me and helping me to raise my head. He brought the glass to my lips and I swallowed some water.

"Thank you," I muttered, and then I started to laugh again.

"Oh, no," he said. "Come on, Ruby, get control of yourself. Come on," he urged. I tried to hold my breath, but the air exploded in my mouth, pushing my lips open. Anything and everything I did made me laugh again and again. Finally, I grew too exhausted, swallowed some of the water, closed my eyes, and took deep breaths.

"I'm sorry," I moaned. "I'm sorry."

"It's all right. I've heard of people having a reaction like that, but I haven't seen it before. You feel a little better?"

"I feel all right. Just tired," I added, and let myself fall back to the pillow.

"You're a real mystery, Ruby," he said. "You seem to know a lot more about things than Gisselle does and yet you seem to know a lot less, too."

"I'm not lying," I said.

"What?"

"I'm not lying. I just met her on the bus."

"Oh." He sat there for a while. I felt his hand brush my hair and then I sensed him leaning over to kiss me softly on my lips. I didn't open my eyes during the kiss, nor did I open them after, and later, when I thought about it, I wasn't sure if it really had happened or it had been just another part of my reaction to the marijuana.

I was sure I felt him stand up, but I was fast asleep before he reached the door and I didn't wake up again until I felt someone shaking my shoulder so vigorously, the entire bed shook along with it. I opened my eyes and looked up at Gisselle.

"Mother sent me up to get you," she complained.

"What?"

"They're waiting at the dinner table, stupid."

I sat up slowly and ground the sleep out of my eyes so I could gaze at the clock.

"I must have passed out," I said, shocked at the time.

"Yeah, you did, but just don't tell them why or anything about what we did, understand?" she said.

"Of course I won't."

"Good." She stared at me a moment and then her lips softened into a sly smile. "Beau seems to like you a lot," she said. "He was very upset over what happened."

I stared back at her, speechless. It was like waiting for the second shoe to drop and then she dropped it. She shrugged.

"I'm getting bored with him anyway," she said. "Maybe I'll let you have him. Later on, you can do something nice for me," she added. "Hurry up and come down."

I watched her leave the room and then I shook my head and wondered why any boy would like a girl who treated his affection so lightly she could give it away at a whim and look for someone else.

Or was she pretending to give away something she was already losing? And more important, was it something I wanted?

16

Fitting In

A few days later, the holidays ended and school resumed. Despite everyone's assurances, including Beau's solemn promise to be at my side as much as he could, and Nina's giving me another good luck charm, I couldn't help but be apprehensive and terribly nervous about entering a new high school, especially a city high school.

Beau came by to pick up Gisselle and take her to school, but on this, my first school morning in New Orleans, both Daphne and my father were going to accompany me to registration.

I let Gisselle choose the skirt and blouse I was going to wear, and once again, she decided she would borrow one of my new outfits until she had gotten Daphne to buy her a dozen or so of her own.

"I can't save you a seat near me in any of our classes," she told me before rushing down to meet Beau. "I'm surrounded by boys, any one of whom would die rather than move. But don't worry. We'll save you a place right next to us in the cafeteria lunch hour," she added breathlessly. She was hurrying because Beau had honked twice and, thanks to her she said, they had been late for school three times this month with a week's detention hovering as punishment on the next tardiness.

"Okay," I called after her. So nervous I felt numb down to my fingertips, I gazed at myself one more time in the mirror, and then went down to wait for my father and Daphne. That was when Nina slipped me my good gris-gris, another section of a black cat's leg bone. Of course, the cat had to have been killed exactly at midnight. I thanked her and stuffed it deep into my pocketbook, alongside the piece of bone Annie Gray had given me. With all this good luck, how could I go wrong? I thought.

A few moments later, Daphne and my father came down the stairs. Daphne looked very chic with her hair brushed back and braided. She wore gold hoop earrings and had chosen to wear an ivory-colored cotton dress that had a belt just under her bosom, long sleeves with frilly cuffs and a high neck. In her high heels and carrying a small parasol that matched her dress, she looked more like a woman dressing for an afternoon lawn party than a mother going to a high school to register her daughter for classes.

My father was full of smiles, but Daphne was very concerned that I begin school in New Orleans with the correct attitude.

"Everyone knows about you by now," she lectured after we got into the car and drove down the driveway. "You've been the topic of conversation at every bridge game, afternoon tea, and dinner in the Garden District as well as other places. So you can expect the children of these people will be curious about you, too.

"The thing to remember is that now you carry the Dumas name. No matter what happens, no matter what anyone says to you, keep that in the forefront of your thoughts. What you do and what you say reflects on all of us. Do you understand, Ruby?"

"Yes, ma'am. I mean Mother," I said quickly. She had begun to grimace, but my speedy correction pleased her.

"It will be fine," my father said. "You'll get along with everyone and make new friends so quickly your head will spin. I'm sure."

"Just be sure you choose the right friends, Ruby," Daphne warned. "Over the last few years, a different class of people has found their way into this district, some without the breeding or background that Creoles of good standing possess."

A flutter of panic crisscrossed my chest. How would I know how to distinguish a Creole of good breeding from anyone else? Daphne sensed my trepidation.

"If you have any doubts, check with Gisselle first," she added.

Gisselle attended and now I was to attend the Beauregard School, named after a Confederate general about whom few of the students knew or cared to know much. A statue of him standing with his sword drawn and held high had fallen victim to an army of vandals over the years, some of it terribly stained, some of it chipped and cracked. It stood at the center of the square in front of the main entrance.

We arrived just after the first bell announcing the start of the day had rung. To me, the redbrick school looked immense and austere, its looming three floors casting a long dark shadow over the hedges, the flowers, sycamore, oak, and magnolia trees. After we parked and entered the building, we found our way to the principal's office. There was an outer office with an elderly lady serving as secretary. She seemed overwhelmed by the pile of paperwork, the ringing of phones, and the demands of other students who paraded up to her desk with a variety of problems. Her fingers were stained blue from running off multiple copies of messages and announcements on the mimeograph machine. She even had a streak of ink along the right side of her chin. I was sure she had arrived looking prim and proper, but right now strands of her blue-gray hair curled out like broken guitar strings and her glasses perched precariously at the bridge of her nose.

When we entered, she looked up, took in Daphne, turned away from the students and immediately began to primp her hair back until she saw the stains on her fingers. Then she sat down and quickly dropped her hands under her desk.

"Good morning, Madame Dumas," she said. "Monsieur." She nodded at my father who smiled and then she flashed a smile at me. "And this is our new student?"

"Yes," Daphne said. "We have an eight o'clock appointment with Dr. Storm," she added, glancing at the wall clock which had just struck eight.

"Of course, madame. I'll inform him you have arrived," she said, rising. She knocked on the inner office door and then created just enough of an opening to slip herself into the principal's office, closing the door quietly behind her.

The students who had been there retreated from the office, their eyes fixed on me so intently, I felt as if I had a wart on the tip of my nose. After they left, I gazed around at the shelves of pamphlets neatly organized, the posters announcing upcoming sporting and dramatics events, and the posted lists of rules and regulations for fire drills, air-raid drills, and accepted behavior in and out of classes. I noted that smoking was expressly forbidden and that vandalism, despite the condition of the Beauregard statue, was an offense punishable with expulsion.

The secretary reappeared and held the door open for us as she declared, "Dr. Storm will see you now."

Three chairs had been arranged for us in front of the principal's desk. I felt like I had swallowed a dozen live butterflies and envied Daphne for her poise and self-assurance as she led the way. The principal rose to greet us.

Dr. Lawrence P. Storm, as his nameplate read, was a short, stout man with a round face, the jowls of which dipped a half inch or so below his jawline. He had thick, rubbery lips and bulging dull brown eyes that reminded me of fish. Later, Daphne, who seemed to know everything about anyone in any position of importance, would tell me he suffered from a thyroid condition but she assured me he was the most impressive high school principal in the city with a doctorate in educational philosophy.

Dr. Storm wore his pale yellow hair brushed flat with a part in the center. He extended his puffy small hand and my father took it quickly.

"Monsieur Dumas and Madame Dumas," he said, nodding to Daphne. "You both look well."

"Thank you, Dr. Storm," my father said, but Daphne, who wasn't hiding her discomfort over having this duty, went right to business.

"We're here to register our daughter. I'm sure you know the details by now," she added.

Dr. Storm's bushy eyebrows rose like two caterpillars nudged.

"Yes, madame. Please, have a seat," he said, and we all sat down. Immediately, he began to shuffle papers. "I have had all the paperwork prepared in anticipation of your arrival. I understand your name is Ruby?" he said, looking at me for the first time.

"Yes, monsieur."

"Dr. Storm," Daphne corrected.

"Dr. Storm," I said. He held a tight smile.

"Well now, Ruby," he continued. "Let me welcome you to our school and say that I hope it will be a truly enjoyable and productive experience for you. I have managed to place you in all of your sister's classes so that she can help you catch up. We will make an attempt to get her transcripts from her previous school," he said, turning to my father, "and any information you can provide to expedite the matter will be appreciated, monsieur."

"Of course," my father said.

"You did attend school this year, did you not, Ruby?" Dr. Storm asked.

"Yes, Dr. Storm. I always attended school," I added pointedly.

"Very good," he said, and then clasped his thick hands together on the desk and leaned forward, his body gliding up into his suit jacket to fill out the shoulders. "But I expect you will find this educational experience somewhat different, my dear. To begin with, the Beauregard School is considered one of the best in the city, one of the most advanced. We have the finest teachers and we have the best results."

He smiled at my father and Daphne and continued.

"Needless to say, you have a rather unique situation here. Your notoriety, the events of your past, have, I am sure, preceded you. You will be the subject of a great deal of curiosity, gossip, etc. In short, you will be the center of attention for some time, which, unfortunately, will make your adjustment that much more difficult.

"But not impossible," he quickly added when he saw the panic written on my face. "I will be available to counsel you and aid you in any way possible. Just come by this office and ask for me whenever you like." His rubbery lips stretched and stretched until they were as thin as pencils and the corners were sharply drawn into his plump cheeks.

"This is your schedule," he said, handing me a sheet of paper. "I have asked one of our honor students, who happens to be in all of your classes, too, to guide you about today." He turned to my father and Daphne.

"It's one of the responsibilities of our honor students. I thought about asking Gisselle, but decided that might just bring more attention to the both of them. I hope you agree."

"Of course, Dr. Storm."

"You understand why we don't have the papers you would ordinarily need for a registration," Daphne said. "This situation has just fallen on us."

"Oh, certainly," Dr. Storm said. "Don't worry about it. I'll take whatever information you have and follow it up like a Sherlock Holmes until we have what we need."

He returned his gaze to me and sat back in his seat.

"Because you are unfamiliar with our rules and regulations and because you will find we do things differently here, I imagine, I have had this pamphlet prepared for you," he said, and held up a packet of stapled papers. "It describes everything—our dress codes, behavior codes, grading systems, in short, what is and what is not expected of you.

"I'm sure," he continued, smiling widely again, "that with your home and your family, none of this will prove difficult for you. However," he added, turning firm, "we do have our standards to maintain and we will maintain them. Do you understand?"

"Yes, sir."

"Dr. Storm," he corrected this time himself.

"Dr. Storm."

He smiled again.

"Well then, no sense in keeping her from starting." He rose from his seat and went to the door. "Mrs. Eltz," he said. "Please send for Caroline Higgins." He returned to his desk. "While she is in class, we can go through whatever you have in terms of information about her and I will take it from there. Please be assured," he added, narrowing his eyes, "that whatever you tell me will be held in the strictest confidence."

"I imagine," Daphne said in an icy voice, "that we won't be telling you anything you don't already know."

Daphne's regal posture and aristocratic tone was like water thrown on a budding fire. Dr. Storm appeared to shrink in his chair. His smile was weaker, his retreat from an important administrator to educational bureaucrat well underway. He stuttered, fumbled through some forms and documents, and looked relieved when Mrs. Eltz knocked on the door to announce Caroline Higgins's arrival.

"Good, good," he said, rising again. "Come along then, Ruby. "Let's get you started." He escorted me into the outer office, welcoming the distraction and the temporary reprieve from Daphne's demanding gaze.

"This is Ruby Dumas, Caroline," he said, introducing me to a slim, dark haired girl with a pale complexion and a homely face with glasses as thick as goggles that made her eyes seem grotesquely large. Her thin mouth turned downward at the corners, giving her a habitually despondent appearance. She flicked a tiny, nervous smile and extended her slight hand. We shook quickly.

"Caroline already knows what has to be done," Dr. Storm said. "What's first, Caroline?" he asked as if to test her.

"English, Dr. Storm."

"Right. Okay, girls, proceed. And remember, Ruby, the door to my office is always open for you."

"Thank you, Dr. Storm," I said, and followed Caroline into the corridor. As soon as we took a half-dozen steps away, she stopped and turned, this time, smiling wider and looking happier.

"Hi. I might as well tell you what everyone calls me so you don't get confused . . . Mookie," she revealed.

"Mookie? Why?"

She shrugged.

"Someone just called me that one day and it stuck like flypaper. If I don't respond when someone calls me that, he or she just doesn't try again," she explained with a tone of resignation. "Anyway, I'm really excited about being your guide. Everyone's been talking about you and Gisselle, and what happened when you were just babies. Mr. Stegman is trying to discuss Edgar Allan Poe, but no one's paying attention. All eyes are on the door and when I was called to come get you, the class started buzzing so much, he had to shout for quiet."

After hearing that preamble, I was terrified of entering the room. But I had to. With my heart pounding so hard that I could feel the thump reverberating down my spine, I followed Mookie, half listening to her description of the school's layout: which corridors were where, where the cafeteria, the gym, and the nurse's office were, and how to get to the ball fields. We paused at the doorway of the English classroom.

"Ready?" she asked.

"No, but I have no choice," I said. She laughed and opened the door.

It was as if a wind had blown into the room and spun everyone's head around. Even the teacher, a tall man with coal black hair and narrow, dark eyes, froze for a moment, his right forefinger up in the air. I searched the sea of curious faces and found Gisselle sitting in the far right corner, a smirk on her face. Just as she had said, she was surrounded by boys, but neither Beau nor Martin were in this class.

"Good morning," Mr. Stegman said, regaining his composure quickly. "Needless to say, we've been expecting you. Please take this seat," he said, indicating the third seat in the row closest to the door. I was surprised there was a desk available that close to the front, but I discovered I was sitting right behind Mookie and imagined it had been prearranged.

"Thank you," I said, and hurried to it, carrying the notebooks, pens, and pencils Daphne had made sure I had.

"My name is Mr. Stegman," he said. "We already know your name, don't we, class?" There was a titter of laughter, all eyes still glued to me. He reached down and picked two textbooks off his desk. "These are yours. I've already copied down the book numbers. This is your grammar book." He held it up. "I suppose I should remind some of you as well. This is the grammar book," he said, and there was more relaxed laughter. "And this is the literature book. We are in the middle of discussing Edgar Allan Poe and his short story, 'The Murders in the Rue Morgue,' a story everyone was supposed to have read over the holidays, I might add," he said, raising his eyes at the class. Some looked very guilty.

He turned back to me.

"For now, you'll just have to listen, but I'd like you to read it tonight."

"Oh, I have read this story, sir," I said.

"What?" He smiled. "You know this story?" I nodded. "And the main character is . . ."

"Dupin, Poe's detective."

"Then you know who the killer is?"

"Yes, sir," I said, smiling.

"And why is this story significant?"

"It's one of the first American detective stories," I said.

"Well, well, well . . . seems our neighbors in the bayou aren't as backward as some of us had anticipated," he said, glaring at the class. "In fact, some of us fit that description more," he said. It seemed to me he was looking at Gisselle. "I sat you across the room from your twin sister because I was afraid I wouldn't be able to tell the difference, but I see I will," he added. There was a lot of laughter this time. I was afraid to look back at Gisselle.

Instead, I looked down, my heart still thumping, as he continued his discussion of the story. Every once in a while, he gazed my way to confirm or reaffirm something he had said, and then he assigned our homework. I turned very slowly and looked at Gisselle. She wore this pained expression, a mixture of surprise and disappointment.

"You made a big hit with Mr. Stegman," Mookie said when the bell rang. "I'm glad you read, too. Everyone makes fun of me for reading so much."

"Why?"

"They just do," Mookie said. Gisselle caught up with us, her flock of girlfriends and boyfriends around her.

"There's no sense introducing you to everyone now," she said. "You'll just forget their names. I'll do it at lunch." Two of her girlfriends groaned and some of the boys looked disappointed. "Oh, all right. Meet Billy, Edward, Charles, and James," she catalogued so quickly I wasn't sure what name belonged to whom. "And this is Claudine and this is Antoinette, my two best friends," she said, indicating a tall brunette and a blonde about our height.

"I can't believe how much you two look alike," Claudine remarked.

"They are twins you know," Antoinette said.

"I know they're twins, but the Gibsons are twins, too, and Mary and Grace look a lot different."

"That's because they're fraternal twins and not identical," Mookie said somewhat pedantically. "They were born together, but they came from separate eggs."

"Oh, please, give us a break, will you, Miss Know-it-all," Claudine said.

"I'm just trying to be helpful," Mookie pleaded.

"Next time we need a walking encyclopedia, we'll call you," Antoinette said. "Don't you have something to look up in the library?" she added.

"I'm supposed to show Ruby around. Dr. Storm assigned me."

"We're reassigning you. Get lost, Mookie," Gisselle said. "I can take my sister around if I want."

"But—"

"I don't want her to get into any trouble, Gisselle," I said. "It's all right." Mookie looked grateful.

"Suit yourself, but don't bring her with you to our table in the cafeteria. She ruins everyone's appetite," Gisselle said, and the girls laughed.

Beau, coming from another part of the building with Martin, hurried to join us.

"How's it going?" he asked.

"Fine," Gisselle replied. "Don't worry, she's in Mookie's hands. Come on," she said, threading her arm through his before he could reply. She started dragging him away.

"But . . . I'll see you at lunch," he called back.

"We better get going or we'll be late for social studies," Mookie said.

"And we don't want to be late for social studies," the girls and boys who were still around us chorused. Her face turned crimson.

"Show me the way," I said quickly, and we walked off. As we moved down the corridor, student after student stared. Some said a quick hello, some smiled, but most just looked at me and whispered to the person beside him or her. Even some of the teachers stood in their doorways to catch sight of me moving down the corridor.

When, I wondered, would I stop being an object of curiosity, and just blend in with everyone else?

In class after class: social studies, science, and math, I found I wasn't as far behind as everyone had anticipated I would be. A large part of the reason was due to the fact that I did a lot of reading on my own. Grandmere Catherine had always emphasized the importance of education, especially reading, and she encouraged me to bring home library books. Instead of finding my teachers at the Beauregard School intimidating, I found them friendly and eager to be helpful. Like Mr.

Stegman, they were impressed with my abilities and with what I already knew. They seemed overjoyed to have someone who took their classes seriously, too.

As the morning went by and my teachers realized what I knew and how vigilantly I did my schoolwork, Gisselle was inevitably compared to me, and reprimanded for not being as serious about her work as I was. Behind their comments and criticism was the thought that her Cajun counterpart was not backward and disadvantaged, but advanced.

I didn't want this to happen. I saw how much it upset her, but there wasn't anything I could do about it. By the time we met at lunch in the cafeteria, she was frustrated and angry, her mood mean and contemptuous of everything and everyone around us.

"I'll see you after lunch," Mookie said, taking one look at Gisselle and then moving to a table of her own.

Beau came up behind me and tickled my ribs before I could object to Mookie's leaving. I squealed and spun around.

"Beau, stop. I'm standing out like crab in a chicken gumbo as it is." He laughed and then beamed his beautiful blue eyes at me softly.

"I hear everyone likes you, especially your teachers," he said. "I knew they would. Come on, let's get some lunch." He escorted me through the line and then we carried our trays to the table at which Gisselle and her friends sat. She was holding court like a queen.

"I was just telling everyone how you had to clean fish and sew little handkerchiefs to sell on the road," she quipped.

There was a titter of laughter.

"Did you also tell them about her artwork and her pictures in the gallery?" Beau asked. Gisselle's smile faded. "In the French Quarter," he added, nodding at Claudine and Antoinette.

"Really?" Claudine said.

"Yes. And she has an instructor from the college now because he thinks she's very talented," Beau added.

"Beau, please," I pleaded.

"No sense being modest anymore," he said. "You're Gisselle's twin sister, aren't you? Act like it," he added. Everyone laughed, but Gisselle fumed.

The questions followed quickly: When did I start painting? What was it like living in the bayou? What was school really like? Did I see alligators often?

With every question and with every answer, Gisselle grew more and more upset. She tried making jokes about my former life, but no one laughed because everyone was more interested in hearing my stories.

Finally, she got up in a huff and declared she was going out for a cigarette.

"Who's coming?" she demanded.

"There's not enough time," Beau said. "And besides, Storm's patrolling the grounds himself these days."

"You were never afraid before, Beau Andreas," she said, flashing her furious eyes at me.

"I'm older and wiser," he quipped. Everyone laughed, but Gisselle pivoted and marched a few steps away before turning around to see who was following. No one had gotten up.

"Suit yourself," she said, and headed for two boys at another table. Their heads lifted in unison when she smiled at them. Then, like bait cast off the fishing boat, she drew them off to follow her outside.

At the end of the day, Beau insisted on taking me home. We waited for Gisselle at his car, but when she didn't show up immediately, Beau decided we would leave without her.

"She's just making me wait for spite," he declared.

"But she'll be so angry, Beau."

"Serves her right. Stop worrying about it," he said, insisting I get in. I looked back when we drove away and thought I saw Gisselle coming out of the doorway. I told Beau, but he only laughed.

"I'll just tell her I thought you were her again," he said, and sped up. With the wind blowing through my hair, the warm sunlight making every leaf, every flower look bright and alive, I couldn't help but feel good. Nina Jackson's cat bone had worked, I thought. My first day at my new school was a big success.

And so too were the days and weeks that followed. I quickly discovered that instead of Gisselle's helping me to catch up, I was helping her, even though she had been the one attending this school and these classes. But this wasn't what she let her friends believe. According to the stories she told each day at lunch, she was spending hours and hours bringing me up-to-date in every subject. One day she giggled and said, "Reviewing everything because of Ruby, I'm starting to do better."

The truth was I ended up doing homework for both of us and as a result, her homework grades did improve. Our teachers wondered aloud about it and gazed at me with knowing glints in their eyes. Gisselle even improved on her test grades because we studied together.

And so my adjustment to the Beauregard School went along far easier than I had imagined it could. I made friends with a number of students, especially a number of boys, and remained very friendly with Mookie, despite Gisselle's and her friends' attitude toward her. I found Mookie to be a very sensitive and very intelligent person, far more sincere than most, if not all, of Gisselle's friends.

I enjoyed my art lessons with Professor Ashbury, who after only two lessons, declared that I had an artistic eye, "The perception that lets you distinguish what is visually significant and what is not."

Once word of my artistic talents spread, I attracted even more attention at school. Mr. Stegman, who was also the newspaper adviser, talked me into becoming the newspaper's art editor and invited me to produce cartoons to accompany the editorials. Mookie was the editor, so we had more time to spend together. Mr. Divito asked me to join the glee club and the following week, I let myself get talked into auditioning for the school play. That afternoon, Beau appeared too, and to my surprise and secret delight, both he and I were chosen to play opposite each other. The whole school was buzzing about it. Only Gisselle appeared annoyed, especially at lunch the following day when Beau jokingly suggested that she become my understudy.

"That way if something happens, no one will know the difference," he added, but before anyone could laugh, Gisselle exploded.

"It doesn't surprise me that you would say that, Beau Andreas," she said, wagging her head. "You wouldn't know the difference between pretend and the real thing."

Everyone roared. Beau flushed and I felt like crawling under the table.

"The truth is," she snapped, poking her thumb between her breasts, "Ruby has been *my* understudy ever since she came wandering back from the swamp." All of her friends smirked and nodded. Satisfied with her results, she continued. "I had to teach her how to bathe, brush her teeth, and wash the mud out of her ears."

"That's not true, Gisselle," I cried, tears suddenly burning behind my eyelids.

"Don't blame me for telling these things. Blame him!" she said, nodding toward Beau. "You're taking advantage of her, Beau, and you know it," she said, now in a more sisterly tone. Then she pulled herself up and added with a sneer, "Just because she came here thinking it was natural for a boy to put his hands in her clothes."

The gasps around the table drew the attention of everyone in the cafeteria.

"Gisselle, that's a horrible lie!" I cried. I got up, grabbed my books and ran from the cafeteria, my tears streaming down my cheeks. For the remainder of the day, I kept my eyes down and barely spoke a word in class. Every time I looked up, I thought the boys in the room were leering at me and the girls were whispering to each other because of what Gisselle had said. I couldn't wait for the end of the day. I knew Beau would be waiting for me by his car, but I felt horribly self-conscious about being seen with him, so I snuck out another entrance and hurried around the block.

I knew my way around enough not to get lost, but the route I took made the trip back home much longer than I had anticipated, and I felt like running away, even returning to the bayou. I strolled down the wide beautiful streets in the Garden District and paused when I saw two little girls, probably no more than six or seven, playing happily together on their swing set. They looked adorable. I was sure they were sisters; there were so many similarities between them. How wonderful it was to grow up with your sister, to be close and loving, to be sensitive to each other's feelings, to comfort each other in sadness, and to reassure each other when childhood fears invaded your world.

I couldn't help but wonder what sort of sisters Gisselle and I would have been like had we been permitted to grow up together. In my put-away heart of hearts, I was positive now that she would have been a better person growing up with me and Grandmere Catherine. It made me so angry. How unfair it was to rip us apart. Even though he didn't know I existed, my Dumas grandfather had had no right to decide Gisselle's future so cavalierly. He'd had no right to play with peoples' lives as if they were no more than cards in a bourré game or checkers on a checkerboard. I couldn't imagine what it was that Daphne had said to my mother to get her to give up Gisselle, but whatever it was, I was sure it was a dreadful lie.

And as far as my father went, I sympathized with him because of the tragedy involving my uncle Jean, and I understood why he would take one look at my mother and fall head over heels in love, but he should have thought more about the consequences and he shouldn't have let my sister be taken away from our mother.

Feeling about as low and miserable as I imagined I could, I finally arrived at our front gate. For a long moment, I gazed up at the great house and wondered if all this wealth and all the advantages it would bring to me was really any better than a simpler life in the bayou. What was it Grandmere Catherine saw in my future? Was it just because she wanted me to get away from Grandpere Jack? Wasn't there a way to live in the bayou and not be under his dirty thumb?

Head down, I walked up the steps and entered the house. It was very quiet, Daddy not yet back from his offices, and Daphne either in the study or up in her suite. I went up the stairs and into my room, quickly closing the door behind me. I threw myself on my bed and buried my face in the pillow. Moments later, I heard a lock opened and turned to see the door adjoining my room and Gisselle's opened for the first time. It had been locked from her side; I had never locked it from mine.

"What do you want?" I said, glaring up at her.

"I'm sorry," she said, looking repentant. It took me by such surprise, I was speechless for a moment. I sat up. "I just lost my temper. I didn't mean to say those terrible things about you, but I lied when I told you I didn't care about Beau anymore and you could have him. All the boys and some of my girlfriends have been teasing me about it."

"I haven't done anything to try and get him to choose me over you," I said.

"I know. It's not your fault and I was stupid to blame you for it. I've already apologized to him for the things I said. He was waiting for you after school."

"I know."

"Where were you?" she asked.

"I just walked around."

She nodded with understanding. "I'm sorry," she repeated. "I'll make sure no one believes the terrible things I said."

Still surprised, but grateful for her change of heart, I smiled. "Thanks."

"Claudine's having a pajama party at her house tomorrow night. Just a bunch of the girls. I'd like you to come with me," she said.

I nodded. "Sure."

"Great. You wanna study for that stupid math test we're having tomorrow?"

"Okay," I said. Was it possible? I wondered. Was there a way for us truly to become the sisters we were meant to be? I hoped so; I hoped so with all my heart.

That night after dinner we did study math. Then we listened to records and Gisselle told me stories about some of the other boys and girls in our so-called group. It was fun gossiping about other kids and talking about music. She promised she would help me memorize my part in the school play, and then she said the nicest thing she had said since I had arrived.

"Now that I've unlocked the door adjoining our two rooms, I want to keep it unlocked. How about you?"

"Sure," I said.

"We don't even have to knock before entering each other's rooms.

Except when one of us has some special visitor," she added with a smile.

The next day we both did well on the math test. When the other students saw us walking and talking together, they stopped gazing at me with suspicious smiles. Beau looked very relieved, too, and we had a good play rehearsal after school. He wanted to take me to a movie that night, but I told him I was going to Claudine's pajama party with Gisselle.

"Really?" he said, concerned. "I haven't heard anything about any pajama party. Usually, we boys find out about those things."

I shrugged.

"Maybe it was a spur-of-the-moment idea. Come by the house tomorrow afternoon," I suggested. He still looked troubled, but he nodded.

I didn't know that Gisselle hadn't gotten permission for us to go to Claudine's pajama party until she brought it up at dinner that night. Daphne complained about not enough notice.

"We just decided today," Gisselle lied, shifting her gaze at me quickly to be sure I didn't disagree. I looked down at my food. "Even if we knew, we couldn't tell you or Daddy before anyway," she whined. "You've both been so busy these last few days."

"I don't see any harm in it, Daphne," Daddy said. "Besides, they deserve some rewards. They've been bringing home some great school grades," he added, winking at me. "I'm very impressed with your improvements, Gisselle," he told her.

"Well," Daphne said, "the Montaigne's are very respectable. I'm glad you've made friends with the right class of people," she told me, and gave us permission.

As soon as dinner was over, we went upstairs to pack our bags. Daddy drove us the three blocks or so to Claudine's home, which was almost as big as ours. Her parents had already gone to some affair outside of the city and wouldn't be back until late. The servants had gone to their quarters so we had the run of the house.

There were two other girls besides Claudine, Gisselle, Antoinette, and I: Theresa Du Pratz and Deborah Tallant. We began by making popcorn and playing records in the enormous family room. Then Claudine suggested we mix vodka and cranberry juice, and I thought, oh, no, here we go again. But all the girls wanted to do it. What was a slumber party without doing something forbidden?

"Don't worry," Gisselle whispered. "I'll mix the drinks and make sure we don't have too much vodka." I watched and saw that she did what she promised, winking at me as she prepared the drinks.

"Did you ever have pajama parties in the bayou?" Deborah asked.

"No. The only parties I attended were parties held in fais dodo halls," I explained, and described them. The girls sat around listening to my descriptions of the food, the music, and the activities.

"What's bourré?" Theresa asked.

"A card game, sort of a cross between poker and bridge. When you lose a hand, you stuff the pot," I said, smiling. Some of the girls smiled.

"We're not that far away and yet it's like we live in another country," Deborah remarked.

"People aren't really all that different," I said. "They all want the same things—love and happiness."

Everyone was quiet a moment.

"This is getting too serious," Gisselle declared, and looked at Claudine and Antoinette, who nodded.

"Let's go up to the attic and get some of my grandmere Montaigne's things and dress up like we lived in the twenties."

It was obviously something the girls had done before.

"We'll put on the old music, too," Claudine added. Antoinette and Gisselle exchanged conspiratorial glances and then we all marched up the stairway. From the doorway of the attic, Claudine cast out garments, assigning what each would wear. I was given an old-fashioned bathing suit.

"We don't want to see what each other looks like until we all come back downstairs," Claudine said. It was as if there were a prescribed procedure for this sort of fun. "Ruby, you can use my room to change." She opened the door to her very pretty room and gestured for me to enter. Then she assigned Gisselle and Antoinette their rooms and told Theresa and Deborah to go downstairs and find places to use. She would use her parents' room. "Everyone meets in the living room in ten minutes."

I closed the door and went into her room. The old-fashioned bathing suit looked so silly when I held it up before me and gazed in Claudine's vanity mirror. It left little really exposed. I imagined people didn't care so much about getting tans in those days.

Envisioning the fun we would have all parading about in old-time clothes, I hurried to get into the bathing suit. I unfastened my skirt, stepped out of it, and unbuttoned my blouse, quickly slipping it off. I started to get into the bathing suit when there was a knock on the door.

"Who is it?"

Claudine peeked in. "How are you doing?"

"Okay. This is going to be big on me."

"My grandmother was a big lady. Oh, you can't wear your bra and panties under a bathing suit. They didn't do that," she said. "Hurry up. Take everything off, get into the suit, and come downstairs."

"But . . ."

She closed the door again. I shrugged to my image in the mirror and unfastened my bra. Then I lowered my panties. Just as they were down to my knees, I heard muffled laughter. A flutter of panic made my heart skip. I spun around to see the sliding closet door thrown open behind me and three boys emerge, laughing hysterically, Billy, Edward, and Charles. I screamed and scrambled for my garments just as a flashbulb went off. Then I charged out the door, another flash following.

Gisselle, Antoinette, and Claudine emerged from her parents' suite, and Deborah and Theresa came up the stairway, big smiles on all their faces.

"What's going on?" Claudine asked, pretending innocence.

"How could you do this?" I cried. The boys followed me to the doorway of Claudine's room and stared out at me, laughing. They were about to take another picture. Panicking, I gazed around for another place to hide and charged through an opened doorway into another room, slamming the door behind me and shutting away their laughter. As quickly as I could, I put on my clothing. The tears of anger and embarrassment streamed down my cheeks and fell off my chin.

Still trembling, but awash in a terrible anger, I took a deep breath and came out to find no one. I took another deep breath and then walked down the stairs. Voices and laughter came from the family room. I paused at the doorway and looked in to see the boys spread out on the floor, drinking the vodka and cranberry juice and the girls around them on the sofas and chairs. I fixed my gaze on Gisselle hatefully.

"How could you let them do this to me?" I demanded.

"Oh, stop being a spoilsport," she said. "It was just a prank."

"Was it?" I cried. "Then let me see you get up and take off your clothes in front of them while they snap pictures. Go on, do it," I challenged. The boys looked up at her expectantly.

"I'm not that stupid," she said, and everyone laughed.

"No, you're not," I admitted. "Because you're not as trusting. Thanks for the lesson, dear sister," I fumed. Then I pivoted and marched to the front door.

"Where are you going? You can't go home now," she cried, charging after me. I turned at the door.

"I'm not staying here," I said. "Not after this."

"Oh, stop acting so babyish. I'm sure you let boys see you naked in the bayou."

"No, I did not. The truth is people have more morals there than you do here," I spit out. She stopped smiling.

"You going to tell?" she asked.

I just shook my head. "What good would it do?" I replied, and walked out.

I hurried over the cobblestone streets and walks, my heart pounding as I practically jogged through the pools of yellow light cast by the street lanterns. I never noticed another pedestrian; I didn't even notice passing cars. I couldn't wait to get home and march up the stairway.

The first thing I was going to do was lock the door again between Gisselle's room and mine.

17

A Formal
Dinner Date

Edgar greeted me at the door, a look of concern on his face when he took one look at mine. I quickly brushed away any lingering tears, but unlike my alligator skinned twin sister, I had a face as thin as cotton. Any mask of deception I tried to wear might as well be made of glass.

"Is everything all right, mademoiselle?" he asked with apprehension.

"Yes, Edgar." I stepped inside. "Is my father downstairs?"

"No, mademoiselle." Something soft and sad in his voice made me turn to meet his eyes. They were dark and full of despair.

"Is something wrong, Edgar?" I asked quickly.

"Monsieur Dumas has retired for the evening," he replied, as if that explained it all.

"And my . . . mother?"

"She, too, has gone to bed, mademoiselle," he said. "Can I get you anything?"

"No, thank you, Edgar," I said. He nodded, then turned and walked away. There was an eerie stillness in the house. Most of the rooms were dark. The teardrop chandeliers above me in the hall were dim and lifeless, making the faces in some of the oil paintings gloomy and ominous. A different sort of panic grew in my chest. It made me feel hollow and terribly alone. A chill shuddered down my spine and sent me to the stairway and the promise of my snug bed waiting upstairs. However, when I reached the landing, I heard it again . . . the sound of sobbing.

Poor Daddy, I thought. How great his sorrow and misery must be to drive him into his brother's room so often and cause him still to cry like a baby after all these years. With pity and compassion in my heart, I approached the door and knocked gently. I wanted to talk to him, not only to comfort him, but to have him comfort me.

"Daddy?"

Just as before, the sobbing stopped, but no one came to the door. I knocked again.

"It's Ruby, Daddy. I came back from the pajama party. I need to talk to you. Please." I listened, my ear to the door. "Daddy?" Hearing nothing, I tried the doorknob and found it would turn. Slowly, I opened the door and peered into the room, a long, dark room with its curtains drawn, but with the light of a dozen candles flickering and casting the shadows of distorted shapes over the bed, the other furniture, and the walls. They performed a ghostly dance, resembling the sort of spirits Grandmere Catherine could drive away with her rituals and prayers. I hesitated, my heart pounding.

"Daddy, are you in here?"

I thought I heard a shuffling to the right and walked farther into the room. I saw no one, but I was drawn to the candles because they were all set up in holders on the dresser and surrounded dozens of pictures in silver and gold frames. All of the pictures were pictures of a handsome young man I could only assume was my uncle Jean. The pictures captured him from boyhood to manhood. My father stood beside him in a few, but most of the pictures were portrait photos, some in color.

He is a very handsome man, I thought, his hair the same sort of blond and brown mixture Paul's is. In every color portrait photo, he had soft bluish-green eyes, a straight nose, not too long or too short, a strong, beautifully drawn mouth that flashed a warm smile full of milk white teeth. From the few full body shots, I saw he had a trim figure, manly and graceful like a bullfighter's with a narrow waist and wide shoulders. In short, my father had not exaggerated when he had described him to me. Uncle Jean was any girl's idea of a dreamboat.

I gazed about the room and even in the dim light saw that nothing had been disturbed or changed since the accident years and years ago. The bed was still made and waiting for someone to sleep in it. It looked dusty and untouched, but everything that had been left on the dressers and nightstands, the desk and armoire was still there. Even a pair of slippers remained at the side of the bed, poised to accept bare feet in the morning.

"Daddy?" I whispered to the darkest corners of the room. "Are you in here?"

"What do you think you're doing?" I heard Daphne demand, and I spun around to see her standing in the doorway, her hands on her hips. "Why are you in there?"

"I . . . thought my father was in here," I said.

"Get out of here this instant," she ordered, and backed away from the door. The moment I stepped out, she reached in and grabbed the doorknob to pull the door shut. "What are you doing home? I thought you and Gisselle were attending a slumber party tonight?"

She scowled at me, then turned her head to look at Gisselle's door. She had a lovely profile, classic, the lines of her face perfect when she burned with anger. I guess I really was an artist at heart. In the midst of this, all I could think of was what it would be like to paint that Grecian visage.

"Is she home, too?" Daphne asked.

"No," I said. She spun on me.

"Then why are you home?" she stormed back.

"I . . . didn't feel well, so I came home," I said quickly. Daphne focused her penetrating gaze on me, making me feel as if she were searching my eyes, maybe even my soul. I was forced to shift my eyes guiltily away.

"Are you sure that's the truth? Are you sure you didn't leave the girls to do something else, maybe something with one of the boys?" she asked suspiciously. Really feeling sick now, I still managed to find a voice.

"Oh, no, I came right home. I just want to go to bed," I said.

She continued to stare at me, her eyes riveted to mine, pinning me to her like butterflies were pinned to a board. She folded her arms under her breasts. She was in her silk robe and slippers and had her hair down, but her face was still made up, her lipstick and rouge fresh. I bit softly on my lower lip. Panic seized me in a tight grip. I imagined I did look quite sick at this point.

"What's wrong with you?" she demanded.

"My stomach," I said quickly. She smirked, but looked a bit more believing.

"They're not drinking liquor over there, are they?" she asked. I shook my head. "You wouldn't tell me if they were, would you?"

"I . . ."

"You don't have to answer. I know what it's like when a group of teenage girls get together. What surprises me is your letting a mere stomachache stop you from having fun," she said.

"I didn't want to spoil anyone else's," I said. She pulled her head back and nodded softly.

"Okay then, go to bed. If you get any sicker . . ."

"I'll be all right," I said quickly.

"Very good." She started to turn away.

"Why are all those candles lit in there?" I risked asking. Slowly, she turned back to me.

"Actually," she said, suddenly changing her tone of voice to a more reasonable and friendlier one, "I'm glad you saw all that, Ruby. Now you have some idea what I have to put up with from time to time. Your father has turned that room into a . . . into a . . . shrine. What's done is done," she said coldly. "Burning candles, mumbling apologies and prayers won't change things. But he's beyond reason. The whole thing is rather embarrassing, so don't discuss it with anyone and especially don't discuss it in front of the servants. I don't want Nina sprinkling voodoo powders and chanting all over the house.

"Is he in there now?"

She looked at the door.

"Yes," she said.

"I want to talk to him."

"He's not in the talking mood. The fact is, he's not himself. You don't want to talk to him or even see him like this. It would upset him afterward more than it would upset you now. Just go to sleep. You can talk to him in the morning," she said, and narrowed her eyes as a new thought crossed her suspicious mind. "Why is it so important for you to talk to him now anyway? What is it you want to tell him that you can't tell me? Have you done something else that's terrible?"

"No," I replied quickly.

"Then what did you want to say to him?" she pursued.

"I just wanted . . . to comfort him."

"He has his priests and his doctors for that," she said. I was surprised she didn't say he had her, too. "Besides, if your stomach's bothering you so much you had to come home, how can you sit around talking to someone?" she followed quickly like a trial lawyer.

"It feels a little better," I said. She looked skeptical again. "But you're right. I'd better go to sleep," I added. She nodded and I walked to my room. She remained in the hallway watching me until I went inside.

I wanted to tell her the truth. I wanted to describe not only what had happened tonight, but the truth about the night with the rum and all the nasty things Gisselle had said and done at school, but I thought once I had drawn so sharp and clear a battle line between us, Gisselle and I would never be the sisters we were meant to be. She would hate me too much. Despite all that had already happened between us, I still clung to the hope that we would bridge the gap that all these years and different ways of living had created. I knew that right now I wanted that to happen more than Gisselle did, but I still thought she would eventually want it as much. In this hard and cruel world, having a sister or a brother, someone to care for you and love you was not something to throw away nonchalantly. I felt confident that someday, Gisselle would understand that.

I went to bed and lay there listening for my father's footsteps. Some time after midnight, I heard them: slow, ponderous steps outside my door. I heard him pause and then I heard him go on to his own room, exhausted, I was sure, from all the sorrow he had expressed in the room he had turned into a memorial to his brother. Why was his sorrow so long and so deep? I wondered. Did he blame himself?

The questions lingered in the darkness waiting for a chance to leap at the answers, like the old marsh hawk, patiently waiting for its prey.

I closed my eyes and rushed headlong into the darkness within me, the darkness that promised some relief.

The next morning it was my father who woke me, knocking on my bedroom door and poking his head in, his face so bright with smiles I wondered if I had dreamt the events of the night before. How could he move from such deep mental anguish to such a jolly mood? I wondered.

"Good morning," he said when I sat up and ground the sleep out of my eyes with my small fists.

"Hi."

"Daphne told me you came home last night because you didn't feel well. How are you this morning?"

"Much better," I said.

"Good. I'll have Nina prepare something soothing and easy to digest for you to have for breakfast. Just take it easy today. You've made quite a beginning with your art instructor, your school-teachers . . . you deserve a day off, a day to do nothing but indulge yourself. Take a lesson from Gisselle," he added with a laugh.

"Daddy," I began. I wanted to tell him everything, to confide in him and develop the sort of relationship in which he wouldn't be afraid to confide in me.

"Yes, Ruby?" He took another step into my bedroom.

"We never talked any more about Uncle Jean. I mean, I would like to go see him with you some day," I added. What I really meant to say was I wanted to share the burden of his sorrow and pain. He gave me a tight smile.

"Well, that's very kind of you, Ruby. It would be a blessed thing to do. Of course," he said, widening his smile, "he would think you were Gisselle. It will take some lengthy explanation to get him to even fathom that he has two different nieces."

"Then he can understand things?" I asked.

"I think so. I hope so," he said, his smile fading. "The doctors aren't as convinced of his improvements as I am, but they don't know him as I know him."

"I'll help you, Daddy," I said eagerly. "I'll go there and read to him and talk to him and spend hours and hours with him, if you like," I blurted.

"That's a very nice thought. The next time I go, I will take you along," he said.

"Promise?"

"Of course, I promise. Now let me go downstairs and order your breakfast," he said. "Oh," he said, turning at the doorway, "Gisselle has phoned already to tell us she will be spending the day with the girls, too. She wanted to know how you were doing. I said I would tell you to call them later, and if you were up to it, I'd bring you back."

"I think I'll just do what you suggested, Daddy, and relax here."

"Fine," he said. "About fifteen minutes?"

"Yes. I'm getting up," I said. He smiled and left.

Maybe what I had suggested I would do would be a wonderful thing. Maybe that was the way to get Daddy out of the melancholia Daphne had described and I had witnessed last night. To Daphne, it was all simply too embarrassing. She had no tolerance for it, and Gisselle certainly couldn't care less. Maybe this was one of the reasons Grandmere Catherine sensed I belonged here. If I could help lift the burden of Daddy's sadness, I could give him something a real daughter should.

Buoyed by these thoughts, I rose quickly and dressed to go down to breakfast. As was proving to be more the rule than the exception, Daddy and I had breakfast together while Daphne remained in bed. I asked Daddy why she rarely joined us.

"Daphne likes to wake up slowly. She watches a little television, reads, and then goes through her detailed morning ministrations, preparing to face each day as if she were making a debut in society," he replied, smiling. "It's the price I pay to have such a beautiful and accomplished wife," he added.

And then he did something rare: he talked about my mother, his eyes dreamy, his gaze far-off.

"Now Gabrielle, Gabrielle was different. She woke like a flower opening itself to the morning sunlight. The brightness in her eyes and the rush of warm blood to her cheeks were all the cosmetics she required to face a day in the bayou. Watching her wake up was like watching the sun rise."

He sighed, quickly realized what he was doing and saying, and snapped the newspaper in front of his face.

I wanted him to tell me so much more. I wanted to ask him a million questions about the mother I had never known. I wanted him to describe her voice, her laugh, even her cry. For now it was only through him that I could know her. But every reference he made to her and every thought he had of her was quickly followed by guilt and fear. The memory of my mother was locked away with so many other forbidden things in the closets of the Dumas past.

After breakfast, I did what my father suggested—I curled up on a bench in the gazebo and read a book. Off, over the Gulf, I could see rain clouds, but they were moving in a different direction. Here, sunlight rained down, occasionally interrupted by the slow journey of a thin cloud nudged by the sea breeze. Two mockingbirds found me a curiosity and landed on the gazebo railing, inching their way closer and closer to me, flying off and then returning. My soft greetings made them tilt their heads and flick their wings, but kept them feeling secure, while a gray squirrel paused near the gazebo steps to sniff the air between us.

Every once in a while, I closed my eyes and lay back and imagined I was floating in my pirogue through the canals, the water lapping softly around me. If there was only some way to marry the best of that world with this one, I thought, my life would be perfect. Maybe that was what Daddy had dreamt would happen when he began his love affair with my mother.

"So there you are," I heard a voice cry out, and I opened my eyes to see Beau approaching. "Edgar said he thought he saw you go out here."

"Hi, Beau. I completely forgot that I suggested you come by today," I said, sitting up. He paused at the gazebo steps.

"I've just come from Claudine's," he said. The look on his face told me he already knew more than I anticipated.

"You know what they did to me, don't you?"

"Yes. Billy told me. The girls were all still asleep, but I had a few words with Gisselle," he replied.

"I suppose everyone's laughing about it," I said. His eyes answered before he did. They were full of pity for me.

"A bunch of sharks, that's all they are," he snapped, the blue in his eyes turning steel cold. "They're jealous of you, jealous of the way everyone has taken to you at school, jealous of your accomplishments," he said, and drew closer. I looked away, the tears welling up.

"I'm so embarrassed, I don't know how I'll go to school," I said.

"You'll go with your head high and ignore their sneers and their laughs," he proclaimed.

"I'd like to be able to say I could do that, Beau, but—"

"But nothing. I'll pick you up in the morning and we'll walk in together. But before that . . ."

"What?"

"I came over here to ask you to dinner," he stated with a polite formality, pulling his shoulders back to assume his young Creole gentleman image.

"Dinner?"

"Yes, a formal dinner date," he said. It was on the tip of my tongue to tell him I had never been on a dinner date before, formal or informal, but I kept silent. "I have already taken the liberty of making reservations at Arnaud's," he added with some pride. I assumed from the way he spoke, this was to be a very special evening.

"I'll have to ask my parents," I said.

"Of course." He looked at his watch. "I have a few errands to run, but I'll call you about noon to confirm the time."

"All right," I said breathlessly. A dinner date, a formal date with Beau . . . everyone would hear about this, too. He wasn't just being nice to me in school or just giving me a ride home.

"Good," he said, smiling. "I'll call you." He started away.

"Beau."

"Yes?"

"You're not doing this just to make me feel better after what they did, are you?" I asked.

"What?" He started to laugh and then turned serious. "Ruby, I just want to be with you and would have asked you for a date whether they pulled that stupid joke on you or not," he declared. "Stop underestimating yourself," he added, turned and walked off leaving me in a whirlpool of mixed emotions that ranged from happiness to terror that I would make an absolute fool of myself and simply add to what had already been done to make me look like I didn't belong.

* * *

"What?" Daphne said, looking up sharply from her cup of coffee. "Beau asked *you* to dinner?"

"Yes. He's calling at noon to see if it's all right for me to go," I said. She looked at my father, who had been sitting with her on the patio, having another cup of coffee. He shrugged.

"Why is that so surprising?" he asked.

"Why? Beau has been seeing Gisselle," she replied.

"Daphne, darling, they weren't engaged. They're just teenagers. Besides," he added, beaming a smile at me, "you hoped the time would come when people would accept Ruby as one of us. Apparently, the way you've dressed her, the advice and instruction you have given her on how to carry herself and speak to people, and the good example you set has had remarkable results. You should be proud, not surprised," he added.

Daphne's eyes narrowed as she thought.

"Where is he taking you?" she asked.

"Arnaud's," I said.

"Arnaud's!" She put her coffee cup down sharply. "That's not just any restaurant. You have to wear the proper things. Many of our friends go to that restaurant and we are friendly with the owners."

"So," my father said. "You'll advise her how to dress."

Daphne wiped her lip with the napkin and considered.

"It's time you went to a beautician and had something done with your hair and your nails," she decided.

"What's wrong with my hair?"

"You need your bangs trimmed and I'd like to see it conditioned. I'll make an appointment for this afternoon. They always find time for me at a moment's notice," she said confidently.

"That's very nice," my father said.

"Then you've made a full recovery from your stomach problem?" Daphne asked me pointedly.

"Yes."

"She looks fine," my father said. "I'm very proud of the way you're adjusting now, Ruby, very proud."

Daphne glared at him.

"You and I haven't been to Arnaud's in months," she remarked.

"Well, I'll make a note of that and we'll go soon. We don't want to go the same night Ruby does. It might make her uncomfortable," he added. She continued to glare.

"I'm glad you're worried about her discomfort, Pierre. Maybe you'll start thinking about mine now," she said, and he reddened.

"I—"

"Go on upstairs, Ruby," she commanded. "I'll be right up to choose your clothes."

"Thank you," I said. I glanced quickly at my father who looked like a little boy who had just been reprimanded, and then I hurriedly left and went up to my room. Why was it that every nice thing that happened to me here always brought along some unpleasantness? I wondered.

Shortly afterward, Daphne came marching into my room.

"You have a two o'clock at the beauty parlor," she said, going to my closet. She threw open the sliding doors and stood back, considering. "I'm glad I thought to buy this," she said, plucking a dress from its hanger, "and the matching shoes." She turned and looked at me. "You're going to need a pair of earrings. I'll let you borrow one of mine and a necklace, too, just so you don't look underdressed."

"Thank you," I said.

"Take special care with them," she warned. She put the dress aside and focused her gaze on me with suspicion again. "Why is Beau taking you to dinner?"

"Why? I don't know. He said he wanted to take me. I didn't ask him to take me, if that's what you mean," I replied.

"No, that's not what I mean. He and Gisselle have been seeing each other for some time now. You come onto the scene and suddenly, he leaves her. What's been going on between you and Beau?" she demanded.

"Going on? I don't know what you mean, Mother."

"Young men, especially young men of Beau's age, are rather sexually driven," she explained. "Their hormones are raging so they look for girls who are more promiscuous, more obliging."

"I'm not one of those girls," I snapped.

"Whether it's true or not," she continued, "Cajun girls have reputations."

"It's not true. The truth is," I fumed, "so-called Creole girls of good breeding are more promiscuous."

"That's ridiculous and I don't want to hear you say such a thing," she replied firmly. I looked down. "I warn you," she continued, "if you did or if you do anything to embarrass me, embarrass the Dumas . . ."

I wrapped my arms around myself and turned away so she couldn't see the tears that clouded my eyes.

"Be ready at one-thirty to go to the beauty parlor," she finally said, and left me trembling with frustration and anger. Was it always going to be this way? Every time I accomplished something or something nice happened to me, she would decide it was because of some indecent reason?

It wasn't until Beau called at noon that I felt better about myself and the promise of the evening. He repeated how much he wanted to take me and was very happy to hear I could go.

"I'll pick you up at seven," he said. "What color is your dress?"

"It's red, like the red dress Gisselle wore to the Mardi Gras Ball."

"Great. See you at seven."

Why he wanted to know the color of my dress didn't occur to me until he came to the door at seven with the corsage of baby white roses. He looked dashing and handsome in his tuxedo. Daphne made a point to appear when Edgar informed me Beau had arrived.

"Good evening, Daphne," he said.

"Beau. You look very handsome," she said.

"Thank you." He turned to me and presented the corsage. "You look great," he said. I saw how nervous he was under Daphne's scrutinizing gaze. His fingers trembled as he opened the box and took out the corsage. "Maybe you'd better put this on her, Daphne. I don't want to stick her."

"You never have trouble doing it for Gisselle," Daphne remarked, but she moved forward and attached the corsage.

"Thank you," I said. She nodded. "Give my regards to the maître d'," she told Beau.

"I will."

I took Beau's arm and eagerly let him lead me out the front door and to his car.

"You look great," he said after we got in.

"So do you."

"Thanks." We pulled away.

"Gisselle didn't come back from Claudine's yet," I told him.

"They're having a party," he said.

"Oh. They called to invite you?"

"Yes." He smiled. "But I told them I had more important things to do," he added, and I laughed, finally feeling as if the heavy cloud of anxiety had begun to move off. It felt good to relax a little and enjoy something for a change.

I couldn't help but be nervous again when we entered the restaurant. It was filled with many fine and distinguished looking men and women, all of whom gazed up from their plates or turned from their conversations to look us over when we entered and were shown our table. I went through the litany of things Daphne had recited to me on the way to and from the beauty parlor—how to sit up straight and hold my silverware, which fork was for what, putting the napkin on my lap, eating slowly with my mouth closed, letting Beau order our dinners . . .

"And if you should drop something, a knife, a spoon, don't you pick it up. That's what the waiters and busboys are there to do," she said. She kept adding new thoughts. "Don't slurp your soup the way they eat gumbo in the bayou."

She made me feel so self-conscious, I was sure I would do something disgraceful and embarrass Beau and myself. I trembled walking through the restaurant, trembled after we were seated, and trembled when it was time to chose my silverware and begin to eat.

Beau did all he could to make me feel relaxed. He continually complimented me and tried telling jokes about other students we both knew. Whenever something was served, he explained what it was and how it had been prepared.

"The only reason I know all this," he said, "is because my mother is amusing herself by learning how to be a gourmet chef. It's driving everyone in the family crazy."

I laughed and ate, remembering Daphne's final warning: "Don't finish everything and wipe the plate clean. It's more feminine to be full faster and not look like some farmhand feeding her face."

Even though the dinner was sumptuous and it was very elegantly served, I was too nervous to really enjoy it and actually felt relieved when the check came and we rose to leave. I had gotten through this elegant dinner date without doing anything Daphne could criticize, I thought. No matter what happened, I would be a success in her eyes, and for some reason, even though she was often unpleasant to me, her admiration and approval remained important. It was as if I wanted to win the respect of royalty.

"It's early," Beau said when we left the restaurant. "Can we take a little ride?"

"Okay."

I had no idea where we were going, but before I knew it, we had left the busier part of the city behind us. Beau talked about places he had been and places he wanted very much to see. When I asked him what he wanted to do with his life, he said he was thinking very seriously of becoming a doctor.

"That would be wonderful, Beau."

"Of course," he added, smiling, "I'm just blowing air right now. Once I find out what's involved, I'll probably back out. I usually do."

"Don't talk about yourself that way, Beau. If you really want to do something, you will."

"You make it sound easy, Ruby. In fact, you have a way of making the most difficult and troubling things look like nothing. Why just look at the way you've already memorized your part in the play and made some of the other students gain confidence in themselves . . . including me, I might add . . ." He shook his head. "Gisselle is always putting things down, belittling things I like. She's so . . . negative sometimes."

"Maybe she's not as happy as she pretends to be," I wondered aloud.

"Yeah, maybe that's it. But you've got every reason to be unhappy and yet, you don't let other people feel you're unhappy."

"My grandmere Catherine taught me that," I said, smiling. "She taught me to be hopeful, to believe in tomorrow."

He grimaced with confusion.

"You make her sound so good and yet she was part of the Cajun family that bought you as a stolen baby, right?" he asked.

"Yes, but . . . she didn't learn about it until years later," I said, quickly covering up. "And by that time, it was too late."

"Oh."

"Where are we?" I asked, looking out the window and seeing we were on a highway now that was surrounded by marshlands.

"Just a nice place we go sometimes. There's a good view up ahead," he said, and turned down a side road that brought us to an open field, looking back at the lights of New Orleans. "Nice, huh?"

"Yes. It's beautiful." I wondered if I would ever get used to the tall buildings and sea of lights. I still felt very much like a stranger.

He turned off his engine, but left the radio playing a soft, romantic song. Although it was mostly cloudy now, stars peeked down through any break in the overcast, twinkling brightly. Beau turned to me and took my hand.

"What sort of dates did you have in the bayou?" he asked.

"I never really went on what you would call a date, I suppose. I went to town for a soda. Once, I went to a fais dodo with a boy. A dance," I added.

"Oh. Oh, yeah."

I couldn't see his face in the darkness and it reminded me of our time in the cabana. Just like then, my heart began to pitter-patter for seemingly no reason. I saw his head and shoulders move toward me until I felt his lips find mine. It was a short kiss, but he followed it with a deep moan and his hands clutched my shoulders and held me tightly.

"Ruby," he whispered. "You look like Gisselle, but you're so much softer, so much lovelier that it's very easy for me to tell the difference between you even with a quick glance." He kissed me again and then kissed the tip of my nose. I had my eyes closed and felt his lips slide softly over my cheeks. He kissed my closed eyes and my forehead and then pulled me closer to him to seal my lips with his in a long, demanding kiss that sent invisible fingers over my breasts and down the small of my stomach, making me tingle to my toes.

"Oh, Ruby, Ruby," he chanted. His lips were on my neck and before I knew it, he brought them to the tops of my breasts, moving quickly to the small valley between them. Whatever resistance was naturally in me, softened. I moaned and let myself sink deeper into the seat as he moved over me, his hands now finding their way over my bosom, his fingers expertly sliding the zipper down until my dress loosened enough for him to bring it lower.

"Oh, Beau, I . . ."

"You're so lovely, lovelier than Gisselle. Your skin is like silk to her sandpaper."

His fingers found the clasp of my bra and almost before I knew it, undid it. Instantly, his mouth moved over my breast, nudging my bra away to expose more and more until he found my nipple, erect, firm, waiting despite the voice within me that tried to keep my body from being so willing. It was truly as though there were two of me: the sensible, quiet, and logical Ruby, and the wild, hungry-for-love-and-affection emotional Ruby.

"I have a blanket in the back," he whispered. "We can spread it out and lie out here under the stars and . . ."

And what? I thought finally. Grope and pet each other until there was no turning back? Suddenly, Daphne's furious face flashed before me and her words resounded: ". . . They look for girls who are more promiscuous, more obliging . . . Whether it is true or not, Cajun girls have reputations."

"No, Beau. We're going too fast and too far. I can't . . ." I cried.

"We'll just sprawl out and be more comfortable," he proposed, keeping his lips close to my ear.

"It would be more than that and you know it, Beau Andreas."

"Come on, Ruby. You've done this before, haven't you?" he said with a sharpness that cut into my heart.

"Never, Beau. Not like you think," I replied with indignation. My tone made him regret his accusation, but he wasn't easily dissuaded.

"Then let me be the first, Ruby. I want to be your first. Please," he pleaded.

"Beau . . ."

He continued moving his lips over my breasts, urging and encouraging me with his fingers, his touch, his tongue, and hot breath, but I firmed up my resistance, a resistance fueled by the memory of Daphne's accusations and expectations. I would not fit the image of the Cajun girl they wanted me to be. I would not give any of them the satisfaction.

"What's wrong, Ruby? Don't you like me?" Beau moaned when I pulled myself back and held my dress against my bosom.

"I do, Beau. I like you a lot, but I don't want to do this now. I don't want to do what everyone expects I would do . . . even you," I added.

Beau sat back abruptly, his frustration quickly turning into anger.

"You led me to believe you really liked me," he said.

"I do, Beau, but why can't we stop when I ask you to stop? Why can't we just—"

"Just torment each other?" he asked caustically. "Is that what you did with your boyfriends in the bayou?"

"I didn't have boyfriends. Not like you think," I said. He was silent for a moment. Then he took a deep breath.

"I'm sorry. I didn't mean to imply you had dozens of boyfriends."

I put my hand on his shoulder. "Can't we get to know each other a little more, Beau?"

"Yes, of course. That's what I want. But there's no better way than making love," he offered, turning back to me. He sounded so convincing. A part of me wanted to be convinced, but I kept that part under tight wraps, locked behind a door. "You're not going to tell me now you just want to be good friends, are you?" he added with obvious sarcasm when I continued to resist.

"No, Beau. I am attracted to you. I would be a liar to say otherwise," I confessed.

"So?"

"So let's not rush into anything and make me regret it," I added. Those words seemed to stop him cold. He froze in the space between us for a moment and then sat back. I began to fasten my bra.

Suddenly, he laughed.

"What?" I asked.

"The first time I took Gisselle out here, she jumped me and not vice versa," he said, starting the engine. "I guess you two really are very, very different."

"I guess we are," I said.

"As my grandfather would say, *viva la difference*," he replied, and laughed again, but I wasn't sure if he meant he liked Gisselle's behavior better or he liked mine.

"All right, Ruby," he said, driving us out of the marshlands, "I'll take your advice and believe what you predicted about me."

"Which is?"

"If I really want to do something," he said, "I will. Eventually." In the glow from the light of oncoming cars, I saw him smiling.

He was so handsome; I did like him; I did want him, but I was glad I had resisted and remained true to myself and not to the image others had of me.

When we arrived at the house, he escorted me to the door and then turned me to him to kiss me good night.

"I'll come by tomorrow afternoon and we can rehearse some of our lines, okay?" he said.

"I'd like that. I had a wonderful time, Beau. Thank you."

He laughed.

"Why do you laugh at everything I say?" I demanded.

"I can't help it. I keep thinking of Gisselle. She would expect me to thank her for permitting me to spend a small fortune on dinner. I'm not laughing at you," he added. "I'm just . . . so surprised by everything you do and say."

"Do you like that, Beau?" I met his blue eyes and felt the heat that sprang up from my heart, hoping for the right answer.

"I think I do. I think I really do," he said, as if first realizing it himself, and then he kissed me again before leaving. I watched him for a moment, my heart now full and happy, and then rang the doorbell for Edgar. He opened it so quickly, I thought he had been standing there on the other side, waiting.

"Good evening, mademoiselle," he said.

"Good evening, Edgar," I sang, and started toward the stairway.

"Mademoiselle."

I turned back, still smiling at my last memories of Beau on the steps.

"Yes, Edgar?"

"I was told to tell you to go straight to the study, mademoiselle," he said.

"Pardon?"

"Your father and mother and Mademoiselle Gisselle are waiting for you," he explained.

"Gisselle's home already?" Surprised, but filled with trepidation, I went to the study. Gisselle was sitting on one of the leather sofas and Daphne was in a leather chair. My father was gazing out the window, his back to me. He turned when Daphne said, "Come in and sit down."

Gisselle was glaring at me, hatefully. Did she think I had told on her? Had my father and Daphne somehow heard about what had occurred at the slumber party?

"Did you have a nice time?" Daphne asked. "Behave properly and do everything as I told you to do it in the restaurant?"

"Yes."

My father looked relieved about that, but he still seemed distant, troubled. My eyes went from him, to Gisselle, who looked away quickly, and then back to Daphne, who folded her hands in her lap.

"Apparently, since your arrival, you haven't told us everything about your sordid past," she said. I gazed at Gisselle again. She was sitting back now, her arms folded, her face full of self-satisfaction.

"I don't understand. What haven't I told you?"

Daphne smirked.

"You haven't told us about the woman you know in Storyville," she said, and for a moment my heart stopped and then started again, this time driven by a combination of fear and anger and utter frustration. I spun on Gisselle.

"What lies did you tell now?" I demanded. She shrugged.

"I just told how you brought us down to Storyville to meet your friend," she explained, throwing a look of pure innocence at Daddy.

"I? Took you? But—" I sputtered.

"How do you know this . . . this prostitute?" Daphne demanded.

"I don't know her," I cried. "Not like she's telling you."

"She knew your name, didn't she? Didn't she?"

"Yes."

"And she knew you were looking for Pierre and me?" Daphne cross-examined.

"That's true, but—"

"How do you know her?" she demanded firmly. A hot rush of blood heated my face.

"I met her on the bus when I came to New Orleans and I didn't know she was a prostitute," I cried. "She told me her name was Annie Gray, and when we arrived in New Orleans, she helped me find this address."

"She knows this address," Daphne said, nodding at Daddy. He closed his eyes and bit down on his lower lip.

"She told me she was coming here to be a singer," I explained. "She's still trying to find a job. Her aunt promised her and—"

"You want us to believe you thought she was only a nightclub singer?"

"It's the truth!" I turned to Daddy. "It is!"

"All right," he said. "Maybe it is."

"What's the difference?" Daphne remarked. "By now the Andreas family and the Montaignes surely know your . . . our daughter has made the acquaintance of such a person."

"We'll explain it," my father insisted.

"You'll explain it," Daphne retorted. Then she turned back to me. "Did she promise to contact you here and give you an address of where she would be in the future?"

I gazed at Gisselle again. She hadn't left out a detail. Wickedly, she grinned.

"Yes, but—"

"Don't you ever so much as nod at this woman if you should see her someplace, much less accept any letters from her or phone calls, understand?"

"Yes, ma'am." I looked down, the tears so cold they made me shiver on their journey down my cheeks.

"You should have told us about this so we could be prepared should it come up. Are there any other sordid secrets?"

I shook my head quickly.

"Very well." She looked at Gisselle. "Both of you go to bed," she commanded.

I rose slowly and without waiting for Gisselle, started toward the stairway. I walked ponderously up the steps, my head down, my heart feeling so heavy in my chest, it was like I was carrying a chunk of lead up with me.

Gisselle came prancing by, her face molded in a smile of self-satisfaction.

"I hope you and Beau had a good time," she quipped as she passed me.

What possible part of my mother and what possible part of my father combined to create someone so hateful and mean? I wondered.

18

A Curse

Gisselle and I didn't speak to each other very much the next day. I finished breakfast before she came down, and soon after she did, she went off with Martin and two of her girlfriends. Daddy left, saying he had to catch up on some work in his office, and I saw Daphne only for a moment before she hurried out to meet some friends for shopping and lunch. I spent the remainder of the morning in my studio, painting. I was still uncomfortable living in such a big house. Despite the many beautiful antiques and works of art, the expensive French furniture and elaborate tapestries and carpets, for me the house remained as empty and as cold as a museum. It was easy to be lonely here, I thought as I wandered back through the long corridors afterward to have my lunch alone.

And so I was glad when Beau arrived in the early afternoon and we went into my art studio to practice our play lines. First, he looked at the pictures I had drawn and painted under Professor Ashbury's tutelage.

"Well?" I said when he went from one to the other without comment.

"How about doing a picture of me?" he suggested, looking up from a watercolor of a bowl of fruit.

"Of you?" The idea startled me. A slow grin appeared on his handsome face.

"Sure. I hope it would be a lot more interesting than something like this." His grin quickly evaporated. Suddenly, those smiling sapphire eyes looked at me as I had never been looked at before. They darkened so with pure desire. "I'd even pose nude, if you like," he said.

I know my cheeks turned crimson.

"Nude! Beau!"

"It's only for the sake of art, right?" he followed quickly. "And an artist has to practice drawing and painting the human body, doesn't she? Even I know that much," he said. "I'm sure your teacher will be taking you to his studio soon and have you do nudes. I hear there are college guys and girls who do it for the money. Or have you already drawn and painted someone in the nude?" he asked with a wry smile.

"Of course not. I'm not ready for that sort of work yet, Beau," I said, my voice nearly failing. He took a few steps toward me.

"You don't think I'm good-looking enough? You think the college guys will look better?"

"No, I don't. It's not that. It's just . . ."

"Just what?"

"I'd be too embarrassed to draw you. Now stop. We came in here to memorize play lines," I said, opening my script. He continued to gaze at me with that look of pure longing on his face, his cerulean eyes darkening. I had to fix my eyes on the pages so he couldn't see the excitement he had stirred in my breast. My heart pitter-pattered when the image of him sprawled nude on a chaise flashed before me. I couldn't help but tremble. I hoped he didn't see the way my fingers fumbled with the pages of my script.

"Are you sure?" he questioned. "You never know about something until you try." I took a deep breath, put the script down, and looked up at him sharply.

"I'm sure, Beau. Besides, all I need is for Daphne to believe one more bad thing about me. She has Daddy nearly convinced that I'm some sort of wicked Cajun girl, thanks to Gisselle."

"What do you mean?" Beau asked, quickly sitting beside me. Breathlessly, I gushed forth, describing how I had been interrogated about Annie Gray.

"Gisselle told on you?" He shook his head. "I guess she's just jealous," he said. "Well, she has reason to be," he added, his eyes continuing to grow warmer. "I'm too fond of you now to turn back. She's going to have to get used to it and behave herself."

We stared into each other's eyes for a moment. Outside, the morning overcast had darkened into rain clouds and a hard downpour began, the drops tapping on the windows and streaking down like tears on someone's cheeks.

Gradually, Beau leaned toward me. I didn't move away and he kissed me softly on the lips. I felt my small wall of resistance start to crumble. Surprising myself, as well as him, I returned his kiss the moment his ended. Neither of us said anything, but we both knew the memorization session was destined to fail. Neither he nor I could concentrate on the play. As soon as I lifted my eyes from the words and met his, my mind stumbled and fumbled.

Finally, he took the play script from my hand and put it aside with his. Then he turned to me.

"Paint me, Ruby," he whispered in a voice as tempting as the serpent's must have been in Paradise. "Draw me and paint me. Let's lock the door and do it," he challenged.

"Beau, I couldn't . . . I just couldn't."

"Why not? You paint animals without clothes," he teased. "And naked fruit, don't you?"

"Stop, Beau."

"It's nothing," he said, growing serious again. "We'll keep it a secret between us," he added. "Why don't we do it right now? There's no one here to disturb us," he said, and began to unbutton his shirt.

"Beau . . ."

With his eyes fixed on me, he stripped off his shirt and then stood up to unfasten his pants.

"Go lock the door," he said, nodding.

"Beau, don't . . ."

"If you don't lock it and someone does walk in . . ."

"Beau Andreas!"

He stepped out of his pants and folded them neatly over the back of the lounge. He stood only in his briefs, his hands on his hips, waiting.

"How should I pose? Sitting? Knees up? On my stomach?"

"Beau, I said I can't . . ."

"The door," he replied, nodding toward it more emphatically. To move me faster, he tucked his thumbs into the elastic of his briefs and began lowering them over his hips. I jumped out of the chair and rushed to the door. The moment I heard the lock click, I knew I had let it go too far. Was it only because I didn't know how to stop him, or did I permit it to happen, want it to happen? I turned and saw him standing with his shorts in his hand, holding them in front of himself.

"How should I pose?" he asked.

"Put your clothes back on this instant, Beau Andreas," I ordered.

"It's done already. It's too late to turn back. Just start."

He sat down on the lounge, still keeping his briefs over his private parts. Then he nonchalantly brought up his feet and sprawled out, facing me. With a quick gesture, he raised his briefs and draped them over the back of the lounge. My mouth gaped.

"Should I lean on my hand like this? This is good, isn't it?"

I shook my head, turned away from him, and sat down quickly in the nearest chair because my pounding heart had turned my legs to marshmallow.

"Do it, Ruby. Draw me," he ordered. "This is a challenge to see if you can really be an artist and look at someone and see only an object to draw and paint, like a doctor separating himself from his patient so he could do what has to be done."

"I can't, Beau. Please. I'm not a doctor and you're not my patient," I insisted, still without looking at him.

"Our secret, Ruby," he whispered. "It will be our secret," he chanted. "Go on. Look at me. You can do it. Look at me," he commanded.

Slowly, like one hypnotized by his words, I turned my head and gazed at him, at his sleek, muscular torso, at the way the lines of his body turned into each other. Could I do what he asked? Could I look at him and detach myself enough to see him only as something to draw?

The artist in me demanded to know, wanted to know. I rose and went to my easel and flipped over the page to work on a blank one. Then I took the drawing pencil in hand and looked at him, drinking him in with long, visual gulps and then turning what I saw into something on the page. My fingers, trembling badly at first, became stronger, firmer as the lines took shape. I took the most time with his face, capturing him as I saw him in my own mind as well as how he looked to others. I drew him with a deep, strong look in his eyes. Satisfied, I moved to his body and soon I had the outline of his shoulders, his sides, his hips, and his legs. I concentrated on his chest and his neck, capturing the strong muscle structure and the smooth lines.

All the while he kept his eyes fixed so firmly on me; it was as if he were a mannequin. I think he was testing himself as much as he was testing me.

"This is hard work," he finally said.

"You want to stop?"

"No. I can go a while longer. I can go as long as you can," he added.

My fingers began to tremble again as I moved down the drawing to the small of his stomach. Now, with every turn of the pencil, I felt I was actually running the tips of my fingers over his body, slowly working my way down until I had to draw his manliness. He knew I had reached that point, for his lips tightened into a sensuous smile.

"If you have to come closer, don't be afraid," he said in a loud whisper.

I dropped my eyes back to the easel and drew quickly, sketching so fast I must have looked like someone in a frenzy. I didn't have to look up at him again. The image of his body lingered on my eyes. I know I was flushed. My heart was pounding so hard, I don't know how I continued, but I did. And when I finally stepped back from the paper, I had drawn a rather detailed picture of him.

"Is it good?" he asked.

"I think so," I said, surprised at how really good it was. I couldn't remember drawing a single line. It was as though I had been possessed.

Suddenly, he rose and stepped up beside me to look at the drawing.

"It is good," he said.

"You can put on your clothes now, Beau," I said, without turning away from the drawing.

"Don't be so nervous," he said, putting his hand on my shoulder.

"Beau . . ."

"You've already seen all there is to see. No reason to be shy anymore," he whispered. When he put his arm around me, I tried to move away; I willed my feet to carry me off, but my command died somewhere on the way and I remained beside him, as pliable as soft clay, permitting him to turn me around so that I faced him and enabled him to kiss me. I felt his nakedness against me, his manliness harden.

"Beau, please . . ."

"Shh," he said, wiping my face softly with his palm. He kissed me tenderly on the lips and then he lifted me into his arms and carried me back to the lounge. As he lowered me onto it, he went to his knees and leaned over to kiss me again. His fingers moved quickly over my clothing, unbuttoning my blouse, unzipping my skirt. He undid my bra and peeled it away. My breasts shuddered, uncovered, but I didn't resist. I kept my eyes closed and only moaned as he kissed me on the neck, the shoulders, and then nibbled gently under and over my breasts. He lifted me gently and slipped my skirt down over my hips, quickly burying his face in the small of my stomach. His kisses were like fire now. Everywhere his lips touched me, I felt the heat build.

"You're wonderful, Ruby, wonderful. You're as pretty as Gisselle on the outside and far more beautiful and lovely on the inside," he said. "I can't help but love you. I can't think of anything else but you. I'm mad for you," he swore.

Wonder filled me. Did he truly love me with such passion? In a moment of exquisite silence, I heard the gentle tapping of the rain and felt a warm shudder pass through my body. His fingers continued to explore me, stir me. I seized his head in my hands, intending to stop him, but instead I kissed his forehead, his hair. I held him against my bosom tightly.

"Your heart's pounding and so is mine," he said. He looked into my eyes. I closed them and then, as in a dream, I felt his soft lips move over my cheek, in my hair, then lightly over my eyelids and finally my lips again. This time, as he kissed me, he slipped his fingers under the waist of my panties and drew them down.

I started to protest, but he quieted me with another kiss.

"It will be wonderful, Ruby," he whispered. "I promise. Besides, you should know what it's like. An artist should know," he said.

"Beau, I'm afraid. Please . . . don't . . ."

"It's all right." He smiled down at me. I was naked below him and his nakedness was against me. I felt him throbbing. It took my breath away, made it harder and harder to talk, to plead. "I want to be your first. I should be your first," he said. "Because I love you."

"Do you, Beau? Do you really?"

"Yes," he swore. Then he returned his lips to mine, slipping himself in between my legs at the same time. I tried to resist, keeping my legs tight, but as he prodded, he continued to kiss me and whisper and nudge me in places I had shown no boy nor man before. I felt like I was trying to hold back a deluge. Wave after wave of excitement washed over me until I was drowning in my own thundering flood of passion. I lost my final desire to resist and felt my thighs and my back relax as he moved with determination to enter me. I cried. I felt my head spin and a delightful dizziness send me reeling back into the echo of my own soft moans. The explosions within me, surprised, frightened, and then pleased me. Finally, his climax came fast, hot, and furious. I felt him shudder and then come to a peaceful stillness, his lips still pressed against my cheek, his breathing still heavy and hard.

"Oh, Ruby," he moaned, "Ruby, you're beautiful, wonderful."

The realization of what had happened, what I had permitted swept over me. I pushed on his shoulders.

"Let me up, Beau. Please," I cried. He sat back and I seized my garments and began putting them on quickly.

"You're not mad at me, are you?" he asked.

"I'm mad at myself," I said.

"Why? Wasn't it wonderful for you, too?"

I buried my face in my hands and began to cry. I couldn't help it. He tried to soothe me, comfort me.

"Ruby, it's all right. Really. Don't cry."

"It's not all right, Beau. It's not. I was hoping I was different," I said.

"Different? From what? From Gisselle?"

"No. From . . ." I couldn't say it. I couldn't tell him I was hoping I wasn't a Landry because he didn't know who my real mother was, but that's what I meant. The blood that ran through my veins was just as hot as the blood that had run through my mother's and had gotten her in trouble with Paul's father and later, with Daddy.

"I don't understand," Beau said. He started to put on his clothes.

"It doesn't matter," I said, regaining control of myself. I turned to him. "I'm not blaming you for anything, Beau. You didn't make me do anything I didn't want to do myself in the end."

"I really care for you, Ruby," he said. "I think I care for you more than I've cared for any other girl."

"Do you, Beau? You didn't just say those things?"

"Of course not. I . . ."

We heard footsteps in the corridor outside my studio. I hurried to finish dressing and he stuffed his shirt into his pants just as someone tried the door. Instantly, there was a pounding. It was Daphne.

"Open this door immediately!" she cried.

I ran to it and unlocked it. She stood there, staring in at us, looking me over with so much disapproval, I couldn't help but tremble.

"What are you doing?" she demanded. "Why was this door locked?"

"We were just studying our play lines and didn't want to be disturbed," I said quickly. My heart was pounding. I was sure my hair was messed and my clothes looked hurriedly put on. She ran her eyes over me again as if I were a slave on an auction block in the antebellum South and then quickly shifted her gaze to Beau. His weak smile reinforced her suspicions.

"Where are your play scripts?" she demanded with a scowl.

"Right here," Beau said, and picked them up to show them to her.

"Hmm," she said, and then flicked her stony eyes at me. "I can't wait to see the result of all this dedicated rehearsal." She pulled herself up into an even straighter, firmer posture. "We're having some dinner guests tonight. Dress more formally," she ordered in a cold, commanding tone. "And fix your hair. Where's your sister?"

"I don't know," I said. "She left earlier and hasn't returned."

"Should she somehow get past me before dinner, inform her of my instructions," she said. She glanced at Beau again, her frown deepening, and then returned her gaze to me and fired her words like bullets. "I don't like locked doors in my house. When people lock doors, they usually have something to hide or they're doing something they don't want anyone else to know," she snapped, and then pivoted and left. It was as if a cold wind had just blown through the room. I let out a breath and so did Beau.

"You better be going, Beau," I said. He nodded.

"I'll pick you up for school tomorrow," he said. "Ruby . . ."

"I hope you really meant what you said, Beau. I hope you really do care for me."

"I do. I swear," he said, and kissed me. "I'll see you in the morning. Bye." He was eager to escape. Daphne's looks were like darts sticking into his facade of innocence.

After he left I sat down for a moment. The events of the last hour seemed more like a dream now. It wasn't until I got up and looked at the drawing I had done of him that I realized none of it was a dream. I covered the picture and hurried out, feeling so light, I thought I might just be carried out an open window by a passing breeze.

Gisselle didn't return home in time for dinner. She phoned to say she was eating with her friends. Daphne was very upset about it, but quickly hid her displeasure when our dinner guests, Monsieur Hamilton Davies and his wife, Beatrice, arrived. Monsieur Davies was a man in his late fifties or early sixties who owned a steamboat company that took tourists up and down the Mississippi River. Daphne had let me know that he was one of the wealthiest men in New Orleans, who they were trying to involve with some of my father's investments. She also let me know in no uncertain terms that it was very important I be on my best behavior and make a good impression.

"Don't speak unless spoken to and when someone does speak to you, answer promptly and briefly. They'll be watching the way you comport yourself so remember everything I taught you about dinner etiquette," she lectured.

"If you're worried about me embarrassing you, maybe I should eat earlier," I suggested.

"Nonsense," she said sharply. "The Davies are here because they want to see you. They're the first of our friends I've invited. They know it's an honor," she added in her most haughty, arrogant tone.

Was I some sort of trophy now, a curiosity she was using to enhance her own importance in the eyes of her friends? I wondered, but dared not ask. Instead, I dressed as she told me to dress and took my place at the table, concentrating on my posture and my manners.

The Davies were pleasant enough, but their interest in my story made me uncomfortable. Madame Davies, especially, asked many detailed questions about my life in the bayou with "those awful Cajuns," and I had to make up answers on the spot, glancing quickly at Daphne after each response to see if I had said the right things.

"Ruby's tolerance for these swamp people is understandable," she told the Davies when I didn't sound bitter enough. "For all of her life, she was led to believe she was one of them and they were her family."

"How tragic," Madame Davies said. "And yet, look at how nice she's turning out. You're doing a wonderful job with her, Daphne."

"Thank you," Daphne said, gloating.

"We oughta get her story into the newspapers, Pierre," Hamilton Davies suggested.

"That would only bring her notoriety, Hamilton dear," Daphne said quickly. "The truth is, we've shared these details solely with our dearest friends," she added. The way she smiled, batted her eyelashes, and turned her shoulders at him made his eyes twinkle with pleasure. "And we've asked everyone to be discreet. No sense in making life any more difficult for the poor child than it already has been," she added.

"Of course," Hamilton said. He smiled at me. "That would be the least desirable thing to do. As usual, Daphne, you're a lot wiser and clearer thinkin' than us Creole men."

Daphne lowered and then raised her eyes flirtatiously. Watching her in action, I felt confident I was watching an expert when it came to manipulating men. All the while my father sat back, a smile of admiration, a look of idolization in his eyes. Even so, I was happy when dinner ended and I was excused.

A few hours later, I heard Gisselle return home and go to her room. I waited to see if she would knock on our adjoining door or try it, but she went right to her telephone. I couldn't hear what she was saying, but I heard her voice drone on well into the night. She seemed to have a slew of friends to call. Naturally, I was curious about what she gossiped, but I didn't want to give her the satisfaction of going to her. I was still very angry over the things she had done.

The next morning, she was all brightness and light, just bubbling over with pleasantness at the breakfast table. I was cordial to her in front of Daddy, but I was determined to see her apologize before I would be as friendly as I had been. To both Beau's and my surprise, she had Martin pick her up for school. Just before she skipped down the steps to get into his car, she turned to me and offered the closest thing to an apology.

"Don't blame me for what happened. Someone else told them we had gone to Storyville and I had to tell them about your friend," she said. "See you at school, sister dear," she added with a smile.

Before I could reply, she was rushing off. A few moments later, I got into Beau's car and we followed. He was still worried about Daphne.

"Did she say or ask you anything else after I left?" he wanted to know.

"No. She was worried only about pleasing our dinner guests."

"Good," he said with visible relief. "My parents have been invited to dinner at your house next weekend. We'll just have to cool it a bit," he suggested.

But cooling things down was not to be my destiny. As soon as we entered the school, I sensed a different atmosphere about me. Beau thought I was imagining it, but it seemed to me that most of the students were looking my way and smiling. Some hid their smirks behind their hands when they whispered, but many didn't try to be discreet. It wasn't until the end of English class that I found out why.

As the class filed out, one of the boys came up beside me and bumped his shoulder against mine.

"Oh, sorry," he said.

"It's all right." I started away, but he seized my arm to pull me back beside him.

"Say, are you smiling in this?" he asked, holding out his hand and unclenching his fist to reveal a picture of me naked in his palm. It was one of the pictures that had been taken at Claudine's slumber party. In it, I had just turned back and wore a look of shock on my face, but most of my body was clearly exposed.

He laughed and hurried on to join a pack of students who had gathered to wait at the corner of the corridor. The collection of both girls and boys gazed over his shoulder to look at the photograph. A kind of paralyzing numbness gripped me. I felt as if my legs had been nailed to the floor. Suddenly, Gisselle joined the group.

"Make sure you tell everyone it's my sister and not me," she quipped, and everyone laughed. She smiled at me and continued on, arm and arm with Martin.

My tears clouded my vision. Everything looked out of focus or hazy. Even Beau coming down the corridor toward me, a look of concern on his face, seemed distant and distorted. I felt something within me crack and suddenly, a shrill scream flowed out of my mouth. Every single person in the corridor, including some teachers, froze and looked my way.

"Ruby!" Beau called.

I shook my head, denying the reality of what was taking place before me. Some students were laughing; some were smiling. Few looked worried or unhappy.

"You . . . animals!" I cried. "You mean, cruel . . . animals!"

I turned and threw my books down and just lunged at the nearest exit.

"RUBY!" Beau cried after me, but I shot through the door and ran down the steps. He came after me, but I was running as hard and as fast as I had ever run. I nearly got hit by a car when I sprinted across the street. The driver put on his brakes and brought it to a screeching stop, but I didn't pause. I ran on and on, not even looking where I was going. I ran until I felt a dozen needles in my side and then, with my lungs bursting, I finally slowed down and collapsed behind an old, large oak tree on someone's front lawn. There, I sobbed and sobbed until my well of tears ran dry and my chest ached with the heaving and crying.

I closed my eyes and tried to imagine myself far away. I saw myself back in the bayou, floating in a pirogue through the canal on a warm, clear spring day.

The clouds above me now disappeared. The grayness of the New Orleans day was replaced by the sunshine in my memory. As my pirogue floated closer to the shore, I heard Grandmere Catherine singing behind the house. She was hanging up some clothes she had washed.

"Grandmere," I called. She leaned to the right and saw me. Her smile was so bright and alive. She looked so young and so beautiful to me.

"Grandmere," I muttered with my eyes still shut tight. "I want to go home. I want to be back in the bayou, living with you. I don't care how poor we were or how hard things were for us. I was still happier. Grandmere, please, make it all right again. Don't be dead and gone. Perform one of your rituals and erase time. Make all this just a nightmare. Let me open my eyes and be beside you in the loom room, working. I'll count to three and it will be true. One . . . two . . ."

"Hey, there," I heard a man call. I opened my eyes. "What do you think you're doing?" An elderly man with wild snow white hair stood in the doorway of the house in front of which I had collapsed. He waved a black cane toward me. "What do you want here?"

"I was just resting, sir," I said.

"This isn't a park, you know," he said. He looked at me more closely. "Shouldn't you be in school?" he demanded.

"Yes, sir," I said and got up. "I'm sorry," I said, and walked off quickly. When I reached the corner, I gathered my bearings and hurried up the next street. Realizing how close I was, I headed for home. When I arrived, Daddy and Daphne were already gone.

"Mademoiselle Ruby?" Edgar said, opening the door and looking out at me. This time I couldn't hide my tear-streaked face or pretend to be all right. He tightened his face into an expression of concern and anger. "Come along," he ordered. I followed him through the corridor to the kitchen. "Nina," he said as soon as we entered. Nina turned around and took one look at me and then at him. She nodded.

"She'll be fine with me," she said, and Edgar, looking satisfied, left. Nina drew closer.

"What happened?" she demanded.

"Oh, Nina," I cried. "No matter what I do, she finds a way to hurt me."

Nina nodded.

"No more. You come with Nina now. This will be stopped. Wait here," she commanded, and left me in the kitchen. I heard her go down the corridor to the stairway. After a minute or so, she returned and took my hand. I thought she was going to take me back to her room again for one of her voodoo rituals. But she surprised me. She threw off her apron and led me to the back door.

"Where are we going, Nina?" I asked as she hurried me through the yard to the street.

"To see Mama Dede. You need very strong gris-gris. Only Mama Dede can do it. Just one thing, child," she said, stopping at the corner and drawing her face closer to mine, her black eyes wide with excitement. "Do not tell Monsieur and Madame Dumas where I'm taking you, okay? This will be our secret only, okay?"

"Who is . . . ?"

"Mama Dede, voodoo queen of all New Orleans now."

"What is Mama Dede going to do?"

"Get your sister to stop hurting you. Drive Papa La Bas out of her heart. Make her be good. You want that?"

"Yes, Nina. I want that," I said.

"Then swear to keep the secret. Swear."

"I swear, Nina."

"Good. Come," she said, and started us down the walk again. I was just angry enough to go anywhere and do anything she wanted.

We took the streetcar and then got off and took a bus to a run-down section of the city in which I had never been, nor even seen. The buildings looked no better than shacks. Black children, most too young to go to school, played on the scarred and bald front yards. Broken-down cars and some that looked like they were about to break down were parked along the streets. The sidewalks were dirty, the gutters full of cans, bottles, and paper. Here and there a lone sycamore or magnolia tree struggled to battle the abused surroundings. To me this looked like a place where the sun itself hated to shine. No matter how bright the day, everything still looked tarnished, rusted, faded.

Nina hurried us along the sidewalk until we reached a shack house no better or no worse than any of the others. The windows all had dark shades drawn and the sidewalk, steps, and even the front door were chipped and cracked. Above the front door hung a string of bones and feathers.

"The queen lives here?" I asked, astounded. I had been expecting another mansion.

"She sure do," Nina said. We went down the narrow walk to the front door and Nina turned the bell key. After a moment a very old black woman, toothless, her hair so thin, I could see the shape and color of her scalp, opened the door and peered out. She wore what looked like a potato sack to me. Stooped, her shoulders turned in sharply, she lifted her tired eyes to gaze at Nina and me. I didn't think she was any more than four feet tall. She wore a pair of men's sneakers, stained, without laces, and no socks.

"Must see Mama Dede," Nina said. The old lady nodded and stepped back so we could enter the small house. The walls were cracked and peeling. The floor looked like it had once been covered with carpet that had just recently been ripped up. Here and there pieces of it remained glued or tacked to the slats. The aroma of something very sweet flowed from the rear of the house. The old lady gestured toward a room on the left and Nina took my hand and we entered.

A half-dozen large candles provided the light. The room looked like a store. It was that full of charms and bones, dolls, and bunches of feathers, hair, and snakeskins. One wall was covered with shelves and shelves of jars of powders. And there were cartons of different color candles on the floor along the far wall.

In the midst of all this clutter were a small settee and two torn easy chairs, the springs popped out of the bottom of one. Between the chairs and the settee was a wooden box. Gold and silver shapes had been etched around it.

"Sit," the old lady commanded. Nina nodded at the easy chair on our left and I went to it. She went to the other.

"Nina . . ." I began.

"Shh," she said and closed her eyes. "Just wait." A moment later, from somewhere else in the house, I heard the sound of a drum. It was a low, steady beat. I couldn't help but become nervous and afraid. Why had I allowed myself to be brought here?

Suddenly, the blanket that hung in the doorway in front of us parted and a much younger looking black woman appeared. She had long, silky black hair gathered in thick ropelike strands around her head, over which she wore a red tignon with seven knots whose points all stuck straight up. She was tall and wore a black robe that flowed all the way down to her bare feet. I thought she had a pretty face, lean with high cheekbones and a nicely shaped mouth, but when she turned to me, I shuddered. Her eyes were as gray as granite.

She was blind.

"Mama Dede, I come for big help," Nina said. Mama Dede nodded and entered the room, moving as if she weren't blind, swiftly and gracefully sitting herself on the settee. She folded her hands in her lap and waited, those seemingly dead eyes turning toward me. I didn't move; I hardly breathed.

"Speak of it, sister," she said.

"This little girl here, she's got a twin sister, jealous and cruel, who does bad things to her causing much pain and grief."

"Give me your hand," Mama Dede said to me, and held hers out. I looked at Nina who nodded. Slowly, I put mine into Mama Dede's. She closed her fingers firmly over mine. They felt hot.

"Your sister," Mama Dede said to me. "You don't know her long and she don't know you long?"

"Yes, that's right," I said amazed.

"And your mother, she can't help you none?"

"No."

"She be dead and gone to the other side," she said, nodding and then she released my hand and turned to Nina.

"Papa La Bas, he eating on her sister's heart," Nina said. "Making her hateful, somethin' terrible. Now we got to protect this baby, Mama. She believes. Her grandmere was a Traiteur lady in the bayou."

Mama Dede nodded softly and then held out her hand again, this time palm up. Nina dug into her pocket and pulled out a silver dollar. She put it in Mama Dede's hand. Mama Dede closed her palm and then turned to the doorway where the old lady stood watching. She came forward and took the silver coin and dropped it in a pocket in her sack dress.

"Burn two yellow candles," she prescribed. The old lady moved to the cartons and plucked out two yellow candles. She set them in holders and then lit their wicks. I thought that might be all there was to it, but suddenly, Mama Dede reached out and seized the top of the ornate box. She lifted it gently and put it beside her on the settee. Nina looked very happy. I waited as Mama Dede concentrated and then dipped her hands into the box. When she brought them up, I nearly fainted.

She was clutching a young python snake. It seemed asleep, barely moving, its eyes just two slits. I gulped to keep down a scream as Mama Dede brought the snake to her face. Instantly, the snake's tongue jetted out and it licked her cheek. As soon as it had, Mama Dede returned it to the box and covered the box again.

"From the snake, Mama Dede gets the power and the vision," Nina whispered. "Old legend say, first man and first woman entered the world blind and were given sight by the snake."

"What's your sister's name, child?" Mama Dede asked. My tongue tightened. I was afraid to give it, afraid now that something terrible might occur.

"You must be the one to give the name," Nina instructed. "Give Mama Dede the name."

"Gisselle," I said. "But . . ."

"Eh! Eh bomba hen hen!" Mama Dede began to chant. As she chanted, she turned and twisted her body under the robe, writhing to the sound of the drum and the rhythm of her own voice.

"Canga bafie te. Danga moune de te. Canga do ki li Gisselle!" she ended with a shout.

My heart was pounding so hard, I had to press the palm of my hand against my breast. Mama Dede turned toward Nina again. She reached into her pocket and produced what I recognized as one of Gisselle's hair ribbons. That was why she had first gone upstairs before we left. I wanted to reach out and stop her before she put it into Mama Dede's hand, but I was too late. The voodoo queen clutched it tightly.

"Wait," I cried, but Mama Dede opened the box and dropped the ribbon into it.

Then she writhed again and began a new chant.

"L'appe vini, Le Grand Zombi. L'appe vini, pou fe gris-gris."

"He is coming," Nina translated. "The Great Zombi, he is coming, to make gris-gris."

Mama Dede paused suddenly and screamed a piercing cry that made my heart stop for a moment. I thought it had risen into my throat. I couldn't swallow; I could barely breathe. She froze and then she fell back against the settee, dropping her head to the side, her eyes closed. For a moment no one moved, no one spoke. Then Nina tapped me on the knee and nodded toward the door. I rose quickly. The old lady moved ahead and opened the front door for us.

"Thank Mama, please, Grandmere," Nina said. The old lady nodded and we left.

My heart didn't stop racing until we reached home again. Nina was so confident everything would be all right now. I couldn't imagine what to expect. But when Gisselle returned from school, she wasn't a bit changed. In fact, she bawled me out for running away and blamed me for everything that happened as a result.

"Because you ran off like that, Beau got into a fight with Billy and they were both taken to the principal," she said, stopping in the doorway of my room. "Beau's parents have to come to school before he can return.

"Everyone thinks you're crazy now. It was all just a joke. But I got called into the principal's office, too, and he's going to call Daddy and Mommy, thanks to you. Now we'll both be in trouble."

I turned to her slowly, my heart so full of anger, I didn't think I would be able to speak without screaming. But I surprised myself and frightened her with the control in my voice.

"I'm sorry Beau got into a fight and into trouble. He was only trying to protect me. But I'm not sorry about you.

"It's true, I lived in a world that most would consider quite backward compared to the one you've lived in, Gisselle. And it's true the people are simpler and things happen that city people think are terrible, crude, and even immoral.

"But the cruel things you've done to me and permitted others to do to me make anything I've seen in the bayou look like child's play. I thought we could be sisters, real sisters who looked out for each other and cared for each other, but you're determined to hurt me any way you can and whenever you can," I said. Tears were streaming down my cheeks now, despite my effort not to cry in front of her.

"Sure," she replied, moans in her voice, too. "You're making me out to be the bad one now. But you're the one who just appeared on our doorstep and turned our world topsy-turvy. You're the one who got everyone to like you more than they like me. You stole Beau, didn't you?"

"I didn't steal him. You told me you didn't care about him anymore anyway," I said.

"Well . . . I don't, but I don't like someone stealing him away," she added. She stood there, fuming for a few moments. "You better not get me in trouble when the principal calls," she warned and marched off.

Dr. Storm did call. After breaking up the fight between Beau and Billy, a teacher had taken the photograph and brought it to the principal. Dr. Storm told Daphne about the picture and she called Gisselle and me into the study just before dinner. She was so full of anger and embarrassment, her face looked distorted: her eyes large and furious, her mouth stretched into a grimace and her nostrils wide.

"Which one of you allowed such a picture to be taken?" she demanded. Gisselle looked down quickly.

"Neither of us allowed it, Mother," I said. "Some boys snuck into Claudine's house without any of us knowing and while I was changing into a costume for a game we were playing, they snapped the picture of me."

"We're the laughingstock of the school community by now, I'm sure," she said. "And the Andreas have to see the principal. I just got off the phone with Edith Andreas. She's beside herself. This is the first time Beau has gotten into serious trouble. And all because of you," she accused.

"But . . ."

"Did you do these sorts of things in the swamp?"

"No. Of course not," I replied quickly.

"I don't know how you get yourself involved in one terrible thing after another so quickly, but you apparently do. Until further notice, you are not to go anywhere, no parties, no dates, no expensive dinners, nothing. Is that understood?"

I choked back my tears. Defending myself was useless. All she could see was how she had been disgraced.

"Yes, Mother."

"Your father doesn't know about this yet. I will tell him calmly when he returns. Go upstairs and remain in your room until it's time to come down for dinner."

I left and went upstairs, feeling strangely numb. It was as if I didn't care anymore. She could do whatever she wanted to do to me. It didn't matter.

Gisselle paused in my doorway on the way back to her room. She flashed a smile of self-satisfaction, but I didn't say a word to her. That night, we had the quietest dinner since I had arrived. My father was subdued by his disappointment and by what I was sure was Daphne's rage. I avoided his eyes and was happy when Gisselle and I were excused. She couldn't wait to get to her telephone to spread the news of what had occurred.

I went to sleep that night, thinking about Mama Dede, the snake, and the ribbon. How I wished there was something to it all. My desire for vengeance was that strong.

But two days later, I regretted it.

19

Fate Keeps On Happening

The following morning I felt like a shadow of myself. With a heart that had a hollow thump, with legs that seemed to glide over the hallways and down the stairs, I went to breakfast. Martin came to take Gisselle to school, but she didn't ask me and I didn't want to go along with them. Beau had to go to school with his parents so I just walked to school, resembling someone in a trance—face forward, eyes moving neither left nor right.

When I arrived at school, I felt like a pariah. Even Mookie was afraid to associate with me and didn't, as usual, meet me at the locker before homeroom to chatter about homework or television shows. I was the victim in all this, the one who had been horribly embarrassed, but no one seemed to feel sorry for me. It was almost as if I had contracted some terrible, infectious disease and instead of people worrying about me, they were worried about themselves.

Later in the day, I ran into Beau rushing down the corridor to class. He and his parents had had their meeting with Dr. Storm.

"I'm on probation," he told me with a frown. "If I do anything else, break the slightest school rule, I'll be suspended and kicked off the baseball team."

"I'm sorry, Beau. I didn't mean for you to do something and get yourself in trouble."

"That's all right. I hated what they did to you," he said, and then he looked down and I knew what was coming. "I had to promise my parents I wouldn't see you for a while. But that's a promise I don't intend to keep," he added, his beautiful blue eyes blazing with defiance and anger.

"No, Beau. Do what they say. You'll only get yourself into more trouble and I'll be blamed for it. Let some time pass."

"It's not fair," he complained.

"What's fair and what isn't doesn't seem to matter, especially where rich Creole reputations are concerned," I told him bitterly. He nodded. The warning bell for the next period sounded.

"I'd better not be late for class," he said.

"Me neither." I started away.

"I'll call you," he cried, but I didn't turn back. I didn't want him to see the tears that had clouded my eyes. I choked them back, took a deep breath, and went on to my next class. In all my classes, I sat quietly, took notes, and answered questions only when I was asked directly. When the period ended and the class was dismissed, I always left the room alone, holding back until most of the students had gone.

The worst time was lunch. No one was eager to sit with me and when I took a seat at a table, the students who were already sitting there moved to another table. Beau sat with his baseball teammates and Gisselle sat with her usual friends. I knew everyone was looking at me, but I didn't return their glances and stares.

Mookie finally had enough nerve to speak to me, but I wished she hadn't, for she brought only bad news.

"Everyone thinks you deliberately did a striptease. Is it true you're good friends with a prostitute?" she asked quickly. A hot rush of blood heated my face.

"First, I didn't do any striptease, and no, I am not good friends with a prostitute. The girls and boys who pulled this horrible prank on me are just spreading stories to try to cover up their own guilt, Mookie. I thought you, of all people, would see that," I snapped.

"Oh, I believe you," she said. "But everyone's talking about you and when I tried to tell my mother you weren't as bad as people were saying, she got furious with me and forbid me to be friends with you. I'm sorry," she added. What she said to me made me stiffen.

"So am I," I replied, and gobbled down the rest of my lunch so I could leave quickly.

At the end of the school day, I went to see Mr. Saxon, the dramatics instructor, and told him I was resigning from the school play. It was obvious from the look on his face that he had heard all about the episode with the photograph.

"That's really not necessary, Ruby," he said, but he looked relieved that I had come forward with the idea. I could tell he had already anticipated my bringing an unwelcome notoriety to the cast which would take away from the performances. People would come just out of curiosity to see the wicked little Cajun girl.

"But if your mind is made up, I do appreciate your doing this before it gets to be too late for me to replace you," he added.

Without saying another thing, I dropped the script on his desk and left to walk home.

Daddy didn't come to dinner that evening. When I came down I found Gisselle and Daphne sitting alone. With her eyes fixed angrily on me, Daphne quickly explained that he had fallen into one of his fits of melancholia.

"The combination of some unfortunate business ventures with the disastrous recent events have pushed him into a deep depression," she continued.

I gazed at Gisselle who continued eating as if she had heard this a hundred times before.

"Shouldn't we call a doctor, get him some medicine?" I asked.

"There is no medicine except filling his life with cheerful news," she replied pointedly. Gisselle jerked her head up.

"I got a ninety on a history test yesterday," she boasted.

"That's very nice, dear. I'll be sure to tell him," Daphne said.

I wanted to say that I had gotten a ninety-five on the same test, but I was sure Gisselle, and maybe even Daphne, would interpret it as my attempt to belittle Gisselle's accomplishment, so I remained silent.

Later that evening, Gisselle stopped by my room. As far as I could tell, even though poor Daddy was quite distraught over all that had occurred, she was completely without guilt or regrets. I had the urge to scream at her and see her poise collapse! I wanted her smiles to peel off like bark from a tree, but I remained silent, afraid of only causing more trouble.

"Deborah Tallant is having a party this weekend," she announced. "I'm going with Martin, and Beau's coming along with us," she added with sadistic pleasure. She looked like she was really enjoying pouring salt on my wounds. "I know he regrets giving me up so quickly now, but I'm not going to make things easy for him. I'm going to let him turn and turn out there like a ball on a string. You know how," she said with an oily, evil smile. "I'll kiss Martin passionately right in front of him, dance so closely with Martin that we look attached . . . that sort of thing."

"Why are you so cruel?" I asked her.

"I'm not so cruel. He deserves it. Anyway, I wish I could take you to the party, but I had to specifically promise Deborah I wouldn't. Her parents wouldn't like it," she said.

"I wouldn't go if she invited me," I replied. A cynical smile twisted her lips.

"Oh, yes you would," she said, laughing. "Yes, you would."

She left me, infuriated. I sat there steaming for a while and then felt myself calm down to a quiet indifference. I lay back in my bed reminiscing and finding some comfort in my beautiful memories living with Grandmere Catherine in the bayou. Paul came to mind and I suddenly felt terrible about the way I had left without saying good-bye to him, even though at the time, it seemed to be the best thing to do.

I sat up quickly and ripped a sheet of paper out of my notebook. Then I went to my desk and began writing him a letter. As I wrote, the tears filled my eyes and my heart contracted into a tight lead fist in my chest.

Dear Paul,

It has been some time now since I left the bayou, but you haven't been out of my thoughts. First, I want to apologize for leaving without saying good-bye to you. The reason why I didn't is simple—it would have been too painful for me, and I was afraid, too painful for you. I'm sure you were just as confused and disturbed about the events that occurred in our pasts as I was, and probably, you were just as angry about it. But fate is something we cannot change. It would be easier to hold back the tide.

Even so, I imagine you've spent a lot of time wondering why I just upped and left the bayou. The immediate reason was Grandpere Jack was arranging my marriage to Buster Trahaw and you know I'd rather be dead than married to him. But there were deeper, even more important reasons, the most important one being that I found out who my real father was and decided to do what Grandmere Catherine had asked as a dying wish—go to him and start a new life.

I have. I now live in an entirely different world in New Orleans. We're rich; we live in a grand house with maids and cooks and butlers. My father is very nice and very concerned about me. One of the first things he did when he discovered my artistic talent was to create a studio for me and hire a college art teacher to give me private lessons. However, the biggest surprise for you to learn is that I have a twin sister!

I wish I could tell you that all is wonderful, that being rich and having so many beautiful things has made my life better. But it hasn't.

My father's life has not been smooth either. The tragedies that befell his younger brother and some of the other things that happened to him have made him a deeply disturbed and sad man. I was hoping that I could change things for him and bring him enough happiness to cure his depression and sadness, but I haven't been successful yet and now I am not sure I can ever be.

In fact, at this very moment I wish I could return to the bayou, return to the time before you and I learned all the terrible things about our own pasts, return to the time before Grandmere Catherine died. But I can't. For better or for worse, as I said, this is my fate and I must learn how to deal with it.

Right now, all I want to do is ask you to forgive me for leaving without saying good-bye, and ask you when you have a chance, in a quiet moment, either in or out of church, to say a little prayer for me.

I do miss you.

God bless.

Love,
Ruby

I put the letter into an envelope and addressed it. The next morning, I mailed it on my way to school. The day wasn't much different from the one before, but I could see that as time went by, the excitement and interest other students had in me and what had occurred would wane. There was nothing as dead as old news. Not that those who had been friendly and interested in me started to be those things again. Oh, no. That would take much longer and only if I made a great effort. For the present, I was treated as if I were invisible.

I saw Beau a few times and every time, he looked at me, he had an expression of shame and regret on his face. I felt more sorry for him than he did for me and tried to avoid him as much as possible so things wouldn't be so hard for him. I knew there were girls and even boys who would rush home to tell their parents if Beau defiantly returned to my side. In a matter of hours, the phones at his house would ring off the hook and his parents would be enraged at him.

But on the way home from school that afternoon, I was surprised when Gisselle and Martin drove up to the curb and called to me. I paused and went over to Martin's car.

"What?" I asked.

"If you want, you can come with us," Gisselle offered, as if she were handing out charity. "Martin's got some good stuff and we're going over to his house. No one's home," she said. I could smell the aroma of the marijuana and knew that they had already started having their so-called good time.

"No, thanks," I said.

"I'm not going to invite you to do things if you keep saying no," Gisselle threatened. "And you'll never get back into the swing of things and have friends again."

"I'm tired and I want to begin my final term paper," I explained.

"What a drag," Gisselle moaned.

Martin puffed on his joint and smiled at me.

"Don't you want to laugh and cry again?" he asked. That set them both laughing and I pulled myself away from the window just as he accelerated and shot off, his tires squealing as he made the turn at the end of the block.

I walked home and went right to my room to do what I had said, begin my homework. But less than an hour later, I heard some shouting coming from downstairs. Curious, I walked out of my room and went to the head of the stairs. Below, in the entryway stood two city policemen, both with their hats off. A few moments later, Daphne came rushing forward, Wendy Williams hurrying with her coat. I took a few steps down.

"What's wrong?" I asked.

Daphne paused in front of the policemen.

"Your sister," she screamed. "She's been in a bad car accident with Martin. Your father's meeting me at the hospital."

"I'll come with you," I cried, and ran down the steps to join her.

"What happened?" I asked, getting into the car with her.

"The police said Martin was smoking that dirty . . . filthy . . . drug stuff. He crashed right into the back of a city bus."

"Oh no." My heart was pounding. I had seen only one car accident before in my life. A man in a pickup truck had gotten drunk and drove off an embankment. When I saw the accident, his bloodied body was still hanging out of the smashed front window, his head dangling.

"What's wrong with you young people today?" Daphne cried. "You have so much, and yet you do these stupid things. Why?" she shrilled. "Why?"

I wanted to say it was because some of us have too much, but I bit down on those thoughts, knowing she would take it as a criticism of her role as mother.

"Did the policemen say how bad they were hurt?" I asked instead.

"Bad," she replied. "Very bad . . ."

Daddy was already waiting for us in the hospital emergency room. He looked terribly distraught, aged and weakened by the events.

"What have you learned?" Daphne asked quickly. He shook his head.

"She's still unconscious. Apparently, she hit the windshield. There are broken bones. They're doing the X rays now."

"Oh, God," Daphne said. "This, on top of everything else."

"What about Martin?" I asked. Daddy lifted his shadowy, sad eyes to me and shook his head. "He's not . . . dead?"

Daddy nodded. My blood ran cold and drained down to my ankles, leaving a hollow ache in my stomach.

"Just a little while ago," he told Daphne. She turned white and clutched his arm.

"Oh, Pierre, how gruesome."

I backed up to a chair by the wall and let myself drop into it. Stunned, I could only sit and stare at the people who rushed to and fro. I waited and watched as Daddy and Daphne spoke with doctors.

When I was about nine, there was a four-year-old boy in the bayou, Dylan Fortier, who had fallen out of a pirogue and drowned. I remember Grandmere Catherine had been called to try to save him and I had gone along with her. The moment she looked at his little withered form on the bank of the canal, she knew it was too late and crossed herself.

At the age of nine, I thought death was something that happened only to old people. We young people were invulnerable, protected by the years we were promised at birth. We wore our youth like a shield. We could get sick, very sick; we could have accidents, even serious ones, or we could be bitten by poisonous things, but somehow, someway there was always something that would save us.

The sight of that little boy, pale and gray, his hair stuck on his forehead, his little fingers clenched into tiny fists, his eyes sewn shut, and his lips blue was a sight that haunted me for years afterward.

All I could think of now was Martin's impish smile when he had pulled away from the curb. What if I had gotten into the car with them, I wondered? Would I be in some hospital emergency room or would I have prevailed and gotten Martin to slow down and drive more carefully?

Fate . . . as I had told Paul in my letter . . . could not be defeated or denied.

Daphne returned first, her face full of agony and emotional fatigue.

"How is she?" I asked, my heart thumping.

"She's regained consciousness, but something is wrong with her spine," she said in a dead, dry tone. She was even paler and held her right palm over her heart.

"What do you mean?" I asked, my voice cracking.

"She can't move her legs," Daphne said. "We're going to have an invalid in the family. Wheelchairs and nurses," she said, grimacing. "Oh, I feel sick," she added quickly. "I'm going to the bathroom. See to your father," she commanded with a wave of her hand.

I looked across the hallway and saw him looking like someone who had been hit by a train. He was standing with the doctor. His back was against the wall and his head was down. The doctor patted him on the shoulder and then walked off, but Daddy didn't move. I rose slowly and started toward him. He raised his head as I approached, the tears streaming from his eyes, his lips quivering.

"My little girl," he said, "my princess . . . is probably going to be crippled for life."

"Oh, Daddy," I shook my head, my own tears rivaling his in quantity now. I rushed to him and embraced him and he buried his face in my hair and sobbed.

"It's my fault," he sobbed. "I'm still being punished for the things I've done."

"Oh, no, Daddy. It's not your fault."

"It is. It is," he insisted. "I'll never be forgiven, never. Everyone I love will suffer."

As we clung to each other tightly, all I could think was . . . this is definitely not his fault. It was my fault . . . my fault. I've got to get Nina to take me back to Mama Dede. I've got to undo the spell.

Daphne and I returned home first. By now, it seemed like half the city had heard of the accident. The phones were ringing off the hook. Daphne went directly up to her suite, telling Edgar to take down the names of those who called, explaining that she wasn't able to speak to anyone just yet. Daddy was even worse, immediately retreating to Uncle Jean's room the moment he stepped through the door. I had a message that Beau had called and I called him back before I went to see Nina.

"I can't believe it," he said, trying to hold back his tears. "I can't believe Martin's dead."

I told him what had happened earlier, how they had approached me on the way home.

"He knew better; he knew you couldn't drive and smoke that stuff or drink."

"Knowing is one thing. Listening to wisdom and obeying it is another," I said dryly.

"Things must be terrible at your house, huh?"

"Yes, Beau."

"My parents will be over to see Daphne and Pierre tonight, I'm sure. I might come along, if they let me," he said.

"I might not be here."

"Where are you going tonight?" he asked, astonished.

"There's someone I have to see."

"Oh."

"It's not another boy, Beau," I said quickly, hearing the disappointment in his voice.

"Well, they probably won't let me come anyway," he said. "I'm feeling sick to my stomach, myself. If I hadn't had baseball practice . . . I would probably have been in that car."

"Fate just didn't point its long, dark finger at you," I told him.

After we spoke I went to find Nina. She, Edgar, and Wendy were consoling each other in the kitchen. As soon as she lifted her eyes and met mine, she knew why I had come.

"This is not your fault, child," she said. "Those who welcome the devil man into their hearts invite the bad gris-gris themselves."

"I want to see Mama Dede, Nina. Right away," I added. She looked at Wendy and Edgar.

"She won't tell you any different," she said.

"I want to see her, Nina," I insisted. "Take me to her," I ordered. She sighed and nodded slowly.

"If the madame or monsieur want something, I'll get it to them," Wendy promised. Nina rose and got her pocketbook. Then we hurried out of the house and met the first streetcar. When we arrived at Mama Dede's, her mother seemed to know why. She and Nina exchanged knowing looks. Once again, we waited in the living room for the voodoo queen to enter. I couldn't take my eyes off the box I knew contained the snake and Gisselle's ribbon.

Mama Dede made her entrance as the drums began. As before, she went to the settee and turned her gray eyes toward me.

"Why you come back to Mama, child?" she asked.

"I didn't want anything this terrible to happen," I cried. "Martin's dead and Gisselle is crippled."

"What you want to happen and what you don't want to happen don't make no difference to the wind. Once you throw your anger in the air, it can't be pulled back."

"It's my fault," I moaned. "I shouldn't have come here. I shouldn't have asked you to do something."

"You came here because you were meant to come here. Zombi bring you to me to do what must be done. You didn't cast the first stone, child. Papa La Bas, he find an open door into your sister's heart and curled himself up comfortable. She let him cast the stones with her name on it, not you."

"Isn't there anything we can do to help her now?" I pleaded.

"When she drive Papa La Bas from her heart completely, you come back and Mama see what Zombi want to do. Not until then," she said with finality.

"I feel terrible," I said, lowering my head. "Please, find a way to help us."

"Give me your hand, child," Mama Dede said. I looked up and gave her my hand. She held it firmly, hers feeling warmer and warmer.

"This all is meant to be, child," she said. "You were brought here by the wind Zombi sent. You want to help your sister now, make her a better person, drive the devil from her heart?"

"Yes," I said.

"Don't be afraid," she said, and pulled my hand slowly toward the box. I looked desperately at Nina who simply closed her eyes and began to rock, mumbling some chant under her breath. "Don't be afraid," Mama Dede repeated, and opened the top of the box. "Now you reach down and take out your sister's ribbon. Take it back and nothing more be happening than has."

I hesitated. Reach into a box that contained a snake? I knew pythons weren't poisonous, but still . . .

Mama Dede released me and sat back, waiting. I thought about Daddy, the sadness in his eyes, the weight on his shoulders and slowly, with my eyes closed, I lowered my hand into the box. My fingers nudged the cold, scaly skin of the sleeping serpent. It began to squirm, but I continued moving my fingers around frantically until I felt the ribbon. Quickly, I seized it and pulled my hand out.

"Be praised," Nina said.

"That ribbon," Mama Dede said. "Its been to the other world and back. You keep it precious, as precious as Rosary beads, and maybe someday, you'll make your sister better." She stood up and turned toward Nina. "Go light me a candle at Marie Laveau's grave."

Nina nodded.

"I'll do that, Mama."

"Child," she said, turning back to me, "the good and the bad, they are sisters, too. Sometimes they twist around each other like strands of rope and make knots in our hearts. Unravel the knots in your own heart first; then help your sister unravel hers."

She turned and walked out through the curtain. The drums got louder.

"Let's go home," Nina said. "Now there's much to do."

When we returned, things hadn't changed very much, except that Edgar had added another dozen or so names to the list of those who had called. Daphne was still resting in her suite and Daddy was still in Uncle Jean's room. But suddenly, a little while later, Daphne emerged looking refreshed and elegant, ready to greet those good friends who were coming to console her and Daddy. She got him to come down to have a little dinner.

I sat quietly and listened while Daphne lectured him firmly about getting himself together.

"This isn't the time to fall apart, Pierre. We have some terrible burdens now and I don't intend to carry them on my shoulders alone the way I've been carrying so many other things," she said. He nodded obediently, looking like a little boy again. "Get a hold of yourself," she ordered. "We have people to greet later and I don't want to add anything to the embarrassment we already have to endure."

"Shouldn't we worry more about Gisselle's condition than how it's all embarrassing us?" I said sharply, unable to contain my anger. I hated the way she spoke down to Daddy, who was already weak and defeated.

"How dare you speak to me that way," she snapped, pulling herself up in the chair.

"I don't mean to be insolent, but—"

"My advice to you, young lady, is to walk the straightest, most narrow line you can these next few weeks. Gisselle hasn't been the same since your arrival and I'm sure the bad things you've done and influenced her to do had something to do with what's happened now."

"That's not true! None of that is true!" I cried. I looked at Daddy.

"Let's not bicker amongst ourselves," he pleaded. He turned to me with his eyes bloodshot from hours and hours of sorrowful crying. "Not now. Please, Ruby. Just listen to your mother." He gazed at Daphne. "At times like this, she is the strongest member of our family. She's always been," he said in a tired, defeated voice.

Daphne beamed with pride and satisfaction. For the remainder of our short meal, we all ate in silence. Later that evening, the Andreas did arrive but without Beau. Other friends followed. I retreated to my room and prayed that God would forgive me for the vengeance I had sought. Then I went to sleep, but for endless hours, I dwelled fitfully on the rim of sleep, never finding the peaceful oblivion I desperately sought.

* * *

An odd thing happened to me at school the next day. The drama and impact of the horrible automobile accident put the entire student body into a state of mourning. Everyone was subdued. Girls who knew Martin well were in tears, comforting each other in the hallways and bathrooms. Dr. Storm got on the public address system and offered prayers and condolences. Our teachers made us do busywork, many unable to carry on as usual and sensitive to the fact that the students weren't with it either.

But the odd thing was I became someone to console and not be ignored or despised. Student after student came up to me to talk and express his or her hope everything would turn out well for Gisselle. Even her good friends, Claudine and Antoinette especially, sought my company and seemed repentant for the pranks and the nasty things they had done and said about me.

Most of all, Beau was at my side. He was a great source of comfort. As one of Martin's best friends, he was the one the other boys came to when they wanted to express their sorrow. At lunch, most of the other students gathered around us, everyone speaking in soft, subdued voices.

After school, Beau and I went directly to the hospital and found Daddy having a cup of coffee in the lounge. He had just met with the specialists.

"Her spine was damaged. It's left her paralyzed from the waist down. All of the other injuries will heal well," he said.

"Is there any possibility she'll be able to walk again," Beau asked softly.

Daddy shook his head. "Most unlikely. She's going to need lots of therapy, and lots of tender loving care," he said. "I'm arranging for a live-in nurse for a while after she comes home."

"When can we see her, Daddy?" I asked.

"She's still in intensive care. Only immediate family can see her," he said, looking at Beau. Beau nodded.

I started for the intensive care room.

"Ruby," Daddy called. I turned. "She doesn't know about Martin," he said. "She thinks he's just badly injured. I didn't want to tell her yet. She's had enough bad news."

"Okay, Daddy," I said, and entered. The nurse showed me to Gisselle's bed. The sight of her lying there, her face all banged up and the IV tubes in her arm made my heart ache. I swallowed back my tears and approached. She opened her eyes and looked up at me.

"How are you, Gisselle?" I asked softly.

"How do I look?" She smirked and turned away. Then she turned back. "I guess you're happy you didn't get into the car with us. I guess you want to say, I told you so, huh?"

"No," I said. "I'm sorry this happened. I feel just terrible about it."

"Why? Now no one will wonder which one of us is you and which one is me. I'm the one who can't walk. That's easy to tell," she said. "I'm the one who can't walk." Her chin quivered.

"Oh, Gisselle, you'll walk again. I'll do everything I can to help you," I promised.

"What can you do . . . mumble some Cajun prayer over my legs? The doctors were here; they told me the ugly truth."

"You can't give up hope. Never give up hope. That's what . . ." I was going to say, that's what Grandmere Catherine taught me, but I hesitated.

"Easy for you to say. You walked in here and you'll walk out," she moaned. Then she took a deep breath and sighed. "Have you seen Martin? How's he doing?"

"No, I haven't seen him. I came right to see you," I said and bit down on my lower lip.

"I remember telling him he was going too fast, but he thought it was funny. Just like you, he thought everything was funny all of a sudden. I bet he's not laughing now. You go see him," she said. "And be sure he knows what's happened to me. Will you go?"

I nodded.

"Good. I hope he feels terrible; I hope . . . oh, what's the difference what I hope?" She gazed up at me. "You're happy this happened to me, aren't you?"

"No. I never wanted this much. I . . . ."

"What do you mean, 'this much'? You wanted something?" She studied my face a moment. "Well?"

"Yes," I said. "I admit it. You were so mean to me, got me into so much trouble and did so many bad things to me, I went to see a voodoo queen."

"What?"

"But she told me it wasn't my fault. It was yours because you had so much hate in your heart," I added quickly.

"I don't care what she said. I'll tell Daddy what you did and he'll hate you forever. Maybe now he'll send you back to the swamps."

"Is that what you want, Gisselle?"

She thought a moment and then smiled, but such a tight, small smile, it sent chills down my spine.

"No. I want you to make it up to me. From now on until I say, you make it up to me."

"What do you want me to do?"

"Anything I ask," she said. "You better."

"I already said I would help you, Gisselle. And I'm going to do it because I want to, not because you threaten me," I told her.

"You're making the pain come back into my head," she moaned.

"I'm sorry. I'll go."

"Not until I tell you to go," she said. I stood there, looking down at her. "All right. Go. But go to Martin and tell him what I told you to tell him and then come back later tonight and tell me what he said. Go on," she commanded, and grimaced with pain. I turned and started away. "Ruby!" she called.

"What?"

"You know the only way we can be twins again?" she asked. I shook my head. She smiled. "I'll tell you. Get crippled," she said, and closed her eyes.

I lowered my head and walked out. Mama Dede's prescription was going to be much more difficult than I could ever imagine. Unravel the sisters of hate and love in Gisselle's heart? I might as well try to hold back night, I thought, and went to join Daddy and Beau who waited in the lounge.

Two days later Gisselle was told about Martin. The news struck her dumb. It was as if she believed that all that had happened to her, the injuries, the paralysis was nothing more than a dream that would soon end. The doctors would give her some pills and send her home to resume her life, just the way she had been living it. But when she was told Martin was dead and in fact the funeral was being held that very day, she withered, grew pale and small, and sealed her lips. She didn't cry in front of Daphne or Daddy and when they left and I remained with her, she didn't cry in front of me either. But as soon as I started away to go with my parents to the funeral, I heard her first sob. I ran back to her.

"Gisselle," I said, stroking her hair. She spun around and looked up at me, but not with gratitude for my returning to comfort her, but with blazing, angry eyes.

"He liked you better, too. He did!" she whined. "Whenever we were together, he talked about you. He was the one who wanted you to come along with us. And now he's dead," she added, as if that were somehow my fault.

"I'm sorry. I wish there was something I could do to change it," I told her.

"Go back to your voodoo queen," she snapped, and turned away from me.

I stood there a moment and then hurried to catch up with Daddy and Daphne.

Martin's funeral was enormous. Many of the students attended. Beau and Martin's teammates were the pallbearers. I felt sick and horrible inside and was glad when Daddy took my hand and led us away.

It rained all that day and the next few. I thought the grayness would never leave our hearts and lives, but one morning I awoke to sunshine and when I arrived at school, I found the cloud of sorrow had moved off. Everyone was back into his or her niche. Claudine appeared to take over the leadership role Gisselle once enjoyed, but I didn't care, for I spent little time with Gisselle's friends. My interest was only in doing well in school and spending whatever time I could with Beau.

Finally, the day arrived when Gisselle could be brought home from the hospital. She had begun some therapy there, but, according to what Daphne said, she was still quite uncooperative. Daddy hired the private nurse, a Mrs. Warren, who had worked in veterans' hospitals and was very familiar with patients who had suffered paralyzing injuries. She was about fifty years old, tall with short dark brown hair and hard, almost manly features. I knew she had strong forearms, for I saw the way her veins bulged the first time she lifted Gisselle to make her more comfortable. She brought some of the military manner with her, barking orders at the servants and snapping at Gisselle as if she were a recruit and not an invalid. I was there when Gisselle complained, but Mrs. Warren wasn't one to tolerate it.

"The time for feeling sorry for yourself has passed," she declared. "Now's the time to work on getting yourself as self-sufficient as possible. You're not going to become a blob in that chair either, so get those thoughts out of your head. Before I'm finished, you'll learn how to do most everything for yourself and you will. Is that understood?"

Gisselle just stared at her a moment and then turned to me.

"Ruby, hand me my hand mirror," she said. "I want to fix my hair. I'm sure some of the boys will be over to see me once they've learned I'm home."

"Get it yourself," Mrs. Warren snapped. "Just wheel yourself over and get it."

"Ruby will get it for me," Gisselle countered. "Won't you, Ruby?" She fixed her steely eyes on me.

I went for the mirror.

"You're not helping her by doing that," Mrs. Warren said.

"I know," I said. But I brought Gisselle the mirror anyway.

"She'll turn the lot of you into her slaves. I warn you."

"Ruby doesn't mind being my slave. We're sisters, right, Ruby?" Gisselle said. "Tell her," she commanded.

"I don't mind," I said.

"Well, I do. Now get out of here while I'm conducting the therapy," she snapped at me.

"I'll tell Ruby when to leave and when not to leave," Gisselle shouted. "Ruby, stay."

"But, Gisselle, if Mrs. Warren thinks it's better for me to go, I'd better go."

Gisselle folded her arms and peered at me with narrow slits. "Don't you move from that spot," she ordered.

"Now see here . . ." Mrs. Warren said.

"All right," Gisselle said, smiling. "You're excused now, Ruby. Oh, and please call Beau and tell him I'm expecting him in an hour."

"Make that two hours," Mrs. Warren advised. I nodded and left. For once I agreed wholeheartedly with Daphne: life was going to get far more complicated and unpleasant with Gisselle as an invalid. The accident, her horrible injury, and the aftermath had done nothing to change her personality. Just as before, she still thought everything was coming to her, even more so now. I realized I should never have confessed to her. She had only taken the opportunity to make me into her slave.

If I had any idea that Gisselle's condition would make her feel less secure about herself when it came to boys, that idea popped out of my head the moment I saw how she reacted when Beau and some of his teammates arrived to visit her. Like some empress who was too divine to have her feet touch the earth, she insisted Beau carry her from room to room, place to place rather than wheel her about. She gathered the young men around her, asking Todd Lambert to massage her feet as she spoke, mainly to complain about Mrs. Warren and the terrible ordeal everyone was putting her through.

"I swear," she said. "If you boys don't visit me every day, I'll go stark raving mad. Will you? Will you promise?" she asked, batting her eyelids at them. Of course, they did. While they were still there, she had to order me about, demanding glasses of water or a pillow for her back, snapping at me as though I really were her little slave.

Afterward, when Beau had carried her back upstairs to her room and each and every one of the boys had been given a kiss good-bye, he and I finally had a moment alone.

"I can see it's going to be particularly hard on you from now on," he said.

"I don't care."

"She doesn't deserve you," he said softly, and leaned toward me to kiss me good-bye. Just at that moment, we heard Daphne's footsteps clicking up the corridor. She marched out of the shadows firmly, but some of the darkness still hovered around her furious eyes. She paused a few feet away from us, her arms folded under her bosom, and glared.

"I want to see you this instant, Ruby," she said. "Beau, I'd like you to leave."

"Leave?"

"This instant," she said, her voice cracking like a bullwhip.

"Is there something wrong?" he asked softly.

"I'll discuss that with your parents," she said. He looked at me and then walked out quickly to join his waiting buddies.

"What's wrong?" I asked Daphne.

"Follow me," she ordered. She pivoted and marched back down the hallway. I tagged along, my heart thumping with anticipation. She paused at the doorway of my studio and turned to me.

"If Beau hadn't deserted Gisselle for you, she would never have been in that car with Martin," she declared. "Why did he leave a sophisticated young Creole girl for an unschooled Cajun so quickly, I've wondered. It came to me last night," she said. "Like divine inspiration. And sure enough, my heartfelt suspicions proved true." She threw the studio door open. "Inside."

"Why?" I asked, but did what she demanded. She stared furiously at me a moment and then followed me in and walked directly to my easel. There she threw back some of my current drawings until she came to the drawing I had done of Beau nude. I gasped.

"This is too good to come just from your sinful imagination," she declared. "Isn't it? Don't lie," she added quickly.

I took a deep breath.

"I've never lied to you, Daphne," I said. "And I won't lie to you now."

"He posed?"

"Yes," I confessed. She nodded. "But—"

"Get out and don't dare set foot in this studio again. The door will be locked forever, as far as I'm concerned. Go," she commanded, her arm extended, finger pointing.

I turned and hurried away. Who was the true invalid in this house, I wondered, Gisselle or me?

20

Bird in a Gilded Cage

Ever since the dreadful car accident, Daddy had been moping about like a man who had lost his desire to live. His shoulders drooped, his face was shadowed, his eyes dull. He ate poorly, grew paler and paler, and even took less care with his appearance. And he spent more and more time alone in Uncle Jean's room.

Daphne's tone was always critical and harsh. Instead of showing him compassion and understanding, she complained about her own new problems and insisted that he was only making things more difficult for her. Never did she first consider him and how he was suffering.

So it came as no surprise to me that she wouldn't waste a moment telling him about what she had found in my art studio and what it meant. I felt sorrier for him than I did for myself, for I knew how devastating this would be on top of what had already occurred. Whipped about by what he considered divine retribution for some past sins, he absorbed Daphne's revelations like a condemned man hearing that his final appeal for mercy had been denied. He offered no resistance to her decision to shut up my art studio and end my private art lessons, nor did he utter a single word of protest when she sentenced me to what amounted to practically house arrest.

Naturally, I was not to see or speak to Beau. In fact, I was forbidden to use the telephone. I was to return home directly from school each and every day and either assist Mrs. Warren with Gisselle's needs or do my homework. To reinforce her ironclad hold over me and Daddy, Daphne called me into the study and cross-examined me in his presence, just to prove to him that beyond a doubt, I was as bad as she had predicted I would be.

"You have conducted yourself like a little tramp," she declared, "even using your art talents as a way to be sexually promiscuous. And in my house!

"Most embarrassing of all, you have corrupted the son of one of the most highly respected Creole families in New Orleans. They are beside themselves with grief over this.

"Have you anything to say in your own defense?" she asked like some high court judge.

I raised my eyes and gazed at Daddy who sat with his hands in his lap, his eyes glassy. The way he was, it made no sense for me to speak. I didn't think he would hear or understand a word and Daphne was sure to belittle and destroy anything I would offer as an excuse or justification. I shook my head and looked down again.

"Then go to your room and be sure you do exactly what I have told you to do," she ordered, and I left.

Beau was punished as well. His parents took away his car and restricted his social activities for a month. When I saw him in school, he looked broken and subdued. His friends had heard he had gotten in trouble, but they didn't know the details.

"I'm sorry," he told me. "This is all my fault. I got you and myself into a pot of boiling water."

"I didn't do anything I didn't want to do, Beau, and you and I do care for each other, don't we?"

"Yes," he said. "But there's not much I can do about it now. At least until everyone calms down, if they ever do. I never saw my father this angry. Daphne really got to him. She put most of the blame on you," he said, quickly adding, ". . . unfairly. But my father thinks you're some kind of seductress. He called you a femme fatale, whatever that means." He gazed about us nervously. "If he even hears I'm talking to you . . ."

"I know," I said sadly, and described my punishments, too. He apologized again and hurried off.

Gisselle was ecstatic. When I saw her after Daphne had told her the details, she was positively buoyant with glee. Even Mrs. Warren said Gisselle was more exuberant and energetic than ever, performing her rituals of therapy without complaint.

"I begged Mother to let me see the drawing," she said. "But she told me she had already destroyed it. You sit right down here and tell me every detail," she ordered. "How did you get him to take off all his clothes? What position was he in when he posed? What did you draw . . . everything?"

"I don't want to talk about it, Gisselle," I said.

"Oh yes you do," she snapped. "I'm stuck in here doing stupid exercises with that grouchy nurse all day or doing the homework the tutor prescribes while you're out there having loads of fun. You have to tell me everything. When did this happen? Recently? After you drew him, what did you do? Did you take off your clothes, too? Answer me!" she screamed.

How I wished I could sit down and talk to her. How I wished I had a sister in whom I could confide, a sister who would give me loving advice and be compassionate and caring. But Gisselle just wanted to be titillated and relish my discomfort and pain.

"I can't talk about it," I insisted, and turned away.

"You'd better!" she screamed after me. "You'd better or I'll tell them about the voodoo queen. Ruby! Ruby, get back in here this instant!"

I knew she would go through with her threat, and that on top of everything else at this point would surely drive poor Daddy into a depression from which he would never emerge. Trapped, chained by my own honest confessions to Gisselle, I returned and let her pump me for the details.

"I knew it," she said, smiling with satisfaction. "I knew he would seduce you some day."

"He didn't seduce me. We care about each other," I insisted, but she just laughed.

"Beau Andreas cares about Beau Andreas. You're a fool, a stupid little Cajun fool," she said. Then she smiled again. "Go get me my bedpan. I have to pee."

"Get it yourself," I retorted, and jumped up.

"Ruby!"

I didn't stop. I ran out of her room this time and into my own where I sprawled on my bed and buried my face in my pillow. Would I have been any more abused by Buster and Grandpere Jack? I wondered.

A few hours later, I was surprised by a knock on my door. I turned, ground away any lingering tears, and called out, "Come in." I was expecting Daddy, but it was Daphne. She stood there with her arms folded, but she didn't look angry this time.

"I've been thinking about you," she said in a calmer tone of voice. "I haven't changed my opinion of you and the things you have done, nor do I intend to lessen your punishments, but I have decided to give you an opportunity to repent for your evil ways and especially make things up to your father. Are you interested?"

"Yes," I said, and held my breath. "What do I have to do?"

"This Saturday is your uncle Jean's birthday. Normally, Pierre would go visit him, but Pierre is not in a state of mind to visit anyone, especially not his mentally handicapped younger brother," she said. "So, as usual, the difficult tasks fall to me. I will be going and I thought it might be decent of you to accompany me and represent your father.

"Of course, Jean won't understand who you really are, but—"

"Oh, yes," I said, hardly containing my excitement. "I've always wanted to do that anyway."

"Have you?" She held me in her critical gaze for a moment, pressing her lips together. "Fine then. We'll leave early in the morning Saturday. Wear something appropriate. I expect you understand what I mean when I say that now," she added.

"Yes, Mother. Thank you."

"Oh, one more thing," she said before turning. "Don't mention this to Pierre. It will only make him feel worse. We'll tell him when we return. Do you understand?"

"Yes," I said.

"I hope I'm doing the right thing," she concluded, and left.

Right thing? Of course she was doing the right thing. Finally, I would be able to make a significant contribution toward my father's happiness. As soon as I returned from the institution, I would run right to him and describe every moment I had spent with Jean in detail. I went right to my closet to decide what would be appropriate to Daphne.

When I told Gisselle about my accompanying Daphne to visit Uncle Jean, she looked very surprised. "Uncle Jean's birthday? Only Mother would remember something like that."

"I think it's nice she asked me," I said.

"I'm glad she didn't ask me to go. I hate that place. It's so depressing. All those disturbed people and young people our age, too."

Nothing she could say would diminish my excitement. When Saturday morning finally arrived, I was dressed hours earlier than I had to be and took extra care with my hair, returning to the mirror a half-dozen times to be sure every strand was in place. I knew how critical Daphne could be.

I was disappointed to discover that Daddy hadn't come down to breakfast. Even though we weren't supposed to tell him where we were going, I wanted him to see how nice I looked.

"Where's Daddy?" I asked Daphne.

"He knows what day it is," she explained after looking me over from head to toe. "It's left him in one of his deeper melancholic states. Wendy will bring a tray up to him later."

We ate and then a short time afterward left for the institute. Daphne was quiet for most of the trip, except when I asked her questions.

"How old is Uncle Jean today?" I queried.

"He's thirty-six," she replied.

"Did you know him before?"

"Of course I knew him," she said. I thought I detected a slight smile on her lips. "I daresay there wasn't an eligible young woman in New Orleans who didn't."

"How long has he been in the institution?"

"Almost fifteen years."

"What's he like? I mean, what's his condition like now?" I pursued. She looked like she wasn't going to reply

Finally, she said, "Why don't you just wait and see. Save your questions for the doctors and nurses," she added, which I thought was a strange thing to say.

The institute was a good twenty miles out of the city. It was off the highway, up a long, winding driveway, but it had beautiful grounds with sprawling weeping willows, rock gardens, and fountains, as well as little walkways that had quaint little wooden benches all along the way. As we approached, I saw some older people being escorted by attendants.

After she pulled our car into a parking space and shut off the engine, Daphne turned to me.

"When we go in there, I don't want you to speak to anyone or ask anyone any questions. This is a mental institution, not a public school. Just follow alongside me and wait. Then do whatever you are told to do. Is that clear?" she demanded.

"Yes," I said. Something in her tone of voice and in her look made my heart race. The four-story, gray stucco structure now loomed above us ominously and cast a long dark shadow over us and our car. As we approached the front entrance, I saw that the windows had bars over them and many had their shades drawn down.

From the highway and even approaching it on the driveway, the institution was very attractive and pleasant, but now, close up, it announced its true purpose and reminded visitors that the people housed within were here because they couldn't function properly in the outside world. The bars on the windows suggested some might even be dangerous to others. I swallowed hard and tracked after Daphne through the front entrance. She walked with her head high as usual, her posture regal stiff. Her heels clicked on the polished marble floor, echoing through the immaculate entryway. At a glass enclosure directly before us, a woman in a white uniform sat writing in charts. She looked up as we approached.

"I'm Daphne Dumas," Daphne declared with an authoritative air. "I'm here to see Dr. Cheryl."

"I'll inform him you've arrived, Madame Dumas," the receptionist said and lifted the receiver at her side immediately. "Take a seat if you like," she added, nodding toward the cushioned benches. Daphne turned and gestured for me to sit down. I hurriedly did so and waited with my hands in my lap, gazing around me. The walls were bare, not a picture, not a clock, nothing.

"Dr. Cheryl will see you now, madame," the receptionist said.

"Ruby," Daphne said, and I stood up and walked with her to the side door. The receptionist buzzed us in. We entered another corridor.

"Right this way," the receptionist said, and led us down the hall to a bank of offices. The first on the right was labeled, Dr. Edward Cheryl, Chief of Administration. The receptionist opened the door for us and we entered the office.

It was a large room with windows that had no bars over them. Right now, the drapes were half-drawn. To the right was a long, light brown leather sofa and to the left was a matching settee. The walls were covered with bookcases and here and there were Impressionistic paintings, mostly of rural scenes. One of a field in the bayou caught my interest.

Behind his desk, Dr. Cheryl had hung all of his diplomas and certificates. Dressed in a lab robe, he rose immediately to greet Daphne. He was a man no more than fifty, fifty-five, with bushy dark brown hair, small chestnut eyes, a small nose, and slight mouth. His chin was so round, it was as if his face had failed to form one. Standing a little under six feet tall, he had a slim build with long arms. His smile was tight and tentative like the smile of an insecure child. It seemed odd to think it, but he looked nervous in Daphne's presence.

"Madame Dumas," he said, extending his hand. When he lifted his arm, the sleeve of his robe slid more than halfway up to his elbow. Daphne took his fingers quickly as if she detested touching him or was afraid he could somehow contaminate her. She nodded and sat down in the bullet leather chair before his desk. I remained standing just behind her.

His attention immediately shifted to me. The intensity of his gaze made me feel self-conscious. Finally, after what seemed an interminable pause, he offered me a smile, too, but one just as tentative.

"And this is the young lady?" he asked, coming around his desk.

"Yes. Ruby," Daphne said, smirking as if my name was the most ridiculous thing she had ever heard. He nodded, but kept his eyes on me. Remembering Daphne's orders, I didn't speak until he spoke to me directly.

"And how are you today, Mademoiselle Ruby?" he asked.

"Fine."

He nodded and turned to Daphne.

"Physically, she is in good health?" he asked. What a strange thing to ask, I thought, knitting my eyebrows together with curiosity.

"Look at her. Does she look like anything's physically wrong with her?" she snapped. She spoke to him as sharply as she would speak to one of our servants, but he didn't seem to mind. He gazed at me again.

"Good. Well, let me begin by showing you around a bit," he said, stepping closer to me and farther away from Daphne. I looked at her, but she kept her gaze fixed ahead. "I'd like you to feel comfortable here," he added. "As comfortable as possible."

His smile widened, but there was still something false about it.

"Thank you," I replied. I didn't know what to say. I knew my father and Daphne made sizeable contributions to the institute, besides paying for Uncle Jean, but it still felt funny being treated like such VIPs.

"I understand you're almost sixteen?" he said.

"Yes, monsieur."

"Please . . . call me Dr. Cheryl. We should be friends, good friends. If that's all right with you," he added.

"Of course, Dr. Cheryl." He nodded.

"Madame?" he said, turning back to Daphne.

"I'll wait right here," she said, without turning around. Why was she behaving so strangely? I wondered.

"Very good, madame. Mademoiselle," he said, indicating a side door to his office. I couldn't help my confusion.

"Where are we going?"

"As I said, I would like to show you around first, if that is all right with you, of course."

"Fine," I said, shrugging. I went to the door and he opened it and led me out through another corridor and then up a short stairway. This place was a maze, I thought as we made another turn and took another corridor in a different direction. We continued until we reached a large window and looked in on what was clearly a recreation room. Patients of all ages, from what looked like teenagers to elderly people played cards, board games, and dominoes. Some watched television, and some did some handicrafts like lanyards, needlework, and crocheting. Others were reading magazines. One boy with sweet potato red hair, who looked about seventeen or eighteen, sat staring at everyone and doing nothing. A half-dozen attendants wandered about the room overlooking all the activities, pausing occasionally to say a few words to one of the patients.

"As you see, this is our recreation area. Patients who are able to can come in here during their free time and do almost anything they like. They can even, as young Lyle Black there, sit and do nothing."

"Does my uncle come in here?" I asked.

"Oh, yes, but right now he's waiting in his room for Madame Dumas. He has a very nice room," Dr. Cheryl added. "Right this way," he indicated. We stopped at another door. It was obviously the library.

"We have over two thousand volumes and we get dozens and dozens of magazines," he explained.

"Very nice," I said.

We continued until we came to what looked like a small gymnasium.

"We don't neglect the patients' physical well-being. This is our exercise room. Every morning, we conduct calisthenics. Some of our patients are even able to swim in our pool, which is located in the rear of the building. Here," he said, taking a few steps and pointing down the corridor to the right, "are our treatment rooms. We have a dentist on a regular basis, as well as general medicine doctors on call. Why, we even have a beauty parlor here," he said, smiling.

"This way," he indicated, pointing down the opposite corridor.

I wondered about Daphne. It surprised me that she would sit back in his office and remain so patient. She had made it perfectly clear to me how much she hated coming here. I was sure she wanted to get in and get out as fast as she could. Now troubled as well as confused, I followed Dr. Cheryl. I didn't want to appear impolite or unappreciative, but I was eager to see my uncle.

We turned a corner and approached what looked like an entirely new administrative area. A nurse sat behind a desk. Two attendants, both big men in their late twenties at least, stood talking to her. They looked up as we approached.

"Morning, Mrs. McDonald," Dr. Cheryl said. The nurse at the desk looked up. She had a softer face than Mrs. Warren, but looked to be the same age with bluish gray hair cut at the nape of her neck.

"Good morning, Doctor."

"Boys," he said to the attendants. "Everything going all right this morning?" They nodded, their eyes fixed on me.

"Very well, Mrs. McDonald. As you know, Madame Dumas has brought her daughter here. This is Ruby," he said, turning to me.

I stared at him a moment. What did he mean, brought her daughter here? Why didn't he finish that and say, brought her daughter to see her uncle Jean?

"Ruby, Mrs. McDonald runs things down here and sees to everyone's needs. She's the finest head nurse on any psychiatric floor in the country. We're mighty proud to have her on our staff."

"I don't understand," I said. "Where's my uncle?"

"Oh, he's on another floor," Dr. Cheryl said, flashing that tight, small smile. "This floor is more or less for our temporaries. We don't expect you to remain here long."

"What?" I stepped back. "Remain here? What do you mean, remain here?"

Mrs. McDonald and Dr. Cheryl exchanged quick looks.

"I thought your mother had explained all of this to you, Ruby," he said.

"Explained? Explained what?"

"You're here for an evaluation, an observation. You didn't agree to it?"

"Are you crazy?" I cried. That brought a smile to the attendants, but Dr. Cheryl straightened up quickly.

"Oh, dear," he said. "I thought this was going to be one of our easier ones."

"I want to go back to my mother," I insisted. I looked back down the corridor, so confused and upset now, I wasn't sure which direction to take.

"Just relax," Dr. Cheryl said, stepping forward.

"Relax? You thought I was coming here to be a patient and you want me to relax?"

"You're not a patient as such," he said, closing and opening his eyes. "You're being evaluated."

"For what?"

"Why don't we just settle you in your room first and then we'll have a talk. If there is nothing to do, why you'll go right home," he said with that small smile again.

"There is nothing to do." I backed away. "I want to go to my mother. Right now. I came here to see my uncle. That's why I came."

Dr. Cheryl looked at Mrs. McDonald and she rose.

"You'll only make things harder for yourself if you become uncooperative, Ruby," she said, coming around her desk. The two attendants moved to follow. I continued to back away, shaking my head.

"This is a mistake. Take me back."

"Just relax," Dr. Cheryl said.

"No. I don't want to relax."

The attendant on my right moved quickly to block my retreat. He didn't touch me, but he stood behind me, intimidating me with his presence. I started to cry.

"Please," I said. "I want to go to my mother. This is a mistake. Just take me back."

"In due time, I promise to do just that," Dr. Cheryl said. "Can we show you your room? Once you see how comfortable it is . . ."

"No. I don't want to see any room."

I spun around and tried to get past the attendant, but he seized my arm and held me so tightly at the wrist, it hurt. I screamed and Mrs. McDonald moved in, too.

"Arnold," she called to the other attendant. He came forward to take my other arm.

"Don't hurt her," Dr. Cheryl said. "Careful now. Ruby, just let them show you your room. Go on, my dear."

I struggled in vain for a moment and then began to sob as they led me forward to another door. Mrs. McDonald pressed a buzzer and the door was opened. My legs didn't want to move, but they were practically carrying me along now. Dr. Cheryl followed right behind. They took me down the dormitory corridor and stopped at an opened door.

"See," Dr. Cheryl said, entering first. "This is one of our best rooms. You have windows facing the west, so you get all the afternoon sunlight and not the sunlight in the morning to wake you too early. And just look at this nice bed," he said, indicating the imitation wood frame bed. "Here's a dresser, a closet, and a private bathroom. This bathroom even has a shower. And you have this small desk and chair. Here is some stationery if you care to write a letter to someone," he added, smiling.

I gazed at the stark floors and walls. How could anyone think this was a nice room? It looked more like a glorified prison cell. The windows had bars, didn't they?

"You can't do this to me," I said. I embraced myself tightly. "Take me back immediately or I swear I'll go to the police the first chance I get."

"Your mother has asked us to evaluate you," he said firmly. "Parents have the right to do this if their children are still legally minors. Now if you cooperate, this will be short and sweet and not painful, but if you persist in fighting everything we do and everything we ask you to do, it will be most unpleasant for all of us, but mostly for you," he threatened. "Now, sit down," he ordered, pointing to the chair. I didn't move. He straightened up as if I had spit in his face.

"We've been told something of your background and know what sort of things you've done and how poorly you've been disciplined, young lady, but I assure you, none of that will be tolerated here. Now you will either listen and do what I tell you or I'll move you to the floor above where the patients are kept restrained in straitjackets a good deal of the time."

With a sinking heart, I moved obediently to the chair and sat down.

"That's better," he said. "I have to see to your mother and her visit and then I will send for you and begin our first interview. In the meantime, I want you to read this little booklet," he said, pulling a yellow, stapled booklet out of the desk drawer. "It explains our institution, our rules, and what we try to do here. We give this only to patients who understand, mostly patients who have committed themselves in fact. It even has a place in the back for you to write in your suggestions. See," he said, opening the booklet to show me. "We consider them, too. Some of our former patients have made excellent suggestions."

"I don't want to make any suggestions. I just want to go home."

"Then cooperate and you will," he said. He started out.

"Why would I be put here? Please, just answer that question before you leave me," I begged. He looked at the two attendants who retreated and then he closed the door and turned to me.

"You have a history of promiscuity, don't you, my dear?"

"What? What do you mean?"

"In psychology, we call it nymphomania. Have you ever heard that term?"

I gasped. "What are you saying about me?" I asked.

"You're having a problem controlling yourself when it comes to relationships with the opposite sex?"

"That's not true, Dr. Cheryl."

"Admitting to your problems is the first step, my dear. After that, it's all downhill. You'll see," he said, smiling.

"But I have no problem to admit to."

He stared at me a moment.

"Okay, we'll see," he said. "That's why you're here. To be evaluated. If you have no problem, I'll send you home directly. Does that sound fair?"

"No. None of this is fair. I'm being held prisoner."

"We are all prisoners of our ailments, Ruby dear. Especially, our mental infirmities. The purpose of this place and my purpose is to free you from the mental aberration that has chained you to this misbehavior and caused you even to hate yourself." He smiled. "We have a good cure rate here. Just give it a chance," he concluded.

"Please, my mother's lying. Daphne's lying! Please," I cried. He closed the door behind him. I knew there was no point in trying, but I did so anyway and discovered that it was locked. Frustrated and defeated, still in a state of utter shock, I sat down and waited. I felt sure Daddy knew nothing about this and wondered what sort of lies Daphne would concoct to explain my disappearance. I imagined, she would tell him I couldn't stand her discipline and decided to run away. Poor Daddy, he would believe it.

Nina Jackson shouldn't have gotten Gisselle's ribbon to throw into the box with the snake, I thought; she should have gotten one of Daphne's instead.

Finally, after what seemed like ages and ages to me, the door was unlocked and Mrs. McDonald appeared.

"Dr. Cheryl can see you now," she said. "If you will just follow me quietly, we can go to him without incident."

I got up quickly, thinking that the first chance I got, I would dart right out. But they anticipated that and one of the attendants was waiting outside to accompany us.

"You people are kidnapping me here," I moaned. "It's nothing less than that."

"Now, now, Ruby, you must not permit yourself to grow paranoid about this. People who care about you, love you, want to see what can be done to make you better, that's all," she said in such a sweet voice it was as if I were walking along with someone's nice old grandmother. "No one's going to do anything to hurt you."

"I'm already hurt beyond repair," I said, but that brought only a smile to her face.

"You young people today are so much more dramatic than we were," she commented. Then she inserted a key in the corridor door and unlocked it. "Right this way."

She led me back to the corridor Dr. Cheryl had described as the treatment area. I gazed down another hallway and considered running, but I remembered all the other doors that had to be buzzed to be opened and I was sure there were no windows without bars. The attendant moved up closer behind me anyway. Finally, we stopped at a door and Mrs. McDonald opened it to lead me into a room that contained only a sofa, two chairs, a table, and what looked like some kind of movie projector on a smaller table. There was a screen on the wall directly across from it. The room had no windows, but there was another door and a wall-size mirror on the right side.

"Just sit here," Mrs. McDonald instructed. I sat in one of the chairs. She went to the other door and knocked gently. Then she opened it and poked her head in to mumble, "She's here, Doctor."

"Very good," I heard Dr. Cheryl say. Mrs. McDonald turned back to me and smiled.

"Remember," she said. "If you're cooperative, everything moves faster." She nodded at the attendant and they started out. "Jack will be right outside should you need him," she said as a veiled threat. I looked at the attendant who returned my gaze with steely dark eyes. Thoroughly intimidated, I sat quietly and waited after they left. A few moments later, Dr. Cheryl appeared.

"Well," he said, beaming a wider smile, "how are we doing now? A little better, I hope?"

"No. Where's Daphne?"

"Your mother is visiting your uncle," he said. He went directly to the projector and put a file down beside it.

"She's not my mother," I declared firmly. If I ever wanted to deny her, I wanted to deny her now.

"I understand how you feel."

"No, you don't understand. She's not my real mother. My real mother is dead."

"However," he said, nodding, "she's trying to be a real mother to you, isn't she?"

"No. She's trying to be what she is . . . a witch," I retorted.

"This anger and aggression you now feel is understandable," he said. "I just want you to recognize it for what it is. You feel this way because you feel threatened. Whenever we try to get a patient to admit to errors or recognize weaknesses and illnesses, it's natural for him or her to first resent it. Believe it or not, many of the people here feel comfortable with their mental and behavioral problems because they've been a part of them so long."

"I don't belong here. I don't have any mental or behavioral problems," I insisted.

"Perhaps not. Let me try something with you to see how you view the world around you, okay? Maybe that's all we'll do today and give you a chance to acclimate yourself to your surroundings more. No rush."

"Yes, there is a rush. I've got to go home."

"All right. We'll begin. I'm going to flash some shapes on the screen in front of you. I want you to tell me what comes to mind instantly when you see each one, okay? Don't think about them, just react as quickly as you can. That's easy, right?"

"I don't need to do this," I moaned.

"Just humor me then," he said, and snapped off the room light. He turned on the projector and put the first shape on the screen. "Please," he said. "The faster we do this, the faster you can relax."

Reluctantly, I responded.

"It looks like the head of an eel."

"An eel, good. And this?"

"Some kind of hose."

"Go on."

"A twisted sycamore limb . . . Spanish Moss . . . An alligator tail . . . A dead fish."

"Why dead?"

"It's not moving," I said.

He laughed. "Of course. And this?"

"A mother and a child."

"What's the child doing?"

"Breast-feeding."

"Yes."

He flashed a half-dozen more pictures and then put on the lights.

"Okay," he said, sitting across from me with his notebook. "I'm going to say a word and you respond immediately again, no thought. Just what comes first to mind, understand?" I just looked down. "Understand?" I nodded.

"Can't we just see Daphne and end this?"

"In due time," he said. "Lips."

"What?"

"What comes to mind first when I say, 'lips'?"

"A kiss."

"Hands."

"Work."

He recited a few dozen words at me, jotting down my reactions and then he sat back, nodding.

"Can I go home now?" I asked.

He smiled and stood up. "We have a few more tests to go through, some talking to do. It won't be too long, I promise. Since you have been cooperative, I'm going to permit you to go to the recreation area before lunch. Find something to read, something to do, and I'll see you again real soon, okay?"

"No, it's not okay," I said. "I want to call my daddy. Can I at least do that?"

"We don't permit patients to use the telephones."

"Will you call him, then? If you just call him, you'll see he doesn't want me to be here," I said.

"I'm sorry, Ruby, but he does," Doctor Cheryl said, and pulled a form out of the file. "See? Here is his signature," he said, and I looked at the line to which he pointed. Pierre Dumas was written there.

"She forged it, I'm sure," I said quickly. "She's going to tell him I ran away. Please, just call him. Will you do that?"

He stood up without replying.

"You've got a little time before lunch. Get acquainted with the facilities. Try to relax. It will help us when we meet again," he said, and opened the door. The attendant was waiting. "Take her to the recreation room," Doctor Cheryl told him. The attendant nodded and looked in at me. Slowly, I rose.

"When my father finds out what she did and what you're doing, you're going to be in a lot of trouble," I threatened. He didn't reply and I had no choice but to follow the attendant back down the corridor to the recreation room.

"Hello, I'm Mrs. Whidden," a woman attendant no more than forty said, greeting me at the door. "Welcome. I'm here to help you. Is there something in particular you would like to do . . . handicrafts, perhaps."

"No," I said.

"Well, why don't you just go about and look over everything until something strikes your fancy. Then I'll help you, okay?" she said. Seeing no point to my constantly protesting, I nodded and entered the room. I walked about, gazing at the patients, some of whom gazed at me with curiosity, some with what looked like anger, and some who didn't seem to see me. The redheaded boy who had been sitting doing nothing was still sitting that way. I noticed that his eyes followed me, however. I went to the window near him and gazed out, longing for my freedom.

"Hate being here?" I heard, and turned. It sounded like he had asked it, but he was still sitting stiffly, staring ahead.

"Did you ask me something?" I inquired. He didn't move, nor did he speak. I shrugged and looked out again, and again, I heard, "Hate being here?" I spun around.

"Pardon me?"

Still, without turning, he spoke again.

"I can tell you don't want to be here."

"I don't. I was kidnapped, locked up before I knew what was happening," I said. That animated his face to the point where he at least raised his eyebrows. He turned to me slowly, only his head moving, and he gazed at me with eyes that seemed as cold and as indifferent as eyes on a mannequin.

"What about your parents?" he asked.

"My father doesn't know what my stepmother has done. I'm sure," I said.

"What's the charge?"

"Pardon?"

"What's the reason you're supposedly here for? You know, your problem?"

"I'd rather not say. It's too embarrassing and ridiculous."

"Paranoia? Schizophrenia? Manic-depression? Am I getting warm?"

"No. Why are you here?" I demanded.

"Immobility," he declared. "I'm unable to make decisions, deal with responsibilities. When confronted with a problem, I simply become immobile. I can't even decide what I want to do in here," he added nonchalantly. "So I sit and wait for the recreation period to end."

"Why are you like this?" I asked. "I mean, you know what's wrong with you, apparently."

"Insecure." He smiled. "My mother, apparently like your stepmother, didn't want me. In her eighth month, she tried to abort me, but I only got born too soon instead. From then on, it was straight downhill: paranoia, autism, learning disabilities," he recited dryly.

"You don't seem like someone with learning disabilities," I said.

"I can't function in a normal school setting. I can't answer questions. I don't raise my hand, and when I'm given a test, I just stare at it. But I read," he added. "That's all I do. It's safe." He raised his eyes to me. "So why did they commit you? You don't have to be afraid of telling me. I won't tell anyone else. But I don't blame you if you don't trust me," he added quickly.

I sighed.

"I've been accused of being too loose with my sexual activities," I said.

"Nymphomania. Great. We don't have any of those."

I couldn't help but laugh.

"You still don't," I said. "It's a lie."

"That's all right. This place flourishes on lies. Patients lie to each other, to themselves, and to the doctors and the doctors lie because they claim they can help you, but they can't. All they can do is keep you comfortable," he said bitterly. He lifted his rust-colored eyes toward me again. "You can tell me your real name or you can lie, if you want."

"My name's Ruby, Ruby Dumas. I know your first name is Lyle, but I forgot your last name."

"Black. Like the bottom of an empty well. Dumas," he said. "Dumas. There's someone else here with that name."

"My uncle," I said. "Jean. I was brought here supposedly to visit him."

"Oh. You're Jean's niece?"

"But I never got to see him."

"I like Jean."

"Does he talk to you? What's he like? How is he?" I hurriedly asked.

"He doesn't talk to anyone, but that doesn't mean he can't. I know he can. He's . . . just very quiet, but as gentle as a little boy and as frightened sometimes. Sometimes, he cries for what seems to be no reason, but I know something's going on in his head to make him cry. Occasionally, I catch him laughing to himself. He won't tell anyone anything, especially the doctors and nurses."

"If I can only see him. At least that would be something good," I said.

"You can. I'm sure he'll be at lunch in the little cafeteria."

"I've never met him before," I said. "Will you point him out to me?"

"Not hard to do. He's the best-dressed and the best-looking guy here. Ruby, huh? Nice," he said, and then tightened his face as if he had said something terrible.

"Thank you." I paused and looked around. "I don't know what I'm going to do now. I've got to get out of here, but this place is worse than a prison—doors that have to be buzzed open, bars on the windows, attendants everywhere . . ."

"Oh, I can get you out," he said casually. "If that's what you really want."

"You can? How?"

"There's a room that has a window without bars on it, the laundry room."

"Really? But how can I get to it?"

"I'll show you . . . later. They let us go outside if we want after lunch and there's a way into the laundry room from the yard."

My heart lifted with hope.

"How do you know all this?"

"I know everything about this place," he replied.

"You do? How long have you been here?" I asked.

"Since I was seven," he said. "Ten years."

"Ten years! Don't you ever want to leave?" I asked. He stared ahead for a moment. A tear escaped his right eye and slid down his cheek.

"No," he said. He turned to me with the saddest eyes. "I belong here. I told you," he continued, "I can't make a decision. I told you I'd help you, but later, when it comes time to do it, I don't know if I can." He stared ahead. "I don't know if I can."

My brightened spirits darkened again when I realized he might just be doing what he said everyone did here—lying.

A bell was rung and Mrs. Whidden announced it was time to go to lunch. I brightened again. At least now, I would see Uncle Jean. Unless of course, that was a lie, too.

21

Betrayed Again

It wasn't a lie and I didn't need to have Uncle Jean pointed out to me. He hadn't changed very much from the young man in the photos, and he was, as Lyle had described, the best-dressed patient in the cafeteria, coming to lunch in a light blue seersucker sports jacket and matching slacks, a white shirt with a blue cravat, and spotless white deck shoes. His golden brown hair was neatly trimmed and brushed back on the sides. I could see that he still had his trim figure. He looked like someone on vacation who had stopped by to visit a sick relative. He ate mechanically and gazed around the cafeteria with little or no interest.

"There he is," Lyle said, nodding in Uncle Jean's direction.

"I know." My heart began to tap a rapid beat on the inside of my chest.

"As you see, despite his problem, whatever that may be," Lyle said dryly, "he remains very concerned about his appearance. You should see his room, how neatly he keeps everything, too. In the beginning, I thought he had a cleanliness fetish or something. If you touch anything in his room, he'll go to it and make sure you didn't smudge it or move it an iota of an inch out of place.

"I'm practically the only one he permits in his room," Lyle added proudly. "He doesn't talk to me as such. He doesn't speak to anyone, but he tolerates me at least. If someone else sits at that table, he'll create a stir."

"What will he do?" I asked.

"He might start beating a spoon on his plate or he might just scream this horrid, beastlike sound until one of the attendants comes over and moves him or the other person away," Lyle explained.

"Maybe I shouldn't go near him," I said fearfully.

"Maybe you shouldn't. Maybe you should. Don't ask me to decide for you, but if you want me to, I'll tell him who you are at least."

"He might recognize me," I said.

"I thought he never saw you."

"He saw my twin sister and will just think that's who I am."

"Really? You have a twin sister? Now that's interesting," Lyle replied.

"If you two want to eat, you had better get in line," an attendant advised us.

"I don't know if I want to eat," Lyle muttered.

"Now, Lyle," the attendant said, "you know you don't have all day to make this decision."

"I'm hungry," I said to help move him along. I went to the stack of trays and got one. Then I started down the line, gazing back once to see Lyle still considering. My action moved him finally and he joined me.

"Please, get two of whatever you choose," he said.

"What if you don't like it?"

"I don't know what I like anymore. It all tastes the same to me," he said.

I chose the stew and got us both some Jell-O for dessert. After we had our food, we turned to decide where to sit and I stared at Uncle Jean, wondering if I should approach him.

"Go on," Lyle said. "I'll sit wherever you want."

With my eyes glued to him, I walked directly toward Uncle Jean. He continued to eat mechanically and move his eyes from side to side, almost in synchronization with each forkful of food. He didn't appear to notice me until I was nearly upon him. Then his eyes stopped scanning the room and he paused, his hand holding the fork about midway between the plate and his mouth. Slowly, he scanned my face. He didn't smile, but it was apparent he recognized me as Gisselle.

"Hello, Uncle Jean," I said, my body trembling. "May I sit with you?"

He didn't respond.

"Tell him who you really are," Lyle coached.

"My name is Ruby. I am not Gisselle. I'm Gisselle's twin sister, someone you've never met."

His eyes blinked rapidly and then he brought the forkful of food to his mouth.

"He's interested or at least amused," Lyle whispered.

"How do you know?"

"If he wasn't, he would be smacking the plate with his fork or starting to scream," Lyle explained. Feeling like the blind led by the blind, I inched my way forward to the table and gently put my tray down. I paused a moment, but Uncle Jean just kept eating, his blue-green eyes fixed on me. Then I sat down.

"Hi, Jean," Lyle said. "The natives appear a bit restless today, huh?" he said, sitting down beside me. Uncle Jean gazed at him, but didn't respond. Then he turned his attention back to me.

"I really am Gisselle's twin sister, Uncle Jean. My parents have told everyone how I was stolen at birth and how I managed to return just recently."

"Is that true?" Lyle asked astonished.

"No. But that's what my parents are telling everyone," I said. Lyle started to eat.

"Why?"

"To cover up the truth," I said, and turned back to Uncle Jean who was blinking rapidly again. "My father, your brother, met my mother in the bayou. They fell in love and she became pregnant. Later, she was talked into giving up the baby, only no one knew there were twins. On the day Gisselle and I were born, my grandmere Catherine kept me when my grandpere Jack took the first baby, Gisselle, out to the limousine where your family was waiting."

"Great story," Lyle said with a wry smile on his face.

"It's true!" I snapped at him, and then turned back to Uncle Jean. "Daphne, Daddy's wife, resents me, Uncle Jean. She's been very cruel to me ever since I arrived. She told me she was bringing me here to see you but secretly she made arrangements with Dr. Cheryl and his staff to keep me here for observation and evaluation. She's doing everything she can to get rid of me. She's—"

"Aaaaa," Uncle Jean cried. I stopped, my heart pounding. Was he about to scream and pound his dish?

"Easy," Lyle warned. "You're going too fast for him."

"I'm sorry, Uncle Jean," I said. "But I wanted to see you and tell you how much Daddy suffers because you're in here. He's so sick with grief, he cries in your room often and in fact, he's been so upset recently, he couldn't come to see you on your birthday."

"His birthday? This isn't his birthday," Lyle said. "They make a big deal over everyone's birthday here. His isn't for another month."

"It doesn't surprise me. Daphne simply lied to get me to come along with her. I would have anyway, Uncle Jean," I said, turning back to him. "I wanted to see you very much."

He stared at me, his mouth open, his eyes wide.

"Start eating," Lyle said. "Pretend it's business as usual."

I did as he advised and Uncle Jean did appear to relax. He lifted his fork, but continued to stare at me instead of continuing to eat. I smiled at him.

"I lived with my grandmere Catherine all my life," I told him. "My mother died shortly after I was born. I never knew who my real father was until recently and I promised my grandmere Catherine I would go to him after she died.

"You can't imagine how surprised everyone was," I said. He started to smile.

"Terrific," Lyle whispered. "He likes you."

"Does he?"

"I can tell. Keep talking," he commanded in a whisper.

"I tried to adjust, to learn how to be a proper young Creole lady, but Gisselle was very jealous of me. She thought I stole her boyfriend and she plotted against me."

"Did you?" Lyle asked.

"Did I what?"

"Steal her boyfriend?"

"No. At least I didn't set out to do anything like that," I said.

"But he liked you more than he liked her?" Lyle pursued.

"It was her own fault. I don't know how anyone could like her. She lies; she likes to see people suffer, and she'll deceive anyone, even herself."

"She sounds like she's the one who belongs in here," he said.

I turned back to Uncle Jean.

"Gisselle wasn't happy unless I was in some sort of trouble," I continued.

Uncle Jean grimaced.

"Daphne always took her side and Daddy . . . Daddy's overwhelmed with problems."

Uncle Jean's grimace deepened. Suddenly, he began to turn angry. He lifted his upper lip and clenched his teeth.

"Uh-oh," Lyle said. "Maybe you'd better stop. It's upsetting him."

"No. He should hear all of it." I turned back to him. "I went to a voodoo queen and asked her to help me. She fixed Gisselle and shortly afterward, Gisselle and another one of her boyfriends got into a dreadful car accident, Uncle Jean. The boy was killed and Gisselle is crippled for life. I feel just terrible about it, and Daddy . . . Daddy's a shadow of himself."

Jean's anger seemed to subside.

"I wish you would say something to me, Uncle Jean. I wish you would tell me something I could tell Daddy when I do get out of here."

I waited, but he just stared at me.

"Don't feel bad. I told you, he doesn't talk to anyone. He—"

"I know, but I want my father to realize I've seen Uncle Jean," I insisted. "I want him to—"

"Ji-ji-ji—"

"What's he trying to say?"

"I don't know," Lyle said.

"Ji-b-b-jib-jib—"

"Jib? What's that mean? Jib?"

Lyle thought a moment.

"Jib? Jib!" His eyes brightened. "It's a sailing term. Is that what you mean, Jean?"

"Jib," Uncle Jean said, nodding. "Jib." He grimaced as if in great pain. Then he sat back, brought his hands to his head, and screamed, "JIB!"

"Oh, no."

"Hey, Jean," the attendant closest to us cried, running over.

"JIB! JIB!"

Another attendant arrived and then another. They helped Uncle Jean to his feet. Around us, the other patients began to become unnerved. Some shouted, some laughed, a young girl, maybe five or six years older than I, began to cry.

Uncle Jean struggled against the attendants for a while and looked at me. Spittle moved down the corners of his mouth as his head shook with the effort to repeat, "Jib, jib." They led him away.

Nurses appeared and more attendants followed to help calm down the patients.

"I feel terrible," I said. "I should have stopped when you told me to."

"Don't blame yourself," Lyle said, "something like that usually happens."

Lyle continued to eat a little more of his stew, but I couldn't put anything in my mouth. I felt so sick inside, so empty and defeated. I had to get out of here; I just had to.

"What happens now?" I asked him. "What will they do to him?"

"Just take him to his room. He usually calms down after that."

"What happens with us after lunch?"

"They'll take us out for a while, but the area is fenced in, so don't think you can just run off."

"Will you show me how to escape then? Will you, Lyle? Please," I begged.

"I don't know. Yes," he said. Then a moment later he said, "I don't know. Don't keep asking me."

"All right, Lyle. I won't," I said quickly. He calmed down and started on his dessert.

Just as he had said, when the lunch hour ended, the attendants directed the patients to their outside time. On my way out with Lyle, the head nurse, Mrs. McDonald, approached me.

"Dr. Cheryl has you scheduled for another hour of evaluation late this afternoon," she said. "I will come for you when it's time. How are you getting along? Make any friends?" she asked, eying Lyle who walked a step or two behind me. I didn't respond. "Hello, Lyle. How are you today?"

"I don't know," he said quickly.

Mrs. McDonald smiled at me and walked on to speak to some other patients.

The yard didn't look much different from the grounds in front of the institution. Like the front, the back had walkways and benches, fountains and flower beds with sprawling magnolia and oak trees providing pools of shade. There was an actual pool for fish and frogs, too. The grounds were obviously well maintained. The rock gardens, blossoms, and polished benches glittered in the warm, afternoon sunlight.

"It's very nice out here," I reluctantly admitted to Lyle.

"They've got to keep it nice. Everyone here comes from a wealthy family. They want to be sure the money continues to flow into the institution. You should see this place when they schedule one of their fetes for the families of patients. Every inch is spick-and-span, not a weed, not a speck of dust, and not a face without a smile," he said, smirking.

"You sound very critical of them, Lyle, yet you want to stay. Why don't you think about trying life on the outside again? You're much brighter than most boys I've met," I said. He blanched but looked away.

"I'm not ready yet," he replied. "But I can tell just from the short time I've been with you that you definitely don't belong here."

"I've got another session scheduled with Dr. Cheryl. He's going to find a way to keep me. I just know it," I moaned. "Daphne gives this place too much money for him not to do what she wants." I embraced myself and looked down as we walked along. Around us and even behind us, the attendants watched.

"You go ask to go to the bathroom," Lyle suddenly said. "It's right off the rear entrance. They won't bother you. To the left of the rest room is a short stairway which goes down to the basement. The second door on the right is the laundry room. They've already done their laundry work for today. They do it in the morning. So there won't be anyone there."

"Are you sure?"

"I told you, I've been here ten years. I know which clocks run slow and which run fast, what door hinges squeak, and where there are windows without bars on them," he added.

"Thank you, Lyle."

He shrugged.

"I haven't done anything yet," he said, as if he wanted to convince himself more than me that he hadn't made a decision.

"You've given me hope, Lyle. That's doing a great deal." I smiled at him. He stared at me a moment, his rust-colored eyes blinking and then he turned away.

"Go on," he said. "Do what I told you."

I went to the female attendant and explained that I had to go to the bathroom.

"I'll show you where it is," she said when we returned to the door.

"I know where it is. Thank you," I replied quickly. She shrugged and left me. I did exactly what Lyle said and scurried down the short flight of steps. The laundry room was a large, long room with cement floors and cement walls lined with washing machines, dryers, and bins. Toward the rear were the windows Lyle had described, but they were high up.

"Quick," I heard him say as he entered behind me. We hurried to the back. "You just snap the hinge in the middle and slide the window to your left," he whispered. "It's not locked."

"How do you know that, Lyle?" I asked suspiciously. He looked down and then up at me quickly.

"I've been here a few times. I even went so far as to stick my foot out, but I . . . I'm not ready," he concluded.

"I hope you will be ready soon, Lyle."

"I'll give you a boost up. Come on, before we're missed," he said, cupping his hands together for my foot.

"I wish you would come with me, Lyle," I said, and put my foot into his hands. He lifted and I clutched at the windowsill to pull myself up. Just as he described, the latch opened easily and I slid the window to the left. I looked down at him.

"Go on," he coached.

"Thank you, Lyle. I know how hard it was for you to do this."

"No it wasn't," he confessed. "I wanted to help you. Go on."

I started to crawl through the window, looking around as I did so to be sure no one was nearby. Across the lawn was a small patch of trees and beyond that, the main highway. Once I was out, I turned and looked back in at him.

"Do you know where to go from here?" he asked me.

"No, but I just want to get away."

"Go south. There's a bus stop there and the bus will take you back to New Orleans. Here," he said, digging into his pants pocket and coming up with a fistful of money. "I don't need this in here."

He handed me the bills.

"Thank you, Lyle."

"Be careful. Don't look suspicious. Smile at people. Act like you're just on an afternoon outing," he advised, telling me things I was sure he had recited to himself a hundred times in vain.

"I'll be back to visit you someday, Lyle. I promise. Unless you're out before then. If you are, call me."

"I haven't used a telephone since I was six years old," he admitted. Looking down at him in the laundry room, I felt so sorry for him. He seemed small and alone now, trapped by his own insecurities. "But," he added, smiling, "if I do get out, I'll call you."

"Good."

"Get going . . . quickly," he said. "Remember, look natural."

He turned and walked away. I stood up, took a deep breath, and started away from the building. When I was no more than a dozen or so feet from it, I looked back and caught sight of someone on the third floor standing in the window. A cloud moved over the sun and the subsequent shade made it possible for me to see beyond the glint of the glass.

It was Uncle Jean!

He looked down at me and then raised his hand slowly. I could just make out the smile on his face. I waved back and then I turned and ran as hard and as fast as I could for the trees, not looking back until I had arrived. The building and the grounds behind me remained calm. I heard no shouting, saw no one running after me. I had slipped away, thanks to Lyle. I focused one more time on the window of Uncle Jean's room, but I couldn't see him anymore. Then I turned and marched through the woods to the highway.

I went south as Lyle had directed and reached the bus station which was just a small quick stop with gas pumps, candies and cakes, homemade pralines and soda. Fortunately, I had to wait only twenty minutes for the next bus to New Orleans. I bought my ticket from the young lady behind the counter and waited inside the store, thumbing through magazines and finally buying one just so I wouldn't be visible outside in case the institute had discovered I was missing and had sent someone looking for me.

I breathed relief when the bus arrived on time. I got on quickly, but following Lyle's advice, I acted as calmly and innocently as I could. I took my seat and sat back with my magazine. Moments later, the bus continued on its journey to New Orleans. We went right past the main entrance of the institution. When it was well behind us, I let out a breath. I was so happy to be free, I couldn't help but cry. Afraid someone would notice, I wiped away my tears quickly and closed my eyes and suddenly thought about Uncle Jean stuttering, "Jib . . . jib . . ."

The rhythm of the tires on the macadam highway beat out the same chant: "Jib . . . jib . . . jib."

What was he trying to tell me? I wondered.

When the New Orleans' skyline came into view, I actually considered not returning to my home and instead returning to the bayou. I wasn't looking forward to the greeting I would receive from Daphne, but then some of Grandmere Catherine's Cajun pride found its way into my backbone and I sat up straight and determined. After all, my father did love me. I was a Dumas and I did belong with him, too. Daphne had no right to do the things she had done to me.

By the time I got on the right city bus and then changed for the streetcar and arrived at the house, I was sure Dr. Cheryl had called Daphne and informed her I was missing. That was confirmed for me the moment Edgar greeted me at the door and I took one look at his face.

"Madame Dumas is waiting for you," he said, shifting his eyes to indicate all was not well. "She's in the parlor."

"Where's my father, Edgar?" I demanded.

He shook his head first and then he replied in a softer voice, "Upstairs, mademoiselle."

"Inform Madame Dumas that I've gone up to see him first," I ordered. Edgar widened his eyes, surprised at my insubordination.

"No, you're not!" Daphne shouted from the parlor doorway the moment I stepped into the entryway. "You're marching yourself right in here first." She stood there, her arm extended, pointing to the room. Her voice was cold, commanding. Edgar quickly moved away and retreated through the door that would take him through the dining room and into the kitchen, where I was sure he would make a report to Nina.

I took a few steps toward Daphne. She kept her arm out, her finger toward the parlor.

"How dare you try to tell me what to do and what not to do after what you've done," I charged, walking toward her slowly, my head high.

"I did what I thought was necessary to protect this family," she replied coldly, lowering her arm slowly.

"No, you didn't. You did what you thought was necessary to get rid of me, to keep me away from my father," I accused, meeting her furious gaze with a furious gaze of my own. She faltered a bit at my aggressive stance, her eyes shifting. "You're jealous of his love for me. You've been jealous ever since I arrived and you hate me because I remind you that he was once more in love with someone else."

"That's ridiculous. That's just another ridiculous Cajun—"

"Stop it!" I shouted. "Stop talking about the Cajun people like that. You know the truth; you know I wasn't kidnapped and sold to any Cajun family. You have no right to act superior. Few Cajun people I've known would stoop to do the sort of deceitful, horrible thing you tried to do to me."

"How dare you shout at me like that?" she said, trying to recover her superior demeanor, but her lips quivered and her body began to tremble. "How dare you!"

"How dare you do what you did at the institution!" I retorted. "My father is going to hear all about it. He's going to know the truth and . . ."

She smiled.

"You little fool. Go on upstairs to him. Go on and gaze upon your savior, your father, who sits in his brother's shrine of a room and moans and groans. I'm thinking about having him committed soon, if you must know. I can't go on like this."

She stepped toward me with renewed confidence.

"Who do you think has been running things around here? Who do you think makes this all possible? Your weak father? Ha! What do you think happens when he falls into one of his melancholic states? Do you think Dumas Enterprises just sits around and waits for him to snap out of it?

"No," she cried, stabbing herself with her thumb so hard it made me wince, "it always falls to me to save the day. I've been conducting business for years. Why, Pierre doesn't even know how much money we have or where it's located."

"I don't believe you," I said, but not with as much confidence as I had at first. She laughed.

"Believe what you like. Go on." She stepped back. "Go up to him and tell him about the horrible thing I tried to do to you," she said, and then stepped toward me again, lowering her voice sharply and narrowing her eyes into hateful slits. "And I'll explain to him and to everyone who wants or has to know how you've been so disruptive since you arrived, you nearly caused a fatal family crisis. I'll force the Andreas boy to confess to your sexual games in the art studio and I'll have Gisselle testify to your friendship with that whore from Story-ville." Her eyes widened and then hardened to rivet on me as she continued.

"I'll have people believing you were a teenage prostitute in the bayou. For all I know, you were."

"That's a lie, a dirty, horrible lie," I cried, but she didn't soften. Her face, the face with the alabaster complexion and those beautiful eyes, turned into the cold visage of a statue as she gazed down at me.

"Is it?" She smiled again, a small, tight smile that drew her lips into thin lines. "I already have Dr. Cheryl's preliminary findings. He thinks you're obsessed with sex and will so testify if I like. And now you've gone and run away from the institution, embarrassing us even further."

I shook my head, but there was no denying her vicious determination to overcome my defiance.

"I'm going to see Daddy," I said in almost a whisper. "I'm going to tell him everything."

"Go on." She lunged forward and grabbed my shoulders to turn me to the stairway. "Go on, you little Cajun fool. Go tell your Daddy." She pushed me toward the steps. I threw her an angry look and then charged up the stairs, my tears flying off my cheeks.

When I got to the upstairs landing, I saw the door to Uncle Jean's room was shut tight, but I had to get Daddy to see me; I had to get him to let me in. I approached slowly and knocked and then pressed my cheek to the door and sobbed.

"Daddy, please . . . please, open up and let me in. Please, let me talk to you and tell you what Daphne did to me. I saw Uncle Jean, Daddy. I was with him. Please," I begged. I continued to sob softly. Finally, when he didn't open the door, I sank to the floor and embraced myself, my shoulders heaving with my deeper sobs. After all that had been done to me and after my great effort to return, I was still shut out; Daphne was still victorious. I sucked in some air and let my head fall back against the door. Then I let it fall back again and again until finally the door was pulled open and I looked up at Daddy.

His eyes were bloodshot, his hair disheveled. His shirt was out of his pants and his tie was loose. He looked like he had slept in his clothes. He had an unshaven face.

I struggled to my feet and ground the tears out of my eyes quickly.

"Daddy, I must talk to you," I said. He threw me a quick glance of deepest despair. Then his shoulders slumped and he backed into the room to let me enter.

The candles were nearly burned out around Uncle Jean's pictures so the room was very dimly lit. Daddy retreated to a chair by the pictures and sat down. His face was shadowed and hidden in the deepening gloom.

"What is it, Ruby?" he said, speaking as though it took all of his strength to pronounce the four words. I rushed to him and seized his hand, falling to my knees at his feet.

"Daddy, she took me to the institution this morning, supposedly to see Uncle Jean for his birthday, but when we got there, she had them lock me up. She tried to have them keep me there. It was horrible, but a nice young man helped me escape."

He raised his head and gazed at me with his sad eyes showing just a hint of surprise. He shook his head in a bewildered fashion, the tears still eking from beneath his lids.

"Who did this?"

"Daphne," I said. "Daphne."

"Daphne?"

"But I got to see Uncle Jean, Daddy. I sat with him and spoke to him."

"You did?" he asked, his interest growing. "How is he?"

"He looks very good," I said, wiping the tears off my cheeks with the back of my hand. "But he's afraid of people and doesn't talk to anyone."

Daddy nodded and lowered his head again.

"Except, I got him to say something, Daddy."

"You did?" he replied, his interest quickly returning.

"Yes. I told him to tell me something I could bring back to you and he said 'jib.' What did he mean, Daddy?"

"Jib? He said that?"

I nodded. Then I had to tell him the rest.

"Afterward, he started to scream and held his head in his hands. They had to take him back to his room."

"Poor Jean," Daddy said. "My poor brother. What have I done?" he asked in a heavy, flat voice. One of the candles went out and a shadow came to darken his eyes even more.

"What do you mean, Daddy? Why did he say 'jib'? Is it what this young man sitting beside me thought . . . something to do with sailing?"

"Yes," Daddy said. He sat back, his gaze far-off now. He looked like he could see into the past. And then he began to speak like one in a trance. "It was a nice day when we started out. I wasn't anxious to go at first. Jean kept taunting me, making fun of me for being so unathletic. 'You're as pale as a bank teller,' he said. 'No wonder Daphne would rather spend her time with me. Come on, get yourself into the fresh air. Let's test those muscles and limbs.'

"Finally, I gave in and accompanied him to the lake. The sky had already begun to change. There were storm clouds hovering along the horizon. I warned him about it, but he laughed and said I was just trying to find another excuse. We started sailing. I wasn't as ignorant about it as I pretended and I didn't like my younger brother telling me to do this or that like some galley slave.

"He seemed particularly arrogant to me that day. How I hated his self-confidence. Why didn't he have any doubts about himself like I had? Why was he so secure in the presence of women, especially Daphne?

"The clouds mounted, expanding, mushrooming, darkening, and the wind grew fiercer. Our sailboat rose and fell as the water became rougher and rougher. Every time I urged Jean to turn us back to shore, he laughed at me for not being adventurous enough.

" 'This is where we test our manhood,' he declared. 'We look Nature in the eye and we don't blink.'

"I pleaded with him to be more sensible and he continued to mock me for being too sensible. 'Women don't like men to be reasonable and sensible and logical all the time, Pierre,' he said. 'They want a little danger, a little insecurity. If you want to win Daphne, take her out here on a day like this and let her scream as the spray hits her face and the sailboat tips and totters like it's doing now,' he cried.

"But the storm grew worse than even he expected. I was angry at him for putting us in this unnecessary danger. I was angry and jealous and during our battle against the storm, when he was struggling with the sail . . ." He sighed, closed his eyes, and then concluded, "I sent the jib flying around and it struck him in the head. It wasn't an accident," he confessed, and lowered his head to his hands.

"Oh, Daddy." I reached up and took his hand as he sobbed. "I'm sure you didn't mean to hurt him so badly. I'm sure you regretted it the moment you did it."

"Yes," he said, lifting his face from his palms. "I did. But that didn't change things and look where he is and what he is now. Look at what he was," he said, lifting one of the silver framed photographs. "My beautiful brother." Tears of remembrance clouded his eyes as he gazed at him. Then he sighed so deeply, I thought his heart had given out, and lowered his chin to his chest.

"He's still your beautiful brother, Daddy. And I think that he could make enough progress to leave that place. I really do. When I spoke to him and told him things, I felt he really understood."

"Did you?" Daddy's eyes lit up as he raised his head again. "Oh, how I wish that were true. I'd give anything now . . . all my wealth, if that were true."

"It is, Daddy. You must go to him more often. Maybe you should get him better treatment, find another doctor, another place," I suggested. "They don't seem to be doing anything more than making him comfortable and taking your money," I said bitterly.

"Yes. Maybe." He paused and looked at me and smiled. "You are a very lovely young lady, Ruby. If I was to believe in any forgiveness, it would be that you were sent here to me as an indication of that. I don't deserve you."

"I was almost shut away, too, Daddy," I said, returning to my original theme.

"Yes," he said. "Tell me more about that."

I described how Daphne had tricked me into accompanying her to the institution and all that had followed afterward. He listened intently, growing more and more upset.

"You've got to get hold of yourself, Daddy," I said. "She just told me she might have you committed, too. Don't let her do these things to you and to me and even to Gisselle."

"Yes," he said. "You're right. I've wallowed in self-pity too long and let things get out of hand."

"We've got to end all the lying, Daddy. We've got to cast the lies off like too much weight on a boat or a canoe. The lies are sinking us," I told him. He nodded. I stood up.

"Gisselle has to know the truth, Daddy, the truth about our birth. Daphne shouldn't be afraid of the truth either. Let her be our mother because of her actions and not because of a mountain of lies."

Daddy sighed.

"You're right." He rose, brushed back his hair, and straightened his tie, tightening the knot. Then he stuffed his shirt into his pants neatly. "I'm going down to speak with Daphne. She won't do anything like this to you again, Ruby. I promise."

"And I'll go in to see Gisselle and tell her the truth, but she won't believe me, Daddy. You'll have to come up and speak with her, too," I told him. He nodded.

"I will." He kissed me and held me for a moment. "Gabrielle would be so proud of you, so proud."

He straightened up, pulled back his shoulders, and left. I gazed at Uncle Jean's photographs for a moment and then I went to tell my sister who her mother really was.

"Where have you been?" Gisselle demanded. "Mother's been home for hours and hours. I kept asking for you and they kept telling me you weren't here. Then Mother came by and told me you ran away. I knew you wouldn't stay away long," she added confidently. "Where would you go, back to the bayou and live with those dirty swamp people?"

Because I didn't say anything immediately, her smile of self-satisfaction evaporated.

"Why are you standing there like that? Where were you?" she wailed. "I needed you. I can't stand that nurse anymore."

"Mother lied to you, Gisselle," I said calmly.

"Lied?"

I walked over to her bed and sat on it to face her in her wheelchair.

"I didn't run away," I said. "Don't you remember? We were going to the institution to see Uncle Jean, only—"

"Only what?"

"She had other intentions. She brought me there to leave me there as a patient," I said. "I was tricked and locked up like some mentally disturbed person."

"You were?" Her eyes widened.

"A nice young man helped me escape. I've already told Daddy what she did."

Gisselle shook her head in disbelief.

"I can't believe she would do such a thing."

"I can," I replied quickly. "Because she's not really our mother."

"What?" Gisselle started to smile, but I stopped her and seized her full attention when I reached out to take her hand into mine.

"You and I were born in the bayou, Gisselle. Years ago, Daddy would go there with our grandfather Dumas to hunt. He saw and fell in love with our real mother, Gabrielle Landry, and he made her pregnant. Grandpere Dumas wanted a grandchild, and Daphne couldn't have any, so he made a bargain with our other grandfather, Grandpere Jack, to buy the child. Only, there were two of us. Grandmere Catherine kept me a secret and Grandpere Jack gave you to the Dumas family."

Gisselle said nothing for a moment and then pulled her hand from mine.

"You are crazy," she said, "if you think I'll ever believe such a story."

"It's true," I said calmly. "The story of the kidnapping was invented after I turned up here to keep people believing Daphne was our real mother."

Gisselle wheeled herself back, shaking her head.

"I'm not a Cajun, too. I'm not," she declared.

"Cajun, Creole, rich, poor, that's not important, Gisselle. The truth is important. It's time to face it and go on," I said dryly. I was very tired now, the heavy weight of one of the most emotional and difficult days of my life finally settling over my shoulders. "I never met our mother because she died right after we were born, but from everything Grandmere Catherine told me about her and from what Daddy told me, I know we would have loved her dearly. She was very beautiful."

Gisselle shook her head, but my quiet revelation had begun to sink in and her lips trembled, too. I saw her eyes begin to cloud.

"Wait," I said, and opened our adjoining door. I went to the nightstand and found Mother's picture and brought it to her. "Her name was Gabrielle," I said, showing the picture to Gisselle. She glanced at it quickly and then turned away.

"I don't want to look at some Cajun woman you say is our mother."

"She is. And what's more . . . she had another child . . . we have a half brother . . . Paul."

"You're crazy. You ARE crazy. You do belong in the institution. I want Daddy. I want Daddy! Daddy! Daddy!" she screamed.

Mrs. Warren came running from her room.

"What's going on now?" she demanded.

"I want my father. Get my father."

"I'm not a maid around here. I'm—"

"GET HIM!" Gisselle cried. Her face turned as red as a beet as she struggled to shout with all her might. Mrs. Warren looked at me.

"I'll get him," I said, and left Gisselle with her nurse cajoling her to calm down.

Daddy and Daphne were down in the parlor. Daphne was sitting on the sofa, looking surprisingly subdued. Daddy stood in front of her, his hands on his hips, looking much stronger. I gazed from him to Daphne, who shifted her eyes from me guiltily.

"I told Gisselle the truth," I said.

"Are you satisfied now?" Daphne fired at Daddy. "I warned you she would eventually destroy the tender fabric that held this family together. I warned you."

"I wanted her to tell Gisselle," he said.

"What?"

"It's time we all faced the truth, no matter how painful, Daphne. Ruby is right. We can't go on living in a world of lies. What you did to her was bad. But what I did to her was even worse. I should never have made her lie, too."

"That's easy for you to say, Pierre," Daphne retorted, her lips trembling and her eyes unexpectedly tearing. "In this society, you will be forgiven for your indiscretion. It's almost expected for you to have an affair, but what about me? How am I to face society now?" she moaned. She was crying. I never thought I'd see tears emerge from those stone cold eyes, but she was feeling so sorry for herself, she couldn't prevent it.

In a way, despite all she had done to me, I felt sorry for her, too. Her world, a world built on falsehoods, on deceits, and propped up with blocks and blocks of fabrications was crumbling right before her eyes and she couldn't stop it.

"We all have a lot of mending to do, Daphne. I, especially, have to find the strength to repair the damage I've done to people I love."

"Yes, you do," she wailed.

He nodded. "But so do you. You know, you're not totally innocent in all this."

She looked up at him sharply.

"We have to find ways to forgive each other if we're to go on," he said.

He pulled back his shoulders.

"I'd better go up to Gisselle," he said. "And then afterward, I'd better go see my brother. I'll go to him as many times as I have to until I've gotten him to forgive me and to start his real recovery."

Daphne looked away. Daddy smiled at me and then left to go up to my sister to confirm and confess the truth.

For a long moment I just stood there looking at my stepmother. Finally, she turned toward me slowly, her eyes no longer clouded with tears, her lips no longer trembling.

"You haven't destroyed me," she said firmly. "Don't think you have."

"I don't want to destroy you, Daphne. I just want you to stop trying to destroy me. I can't say I forgive you for the dreadful thing you tried to do to me, but I'm willing to start anew and try to get along with you. If for no other reason than to make my father happy," I said.

"And maybe someday," I added, although it seemed impossible to me at the moment, "I'll call you Mother and be able to mean it."

She turned back to me, her eyes narrow, her face taut.

"You've charmed everyone you've met. Would you try to charm me, even after today?"

"That's really up to you, isn't it . . . Mother?" I said, and turned away to leave her pondering the future of the Dumas.

EPILOGUE

Truth, like a foundation in the bayou, has to be driven deeply to take hold, especially in a world where lies could storm in and wash away the paper-thin walls of illusion any time. Grandmere Catherine used to say the strongest trees are the ones whose roots go the deepest. "Nature has a way of finding out which ones don't go deep enough and they get washed away in the floods and the winds. But that ain't all bad because it leaves us with a world in which we can feel more secure, a world on which we can depend. Drive your roots deep, child. Drive your roots deep."

For better or for worse, my roots were now set in the garden of the Dumas family, and I had come from the timid, insecure Cajun girl who trembled on the family doorstep to the girl who had begun to understand a little more about who she really was.

In the days that followed, Gisselle grew strangely weaker and far more dependent on me than ever. I found her crying often and consoled her. She resisted learning about our Cajun background at first, and then, slowly, she began to ask a question here and there that led to my describing places and people. Of course, she was uncomfortable with the truth and made me swear dozens of times in dozens of ways never to tell anyone until she was ready for it to be told. I swore.

And then, one afternoon while I was up in Gisselle's room telling her about something that had happened during final exams at school, Edgar appeared.

"Pardon me, Mademoiselle Ruby," he said, after knocking on the doorjamb to get our attention, "but there is someone here to see you. A young man."

"A young man?" Gisselle quipped before I could respond. "What's his name, Edgar?"

"He says his name is Paul, Paul Tate."

The blood left my face for a moment and then rushed back in so quickly, I grew faint.

"Paul?"

"Who's Paul?" Gisselle demanded.

"Paul's our half brother," I told her. Her eyes widened.

"Bring him up here," she ordered.

I hurried down and found him standing in the entryway. He looked so much older to me and a good six inches taller, and far more handsome than I could recall.

"Hi, Ruby," he said, beaming a wide, happy smile.

"How did you find me?" I gasped. I hadn't left a return address on the letter I had written because I didn't want him to find me.

"It wasn't all that hard. After I got your letter and knew you were in New Orleans at least, I went to Grandpere Jack with a bottle of bourbon one night."

"You wicked boy," I chastised. "Taking advantage of a drunk like that."

"I would have drunk with the devil if it meant I could find you, Ruby." We gazed at each other for a moment, our eyes locked.

"Can I give you a hello kiss?" he asked.

"Yes. Of course."

He kissed me on the cheek and then stepped back to look around.

"You weren't exaggerating, you are rich. Have things gotten any better for you here since you wrote me that letter?"

"Yes," I said. He looked disappointed.

"I was hoping you would say no and I'd talk you into returning to the bayou, but I don't blame you for not wanting to leave this."

"My family is here, too, Paul."

"Right. So. Where is this twin sister?" he asked. I quickly told him about the automobile accident. "Oh," he moaned. "I'm sorry. Is she still in the hospital?"

"No. She's upstairs, dying to meet you. I've told her all about you," I said.

"You have?"

"Come on. She's probably tearing up the room because I've taken so long."

I led him upstairs. On the way he told me that Grandpere Jack was the same.

"You wouldn't recognize the house, of course. He's made it into the same pigsty he had in the swamps. And the grounds are peppered with holes. He's still looking for the buried money.

"For a time, after you had left, the authorities thought he might have done something to you. It was something of a scandal, but when nothing to lead anyone to believe it was found, the police stopped hounding him. Of course, some people still believe it."

"Oh. That's terrible. I'll have to write to Grandmere's friends and let them know where I am and that everything is fine."

He nodded and I showed him into Gisselle's room.

Nothing brought the tint back into Gisselle's cheeks and the glint back into her eyes as much as a handsome young man did. We weren't sitting and talking five minutes before she was flirting, batting her eyelashes, swinging her shoulders, and smiling at him. Paul was amused, maybe even a bit overwhelmed with such feminine attention.

Toward the end of the visit, Gisselle surprised me by suggesting that we go visit him in the bayou one of these days soon.

"Would you?" Paul beamed. "I'd show you around, show you things that would make your eyes pop. I've got my own boat and now I have horses and—"

"I don't know if I could sit on a horse," Gisselle moaned.

"Of course you can," Paul said. "And if you couldn't, I'd sit with you."

She liked that idea.

"Now that you know where we are, you don't be a stranger either," Gisselle told him. "We've got to get to know each other more and more."

"I will. I mean, thanks."

"Are you going to stay for dinner?" she asked.

"Oh, no. I got a ride in with someone and I've got to meet him real soon," he said. I could tell he was making that up, but I didn't say anything. Gisselle was disappointed but she lit right up when he leaned over to kiss her good-bye.

"You come back real soon, hear?" she called as we started out.

"You could have stayed for dinner," I told him. "I'm sure Daddy would like to meet you. My stepmother Daphne is snobby, but she wouldn't be impolite."

"No. I really do have to get back. No one knows I came here," he confessed.

"Oh."

"But now that I know where you are and I've met my other half sister, I won't be a stranger. That is, if you don't want me to be."

"Of course I don't. And one day soon, I will bring Gisselle out to the bayou."

"That would be great," Paul said. He looked down for a moment and then looked up quickly. "There hasn't been anyone else for me since you," he confessed.

"That's not right, Paul."

"I just can't help it," he said.

"Try. Please," I begged him. He nodded. Then he leaned forward quickly and kissed me. A moment later, like some memory from the past that had flowed through my thoughts, he was gone.

Rather than go right back to Gisselle, I went out to the garden. It was still a very beautiful day with the azure sky looking like an artist's canvas, sprinkled here and there with dabs of puffy white clouds. I closed my eyes and I might have fallen asleep had I not heard Daddy's voice.

"Somehow I thought I would find you out here," he declared. "I took one look at that blue sky and said to myself, Ruby's somewhere outside enjoying the late afternoon."

"It is a pretty day, Daddy. How was your day?"

"Good. Ruby," he said, sitting down across from me and looking very serious, "I've made a decision. I want you and Gisselle to attend a private school next year. She needs special attention and . . . frankly, she needs you. Although she'd never confess that."

"Private school?" I thought about it, thought about leaving the few friends I had made, and especially, thought about leaving Beau. Things were still difficult between us because of what Daphne had told his parents, but we were finding ways to see each other from time to time.

"It would be better for everyone if you two attended a live-in, private school," he added, his meaning quite clear. "I will miss you both terribly, but I'll try to be there often," he promised. "It won't be far from New Orleans. Will you do it?"

"A school full of snobby rich Creoles?" I asked.

"Probably," he admitted. "But somehow, I don't think you're afraid of that anymore. You'll change them before they change you," he predicted. "It's the kind of place where you'll have great balls and parties, travel excursions, the best teachers and facilities, and most importantly, you'll get back to your art. And Gisselle will have the special care she needs."

"All right, Daddy," I said. "If you think that would be best."

"I do. I knew I could count on you. So," he said. "What's your sister doing? How come she let you get some free time?" he joked.

"She's probably brushing her hair and talking on the phone about our male visitor," I said.

"Male visitor?"

I had never told him about Paul, and when I began, he surprised me by telling me he already knew.

"Gabrielle wasn't one to hide such a thing," he said. "I'm sorry I missed him."

"He'll be back and we promised to visit someday," I said.

"I'd like that. I haven't been to the bayou ever since . . . ever since." He got up.

"I'd better go see my other princess," he declared. "Coming?"

"I just want to sit here a while longer, Daddy."

"Sure," he said. He leaned over and kissed me and then he went back in to see my sister.

I sat back and looked over the grounds, but I didn't see the beautifully manicured flowers and trees. Instead, I saw the bayou. I saw Paul and I, the two of us, young and innocent, in a pirogue, Paul poling, me leaning back, the Gulf breeze flowing over my face and lifting strands of my hair. We turned a corner and the marsh hawk was there on a branch looking down at us. He lifted his wings as if to greet us and welcome us into the secret world that lay within our most cherished dreams and deep down in the softness of our hearts.

And then he dove off the branch and flew above the trees toward the blue sky and left us alone, drifting toward tomorrow.